THE COMPLETE SHORT STORIES
OF
W. SOMERSET MAUGHAM
I

Books by
W. SOMERSET MAUGHAM

Novels

CATALINA
ASHENDEN
THEN AND NOW
THE RAZOR'S EDGE
THE HOUR BEFORE THE DAWN
THE MOON AND SIXPENCE
UP AT THE VILLA
MRS. CRADDOCK
CHRISTMAS HOLIDAY
CAKES AND ALE
THEATRE
THE PAINTED VEIL
THE NARROW CORNER
OF HUMAN BONDAGE
LIZA OF LAMBETH

Short Stories

ENCORE
TRIO
QUARTET
CREATURES OF CIRCUMSTANCE
THE TREMBLING OF A LEAF
THE MIXTURE AS BEFORE
AH KING
COSMOPOLITANS
THE CASUARINA TREE
FIRST PERSON SINGULAR
EAST AND WEST
THE WORLD OVER

Essays

FRANCE AT WAR
STRICTLY PERSONAL

THE SUMMING UP
BOOKS AND YOU
A WRITER'S NOTEBOOK
THE MAUGHAM READER

Travel

ON A CHINESE SCREEN
DON FERNANDO
THE GENTLEMAN IN THE
   PARLOUR
THE LAND OF THE BLESSED
   VIRGIN

Plays

FOR SERVICES RENDERED
A MAN OF HONOUR
THE BREADWINNER
PENELOPE
THE SACRED FLAME
JACK STRAW
SHEPPEY
LADY FREDERICK
THE CONSTANT WIFE
THE TENTH MAN
THE CIRCLE
LANDED GENTRY
THE EXPLORER
THE UNKNOWN MRS. DOT
   SMITH
OUR BETTERS
THE LAND OF PROMISE
SIX COMEDIES

The Complete Short Stories of

W. SOMERSET MAUGHAM

I
East and West

DOUBLEDAY & COMPANY, INC.

Garden City, New York

LIBRARY OF CONGRESS CATALOG CARD NUMBER 52–11626

W

COPYRIGHT, 1921, 1934
BY DOUBLEDAY & COMPANY, INC.
COPYRIGHT, 1923, 1924, 1926, 1927, 1928, 1930, 1931, 1932
BY W. SOMERSET MAUGHAM
ALL RIGHTS RESERVED

This book was published in England under the title of *Altogether*

PREFACE

THIS book contains thirty stories. They are all about the same length and on the same scale. The first was written in 1919 and the last in 1931. Though in early youth I had written a number of short stories, for a long time, twelve or fifteen years at least, occupied with the drama, I had ceased to do so; and when a journey to the South Seas unexpectedly provided me with themes that seemed to suit this medium, it was as a beginner of over forty that I wrote the story which is now called *Rain*. Since it caused some little stir the reader of this preface will perhaps have patience with me if I transcribe the working notes, made at the time, on which it was constructed. They are written in hackneyed and slipshod phrases, without grace; for nature has not endowed me with the happy gift of hitting instinctively upon the perfect word to indicate an object and the unusual but apt adjective to describe it. I was travelling from Honolulu to Pago Pago and, hoping they might at some time be of service, I jotted down as usual my impressions of such of my fellow-passengers as attracted my attention. This is what I said of Miss Thompson: "Plump, pretty in a coarse fashion, perhaps not more than twenty-seven. She wore a white dress and a large white hat, long white boots from which the calves bulged in cotton stockings." There had been a raid on the Red Light district in Honolulu just before we sailed and the gossip of the ship spread the report that she was making the journey to escape arrest. My notes go on: "*W. The Missionary.* He was a tall thin man, with long limbs loosely jointed, he had

v

hollow cheeks and high cheek bones, his fine, large, dark eyes
were deep in their sockets, he had full sensual lips, he wore his
hair rather long. He had a cadaverous air and a look of suppressed fire. His hands were large, with long fingers, rather finely
shaped. His naturally pale skin was deeply burned by the
tropical sun. *Mrs. W. His Wife.* She was a little woman with
her hair very elaborately done, New England; not prominent
blue eyes behind gold-rimmed pince-nez, her face was long
like a sheep's, but she gave no impression of foolishness, rather
of extreme alertness. She had the quick movements of a bird.
The most noticeable thing about her was her voice, high, metallic, and without inflection; it fell on the ear with a hard
monotony, irritating to the nerves like the ceaseless clamour
of a pneumatic drill. She was dressed in black and wore round
her neck a gold chain from which hung a small cross. She told
me that W. was a missionary on the Gilberts and his district
consisting of widely separated islands he frequently had to go
distances by canoe. During this time she remained at headquarters and managed the mission. Often the seas were very
rough and the journeys were not without peril. He was a
medical missionary. She spoke of the depravity of the natives
in a voice which nothing could hush, but with a vehement, unctuous horror, telling me of their marriage customs which were
obscene beyond description. She said, when first they went it
was impossible to find a single good girl in any of the villages.
She inveighed against dancing. I talked with the missionary
and his wife but once, and with Miss Thompson not at all.
Here is the note for the story: "A prostitute, flying from Honolulu after a raid, lands at Pago Pago. There lands there also a
missionary and his wife. Also the narrator. All are obliged to
stay there owing to an outbreak of measles. The missionary
finding out her profession persecutes her. He reduces her to
misery, shame, and repentance, he has no mercy on her. He
induces the governor to order her return to Honolulu. One
morning he is found with his throat cut by his own hand and
she is once more radiant and self-possessed. She looks at men
and scornfully exclaims: dirty pigs."

An intelligent critic, who combines wide reading and a sensitive taste with a knowledge of the world rare among those who
follow his calling, has found in my stories the influence of Guy
de Maupassant. That is not strange. When I was a boy he was
considered the best short story writer in France and I read his

works with avidity. From the age of fifteen whenever I went to
Paris I spent most of my afternoons poring over the books in
the galleries of the Odéon. I have never passed more enchanted
hours. The attendants in their long smocks were indifferent to
the people who sauntered about looking at the books and they
would let you read for hours without bothering. There was a
shelf filled with the works of Guy de Maupassant, but they cost
three francs fifty a volume and that was not a sum I was prepared to spend. I had to read as best I could standing up and
peering between the uncut pages. Sometimes when no attendant
was looking I would hastily cut a page and thus read more
conveniently. Fortunately some of them were issued in a cheap
edition at seventy-five centimes and I seldom came away without one of these. In this manner, before I was eighteen, I had
read all the best stories. It is natural enough that when at that
age I began writing stories myself I should unconsciously have
chosen those little masterpieces as a model. I might very well
have hit upon a worse.

Maupassant's reputation does not stand as high as it did,
and it is evident now that there is much in his work to repel.
He was a Frenchman of his period in violent reaction against
the romantic age which was finishing in the saccharine sentimentality of Octave Feuillet (admired by Matthew Arnold)
and in the impetuous slop of George Sand. He was a naturalist,
aiming at truth at all costs, but the truth he achieved looks to us
now a trifle superficial. He does not analyse his characters. He
takes little interest in the reason why. They act, but wherefore
he does not know. "For me," he says, "psychology in a novel
or in a story consists in this: to show the inner man by his life."
That is very well, that is what we all try to do, but the gesture
will not by itself always indicate the motive. The result with
Maupassant was a simplification of character which is effective
enough in a short story, but on reflection leaves you unconvinced. There is more in men than that, you say. Again, he was
obsessed by the tiresome notion, common then to his countrymen, that it was a duty a man owed himself to hop into bed
with every woman under forty that he met. His characters indulge their sexual desire to gratify their self-esteem. They are
like the people who eat caviare when they are not hungry because it is expensive. Perhaps the only human emotion that
affects his characters with passion is avarice. This he can understand; it fills him with horror, but notwithstanding he has a

sneaking sympathy with it. He was slightly common. But for
all this it would be foolish to deny his excellence. An author has
the right to be judged by his best work. No author is perfect.
You must accept his defects; they are often the necessary com-
plement of his merits; and this may be said in gratitude to
posterity that it is very willing to do this. It takes what is good
in a writer and is not troubled by what is bad. It goes so far
sometimes, to the confusion of the candid reader, as to claim a
profound significance for obvious faults. So you will see the
critics (the awe-inspiring voice of posterity) find subtle reasons
to explain to his credit something in a play of Shakespeare's
that any dramatist could tell them needed no other explanation
than haste, indifference or wilfulness. Maupassant's stories are
good stories. The anecdote is interesting apart from the narration so that it would secure attention if it were told over the
dinner-table; and that seems to me a very great merit indeed.
However halting your words and insipid your rendering, you
could not fail to interest your listeners if you told them the
bare story of *Boule de Suif*, *L'Héritage* or *La Parure*. These
stories have a beginning, a middle and an end. They do not
wander along an uncertain line so that you cannot see whither
they are leading, but follow without hesitation, from exposition
to climax, a bold and vigorous curve. It may be that they have
no great spiritual significance. Maupassant did not aim at that.
He looked upon himself as a plain man; no good writer was ever
less a man of letters. He did not pretend to be a philosopher,
and here he was well-advised, for when he indulges in reflection
he is commonplace. But within his limits he is admirable. He
has an astonishing capacity for creating living people. He can
afford little space, but in a few pages can set before you half
a dozen persons so sharply seen and vividly described that you
know all about them that you need. Their outline is clear; they
are distinguishable from one another; and they breathe the
breath of life. They have no complexity, they lack strangely the
indecision, the unexpectedness, the mystery that we see in
human beings; they are in fact simplified for the purposes of
the story. But they are not deliberately simplified: those keen
eyes of his saw clearly, but they did not see profoundly; it is a
happy chance that they saw all that was necessary for him to
achieve the aim he had in view. He treats the surroundings in
the same way, he sets his scene accurately, briefly and effectively; but whether he is describing the charming landscape of

Normandy or the stuffy, overcrowded drawing-rooms of the
eighties his object is the same, to get on with the story. On his
own lines I do not think that Maupassant is likely to be surpassed. If his excellence is not at the moment so apparent it is
because what he wrote must now stand comparison with the
very different, more subtle and moving work of Chekov.

No one's stock to-day stands higher with the best critics
than Chekov's. In fact he has put every other story-teller's nose
out of joint. To admire him is a proof of good taste; not to like
him is to declare yourself a philistine. His stories are the models
that young writers naturally take. This is understandable. On
the face of it it is easier to write stories like Chekov's than
stories like Maupassant's. To invent a story interesting in itself
apart from the telling is a difficult thing, the power to do it is
a gift of nature, it cannot be acquired by taking thought, and
it is a gift that very few people have. Chekov had many gifts,
but not this one. If you try to tell one of his stories you will
find that there is nothing to tell. The anecdote, stripped of its
trimmings, is insignificant and often inane. It was grand for
people who wanted to write a story and couldn't think of a plot
to discover that you could very well manage without one. If
you could take two or three persons, describe their mutual
relations and leave it at that, why then it wasn't so hard to
write a story; and if you could flatter yourself that this really
was art, what could be more charming?

But I am not quite sure that it is wise to found a technique
on a writer's defects. I have little doubt that Chekov would
have written stories with an ingenious, original and striking
plot if he had been able to think of them. It was not in his
temperament. Like all good writers he made a merit of his
limitations. Was it not Goethe who said that an artist only
achieves greatness when he recognises them? If a short story
is a piece of prose dealing with more or less imaginary persons
no one wrote better short stories than Chekov. If, however,
as some think, it should be the representation of an action,
complete in itself and of a certain limited length, he leaves
something to be desired. He put his own idea clearly enough
in these words: "Why write about a man getting into a sub-
marine and going to the North Pole to reconcile himself to the
world, while his beloved at that moment throws herself with a
hysterical shriek from the belfry? All this is untrue and does
not happen in real life. One must write about simple things:

how Peter Semionovitch married Maria Ivanovna. That is all."
But there is no reason why a writer should not make a story of
an unusual incident. The fact that something happens every
day does not make it more important. The pleasure of recognition, which is the pleasure thus aimed at, is the lowest of the
aesthetic pleasures. It is not a merit in a story that it is un-
dramatic. Maupassant chose very ordinary people and sought
to show what there was of drama in the common happenings of
their lives. He chose the significant incident and extracted
from it all the drama possible. It is a method as praiseworthy
as another; it tends to make a story more absorbing. Probability
is not the only test; and probability is a constantly changing
thing. At one time it was accepted that the "call of the blood"
should enable long-lost children to recognize their parents and
that a woman only had to get into men's clothes to pass as
a man. Probability is what you can get the readers of your
time to swallow. Nor did Chekov, notwithstanding his principles, adhere to his canon unless it suited him. Take one of
the most beautiful and touching of his stories, *The Bishop*.
It describes the approach of death with great tenderness, but
there is no reason for the Bishop to die, and a better tech-
nician would have made the cause of death an integral part of
the story. "Everything that has no relation to the story must
be ruthlessly thrown away," he says in his advice to Schoukin.
"If in the first chapter you say that a gun hung on the wall,
in the second or third chapter it must without fail be discharged." So when the Bishop eats some tainted fish and a few
days later dies of typhoid we may suppose that it was the
tainted fish that killed him. If that is so he did not die of typhoid, but of ptomaine poisoning, and the symptoms were not
as described. But of course Chekov did not care. He was determined that his good and gentle bishop should die and for his
own purposes he wanted him to die in a particular way. I do
not understand the people who say of Chekov's stories that
they are slices of life, I do not understand, that is, if they mean
that they offer a true and typical picture of life. I do not believe
they do that, nor do I believe they ever did. I think they are
marvellously lifelike, owing to the writer's peculiar talent, but
I think they are deliberately chosen to square with the pre-
possessions of a sick, sad and overworked, gray-minded man.
I do not blame them for that. Every writer sees the world in
his own way and gives you his own picture of it. The imitation

of life is not a reasonable aim of art; it is a discipline to which the artist from time to time subjects himself when the stylization of life has reached an extravagance that outrages common sense. For Chekov life is like a game of billiards in which you never pot the red, bring off a losing hazard or make a cannon, and should you by a miraculous chance get a fluke you will almost certainly cut the cloth. He sighs sadly because the futile do not succeed, the idle do not work, liars do not speak the truth, drunkards are not sober and the ignorant have no culture. I suppose that it is this attitude that makes his chief characters somewhat indistinct. He can give you a striking portrait of a man in two lines, as much as can be said of anyone in two lines to set before you a living person, but with elaboration he seems to lose his grasp of the individual. His men are shadowy creatures, with vague impulses to good, but without will-power, shiftless, untruthful, fond of fine words, often with great ideals, but with no power of action. His women are lachrymose, slatternly and feeble-minded. Though they think it a sin they will commit fornication with anyone who asks them, not because they have passion, not even because they want to, but because it is too much trouble to refuse. It is only in his description of young girls that he seems touched with a tender indulgence. "Alas! regardless of their doom, the little victims play." He is moved by their charm, the gaiety of their laughter, their ingenuousness and their vitality; but it all leads to nothing. They make no effort to conquer their happiness, but yield passively to the first obstacle in the way.

But if I have ventured to make these observations I beg the reader not to think that I have anything but a very great admiration for Chekov. No writer, I repeat, is faultless. It is well to admire him for his merits. Not to recognize his imperfections, but rather to insist that they are excellencies, can in the long run only hurt his reputation. Chekov is extremely readable. That is a writer's supreme virtue and one upon which sufficient stress is often not laid. He shared it with Maupassant. Both of them were professional writers who turned out stories at more or less regular intervals to earn their living. They wrote as a doctor visits his patients or a solicitor sees his clients. It was part of the day's work. They had to please their readers. They were not always inspired, it was only now and then that they produced a masterpiece, but it is very seldom that they wrote anything that did not hold the reader's attention to the last

line. They both wrote for papers and magazines. Sometimes a
critic will describe a book of short stories as magazine stories
and thus in his own mind damn them. That is foolish. No form
of art is produced unless there is a demand for it and if newspapers and magazines did not publish short stories they would
not be written. All stories are magazine stories or newspaper
stories. The writers must accept certain (but constantly changing) conditions; it has never been known yet that a good writer
was unable to write his best owing to the conditions under
which alone he could gain a public for his work. That has never
been anything but an excuse of the second-rate. I suspect that
Chekov's great merit of concision is due to the fact that the
newspapers for which he habitually wrote could only give him
a certain amount of space. He said that stories should have
neither a beginning nor an end. He could not have meant that
literally. You might as well ask of a fish that it should have
neither head nor tail. It would not be a fish if it hadn't. The
way Chekov in reality begins a story is wonderfully good. He
gives the facts at once, in a few lines; he has an unerring feeling
for the essential statements, and he sets them down baldly,
but with great precision, so that you know at once whom you
have to deal with and what the circumstances are. Maupassant
often started his stories with an introduction designed to put
the reader in a certain frame of mind. It is a dangerous method
only justified by success. It may be dull. It may throw the
reader off the scent; you have won his interest in certain
characters and then instead of being told what you would like
to know about them, your interest is claimed for other people
in other circumstances. Chekov preached compactness. In his
longer stories he did not always achieve it. He was distressed
by the charge brought against him that he was indifferent to
moral and sociological questions and when he had ample space
at his command he seized the opportunity to show that they
meant as much to him as to any other right-thinking person.
Then in long and somewhat tedious conversations he would
make his characters express his own conviction that, whatever
the conditions of things might be then, at some not far distant
date (say 1934) the Russians would be free, tyranny would exist
no longer, the poor would hunger no more and happiness, peace
and brotherly love rule in the vast empire. But these were
aberrations forced upon him by the pressure of opinion (common in all countries) that the writer of fiction should be a

prophet, a social reformer and a philosopher. In his shorter
stories Chekov attained the concision he aimed at in a manner
that is almost miraculous.

And no one had a greater gift than he for giving you the
intimate feeling of a place, a landscape, a conversation or
(within his limited range) a character. I suppose this is what
people mean by the vague word atmosphere. Chekov seems to
have achieved it very simply, without elaborate explanation or
long description, by a precise narration of facts; and I think it
was due with him to a power of seeing things with amazing
naïvety. The Russians are a semi-barbarous people and they
seem to have retained the power of seeing things naturally, as
though they existed in a vacuum; while we in the West, with
our complicated culture behind us, see things with the associations they have gathered during long centuries of civilization.
They almost seem to see the thing in itself. Most writers, especially those living abroad, have in the last few years been shown
numbers of stories by Russian refugees who vainly hope to
earn a few guineas by placing them somewhere. Though dealing
with the present day they might very well be stories by Chekov
not at his best; they all have that direct, sincere vision. It is a
national gift. In no one was it more acutely developed than in
Chekov.

But I have not yet pointed out what to my mind is Chekov's
greatest merit. Since I am not a critic and do not know the
proper critical expressions I am obliged to describe this as best
I can in terms of my own feeling. Chekov had an amazing
power of surrounding people with air so that, though he does
not put them before you in the round and they lack the coarse,
often brutal vitality of Maupassant's figures, they live with
a strange and unearthly life. They are not lit by the hard light
of common day but suffused in a mysterious grayness. They
move in this as though they were disembodied spirits. It is their
souls that you seem to see. The subconscious seems to come to
the surface and they communicate with one another directly
without the impediment of speech. Strange, futile creatures,
with descriptions of their outward seeming tacked on them like
a card on an exhibit in a museum, they move as mysteriously
as the tortured souls who crowded about Dante when he walked
in Hell. You have the feeling of a vast, gray, lost throng
wandering aimless in some dim underworld. It fills you with
awe and with uneasiness. I have hinted that Chekov had no

great talent for inventing a multiplicity of persons. Under different names, with different environment, the same characters recur. It is as though, when you looked at the soul, the superficial difference vanishes and everyone is more or less the same. His people seem strangely to slip into one another as though they were not distinct individuals, but temporary fictions, and as though in truth they were all part of one another. The importance of a writer in the long run rests on his uniqueness. I do not know that anyone but Chekov has so poignantly been able to represent spirit communing with spirit. It is this that makes one feel that Maupassant in comparison is obvious and vulgar. The strange, the terrible thing is that, looking at man in their different ways, these two great writers, Maupassant and Chekov, saw eye to eye. One was content to look upon the flesh, the other, more nobly and subtly, surveyed the spirit; but they agreed that life was tedious and insignificant and that men were base, unintelligent and pitiful.

I hope the reader will not be impatient with me because in an introduction to my own stories I have dwelt at length on these remarkable writers. Maupassant and Chekov are the two authors of short stories whose influence survives to the present day and all of us who cultivate the medium must in the end be judged by the standards they have set.

So far as I could remember it I have placed the stories in this volume in the order in which they were written. I thought it might possibly interest the reader to see how I had progressed from the tentativeness of the first ones, when I was very much at the mercy of my anecdote, to the relative certainty of the later ones when I had learnt so to arrange my material as to attain the result I wanted. Though all but two have been published in a magazine these stories were not written with that end in view. When I began to write them I was fortunately in a position of decent independence and I wrote them as a relief from work which I thought I had been too long concerned with. It is often said that stories are no better than they are because the editors of magazines insist on their being written to a certain pattern. This has not been my experience. All but *Rain* and *The Book-Bag* were published in the Cosmopolitan Magazine and Ray Long, the Editor, never put pressure on me to write other than as I wished. Sometimes the stories were cut and this is reasonable since no editor can afford one contributor more than a certain amount of space; but I was never asked to make the smallest alteration to suit what might be supposed to be the taste of the readers. Ray Long paid me for them not only with good money, but with generous appreciation. I did not value this less. We authors are simple, childish creatures and we treasure a word of praise from those who buy our wares. Most of them were written in groups from notes made as they occurred to me, and in each group I left naturally enough to the last those that seemed most difficult to write. A story is difficult to write when you do not know *all* about it from the beginning, but for part of it must trust to your imagination and experience. Sometimes the curve does not intuitively present itself and you have to resort to this method and that to get the appropriate line.

I beg the reader not to be deceived by the fact that a good many of these stories are told in the first person into thinking that they are experiences of my own. This is merely a device to gain verisimilitude. It is one that has its defects, for it may strike the reader that the narrator could not know all the events he sets forth; and when he tells a story in the first person at one remove, when he reports, I mean, a story that someone tells him, it may very well seem that the speaker, a police officer, for example, or a sea-captain, could never have expressed himself with such facility and with such elaboration. Every convention has its disadvantages. These must be as far as possible disguised and what cannot be disguised must be accepted. The advantage of this one is its directness. It makes it possible for the writer to tell no more than he knows. Making no claim to omniscience, he can frankly say when a motive or an occurrence is unknown to him, and thus often give his story a plausibility that it might otherwise lack. It tends also to put the reader on intimate terms with the author. Since Maupassant and Chekov, who tried so hard to be objective, nevertheless are so nakedly personal, it has sometimes seemed to me that if the author can in no way keep himself out of his work it might be better if he put in as much of himself as possible. The danger is that he may put in too much and thus be as boring as a talker who insists on monopolizing the conversation. Like all conventions this one must be used with discretion. The reader may have observed that in the original note of *Rain* the narrator was introduced, but in the story as written omitted.

Three of the stories in this volume were told me and I had nothing to do but make them probable, coherent and dramatic.

They are *The Letter, Footprints in the Jungle* and *The Book-Bag*.
The rest were invented, as I have shown *Rain* was, by the accident of my happening upon persons here and there, who in themselves or from something I heard about them suggested a theme
that seemed suitable for a short story. This brings me to a topic
that has always concerned writers and that has at times given
the public, the writer's raw material, some uneasiness. There
are authors who state that they never have a living model in
mind when they create a character. I think they are mistaken.
They are of this opinion because they have not scrutinized with
sufficient care the recollections and impressions upon which
they have constructed the person who, they fondly imagine,
is of their invention. If they did they would discover that, unless he was taken from some book they had read, a practise by
no means uncommon, he was suggested by one or more persons
they had at one time known or seen. The great writers of the
past made no secret of the fact that their characters were
founded on living people. We know that the good Sir Walter
Scott, a man of the highest principles, portrayed his father,
with sharpness first and then, when the passage of years had
changed his temper, with tolerance; Henri Beyle, in the manu-
script of at least one of his novels, has written in at the side
the names of the real persons who were his models; and this is
what Turgenev himself says: "For my part, I ought to confess
that I never attempted to create a type without having, not an
idea, but a living person, in whom the various elements were
harmonized together, to work from. I have always needed some
groundwork on which I could tread firmly." With Flaubert it
is the same story; that Dickens used his friends and relations
freely is notorious; and if you read the Journal of Jules Renard,
a most instructive book to anyone who wishes to know how a
writer works, you will see the care with which he set down every
little detail about the habits, ways of speech and appearance
of the persons he knew. When he came to write a novel he made
use of this storehouse of carefully collected information. In
Chekov's diary you will find notes which were obviously made
for use at some future time, and in the recollections of his friends
there are frequent references to the persons who were the originals of certain of his characters. It looks as though the practice
were very common. I should have said it was necessary and
inevitable. Its convenience is obvious. You are much more
likely to depict a character who is a recognizable human being,

with his own individuality, if you have a living model. The imagination can create nothing out of the void. It needs the stimulus of sensation. The writer whose creative faculty has been moved by something peculiar in a person (peculiar perhaps only to the writer) falsifies his idea if he attempts to describe that person other than as he sees him. Character hangs together and if you try to throw people off the scent, by making a short man tall for example (as though stature had no effect on character) or by making him choleric when he has the concomitant traits of an equable temper, you will destroy the plausible harmony (to use the beautiful phrase of Baltasar Gracian) of which it consists. The whole affair would be plain sailing if it were not for the feelings of the persons concerned. The writer has to consider the vanity of the human race and the Schadenfreude which is one of its commonest and most detestable failings. A man's friends will find pleasure in recognizing him in a book and though the author may never even have seen him will point out to him, especially if it is unflattering, what they consider his living image. Often someone will recognize a trait he knows in himself or a description of the place he lives in and in his conceit jumps to the conclusion that the character described is a portrait of himself. Thus in the story called *The Outstation* the Resident was suggested by a British Consul I had once known in Spain and it was written ten years after his death, but I have heard that the Resident of a district in Sarawak, which I described in the story, was much affronted because he thought I had had him in mind. The two men had not a trait in common. I do not suppose any writer attempts to draw an exact portrait. Nothing, indeed, is so unwise as to put into a work of fiction a person drawn line by line from life. His values are all wrong, and, strangely enough, he does not make the other characters in the story seem false, but himself. He never convinces. That is why the many writers who have been attracted by the singular and powerful figure of the late Lord Northcliffe have never succeeded in presenting a credible personage. The model a writer chooses is seen through his own temperament and if he is a writer of any originality what he sees need have little relation with the facts. He may see a tall man short or a generous one avaricious; but, I repeat, if he sees him tall, tall he must remain. He takes only what he wants of the living man. He uses him as a peg on which to hang his own fancies. To achieve his end (the plausible harmony that

nature so seldom provides) he gives him traits that the model
does not possess. He makes him coherent and substantial. The
created character, the result of imagination founded on fact,
is art, and life in the raw, as we know, is of this only the material. The odd thing is that when the charge is made that an
author has copied this person or the other from life, emphasis is
laid only on his less praiseworthy characteristics. If you
say of a character that he is kind to his mother, but beats
his wife, everyone will cry: Ah, that's Brown, how beastly to say
he beats his wife; and no one thinks for a moment of Jones and
Robinson who are notoriously kind to their mothers. I draw
from this the somewhat surprising conclusion that we know our
friends by their vices and not by their virtues. I have stated
that I never even spoke to Miss Thompson in *Rain*. This is a
character that the world has not found wanting in vividness.
Though but one of a multitude of writers my practise is doubtless common to most, so that I may be permitted to give another instance of it. I was once asked to meet at dinner two
persons, a husband and wife, of whom I was told only what the
reader will shortly read. I think I never knew their names. I
should certainly not recognize them if I met them in the street.
Here are the notes I made at the time. "A stout, rather pompous man of fifty, with pince-nez, gray-haired, a florid complexion, blue eyes, a neat gray moustache. He talks with assurance.
He is resident of an outlying district and is somewhat impressed
with the importance of his position. He despises the men who
have let themselves go under the influence of the climate and
the surroundings. He has travelled extensively during his short
leaves in the East and knows Java, the Philippines, the coast of
China and the Malay Peninsula. He is very British, very patriotic; he takes a great deal of exercise. He has been a very
heavy drinker and always took a bottle of whiskey to bed with
him. His wife has entirely cured him and now he drinks nothing
but water. She is a little insignificant woman, with sharp features, thin, with a sallow skin and a flat chest. She is very badly
dressed. She has all the prejudices of an Englishwoman. All her
family for generations have been in second-rate regiments.
Except that you know that she has caused her husband to cease
drinking entirely you would think her quite colourless and un-
important." On these materials I invented the story which is
called *Before the Party*. I do not believe that any candid person
could think that these two people had cause for complaint be-

cause they had been made use of. It is true that I should never
have thought of the story if I had not met them, but anyone
who takes the trouble to read it will see how insignificant was
the incident (the taking of the bottle to bed) that suggested it
and how differently the two chief characters have in the course
of writing developed from the brief sketch which was their
foundation.

"Critics are like horse-flies which prevent the horse from
ploughing," said Chekov. "For over twenty years I have read
criticisms of my stories, and I do not remember a single remark
of any value or one word of valuable advice. Only once Ska-
bichevsky wrote something which made an impression on me.
He said I would die in a ditch, drunk." He was writing for
twenty-five years and during that time his writing was constantly attacked. I do not know whether the critics of the present day are naturally of a less ferocious temper; I must allow
that on the whole the judgment that has been passed on the
stories in this volume when from time to time a collection has
been published in book form has been favourable. One epithet,
however, has been much applied to them, which has puzzled
me; they have been described with disconcerting frequency as
"competent." Now on the face of it I might have thought this
laudatory, for to do a thing competently is certainly more de-
serving of praise than to do it incompetently, but the adjective
has been used in a disparaging sense and, anxious to learn and
if possible to improve, I have asked myself what was in the
mind of the critics who thus employed it. Of course none of
us is liked by everybody and it is necessary that a man's writing,
which is so intimate a revelation of himself, should be repulsive
to persons who are naturally antagonistic to the creature he is.
This should leave him unperturbed. But when an author's
work is somewhat commonly found to have a quality that is
unattractive to many it is sensible of him to give the matter
his attention. There is evidently something that a number of
people do not like in my stories and it is this they try to express
when they damn them with the faint praise of competence. I
have a notion that it is the definiteness of their form. I hazard
the suggestion (perhaps unduly flattering to myself) because
this particular criticism has never been made in France where
my stories have had with the critics and the public much
greater success than they have had in England. The French,
with their classical sense and their orderly minds, demand a

precise form and are exasperated by a work in which the ends
are left lying about, themes are propounded and not resolved
and a climax is foreseen and then eluded. This precision on the
other hand has always been slightly antipathetic to the English.
Our great novels have been shapeless and this, far from disconcerting their readers, has given them a sense of security.
This is the life we know, they have thought, with its arbitrari-
ness and inconsequence; we can put out of our minds the irritating thought that two and two make four. If I am right in this
surmise I can do nothing about it and I must resign myself to
being called competent for the rest of my days. My preposses-
sions in the arts are on the side of law and order. I like a story
that fits. I did not take to writing stories seriously till I had had
much experience as a dramatist, and this experience taught me
to leave out everything that did not serve the dramatic value
of my story. It taught me to make incident follow incident in
such a manner as to lead up to the climax I had in mind. I am
not unaware of the disadvantages of this method. It gives a
tightness of effect that is sometimes disconcerting. You feel
that life does not dovetail into its various parts with such neatness. In life stories straggle, they begin nowhere and tail off
without a point. That is probably what Chekov meant when he
said that stories should have neither a beginning nor an end.
It is certain that sometimes it gives you a sensation of airless-
ness when you see persons who behave so exactly according to
character, and incidents that fall into place with such perfect
convenience. The story-teller of this kind aims not only at
giving his own feelings about life, but at a formal decoration.
He arranges life to suit his purposes. He follows a design in his
mind, leaving out this and changing that; he distorts facts to
his advantage, according to his plan; and when he attains his
object produces a work of art. It may be that life slips through
his fingers; then he has failed; it may be that he seems sometimes so artificial that you cannot believe him, and when you
do not believe a story-teller he is done. When he succeeds he
has forced you for a time to accept his view of the universe and
has given you the pleasure of following out the pattern he
has drawn on the surface of chaos. But he seeks to prove nothing. He paints a picture and sets it before you. You can take it
or leave it.

CONTENTS

Contents

THE COMPLETE SHORT STORIES
OF
W. SOMERSET MAUGHAM
I

RAIN

It was nearly bed-time and when they awoke next morning land would be in sight. Dr. Macphail lit his pipe and, leaning over the rail, searched the heavens for the Southern Cross. After two years at the front and a wound that had taken longer to heal than it should, he was glad to settle down quietly at Apia for twelve months at least, and he felt already better for the journey. Since some of the passengers were leaving the ship next day at Pago-Pago they had had a little dance that evening and in his ears hammered still the harsh notes of the mechanical piano. But the deck was quiet at last. A little way off he saw his wife in a long chair talking with the Davidsons, and he strolled over to her. When he sat down under the light and took off his hat you saw that he had very red hair, with a bald patch on the crown, and the red, freckled skin which accompanies red hair; he was a man of forty, thin, with a pinched face, precise and rather pedantic; and he spoke with a Scots accent in a very low, quiet voice.

Between the Macphails and the Davidsons, who were missionaries, there had arisen the intimacy of shipboard, which is due to propinquity rather than to any community of taste. Their chief tie was the disapproval they shared of the men who spent their days and nights in the smoking-room playing poker or bridge and drinking. Mrs. Macphail was not a little flattered to think that she and her husband were the only people on board with whom the Davidsons were willing to associate, and even the doctor, shy but no fool, half unconsciously acknowledged

the compliment. It was only because he was of an argumentative mind that in their cabin at night he permitted himself to
carp.

"Mrs. Davidson was saying she didn't know how they'd have
got through the journey if it hadn't been for us," said Mrs.
Macphail, as she neatly brushed out her transformation. "She
said we were really the only people on the ship they cared to
know."

"I shouldn't have thought a missionary was such a big bug
that he could afford to put on frills."

"It's not frills. I quite understand what she means. It
wouldn't have been very nice for the Davidsons to have to mix
with all that rough lot in the smoking-room."

"The founder of their religion wasn't so exclusive," said
Dr. Macphail with a chuckle.

"I've asked you over and over again not to joke about
religion," answered his wife. "I shouldn't like to have a nature
like yours, Alec. You never look for the best in people."

He gave her a sidelong glance with his pale, blue eyes, but
did not reply. After many years of married life he had learned
that it was more conducive to peace to leave his wife with the
last word. He was undressed before she was, and climbing into
the upper bunk he settled down to read himself to sleep.

When he came on deck next morning they were close to land.
He looked at it with greedy eyes. There was a thin strip of
silver beach rising quickly to hills covered to the top with
luxuriant vegetation. The coconut trees, thick and green, came
nearly to the water's edge, and among them you saw the grass
houses of the Samoans; and here and there, gleaming white, a
little church. Mrs. Davidson came and stood beside him. She
was dressed in black and wore round her neck a gold chain,
from which dangled a small cross. She was a little woman, with
brown, dull hair very elaborately arranged, and she had
prominent blue eyes behind invisible *pince-nez*. Her face was
long, like a sheep's, but she gave no impression of foolishness,
rather of extreme alertness; she had the quick movements of a
bird. The most remarkable thing about her was her voice, high,
metallic, and without inflection; it fell on the ear with a hard
monotony, irritating to the nerves like the pitiless clamour of
the pneumatic drill.

"This must seem like home to you," said Dr. Macphail, with
his thin, difficult smile.

"Ours are low islands, you know, not like these. Coral. These are volcanic. We've got another ten days' journey to reach them."

"In these parts that's almost like being in the next street at home," said Dr. Macphail facetiously.

"Well, that's rather an exaggerated way of putting it, but one does look at distances differently in the South Seas. So far you're right."

Dr. Macphail sighed faintly.

"I'm glad we're not stationed here," she went on. "They say this is a terribly difficult place to work in. The steamers' touching makes the people unsettled; and then there's the naval station; that's bad for the natives. In our district we don't have difficulties like that to contend with. There are one or two traders, of course, but we take care to make them behave, and if they don't we make the place so hot for them they're glad to go."

Fixing the glasses on her nose she looked at the green island with a ruthless stare.

"It's almost a hopeless task for the missionaries here. I can never be sufficiently thankful to God that we are at least spared that."

Davidson's district consisted of a group of islands to the North of Samoa; they were widely separated and he had frequently to go long distances by canoe. At these times his wife remained at their headquarters and managed the mission. Dr. Macphail felt his heart sink when he considered the efficiency with which she certainly managed it. She spoke of the depravity of the natives in a voice which nothing could hush, but with a vehemently unctuous horror. Her sense of delicacy was singular. Early in their acquaintance she had said to him:

"You know, their marriage customs when we first settled in the islands were so shocking that I couldn't possibly describe them to you. But I'll tell Mrs. Macphail and she'll tell you."

Then he had seen his wife and Mrs. Davidson, their deck-chairs close together, in earnest conversation for about two hours. As he walked past them backwards and forwards for the sake of exercise, he had heard Mrs. Davidson's agitated whisper, like the distant flow of a mountain torrent, and he saw by his wife's open mouth and pale face that she was enjoying an alarming experience. At night in their cabin she repeated to him with bated breath all she had heard.

"Well, what did I say to you?" cried Mrs. Davidson, exult-ant, next morning. "Did you ever hear anything more dreadful? You don't wonder that I couldn't tell you myself, do you? Even though you are a doctor."

Mrs. Davidson scanned his face. She had a dramatic eager-ness to see that she had achieved the desired effect.

"Can you wonder that when we first went there our hearts sank? You'll hardly believe me when I tell you it was im-possible to find a single good girl in any of the villages."

She used the word *good* in a severely technical manner.

"Mr. Davidson and I talked it over, and we made up our minds the first thing to do was to put down the dancing. The natives were crazy about dancing."

"I was not averse to it myself when I was a young man." said Dr. Macphail.

"I guessed as much when I heard you ask Mrs. Macphail to have a turn with you last night. I don't think there's any real harm if a man dances with his wife, but I was relieved that she wouldn't. Under the circumstances I thought it better that we should keep ourselves to ourselves."

"Under what circumstances?"

Mrs. Davidson gave him a quick look through her *pince-nez,* but did not answer his question.

"But among white people it's not quite the same," she went on, "though I must say I agree with Mr. Davidson, who says he can't understand how a husband can stand by and see his wife in another man's arms, and as far as I'm concerned I've never danced a step since I married. But the native dancing is quite another matter. It's not only immoral in itself, but it dis-tinctly leads to immorality. However, I'm thankful to God that we stamped it out, and I don't think I'm wrong in saying that no one has danced in our district for eight years."

But now they came to the mouth of the harbour and Mrs. Macphail joined them. The ship turned sharply and steamed slowly in. It was a great land-locked harbour big enough to hold a fleet of battleships; and all around it rose, high and steep, the green hills. Near the entrance, getting such breeze as blew from the sea, stood the governor's house in a garden. The Stars and Stripes dangled languidly from a flagstaff. They passed two or three trim bungalows, and a tennis court, and then they came to the quay with its warehouses. Mrs. David-son pointed out the schooner, moored two or three hundred yards from the side, which was to take them to Apia. There was a crowd of eager, noisy, and good-humoured natives come from all parts of the island, some from curiosity, others to barter with the travellers on their way to Sydney; and they brought pineapples and huge bunches of bananas, *tapa* cloths, necklaces of shells or sharks' teeth, *kava*-bowls, and models of war canoes. American sailors, neat and trim, clean-shaven and frank of face, sauntered among them, and there was a little group of officials. While their luggage was being landed the Macphails and Mrs. Davidson watched the crowd. Dr. Macphail looked at the yaws from which most of the children and the young boys seemed to suffer, disfiguring sores like torpid ulcers, and his professional eyes glistened when he saw for the first time in his experience cases of elephantiasis, men going about with a huge, heavy arm or dragging along a grossly disfigured leg. Men and women wore the *lava-lava*.

"It's a very indecent costume," said Mrs. Davidson. "Mr. Davidson thinks it should be prohibited by law. How can you expect people to be moral when they wear nothing but a strip of red cotton round their loins?"

"It's suitable enough to the climate," said the doctor, wiping the sweat off his head.

Now that they were on land the heat, though it was so early in the morning, was already oppressive. Closed in by its hills, not a breath of air came in to Pago-Pago.

"In our islands," Mrs. Davidson went on in her high-pitched tones, "we've practically eradicated the *lava-lava*. A few old men still continue to wear it, but that's all. The women have all taken to the Mother Hubbard, and the men wear trousers and singlets. At the very beginning of our stay Mr. Davidson said in one of his reports: the inhabitants of these islands will never be thoroughly Christianized till every boy of more than ten years is made to wear a pair of trousers."

But Mrs. Davidson had given two or three of her birdlike glances at heavy grey clouds that came floating over the mouth of the harbour. A few drops began to fall.

"We'd better take shelter," she said.

They made their way with all the crowd to a great shed of corrugated iron, and the rain began to fall in torrents. They stood there for some time and then were joined by Mr. Davidson. He had been polite enough to the Macphails during the journey, but he had not his wife's sociability, and had spent much of his time reading. He was a silent, rather sullen man, and you felt that his affability was a duty that he imposed upon himself Christianly; he was by nature reserved and even morose. His appearance was singular. He was very tall and thin, with long limbs loosely jointed; hollow cheeks and curiously high cheek-bones; he had so cadaverous an air that it surprised you to notice how full and sensual were his lips. He wore his hair very long. His dark eyes, set deep in their sockets, were large and tragic; and his hands with their big, long fingers, were finely shaped; they gave him a look of great strength. But the most striking thing about him was the feeling he gave you of suppressed fire. It was impressive and vaguely troubling. He was not a man with whom any intimacy was possible.

He brought now unwelcome news. There was an epidemic of measles, a serious and often fatal disease among the Kanakas, on the island, and a case had developed among the crew of the schooner which was to take them on their journey. The sick man had been brought ashore and put in hospital on the quarantine station, but telegraphic instructions had been sent from Apia to say that the schooner would not be allowed to enter the harbour till it was certain no other member of the crew was affected.

"It means we shall have to stay here for ten days at least."

"But I'm urgently needed at Apia," said Dr. Macphail.

"That can't be helped. If no more cases develop on board, the schooner will be allowed to sail with white passengers, but all native traffic is prohibited for three months."

"Is there a hotel here?" asked Mrs. Macphail.

Davidson gave a low chuckle.

"There's not."

"What shall we do then?"

"I've been talking to the governor. There's a trader along the front who has rooms that he rents, and my proposition is that as soon as the rain lets up we should go along there and see what we can do. Don't expect comfort. You've just got to be thankful if we get a bed to sleep on and a roof over our heads."

But the rain showed no sign of stopping, and at length with umbrellas and waterproofs they set out. There was no town but merely a group of official buildings, a store or two, and at the back, among the coconut trees and plantains, a few native dwellings. The house they sought was about five minutes' walk from the wharf. It was a frame house of two storeys, with broad verandahs on both floors and a roof of corrugated iron. The owner was a half-caste named Horn, with a native wife surrounded by little brown children, and on the ground-floor he had a store where he sold canned goods and cottons. The rooms he showed them were almost bare of furniture. In the Macphails' there was nothing but a poor, worn bed with a ragged mosquito net, a rickety chair, and a washstand. They looked round with dismay. The rain poured down without ceasing.

"I'm not going to unpack more than we actually need," said Mrs. Macphail.

Mrs. Davidson came into the room as she was unlocking a portmanteau. She was very brisk and alert. The cheerless surroundings had no effect on her.

"If you'll take my advice you'll get a needle and cotton and start right in to mend the mosquito net," she said, "or you'll not be able to get a wink of sleep to-night."

"Will they be very bad?" asked Dr. Macphail.

"This is the season for them. When you're asked to a party at Government House at Apia you'll notice that all the ladies are given a pillow-slip to put their—their lower extremities in."

"I wish the rain would stop for a moment," said Mrs. Macphail. "I could try to make the place comfortable with more heart if the sun were shining."

"Oh, if you wait for that, you'll wait a long time. Pago-Pago is about the rainiest place in the Pacific. You see, the hills, and that bay, they attract the water, and one expects rain at this time of year anyway."

She looked from Macphail to his wife, standing helplessly in different parts of the room, like lost souls, and she pursed her lips. She saw that she must take them in hand. Feckless people like that made her impatient, but her hands itched to put everything in order which came so naturally to her.

"Here, you give me a needle and cotton and I'll mend that net of yours, while you go on with your unpacking. Dinner's at one. Dr. Macphail, you'd better go down to the wharf and see that your heavy luggage has been put in a dry place. You know what these natives are, they're quite capable of storing it where the rain will beat in on it all the time."

The doctor put on his waterproof again and went downstairs. At the door Mr. Horn was standing in conversation with the quartermaster of the ship they had just arrived in and a second-class passenger whom Dr. Macphail had seen several times on

board. The quartermaster, a little, shrivelled man, extremely
dirty, nodded to him as he passed.

"This is a bad job about the measles, doc," he said. "I see
you've fixed yourself up already."

Dr. Macphail thought he was rather familiar, but he was a
timid man and he did not take offence easily.

"Yes, we've got a room upstairs."

"Miss Thompson was sailing with you to Apia, so I've
brought her along here."

The quartermaster pointed with his thumb to the woman
standing by his side. She was twenty-seven perhaps, plump,
and in a coarse fashion pretty. She wore a white dress and a
large white hat. Her fat calves in white cotton stockings bulged
over the tops of long white boots in glacé kid. She gave Macphail an ingratiating smile.

"The feller's tryin' to soak me a dollar and a half a day
for the meanest sized room," she said in a hoarse voice.

"I tell you she's a friend of mine, Jo," said the quartermaster.
"She can't pay more than a dollar, and you've sure got to take
her for that."

The trader was fat and smooth and quietly smiling.

"Well, if you put it like that, Mr. Swan, I'll see what I can
do about it. I'll talk to Mrs. Horn and if we think we can make
a reduction we will."

"Don't try to pull that stuff with me," said Miss Thompson.
"We'll settle this right now. You get a dollar a day for the room
and not one bean more."

Dr. Macphail smiled. He admired the effrontery with which
she bargained. He was the sort of man who always paid what
he was asked. He preferred to be over-charged than to haggle.
The trader sighed.

"Well, to oblige Mr. Swan I'll take it."

"That's the goods," said Miss Thompson. "Come right in
and have a shot of hooch. I've got some real good rye in that
grip if you'll bring it along, Mr. Swan. You come along too,
doctor."

"Oh, I don't think I will, thank you," he answered. "I'm
just going down to see that our luggage is all right."

He stepped out into the rain. It swept in from the opening
of the harbour in sheets and the opposite shore was all blurred.
He passed two or three natives clad in nothing but the *lava-lava*,
with huge umbrellas over them. They walked finely, with

leisurely movements, very upright; and they smiled and greeted him in a strange tongue as they went by.

It was nearly dinner-time when he got back, and their meal was laid in the trader's parlour. It was a room designed not to live in but for purposes of prestige, and it had a musty, melancholy air. A suite of stamped plush was arranged neatly round the walls, and from the middle of the ceiling, protected from the flies by yellow tissue paper, hung a gilt chandelier. Davidson did not come.

"I know he went to call on the governor," said Mrs. Davidson, "and I guess he's kept him to dinner."

A little native girl brought them a dish of Hamburger steak, and after a while the trader came up to see that they had everything they wanted.

"I see we have a fellow lodger, Mr. Horn," said Dr. Macphail.

"She's taken a room, that's all," answered the trader. "She's getting her own board."

He looked at the two ladies with an obsequious air.

"I put her downstairs so she shouldn't be in the way. She won't be any trouble to you."

"Is it someone who was on the boat?" asked Mrs. Macphail.

"Yes, ma'am, she was in the second cabin. She was going to Apia. She has a position as cashier waiting for her."

"Oh!"

When the trader was gone Macphail said:

"I shouldn't think she'd find it exactly cheerful having her meals in her room."

"If she was in the second cabin I guess she'd rather," answered Mrs. Davidson. "I don't exactly know who it can be."

"I happened to be there when the quartermaster brought her along. Her name's Thompson."

"It's not the woman who was dancing with the quartermaster last night?" asked Mrs. Davidson.

"That's who it must be," said Mrs. Macphail. "I wondered at the time what she was. She looked rather fast to me."

"Not good style at all," said Mrs. Davidson.

They began to talk of other things, and after dinner, tired with their early rise, they separated and slept. When they awoke, though the sky was still grey and the clouds hung low, it was not raining and they went for a walk on the high road which the Americans had built along the bay.

On their return they found that Davidson had just come in.

"We may be here for a fortnight," he said irritably. "I've argued it out with the governor, but he says there is nothing to be done."

"Mr. Davidson's just longing to get back to his work," said his wife, with an anxious glance at him.

"We've been away for a year," he said, walking up and down the verandah. "The mission has been in charge of native missionaries and I'm terribly nervous that they've let things slide. They're good men, I'm not saying a word against them, God-fearing, devout, and truly Christian men—their Christianity would put many so-called Christians at home to the blush—but they're pitifully lacking in energy. They can make a stand once, they can make a stand twice, but they can't make a stand all the time. If you leave a mission in charge of a native missionary, no matter how trustworthy he seems, in course of time you'll find he's let abuses creep in."

Mr. Davidson stood still. With his tall, spare form, and his great eyes flashing out of his pale face, he was an impressive figure. His sincerity was obvious in the fire of his gestures and in his deep, ringing voice.

"I expect to have my work cut out for me. I shall act and I shall act promptly. If the tree is rotten it shall be cut down and cast into the flames."

And in the evening after the high tea which was their last meal, while they sat in the stiff parlour, the ladies working and Dr. Macphail smoking his pipe, the missionary told them of his work in the islands.

"When we went there they had no sense of sin at all," he said. "They broke the commandments one after the other and never knew they were doing wrong. And I think that was the most difficult part of my work, to instil into the natives the sense of sin."

The Macphails knew already that Davidson had worked in the Solomons for five years before he met his wife. She had been a missionary in China, and they had become acquainted in Boston, where they were both spending part of their leave to attend a missionary congress. On their marriage they had been appointed to the islands in which they had laboured ever since.

In the course of all the conversations they had had with Mr. Davidson one thing had shone out clearly and that was the man's unflinching courage. He was a medical missionary, and he was liable to be called at any time to one or other of the islands in the group. Even the whaleboat is not so very safe a conveyance in the stormy Pacific of the wet season, but often he would be sent for in a canoe, and then the danger was great. In cases of illness or accident he never hesitated. A dozen times he had spent the whole night baling for his life, and more than once Mrs. Davidson had given him up for lost.

"I'd beg him not to go sometimes," she said, "or at least to wait till the weather was more settled, but he'd never listen. He's obstinate, and when he's once made up his mind, nothing can move him."

"How can I ask the natives to put their trust in the Lord if I am afraid to do so myself?" cried Davidson. "And I'm not, I'm not. They know that if they send for me in their trouble I'll come if it's humanly possible. And do you think the Lord is going to abandon me when I am on his business? The wind blows at his bidding and the waves toss and rage at his word."

Dr. Macphail was a timid man. He had never been able to get used to the hurtling of the shells over the trenches, and when he was operating in an advanced dressing-station the sweat poured from his brow and dimmed his spectacles in the effort he made to control his unsteady hand. He shuddered a little as he looked at the missionary.

"I wish I could say that I've never been afraid," he said.

"I wish you could say that you believed in God," retorted the other.

But for some reason, that evening the missionary's thoughts travelled back to the early days he and his wife had spent on the islands.

"Sometimes Mrs. Davidson and I would look at one another and the tears would stream down our cheeks. We worked without ceasing, day and night, and we seemed to make no progress. I don't know what I should have done without her then. When I felt my heart sink, when I was very near despair, she gave me courage and hope."

Mrs. Davidson looked down at her work, and a slight colour rose to her thin cheeks. Her hands trembled a little. She did not trust herself to speak.

"We had no one to help us. We were alone, thousands of miles from any of our own people, surrounded by darkness. When I was broken and weary she would put her work aside and take the Bible and read to me till peace came and settled upon me like sleep upon the eyelids of a child, and when at last she closed the book she'd say: 'We'll save them in spite of themselves.' And I felt strong again in the Lord, and I answered: 'Yes, with God's help I'll save them. I must save them.'"

He came over to the table and stood in front of it as though it were a lectern.

"You see, they were so naturally depraved that they couldn't be brought to see their wickedness. We had to make sins out of what they thought were natural actions. We had to make it a sin, not only to commit adultery and to lie and thieve, but to expose their bodies, and to dance and not to come to church. I made it a sin for a girl to show her bosom and a sin for a man not to wear trousers."

"How?" asked Dr. Macphail, not without surprise.

"I instituted fines. Obviously the only way to make people realize that an action is sinful is to punish them if they commit it. I fined them if they didn't come to church, and I fined them if they danced. I fined them if they were improperly dressed. I had a tariff, and every sin had to be paid for either in money or work. And at last I made them understand."

"But did they never refuse to pay?"

"How could they?" asked the missionary.

"It would be a brave man who tried to stand up against Mr. Davidson," said his wife, tightening her lips.

Dr. Macphail looked at Davidson with troubled eyes. What he heard shocked him, but he hesitated to express his disapproval.

"You must remember that in the last resort I could expel them from their church membership."

"Did they mind that?"

Davidson smiled a little and gently rubbed his hands.

"They couldn't sell their copra. When the men fished they got no share of the catch. It meant something very like starvation. Yes, they minded quite a lot."

"Tell him about Fred Ohlson," said Mrs. Davidson.

The missionary fixed his fiery eyes on Dr. Macphail.

"Fred Ohlson was a Danish trader who had been in the islands a good many years. He was a pretty rich man as traders go, and he wasn't very pleased when we came. You see, he'd had things very much his own way. He paid the natives what he liked for their copra, and he paid in goods and whiskey. He had a native wife, but he was flagrantly unfaithful to her. He was a drunkard. I gave him a chance to mend his ways, but he wouldn't take it. He laughed at me."

Davidson's voice fell to a deep bass as he said the last words, and he was silent for a minute or two. The silence was heavy with menace.

"In two years he was a ruined man. He'd lost everything he'd saved in a quarter of a century. I broke him, and at last he was forced to come to me like a beggar and beseech me to give him a passage back to Sydney."

"I wish you could have seen him when he came to see Mr. Davidson," said the missionary's wife. "He had been a fine, powerful man, with a lot of fat on him, and he had a great big voice, but now he was half the size, and he was shaking all over. He'd suddenly become an old man."

With abstracted gaze Davidson looked out into the night. The rain was falling again.

Suddenly from below came a sound, and Davidson turned and looked questioningly at his wife. It was the sound of a gramophone, harsh and loud, wheezing out a syncopated tune.

"What's that?" he asked.

Mrs. Davidson fixed her *pince-nez* more firmly on her nose.

"One of the second-class passengers has a room in the house. I guess it comes from there."

They listened in silence, and presently they heard the sound of dancing. Then the music stopped, and they heard the popping of corks and voices raised in animated conversation.

"I daresay she's giving a farewell party to her friends on board," said Dr. Macphail. "The ship sails at twelve, doesn't it?"

Davidson made no remark, but he looked at his watch.

"Are you ready?" he asked his wife.

She got up and folded her work.

"Yes, I guess I am," she answered.

"It's early to go to bed yet, isn't it?" said the doctor.

"We have a good deal of reading to do," explained Mrs. Davidson. "Wherever we are, we read a chapter of the Bible before retiring for the night and we study it with the commentaries, you know, and discuss it thoroughly. It's a wonderful training for the mind."

The two couples bade one another good-night. Dr. and Mrs. Macphail were left alone. For two or three minutes they did not speak.

"I think I'll go and fetch the cards," the doctor said at last. Mrs. Macphail looked at him doubtfully. Her conversation with the Davidsons had left her a little uneasy, but she did not like to say that she thought they had better not play cards when the Davidsons might come in at any moment. Dr. Macphail brought them and she watched him, though with a vague sense of guilt, while he laid out his patience. Below the sound of revelry continued.

It was fine enough next day, and the Macphails, condemned to spend a fortnight of idleness at Pago-Pago, set about making the best of things. They went down to the quay and got out of their boxes a number of books. The doctor called on the chief surgeon of the naval hospital and went round the beds with him. They left cards on the governor. They passed Miss Thompson on the road. The doctor took off his hat, and she gave him a "Good morning, doc," in a loud, cheerful voice. She was dressed as on the day before, in a white frock, and her shiny white boots with their high heels, her fat legs bulging over the tops of them, were strange things on that exotic scene.

"I don't think she's very suitably dressed, I must say," said Mrs. Macphail. "She looks extremely common to me."

When they got back to their house, she was on the verandah playing with one of the trader's dark children.

"Say a word to her," Dr. Macphail whispered to his wife. "She's all alone here, and it seems rather unkind to ignore her."

Mrs. Macphail was shy, but she was in the habit of doing what her husband bade her.

"I think we're fellow lodgers here," she said, rather foolishly.

"Terrible, ain't it, bein' cooped up in a one-horse burg like this?" answered Miss Thompson. "And they tell me I'm lucky to have gotten a room. I don't see myself livin' in a native house, and that's what some have to do. I don't know why they don't have a hotel."

They exchanged a few more words. Miss Thompson, loud-voiced and garrulous, was evidently quite willing to gossip, but Mrs. Macphail had a poor stock of small talk and presently she said:

"Well, I think we must go upstairs."

In the evening when they sat down to their high-tea Davidson on coming in said:

"I see that woman downstairs has a couple of sailors sitting there. I wonder how she's gotten acquainted with them."

"She can't be very particular," said Mrs. Davidson.

They were all rather tired after the idle, aimless day.

"If there's going to be a fortnight of this I don't know what we shall feel like at the end of it," said Dr. Macphail.

"The only thing to do is to portion out the day to different activities," answered the missionary. "I shall set aside a certain number of hours to study and a certain number to exercise, rain or fine—in the wet season you can't afford to pay any attention to the rain—and a certain number to recreation."

Dr. Macphail looked at his companion with misgiving. Davidson's programme oppressed him. They were eating Hamburger steak again. It seemed the only dish the cook knew how to make. Then below the gramophone began. Davidson started nervously when he heard it, but said nothing. Men's voices floated up. Miss Thompson's guests were joining in a well-known song and presently they heard her voice too, hoarse and loud. There was a good deal of shouting and laughing. The four people upstairs, trying to make conversation, listened despite themselves to the clink of glasses and the scrape of chairs. More people had evidently come. Miss Thompson was giving a party.

"I wonder how she gets them all in," said Mrs. Macphail, suddenly breaking into a medical conversation between the missionary and her husband.

It showed whither her thoughts were wandering. The twitch of Davidson's face proved that, though he spoke of scientific things, his mind was busy in the same direction. Suddenly, while the doctor was giving some experience of practice on the Flanders front, rather prosily, he sprang to his feet with a cry.

"What's the matter, Alfred?" asked Mrs. Davidson.

"Of course! It never occurred to me. She's out of Iwelei."

"She can't be."

"She came on board at Honolulu. It's obvious. And she's carrying on her trade here. Here."

He uttered the last word with a passion of indignation.

"What's Iwelei?" asked Mrs. Macphail.

He turned his gloomy eyes on her and his voice trembled with horror.

"The plague spot of Honolulu. The Red Light district. It was a blot on our civilization."

Iwelei was on the edge of the city. You went down side streets

by the harbour, in the darkness, across a rickety bridge, till
you came to a deserted road, all ruts and holes, and then suddenly you came out into the light. There was parking room
for motors on each side of the road, and there were saloons,
tawdry and bright, each one noisy with its mechanical piano,
and there were barbers' shops and tobacconists. There was a
stir in the air and a sense of expectant gaiety. You turned down
a narrow alley, either to the right or to the left, for the road
divided Iwelei into two parts, and you found yourself in the
district. There were rows of little bungalows, trim and neatly
painted in green, and the pathway between them was broad,
and straight. It was laid out like a garden-city. In its respectable
regularity, its order and spruceness, it gave an impression of
sardonic horror; for never can the search for love have been so
systematized and ordered. The pathways were lit by a rare
lamp, but they would have been dark except for the lights that
came from the open windows of the bungalows. Men wandered
about, looking at the women who sat at their windows, reading
or sewing, for the most part taking no notice of the passers-by;
and like the women they were of all nationalities. There were
Americans, sailors from the ships in port, enlisted men off the
gunboats, sombrely drunk, and soldiers from the regiments,
white and black, quartered on the island; there were Japanese,
walking in twos and threes; Hawaiians, Chinese in long robes,
and Filipinos in preposterous hats. They were silent and as it
were oppressed. Desire is sad.

"It was the most crying scandal of the Pacific," exclaimed
Davidson vehemently. "The missionaries had been agitating
against it for years, and at last the local press took it up. The
police refused to stir. You know their argument. They say that
vice is inevitable and consequently the best thing is to localize
and control it. The truth is, they were paid. Paid. They were
paid by the saloon-keepers, paid by the bullies, paid by the
women themselves. At last they were forced to move."

"I read about it in the papers that came on board in Honolulu," said Dr. Macphail.

"Iwelei, with its sin and shame, ceased to exist on the very
day we arrived. The whole population was brought before the
justices. I don't know why I didn't understand at once what
that woman was."

"Now you come to speak of it," said Mrs. Macphail, "I
remember seeing her come on board only a few minutes before

the boat sailed. I remember thinking at the time she was cutting it rather fine."

"How dare she come here!" cried Davidson indignantly. "I'm not going to allow it."

He strode towards the door.

"What are you going to do?" asked Macphail.

"What do you expect me to do? I'm going to stop it. I'm not going to have this house turned into—into . . ."

He sought for a word that should not offend the ladies' ears. His eyes were flashing and his pale face was paler still in his emotion.

"It sounds as though there were three or four men down there," said the doctor. "Don't you think it's rather rash to go in just now?"

The missionary gave him a contemptuous look and without a word flung out of the room.

"You know Mr. Davidson very little if you think the fear of personal danger can stop him in the performance of his duty," said his wife.

She sat with her hands nervously clasped, a spot of colour on her high cheek bones, listening to what was about to happen below. They all listened. They heard him clatter down the wooden stairs and throw open the door. The singing stopped suddenly, but the gramophone continued to bray out its vulgar tune. They heard Davidson's voice and then the noise of something heavy falling. The music stopped. He had hurled the gramophone on the floor. Then again they heard Davidson's voice, they could not make out the words, then Miss Thompson's, loud and shrill, then a confused clamour as though several people were shouting together at the top of their lungs. Mrs. Davidson gave a little gasp, and she clenched her hands more tightly. Dr. Macphail looked uncertainly from her to his wife. He did not want to go down, but he wondered if they expected him to. Then there was something that sounded like a scuffle. The noise now was more distinct. It might be that Davidson was being thrown out of the room. The door was slammed. There was a moment's silence and they heard Davidson come up the stairs again. He went to his room.

"I think I'll go to him," said Mrs. Davidson.

She got up and went out.

"If you want me, just call," said Mrs. Macphail, and then when the other was gone: "I hope he isn't hurt."

"Why couldn't he mind his own business?" said Dr. Macphail.

They sat in silence for a minute or two and then they both
started, for the gramophone began to play once more, defiantly,
and mocking voices shouted hoarsely the words of an obscene
song.

Next day Mrs. Davidson was pale and tired. She complained
of headache, and she looked old and wizened. She told Mrs.
Macphail that the missionary had not slept at all; he had
passed the night in a state of frightful agitation and at five had
got up and gone out. A glass of beer had been thrown over him
and his clothes were stained and stinking. But a sombre fire
glowed in Mrs. Davidson's eyes when she spoke of Miss
Thompson.

"She'll bitterly rue the day when she flouted Mr. Davidson," she said. "Mr. Davidson has a wonderful heart and no
one who is in trouble has ever gone to him without being comforted, but he has no mercy for sin, and when his righteous
wrath is excited he's terrible."

"Why, what will he do?" asked Mrs. Macphail.

"I don't know, but I wouldn't stand in that creature's shoes
for anything in the world."

Mrs. Macphail shuddered. There was something positively
alarming in the triumphant assurance of the little woman's
manner. They were going out together that morning, and they
went down the stairs side by side. Miss Thompson's door was
open, and they saw her in a bedraggled dressing-gown, cooking
something in a chafing-dish.

"Good morning," she called. "Is Mr. Davidson better this
morning?"

They passed her in silence, with their noses in the air, as if
she did not exist. They flushed, however, when she burst into a
shout of derisive laughter. Mrs. Davidson turned on her suddenly.

"Don't you dare to speak to me," she screamed. "If you
insult me I shall have you turned out of here."

"Say, did I ask Mr. Davidson to visit with me?"

"Don't answer her," whispered Mrs. Macphail hurriedly.

They walked on till they were out of earshot.

"She's brazen, brazen," burst from Mrs. Davidson.

Her anger almost suffocated her.

And on their way home they met her strolling towards the

quay. She had all her finery on. Her great white hat with its vulgar, showy flowers was an affront. She called out cheerily to them as she went by, and a couple of American sailors who were standing there grinned as the ladies set their faces to an icy stare. They got in just before the rain began to fall again.

"I guess she'll get her fine clothes spoilt," said Mrs. Davidson with a bitter sneer.

Davidson did not come in till they were half way through dinner. He was wet through, but he would not change. He sat, morose and silent, refusing to eat more than a mouthful, and he stared at the slanting rain. When Mrs. Davidson told him of their two encounters with Miss Thompson he did not answer. His deepening frown alone showed that he had heard.

"Don't you think we ought to make Mr. Horn turn her out of here?" asked Mrs. Davidson. "We can't allow her to insult us."

"There doesn't seem to be any other place for her to go," said Macphail.

"She can live with one of the natives."

"In weather like this a native hut must be a rather uncomfortable place to live in."

"I lived in one for years," said the missionary.

When the little native girl brought in the fried bananas which formed the sweet they had every day, Davidson turned to her.

"Ask Miss Thompson when it would be convenient for me to see her," he said.

The girl nodded shyly and went out.

"What do you want to see her for, Alfred?" asked his wife.

"It's my duty to see her. I won't act till I've given her every chance."

"You don't know what she is. She'll insult you."

"Let her insult me. Let her spit on me. She has an immortal soul, and I must do all that is in my power to save it."

Mrs. Davidson's ears rang still with the harlot's mocking laughter.

"She's gone too far."

"Too far for the mercy of God?" His eyes lit up suddenly and his voice grew mellow and soft. "Never. The sinner may be deeper in sin than the depth of hell itself, but the love of the Lord Jesus can reach him still."

The girl came back with the message.

"Miss Thompson's compliments and as long as Rev. David-

son don't come in business hours she'll be glad to see him any
time."

The party received it in stony silence, and Dr. Macphail
quickly effaced from his lips the smile which had come upon
them. He knew his wife would be vexed with him if he found
Miss Thompson's effrontery amusing.

They finished the meal in silence. When it was over the two
ladies got up and took their work, Mrs. Macphail was making
another of the innumerable comforters which she had turned
out since the beginning of the war, and the doctor lit his pipe.
But Davidson remained in his chair and with abstracted eyes
stared at the table. At last he got up and without a word went
out of the room. They heard him go down and they heard Miss
Thompson's defiant "Come in" when he knocked at the door.
He remained with her for an hour. And Dr. Macphail watched
the rain. It was beginning to get on his nerves. It was not like
our soft English rain that drops gently on the earth; it was
unmerciful and somehow terrible; you felt in it the malignancy
of the primitive powers of nature. It did not pour, it flowed.
It was like a deluge from heaven, and it rattled on the roof of
corrugated iron with a steady persistence that was maddening.
It seemed to have a fury of its own. And sometimes you felt
that you must scream if it did not stop, and then suddenly you
felt powerless, as though your bones had suddenly become soft;
and you were miserable and hopeless.

Macphail turned his head when the missionary came back.
The two women looked up.

"I've given her every chance. I have exhorted her to repent.
She is an evil woman."

He paused, and Dr. Macphail saw his eyes darken and his
pale face grow hard and stern.

"Now I shall take the whips with which the Lord Jesus
drove the usurers and the money changers out of the Temple
of the Most High."

He walked up and down the room. His mouth was close set,
and his black brows were frowning.

"If she fled to the uttermost parts of the earth I should pursue her."

With a sudden movement he turned round and strode out of
the room. They heard him go downstairs again.

"What is he going to do?" asked Mrs. Macphail.

"I don't know." Mrs. Davidson took off her *pince-nez* and

wiped them. "When he is on the Lord's work I never ask him
questions."

She sighed a little.

"What is the matter?"

"He'll wear himself out. He doesn't know what it is to spare
himself."

Dr. Macphail learnt the first results of the missionary's
activity from the half-caste trader in whose house they lodged.
He stopped the doctor when he passed the store and came out to
speak to him on the stoop. His fat face was worried.

"The Rev. Davidson has been at me for letting Miss Thompson have a room here," he said, "but I didn't know what she
was when I rented it to her. When people come and ask if I can
rent them a room all I want to know is if they've the money to
pay for it. And she paid me for hers a week in advance."

Dr. Macphail did not want to commit himself.

"When all's said and done it's your house. We're very much
obliged to you for taking us in at all."

Horn looked at him doubtfully. He was not certain yet how
definitely Macphail stood on the missionary's side.

"The missionaries are in with one another," he said, hesitatingly. "If they get it in for a trader he may just as well shut
up his store and quit."

"Did he want you to turn her out?"

"No, he said so long as she behaved herself he couldn't ask
me to do that. He said he wanted to be just to me. I promised
she shouldn't have no more visitors. I've just been and told
her."

"How did she take it?"

"She gave me Hell."

The trader squirmed in his old ducks. He had found Miss
Thompson a rough customer.

"Oh, well, I daresay she'll get out. I don't suppose she wants
to stay here if she can't have anyone in."

"There's nowhere she can go, only a native house, and no
native'll take her now, not now that the missionaries have got
their knife in her."

Dr. Macphail looked at the falling rain.

"Well, I don't suppose it's any good waiting for it to clear
up."

In the evening when they sat in the parlour Davidson talked
to them of his early days at college. He had had no means and

had worked his way through by doing odd jobs during the vacations. There was silence downstairs. Miss Thompson was sitting in her little room alone. But suddenly the gramophone began to play. She had set it on in defiance, to cheat her loneliness, but there was no one to sing, and it had a melancholy note. It was like a cry for help. Davidson took no notice. He was in the middle of a long anecdote and without change of expression went on. The gramophone continued. Miss Thompson put on one reel after another. It looked as though the silence of the night were getting on her nerves. It was breathless and sultry. When the Macphails went to bed they could not sleep. They lay side by side with their eyes wide open, listening to the cruel singing of the mosquitoes outside their curtain.

"What's that?" whispered Mrs. Macphail at last.

They heard a voice, Davidson's voice, through the wooden partition. It went on with a monotonous, earnest insistence. He was praying aloud. He was praying for the soul of Miss Thompson.

Two or three days went by. Now when they passed Miss Thompson on the road she did not greet them with ironic cordiality or smile; she passed with her nose in the air, a sulky look on her painted face, frowning, as though she did not see them. The trader told Macphail that she had tried to get lodging elsewhere, but had failed. In the evening she played through the various reels of her gramophone, but the pretence of mirth was obvious now. The ragtime had a cracked, heartbroken rhythm as though it were a one-step of despair. When she began to play on Sunday Davidson sent Horn to beg her to stop at once since it was the Lord's day. The reel was taken off and the house was silent except for the steady pattering of the rain on the iron roof.

"I think she's getting a bit worked up," said the trader next day to Macphail. "She don't know what Mr. Davidson's up to and it makes her scared."

Macphail had caught a glimpse of her that morning and it struck him that her arrogant expression had changed. There was in her face a hunted look. The half-caste gave him a sidelong glance.

"I suppose you don't know what Mr. Davidson is doing about it?" he hazarded.

"No, I don't."

It was singular that Horn should ask him that question, for he also had the idea that the missionary was mysteriously at work. He had an impression that he was weaving a net around the woman, carefully, systematically, and suddenly, when everything was ready, would pull the strings tight.

"He told me to tell her," said the trader, "that if at any time she wanted him she only had to send and he'd come."

"What did she say when you told her that?"

"She didn't say nothing. I didn't stop. I just said what he said I was to and then I beat it. I thought she might be going to start weepin'."

"I have no doubt the loneliness is getting on her nerves," said the doctor. "And the rain—that's enough to make anyone jumpy," he continued irritably. "Doesn't it ever stop in this confounded place?"

"It goes on pretty steady in the rainy season. We have three hundred inches in the year. You see, it's the shape of the bay. It seems to attract the rain from all over the Pacific."

"Damn the shape of the bay," said the doctor.

He scratched his mosquito bites. He felt very short-tempered. When the rain stopped and the sun shone, it was like a hothouse, seething, humid, sultry, breathless, and you had a strange feeling that everything was growing with a savage violence. The natives, blithe and childlike by reputation, seemed then, with their tattooing and their dyed hair, to have something sinister in their appearance; and when they pattered along at your heels with their naked feet you looked back instinctively. You felt they might at any moment come behind you swiftly and thrust a long knife between your shoulder blades. You could not tell what dark thoughts lurked behind their wide-set eyes. They had a little the look of ancient Egyptians painted on a temple wall, and there was about them the terror of what is immeasurably old.

The missionary came and went. He was busy, but the Macphails did not know what he was doing. Horn told the doctor that he saw the governor every day, and once Davidson mentioned him.

"He looks as if he had plenty of determination," he said, "but when you come down to brass tacks he has no backbone."

"I suppose that means he won't do exactly what you want," suggested the doctor facetiously.

The missionary did not smile.

"I want him to do what's right. It shouldn't be necessary to persuade a man to do that."

"But there may be differences of opinion about what is right."

"If a man had a gangrenous foot would you have patience with anyone who hesitated to amputate it?"

"Gangrene is a matter of fact."

"And Evil?"

What Davidson had done soon appeared. The four of them had just finished their midday meal, and they had not yet separated for the siesta which the heat imposed on the ladies and on the doctor. Davidson had little patience with the slothful habit. The door was suddenly flung open and Miss Thompson came in. She looked round the room and then went up to Davidson.

"You low-down skunk, what have you been saying about me to the governor?"

She was spluttering with rage. There was a moment's pause. Then the missionary drew forward a chair.

"Won't you be seated, Miss Thompson? I've been hoping to have another talk with you."

"You poor low-life bastard."

She burst into a torrent of insult, foul and insolent. Davidson kept his grave eyes on her.

"I'm indifferent to the abuse you think fit to heap on me, Miss Thompson," he said, "but I must beg you to remember that ladies are present."

Tears by now were struggling with her anger. Her face was red and swollen as though she were choking.

"What has happened?" asked Dr. Macphail.

"A feller's just been in here and he says I gotter beat it on the next boat."

Was there a gleam in the missionary's eyes? His face remained impassive.

"You could hardly expect the governor to let you stay here under the circumstances."

"You done it," she shrieked. "You can't kid me. You done it."

"I don't want to deceive you. I urged the governor to take the only possible step consistent with his obligations."

"Why couldn't you leave me be? I wasn't doin' you no harm."

"You may be sure that if you had I should be the last man to resent it."

"Do you think I want to stay on in this poor imitation of a burg? I don't look no busher, do I?"

"In that case I don't see what cause of complaint you have," he answered.

She gave an inarticulate cry of rage and flung out of the room. There was a short silence.

"It's a relief to know that the governor has acted at last," said Davidson finally. "He's a weak man and he shilly-shallied. He said she was only here for a fortnight anyway, and if she went on to Apia that was under British jurisdiction and had nothing to do with him."

The missionary sprang to his feet and strode across the room.

"It's terrible the way the men who are in authority seek to evade their responsibility. They speak as though evil that was out of sight ceased to be evil. The very existence of that woman is a scandal and it does not help matters to shift it to another of the islands. In the end I had to speak straight from the shoulder."

Davidson's brow lowered, and he protruded his firm chin. He looked fierce and determined.

"What do you mean by that?"

"Our mission is not entirely without influence at Washington. I pointed out to the governor that it wouldn't do him any good if there was a complaint about the way he managed things here."

"When has she got to go?" asked the doctor, after a pause.

"The San Francisco boat is due here from Sydney next Tuesday. She's to sail on that."

That was in five days' time. It was next day, when he was coming back from the hospital where for want of something better to do Macphail spent most of his mornings, that the half-caste stopped him as he was going upstairs.

"Excuse me, Dr. Macphail, Miss Thompson's sick. Will you have a look at her?"

"Certainly."

Horn led him to her room. She was sitting in a chair idly, neither reading nor sewing, staring in front of her. She wore her white dress and the large hat with the flowers on it. Macphail noticed that her skin was yellow and muddy under her powder, and her eyes were heavy.

"I'm sorry to hear you're not well," he said.

"Oh, I ain't sick really. I just said that, because I just had to see you. I've got to clear on a boat that's going to 'Frisco."

She looked at him and he saw that her eyes were suddenly startled. She opened and clenched her hands spasmodically. The trader stood at the door, listening.

"So I understand," said the doctor.

She gave a little gulp.

"I guess it ain't very convenient for me to go to 'Frisco just now. I went to see the governor yesterday afternoon, but I couldn't get to him. I saw the secretary, and he told me I'd got to take that boat and that was all there was to it. I just had to see the governor, so I waited outside his house this morning, and when he come out I spoke to him. He didn't want to speak to me, I'll say, but I wouldn't let him shake me off, and at last he said he hadn't no objection to my staying here till the next boat to Sydney if the Rev. Davidson will stand for it."

She stopped and looked at Dr. Macphail anxiously.

"I don't know exactly what I can do," he said.

"Well, I thought maybe you wouldn't mind asking him. I swear to God I won't start anything here if he'll just only let me stay. I won't go out of the house if that'll suit him. It's no more'n a fortnight."

"I'll ask him."

"He won't stand for it," said Horn. "He'll have you out on Tuesday, so you may as well make up your mind to it."

"Tell him I can get work in Sydney, straight stuff, I mean. 'Tain't asking very much."

"I'll do what I can."

"And come and tell me right away, will you? I can't set down to a thing till I get the dope one way or the other."

It was not an errand that much pleased the doctor, and, characteristically perhaps, he went about it indirectly. He told his wife what Miss Thompson had said to him and asked her to speak to Mrs. Davidson. The missionary's attitude seemed rather arbitrary and it could do no harm if the girl were allowed to stay in Pago-Pago another fortnight. But he was not prepared for the result of his diplomacy. The missionary came to him straightway.

"Mrs. Davidson tells me that Thompson has been speaking to you."

Dr. Macphail thus directly tackled, had the shy man's

resentment at being forced out into the open. He felt his temper rising, and he flushed.

"I don't see that it can make any difference if she goes to Sydney rather than to San Francisco, and so long as she promises to behave while she's here it's dashed hard to persecute her."

The missionary fixed him with his stern eyes.

"Why is she unwilling to go back to San Francisco?"

"I didn't enquire," answered the doctor with some asperity. "And I think one does better to mind one's own business."

Perhaps it was not a very tactful answer.

"The governor has ordered her to be deported by the first boat that leaves the island. He's only done his duty and I will not interfere. Her presence is a peril here."

"I think you're very harsh and tyrannical."

The two ladies looked up at the doctor with some alarm, but they need not have feared a quarrel, for the missionary smiled gently.

"I'm terribly sorry you should think that of me, Dr. Macphail. Believe me, my heart bleeds for that unfortunate woman, but I'm only trying to do my duty."

The doctor made no answer. He looked out of the window sullenly. For once it was not raining and across the bay you saw nestling among the trees the huts of a native village.

"I think I'll take advantage of the rain stopping to go out," he said.

"Please don't bear me malice because I can't accede to your wish," said Davidson, with a melancholy smile. "I respect you very much, doctor, and I should be sorry if you thought ill of me."

"I have no doubt you have a sufficiently good opinion of yourself to bear mine with equanimity," he retorted.

"That's one on me," chuckled Davidson.

When Dr. Macphail, vexed with himself because he had been uncivil to no purpose, went downstairs, Miss Thompson was waiting for him with her door ajar.

"Well," she said, "have you spoken to him?"

"Yes, I'm sorry, he won't do anything," he answered, not looking at her in his embarrassment.

But then he gave her a quick glance, for a sob broke from her. He saw that her face was white with fear. It gave him a shock of dismay. And suddenly he had an idea.

"But don't give up hope yet. I think it's a shame the way they're treating you and I'm going to see the governor myself."

"Now?"

He nodded. Her face brightened.

"Say, that's real good of you. I'm sure he'll let me stay if you speak for me. I just won't do a thing I didn't ought all the time I'm here."

Dr. Macphail hardly knew why he had made up his mind to appeal to the governor. He was perfectly indifferent to Miss Thompson's affairs, but the missionary had irritated him, and with him temper was a smouldering thing. He found the governor at home. He was a large, handsome man, a sailor, with a grey toothbrush moustache; and he wore a spotless uniform of white drill.

"I've come to see you about a woman who's lodging in the same house as we are," he said. "Her name's Thompson."

"I guess I've heard nearly enough about her, Dr. Macphail," said the governor, smiling. "I've given her the order to get out next Tuesday and that's all I can do."

"I wanted to ask you if you couldn't stretch a point and let her stay here till the boat comes in from San Francisco so that she can go to Sydney. I will guarantee her good behaviour."

The governor continued to smile, but his eyes grew small and serious.

"I'd be very glad to oblige you, Dr. Macphail, but I've given the order and it must stand."

The doctor put the case as reasonably as he could, but now the governor ceased to smile at all. He listened sullenly, with averted gaze. Macphail saw that he was making no impression.

"I'm sorry to cause any lady inconvenience, but she'll have to sail on Tuesday and that's all there is to it."

"But what difference can it make?"

"Pardon me, doctor, but I don't feel called upon to explain my official actions except to the proper authorities."

Macphail looked at him shrewdly. He remembered Davidson's hint that he had used threats, and in the governor's attitude he read a singular embarrassment.

"Davidson's a damned busybody," he said hotly.

"Between ourselves, Dr. Macphail, I don't say that I have formed a very favourable opinion of Mr. Davidson, but I am bound to confess that he was within his rights in pointing out to me the danger that the presence of a woman of Miss Thomp-

son's character was to a place like this where a number of enlisted men are stationed among a native population."

He got up and Dr. Macphail was obliged to do so too.

"I must ask you to excuse me. I have an engagement. Please
give my respects to Mrs. Macphail."

The doctor left him crest-fallen. He knew that Miss Thompson would be waiting for him, and unwilling to tell her himself
that he had failed, he went into the house by the back door and
sneaked up the stairs as though he had something to hide.

At supper he was silent and ill-at-ease, but the missionary
was jovial and animated. Dr. Macphail thought his eyes rested
on him now and then with triumphant good-humour. It struck
him suddenly that Davidson knew of his visit to the governor
and of its ill success. But how on earth could he have heard of
it? There was something sinister about the power of that man.
After supper he saw Horn on the verandah and, as though to
have a casual word with him, went out.

"She wants to know if you've seen the governor," the trader
whispered.

"Yes. He wouldn't do anything. I'm awfully sorry, I can't
do anything more."

"I knew he wouldn't. They daren't go against the missionaries."

"What are you talking about?" said Davidson affably, coming out to join them.

"I was just saying there was no chance of your getting over
to Apia for at least another week," said the trader glibly.

He left them, and the two men returned into the parlour.
Mr. Davidson devoted one hour after each meal to recreation.
Presently a timid knock was heard at the door.

"Come in," said Mrs. Davidson, in her sharp voice.

The door was not opened. She got up and opened it. They
saw Miss Thompson standing at the threshold. But the change
in her appearance was extraordinary. This was no longer the
flaunting hussy who had jeered at them in the road, but a
broken, frightened woman. Her hair, as a rule so elaborately
arranged, was tumbling untidily over her neck. She wore bedroom slippers and a skirt and blouse. They were unfresh and
bedraggled. She stood at the door with the tears streaming down
her face and did not dare to enter.

"What do you want?" said Mrs. Davidson harshly.

"May I speak to Mr. Davidson?" she said in a choking voice.

The missionary rose and went towards her.

"Come right in, Miss Thompson," he said in cordial tones. "What can I do for you?"

She entered the room.

"Say, I'm sorry for what I said to you the other day an' for— for everythin' else. I guess I was a bit lit up. I beg pardon."

"Oh, it was nothing. I guess my back's broad enough to bear a few hard words."

She stepped towards him with a movement that was horribly cringing.

"You've got me beat. I'm all in. You won't make me go back to 'Frisco?"

His genial manner vanished and his voice grew on a sudden hard and stern.

"Why don't you want to go back there?"

She cowered before him.

"I guess my people live there. I don't want them to see me like this. I'll go anywhere else you say."

"Why don't you want to go back to San Francisco?"

"I've told you."

He leaned forward, staring at her, and his great, shining eyes seemed to try to bore into her soul. He gave a sudden gasp.

"The penitentiary."

She screamed, and then she fell at his feet, clasping his legs.

"Don't send me back there. I swear to you before God I'll be a good woman. I'll give all this up."

She burst into a torrent of confused supplication and the tears coursed down her painted cheeks. He leaned over her and, lifting her face, forced her to look at him.

"Is that it, the penitentiary?"

"I beat it before they could get me," she gasped. "If the bulls grab me it's three years for mine."

He let go his hold of her and she fell in a heap on the floor, sobbing bitterly. Dr. Macphail stood up.

"This alters the whole thing," he said. "You can't make her go back when you know this. Give her another chance. She wants to turn over a new leaf."

"I'm going to give her the finest chance she's ever had. If she repents let her accept her punishment."

She misunderstood the words and looked up. There was a gleam of hope in her heavy eyes.

"You'll let me go?"

"No. You shall sail for San Francisco on Tuesday."

She gave a groan of horror and then burst into low, hoarse shrieks which sounded hardly human, and she beat her head passionately on the ground. Dr. Macphail sprang to her and lifted her up.

"Come on, you mustn't do that. You'd better go to your room and lie down. I'll get you something."

He raised her to her feet and partly dragging her, partly carrying her, got her downstairs. He was furious with Mrs. Davidson and with his wife because they made no effort to help. The half-caste was standing on the landing and with his assistance he managed to get her on the bed. She was moaning and crying. She was almost insensible. He gave her a hypodermic injection. He was hot and exhausted when he went upstairs again.

"I've got her to lie down."

The two women and Davidson were in the same positions as when he had left them. They could not have moved or spoken since he went.

"I was waiting for you," said Davidson, in a strange, distant voice. "I want you all to pray with me for the soul of our erring sister."

He took the Bible off a shelf, and sat down at the table at which they had supped. It had not been cleared, and he pushed the tea-pot out of the way. In a powerful voice, resonant and deep, he read to them the chapter in which is narrated the meeting of Jesus Christ with the woman taken in adultery.

"Now kneel with me and let us pray for the soul of our dear sister, Sadie Thompson."

He burst into a long, passionate prayer in which he implored God to have mercy on the sinful woman. Mrs. Macphail and Mrs. Davidson knelt with covered eyes. The doctor, taken by surprise, awkward and sheepish, knelt too. The missionary's prayer had a savage eloquence. He was extraordinarily moved, and as he spoke the tears ran down his cheeks. Outside, the pitiless rain fell, fell steadily, with a fierce malignity that was all too human.

At last he stopped. He paused for a moment and said:

"We will now repeat the Lord's prayer."

They said it and then, following him, they rose from their

knees. Mrs. Davidson's face was pale and restful. She was comforted and at peace, but the Macphails felt suddenly bashful. They did not know which way to look.

"I'll just go down and see how she is now," said Dr. Macphail.

When he knocked at her door it was opened for him by Horn. Miss Thompson was in a rocking-chair, sobbing quietly.

"What are you doing there?" exclaimed Macphail. "I told you to lie down."

"I can't lie down. I want to see Mr. Davidson."

"My poor child, what do you think is the good of it? You'll never move him."

"He said he'd come if I sent for him."

Macphail motioned to the trader.

"Go and fetch him."

He waited with her in silence while the trader went upstairs. Davidson came in.

"Excuse me for asking you to come here," she said, looking at him sombrely.

"I was expecting you to send for me. I knew the Lord would answer my prayer."

They stared at one another for a moment and then she looked away. She kept her eyes averted when she spoke.

"I've been a bad woman. I want to repent."

"Thank God! thank God! He has heard our prayers."

He turned to the two men.

"Leave me alone with her. Tell Mrs. Davidson that our prayers have been answered."

They went out and closed the door behind them.

"Gee whizz," said the trader.

That night Dr. Macphail could not get to sleep till late, and when he heard the missionary come upstairs he looked at his watch. It was two o'clock. But even then he did not go to bed at once, for through the wooden partition that separated their rooms he heard him praying aloud, till he himself, exhausted, fell asleep.

When he saw him next morning he was surprised at his appearance. He was paler than ever, tired, but his eyes shone with an inhuman fire. It looked as though he were filled with an overwhelming joy.

"I want you to go down presently and see Sadie," he said.

"I can't hope that her body is better, but her soul—her soul is transformed."

The doctor was feeling wan and nervous.

"You were with her very late last night," he said.

"Yes, she couldn't bear to have me leave her."

"You look as pleased as Punch," the doctor said irritably.

Davidson's eyes shone with ecstasy.

"A great mercy has been vouchsafed me. Last night I was privileged to bring a lost soul to the loving arms of Jesus."

Miss Thompson was again in the rocking-chair. The bed had not been made. The room was in disorder. She had not troubled to dress herself, but wore a dirty dressing-gown, and her hair was tied in a sluttish knot. She had given her face a dab with a wet towel, but it was all swollen and creased with crying. She looked a drab.

She raised her eyes dully when the doctor came in. She was cowed and broken.

"Where's Mr. Davidson?" she asked.

"He'll come presently if you want him," answered Macphail acidly. "I came here to see how you were."

"Oh, I guess I'm O. K. You needn't worry about that."

"Have you had anything to eat?"

"Horn brought me some coffee."

She looked anxiously at the door.

"D'you think he'll come down soon? I feel as if it wasn't so terrible when he's with me."

"Are you still going on Tuesday?"

"Yes, he says I've got to go. Please tell him to come right along. You can't do me any good. He's the only one as can help me now."

"Very well," said Dr. Macphail.

During the next three days the missionary spent almost all his time with Sadie Thompson. He joined the others only to have his meals. Dr. Macphail noticed that he hardly ate.

"He's wearing himself out," said Mrs. Davidson pitifully. "He'll have a breakdown if he doesn't take care, but he won't spare himself."

She herself was white and pale. She told Mrs. Macphail that she had had no sleep. When the missionary came upstairs from Miss Thompson he prayed till he was exhausted, but even then he did not sleep for long. After an hour or two he got up and dressed himself, and went for a tramp along the bay. He had strange dreams.

"This morning he told me that he'd been dreaming about the mountains of Nebraska," said Mrs. Davidson.

"That's curious," said Dr. Macphail.

He remembered seeing them from the windows of the train when he crossed America. They were like huge mole-hills, rounded and smooth, and they rose from the plain abruptly. Dr. Macphail remembered how it struck him that they were like a woman's breasts.

Davidson's restlessness was intolerable even to himself. But he was buoyed up by a wonderful exhilaration. He was tearing out by the roots the last vestiges of sin that lurked in the hidden corners of that poor woman's heart. He read with her and prayed with her.

"It's wonderful," he said to them one day at supper. "It's a true rebirth. Her soul, which was black as night, is now pure and white like the new-fallen snow. I am humble and afraid. Her remorse for all her sins is beautiful. I am not worthy to touch the hem of her garment."

"Have you the heart to send her back to San Francisco?" said the doctor. "Three years in an American prison. I should have thought you might have saved her from that."

"Ah, but don't you see? It's necessary. Do you think my heart doesn't bleed for her? I love her as I love my wife and my sister. All the time that she is in prison I shall suffer all the pain that she suffers."

"Bunkum," cried the doctor impatiently.

"You don't understand because you're blind. She's sinned, and she must suffer. I know what she'll endure. She'll be starved and tortured and humiliated. I want her to accept the punishment of man as a sacrifice to God. I want her to accept it joyfully. She has an opportunity which is offered to very few of us. God is very good and very merciful."

Davidson's voice trembled with excitement. He could hardly articulate the words that tumbled passionately from his lips.

"All day I pray with her and when I leave her I pray again. I pray with all my might and main, so that Jesus may grant her this great mercy. I want to put in her heart the passionate desire to be punished so that at the end, even if I offered to let her go, she would refuse. I want her to feel that the bitter

had to go back - revenge

punishment of prison is the thank-offering that she places at the
feet of our Blessed Lord, who gave his life for her."

The days passed slowly. The whole household, intent on the
wretched, tortured woman downstairs, lived in a state of unnatural excitement. She was like a victim that was being prepared for the savage rites of a bloody idolatry. Her terror
numbed her. She could not bear to let Davidson out of her
sight; it was only when he was with her that she had courage,
and she hung upon him with a slavish dependence. She cried a
great deal, and she read the Bible, and prayed. Sometimes she
was exhausted and apathetic. Then she did indeed look forward
to her ordeal, for it seemed to offer an escape, direct and concrete, from the anguish she was enduring. She could not bear
much longer the vague terrors which now assailed her. With her
sins she had put aside all personal vanity, and she slopped about
her room, unkempt and dishevelled, in her tawdry dressing-
gown. She had not taken off her night-dress for four days, nor
put on stockings. Her room was littered and untidy. Meanwhile the rain fell with a cruel persistence. You felt that the
heavens must at last be empty of water, but still it poured
down, straight and heavy, with a maddening iteration, on the
iron roof. Everything was damp and clammy. There was mil-
dew on the walls and on the boots that stood on the floor.
Through the sleepless nights the mosquitoes droned their angry
chant.

"If it would only stop raining for a single day it wouldn't be
so bad," said Dr. Macphail.

They all looked forward to the Tuesday when the boat for
San Francisco was to arrive from Sydney. The strain was intolerable. So far as Dr. Macphail was concerned, his pity and
his resentment were alike extinguished by his desire to be rid
of the unfortunate woman. The inevitable must be accepted.
He felt he would breathe more freely when the ship had sailed.
Sadie Thompson was to be escorted on board by a clerk in the
governor's office. This person called on the Monday evening
and told Miss Thompson to be prepared at eleven in the morning. Davidson was with her.

"I'll see that everything is ready. I mean to come on board
with her myself."

Miss Thompson did not speak.

When Dr. Macphail blew out his candle and crawled cautiously under his mosquito curtains, he gave a sigh of relief.

"Well, thank God that's over. By this time tomorrow she'll be gone."

"Mrs. Davidson will be glad too. She says he's wearing himself to a shadow," said Mrs. Macphail. "She's a different woman."

"Who?"

"Sadie. I should never have thought it possible. It makes one humble."

Dr. Macphail did not answer, and presently he fell asleep. He was tired out, and he slept more soundly than usual.

He was awakened in the morning by a hand placed on his arm, and, starting up, saw Horn by the side of his bed. The trader put his finger on his mouth to prevent any exclamation from Dr. Macphail and beckoned to him to come. As a rule he wore shabby ducks, but now he was barefoot and wore only the *lava-lava* of the natives. He looked suddenly savage, and Dr. Macphail, getting out of bed, saw that he was heavily tattooed. Horn made him a sign to come on to the verandah. Dr. Macphail got out of bed and followed the trader out.

"Don't make a noise," he whispered. "You're wanted. Put on a coat and some shoes. Quick."

Dr. Macphail's first thought was that something had happened to Miss Thompson.

"What is it? Shall I bring my instruments?"

"Hurry, please, hurry."

Dr. Macphail crept back into the bedroom, put on a waterproof over his pyjamas, and a pair of rubber-soled shoes. He rejoined the trader, and together they tiptoed down the stairs. The door leading out to the road was open and at it were standing half a dozen natives.

"What is it?" repeated the doctor.

"Come along with me," said Horn.

He walked out and the doctor followed him. The natives came after them in a little bunch. They crossed the road and came on to the beach. The doctor saw a group of natives standing round some object at the water's edge. They hurried along, a couple of dozen yards perhaps, and the natives opened out as the doctor came up. The trader pushed him forwards. Then he saw, lying half in the water and half out, a dreadful object, the body of Davidson. Dr. Macphail bent down—he was not a man to lose his head in an emergency—and turned the body over.

The throat was cut from ear to ear, and in the right hand was still the razor with which the deed was done.

"He's quite cold," said the doctor. "He must have been dead some time."

"One of the boys saw him lying there on his way to work just now and came and told me. Do you think he did it himself?"

"Yes. Someone ought to go for the police."

Horn said something in the native tongue, and two youths started off.

"We must leave him here till they come," said the doctor.

"They mustn't take him into my house. I won't have him in my house."

"You'll do what the authorities say," replied the doctor sharply. "In point of fact I expect they'll take him to the mortuary."

They stood waiting where they were. The trader took a cigarette from a fold in his *lava-lava* and gave one to Dr. Macphail. They smoked while they stared at the corpse. Dr. Macphail could not understand.

"Why do you think he did it?" asked Horn.

The doctor shrugged his shoulders. In a little while native police came along, under the charge of a marine, with a stretcher, and immediately afterwards a couple of naval officers and a naval doctor. They managed everything in a businesslike manner.

"What about the wife?" said one of the officers.

"Now that you've come I'll go back to the house and get some things on. I'll see that it's broken to her. She'd better not see him till he's been fixed up a little."

"I guess that's right," said the naval doctor.

When Dr. Macphail went back he found his wife nearly dressed.

"Mrs. Davidson's in a dreadful state about her husband," she said to him as soon as he appeared. "He hasn't been to bed all night. She heard him leave Miss Thompson's room at two, but he went out. If he's been walking about since then he'll be absolutely dead."

Dr. Macphail told her what had happened and asked her to break the news to Mrs. Davidson.

"But why did he do it?" she asked, horror-stricken.

"I don't know."

"But I can't. I can't."

"You must."

She gave him a frightened look and went out. He heard her go into Mrs. Davidson's room. He waited a minute to gather himself together and then began to shave and wash. When he was dressed he sat down on the bed and waited for his wife. At last she came.

"She wants to see him," she said.

"They've taken him to the mortuary. We'd better go down with her. How did she take it?"

"I think she's stunned. She didn't cry. But she's trembling like a leaf."

"We'd better go at once."

When they knocked at her door Mrs. Davidson came out. She was very pale, but dry-eyed. To the doctor she seemed unnaturally composed. No word was exchanged, and they set out in silence down the road. When they arrived at the mortuary Mrs. Davidson spoke.

"Let me go in and see him alone."

They stood aside. A native opened a door for her and closed it behind her. They sat down and waited. One or two white men came and talked to them in undertones. Dr. Macphail told them again what he knew of the tragedy. At last the door was quietly opened and Mrs. Davidson came out. Silence fell upon them.

"I'm ready to go back now," she said.

Her voice was hard and steady. Dr. Macphail could not understand the look in her eyes. Her pale face was very stern. They walked back slowly, never saying a word, and at last they came round the bend on the other side of which stood their house. Mrs. Davidson gave a gasp, and for a moment they stopped still. An incredible sound assaulted their ears. The gramophone which had been silent for so long was playing, playing ragtime loud and harsh.

"What's that?" cried Mrs. Macphail with horror.

"Let's go on," said Mrs. Davidson.

They walked up the steps and entered the hall. Miss Thompson was standing at her door, chatting with a sailor. A sudden change had taken place in her. She was no longer the cowed drudge of the last days. She was dressed in all her finery, in her white dress, with the high shiny boots over which her fat legs bulged in their cotton stockings; her hair was elaborately arranged; and she wore that enormous hat covered with gaudy flowers. Her face was painted, her eyebrows were boldly black, and her lips were scarlet. She held herself erect. She was the flaunting quean that they had known at first. As they came in she broke into a loud, jeering laugh; and then, when Mrs. Davidson involuntarily stopped, she collected the spittle in her mouth and spat. Mrs. Davidson cowered back, and two red spots rose suddenly to her cheeks. Then, covering her face with her hands, she broke away and ran quickly up the stairs. Dr. Macphail was outraged. He pushed past the woman into her room.

"What the devil are you doing?" he cried. "Stop that damned machine."

He went up to it and tore the record off. She turned on him.

"Say, doc, you can that stuff with me. What the hell are you doin' in my room?"

"What do you mean?" he cried. "What d'you mean?"

She gathered herself together. No one could describe the scorn of her expression or the contemptuous hatred she put into her answer.

"You men! You filthy, dirty pigs! You're all the same, all of you. Pigs! Pigs!"

Dr. Macphail gasped. He understood.

THE FALL OF EDWARD BARNARD

BATEMAN HUNTER slept badly. For a fortnight on the boat that brought him from Tahiti to San Francisco he had been thinking of the story he had to tell, and for three days on the train he had repeated to himself the words in which he meant to tell it. But in a few hours now he would be in Chicago, and doubts assailed him. His conscience, always very sensitive, was not at ease. He was uncertain that he had done all that was possible, it was on his honour to do much more than the possible, and the thought was disturbing that, in a matter which so nearly touched his own interest, he had allowed his interest to prevail over his quixotry. Self-sacrifice appealed so keenly to his imagination that the inability to exercise it gave him a sense of disillusion. He was like the philanthropist who with altruistic motives builds model dwellings for the poor and finds that he has made a lucrative investment. He cannot prevent the satisfaction he feels in the ten per cent which rewards the bread he had cast upon the waters, but he has an awkward feeling that it detracts somewhat from the savour of his virtue. Bateman Hunter knew that his heart was pure, but he was not quite sure how steadfastly, when he told her his story, he would endure the scrutiny of Isabel Longstaffe's cool grey eyes. They were far-seeing and wise. She measured the standards of others by her own meticulous uprightness and there could be no greater censure than the cold silence with which she expressed her disapproval of a conduct that did not satisfy her exacting code. There was no appeal from her judgment, for, having made up her mind, she never changed it. But Bateman would not have had her different. He loved not only the beauty of her person, slim and straight, with the proud carriage of her head, but still more the beauty of her soul. With her truthfulness, her rigid sense of honour, her fearless outlook, she seemed to him to collect in herself all that was most admirable in his country-women. But he saw in her something more than the perfect type of the American girl, he felt that her exquisiteness was peculiar in a way to her environment, and he was assured that no city in the world could have produced her but Chicago. A pang seized him when he remembered that he must deal so bitter a blow to her pride, and anger flamed up in his heart when he thought of Edward Barnard.

But at last the train steamed in to Chicago and he exulted when he saw the long streets of grey houses. He could hardly bear his impatience at the thought of State and Wabash with their crowded pavements, their hustling traffic, and their noise. He was at home. And he was glad that he had been born in the most important city in the United States. San Francisco was provincial, New York was effete; the future of America lay in the development of its economic possibilities, and Chicago, by its position and by the energy of its citizens, was destined to become the real capital of the country.

"I guess I shall live long enough to see it the biggest city in the world," Bateman said to himself as he stepped down to the platform.

His father had come to meet him, and after a hearty hand-shake, the pair of them, tall, slender, and well-made, with the same fine, ascetic features and thin lips, walked out of the station. Mr. Hunter's automobile was waiting for them and they got in. Mr. Hunter caught his son's proud and happy glance as he looked at the street.

"Glad to be back, son?" he asked.

"I should just think I was," said Bateman.

His eyes devoured the restless scene.

"I guess there's a bit more traffic here than in your South Sea island," laughed Mr. Hunter. "Did you like it there?"

"Give me Chicago, dad," answered Bateman.

"You haven't brought Edward Barnard back with you."

"No."

"How was he?"

Bateman was silent for a moment, and his handsome, sensitive face darkened.

"I'd sooner not speak about him, dad," he said at last.

"That's all right, my son. I guess your mother will be a happy woman to-day."

They passed out of the crowded streets in the Loop and drove along the lake till they came to the imposing house, an exact copy of a château on the Loire, which Mr. Hunter had built himself some years before. As soon as Bateman was alone in his room he asked for a number on the telephone. His heart leaped when he heard the voice that answered him.

"Good-morning, Isabel," he said gaily.

"Good-morning, Bateman."

"How did you recognize my voice?"

"It is not so long since I heard it last. Besides, I was expecting you."

"When may I see you?"

"Unless you have anything better to do perhaps you'll dine with us to-night."

"You know very well that I couldn't possibly have anything better to do."

"I suppose that you're full of news?"

He thought he detected in her voice a note of apprehension.

"Yes," he answered.

"Well, you must tell me to-night. Good-bye."

She rang off. It was characteristic of her that she should be able to wait so many unnecessary hours to know what so immensely concerned her. To Bateman there was an admirable fortitude in her restraint.

At dinner, at which beside himself and Isabel no one was present but her father and mother, he watched her guide the conversation into the channels of an urbane small-talk, and it occurred to him that in just such a manner would a marquise under the shadow of the guillotine toy with the affairs of a day that would know no morrow. Her delicate features, the aristocratic shortness of her upper lip, and her wealth of fair hair suggested the marquise again, and it must have been obvious, even if it were not notorious, that in her veins flowed the best blood in Chicago. The dining-room was a fitting frame to her fragile beauty, for Isabel had caused the house, a replica of a palace on the Grand Canal at Venice, to be furnished by an English expert in the style of Louis XV; and the graceful decoration linked with the name of that amorous monarch enhanced her loveliness and at the same time acquired from it a more profound significance. For Isabel's mind was richly stored, and her conversation, however light, was never flippant. She spoke now of the *Musicale* to which she and her mother had been in the afternoon, of the lectures which an English poet was giving at the Auditorium, of the political situation, and of the Old Master which her father had recently bought for fifty thousand dollars in New York. It comforted Bateman to hear her. He felt that he was once more in the civilized world, at the centre of culture and distinction; and certain voices, troubling and yet against his will refusing to still their clamour, were at last silent in his heart.

"Gee, but it's good to be back in Chicago," he said.

At last dinner was over, and when they went out of the dining-room Isabel said to her mother:

"I'm going to take Bateman along to my den. We have various things to talk about."

"Very well, my dear," said Mrs. Longstaffe. "You'll find your father and me in the Madame du Barry room when you're through."

Isabel led the young man upstairs and showed him into the room of which he had so many charming memories. Though he knew it so well he could not repress the exclamation of delight which it always wrung from him. She looked round with a smile.

"I think it's a success," she said. "The main thing is that it's right. There's not even an ash-tray that isn't of the period."

"I suppose that's what makes it so wonderful. Like all you do it's so superlatively right."

They sat down in front of a log fire and Isabel looked at him with calm grave eyes.

"Now what have you to say to me?" she asked.

"I hardly know how to begin."

"Is Edward Barnard coming back?"

"No."

There was a long silence before Bateman spoke again, and with each of them it was filled with many thoughts. It was a difficult story he had to tell, for there were things in it which were so offensive to her sensitive ears that he could not bear to tell them, and yet in justice to her, no less than in justice to himself, he must tell her the whole truth.

It had all begun long ago when he and Edward Barnard, still at college, had met Isabel Longstaffe at the tea-party given to introduce her to society. They had both known her when she was a child and they long-legged boys, but for two years she had been in Europe to finish her education and it was with a surprised delight that they renewed acquaintance with the lovely girl who returned. Both of them fell desperately in love with her, but Bateman saw quickly that she had eyes only for Edward, and, devoted to his friend, he resigned himself to the rôle of confidant. He passed bitter moments, but he could not deny that Edward was worthy of his good fortune, and, anxious that nothing should impair the friendship he so greatly valued, he took care never by a hint to disclose his own feelings. In six months the young couple were engaged. But they were very young and Isabel's father decided that they should not marry at least till Edward graduated. They had to wait a year. Bateman remembered the winter at the end of which Isabel and Edward were to be married, a winter of dances and theatre-parties and of informal gaieties at which he, the constant third, was always present. He loved her no less because she would shortly be his friend's wife; her smile, a gay word she flung him, the confidence of her affection, never ceased to delight him; and he congratulated himself, somewhat complacently, because he did not envy them their happiness. Then an accident happened. A great bank failed, there was a panic on the exchange, and Edward Barnard's father found himself a ruined man. He came home one night, told his wife that he was penniless, and after dinner, going into his study, shot himself.

A week later, Edward Barnard, with a tired, white face, went to Isabel and asked her to release him. Her only answer was to throw her arms round his neck and burst into tears.

"Don't make it harder for me, sweet," he said.

"Do you think I can let you go now? I love you."

"How can I ask you to marry me? The whole thing's hopeless. Your father would never let you. I haven't a cent."

"What do I care? I love you."

He told her his plans. He had to earn money at once, and George Braunschmidt, an old friend of his family, had offered to take him into his own business. He was a South Sea merchant, and he had agencies in many of the islands of the Pacific. He had suggested that Edward should go to Tahiti for a year or two, where under the best of his managers he could learn the details of that varied trade, and at the end of that time he promised the young man a position in Chicago. It was a wonderful opportunity, and when he had finished his explanations Isabel was once more all smiles.

"You foolish boy, why have you been trying to make me miserable?"

His face lit up at her words and his eyes flashed.

"Isabel, you don't mean to say you'll wait for me?"

"Don't you think you're worth it?" she smiled.

"Ah, don't laugh at me now. I beseech you to be serious. It may be for two years."

"Have no fear. I love you, Edward. When you come back I will marry you."

Edward's employer was a man who did not like delay and he had told him that if he took the post he offered he must sail that day week from San Francisco. Edward spent his last evening with Isabel. It was after dinner that Mr. Longstaffe, saying he wanted a word with Edward, took him into the smoking-room. Mr. Longstaffe had accepted good-naturedly the arrangement which his daughter had told him of and Edward could not imagine what mysterious communication he had now to make. He was not a little perplexed to see that his host was embarrassed. He faltered. He talked of trivial things. At last he blurted it out.

"I guess you've heard of Arnold Jackson," he said, looking at Edward with a frown.

Edward hesitated. His natural truthfulness obliged him to admit a knowledge he would gladly have been able to deny.

"Yes, I have. But it's a long time ago. I guess I didn't pay very much attention."

"There are not many people in Chicago who haven't heard of Arnold Jackson," said Mr. Longstaffe bitterly, "and if there are they'll have no difficulty in finding someone who'll be glad to tell them. Did you know he was Mrs. Longstaffe's brother?"

"Yes, I knew that."

"Of course we've had no communication with him for many years. He left the country as soon as he was able to, and I guess the country wasn't sorry to see the last of him. We understand he lives in Tahiti. My advice to you is to give him a wide berth, but if you do hear anything about him Mrs. Longstaffe and I would be very glad if you'd let us know."

"Sure."

"That was all I wanted to say to you. Now I daresay you'd like to join the ladies."

There are few families that have not among their members one whom, if their neighbours permitted, they would willingly forget, and they are fortunate when the lapse of a generation or two has invested his vagaries with a romantic glamour. But when he is actually alive, if his peculiarities are not of the kind that can be condoned by the phrase, "he is nobody's enemy but his own," a safe one when the culprit has no worse to answer for than alcoholism or wandering affections, the only possible course is silence. And it was this which the Longstaffes had adopted towards Arnold Jackson. They never talked of him. They would not even pass through the street in which he had lived. Too kind to make his wife and children suffer for his misdeeds, they had supported them for years, but on the understanding that they should live in Europe. They did everything they could to blot out all recollection of Arnold Jackson and yet were conscious that the story was as fresh in the public mind as when first the scandal burst upon a gaping world. Arnold Jackson was as black a sheep as any family could suffer from. A wealthy banker, prominent in his church, a philanthropist, a man respected by all, not only for his connections (in his veins ran the blue blood of Chicago), but also for his upright character, he was arrested one day on a charge of fraud; and the dishonesty which the trial brought to light was not of the sort which could be explained by a sudden temptation; it was deliberate and systematic. Arnold Jackson was a rogue. When he was sent to the penitentiary for seven years there were few who did not think he had escaped lightly.

When at the end of this last evening the lovers separated it was with many protestations of devotion. Isabel, all tears, was consoled a little by her certainty of Edward's passionate love. It was a strange feeling that she had. It made her wretched to part from him and yet she was happy because he adored her.

This was more than two years ago.

He had written to her by every mail since then, twenty-four letters in all, for the mail went but once a month, and his letters had been all that a lover's letters should be. They were intimate and charming, humorous sometimes, especially of late, and tender. At first they suggested that he was homesick, they were full of his desire to get back to Chicago and Isabel; and, a little anxiously, she wrote begging him to persevere. She was afraid that he might throw up his opportunity and come racing back. She did not want her lover to lack endurance and she quoted to him the lines:

> "*I could not love thee, dear, so much,*
> *Loved I not honour more.*"

But presently he seemed to settle down and it made Isabel very happy to observe his growing enthusiasm to introduce American methods into that forgotten corner of the world. But she knew him, and at the end of the year, which was the shortest time he could possibly stay in Tahiti, she expected to have to use all her influence to dissuade him from coming home. It was much better that he should learn the business thoroughly, and if they had been able to wait a year there seemed no reason why they should not wait another. She talked it over with Bateman Hunter, always the most generous of friends (during those first few days after Edward went she did not know what she would have done without him), and they decided that Edward's future must stand before everything. It was with relief that she found as the time passed that he made no suggestion of returning.

"He's splendid, isn't he?" she exclaimed to Bateman.

"He's white, through and through."

"Reading between the lines of his letter I know he hates it over there, but he's sticking it out because . . ."

She blushed a little and Bateman, with the grave smile which was so attractive in him, finished the sentence for her.

"Because he loves you."

"It makes me feel so humble," she said.

"You're wonderful, Isabel, you're perfectly wonderful."

But the second year passed and every month Isabel continued to receive a letter from Edward, and presently it began to seem a little strange that he did not speak of coming back. He wrote as though he were settled definitely in Tahiti, and what was more, comfortably settled. She was surprised. Then she read his letters again, all of them, several times; and now, reading between the lines indeed, she was puzzled to notice a change which had escaped her. The later letters were as tender and as delightful as the first, but the tone was different. She was vaguely suspicious of their humour, she had the instinctive mistrust of her sex for that unaccountable quality, and she dis-

cerned in them now a flippancy which perplexed her. She was
not quite certain that the Edward who wrote to her now was
the same Edward that she had known. One afternoon, the day
after a mail had arrived from Tahiti, when she was driving with
Bateman he said to her:

"Did Edward tell you when he was sailing?"

"No, he didn't mention it. I thought he might have said
something to you about it."

"Not a word."

"You know what Edward is," she laughed in reply, "he has
no sense of time. If it occurs to you next time you write you
might ask him when he's thinking of coming."

Her manner was so unconcerned that only Bateman's acute
sensitiveness could have discerned in her request a very urgent
desire. He laughed lightly.

"Yes. I'll ask him. I can't imagine what he's thinking about."

A few days later, meeting him again, she noticed that something troubled him. They had been much together since Edward left Chicago; they were both devoted to him and each in
his desire to talk of the absent one found a willing listener; the
consequence was that Isabel knew every expression of Bateman's
face, and his denials now were useless against her keen instinct.
Something told her that his harassed look had to do with Edward and she did not rest till she had made him confess.

"The fact is," he said at last, "I heard in a roundabout way
that Edward was no longer working for Braunschmidt and Co.,
and yesterday I took the opportunity to ask Mr. Braunschmidt
himself."

"Well?"

"Edward left his employment with them nearly a year ago."

"How strange he should have said nothing about it!"

Bateman hesitated, but he had gone so far now that he was
obliged to tell the rest. It made him feel dreadfully embarrassed.

"He was fired."

"In heaven's name what for?"

"It appears they warned him once or twice, and at last they
told him to get out. They say he was lazy and incompetent."

"Edward?"

They were silent for a while, and then he saw that Isabel was
crying. Instinctively he seized her hand.

"Oh, my dear, don't, don't," he said. "I can't bear to see it."

She was so unstrung that she let her hand rest in his. He tried to console her.

"It's incomprehensible, isn't it? It's so unlike Edward. I can't help feeling there must be some mistake."

She did not say anything for a while, and when she spoke it was hesitatingly.

"Has it struck you that there was anything queer in his letters lately?" she asked, looking away, her eyes all bright with tears.

He did not quite know how to answer.

"I have noticed a change in them," he admitted. "He seems to have lost that high seriousness which I admired so much in him. One would almost think that the things that matter— well, don't matter."

Isabel did not reply. She was vaguely uneasy.

"Perhaps in his answer to your letter he'll say when he's coming home. All we can do is to wait for that."

Another letter came from Edward for each of them, and still he made no mention of his return; but when he wrote he could not have received Bateman's enquiry. The next mail would bring them an answer to that. The next mail came, and Bateman brought Isabel the letter he had just received; but the first glance of his face was enough to tell her that he was disconcerted. She read it through carefully and then, with slightly tightened lips, read it again.

"It's a very strange letter," she said. "I don't quite understand it."

"One might almost think that he was joshing me," said Bateman, flushing.

"It reads like that, but it must be unintentional. That's so unlike Edward."

"He says nothing about coming back."

"If I weren't so confident of his love I should think . . . I hardly know what I should think."

It was then that Bateman had broached the scheme which during the afternoon had formed itself in his brain. The firm, founded by his father, in which he was now a partner, a firm which manufactured all manner of motor vehicles, was about to establish agencies in Honolulu, Sydney, and Wellington; and Bateman proposed that himself should go instead of the manager who had been suggested. He could return by Tahiti; in fact, travelling from Wellington, it was inevitable to do so; and he could see Edward.

"There's some mystery and I'm going to clear it up. That's the only way to do it."

"Oh, Bateman, how can you be so good and kind?" she exclaimed.

"You know there's nothing in the world I want more than your happiness, Isabel."

She looked at him and she gave him her hands.

"You're wonderful, Bateman. I didn't know there was anyone in the world like you. How can I ever thank you?"

"I don't want your thanks. I only want to be allowed to help you."

She dropped her eyes and flushed a little. She was so used to him that she had forgotten how handsome he was. He was as tall as Edward and as well made, but he was dark and pale of face, while Edward was ruddy. Of course she knew he loved her. It touched her. She felt very tender towards him.

It was from this journey that Bateman Hunter was now returned.

The business part of it took him somewhat longer than he expected and he had much time to think of his two friends. He had come to the conclusion that it could be nothing serious that prevented Edward from coming home, a pride, perhaps, which made him determined to make good before he claimed the bride he adored; but it was a pride that must be reasoned with. Isabel was unhappy. Edward must come back to Chicago with him and marry her at once. A position could be found for him in the works of the Hunter Motor Traction and Automobile Company. Bateman, with a bleeding heart, exulted at the prospect of giving happiness to the two persons he loved best in the world at the cost of his own. He would never marry. He would be godfather to the children of Edward and Isabel, and many years later when they were both dead he would tell Isabel's daughter how long, long ago he had loved her mother. Bateman's eyes were veiled with tears when he pictured this scene to himself.

Meaning to take Edward by surprise he had not cabled to announce his arrival, and when at last he landed at Tahiti he allowed a youth, who said he was the son of the house, to lead him to the Hotel de la Fleur. He chuckled when he thought of his friend's amazement on seeing him, the most unexpected of visitors, walk into his office.

"By the way," he asked, as they went along, "can you tell me where I shall find Mr. Edward Barnard?"

"Barnard?" said the youth. "I seem to know the name."

"He's an American. A tall fellow with light brown hair and blue eyes. He's been here over two years."

"Of course. Now I know who you mean. You mean Mr. Jackson's nephew."

"Whose nephew?"

"Mr. Arnold Jackson."

"I don't think we're speaking of the same person," answered Bateman, frigidly.

He was startled. It was queer that Arnold Jackson, known apparently to all and sundry, should live here under the disgraceful name in which he had been convicted. But Bateman could not imagine whom it was that he passed off as his nephew. Mrs. Longstaffe was his only sister and he had never had a brother. The young man by his side talked volubly in an English that had something in it of the intonation of a foreign tongue, and Bateman, with a sidelong glance, saw, what he had not noticed before, that there was in him a good deal of native blood. A touch of hauteur involuntarily entered into his manner. They reached the hotel. When he had arranged about his room Bateman asked to be directed to the premises of Braunschmidt & Co. They were on the front, facing the lagoon, and, glad to feel the solid earth under his feet after eight days at sea, he sauntered down the sunny road to the water's edge. Having found the place he sought, Bateman sent in his card to the manager and was led through a lofty barn-like room, half store and half warehouse, to an office in which sat a stout, spectacled, bald-headed man.

"Can you tell me where I shall find Mr. Edward Barnard? I understand he was in this office for some time."

"That is so. I don't know just where he is."

"But I thought he came here with a particular recommendation from Mr. Braunschmidt. I know Mr. Braunschmidt very well."

The fat man looked at Bateman with shrewd, suspicious eyes. He called to one of the boys in the warehouse.

"Say, Henry, where's Barnard now, d'you know?"

"He's working at Cameron's, I think," came the answer from someone who did not trouble to move.

The fat man nodded.

"If you turn to your left when you get out of here you'll come to Cameron's in about three minutes."

Bateman hesitated.

"I think I should tell you that Edward Barnard is my greatest friend. I was very much surprised when I heard he'd left Braunschmidt & Co."

The fat man's eyes contracted till they seemed like pin-points, and their scrutiny made Bateman so uncomfortable that he felt himself blushing.

"I guess Braunschmidt & Co. and Edward Barnard didn't see eye to eye on certain matters," he replied.

Bateman did not quite like the fellow's manner, so he got up, not without dignity, and with an apology for troubling him bade him good-day. He left the place with a singular feeling that the man he had just interviewed had much to tell him, but no intention of telling it. He walked in the direction indicated and soon found himself at Cameron's. It was a trader's store, such as he had passed half a dozen of on his way, and when he entered the first person he saw, in his shirt sleeves, measuring out a length of trade cotton, was Edward. It gave him a start to see him engaged in so humble an occupation. But he had scarcely appeared when Edward, looking up, caught sight of him, and gave a joyful cry of surprise.

"Bateman! Who ever thought of seeing you here?"

He stretched his arm across the counter and wrung Bateman's hand. There was no self-consciousness in his manner and the embarrassment was all on Bateman's side.

"Just wait till I've wrapped this package."

With perfect assurance he ran his scissors across the stuff, folded it, made it into a parcel, and handed it to the dark-skinned customer.

"Pay at the desk, please."

Then, smiling, with bright eyes, he turned to Bateman.

"How did you show up here? Gee, I am delighted to see you. Sit down, old man. Make yourself at home."

"We can't talk here. Come along to my hotel. I suppose you can get away?"

This he added with some apprehension.

"Of course I can get away. We're not so businesslike as all

that in Tahiti." He called out to a Chinese who was standing behind the opposite counter. "Ah-Ling, when the boss comes tell him a friend of mine's just arrived from America and I've gone out to have a drain with him."

"All-light," said the Chinese, with a grin.

Edward slipped on a coat and, putting on his hat, accompanied Bateman out of the store. Bateman attempted to put the matter facetiously.

"I didn't expect to find you selling three and a half yards of rotten cotton to a greasy nigger," he laughed.

"Braunschmidt fired me, you know, and I thought that would do as well as anything else."

Edward's candour seemed to Bateman very surprising, but he thought it indiscreet to pursue the subject.

"I guess you won't make a fortune where you are," he answered, somewhat dryly.

"I guess not. But I earn enough to keep body and soul together, and I'm quite satisfied with that."

"You wouldn't have been two years ago."

"We grow wiser as we grow older," retorted Edward, gaily.

Bateman took a glance at him. Edward was dressed in a suit of shabby white ducks, none too clean, and a large straw hat of native make. He was thinner than he had been, deeply burned by the sun, and he was certainly better looking than ever. But there was something in his appearance that disconcerted Bateman. He walked with a new jauntiness; there was a carelessness in his demeanour, a gaiety about nothing in particular, which Bateman could not precisely blame, but which exceedingly puzzled him.

"I'm blest if I can see what he's got to be so darned cheerful about," he said to himself.

They arrived at the hotel and sat on the terrace. A Chinese boy brought them cocktails. Edward was most anxious to hear all the news of Chicago and bombarded his friend with eager questions. His interest was natural and sincere. But the odd thing was that it seemed equally divided among a multitude of subjects. He was as eager to know how Bateman's father was as what Isabel was doing. He talked of her without a shade of embarrassment, but she might just as well have been his sister as his promised wife; and before Bateman had done analyzing the exact meaning of Edward's remarks he found that the conversation had drifted to his own work and the buildings his father had lately erected. He was determined to bring the conversation back to Isabel and was looking for the occasion when he saw Edward wave his hand cordially. A man was advancing towards them on the terrace, but Bateman's back was turned to him and he could not see him.

"Come and sit down," said Edward gaily.

The new-comer approached. He was a very tall, thin man, in white ducks, with a fine head of curly white hair. His face was thin too, long, with a large, hooked nose and a beautiful, expressive mouth.

"This is my old friend Bateman Hunter. I've told you about him," said Edward, his constant smile breaking on his lips.

"I'm pleased to meet you, Mr. Hunter. I used to know your father."

The stranger held out his hand and took the young man's in a strong, friendly grasp. It was not till then that Edward mentioned the other's name.

"Mr. Arnold Jackson."

Bateman turned white and he felt his hands grow cold. This was the forger, the convict, this was Isabel's uncle. He did not know what to say. He tried to conceal his confusion. Arnold Jackson looked at him with twinkling eyes.

"I daresay my name is familiar to you."

Bateman did not know whether to say yes or no, and what made it more awkward was that both Jackson and Edward seemed to be amused. It was bad enough to have forced on him the acquaintance of the one man on the island he would rather have avoided, but worse to discern that he was being made a fool of. Perhaps, however, he had reached this conclusion too quickly, for Jackson, without a pause, added:

"I understand you're very friendly with the Longstaffes. Mary Longstaffe is my sister."

Now Bateman asked himself if Arnold Jackson could think him ignorant of the most terrible scandal that Chicago had ever known. But Jackson put his hand on Edward's shoulder.

"I can't sit down, Teddie," he said. "I'm busy. But you two boys had better come up and dine tonight."

"That'll be fine," said Edward.

"It's very kind of you, Mr. Jackson," said Bateman, frigidly, "but I'm here for so short a time; my boat sails to-morrow, you know; I think if you'll forgive me, I won't come."

"Oh, nonsense. I'll give you a native dinner. My wife's a wonderful cook. Teddie will show you the way. Come early so as to see the sunset. I can give you both a shake-down if you like."

"Of course we'll come," said Edward. "There's always the devil of a row in the hotel on the night a boat arrives and we can have a good yarn up at the bungalow."

"I can't let you off, Mr. Hunter," Jackson continued with the utmost cordiality. "I want to hear all about Chicago and Mary."

He nodded and walked away before Bateman could say another word.

"We don't take refusals in Tahiti," laughed Edward. "Besides, you'll get the best dinner on the island."

"What did he mean by saying his wife was a good cook? I happen to know his wife's in Geneva."

"That's a long way off for a wife, isn't it?" said Edward. "And it's a long time since he saw her. I guess it's another wife he's talking about."

For some time Bateman was silent. His face was set in grave lines. But looking up he caught the amused look in Edward's eyes, and he flushed darkly.

"Arnold Jackson is a despicable rogue," he said.

"I greatly fear he is," answered Edward, smiling.

"I don't see how any decent man can have anything to do with him."

"Perhaps I'm not a decent man."

"Do you see much of him, Edward?"

"Yes, quite a lot. He's adopted me as his nephew."

Bateman leaned forward and fixed Edward with his searching eyes.

"Do you like him?"

"Very much."

"But don't you know, doesn't everyone here know, that he's a forger and that he's been a convict? He ought to be hounded out of civilized society."

Edward watched a ring of smoke that floated from his cigar into the still, scented air.

"I suppose he is a pretty unmitigated rascal," he said at last. "And I can't flatter myself that any repentance for his misdeeds offers one an excuse for condoning them. He was a swindler and a hypocrite. You can't get away from it. I never met a more agreeable companion. He's taught me everything I know."

"What has he taught you?" cried Bateman in amazement.

"How to live."

Bateman broke into ironical laughter.

"A fine master. Is it owing to his lessons that you lost the chance of making a fortune and earn your living now by serving behind a counter in a ten cent store?"

"He has a wonderful personality," said Edward, smiling good-naturedly. "Perhaps you'll see what I mean to-night."

"I'm not going to dine with him if that's what you mean. Nothing would induce me to set foot within that man's house."

"Come to oblige me, Bateman. We've been friends for so many years, you won't refuse me a favour when I ask it."

Edward's tone had in it a quality new to Bateman. Its gentleness was singularly persuasive.

"If you put it like that, Edward, I'm bound to come," he smiled.

Bateman reflected, moreover, that it would be as well to learn what he could about Arnold Jackson. It was plain that he had a great ascendency over Edward, and if it was to be combated it was necessary to discover in what exactly it consisted. The more he talked with Edward the more conscious he became that a change had taken place in him. He had an instinct that it behooved him to walk warily, and he made up his mind not to broach the real purport of his visit till he saw his way more clearly. He began to talk of one thing and another, of his journey and what he had achieved by it, of politics in Chicago, of this common friend and that, of their days together at college.

At last Edward said he must get back to his work and proposed that he should fetch Bateman at five so that they could drive out together to Arnold Jackson's house.

"By the way, I rather thought you'd be living at this hotel," said Bateman, as he strolled out of the garden with Edward. "I understand it's the only decent one here."

"Not I," laughed Edward. "It's a deal too grand for me. I rent a room just outside the town. It's cheap and clean."

"If I remember right those weren't the points that seemed most important to you when you lived in Chicago."

"Chicago!"

"I don't know what you mean by that, Edward. It's the greatest city in the world."

"I know," said Edward.

Bateman glanced at him quickly, but his face was inscrutable. "When are you coming back to it?"

"I often wonder," smiled Edward.

This answer, and the manner of it, staggered Bateman, but before he could ask for an explanation Edward waved to a half-caste who was driving a passing motor.

"Give us a ride down, Charlie," he said.

He nodded to Bateman, and ran after the machine that had pulled up a few yards in front. Bateman was left to piece together a mass of perplexing impressions.

Edward called for him in a rickety trap drawn by an old mare, and they drove along a road that ran by the sea. On each side of it were plantations, coconut and vanilla; and now and then they saw a great mango, its fruit yellow and red and purple among the massy green of the leaves; now and then they had a glimpse of the lagoon, smooth and blue, with here and there a tiny islet graceful with tall palms. Arnold Jackson's house stood on a little hill and only a path led to it, so they unharnessed the mare and tied her to a tree, leaving the trap by the side of the road. To Bateman it seemed a happy-go-lucky way of doing things. But when they went up to the house they were met by a tall, handsome native woman, no longer young, with whom Edward cordially shook hands. He introduced Bateman to her.

"This is my friend Mr. Hunter. We're going to dine with you, Lavina."

"All right," she said, with a quick smile. "Arnold ain't back yet."

"We'll go down and bathe. Let us have a couple of *pareos*."

The woman nodded and went into the house.

"Who is that?" asked Bateman.

"Oh, that's Lavina. She's Arnold's wife."

Bateman tightened his lips, but said nothing. In a moment the woman returned with a bundle, which she gave to Edward; and the two men, scrambling down a steep path, made their way to a grove of coconut trees on the beach. They undressed and Edward showed his friend how to make the strip of red trade cotton which is called a *pareo* into a very neat pair of bathing-drawers. Soon they were splashing in the warm, shallow water. Edward was in great spirits. He laughed and shouted and sang. He might have been fifteen. Bateman had never seen him so gay, and afterwards when they lay on the beach, smoking cigarettes, in the limpid air, there was such an irresistible light-heartedness in him that Bateman was taken aback.

"You seem to find life mighty pleasant," said he.

"I do."

They heard a soft movement and looking round saw that Arnold Jackson was coming towards them.

"I thought I'd come down and fetch you two boys back," he said. "Did you enjoy your bath, Mr. Hunter?"

"Very much," said Bateman.

Arnold Jackson, no longer in spruce ducks, wore nothing but a *pareo* round his loins and walked barefoot. His body was deeply browned by the sun. With his long, curling white hair and his ascetic face he made a fantastic figure in the native dress, but he bore himself without a trace of self-consciousness.

"If you're ready we'll go right up," said Jackson.

"I'll just put on my clothes," said Bateman.

"Why, Teddie, didn't you bring a *pareo* for your friend?"

"I guess he'd rather wear clothes," smiled Edward.

"I certainly would," answered Bateman, grimly, as he saw Edward gird himself in the loincloth and stand ready to start before he himself had got his shirt on.

"Won't you find it rough walking without your shoes?" he asked Edward. "It struck me the path was a trifle rocky."

"Oh, I'm used to it."

"It's a comfort to get into a *pareo* when one gets back from town," said Jackson. "If you were going to stay here I should strongly recommend you to adopt it. It's one of the most sensible costumes I have ever come across. It's cool, convenient, and inexpensive."

They walked up to the house, and Jackson took them into a large room with white-washed walls and an open ceiling in which a table was laid for dinner. Bateman noticed that it was set for five.

"Eva, come and show yourself to Teddie's friend, and then shake us a cocktail," called Jackson.

Then he led Bateman to a long low window.

"Look at that," he said, with a dramatic gesture. "Look well."

Below them coconut trees tumbled down steeply to the lagoon, and the lagoon in the evening light had the colour, tender and varied, of a dove's breast. On a creek, at a little distance, were the clustered huts of a native village, and towards the reef was a canoe, sharply-silhouetted, in which were a couple of natives fishing. Then, beyond, you saw the vast calmness of the Pacific and twenty miles away, airy and unsubstantial like the fabric of a poet's fancy, the unimaginable beauty of the island which is called Murea. It was all so lovely that Bateman stood abashed.

"I've never seen anything like it," he said at last.

Arnold Jackson stood staring in front of him, and in his eyes was a dreamy softness. His thin, thoughtful face was very grave. Bateman, glancing at it, was once more conscious of its intense spirituality.

"Beauty," murmured Arnold Jackson. "You seldom see beauty face to face. Look at it well, Mr. Hunter, for what you see now you will never see again, since the moment is transitory, but it will be an imperishable memory in your heart. You touch eternity."

His voice was deep and resonant. He seemed to breathe forth' the purest idealism, and Bateman had to urge himself to remember that the man who spoke was a criminal and a cruel cheat. But Edward, as though he heard a sound, turned round quickly.

"Here is my daughter. Mr. Hunter."

Bateman shook hands with her. She had dark, splendid eyes and a red mouth tremulous with laughter; but her skin was brown, and her curling hair, rippling down her shoulders, was coal black. She wore but one garment, a Mother Hubbard of pink cotton, her feet were bare, and she was crowned with a wreath of white scented flowers. She was a lovely creature. She was like a goddess of the Polynesian spring.

She was a little shy, but not more shy than Bateman, to whom the whole situation was highly embarrassing, and it did not put him at his ease to see this sylph-like thing take a shaker and with a practiced hand mix three cocktails.

"Let us have a kick in them, child," said Jackson.

She poured them out and smiling delightfully handed one to each of the men. Bateman flattered himself on his skill in the subtle art of shaking cocktails and he was not a little astonished, on tasting this one, to find that it was excellent. Jackson laughed proudly when he saw his guest's involuntary look of appreciation.

"Not bad, is it? I taught the child myself, and in the old days in Chicago I considered that there wasn't a bar-tender in the city that could hold a candle to me. When I had nothing better to do in the penitentiary I used to amuse myself by thinking out new cocktails, but when you come down to brass-tacks there's nothing to beat a dry Martini."

Bateman felt as though someone had given him a violent blow on the funny-bone and he was conscious that he turned red and then white. But before he could think of anything to say a native boy brought in a great bowl of soup and the whole party sat down to dinner. Arnold Jackson's remark seemed to have aroused in him a train of recollections, for he began to talk of his prison days. He talked quite naturally, without malice, as though he were relating his experiences at a foreign university. He addressed himself to Bateman and Bateman was confused and then confounded. He saw Edward's eyes fixed on him and there was in them a flicker of amusement. He blushed scarlet, for it struck him that Jackson was making a fool of him, and then because he felt absurd—and knew there was no reason why he should—he grew angry. Arnold Jackson was impudent—there was no other word for it—and his callousness, whether assumed or not, was outrageous. The dinner proceeded. Bateman was asked to eat sundry messes, raw fish and he knew not what, which only his civility induced him to swallow, but which he was amazed to find very good eating. Then an incident happened which to Bateman was the most mortifying experience of the evening. There was a little circlet of flowers in front of him, and for the sake of conversation he hazarded a remark about it.

"It's a wreath that Eva made for you," said Jackson, "but I guess she was too shy to give it you."

Bateman took it up in his hand and made a polite little speech of thanks to the girl.

"You must put it on," she said, with a smile and a blush.

"I? I don't think I'll do that."

"It's the charming custom of the country," said Arnold Jackson.

There was one in front of him and he placed it on his hair. Edward did the same.

"I guess I'm not dressed for the part," said Bateman, uneasily.

"Would you like a *pareo?*" said Eva quickly. "I'll get you one in a minute."

"No, thank you. I'm quite comfortable as I am."

"Show him how to put it on, Eva," said Edward.

At that moment Bateman hated his greatest friend. Eva got up from the table and with much laughter placed the wreath on his black hair.

"It suits you very well," said Mrs. Jackson. "Don't it suit him, Arnold?"

"Of course it does."

Bateman sweated at every pore.

"Isn't it a pity it's dark?" said Eva. "We could photograph you all three together."

Bateman thanked his stars it was. He felt that he must look prodigiously foolish in his blue serge suit and high collar—very neat and gentlemanly—with that ridiculous wreath of flowers on his head. He was seething with indignation, and he had never in his life exercised more self-control than now when he presented an affable exterior. He was furious with that old man, sitting at the head of the table, half-naked, with his saintly face and the flowers on his handsome white locks. The whole position was monstrous.

Then dinner came to an end, and Eva and her mother remained to clear away while the three men sat on the verandah. It was very warm and the air was scented with the white flowers of the night. The full moon, sailing across an unclouded sky, made a pathway on the broad sea that led to the boundless realms of Forever. Arnold Jackson began to talk. His voice was rich and musical. He talked now of the natives and of the old legends of the country. He told strange stories of the past, stories of hazardous expeditions into the unknown, of love and death, of hatred and revenge. He told of the adventurers who had discovered those distant islands, of the sailors who, settling in them, had married the daughters of great chieftains, and of the beach-combers who had led their varied lives on those silvery shores. Bateman, mortified and exasperated, at first listened sullenly, but presently some magic in the words possessed him and he sat entranced. The mirage of romance obscured the light of common day. Had he forgotten that Arnold Jackson had a tongue of silver, a tongue by which he had charmed vast sums out of the credulous public, a tongue which very nearly enabled him to escape the penalty of his crimes? No one had a sweeter eloquence, and no one had a more acute sense of climax. Suddenly he rose.

"Well, you two boys haven't seen one another for a long time. I shall leave you to have a yarn. Teddie will show you your quarters when you want to go to bed."

"Oh, but I wasn't thinking of spending the night, Mr. Jackson," said Bateman.

"You'll find it more comfortable. We'll see that you're called in good time."

Then with a courteous shake of the hand, stately as though he were a bishop in canonicals, Arnold Jackson took leave of his guest.

"Of course I'll drive you back to Papeete if you like," said Edward, "but I advise you to stay. It's bully driving in the early morning."

For a few minutes neither of them spoke. Bateman wondered how he should begin on the conversation which all the events of the day made him think more urgent.

"When are you coming back to Chicago?" he asked, suddenly.

For a moment Edward did not answer. Then he turned rather lazily to look at his friend and smiled.

"I don't know. Perhaps never."

"What in heaven's name do you mean?" cried Bateman.

"I'm very happy here. Wouldn't it be folly to make a change?"

"Man alive, you can't live here all your life. This is no life for a man. It's a living death. Oh, Edward, come away at once, before it's too late. I've felt that something was wrong. You're infatuated with the place, you've succumbed to evil influences, but it only requires a wrench, and when you're free from these surroundings you'll thank all the gods there be. You'll be like a dope-fiend when he's broken from his drug. You'll see then that for two years you've been breathing poisoned air. You can't imagine what a relief it will be when you fill your lungs once more with the fresh, pure air of your native country."

He spoke quickly, the words tumbling over one another in his excitement, and there was in his voice sincere and affectionate emotion. Edward was touched.

"It is good of you to care so much, old friend."

"Come with me to-morrow, Edward. It was a mistake that you ever came to this place. This is no life for you."

"You talk of this sort of life and that. How do you think a man gets the best out of life?"

"Why, I should have thought there could be no two answers to that. By doing his duty, by hard work, by meeting all the obligations of his state and station."

"And what is his reward?"

"His reward is the consciousness of having achieved what he set out to do."

"It all sounds a little portentous to me," said Edward, and in the lightness of the night Bateman could see that he was smiling. "I'm afraid you'll think I've degenerated sadly. There are several things I think now which I daresay would have seemed outrageous to me three years ago."

"Have you learnt them from Arnold Jackson?" asked Bateman, scornfully.

"You don't like him? Perhaps you couldn't be expected to. I didn't when I first came. I had just the same prejudice as you. He's a very extraordinary man. You saw for yourself that he makes no secret of the fact that he was in a penitentiary. I do not know that he regrets it or the crimes that led him there. The only complaint he ever made in my hearing was that when he came out his health was impaired. I think he does not know what remorse is. He is completely unmoral. He accepts everything and he accepts himself as well. He's generous and kind."

"He always was," interrupted Bateman, "on other people's money."

"I've found him a very good friend. Is it unnatural that I should take a man as I find him?"

"The result is that you lose the distinction between right and wrong."

"No, they remain just as clearly divided in my mind as before, but what has become a little confused in me is the distinction between the bad man and the good one. Is Arnold Jackson a bad man who does good things or a good man who does bad things? It's a difficult question to answer. Perhaps we make too much of the difference between one man and another. Perhaps even the best of us are sinners and the worst of us are saints. Who knows?"

"You will never persuade me that white is black and that black is white," said Bateman.

"I'm sure I shan't, Bateman."

Bateman could not understand why the flicker of a smile crossed Edward's lips when he thus agreed with him. Edward was silent for a minute.

"When I saw you this morning, Bateman," he said then, "I seemed to see myself as I was two years ago. The same collar, and the same shoes, the same blue suit, the same energy. The same determination. By God, I was energetic. The sleepy methods of this place made my blood tingle. I went about and everywhere I saw possibilities for development and enterprise. There were fortunes to be made here. It seemed to me absurd that the copra should be taken away from here in sacks and the oil extracted in America. It would be far more economical to do all that on the spot, with cheap labour, and save freight, and I saw already the vast factories springing up on the island. Then the way they extracted it from the coconut seemed to me hopelessly inadequate, and I invented a machine which divided the nut and scooped out the meat at the rate of two hundred and forty an hour. The harbour was not large enough. I made plans to enlarge it, then to form a syndicate to buy land, put up two or three large hotels, and bungalows for occasional residents; I had a scheme for improving the steamer service in order to attract visitors from California. In twenty years, instead of this half French, lazy little town of Papeete I saw a great American city with ten-story buildings and street-cars, a theatre and an opera house, a stock exchange and a mayor."

"But go ahead, Edward," cried Bateman, springing up from the chair in excitement. "You've got the ideas and the capacity. Why, you'll become the richest man between Australia and the States."

Edward chuckled softly.

"But I don't want to," he said.

"Do you mean to say you don't want money, big money, money running into millions? Do you know what you can do with it? Do you know the power it brings? And if you don't care about it for yourself think what you can do, opening new channels for human enterprise, giving occupation to thousands. My brain reels at the visions your words have conjured up."

"Sit down, then, my dear Bateman," laughed Edward. "My machine for cutting the coconuts will always remain unused, and so far as I'm concerned street-cars shall never run in the idle streets of Papeete."

Bateman sank heavily into his chair.

"I don't understand you," he said.

"It came upon me little by little. I came to like the life here, with its ease and its leisure, and the people, with their good-nature and their happy smiling faces. I began to think. I'd never had time to do that before. I began to read."

"You always read."

"I read for examinations. I read in order to be able to hold my own in conversation. I read for instruction. Here I learned to read for pleasure. I learned to talk. Do you know that conversation is one of the greatest pleasures in life? But it wants leisure. I'd always been too busy before. And gradually all the life that had seemed so important to me began to seem rather trivial and vulgar. What is the use of all this hustle and this constant striving? I think of Chicago now and I see a dark, grey city, all stone—it is like a prison—and a ceaseless turmoil. And what does all that activity amount to? Does one get there the best out of life? Is that what we come into the world for, to hurry to an office, and work hour after hour till night, then hurry home and dine and go to a theatre? Is that how I must spend my youth? Youth lasts so short a time, Bateman. And when I am old, what have I to look forward to? To hurry from my home in the morning to my office and work hour after hour till night, and then hurry again, and dine and go to a theatre? That may be worth while if you make a fortune; I don't know, it depends on your nature; but if you don't, is it worth while then? I want to make more out of my life than that, Bateman.'

"What do you value in life then?"

"I'm afraid you'll laugh at me. Beauty, truth, and goodness."

"Don't you think you can have those in Chicago?"

"Some men can, perhaps, but not I." Edward sprang up now. 'I tell you when I think of the life I led in the old days I am filled with horror," he cried violently. "I tremble with fear when I think of the danger I have escaped. I never knew I had a soul till I found it here. If I had remained a rich man I might have lost it for good and all."

"I don't know how you can say that," cried Bateman indignantly. "We often used to have discussions about it."

"Yes, I know. They were about as effectual as the discussions of deaf mutes about harmony. I shall never come back to Chicago, Bateman."

"And what about Isabel?"

Edward walked to the edge of the verandah and leaning over looked intently at the blue magic of the night. There was a slight smile on his face when he turned back to Bateman.

"Isabel is infinitely too good for me. I admire her more than any woman I have ever known. She has a wonderful brain and she's as good as she's beautiful. I respect her energy and her ambition. She was born to make a success of life. I am entirely unworthy of her."

"She doesn't think so."

"But you must tell her so, Bateman."

"I?" cried Bateman. "I'm the last person who could ever do that."

Edward had his back to the vivid light of the moon and his face could not be seen. Is it possible that he smiled again?

"It's no good your trying to conceal anything from her, Bateman. With her quick intelligence she'll turn you inside out in five minutes. You'd better make a clean breast of it right away."

"I don't know what you mean. Of course I shall tell her I've seen you." Bateman spoke in some agitation. "Honestly I don't know what to say to her."

"Tell her that I haven't made good. Tell her that I'm not only poor, but that I'm content to be poor. Tell her I was fired from my job because I was idle and inattentive. Tell her all you've seen to-night and all I've told you."

The idea which on a sudden flashed through Bateman's brain brought him to his feet and in uncontrollable perturbation he faced Edward.

"Man alive, don't you want to marry her?"

Edward looked at him gravely.

"I can never ask her to release me. If she wishes to hold me to my word I will do my best to make her a good and loving husband."

"Do you wish me to give her that message, Edward? Oh, I can't. It's terrible. It's never dawned on her for a moment that you don't want to marry her. She loves you. How can I inflict such a mortification on her?"

Edward smiled again.

"Why don't you marry her yourself, Bateman? You've been in love with her for ages. You're perfectly suited to one another. You'll make her very happy."

"Don't talk to me like that. I can't bear it."

"I resign in your favour, Bateman. You are the better man."

There was something in Edward's tone that made Bateman look up quickly, but Edward's eyes were grave and unsmiling. Bateman did not know what to say. He was disconcerted. He wondered whether Edward could possibly suspect that he had come to Tahiti on a special errand. And though he knew it was horrible he could not prevent the exultation in his heart.

"What will you do if Isabel writes and puts an end to her engagement with you?" he said, slowly.

"Survive," said Edward.

Bateman was so agitated that he did not hear the answer.

"I wish you had ordinary clothes on," he said, somewhat irritably. "It's such a tremendously serious decision you're taking. That fantastic costume of yours makes it seem terribly casual."

"I assure you, I can be just as solemn in a *parco* and a wreath of roses, as in a high hat and a cutaway coat."

Then another thought struck Bateman.

"Edward, it's not for my sake you're doing this? I don't know, but perhaps this is going to make a tremendous difference to my future. You're not sacrificing yourself for me? I couldn't stand for that, you know."

"No, Bateman, I have learnt not to be silly and sentimental here. I should like you and Isabel to be happy, but I have not the least wish to be unhappy myself."

The answer somewhat chilled Bateman. It seemed to him a little cynical. He would not have been sorry to act a noble part.

"Do you mean to say you're content to waste your life here? It's nothing less than suicide. When I think of the great hopes you had when we left college it seems terrible that you should be content to be no more than a salesman in a cheap-John store."

"Oh, I'm only doing that for the present, and I'm gaining a great deal of valuable experience. I have another plan in my head. Arnold Jackson has a small island in the Paumotas, about a thousand miles from here, a ring of land round a lagoon. He's planted coconut there. He's offered to give it to me."

"Why should he do that?" asked Bateman.

"Because if Isabel releases me I shall marry his daughter."

"You?" Bateman was thunderstruck. "You can't marry a half-caste. You wouldn't be so crazy as that."

"She's a good girl, and she has a sweet and gentle nature. I think she would make me very happy."

"Are you in love with her?"

"I don't know," answered Edward reflectively. "I'm not in love with her as I was in love with Isabel. I worshipped Isabel. I thought she was the most wonderful creature I had ever seen. I was not half good enough for her. I don't feel like that with Eva. She's like a beautiful exotic flower that must be sheltered from bitter winds. I want to protect her. No one ever thought of protecting Isabel. I think she loves me for myself and not for what I may become. Whatever happens to me I shall never disappoint her. She suits me."

Bateman was silent.

"We must turn out early in the morning," said Edward at last. "It's really about time we went to bed."

Then Bateman spoke and his voice had in it a genuine distress.

"I'm so bewildered, I don't know what to say. I came here because I thought something was wrong. I thought you hadn't succeeded in what you set out to do and were ashamed to come back when you'd failed. I never guessed I should be faced with this. I'm so desperately sorry, Edward. I'm so disappointed. I hoped you would do great things. It's almost more than I can bear to think of you wasting your talents and your youth and your chance in this lamentable way."

"Don't be grieved, old friend," said Edward. "I haven't failed. I've succeeded. You can't think with what zest I look forward to life, how full it seems to me and how significant. Sometimes, when you are married to Isabel, you will think of me. I shall build myself a house on my coral island and I shall live there, looking after my trees—getting the fruit out of the nuts in the same old way that they have done for unnumbered years—I shall grow all sorts of things in my garden, and I shall fish. There will be enough work to keep me busy and not enough to make me dull. I shall have my books and Eva, children, I hope, and above all, the infinite variety of the sea and the sky, the freshness of the dawn and the beauty of the sunset, and the rich magnificence of the night. I shall make a garden out of what so short a while ago was a wilderness. I shall have created something. The years will pass insensibly, and when I am an old man I hope that I shall be able to look back on a happy, simple, peaceful life. In my small way I too shall have lived in beauty. Do you think it is so little to have enjoyed contentment? We know that it will profit a man little if he gain the whole world and lose his soul. I think I have won mine.''

Edward led him to a room in which there were two beds and he threw himself on one of them. In ten minutes Bateman knew by his regular breathing, peaceful as a child's, that Edward was asleep. But for his part he had no rest, he was disturbed in mind, and it was not till the dawn crept into the room, ghostlike and silent, that he fell asleep.

Bateman finished telling Isabel his long story. He had hidden nothing from her except what he thought would wound her or what made himself ridiculous. He did not tell her that he had been forced to sit at dinner with a wreath of flowers round his head and he did not tell her that Edward was prepared to marry her uncle's half-caste daughter the moment she set him free. But perhaps Isabel had keener intuitions than he knew, for as he went on with his tale her eyes grew colder and her lips closed upon one another more tightly. Now and then she looked at him closely, and if he had been less intent on his narrative he might have wondered at her expression.

"What was this girl like?" she asked when he finished. "Uncle Arnold's daughter. Would you say there was any resemblance between her and me?"

Bateman was surprised at the question.

"It never struck me. You know I've never had eyes for anyone but you and I could never think that anyone was like you. Who could resemble you?"

"Was she pretty?" said Isabel, smiling slightly at his words.

"I suppose so. I daresay some men would say she was very beautiful."

"Well, it's of no consequence. I don't think we need give her any more of our attention."

"What are you going to do, Isabel?" he asked then.

Isabel looked down at the hand which still bore the ring Edward had given her on their betrothal.

"I wouldn't let Edward break our engagement because I thought it would be an incentive to him. I wanted to be an inspiration to him. I thought if anything could enable him to achieve success it was the thought that I loved him. I have done all I could. It's hopeless. It would only be weakness on my part not to recognize the facts. Poor Edward, he's nobody's enemy but his own. He was a dear, nice fellow, but there was something lacking in him, I suppose it was backbone. I hope he'll be happy."

She slipped the ring off her finger and placed it on the table. Bateman watched her with a heart beating so rapidly that he could hardly breathe.

"You're wonderful, Isabel, you're simply wonderful."

She smiled, and, standing up, held out her hand to him.

"How can I ever thank you for what you've done for me?" she said. "You've done me a great service. I knew I could trust you."

He took her hand and held it. She had never looked more beautiful.

"Oh, Isabel, I would do so much more for you than that. You know that I only ask to be allowed to love and serve you."

"You're so strong, Bateman," she sighed. "It gives me such a delicious feeling of confidence."

"Isabel, I adore you."

He hardly knew how the inspiration had come to him, but suddenly he clasped her in his arms, and she, all unresisting, smiled into his eyes.

"Isabel, you know I wanted to marry you the very first day I saw you," he cried passionately.

"Then why on earth didn't you ask me?" she replied.

She loved him. He could hardly believe it was true. She gave him her lovely lips to kiss. And as he held her in his arms he had a vision of the works of the Hunter Motor Traction and Automobile Company growing in size and importance till they covered a hundred acres, and of the millions of motors they would turn out, and of the great collection of pictures he would form which should beat anything they had in New York. He would wear horn spectacles. And she, with the delicious pressure of his arms about her, sighed with happiness, for she thought of the exquisite house she would have, full of antique furniture, and of the concerts she would give, and of the *thés dansants*, and the dinners to which only the most cultured people would come. Bateman should wear horn spectacles.

"Poor Edward," she sighed.

MACKINTOSH

HE SPLASHED about for a few minutes in the sea; it was too
shallow to swim in and for fear of sharks he could not go out
of his depth; then he got out and went into the bath-house for
a shower. The coldness of the fresh water was grateful after
the heavy stickiness of the salt Pacific, so warm, though it was
only just after seven, that to bathe in it did not brace you
but rather increased your languor; and when he had dried
himself, slipping into a bath-gown, he called out to the Chinese
cook that he would be ready for breakfast in five minutes. He
walked barefoot across the patch of coarse grass which Walker,
the administrator, proudly thought was a lawn, to his own
quarters and dressed. This did not take long, for he put on
nothing but a shirt and a pair of duck trousers and then went
over to his chief's house on the other side of the compound.
The two men had their meals together, but the Chinese cook
told him that Walker had set out on horseback at five and
would not be back for another hour.

Mackintosh had slept badly and he looked with distaste
at the paw-paw and the eggs and bacon which were set before
him. The mosquitoes had been maddening that night; they flew
about the net under which he slept in such numbers that their
humming, pitiless and menacing, had the effect of a note, infinitely drawn out, played on a distant organ, and whenever
he dozed off he awoke with a start in the belief that one had
found its way inside his curtains. It was so hot that he lay
naked. He turned from side to side. And gradually the dull

roar of the breakers on the reef, so unceasing and so regular that generally you did not hear it, grew distinct on his consciousness, its rhythm hammered on his tired nerves and he held himself with clenched hands in the effort to bear it. The thought that nothing could stop that sound, for it would continue to all eternity, was almost impossible to bear, and, as though his strength were a match for the ruthless forces of nature, he had an insane impulse to do some violent thing. He felt he must cling to his self-control or he would go mad. And now, looking out of the window at the lagoon and the strip of foam which marked the reef, he shuddered with hatred of the brilliant scene. The cloudless sky was like an inverted bowl that hemmed it in. He lit his pipe and turned over the pile of Auckland papers that had come over from Apia a few days before. The newest of them was three weeks old. They gave an impression of incredible dullness.

Then he went into the office. It was a large, bare room with two desks in it and a bench along one side. A number of natives were seated on this, and a couple of women. They gossiped while they waited for the administrator, and when Mackintosh came in they greeted him.

"*Talofa li.*"

He returned their greeting and sat down at his desk. He began to write, working on a report which the governor of Samoa had been clamouring for and which Walker, with his usual dilatoriness, had neglected to prepare. Mackintosh as he made his notes reflected vindictively that Walker was late with his report because he was so illiterate that he had an invincible distaste for anything to do with pens and paper; and now when it was at last ready, concise and neatly official, he would accept his subordinate's work without a word of appreciation, with a sneer rather or a gibe, and send it on to his own superior as though it were his own composition. He could not have written a word of it. Mackintosh thought with rage that if his chief pencilled in some insertion it would be childish in expression and faulty in language. If he remonstrated or sought to put his meaning into an intelligible phrase, Walker would fly into a passion and cry:

"What the hell do I care about grammar? That's what I want to say and that's how I want to say it."

At last Walker came in. The natives surrounded him as he entered, trying to get his immediate attention, but he turned ι ι them roughly and told them to sit down and hold their tongues. He threatened that if they were not quiet he would have them all turned out and see none of them that day. He nodded to Mackintosh.

"Hulloa, Mac; up at last? I don't know how you can waste the best part of the day in bed. You ought to have been up before dawn like me. Lazy beggar."

He threw himself heavily into his chair and wiped his face with a large bandana.

"By heaven, I've got a thirst."

He turned to the policeman who stood at the door, a picturesque figure in his white jacket and *lava-lava*, the loin cloth of the Samoan, and told him to bring *kava*. The *kava* bowl stood on the floor in the corner of the room, and the policeman filled a half coconut shell and brought it to Walker. He poured a few drops on the ground, murmured the customary words to the company, and drank with relish. Then he told the policeman to serve the waiting natives, and the shell was handed to each one in order of birth or importance and emptied with the same ceremonies.

Then he set about the day's work. He was a little man, considerably less than of middle height, and enormously stout; he had a large, fleshy face, clean-shaven, with the cheeks hanging on each side in great dew-laps, and three vast chins; his small features were all dissolved in fat; and, but for a crescent of white hair at the back of his head, he was completely bald. He reminded you of Mr. Pickwick. He was grotesque, a figure of fun, and yet, strangely enough, not without dignity. His blue eyes, behind large gold-rimmed spectacles, were shrewd and vivacious, and there was a great deal of determination in his face. He was sixty, but his native vitality triumphed over advancing years. Notwithstanding his corpulence his movements were quick, and he walked with a heavy, resolute tread as though he sought to impress his weight upon the earth. He spoke in a loud, gruff voice.

It was two years now since Mackintosh had been appointed Walker's assistant. Walker, who had been for a quarter of a century administrator of Talua, one of the larger islands in the Samoan group, was a man known in person or by report through the length and breadth of the South Seas; and it was with lively curiosity that Mackintosh looked forward to his first meeting with him. For one reason or another he stayed

a couple of weeks at Apia before he took up his post and both
at Chaplin's hotel and at the English club he heard innumerable
stories about the administrator. He thought now with irony
of his interest in them. Since then he had heard them a hundred
times from Walker himself. Walker knew that he was a character, and, proud of his reputation, deliberately acted up to it.
He was jealous of his "legend" and anxious that you should
know the exact details of any of the celebrated stories that were
told of him. He was ludicrously angry with anyone who had
told them to the stranger incorrectly.

There was a rough cordiality about Walker which Mackintosh at first found not unattractive, and Walker, glad to have a
listener to whom all he said was fresh, gave of his best. He was
good-humoured, hearty, and considerate. To Mackintosh, who
had lived the sheltered life of a government official in London
till at the age of thirty-four an attack of pneumonia, leaving
him with the threat of tuberculosis, had forced him to seek a
post in the Pacific, Walker's existence seemed extraordinarily
romantic. The adventure with which he started on his conquest
of circumstance was typical of the man. He ran away to sea
when he was fifteen and for over a year was employed in
shovelling coal on a collier. He was an undersized boy and both
men and mates were kind to him, but the captain for some
reason conceived a savage dislike of him. He used the lad cruelly
so that, beaten and kicked, he often could not sleep for the pain
that racked his limbs. He loathed the captain with all his
soul. Then he was given a tip for some race and managed to
borrow twenty-five pounds from a friend he had picked up in
Belfast. He put it on the horse, an outsider, at long odds. He
had no means of repaying the money if he lost, but it never
occurred to him that he could lose. He felt himself in luck. The
horse won and he found himself with something over a thousand pounds in hard cash. Now his chance had come. He found
out who was the best solicitor in the town—the collier lay
then somewhere on the Irish coast—went to him, and, telling
him that he heard the ship was for sale, asked him to arrange
the purchase for him. The solicitor was amused at his small
client, he was only sixteen and did not look so old, and, moved
perhaps by sympathy, promised not only to arrange the matter
for him but to see that he made a good bargain. After a little
while Walker found himself the owner of the ship. He went
back to her and had what he described as the most glorious

moment of his life when he gave the skipper notice and told
him that he must get off *his* ship in half an hour. He made the
mate captain and sailed on the collier for another nine months,
at the end of which he sold her at a profit.

He came out to the islands at the age of twenty-six as a
planter. He was one of the few white men settled in Talua at
the time of the German occupation and had then already some
influence with the natives. The Germans made him administrator, a position which he occupied for twenty years, and
when the island was seized by the British he was confirmed in
his post. He ruled the island despotically, but with complete
success. The prestige of this success was another reason for the
interest that Mackintosh took in him.

But the two men were not made to get on. Mackintosh was
an ugly man, with ungainly gestures, a tall thin fellow, with a
narrow chest and bowed shoulders. He had sallow, sunken
cheeks, and his eyes were large and sombre. He was a great
reader, and when his books arrived and were unpacked Walker
came over to his quarters and looked at them. Then he turned
to Mackintosh with a coarse laugh.

"What in Hell have you brought all this muck for?" he
asked.

Mackintosh flushed darkly.

"I'm sorry you think it muck. I brought my books because
I want to read them."

"When you said you'd got a lot of books coming I thought
there'd be something for me to read. Haven't you got any detective stories?"

"Detective stories don't interest me."

"You're a damned fool then."

"I'm content that you should think so."

Every mail brought Walker a mass of periodical literature,
papers from New Zealand and magazines from America, and
it exasperated him that Mackintosh showed his contempt for
these ephemeral publications. He had no patience with the
books that absorbed Mackintosh's leisure and thought it only
a pose that he read Gibbon's *Decline and Fall* or Burton's
Anatomy of Melancholy. And since he had never learned to
put any restraint on his tongue, he expressed his opinion of
his assistant freely. Mackintosh began to see the real man, and
under the boisterous good-humour he discerned a vulgar cunning which was hateful; he was vain and domineering, and it

was strange that he had notwithstanding a shyness which
made him dislike people who were not quite of his kidney.
He judged others, naïvely, by their language, and if it was
free from the oaths and the obscenity which made up the
greater part of his own conversation, he looked upon them
with suspicion. In the evening the two men played piquet. He
played badly but vaingloriously, crowing over his opponent
when he won and losing his temper when he lost. On rare
occasions a couple of planters or traders would drive over to
play bridge, and then Walker showed himself in what Mackintosh considered a characteristic light. He played regardless of
his partner, calling up in his desire to play the hand, and argued
interminably, beating down opposition by the loudness of his
voice. He constantly revoked, and when he did so said with
an ingratiating whine: "Oh, you wouldn't count it against an
old man who can hardly see." Did he know that his opponents
thought it as well to keep on the right side of him and hesitated to insist on the rigour of the game? Mackintosh watched
him with an icy contempt. When the game was over, while
they smoked their pipes and drank whisky, they would begin
telling stories. Walker told with gusto the story of his marriage.
He had got so drunk at the wedding feast that the bride had
fled and he had never seen her since. He had had numberless
adventures, commonplace and sordid, with the women of the
island and he described them with a pride in his own prowess
which was an offence to Mackintosh's fastidious ears. He was
a gross, sensual old man. He thought Mackintosh a poor fellow
because he would not share his promiscuous amours and remained sober when the company was drunk.

He despised him also for the orderliness with which he did
his official work. Mackintosh liked to do everything just so.
His desk was always tidy, his papers were always neatly dock-
eted, he could put his hand on any document that was needed,
and he had at his fingers' ends all the regulations that were
required for the business of their administration.

"Fudge, fudge," said Walker. "I've run this island for
twenty years without red tape, and I don't want it now."

"Does it make it any easier for you that when you want
a letter you have to hunt half an hour for it?" answered Mackintosh.

"You're nothing but a damned official. But you're not a
bad fellow: when you've been out here a year or two you'll be

all right. What's wrong about you is that you won't drink. You wouldn't be a bad sort if you got soused cnce a week."

The curious thing was that Walker remained perfectly unconscious of the dislike for him which every month increased in the breast of his subordinate. Although he laughed at him, as he grew accustomed to him, he began almost to like him. He had a certain tolerance for the peculiarities of others, and he accepted Mackintosh as a queer fish. Perhaps he liked him, unconsciously, because he could chaff him. His humour consisted of coarse banter and he wanted a butt. Mackintosh's exactness, his morality, his sobriety, were all fruitful subjects; his Scot's name gave an opportunity for the usual jokes about Scotland; he enjoyed himself thoroughly when two or three men were there and he could make them all laugh at the expense of Mackintosh. He would say ridiculous things about him to the natives, and Mackintosh, his knowledge of Samoan still imperfect, would see their unrestrained mirth when Walker had made an obscene reference to him. He smiled good-humouredly.

"I'll say this for you, Mac," Walker would say in his gruff loud voice, "you can take a joke."

"Was it a joke?" smiled Mackintosh. "I didn't know."

"Scots wha hae!" shouted Walker, with a bellow of laughter. "There's only one way to make a Scotchman see a joke and that's by a surgical operation."

Walker little knew that there was nothing Mackintosh could stand less than chaff. He would wake in the night, the breathless night of the rainy season, and brood sullenly over the gibe that Walker had uttered carelessly days before. It rankled. His heart swelled with rage, and he pictured to himself ways in which he might get even with the bully. He had tried answering him, but Walker had a gift of repartee, coarse and obvious, which gave him an advantage. The dullness of his intellect made him impervious to a delicate shaft. His self-satisfaction made it impossible to wound him. His loud voice, his bellow of laughter, were weapons against which Mackintosh had nothing to counter, and he learned that the wisest thing was never to betray his irritation. He learned to control himself. But his hatred grew till it was a monomania. He watched Walker with an insane vigilance. He fed his own self-esteem by every instance of meanness on Walker's part, by every exhibition of childish vanity, of cunning and of vulgarity. Walker ate greedily, noisily, filthily, and Mackintosh watched him with satisfaction. He took note of the foolish things he said and of his mistakes in grammar. He knew that Walker held him in small esteem, and he found a bitter satisfaction in his chief's opinion of him; it increased his own contempt for the narrow, complacent old man. And it gave him a singular pleasure to know that Walker was entirely unconscious of the hatred he felt for him. He was a fool who liked popularity, and he blandly fancied that everyone admired him. Once Mackintosh had overheard Walker speaking of him.

"He'll be all right when I've licked him into shape," he said. "He's a good dog and he loves his master."

Mackintosh silently, without a movement of his long, sallow face, laughed long and heartily.

But his hatred was not blind; on the contrary, it was peculiarly clear-sighted, and he judged Walker's capabilities with precision. He ruled his small kingdom with efficiency. He was just and honest. With opportunities to make money he was a poorer man than when he was first appointed to his post, and his only support for his old age was the pension which he expected when at last he retired from official life. His pride was that with an assistant and a half-caste clerk he was able to administer the island more competently than Upolu, the island of which Apia is the chief town, was administered with its army of functionaries. He had a few native policemen to sustain his authority, but he made no use of them. He governed by bluff and his Irish humour.

"They insisted on building a jail for me," he said. "What the devil do I want a jail for? I'm not going to put the natives in prison. If they do wrong I know how to deal with them."

One of his quarrels with the higher authorities at Apia was that he claimed entire jurisdiction over the natives of his island. Whatever their crimes he would not give them up to courts competent to deal with them, and several times an angry correspondence had passed between him and the Governor at Upolu. For he looked upon the natives as his children. And that was the amazing thing about this coarse, vulgar, selfish man; he loved the island on which he had lived so long with passion, and he had for the natives a strange rough tenderness which was quite wonderful.

He loved to ride about the island on his old grey mare and he was never tired of its beauty. Sauntering along the

grassy roads among the coconut trees he would stop every
now and then to admire the loveliness of the scene. Now and
then he would come upon a native village and stop while
the head man brought him a bowl of *kava*. He would look at the
little group of bell-shaped huts with their high thatched roofs,
like beehives, and a smile would spread over his fat face. His
eyes rested happily on the spreading green of the breadfruit
trees.

"By George, it's like the garden of Eden."

Sometimes his rides took him along the coast and through
the trees he had a glimpse of the wide sea, empty, with never a
sail to disturb the loneliness; sometimes he climbed a hill so
that a great stretch of country, with little villages nestling
among the tall trees, was spread out before him like the kingdom of the world, and he would sit there for an hour in an ecstasy of delight. But he had no words to express his feelings and
to relieve them would utter an obscene jest; it was as though
his emotion was so violent that he needed vulgarity to break
the tension.

Mackintosh observed this sentiment with an icy disdain.
Walker had always been a heavy drinker, he was proud of his
capacity to see men half his age under the table when he spent
a night in Apia, and he had the sentimentality of the toper.
He could cry over the stories he read in his magazines and yet
would refuse a loan to some trader in difficulties whom he
had known for twenty years. He was close with his money.
Once Mackintosh said to him:

"No one could accuse you of giving money away."

He took it as a compliment. His enthusiasm for nature was
but the drivelling sensibility of the drunkard. Nor had Mackintosh any sympathy for his chief's feelings towards the natives.
He loved them because they were in his power, as a selfish man
loves his dog, and his mentality was on a level with theirs.
Their humour was obscene and he was never at a loss for the
lewd remark. He understood them and they understood him.
He was proud of his influence over them. He looked upon them
as his children and he mixed himself in all their affairs. But he
was very jealous of his authority; if he ruled them with a
rod of iron, brooking no contradiction, he would not suffer any
of the white men on the island to take advantage of them.
He watched the missionaries suspiciously and, if they did
anything of which he disapproved. was able to make life so

unendurable to them that if he could not get them removed
they were glad to go of their own accord. His power over the
natives was so great that on his word they would refuse labour
and food to their pastor. On the other hand he showed the
traders no favour. He took care that they should not cheat
the natives; he saw that they got a fair reward for their work
and their copra and that the traders made no extravagant profit
on the wares they sold them. He was merciless to a bargain
that he thought unfair. Sometimes the traders would complain
at Apia that they did not get fair opportunities. They suffered
for it. Walker then hesitated at no calumny, at no outrageous
lie, to get even with them, and they found that if they wanted
not only to live at peace, but to exist at all, they had to accept
the situation on his own terms. More than once the store of a
trader obnoxious to him had been burned down, and there was
only the appositeness of the event to show that the administrator had instigated it. Once a Swedish half-caste, ruined by
the burning, had gone to him and roundly accused him of
arson. Walker laughed in his face.

"You dirty dog. Your mother was a native and you try
to cheat the natives. If your rotten old store is burned down
it's a judgment of Providence; that's what it is, a judgment of
Providence. Get out."

And as the man was hustled out by two native policemen the
administrator laughed fatly.

"A judgment of Providence."

And now Mackintosh watched him enter upon the day's
work. He began with the sick, for Walker added doctoring to
his other activities, and he had a small room behind the office
full of drugs. An elderly man came forward, a man with a crop
of curly grey hair, in a blue *lava-lava*, elaborately tatooed, with
the skin of his body wrinkled like a wine-skin.

"What have you come for?" Walker asked him abruptly.

In a whining voice the man said that he could not eat without vomiting and that he had pains here and pains there.

"Go to the missionaries," said Walker. "You know that
I only cure children."

"I have been to the missionaries and they do me no good."

"Then go home and prepare yourself to die. Have you lived
so long and still want to go on living? You're a fool."

The man broke into querulous expostulation, but Walker,
pointing to a woman with a sick child in her arms, told her to

bring it to his desk. He asked her questions and looked at the child.

"I will give you medicine," he said. He turned to the half-caste clerk. "Go into the dispensary and bring me some calomel pills."

He made the child swallow one there and then and gave another to the mother.

"Take the child away and keep it warm. Tomorrow it wil' be dead or better."

He leaned back in his chair and lit his pipe.

"Wonderful stuff, calomel. I've saved more lives with it than all the hospital doctors at Apia put together."

Walker was very proud of his skill, and with the dogmatism of ignorance had no patience with the members of the medical profession.

"The sort of case I like," he said, "is the one that all the doctors have given up as hopeless. When the doctors have said they can't cure you, I say to them, 'come to me.' Did I ever tell you about the fellow who had a cancer?"

"Frequently," said Mackintosh.

"I got him right in three months."

"You've never told me about the people you haven't cured."

He finished this part of the work and went on to the rest. It was a queer medley. There was a woman who could not get on with her husband and a man who complained that his wife had run away from him.

"Lucky dog," said Walker. "Most men wish their wives would too."

There was a long complicated quarrel about the ownership of a few yards of land. There was a dispute about the sharing out of a catch of fish. There was a complaint against a white trader because he had given short measure. Walker listened attentively to every case, made up his mind quickly, and gave his decision. Then he would listen to nothing more; if the complainant went on he was hustled out of the office by a policeman. Mackintosh listened to it all with sullen irritation. On the whole, perhaps, it might be admitted that rough justice was done, but it exasperated the assistant that his chief trusted his instinct rather than the evidence. He would not listen to reason. He browbeat the witnesses and when they did not see what he wished them to called them thieves and liars.

He left to the last a group of men who were sitting in the

corner of the room. He had deliberately ignored them. The party consisted of an old chief, a tall, dignified man with short, white hair, in a new *lava-lava*, bearing a huge fly wisp as a badge of office, his son, and half a dozen of the important men of the village. Walker had had a feud with them and had beaten them. As was characteristic of him he meant now to rub in his victory, and because he had them down to profit by their helplessness. The facts were peculiar. Walker had a passion for building roads. When he had come to Talua there were but a few tracks here and there, but in course of time he had cut roads through the country, joining the villages together, and it was to this that a great part of the island's prosperity was due. Whereas in the old days it had been impossible to get the produce of the land, copra chiefly, down to the coast where it could be put on schooners or motor launches and so taken to Apia, now transport was easy and simple. His ambition was to make a road right round the island and a great part of it was already built.

"In two years I shall have done it, and then I can die or they can fire me, I don't care."

His roads were the joy of his heart and he made excursions constantly to see that they were kept in order. They were simple enough, wide tracks, grass covered, cut through the scrub or through the plantations; but trees had to be rooted out, rocks dug up or blasted, and here and there levelling had been necessary. He was proud that he had surmounted by his own skill such difficulties as they presented. He rejoiced in his disposition of them so that they were not only convenient, but showed off the beauties of the island which his soul loved. When he spoke of his roads he was almost a poet. They meandered through those lovely scenes, and Walker had taken care that here and there they should run in a straight line, giving you a green vista through the tall trees, and here and there should turn and curve so that the heart was rested by the diversity. It was amazing that this coarse and sensual man should exercise so subtle an ingenuity to get the effects which his fancy suggested to him. He had used in making his roads all the fantastic skill of a Japanese gardener. He received a grant from headquarters for the work but took a curious pride in using but a small part of it, and the year before had spent only a hundred pounds of the thousand assigned to him.

"What do they want money for?" he boomed. "They'll

only spend it on all kinds of muck they don't want; what the missionaries leave them, that is to say."

For no particular reason, except perhaps pride in the economy of his administration and the desire to contrast his efficiency with the wasteful methods of the authorities at Apia, he got the natives to do the work he wanted for wages that were almost nominal. It was owing to this that he had lately had difficulty with the village whose chief men now were come to see him. The chief's son had been in Upolu for a year and on coming back had told his people of the large sums that were paid at Apia for the public works. In long, idle talks he had inflamed their hearts with the desire for gain. He held out to them visions of vast wealth and they thought of the whisky they could buy—it was dear, since there was a law that it must not be sold to natives, and so it cost them double what the white man had to pay for it—they thought of the great sandal-wood boxes in which they kept their treasures, and the scented soap and potted salmon, the luxuries for which the Kanaka will sell his soul; so that when the administrator sent for them and told them he wanted a road made from their village to a certain point along the coast and offered them twenty pounds, they asked him a hundred. The chief's son was called Manuma. He was a tall, handsome fellow, copper-coloured, with his fuzzy hair dyed red with lime, a wreath of red berries round his neck, and behind his ear a flower like a scarlet flame against his brown face. The upper part of his body was naked, but to show that he was no longer a savage, since he had lived in Apia, he wore a pair of dungarees instead of a *lava-lava*. He told them that if they held together the administrator would be obliged to accept their terms. His heart was set on building the road and when he found they would not work for less he would give them what they asked. But they must not move; whatever he said they must not abate their claim; they had asked a hundred and that they must keep to. When they mentioned the figure, Walker burst into a shout of his long, deep-voiced laughter. He told them not to make fools of themselves, but to set about the work at once. Because he was in a good humour that day he promised to give them a feast when the road was finished. But when he found that no attempt was made to start work, he went to the village and asked the men what silly game they were playing. Manuma had coached them well. They were quite calm, they did not

attempt to argue—and argument is a passion with the Kanaka
—they merely shrugged their shoulders: they would do it for
a hundred pounds, and if he would not give them that they
would do no work. He could please himself. They did not care.
Then Walker flew into a passion. He was ugly then. His short
fat neck swelled ominously, his red face grew purple, he foamed
at the mouth. He set upon the natives with invective. He knew
well how to wound and how to humiliate. He was terrifying.
The older men grew pale and uneasy. They hesitated. If it
had not been for Manuma, with his knowledge of the great
world, and their dread of his ridicule, they would have yielded.
It was Manuma who answered Walker.

"Pay us a hundred pounds and we will work."

Walker, shaking his fist at him, called him every name he
could think of. He riddled him with scorn. Manuma sat still
and smiled. There may have been more bravado than confidence in his smile, but he had to make a good show before the
others. He repeated his words.

"Pay us a hundred pounds and we will work."

They thought that Walker would spring on him. It would
not have been the first time that he had thrashed a native with
his own hands; they knew his strength, and though Walker
was three times the age of the young man and six inches shorter
they did not doubt that he was more than a match for Manuma.
No one had ever thought of resisting the savage onslaught of
the administrator. But Walker said nothing. He chuckled.

"I am not going to waste my time with a pack of fools,"
he said. "Talk it over again. You know what I have offered.
If you do not start in a week, take care."

He turned round and walked out of the chief's hut. He untied
his old mare and it was typical of the relations between him
and the natives that one of the elder men hung on to the off
stirrup while Walker from a convenient boulder hoisted himself heavily into the saddle.

That same night when Walker according to his habit was
strolling along the road that ran past his house, he heard
something whizz past him and with a thud strike a tree. Something had been thrown at him. He ducked instinctively. With
a shout, "Who's that"? he ran towards the place from which
the missile had come and he heard the sound of a man escaping
through the bush. He knew it was hopeless to pursue in the
darkness, and besides he was soon out of breath, so he stopped

and made his way back to the road. He looked about for what
had been thrown, but could find nothing. It was quite dark.
He went quickly back to the house and called Mackintosh and
the Chinese boy.

"One of those devils has thrown something at me. Come
along and let's find out what it was."

He told the boy to bring a lantern and the three of them
made their way back to the place. They hunted about the
ground, but could not find what they sought. Suddenly the
boy gave a guttural cry. They turned to look. He held up the
lantern, and there, sinister in the light that cut the surrounding darkness, was a long knife sticking into the trunk of a
coconut tree. It had been thrown with such force that it required quite an effort to pull it out.

"By George, if he hadn't missed me I'd have been in a
nice state."

Walker handled the knife. It was one of those knives, made
in imitation of the sailor knives brought to the islands a
hundred years before by the first white men, used to divide the
coconuts in two so that the copra might be dried. It was a
murderous weapon, and the blade, twelve inches long, was
very sharp. Walker chuckled softly.

"The devil, the impudent devil."

He had no doubt it was Manuma who had flung the knife.
He had escaped death by three inches. He was not angry. On
the contrary, he was in high spirits; the adventure exhilarated
him, and when they got back to the house, calling for drinks,
he rubbed his hands gleefully.

"I'll make them pay for this!"

His little eyes twinkled. He blew himself out like a turkey-
cock, and for the second time within half an hour insisted on
telling Mackintosh every detail of the affair. Then he asked
him to play piquet, and while they played he boasted of his
intentions. Mackintosh listened with tightened lips.

"But why should you grind them down like this?" he asked.
"Twenty pounds is precious little for the work you want them
to do."

"They ought to be precious thankful I give them anything."

"Hang it all, it's not your own money. The government
allots you a reasonable sum. They won't complain if you spend
it."

"They're a bunch of fools at Apia."

Mackintosh saw that Walker's motive was merely vanity. He shrugged his shoulders.

"It won't do you much good to score off the fellows at Apia at the cost of your life."

"Bless you, they wouldn't hurt me, these people. They couldn't do without me. They worship me. Manuma is a fool. He only threw that knife to frighten me."

The next day Walker rode over again to the village. It was called Matautu. He did not get off his horse. When he reached the chief's house he saw that the men were sitting round the floor in a circle, talking, and he guessed they were discussing again the question of the road. The Samoan huts are formed in this way: Trunks of slender trees are placed in a circle at intervals of perhaps five or six feet; a tall tree is set in the middle and from this downwards slopes the thatched roof. Venetian blinds of coconut leaves can be pulled down at night or when it is raining. Ordinarily the hut is open all round so that the breeze can blow through freely. Walker rode to the edge of the hut and called out to the chief.

"Oh, there, Tangatu, your son left his knife in a tree last night. I have brought it back to you."

He flung it down on the ground in the midst of the circle, and with a low burst of laughter ambled off.

On Monday he went out to see if they had started work. There was no sign of it. He rode through the village. The inhabitants were about their ordinary avocations. Some were weaving mats of the pandanus leaf, one old man was busy with a *kava* bowl, the children were playing, the women went about their household chores. Walker, a smile on his lips, came to the chief's house.

"*Talofa-li*," said the chief.

"*Talofa*," answered Walker.

Manuma was making a net. He sat with a cigarette between his lips and looked up at Walker with a smile of triumph.

"You have decided that you will not make the road?"

The chief answered.

"Not unless you pay us one hundred pounds."

"You will regret it." He turned to Manuma. "And you, my lad, I shouldn't wonder if your back was very sore before you're much older."

He rode away chuckling. He left the natives vaguely uneasy. They feared the fat sinful old man, and neither the missionaries'

abuse of him nor the scorn which Manuma had learnt in Apia
made them forget that he had a devilish cunning and that
no man had ever braved him without in the long run suffering
for it. They found out within twenty-four hours what scheme
he had devised. It was characteristic. For next morning a great
band of men, women, and children came into the village and
the chief men said that they had made a bargain with Walker
to build the road. He had offered them twenty pounds and they
had accepted. Now the cunning lay in this, that the Polynesians
have rules of hospitality which have all the force of laws; an
etiquette of absolute rigidity made it necessary for the people
of the village not only to give lodging to the strangers, but to
provide them with food and drink as long as they wished to
stay. The inhabitants of Matautu were outwitted. Every
morning the workers went out in a joyous band, cut down
trees, blasted rocks, levelled here and there and then in the
evening tramped back again, and ate and drank, ate heartily,
danced, sang hymns, and enjoyed life. For them it was a picnic.
But soon their hosts began to wear long faces; the strangers
had enormous appetites, and the plantains and the breadfruit vanished before their rapacity; the alligator-pear trees,
whose fruit sent to Apia might sell for good money, were
stripped bare. Ruin stared them in the face. And then they
found that the strangers were working very slowly. Had they
received a hint from Walker that they might take their time?
At this rate by the time the road was finished there would not
be a scrap of food in the village. And worse than this, they
were a laughing-stock; when one or other of them went to some
distant hamlet on an errand he found that the story had got
there before him, and he was met with derisive laughter. There
is nothing the Kanaka can endure less than ridicule. It was
not long before much angry talk passed among the sufferers.
Manuma was no longer a hero; he had to put up with a good
deal of plain speaking, and one day what Walker had suggested came to pass: a heated argument turned into a quarrel
and half a dozen of the young men set upon the chief's son and
gave him such a beating that for a week he lay bruised and sore
on the pandanus mats. He turned from side to side and could
find no ease. Every day or two the administrator rode over on
his old mare and watched the progress of the road. He was not
a man to resist the temptation of taunting the fallen foe, and
he missed no opportunity to rub into the shamed inhabitants

of Matautu the bitterness of their humiliation. He broke their
spirit. And one morning, putting their pride in their pockets,
a figure of speech, since pockets they had not, they all set out
with the strangers and started working on the road. It was
urgent to get it done quickly if they wanted to save any food
at all, and the whole village joined in. But they worked silently,
with rage and mortification in their hearts, and even the
children toiled in silence. The women wept as they carried
away bundles of brushwood. When Walker saw them he
laughed so much that he almost rolled out of his saddle. The
news spread quickly and tickled the people of the island to
death. This was the greatest joke of all, the crowning triumph
of that cunning old white man whom no Kanaka had ever been
able to circumvent; and they came from distant villages, with
their wives and children, to look at the foolish folk who had
refused twenty pounds to make the road and now were forced
to work for nothing. But the harder they worked the more
easily went the guests. Why should they hurry, when they
were getting good food for nothing and the longer they took
about the job the better the joke became? At last the wretched
villagers could stand it no longer, and they were come this
morning to beg the administrator to send the strangers back
to their own homes. If he would do this they promised to finish
the road themselves for nothing. For him it was a victory
complete and unqualified. They were humbled. A look of arrogant complacence spread over his large, naked face, and he
seemed to swell in his chair like a great bullfrog. There was
something sinister in his appearance, so that Mackintosh
shivered with disgust. Then in his booming tones he began to
speak.

"Is it for my good that I make the road? What benefit do
you think I get out of it? It is for you, so that you can walk
in comfort and carry your copra in comfort. I offered to pay
you for your work, though it was for your own sake the work
was done. I offered to pay you generously. Now *you* must pay.
I will send the people of Manua back to their homes if you
will finish the road and pay the twenty pounds that I have to
pay them."

There was an outcry. They sought to reason with him. They
told him they had not the money. But to everything they said
he replied with brutal gibes. Then the clock struck.

"Dinner time," he said. "Turn them all out."

He raised himself heavily from his chair and walked out of the room. When Mackintosh followed him he found him already seated at table, a napkin tied round his neck, holding his knife and fork in readiness for the meal the Chinese cook was about to bring. He was in high spirits.

"I did 'em down fine," he said, as Mackintosh sat down. "I shan't have much trouble with the roads after this."

"I suppose you were joking," said Mackintosh icily.

"What do you mean by that?"

"You're not really going to make them pay twenty pounds?"

"You bet your life I am."

"I'm not sure you've got any right to."

"Ain't you? I guess I've got the right to do any damned thing I like on this island."

"I think you've bullied them quite enough."

Walker laughed fatly. He did not care what Mackintosh thought.

"When I want your opinion I'll ask for it."

Mackintosh grew very white. He knew by bitter experience that he could do nothing but keep silence, and the violent effort at self-control made him sick and faint. He could not eat the food that was before him and with disgust he watched Walker shovel meat into his vast mouth. He was a dirty feeder, and to sit at table with him needed a strong stomach. Mackintosh shuddered. A tremendous desire seized him to humiliate that gross and cruel man; he would give anything in the world to see him in the dust, suffering as much as he had made others suffer. He had never loathed the bully with such loathing as now.

The day wore on. Mackintosh tried to sleep after dinner, but the passion in his heart prevented him; he tried to read, but the letters swam before his eyes. The sun beat down pitilessly, and he longed for rain; but he knew that rain would bring no coolness; it would only make it hotter and more steamy. He was a native of Aberdeen and his heart yearned suddenly for the icy winds that whistled through the granite streets of that city. Here he was a prisoner, imprisoned not only by that placid sea, but by his hatred for that horrible old man. He pressed his hands to his aching head. He would like to kill him. But he pulled himself together. He must do something to distract his mind, and since he could not read he thought he would set his private papers in order. It was a job

which he had long meant to do and which he had constantly
put off. He unlocked the drawer of his desk and took out a
handful of letters. He caught sight of his revolver. An impulse,
no sooner realized than set aside, to put a bullet through his
head and so escape from the intolerable bondage of life flashed
through his mind. He noticed that in the damp air the revolver
was slightly rusted, and he got an oil rag and began to clean
it. It was while he was thus occupied that he grew aware of
someone slinking round the door. He looked up and called:

"Who is there?"

There was a moment's pause, then Manuma showed himself.

"What do you want?"

The chief's son stood for a moment, sullen and silent, and
when he spoke it was with a strangled voice.

"We can't pay twenty pounds. We haven't the money."

"What am I to do?" said Mackintosh. "You heard what
Mr. Walker said."

Manuma began to plead, half in Samoan and half in English.
It was a sing-song whine, with the quavering intonations of a
beggar, and it filled Mackintosh with disgust. It outraged
him that the man should let himself be so crushed. He was a
pitiful object.

"I can do nothing," said Mackintosh irritably. "You know
that Mr. Walker is master here."

Manuma was silent again. He still stood in the doorway.

"I am sick," he said at last. "Give me some medicine."

"What is the matter with you?"

"I do not know. I am sick. I have pains in my body."

"Don't stand there," said Mackintosh sharply. "Come in
and let me look at you."

Manuma entered the little room and stood before the desk.

"I have pains here and here."

He put his hands to his loins and his face assumed an expression of pain. Suddenly Mackintosh grew conscious that the
boy's eyes were resting on the revolver which he had laid on
the desk when Manuma appeared in the doorway. There
was a silence between the two which to Mackintosh was endless. He seemed to read the thoughts which were in the Kanaka's mind. His heart beat violently. And then he felt as
though something possessed him so that he acted under the
compulsion of a foreign will. Himself did not make the movements of his body, but a power that was strange to him. His

throat was suddenly dry, and he put his hand to it mechanically
in order to help his speech. He was impelled to avoid Manuma's eyes.

"Just wait here," he said, his voice sounding as though someone had seized him by the windpipe, "and I'll fetch you something from the dispensary."

He got up. Was it his fancy that he staggered a little? Manuma stood silently, and though he kept his eyes averted,
Mackintosh knew that he was looking dully out of the door.
It was this other person that possessed him, that drove him
out of the room, but it was himself that took a handful of
muddled papers and threw them on the revolver in order to
hide it from view. He went to the dispensary. He got a pill
and poured out some blue draught into a small bottle, and then
came out into the compound. He did not want to go back into
his own bungalow, so he called to Manuma.

"Come here."

He gave him the drugs and instructions how to take them.
He did not know what it was that made it impossible for him
to look at the Kanaka. While he was speaking to him he kept
his eyes on his shoulder. Manuma took the medicine and slunk
out of the gate.

Mackintosh went into the dining-room and turned over
once more the old newspapers. But he could not read them.
The house was very still. Walker was upstairs in his room
asleep, the Chinese cook was busy in the kitchen, the two
policemen were out fishing. The silence that seemed to brood
over the house was unearthly, and there hammered in Mackintosh's head the question whether the revolver still lay where
he had placed it. He could not bring himself to look. The
uncertainty was horrible, but the certainty would be more
horrible still. He sweated. At last he could stand the silence no
longer, and he made up his mind to go down the road to the
trader's, a man named Jervis, who had a store about a mile
away. He was a half-caste, but even that amount of white
blood made him possible to talk to. He wanted to get away
from his bungalow, with the desk littered with untidy papers,
and underneath them something, or nothing. He walked along
the road. As he passed the fine hut of a chief a greeting was
called out to him. Then he came to the store. Behind the
counter sat the trader's daughter, a swarthy broad-featured
girl in a pink blouse and a white drill skirt. Jervis hoped he

would marry her. He had money, and he had told Mackintosh
that his daughter's husband would be well-to-do. She flushed
a little when she saw Mackintosh.

"Father's just unpacking some cases that have come in this
morning. I'll tell him you're here."

He sat down and the girl went out behind the shop. In a
moment her mother waddled in, a huge old woman, a chiefess,
who owned much land in her own right; and gave him her hand.
Her monstrous obesity was an offence, but she managed to
convey an impression of dignity. She was cordial without
obsequiousness; affable, but conscious of her station.

"You're quite a stranger, Mr. Mackintosh. Teresa was
saying only this morning: 'Why, we never see Mr. Mackintosh
now.'"

He shuddered a little as he thought of himself as that old
native's son-in-law. It was notorious that she ruled her husband, notwithstanding his white blood, with a firm hand. Hers
was the authority and hers the business head. She might be
no more than Mrs. Jervis to the white people, but her father
had been a chief of the blood royal, and his father and his
father's father had ruled as kings. The trader came in, small
beside his imposing wife, a dark man with a black beard going
grey, in ducks, with handsome eyes and flashing teeth. He
was very British, and his conversation was slangy, but you
felt he spoke English as a foreign tongue; with his family he
used the language of his native mother. He was a servile man,
cringing and obsequious.

"Ah, Mr. Mackintosh, this is a joyful surprise. Get the
whisky, Teresa; Mr. Mackintosh will have a gargle with us."

He gave all the latest news of Apia, watching his guest's
eyes the while, so that he might know the welcome thing to
say.

"And how is Walker? We've not seen him just lately. Mrs.
Jervis is going to send him a sucking-pig one day this week."

"I saw him riding home this morning," said Teresa.

"Here's how," said Jervis, holding up his whisky.

Mackintosh drank. The two women sat and looked at him,
Mrs. Jervis in her black Mother Hubbard, placid and haughty,
and Teresa, anxious to smile whenever she caught his eye,
while the trader gossiped insufferably.

"They were saying in Apia it was about time Walker retired. He ain't so young as he was. Things have changed since he first come to the islands and he ain't changed with them."

"He'll go too far," said the old chiefess. "The natives aren't satisfied."

"That was a good joke about the road," laughed the trader. "When I told them about it in Apia they fair split their sides with laughing. Good old Walker."

Mackintosh looked at him savagely. What did he mean by talking of him in that fashion? To a half-caste trader he was Mr. Walker. It was on his tongue to utter a harsh rebuke for the impertinence. He did not know what held him back.

"When he goes I hope you'll take his place, Mr. Mackintosh," said Jervis. "We all like you on the island. You understand the natives. They're educated now, they must be treated differently to the old days. It wants an educated man to be administrator now. Walker was only a trader same as I am."

Teresa's eyes glistened.

"When the time comes if there's anything anyone can do here, you bet your bottom dollar we'll do it. I'd get all the chiefs to go over to Apia and make a petition."

Mackintosh felt horribly sick. It had not struck him that if anything happened to Walker it might be he who would succeed him. It was true that no one in his official position knew the island so well. He got up suddenly and scarcely taking his leave walked back to the compound. And now he went straight to his room. He took a quick look at his desk. He rummaged among the papers.

The revolver was not there.

His heart thumped violently against his ribs. He looked for the revolver everywhere. He hunted in the chairs and in the drawers. He looked desperately, and all the time he knew he would not find it. Suddenly he heard Walker's gruff, hearty voice.

"What the devil are you up to, Mac?"

He started. Walker was standing in the doorway and instinctively he turned round to hide what lay upon his desk.

"Tidying up?" quizzed Walker. "I've told 'em to put the grey in the trap. I'm going down to Tafoni to bathe. You'd better come along."

"All right," said Mackintosh.

So long as he was with Walker nothing could happen.

The place they were bound for was about three miles away, and there was a fresh-water pool, separated by a thin barrier of rock from the sea, which the administrator had blasted out for the natives to bathe in. He had done this at spots round the island, wherever there was a spring; and the fresh water, compared with the sticky warmth of the sea, was cool and invigorating. They drove along the silent grassy road, splashing now and then through fords, where the sea had forced its way in, past a couple of native villages, the bell-shaped huts spaced out roomily and the white chapel in the middle, and at the third village they got out of the trap, tied up the horse, and walked down to the pool. They were accompanied by four or five girls and a dozen children. Soon they were all splashing about, shouting and laughing, while Walker, in a *lava-lava*, swam to and fro like an unwieldy porpoise. He made lewd jokes with the girls, and they amused themselves by diving under him and wriggling away when he tried to catch them. When he was tired he lay down on a rock, while the girls and children surrounded him; it was a happy family; and the old man, huge, with his crescent of white hair and his shining bald crown, looked like some old sea god. Once Mackintosh caught a queer soft look in his eyes.

"They're dear children," he said. "They look upon me as their father."

And then without a pause he turned to one of the girls and made an obscene remark which sent them all into fits of laughter. Mackintosh started to dress. With his thin legs and thin arms he made a grotesque figure, a sinister Don Quixote, and Walker began to make coarse jokes about him. They were acknowledged with little smothered laughs. Mackintosh struggled with his shirt. He knew he looked absurd, but he hated being laughed at. He stood silent and glowering.

"If you want to get back in time for dinner you ought to come soon."

"You're not a bad fellow, Mac. Only you're a fool. When you're doing one thing you always want to do another. That's not the way to live."

But all the same he raised himself slowly to his feet and began to put on his clothes. They sauntered back to the village, drank a bowl of *kava* with the chief, and then, after a joyful farewell from all the lazy villagers, drove home.

After dinner, according to his habit, Walker, lighting his

cigar, prepared to go for a stroll. Mackintosh was suddenly seized with fear.

"Don't you think it's rather unwise to go out at night by yourself just now?"

Walker stared at him with his round blue eyes.

"What the devil do you mean?"

"Remember the knife the other night. You've got those fellows' backs up."

"Pooh! They wouldn't dare."

"Someone dared before."

"That was only a bluff. They wouldn't hurt me. They look upon me as a father. They know that whatever I do is for their own good."

Mackintosh watched him with contempt in his heart. The man's self-complacency outraged him, and yet something, he knew not what, made him insist.

"Remember what happened this morning. It wouldn't hurt you to stay at home just to-night. I'll play piquet with you."

"I'll play piquet with you when I come back. The Kanaka isn't born yet who can make me alter my plans."

"You'd better let me come with you."

"You stay where you are."

Mackintosh shrugged his shoulders. He had given the man full warning. If he did not heed it that was his own lookout. Walker put on his hat and went out. Mackintosh began to read; but then he thought of something; perhaps it would be as well to have his own whereabouts quite clear. He crossed over to the kitchen and, inventing some pretext, talked for a few minutes with the cook. Then he got out the gramophone and put a record on it, but while it ground out its melancholy tune, some comic song of a London music-hall, his ear was strained for ¬ sound away there in the night. At his elbow the record reeled out its loudness, the words were raucous, but notwithstanding he seemed to be surrounded by an unearthly silence. He heard the dull roar of the breakers against the reef. He heard the breeze sigh, far up, in the leaves of the coconut trees. How long would it be? It was awful.

He heard a hoarse laugh.

"Wonders will never cease. It's not often you play yourself a tune, Mac."

Walker stood at the window, red-faced, bluff and jovial.

"Well, you see I'm alive and kicking. What were you playing for?"

Walker came in.

"Nerves a bit dicky, eh? Playing a tune to keep your pecker up?"

"I was playing your requiem."

"What the devil's that?"

"'Alf o' bitter an' a pint of stout."

"A rattling good song too. I don't mind how often I hear it. Now I'm ready to take your money off you at piquet."

They played and Walker bullied his way to victory, bluffing his opponent, chaffing him, jeering at his mistakes, up to every dodge, browbeating him, exulting. Presently Mackintosh recovered his coolness, and standing outside himself, as it were, he was able to take a detached pleasure in watching the overbearing old man and in his own cold reserve. Somewhere Manuma sat quietly and awaited his opportunity.

Walker won game after game and pocketed his winnings at the end of the evening in high good humour.

"You'll have to grow a little bit older before you stand much chance against me, Mac. The fact is I have a natural gift for cards."

"I don't know that there's much gift about it when I happen to deal you fourteen aces."

"Good cards come to good players," retorted Walker. "I'd have won if I'd had your hands."

He went on to tell long stories of the various occasions on which he had played cards with notorious sharpers and to their consternation had taken all their money from them. He boasted. He praised himself. And Mackintosh listened with absorption. He wanted now to feed his hatred; and everything Walker said, every gesture, made him more detestable. At last Walker got up.

"Well, I'm going to turn in," he said with a loud yawn. "I've got a long day to-morrow."

"What are you going to do?"

"I'm driving over to the other side of the island. I'll start at five, but I don't expect I shall get back to dinner till late."

They generally dined at seven.

"We'd better make it half-past seven then."

"I guess it would be as well."

Mackintosh watched him knock the ashes out of his pipe.

His vitality was rude and exuberant. It was strange to think that death hung over him. A faint smile flickered in Mackintosh's cold, gloomy eyes.

"Would you like me to come with you?"

"What in God's name should I want that for? I'm using the mare and she'll have enough to do to carry me; she don't want to drag you over thirty miles of road."

"Perhaps you don't quite realize what the feeling is at Matautu. I think it would be safer if I came with you."

Walker burst into contemptuous laughter.

"You'd be a fine lot of use in a scrap. I'm not a great hand at getting the wind up."

Now the smile passed from Mackintosh's eyes to his lips. It distorted them painfully.

"*Quem deus vult perdere prius dementat.*"

"What the hell is that?" said Walker.

"Latin," answered Mackintosh as he went out.

And now he chuckled. His mood had changed. He had done all he could and the matter was in the hands of fate. He slept more soundly than he had done for weeks. When he awoke next morning he went out. After a good night he found a pleasant exhilaration in the freshness of the early air. The sea was a more vivid blue, the sky more brilliant, than on most days, the trade wind was fresh, and there was a ripple on the lagoon as the breeze brushed over it like velvet brushed the wrong way. He felt himself stronger and younger. He entered upon the day's work with zest. After luncheon he slept again, and as evening drew on he had the bay saddled and sauntered through the bush. He seemed to see it all with new eyes. He felt more normal. The extraordinary thing was that he was able to put Walker out of his mind altogether. So far as he was concerned he might never have existed.

He returned late, hot after his ride, and bathed again. Then he sat on the verandah, smoking his pipe, and looked at the day declining over the lagoon. In the sunset the lagoon, rosy and purple and green, was very beautiful. He felt at peace with the world and with himself. When the cook came out to say that dinner was ready and to ask whether he should wait, Mackintosh smiled at him with friendly eyes. He looked at his watch.

"It's half-past seven. Better not wait. One can't tell when the boss'll be back."

The boy nodded, and in a moment Mackintosh saw him carry across the yard a bowl of steaming soup. He got up lazily, went into the dining-room, and ate his dinner. Had it happened? The uncertainty was amusing and Mackintosh chuckled in the silence. The food did not seem so monotonous as usual, and even though there was Hamburger steak, the cook's invariable dish when his poor invention failed him, it tasted by some miracle succulent and spiced. After dinner he strolled over lazily to his bungalow to get a book. He liked the intense stillness, and now that the night had fallen the stars were blazing in the sky. He shouted for a lamp and in a moment the Chink pattered over on his bare feet, piercing the darkness with a ray of light. He put the lamp on the desk and noiselessly slipped out of the room. Mackintosh stood rooted to the floor, for there, half hidden by untidy papers, was his revolver. His heart throbbed painfully, and he broke into a sweat. It was done then.

He took up the revolver with a shaking hand. Four of the chambers were empty. He paused a moment and looked suspiciously out into the night, but there was no one there. He quickly slipped four cartridges into the empty chambers and locked the revolver in his drawer.

He sat down to wait.

An hour passed, a second hour passed. There was nothing. He sat at his desk as though he were writing, but he neither wrote nor read. He merely listened. He strained his ears for a sound travelling from a far distance. At last he heard hesitating footsteps and knew it was the Chinese cook.

"Ah-Sung," he called.

The boy came to the door.

"Boss velly late," he said. "Dinner no good."

Mackintosh stared at him, wondering whether he knew what had happened, and whether, when he knew, he would realize on what terms he and Walker had been. He went about his work, sleek, silent, and smiling, and who could tell his thoughts?

"I expect he's had dinner on the way, but you must keep the soup hot at all events."

The words were hardly out of his mouth when the silence was suddenly broken into by a confusion, cries, and a rapid patter of naked feet. A number of natives ran into the compound, men and women and children; they crowded round

Mackintosh and they all talked at once. They were unintelligible. They were excited and frightened and some of them were crying. Mackintosh pushed his way through them and went to the gateway. Though he had scarcely understood what they said he knew quite well what had happened. And as he reached the gate the dog-cart arrived. The old mare was being led by a tall Kanaka, and in the dog-cart crouched two men, trying to hold Walker up. A little crowd of natives surrounded it.

The mare was led into the yard and the natives surged in after it. Mackintosh shouted to them to stand back and the two policemen, sprang suddenly from God knows where, pushed them violently aside. By now he had managed to understand that some lads who had been fishing, on their way back to their village had come across the cart on the home side of the ford. The mare was nuzzling about the herbage and in the darkness they could just see the great white bulk of the old man sunk between the seat and the dashboard. At first they thought he was drunk and they peered in, grinning, but then they heard him groan, and guessed that something was amiss. They ran to the village and called for help. It was when they returned, accompanied by half a hundred people, that they discovered Walker had been shot.

With a sudden thrill of horror Mackintosh asked himself whether he was already dead. The first thing at all events was to get him out of the cart, and that, owing to Walker's corpulence, was a difficult job. It took four strong men to lift him. They jolted him and he uttered a dull groan. He was still alive. At last they carried him into the house, up the stairs, and placed him on his bed. Then Mackintosh was able to see him, for in the yard, lit only by half a dozen hurricane lamps, everything had been obscured. Walker's white ducks were stained with blood, and the men who had carried him wiped their hands, red and sticky, on their *lava-lavas*. Mackintosh held up the lamp. He had not expected the old man to be so pale. His eyes were closed. He was breathing still, his pulse could be just felt, but it was obvious that he was dying. Mackintosh had not bargained for the shock of horror that convulsed him. He saw that the native clerk was there, and in a voice hoarse with fear told him to go into the dispensary and get what was necessary for a hypodermic injection. One of the policemen had brought up the whisky, and Mackintosh forced a little into the old man's mouth. The room was crowded with natives. They sat about the floor, speechless now and terrified, and every now and then one wailed aloud. It was very hot, but Mackintosh felt cold, his hands and his feet were like ice, and he had to make a violent effort not to tremble in all his limbs. He did not know what to do. He did not know if Walker was bleeding still, and if he was, how he could stop the bleeding.

The clerk brought the hypodermic needle.

"You give it to him," said Mackintosh. "You're more used to that sort of thing than I am."

His head ached horribly. It felt as though all sorts of little savage things were beating inside it, trying to get out. They watched for the effect of the injection. Presently Walker opened his eyes slowly. He did not seem to know where he was.

"Keep quiet," said Mackintosh. "You're at home. You're quite safe."

Walker's lips outlined a shadowy smile.

"They've got me," he whispered.

"I'll get Jervis to send his motor-boat to Apia at once. We'll get a doctor out by to-morrow afternoon."

There was a long pause before the old man answered,

"I shall be dead by then."

A ghastly expression passed over Mackintosh's pale face. He forced himself to laugh.

"What rot! You keep quiet and you'll be as right as rain."

"Give me a drink," said Walker. "A stiff one."

With shaking hand Mackintosh poured out whisky and water, half and half, and held the glass while Walker drank greedily. It seemed to restore him. He gave a long sigh and a little colour came into his great fleshy face. Mackintosh felt extraordinarily helpless. He stood and stared at the old man.

"If you'll tell me what to do I'll do it," he said.

"There's nothing to do. Just leave me alone. I'm done for."

He looked dreadfully pitiful as he lay on the great bed, a huge, bloated, old man; but so wan, so weak, it was heart-rending. As he rested, his mind seemed to grow clearer.

"You were right, Mac," he said presently. "You warned me."

"I wish to God I'd come with you."

"You're a good chap, Mac, only you don't drink."

There was another long silence, and it was clear that Walker was sinking. There was an internal hæmorrhage and even Mackintosh in his ignorance could not fail to see that his chief had but an hour or two to live. He stood by the side of the bed stock still. For half an hour perhaps Walker lay with his eyes closed, then he opened them.

"They'll give you my job," he said, slowly. "Last time I was in Apia I told them you were all right. Finish my road. I want to think that'll be done. All round the island."

"I don't want your job. You'll get all right."

Walker shook his head wearily.

"I've had my day. Treat them fairly, that's the great thing. They're children. You must always remember that. You must be firm with them, but you must be kind. And you must be just. I've never made a bob out of them. I haven't saved a hundred pounds in twenty years. The road's the great thing. Get the road finished."

Something very like a sob was wrung from Mackintosh.

"You're a good fellow, Mac. I always liked you."

He closed his eyes, and Mackintosh thought that he would never open them again. His mouth was so dry that he had to get himself something to drink. The Chinese cook silently put a chair for him. He sat down by the side of the bed and waited. He did not know how long a time passed. The night was endless. Suddenly one of the men sitting there broke into uncontrollable sobbing, loudly, like a child, and Mackintosh grew aware that the room was crowded by this time with natives. They sat all over the floor on their haunches, men and women, staring at the bed.

"What are all these people doing here?" said Mackintosh. "They've got no right. Turn them out, turn them out, all of them."

His words seemed to rouse Walker, for he opened his eyes once more, and now they were all misty. He wanted to speak, but he was so weak that Mackintosh had to strain his ears to catch what he said.

"Let them stay. They're my children. They ought to be here."

Mackintosh turned to the natives.

"Stay where you are. He wants you. But be silent."

A faint smile came over the old man's white face.

"Come nearer," he said.

Mackintosh bent over him. His eyes were closed and the
words he said were like a wind sighing through the fronds of
the coconut trees.

"Give me another drink. I've got something to say."

This time Mackintosh gave him his whisky neat. Walker
collected his strength in a final effort of will.

"Don't make a fuss about this. In 'ninety-five when there
were troubles white men were killed, and the fleet came and
shelled the villages. A lot of people were killed who'd had
nothing to do with it. They're damned fools at Apia. If they
make a fuss they'll only punish the wrong people. I don't want
anyone punished."

He paused for a while to rest.

"You must say it was an accident. No one's to blame.
Promise me that."

"I'll do anything you like," whispered Mackintosh.

"Good chap. One of the best. They're children. I'm their
father. A father don't let his children get into trouble if he can
help it."

A ghost of a chuckle came out of his throat. It was astonishingly weird and ghastly.

"You're a religious chap, Mac. What's that about forgiving
them? You know."

For a while Mackintosh did not answer. His lips trembled.

"Forgive them, for they know not what they do?"

"That's right. Forgive them. I've loved them, you know,
always loved them."

He sighed. His lips faintly moved, and now Mackintosh
had to put his ears quite close to them in order to hear.

"Hold my hand," he said.

Mackintosh gave a gasp. His heart seemed wrenched. He
took the old man's hand, so cold and weak, a coarse, rough
hand, and held it in his own. And thus he sat until he nearly
started out of his seat, for the silence was suddenly broken
by a long rattle. It was terrible and unearthly. Walker was dead.
Then the natives broke out with loud cries. The tears ran down
their faces, and they beat their breasts.

Mackintosh disengaged his hand from the dead man's,
and staggering like one drunk with sleep he went out of the
room. He went to the locked drawer in his writing-desk and
took out the revolver. He walked down to the sea and walked

into the lagoon; he waded out cautiously, so that he should not trip against a coral rock, till the water came to his armpits. Then he put a bullet through his head.

An hour later half a dozen slim brown sharks were splashing and struggling at the spot where he fell.

RED

THE skipper thrust his hand into one of his trouser pockets and with difficulty, for they were not at the sides but in front and he was a portly man, pulled out a large silver watch. He looked at it and then looked again at the declining sun. The Kanaka at the wheel gave him a glance, but did not speak. The skipper's eyes rested on the island they were approaching. A white line of foam marked the reef. He knew there was an opening large enough to get his ship through, and when they came a little nearer he counted on seeing it. They had nearly an hour of daylight still before them. In the lagoon the water was deep and they could anchor comfortably. The chief of the village which he could already see among the coconut trees was a friend of the mate's, and it would be pleasant to go ashore for the night. The mate came forward at that minute and the skipper turned to him.

"We'll take a bottle of booze along with us and get some girls in to dance," he said.

"I don't see the opening," said the mate.

He was a Kanaka, a handsome, swarthy fellow, with somewhat the look of a later Roman emperor, inclined to stoutness; but his face was fine and clean-cut.

"I'm dead sure there's one right here," said the captain, looking through his glasses. "I can't understand why I can't pick it up. Send one of the boys up the mast to have a look."

The mate called one of the crew and gave him the order. The captain watched the Kanaka climb and waited for him to speak. But the Kanaka shouted down that he could see nothing but the unbroken line of foam. The captain spoke Samoan like a native, and he cursed him freely.

"Shall he stay up there?" asked the mate.

"What the hell good does that do?" answered the captain. "The blame fool can't see worth a cent. You bet your sweet life I'd find the opening if I was up there."

He looked at the slender mast with anger. It was all very well for a native who had been used to climbing up coconut trees all his life. He was fat and heavy.

"Come down," he shouted. "You're no more use than a dead dog. We'll just have to go along the reef till we find the opening."

It was a seventy-ton schooner with paraffin auxiliary, and it ran, when there was no head wind, between four and five knots an hour. It was a bedraggled object; it had been painted white a very long time ago, but it was now dirty, dingy, and mottled. It smelt strongly of paraffin and of the copra which was its usual cargo. They were within a hundred feet of the reef now and the captain told the steersman to run along it till they came to the opening. But when they had gone a couple of miles he realized that they had missed it. He went about and slowly worked back again. The white foam of the reef continued without interruption and now the sun was setting. With a curse at the stupidity of the crew the skipper resigned himself to waiting till next morning.

"Put her about," he said. "I can't anchor here."

They went out to sea a little and presently it was quite dark. They anchored. When the sail was furled the ship began to roll a good deal. They said in Apia that one day she would roll right over; and the owner, a German-American who managed one of the largest stores, said that no money was big enough to induce him to go out in her. The cook, a Chinese in white trousers, very dirty and ragged, and a thin white tunic, came to say that supper was ready, and when the skipper went into the cabin he found the engineer already seated at table. The engineer was a long, lean man with a scraggy neck. He was dressed in blue overalls and a sleeveless jersey which showed his thin arms tatooed from elbow to wrist.

"Hell, having to spend the night outside," said the skipper.

The engineer did not answer, and they ate their supper in silence. The cabin was lit by a dim oil lamp. When they had eaten the canned apricots with which the meal finished the Chink brought them a cup of tea. The skipper lit a cigar and went on the upper deck. The island now was only a darker mass against the night. The stars were very bright. The only sound was the ceaseless breaking of the surf. The skipper sank into a deck-chair and smoked idly. Presently three or four members of the crew came up and sat down. One of them had a banjo and another a concertina. They began to play, and one of them sang. The native song sounded strange on these instruments. Then to the singing a couple began to dance. It was a barbaric dance, savage and primeval, rapid, with quick movements of the hands and feet and contortions of the body; it was sensual, sexual even, but sexual without passion. It was very animal, direct, weird without mystery, natural in short, and one might almost say childlike. At last they grew tired. They stretched themselves on the deck and slept, and all was silent. The skipper lifted himself heavily out of his chair and clambered down the companion. He went into his cabin and got out of his clothes. He climbed into his bunk and lay there. He panted a little in the heat of the night.

But next morning, when the dawn crept over the tranquil sea, the opening in the reef which had eluded them the night before was seen a little to the east of where they lay. The schooner entered the lagoon. There was not a ripple on the surface of the water. Deep down among the coral rocks you saw little coloured fish swim. When he had anchored his ship the skipper ate his breakfast and went on deck. The sun shone from an unclouded sky, but in the early morning the air was grateful and cool. It was Sunday, and there was a feeling of quietness, a silence as though nature were at rest, which gave him a peculiar sense of comfort. He sat, looking at the wooded coast, and felt lazy and well at ease. Presently a slow smile moved his lips and he threw the stump of his cigar into the water.

"I guess I'll go ashore," he said. "Get the boat out."

He climbed stiffly down the ladder and was rowed to a little cove. The coconut trees came down to the water's edge, not in rows, but spaced out with an ordered formality. They were like a ballet of spinsters, elderly but flippant, standing in affected attitudes with the simpering graces of a bygone age. He sauntered idly through them, along a path that could be just seen winding its tortuous way, and it led him presently to a broad creek. There was a bridge across it, but a bridge constructed of single trunks of coconut trees, a dozen of them, placed end to end and supported where they met by a forked branch driven into the bed of the creek. You walked on a smooth, round surface, narrow and slippery, and there was no support for the hand. To cross such a bridge required sure feet and a stout heart. The skipper hesitated. But he saw on the other side, nestling among the trees, a white man's house; he made up his mind and, rather gingerly, began to walk. He watched his feet carefully, and where one trunk joined on to the next and there was a difference of level, he tottered a little. It was with a gasp of relief that he reached the last tree and finally set his feet on the firm ground of the other side. He had been so intent on the difficult crossing that he never noticed anyone was watching him, and it was with surprise that he heard himself spoken to.

"It takes a bit of nerve to cross these bridges when you're not used to them."

He looked up and saw a man standing in front of him. He had evidently come out of the house which he had seen.

"I saw you hesitate," the man continued, with a smile on his lips, "and I was watching to see you fall in."

"Not on your life," said the captain, who had now recovered his confidence.

"I've fallen in myself before now. I remember, one evening I came back from shooting, and I fell in, gun and all. Now I get a boy to carry my gun for me."

He was a man no longer young, with a small beard, now somewhat grey, and a thin face. He was dressed in a singlet, without arms, and a pair of duck trousers. He wore neither shoes nor socks. He spoke English with a slight accent.

"Are you Neilson?" asked the skipper.

"I am."

"I've heard about you. I thought you lived somewheres round here."

The skipper followed his host into the little bungalow and sat down heavily in the chair which the other motioned him to take. While Neilson went out to fetch whisky and glasses he took a look round the room. It filled him with amazement. He had never seen so many books. The shelves reached from floor to ceiling on all four walls, and they were closely packed. There was a grand piano littered with music, and a large table

on which books and magazines lay in disorder. The room made
him feel embarrassed. He remembered that Neilson was a queer
fellow. No one knew very much about him, although he had
been in the islands for so many years, but those who knew
him agreed that he was queer. He was a Swede.

"You've got one big heap of books here," he said, when Neilson returned.

"They do no harm," answered Neilson with a smile.

"Have you read them all?" asked the skipper.

"Most of them."

"I'm a bit of a reader myself. I have the *Saturday Evening
Post* sent me regler."

Neilson poured his visitor a good stiff glass of whisky and
gave him a cigar. The skipper volunteered a little information.

"I got in last night, but I couldn't find the opening, so I had
to anchor outside. I never been this run before, but my people
had some stuff they wanted to bring over here. Gray, d'you
know him?"

"Yes, he's got a store a little way along."

"Well, there was a lot of canned stuff that he wanted over,
an' he's got some copra. They thought I might just as well come
over as lie idle at Apia. I run between Apia and Pago-Pago
mostly, but they've got smallpox there just now, and there's
nothing stirring."

He took a drink of his whisky and lit a cigar. He was a taciturn man, but there was something in Neilson that made him
nervous, and his nervousness made him talk. The Swede was
looking at him with large dark eyes in which there was an expression of faint amusement.

"This is a tidy little place you've got here."

"I've done my best with it."

"You must do pretty well with your trees. They look fine.
With copra at the price it is now. I had a bit of a plantation
myself once, in Upolu it was, but I had to sell it."

He looked round the room again, where all those books gave
him a feeling of something incomprehensible and hostile.

"I guess you must find it a bit lonesome here though," he
said.

"I've got used to it. I've been here for twenty-five years."

Now the captain could think of nothing more to say, and he
smoked in silence. Neilson had apparently no wish to break it.
He looked at his guest with a meditative eye. He was a tall man,

more than six feet high, and very stout. His face was red and blotchy, with a network of little purple veins on the cheeks, and his features were sunk into its fatness. His eyes were bloodshot. His neck was buried in rolls of fat. But for a fringe of long curly hair, nearly white, at the back of his head, he was quite bald; and that immense, shiny surface of forehead, which might have given him a false look of intelligence, on the contrary gave him one of peculiar imbecility. He wore a blue flannel shirt, open at the neck and showing his fat chest covered with a mat of reddish hair, and a very old pair of blue serge trousers. He sat in his chair in a heavy ungainly attitude, his great belly thrust forward and his fat legs uncrossed. All elasticity had gone from his limbs. Neilson wondered idly what sort of man he had been in his youth. It was almost impossible to imagine that this creature of vast bulk had ever been a boy who ran about. The skipper finished his whisky, and Neilson pushed the bottle towards him.

"Help yourself."

The skipper leaned forward and with his great hand seized it.

"And how come you in these parts anyways?" he said.

"Oh, I came out to the islands for my health. My lungs were bad and they said I hadn't a year to live. You see they were wrong."

"I meant, how come you to settle down right here?"

"I am a sentimentalist."

"Oh!"

Neilson knew that the skipper had not an idea what he meant, and he looked at him with an ironical twinkle in his dark eyes. Perhaps just because the skipper was so gross and dull a man the whim seized him to talk further.

"You were too busy keeping your balance to notice, when you crossed the bridge, but this spot is generally considered rather pretty."

"It's a cute little house you've got here."

"Ah, that wasn't here when I first came. There was a native hut, with its beehive roof and its pillars, overshadowed by a great tree with red flowers; and the croton bushes, their leaves yellow and red and golden, made a pied fence around it. And then all about were the coconut trees, as fanciful as women, and as vain. They stood at the water's edge and spent all day looking at their reflections. I was a young man then—Good Heav-

ens, it's a quarter of a century ago—and I wanted to enjoy
all the loveliness of the world in the short time allotted to me
before I passed into the darkness. I thought it was the most
beautiful spot I had ever seen. The first time I saw it I had a
catch at my heart, and I was afraid I was going to cry. I wasn't
more than twenty-five, and though I put the best face I could
on it, I didn't want to die. And somehow it seemed to me that
the very beauty of this place made it easier for me to accept
my fate. I felt when I came here that all my past life had fallen
away, Stockholm and its University, and then Bonn: it all
seemed the life of somebody else, as though now at last I had
achieved the reality which our doctors of philosophy—I am
one myself, you know—had discussed so much. 'A year,' I
cried to myself. 'I have a year. I will spend it here and then I
am content to die.'

"We are foolish and sentimental and melodramatic at
twenty-five, but if we weren't perhaps we should be less wise at
fifty.

"Now drink, my friend. Don't let the nonsense I talk interfere with you."

He waved his thin hand towards the bottle, and the skipper
finished what remained in his glass.

"You ain't drinking nothin'," he said, reaching for the
whisky.

"I am of a sober habit," smiled the Swede. "I intoxicate myself in ways which I fancy are more subtle. But perhaps that
is only vanity. Anyhow, the effects are more lasting and the results less deleterious."

"They say there's a deal of cocaine taken in the States now,"
said the captain.

Neilson chuckled.

"But I do not see a white man often," he continued, "and
for once I don't think a drop of whisky can do me any harm."

He poured himself out a little, added some soda, and took a
sip.

"And presently I found out why the spot had such an unearthly loveliness. Here love had tarried for a moment like a
migrant bird that happens on a ship in mid-ocean and for a
little while folds its tired wings. The fragrance of a beautiful
passion hovered over it like the fragrance of hawthorn in May in
the meadows of my home. It seems to me that the places where
men have loved or suffered keep about them always some faint

aroma of something that has not wholly died. It is as though they had acquired a spiritual significance which mysteriously affects those who pass. I wish I could make myself clear." He smiled a little. "Though I cannot imagine that if I did you would understand."

He paused.

"I think this place was beautiful because here had been loved beautifully." And now he shrugged his shoulders. "But perhaps it is only that my æsthetic sense is gratified by the happy conjunction of young love and a suitable setting."

Even a man less thick-witted than the skipper might have been forgiven if he were bewildered by Neilson's words. For he seemed faintly to laugh at what he said. It was as though he spoke from emotion which his intellect found ridiculous. He had said himself that he was a sentimentalist, and when sentimentality is joined with scepticism there is often the devil to pay.

He was silent for an instant and looked at the captain with eyes in which there was a sudden perplexity.

"You know, I can't help thinking that I've seen you before, somewhere or other," he said.

"I couldn't say as I remember you," returned the skipper.

"I have a curious feeling as though your face were familiar to me. It's been puzzling me for some time. But I can't situate my recollection in any place or at any time."

The skipper massively shrugged his heavy shoulders.

"It's thirty years since I first come to the islands. A man can't figure on remembering all the folk he meets in a while like that."

The Swede shook his head.

"You know how one sometimes has the feeling that a place one has never been to before is strangely familiar. That's how I seem to see you." He gave a whimsical smile. "Perhaps I knew you in some past existence. Perhaps, perhaps you were the master of a galley in ancient Rome and I was a slave at the oar. Thirty years have you been here?"

"Every bit of thirty years."

"I wonder if you knew a man called Red?"

"Red?"

"That is the only name I've ever known him by. I never knew him personally. I never even set eyes on him. And yet I seem to see him more clearly than many men, my brothers, for instance, with whom I passed my daily life for many years. He lives in my imagination with the distinctness of a Paolo Malatesta or a Romeo. But I daresay you have never read Dante or Shakespeare?"

"I can't say as I have," said the captain.

Neilson, smoking a cigar, leaned back in his chair and looked vacantly at the ring of smoke which floated in the still air. A smile played on his lips, but his eyes were grave. Then he looked at the captain. There was in his gross obesity something extraordinarily repellent. He had the plethoric self-satisfaction of the very fat. It was an outrage. It set Neilson's nerves on edge. But the contrast between the man before him and the man he had in mind was pleasant.

"It appears that Red was the most comely thing you ever saw. I've talked to quite a number of people who knew him in those days, white men, and they all agree that the first time you saw him his beauty just took your breath away. They called him Red on account of his flaming hair. It had a natural wave and he wore it long. It must have been of that wonderful colour that the pre-Raphaelites raved over. I don't think he was vain of it, he was much too ingenuous for that, but no one could have blamed him if he had been. He was tall, six feet and an inch or two—in the native house that used to stand here was the mark of his height cut with a knife on the central trunk that supported the roof—and he was made like a Greek god, broad in the shoulders and thin in the flanks; he was like Apollo, with just that soft roundness which Praxiteles gave him, and that suave, feminine grace which has in it something troubling and mysterious. His skin was dazzling white, milky, like satin; his skin was like a woman's."

"I had kind of a white skin myself when I was a kiddie," said the skipper, with a twinkle in his bloodshot eyes.

But Neilson paid no attention to him. He was telling his story now and interruption made him impatient.

"And his face was just as beautiful as his body. He had large blue eyes, very dark, so that some say they were black, and unlike most red-haired people he had dark eyebrows and long dark lashes. His features were perfectly regular and his mouth was like a scarlet wound. He was twenty."

On these words the Swede stopped with a certain sense of the dramatic. He took a sip of whisky.

"He was unique. There never was anyone more beautiful.

There was no more reason for him than for a wonderful blossom
to flower on a wild plant. He was a happy accident of nature.

"One day he landed at that cove into which you must have
put this morning. He was an American sailor, and he had
deserted from a man-of-war in Apia. He had induced some good-
humoured native 'o give him a passage on a cutter that happened to be sailing from Apia to Safoto, and he had been put
ashore here in a dugout. I do not know why he deserted. Perhaps life on a man-of-war with its restrictions irked him, perhaps he was in trouble, and perhaps it was the South Seas and
these romantic islands that got into his bones. Every now and
then they take a man strangely, and he finds himself like a fly
in a spider's web. It may be that there was a softness of fibre
in him, and these green hills with their soft airs, this blue sea,
took the northern strength from him as Delilah took the Naza-
rite's. Anyhow, he wanted to hide himself, and he thought he
would be safe in this secluded nook till his ship had sailed from
Samoa.

"There was a native hut at the cove and as he stood there,
wondering where exactly he should turn his steps, a young girl
came out and invited him to enter. He knew scarcely two words
of the native tongue and she as little English. But he understood well enough what her smiles meant, and her pretty
gestures, and he followed her. He sat down on a mat and she
gave him slices of pineapple to eat. I can speak of Red only
from hearsay, but I saw the girl three years after he first met
her, and she was scarcely nineteen then. You cannot imagine
how exquisite she was. She had the passionate grace of the
hibiscus and the rich colour. She was rather tall, slim, with the
delicate features of her race, and large eyes like pools of still
water under the palm trees; her hair, black and curling, fell
down her back, and she wore a wreath of scented flowers. Her
hands were lovely. They were so small, so exquisitely formed,
they gave your heart-strings a wrench. And in those days she
laughed easily. Her smile was so delightful that it made your
knees shake. Her skin was like a field of ripe corn on a summer
day. Good Heavens, how can I describe her? She was too beautiful to be real.

"And these two young things, she was sixteen and he was
twenty, fell in love with one another at first sight. That is the
real love, not the love that comes from sympathy, common
interests, or intellectual community, but love pure and simple.

That is the love that Adam felt for Eve when he awoke and
found her in the garden gazing at him with dewy eyes. That is
the love that draws the beasts to one another, and the Gods.
That is the love that makes the world a miracle. That is the
love which gives life its pregnant meaning. You have never
heard of the wise, cynical French duke who said that with two
lovers there is always one who loves and one who lets himself
be loved; it is a bitter truth to which most of us have to resign
ourselves; but now and then there are two who love and two
who let themselves be loved. Then one might fancy that the
sun stands still as it stood when Joshua prayed to the God of
Israel.

"And even now after all these years, when I think of these
two, so young, so fair, so simple, and of their love, I feel a pang.
It tears my heart just as my heart is torn when on certain
nights I watch the full moon shining on the lagoon from an
unclouded sky. There is always pain in the contemplation of
perfect beauty.

"They were children. She was good and sweet and kind.
I know nothing of him, and I like to think that then at all
events he was ingenuous and frank. I like to think that his soul
was as comely as his body. But I daresay he had no more soul
than the creatures of the woods and forests who made pipes
from reeds and bathed in the mountain streams when the
world was young, and you might catch sight of little fawns
galloping through the glade on the back of a bearded centaur.
A soul is a troublesome possession and when man developed
it he lost the Garden of Eden.

"Well, when Red came to the island it had recently been
visited by one of those epidemics which the white man has
brought to the South Seas, and one third of the inhabitants had
died. It seems that the girl had lost all her near kin and she
lived now in the house of distant cousins. The household consisted of two ancient crones, bowed and wrinkled, two younger
women, and a man and a boy. For a few days he stayed there.
But perhaps he felt himself too near the shore, with the possibility that he might fall in with white men who would reveal
his hiding-place; perhaps the lovers could not bear that the
company of others should rob them for an instant of the delight of being together. One morning they set out, the pair of
them, with the few things that belonged to the girl, and walked
along a grassy path under the coconuts, till they came to the

creek you see. They had to cross the bridge you crossed, and
the girl laughed gleefully because he was afraid. She held his
hand till they came to the end of the first tree, and then his
courage failed him and he had to go back. He was obliged to
take off all his clothes before he could risk it, and she carried
them over for him on her head. They settled down in the empty
hut that stood here. Whether she had any rights over it (land
tenure is a complicated business in the islands), or whether the
owner had died during the epidemic, I do not know, but anyhow no one questioned them, and they took possession. Their
furniture consisted of a couple of grass mats on which they
slept, a fragment of looking-glass, and a bowl or two. In this
pleasant land that is enough to start housekeeping on.

"They say that happy people have no history, and certainly
a happy love has none. They did nothing all day long and yet
the days seemed all too short. The girl had a native name, but
Red called her Sally. He picked up the easy language very
quickly, and he used to lie on the mat for hours while she
chattered gaily to him. He was a silent fellow, and perhaps his
mind was lethargic. He smoked incessantly the cigarettes
which she made him out of the native tobacco and pandanus
leaf, and he watched her while with deft fingers she made grass
mats. Often natives would come in and tell long stories of the
old days when the island was disturbed by tribal wars. Sometimes he would go fishing on the reef, and bring home a basket
full of coloured fish. Sometimes at night he would go out with
a lantern to catch lobster. There were plantains round the hut
and Sally would roast them for their frugal meal. She knew how
to make delicious messes from coconuts, and the breadfruit
tree by the side of the creek gave them its fruit. On feast-days
they killed a little pig and cooked it on hot stones. They bathed
together in the creek; and in the evening they went down to the
lagoon and paddled about in a dugout, with its great outrigger.
The sea was deep blue, wine-coloured at sundown, like the sea
of Homeric Greece; but in the lagoon the colour had an infinite
variety, aquamarine and amethyst and emerald; and the setting
sun turned it for a short moment to liquid gold. Then there was
the colour of the coral, brown, white, pink, red, purple; and
the shapes it took were marvellous. It was like a magic garden,
and the hurrying fish were like butterflies. It strangely lacked
reality. Among the coral were pools with a floor of white sand
and here, where the water was dazzling clear, it was very

good to bathe. Then, cool and happy, they wandered back in
the gloaming over the soft grass road to the creek, walking
hand in hand, and now the mynah birds filled the coconut
trees with their clamour. And then the night, with that great
sky shining with gold, that seemed to stretch more widely
than the skies of Europe, and the soft airs that blew gently
through the open hut, the long night again was all too short.
She was sixteen and he was barely twenty. The dawn crept in
among the wooden pillars of the hut and looked at those lovely
children sleeping in one another's arms. The sun hid behind the
great tattered leaves of the plantains so that it might not
disturb them, and then, with playful malice, shot a golden ray,
like the outstretched paw of a Persian cat, on their faces. They
opened their sleepy eyes and they smiled to welcome another
day. The weeks lengthened into months, and a year passed.
They seemed to love one another as—I hesitate to say passionately, for passion has in it always a shade of sadness, a touch of
bitterness or anguish, but as whole heartedly, as simply and
naturally as on that first day on which, meeting, they had
recognized that a god was in them.

"If you had asked them I have no doubt that they would
have thought it impossible to suppose their love could ever
cease. Do we not know that the essential element of love is a
belief in its own eternity? And yet perhaps in Red there was
already a very little seed, unknown to himself and unsuspected
by the girl, which would in time have grown to weariness. For
one day one of the natives from the cove told them that some
way down the coast at the anchorage was a British whaling-
ship.

"'Gee,' he said, 'I wonder if I could make a trade of some
nuts and plantains for a pound or two of tobacco.'

"The pandanus cigarettes that Sally made him with untiring
hands were strong and pleasant enough to smoke, but they
left him unsatisfied; and he yearned on a sudden for real
tobacco, hard, rank, and pungent. He had not smoked a pipe
for many months. His mouth watered at the thought of it.
One would have thought some premonition of harm would have
made Sally seek to dissuade him, but love possessed her so
completely that it never occurred to her any power on earth
could take him from her. They went up into the hills together
and gathered a great basket of wild oranges, green, but sweet
and juicy; and they picked plantains from around the hut, and

coconuts from their trees, and breadfruit and mangoes; and they carried them down to the cove. They loaded the unstable canoe with them, and Red and the native boy who had brought them the news of the ship paddled along outside the reef.

"It was the last time she ever saw him.

"Next day the boy came back alone. He was all in tears. This is the story he told. When after their long paddle they reached the ship and Red hailed it, a white man looked over the side and told them to come on board. They took the fruit they had brought with them and Red piled it up on the deck. The white man and he began to talk, and they seemed to come to some agreement. One of them went below and brought up tobacco. Red took some at once and lit a pipe. The boy imitated the zest with which he blew a great cloud of smoke from his mouth. Then they said something to him and he went into the cabin. Through the open door the boy, watching curiously, saw a bottle brought out and glasses. Red drank and smoked. They seemed to ask him something, for he shook his head and laughed. The man, the first man who had spoken to them, laughed too, and he filled Red's glass once more. They went on talking and drinking, and presently, growing tired of watching a sight that meant nothing to him, the boy curled himself up on the deck and slept. He was awakened by a kick; and, jumping to his feet, he saw that the ship was slowly sailing out of the lagoon. He caught sight of Red seated at the table, with his head resting heavily on his arms, fast asleep. He made a movement towards him, intending to wake him, but a rough hand seized his arm, and a man, with a scowl and words which he did not understand, pointed to the side. He shouted to Red, but in a moment he was seized and flung overboard. Helpless, he swam round to his canoe which was drifting a little way off, and pushed it on to the reef. He climbed in and, sobbing all the way, paddled back to shore.

"What had happened was obvious enough. The whaler, by desertion or sickness, was short of hands, and the captain when Red came aboard had asked him to sign on; on his refusal he had made him drunk and kidnapped him.

"Sally was beside herself with grief. For three days she screamed and cried. The natives did what they could to comfort her, but she would not be comforted. She would not eat. And then, exhausted, she sank into a sullen apathy. She spent long days at the cove, watching the lagoon, in the vain hope

that Red somehow or other would manage to escape. She sat on
the white sand, hour after hour, with the tears running down her
cheeks, and at night dragged herself wearily back across the
creek to the little hut where she had been happy. The people
with whom she had lived before Red came to the island wished
her to return to them, but she would not; she was convinced
that Red would come back, and she wanted him to find her
where he had left her. Four months later she was delivered of a
still-born child, and the old woman who had come to help her
through her confinement remained with her in the hut. All joy
was taken from her life. If her anguish with time became less
intolerable it was replaced by a settled melancholy. You would
not have thought that among these people, whose emotions,
though so violent, are very transient, a woman could be found
capable of so enduring a passion. She never lost the profound
conviction that sooner or later Red would come back. She
watched for him, and every time someone crossed this slender
little bridge of coconut trees she looked. It might at last be he."

Neilson stopped talking and gave a faint sigh.

"And what happened to her in the end?" asked the skipper.
Neilson smiled bitterly.

"Oh, three years afterwards she took up with another white
man."

The skipper gave a fat, cynical chuckle.

"That's generally what happens to them," he said.

The Swede shot him a look of hatred. He did not know why
that gross, obese man excited in him so violent a repulsion.
But his thoughts wandered and he found his mind filled with
memories of the past. He went back five and twenty years. It
was when he first came to the island, weary of Apia, with its
heavy drinking, its gambling and coarse sensuality, a sick man,
trying to resign himself to the loss of the career which had fired
his imagination with ambitious thoughts. He set behind him
resolutely all his hopes of making a great name for himself and
strove to content himself with the few poor months of careful
life which was all that he could count on. He was boarding with
a half-caste trader who had a store a couple of miles along the
coast at the edge of a native village; and one day, wandering
aimlessly along the grassy paths of the coconut groves, he had
come upon the hut in which Sally lived. The beauty of the spot
had filled him with a rapture so great that it was almost painful,
and then he had seen Sally. She was the loveliest creature he

had ever seen, and the sadness in those dark, magnificent eyes
of hers affected him strangely. The Kanakas were a handsome
race, and beauty was not rare among them, but it was the
beauty of shapely animals. It was empty. But those tragic eyes
were dark with mystery, and you felt in them the bitter complexity of the groping, human soul. The trader told him the
story and it moved him.

"Do you think he'll ever come back?" asked Neilson.

"No fear. Why, it'll be a couple of years before the ship is
paid off, and by then he'll have forgotten all about her. I bet
he was pretty mad when he woke up and found he'd been
shanghaied, and I shouldn't wonder but he wanted to fight
somebody. But he'd got to grin and bear it, and I guess in a
month he was thinking it the best thing that had ever happened
to him that he got away from the island."

But Neilson could not get the story out of his head. Perhaps
because he was sick and weakly, the radiant health of Red
appealed to his imagination. Himself an ugly man, insignificant
of appearance, he prized very highly comeliness in others. He
had never been passionately in love, and certainly he had never
been passionately loved. The mutual attraction of those two
young things gave him a singular delight. It had the ineffable
beauty of the Absolute. He went again to the little hut by the
creek. He had a gift for languages and an energetic mind,
accustomed to work, and he had already given much time to
the study of the local tongue. Old habit was strong in him and
he was gathering together material for a paper on the Samoan
speech. The old crone who shared the hut with Sally invited
him to come in and sit down. She gave him *kava* to drink and
cigarettes to smoke. She was glad to have someone to chat with
and while she talked he looked at Sally. She reminded him of
the Psyche in the museum at Naples. Her features had the
same clear purity of line, and though she had borne a child
she had still a virginal aspect.

It was not till he had seen her two or three times that he
induced her to speak. Then it was only to ask him if he had seen
in Apia a man called Red. Two years had passed since his disap-
pearance, but it was plain that she still thought of him incessantly.

It did not take Neilson long to discover that he was in love
with her. It was only by an effort of will now that he prevented
himself from going every day to the creek, and when he was not

with Sally his thoughts were. At first, looking upon himself as a dying man, he asked only to look at her, and occasionally hear her speak, and his love gave him a wonderful happiness. He exulted in its purity. He wanted nothing from her but the opportunity to weave around her graceful person a web of beautiful fancies. But the open air, the equable temperature, the rest, the simple fare, began to have an unexpected effect on his health. His temperature did not soar at night to such alarming heights, he coughed less and began to put on weight; six months passed without his having a hæmorrhage; and on a sudden he saw the possibility that he might live. He had studied his disease carefully, and the hope dawned upon him that with great care he might arrest its course. It exhilarated him to look forward once more to the future. He made plans. It was evident that any active life was out of the question, but he could live on the islands, and the small income he had, insufficient elsewhere, would be ample to keep him. He could grow coconuts; that would give him an occupation; and he would send for his books and a piano; but his quick mind saw that in all this he was merely trying to conceal from himself the desire which obsessed him.

He wanted Sally. He loved not only her beauty, but that dim soul which he divined behind her suffering eyes. He would intoxicate her with his passion. In the end he would make her forget. And in an ecstasy of surrender he fancied himself giving her too the happiness which he had thought never to know again, but had now so miraculously achieved.

He asked her to live with him. She refused. He had expected that and did not let it depress him, for he was sure that sooner or later she would yield. His love was irresistible. He told the old woman of his wishes, and found somewhat to his surprise that she and the neighbours, long aware of them, were strongly urging Sally to accept his offer. After all, every native was glad to keep house for a white man, and Neilson according to the standards of the island was a rich one. The trader with whom he boarded went to her and told her not to be a fool; such an opportunity would not come again, and after so long she could not still believe that Red would ever return. The girl's resistance only increased Neilson's desire, and what had been a very pure love now became an agonizing passion. He was determined that nothing should stand in his way. He gave Sally no peace. At last, worn out by his persistence and the persuasions, by turns pleading and angry, of everyone around her, she consented. But the day after when, exultant, he went to see her he found that in the night she had burnt down the hut in which she and Red had lived together. The old crone ran towards him full of angry abuse of Sally, but he waved her aside; it did not matter; they would build a bungalow on the place where the hut had stood. A European house would really be more convenient if he wanted to bring out a piano and a vast number of books.

And so the little wooden house was built in which he had now lived for many years, and Sally became his wife. But after the first few weeks of rapture, during which he was satisfied with what she gave him, he had known little happiness. She had yielded to him, through weariness, but she had only yielded what she set no store on. The soul which he had dimly glimpsed escaped him. He knew that she cared nothing for him. She still loved Red, and all the time she was waiting for his return. At a sign from him, Neilson knew that, notwithstanding his love, his tenderness, his sympathy, his generosity, she would leave him without a moment's hesitation. She would never give a thought to his distress. Anguish seized him and he battered at that impenetrable self of hers which sullenly resisted him. His love became bitter. He tried to melt her heart with kindness, but it remained as hard as before; he feigned indifference, but she did not notice it. Sometimes he lost his temper and abused her, and then she wept silently. Sometimes he thought she was nothing but a fraud, and that soul simply an invention of his own, and that he could not get into the sanctuary of her heart because there was no sanctuary there. His love became a prison from which he longed to escape, but he had not the strength merely to open the door—that was all it needed—and walk out into the open air. It was torture and at last he became numb and hopeless. In the end the fire burnt itself out and, when he saw her eyes rest for an instant on the slender bridge, it was no longer rage that filled his heart but impatience. For many years now they had lived together bound by the ties of habit and convenience, and it was with a smile that he looked back on his old passion. She was an old woman, for the women on the islands age quickly, and if he had no love for her any more he had tolerance. She left him alone. He was contented with his piano and his books.

His thoughts led him to a desire for words.

"When I look back now and reflect on that brief passionate

love of Red and Sally, I think that perhaps they should thank
the ruthless fate that separated them when their love seemed
still to be at its height. They suffered, but they suffered in
beauty. They were spared the real tragedy of love."

"I don't know exactly as I get you," said the skipper.

"The tragedy of love is not death or separation. How long
do you think it would have been before one or other of them
ceased to care? Oh, it is dreadfully bitter to look at a woman
whom you have loved with all your heart and soul, so that you
felt you could not bear to let her out of your sight, and realize
that you would not mind if you never saw her again. The
tragedy of love is indifference."

But while he was speaking a very extraordinary thing happened. Though he had been addressing the skipper he had not
been talking to him, he had been putting his thoughts into words
for himself, and with his eyes fixed on the man in front of him
he had not seen him. But now an image presented itself to
them, an image not of the man he saw, but of another man. It
was as though he were looking into one of those distorting
mirrors that make you extraordinarily squat or outrageously
elongate, but here exactly the opposite took place, and in the
obese, ugly old man he caught the shadowy glimpse of a
stripling. He gave him now a quick, searching scrutiny. Why
had a haphazard stroll brought him just to this place? A sudden
tremor of his heart made him slightly breathless. An absurd
suspicion seized him. What had occurred to him was impossible,
and yet it might be a fact.

"What is your name?" he asked abruptly.

The skipper's face puckered and he gave a cunning chuckle.
He looked then malicious and horribly vulgar.

"It's such a damned long time since I heard it that I almost
forget it myself. But for thirty years now in the islands they've
always called me Red."

His huge form shook as he gave a low, almost silent laugh.
It was obscene. Neilson shuddered. Red was hugely amused,
and from his bloodshot eyes tears ran down his cheeks.

Neilson gave a gasp, for at that moment a woman came in.
She was a native, a woman of somewhat commanding presence,
stout without being corpulent, dark, for the natives grow darker
with age, with very grey hair. She wore a black Mother Hubbard, and its thinness showed her heavy breasts. The moment
had come.

She made an observation to Neilson about some household matter and he answered. He wondered if his voice sounded as unnatural to her as it did to himself. She gave the man who was sitting in the chair by the window an indifferent glance, and went out of the room. The moment had come and gone.

Neilson for a moment could not speak. He was strangely shaken. Then he said:

"I'd be very glad if you'd stay and have a bit of dinner with me. Pot luck."

"I don't think I will," said Red. "I must go after this fellow Gray. I'll give him his stuff and then I'll get away. I want to be back in Apia to-morrow."

"I'll send a boy along with you to show you the way."

"That'll be fine."

Red heaved himself out of his chair, while the Swede called one of the boys who worked on the plantation. He told him where the skipper wanted to go, and the boy stepped along the bridge. Red prepared to follow him.

"Don't fall in," said Neilson.

"Not on your life."

Neilson watched him make his way across and when he had disappeared among the coconuts he looked still. Then he sank heavily in his chair. Was that the man who had prevented him from being happy? Was that the man whom Sally had loved all these years and for whom she had waited so desperately? It was grotesque. A sudden fury seized him so that he had an instinct to spring up and smash everything around him. He had been cheated. They had seen each other at last and had not known it. He began to laugh, mirthlessly, and his laughter grew till it became hysterical. The Gods had played him a cruel trick. And he was old now.

At last Sally came in to tell him dinner was ready. He sat down in front of her and tried to eat. He wondered what she would say if he told her now that the fat old man sitting in the chair was the lover whom she remembered still with the passionate abandonment of her youth. Years ago, when he hated her because she made him so unhappy, he would have been glad to tell her. He wanted to hurt her then as she hurt him, because his hatred was only love. But now he did not care. He shrugged his shoulders listlessly.

"What did that man want?" she asked presently.

He did not answer at once. She was old too, a fat old native woman. He wondered why he had ever loved her so madly. He had laid at her feet all the treasures of his soul, and she had cared nothing for them. Waste, what waste! And now, when he looked at her, he felt only contempt. His patience was at last exhausted. He answered her question.

"He's the captain of a schooner. He's come from Apia."

"Yes."

"He brought me news from home. My eldest brother is very ill and I must go back."

"Will you be gone long?"

He shrugged his shoulders.

HONOLULU

THE wise traveller travels only in imagination. An old Frenchman (he was really a Savoyard) once wrote a book called *Voyage
autour de ma Chambre*. I have not read it and do not even know
what it is about, but the title stimulates my fancy. In such a
journey I could circumnavigate the globe. An eikon by the
chimneypiece can take me to Russia with its great forests of
birch and its white, domed churches. The Volga is wide, and at
the end of a straggling village, in the wine-shop, bearded men
in rough sheepskin coats sit drinking. I stand on the little hill
from which Napoleon first saw Moscow and I look upon the
vastness of the city. I will go down and see the people whom I
know more intimately than so many of my friends, Alyosha,
and Vronsky, and a dozen more. But my eyes fall on a piece of
porcelain and I smell the acrid odours of China. I am borne in
a chair along a narrow causeway between the padi fields, or else
I skirt a tree-clad mountain. My bearers chat gaily as they
trudge along in the bright morning and every now and then,
distant and mysterious, I hear the deep sound of a monastery
bell. In the streets of Peking there is a motley crowd and it
scatters to allow passage to a string of camels, stepping delicately, that bring skins and strange drugs from the stony deserts
of Mongolia. In England, in London, there are certain afternoons in winter when the clouds hang heavy and low and the
light is so bleak that your heart sinks, but then you can look
out of your window, and you see the coconut trees crowded upon
the beach of a coral island. The sand is silvery and when you

walk along in the sunshine it is so dazzling that you can hardly
bear to look at it. Overhead the mynah birds are making a great
to-do, and the surf beats ceaselessly against the reef. Those are
the best journeys, the journeys that you take at your own fireside, for then you lose none of your illusions.

But there are people who take salt in their coffee. They say
it gives it a tang, a savour, which is peculiar and fascinating.
In the same way there are certain places, surrounded by a halo
of romance, to which the inevitable disillusionment which you
must experience on seeing them gives a singular spice. You
had expected something wholly beautiful and you get an impression which is infinitely more complicated than any that
beauty can give you. It is like the weakness in the character of
a great man which may make him less admirable but certainly
makes him more interesting.

Nothing had prepared me for Honolulu. It is so far away
from Europe, it is reached after so long a journey from San
Francisco, so strange and so charming associations are attached
to the name, that at first I could hardly believe my eyes. I do
not know that I had formed in my mind any very exact picture
of what I expected, but what I found caused me a great surprise. It is a typical western city. Shacks are cheek by jowl with
stone mansions; dilapidated frame houses stand next door to
smart stores with plate glass windows; electric cars rumble
noisily along the streets; and motors, Fords, Buicks, Packards,
line the pavement. The shops are filled with all the necessities
of American civilization. Every third house is a bank and every
fifth the agency of a steamship company.

Along the streets crowd an unimaginable assortment of people. The Americans, ignoring the climate, wear black coats and
high, starched collars, straw hats, soft hats, and bowlers. The
Kanakas, pale brown, with crisp hair, have nothing on but a
shirt and a pair of trousers; but the half-breeds are very smart
with flaring ties and patent-leather boots. The Japanese, with
their obsequious smile, are neat and trim in white duck, while
their women walk a step or two behind them, in native dress,
with a baby on their backs. The Japanese children, in bright
coloured frocks, their little heads shaven, look like quaint dolls.
Then there are the Chinese. The men, fat and prosperous, wear
their American clothes oddly, but the women are enchanting
with their tightly-dressed black hair, so neat that you feel it can
never be disarranged, and they are very clean in their tunics

and trousers, white, or powder blue, or black. Lastly there are
the Filipinos, the men in huge straw hats, the women in bright
yellow muslin with great puffed sleeves.

It is the meeting-place of East and West. The very new rubs
shoulders with the immeasurably old. And if you have not found
the romance you expected you have come upon something
singularly intriguing. All these strange people live close to each
other with different languages and different thoughts; they
believe in different gods and they have different values; two
passions alone they share, love and hunger. And somehow as
you watch them you have an impression of extraordinary
vitality. Though the air is so soft and the sky so blue, you have,
I know not why, a feeling of something hotly passionate that
beats like a throbbing pulse through the crowd. Though the
native policeman at the corner, standing on a platform, with a
white club to direct the traffic, gives the scene an air of respectability, you cannot but feel that it is a respectability only of the
surface; a little below there is darkness and mystery. It gives
you just that thrill, with a little catch at the heart, that you
have when at night in the forest the silence trembles on a sudden
with the low, insistent beating of a drum. You are all expectant
of I know not what.

If I have dwelt on the incongruity of Honolulu, it is because
just this, to my mind, gives its point to the story I want to tell.
It is a story of primitive superstition, and it startles me that
anything of the sort should survive in a civilization which, if not
very distinguished, is certainly very elaborate. I cannot get
over the fact that such incredible things should happen, or at
least be thought to happen, right in the middle, so to speak, of
telephones, tram-cars, and daily papers. And the friend who
showed me Honolulu had the same incongruity which I felt
from the beginning was its most striking characteristic.

He was an American named Winter and I had brought a letter of introduction to him from an acquaintance in New York.
He was a man between forty and fifty, with scanty black hair,
grey at the temples, and a sharp-featured, thin face. His eyes
had a twinkle in them and his large horn spectacles gave him a
demureness which was not a little diverting. He was tall rather
than otherwise and very spare. He was born in Honolulu and
his father had a large store which sold hosiery and all such
goods, from tennis racquets to tarpaulins, as a man of fashion
could require. It was a prosperous business and I could well

understand the indignation of Winter *père* when his son, refusing
to go into it, had announced his determination to be an actor.
My friend spent twenty years on the stage, sometimes in New
York, but more often on the road, for his gifts were small; but
at last, being no fool, he came to the conclusion that it was
better to sell sock-suspenders in Honolulu than to play small
parts in Cleveland, Ohio. He left the stage and went into the
business. I think after the hazardous existence he had lived so
long, he thoroughly enjoyed the luxury of driving a large car
and living in a beautiful house near the golf-course, and I am
quite sure, since he was a man of parts, he managed the business competently. But he could not bring himself entirely to
break his connection with the arts and since he might no longer
act he began to paint. He took me to his studio and showed me
his work. It was not at all bad, but not what I should have expected from him. He painted nothing but still life, very small
pictures, perhaps eight by ten; and he painted very delicately,
with the utmost finish. He had evidently a passion for detail.
His fruit pieces reminded you of the fruit in a picture by Ghir-
landajo. While you marvelled a little at his patience, you could
not help being impressed by his dexterity. I imagine that he
failed as an actor because his effects, carefully studied, were
neither bold nor broad enough to get across the footlights.

I was entertained by the proprietary, yet ironical air with
which he showed me the city. He thought in his heart that there
was none in the United States to equal it, but he saw quite
clearly that his attitude was comic. He drove me round to the
various buildings and swelled with satisfaction when I expressed
a proper admiration for their architecture. He showed me the
houses of rich men.

"That's the Stubbs' house," he said. "It cost a hundred
thousand dollars to build. The Stubbs are one of our best families. Old man Stubbs came here as a missionary more than
seventy years ago."

He hesitated a little and looked at me with twinkling eyes
through his big round spectacles.

"All our best families are missionary families," he said.
"You're not very much in Honolulu unless your father or your
grandfather converted the heathen."

"Is that so?"

"Do you know your Bible?"

"Fairly," I answered.

"There is a text which says: The fathers have eaten sour grapes and the children's teeth are set on edge. I guess it runs differently in Honolulu. The fathers brought Christianity to the Kanaka and the children jumped his land."

"Heaven helps those who help themselves," I murmured.

"It surely does. By the time the natives of this island had embraced Christianity they had nothing else they could afford to embrace. The kings gave the missionaries land as a mark of esteem, and the missionaries bought land by way of laying up treasure in heaven. It surely was a good investment. One missionary left the business—I think one may call it a business without offence—and became a land agent, but that is an exception. Mostly it was their sons who looked after the commercial side of the concern. Oh, it's a fine thing to have a father who came here fifty years ago to spread the faith."

But he looked at his watch.

"Gee, it's stopped. That means it's time to have a cocktail."

We sped along an excellent road, bordered with red hibiscus, and came back into the town.

"Have you been to the Union Saloon?"

"Not yet."

"We'll go there."

I knew it was the most famous spot in Honolulu and I entered it with a lively curiosity. You get to it by a narrow passage from King Street, and in the passage are offices, so that thirsty souls may be supposed bound for one of these just as well as for the saloon. It is a large square room, with three entrances, and opposite the bar, which runs the length of it, two corners have been partitioned off into little cubicles. Legend states that they were built so that King Kalakaua might drink there without being seen by his subjects, and it is pleasant to think that in one or other of these he may have sat over his bottle, a coal-black potentate, with Robert Louis Stevenson. There is a portrait of him, in oils, in a rich gold frame; but there are also two prints of Queen Victoria. On the walls, besides, are old line engravings of the eighteenth century, one of which, and heaven knows how it got there, is after a theatrical picture by De Wilde; and there are oleographs from the Christmas supplements of the *Graphic* and the *Illustrated London News* of twenty years ago. Then there are advertisements of whisky, gin, champagne, and beer; and photographs of baseball teams and of native orchestras.

The place seemed to belong not to the modern, hustling world that I had left in the bright street outside, but to one that was dying. It had the savour of the day before yesterday. Dingy and dimly lit, it had a vaguely mysterious air and you could imagine that it would be a fit scene for shady transactions. It suggested a more lurid time, when ruthless men carried their lives in their hands, and violent deeds diapered the monotony of life.

When I went in the saloon was fairly full. A group of business men stood together at the bar, discussing affairs, and in a corner two Kanakas were drinking. Two or three men who might have been store-keepers were shaking dice. The rest of the company plainly followed the sea; they were captains of tramps, first mates, and engineers. Behind the bar, busily making the Honolulu cocktail for which the place was famous, served two large half-castes, in white, fat, clean-shaven and dark skinned, with thick, curly hair and large bright eyes.

Winter seemed to know more than half the company, and when we made our way to the bar a little fat man in spectacles, who was standing by himself, offered him a drink.

"No, you have one with me, Captain," said Winter.

He turned to me.

"I want you to know Captain Butler."

The little man shook hands with me. We began to talk, but, my attention distracted by my surroundings, I took small notice of him, and after we had each ordered a cocktail we separated. When we had got into the motor again and were driving away, Winter said to me:

"I'm glad we ran up against Butler. I wanted you to meet him. What did you think of him?"

"I don't know that I thought very much of him at all," I answered.

"Do you believe in the supernatural?"

"I don't exactly know that I do," I smiled.

"A very queer thing happened to him a year or two ago. You ought to have him tell you about it."

"What sort of thing?"

Winter did not answer my question.

"I have no explanation of it myself," he said. "But there's no doubt about the facts. Are you interested in things like that?"

"Things like what?"

"Spells and magic and all that."

"I've never met anyone who wasn't."

Winter paused for a moment.

"I guess I won't tell you myself. You ought to hear it from his own lips so that you can judge. How are you fixed up for to-night?"

"I've got nothing on at all."

"Well, I'll get hold of him between now and then and see if we can't go down to his ship."

Winter told me something about him. Captain Butler had spent all his life on the Pacific. He had been in much better circumstances than he was now, for he had been first officer and then captain of a passenger-boat plying along the coast of California, but he had lost his ship and a number of passengers had been drowned.

"Drink, I guess," said Winter.

Of course there had been an enquiry, which had cost him his certificate, and then he drifted further afield. For some years he had knocked about the South Seas, but he was now in command of a small schooner which sailed between Honolulu and the various islands of the group. It belonged to a Chinese to whom the fact that his skipper had no certificate meant only that he could be had for lower wages, and to have a white man in charge was always an advantage.

And now that I had heard this about him I took the trouble to remember more exactly what he was like. I recalled his round spectacles and the round blue eyes behind them, and so gradually reconstructed him before my mind. He was a little man, without angles, plump, with a round face like the full moon and a little fat round nose. He had fair short hair, and he was red-faced and clean shaven. He had plump hands, dimpled on the knuckles, and short fat legs. He was a jolly soul, and the tragic experience he had gone through seemed to have left him unscarred. Though he must have been thirty-four or thirty-five he looked much younger. But after all I had given him but a superficial attention, and now that I knew of this catastrophe, which had obviously ruined his life, I promised myself that when I saw him again I would take more careful note of him. It is very curious to observe the differences of emotional response that you find in different people. Some can go through terrific battles, the fear of imminent death and unimaginable horrors, and preserve their soul unscathed, while with

others the trembling of the moon on a solitary sea or the song
of a bird in a thicket will cause a convulsion great enough to
transform their entire being. Is it due to strength or weakness,
want of imagination or instability of character? I do not know.
When I called up in my fancy that scene of shipwreck, with the
shrieks of the drowning and the terror, and then later, the ordeal
of the enquiry, the bitter grief of those who sorrowed for the
lost, and the harsh things he must have read of himself in the
papers, the shame and the disgrace, it came to me with a shock
to remember that Captain Butler had talked with the frank
obscenity of a schoolboy of the Hawaiian girls and of Ewelei,
the Red Light district, and of his successful adventures. He
laughed readily, and one would have thought he could never
laugh again. I remembered his shining, white teeth; they were
his best feature. He began to interest me, and thinking of him
and of his gay insouciance I forgot the particular story, to hear
which I was to see him again. I wanted to see him rather to
find out if I could a little more what sort of man he was.

Winter made the necessary arrangements and after dinner
we went down to the water front. The ship's boat was waiting
for us and we rowed out. The schooner was anchored some way
across the harbour, not far from the breakwater. We came
alongside, and I heard the sound of a ukulele. We clambered
up the ladder.

"I guess he's in the cabin," said Winter, leading the way.

It was a small cabin, bedraggled and dirty, with a table
against one side and a broad bench all round upon which slept,
I supposed, such passengers as were ill-advised enough to travel
in such a ship. A petroleum lamp gave a dim light. The ukulele
was being played by a native girl and Butler was lolling on the
seat, half lying, with his head on her shoulder and an arm round
her waist.

"Don't let us disturb you, Captain," said Winter, facetiously.

"Come right in," said Butler, getting up and shaking hands
with us. "What'll you have?"

It was a warm night, and through the open door you saw
countless stars in a heaven that was still almost blue. Captain
Butler wore a sleeveless undershirt, showing his fat white arms,
and a pair of incredibly dirty trousers. His feet were bare, but
on his curly head he wore a very old, a very shapeless felt hat.

"Let me introduce you to my girl. Ain't she a peach?"

We shook hands with a very pretty person. She was a good

deal taller than the captain, and even the Mother Hubbard, which the missionaries of a past generation had, in the interests of decency, forced on the unwilling natives, could not conceal the beauty of her form. One could not but suspect that age would burden her with a certain corpulence, but now she was graceful and alert. Her brown skin had an exquisite translucency and her eyes were magnificent. Her black hair, very thick and rich, was coiled round her head in a massive plait. When she smiled in a greeting that was charmingly natural, she showed teeth that were small, even, and white. She was certainly a most attractive creature. It was easy to see that the captain was madly in love with her. He could not take his eyes off her; he wanted to touch her all the time. That was very easy to understand; but what seemed to me stranger was that the girl was apparently in love with him. There was a light in her eyes that was unmistakable, and her lips were slightly parted as though in a sigh of desire. It was thrilling. It was even a little moving, and I could not help feeling somewhat in the way. What had a stranger to do with this lovesick pair? I wished that Winter had not brought me. And it seemed to me that the dingy cabin was transfigured and now it seemed a fit and proper scene for such an extremity of passion. I thought I should never forget that schooner in the harbour of Honolulu, crowded with shipping, and yet, under the immensity of the starry sky, remote from all the world. I liked to think of those lovers sailing off together in the night over the empty spaces of the Pacific from one green, hilly island to another. A faint breeze of romance softly fanned my cheek.

And yet Butler was the last man in the world with whom you would have associated romance, and it was hard to see what there was in him to arouse love. In the clothes he wore now he looked podgier than ever, and his round spectacles gave his round face the look of a prim cherub. He suggested rather a curate who had gone to the dogs. His conversation was peppered with the quaintest Americanisms, and it is because I despair of reproducing these that, at whatever loss of vividness, I mean to narrate the story he told me a little later in my own words. Moreover he was unable to frame a sentence without an oath, though a good-natured one, and his speech, albeit offensive only to prudish ears, in print would seem coarse. He was a mirth-loving man, and perhaps that accounted not a little for his successful amours; since women, for the most part frivolous creatures, are excessively bored by the seriousness with which men treat them, and they can seldom resist the buffoon who makes them laugh. Their sense of humour is crude. Diana of Ephesus is always prepared to fling prudence to the winds for the red-nosed comedian who sits on his hat. I realized that Captain Butler had charm. If I had not known the tragic story of the shipwreck I should have thought he had never had a care in his life.

Our host had rung the bell on our entrance and now a Chinese cook came in with more glasses and several bottles of soda. The whisky and the captain's empty glass stood already on the table. But when I saw the Chinese I positively started, for he was certainly the ugliest man I had ever seen. He was very short, but thick-set, and he had a bad limp. He wore a singlet and a pair of trousers that had been white, but were now filthy, and, perched on a shock of bristly, grey hair, an old tweed deer-stalker. It would have been grotesque on any Chinese, but on him it was outrageous. His broad, square face was very flat as though it had been bashed in by a mighty fist, and it was deeply pitted with smallpox; but the most revolting thing in him was a very pronounced harelip which had never been operated on, so that his upper lip, cleft, went up in an angle to his nose, and in the opening was a huge yellow fang. It was horrible. He came in with the end of a cigarette at the corner of his mouth, and this, I do not know why, gave him a devilish expression.

He poured out the whisky and opened a bottle of soda.

"Don't drown it, John," said the captain.

He said nothing, but handed a glass to each of us. Then he went out.

"I saw you lookin' at my Chink," said Butler, with a grin on his fat, shining face.

"I should hate to meet him on a dark night," I said.

"He sure is homely," said the captain, and for some reason he seemed to say it with a peculiar satisfaction. "But he's fine for one thing, I'll tell the world; you just have to have a drink every time you look at him."

But my eyes fell on a calabash that hung against the wall over the table, and I got up to look at it. I had been hunting for an old one and this was better than any I had seen outside the museum.

"It was given me by a chief over on one of the islands," said the captain, watching me. "I done him a good turn and he wanted to give me something good."

"He certainly did," I answered.

I was wondering whether I could discreetly make Captain Butler an offer for it, I could not imagine that he set any store on such an article, when, as though he read my thoughts, he said:

"I wouldn't sell that for ten thousand dollars."

"I guess not," said Winter. "It would be a crime to sell it."

"Why?" I asked.

"That comes into the story," returned Winter. "Doesn't it, Captain?"

"It surely does."

"Let's hear it then."

"The night's young yet," he answered.

The night distinctly lost its youth before he satisfied my curiosity, and meanwhile we drank a great deal too much whisky while Captain Butler narrated his experiences of San Francisco in the old days and of the South Seas. At last the girl fell asleep. She lay curled up on the seat, with her face on her brown arm, and her bosom rose and fell gently with her breathing. In sleep she looked sullen, but darkly beautiful.

He had found her on one of the islands in the group among which, whenever there was cargo to be got, he wandered with his crazy old schooner. The Kanakas have little love for work, and the laborious Chinese, the cunning Japs, have taken the trade out of their hands. Her father had a strip of land on which he grew taro and bananas and he had a boat in which he went fishing. He was vaguely related to the mate of the schooner, and it was he who took Captain Butler up to the shabby little frame house to spend an idle evening. They took a bottle of whisky with them and the ukulele. The captain was not a shy man and when he saw a pretty girl he made love to her. He could speak the native language fluently and it was not long before he had overcome the girl's timidity. They spent the evening singing and dancing, and by the end of it she was sitting by his side and he had his arm round her waist. It happened that they were delayed on the island for several days and the captain, at no time a man to hurry, made no effort to shorten his stay. He was very comfortable in the snug little harbour and life was long. He had a swim round his ship in the morning and another in the evening. There was a chandler's shop on the

water front where sailormen could get a drink of whisky, and
he spent the best part of the day there, playing cribbage with
the half-caste who owned it. At night the mate and he went up
to the house where the pretty girl lived and they sang a song
or two and told stories. It was the girl's father who suggested
that he should take her away with him. They discussed the
matter in a friendly fashion, while the girl, nestling against the
captain, urged him by the pressure of her hands and her soft,
smiling glances. He had taken a fancy to her and he was a
domestic man. He was a little dull sometimes at sea and it would
be very pleasant to have a pretty little creature like that about
the old ship. He was of a practical turn too, and he recognized
that it would be useful to have someone around to darn his
socks and look after his linen. He was tired of having his things
washed by a Chink who tore everything to pieces; the natives
washed much better, and now and then when the captain went
ashore at Honolulu he liked to cut a dash in a smart duck suit.
It was only a matter of arranging a price. The father wanted
two hundred and fifty dollars, and the captain, never a thrifty
man, could not put his hand on such a sum. But he was a generous one, and with the girl's soft face against his, he was not
inclined to haggle. He offered to give a hundred and fifty dollars
there and then and another hundred in three months. There
was a good deal of argument and the parties could not come to
any agreement that night, but the idea had fired the captain,
and he could not sleep as well as usual. He kept dreaming of the
lovely girl and each time he awoke it was with the pressure of
her soft, sensual lips on his. He cursed himself in the morning
because a bad night at poker the last time he was at Honolulu
had left him so short of ready money. And if the night before
he had been in love with the girl, this morning he was crazy
about her.

"See here, Bananas," he said to the mate, "I've got to have
that girl. You go and tell the old man I'll bring the dough up
to-night and she can get fixed up. I figure we'll be ready to sail
at dawn."

I have no idea why the mate was known by that eccentric
name. He was called Wheeler, but though he had that English
surname there was not a drop of white blood in him. He was a
tall man, and well-made though inclined to stoutness, but
much darker than is usual in Hawaii. He was no longer young,
and his crisply curling, thick hair was grey. His upper front

teeth were cased in gold. He was very proud of them. He had a marked squint and this gave him a saturnine expression. The captain, who was fond of a joke, found in it a constant source of humour and hesitated the less to rally him on the defect because he realized that the mate was sensitive about it. Bananas, unlike most of the natives, was a taciturn fellow and Captain Butler would have disliked him if it had been possible for a man of his good nature to dislike anyone. He liked to be at sea with someone he could talk to, he was a chatty, sociable creature, and it was enough to drive a missionary to drink to live there day after day with a chap who never opened his mouth. He did his best to wake the mate up, that is to say, he chaffed him without mercy, but it was poor fun to laugh by oneself, and he came to the conclusion that, drunk or sober, Bananas was no fit companion for a white man. But he was a good seaman and the captain was shrewd enough to know the value of a mate he could trust. It was not rare for him to come aboard, when they were sailing, fit for nothing but to fall into his bunk, and it was worth something to know that he could stay there till he had slept his liquor off, since Bananas could be relied on. But he was an unsociable devil, and it would be a treat to have someone he could talk to. That girl would be fine. Besides, he wouldn't be so likely to get drunk when he went ashore if he knew there was a little girl waiting for him when he came on board again.

He went to his friend the chandler and over a peg of gin asked him for a loan. There were one or two useful things a ship's captain could do for a ship's chandler, and after a quarter of an hour's conversation in low tones (there is no object in letting all and sundry know your business), the captain crammed a wad of notes in his hip-pocket, and that night, when he went back to his ship, the girl went with him.

What Captain Butler, seeking for reasons to do what he had already made up his mind to, had anticipated, actually came to pass. He did not give up drinking, but he ceased to drink to excess. An evening with the boys, when he had been away from town two or three weeks, was pleasant enough, but it was pleasant too to get back to his little girl; he thought of her, sleeping so softly, and how, when he got into his cabin and leaned over her, she would open her eyes lazily and stretch out her arms for him: it was as good as a full hand. He found he was saving money, and since he was a generous man he did the right thing by the little girl: he gave her some silver-backed brushes for her long hair, and a gold chain, and a reconstructed ruby for her finger. Gee, but it was good to be alive.

A year went by, a whole year, and he was not tired of her yet. He was not a man who analyzed his feelings, but this was so surprising that it forced itself upon his attention. There must be something very wonderful about that girl. He couldn't help seeing that he was more wrapped up in her than ever, and sometimes the thought entered his mind that it might not be a bad thing if he married her.

Then, one day the mate did not come in to dinner or to tea. Butler did not bother himself about his absence at the first meal, but at the second he asked the Chinese cook:

"Where's the mate? He no come tea?"

"No wantchee," said the Chink.

"He ain't sick?"

"No savvy."

Next day Bananas turned up again, but he was more sullen than ever, and after dinner the captain asked the girl what was the matter with him. She smiled and shrugged her pretty shoulders. She told the captain that Bananas had taken a fancy to her and he was sore because she had told him off. The captain was a good-humoured man and he was not of a jealous nature; it struck him as exceeding funny that Bananas should be in love. A man who had a squint like that had a precious poor chance. When tea came round he chaffed him gaily. He pretended to speak in the air, so that the mate should not be certain that he knew anything, but he dealt him some pretty shrewd blows. The girl did not think him as funny as he thought himself, and afterwards she begged him to say nothing more. He was surprised at her seriousness. She told him he did not know her people. When their passion was aroused they were capable of anything. She was a little frightened. This was so absurd to him that he laughed heartily.

"If he comes bothering round you, you just threaten to tell me. That'll fix him."

"Better fire him, I think."

"Not on your sweet life. I know a good sailor when I see one. But if he don't leave you alone I'll give him the worst licking he's ever had."

Perhaps the girl had a wisdom unusual in her sex. She knew that it was useless to argue with a man when his mind was made up, for it only increased his stubbornness, and she held her peace. And now on the shabby schooner, threading her way across the silent sea, among those lovely islands, was enacted a dark, tense drama of which the fat little captain remained entirely ignorant. The girl's resistance fired Bananas so that he ceased to be a man, but was simply blind desire. He did not make love to her gently or gaily, but with a black and savage ferocity. Her contempt now was changed to hatred and when he besought her she answered him with bitter, angry taunts. But the struggle went on silently, and when the captain asked her after a little while whether Bananas was bothering her, she lied.

But one night, when they were in Honolulu, he came on board only just in time. They were sailing at dawn. Bananas had been ashore, drinking some native spirit, and he was drunk. The captain, rowing up, heard sounds that surprised him. He scrambled up the ladder. He saw Bananas, beside himself, trying to wrench open the cabin door. He was shouting at the girl. He swore he would kill her if she did not let him in.

"What in hell are you up to?" cried Butler.

The mate let go the handle, gave the captain a look of savage hate, and without a word turned away.

"Stop here. What are you doing with that door?"

The mate still did not answer. He looked at him with sullen, bootless rage.

"I'll teach you not to pull any of your queer stuff with me, you dirty, cross-eyed nigger," said the captain.

He was a good foot shorter than the mate and no match for him, but he was used to dealing with native crews, and he had his knuckle-duster handy. Perhaps it was not an instrument that a gentleman would use, but then Captain Butler was not a gentleman. Nor was he in the habit of dealing with gentlemen. Before Bananas knew what the captain was at, his right arm had shot out and his fist, with its ring of steel, caught him fair and square on the jaw. He fell like a bull under the pole-axe.

"That'll learn him," said the captain.

Bananas did not stir. The girl unlocked the cabin door and came out.

"Is he dead?"

"He ain't."

He called a couple of men and told them to carry the mate to his bunk. He rubbed his hands with satisfaction and his round blue eyes gleamed behind his spectacles. But the girl was strangely silent. She put her arms round him as though to protect him from invisible harm.

It was two or three days before Bananas was on his feet again, and when he came out of his cabin his face was torn and swollen. Through the darkness of his skin you saw the livid bruise. Butler saw him slinking along the deck and called him. The mate went to him without a word.

"See here, Bananas," he said to him, fixing his spectacles on his slippery nose, for it was very hot. "I ain't going to fire you for this, but you know now that when I hit, I hit hard. Don't forget it and don't let me have any more funny business."

Then he held out his hand and gave the mate that good-humoured, flashing smile of his which was his greatest charm. The mate took the outstretched hand and twitched his swollen lips into a devilish grin. The incident in the captain's mind was so completely finished that when the three of them sat at dinner he chaffed Bananas on his appearance. He was eating with difficulty and, his swollen face still more distorted by pain, he looked truly a repulsive object.

That evening, when he was sitting on the upper deck, smoking his pipe, a shiver passed through the captain.

"I don't know what I should be shiverin' for on a night like this," he grumbled. "Maybe I've gotten a dose of fever. I've been feelin' a bit queer all day."

When he went to bed he took some quinine, and next morning he felt better, but a little washed out, as though he were recovering from a debauch.

"I guess my liver's out of order," he said, and he took a pill.

He had not much appetite that day and towards evening he began to feel very unwell. He tried the next remedy he knew, which was to drink two or three hot whiskies, but that did not seem to help him much, and when in the morning he surveyed himself in the glass he thought he was not looking quite the thing.

"If I ain't right by the time we get back to Honolulu I'll just give Dr. Denby a call. He'll sure fix me up."

He could not eat. He felt a great lassitude in all his limbs. He slept soundly enough, but he awoke with no sense of refreshment; on the contrary he felt a peculiar exhaustion. And the energetic little man, who could not bear the thought of lying in bed, had to make an effort to force himself out of his bunk.

After a few days he found it impossible to resist the languor that oppressed him, and he made up his mind not to get up.

"Bananas can look after the ship," he said. "He has before now."

He laughed a little to himself as he thought how often he had lain speechless in his bunk after a night with the boys. That was before he had his girl. He smiled at her and pressed her hand. She was puzzled and anxious. He saw that she was concerned about him and tried to reassure her. He had never had a day's illness in his life and in a week at the outside he would be as right as rain.

"I wish you'd fired Bananas," she said. "I've got a feeling that he's at the bottom of this."

"Damned good thing I didn't, or there'd be no one to sail the ship. I know a good sailor when I see one." His blue eyes, rather pale now, with the whites all yellow, twinkled. "You don't think he's trying to poison me, little girl?"

She did not answer, but she had one or two talks with the Chinese cook, and she took great care with the captain's food. But he ate little enough now, and it was only with the greatest difficulty that she persuaded him to drink a cup of soup two or three times a day. It was clear that he was very ill, he was losing weight quickly; and his chubby face was pale and drawn. He suffered no pain, but merely grew every day weaker and more languid. He was wasting away. The round trip on this occasion lasted about four weeks and by the time they came to Honolulu the captain was a little anxious about himself. He had not been out of his bed for more than a fortnight and really he felt too weak to get up and go to the doctor. He sent a message asking him to come on board. The doctor examined him, but could find nothing to account for his condition. His temperature was normal.

"See here, Captain," he said, "I'll be perfectly frank with you. I don't know what's the matter with you, and just seeing you like this don't give me a chance. You come into the hospital so that we can keep you under observation. There's nothing organically wrong with you, I know that, and my impression is that a few weeks in hospital ought to put you to rights."

"I ain't going to leave my ship."

Chinese owners were queer customers, he said; if he left his ship because he was sick, his owner might fire him, and he couldn't afford to lose his job. So long as he stayed where he was his contract safeguarded him, and he had a first-rate mate. Besides, he couldn't leave his girl. No man could want a better nurse; if anyone could pull him through she would. Every man had to die once and he only wished to be left in peace. He would not listen to the doctor's expostulations, and finally the doctor gave in.

"I'll write you a prescription," he said doubtfully, "and see if it does you any good. You'd better stay in bed for a while."

"There ain't much fear of my getting up, doc," answered the captain. "I feel as weak as a cat."

But he believed in the doctor's prescription as little as did the doctor himself, and when he was alone amused himself by lighting his cigar with it. He had to get amusement out of something, for his cigar tasted like nothing on earth, and he smoked only to persuade himself that he was not too ill to. That evening a couple of friends of his, masters of tramp steamers, hearing he was sick came to see him. They discussed his case over a bottle of whisky and a box of Philippine cigars. One of them remembered how a mate of his had been taken queer just like that and not a doctor in the United States had been able to cure him. He had seen in the paper an advertisement of a patent medicine, and thought there'd be no harm in trying it. That man was as strong as ever he'd been in his life after two bottles. But his illness had given Captain Butler a lucidity which was new and strange, and while they talked he seemed to read their minds. They thought he was dying. And when they left him he was afraid.

The girl saw his weakness. This was her opportunity. She had been urging him to let a native doctor see him, and he had stoutly refused; but now she entreated him. He listened with harassed eyes. He wavered. It was very funny that the American doctor could not tell what was the matter with him. But he did not want her to think that he was scared. If he let a damned nigger come along and look at him, it was to comfort *her*. He told her to do what she liked.

The native doctor came the next night. The captain was lying alone, half awake, and the cabin was dimly lit by an oil lamp. The door was softly opened and the girl came in on tip-toe. She held the door open and someone slipped in silently behind her. The captain smiled at this mystery, but he was so weak now, the smile was no more than a glimmer in his eyes. The doctor was a little, old man, very thin and very wrinkled, with a completely bald head, and the face of a monkey. He was bowed and gnarled like an old tree. He looked hardly human, but his eyes were very bright, and in the half darkness, they seemed to glow with a reddish light. He was dressed filthily in a pair of ragged dungarees, and the upper part of his body was naked. He sat down on his haunches and for ten minutes looked at the captain. Then he felt the palms of his hands and the soles of his feet. The girl watched him with frightened eyes. No word was spoken. Then he asked for something that the captain had worn. The girl gave him the old felt hat which the captain used constantly and taking it he sat down again on the floor, clasping it firmly with both hands; and rocking backwards and forwards slowly he muttered some gibberish in a very low tone.

At last he gave a little sigh and dropped the hat. He took an old pipe out of his trouser pocket and lit it. The girl went over to him and sat by his side. He whispered something to her, and she started violently. For a few minutes they talked in hurried undertones, and then they stood up. She gave him money and opened the door for him. He slid out as silently as he had come in. Then she went over to the captain and leaned over him so that she could speak into his ear.

"It's an enemy praying you to death."

"Don't talk fool stuff, girlie," he said impatiently.

"It's truth. It's God's truth. That's why the American doctor couldn't do anything. Our people can do that. I've seen it done. I thought you were safe because you were a white man."

"I haven't an enemy."

"Bananas."

"What's he want to pray me to death for?"

"You ought to have fired him before he had a chance."

"I guess if I ain't got nothing more the matter with me than Bananas' hoodoo I shall be sitting up and taking nourishment in a very few days."

She was silent for a while and she looked at him intently.

"Don't you know you're dying?" she said to him at last.

That was what the two skippers had thought, but they hadn't said it. A shiver passed across the captain's wan face.

"The doctor says there ain't nothing really the matter with me. I've only to lie quiet for a bit and I shall be all right."

She put her lips to his ear as if she were afraid that the air itself might hear.

"You're dying, dying, dying. You'll pass out with the old moon."

"That's something to know."

"You'll pass out with the old moon unless Bananas dies before."

He was not a timid man and he had recovered already from the shock her words, and still more her vehement, silent manner, had given him. Once more a smile flickered in his eyes.

"I guess I'll take my chance, girlie."

"There's twelve days before the new moon."

There was something in her tone that gave him an idea.

"See here, my girl, this is all bunk. I don't believe a word of it. But I don't want you to try any of your monkey tricks with Bananas. He ain't a beauty, but he's a first-rate mate."

He would have said a good deal more, but he was tired out. He suddenly felt very weak and faint. It was always at that hour that he felt worse. He closed his eyes. The girl watched him for a minute and then slipped out of the cabin. The moon, nearly full, made a silver pathway over the dark sea. It shone from an unclouded sky. She looked at it with terror, for she knew that with its death the man she loved would die. His life was in her hands. She could save him, she alone could save him, but the enemy was cunning, and she must be cunning too. She felt that someone was looking at her, and without turning, by the sudden fear that seized her, knew that from the shadow the burning eyes of the mate were fixed upon her. She did not know what he could do; if he could read her thoughts she was defeated already, and with a desperate effort she emptied her mind of all content. His death alone could save her lover, and she could bring his death about. She knew that if he could be brought to look into a calabash in which was water so that a reflection of him was made, and the reflection were broken by hurtling the water, he would die as though he had been struck by lightning; for the reflection was his soul. But none knew better than he the danger, and he could be made to look only by a guile which had lulled his least suspicion. He must never think that he had an enemy who was on the watch to cause his destruction. She knew what she had to do. But the time was short, the time was terribly short. Presently she realized that the mate had gone. She breathed more freely.

Two days later they sailed, and there were ten now before the new moon. Captain Butler was terrible to see. He was noth-

ing but skin and bone, and he could not move without help. He
could hardly speak. But she dared do nothing yet. She knew
that she must be patient. The mate was cunning, cunning.
They went to one of the smaller islands of the group and discharged cargo, and now there were only seven days more. The
moment had come to start. She brought some things out of the
cabin she shared with the captain and made them into a bundle.
She put the bundle in the deck cabin where she and Bananas
ate their meals, and at dinner time, when she went in, he turned
quickly and she saw that he had been looking at it. Neither
of them spoke, but she knew what he suspected. She was making
her preparations to leave the ship. He looked at her mockingly.
Gradually, as though to prevent the captain from knowing
what she was about, she brought everything she owned into
the cabin, and some of the captain's clothes, and made them
all into bundles. At last Bananas could keep silence no longer.
He pointed to a suit of ducks.

"What are you going to do with that?" he asked.

She shrugged her shoulders.

"I'm going back to my island."

He gave a laugh that distorted his grim face. The captain
was dying and she meant to get away with all she could lay
hands on.

"What'll you do if I say you can't take those things? They're
the captain's."

"They're no use to you," she said.

There was a calabash hanging on the wall. It was the very
calabash I had seen when I came into the cabin and which
we had talked about. She took it down. It was all dusty, so
she poured water into it from the water-bottle, and rinsed it
with her fingers.

"What are you doing with that?"

"I can sell it for fifty dollars," she said.

"If you want to take it you'll have to pay me."

"What d'you want?"

"You know what I want."

She allowed a fleeting smile to play on her lips. She flashed a
quick look at him and quickly turned away. He gave a gasp of
desire. She raised her shoulders in a little shrug. With a savage
bound he sprang upon her and seized her in his arms. Then
she laughed. She put her arms, her soft, round arms, about his
neck, and surrendered herself to him voluptuously.

When the morning came she roused him out of a deep sleep. The early rays of the sun slanted into the cabin. He pressed her to his heart. Then he told her that the captain could not last more than a day or two, and the owner wouldn't so easily find another white man to command the ship. If Bananas offered to take less money he would get the job and the girl could stay with him. He looked at her with love-sick eyes. She nestled up against him. She kissed his lips, in the foreign way, in the way the captain had taught her to kiss. And she promised to stay. Bananas was drunk with happiness.

It was now or never.

She got up and went to the table to arrange her hair. There was no mirror and she looked into the calabash, seeking for her reflection. She tidied her beautiful hair. Then she beckoned to Bananas to come to her. She pointed to the calabash.

"There's something in the bottom of it," she said.

Instinctively, without suspecting anything, Bananas looked full into the water. His face was reflected in it. In a flash she beat upon it violently, with both her hands, so that they pounded on the bottom and the water splashed up. The reflection was broken in pieces. Bananas started back with a sudden hoarse cry and he looked at the girl. She was standing there with a look of triumphant hatred on her face. A horror came into his eyes. His heavy features were twisted in agony, and with a thud, as though he had taken a violent poison, he crumpled up on to the ground. A great shudder passed through his body and he was still. She leaned over him callously. She put her hand on his heart and then she pulled down his lower eyelid. He was quite dead.

She went into the cabin in which lay Captain Butler. There was a faint colour in his cheeks and he looked at her in a startled way.

"What's happened?" he whispered.

They were the first words he had spoken for forty-eight hours.

"Nothing's happened," she said.

"I feel all funny."

Then his eyes closed and he fell asleep. He slept for a day and a night, and when he awoke he asked for food. In a fortnight he was well.

It was past midnight when Winter and I rowed back to shore and we had drunk innumerable whiskies and sodas.

"What do you think of it all?" asked Winter.

"What a question! If you mean, have I any explanation to suggest, I haven't."

"The captain believes every word of it."

"That's obvious; but you know that's not the part that interests me most, whether it's true or not, and what it all means; the part that interests me is that such things should happen to such people. I wonder what there is in that commonplace little man to arouse such a passion in that lovely creature. As I watched her, asleep there, while he was telling the story I had some fantastic idea about the power of love being able to work miracles."

"But that's not the girl," said Winter.

"What on earth do you mean?"

"Didn't you notice the cook?"

"Of course I did. He's the ugliest man I ever saw."

"That's why Butler took him. The girl ran away with the Chinese cook last year. This is a new one. He's only had her there about two months."

"Well, I'm hanged."

"He thinks this cook is safe. But I wouldn't be too sure in his place. There's something about a Chink, when he lays himself out to please a woman she can't resist him."

THE POOL

WHEN I was introduced to Lawson by Chaplin, the owner of the Hotel Metropole at Apia, I paid no particular attention to him. We were sitting in the lounge over an early cocktail and I was listening with amusement to the gossip of the island.

Chaplin entertained me. He was by profession a mining engineer and perhaps it was characteristic of him that he had settled in a place where his professional attainments were of no possible value. It was, however, generally reported that he was an extremely clever mining engineer. He was a small man, neither fat nor thin, with black hair, scanty on the crown, turning grey, and a small, untidy moustache; his face, partly from the sun and partly from liquor, was very red. He was but a figurehead, for the hotel, though so grandly named but a frame building of two storeys, was managed by his wife, a tall, gaunt Australian of five and forty, with an imposing presence and a determined air. The little man, excitable and often tipsy, was terrified of her, and the stranger soon heard of domestic quarrels in which she used her fist and her foot in order to keep him in subjection. She had been known after a night of drunkenness to confine him for twenty-four hours to his own room, and then he could be seen, afraid to leave his prison, talking somewhat pathetically from his verandah to people in the street below.

He was a character, and his reminiscences of a varied life, whether true or not, made him worth listening to, so that when Lawson strolled in I was inclined to resent the interruption. Although not midday, it was clear that he had had enough to drink, and it was without enthusiasm that I yielded to his persistence and accepted his offer of another cocktail. I knew already that Chaplin's head was weak. The next round which in common politeness I should be forced to order would be enough to make him lively, and then Mrs. Chaplin would give me black looks.

Nor was there anything attractive in Lawson's appearance. He was a little thin man, with a long, sallow face and a narrow, weak chin, a prominent nose, large and bony, and great shaggy black eyebrows. They gave him a peculiar look. His eyes, very large and very dark, were magnificent. He was jolly, but his jollity did not seem to me sincere; it was on the surface, a mask which he wore to deceive the world, and I suspected that it concealed a mean nature. He was plainly anxious to be thought a "good sport" and he was hail-fellow-well-met; but, I do not know why, I felt that he was cunning and shifty. He talked a great deal in a raucous voice, and he and Chaplin capped one another's stories of beanos which had become legendary, stories of "wet" nights at the English Club, of shooting expeditions where an incredible amount of whisky had been consumed, and of jaunts to Sydney of which their pride was that they could remember nothing from the time they landed till the time they sailed. A pair of drunken swine. But even in their intoxication, for by now after four cocktails each, neither was sober, there was a great difference between Chaplin, rough and vulgar, and Lawson: Lawson might be drunk, but he was certainly a gentleman.

At last he got out of his chair, a little unsteadily.

"Well, I'll be getting along home," he said. "See you before dinner."

"Missus all right?" said Chaplin.

"Yes."

He went out. There was a peculiar note in the monosyllable of his answer which made me look up.

"Good chap," said Chaplin flatly, as Lawson went out of the door into the sunshine. "One of the best. Pity he drinks."

This from Chaplin was an observation not without humour.

"And when he's drunk he wants to fight people."

"Is he often drunk?"

"Dead drunk, three or four days a week. It's the island done it, and Ethel."

"Who's Ethel?"

"Ethel's his wife. Married a half-caste. Old Brevald's daughter. Took her away from here. Only thing to do. But she couldn't
stand it, and now they're back again. He'll hang himself one of
these days, if he don't drink himself to death before. Good chap,
Nasty when he's drunk."

Chaplin belched loudly.

"I'll go and put my head under the shower. I oughtn't to
have had that last cocktail. It's always the last one that does
you in."

He looked uncertainly at the staircase as he made up his
mind to go to the cubby hole in which was the shower, and
then with unnatural seriousness got up.

"Pay you to cultivate Lawson," he said. "A well read chap.
You'd be surprised when he's sober. Clever too. Worth talking
to."

Chaplin had told me the whole story in these few speeches.

When I came in towards evening from a ride along the sea-
shore Lawson was again in the hotel. He was heavily sunk in
one of the cane chairs in the lounge and he looked at me with
glassy eyes. It was plain that he had been drinking all the afternoon. He was torpid, and the look on his face was sullen and
vindictive. His glance rested on me for a moment, but I could
see that he did not recognize me. Two or three other men were
sitting there, shaking dice, and they took no notice of him. His
condition was evidently too usual to attract attention. I sat
down and began to play.

"You're a damned sociable lot," said Lawson suddenly.

He got out of his chair and waddled with bent knees
towards the door. I do not know whether the spectacle was
more ridiculous than revolting. When he had gone one of the
men sniggered.

"Lawson's fairly soused to-day," he said.

"If I couldn't carry my liquor better than that," said another, "I'd climb on the waggon and stay there."

Who would have thought that this wretched object was in
his way a romantic figure or that his life had in it those elements
of pity and terror which the theorist tells us are necessary to
achieve the effect of tragedy?

I did not see him again for two or three days.

I was sitting one evening on the first floor of the hotel on a
verandah that overlooked the street when Lawson came up and
sank into a chair beside me. He was quite sober. He made a

casual remark and then, when I had replied somewhat indifferently, added with a laugh which had in it an apologetic tone:

"I was devilish soused the other day."

I did not answer. There was really nothing to say. I pulled
away at my pipe in the vain hope of keeping the mosquitoes
away, and looked at the natives going home from their work.
They walked with long steps, slowly, with care and dignity,
and the soft patter of their naked feet was strange to hear.
Their dark hair, curling or straight, was often white with lime,
and then they had a look of extraordinary distinction. They
were tall and finely built. Then a gang of Solomon Islanders,
indentured labourers, passed by, singing; they were shorter and
slighter than the Samoans, coal black, with great heads of fuzzy
hair dyed red. Now and then a white man drove past in his
buggy or rode into the hotel yard. In the lagoon two or three
schooners reflected their grace in the tranquil water.

"I don't know what there is to do in a place like this except
to get soused," said Lawson at last.

"Don't you like Samoa?" I asked casually, for something to
say.

"It's pretty, isn't it?"

The word he chose seemed so inadequate to describe the
unimaginable beauty of the island, that I smiled, and smiling I
turned to look at him. I was startled by the expression in those
fine sombre eyes of his, an expression of intolerable anguish;
they betrayed a tragic depth of emotion of which I should
never have thought him capable. But the expression passed
away and he smiled. His smile was simple and a little naïve. It
changed his face so that I wavered in my first feeling of aversion
from him.

"I was all over the place when I first came out," he said.

He was silent for a moment.

"I went away for good about three years ago, but I came
back." He hesitated. "My wife wanted to come back. She was
born here, you know."

"Oh, yes."

He was silent again, and then hazarded a remark about
Robert Louis Stevenson. He asked me if I had been up to
Vailima. For some reason he was making an effort to be agreeable to me. He began to talk of Stevenson's books, and presently the conversation drifted to London.

"I suppose Covent Garden's still going strong," he said.

"I think I miss the opera as much as anything here. Have you seen *Tristan and Isolde?*"

He asked me the question as though the answer were really important to him, and when I said, a little casually, I daresay, that I had, he seemed pleased. He began to speak of Wagner, not as a musician, but as the plain man who received from him an emotional satisfaction that he could not analyze.

"I suppose Bayreuth was the place to go really," he said. "I never had the money, worse luck. But of course one might do worse than Covent Garden, all the lights and the women dressed up to the nines, and the music. The first act of the *Walküre's* all right, isn't it? And the end of *Tristan.* Golly!"

His eyes were flashing now and his face was lit up so that he hardly seemed the same man. There was a flush on his sallow, thin cheeks, and I forgot that his voice was harsh and unpleasant. There was even a certain charm about him.

"By George, I'd like to be in London to-night. Do you know the Pall Mall restaurant? I used to go there a lot. Piccadilly Circus with the shops all lit up, and the crowd. I think it's stunning to stand there and watch the buses and taxis streaming along as though they'd never stop. And I like the Strand too. What are those lines about God and Charing Cross?"

I was taken aback.

"Thompson's, d'you mean?" I asked.

I quoted them.

> "*And when so sad, thou canst not sadder,*
> *Cry, and upon thy so sore loss*
> *Shall shine the traffic of Jacob's ladder*
> *Pitched between Heaven and Charing Cross.*"

He gave a faint sigh.

"I've read *The Hound of Heaven.* It's a bit of all right."

"It's generally thought so," I murmured.

"You don't meet anybody here who's read anything. They think it's swank."

There was a wistful look on his face, and I thought I divined the feeling that made him come to me. I was a link with the world he regretted and a life that he would know no more. Because not so very long before I had been in the London which he loved, he looked upon me with awe and envy. He had not

spoken for five minutes perhaps when he broke out with words
that startled me by their intensity.

"I'm fed up," he said. "I'm fed up."

"Then why don't you clear out?" I asked.

His face grew sullen.

"My lungs are a bit dicky. I couldn't stand an English winter
now."

At that moment another man joined us on the verandah and
Lawson sank into a moody silence.

"It's about time for a drain," said the newcomer. "Who'll
have a drop of Scotch with me? Lawson?"

Lawson seemed to arise from a distant world. He got up.

"Let's go down to the bar," he said.

When he left me I remained with a more kindly feeling
towards him than I should have expected. He puzzled and interested me. And a few days later I met his wife. I knew they
had been married for five or six years, and I was surprised to see
that she was still extremely young. When he married her she
could not have been more than sixteen. She was adorably
pretty. She was no darker than a Spaniard, small and very
beautifully made, with tiny hands and feet, and a slight, lithe
figure. Her features were lovely; but I think what struck me
most was the delicacy of her appearance; the half-caste as a
rule have a certain coarseness, they seem a little roughly
formed, but she had an exquisite daintiness which took your
breath away. There was something extremely civilized about
her, so that it surprised you to see her in those surroundings,
and you thought of those famous beauties who had set all the
world talking at the Court of the Emperor Napoleon III.
Though she wore but a muslin frock and a straw hat she wore
them with an elegance that suggested the woman of fashion.
She must have been ravishing when Lawson first saw her.

He had but lately come out from England to manage the
local branch of an English bank, and, reaching Samoa at the
beginning of the dry season, he had taken a room at the hotel.
He quickly made the acquaintance of all and sundry. The life
of the island is pleasant and easy. He enjoyed the long idle
talks in the lounge of the hotel and the gay evenings at the
English Club when a group of fellows would play pool. He liked
Apia straggling along the edge of the lagoon, with its stores and
bungalows, and its native village. Then there were week-ends
when he would ride over to the house of one planter or another

and spend a couple of nights on the hills. He had never before known freedom or leisure. And he was intoxicated by the sunshine. When he rode through the bush his head reeled a little at the beauty that surrounded him. The country was indescribably fertile. In parts the forest was still virgin, a tangle of strange trees, luxuriant undergrowth, and vine; it gave an impression that was mysterious and troubling.

But the spot that entranced him was a pool a mile or two away from Apia to which in the evenings he often went to bathe. There was a little river that bubbled over the rocks in a swift stream, and then, after forming the deep pool, ran on, shallow and crystalline, past a ford made by great stones where the natives came sometimes to bathe or to wash their clothes. The coconut trees, with their frivolous elegance, grew thickly on the banks, all clad with trailing plants, and they were reflected in the green water. It was just such a scene as you might see in Devonshire among the hills, and yet with a difference, for it had a tropical richness, a passion, a scented languor which seemed to melt the heart. The water was fresh, but not cold; and it was delicious after the heat of the day. To bathe there refreshed not only the body but the soul.

At the hour when Lawson went, there was not a soul and he lingered for a long time, now floating idly in the water, now drying himself in the evening sun, enjoying the solitude and the friendly silence. He did not regret London then, nor the life that he had abandoned, for life as it was seemed complete and exquisite.

It was here that he first saw Ethel.

Occupied till late by letters which had to be finished for the monthly sailing of the boat next day, he rode down one evening to the pool when the light was almost failing. He tied up his horse and sauntered to the bank. A girl was sitting there. She glanced round as he came and noiselessly slid into the water. She vanished like a naiad startled by the approach of a mortal. He was surprised and amused. He wondered where she had hidden herself. He swam downstream and presently saw her sitting on a rock. She looked at him with uncurious eyes. He called out a greeting in Samoan.

"*Talofa.*"

She answered him, suddenly smiling, and then let herself into the water again. She swam easily and her hair spread out behind her. He watched her cross the pool and climb out on the

bank. Like all the natives she bathed in a Mother Hubbard,
and the water had made it cling to her slight body. She wrung
out her hair, and as she stood there, unconcerned, she looked
more than ever like a wild creature of the water or the woods.
He saw now that she was half-caste. He swam towards her and,
getting out, addressed her in English.

"You're having a late swim."

She shook back her hair and then let it spread over her
shoulders in luxuriant curls.

"I like it when I'm alone," she said.

"So do I."

She laughed with the childlike frankness of the native. She
slipped a dry Mother Hubbard over her head and, letting down
the wet one, stepped out of it. She wrung it out and was ready
to go. She paused a moment irresolutely and then sauntered
off. The night fell suddenly.

Lawson went back to the hotel and, describing her to the
men who were in the lounge shaking dice for drinks, soon discovered who she was. Her father was a Norwegian called
Brevald who was often to be seen in the bar of the Hotel
Metropole drinking rum and water. He was a little old man,
knotted and gnarled like an ancient tree, who had come out
to the islands forty years before as mate of a sailing vessel.
He had been a blacksmith, a trader, a planter, and at one time
fairly well-to-do; but, ruined by the great hurricane of the
nineties, he had now nothing to live on but a small plantation of
coconut trees. He had had four native wives and, as he told you
with a cracked chuckle, more children than he could count. But
some had died and some had gone out into the world, so that
now the only one left at home was Ethel.

"She's a peach," said Nelson, the supercargo of the *Moana*.
"I've given her the glad eye once or twice, but I guess there's
nothing doing."

"Old Brevald's not that sort of a fool, sonny," put in another, a man called Miller. "He wants a son-in-law who's prepared to keep him in comfort for the rest of his life."

It was distasteful to Lawson that they should speak of the
girl in that fashion. He made a remark about the departing mail
and so distracted their attention. But next evening he went
again to the pool. Ethel was there; and the mystery of the sunset, the deep silence of the water, the lithe grace of the coconut
trees, added to her beauty, giving it a profundity, a magic,

which stirred the heart to unknown emotions. For some reason
that time he had the whim not to speak to her. She took no
notice of him. She did not even glance in his direction. She
swam about the green pool. She dived, she rested on the bank,
as though she were quite alone: he had a queer feeling that he
was invisible. Scraps of poetry, half forgotten, floated across his
memory, and vague recollections of the Greece he had negli-
gently studied in his school days. When she had changed her wet
clothes for dry ones and sauntered away he found a scarlet
hibiscus where she had been. It was a flower that she had worn
in her hair when she came to bathe and, having taken it out on
getting into the water, had forgotten or not cared to put in
again. He took it in his hands and looked at it with a singular
emotion. He had an instinct to keep it, but his sentimentality
irritated him, and he flung it away. It gave him quite a little
pang to see it float down the stream.

He wondered what strangeness it was in her nature that
urged her to go down to this hidden pool when there was no
likelihood that anyone should be there. The natives of the
islands are devoted to the water. They bathe, somewhere or
other, every day, once always, and often twice; but they bathe
in bands, laughing and joyous, a whole family together; and
you often saw a group of girls, dappled by the sun shining
through the trees, with the half-castes among them, splashing
about the shallows of the stream. It looked as though there
were in this pool some secret which attracted Ethel against her
will.

Now the night had fallen, mysterious and silent, and he let
himself down in the water softly, in order to make no sound,
and swam lazily in the warm darkness. The water seemed
fragrant still from her slender body. He rode back to the town
under the starry sky. He felt at peace with the world.

Now he went every evening to the pool and every evening he
saw Ethel. Presently he overcame her timidity. She became
playful and friendly. They sat together on the rocks above the
pool, where the water ran fast, and they lay side by side on the
ledge that overlooked it, watching the gathering dusk envelop
it with mystery. It was inevitable that their meetings should
become known—in the South Seas everyone seems to know
everyone's business—and he was subjected to much rude chaff
by the men at the hotel. He smiled and let them talk. It was not

even worth while to deny their coarse suggestions. His feelings were absolutely pure. He loved Ethel as a poet might love the moon. He thought of her not as a woman but as something not of this earth. She was the spirit of the pool.

One day at the hotel, passing through the bar, he saw that old Brevald, as ever in his shabby blue overalls, was standing there. Because he was Ethel's father he had a desire to speak to him, so he went in, nodded and, ordering his own drink, casually turned and invited the old man to have one with him. They chatted for a few minutes of local affairs, and Lawson was uneasily conscious that the Norwegian was scrutinizing him with sly blue eyes. His manner was not agreeable. It was sycophantic, and yet behind the cringing air of an old man who had been worsted in his struggle with fate was a shadow of old truculence. Lawson remembered that he had once been captain of a schooner engaged in the slave trade, a blackbirder they call it in the Pacific, and he had a large hernia in the chest which was the result of a wound received in a scrap with Solomon Islanders. The bell rang for luncheon.

"Well, I must be off," said Lawson.

"Why don't you come along to my place one time?" said Brevald, in his wheezy voice. "It's not very grand, but you'll be welcome. You know Ethel."

"I'll come with pleasure."

"Sunday afternoon's the best time."

Brevald's bungalow, shabby and bedraggled, stood among the coconut trees of the plantation, a little away from the main road that ran up to Vailima. Immediately around it grew huge plantains. With their tattered leaves they had the tragic beauty of a lovely woman in rags. Everything was slovenly and neglected. Little black pigs, thin and high-backed, rooted about, and chickens clucked noisily as they picked at the refuse scattered here and there. Three or four natives were lounging about the verandah. When Lawson asked for Brevald the old man's cracked voice called out to him, and he found him in the sitting-room smoking an old briar pipe.

"Sit down and make yerself at home," he said. "Ethel's just titivating."

She came in. She wore a blouse and skirt and her hair was done in the European fashion. Although she had not the wild, timid grace of the girl who came down every evening to the

pool, she seemed now more usual and consequently more ap-
proachable. She shook hands with Lawson. It was the first time
he had touched her hand.

"I hope you'll have a cup of tea with us," she said.

He knew she had been at a mission school, and he was
amused, and at the same time touched, by the company manners she was putting on for his benefit. Tea was already set out
on the table and in a minute old Brevald's fourth wife brought
in the tea-pot. She was a handsome native, no longer very
young, and she spoke but a few words of English. She smiled
and smiled. Tea was rather a solemn meal, with a great deal of
bread and butter and a variety of very sweet cakes, and the
conversation was formal. Then a wrinkled old woman came in
softly.

"That's Ethel's granny," said old Brevald, noisily spitting on
the floor.

She sat on the edge of a chair, uncomfortably, so that you
saw it was unusual for her and she would have been more at
ease on the ground, and remained silently staring at Lawson
with fixed, shining eyes. In the kitchen behind the bungalow
someone began to play the concertina and two or three voices
were raised in a hymn. But they sang for the pleasure of the
sounds rather than from piety.

When Lawson walked back to the hotel he was strangely
happy. He was touched by the higgledy-piggledy way in which
those people lived; and in the smiling good-nature of Mrs.
Brevald, in the little Norwegian's fantastic career, and in the
shining mysterious eyes of the old grandmother, he found
something unusual and fascinating. It was a more natural life
than any he had known, it was nearer to the friendly, fertile
earth; civilization repelled him at that moment, and by mere
contact with these creatures of a more primitive nature he felt a
greater freedom.

He saw himself rid of the hotel which already was beginning
to irk him, settled in a little bungalow of his own, trim and
white, in front of the sea so that he had before his eyes always
the multicoloured variety of the lagoon. He loved the beautiful
island. London and England meant nothing to him any more,
he was content to spend the rest of his days in that forgotten
spot, rich in the best of the world's goods, love and happiness.
He made up his mind that whatever the obstacles nothing
should prevent him from marrying Ethel.

But there were no obstacles. He was always welcome at the
Brevalds' house. The old man was ingratiating and Mrs.
Brevald smiled without ceasing. He had brief glimpses of natives who seemed somehow to belong to the establishment, and
once he found a tall youth in a *lava-lava*, his body tattooed, his
hair white with lime, sitting with Brevald, and was told he was
Mrs. Brevald's brother's son; but for the most part they kept
out of his way. Ethel was delightful with him. The light in her
eyes when she saw him filled him with ecstasy. She was charming and naïve. He listened enraptured when she told him of the
mission school at which she was educated, and of the sisters.
He went with her to the cinema which was given once a fortnight and danced with her at the dance which followed it. They
came from all parts of the island for this, since gaieties are few
in Upolu; and you saw there all the society of the place, the
white ladies keeping a good deal to themselves, the half-castes
very elegant in American clothes, the natives, strings of dark
girls in white Mother Hubbards and young men in unaccustomed ducks and white shoes. It was all very smart and gay.
Ethel was pleased to show her friends the white admirer who
did not leave her side. The rumour was soon spread that he
meant to marry her and her friends looked at her with envy. It
was a great thing for a half-caste to get a white man to marry
her, even the less regular relation was better than nothing, but
one could never tell what it would lead to; and Lawson's position as manager of the bank made him one of the catches of the
island. If he had not been so absorbed in Ethel he would have
noticed that many eyes were fixed on him curiously, and he
would have seen the glances of the white ladies and noticed how
they put their heads together and gossiped.

Afterwards, when the men who lived at the hotel were having
a whisky before turning in, Nelson burst out with:

"Say, they say Lawson's going to marry that girl."

"He's a damned fool then," said Miller.

Miller was a German-American who had changed his name
from Müller, a big man, fat and bald-headed, with a round,
clean-shaven face. He wore large gold-rimmed spectacles, which
gave him a benign look, and his ducks were always clean and
white. He was a heavy drinker, invariably ready to stay up all
night with the "boys," but he never got drunk; he was jolly
and affable, but very shrewd. Nothing interfered with his business; he represented a firm in San Francisco, jobbers of the

goods sold in the islands, calico, machinery and what not; and
his good-fellowship was part of his stock-in-trade.

"He don't know what he's up against," said Nelson. "Someone ought to put him wise."

"If you'll take my advice you won't interfere in what don't
concern you," said Miller. "When a man's made up his mind
to make a fool of himself, there's nothing like letting him."

"I'm all for having a good time with the girls out here, but
when it comes to marrying them—this child ain't taking any,
I'll tell the world."

Chaplin was there, and now he had his say.

"I've seen a lot of fellows do it, and it's no good."

"You ought to have a talk with him, Chaplin," said Nelson.
"You know him better than anyone else does."

"My advice to Chaplin is to leave it alone," said Miller.

Even in those days Lawson was not popular and really no
one took enough interest in him to bother. Mrs. Chaplin talked
it over with two or three of the white ladies, but they contented
themselves with saying that it was a pity; and when he told her
definitely that he was going to be married it seemed too late
to do anything.

For a year Lawson was happy. He took a bungalow at the
point of the bay round which Apia is built, on the borders of a
native village. It nestled charmingly among the coconut trees
and faced the passionate blue of the Pacific. Ethel was lovely as
she went about the little house, lithe and graceful like some
young animal of the woods, and she was gay. They laughed a
great deal. They talked nonsense. Sometimes one or two of the
men at the hotel would come over and spend the evening, and
often on a Sunday they would go for a day to some planter who
had married a native; now and then one or other of the half-
caste traders who had a store in Apia would give a party and
they went to it. The half-castes treated Lawson quite differently
now. His marriage had made him one of themselves and they
called him Bertie. They put their arms through his and smacked
him on the back. He liked to see Ethel at these gatherings. Her
eyes shone and she laughed. It did him good to see her radiant
happiness. Sometimes Ethel's relations would come to the
bungalow, old Brevald of course, and her mother, but cousins
too, vague native women in Mother Hubbards and men and
boys in *lava-lavas*, with their hair dyed red and their bodies

elaborately tattooed. He would find them sitting there when
he got back from the bank. He laughed indulgently.

"Don't let them eat us out of hearth and home," he said.

"They're my own family. I can't help doing something for
them when they ask me."

He knew that when a white man marries a native or a half-
caste he must expect her relations to look upon him as a gold
mine. He took Ethel's face in his hands and kissed her red lips.
Perhaps he could not expect her to understand that the salary
which had amply sufficed for a bachelor must be managed with
some care when it had to support a wife and a house. Then
Ethel was delivered of a son.

It was when Lawson first held the child in his arms that a
sudden pang shot through his heart. He had not expected it to
be so dark. After all it had but a fourth part of native blood,
and there was no reason really why it should not look just
like an English baby; but, huddled together in his arms, sallow,
its head covered already with black hair, with huge black eyes,
it might have been a native child. Since his marriage he had
been ignored by the white ladies of the colony. When he came
across men in whose houses he had been accustomed to dine as a
bachelor, they were a little self-conscious with him; and they
sought to cover their embarrassment by an exaggerated cordiality.

"Mrs. Lawson well?" they would say. "You're a lucky fellow. Damned pretty girl."

But if they were with their wives and met him and Ethel
they would feel it awkward when their wives gave Ethel a
patronizing nod. Lawson had laughed.

"They're as dull as ditchwater, the whole gang of them," he
said. "It's not going to disturb my night's rest if they don't
ask me to their dirty parties."

But now it irked him a little.

The little dark baby screwed up its face. That was his son.
He thought of the half-caste children in Apia. They had an
unhealthy look, sallow and pale, and they were odiously precocious. He had seen them on the boat going to school in New
Zealand, and a school had to be chosen which took children
with native blood in them; they were huddled together, brazen
and yet timid, with traits which set them apart strangely from
white people. They spoke the native language among them-

selves. And when they grew up the men accepted smaller sala-
ries because of their native blood; girls might marry a white man,
but boys had no chance; they must marry a half-caste like themselves or a native. Lawson made up his mind passionately that
he would take his son away from the humiliation of such a life.
At whatever cost he must get back to Europe. And when he
went in to see Ethel, frail and lovely in her bed, surrounded by
native women, his determination was strengthened. If he took
her away among his own people she would belong more completely to him. He loved her so passionately, he wanted her to
be one soul and one body with him; and he was conscious that
here, with those deep roots attaching her to the native life, she
would always keep something from him.

He went to work quietly, urged by an obscure instinct of
secrecy, and wrote to a cousin who was partner in a shipping
firm in Aberdeen, saying that his health (on account of which
like so many more he had come out to the islands) was so
much better, there seemed no reason why he should not return
to Europe. He asked him to use what influence he could to get
him a job, no matter how poorly paid, on Deeside, where the
climate was particularly suitable to such as suffered from dis-
eases of the lungs. It takes five or six weeks for letters to get
from Aberdeen to Samoa, and several had to be exchanged. He
had plenty of time to prepare Ethel. She was as delighted as a
child. He was amused to see how she boasted to her friends that
she was going to England; it was a step up for her; she would
be quite English there; and she was excited at the interest the
approaching departure gave her. When at length a cable came
offering him a post in a bank in Kincardineshire she was beside
herself with joy.

When, their long journey over, they were settled in the little
Scots town with its granite houses Lawson realized how much
it meant to him to live once more among his own people. He
looked back on the three years he had spent in Apia as exile,
and returned to the life that seemed the only normal one with a
sigh of relief. It was good to play golf once more, and to fish—to
fish properly, that was poor fun in the Pacific when you just
threw in your line and pulled out one big sluggish fish after another from the crowded sea—and it was good to see a paper
every day with that day's news, and to meet men and women
of your own sort, people you could talk to; and it was good to
eat meat that was not frozen and to drink milk that was not

canned. They were thrown upon their own resources much more than in the Pacific, and he was glad to have Ethel exclusively to himself. After two years of marriage he loved her more devotedly than ever, he could hardly bear her out of his sight, and the need in him grew urgent for a more intimate communion between them. But it was strange that after the first excitement of arrival she seemed to take less interest in the new life than he had expected. She did not accustom herself to her surroundings. She was a little lethargic. As the fine autumn darkened into winter she complained of the cold. She lay half the morning in bed and the rest of the day on a sofa, reading novels sometimes, but more often doing nothing. She looked pinched.

"Never mind, darling," he said. "You'll get used to it very soon. And wait till the summer comes. It can be almost as hot as in Apia."

He felt better and stronger than he had done for years.

The carelessness with which she managed her house had not mattered in Samoa, but here it was out of place. When anyone came he did not want the place to look untidy; and, laughing, chaffing Ethel a little, he set about putting things in order. Ethel watched him indolently. She spent long hours playing with her son. She talked to him in the baby language of her own country. To distract her, Lawson bestirred himself to make friends among the neighbours, and now and then they went to little parties where the ladies sang drawing-room ballads and the men beamed in silent good nature. Ethel was shy. She seemed to sit apart. Sometimes Lawson, seized with a sudden anxiety, would ask her if she was happy.

"Yes, I'm quite happy," she answered.

But her eyes were veiled by some thought he could not guess. She seemed to withdraw into herself so that he was conscious that he knew no more of her than when he had first seen her bathing in the pool. He had an uneasy feeling that she was concealing something from him, and because he adored her it tortured him.

"You don't regret Apia, do you?" he asked her once.

"Oh, no—I think it's very nice here."

An obscure misgiving drove him to make disparaging remarks about the island and the people there. She smiled and did not answer. Very rarely she received a bundle of letters from Samoa and then she went about for a day or two with a set, pale face.

"Nothing would induce me ever to go back there," he said once. "It's no place for a white man."

But he grew conscious that sometimes, when he was away, Ethel cried. In Apia she had been talkative, chatting volubly about all the little details of their common life, the gossip of the place; but now she gradually became silent, and, though he increased his efforts to amuse her, she remained listless. It seemed to him that her recollections of the old life were drawing her away from him, and he was madly jealous of the island and of the sea, of Brevald, and all the dark-skinned people whom he remembered now with horror. When she spoke of Samoa he was bitter and satirical. One evening late in the spring when the birch trees were bursting into leaf, coming home from a round of golf, he found her not as usual lying on the sofa, but at the window, standing. She had evidently been waiting for his return. She addressed him the moment he came into the room. To his amazement she spoke in Samoan.

"I can't stand it. I can't live here any more. I hate it. I hate it."

"For God's sake speak in a civilized language," he said irritably.

She went up to him and clasped her arms around his body awkwardly, with a gesture that had in it something barbaric.

"Let's go away from here. Let's go back to Samoa. If you make me stay here I shall die. I want to go home."

Her passion broke suddenly and she burst into tears. His anger vanished and he drew her down on his knees. He explained to her that it was impossible for him to throw up his job, which after all meant his bread and butter. His place in Apia was long since filled. He had nothing to go back to there. He tried to put it to her reasonably, the inconveniences of life there, the humiliation to which they must be exposed, and the bitterness it must cause their son.

"Scotland's wonderful for education and that sort of thing. Schools are good and cheap, and he can go to the University at Aberdeen. I'll make a real Scot of him."

They had called him Andrew. Lawson wanted him to become a doctor. He would marry a white woman.

"I'm not ashamed of being half native," Ethel said sullenly.

"Of course not, darling. There's nothing to be ashamed of."

With her soft cheek against his he felt incredibly weak.

"You don't know how much I love you," he said. "I'd give

anything in the world to be able to tell you what I've got in my heart."

He sought her lips.

The summer came. The highland valley was green and fragrant, and the hills were gay with the heather. One sunny day followed another in that sheltered spot, and the shade of the birch trees was grateful after the glare of the high road. Ethel spoke no more of Samoa and Lawson grew less nervous. He thought that she was resigned to her surroundings, and he felt that his love for her was so passionate that it could leave no room in her heart for any longing. One day the local doctor stopped him in the street.

"I say, Lawson, your missus ought to be careful how she bathes in our highland streams. It's not like the Pacific, you know."

Lawson was surprised, and had not the presence of mind to conceal the fact.

"I didn't know she was bathing."

The doctor laughed.

"A good many people have seen her. It makes them talk a bit, you know, because it seems a rum place to choose, the pool up above the bridge, and bathing isn't allowed there, but there's no harm in that. I don't know how she can stand the water."

Lawson knew the pool the doctor spoke of, and suddenly it occurred to him that in a way it was just like that pool at Upolu where Ethel had been in the habit of bathing every evening. A clear highland stream ran down a sinuous course, rocky, splashing gaily, and then formed a deep, smooth pool, with a little sandy beach. Trees overshadowed it thickly, not coconut trees, but beeches, and the sun played fitfully through the leaves on the sparkling water. It gave him a shock. With his imagination he saw Ethel go there every day and undress on the bank and slip into the water, cold, colder than that of the pool she loved at home, and for a moment regain the feeling of the past. He saw her once more as the strange, wild spirit of the stream, and it seemed to him fantastically that the running water called her. That afternoon he went along to the river. He made his way cautiously among the trees and the grassy path deadened the sound of his steps. Presently he came to a spot from which he could see the pool. Ethel was sitting on the bank, looking down at the water. She sat quite still. It seemed as though the water

drew her irresistibly. He wondered what strange though
wandered through her head. At last she got up, and for a minu
or two she was hidden from his gaze; then he saw her agai
wearing a Mother Hubbard, and with her little bare feet sl
stepped delicately over the mossy bank. She came to tl
water's edge, and softly, without a splash, let herself dow
She swam about quietly, and there was something not quite of
human being in the way she swam. He did not know why
affected him so queerly. He waited till she clambered out. Sl
stood for a moment with the wet folds of her dress clinging t
her body, so that its shape was outlined, and then, passing h
hands slowly over her breasts, gave a little sigh of deligh
Then she disappeared. Lawson turned away and walked bac
to the village. He had a bitter pain in his heart, for he knew tha
she was still a stranger to him and his hungry love was destine
ever to remain unsatisfied.

He did not make any mention of what he had seen. H
ignored the incident completely, but he looked at her curiousl
trying to divine what was in her mind. He redoubled the tende
ness with which he used her. He sought to make her forge
the deep longing of her soul by the passion of his love.

Then one day, when he came home, he was astonished t
find her not in the house.

"Where's Mrs. Lawson?" he asked the maid.

"She went into Aberdeen, Sir, with the baby," the mai
answered, a little surprised at the question. "She said she woul
not be back till the last train."

"Oh, all right."

He was vexed that Ethel had said nothing to him about th
excursion, but he was not disturbed, since of late she had bee
in now and again to Aberdeen, and he was glad that she shoul
look at the shops and perhaps visit a cinema. He went to mee
the last train, but when she did not come he grew suddenl
frightened. He went up to the bedroom and saw at once tha
her toilet things were no longer in their place. He opened th
wardrobe and the drawers. They were half empty. She ha
bolted.

He was seized with a passion of anger. It was too late tha
night to telephone to Aberdeen and make enquiries, but h
knew already all that his enquiries might have taught him
With fiendish cunning she had chosen a time when they wer
making up their periodical accounts at the bank and there wa

no chance that he could follow her. He was imprisoned by his work. He took up a paper and saw that there was a boat sailing for Australia next morning. She must be now well on the way to London. He could not prevent the sobs that were wrung painfully from him.

"I've done everything in the world for her," he cried, "and she had the heart to treat me like this. How cruel, how monstrously cruel!"

After two days of misery he received a letter from her. It was written in her school-girl hand. She had always written with difficulty:

Dear Bertie:
    I couldn't stand it any more. I'm going back home. Good-bye.
                                      Ethel.

She did not say a single word of regret. She did not even ask him to come too. Lawson was prostrated. He found out where the ship made its first stop and, though he knew very well she would not come, sent a cable beseeching her to return. He waited with pitiful anxiety. He wanted her to send him just one word of love; she did not even answer. He passed through one violent phase after another. At one moment he told himself that he was well rid of her, and at the next that he would force her to return by withholding money. He was lonely and wretched. He wanted his boy and he wanted her. He knew that, whatever he pretended to himself, there was only one thing to do and that was to follow her. He could never live without her now. All his plans for the future were like a house of cards and he scattered them with angry impatience. He did not care whether he threw away his chances for the future, for nothing in the world mattered but that he should get Ethel back again. As soon as he could he went into Aberdeen and told the manager of his bank that he meant to leave at once. The manager remonstrated. The short notice was inconvenient. Lawson would not listen to reason. He was determined to be free before the next boat sailed; and it was not until he was on board of her, having sold everything he possessed, that in some measure he regained his calm. Till then to those who had come in contact with him he seemed hardly sane. His last action in England was to cable to Ethel at Apia that he was joining her.

He sent another cable from Sydney, and when at last with the

dawn his boat crossed the bar at Apia and he saw once more
the white houses straggling along the bay he felt an immense
relief. The doctor came on board and the agent. They were
both old acquaintances and he felt kindly towards their familiar
faces. He had a drink or two with them for old times' sake, and
also because he was desperately nervous. He was not sure if
Ethel would be glad to see him. When he got into the launch
and approached the wharf he scanned anxiously the little
crowd that waited. She was not there and his heart sank, but
then he saw Brevald, in his old blue clothes, and his heart
warmed towards him.

"Where's Ethel?" he said, as he jumped on shore.

"She's down at the bungalow. She's living with us."

Lawson was dismayed, but he put on a jovial air.

"Well, have you got room for me? I daresay it'll take a week
or two to fix ourselves up."

"Oh, yes, I guess we can make room for you."

After passing through the custom-house they went to the
hotel and there Lawson was greeted by several of his old
friends. There were a good many rounds of drinks before it
seemed possible to get away and when they did go out at last to
Brevald's house they were both rather gay. He clasped Ethel
in his arms. He had forgotten all his bitter thoughts in the joy
of beholding her once more. His mother-in-law was pleased to
see him, and so was the old, wrinkled beldame, her mother;
natives and half-castes came in, and they all sat round, beaming
on him. Brevald had a bottle of whisky and everyone who
came was given a nip. Lawson sat with his little dark-skinned
boy on his knees, they had taken his English clothes off him
and he was stark, with Ethel by his side in a Mother Hubbard.
He felt like a returning prodigal. In the afternoon he went down
to the hotel again and when he got back he was more than gay,
he was drunk. Ethel and her mother knew that white men got
drunk now and then, it was what you expected of them, and
they laughed good-naturedly as they helped him to bed.

But in a day or two he set about looking for a job. He knew
that he could not hope for such a position as that which he had
thrown away to go to England; but with his training he could
not fail to be useful to one of the trading firms, and perhaps in
the end he would not lose by the change.

"After all, you can't make money in a bank," he said.
"Trade's the thing."

He had hopes that he would soon make himself so indispensable that he would get someone to take him into partnership, and there was no reason why in a few years he should not be a rich man.

"As soon as I'm fixed up we'll find ourselves a shack," he told Ethel. "We can't go on living here."

Brevald's bungalow was so small that they were all piled on one another, and there was no chance of ever being alone. There was neither peace nor privacy.

"Well, there's no hurry. We shall be all right here till we find just what we want."

It took him a week to get settled and then he entered the firm of a man called Bain. But when he talked to Ethel about moving she said she wanted to stay where she was till her baby was born, for she was expecting another child. Lawson tried to argue with her.

"If you don't like it," she said, "go and live at the hotel."

He grew suddenly pale.

"Ethel, how can you suggest that!"

She shrugged her shoulders.

"What's the good of having a house of our own when we can live here?"

He yielded.

When Lawson, after his work, went back to the bungalow he found it crowded with natives. They lay about smoking, sleeping, drinking *kava;* and they talked incessantly. The place was grubby and untidy. His child crawled about, playing with native children, and it heard nothing spoken but Samoan. He fell into the habit of dropping into the hotel on his way home to have a few cocktails, for he could only face the evening and the crowd of friendly natives when he was fortified with liquor. And all the time, though he loved her more passionately than ever, he felt that Ethel was slipping away from him. When the baby was born he suggested that they should get into a house of their own, but Ethel refused. Her stay in Scotland seemed to have thrown her back on her own people, now that she was once more among them, with a passionate zest, and she turned to her native ways with abandon. Lawson began to drink more. Every Saturday night he went to the English Club and got blind drunk.

He had the peculiarity that as he grew drunk he grew quarrelsome and once he had a violent dispute with Bain, his employer.

Bain dismissed him, and he had to look out for another job. He
was idle for two or three weeks and during these, sooner than
sit in the bungalow, he lounged about in the hotel or at the
English Club, and drank. It was more out of pity than anything
else that Miller, the German-American, took him into his office;
but he was a business man, and though Lawson's financial
skill made him valuable, the circumstances were such that he
could hardly refuse a smaller salary than he had had before,
and Miller did not hesitate to offer it to him. Ethel and Brevald
blamed him for taking it, since Pedersen, the half-caste, offered
him more. But he resented bitterly the thought of being under
the orders of a half-caste. When Ethel nagged him he burst out
furiously:

"I'll see myself dead before I work for a nigger."

"You may have to," she said.

And in six months he found himself forced to this final humiliation. The passion for liquor had been gaining on him, he was
often heavy with drink, and he did his work badly. Miller
warned him once or twice and Lawson was not the man to accept remonstrance easily. One day in the midst of an altercation
he put on his hat and walked out. But by now his reputation
was well known and he could find no one to engage him. For a
while he idled, and then he had an attack of *delirium tremens.*
When he recovered, shameful and weak, he could no longer
resist the constant pressure, and he went to Pedersen and asked
him for a job. Pedersen was glad to have a white man in his
store and Lawson's skill at figures made him useful.

From that time his degeneration was rapid. The white people
gave him the cold shoulder. They were only prevented from
cutting him completely by disdainful pity and by a certain
dread of his angry violence when he was drunk. He became
extremely susceptible and was always on the lookout for
affront.

He lived entirely among the natives and half-castes, but he
had no longer the prestige of the white man. They felt his
loathing for them and they resented his attitude of superiority.
He was one of themselves now and they did not see why he
should put on airs. Brevald, who had been ingratiating and
obsequious, now treated him with contempt. Ethel had made a
bad bargain. There were disgraceful scenes and once or twice
the two men came to blows. When there was a quarrel Ethel
took the part of her family. They found he was better drunk

than sober, for when he was drunk he would lie on the bed or on
the floor, sleeping heavily.

Then he became aware that something was being hidden
from him.

When he got back to the bungalow for the wretched, half-
native supper which was his evening meal, often Ethel was not
in. If he asked where she was Brevald told him she had gone to
spend the evening with one or other of her friends. Once he
followed her to the house Brevald had mentioned and found
she was not there. On her return he asked where she had been
and she told him her father had made a mistake; she had been
to so-and-so's. But he knew that she was lying. She was in her
best clothes; her eyes were shining, and she looked lovely.

"Don't try any monkey tricks on me, my girl," he said, "or
I'll break every bone in your body."

"You drunken beast," she said, scornfully.

He fancied that Mrs. Brevald and the old grandmother
looked at him maliciously and he ascribed Brevald's good-humour with him, so unusual those days, to his satisfaction at having something up his sleeve against his son-in-law. And then,
his suspicions aroused, he imagined that the white men gave
him curious glances. When he came into the lounge of the hotel
the sudden silence which fell upon the company convinced him
that he had been the subject of the conversation. Something was
going on and everyone knew it but himself. He was seized
with furious jealousy. He believed that Ethel was carrying on
with one of the white men, and he looked at one after the
other with scrutinizing eyes; but there was nothing to give him
even a hint. He was helpless. Because he could find no one on
whom definitely to fix his suspicions, he went about like a
raving maniac, looking for someone on whom to vent his wrath.
Chance caused him in the end to hit upon the man who of all
others least deserved to suffer from his violence. One afternoon, when he was sitting in the hotel by himself, moodily,
Chaplin came in and sat down beside him. Perhaps Chaplin
was the only man on the island who had any sympathy for him.
They ordered drinks and chatted a few minutes about the races
that were shortly to be run. Then Chaplain said:

"I guess we shall all have to fork out money for new dresses."

Lawson sniggered. Since Mrs. Chaplin held the purse-strings
if she wanted a new frock for the occasion she would certainly
not ask her husband for the money.

"How is your missus?" asked Chaplin, desiring to be friendly.

"What the hell's that got to do with you?" said Lawson, knitting his dark brows.

"I was only asking a civil question."

"Well, keep your civil questions to yourself."

Chaplin was not a patient man; his long residence in the tropics, the whisky bottle, and his domestic affairs had given him a temper hardly more under control than Lawson's.

"Look here, my boy, when you're in my hotel you behave like a gentleman or you'll find yourself in the street before you can say knife."

Lawson's lowering face grew dark and red.

"Let me just tell you once for all and you can pass it on to the others," he said, panting with rage. "If any of you fellows come messing round with my wife he'd better look out."

"Who do you think wants to mess around with your wife?"

"I'm not such a fool as you think. I can see a stone wall in front of me as well as most men, and I warn you straight, that's all. I'm not going to put up with any hanky-panky, not on your life."

"Look here, you'd better clear out of here, and come back when you're sober."

"I shall clear out when I choose and not a minute before," said Lawson.

It was an unfortunate boast, for Chaplin in the course of his experience as a hotel-keeper had acquired a peculiar skill in dealing with gentlemen whose room he preferred to their company, and the words were hardly out of Lawson's mouth before he found himself caught by the collar and arm and hustled not without force into the street. He stumbled down the steps into the blinding glare of the sun.

It was in consequence of this that he had his first violent scene with Ethel. Smarting with humiliation and unwilling to go back to the hotel, he went home that afternoon earlier than usual. He found Ethel dressing to go out. As a rule she lay about in a Mother Hubbard, barefoot, with a flower in her dark hair; but now, in white silk stockings and high-heeled shoes, she was doing up a pink muslin dress which was the newest she had.

"You're making yourself very smart," he said. "Where are you going?"

"I'm going to the Crossleys'."

"I'll come with you."

"Why?" she asked coolly.

"I don't want you to gad about by yourself all the time."

"You're not asked."

"I don't care a damn about that. You're not going without me."

"You'd better lie down till I'm ready."

She thought he was drunk and if he once settled himself on the bed would quickly drop off to sleep. He sat down on a chair and began to smoke a cigarette. She watched him with increasing irritation. When she was ready he got up. It happened by an unusual chance that there was no one in the bungalow. Brevald was working on the plantation and his wife had gone into Apia. Ethel faced him.

"I'm not going with you. You're drunk."

"That's a lie. You're not going without me."

She shrugged her shoulders and tried to pass him, but he caught her by the arm and held her.

"Let me go, you devil," she said, breaking into Samoan.

"Why do you want to go without me? Haven't I told you I'm not going to put up with any monkey tricks?"

She clenched her fist and hit him in the face. He lost all control of himself. All his love, all his hatred, welled up in him and he was beside himself.

"I'll teach you," he shouted. "I'll teach you."

He seized a riding-whip which happened to be under his hand, and struck her with it. She screamed, and the scream maddened him so that he went on striking her, again and again. Her shrieks rang through the bungalow and he cursed her as he hit. Then he flung her on the bed. She lay there sobbing with pain and terror. He threw the whip away from him and rushed out of the room. Ethel heard him go and she stopped crying. She looked round cautiously, then she raised herself. She was sore, but she had not been badly hurt, and she looked at her dress to see if it was damaged. The native women are not unused to blows. What he had done did not outrage her. When she looked at herself in the glass and arranged her hair, her eyes were shining. There was a strange look in them. Perhaps then she was nearer loving him than she had ever been before.

But Lawson, driven forth blindly, stumbled through the plantation and suddenly exhausted, weak as a child, flung himself on the ground at the foot of a tree. He was miserable and ashamed. He thought of Ethel, and in the yielding tenderness of his love all his bones seemed to grow soft within him. He thought of the past, and of his hopes, and he was aghast at what he had done. He wanted her more than ever. He wanted to take her in his arms. He must go to her at once. He got up. He was so weak that he staggered as he walked. He went into the house and she was sitting in their cramped bedroom in front of her looking-glass.

"Oh, Ethel, forgive me. I'm so awfully ashamed of myself. I didn't know what I was doing."

He fell on his knees before her and timidly stroked the skirt of her dress.

"I can't bear to think of what I did. It's awful. I think I was mad. There's no one in the world I love as I love you. I'd do anything to save you from pain and I've hurt you. I can never forgive myself, but for God's sake say you forgive me."

He heard her shrieks still. It was unendurable. She looked at him silently. He tried to take her hands and the tears streamed from his eyes. In his humiliation he hid his face in her lap and his frail body shook with sobs. An expression of utter contempt came over her face. She had the native woman's disdain of a man who abased himself before a woman. A weak creature! And for a moment she had been on the point of thinking there was something in him. He grovelled at her feet like a cur. She gave him a little scornful kick.

"Get out," she said. "I hate you."

He tried to hold her, but she pushed him aside. She stood up. She began to take off her dress. She kicked off her shoes and slid the stockings off her feet, then she slipped on her old Mother Hubbard.

"Where are you going?"

"What's that got to do with you? I'm going down to the pool."

"Let me come too," he said.

He asked as though he were a child.

"Can't you even leave me that?"

He hid his face in his hands, crying miserably, while she, her eyes hard and cold, stepped past him and went out.

From that time she entirely despised him; and though, herded together in the small bungalow, Lawson and Ethel with her two children, Brevald, his wife and her mother, and the vague relations and hangers-on who were always in and about, they had to live cheek by jowl, Lawson, ceasing to be of any account, was hardly noticed. He left in the morning after breakfast, and came back only to have supper. He gave up the struggle, and when for want of money he could not go to the English Club he spent the evening playing hearts with old Brevald and the natives. Except when he was drunk he was cowed and listless. Ethel treated him like a dog. She submitted at times to his fits of wild passion, and she was frightened by the gusts of hatred with which they were followed; but when, afterwards, he was cringing and lachrymose she had such a contempt for him that she could have spat in his face. Sometimes he was violent, but now she was prepared for him, and when he hit her she kicked and scratched and bit. They had horrible battles in which he had not always the best of it. Very soon it was known all over Apia that they got on badly. There was little sympathy for Lawson, and at the hotel the general surprise was that old Brevald did not kick him out of the place.

"Brevald's a pretty ugly customer," said one of the men. "I shouldn't be surprised if he put a bullet into Lawson's carcass one of these days."

Ethel still went in the evenings to bathe in the silent pool. It seemed to have an attraction for her that was not quite human, just that attraction you might imagine that a mermaid who had won a soul would have for the cool salt waves of the sea; and sometimes Lawson went also. I do not know what urged him to go, for Ethel was obviously irritated by his presence; perhaps it was because in that spot he hoped to regain the clean rapture which had filled his heart when first he saw her; perhaps only, with the madness of those who love them that love them not, from the feeling that his obstinacy could force love. One day he strolled down there with a feeling that was rare with him now. He felt suddenly at peace with the world. The evening was drawing in and the dusk seemed to cling to the leaves of the coconut trees like a little thin cloud. A faint breeze stirred them noiselessly. A crescent moon hung just over their tops. He made his way to the bank. He saw Ethel in the water floating on her back. Her hair streamed out all round her, and she was holding in her hand a large hibiscus. He stopped a moment to admire her; she was like Ophelia.

"Hulloa, Ethel," he cried joyfully.

She made a sudden movement and dropped the red flower. It floated idly away. She swam a stroke or two till she knew there was ground within her depth and then stood up.

"Go away," she said. "Go away."

He laughed.

"Don't be selfish. There's plenty of room for both of us."

"Why can't you leave me alone? I want to be by myself."

"Hang it all, I want to bathe," he answered, good-humouredly.

"Go down to the bridge. I don't want you here."

"I'm sorry for that," he said, smiling still.

He was not in the least angry, and he hardly noticed that she was in a passion. He began to take off his coat.

"Go away," she shrieked. "I won't have you here. Can't you even leave me this? Go away."

"Don't be silly, darling."

She bent down and picked up a sharp stone and flung it quickly at him. He had no time to duck. It hit him on the temple. With a cry he put his hand to his head and when he took it away it was wet with blood. Ethel stood still, panting with rage. He turned very pale, and without a word, taking up his coat, went away. Ethel let herself fall back into the water and the stream carried her slowly down to the ford.

The stone had made a jagged wound and for some days Lawson went about with a bandaged head. He had invented a likely story to account for the accident when the fellows at the club asked him about it, but he had no occasion to use it. No one referred to the matter. He saw them cast surreptitious glances at his head, but not a word was said. The silence could only mean that they knew how he came by his wound. He was certain now that Ethel had a lover, and they all knew who it was. But there was not the smallest indication to guide him. He never saw Ethel with anyone; no one showed a wish to be with her, or treated him in a manner that seemed strange. Wild rage seized him, and having no one to vent it on he drank more and more heavily. A little while before I came to the island he had had another attack of *delirium tremens*.

I met Ethel at the house of a man called Caster, who lived two or three miles from Apia with a native wife. I had been playing tennis with him and when we were tired he suggested a cup of tea. We went into the house and in the untidy living-room found Ethel chatting with Mrs. Caster.

"Hulloa, Ethel," he said, "I didn't know you were here."

I could not help looking at her with curiosity. I tried to see what there was in her to have excited in Lawson such a devas-

tating passion. But who can explain these things? It was true
that she was lovely; she reminded one of the red hibiscus, the
common flower of the hedgerow in Samoa, with its grace and
its languor and its passion; but what surprised me most, taking
into consideration the story I knew even then a good deal of,
was her freshness and simplicity. She was quiet and a little
shy. There was nothing coarse or loud about her; she had not
the exuberance common to the half-caste; and it was almost
impossible to believe that she could be the virago that the
horrible scenes between husband and wife, which were now
common knowledge, indicated. In her pretty pink frock and
high-heeled shoes she looked quite European. You could hardly
have guessed at that dark background of native life in which
she felt herself so much more at home. I did not imagine that
she was at all intelligent, and I should not have been surprised
if a man, after living with her for some time, had found the
passion which had drawn him to her sink into boredom. It suggested itself to me that in her elusiveness, like a thought that
presents itself to consciousness and vanishes before it can be
captured by words, lay her peculiar charm; but perhaps that
was merely fancy, and if I had known nothing about her I
should have seen in her only a pretty little half-caste like another.

She talked to me of the various things which they talk of to
the stranger in Samoa, of the journey, and whether I had slid
down the water rock at Papaseea, and if I meant to stay in a
native village. She talked to me of Scotland, and perhaps I
noticed in her a tendency to enlarge on the sumptuousness of
her establishment there. She asked me naïvely if I knew Mrs.
This and Mrs. That, with whom she had been acquainted when
she lived in the north.

Then Miller, the fat German-American, came in. He shook
hands all round very cordially and sat down, asking in his loud,
cheerful voice for a whisky and soda. He was very fat and he
sweated profusely. He took off his gold-rimmed spectacles and
wiped them; you saw then that his little eyes, benevolent behind
the large round glasses, were shrewd and cunning; the party had
been somewhat dull till he came, but he was a good story-teller
and a jovial fellow. Soon he had the two women, Ethel and my
friend's wife, laughing delightedly at his sallies. He had a reputation on the island of a lady's man, and you could see how
this fat, gross fellow, old and ugly, had yet the possibility of

fascination. His humour was on a level with the understanding
of his company, an affair of vitality and assurance, and his
Western accent gave a peculiar point to what he said. At last
he turned to me:

"Well, if we want to get back for dinner we'd better be getting. I'll take you along in my machine if you like."

I thanked him and got up. He shook hands with the others,
went out of the room, massive and strong in his walk, and
climbed into his car.

"Pretty little thing, Lawson's wife," I said, as we drove
along.

"Too bad the way he treats her. Knocks her about. Gets my
dander up when I hear of a man hitting a woman."

We went on a little. Then he said:

"He was a darned fool to marry her. I said so at the time.
If he hadn't, he'd have had the whip hand over her. He's yaller,
that's what he is, yaller."

The year was drawing to its end and the time approached
when I was to leave Samoa. My boat was scheduled to sail for
Sydney on the fourth of January. Christmas Day had been
celebrated at the hotel with suitable ceremonies, but it was
looked upon as no more than a rehearsal for New Year, and the
men who were accustomed to foregather in the lounge determined on New Year's Eve to make a night of it. There was an
uproarious dinner, after which the party sauntered down to the
English Club, a simple little frame house, to play pool. There
was a great deal of talking, laughing, and betting, but some very
poor play, except on the part of Miller, who had drunk as much
as any of them, all far younger than he, but had kept unimpaired the keenness of his eye and the sureness of his hand. He
pocketed the young men's money with humour and urbanity.
After an hour of this I grew tired and went out. I crossed the
road and came on to the beach. Three coconut trees grew there,
like three moon maidens waiting for their lovers to ride out of
the sea, and I sat at the foot of one of them, watching the
lagoon and the nightly assemblage of the stars.

I do not know where Lawson had been during the evening,
but between ten and eleven he came along to the club. He
shambled down the dusty, empty road, feeling dull and bored,
and when he reached the club, before going into the billiard-
room, went into the bar to have a drink by himself. He had a
shyness now about joining the company of white men when

there were a lot of them together and needed a stiff dose of whisky to give him confidence. He was standing with the glass in his hand when Miller came in to him. He was in his shirt sleeves and still held his cue. He gave the bar-tender a glance. "Get out, Jack," he said.

The bar-tender, a native in a white jacket and a red *lava-lava,* without a word slid out of the small room.

"Look here, I've been wanting to have a few words with you, Lawson," said the big American.

"Well, that's one of the few things you can have free, gratis, and for nothing on this damned island."

Miller fixed his gold spectacles more firmly on his nose and held Lawson with his cold determined eyes.

"See here, young fellow, I understand you've been knocking Mrs. Lawson about again. I'm not going to stand for that. If you don't stop it right now I'll break every bone of your dirty little body."

Then Lawson knew what he had been trying to find out so long. It was Miller. The appearance of the man, fat, bald-headed, with his round bare face and double chin and the gold spectacles, his age, his benign, shrewd look, like that of a rene-gade priest, and the thought of Ethel, so slim and virginal, filled him with a sudden horror. Whatever his faults Lawson was no coward, and without a word he hit out violently at Miller. Miller quickly warded the blow with the hand that held the cue, and then with a great swing of his right arm brought his fist down on Lawson's ear. Lawson was four inches shorter than the American and he was slightly built, frail and weakened not only by illness and the enervating tropics, but by drink. He fell like a log and lay half dazed at the foot of the bar. Miller took off his spectacles and wiped them with his handkerchief.

"I guess you know what to expect now. You've had your warning and you'd better take it."

He took up his cue and went back into the billiard-room. There was so much noise there that no one knew what had happened. Lawson picked himself up. He put his hand to his ear, which was singing still. Then he slunk out of the club.

I saw a man cross the road, a patch of white against the dark-ness of the night, but did not know who it was. He came down to the beach, passed me sitting at the foot of the tree, and looked down. I saw then that it was Lawson, but since he was doubtless drunk, did not speak. He went on, walked irresolutely two or three steps, and turned back. He came up to me and bending down stared in my face.

"I thought it was you," he said.

He sat down and took out his pipe.

"It was hot and noisy in the club," I volunteered.

"Why are you sitting here?"

"I was waiting about for the midnight mass at the Cathedral."

"If you like I'll come with you."

Lawson was quite sober. We sat for a while smoking in silence. Now and then in the lagoon was the splash of some big fish, and a little way out towards the opening in the reef was the light of a schooner.

"You're sailing next week, aren't you?" he said.

"Yes."

"It would be jolly to go home once more. But I could never stand it now. The cold, you know."

"It's odd to think that in England now they're shivering round the fire," I said.

There was not even a breath of wind. The balminess of the night was like a spell. I wore nothing but a thin shirt and a suit of ducks. I enjoyed the exquisite languor of the night, and stretched my limbs voluptuously.

"This isn't the sort of New Year's Eve that persuades one to make good resolutions for the future," I smiled.

He made no answer, but I do not know what train of thought my casual remark had suggested in him, for presently he began to speak. He spoke in a low voice, without any expression, but his accents were educated, and it was a relief to hear him after the twang and the vulgar intonations which for some time had wounded my ears.

"I've made an awful hash of things. That's obvious, isn't it? I'm right down at the bottom of the pit and there's no getting out for me. '*Black as the pit from pole to pole.*'" I felt him smile as he made the quotation. "And the strange thing is that I don't see how I went wrong."

I held my breath, for to me there is nothing more awe-inspiring than when a man discovers to you the nakedness of his soul. Then you see that no one is so trivial or debased but that in him is a spark of something to excite compassion.

"It wouldn't be so rotten if I could see that it was all my own fault. It's true I drink, but I shouldn't have taken to that if things had gone differently. I wasn't really fond of liquor. I suppose I ought not to have married Ethel. If I'd kept her it would be all right. But I did love her so."

His voice faltered.

"She's not a bad lot, you know, not really. It's just rotten luck. We might have been as happy as lords. When she bolted I suppose I ought to have let her go, but I couldn't do that—I was dead stuck on her then; and there was the kid."

"Are you fond of the kid?" I asked.

"I was. There are two, you know. But they don't mean so much to me now. You'd take them for natives anywhere. I have to talk to them in Samoan."

"Is it too late for you to start fresh? Couldn't you make a dash for it and leave the place?"

"I haven't the strength. I'm done for."

"Are you still in love with your wife?"

"Not now. Not now." He repeated the two words with a kind of horror in his voice. "I haven't even got that now. I'm down and out."

The bells of the Cathedral were ringing.

"If you really want to come to the midnight mass we'd better go along," I said.

"Come on."

We got up and walked along the road. The Cathedral, all white, stood facing the sea not without impressiveness, and beside it the Protestant chapels had the look of meeting-houses. In the road were two or three cars, and a great number of traps, and traps were put up against the walls at the side. People had come from all parts of the island for the service, and through the great open doors we saw that the place was crowded. The high altar was all ablaze with light. There were a few whites and a good many half-castes, but the great majority were natives. All the men wore trousers, for the Church has decided that the *lava-lava* is indecent. We found chairs at the back, near the open door, and sat down. Presently, following Lawson's eyes, I saw Ethel come in with a party of half-castes. They were all very much dressed up, the men in high, stiff collars and shiny boots, the women in large, gay hats. Ethel nodded and smiled to her friends as she passed up the aisle. The service began.

When it was over Lawson and I stood on one side for awhile to watch the crowd stream out, then he held out his hand.

"Good-night," he said. "I hope you'll have a pleasant journey home."

"Oh, but I shall see you before I go."

He sniggered.

"The question is if you'll see me drunk or sober."

He turned and left me. I had a recollection of those very large black eyes, shining wildly under the shaggy brows. I paused irresolutely. I did not feel sleepy and I thought I would at all events go along to the club for an hour before turning in. When I got there I found the billiard-room empty, but half-a-dozen men were sitting round a table in the lounge, playing poker. Miller looked up as I came in

"Sit down and take a hand," he said.

"All right."

I bought some chips and began to play. Of course it is the most fascinating game in the world and my hour lengthened out to two, and then to three. The native bar-tender, cheer'' and wide-awake notwithstanding the time, was at our elbow to supply us with drinks and from somewhere or other he produced a ham and a loaf of bread. We played on. Most of the party had drunk more than was good for them and the play was high and reckless. I played modestly, neither wishing to win nor anxious to lose, but I watched Miller with a fascinated interest. He drank glass for glass with the rest of the company, but remained cool and level-headed. His pile of chips increased in size and he had a neat little paper in front of him on which he had marked various sums lent to players in distress. He beamed amiably at the young men whose money he was taking. He kept up interminably his stream of jest and anecdote, but he never missed a draw, he never let an expression of the face pass him. At last the dawn crept into the windows, gently, with a sort of deprecating shyness, as though it had no business there, and then it was day.

"Well," said Miller, "I reckon we've seen the old year out in style. Now let's have a round of jackpots and me for my mosquito net. I'm fifty, remember, I can't keep these late hours."

The morning was beautiful and fresh when we stood on the verandah, and the lagoon was like a sheet of multicoloured glass. Someone suggested a dip before going to bed, but none cared to bathe in the lagoon, sticky and treacherous to the feet. Miller had his car at the door and he offered to take us down to the pool. We jumped in and drove along the deserted road. When we reached the pool it seemed as though the day had hardly risen there yet. Under the trees the water was all in shadow and the night had the effect of lurking still. We were in great spirits. We had no towels or any costume and in my prudence I wondered how we were going to dry ourselves. None of us had much on and it did not take us long to snatch off our clothes. Nelson, the little supercargo, was stripped first.

"I'm going down to the bottom," he said.

He dived and in a moment another man dived too, but shallow, and was out of the water before him. Then Nelson came up and scrambled to the side.

"I say, get me out," he said.

"What's up?"

Something was evidently the matter. His face was terrified. Two fellows gave him their hands and he slithered up.

"I say, there's a man down there."

"Don't be a fool. You're drunk."

"Well, if there isn't I'm in for D. T.'s. But I tell you there's a man down there. It just scared me out of my wits."

Miller looked at him for a moment. The little man was all white. He was actually trembling.

"Come on, Caster," said Miller to the big Australian, "we'd better go down and see."

"He was standing up," said Nelson, "all dressed. I saw him. He tried to catch hold of me."

"Hold your row," said Miller. "Are you ready?"

They dived in. We waited on the bank, silent. It really seemed as though they were under water longer than any men could breathe. Then Caster came up, and immediately after him, red in the face as though he were going to have a fit, Miller. They were pulling something behind them. Another man jumped in to help them, and the three together dragged their burden to the side. They shoved it up. Then we saw that it was Lawson, with a great stone tied up in his coat and bound to his feet.

"He was set on making a good job of it," said Miller, as he wiped the water from his short-sighted eyes.

THE LETTER

OUTSIDE on the quay the sun beat fiercely. A stream of motors, lorries and buses, private cars and hirelings, sped up and down the crowded thoroughfare, and every chauffeur blew his horn; rickshaws threaded their nimble path amid the throng, and the panting coolies found breath to yell at one another; coolies, carrying heavy bales, sidled along with their quick jog-trot and shouted to the passer-by to make way; itinerant vendors proclaimed their wares. Singapore is the meeting-place of a hundred peoples; and men of all colours, black Tamils, yellow Chinks, brown Malays, Armenians, Jews and Bengalis, called to one another in raucous tones. But inside the office of Messrs. Ripley, Joyce & Naylor it was pleasantly cool; it was dark after the dusty glitter of the street and agreeably quiet after its unceasing din. Mr. Joyce sat in his private room, at the table, with an electric fan turned full on him. He was leaning back, his elbows on the arms of the chair, with the tips of the outstretched fingers of one hand resting neatly against the tips of the outstretched fingers of the other. His gaze rested on the battered volumes of the Law Reports which stood on a long shelf in front of him. On the top of a cupboard were square boxes of japanned tin on which were painted the names of various clients.

There was a knock at the door.

"Come in."

A Chinese clerk, very neat in his white ducks, opened it

"Mr. Crosbie is here, sir."

He spoke beautiful English, accenting each word with precision, and Mr. Joyce had often wondered at the extent of his vocabulary. Ong Chi Seng was a Cantonese, and he had studied law at Gray's Inn. He was spending a year or two with Messrs. Ripley, Joyce & Naylor in order to prepare himself for practice on his own account. He was industrious, obliging, and of exemplary character.

"Show him in," said Mr. Joyce.

He rose to shake hands with his visitor and asked him to sit down. The light fell on him as he did so. The face of Mr. Joyce remained in shadow. He was by nature a silent man, and now he looked at Robert Crosbie for quite a minute without speaking. Crosbie was a big fellow well over six feet high, with broad shoulders, and muscular. He was a rubber-planter, hard with the constant exercise of walking over the estate and with the tennis which was his relaxation when the day's work was over. He was deeply sunburned. His hairy hands, his feet in clumsy boots, were enormous, and Mr. Joyce found himself thinking that a blow of that great fist would easily kill the fragile Tamil. But there was no fierceness in his blue eyes; they were confiding and gentle; and his face, with its big, undistinguished features, was open, frank and honest. But at this moment it bore a look of deep distress. It was drawn and haggard.

"You look as though you hadn't had much sleep the last night or two," said Mr. Joyce.

"I haven't."

Mr. Joyce noticed now the old felt hat, with its broad double brim, which Crosbie had placed on the table; and then his eyes travelled to the khaki shorts he wore, showing his red hairy thighs, the tennis shirt open at the neck, without a tie, and the dirty khaki jacket with the ends of the sleeves turned up. He looked as though he had just come in from a long tramp among the rubber trees. Mr. Joyce gave a slight frown.

"You must pull yourself together, you know. You must keep your head."

"Oh, I'm all right."

"Have you seen your wife to-day?"

"No, I'm to see her this afternoon. You know, it is a damned shame that they should have arrested her."

"I think they had to do that," Mr. Joyce answered in his level, soft tone.

"I should have thought they'd have let her out on bail."

"It's a very serious charge."

"It is damnable. She did what any decent woman would

do in her place. Only, nine women out of ten wouldn't have the
pluck. Leslie's the best woman in the world. She wouldn't
hurt a fly. Why, hang it all, man, I've been married to her for
twelve years, do you think I don't know her? God, if I'd got hold
of the man I'd have wrung his neck. I'd have killed him without
a moment's hesitation. So would you."

"My dear fellow, everybody's on your side. No one has a good
word to say for Hammond. We're going to get her off. I don't
suppose either the assessors or the judge will go into court
without having already made up their minds to bring in a
verdict of not guilty."

"The whole thing's a farce," said Crosbie violently. "She
ought never to have been arrested in the first place, and then
it's terrible, after all the poor girl's gone through, to subject
her to the ordeal of a trial. There's not a soul I've met since I've
been in Singapore, man or woman, who hasn't told me that
Leslie was absolutely justified. I think it's awful to keep her in
prison all these weeks."

"The law is the law. After all, she confesses that she killed
the man. It is terrible, and I'm dreadfully sorry both for you
and for her."

"I don't matter a hang," interrupted Crosbie.

"But the fact remains that murder has been committed, and
in a civilized community a trial is inevitable."

"Is it murder to exterminate noxious vermin? She shot him
as she would have shot a mad dog."

Mr. Joyce leaned back again in his chair and once more
placed the tips of his ten fingers together. The little construction
he formed looked like the skeleton of a roof. He was silent for
a moment.

"I should be wanting in my duty as your legal adviser," he
said at last, in an even voice, looking at his client with his cool,
brown eyes, "if I did not tell you that there is one point which
causes me just a little anxiety. If your wife had only shot Hammond once, the whole thing would be absolutely plain sailing.
Unfortunately she fired six times."

"Her explanation is perfectly simple. In the circumstances
any one would have done the same."

"I daresay," said Mr. Joyce, "and of course I think the explanation is very reasonable. But it's no good closing our eyes
to the facts. It's always a good plan to put yourself in another
man's place, and I can't deny that if I were prosecuting for the

Crown that's the point on which I should centre my enquiry."

"My dear fellow, that's perfectly idiotic."

Mr. Joyce shot a sharp glance at Robert Crosbie. The shadow of a smile hovered over his shapely lips. Crosbie was a good fellow, but he could hardly be described as intelligent.

"I daresay it's of no importance," answered the lawyer, "I just thought it was a point worth mentioning. You haven't got very long to wait now, and when it's all over I recommend you to go off somewhere with your wife on a trip and forget all about it. Even though we are almost dead certain to get an acquittal, a trial of that sort is anxious work and you'll both want a rest."

For the first time Crosbie smiled, and his smile strangely changed his face. You forgot the uncouthness and saw only the goodness of his soul.

"I think I shall want it more than Leslie. She's borne up wonderfully. By God, there's a plucky little woman for you."

"Yes, I've been very much struck by her self-control," said the lawyer. "I should never have guessed that she was capable of such determination."

His duties as her counsel had made it necessary for him to have a good many interviews with Mrs. Crosbie since her arrest. Though things had been made as easy as could be for her, the fact remained that she was in jail, awaiting her trial for murder, and it would not have been surprising if her nerves had failed her. She appeared to bear her ordeal with composure. She read a great deal, took such exercise as was possible, and by favour of the authorities worked at the pillow lace which had always formed the entertainment of her long hours of leisure. When Mr. Joyce saw her she was neatly dressed in cool, fresh, simple frocks, her hair was carefully arranged, and her nails were manicured. Her manner was collected. She was able even to jest upon the little inconveniences of her position. There was something casual about the way in which she spoke of the tragedy, which suggested to Mr. Joyce that only her good breeding prevented her from finding something a trifle ludicrous in a situation which was eminently serious. It surprised him, for he had never thought that she had a sense of humour.

He had known her off and on for a good many years. When she paid visits to Singapore she generally came to dine with his wife and himself, and once or twice she had passed a week-end with them at their bungalow by the sea. His wife had spent a fortnight with her on the estate and had met Geoffrey Hammond several times. The two couples had been on friendly, if not on intimate, terms, and it was on this account that Robert Crosbie had rushed over to Singapore immediately after the catastrophe and begged Mr. Joyce to take charge personally of his unhappy wife's defence.

The story she told him the first time he saw her, she had never varied in the smallest detail. She told it as coolly then, a few hours after the tragedy, as she told it now. She told it connectedly, in a level, even voice, and her only sign of confusion was when a slight colour came into her cheeks as she described one or two of its incidents. She was the last woman to whom one would have expected such a thing to happen. She was in the early thirties, a fragile creature, neither short nor tall, and graceful rather than pretty. Her wrists and ankles were very delicate, but she was extremely thin and you could see the bones of her hands through the white skin, and the veins were large and blue. Her face was colourless, slightly sallow, and her lips were pale. You did not notice the colour of her eyes. She had a great deal of light brown hair and it had a slight natural wave; it was the sort of hair that with a little touching-up would have been very pretty, but you could not imagine that Mrs. Crosbie would think of resorting to any such device. She was a quiet, pleasant, unassuming woman. Her manner was engaging and if she was not very popular it was because she suffered from a certain shyness. This was comprehensible enough, for the planter's life is lonely, and in her own house, with people she knew, she was in her quiet way charming. Mrs. Joyce after her fortnight's stay had told her husband that Leslie was a very agreeable hostess. There was more in her, she said, than people thought; and when you came to know her you were surprised how much she had read and how entertaining she could be.

She was the last woman in the world to commit murder.

Mr. Joyce dismissed Robert Crosbie with such reassuring words as he could find and, once more alone in his office, turned over the pages of the brief. But it was a mechanical action, for all its details were familiar to him. The case was the sensation of the day, and it was discussed in all the clubs, at all the dinner tables, up and down the Peninsula from Singapore to Penang. The facts that Mrs. Crosbie gave were simple. Her husband had gone to Singapore on business and she was alone for the night. She dined by herself, late, at a quarter to nine, and after dinner sat in the sitting-room working at her lace. It opened on to the verandah. There was no one in the bungalow, for the servants had retired to their own quarters at the back of the compound. She was surprised to hear a step on the gravel path in the garden, a booted step which suggested a white man rather than a native, for she had not heard a motor drive up and she could not imagine who could be coming to see her at that time of night. Someone ascended the few stairs that led up to the bungalow, walked across the verandah, and appeared at the door of the room in which she sat. At the first moment she did not recognize the visitor. She sat with a shaded lamp and he stood with his back to the darkness.

"May I come in?" he said.

She did not even recognize the voice.

"Who is it?" she asked.

She worked with spectacles, and she took them off as she spoke.

"Geoff. Hammond."

"Of course. Come in and have a drink."

She rose and shook hands with him cordially. She was a little surprised to see him, for though he was a neighbour neither she nor Robert had been lately on very intimate terms with him, and she had not seen him for some weeks. He was the manager of a rubber estate nearly eight miles from theirs and she wondered why he had chosen this late hour to come and see them.

"Robert's away," she said. "He had to go to Singapore for the night."

Perhaps he thought his visit called for some explanation, for he said:

"I'm sorry. I felt rather lonely to-night, so I thought I'd just come along and see how you were getting on."

"How on earth did you come? I never heard a car."

"I left it down the road. I thought you might both be in bed and asleep."

This was natural enough. The planter gets up at dawn in order to take the roll-call of the workers, and soon after dinner he is glad to go to bed. Hammond's car was in point of fact found next day a quarter of a mile from the bungalow.

Since Robert was away there was no whisky and soda in

the room. Leslie did not call the boy, since he was probably asleep, but fetched it herself. Her guest mixed himself a drink and filled his pipe.

Geoff. Hammond had a host of friends in the colony. He was at this time in the late thirties, but he had come out as a lad. He had been one of the first to volunteer on the outbreak of war, and had done very well. A wound in the knee caused him to be invalided out of the army after two years, but he returned to the Federated Malay States with a D.S.O. and an M.C. He was one of the best billiard players in the colony. He had been a beautiful dancer and a fine tennis player, but, though able no longer to dance, and his tennis, with a stiff knee, was not so good as it had been, he had the gift of popularity and was universally liked. He was a tall, good-looking fellow, with attractive blue eyes and a fine head of black, curling hair. Old stagers said his only fault was that he was too fond of the girls, and after the catastrophe they shook their heads and vowed that they had always known this would get him into trouble.

He began now to talk to Leslie about the local affairs, the forthcoming races in Singapore, the price of rubber, and his chances of killing a tiger which had been lately seen in the neighbourhood. She was anxious to finish by a certain date the piece of lace on which she was working, for she wanted to send it home for her mother's birthday, and so put on her spectacles again and drew towards her chair the little table on which stood the pillow.

"I wish you wouldn't wear those great horn-spectacles," he said. "I don't know why a pretty woman should do her best to look plain."

She was a trifle taken aback at this remark. He had never used that tone with her before. She thought the best thing was to make light of it.

"I have no pretensions to being a raving beauty, you know, and, if you ask me point blank, I'm bound to tell you that I don't care two pins if you think me plain or not."

"I don't think you're plain. I think you're awfully pretty."

"Sweet of you," she answered ironically. "But in that case I can only think you half-witted."

He chuckled. But he rose from his chair and sat down in another by her side.

"You're not going to have the face to deny that you have the prettiest hands in the world," he said.

He made a gesture as though to take one of them. She gave him a little tap.

"Don't be an idiot. Sit down where you were before and talk sensibly, or else I shall send you home."

He did not move.

"Don't you know that I'm awfully in love with you?" he said.

She remained quite cool.

"I don't. I don't believe it for a minute, and even if it were true I don't want you to say it."

She was the more surprised at what he was saying, since during the seven years she had known him he had never paid her any particular attention. When he came back from the war they had seen a good deal of one another, and once when he was ill Robert had gone over and brought him back to their bungalow in his car. He had stayed with them then for a fortnight. But their interests were dissimilar and the acquaintance had never ripened into friendship. For the last two or three years they had seen little of him. Now and then he came over to play tennis, now and then they met him at some planter's who was giving a party, but it often happened that they did not set eyes on him for a month at a time.

Now he took another whisky and soda. Leslie wondered if he had been drinking before. There was something odd about him, and it made her a trifle uneasy. She watched him help himself with disapproval.

"I wouldn't drink any more if I were you," she said, good-humouredly still.

He emptied his glass and put it down.

"Do you think I'm talking to you like this because I'm drunk?" he asked abruptly.

"That is the most obvious explanation, isn't it?"

"Well, it's a lie. I've loved you ever since I first knew you. I've held my tongue as long as I could, and now it's got to come out. I love you, I love you, I love you."

She rose and carefully put aside the pillow.

"Good-night," she said.

"I'm not going now."

At last she began to lose her temper.

"But, you poor fool, don't you know that I've never loved any one but Robert, and even if I didn't love Robert you're the last man I should care for."

"What do I care? Robert's away."

"If you don't go away this minute I shall call the boys and have you thrown out."

"They're out of earshot."

She was very angry now. She made a movement as though to go on to the verandah from which the house-boy would certainly hear her, but he seized her arm.

"Let me go," she cried furiously.

"Not much. I've got you now."

She opened her mouth and called "Boy, boy," but with a quick gesture he put his hand over it. Then before she knew what he was about he had taken her in his arms and was kissing her passionately. She struggled, turning her lips away from his burning mouth.

"No, no, no," she cried. "Leave me alone. I won't."

She grew confused about what happened then. All that had been said before she remembered accurately, but now his words assailed her ears through a mist of horror and fear. He seemed to plead for her love. He broke into violent protestations of passion. And all the time he held her in his tempestuous embrace. She was helpless, for he was a strong, powerful man, and her arms were pinioned to her sides; her struggles were unavailing and she felt herself growing weaker; she was afraid she would faint, and his hot breath on her face made her feel desperately sick. He kissed her mouth, her eyes, her cheeks, her hair. The pressure of his arms was killing her. He lifted her off her feet. She tried to kick him, but he only held her more closely. He was carrying her now. He wasn't speaking any more, but she knew that his face was pale and his eyes hot with desire. He was taking her into the bedroom. He was no longer a civilized man, but a savage. And as he ran he stumbled against a table which was in the way. His stiff knee made him a little awkward on his feet, and with the burden of the woman in his arms he fell. In a moment she had snatched herself away from him. She ran round the sofa. He was up in a flash and flung himself towards her. There was a revolver on the desk. She was not a nervous woman, but Robert was to be away for the night and she had meant to take it into her room when she went to bed. That was why it happened to be there. She was frantic with terror now. She did not know what she was doing. She heard a report. She saw Hammond stagger. He gave a cry. He said something, she didn't know what. He lurched out of the room.

on to the verandah. She was in a frenzy now, she was beside herself, she followed him out, yes, that was it, she must have followed him out, though she remembered nothing of it, she followed firing automatically shot after shot till the six chambers were empty. Hammond fell down on the floor of the verandah. He crumpled up into a bloody heap.

When the boys, startled by the reports, rushed up, they found her standing over Hammond with the revolver still in her hand, and Hammond lifeless. She looked at them for a moment without speaking. They stood in a frightened, huddled bunch. She let the revolver fall from her hand and without a word turned and went into the sitting-room. They watched her go into her bedroom and turn the key in the lock. They dared not touch the dead body, but looked at it with terrified eyes, talking excitedly to one another in undertones. Then the head-boy collected himself; he had been with them for many years, he was Chinese and a level-headed fellow. Robert had gone into Singapore on his motor-cycle and the car stood in the garage. He told the seis to get it out; they must go at once to the Assistant District Officer and tell him what had happened. He picked up the revolver and put it in his pocket. The A.D.O., a man called Withers, lived on the outskirts of the nearest town, which was about thirty-five miles away. It took them an hour and a half to reach him. Every one was asleep, and they had to rouse the boys. Presently Withers came out and they told him their errand. The head-boy showed him the revolver in proof of what he said. The A.D.O. went into his room to dress, sent for his car, and in a little while was following them back along the deserted road. The dawn was just breaking as he reached the Crosbies' bungalow. He ran up the steps of the verandah, and stopped short as he saw Hammond's body lying where he fell. He touched the face. It was quite cold.

"Where's mem?" he asked the house-boy.

The Chinese pointed to the bedroom. Withers went to the door and knocked. There was no answer. He knocked again.

"Mrs. Crosbie," he called.

"Who is it?"

"Withers."

There was another pause. Then the door was unlocked and slowly opened. Leslie stood before him. She had not been to bed and wore the tea-gown in which she had dined. She stood and looked silently at the A.D.O.

"Your house-boy fetched me," he said. "Hammond. What have you done?"

"He tried to rape me and I shot him."

"My God! I say, you'd better come out here. You must tell me exactly what happened."

"Not now. I can't. You must give me time. Send for my husband."

Withers was a young man, and he did not know exactly what to do in an emergency which was so out of the run of his duties. Leslie refused to say anything till at last Robert arrived. Then she told the two men the story, from which since then, though she had repeated it over and over again, she had never in the slightest degree diverged.

The point to which Mr. Joyce recurred was the shooting. As a lawyer he was bothered that Leslie had fired not once but six times, and the examination of the dead man showed that four of the shots had been fired close to the body. One might almost have thought that when the man fell she stood over him and emptied the contents of the revolver into him. She confessed that her memory, so accurate for all that had preceded, failed her here. Her mind was blank. It pointed to an uncontrollable fury; but uncontrollable fury was the last thing you would have expected from this quiet and demure woman. Mr. Joyce had known her a good many years, and had always thought her an unemotional person; during the weeks that had passed since the tragedy her composure had been amazing.

Mr. Joyce shrugged his shoulders.

"The fact is, I suppose," he reflected, "that you can never tell what hidden possibilities of savagery there are in the most respectable of women."

There was a knock at the door.

"Come in."

The Chinese clerk entered and closed the door behind him. He closed it gently, with deliberation, but decidedly, and advanced to the table at which Mr. Joyce was sitting.

"May I trouble you, sir, for a few words' private conversation?" he said.

The elaborate accuracy with which the clerk expressed himself always faintly amused Mr. Joyce, and now he smiled.

"It's no trouble, Chi Seng," he replied.

"The matter on which I desire to speak to you, sir, is delicate and confidential."

"Fire away."

Mr. Joyce met his clerk's shrewd eyes. As usual Ong Chi Seng was dressed in the height of local fashion. He wore very shiny patent-leather shoes and gay silk socks. In his black tie was a pearl and ruby pin, and on the fourth finger of his left hand a diamond ring. From the pocket of his neat white coat protruded a gold fountain pen and a gold pencil. He wore a gold wrist-watch, and on the bridge of his nose invisible pince-nez. He gave a little cough.

"The matter has to do with the case R. v. Crosbie, sir."

"Yes?"

"A circumstance has come to my knowledge, sir, which seems to me to put a different complexion on it."

"What circumstance?"

"It has come to my knowledge, sir, that there is a letter in existence from the defendant to the unfortunate victim of the tragedy."

"I shouldn't be at all surprised. In the course of the last seven years I have no doubt that Mrs. Crosbie often had occasion to write to Mr. Hammond."

Mr. Joyce had a high opinion of his clerk's intelligence and his words were designed to conceal his thoughts.

"That is very probable, sir. Mrs. Crosbie must have communicated with the deceased frequently, to invite him to dine with her for example, or to propose a tennis game. That was my first thought when the matter was brought to my notice. This letter, however, was written on the day of the late Mr. Hammond's death."

Mr. Joyce did not flicker an eyelash. He continued to look at Ong Chi Seng with the smile of faint amusement with which he generally talked to him.

"Who has told you this?"

"The circumstances were brought to my knowledge, sir, by a friend of mine."

Mr. Joyce knew better than to insist.

"You will no doubt recall, sir, that Mrs. Crosbie has stated that until the fatal night she had had no communication with the deceased for several weeks."

"Have you got the letter?"

"No, sir."

"What are its contents?"

"My fliend gave me a copy. Would you like to peruse it, sir?"

"I should."

Ong Chi Seng took from an inside pocket a bulky wallet. It was filled with papers, Singapore dollar notes and cigarette cards. From the confusion he presently extracted a half sheet of thin note-paper and placed it before Mr. Joyce. The letter read as follows:

> *R. will be away for the night. I absolutely must see you. I shall expect you at eleven. I am desperate and if you don't come I won't answer for the consequences. Don't drive up.—L.*

It was written in the flowing hand which the Chinese were taught at the foreign schools. The writing, so lacking in character, was oddly incongruous with the ominous words.

"What makes you think that this note was written by Mrs. Crosbie?"

"I have every confidence in the veracity of my informant, sir," replied Ong Chi Seng. "And the matter can very easily be put to the proof. Mrs. Crosbie will no doubt be able to tell you at once whether she wrote such a letter or not."

Since the beginning of the conversation Mr. Joyce had not taken his eyes off the respectful countenance of his clerk. He wondered now if he discerned in it a faint expression of mockery.

"It is inconceivable that Mrs. Crosbie should have written such a letter," said Mr. Joyce.

"If that is your opinion, sir, the matter is of course ended. My fliend spoke to me on the subject only because he thought, as I was in your office, you might like to know of the existence of this letter before a communication was made to the Deputy Public Prosecutor."

"Who has the original?" asked Mr. Joyce sharply.

Ong Chi Seng made no sign that he perceived in this question and its manner a change of attitude.

"You will remember, sir, no doubt, that after the death of Mr. Hammond it was discovered that he had had relations with a Chinese woman. The letter is at present in her possession."

That was one of the things which had turned public opinion most vehemently against Hammond. It came to be known that for several months he had had a Chinese woman living in his house.

For a moment neither of them spoke. Indeed everything had been said and each understood the other perfectly.

"I'm obliged to you, Chi Seng. I will give the matter my consideration."

"Very good, sir. Do you wish me to make a communication to that effect to my friend?"

"I daresay it would be as well if you kept in touch with him," Mr. Joyce answered with gravity.

"Yes, sir."

The clerk noiselessly left the room, shutting the door again with deliberation, and left Mr. Joyce to his reflections. He stared at the copy, in its neat, impersonal writing, of Leslie's letter. Vague suspicions troubled him. They were so disconcerting that he made an effort to put them out of his mind. There must be a simple explanation of the letter, and Leslie without doubt could give it at once, but, by heaven, an explanation was needed. He rose from his chair, put the letter in his pocket, and took his topee. When he went out Ong Chi Seng was busily writing at his desk.

"I'm going out for a few minutes, Chi Seng," he said.

"Mr. George Reed is coming by appointment at twelve o'clock, sir. Where shall I say you've gone?"

Mr. Joyce gave him a thin smile.

"You can say that you haven't the least idea."

But he knew perfectly well that Ong Chi Seng was aware that he was going to the jail. Though the crime had been committed in Belanda and the trial was to take place at Belanda Bharu, since there was in the jail there no convenience for the detention of a white woman Mrs. Crosbie had been brought to Singapore.

When she was led into the room in which he waited she held out her thin, distinguished hand, and gave him a pleasant smile. She was as ever neatly and simply dressed and her abundant, pale hair was arranged with care.

"I wasn't expecting to see you this morning," she said graciously.

She might have been in her own house, and Mr. Joyce almost expected to hear her call the boy and tell him to bring the visitor a gin pahit.

"How are you?" he asked.

"I'm in the best of health, thank you." A flicker of amusement flashed across her eyes. "This is a wonderful place for a rest cure."

The attendant withdrew and they were left alone.

"Do sit down," said Leslie.

He took a chair. He did not quite know how to begin. She was so cool that it seemed almost impossible to say to her the thing he had come to say. Though she was not pretty there was something agreeable in her appearance. She had elegance, but it was the elegance of good breeding in which there was nothing of the artifice of society. You had only to look at her to know what sort of people she had and what kind of surroundings she had lived in. Her fragility gave her a singular refinement. It was impossible to associate her with the vaguest idea of grossness.

"I'm looking forward to seeing Robert this afternoon," she said, in her good-humoured, easy voice. (It was a pleasure to hear her speak, her voice and her accent were so distinctive of her class.) "Poor dear, it's been a great trial to his nerves. I'm thankful it'll all be over in a few days."

"It's only five days now."

"I know. Each morning when I awake I say to myself, 'one less.'" She smiled then. "Just as I used to do at school and the holidays were coming."

"By the way, am I right in thinking that you had no communication whatever with Hammond for several weeks before the catastrophe?"

"I'm quite positive of that. The last time we met was at a tennis-party at the MacFarrens'. I don't think I said more than two words to him. They have two courts, you know, and we didn't happen to be in the same sets."

"And you haven't written to him?"

"Oh, no."

"Are you quite sure of that?"

"Oh, quite," she answered, with a little smile. "There was nothing I should write to him for except to ask him to dine or to play tennis, and I hadn't done either for months."

"At one time you'd been on fairly intimate terms with him. How did it happen that you had stopped asking him to anything?"

Mrs. Crosbie shrugged her thin shoulders.

"One gets tired of people. We hadn't anything very much in common. Of course, when he was ill Robert and I did everything we could for him, but the last year or two he'd been quite well, and he was very popular. He had a good many calls on his time, and there didn't seem to be any need to shower invitations upon him."

"Are you quite certain that was all?"

Mrs. Crosbie hesitated for a moment.

"Well, I may just as well tell you. It had come to our ears that he was living with a Chinese woman, and Robert said he wouldn't have him in the house. I had seen her myself."

Mr. Joyce was sitting in a straight-backed arm-chair, resting his chin on his hand, and his eyes were fixed on Leslie. Was it his fancy that as she made this remark her black pupils were filled on a sudden, for the fraction of a second, with a dull red light? The effect was startling. Mr. Joyce shifted in his chair. He placed the tips of his ten fingers together. He spoke very slowly, choosing his words.

"I think I should tell you that there is in existence a letter in your handwriting to Geoff. Hammond."

He watched her closely. She made no movement, nor did her face change colour, but she took a noticeable time to reply.

"In the past I've often sent him little notes to ask him to something or other, or to get me something when I knew he was going to Singapore."

"This letter asks him to come and see you because Robert was going to Singapore."

"That's impossible. I never did anything of the kind."

"You'd better read it for yourself."

He took it out of his pocket and handed it to her. She gave it a glance and with a smile of scorn handed it back to him.

"That's not my handwriting."

"I know, it's said to be an exact copy of the original."

She read the words now, and as she read a horrible change came over her. Her colourless face grew dreadful to look at. It turned green. The flesh seemed on a sudden to fall away and her skin was tightly stretched over the bones. Her lips receded, showing her teeth, so that she had the appearance of making a grimace. She stared at Mr. Joyce with eyes that started from their sockets. He was looking now at a gibbering death's head.

"What does it mean?" she whispered.

Her mouth was so dry that she could utter no more than a hoarse sound. It was no longer a human voice.

"That is for you to say," he answered.

"I didn't write it. I swear I didn't write it."

"Be very careful what you say. If the original is in your handwriting it would be useless to deny it."

"It would be a forgery."

"It would be difficult to prove that. It would be easy to prove that it was genuine."

A shiver passed through her lean body. But great beads of sweat stood on her forehead. She took a handkerchief from her bag and wiped the palms of her hands. She glanced at the letter again and gave Mr. Joyce a sidelong look.

"It's not dated. If I had written it and forgotten all about it, it might have been written years ago. If you'll give me time, I'll try and remember the circumstances."

"I noticed there was no date. If this letter were in the hands of the prosecution they would cross-examine the boys. They would soon find out whether someone took a letter to Hammond on the day of his death."

Mrs. Crosbie clasped her hands violently and swayed in her chair so that he thought she would faint.

"I swear to you that I didn't write that letter."

Mr. Joyce was silent for a little while. He took his eyes from her distraught face, and looked down on the floor. He was reflecting.

"In these circumstances we need not go into the matter further," he said slowly, at last breaking the silence. "If the possessor of this letter sees fit to place it in the hands of the prosecution you will be prepared."

His words suggested that he had nothing more to say to her, but he made no movement of departure. He waited. To himself he seemed to wait a very long time. He did not look at Leslie, but he was conscious that she sat very still. She made no sound. At last it was he who spoke.

"If you have nothing more to say to me I think I'll be getting back to my office."

"What would anyone who read the letter be inclined to think that it meant?" she asked then.

"He'd know that you had told a deliberate lie," answered Mr. Joyce sharply.

"When?"

"You have stated definitely that you had had no communication with Hammond for at least three months."

"The whole thing has been a terrible shock to me. The events of that dreadful night have been a nightmare. It's not very strange if one detail has escaped my memory."

"It would be very unfortunate when your memory has reproduced so exactly every particular of your interview with

Hammond, that you should have forgotten so important a point as that he came to see you in the bungalow on the night of his death at your express desire."

"I hadn't forgotten. After what happened I was afraid to mention it. I thought you'd none of you believe my story if I admitted that he'd come at my invitation. I daresay it was stupid of me; but I lost my head, and after I'd said once that I'd had no communication with Hammond I was obliged to stick to it."

By now Leslie had recovered her admirable composure, and she met Mr. Joyce's appraising glance with candour. Her gentleness was very disarming.

"You will be required to explain, then, *why* you asked Hammond to come and see you when Robert was away for the night."

She turned her eyes full on the lawyer. He had been mistaken in thinking them insignificant, they were rather fine eyes, and unless he was mistaken they were bright now with tears. Her voice had a little break in it.

"It was a surprise I was preparing for Robert. His birthday is next month. I knew he wanted a new gun and you know I'm dreadfully stupid about sporting things. I wanted to talk to Geoff. about it. I thought I'd get him to order it for me."

"Perhaps the terms of the letter are not very clear to your recollection. Will you have another look at it?"

"No, I don't want to," she said quickly.

"Does it seem to you the sort of letter a woman would write to a somewhat distant acquaintance because she wanted to consult him about buying a gun?"

"I daresay it's rather extravagant and emotional. I do express myself like that, you know. I'm quite prepared to admit it's very silly." She smiled. "And after all, Geoff. Hammond wasn't quite a distant acquaintance. When he was ill I'd nursed him like a mother. I asked him to come when Robert was away, because Robert wouldn't have him in the house."

Mr. Joyce was tired of sitting so long in the same position. He rose and walked once or twice up and down the room, choosing the words he proposed to say; then he leaned over the back of the chair in which he had been sitting. He spoke slowly in a tone of deep gravity.

"Mrs. Crosbie, I want to talk to you very, very seriously. This case was comparatively plain sailing. There was only one point which seemed to me to require explanation: as far as I could judge, you had fired no less than four shots into Hammond when he was lying on the ground. It was hard to accept the possibility that a delicate, frightened, and habitually self-controlled woman, of gentle nurture and refined instincts, should have surrendered to an absolutely uncontrolled frenzy. But of course it was admissible. Although Geoffrey Hammond was much liked and on the whole thought highly of, I was prepared to prove that he was the sort of man who might be guilty of the crime which in justification of your act you accused him of. The fact, which was discovered after his death, that he had been living with a Chinese woman gave us something very definite to go upon. That robbed him of any sympathy which might have been felt for him. We made up our minds to make use of the odium which such a connection cast upon him in the minds of all respectable people. I told your husband this morning that I was certain of an acquittal, and I wasn't just telling him that to give him heart. I do not believe the assessors would have left the court."

They looked into one another's eyes. Mrs. Crosbie was strangely still. She was like a little bird paralyzed by the fascination of a snake. He went on in the same quiet tones.

"But this letter has thrown an entirely different complexion on the case. I am your legal adviser, I shall represent you in Court. I take your story as you tell it me, and I shall conduct your defence according to its terms. It may be that I believe your statements, and it may be that I doubt them. The duty of counsel is to persuade the Court that the evidence placed before it is not such as to justify it in bringing in a verdict of guilty, and any private opinion he may have of the guilt or innocence of his client is entirely beside the point."

He was astonished to see in Leslie's eyes the flicker of a smile. Piqued, he went on somewhat dryly.

"You're not going to deny that Hammond came to your house at your urgent, and I may even say, hysterical, invitation?"

Mrs. Crosbie, hesitating for an instant, seemed to consider.

"They can prove that the letter was taken to his bungalow by one of the house-boys. He rode over on his bicycle."

"You mustn't expect other people to be stupider than you. The letter will put them on the track of suspicions which have entered nobody's head. I will not tell you what I personally thought when I saw the copy. I do not wish you to tell me anything but what is needed to save your neck."

Mrs. Crosbie gave a shrill cry. She sprang to her feet, white with terror.

"You don't think they'd hang me?"

"If they came to the conclusion that you hadn't killed Hammond in self-defence, it would be the duty of the assessors to bring in a verdict of guilty. The charge is murder. It would be the duty of the judge to sentence you to death."

"But what can they prove?" she gasped.

"I don't know what they can prove. You know. I don't want to know. But if their suspicions are aroused, if they begin to make enquiries, if the natives are questioned—what is it that can be discovered?"

She crumpled up suddenly. She fell on the floor before he could catch her. She had fainted. He looked round the room for water, but there was none there, and he did not want to be disturbed. He stretched her out on the floor and kneeling beside her waited for her to recover. When she opened her eyes he was disconcerted by the ghastly fear that he saw in them.

"Keep quite still," he said. "You'll be better in a moment."

"You won't let them hang me," she whispered.

She began to cry, hysterically, while in undertones he sought to quieten her.

"For goodness' sake, pull yourself together," he said.

"Give me a minute."

Her courage was amazing. He could see the effort she made to regain her self-control, and soon she was once more calm.

"Let me get up now."

He gave her his hand and helped her to her feet. Taking her arm, he led her to the chair. She sat down wearily.

"Don't talk to me for a minute or two," she said.

"Very well."

When at last she spoke it was to say something which he did not expect. She gave a little sigh.

"I'm afraid I've made rather a mess of things," she said.

He did not answer, and once more there was a silence.

"Isn't it possible to get hold of the letter?" she said at last.

"I do not think anything would have been said to me about it if the person in whose possession it is was not prepared to sell it."

"Who's got it?"

"The Chinese woman who was living in Hammond's house."

A spot of colour flickered for an instant on Leslie's cheek-bones.

"Does she want an awful lot for it?"

"I imagine that she has a very shrewd idea of its value. I doubt if it would be possible to get hold of it except for a very large sum."

"Are you going to let me be hanged?"

"Do you think it's so simple as all that to secure possession of an unwelcome piece of evidence? It's no different from suborning a witness. You have no right to make any such suggestion to me."

"Then what is going to happen to me?"

"Justice must take its course."

She grew very pale. A little shudder passed through her body.

"I put myself in your hands. Of course I have no right to ask you to do anything that isn't proper."

Mr. Joyce had not bargained for the little break in her voice which her habitual self-restraint made quite intolerably moving. She looked at him with humble eyes and he thought that if he rejected their appeal they would haunt him for the rest of his life. After all, nothing could bring poor Hammond back to life again. He wondered what really was the explanation of that letter. It was not fair to conclude from it that she had killed Hammond without provocation. He had lived in the East a long time and his sense of professional honour was not perhaps so acute as it had been twenty years before. He stared at the floor. He made up his mind to do something which he knew was unjustifiable, but it stuck in his throat and he felt dully resentful towards Leslie. It embarrassed him a little to speak.

"I don't know exactly what your husband's circumstances are?"

Flushing a rosy red, she shot a swift glance at him.

"He has a good many tin shares and a small share in two or three rubber estates. I suppose he could raise money."

"He would have to be told what it was for."

She was silent for a moment. She seemed to think.

"He's in love with me still. He would make any sacrifice to save me. Is there any need for him to see the letter?"

Mr. Joyce frowned a little, and, quick to notice, she went on.

"Robert is an old friend of yours. I'm not asking you to do anything for me, I'm asking you to save a rather simple, kind man who never did you any harm from all the pain that's possible."

Mr. Joyce did not reply. He rose to go and Mrs. Crosbie, with the grace that was natural to her, held out her hand. She was shaken by the scene, and her look was haggard, but she made a brave attempt to speed him with courtesy.

"It's so good of you to take all this trouble for me. I can't begin to tell you how grateful I am."

Mr. Joyce returned to his office. He sat in his own room, quite still, attempting to do no work, and pondered. His imagination brought him many strange ideas. He shuddered a little. At last there was the discreet knock on the door which he was expecting. Ong Chi Seng came in.

"I was just going out to have my tiffin, sir," he said.

"All right."

"I didn't know if there was anything you wanted before I went, sir."

"I don't think so. Did you make another appointment for Mr. Reed?"

"Yes, sir. He will come at three o'clock."

"Good."

Ong Chi Seng turned away, walked to the door, and put his long slim fingers on the handle. Then, as though on an afterthought, he turned back.

"Is there anything you wish me to say to my fliend, sir?"

Although Ong Chi Seng spoke English so admirably he had still a difficulty with the letter r, and he pronounced it "fliend."

"What friend?"

"About the letter Mrs. Crosbie wrote to Hammond deceased, sir."

"Oh! I'd forgotten about that. I mentioned it to Mrs. Crosbie and she denies having written anything of the sort. It's evidently a forgery."

Mr. Joyce took the copy from his pocket and handed it to Ong Chi Seng. Ong Chi Seng ignored the gesture.

"In that case, sir, I suppose there would be no objection if my fliend delivered the letter to the Deputy Public Prosecutor."

"None. But I don't quite see what good that would do your friend."

"My fliend, sir, thought it was his duty in the interests of justice."

"I am the last man in the world to interfere with any one who wishes to do his duty, Chi Seng."

The eyes of the lawyer and of the Chinese clerk met. Not the shadow of a smile hovered on the lips of either, but they understood each other perfectly.

"I quite understand, sir," said Ong Chi Seng, "but from my study of the case R. v. Crosbie I am of opinion that the production of such a letter would be damaging to our client."

"I have always had a very high opinion of your legal acumen, Chi Seng."

"It has occurred to me, sir, that if I could persuade my fliend to induce the Chinese woman who has the letter to deliver it into our hands it would save a great deal of trouble."

Mr. Joyce idly drew faces on his blotting-paper.

"I suppose your friend is a business man. In what circumstances do you think he would be induced to part with the letter?"

"He has not got the letter. The Chinese woman has the letter. He is only a relation of the Chinese woman. She is an ignorant woman; she did not know the value of the letter till my fliend told her."

"What value did he put on it?"

"Ten thousand dollars, sir."

"Good God! Where on earth do you suppose Mrs. Crosbie can get ten thousand dollars! I tell you the letter's a forgery."

He looked up at Ong Chi Seng as he spoke. The clerk was unmoved by the outburst. He stood at the side of the desk, civil, cool and observant.

"Mr. Crosbie owns an eighth share of the Betong Rubber Estate and a sixth share of the Selantan River Rubber Estate. I have a fliend who will lend him the money on the security of his properties."

"You have a large circle of acquaintance, Chi Seng."

"Yes, sir."

"Well, you can tell them to go to hell. I would never advise Mr. Crosbie to give a penny more than five thousand for a letter that can be very easily explained."

"The Chinese woman does not want to sell the letter, sir. My fliend took a long time to persuade her. It is useless to offer her less than the sum mentioned."

Mr. Joyce looked at Ong Chi Seng for at least three minutes. The clerk bore the searching scrutiny without embarrassment.

He stood in a respectful attitude with downcast eyes. Mr. Joyce knew his man. Clever fellow, Chi Seng, he thought, I wonder how much he's going to get out of it.

"Ten thousand dollars is a very large sum."

"Mr. Crosbie will certainly pay it rather than see his wife hanged, sir."

Again Mr. Joyce paused. What more did Chi Seng know than he had said? He must be pretty sure of his ground if he was obviously so unwilling to bargain. That sum had been fixed because whoever it was that was managing the affair knew it was the largest amount that Robert Crosbie could raise.

"Where is the Chinese woman now?" asked Mr. Joyce.

"She is staying at the house of my fliend, sir."

"Will she come here?"

"I think it more better if you go to her, sir. I can take you to the house to-night and she will give you the letter. She is a very ignorant woman, sir, and she does not understand cheques."

"I wasn't thinking of giving her a cheque. I will bring bank-notes with me."

"It would only be waste of valuable time to bring less than ten thousand dollars, sir."

"I quite understand."

"I will go and tell my fliend after I have had my tiffin, sir."

"Very good. You'd better meet me outside the club at ten o'clock to-night."

"With pleasure, sir," said Ong Chi Seng.

He gave Mr. Joyce a little bow and left the room. Mr. Joyce went out to have luncheon too. He went to the club and here, as he had expected, he saw Robert Crosbie. He was sitting at a crowded table, and as he passed him, looking for a place, Mr. Joyce touched him on the shoulder.

"I'd like a word or two with you before you go," he said.

"Right you are. Let me know when you're ready."

Mr. Joyce had made up his mind how to tackle him. He played a rubber of bridge after luncheon in order to allow time for the club to empty itself. He did not want on this particular matter to see Crosbie in his office. Presently Crosbie came into the card-room and looked on till the game was finished. The other players went on their various affairs, and the two were left alone.

"A rather unfortunate thing has happened, old man," said

Mr. Joyce, in a tone which he sought to render as casual a
possible. "It appears that your wife sent a letter to Hammon
asking him to come to the bungalow on the night he wa
killed."

"But that's impossible," cried Crosbie. "She's always state
that she had had no communication with Hammond. I kno
from my own knowledge that she hadn't set eyes on him for
couple of months."

"The fact remains that the letter exists. It's in the possessio
of the Chinese woman Hammond was living with. Your wif
meant to give you a present on your birthday, and she wante
Hammond to help her to get it. In the emotional excitemen
that she suffered from after the tragedy, she forgot all about it
and having once denied having any communication with Ham
mond, she was afraid to say that she had made a mistake. I
was of course very unfortunate, but I daresay it was not un
natural."

Crosbie did not speak. His large, red face bore an expressio
of complete bewilderment, and Mr. Joyce was at once relieve
and exasperated by his lack of comprehension. He was
stupid man, and Mr. Joyce had no patience with stupidity
But his distress since the catastrophe had touched a soft spo
in the lawyer's heart; and Mrs. Crosbie had struck the righ
note when she asked him to help her, not for her sake, but fo
her husband's.

"I need not tell you that it would be very awkward if thi
letter found its way into the hands of the prosecution. You
wife has lied, and she would be asked to explain the lie. I
alters things a little if Hammond did not intrude, an unwante
guest, but came to your house by invitation. It would be eas
to arouse in the assessors a certain indecision of mind."

Mr. Joyce hesitated. He was face to face now with his de
cision. If it had been a time for humour, he could have smile
at the reflection that he was taking so grave a step, and tha
the man for whom he was taking it had not the smallest con
ception of its gravity. If he gave the matter a thought, h
probably imagined that what Mr. Joyce was doing was wha
any lawyer did in the ordinary run of business.

"My dear Robert, you are not only my client, but my friend
I think we must get hold of that letter. It'll cost a good deal o
money. Except for that I should have preferred to say nothing
to you about it."

"How much?"

"Ten thousand dollars."

"That's a devil of a lot. With the slump and one thing and another it'll take just about all I've got."

"Can you get it at once?"

"I suppose so. Old Charlie Meadows will let me have it on my tin shares and on those two estates I'm interested in."

"Then will you?"

"Is it absolutely necessary?"

"If you want your wife to be acquitted."

Crosbie grew very red. His mouth sagged strangely.

"But . . ." He could not find words, his face now was purple. "But I don't understand. She can explain. You don't mean to say they'd find her guilty? They couldn't hang her for putting a noxious vermin out of the way."

"Of course they wouldn't hang her. They might only find her guilty of manslaughter. She'd probably get off with two or three years."

Crosbie started to his feet and his red face was distraught with horror.

"Three years."

Then something seemed to dawn in that slow intelligence of his. His mind was darkness across which shot suddenly a flash of lightning, and though the succeeding darkness was as profound, there remained the memory of something not seen but perhaps just descried. Mr. Joyce saw that Crosbie's big red hands, coarse and hard with all the odd jobs he had set them to, trembled.

"What was the present she wanted to make me?"

"She says she wanted to give you a new gun."

Once more that great red face flushed a deeper red.

"When have you got to have the money ready?"

There was something odd in his voice now. It sounded as though he spoke with invisible hands clutching at his throat.

"At ten o'clock to-night. I thought you could bring it to my office at about six."

"Is the woman coming to you?"

"No, I'm going to her."

"I'll bring the money. I'll come with you."

Mr. Joyce looked at him sharply.

"Do you think there's any need for you to do that? I think

it would be better if you left me to deal with this matter by myself."

"It's my money, isn't it? I'm going to come."

Mr. Joyce shrugged his shoulders. They rose and shook hands. Mr. Joyce looked at him curiously.

At ten o'clock they met in the empty club.

"Everything all right?" asked Mr. Joyce.

"Yes. I've got the money in my pocket."

"Let's go then."

They walked down the steps. Mr. Joyce's car was waiting for them in the square, silent at that hour, and as they came to it Ong Chi Seng stepped out of the shadow of a house. He took his seat beside the driver and gave him a direction. They drove past the Hotel de l'Europe and turned up by the Sailors' Home to get into Victoria Street. Here the Chinese shops were open still, idlers lounged about, and in the roadway rickshaws and motor-cars and gharries gave a busy air to the scene. Suddenly their car stopped and Chi Seng turned round.

"I think it more better if we walk here, sir," he said.

They got out and he went on. They followed a step or two behind. Then he asked them to stop.

"You wait here, sir. I go in and speak to my fliend."

He went into a shop, open to the street, where three or four Chinese were standing behind the counter. It was one of those strange shops where nothing was on view and you wondered what it was they sold there. They saw him address a stout man in a duck suit with a large gold chain across his breast and the man shot a quick glance out into the night. He gave Chi Seng a key and Chi Seng came out. He beckoned to the two men waiting and slid into a doorway at the side of the shop. They followed him and found themselves at the foot of a flight of stairs.

"If you wait a minute I will light a match," he said, always resourceful. "You come upstairs, please."

He held a Japanese match in front of them, but it scarcely dispelled the darkness and they groped their way up behind him. On the first floor he unlocked a door and going in lit a gas-jet.

"Come in, please," he said.

It was a small square room, with one window, and the only furniture consisted of two low Chinese beds covered with matting. In one corner was a large chest, with an elaborate lock, and on this stood a shabby tray with an opium pipe on it and a lamp. There was in the room the faint, acrid scent of the drug. They sat down and Ong Chi Seng offered them cigarettes. In a moment the door was opened by the fat Chinaman whom they had seen behind the counter. He bade them good evening in very good English and sat down by the side of his fellow-countryman.

"The Chinese woman is just coming," said Chi Seng.

A boy from the shop brought in a tray with a tea-pot and cups and the Chinaman offered them a cup of tea. Crosbie refused. The Chinese talked to one another in undertones, but Crosbie and Mr. Joyce were silent. At last there was the sound of a voice outside; some one was calling in a low tone; and the Chinaman went to the door. He opened it, spoke a few words, and ushered a woman in. Mr. Joyce looked at her. He had heard much about her since Hammond's death, but he had never seen her. She was a stoutish person, not very young, with a broad, phlegmatic face. She was powdered and rouged and her eyebrows were a thin black line, but she gave you the impression of a woman of character. She wore a pale blue jacket and a white skirt, her costume was not quite European nor quite Chinese, but on her feet were little Chinese silk slippers. She wore heavy gold chains round her neck, gold bangles on her wrists, gold ear-rings and elaborate gold pins in her black hair. She walked in slowly, with the air of a woman sure of herself, but with a certain heaviness of tread, and sat down on the bed beside Ong Chi Seng. He said something to her and nodding she gave an incurious glance at the two white men.

"Has she got the letter?" asked Mr. Joyce.

"Yes, sir."

Crosbie said nothing, but produced a roll of five-hundred-dollar notes. He counted out twenty and handed them to Chi Seng.

"Will you see if that is correct?"

The clerk counted them and gave them to the fat Chinaman.

"Quite correct, sir."

The Chinaman counted them once more and put them in his pocket. He spoke again to the woman and she drew from her bosom a letter. She gave it to Chi Seng who cast his eyes over it.

"This is the right document, sir," he said, and was about to give it to Mr. Joyce when Crosbie took it from him.

"Let me look at it," he said.

Mr. Joyce watched him read and then held out his hand for it.

"You'd better let me have it."

Crosbie folded it up deliberately and put it in his pocket.

"No, I'm going to keep it myself. It's cost me enough money."

Mr. Joyce made no rejoinder. The three Chinese watched the little passage, but what they thought about it, or whether they thought, it was impossible to tell from their impassive countenances. Mr. Joyce rose to his feet.

"Do you want me any more to-night, sir?" said Ong Chi Seng.

"No." He knew that the clerk wished to stay behind in order to get his agreed share of the money, and he turned to Crosbie. "Are you ready?"

Crosbie did not answer, but stood up. The Chinaman went to the door and opened it for them. Chi Seng found a bit of candle and lit it in order to light them down, and the two Chinese accompanied them to the street. They left the woman sitting quietly on the bed smoking a cigarette. When they reached the street the Chinese left them and went once more upstairs.

"What are you going to do with that letter?" asked Mr. Joyce.

"Keep it."

They walked to where the car was waiting for them and here Mr. Joyce offered his friend a lift. Crosbie shook his head.

"I'm going to walk." He hesitated a little and shuffled his feet. "I went to Singapore on the night of Hammond's death partly to buy a new gun that a man I knew wanted to dispose of. Good-night."

He disappeared quickly into the darkness.

Mr. Joyce was quite right about the trial. The assessors went into court fully determined to acquit Mrs. Crosbie. She gave evidence on her own behalf. She told her story simply add with straightforwardness. The D.P.P. was a kindly man and it was plain that he took no great pleasure in his task. He asked the necessary questions in a deprecating manner. His speech for the prosecution might really have been a speech for the defence, and the assessors took less than five minutes to consider their popular verdict. It was impossible to prevent

the great outburst of applause with which it was received by
the crowd that packed the court-house. The judge congratulated Mrs. Crosbie and she was a free woman.

No one had expressed a more violent disapprobation of
Hammond's behaviour than Mrs. Joyce; she was a woman loyal
to her friends and she had insisted on the Crosbies staying
with her after the trial, for she in common with every one else
had no doubt of the result, till they could make arrangements to
go away. It was out of the question for poor, dear, brave Leslie
to return to the bungalow at which the horrible catastrophe
had taken place. The trial was over by half-past twelve and
when they reached the Joyces' house a grand luncheon was
awaiting them. Cocktails were ready, Mrs. Joyce's million-
dollar cocktail was celebrated through all the Malay States,
and Mrs. Joyce drank Leslie's health. She was a talkative,
vivacious woman, and now she was in the highest spirits. It
was fortunate, for the rest of them were silent. She did not
wonder, her husband never had much to say, and the other two
were naturally exhausted from the long strain to which they
had been subjected. During luncheon she carried on a bright
and spirited monologue. Then coffee was served.

"Now, children," she said in her gay, bustling fashion, "you
must have a rest and after tea I shall take you both for a drive
to the sea."

Mr. Joyce, who lunched at home only by exception, had of
course to go back to his office.

"I'm afraid I can't do that, Mrs. Joyce," said Crosbie. "I've
got to get back to the estate at once."

"Not to-day?" she cried.

"Yes, now. I've neglected it for too long and I have urgent
business. But I shall be very grateful if you will keep Leslie
until we have decided what to do."

Mrs. Joyce was about to expostulate, but her husband prevented her.

"If he must go, he must, and there's an end of it."

There was something in the lawyer's tone which made her
look at him quickly. She held her tongue and there was a
moment's silence. Then Crosbie spoke again.

"If you'll forgive me, I'll start at once so that I can get there
before dark." He rose from the table. "Will you come and
see me off, Leslie?"

"Of course."

They went out of the dining-room together.

"I think that's rather inconsiderate of him," said Mrs. Joyce. "He must know that Leslie wants to be with him just now."

"I'm sure he wouldn't go if it wasn't absolutely necessary."

"Well, I'll just see that Leslie's room is ready for her. She wants a complete rest, of course, and then amusement."

Mrs. Joyce left the room and Joyce sat down again. In a short time he heard Crosbie start the engine of his motor-cycle and then noisily scrunch over the gravel of the garden path. He got up and went into the drawing-room. Mrs. Crosbie was standing in the middle of it, looking into space, and in her hand was an open letter. He recognized it. She gave him a glance as he came in and he saw that she was deathly pale.

"He knows," she whispered.

Mr. Joyce went up to her and took the letter from her hand. He lit a match and set the paper afire. She watched it burn. When he could hold it no longer he dropped it on the tiled floor and they both looked at the paper curl and blacken. Then he trod it into ashes with his foot.

"What does he know?"

She gave him a long, long stare and into her eyes came a strange look. Was it contempt or despair? Mr. Joyce could not tell.

"He knows that Geoff. was my lover."

Mr. Joyce made no movement and uttered no sound.

"He'd been my lover for years. He became my lover almost immediately after he came back from the war. We knew how careful we must be. When we became lovers I pretended I was tired of him, and he seldom came to the house when Robert was there. I used to drive out to a place we knew and he met me, two or three times a week, and when Robert went to Singapore he used to come to the bungalow late, when the boys had gone for the night. We saw one another constantly, all the time, and not a soul had the smallest suspicion of it. And then lately, a year ago, he began to change. I didn't know what was the matter. I couldn't believe that he didn't care for me any more. He always denied it. I was frantic. I made him scenes. Sometimes I thought he hated me. Oh, if you knew what agonies I endured. I passed through hell. I knew he didn't want me any more and I wouldn't let him go. Misery! Misery! I loved him. I'd given him everything. He was all my life. And then I heard

he was living with a Chinese woman. I couldn't believe it. I
wouldn't believe it. At last I saw her, I saw her with my own
eyes, walking in the village, with her gold bracelets and her
necklaces, an old, fat, Chinese woman. She was older than I
was. Horrible! They all knew in the kampong that she was his
mistress. And when I passed her, she looked at me and I knew
that she knew 1 was his mistress too. I sent for him. I told him
I must see him. You've read the letter. I was mad to write it.
I didn't know what I was doing. I didn't care. I hadn't seen
him for ten days. It was a lifetime. And when last we'd parted
he took me in his arms and kissed me and told me not to worry.
And he went straight from my arms to hers."

She had been speaking in a low voice, vehemently, and now
she stopped and wrung her hands.

"That damned letter. We'd always been so careful. He always tore up any word I wrote to him the moment he'd read
it. How was I to know he'd leave that one? He came and I told
him I knew about the Chinawoman. He denied it. He said it
was only scandal. I was beside myself. I don't know what I
said to him. Oh, I hated him then. I tore him limb from limb.
I said everything I could to wound him. I insulted him. I could
have spat in his face. And at last he turned on me. He told me
he was sick and tired of me and never wanted to see me again.
He said I bored him to death. And then he acknowledged that
it was true about the Chinawoman. He said he'd known her for
years, before the war, and she was the only woman who really
meant anything to him, and the rest was just pastime. And he
said he was glad I knew, and now at last I'd leave him alone.
And then I don't know what happened, I was beside myself, I
saw red. I seized the revolver and I fired. He gave a cry and
I saw I'd hit him. He staggered and rushed for the verandah.
I ran after him and fired again. He fell, and then I stood over
him and I fired and fired till the revolver went click, click, and
I knew there were no more cartridges."

At last she stopped, panting. Her face was no longer human,
it was distorted with cruelty, and rage and pain. You would
never have thought that this quiet, refined woman was capable
of such a fiendish passion. Mr. Joyce took a step backwards.
He was absolutely aghast at the sight of her. It was not a face,
it was a gibbering, hideous mask. Then they heard a voice
calling from another room. a loud, friendly, cheerful voice.
It was Mrs. Joyce.

"Come along, Leslie darling, your room's ready. You must be dropping with sleep."

Mrs. Crosbie's features gradually composed themselves. Those passions, so clearly delineated, were smoothed away as with your hand you would smooth a crumpled paper, and in a minute the face was cool and calm and unlined. She was a trifle pale, but her lips broke into a pleasant, affable smile. She was once more the well-bred and even distinguished woman.

"I'm coming, Dorothy dear. I'm sorry to give you so much trouble."

BEFORE THE PARTY

Mrs. SKINNER liked to be in good time. She was already dressed, in black silk as befitted her age and the mourning she wore for her son-in-law, and now she put on her toque. She was a little uncertain about it, since the egrets' feathers which adorned it might very well arouse in some of the friends she would certainly meet at the party acid expostulations; and of course it was shocking to kill those beautiful white birds, in the mating season too, for the sake of their feathers; but there they were, so pretty and stylish, and it would have been silly to refuse them, and it would have hurt her son-in-law's feelings. He had brought them all the way from Borneo and he expected her to be so pleased with them. Kathleen had made herself rather unpleasant about them, she must wish she hadn't now, after what had happened, but Kathleen had never really liked Harold. Mrs. Skinner, standing at her dressing-table, placed the toque on her head, it was after all the only nice hat she had, and put in a pin with a large jet knob. If anybody spoke to her about the ospreys she had her answer.

"I know it's dreadful," she would say, "and I wouldn't dream of buying them, but my poor son-in-law brought them back the last time he was home on leave."

That would explain her possession of them and excuse their use. Every one had been very kind. Mrs. Skinner took a clean handkerchief from a drawer and sprinkled a little *Eau de Cologne* on it. She never used scent, and she had always thought it rather fast, but *Eau de Cologne* was so refreshing.

217

She was very nearly ready now and her eyes wandered out of the window behind her looking-glass. Canon Heywood had a beautiful day for his garden-party. It was warm and the sky was blue; the trees had not yet lost the fresh green of the spring. She smiled as she saw her little granddaughter in the strip of garden behind the house busily raking her very own flower-bed. Mrs. Skinner wished Joan were not quite so pale, it was a mistake to have kept her so long in the tropics; and she was so grave for her age, you never saw her run about; she played quiet games of her own invention and watered her garden. Mrs. Skinner gave the front of her dress a little pat, took up her gloves, and went down-stairs.

Kathleen was at the writing-table in the window busy with lists she was making, for she was honorary secretary of the Ladies' Golf Club and when there were competitions had a good deal to do. But she too was ready for the party.

"I see you've put on your jumper after all," said Mrs. Skinner.

They had discussed at luncheon whether Kathleen should wear her jumper or her black chiffon. The jumper was black and white, and Kathleen thought it rather smart, but it was hardly mourning. Millicent, however, was in favour of it.

"There's no reason why we should all look as if we'd just come from a funeral," she said. "Harold's been dead eight months." ·

To Mrs. Skinner it seemed rather unfeeling to talk like that. Millicent was strange since her return from Borneo.

"You're not going to leave off your weeds yet, darling?" she asked.

Millicent did not give a direct answer.

"People don't wear mourning in the way they used," she said. She paused a little and when she went on there was a tone in her voice which Mrs. Skinner thought quite peculiar. It was plain that Kathleen noticed it too, for she gave her sister a curious look. "I'm sure Harold wouldn't wish me to wear mourning for him indefinitely."

"I dressed early because I wanted to say something to Millicent," said Kathleen in reply to her mother's observation. "Oh?"

Kathleen did not explain. But she put her lists aside and with knitted brows read for the second time a letter from a lady who complained that the committee had most unfairly marked down her handicap from twenty-four to eighteen. It requires a good deal of tact to be Honorary Secretary to a ladies' golf club. Mrs. Skinner began to put on her new gloves. The sun-blinds kept the room cool and dark. She looked at the great wooden hornbill, gaily painted, which Harold had left in her safe-keeping; and it seemed a little odd and barbaric to her, but he had set much store on it. It had some religious significance and Canon Heywood had been greatly struck by it. On the wall, over the sofa, were Malay weapons, she forgot what they were called, and here and there on occasional tables pieces of silver and brass which Harold at various times had sent to them. She had liked Harold and involuntarily her eyes sought his photograph which stood on the piano with photographs of her two daughters, her grandchild, her sister and her sister's son.

"Why, Kathleen, where's Harold's photograph?" she asked.

Kathleen looked round. It no longer stood in its place.

"Some one's taken it away," said Kathleen.

Surprised and puzzled, she got up and went over to the piano. The photographs had been rearranged so that no gap should show.

"Perhaps Millicent wanted to have it in her bedroom," said Mrs. Skinner.

"I should have noticed it. Besides, Millicent has several photographs of Harold. She keeps them locked up."

Mrs. Skinner had thought it very peculiar that her daughter should have no photographs of Harold in her room. Indeed she had spoken of it once, but Millicent had made no reply. Millicent had been strangely silent since she came back from Borneo, and had not encouraged the sympathy Mrs. Skinner would have been so willing to show her. She seemed unwilling to speak of her great loss. Sorrow took people in different ways. Her husband had said the best thing was to leave her alone. The thought of him turned her ideas to the party they were going to.

"Father asked if I thought he ought to wear a top-hat," she said. "I said I thought it was just as well to be on the safe side."

It was going to be quite a grand affair. They were having ices, strawberry and vanilla, from Boddy, the confectioner, but the Heywoods were making the iced coffee at home. Every one would be there. They had been asked to meet the Bishop of Hong-Kong, who was staying with the Canon, an old college friend of his, and he was going to speak on the Chinese missions. Mrs. Skinner, whose daughter had lived in the East for eight years and whose son-in-law had been Resident of a district in Borneo, was in a flutter of interest. Naturally it meant more to her than to people who had never had anything to do with the Colonies and that sort of thing.

"What can they know of England who only England know?" as Mr. Skinner said.

He came into the room at that moment. He was a lawyer, as his father had been before him, and he had offices in Lincoln's Inn Fields. He went up to London every morning and came down every evening. He was only able to accompany his wife and daughters to the Canon's garden-party because the Canon had very wisely chosen a Saturday to have it on. Mr. Skinner looked very well in his tail-coat and pepper-and-salt trousers. He was not exactly dressy, but he was neat. He looked like a respectable family solicitor, which indeed he was; his firm never touched work that was not perfectly above board, and if a client went to him with some trouble that was not quite nice, Mr. Skinner would look grave.

"I don't think this is the sort of case that we very much care to undertake," he said. "I think you'd do better to go elsewhere."

He drew towards him his writing-block and scribbled a name and address on it. He tore off a sheet of paper and handed it to his client.

"If I were you I think I would go and see these people. If you mention my name I believe they'll do anything they can for you."

Mr. Skinner was clean-shaven and very bald. His pale lips were tight and thin, but his blue eyes were shy. He had no colour in his cheeks and his face was much lined.

"I see you've put on your new trousers," said Mrs. Skinner.

"I thought it would be a good opportunity," he answered. "I was wondering if I should wear a buttonhole."

"I wouldn't, father," said Kathleen. "I don't think it's awfully good form."

"A lot of people will be wearing them," said Mrs. Skinner.

"Only clerks and people like that," said Kathleen. "The Heywoods have had to ask everybody, you know. And besides, we are in mourning."

"I wonder if there'll be a collection after the Bishop's address," said Mr. Skinner.

"I should hardly think so," said Mrs. Skinner.

"I think it would be rather bad form," agreed Kathleen.

"It's as well to be on the safe side," said Mr. Skinner. "I'll give for all of us. I was wondering if ten shillings would be enough or if I must give a pound."

"If you give anything I think you ought to give a pound, father," said Kathleen.

"I'll see when the time comes. I don't want to give less than any one else, but on the other hand I see no reason to give more than I need."

Kathleen put away her papers in the drawer of the writing-table and stood up. She looked at her wrist-watch.

"Is Millicent ready?" asked Mrs. Skinner.

"There's plenty of time. We're only asked at four and I don't think we ought to arrive much before half-past. I told Davis to bring the car round at four-fifteen."

Generally Kathleen drove the car, but on grand occasions like this Davis, who was the gardener, put on his uniform and acted as chauffeur. It looked better when you drove up and naturally Kathleen didn't much want to drive herself when she was wearing her new jumper. The sight of her mother forcing her fingers one by one into her new gloves reminded her that she must put on her own. She smelt them to see if any odour of the cleaning still clung to them. It was very slight. She didn't believe any one would notice.

At last the door opened and Millicent came in. She wore her widow's weeds. Mrs. Skinner never could get used to them, but of course she knew that Millicent must wear them for a year. It was a pity they didn't suit her; they suited some people. She had tried on Millicent's bonnet once, with its white band and long veil, and thought she looked very well in it. Of course she hoped dear Alfred would survive her, but if he didn't she would never go out of weeds. Queen Victoria never had. It was different for Millicent; Millicent was a much younger woman; she was only thirty-six; it was very sad to be a widow at thirty-six. And there wasn't much chance of her marrying again. Kathleen wasn't very likely to marry now, she was thirty-five; last time Millicent and Harold had come home she had suggested that they should have Kathleen to stay with them; Harold had seemed willing enough, but

Millicent said it wouldn't do. Mrs. Skinner didn't know wh;
not. It would give her a chance. Of course they didn't want t
get rid of her, but a girl ought to marry, and somehow al
the men they knew at home were married already. Millicen
said the climate was trying. It was true she was a bad colour
No one would think now that Millicent had been the prettie
of the two. Kathleen had fined down as she grew older (o
course some people said she was too thin) but now that sh
had cut her hair, with her cheeks red from playing golf i
all weathers, Mrs. Skinner thought her quite pretty. No on
could say that of poor Millicent; she had lost her figure com
pletely; she had never been tall and now that she had filled
out she looked stocky. She was a good deal too fat; Mrs
Skinner supposed it was due to the tropical heat that pre
vented her from taking exercise. Her skin was sallow an
muddy; and her blue eyes, which had been her best feature
had gone quite pale.

"She ought to do something about her neck," Mrs. Skinne
reflected. "She's becoming dreadfully jowly."

She had spoken of it once or twice to her husband. He re
marked that Millicent wasn't as young as she was: that migh
be, but she needn't let herself go altogether. Mrs. Skinne
made up her mind to talk to her daughter seriously, but o
course she must respect her grief and she would wait till th
year was up. She was just as glad to have this reason to put of
a conversation the thought of which made her slightly nervous
For Millicent was certainly changed. There was something
sullen in her face which made her mother not quite at home
with her. Mrs. Skinner liked to say aloud all the thoughts that
passed through her head, but Millicent when you made a
remark (just to say something, you know), had an awkward
habit of not answering so that you wondered whether she
had heard. Sometimes Mrs. Skinner found it so irritating, that
not to be quite sharp with Millicent she had to remind hersel
that poor Harold had only been dead eight months.

The light from the window fell on the widow's heavy face
as she advanced silently, but Kathleen stood with her back
to it. She watched her sister for a moment.

"Millicent, there's something I want to say to you," she
said. "I was playing golf with Gladys Heywood this morning.'

"Did you beat her?" asked Millicent.

Gladys Heywood was the Canon's only unmarried daughter.

"She told me something about you which I think you ought
to know."

Millicent's eyes passed beyond her sister to the little girl
watering flowers in the garden.

"Have you told Annie to give Joan her tea in the kitchen,
mother?" she said.

"Yes, she'll have it when the servants have theirs."

Kathleen looked at her sister coolly.

"The Bishop spent two or three days at Singapore on his
way home," she went on. "He's very fond of travelling. He's
been to Borneo and he knows a good many of the people that
you know."

"He'll be interested to see you, dear," said Mrs. Skinner.
"Did he know poor Harold?"

"Yes, he met him at Kuala Solor. He remembers him very
well. He says he was shocked to hear of his death."

Millicent sat down and began to put on her black gloves.
It seemed strange to Mrs. Skinner that she received these
remarks with complete silence.

"Oh, Millicent," she said, "Harold's photo has disappeared.
Have you taken it?"

"Yes, I put it away."

"I should have thought you'd like to have it out."

Once more Millicent said nothing. It really was an exasperating habit.

Kathleen turned slightly in order to face her sister.

"Millicent, why did you tell us that Harold died of fever?"

The widow made no gesture, she looked at Kathleen with
steady eyes, but her sallow skin darkened with a flush. She
did not reply.

"What *do* you mean, Kathleen?" asked Mr. Skinner, with
surprise.

"The Bishop says that Harold committed suicide."

Mrs. Skinner gave a startled cry, but her husband put out
a deprecating hand.

"Is it true, Millicent?"

"It is."

"But why didn't you tell us?"

Millicent paused for an instant. She fingered idly a piece of
Brunei brass which stood on the table by her side. That too
had been a present from Harold.

"I thought it better for Joan that her father should be

thought to have died of fever. I didn't want her to know anything about it."

"You've put us in an awfully awkward position," said Kathleen, frowning a little. "Gladys Heywood said she thought it rather nasty of me not to have told her the truth. I had the greatest difficulty in getting her to believe that I knew absolutely nothing about it. She said her father was rather put out. He says, after all the years we've known one another, and considering that he married you, and the terms we've been on, and all that, he does think we might have had confidence in him. And at all events if we didn't want to tell him the truth we needn't have told him a lie."

"I must say I sympathize with him there," said Mr. Skinner acidly.

"Of course I told Gladys that we weren't to blame. We only told them what you told us."

"I hope it didn't put you off your game," said Millicent.

"Really, my dear, I think that is a most improper observation," exclaimed her father.

He rose from his chair, walked over to the empty fireplace, and from force of habit stood in front of it with parted coattails.

"It was my business," said Millicent, "and if I chose to keep it to myself I didn't see why I shouldn't."

"It doesn't look as if you had any affection for your mother if you didn't even tell her," said Mrs. Skinner.

Millicent shrugged her shoulders.

"You might have known it was bound to come out," said Kathleen.

"Why? I didn't expect that two gossiping old parsons would have nothing else to talk about than me."

"When the Bishop said he'd been to Borneo it's only natural that the Heywoods should ask him if he knew you and Harold."

"All that's neither here nor there," said Mr. Skinner. "I think you should certainly have told us the truth and we could have decided what was the best thing to do. As a solicitor I can tell you that in the long run it only makes things worse if you attempt to hide them."

"Poor Harold," said Mrs. Skinner, and the tears began to trickle down her raddled cheeks. "It seems dreadful. He was always a good son-in-law to me. Whatever induced him to do such a dreadful thing?"

"The climate."

"I think you'd better give us all the facts, Millicent," said her father.

"Kathleen will tell you."

Kathleen hesitated. What she had to say really was rather dreadful. It seemed terrible that such things should happen to a family like theirs.

"The Bishop says he cut his throat."

Mrs. Skinner gasped and she went impulsively up to her bereaved daughter. She wanted to fold her in her arms.

"My poor child," she sobbed.

But Millicent withdrew herself.

"Please don't fuss me, mother. I really can't stand being mauled about."

"Really, Millicent," said Mr. Skinner, with a frown.

He did not think she was behaving very nicely.

Mrs. Skinner dabbed her eyes carefully with her handkerchief and with a sigh and a little shake of the head returned to her chair. Kathleen fidgeted with the long chain she wore round her neck.

"It does seem rather absurd that I should have to be told the details of my brother-in-law's death by a friend. It makes us all look such fools. The Bishop wants very much to see you, Millicent; he wants to tell you how much he feels for you." She paused, but Millicent did not speak. "He says that Millicent had been away with Joan and when she came back she found poor Harold lying dead on his bed."

"It must have been a great shock," said Mr. Skinner.

Mrs. Skinner began to cry again, but Kathleen put her hand gently on her shoulder.

"Don't cry, mother," she said. "It'll make your eyes red and people will think it so funny."

They were all silent while Mrs. Skinner, drying her eyes, made a successful effort to control herself. It seemed very strange to her that at this very moment she should be wearing in her toque the ospreys that poor Harold had given her.

"There's something else I ought to tell you," said Kathleen.

Millicent looked at her sister again, without haste, and her eyes were steady, but watchful. She had the look of a person who is waiting for a sound which he is afraid of missing.

"I don't want to say anything to wound you, dear," Kath-

leen went on, "but there's something else and I think you
ought to know it. The Bishop says that Harold drank."

"Oh, my dear, how dreadful!" cried Mrs. Skinner. "What a
shocking thing to say. Did Gladys Heywood tell you? What
did you say?"

"I said it was entirely untrue."

"This is what comes of making secrets of things," said Mr.
Skinner irritably. "It's always the same. If you try and hush
a thing up all sorts of rumours get about which are ten times
worse than the truth."

"They told the Bishop in Singapore that Harold had killed
himself while he was suffering from *delirium tremens*. I think
for all our sakes you ought to deny that, Millicent."

"It's such a dreadful thing to have said about any one
who's dead," said Mrs. Skinner. "And it'll be so bad for Joan
when she grows up."

"But what is the foundation of this story, Millicent?"
asked her father. "Harold was always very abstemious."

"Here," said the widow.

"Did he drink?"

"Like a fish."

The answer was so unexpected, and the tone so sardonic,
that all three of them were startled.

"Millicent, how can you talk like that of your husband
when he's dead?" cried her mother, clasping her neatly gloved
hands. "I can't understand you. You've been so strange since
you came back. I could never have believed that a girl of mine
could take her husband's death like that."

"Never mind about that, mother," said Mr. Skinner. "We
can go into all that later."

He walked to the window and looked out at the sunny
little garden, and then walked back into the room. He took
his pince-nez out of his pocket and, though he had no intention
of putting them on, wiped them with his handkerchief. Millicent looked at him and in her eyes, unmistakably, was a look
of irony which was quite cynical. Mr. Skinner was vexed. He
had finished his week's work and he was a free man till Monday
morning. Though he had told his wife that this garden-party
was a great nuisance and he would much sooner have tea
quietly in his own garden, he had been looking forward to it.
He did not care very much about Chinese missions, but it
would be interesting to meet the Bishop. And now this! It

was not the kind of thing he cared to be mixed up in; it was
most unpleasant to be told on a sudden that his son-in-law
was a drunkard and a suicide. Millicent was thoughtfully
smoothing her white cuffs. Her coolness irritated him; but instead of addressing her he spoke to his younger daughter.

"Why don't you sit down, Kathleen? Surely there are
plenty of chairs in the room."

Kathleen drew forward a chair and without a word seated
herself. Mr. Skinner stopped in front of Millicent and faced
her.

"Of course I see why you told us Harold had died of fever.
I think it was a mistake, because that sort of thing is bound
to come out sooner or later. I don't know how far what the
Bishop has told the Heywoods coincides with the facts, but
if you will take my advice you will tell us everything as cir-
cumstantially as you can, then we can see. We can't hope that
it will go no further now that Canon Heywood and Gladys
know. In a place like this people are bound to talk. It will
make it easier for all of us if we at all events know the exact
truth."

Mrs. Skinner and Kathleen thought he put the matter very
well. They waited for Millicent's reply. She had listened with
an impassive face; that sudden flush had disappeared and it
was once more, as usual, pasty and sallow.

"I don't think you'll much like the truth if I tell it you,"
she said.

"You must know that you can count on our sympathy and
understanding," said Kathleen gravely.

Millicent gave her a glance and the shadow of a smile flickered across her set mouth. She looked slowly at the three of
them. Mrs. Skinner had an uneasy impression that she looked
at them as though they were mannequins at a dressmaker's.
She seemed to live in a different world from theirs and to have
no connection with them.

"You know, I wasn't in love with Harold when I married
him," she said reflectively.

Mrs. Skinner was on the point of making an exclamation
when a rapid gesture of her husband, barely indicated, but
after so many years of married life perfectly significant, stopped
her. Millicent went on. She spoke with a level voice, slowly,
and there was little change of expression in her tone.

"I was twenty-seven, and no one else seemed to want to

marry me. It's true he was forty-four, and it seemed rather old, but he had a very good position, hadn't he? I wasn't likely to get a better chance."

Mrs. Skinner felt inclined to cry again, but she remembered the party.

"Of course I see now why you took his photograph away," she said dolefully.

"Don't, mother," exclaimed Kathleen.

It had been taken when he was engaged to Millicent and was a very good photograph of Harold. Mrs. Skinner had always thought him quite a fine man. He was heavily built, tall and perhaps a little too fat, but he held himself well, and his presence was imposing. He was inclined to be bald, even then, but men did go bald very early nowadays, and he said that topees, sun-helmets, you know, were very bad for the hair. He had a small dark moustache and his face was deeply burned by the sun. Of course his best feature was his eyes; they were brown and large, like Joan's. His conversation was interesting. Kathleen said he was pompous, but Mrs. Skinner didn't think him so, she didn't mind it if a man laid down the law; and when she saw, as she very soon did, that he was attracted by Millicent she began to like him very much. He was always very attentive to Mrs. Skinner and she listened as though she were really interested when he spoke of his district and told her of the big game he had killed. Kathleen said he had a pretty good opinion of himself, but Mrs. Skinner came of a generation which accepted without question the good opinion that men had of themselves. Millicent saw very soon which way the wind blew and, though she said nothing to her mother, her mother knew that if Harold asked her she was going to accept him.

Harold was staying with some people who had been thirty years in Borneo and they spoke well of the country. There was no reason why a woman shouldn't live there comfortably; of course the children had to come home when they were seven; but Mrs. Skinner thought it unnecessary to trouble about that yet. She asked Harold to dine and she told him they were always in to tea. He seemed to be at a loose end and when his visit to his old friends was drawing to a close she told him they would be very much pleased if he would come and spend a fortnight with them. It was towards the end of this that Harold and Millicent became engaged. They had a very pretty wedding, they went to Venice for their honeymoon, and then they started for the East. Millicent wrote from the various ports at which the ship touched. She seemed happy.

"People were very nice to me at Kuala Solor," she said. Kuala Solor was the chief town of the state of Sembulu. "We stayed with the Resident and every one asked us to dinner. Once or twice I heard men ask Harold to have a drink but he refused; he said he had turned over a new leaf now he was a married man. I didn't know why they laughed. Mrs. Gray, the Resident's wife, told me they were all so glad Harold was married. She said it was dreadfully lonely for a bachelor on one of the out-stations. When we left Kuala Solor Mrs. Gray said good-bye to me so funnily that I was quite surprised. It was as if she was solemnly putting Harold in my charge."

They listened to her in silence. Kathleen never took her eyes off her sister's impassive face, but Mr. Skinner stared straight in front of him at the Malay arms, krises and parangs, which hung on the wall above the sofa on which his wife sat.

"It wasn't till I went back to Kuala Solor a year and a half later that I found out why their manner had seemed so odd." Millicent gave a queer little sound like the echo of a scornful laugh. "I knew then a good deal that I hadn't known before. Harold came to England that time in order to marry. He didn't much mind who it was. Do you remember how we spread ourselves out to catch him, mother? We needn't have taken so much trouble."

"I don't know what you mean, Millicent," said Mrs. Skinner, not without acerbity, for the insinuation of scheming did not please her. "I saw he was attracted by you."

Millicent shrugged her heavy shoulders.

"He was a confirmed drunkard. He used to go to bed every night with a bottle of whisky and empty it before morning. The Chief Secretary told him he'd have to resign unless he stopped drinking. He said he'd give him one more chance. He could take his leave then and go to England. He advised him to marry so that when he got back he'd have some one to look after him. Harold married me because he wanted a keeper. They took bets in Kuala Solor on how long I'd make him stay sober."

"But he was in love with you," Mrs. Skinner interrupted. "You don't know how he used to speak to me about you, and at that time you're speaking of, when you went to Kuala Solor to have Joan, he wrote me such a charming letter about you."

Millicent looked at her mother again and a deep colour dyed her sallow skin. Her hands, lying on her lap, began to tremble a little. She thought of those first months of her married life. The Government launch took them to the mouth of the river and they spent the night at the bungalow which Harold said jokingly was their seaside residence. Next day they went up-stream in a prahu. From the novels she had read she expected the rivers of Borneo to be dark and strangely sinister, but the sky was blue, dappled with little white clouds, and the green of the mangroves and the nipas, washed by the flowing water, glistened in the sun. On each side stretched the pathless jungle, and in the distance, silhouetted against the sky, was the rugged outline of a mountain. The air in the early morning was fresh and buoyant. She seemed to enter upon a friendly, fertile land, and she had a sense of spacious freedom. They watched the banks for monkeys sitting on the branches of the tangled trees and once Harold pointed out something that looked like a log and said it was a crocodile. The Assistant Resident, in ducks and a topee, was at the landing-stage to meet them, and a dozen trim little soldiers were lined up to do them honour. The Assistant Resident was introduced to her. His name was Simpson.

"By Jove, sir," he said to Harold, "I'm glad to see you back. It's been deuced lonely without you."

The Resident's bungalow, surrounded by a garden in which grew wildly all manner of gay flowers, stood on the top of a low hill. It was a trifle shabby and the furniture was sparse, but the rooms were cool and of generous size.

"The kampong is down there," said Harold, pointing.

Her eyes followed his gesture, and from among the coconut trees rose the beating of a gong. It gave her a queer little sensation in the heart.

Though she had nothing much to do the days passed easily enough. At dawn a boy brought them their tea and they lounged about the verandah, enjoying the fragrance of the morning (Harold in a singlet and a sarong, she in a dressing-gown), till it was time to dress for breakfast. Then Harold went to his office and she spent an hour or two learning Malay. After tiffin he went back to his office while she slept. A cup of tea

revived them both and they went for a walk or played golf on
the nine-hole links which Harold had made on a level piece of
cleared jungle below the bungalow. Night fell at six and Mr.
Simpson came along to have a drink. They chatted till their
late dinner hour, and sometimes Harold and Mr. Simpson
played chess. The balmy evenings were enchanting. The fire-
flies turned the bushes just below the verandah into coldly
sparkling, tremulous beacons, and flowering trees scented the
air with sweet odours. After dinner they read the papers which
had left London six weeks before and presently went to bed.
Millicent enjoyed being a married woman, with a house of her
own, and she was pleased with the native servants, in their
gay sarongs, who went about the bungalow, with bare feet,
silent but friendly. It gave her a pleasant sense of importance
to be the wife of the Resident. Harold impressed her by the
fluency with which he spoke the language, by his air of command, and by his dignity. She went into the court-house now
and then to hear him try cases. The multifariousness of his
duties and the competent way in which he performed them
aroused her respect. Mr. Simpson told her that Harold understood the natives as well as any man in the country. He had
the combination of firmness, tact, and good humour which
was essential in dealing with that timid, revengeful, and suspicious race. Millicent began to feel a certain admiration for
her husband.

They had been married nearly a year when two English
naturalists came to stay with them for a few days on their
way to the interior. They brought a pressing recommendation
from the Governor and Harold said he wanted to do them
proud. Their arrival was an agreeable change. Millicent asked
Mr. Simpson to dinner (he lived at the Fort and only dined
with them on Sunday nights) and after dinner the men sat
down to play bridge. Millicent left them presently and went
to bed, but they were so noisy that for some time she could
not get to sleep. She did not know at what hour she was awakened by Harold staggering into the room. She kept silent. He
made up his mind to have a bath before getting into bed; the
bath-house was just below their room and he went down the
steps that led to it. Apparently he slipped, for there was a
great clatter, and he began to swear. Then he was violently
sick. She heard him sluice the buckets of water over himself
and in a little while, walking very cautiously this time, he

crawled up the stairs and slipped into bed. Millicent pretende
to be asleep. She was disgusted. Harold was drunk. She mac
up her mind to speak about it in the morning. What would tl
naturalists think of him? But in the morning Harold was s
dignified that she hadn't quite the determination to refer t
the matter. At eight Harold and she, with their two guest
sat down to breakfast. Harold looked round the table.

"Porridge," he said. "Millicent, your guests might manaで
a little Worcester Sauce for breakfast, but I don't think they'
much fancy anything else. Personally I shall content myse
with a whisky and soda."

The naturalists laughed, but shamefacedly.

"Your husband's a terror," said one of them.

"I should not think I had properly performed the duties の
hospitality if I sent you sober to bed on the first night of you
visit," said Harold, with his round, stately way of puttin
things.

Millicent, smiling acidly, was relieved to think that he
guests had been as drunk as her husband. The next evenin
she sat up with them and the party broke up at a reasonabl
hour. But she was glad when the strangers went on with thei
journey. Their life resumed its placid course. Some month
later Harold went on a tour of inspection of his district an
came back with a bad attack of malaria. This was the firs
time she had seen the disease of which she had heard so mucl
and when he recovered it did not seem strange to her tha
Harold was very shaky. She found his manner peculiar. H
would come back from the office and stare at her with glaze
eyes; he would stand on the verandah, swaying slightly, bu
still dignified, and make long harangues about the politica
situation in England; losing the thread of his discourse, h
would look at her with an archness which his natural statelines
made somewhat disconcerting and say:

"Pulls you down dreadfully, this confounded malaria. Ah
little woman, you little know the strain it puts upon a man t
be an empire builder."

She thought that Mr. Simpson began to look worried, an
once or twice, when they were alone, he seemed on the poin
of saying something to her which his shyness at the last mo
ment prevented. The feeling grew so strong that it made he
nervous and one evening when Harold, she knew not why
had remained later than usual at the office she tackled him.

"What have you got to say to me, Mr. Simpson?" she broke out suddenly.

He blushed and hesitated.

"Nothing. What makes you think I have anything in particular to say to you?"

Mr. Simpson was a thin, weedy youth of four and twenty, with a fine head of waving hair which he took great pains to plaster down very flat. His wrists were swollen and scarred with mosquito bites. Millicent looked at him steadily.

"If it's something to do with Harold, don't you think it would be kinder to tell me frankly?"

He grew scarlet now. He shuffled uneasily on his rattan chair. She insisted.

"I'm afraid you'll think it awful cheek," he said at last. "It's rotten of me to say anything about my chief behind his back. Malaria's a rotten thing and after one's had a bout of it one feels awfully down and out."

He hesitated again. The corners of his mouth sagged as if he were going to cry. To Millicent he seemed like a little boy.

"I'll be as silent as the grave," she said with a smile, trying to conceal her apprehension. "Do tell me."

"I think it's a pity your husband keeps a bottle of whisky at the office. He's apt to take a nip more often than he otherwise would."

Mr. Simpson's voice was hoarse with agitation. Millicent felt a sudden coldness shiver through her. She controlled herself, for she knew that she must not frighten the boy if she were to get out of him all there was to tell. He was unwilling to speak. She pressed him, wheedling, appealing to his sense of duty, and at last she began to cry. Then he told her that Harold had been drunk more or less for the last fortnight, the natives were talking about it, and they said that soon he would be as bad as he had been before his marriage. He had been in the habit of drinking a good deal too much then, but details of that time, notwithstanding all her attempts, Mr. Simpson resolutely declined to give her.

"Do you think he's drinking now?" she asked.

"I don't know."

Millicent felt herself on a sudden hot with shame and anger. The Fort, as it was called because the rifles and the ammunition were kept there, was also the court-house. It stood opposite the Resident's bungalow in a garden of its own. The sun was just about to set and she did not need a hat. She got up and walked across. She found Harold sitting in the office behind the large hall in which he administered justice. There was a bottle of whisky in front of him. He was smoking cigarettes and talking to three or four Malays who stood in front of him listening with obsequious and at the same time scornful smiles. His face was red.

The natives vanished.

"I came to see what you were doing," she said.

He rose, for he always treated her with elaborate politeness, and lurched. Feeling himself unsteady he assumed an elaborate stateliness of demeanour.

"Take a seat, my dear, take a seat. I was detained by press of work."

She looked at him with angry eyes.

"You're drunk," she said.

He stared at her, his eyes bulging a little, and a haughty look gradually traversed his large and fleshy face.

"I haven't the remotest idea what you mean," he said.

She had been ready with a flow of wrathful expostulation, but suddenly she burst into tears. She sank into a chair and hid her face. Harold looked at her for an instant, then the tears began to trickle down his cheeks; he came towards her with outstretched arms and fell heavily on his knees. Sobbing, he clasped her to him.

"Forgive me, forgive me," he said. "I promise you it shall not happen again. It was that damned malaria."

"It's so humiliating," she moaned.

He wept like a child. There was something very touching in the self-abasement of that big dignified man. Presently Millicent looked up. His eyes, appealing and contrite, sought hers.

"Will you give me your word of honour that you'll never touch liquor again?"

"Yes, yes. I hate it."

It was then she told him that she was with child. He was overjoyed.

"That is the one thing I wanted. That'll keep me straight."

They went back to the bungalow. Harold bathed himself and had a nap. After dinner they talked long and quietly. He admitted that before he married her he had occasionally drunk more than was good for him: in outstations it was easy to fall into bad habits. He agreed to everything that Millicent asked. And during the months before it was necessary for her to go to Kuala Solor for her confinement Harold was an excellent husband, tender, thoughtful, proud and affectionate: he was irreproachable. A launch came to fetch her, she was to leave him for six weeks, and he promised faithfully to drink nothing during her absence. He put his hands on her shoulders.

"I never break a promise," he said in his dignified way. "But even without it, can you imagine that while you are going through so much, I should do anything to increase your troubles?"

Joan was born. Millicent stayed at the Resident's and Mrs. Gray, his wife, a kindly creature of middle age, was very good to her. The two women had little to do during the long hours they were alone but to talk, and in course of time Millicent learnt everything there was to know of her husband's alcoholic past. The fact which she found most difficult to reconcile herself to was that Harold had been told that the only condition upon which he would be allowed to keep his post was that he should bring back a wife. It caused in her a dull feeling of resentment. And when she discovered what a persistent drunkard he had been she felt vaguely uneasy. She had a horrid fear that during her absence he would not have been able to resist the craving. She went home with her baby and a nurse. She spent a night at the mouth of the river and sent a messenger in a canoe to announce her arrival. She scanned the landing-stage anxiously as the launch approached it. Harold and Mr. Simpson were standing there. The trim little soldiers were lined up. Her heart sank, for Harold was swaying slightly, like a man who seeks to keep his balance on a rolling ship, and she knew he was drunk.

It wasn't a very pleasant home-coming. She had almost forgotten her mother and father and her sister who sat there silently listening to her. Now she roused herself and became once more aware of their presence. All that she spoke of seemed very far away.

"I knew that I hated him then," she said. "I could have killed him."

"Oh, Millicent, don't say that," cried her mother. "Don't forget that he's dead, poor man."

Millicent looked at her mother, and for a moment a scowl darkened her impassive face. Mr. Skinner moved uneasily.

"Go on," said Kathleen.

"When he found out that I knew all about him he didn'
bother very much more. In three months he had another at
tack of D. T.'s."

"Why didn't you leave him?" said Kathleen.

"What would have been the good of that? He would hav
been dismissed from the service in a fortnight. Who was t
keep me and Joan? I had to stay. And when he was sober
had nothing to complain of. He wasn't in the least in wit
me, but he was fond of me: I hadn't married him because
was in love with him but because I wanted to be married.
did everything I could to keep liquor from him; I managec
to get Mr. Gray to prevent whisky being sent from Kual
Solor, but he got it from the Chinese. I watched him as a ca
watches a mouse. He was too cunning for me. In a little whil
he had another outbreak. He neglected his duties. I was afrai
complaints would be made. We were two days from Kual
Solor and that was our safeguard, but I suppose something
was said, for Mr. Gray wrote a private letter of warning tc
me. I showed it to Harold. He stormed and blustered, but I
saw he was frightened, and for two or three months he wa
quite sober. Then he began again. And so it went on till ou
leave became due.

"Before we came to stay here I begged and prayed him tc
be careful. I didn't want any of you to know what sort of a
man I had married. All the time he was in England he was al
right and before we sailed I warned him. He'd grown to be
very fond of Joan, and very proud of her, and she was de
voted to him. She always liked him better than she liked me
I asked him if he wanted to have his child grow up knowing
that he was a drunkard, and I found out that at last I'd got a
hold on him. The thought terrified him. I told him that I
wouldn't allow it, and if he ever let Joan see him drunk I'd
take her away from him at once. Do you know, he grew quite
pale when I said it. I fell on my knees that night and thanked
God because I'd found a way of saving my husband.

"He told me that if I would stand by him he would have
another try. We made up our minds to fight the thing together.
And he tried so hard. When he felt as though he *must* drink
he came to me. You know he was inclined to be rather pompous:
with me he was so humble, he was like a child; he depended

on me. Perhaps he didn't love me when he married me, but he loved me then, me and Joan. I'd hated him, because of the humiliation, because when he was drunk and tried to be dignified and impressive he was loathsome; but now I got a strange feeling in my heart. It wasn't love, but it was a queer, shy tenderness. He was something more than my husband, he was like a child that I'd carried under my heart for long and weary months. He was so proud of me and you know, I was proud too. His long speeches didn't irritate me any more and I only thought his stately ways rather funny and charming. At last we won. For two years he never touched a drop. He lost his craving entirely. He was even able to joke about it.

"Mr. Simpson had left us then and we had another young man called Francis.

"'I'm a reformed drunkard you know, Francis,' Harold said to him once. 'If it hadn't been for my wife I'd have been sacked long ago. I've got the best wife in the world, Francis.'

"You don't know what it meant to me to hear him say that. I felt that all I'd gone through was worth while. I was so happy."

She was silent. She thought of the broad, yellow and turbid river on whose banks she had lived so long. The egrets, white and gleaming in the tremulous sunset, flew down the stream in a flock, flew low and swift, and scattered. They were like a ripple of snowy notes, sweet and pure and spring-like, which an unseen hand drew forth, a divine arpeggio, from an unseen harp. They fluttered along between the green banks, wrapped in the shadows of evening, like the happy thoughts of a contented mind.

"Then Joan fell ill. For three weeks we were very anxious. There was no doctor nearer than Kuala Solor and we had to put up with the treatment of a native dispenser. When she grew well again I took her down to the mouth of the river in order to give her a breath of sea air. We stayed there a week. It was the first time I had been separated from Harold since I went away to have Joan. There was a fishing village, on piles, not far from us, but really we were quite alone. I thought a great deal about Harold, so tenderly, and all at once I knew that I loved him. I was so glad when the prahu came to fetch us back, because I wanted to tell him. I thought it would mean a good deal to him. I can't tell you how happy I was. As we

rowed up-stream the headman told me that Mr. Francis ha
had to go up-country to arrest a woman who had murdere
her husband. He had been gone a couple of days.

"I was surprised that Harold was not on the landing
stage to meet me; he was always very punctilious about tha
sort of thing; he used to say that husband and wife shoul
treat one another as politely as they treated acquaintances
and I could not imagine what business had prevented him.
walked up the little hill on which the bungalow stood. Th
ayah brought Joan behind me. The bungalow was strangel
silent. There seemed to be no servants about and I could no
make it out; I wondered if Harold hadn't expected me so soo
and was out. I went up the steps. Joan was thirsty and th
ayah took her to the servants' quarters to give her somethin
to drink. Harold was not in the sitting-room. I called him, bu
there was no answer. I was disappointed, because I shoul
have liked him to be there. I went into our bedroom. Harol
wasn't out after all: he was lying on the bed asleep. I was reall
very much amused because he always pretended he never slep
in the afternoon. He said it was an unnecessary habit tha
we white people got into. I went up to the bed softly. I though
I would have a joke with him. I opened the mosquito curtains
He was lying on his back, with nothing on but a sarong
and there was an empty whisky bottle by his side. He wa
drunk.

"It had begun again. All my struggles for so many year
were wasted. My dream was shattered. It was all hopeless. I
was seized with rage."

Millicent's face grew once again darkly red and she clenched
the arms of the chair she sat in.

"I took him by the shoulders and shook him with all my
might. 'You beast,' I cried, 'you beast.' I was so angry I don't
know what I did, I don't know what I said. I kept on shaking
him. You don't know how loathsome he looked, that large
fat man, half naked; he hadn't shaved for days, and his face
was bloated and purple. He was breathing heavily. I shouted
at him, but he took no notice. I tried to drag him out of bed,
but he was too heavy. He lay there like a log. 'Open your
eyes,' I screamed. I shook him again. I hated him. I hated him
all the more because for a week I'd loved him with all my
heart. He'd let me down. He'd let me down. I wanted to tell
him what a filthy beast he was. I could make no impression

on him. 'You shall open your eyes,' I cried. I was determined
to make him look at me."

The widow licked her dry lips. Her breath seemed hurried.
She was silent.

"If he was in that state I should have thought it best to
have let him go on sleeping," said Kathleen.

"There was a parang on the wall by the side of the bed.
You know how fond Harold was of curios."

"What's a parang?" said Mrs. Skinner.

"Don't be silly, mother," her husband replied irritably.
"There's one on the wall immediately behind you."

He pointed to the Malay sword on which for some reason
his eyes had been unconsciously resting. Mrs. Skinner drew
quickly into the corner of the sofa, with a little frightened
gesture, as though she had been told that a snake lay curled
up beside her.

"Suddenly the blood spurted out from Harold's throat.
There was a great red gash right across it."

"Millicent," cried Kathleen, springing up and almost leaping
towards her, "what in God's name do you mean?"

Mrs. Skinner stood staring at her with wide startled eyes,
her mouth open.

"The parang wasn't on the wall any more. It was on the
bed. Then Harold opened his eyes. They were just like Joan's."

"I don't understand," said Mr. Skinner. "How could he
have committed suicide if he was in the state you describe?"

Kathleen took her sister's arm and shook her angrily.

"Millicent, for God's sake, explain."

Millicent released herself.

"The parang was on the wall, I told you. I don't know what
happened. There was all the blood and Harold opened his eyes.
He died almost at once. He never spoke, but he gave a sort of
gasp."

At last Mr. Skinner found his voice.

"But, you wretched woman, it was murder."

Millicent, her face mottled with red, gave him such a look
of scornful hatred that he shrank back. Mrs. Skinner cried out.

"Millicent, you didn't do it, did you?"

Then Millicent did something that made them all feel as
though their blood were turned to ice in their veins. She
chuckled.

"I don't know who else did," she said.

"My God," muttered Mr. Skinner.

Kathleen had been standing bolt upright, with her hands to her heart, as though its beating were intolerable.

"And what happened then?" she said.

"I screamed. I went to the window and flung it open. I called for the ayah. She came across the compound with Joan. 'Not Joan,' I cried. 'Don't let her come.' She called the cook and told him to take the child. I cried to her to hurry. And when she came I showed her Harold. 'The Tuan's killed himself!' I cried. She gave a scream and ran out of the house.

"No one would come near. They were all frightened out of their wits. I wrote a letter to Mr. Francis, telling him what had happened, and asking him to come at once."

"How do you mean you told him what had happened?"

"I said, on my return from the mouth of the river, I'd found Harold with his throat cut. You know, in the tropics you have to bury people quickly. I got a Chinese coffin, and the soldiers dug a grave behind the Fort. When Mr. Francis came Harold had been buried for nearly two days. He was only a boy. I could do anything I wanted with him. I told him I'd found the parang in Harold's hand and there was no doubt he'd killed himself in an attack of *delirium tremens*. I showed him the empty bottle. The servants said he'd been drinking hard ever since I left to go to the sea. I told the same story at Kuala Solor. Every one was very kind to me, and the Government granted me a pension."

For a little while nobody spoke. At last Mr. Skinner gathered himself together.

"I am a member of the legal profession. I'm a solicitor. I have certain duties. We've always had a most respectable practice. You've put me in a monstrous position."

He fumbled, searching for the phrases that played at hide and seek in his scattered wits. Millicent looked at him with scorn.

"What are you going to do about it?"

"It was murder, that's what it was; do you think I can possibly connive at it?"

"Don't talk nonsense, father," said Kathleen sharply "You can't give your own daughter up."

"You've put me in a monstrous position," he repeated.

Millicent shrugged her shoulders again.

"You made me tell you. And I've borne it long enough by myself. It was time that all of you bore it too."

At that moment the door was opened by the maid.

"Davis has brought the car round, sir," she said.

Kathleen had the presence of mind to say something, and the maid withdrew.

"We'd better be starting," said Millicent.

"I can't go to the party now," cried Mrs. Skinner, with horror. "I'm far too upset. How can we face the Heywoods? And the Bishop will want to be introduced to you."

Millicent made a gesture of indifference. Her eyes held their ironical expression.

"We must go, mother," said Kathleen. "It would look so funny if we stayed away." She turned on Millicent furiously. "Oh, I think the whole thing is such frightfully bad form."

Mrs. Skinner looked helplessly at her husband. He went to her and gave her his hand to help her up from the sofa.

"I'm afraid we must go, mother," he said.

"And me with the ospreys in my toque that Harold gave me with his own hands," she moaned.

He led her out of the room, Kathleen followed close on their heels, and a step or two behind came Millicent.

"You'll get used to it, you know," she said quietly. "At first I thought of it all the time, but now I forget it for two or three days together. It's not as if there was any danger."

They did not answer. They walked through the hall and out of the front door. The three ladies got into the back of the car and Mr. Skinner seated himself beside the driver. They had no self-starter; it was an old car, and Davis went to the bonnet to crank it up. Mr. Skinner turned round and looked petulantly at Millicent.

"I ought never to have been told," he said. "I think it was most selfish of you."

Davis took his seat and they drove off to the Canon's garden-party.

THE FORCE OF CIRCUM-
STANCE

SHE was sitting on the verandah waiting for her husband to
come in for luncheon. The Malay boy had drawn the blinds
when the morning lost its freshness, but she had partly raised
one of them so that she could look at the river. Under the
breathless sun of midday it had the white pallor of death. A
native was paddling along in a dug-out so small that it hardly
showed above the surface of the water. The colours of the day
were ashy and wan. They were but the various tones of the heat.¹
(It was like an Eastern melody, in the minor key, which exacer-
bates the nerves by its ambiguous monotony; and the ear awaits
impatiently a resolution, but waits in vain.) The cicadas sang
their grating song with a frenzied energy: it was as continual
and monotonous as the rustling of a brook over the stones; but
on a sudden it was drowned by the loud singing of a bird, mellif-
luous and rich; and for an instant, with a catch at her heart,
she thought of the English blackbird.

Then she heard her husband's step on the gravel path behind
the bungalow, the path that led to the court-house in which
he had been working, and she rose from her chair to greet him.
He ran up the short flight of steps, for the bungalow was built on
piles, and at the door the boy was waiting to take his topee.
He came into the room which served them as dining-room and
parlour, and his eyes lit up with pleasure as he saw her.

"Hulloa, Doris. Hungry?"

"Ravenous."

"It'll only take me a minute to have a bath and then I'm ready."

"Be quick," she smiled.

He disappeared into his dressing-room and she heard him whistling cheerily while, with the carelessness with which she was always remonstrating, he tore off his clothes and flung them on the floor. He was twenty-nine, but he was still a schoolboy; he would never grow up. That was why she had fallen in love with him, perhaps, for no amount of affection could persuade her that he was good-looking. He was a little round man, with a red face like the full moon, and blue eyes. He was rather pimply. She had examined him carefully and had been forced to confess to him that he had not a single feature which she could praise. She had told him often that he wasn't her type at all.

"I never said I was a beauty," he laughed.

"I can't think what it is I see in you."

But of course she knew perfectly well. He was a gay, jolly little man, who took nothing very solemnly, and he was constantly laughing. He made her laugh too. He found life an amusing rather than a serious business, and he had a charming smile. When she was with him she felt happy and good-tempered. And the deep affection which she saw in those merry blue eyes of his touched her. It was very satisfactory to be loved like that. Once, sitting on his knees, during their honeymoon she had taken his face in her hands and said to him:

"You're an ugly, little fat man, Guy, but you've got charm. I can't help loving you."

A wave of emotion swept over her and her eyes filled with tears. She saw his face contorted for a moment with the extremity of his feeling and his voice was a little shaky when he answered.

"It's a terrible thing for me to have married a woman who's mentally deficient," he said.

She chuckled. It was the characteristic answer which she would have liked him to make.

It was hard to realize that nine months ago she had never even heard of him. She had met him at a small place by the sea-side where she was spending a month's holiday with her mother. Doris was secretary to a member of parliament. Guy was home on leave. They were staying at the same hotel, and he quickly told her all about himself. He was born in Sembulu, where his father had served for thirty years under the second Sultan, and on leaving school he had entered the same service. He was devoted to the country.

"After all, England's a foreign land to me," he told her. "My home's Sembulu."

And now it was her home too. He asked her to marry him at the end of the month's holiday. She had known he was going to, and had decided to refuse him. She was her widowed mother's only child and she could not go so far away from her, but when the moment came she did not quite know what happened to her, she was carried off her feet by an unexpected emotion, and she accepted him. They had been settled now for four months in the little outstation of which he was in charge. She was very happy.

She told him once that she had quite made up her mind to refuse him.

"Are you sorry you didn't?" he asked, with a merry smile in his twinkling blue eyes.

"I should have been a perfect fool if I had. What a bit of luck that fate or chance or whatever it was stepped in and took the matter entirely out of my hands!"

Now she heard Guy clatter down the steps to the bath-house. He was a noisy fellow and even with bare feet he could not be quiet. But he uttered an exclamation. He said two or three words in the local dialect and she could not understand. Then she heard some one speaking to him, not aloud, but in a sibilant whisper. Really it was too bad of people to waylay him when he was going to have his bath. He spoke again and though his voice was low she could hear that he was vexed. The other voice was raised now; it was a woman's. Doris supposed it was some one who had a complaint to make. It was like a Malay woman to come in that surreptitious way. But she was evidently getting very little from Guy, for she heard him say: get out. That at all events she understood, and then she heard him bolt the door. There was a sound of the water he was throwing over himself (the bathing arrangements still amused her, the bath-houses were under the bedrooms, on the ground; you had a large tub of water and you sluiced yourself with a little tin pail) and in a couple of minutes he was back again in the dining-room. His hair was still wet. They sat down to luncheon.

"It's lucky I'm not a suspicious or a jealous person," she laughed. "I don't know that I should altogether approve of

your having animated conversations with ladies while you're
having your bath."

His face, usually so cheerful, had borne a sullen look when he
came in, but now it brightened.

"I wasn't exactly pleased to see her."

"So I judged by the tone of your voice. In fact, I thought
you were rather short with the young person."

"Damned cheek, waylaying me like that!"

"What did she want?"

"Oh, I don't know. It's a woman from the kampong. She's
had a row with her husband or something."

"I wonder if it's the same one who was hanging about this
morning."

He frowned a little.

"Was there some one hanging about?"

"Yes, I went into your dressing-room to see that everything
was nice and tidy, and then I went down to the bath-house. I
saw some one slink out of the door as I went down the steps
and when I looked out I saw a woman standing there."

"Did you speak to her?"

"I asked her what she wanted and she said something, but
I couldn't understand."

"I'm not going to have all sorts of stray people prowling
about here," he said. "They've got no right to come."

He smiled, but Doris, with the quick perception of a woman
in love, noticed that he smiled only with his lips, not as usual
with his eyes also, and wondered what it was that troubled him.

"What have you been doing this morning?" he asked.

"Oh, nothing much. I went for a little walk."

"Through the kampong?"

"Yes. I saw a man send a chained monkey up a tree to pick
coconuts, which rather thrilled me."

"It's rather a lark, isn't it?"

"Oh, Guy, there were two little boys watching him who were
much whiter than the others. I wondered if they were half-
castes. I spoke to them, but they didn't know a word of English."

"There are two or three half-caste children in the kampong,"
he answered.

"Who do they belong to?"

"Their mother is one of the village girls."

"Who is their father?"

"Oh, my dear, that's the sort of question we think it a little dangerous to ask out here." He paused. "A lot of fellows have native wives, and then when they go home or marry, they pension them off and send them back to their village."

Doris was silent. The indifference with which he spoke seemed a little callous to her. There was almost a frown on her frank, open, pretty English face when she replied.

"But what about the children?"

"I have no doubt they're properly provided for. Within his means, a man generally sees that there's enough money to have them decently educated. They get jobs as clerks in a Government office, you know; they're all right."

She gave him a slightly rueful smile.

"You can't expect me to think it's a very good system."

"You mustn't be too hard," he smiled back.

"I'm not hard. But I'm thankful you never had a Malay wife. I should have hated it. Just think if those two little brats were yours."

The boy changed their plates. There was never much variety in their menu. They started luncheon with river fish, dull and insipid, so that a good deal of tomato ketchup was needed to make it palatable, and then went on to some kind of stew. Guy poured Worcester Sauce over it.

"The old Sultan didn't think it was a white woman's country," he said presently. "He rather encouraged people to—keep house with native girls. Of course things have changed now. The country's perfectly quiet and I suppose we know better how to cope with the climate."

"But, Guy, the eldest of those boys wasn't more than seven or eight and the other was about five."

"It's awfully lonely on an outstation. Why, often one doesn't see another white man for six months on end. A fellow comes out here when he's only a boy." He gave her that charming smile of his which transfigured his round, plain face. "There are excuses, you know."

She always found that smile irresistible. It was his best argument. Her eyes grew once more soft and tender.

"I'm sure there are." She stretched her hand across the little table and put it on his. "I'm very lucky to have caught you so young. Honestly, it would upset me dreadfully if I were told that you had lived like that."

He took her hand and pressed it.

"Are you happy here, darling?"

"Desperately."

She looked very cool and fresh in her linen frock. The heat did not distress her. She had no more than the prettiness of youth, though her brown eyes were fine; but she had a pleasing frankness of expression, and her dark, short hair was neat and glossy. She gave you the impression of a girl of spirit and you felt sure that the member of parliament for whom she had worked had in her a very competent secretary.

"I loved the country at once," she said. "Although I'm alone so much I don't think I've ever once felt lonely."

Of course she had read novels about the Malay Archipelago and she had formed an impression of a sombre land with great ominous rivers and a silent, impenetrable jungle. When the little coasting steamer set them down at the mouth of the river, where a large boat, manned by a dozen Dyaks, was waiting to take them to the station, her breath was taken away by the beauty, friendly rather than awe-inspiring, of the scene. It had a gaiety, like the joyful singing of birds in the trees, which she had never expected. On each bank of the river were mangroves and nipa palms, and behind them the dense green of the forest. In the distance stretched blue mountains, range upon range, as far as the eye could see. She had no sense of confinement nor of gloom, but rather of openness and wide spaces where the exultant fancy could wander with delight. The green glittered in the sunshine and the sky was blithe and cheerful. The gracious land seemed to offer her a smiling welcome.

They rowed on, hugging a bank, and high overhead flew a pair of doves. A flash of colour, like a living jewel, dashed across their path. It was a kingfisher. Two monkeys, with their dangling tails, sat side by side on a branch. On the horizon, over there on the other side of the broad and turbid river, beyond the jungle, was a row of little white clouds, the only clouds in the sky, and they looked like a row of ballet-girls, dressed in white, waiting at the back of the stage, alert and merry, for the curtain to go up. Her heart was filled with joy; and now, remembering it all, her eyes rested on her husband with a grateful, assured affection.

And what fun it had been to arrange their living-room! It was very big. On the floor, when she arrived, was a torn and dirty matting; on the walls of unpainted wood hung (much too high up) photogravures of Academy pictures, Dyak shields and parangs. The tables were covered with Dyak cloth in sombre colours, and on them stood pieces of Brunei brassware, much in need of cleaning, empty cigarette tins and bits of Malay silver. There was a rough wooden shelf with cheap editions of novels and a number of old travel books in battered leather; and another shelf was crowded with empty bottles. It was a bachelor's room, untidy but stiff; and though it amused her she found it intolerably pathetic. It was a dreary, comfortless life that Guy had led there, and she threw her arms round his neck and kissed him.

"You poor darling," she laughed.

She had deft hands and she soon made the room habitable. She arranged this and that, and what she could not do with she turned out. Her wedding-presents helped. Now the room was friendly and comfortable. In glass vases were lovely orchids and in great bowls huge masses of flowering shrubs. She felt an inordinate pride because it was her house (she had never in her life lived in anything but a poky flat) and she had made it charming for him.

"Are you pleased with me?" she asked when she had finished.

"Quite," he smiled.

The deliberate understatement was much to her mind. How jolly it was that they should understand each other so well! They were both of them shy of displaying emotion, and it was only at rare moments that they used with one another anything but ironic banter.

They finished luncheon and he threw himself into a long chair to have a sleep. She went towards her room. She was a little surprised that he drew her to him as she passed and, making her bend down, kissed her lips. They were not in the habit of exchanging embraces at odd hours of the day.

"A full tummy is making you sentimental, my poor lamb," she chaffed him.

"Get out and don't let me see you again for at least two hours."

"Don't snore."

She left him. They had risen at dawn and in five minutes were fast asleep.

Doris was awakened by the sound of her husband's splashing in the bath-house. The walls of the bungalow were like a sounding-board and not a thing that one of them did escaped the other. She felt too lazy to move, but she heard the boy brin[/] the tea things in, so she jumped up and ran down into her own bath-house. The water, not cold but cool, was deliciously refreshing. When she came into the sitting-room Guy was taking the rackets out of the press, for they played tennis in the short cool of the evening. The night fell at six.

The tennis-court was two or three hundred yards from the bungalow and after tea, anxious not to lose time, they strolled down to it.

"Oh, look," said Doris, "there's that girl that I saw this morning."

Guy turned quickly. His eyes rested for a moment on a native woman, but he did not speak.

"What a pretty sarong she's got," said Doris. "I wonder where it comes from."

They passed her. She was slight and small, with the large, dark, starry eyes of her race and a mass of raven hair. She did not stir as they went by, but stared at them strangely. Doris saw then that she was not quite so young as she had at first thought. Her features were a trifle heavy and her skin was dark, but she was very pretty. She held a small child in her arms. Doris smiled a little as she saw it, but no answering smile moved the woman's lips. Her face remained impassive. She did not look at Guy, she looked only at Doris, and he walked on as though he did not see her. Doris turned to him.

"Isn't that baby a duck?"

"I didn't notice."

She was puzzled by the look of his face. It was deathly white, and the pimples which not a little distressed her were more than commonly red.

"Did you notice her hands and feet? She might be a duchess."

"All natives have good hands and feet," he answered, but not jovially as was his wont; it was as though he forced himself to speak.

But Doris was not intrigued.

"Who is she, d'you know?"

"She's one of the girls in the kampong."

They had reached the court now. When Guy went up to the net to see that it was taut he looked back. The woman was still standing where they had passed her. Their eyes met.

"Shall I serve?" said Doris.

"Yes, you've got the balls on your side."

He played very badly. Generally he gave her fifteen and beat her, but to-day she won easily. And he played silently. Generally he was a noisy player, shouting all the time, cursing his foolishness when he missed a ball and chaffing her when he placed one out of her reach.

"You're off your game, young man," she cried.

"Not a bit," he said.

He began to slam the balls, trying to beat her, and sent one after the other into the net. She had never seen him with that set face. Was it possible that he was a little out of temper because he was not playing well? The light fell, and they ceased to play. The woman whom they had passed stood in exactly the same position as when they came and once more, with expressionless face, she watched them go.

The blinds on the verandah were raised now and on the table between their two long chairs were bottles and soda-water. This was the hour at which they had the first drink of the day and Guy mixed a couple of gin slings. The river stretched widely before them and on the further bank the jungle was wrapped in the mystery of the approaching night. A native was silently rowing up-stream, standing at the bow of the boat, with two oars.

"I played like a fool," said Guy, breaking a silence. "I'm feeling a bit under the weather."

"I'm sorry. You're not going to have fever, are you?"

"Oh, no. I shall be all right to-morrow."

Darkness closed in upon them. The frogs croaked loudly and now and then they heard a few short notes from some singing bird of the night. Fireflies flitted across the verandah and they made the trees that surrounded it look like Christmas trees lit with tiny candles. They sparkled softly. Doris thought she heard a little sigh. It vaguely disturbed her. Guy was always so full of gaiety.

"What is it, old man?" she said gently. "Tell mother."

"Nothing. Time for another drink," he answered breezily.

Next day he was as cheerful as ever and the mail came. The coasting steamer passed the mouth of the river twice a month, once on its way to the coal-fields and once on its way back. On the outward journey it brought mail, which Guy sent a boat down to fetch. Its arrival was the excitement of their uneventful lives. For the first day or two they skimmed rapidly all that had come, letters, English papers and papers from

Singapore, magazines and books, leaving for the ensuing weeks a more exact perusal. They snatched the illustrated papers from one another. If Doris had not been so absorbed she might have noticed that there was a change in Guy. She would have found it hard to describe and harder still to explain. There was in his eyes a sort of watchfulness and in his mouth a slight droop of anxiety.

Then, perhaps a week later, one morning when she was sitting in the shaded room studying a Malay grammar, for she was industriously learning the language, she heard a commotion in the compound. She heard the house-boy's voice, he was speaking angrily, the voice of another man, perhaps it was the water-carrier's, and then a woman's, shrill and vituperative. There was a scuffle. She went to the window and opened the shutters. The water-carrier had hold of a woman's arm and was dragging her along, while the house-boy was pushing her from behind with both hands. Doris recognized her at once as the woman she had seen one morning loitering in the compound and later in the day outside the tennis-court. She was holding a baby against her breast. All three were shouting angrily.

"Stop," cried Doris. "What are you doing?"

At the sound of her voice the water-carrier let go suddenly and the woman, still pushed from behind, fell to the ground. There was a sudden silence and the house-boy looked sullenly into space. The water-carrier hesitated a moment and then slunk away. The woman raised herself slowly to her feet, arranged the baby on her arm, and stood impassive, staring at Doris. The boy said something to her which Doris could not have heard even if she had understood; the woman by no change of face showed that his words meant anything to her; but she slowly strolled away. The boy followed her to the gate of the compound. Doris called to him as he walked back, but he pretended not to hear. She was growing angry now and she called more sharply.

"Come here at once," she cried.

Sullenly, avoiding her wrathful glance, he came towards the bungalow. He came in and stood at the door. He looked at her sulkily.

"What were you doing with that woman?" she asked abruptly.

"Tuan say she no come here."

"You mustn't treat a woman like that. I won't have it. I shall tell the tuan exactly what I saw."

The boy did not answer. He looked away, but she felt that he was watching her through his long eyelashes. She dismissed him.

"That'll do."

Without a word he turned and went back to the servants' quarters. She was exasperated and she found it impossible to give her attention once more to the Malay exercises. In a little while the boy came in to lay the cloth for luncheon. On a sudden he went to the door.

"What is it?" she asked.

"Tuan just coming."

He went out to take Guy's hat from him. His quick ears had caught the footsteps before they were audible to her. Guy did not as usual come up the steps immediately; he paused, and Doris at once surmised that the boy had gone down to meet him in order to tell him of the morning's incident. She shrugged her shoulders. The boy evidently wanted to get his story in first. But she was astonished when Guy came in. His face was ashy.

"Guy, what on earth's the matter?"

He flushed a sudden hot red.

"Nothing. Why?"

She was so taken aback that she let him pass into his room without a word of what she had meant to speak of at once. It took him longer than usual to have his bath and change his clothes, and luncheon was served when he came in.

"Guy," she said, as they sat down, "that woman we saw the other day was here again this morning."

"So I've heard," he answered.

"The boys were treating her brutally. I had to stop them. You must really speak to them about it."

Though the Malay understood every word she said, he made no sign that he heard. He handed her the toast.

"She's been told not to come here. I gave instructions that if she showed herself again she was to be turned out."

"Were they obliged to be so rough?"

"She refused to go. I don't think they were any rougher than they could help."

"It was horrible to see a woman treated like that. She had a baby in her arms."

"Hardly a baby. It's three years old."

"How d'you know?"

"I know all about her. She hasn't the least right to come here pestering everybody."

"What does she want?"

"She wants to do exactly what she did. She wants to make a disturbance."

For a little while Doris did not speak. She was surprised at her husband's tone. He spoke tersely. He spoke as though all this were no concern of hers. She thought him a little unkind. He was nervous and irritable.

"I doubt if we shall be able to play tennis this afternoon," he said. "It looks to me as though we were going to have a storm."

The rain was falling when she awoke and it was impossible to go out. During tea Guy was silent and abstracted. She got her sewing and began to work. Guy sat down to read such of the English papers as he had not yet gone through from cover to cover; but he was restless; he walked up and down the large room and then went out on the verandah. He looked at the steady rain. What was he thinking of? Doris was vaguely uneasy.

It was not till after dinner that he spoke. During the simple meal he had exerted himself to be his usual gay self, but the exertion was apparent. The rain had ceased and the night was starry. They sat on the verandah. In order not to attract insects they had put out the lamp in the sitting-room. At their feet, with a mighty, formidable sluggishness, silent, mysterious and fatal, flowed the river. It had the terrible deliberation and the relentlessness of destiny.

"Doris, I've got something to say to you," he said suddenly.

His voice was very strange. Was it her fancy that he had difficulty in keeping it quite steady? She felt a little pang in her heart because he was in distress, and she put her hand gently into his. He drew it away.

"It's rather a long story. I'm afraid it's not a very nice one and I find it rather difficult to tell. I'm going to ask you not to interrupt me, or to say anything, till I've finished."

In the darkness she could not see his face, but she felt that it was haggard. She did not answer. He spoke in a voice so low that it hardly broke the silence of the night.

"I was only eighteen when I came out here. I came straight

from school. I spent three months in Kuala Solor, and then I was sent to a station up the Sembulu River. Of course there was a Resident there and his wife. I lived in the court-house, but I used to have my meals with them and spend the evening with them. I had an awfully good time. Then the fellow who was here fell ill and had to go home. We were short of men on account of the war and I was put in charge of this place. Of course I was very young, but I spoke the language like a native, and they remembered my father. I was as pleased as Punch to be on my own."

He was silent while he knocked the ashes out of his pipe and refilled it. When he lit a match Doris, without looking at him, noticed that his hand was unsteady.

"I'd never been alone before. Of course at home there'd been father and mother and generally an assistant. And then at school naturally there were always fellows about. On the way out, on the boat, there were people all the time, and at K.S., and the same at my first post. The people there were almost like my own people. I seemed always to live in a crowd. I like people. I'm a noisy blighter. I like to have a good time. All sorts of things make me laugh and you must have somebody to laugh with. But it was different here. Of course it was all right in the daytime; I had my work and I could talk to the Dyaks. Although they were head-hunters in those days and now and then I had a bit of trouble with them, they were an awfully decent lot of fellows. I got on very well with them. Of course I should have liked a white man to gas to, but they were better than nothing, and it was easier for me because they didn't look upon me quite as a stranger. I like the work too. It was rather lonely in the evening to sit on the verandah and drink a gin and bitters by myself, but I could read. And the boys were about. My own boy was called Abdul. He'd known my father. When I got tired of reading I could give him a shout and have a bit of a jaw with him.

"It was the nights that did for me. After dinner the boys shut up and went away to sleep in the kampong. I was all alone. There wasn't a sound in the bungalow except now and then the croak of the chik-chak. It used to come out of the silence, suddenly, so that it made me jump. Over in the kampong I heard the sound of a gong or fire-crackers. They were having a good time, they weren't so far away, but I had to stay where I was.

I was tired of reading. I couldn't have been more of a prisoner
if I'd been in jail. Night after night it was the same. I tried
drinking three or four whiskies, but it's poor fun drinking alone,
and it didn't cheer me up; it only made me feel rather rotten
next day. I tried going to bed immediately after dinner, but
I couldn't sleep. I used to lie in bed, getting hotter and hotter,
and more wide awake, till I didn't know what to do with myself. By George, those nights were long. D'you know, I got so
low, I was so sorry for myself that sometimes—it makes me
laugh now when I think of it, but I was only nineteen and a
half—sometimes I used to cry.

"Then, one evening, after dinner, Abdul had cleared away
and was just going off, when he gave a little cough. He said,
wasn't I lonely in the house all night by myself? 'Oh, no, that's
all right,' I said. I didn't want him to know what a damned fool
I was, but I expect he knew all right. He stood there without
speaking, and I knew he wanted to say something to me.
'What is it?' I said. 'Spit it out.' Then he said that if I'd like
to have a girl to come and live with me he knew one who was
willing. She was a very good girl and he could recommend
her. She'd be no trouble and it would be some one to have
about the bungalow. She'd mend my things for me. . . . I felt
awfully low. It had been raining all day and I hadn't been able
to get any exercise. I knew I shouldn't go to sleep for hours. It
wouldn't cost me very much money, he said, her people were
poor and they'd be quite satisfied with a small present. Two
hundred Straits dollars. 'You look,' he said. 'If you don't like
her you send her away.' I asked him where she was. 'She's
here,' he said. 'I call her.' He went to the door. She'd been
waiting on the steps with her mother. They came in and sat
down on the floor. I gave them some sweets. She was shy, of
course, but cool enough, and when I said something to her she
gave me a smile. She was very young, hardly more than a child,
they said she was fifteen. She was awfully pretty, and she had
her best clothes on. We began to talk. She didn't say much,
but she laughed a lot when I chaffed her. Abdul said I'd find
she had plenty to say for herself when she got to know me. He
told her to come and sit by me. She giggled and refused, but
her mother told her to come, and I made room for her on the
chair. She blushed and laughed, but she came, and then she
snuggled up to me. The boy laughed too. 'You see, she's taken

to you already,' he said. 'Do you want her to stay?' he asked. 'Do you want to?' I said to her. She hid her face, laughing, on my shoulder. She was very soft and small. 'Very well,' I said, 'let her stay.'"

Guy leaned forward and helped himself to a whisky and soda.

"May I speak now?" asked Doris.

"Wait a minute, I haven't finished yet. I wasn't in love with her, not even at the beginning. I only took her so as to have somebody about the bungalow. I think I should have gone mad if I hadn't, or else taken to drink. I was at the end of my tether. I was too young to be quite alone. I was never in love with any one but you." He hesitated a moment. "She lived here till I went home last year on leave. It's the woman you've seen hanging about."

"Yes, I guessed that. She had a baby in her arms. Is that your child?"

"Yes. It's a little girl."

"Is it the only one?"

"You saw the two small boys the other day in the kampong. You mentioned them."

"She has three children then?"

"Yes."

"It's quite a family you've got."

She felt the sudden gesture which her remark forced from him, but he did not speak.

"Didn't she know that you were married till you suddenly turned up here with a wife?" asked Doris.

"She knew I was going to be married."

"When?"

"I sent her back to the village before I left here. I told her it was all over. I gave her what I'd promised. She always knew it was only a temporary arrangement. I was fed up with it. I told her I was going to marry a white woman."

"But you hadn't even seen me then."

"No, I know. But I'd made up my mind to marry when I was home." He chuckled in his old manner. "I don't mind telling you that I was getting rather despondent about it when I met you. I fell in love with you at first sight and then I knew it was either you or nobody."

"Why didn't you tell me? Don't you think it would have been only fair to give me a chance of judging for myself? It might have occurred to you that it would be rather a shock to a girl to find out that her husband had lived for ten years with another girl and had three children."

"I couldn't expect you to understand. The circumstances out here are peculiar. It's the regular thing. Five men out of six do it. I thought perhaps it would shock you and I didn't want to lose you. You see, I was most awfully in love with you. I am now, darling. There was no reason that you should ever know. I didn't expect to come back here. One seldom goes back to the same station after home leave. When we came here I offered her money if she'd go to some other village. First she said she would and then she changed her mind."

"Why have you told me now?"

"She's been making the most awful scenes. I don't know how she found out that you knew nothing about it. As soon as she did she began to blackmail me. I've had to give her an awful lot of money. I gave orders that she wasn't to be allowed in the compound. This morning she made that scene just to attract your attention. She wanted to frighten me. I couldn't go on like that. I thought the only thing was to make a clean breast of it."

There was a long silence as he finished. At last he put his hand on hers.

"You do understand, Doris, don't you? I know I've been to blame."

She did not move her hand. He felt it cold beneath his.

"Is she jealous?"

"I daresay there were all sorts of perks when she was living here, and I don't suppose she much likes not getting them any longer. But she was never in love with me any more than I was in love with her. Native women never do really care for white men, you know."

"And the children?"

"Oh, the children are all right. I've provided for them. As soon as the boys are old enough I shall send them to school at Singapore."

"Do they mean nothing to you at all?"

He hesitated.

"I want to be quite frank with you. I should be sorry if anything happened to them. When the first one was expected I thought I'd be much fonder of it than I ever had been of its mother. I suppose I should have been if it had been white. Of course, when it was a baby it was rather funny and touching, but I had no particular feeling that it was mine. I think that's what it is; you see, I have no sense of their belonging to me. I've reproached myself sometimes, because it seemed rather unnatural, but the honest truth is that they're no more to me than if they were somebody else's children. Of course a lot of slush is talked about children by people who haven't got any."

Now she had heard everything. He waited for her to speak, but she said nothing. She sat motionless.

"Is there anything more you want to ask me, Doris?" he said at last.

"No, I've got rather a headache. I think I shall go to bed." Her voice was as steady as ever. "I don't quite know what to say. Of course it's been all very unexpected. You must give me a little time to think."

"Are you very angry with me?"

"No. Not at all. Only—only I must be left to myself for a while. Don't move. I'm going to bed."

She rose from her long chair and put her hand on his shoulder.

"It's so very hot to-night. I wish you'd sleep in your dressing-room. Good night."

She was gone. He heard her lock the door of her bedroom.

She was pale next day and he could see that she had not slept. There was no bitterness in her manner, she talked as usual, but without ease; she spoke of this and that as though she were making conversation with a stranger. They had never had a quarrel, but it seemed to Guy that so would she talk if they had had a disagreement and the subsequent reconciliation had left her still wounded. The look in her eyes puzzled him; he seemed to read in them a strange fear. Immediately after dinner she said:

"I'm not feeling very well to-night. I think I shall go straight to bed."

"Oh, my poor darling, I'm so sorry," he cried.

"It's nothing. I shall be all right in a day or two."

"I shall come in and say good night to you later."

"No, don't do that. I shall try and get straight off to sleep."

"Well, then, kiss me before you go."

He saw that she flushed. For an instant she seemed to hesitate; then, with averted eyes, she leaned towards him. He took her in his arms and sought her lips, but she turned her face away and he kissed her cheek. She left him quickly and again he heard the key turn softly in the lock of her door. He flung himself heavily on the chair. He tried to read, but his ear was attentive to the smallest sound in his wife's room. She had said she was going to bed, but he did not hear her move. The silence in there made him unaccountably nervous. Shading the lamp with his hand he saw that there was a glimmer under her door; she had not put out her light. What on earth was she doing? He put down his book. It would not have surprised him if she had been angry and had made him a scene, or if she had cried; he could have coped with that; but her calmness frightened him. And then what was that fear which he had seen so plainly in her eyes? He thought once more over all he had said to her on the previous night. He didn't know how else he could have put it. After all, the chief point was that he'd done the same as everybody else, and it was all over long before he met her. Of course as things turned out he had been a fool, but any one could be wise after the event. He put his hand to his heart. Funny how it hurt him there!

"I suppose that's the sort of thing people mean when they say they're heart-broken," he said to himself. "I wonder how long it's going on like this?"

Should he knock at the door and tell her he must speak to her? It was better to have it out. He *must* make her understand. But the silence scared him. Not a sound! Perhaps it was better to leave her alone. Of course it had been a shock. He must give her as long as she wanted. After all, she knew how devotedly he loved her. Patience, that was the only thing; perhaps she was fighting it out with herself; he must give her time; he must have patience.

Next morning he asked her if she had slept better.

"Yes, much," she said.

"Are you very angry with me?" he asked piteously.

She looked at him with candid, open eyes.

"Not a bit."

"Oh, my dear, I'm so glad. I've been a brute and a beast. I know it's been hateful for you. But do forgive me. I've been so miserable."

"I do forgive you. I don't even blame you."

He gave her a little rueful smile, and there was in his eyes the look of a whipped dog.

"I haven't much liked sleeping by myself the last two nights."

She glanced away. Her face grew a trifle paler.

"I've had the bed in my room taken away. It took up so much space. I've had a little camp bed put there instead."

"My dear, what are you talking about?"

Now she looked at him steadily.

"I'm not going to live with you as your wife again."

"Never?"

She shook her head. He looked at her in a puzzled way. He could hardly believe he had heard aright and his heart began to beat painfully.

"But that's awfully unfair to me, Doris."

"Don't you think it was a little unfair to me to bring me out here in the circumstances?"

"But you just said you didn't blame me."

"That's quite true. But the other's different. I can't do it."

"But how are we going to live together like that?"

She stared at the floor. She seemed to ponder deeply.

"When you wanted to kiss me on the lips last night I—it almost made me sick."

"Doris."

She looked at him suddenly and her eyes were cold and hostile.

"That bed I slept on, is that the bed in which she had her children?" She saw him flush deeply. "Oh, it's horrible. How could you?" She wrung her hands, and her twisting, tortured fingers looked like little writhing snakes. But she made a great effort and controlled herself. "My mind is quite made up. I don't want to be unkind to you, but there are some things that you can't ask me to do. I've thought it all over. I've been thinking of nothing else since you told me, night and day, till I'm exhausted. My first instinct was to get up and go. At once. The steamer will be here in two or three days."

"Doesn't it mean anything to you that I love you?"

"Oh, I know you love me. I'm not going to do that. I want to give us both a chance. I have loved you so, Guy." Her voice broke, but she did not cry. "I don't want to be unreasonable. Heaven knows, I don't want to be unkind. Guy, will you give me time?"

"I don't know quite what you mean."

"I just want you to leave me alone. I'm frightened by the feelings that I have."

He had been right then; she was afraid.

"What feelings?"

"Please don't ask me. I don't want to say anything to wound you. Perhaps I shall get over them. Heaven knows, I want to. I'll try, I promise you. I'll try. Give me six months. I'll do everything in the world for you, but just that one thing." She made a little gesture of appeal. "There's no reason why we shouldn't be happy enough together. If you really love me you'll—you'll have patience."

He sighed deeply.

"Very well," he said. "Naturally I don't want to force you to do anything you don't like. It shall be as you say."

He sat heavily for a little, as though, on a sudden grown old, it was an effort to move; then he got up.

"I'll be getting along to the office."

He took his topee and went out.

A month passed. Women conceal their feelings better than men and a stranger visiting them would never have guessed that Doris was in any way troubled. But in Guy the strain was obvious; his round, good-natured face was drawn, and in his eyes was a hungry, harassed look. He watched Doris. She was gay and she chaffed him as she had been used to do; they played tennis together; they chatted about one thing and another. But it was evident that she was merely playing a part, and at last, unable to contain himself, he tried to speak again of his connection with the Malay woman.

"Oh, Guy, there's no object in going back on all that," she answered breezily. "We've said all we had to say about it and I don't blame you for anything."

"Why do you punish me then?"

"My poor boy, I don't want to punish you. It's not my fault if . . ." She shrugged her shoulders. "Human nature is very odd."

"I don't understand."

"Don't try."

The words might have been harsh, but she softened them with a pleasant, friendly smile. Every night when she went to bed she leaned over Guy and lightly kissed his cheek. Her lips only touched it. It was as though a moth had just brushed his face in its flight.

A second month passed, then a third, and suddenly the six months which had seemed so interminable were over. Guy asked himself whether she remembered. He gave a strained attention now to everything she said, to every look on her face and to every gesture of her hands. She remained impenetrable. She had asked him to give her six months; well, he had.

The coasting steamer passed the mouth of the river, dropped their mail, and went on its way. Guy busily wrote the letter which it would pick up on the return journey. Two or three days passed by. It was a Tuesday and the prahu was to start at dawn on Thursday to await the steamer. Except at meal time when Doris exerted herself to make conversation they had not of late talked very much together; and after dinner as usual they took their books and began to read; but when the boy had finished clearing away and was gone for the night Doris put down hers.

"Guy, I have something I want to say to you," she murmured.

His heart gave a sudden thud against his ribs and he felt himself change colour.

"Oh, my dear, don't look like that, it's not so very terrible," she laughed.

But he thought her voice trembled a little.

"Well?"

"I want you to do something for me."

"My darling, I'll do anything in the world for you."

He put out his hand to take hers, but she drew it away.

"I want you to let me go home."

"You?" he cried, aghast. "When? Why?"

"I've borne it as long as I can. I'm at the end of my tether."

"How long do you want to go for? For always?"

"I don't know. I think so." She gathered determination. "Yes, for always."

"Oh, my God!"

His voice broke and she thought he was going to cry.

"Oh, Guy, don't blame me. It really is not my fault. I can't help myself."

"You asked me for six months. I accepted your terms. You can't say I've made a nuisance of myself."

"No, no."

"I've tried not to let you see what a rotten time I was having."

"I know. I'm very grateful to you. You've been awfully kind to me. Listen, Guy, I want to tell you again that I don't blame you for a single thing you did. After all, you were only a boy, and you did no more than the others; I know what the loneliness is here. Oh, my dear, I'm so dreadfully sorry for you. I knew all that from the beginning. That's why I asked you for six months. My common sense tells me that I'm making a mountain out of a molehill. I'm unreasonable; I'm being unfair to you. But, you see, common sense has nothing to do with it; my whole soul is in revolt. When I see the woman and her children in the village I just feel my legs shaking. Everything in this house; when I think of that bed I slept in, it gives me gooseflesh. . . . You don't know what I've endured."

"I think I've persuaded her to go away. And I've applied for a transfer."

"That wouldn't help. She'd be there always. You belong to them, you don't belong to me. I think perhaps I could have stood it if there'd only been one child, but three; and the boys are quite big boys. For ten years you lived with her." And now she came out with what she had been working up to. She was desperate. "It's a physical thing, I can't help it, it's stronger than I am. I think of those thin, black arms of hers round you and it fills me with a physical nausea. I think of you holding those little black babies in your arms. Oh, it's loathsome. The touch of you is odious to me. Each night, when I've kissed you, I've had to brace myself up to it. I've had to clench my hands and force myself to touch your cheek." Now she was clasping and unclasping her fingers in a nervous agony and her voice was out of control. "I know it's I who am to blame now. I'm a silly, hysterical woman. I thought I'd get over it. I can't, and now I never shall. I've brought it all on myself; I'm willing to take the consequences; if you say I must stay here, I'll stay, but if I stay I shall die. I beseech you to let me go."

And now the tears which she had restrained so long overflowed and she wept broken-heartedly. He had never seen her cry before.

"Of course I don't want to keep you here against your will," he said hoarsely.

Exhausted, she leaned back in her chair. Her features were all twisted and awry. It was horribly painful to see the abandonment of grief on that face which was habitually so placid.

"I'm so sorry, Guy. I've broken your life, but I've broken mine too. And we might have been so happy."

"When do you want to go? On Thursday?"

"Yes."

She looked at him piteously. He buried his face in his hand
At last he looked up.

"I'm tired out," he muttered.

"May I go?"

"Yes."

For two minutes perhaps they sat there without a wor
She started when the chik-chak gave its piercing, hoarse an
strangely human cry. Guy rose and went out on to the veran
dah. He leaned against the rail and looked at the softly flowin
water. He heard Doris go into her room.

Next morning, up earlier than usual, he went to her doo
and knocked.

"Yes?"

"I have to go up-river to-day. I shan't be back till late."

"All right."

She understood. He had arranged to be away all day in orde
not to be about while she was packing. It was heart-breakin
work. When she had packed her clothes she looked round th
sitting-room at the things that belonged to her. It seemed dreac
ful to take them. She left everything but the photograph of he
mother. Guy did not come in till ten o'clock at night.

"I'm sorry I couldn't get back to dinner," he said. "Th
headman at the village I had to go to had a lot of things fo
me to attend to."

She saw his eyes wander about the room and notice that he
mother's photograph no longer stood in its place.

"Is everything quite ready?" he asked. "I've ordered th
boatman to be at the steps at dawn."

"I told the boy to wake me at five."

"I'd better give you some money." He went to his desk an
wrote out a cheque. He took some notes from a drawer. "Here'
some cash to take you as far as Singapore and at Singapor
you'll be able to change the cheque."

"Thank you."

"Would you like me to come to the mouth of the river with
you?"

"Oh, I think it would be better if we said good-bye here."

"All right. I think I shall turn in. I've had a long day an
I'm dead beat."

He did not even touch her hand. He went into his room. I
a few minutes she heard him throw himself on his bed. For a
little while she sat looking for the last time around that room

in which she had been so happy and so miserable. She sighed deeply. She got up and went into her own room. Everything was packed except the one or two things she needed for the night.

It was dark when the boy awakened them. They dressed hurriedly and when they were ready breakfast was waiting for them. Presently they heard the boat row up to the landing-stage below the bungalow, and then the servants carried down her luggage. It was a poor pretence they made at eating. The darkness thinned away and the river was ghostly. It was not yet day, but it was no longer night. In the silence the voices of the natives at the landing-stage were very clear. Guy glanced at his wife's untouched plate.

"If you've finished we might stroll down. I think you ought to be starting."

She did not answer. She rose from the table. She went into her room to see that nothing had been forgotten and then side by side with him walked down the steps. A little winding path led them to the river. At the landing-stage the native guards in their smart uniforms were lined up and they presented arms as Guy and Doris passed. The head boatman gave her his hand as she stepped into the boat. She turned and looked at Guy. She wanted desperately to say one last word of comfort, once more to ask for his forgiveness, but she seemed to be struck dumb.

He stretched out his hand.

"Well, good-bye, I hope you'll have a jolly journey."

They shook hands.

Guy nodded to the head boatman and the boat pushed off. The dawn now was creeping along the river mistily, but the night lurked still in the dark trees of the jungle. He stood at the landing-stage till the boat was lost in the shadows of the morning. With a sigh he turned away. He nodded absent-mindedly when the guard once more presented arms. But when he reached the bungalow he called the boy. He went round the room picking out everything that had belonged to Doris.

"Pack all these things up," he said. "It's no good leaving them about."

Then he sat down on the verandah and watched the day advance gradually like a bitter, an unmerited and an over-whelming sorrow. At last he looked at his watch. It was time for him to go to the office.

In the afternoon he could not sleep, his head ached miserably, so he took his gun and went for a tramp in the jungle. He shot nothing, but he walked in order to tire himself out. Towards sunset he came back and had two or three drinks, and then it was time to dress for dinner. There wasn't much use in dressing now; he might just as well be comfortable; he put on a loose native jacket and a sarong. That was what he had been accustomed to wear before Doris came. He was barefoot. He ate his dinner listlessly and the boy cleared away and went He sat down to read The Tatler. The bungalow was very silent He could not read and let the paper fall on his knees. He was exhausted. He could not think and his mind was strangely vacant. The chik-chak was noisy that night and its hoarse and sudden cry seemed to mock him. You could hardly believe that this reverberating sound came from so small a throat. Presently he heard a discreet cough.

"Who's there?" he cried.

There was a pause. He looked at the door. The chik-chak laughed harshly. A small boy sidled in and stood on the threshold. It was a little half-caste boy in a tattered singlet and a sarong. It was the elder of his two sons.

"What do you want?" said Guy.

The boy came forward into the room and sat down, tucking his legs away under him.

"Who told you to come here?"

"My mother sent me. She says, do you want anything?"

Guy looked at the boy intently. The boy said nothing more. He sat and waited, his eyes cast down shyly. Then Guy in deep and bitter reflection buried his face in his hands. What was the use? It was finished. Finished! He surrendered. He sat back in his chair and sighed deeply.

"Tell your mother to pack up her things and yours. She can come back."

"When?" asked the boy impassively.

Hot tears trickled down Guy's funny, round, spotty face.

"To-night."

THE OUTSTATION

The new assistant arrived in the afternoon. When the Resident, Mr. Warburton, was told that the prahu was in sight he put on his solar topee and went down to the landing-stage. The guard, eight little Dyak soldiers, stood to attention as he passed. He noted with satisfaction that their bearing was martial, their uniforms neat and clean, and their guns shining. They were a credit to him. From the landing-stage he watched the bend of the river round which in a moment the boat would sweep. He looked very smart in his spotless ducks and white shoes. He held under his arm a gold-headed Malacca cane which had been given him by the Sultan of Perak. He awaited the new-comer with mingled feelings. There was more work in the district than one man could properly do, and during his period-ical tours of the country under his charge it had been incon-venient to leave the station in the hands of a native clerk, but he had been so long the only white man there that he could not face the arrival of another without misgiving. He was accus-tomed to loneliness. During the war he had not seen an English face for three years; and once when he was instructed to put up an afforestation officer he was seized with panic, so that when the stranger was due to arrive, having arranged every-thing for his reception, he wrote a note telling him he was obliged to go up-river, and fled; he remained away till he was informed by a messenger that his guest had left.

Now the prahu appeared in the broad reach. It was manned by prisoners, Dyaks under various sentences, and a couple of

warders were waiting on the landing-stage to take them back
to jail. They were sturdy fellows, used to the river, and they
rowed with a powerful stroke. As the boat reached the side a
man got out from under the attap awning and stepped on shore.
The guard presented arms.

"Here we are at last. By God, I'm as cramped as the devil.
I've brought you your mail."

He spoke with exuberant joviality. Mr. Warburton politely
held out his hand.

"Mr. Cooper, I presume?"

"That's right. Were you expecting any one else?"

The question had a facetious intent, but the Resident did
not smile.

"My name is Warburton. I'll show you your quarters. They'll
bring your kit along."

He preceded Cooper along the narrow pathway and they
entered a compound in which stood a small bungalow.

"I've had it made as habitable as I could, but of course no
one has lived in it for a good many years."

It was built on piles. It consisted of a long living-room which
opened on to a broad verandah, and behind, on each side of a
passage, were two bedrooms.

"This'll do me all right," said Cooper.

"I daresay you want to have a bath and a change. I shall
be very much pleased if you'll dine with me to-night. Will eight
o'clock suit you?"

"Any old time will do for me."

The Resident gave a polite, but slightly disconcerted, smile
and withdrew. He returned to the Fort where his own residence
was. The impression which Allen Cooper had given him was
not very favourable, but he was a fair man, and he knew that
it was unjust to form an opinion on so brief a glimpse. Cooper
seemed to be about thirty. He was a tall, thin fellow, with a
sallow face in which there was not a spot of colour. It was a
face all in one tone. He had a large, hooked nose and blue eyes.
When, entering the bungalow, he had taken off his topee and
flung it to a waiting boy, Mr. Warburton noticed that his large
skull, covered with short, brown hair, contrasted somewhat
oddly with a weak, small chin. He was dressed in khaki shorts
and a khaki shirt, but they were shabby and soiled; and his
battered topee had not been cleaned for days. Mr. Warburton
reflected that the young man had spent a week on a coasting

steamer and had passed the last forty-eight hours lying in the bottom of a prahu.

"We'll see what he looks like when he comes in to dinner."

He went into his room where his things were as neatly laid out as if he had an English valet, undressed, and, walking down the stairs to the bath-house, sluiced himself with cool water. The only concession he made to the climate was to wear a white dinner-jacket; but otherwise, in a boiled shirt and a high collar, silk socks and patent-leather shoes, he dressed as formally as though he were dining at his club in Pall Mall. A careful host, he went into the dining-room to see that the table was properly laid. It was gay with orchids and the silver shone brightly. The napkins were folded into elaborate shapes. Shaded candles in silver candlesticks shed a soft light. Mr. Warburton smiled his approval and returned to the sitting-room to await his guest. Presently he appeared. Cooper was wearing the khaki shorts, the khaki shirt, and the ragged jacket in which he had landed. Mr. Warburton's smile of greeting froze on his face.

"Hulloa, you're all dressed up," said Cooper. "I didn't know you were going to do that. I very nearly put on a sarong."

"It doesn't matter at all. I daresay your boys were busy."

"You needn't have bothered to dress on my account, you know."

"I didn't. I always dress for dinner."

"Even when you're alone?"

"Especially when I'm alone," replied Mr. Warburton, with a frigid stare.

He saw a twinkle of amusement in Cooper's eyes, and he flushed an angry red. Mr. Warburton was a hot-tempered man; you might have guessed that from his red face with its pugnacious features and from his red hair, now growing white; his blue eyes, cold as a rule and observing, could flush with sudden wrath; but he was a man of the world and he hoped a just one. He must do his best to get on with this fellow.

"When I lived in London I moved in circles in which it would have been just as eccentric not to dress for dinner every night as not to have a bath every morning. When I came to Borneo I saw no reason to discontinue so good a habit. For three years, during the war, I never saw a white man. I never omitted to dress on a single occasion on which I was well enough to come in to dinner. You have not been very long in this country; believe me, there is no better way to maintain the proper pride which you should have in yourself. When a white man surrenders in the slightest degree to the influences that surround him he very soon loses his self-respect, and when he loses his self-respect you may be quite sure that the natives will soon cease to respect him."

"Well, if you expect me to put on a boiled shirt and a stiff collar in this heat I'm afraid you'll be disappointed."

"When you are dining in your own bungalow you will, of course, dress as you think fit, but when you do me the pleasure of dining with me, perhaps you will come to the conclusion that it is only polite to wear the costume usual in civilized society."

Two Malay boys, in sarongs and songkoks, with smart white coats and brass buttons, came in, one bearing gin pahits, and the other a tray on which were olives and anchovies. Then they went in to dinner. Mr. Warburton flattered himself that he had the best cook, a Chinese, in Borneo, and he took great trouble to have as good food as in the difficult circumstances was possible. He exercised much ingenuity in making the best of his materials.

"Would you care to look at the menu?" he said, handing it to Cooper.

It was written in French and the dishes had resounding names. They were waited on by the two boys. In opposite corners of the room two more waved immense fans, and so gave movement to the sultry air. The fare was sumptuous and the champagne excellent.

"Do you do yourself like this every day?" said Cooper.

Mr. Warburton gave the menu a careless glance.

"I have not noticed that the dinner is any different from usual," he said. "I eat very little myself, but I make a point of having a proper dinner served to me every night. It keeps the cook in practice and it's good discipline for the boys."

The conversation proceeded with effort. Mr. Warburton was elaborately courteous, and it may be that he found a slightly malicious amusement in the embarrassment which he thereby occasioned in his companion. Cooper had not been more than a few months in Sembulu, and Mr. Warburton's enquiries about friends of his in Kuala Solor were soon exhausted.

"By the way," he said presently, "did you meet a lad called Hennerley? He's come out recently, I believe."

"Oh, yes, he's in the police. A rotten bounder."

"I should hardly have expected him to be that. His uncle is my friend Lord Barraclough. I had a letter from Lady Barraclough only the other day asking me to look out for him."

"I heard he was related to somebody or other. I suppose that's how he got the job. He's been to Eton and Oxford and he doesn't forget to let you know it."

"You surprise me," said Mr. Warburton. "All his family have been at Eton and Oxford for a couple of hundred years. I should have expected him to take it as a matter of course."

"I thought him a damned prig."

"To what school did you go?"

"I was born in Barbadoes. I was educated there."

"Oh, I see."

Mr. Warburton managed to put so much offensiveness into his brief reply that Cooper flushed. For a moment he was silent.

"I've had two or three letters from Kuala Solor," continued Mr. Warburton, "and my impression was that young Hennerley was a great success. They say he's a first-rate sportsman."

"Oh, yes, he's very popular. He's just the sort of fellow they would like in K.S. I haven't got much use for the first-rate sportsman myself. What does it amount to in the long run that a man can play golf and tennis better than other people? And who cares if he can make a break of seventy-five at billiards? They attach a damned sight too much importance to that sort of thing in England."

"Do you think so? I was under the impression that the first-rate sportsman had come out of the war certainly no worse than any one else."

"Oh, if you're going to talk of the war then I do know what I'm talking about. I was in the same regiment as Hennerley and I can tell you that the men couldn't stick him at any price."

"How do you know?"

"Because I was one of the men."

"Oh, you hadn't got a commission."

"A fat chance I had of getting a commission. I was what was called a Colonial. I hadn't been to a public school and I had no influence. I was in the ranks the whole damned time."

Cooper frowned. He seemed to have difficulty in preventing himself from breaking into violent invective. Mr. Warburton watched him, his little blue eyes narrowed, watched him and formed his opinion. Changing the conversation, he began to

speak to Cooper about the work that would be required of
him, and as the clock struck ten he rose.

"Well, I won't keep you any more. I daresay you're tired by
your journey."

They shook hands.

"Oh, I say, look here," said Cooper, "I wonder if you can
find me a boy. The boy I had before never turned up when I
was starting from K.S. He took my kit on board and all that
and then disappeared. I didn't know he wasn't there till we
were out of the river."

"I'll ask my head-boy. I have no doubt he can find you some
one."

"All right. Just tell him to send the boy along and if I like
the look of him I'll take him."

There was a moon, so that no lantern was needed. Cooper
walked across from the Fort to his bungalow.

"I wonder why on earth they've sent me a fellow like that?"
reflected Mr. Warburton. "If that's the kind of man they're
going to get out now I don't think much of it."

He strolled down his garden. The Fort was built on the top
of a little hill and the garden ran down to the river's edge; on
the bank was an arbour, and hither it was his habit to come
after dinner to smoke a cheroot. And often from the river that
flowed below him a voice was heard, the voice of some Malay
too timorous to venture into the light of day, and a complaint
or an accusation was softly wafted to his ears, a piece of information was whispered to him or a useful hint, which otherwise would never have come into his official ken. He threw
himself heavily into a long rattan chair. Cooper! An envious,
ill-bred fellow, bumptious, self-assertive and vain. But Mr.
Warburton's irritation could not withstand the silent beauty
of the night. The air was scented with the sweet-smelling flowers
of a tree that grew at the entrance to the arbour, and the
fireflies, sparkling dimly, flew with their slow and silvery flight.
The moon made a pathway on the broad river for the light feet
of Siva's bride, and on the further bank a row of palm trees
was delicately silhouetted against the sky. Peace stole into the
soul of Mr. Warburton.

He was a queer creature and he had had a singular career.
At the age of twenty-one he had inherited a considerable
fortune, a hundred thousand pounds, and when he left Oxford
he threw himself into the gay life which in those days (now Mr.

Warburton was a man of four and fifty) offered itself to the
young man of good family. He had his flat in Mount Street, his
private hansom, and his hunting-box in Warwickshire. He
went to all the places where the fashionable congregate. He
was handsome, amusing and generous. He was a figure in the
society of London in the early nineties, and society then had
not lost its exclusiveness nor its brilliance. The Boer War which
shook it was unthought of; the Great War which destroyed it
was prophesied only by the pessimists. It was no unpleasant
thing to be a rich young man in those days, and Mr. Warburton's chimney-piece during the season was packed with cards
for one great function after another. Mr. Warburton displayed
them with complacency. For Mr. Warburton was a snob. He
was not a timid snob, a little ashamed of being impressed by
his betters, nor a snob who sought the intimacy of persons who
had acquired celebrity in politics or notoriety in the arts, nor
the snob who was dazzled by riches; he was the naked, unadul-
terated common snob who dearly loved a lord. He was touchy
and quick-tempered, but he would much rather have been
snubbed by a person of quality than flattered by a commoner.
His name figured insignificantly in Burke's Peerage, and it was
marvellous to watch the ingenuity he used to mention his distant relationship to the noble family he belonged to; but never
a word did he say of the honest Liverpool manufacturer from
whom, through his mother, a Miss Gubbins, he had come by
his fortune. It was the terror of his fashionable life that at
Cowes, maybe, or at Ascot, when he was with a duchess or even
with a prince of the blood, one of these relatives would claim
acquaintance with him.

His failing was too obvious not soon to become notorious,
but its extravagance saved it from being merely despicable.
The great whom he adored laughed at him, but in their hearts
felt his adoration not unnatural. Poor Warburton was a dreadful snob, of course, but after all he was a good fellow. He was
always ready to back a bill for an impecunious nobleman, and
if you were in a tight corner you could safely count on him for
a hundred pounds. He gave good dinners. He played whist
badly, but never minded how much he lost if the company was
select. He happened to be a gambler, an unlucky one, but he
was a good loser, and it was impossible not to admire the coolness with which he lost five hundred pounds at a sitting. His
passion for cards, almost as strong as his passion for titles,

was the cause of his undoing. The life he led was expensive and his gambling losses were formidable. He began to plunge more heavily, first on horses, and then on the Stock Exchange. He had a certain simplicity of character and the unscrupulous found him an ingenuous prey. I do not know if he ever realized that his smart friends laughed at him behind his back, but I think he had an obscure instinct that he could not afford to appear other than careless of his money. He got into the hands of money-lenders. At the age of thirty-four he was ruined.

He was too much imbued with the spirit of his class to hesitate in the choice of his next step. When a man in his set had run through his money he went out to the colonies. No one heard Mr. Warburton repine. He made no complaint because a noble friend had advised a disastrous speculation, he pressed nobody to whom he had lent money to repay it, he paid his debts (if he had only known it, the despised blood of the Liverpool manufacturer came out in him there), sought help from no one, and, never having done a stroke of work in his life, looked for a means of livelihood. He remained cheerful, unconcerned and full of humour. He had no wish to make any one with whom he happened to be uncomfortable by the recital of his misfortune. Mr. Warburton was a snob, but he was also a gentleman.

The only favour he asked of any of the great friends in whose daily company he had lived for years was a recommendation. The able man who was at that time Sultan of Sembulu took him into his service. The night before he sailed he dined for the last time at his club.

"I hear you're going away, Warburton," the old Duke of Hereford said to him.

"Yes, I'm going to Borneo."

"Good God, what are you going there for?"

"Oh, I'm broke."

"Are you? I'm sorry. Well, let us know when you come back. I hope you have a good time."

"Oh, yes. Lots of shooting, you know."

The Duke nodded and passed on. A few hours later Mr. Warburton watched the coast of England recede into the mist, and he left behind everything which to him made life worth living.

Twenty years had passed since then. He kept up a busy correspondence with various great ladies and his letters were amusing and chatty. He never lost his love for titled persons and paid careful attention to the announcements in The Times (which reached him six weeks after publication) of their comings and goings. He perused the column which records births, deaths, and marriages, and he was always ready with his letter of congratulation or condolence. The illustrated papers told him how people looked and on his periodical visits to England, able to take up the threads as though they had never been broken, he knew all about any new person who might have appeared on the social surface. His interest in the world of fashion was as vivid as when himself had been a figure in it. It still seemed to him the only thing that mattered.

But insensibly another interest had entered into his life. The position he found himself in flattered his vanity; he was 'no longer the sycophant craving the smiles of the great, he was the master whose word was law. He was gratified by the guard of Dyak soldiers who presented arms as he passed. He liked to sit in judgment on his fellow men. It pleased him to compose quarrels between rival chiefs. When the head-hunters were troublesome in the old days he set out to chastise them with a thrill of pride in his own behaviour. He was too vain not to be of dauntless courage, and a pretty story was told of his coolness in adventuring single-handed into a stockaded village and demanding the surrender of a bloodthirsty pirate. He became a skilful administrator. He was strict, just and honest.

And little by little he conceived a deep love for the Malays. He interested himself in their habits and customs. He was never tired of listening to their talk. He admired their virtues, and with a smile and a shrug of the shoulders condoned their vices.

"In my day," he would say, "I have been on intimate terms with some of the greatest gentlemen in England, but I have never known finer gentlemen than some well-born Malays whom I am proud to call my friends."

He liked their courtesy and their distinguished manners, their gentleness and their sudden passions. He knew by instinct exactly how to treat them. He had a genuine tenderness for them. But he never forgot that he was an English gentleman' and he had no patience with the white men who yielded to native customs. He made no surrenders. And he did not imitate so many of the white men in taking a native woman to wife, for an intrigue of this nature, however sanctified by custom,

seemed to him not only shocking but undignified. A man who
had been called George by Albert Edward, Prince of Wales,
could hardly be expected to have any connection with a native.
And when he returned to Borneo from his visits to England
it was now with something like relief. His friends, like himself,
were no longer young, and there was a new generation which
looked upon him as a tiresome old man. It seemed to him that
the England of to-day had lost a good deal of what he had
loved in the England of his youth. But Borneo remained the
same. It was home to him now. He meant to remain in the service as long as was possible, and the hope in his heart was that
he would die before at last he was forced to retire. He had stated
in his will that wherever he died he wished his body to be
brought back to Sembulu and buried among the people he
loved within sound of the softly flowing river.

But these emotions he kept hidden from the eyes of men;
and no one, seeing this spruce, stout, well-set-up man, with his
clean-shaven strong face and his whitening hair, would have
dreamed that he cherished so profound a sentiment.

He knew how the work of the station should be done, and
during the next few days he kept a suspicious eye on his
assistant. He saw very soon that he was painstaking and competent. The only fault he had to find with him was that he was
brusque with the natives.

"The Malays are shy and very sensitive," he said to him. "I
think you will find that you will get much better results if you
take care always to be polite, patient and kindly."

Cooper gave a short, grating laugh.

"I was born in Barbadoes and I was in Africa in the war.
I don't think there's much about niggers that I don't know."

"I know nothing," said Mr. Warburton acidly. "But we
were not talking of them. We were talking of Malays."

"Aren't they niggers?"

"You are very ignorant," replied Mr. Warburton.

He said no more.

On the first Sunday after Cooper's arrival he asked him to
dinner. He did everything ceremoniously, and though they had
met on the previous day in the office and later, on the Fort
verandah where they drank a gin and bitters together at six
o'clock, he sent a polite note across to the bungalow by a boy.
Cooper, however unwillingly, came in evening dress and Mr.
Warburton, though gratified that his wish was respected,

noticed with disdain that the young man's clothes were badly cut and his shirt ill-fitting. But Mr. Warburton was in a good temper that evening.

"By the way," he said to him, as he shook hands, "I've talked to my head-boy about finding you some one and he recommends his nephew. I've seen him and he seems a bright and willing lad. Would you like to see him?"

"I don't mind."

"He's waiting now."

Mr. Warburton called his boy and told him to send for his nephew. In a moment a tall, slender youth of twenty appeared. He had large dark eyes and a good profile. He was very neat in his sarong, a little white coat, and a fez, without a tassel, of plum-coloured velvet. He answered to the name of Abas. Mr. Warburton looked on him with approval, and his manner insensibly softened as he spoke to him in fluent and idiomatic Malay. He was inclined to be sarcastic with white people, but with the Malays he had a happy mixture of condescension and kindliness. He stood in the place of the Sultan. He knew perfectly how to preserve his own dignity, and at the same time put a native at his ease.

"Will he do?" said Mr. Warburton, turning to Cooper.

"Yes, I daresay he's no more of a scoundrel than any of the rest of them."

Mr. Warburton informed the boy that he was engaged and dismissed him.

"You're very lucky to get a boy like that," he told Cooper. "He belongs to a very good family. They came over from Malacca nearly a hundred years ago."

"I don't much mind if the boy who cleans my shoes and brings me a drink when I want it has blue blood in his veins or not. All I ask is that he should do what I tell him and look sharp about it."

Mr. Warburton pursed his lips, but made no reply.

They went in to dinner. It was excellent, and the wine was good. Its influence presently had its effect on them and they talked not only without acrimony, but even with friendliness. Mr. Warburton liked to do himself well, and on Sunday night he made it a habit to do himself even a little better than usual. He began to think he was unfair to Cooper. Of course he was not a gentleman, but that was not his fault, and when you got to know him it might be that he would turn out a very good fellow. His faults, perhaps, were faults of manner. And he was certainly good at his work, quick, conscientious and thorough. When they reached the dessert Mr. Warburton was feeling kindly disposed towards all mankind.

"This is your first Sunday and I'm going to give you a very special glass of port. I've only got about two dozen of it left and I keep it for special occasions."

He gave his boy instructions and presently the bottle was brought. Mr. Warburton watched the boy open it.

"I got this port from my old friend Charles Hollington. He'd had it for forty years and I've had it for a good many. He was well known to have the best cellar in England."

"Is he a wine merchant?"

"Not exactly," smiled Mr. Warburton. "I was speaking of Lord Hollington of Castle Reagh. He's one of the richest peers in England. A very old friend of mine. I was at Eton with his brother."

This was an opportunity that Mr. Warburton could never resist and he told a little anecdote of which the only point seemed to be that he knew an earl. The port was certainly very good; he drank a glass and then a second. He lost all caution. He had not talked to a white man for months. He began to tell stories. He showed himself in the company of the great. Hearing him you would have thought that at one time ministries were formed and policies decided on his suggestion whispered into the ear of a duchess or thrown over the dinner-table to be gratefully acted on by the confidential adviser of the sovereign. The old days at Ascot, Goodwood and Cowes lived again for him. Another glass of port. There were the great house-parties in Yorkshire and in Scotland to which he went every year.

"I had a man called Foreman then, the best valet I ever had, and why do you think he gave me notice? You know in the Housekeeper's Room the ladies' maids and the gentlemen's gentlemen sit according to the precedence of their masters. He told me he was sick of going to party after party at which I was the only commoner. It meant that he always had to sit at the bottom of the table and all the best bits were taken before a dish reached him. I told the story to the old Duke of Hereford and he roared. 'By God, sir,' he said, 'if I were King of England I'd make you a viscount just to give your man a chance.' 'Take him yourself, Duke,' I said. 'He's the best valet

I've ever had.' 'Well, Warburton,' he said, 'if he's good enough for you he's good enough for me. Send him along.'"

Then there was Monte Carlo where Mr. Warburton and the Grand Duke Fyodor, playing in partnership, had broken the bank one evening; and there was Marienbad. At Marienbad Mr. Warburton had played baccarat with Edward VII.

"He was only Prince of Wales then, of course. I remember him saying to me, 'George, if you draw on a five you'll lose your shirt.' He was right; I don't think he ever said a truer word in his life. He was a wonderful man. I always said he was the greatest diplomatist in Europe. But I was a young fool in those days, I hadn't the sense to take his advice. If I had, if I'd never drawn on a five, I daresay I shouldn't be here to-day."

Cooper was watching him. His blue eyes, deep in their sockets, were hard and supercilious, and on his lips was a mocking smile. He had heard a good deal about Mr. Warburton in Kuala Solor. Not a bad sort, and he ran his district like clockwork, they said, but by heaven, what a snob! They laughed at him good-naturedly, for it was impossible to dislike a man who was so generous and so kindly, and Cooper had already heard the story of the Prince of Wales and the game of baccarat. But Cooper listened without indulgence. From the beginning he had resented the Resident's manner. He was very sensitive and he writhed under Mr. Warburton's polite sarcasms. Mr. Warburton had a knack of receiving a remark of which he disapproved with a devastating silence. Cooper had lived little in England and he had a peculiar dislike of the English. He resented especially the public-school boy since he always feared that he was going to patronize him. He was so much afraid of others putting on airs with him that, in order as it were to get in first, he put on such airs as to make every one think him insufferably conceited.

"Well, at all events the war has done one good thing for us," he said at last. "It's smashed up the power of the aristocracy. The Boer War started it, and 1914 put the lid on."

"The great families of England are doomed," said Mr. Warburton with the complacent melancholy of an *émigré* who remembered the court of Louis XV. "They cannot afford any longer to live in their splendid palaces and their princely hospitality will soon be nothing but a memory."

"And a damned good job too in my opinion."

"My poor Cooper, what can you know of the glory that was Greece and the grandeur that was Rome?"

Mr. Warburton made an ample gesture. His eyes for an instant grew dreamy with a vision of the past.

"Well, believe me, we're fed up with all that rot. What we want is a business government by business men. I was born in a Crown Colony and I've lived practically all my life in the colonies. I don't give a row of pins for a lord. What's wrong with England is snobbishness. And if there's anything that gets my goat it's a snob."

A snob! Mr. Warburton's face grew purple and his eyes blazed with anger. That was a word that had pursued him all his life. The great ladies whose society he had enjoyed in his youth were not inclined to look upon his appreciation of themselves as unworthy, but even great ladies are sometimes out of temper and more than once Mr. Warburton had had the dreadful word flung in his teeth. He knew, he could not help knowing, that there were odious people who called him a snob. How unfair it was! Why, there was no vice he found so detestable as snobbishness. After all, he liked to mix with people of his own class, he was only at home in their company, and how in heaven's name could any one say that was snobbish? Birds of a feather.

"I quite agree with you," he answered. "A snob is a man who admires or despises another because he is of a higher social rank than his own. It is the most vulgar failing of our English middle class."

He saw a flicker of amusement in Cooper's eyes. Cooper put up his hand to hide the broad smile that rose to his lips, and so made it more noticeable. Mr. Warburton's hands trembled a little.

Probably Cooper never knew how greatly he had offended his chief. A sensitive man himself he was strangely insensitive to the feelings of others.

Their work forced them to see one another for a few minutes now and then during the day, and they met at six to have a drink on Mr. Warburton's verandah. This was an old-established custom of the country which Mr. Warburton would not for the world have broken. But they ate their meals separately, Cooper in his bungalow and Mr. Warburton at the Fort. After the office work was over they walked till dusk fell, but they walked apart. There were but few paths in this country, where the jungle pressed close upon the plantations of the village, and when Mr. Warburton caught sight of his assistant passing along with his loose stride, he would make a circuit in order to avoid him. Cooper, with his bad manners, his conceit in his own judgment and his intolerance, had already got on his nerves; but it was not till Cooper had been on the station for a couple of months that an incident happened which turned the Resident's dislike into bitter hatred.

Mr. Warburton was obliged to go up-country on a tour of inspection, and he left the station in Cooper's charge with more confidence, since he had definitely come to the conclusion that he was a capable fellow. The only thing he did not like was that he had no indulgence. He was honest, just and painstaking, but he had no sympathy for the natives. It bitterly amused Mr. Warburton to observe that this man, who looked upon himself as every man's equal, should look upon so many men as his own inferiors. He was hard, he had no patience with the native mind, and he was a bully. Mr. Warburton very quickly realized that the Malays disliked and feared him. He was not altogether displeased. He would not have liked it very much if his assistant had enjoyed a popularity which might rival his own. Mr. Warburton made his elaborate preparations, set out on his expedition, and in three weeks returned. Meanwhile the mail had arrived. The first thing that struck his eyes when he entered his sitting-room was a great pile of open newspapers. Cooper had met him, and they went into the room together. Mr. Warburton turned to one of the servants who had been left behind and sternly asked him what was the meaning of those open papers. Cooper hastened to explain.

"I wanted to read all about the Wolverhampton murder and so I borrowed your Times. I brought them back again. I knew you wouldn't mind."

Mr. Warburton turned on him, white with anger.

"But I do mind. I mind very much."

"I'm sorry," said Cooper, with composure. "The fact is, I simply couldn't wait till you came back."

"I wonder you didn't open my letters as well."

Cooper, unmoved, smiled at his chief's exasperation.

"Oh, that's not quite the same thing. After all, I couldn't imagine you'd mind my looking at your newspapers. There's nothing private in them."

"I very much object to any one reading my paper before

me." He went up to the pile. There were nearly thirty numbers there. "I think it extremely impertinent of you. They're all mixed up."

"We can easily put them in order," said Cooper, joining him at the table.

"Don't touch them," cried Mr. Warburton.

"I say, it's childish to make a scene about a little thing like that."

"How dare you speak to me like that?"

"Oh, go to hell," said Cooper, and he flung out of the room.

Mr. Warburton, trembling with passion, was left contemplating his papers. His greatest pleasure in life had been destroyed by those callous, brutal hands. Most people living in out-of-the-way places when the mail comes tear open impatiently their papers and taking the last ones first glance at the latest news from home. Not so Mr. Warburton. His newsagent had instructions to write on the outside of the wrapper the date of each paper he despatched and when the great bundle arrived Mr. Warburton looked at these dates and with his blue pencil numbered them. His head-boy's orders were to place one on the table every morning in the verandah with the early cup of tea, and it was Mr. Warburton's especial delight to break the wrapper as he sipped his tea, and read the morning paper. It gave him the illusion of living at home. Every Monday morning he read the Monday Times of six weeks back and so went through the week. On Sunday he read The Observer. Like his habit of dressing for dinner it was a tie to civilization. And it was his pride that no matter how exciting the news was he had never yielded to the temptation of opening a paper before its allotted time. During the war the suspense sometimes had been intolerable, and when he read one day that a push was begun he had undergone agonies of suspense which he might have saved himself by the simple expedient of opening a later paper which lay waiting for him on a shelf. It had been the severest trial to which he had ever exposed himself, but he victoriously surmounted it. And that clumsy fool had broken open those neat tight packages because he wanted to know whether some horrid woman had murdered her odious husband.

Mr. Warburton sent for his boy and told him to bring wrappers. He folded up the papers as neatly as he could, placed a wrapper round each and numbered it. But it was a melancholy task.

"I shall never forgive him," he said. "Never."

Of course his boy had been with him on his expedition; he never travelled without him, for his boy knew exactly how he liked things, and Mr. Warburton was not the kind of jungle traveller who was prepared to dispense with his comforts; but in the interval since their arrival he had been gossiping in the servants' quarters. He had learnt that Cooper had had trouble with his boys. All but the youth Abas had left him. Abas had desired to go too, but his uncle had placed him there on the instructions of the Resident, and he was afraid to leave without his uncle's permission.

"I told him he had done well, Tuan," said the boy. "But he is unhappy. He says it is not a good house and he wishes to know if he may go as the others have gone."

"No, he must stay. The tuan must have servants. Have those who went been replaced?"

"No, Tuan, no one will go."

Mr. Warburton frowned. Cooper was an insolent fool, but he had an official position and must be suitably provided with servants. It was not seemly that his house should be improperly conducted.

"Where are the boys who ran away?"

"They are in the kampong, Tuan."

"Go and see them to-night and tell them that I expect them to be back in Tuan Cooper's house at dawn to-morrow."

"They say they will not go, Tuan."

"On my order?"

The boy had been with Mr. Warburton for fifteen years, and he knew every intonation of his master's voice. He was not afraid of him, they had gone through too much together, once in the jungle the Resident had saved his life and once, upset in some rapids, but for him the Resident would have been drowned; but he knew when the Resident must be obeyed without question.

"I will go to the kampong," he said.

Mr. Warburton expected that his subordinate would take the first opportunity to apologize for his rudeness, but Cooper had the ill-bred man's inability to express regret; and when they met next morning in the office he ignored the incident. Since Mr. Warburton had been away for three weeks it was necessary for them to have a somewhat prolonged interview. At the end of it Mr. Warburton dismissed him.

"I don't think there's anything else, thank you." Cooper turned to go, but Mr. Warburton stopped him. "I understand you've been having some trouble with your boys."

Cooper gave a harsh laugh.

"They tried to blackmail me. They had the damned cheek to run away, all except that incompetent fellow Abas—he knew when he was well off—but I just sat tight. They've all come to heel again."

"What do you mean by that?"

"This morning they were all back on their jobs, the Chinese cook and all. There they were, as cool as cucumbers; you would have thought they owned the place. I suppose they'd come to the conclusion that I wasn't such a fool as I looked."

"By no means. They came back on my express order."

Cooper flushed slightly.

"I should be obliged if you wouldn't interfere with my private concerns."

"They're not your private concerns. When your servants run away it makes you ridiculous. You are perfectly free to make a fool of yourself, but I cannot allow you to be made a fool of. It is unseemly that your house should not be properly staffed. As soon as I heard that your boys had left you, I had them told to be back in their places at dawn. That'll do."

Mr. Warburton nodded to signify that the interview was at an end. Cooper took no notice.

"Shall I tell you what I did? I called them and gave the whole bally lot the sack. I gave them ten minutes to get out of the compound."

Mr. Warburton shrugged his shoulders.

"What makes you think you can get others?"

"I've told my own clerk to see about it."

Mr. Warburton reflected for a moment.

"I think you behaved very foolishly. You will do well to remember in future that good masters make good servants."

"Is there anything else you want to teach me?"

"I should like to teach you manners, but it would be an arduous task, and I have not the time to waste. I will see that you get boys."

"Please don't put yourself to any trouble on my account. I'm quite capable of getting them for myself."

Mr. Warburton smiled acidly. He had an inkling that Cooper disliked him as much as he disliked Cooper, and he knew that nothing is more galling than to be forced to accept the favours of a man you detest.

"Allow me to tell you that you have no more chance of getting Malay or Chinese servants here now than you have of getting an English butler or a French chef. No one will come to you except on an order from me. Would you like me to give it?"

"No."

"As you please. Good morning."

Mr. Warburton watched the development of the situation with acrid humour. Cooper's clerk was unable to persuade Malay, Dyak or Chinese to enter the house of such a master. Abas, the boy who remained faithful to him, knew how to cook only native food, and Cooper, a coarse feeder, found his gorge rise against the everlasting rice. There was no water-carrier, and in that great heat he needed several baths a day. He cursed Abas, but Abas opposed him with sullen resistance and would not do more than he chose. It was galling to know that the lad stayed with him only because the Resident insisted. This went on for a fortnight and then, one morning, he found in his house the very servants whom he had previously dismissed. He fell into a violent rage, but he had learnt a little sense, and this time, without a word, he let them stay. He swallowed his humiliation, but the impatient contempt he had felt for Mr. Warburton's idiosyncrasies changed into a sullen hatred; the Resident with this malicious stroke had made him the laughing-stock of all the natives.

The two men now held no communication with one another. They broke the time-honoured custom of sharing, notwithstanding personal dislike, a drink at six o'clock with any white man who happened to be at the station. Each lived in his own house as though the other did not exist. Now that Cooper had fallen into the work, it was necessary for them to have little to do with one another in the office. Mr. Warburton used his orderly to send any message he had to give his assistant, and his instructions he sent by formal letter. They saw one another constantly, that was inevitable, but did not exchange half a dozen words in a week. The fact that they could not avoid catching sight of one another got on their nerves. They brooded over their antagonism and Mr. Warburton, taking his daily walk, could think of nothing but how much he detested his assistant.

And the dreadful thing was that in all probability they would remain thus, facing each other in deadly enmity, till Mr. Warburton went on leave. It might be three years. He had no reason to send in a complaint to headquarters: Cooper did his work very well, and at that time men were hard to get. True, vague complaints reached him and hints that the natives found Cooper harsh. There was certainly a feeling of dissatisfaction among them. But when Mr. Warburton looked into specific cases, all he could say was that Cooper had shown severity where mildness would not have been misplaced and had been unfeeling when himself would have been sympathetic. He had done nothing for which he could be taken to task. But Mr. Warburton watched him. Hatred will often make a man clear-sighted, and he had a suspicion that Cooper was using the natives without consideration, yet keeping within the law, because he felt that thus he could exasperate his chief. One day perhaps he would go too far. None knew better than Mr. Warburton how irritable the incessant heat could make a man and how difficult it was to keep one's self-control after a sleepless night. He smiled softly to himself. Sooner or later Cooper would deliver himself into his hand.

When at last the opportunity came Mr. Warburton laughed aloud. Cooper had charge of the prisoners; they made roads, built sheds, rowed when it was necessary to send the prahu up- or down-stream, kept the town clean and otherwise usefully employed themselves. If well-behaved they even on occasion served as house-boys. Cooper kept them hard at it. He liked to see them work. He took pleasure in devising tasks for them; and seeing quickly enough that they were being made to do useless things the prisoners worked badly. He punished them by lengthening their hours. This was contrary to the regulations, and as soon as it was brought to the attention of Mr. Warburton, without referring the matter back to his subordinate, he gave instructions that the old hours should be kept; Cooper, going out for his walk, was astounded to see the prisoners strolling back to the jail; he had given instructions that they were not to knock off till dusk. When he asked the warder in charge why they had left off work he was told that it was the Resident's bidding.

White with rage he strode to the Fort. Mr. Warburton, in his spotless white ducks and his neat topee, with a walking-stick in his hand, followed by his dogs, was on the point of

starting out on his afternoon stroll. He had watched Cooper
go and knew that he had taken the road by the river. Cooper
jumped up the steps and went straight up to the Resident.

"I want to know what the hell you mean by countermanding
my order that the prisoners were to work till six," he burst
out, beside himself with fury.

Mr. Warburton opened his cold blue eyes very wide and
assumed an expression of great surprise.

"Are you out of your mind? Are you so ignorant that you do
not know that that is not the way to speak to your official
superior?"

"Oh, go to hell. The prisoners are my pidgin and you've
got no right to interfere. You mind your business and I'll mind
mine. I want to know what the devil you mean by making a
damned fool of me. Every one in the place will know that you've
countermanded my order."

Mr. Warburton kept very cool.

"You had no power to give the order you did. I countermanded it because it was harsh and tyrannical. Believe me, I
have not made half such a damned fool of you as you have
made of yourself."

"You disliked me from the first moment I came here. You've
done everything you could to make the place impossible for me
because I wouldn't lick your boots for you. You got your knife
into me because I wouldn't flatter you."

Cooper, spluttering with rage, was nearing dangerous ground,
and Mr. Warburton's eyes grew on a sudden colder and more
piercing.

"You are wrong. I thought you were a cad, but I was perfectly satisfied with the way you did your work."

"You snob. You damned snob. You thought me a cad because I hadn't been to Eton. Oh, they told me in K.S. what to
expect. Why, don't you know that you're the laughing-stock
of the whole country? I could hardly help bursting into a roar
of laughter when you told your celebrated story about the
Prince of Wales. My God, how they shouted at the club when
they told it. By God, I'd rather be the cad I am than the snob
you are."

He got Mr. Warburton on the raw.

"If you don't get out of my house this minute I shall knock
you down," he cried.

The other came a little closer to him and put his face in his.

"Touch me, touch me," he said. "By God, I'd like to see you hit me. Do you want me to say it again? Snob. Snob."

Cooper was three inches taller than Mr. Warburton, a strong, muscular young man. Mr. Warburton was fat and fifty-four. His clenched fist shot out. Cooper caught him by the arm and pushed him back.

"Don't be a damned fool. Remember I'm not a gentleman. I know how to use my hands."

He gave a sort of hoot, and, grinning all over his pale, sharp face, jumped down the verandah steps. Mr. Warburton, his heart in his anger pounding against his ribs, sank exhausted into a chair. His body tingled as though he had prickly heat. For one horrible moment he thought he was going to cry. But suddenly he was conscious that his head-boy was on the verandah and instinctively regained control of himself. The boy came forward and filled him a glass of whisky and soda. Without a word Mr. Warburton took it and drank it to the dregs.

"What do you want to say to me?" asked Mr. Warburton, trying to force a smile on to his strained lips.

"Tuan, the assistant tuan is a bad man. Abas wishes again to leave him."

"Let him wait a little. I shall write to Kuala Solor and ask that Tuan Cooper should go elsewhere."

"Tuan Cooper is not good with the Malays."

"Leave me."

The boy silently withdrew. Mr. Warburton was left alone with his thoughts. He saw the club at Kuala Solor, the men sitting round the table in the window in their flannels, when the night had driven them in from golf and tennis, drinking whiskies and gin pahits and laughing when they told the celebrated story of the Prince of Wales and himself at Marienbad. He was hot with shame and misery. A snob! They all thought him a snob. And he had always thought them very good fellows, he had always been gentleman enough to let it make no difference to him that they were of very second-rate position. He hated them now. But his hatred for them was nothing compared with his hatred for Cooper. And if it had come to blows Cooper could have thrashed him. Tears of mortification ran down his red, fat face. He sat there for a couple of hours smoking cigarette after cigarette, and he wished he were dead.

At last the boy came back and asked him if he would dress

for dinner. Of course! He always dressed for dinner. He rose
wearily from his chair and put on his stiff shirt and the high
collar. He sat down at the prettily decorated table and was
waited on as usual by the two boys while two others waved
their great fans. Over there in the bungalow, two hundred
yards away, Cooper was eating a filthy meal clad only in a
sarong and a baju. His feet were bare and while he ate he
probably read a detective story. After dinner Mr. Warburton
sat down to write a letter. The Sultan was away, but he wrote,
privately and confidentially, to his representative. Cooper did
his work very well, he said, but the fact was that he couldn't
get on with him. They were getting dreadfully on each other's
nerves and he would look upon it as a very great favour if
Cooper could be transferred to another post.

He despatched the letter next morning by special messenger.
The answer came a fortnight later with the month's mail. It
was a private note and ran as follows:

My dear Warburton:—

*I do not want to answer your letter officially and so I am
writing you a few lines myself. Of course if you insist I will
put the matter up to the Sultan, but I think you would be much
wiser to drop it. I know Cooper is a rough diamond, but he is
capable, and he had a pretty thin time in the war, and I think
he should be given every chance. I think you are a little too much
inclined to attach importance to a man's social position. You
must remember that times have changed. Of course it's a very
good thing for a man to be a gentleman, but it's better that he
should be competent and hard-working. I think if you'll exercise
a little tolerance you'll get on very well with Cooper.*

Yours very sincerely

Richard Temple.

The letter dropped from Mr. Warburton's hand. It was
easy to read between the lines. Dick Temple, whom he had
known for twenty years, Dick Temple, who came from quite
a good county family, thought him a snob and for that reason
had no patience with his request. Mr. Warburton felt on a sudden discouraged with life. The world of which he was a part
had passed away, and the future belonged to a meaner generation. Cooper represented it and Cooper he hated with all his
heart. He stretched out his hand to fill his glass and at the
gesture his head-boy stepped forward.

"I didn't know you were there."

The boy picked up the official letter. Ah, that was why he was waiting.

"Does Tuan Cooper go, Tuan?"

"No."

"There will be a misfortune."

For a moment the words conveyed nothing to his lassitude. But only for a moment. He sat up in his chair and looked at the boy. He was all attention.

"What do you mean by that?"

"Tuan Cooper is not behaving rightly with Abas."

Mr. Warburton shrugged his shoulders. How should a man like Cooper know how to treat servants? Mr. Warburton knew the type: he would be grossly familiar with them at one moment and rude and inconsiderate the next.

"Let Abas go back to his family."

"Tuan Cooper holds back his wages so that he may not run away. He has paid him nothing for three months. I tell him to be patient. But he is angry, he will not listen to reason. If the tuan continues to use him ill there will be a misfortune."

"You were right to tell me."

The fool! Did he know so little of the Malays as to think he could safely injure them? It would serve him damned well right if he got a kris in his back. A kris. Mr. Warburton's heart seemed on a sudden to miss a beat. He had only to let things take their course and one fine day he would be rid of Cooper. He smiled faintly as the phrase, a masterly inactivity, crossed his mind. And now his heart beat a little quicker, for he saw the man he hated lying on his face in a pathway of the jungle with a knife in his back. A fit end for the cad and the bully. Mr. Warburton sighed. It was his duty to warn him and of course he must do it. He wrote a brief and formal note to Cooper asking him to come to the Fort at once.

In ten minutes Cooper stood before him. They had not spoken to one another since the day when Mr. Warburton had nearly struck him. He did not now ask him to sit down.

"Did you wish to see me?" Cooper asked.

He was untidy and none too clean. His face and hands were covered with little red blotches where mosquitoes had bitten him and he had scratched himself till the blood came. His long, thin face bore a sullen look.

"I understand that you are again having trouble with your

servants. Abas, my head-boy's nephew, complains that you have held back his wages for three months. I consider it a most arbitrary proceeding. The lad wishes to leave you, and I certainly do not blame him. I must insist on your paying what is due to him."

"I don't choose that he should leave me. I am holding back his wages as a pledge of his good behaviour."

"You do not know the Malay character. The Malays are very sensitive to injury and ridicule. They are passionate and revengeful. It is my duty to warn you that if you drive this boy beyond a certain point you run a great risk."

Cooper gave a contemptuous chuckle.

"What do you think he'll do?"

"I think he'll kill you."

"Why should you mind?"

"Oh, I wouldn't," replied Mr. Warburton, with a faint laugh. "I should bear it with the utmost fortitude. But I feel the official obligation to give you a proper warning."

"Do you think I'm afraid of a damned nigger?"

"It's a matter of entire indifference to me."

"Well, let me tell you this, I know how to take care of myself; that boy Abas is a dirty, thieving rascal, and if he tries any monkey tricks on me, by God, I'll wring his bloody neck."

"That was all I wished to say to you," said Mr. Warburton. "Good evening."

Mr. Warburton gave him a little nod of dismissal. Cooper flushed, did not for a moment know what to say or do, turned on his heel and stumbled out of the room. Mr. Warburton watched him go with an icy smile on his lips. He had done his duty. But what would he have thought had he known that when Cooper got back to his bungalow, so silent and cheerless, he threw himself down on his bed and in his bitter loneliness on a sudden lost all control of himself? Painful sobs tore his chest and heavy tears rolled down his thin cheeks.

After this Mr. Warburton seldom saw Cooper, and never spoke to him. He read his Times every morning, did his work at the office, took his exercise, dressed for dinner, dined and sat by the river smoking his cheroot. If by chance he ran across Cooper he cut him dead. Each, though never for a moment unconscious of the propinquity, acted as though the other did not exist. Time did nothing to assuage their animosity. They watched one another's actions and each knew what the other did. Though Mr. Warburton had been a keen shot in his youth, with age he had acquired a distaste for killing the wild things of the jungle, but on Sundays and holidays Cooper went out with his gun: if he got something it was a triumph over Mr. Warburton; if not, Mr. Warburton shrugged his shoulders and chuckled. These counter-jumpers trying to be sportsmen! Christmas was a bad time for both of them: they ate their dinners alone, each in his own quarters, and they got deliberately drunk. They were the only white men within two hundred miles and they lived within shouting distance of each other. At the beginning of the year Cooper went down with fever, and when Mr. Warburton caught sight of him again he was surprised to see how thin he had grown. He looked ill and worn. The solitude, so much more unnatural because it was due to no necessity, was getting on his nerves. It was getting on Mr. Warburton's too, and often he could not sleep at night. He lay awake brooding. Cooper was drinking heavily and surely the breaking point was near; but in his dealings with the natives he took care to do nothing that might expose him to his chief's rebuke. They fought a grim and silent battle with one another. It was a test of endurance. The months passed, and neither gave sign of weakening. They were like men dwelling in regions of eternal night, and their souls were oppressed with the knowledge that never would the day dawn for them. It looked as though their lives would continue for ever in this dull and hideous monotony of hatred.

And when at last the inevitable happened it came upon Mr. Warburton with all the shock of the unexpected. Cooper accused the boy Abas of stealing some of his clothes, and when the boy denied the theft took him by the scruff of the neck and kicked him down the steps of the bungalow. The boy demanded his wages, and Cooper flung at his head every word of abuse he knew. If he saw him in the compound in an hour he would hand him over to the police. Next morning the boy waylaid him outside the Fort when he was walking over to his office, and again demanded his wages. Cooper struck him in the face with his clenched fist. The boy fell to the ground and got up with blood streaming from his nose.

Cooper walked on and set about his work. But he could not attend to it. The blow had calmed his irritation, and he knew that he had gone too far. He was worried. He felt ill, miserable and discouraged. In the adjoining office sat Mr. Warburton, and

his impulse was to go and tell him what he had done; he made
a movement in his chair, but he knew with what icy scorn he
would listen to the story. He could see his patronizing smile.
For a moment he had an uneasy fear of what Abas might do.
Warburton had warned him all right. He sighed. What a fool
he had been! But he shrugged his shoulders impatiently. He
did not care; a fat lot he had to live for. It was all Warburton's
fault; if he hadn't put his back up nothing like this would have
happened. Warburton had made life a hell for him from the
start. The snob. But they were all like that: it was because he
was a Colonial. It was a damned shame that he had never got
his commission in the war; he was as good as any one else. They
were a lot of dirty snobs. He was damned if he was going to
knuckle under now. Of course Warburton would hear of what
had happened; the old devil knew everything. He wasn't afraid.
He wasn't afraid of any Malay in Borneo, and Warburton could
go to blazes.

He was right in thinking that Mr. Warburton would know
what had happened. His head-boy told him when he went in
to tiffin.

"Where is your nephew now?"

"I do not know, Tuan. He has gone."

Mr. Warburton remained silent. After luncheon as a rule
he slept a little, but to-day he found himself very wide awake.
His eyes involuntarily sought the bungalow where Cooper was
now resting.

The idiot! Hesitation for a little was in Mr. Warburton's
mind. Did the man know in what peril he was? He supposed he
ought to send for him. But each time he had tried to reason with
Cooper, Cooper had insulted him. Anger, furious anger welled
up suddenly in Mr. Warburton's heart, so that the veins on his
temples stood out and he clenched his fists. The cad had had his
warning. Now let him take what was coming to him. It was
no business of his and if anything happened it was not his fault.
But perhaps they would wish in Kuala Solor that they had
taken his advice and transferred Cooper to another station.

He was strangely restless that night. After dinner he walked
up and down the verandah. When the boy went away to his
own quarters, Mr. Warburton asked him whether anything
had been seen of Abas.

"No, Tuan, I think maybe he has gone to the village of his
mother's brother."

Mr. Warburton gave him a sharp glance, but the boy was looking down and their eyes did not meet. Mr. Warburton went down to the river and sat in his arbour. But peace was denied him. The river flowed ominously silent. It was like a great serpent gliding with sluggish movement towards the sea. And the trees of the jungle over the water were heavy with a breathless menace. No bird sang. No breeze ruffled the leaves of the cassias. All around him it seemed as though something waited.

He walked across the garden to the road. He had Cooper's bungalow in full view from there. There was a light in his sitting-room and across the road floated the sound of rag-time. Cooper was playing his gramophone. Mr. Warburton shuddered; he had never got over his instinctive dislike of that instrument. But for that he would have gone over and spoken to Cooper. He turned and went back to his own house. He read late into the night, and at last he slept. But he did not sleep very long, he had terrible dreams, and he seemed to be awakened by a cry. Of course that was a dream too, for no cry—from the bungalow for instance—could be heard in his room. He lay awake till dawn. Then he heard hurried steps and the sound of voices, his head-boy burst suddenly into the room without his fez, and Mr. Warburton's heart stood still.

"Tuan, Tuan."

Mr. Warburton jumped out of bed.

"I'll come at once."

He put on his slippers, and in his sarong and pyjama-jacket walked across his compound and into Cooper's. Cooper was lying in bed, with his mouth open, and a kris sticking in his heart. He had been killed in his sleep. Mr. Warburton started, but not because he had not expected to see just such a sight, he started because he felt in himself a sudden glow of exultation. A great burden had been lifted from his shoulders.

Cooper was quite cold. Mr. Warburton took the kris out of the wound, it had been thrust in with such force that he had to use an effort to get it out, and looked at it. He recognized it. It was a kris that a dealer had offered him some weeks before and which he knew Cooper had bought.

"Where is Abas?" he asked sternly.

"Abas is at the village of his mother's brother."

The sergeant of the native police was standing at the foot of the bed.

"Take two men and go to the village and arrest him."

Mr. Warburton did what was immediately necessary. With set face he gave orders. His words were short and peremptory. Then he went back to the Fort. He shaved and had his bath, dressed and went into the dining-room. By the side of his plate The Times in its wrapper lay waiting for him. He helped himself to some fruit. The head-boy poured out his tea while the second handed him a dish of eggs. Mr. Warburton ate with a good appetite. The head-boy waited.

"What is it?" asked Mr. Warburton.

"Tuan, Abas, my nephew, was in the house of his mother's brother all night. It can be proved. His uncle will swear that he did not leave the kampong."

Mr. Warburton turned upon him with a frown.

"Tuan Cooper was killed by Abas. You know it as well as I know it. Justice must be done."

"Tuan, you would not hang him?"

Mr. Warburton hesitated an instant, and though his voice remained set and stern a change came into his eyes. It was a flicker which the Malay was quick to notice and across his own eyes flashed an answering look of understanding.

"The provocation was very great. Abas will be sentenced to a term of imprisonment." There was a pause while Mr. Warburton helped himself to marmalade. "When he has served a part of his sentence in prison I will take him into this house as a boy. You can train him in his duties. I have no doubt that in the house of Tuan Cooper he got into bad habits."

"Shall Abas give himself up, Tuan?"

"It would be wise of him."

The boy withdrew. Mr. Warburton took his Times and neatly slit the wrapper. He loved to unfold the heavy, rustling pages. The morning, so fresh and cool, was delicious and for a moment his eyes wandered out over his garden with a friendly glance. A great weight had been lifted from his mind. He turned to the columns in which were announced the births, deaths, and marriages. That was what he always looked at first. A name he knew caught his attention. Lady Ormskirk had had a son at last. By George, how pleased the old dowager must be! He would write her a note of congratulation by the next mail.

Abas would make a very good house-boy.

That fool Cooper!

THE YELLOW STREAK

THE two prahus were dropping easily down-stream, one a few yards ahead of the other, and in the first sat the two white men. After seven weeks on the rivers they were glad to know that they would lodge that night in a civilized house. To Izzart, who had been in Borneo since the war, the Dyak houses and their feasts were of course an old story; but Campion, though new to the country and at first amused by the strangeness, hankered too now for chairs to sit on and a bed to sleep in. The Dyaks were hospitable, but no one could say that there was much comfort to be found in their houses, and there was a monotony in the entertainment they offered a guest which presently grew somewhat wearisome. Every evening, as the travellers reached the landing-place, the headman, bearing a flag, and the more important members of the household, came down to the river to fetch them. They were led up to the long-house—a village really under one roof, built on piles, to which access was obtained by climbing up the trunk of a tree rudely notched into steps—and to the beating of drums and gongs walked up and down the whole length of it in long procession. On both sides serried throngs of brown people sat on their haunches and stared silently as the white men passed. Clean mats were unrolled and the guests seated themselves. The headman brought a live chicken and, holding it by the legs, waved it three times over their heads, called the spirits loudly to witness and uttered an invocation. Then various persons brought eggs. Arak was drunk. A girl, a very small shy thing with the grace of a flower but with something hieratic in her immobile face, held a cup to the white man's lips till it was empty and then a great shout arose. The men began to dance, one after the other, each treading his little measure, with his shield and his parang, to the accompaniment of drum and gong. After this had gone on for some time the visitors were taken into one of the rooms that led off the long platform on which was led the common life of the household and found their supper prepared for them. The girls fed them with Chinese spoons. Then every one grew a little drunk and they all talked till the early hours of the morning.

But now their journey was done and they were on their way to the coast. They had started at dawn. The river then was very shallow and ran clear and bright over a shingly bottom; the trees leaned over it so that above there was only a strip of blue sky; but now it had broadened out, and the men were poling no longer but paddling. The trees, bamboos, wild sago like huge bunches of ostrich feathers, trees with enormous leaves and trees with feathery foliage like the acacia, coconut trees and areca palms, with their long straight white stems, the trees on the banks were immensely and violently luxuriant. Here and there, gaunt and naked, was the bare skeleton of a tree struck by lightning or dead of old age, and its whiteness against all that green was vivid. Here and there, rival kings of the forest, tall trees soared above the common level of the jungle. Then there were the parasites; in the fork of two branches great tufts of lush green leaves, or flowering creepers that covered the spreading foliage like a bride's veil; sometimes they wound round a tall trunk, a sheath of splendour, and threw long flowering arms from branch to branch. There was something thrilling in the passionate wildness of that eager growth; it had the daring abandon of the nomad rioting in the train of the god.

The day wore on and now the heat was no longer so oppressive. Campion looked at the shabby silver watch on his wrist. It could not be long now before they reached their destination.

"What sort of a chap is Hutchinson?" he asked.

"I don't know him. I believe he's a very good sort."

Hutchinson was the Resident in whose house they were to spend the night and they had sent on a Dyak in a canoe to announce their arrival.

"Well, I hope he's got some whisky. I've drunk enough Arak to last me a lifetime."

Campion was a mining engineer, whom the Sultan on his way to England had met at Singapore and finding him at a loose end had commissioned to go to Sembulu and see whether he could discover any mineral which might be profitably worked. He sent Willis, the Resident at Kuala Solor, instructions to afford him every facility and Willis had put him in the care of Izzart because Izzart spoke both Malay and Dyak like a native. This was the third trip they had made into the interior and now Campion was to go home with his reports. They were to catch the Sultan Ahmed which was due to pass the mouth of the river at dawn on the next day but one, and with any luck should reach Kuala Solor on the same afternoon. They were both glad to get back to it. There was tennis and golf there, and the club with its billiard tables, food which was relatively good, and the comforts of civilization. Izzart was glad too that he would have other society than Campion's. He gave him a sidelong glance. He was a little man with a big, bald head, and though certainly fifty, strong and wiry; he had quick, shining blue eyes and a stubbly, grey moustache. He was seldom without an old briar pipe between his broken and discoloured teeth. He was neither clean nor neat, his khaki shorts were ragged and his singlet torn; he was wearing now a battered topee. He had knocked about the world since he was eighteen and had been in South Africa, in China and in Mexico. He was good company; he could tell a story well, and he was prepared to drink and drink again with any one he met. They had got on very well together, but Izzart had never felt quite at home with him. Though they joked and laughed together, got drunk together, Izzart felt that there was no intimacy between them: for all the cordiality of their relations they remained nothing but acquaintances. He was very sensitive to the impression he made on others, and behind Campion's joviality he had felt a certain coolness; those shining blue eyes had summed him up; and it vaguely irritated Izzart that Campion had formed an opinion of him, and he did not quite know what it was. He was exasperated by the possibility that this common little man did not think entirely well of him. He desired to be liked and admired. He wanted to be popular. He wished the people he met to take an inordinate fancy to him so that he could either reject them or a trifle condescendingly bestow his friendship on them. His inclination was to be familiar with all and sundry, but he was held back by the fear of a rebuff; sometimes he had been uneasily conscious that his effusiveness surprised the persons he lavished it on.

By some chance he had never met Hutchinson, though of course he knew all about him just as Hutchinson knew all about *him*, and they would have many common friends to talk of. Hutchinson had been at Winchester, and Izzart was glad that he could tell him that he had been at Harrow.

The prahu rounded a bend in the river and suddenly, standing on a slight eminence, they saw the bungalow. In a few minutes they caught sight of the landing-stage and on it, among a little group of natives, a figure in white waving to them.

Hutchinson was a tall, stout man with a red face. His appearance led you to expect that he was breezy and self-confident, so that it was not a little surprising to discover quickly that he was diffident and even a trifle shy. When he shook hands with his guests—Izzart introduced himself and then Campion —and led them up the pathway to the bungalow, though he was plainly anxious to be civil it was not hard to see that he found it difficult to make conversation. He took them out on to the verandah and here they found on the table glasses and whisky and soda. They made themselves comfortable on long chairs. Izzart, conscious of Hutchinson's slight embarrassment with strangers, expanded; he was very hearty and voluble. He began to speak of their common acquaintances at Kuala Solor, and he managed very soon to slip in casually the information that he had been at Harrow.

"You were at Winchester, weren't you?" he asked.

"Yes."

"I wonder if you knew George Parker. He was in my regiment. He was at Winchester. I daresay he was younger than you."

Izzart felt that it was a bond between them that they had been at these particular schools and it excluded Campion, who obviously had enjoyed no such advantage. They drank two or three whiskies. Izzart in half an hour began to call his host Hutchie. He talked a good deal about "my regiment" in which he had got his company during the war, and what good fellows his brother officers were. He mentioned two or three names which could hardly be unknown to Hutchinson. They were not the sort of people that Campion was likely to have come across and he was not sorry to administer to him a neat snub when he claimed acquaintance with some one he spoke of.

"Billie Meadows? I knew a fellow called Billie Meadows in Sinaloa many years ago," said Campion.

"Oh, I shouldn't think it could be the same," said Izzart, with a smile. "Billie's by way of being a peer of the realm. He's the Lord Meadows who races. Don't you remember, he owned Spring Carrots?"

Dinner-time was approaching and after a wash and brush-up they drank a couple of gin pahits. They sat down. Hutchinson had not been to Kuala Solor for the best part of a year, and had not seen another white man for three months. He was anxious to make the most of his visitors. He could give them no wine, but there was plenty of whisky and after dinner he brought out a precious bottle of Benedictine. They were very gay. They laughed and talked a great deal. Izzart was getting on famously. He thought he had never liked a fellow more than Hutchinson and he pressed him to come down to Kuala Solor as soon as he could. They would have a wonderful beano. Campion was left out of the conversation by Izzart with the faintly malicious intention of putting him in his place, and by Hutchinson through shyness; and presently, after yawning a good deal, he said he would go to bed. Hutchinson showed him to his room and when he returned Izzart said to him:

"You don't want to turn in yet, do you?"

"Not on your life. Let's have another drink."

They sat and talked. They both grew a little drunk. Presently Hutchinson told Izzart that he lived with a Malay girl and had a couple of children by her. He had told them to keep out of sight while Campion was there.

"I expect she's asleep now," said Hutchinson, with a glance at the door which Izzart knew led into his room, "but I'd like you to see the kiddies in the morning."

Just then a faint wail was heard and Hutchinson, with a "Hulloa, the little devil's awake," went to the door and opened it. In a moment or two he came out of the room with a child in his arms. A woman followed him.

"He's cutting his teeth," said Hutchinson. "It makes him restless."

The woman wore a sarong and a thin white jacket and she was barefoot. She was young, with fine dark eyes, and she gave Izzart when he spoke to her a bright and pleasant smile. She sat down and lit a cigarette. She answered the civil questions Izzart put to her without embarrassment but also without effusion. Hutchinson asked her if she would have a whisky and soda, but she refused. When the two men began to talk again in English she sat on quite quietly, faintly rocking herself in her chair, and occupied with none could tell what calm thoughts.

"She's a very good girl," said Hutchinson. "She looks after the house and she's no trouble. Of course it's the only thing to do in a place like this."

"I shall never do it myself," said Izzart. "After all, one may want to get married and then it means all sorts of botherations."

"But who wants to get married? What a life for a white woman. I wouldn't ask a white woman to live here for anything in the world."

"Of course it's a matter of taste. If I have any kiddies I'm going to see that they have a white mother."

Hutchinson looked down at the little dark-skinned child he held in his arms. He gave a faint smile.

"It's funny how you get to like them," he said. "When they're your own it doesn't seem to matter that they've got a touch of the tar-brush."

The woman gave the child a look and getting up said she would take it back to bed.

"I should think we'd better all turn in," said Hutchinson. "God knows what the time is."

Izzart went to his room and threw open the shutters which his boy Hassan, whom he was travelling with, had closed. Blowing out the candle so that it should not attract the mosquitoes, he sat down at the window and looked at the soft night. The whisky he had drunk made him feel very wide awake, and he was not inclined to go to bed. He took off his ducks, put on a sarong and lit a cheroot. His good-humour was gone. It was the sight of Hutchinson looking fondly at the half-caste child which had upset him.

"They've got no right to have them," he said to himself. "They've got no chance in the world. Ever."

He passed his hands reflectively along his bare and hairy legs. He shuddered a little. Though he had done everything he could to develop the calves, his legs were like broomsticks.

He hated them. He was uneasily conscious of them all the time. They were like a native's. Of course they were the very legs for a top-boot. In his uniform he had looked very well. He was a tall, powerful man, over six feet high, and he had a neat black moustache and neat black hair. His dark eyes were fine and mobile. He was a good-looking fellow and he knew it, and he dressed well, shabbily when shabbiness was good form, and smartly when the occasion demanded. He had loved the army, and it was a bitter blow to him when, at the end of the war, he could not remain in it. His ambitions were simple. He wanted to have two thousand a year, give smart little dinners, go to parties and wear a uniform. He hankered after London.

Of course his mother lived there, and his mother cramped his style. He wondered how on earth he could produce her if ever he got engaged to the girl of good family (with a little money) whom he was looking for to make his wife. Because his father had been dead so long and during the later part of his career was stationed in the most remote of the Malay States, Izzart felt fairly sure that no one in Sembulu knew anything about her, but he lived in terror lest some one, running across her in London, should write over to tell people that she was a half-caste. She had been a beautiful creature when Izzart's father, an engineer in the Government Service, had married her; but now she was a fat old woman with grey hair who sat about all day smoking cigarettes. Izzart was twelve years old when his father died and then he could speak Malay much more fluently than English. An aunt offered to pay for his education and Mrs. Izzart accompanied her son to England. She lived habitually in furnished apartments, and her rooms with their Oriental draperies and Malay silver were over-heated and stuffy. She was for ever in trouble with her land-ladies because she would leave cigarette-ends about. Izzart hated the way she made friends with them: she would be shockingly familiar with them for a time, then there would be a falling-out, and after a violent scene she would flounce out of the house. Her only amusement was the pictures, and to these she went every day in the week. At home she wore an old and tawdry dressing-gown, but when she went out she dressed herself—but, oh, how untidily—in extravagant colours, so that it was a mortification to her dapper son. He quarrelled with her frequently, she made him impatient and he was ashamed of her; and yet he felt for her a deep tenderness; it was almost a physical bond between them, something stronger than the ordinary feeling of mother and son, so that notwithstanding the failings that exasperated him she was the only person in the world with whom he felt entirely at home.

It was owing to his father's position and his own knowledge of Malay, for his mother always spoke it to him, that after the war, finding himself with nothing to do, he had managed to enter the service of the Sultan of Sembulu. He had been a success. He played games well, he was strong and a good athlete; in the rest-house at Kuala Solor were the cups which he had won at Harrow for running and jumping, and to these he had added since others for golf and tennis. With his abundant fund of small-talk he was an asset at parties and his cheeriness made things go. He ought to have been happy and he was wretched. He wanted so much to be popular, and he had an impression, stronger than ever at this moment, that popularity escaped him. He wondered whether by any chance the men at Kuala Solor with whom he was so hail fellow well met suspected that he had native blood in him. He knew very well what to expect if they ever found out. They wouldn't say he was gay and friendly then, they would say he was damned familiar; and they would say he was inefficient and careless, as the half-castes were, and when he talked of marrying a white woman they would snigger. Oh, it was so unfair! What difference could it make, that drop of native blood in his veins, and yet because of it they would always be on the watch for the expected failure at the critical moment. Every one knew that you couldn't rely on Eurasians, sooner or later they would let you down; he knew it too, but now he asked himself whether they didn't fail because failure was expected of them. They were never given a chance, poor devils.

But a cock crew loudly. It must be very late and he was beginning to feel chilly. He got into bed. When Hassan brought him his tea next morning he had a racking headache and when he went in to breakfast he could not look at the porridge and the bacon and eggs which were set before him. Hutchinson too was feeling none too well.

"I fancy we made rather a night of it," said his host, with a smile to conceal his faint embarrassment.

"I feel like hell, ' said Izzart.

"I'm going to breakfast off a whisky and soda myself," added Hutchinson.

Izzart asked for nothing better, and it was with distaste that they watched Campion eat with healthy appetite a substantial meal. Campion chaffed them.

"By God, Izzart, you're looking green about the gills," he said. "I never saw such a filthy colour."

Izzart flushed. His swarthiness was always a sensitive point with him. But he forced himself to give a cheery laugh.

"You see, I had a Spanish grandmother," he answered, "and when I'm under the weather it always comes out. I remember at Harrow I fought a boy and licked him because he called me a damned half-caste."

"You are dark," said Hutchinson. "Do Malays ever ask you if you have any native blood in you?"

"Yes, damn their impudence."

A boat with their kit had started early in the morning in order to get to the mouth of the river before them and tell the skipper of the Sultan Ahmed, if by chance he arrived before he was due, that they were on their way. Campion and Izzart were to set out immediately after tiffin in order to arrive at the place where they were to spend the night before the Bore passed. A Bore is a tidal wave that, by reason of a peculiarity in the lie of the land, surges up certain rivers, and there happened to be one on the river on which they were travelling. Hutchinson had talked to them of it the night before and Campion, who had never seen such a thing, was much interested.

"This is one of the best in Borneo. It's worth looking at," said Hutchinson.

He told them how the natives, waiting the moment, rode it and were borne up the river on its crest at a breathless and terrifying speed. He had done it once himself.

"Never no more for me," he said. "I was scared out of my wits."

"I should like to try it once," said Izzart.

"It's exciting enough, but my word, when you're in a flimsy dug-out and you know that if the native doesn't get the right moment you'll be flung out in that seething torrent and you won't have a chance in a million . . . no, it's not my idea of sport."

"I've shot a good many rapids in my day," said Campion.

"Rapids be damned. You wait till you see the Bore. It's one of the most terrifying things I know. D'you know that at least a dozen natives are drowned in it in this river alone every year?"

They lounged about on the verandah most of the morning and Hutchinson showed them the court-house. Then gin pahits were served. They drank two or three. Izzart began to feel himself, and when at length tiffin was ready he found that he had an excellent appetite. Hutchinson had boasted of his Malay curry and when the steaming, succulent dishes were placed before them they all set to ravenously. Hutchinson pressed them to drink.

"You've got nothing to do but sleep. Why shouldn't you get drunk?"

He could not bear to let them go so soon, it was good after so long to have white men to talk to, and he lingered over the meal. He urged them to eat. They would have a filthy meal that night at the long-house and nothing to drink but Arak. They had better make hay while the sun shone. Campion suggested once or twice that they should start, but Hutchinson, and Izzart too, for now he was feeling very happy and comfortable, assured him there was plenty of time. Hutchinson sent for his precious bottle of Benedictine. They had made a hole in it last night; they might as well finish it before they went.

When at last he walked down with them to the river they were all very merry and none of them was quite steady on his legs. Over the middle of the boat was an attap awning and under this Hutchinson had had a mattress laid. The crew were prisoners who had been marched down from the jail to row the white men, and they wore dingy sarongs with the prison mark. They waited at their oars. Izzart and Campion shook hands with Hutchinson and threw themselves down on the mattress. The boat pushed off. The turbid river, wide and placid, glistened in the heat of that brilliant afternoon like polished brass. In the distance ahead of them they could see the bank with its tangle of green trees. They felt drowsy, but Izzart at least found a curious enjoyment in resisting for a little while the heaviness that was creeping over him, and he made up his mind that he would not let himself fall asleep till he had finished his cheroot. At last the stub began to burn his fingers and he flung it into the river.

"I'm going to have a wonderful snooze," he said.

"What about the Bore?" asked Campion.

"Oh, that's all right. We needn't worry about that."

He gave a long and noisy yawn. His limbs felt like lead. He had one moment in which he was conscious of his delicious drowsiness and then he knew nothing more. Suddenly he was awakened by Campion shaking him.

"I say, what's that?"

"What's what?"

He spoke irritably, for sleep was still heavy upon him, but with his eyes he followed Campion's gesture. He could hear nothing, but a good way off he saw two or three white-crested waves following one another. They did not look very alarming.

"Oh, I suppose that's the Bore."

"What are we going to do about it?" cried Campion.

Izzart was scarcely yet quite awake. He smiled at the concern in Campion's voice.

"Don't worry. These fellows know all about it. They know exactly what to do. We may get a bit splashed."

But while they were saying these few words the Bore came nearer, very quickly, with a roar like the roar of an angry sea, and Izzart saw that the waves were much higher than he had thought. He did not like the look of them and he tightened his belt so that his shorts should not slip down if the boat were upset. In a moment the waves were upon them. It was a great wall of water that seemed to tower over them, and it might have been ten or twelve feet high, but you could measure it only with your horror. It was quite plain that no boat could weather it. The first wave dashed over them, drenching them all, half filling the boat with water, and then immediately another wave struck them. The boatmen began to shout. They pulled madly at their oars and the steersman yelled an order. But in that surging torrent they were helpless, and it was frightening to see how soon they lost all control of the boat. The force of the water turned it broadside on and it was carried along, helter-skelter, upon the crest of the Bore. Another great wave dashed over them and the boat began to sink. Izzart and Campion scrambled out of the covered place in which they had been lying and suddenly the boat gave way under their feet and they found themselves struggling in the water. It surged and stormed around them. Izzart's first impulse was to swim for the shore, but his boy, Hassan, shouted

to him to cling to the boat. For a minute or two they all did
this.

"Are you all right?" Campion shouted to him.

"Yes, enjoying the bath," said Izzart.

He imagined that the waves would pass by as the Bore
ascended the river and in a few minutes at the outside they
would find themselves in calm water once more. He forgot
that they were being carried along on its crest. The waves
dashed over them. They clung to the gunwale and the base of
the structure which supported the attap awning. Then a
larger wave caught the boat and it turned over, falling upon
them so that they lost their hold; there seemed nothing but a
slippery bottom to cling to and Izzart's hands slithered helplessly on the greasy surface. But the boat continued to turn
and he made a desperate grab at the gunwale, only to feel
it slip out of his hands as the turn went on, then he caught the
framework of the awning, and still it turned, turned slowly
right round and once more he sought for a hand-hold on the
bottom. The boat went round and round with a horrible regularity. He thought this must be because every one was clinging to one side of it, and he tried to make the crew go round to
the other. He could not make them undertand. Every one was
shouting and the waves beat against them with a dull and
angry roar. Each time the boat rolled over on them Izzart
was pushed under water, only to come up again as the gunwale
and the framework of the awning gave him something to cling
to. The struggle was awful. Presently he began to get terribly
out of breath, and he felt his strength leaving him. He knew
that he could not hold on much longer, but he did not feel
frightened, for his fatigue by now was so great that he did not
very much care what happened. Hassan was by his side and he
told him he was growing very tired. He thought the best thing
was to make a dash for the shore, it did not look more than
sixty yards away, but Hassan begged him not to. Still they
were being carried along amid those seething, pounding waves.
The boat went round and round and they scrambled over it
like squirrels in a cage. Izzart swallowed a lot of water. He felt
he was very nearly done. Hassan could not help him, but it
was a comfort that he was there, for Izzart knew that his
boy, used to the water all his life, was a powerful swimmer.
Then, Izzart did not know why, for a minute or two the boat
held bottom downwards, so that he was able to hold on to

the gunwale. It was a precious thing to be able to get his breath. At that moment two dug-outs, with Malays in them riding the Bore, passed swiftly by them. They shouted for help, but the Malays averted their faces and went on. They saw the white men and did not want to be concerned in any trouble that might befall them. It was agonizing to see them go past, callous and indifferent in their safety. But on a sudden the boat rolled round again, round and round, slowly, and the miserable, exhausting scramble repeated itself. It took the heart out of you. But the short respite had helped Izzart and he was able to struggle a little longer. Then once more he found himself so terribly out of breath that he thought his chest would burst. His strength was all gone and he did not know now whether he had enough to try to swim for the shore. Suddenly he heard a cry.

"Izzart, Izzart. Help. Help."

It was Campion's voice. It was a scream of agony. It sent a shock all through Izzart's nerves. Campion, Campion, what did he care for Campion? Fear seized him, a blind, animal fear, and it gave him a new strength. He did not answer.

"Help me, quick, quick," he said to Hassan.

Hassan understood him at once. By a miracle one of the oars was floating quite close to them and he pushed it into Izzart's reach. He placed a hand under Izzart's arm and they struck away from the boat. Izzart's heart was pounding and his breath came with difficulty. He felt horribly weak. The waves beat in his face. The bank looked dreadfully far away. He did not think he could ever reach it. Suddenly the boy cried that he could touch bottom and Izzart put down his legs; but he could feel nothing; he swam a few more exhausted strokes, his eyes fixed on the bank, and then, trying again, felt his feet sink into thick mud. He was thankful. He floundered on and there was the bank within reach of his hands, black mud in which he sank to his knees; he scrambled up, desperate to get out of the cruel water, and when he came to the top he found a little flat with tall rank grass all about it. He and Hassan sank down on it and lay for a while stretched out like dead men. They were so tired that they could not move. They were covered with black mud from head to foot.

But presently Izzart's mind began to work, and a pang of anguish on a sudden shook him. Campion was drowned. It was awful. He did not know how he was going to explain the disaster when he got back to Kuala Solor. They would blame him for it; he ought to have remembered the Bore and told the steersman to make for the bank and tie up the boat when he saw it coming. It wasn't his fault, it was the steersman's, he knew the river: why in God's name hadn't he had the sense to get into safety? How could he have expected that it was possible to ride that horrible torrent? Izzart's limbs shook as he remembered the wall of seething water that rushed down upon them. He must get the body and take it back to Kuala Solor. He wondered whether any of the crew were drowned too. He felt too weak to move, but Hassan now rose and wrung the water out of his sarong; he looked over the river and quickly turned to Izzart.

"Tuan, a boat is coming."

The lalang grass prevented Izzart from seeing anything.

"Shout to them," he said.

Hassan slipped out of view and made his way along the branch of a tree that overhung the water; he cried out and waved. Presently Izzart heard voices. There was a rapid conversation between the boy and the occupants of the boat and then the boy came back.

"They saw us capsize, Tuan," he said, "and they came as soon as the Bore passed. There's a long-house on the other side. If you will cross the river they will give us sarongs and food and we can sleep there."

Izzart for a moment felt that he could not again trust himself on the face of the treacherous water.

"What about the other tuan?" he asked.

"They do not know."

"If he's drowned they must find the body."

"Another boat has gone up-stream."

Izzart did not know what to do. He was numb. Hassan put his arm round his shoulder and raised him to his feet. He made his way through the thick grass to the edge of the water and there he saw a dug-out with two Dyaks in it. The river now once more was calm and sluggish; the great wave had passed and no one would have dreamed that so short a while before the placid surface was like a stormy sea. The Dyaks repeated to him what they had already told the boy. Izzart could not bring himself to speak. He felt that if he said a word he would burst out crying. Hassan helped him to get in, and the Dyaks began to pull across. He fearfully wanted something to smoke.

but his cigarettes and his matches, both in a hip-pocket, were soaking. The passage of the river seemed endless. The night fell and when they reached the bank the first stars were shining. He stepped ashore and one of the Dyaks took him up to the long-house. But Hassan seized the paddle he had dropped and with the other pushed out into the stream. Two or three men and some children came down to meet Izzart and he climbed to the house amid a babel of conversation. He went up the ladder and was led with greetings and excited comment to the space where the young men slept. Rattan mats were hurriedly laid to make him a couch and he sank down on them. Some one brought him a jar of Arak and he took a long drink; it was rough and fiery, burning his throat, but it warmed his heart. He slipped off his shirt and trousers and put on a dry sarong which some one lent him. By chance he caught sight of the yellow new moon lying on her back, and it gave him a keen, almost a sensual, pleasure. He could not help thinking that he might at that moment be a corpse floating up the river with the tide. The moon had never looked to him more lovely. He began to feel hungry and he asked for rice. One of the women went into a room to prepare it. He was more himself now and he began to think again of the explanations he would make at Kuala Solor. No one could really blame him because he had gone to sleep; he certainly wasn't drunk, Hutchinson would bear him out there, and how was he to suspect that the steersman would be such a damned fool? It was just rotten luck. But he couldn't think of Campion without a shudder. At last a platter of rice was brought him and he was just about to start eating when a man ran hurriedly along and came up to him.

"The tuan's come," he cried.

"What tuan?"

He jumped up. There was a commotion about the doorway and he stepped forward. Hassan was coming quickly towards him out of the darkness, and then he heard a voice.

"Izzart: Are you there?"

Campion advanced towards him.

"Well, here we are again. By God, that was a pretty near thing, wasn't it? You seem to have made yourself nice and comfortable. My heavens, I could do with a drink."

His dank clothes clung round him and he was muddy and dishevelled. But he was in excellent spirits.

"I didn't know where the hell they were bringing me. I'd

made up my mind that I should have to spend the night on
the bank. I thought you were drowned."

"Here's some Arak," said Izzart.

Campion put his mouth to the jar and drank and spluttered
and drank again.

"Muck, but by God it's strong." He looked at Izzart with
a grin of his broken and discoloured teeth. "I say, old man,
you look as though you'd be all the better for a wash."

"I'll wash later."

"All right, so will I. Tell them to get me a sarong. How did
you get out?" He did not wait for an answer. "I thought I
was done for. I owe my life to these two sportsmen here." He
indicated with a cheery nod two of the Dyak prisoners whom
Izzart vaguely recognized as having been part of their crew.
"They were hanging on to that blasted boat on each side of
me and somehow they cottoned on to it that I was down and
out. I couldn't have lasted another minute. They made signs
to me that we could risk having a shot at getting to the bank,
but I didn't think I had the strength. By George, I've never
been so blown in all my life. I don't know how they managed
it, but somehow they got hold of the mattress we'd been lying
on, and they made it into a roll. They're sportsmen, they are.
I don't know why they didn't just save themselves without
bothering about me. They gave it me. I thought it a damned
poor lifebelt, but I saw the force of the proverb about a drowning man clutching at a straw. I caught hold of the damned
thing and between them somehow or other they dragged me
ashore."

The danger from which he had escaped made Campion excited and voluble; but Izzart hardly listened to what he said.
He heard once more, as distinctly as though the words rang
now through the air, Campion's agonized cry for help. and he
felt sick with terror. The blind panic raced down his nerves.
Campion was talking still, but was he talking to conceal his
thoughts? Izzart looked into those bright blue eyes and sought
to read the sense behind the flow of words. Was there a hard
glint in them or something of cynical mockery? Did he know
that Izzart, leaving him to his fate, had cut and run? He
flushed deeply. After all, what was there that he could have
done? At such a moment it was each for himself and the devil
take the hindmost. But what would they say in Kuala Solor if
Campion told them that Izzart had deserted him? He ought

to have stayed, he wished now with all his heart that he had, but then, then it was stronger than himself, he couldn't. Could any one blame him? No one who had seen that fierce and seething torrent. Oh, the water and the exhaustion, so that he could have cried!

"If you're as hungry as I am you'd better have a tuck in at this rice," he said.

Campion ate voraciously, but when Izzart had taken a mouthful or two he found that he had no appetite. Campion talked and talked. Izzart listened suspiciously. He felt that he must be alert and he drank more Arak. He began to feel a little drunk.

"I shall get into the devil of a row at K.S.," he said tentatively.

"I don't know why."

"I was told off to look after you. They won't think it was very clever of me to let you get nearly drowned."

"It wasn't your fault. It was the fault of the damned fool of a steersman. After all, the important thing is that we're saved. By George, I thought I was finished once. I shouted out to you. I don't know if you heard me."

"No, I didn't hear anything. There was such a devil of a row, wasn't there?"

"Perhaps you'd got away before. I don't know exactly when you did get away."

Izzart looked at him sharply. Was it his fancy that there was an odd look in Campion's eyes?

"There was such an awful confusion," he said. "I was just about down and out. My boy threw me over an oar. He gave me to understand you were all right. He told me you'd got ashore."

The oar! He ought to have given Campion the oar and told Hassan, the strong swimmer, to give *him* his help. Was it his fancy again that Campion gave him a quick and searching glance?

"I wish I could have been of more use to you," said Izzart.

"Oh, I'm sure you had enough to do to look after yourself," answered Campion.

The headman brought them cups of Arak, and they both drank a great deal. Izzart's head began to spin and he suggested that they should turn in. Beds had been prepared for them and mosquito nets fixed. They were to set out at dawn

on the rest of their journey down the river. Campion's bed was
next to his, and in a few minutes he heard him snoring. He had
fallen asleep the moment he lay down. The young men of the
long-house and the prisoners of the boat's crew went on talking
late into the night. Izzart's head now was aching horribly and
he could not think. When Hassan roused him as day broke
it seemed to him that he had not slept at all. Their clothes
had been washed and dried, but they were bedraggled objects
as they walked along the narrow pathway to the river where
the prahu was waiting for them. They rowed leisurely. The
morning was lovely and the great stretch of placid water
gleamed in the early light.

"By George, it's fine to be alive," said Campion.

He was grubby and unshaved. He took long breaths and
his twisted mouth was half open with a grin. You could tell
that he found the air singularly good to breathe. He was delighted with the blue sky and the sunshine and the greenness
of the trees. Izzart hated him. He was sure that this morning
there was a difference in his manner. He did not know what
to do. He had a mind to throw himself on his mercy. He had
behaved like a cad, but he was sorry, he would give anything
to have the chance again, but any one might have done what
he did, and if Campion gave him away he was ruined. He could
never stay in Sembulu; his name would be mud in Borneo and
the Straits Settlements. If he made his confession to Campion
he could surely get Campion to promise to hold his tongue.
But would he keep his promise? He looked at him, a shifty
little man; how could he be relied on? Izzart thought of what
he had said the night before. It wasn't the truth, of course,
but who could know that? At all events who could prove that
he hadn't honestly thought that Campion was safe? Whatever
Campion said it was only his word against Izzart's; he could
laugh and shrug his shoulders and say that Campion had lost
his head and didn't know what he was talking about. Besides,
it wasn't certain that Campion hadn't accepted his story; in
that frightful struggle for life he could be very sure of nothing.
He had a temptation to go back to the subject, but was afraid
if he did that he would excite suspicion in Campion's mind. He
must hold his tongue. That was his only chance of safety. And
when they got to K.S. he would get in his story first.

"I should be completely happy now," said Campion, "if I
only had something to smoke."

"We shall be able to get some stinkers on board."

Campion gave a little laugh.

"Human beings are very unreasonable," he said. "At the first moment I was so glad to be alive that I thought of nothing else, but now I'm beginning to regret the loss of my notes and my photographs and my shaving tackle."

Izzart formulated the thought which had lurked at the back of his mind, but which all through the night he had refused to admit into his consciousness.

"I wish to God he'd been drowned. Then I'd have been safe."

"There she is," cried Campion suddenly.

Izzart looked round. They were at the mouth of the river and there was the Sultan Ahmed waiting for them. Izzart's heart sank: he had forgotten that she had an English skipper and that he would have to be told the story of their adventure. What would Campion say? The skipper was called Bredon and Izzart had met him often at Kuala Solor. He was a little bluff man, with a black moustache, and a breezy manner.

"Hurry up," he called out to them, as they rowed up, "I've been waiting for you since dawn." But when they climbed on board his face fell. "Hulloa, what's the matter with you?"

"Give us a drink and you shall hear all about it," said Campion, with his crooked grin.

"Come along."

They sat down under the awning. On a table were glasses, a bottle of whisky and soda water. The skipper gave an order and in a few minutes they were noisily under way.

"We were caught in the Bore," said Izzart.

He felt he must say something. His mouth was horribly dry notwithstanding the drink.

"Were you, by Jove? You're lucky not to have been drowned. What happened?"

He addressed himself to Izzart because he knew him, but it was Campion who answered. He related the whole incident, accurately, and Izzart listened with strained attention. Campion spoke in the plural when he told the early part of the story, and then, as he came to the moment when they were thrown into the water, changed to the singular. At first it was what *they* had done and now it was what happened to *him*. He left Izzart out of it. Izzart did not know whether to be relieved or alarmed. Why did he not mention him? Was it because in that mortal struggle for life he had thought of nothing but himself or—did he *know?*

"And what happened to you?" said Captain Bredon, turning to Izzart.

Izzart was about to answer when Campion spoke.

"Until I got over to the other side of the river I thought he was drowned. I don't know how he got out. I expect he hardly knows himself."

"It was touch and go," said Izzart, with a laugh.

Why had Campion said that? He caught his eye. He was sure now that there was a gleam of amusement in it. It was awful not to be certain. He was frightened. He was ashamed. He wondered if he could not so guide the conversation, either now or later, as to ask Campion whether that was the story he was going to tell in Kuala Solor. There was nothing in it to excite any one's suspicions. But if nobody else knew, Campion knew. He could have killed him.

"Well, I think you're both of you damned lucky to be alive," said the skipper.

It was but a short run to Kuala Solor, and as they steamed up the Sembulu River Izzart moodily watched the banks. On each side were the mangroves and the nipas washed by the water, and behind, the dense green of the jungle; here and there, among fruit trees, were Malay houses on piles. Night fell as they docked. Goring, of the police, came on board and shook hands with them. He was living at the rest-house just then, and as he set about his work of seeing the native passengers he told them that they would find another man, Porter by name, staying there too. They would all meet at dinner. The boys took charge of their kit, and Campion and Izzart strolled along. They bathed and changed and at half-past eight the four of them assembled in the common-room for gin pahits.

"I say, what's this Bredon tells me about your being nearly drowned?" said Goring as he came in.

Izzart felt himself flush, but before he could answer Campion broke in, and it seemed certain to Izzart that he spoke in order to give the story as he chose. He felt hot with shame. Not a word was spoken in disparagement of him, not a word was said of him at all; he wondered if those two men who listened, Goring and Porter, thought it strange that he should be left out. He looked at Campion intently as he proceeded with his narration; he told it rather humorously; he did not disguise the danger in which they had been, but he made a joke of it, so that the two listeners laughed at the quandary in which they had found themselves.

"A thing that's tickled me since," said Campion, "is that when I got over to the other bank I was black with mud from head to foot. I felt I really ought to jump in the river and have a wash, but you know I felt I'd been in that damned river as much as ever I wanted, and I said to myself: No, by George, I'll go dirty. And when I got into the long-house and saw Izzart as black as I was, I knew he'd felt just like I did."

They laughed and Izzart forced himself to laugh too. He noticed that Campion had told the story in precisely the same words as he had used when he told it to the skipper of the Sultan Ahmed. There could be only one explanation of that; he knew, he knew everything, and had made up his mind exactly what story to tell. The ingenuity with which Campion gave the facts and yet left out what must be to Izzart's discredit was devilish. But why was he holding his hand? It wasn't in him not to feel contempt and resentment for the man who had callously deserted him in that moment of dreadful peril. Suddenly, in a flash of inspiration Izzart understood: he was keeping the truth to tell to Willis, the Resident. Izzart had gooseflesh as he thought of confronting Willis. He could deny, but would his denials serve him? Willis was no fool and he would get at Hassan; Hassan could not be trusted to be silent; Hassan would give him away. Then he would be done for. Willis would suggest that he had better go home.

He had a racking headache and after dinner he went to his room, for he wanted to be alone so that he could devise a plan of action. And then a thought came to him which made him go hot and cold; he knew that the secret which he had guarded so long was a secret to nobody. He was on a sudden certain of it. Why should he have those bright eyes and that swarthy skin? Why should he speak Malay with such ease and have learned Dyak so quickly? Of course they knew. What a fool he was ever to think that they believed that story of his, about the Spanish grandmother! They must have laughed up their sleeves when he told it, and behind his back they had called him a damned nigger. And now another thought came to him, torturing, and he asked himself whether it was on account of that wretched drop of native blood in him that when he heard Campion cry out his nerve failed him. After all, any one might at that moment have been seized with panic; and why in God's name should he sacrifice his life to save a man's, whom he cared nothing for? It was insane. But of course in K.S. they would say it was only what they expected; they would make no allowances.

At last he went to bed, but when, after tossing about restlessly for God knows how long, he fell asleep, he was awakened by a fearful dream; he seemed to be once more in that raging torrent, with the boat turning, turning; and then there was the desperate clutching at the gunwale, and the agony as it slipped out of his hands, and the water that roared over him. He was wide awake before dawn. His only chance was to see Willis and get his story in first; and he thought over carefully what he was going to say and chose the very words he meant to use.

He got up early, and in order not to see Campion went out, without breakfast. He walked along the highroad till such time as he knew the Resident would be in his office and then walked back again. He sent in his name and was ushered into Willis's room. He was a little elderly man with thin grey hair and a long yellow face.

"I'm glad to see you back safe and sound," he said, shaking hands with Izzart. "What's this I hear about your being nearly drowned?"

Izzart, in clean ducks, his topee spotless, was a fine figure of a man. His black hair was neatly brushed and his moustache was trimmed. He had an upright and soldierly bearing.

"I thought I'd better come and tell you at once, sir, as you told me to look after Campion."

"Fire away."

Izzart told his story. He made light of the danger. He gave Willis to understand that it had not been very great. They would never have been upset if they had not started so late.

"I tried to get Campion away earlier, but he'd had two or three drinks and the fact is, he didn't want to move."

"Was he tight?"

"I don't know about that," smiled Izzart good-humouredly. "I shouldn't say he was cold sober."

He went on with his story. He managed to insinuate that

Campion had lost his head a little. Of course it was a very frightening business to a man who wasn't a decent swimmer: he, Izzart, had been more concerned for Campion than for himself; he knew the only chance was to keep cool, and the moment they were upset he saw that Campion had got the wind up.

"You can't blame him for that," said the Resident.

"Of course I did everything I possibly could for him, sir, but the fact is, there wasn't anything much I could do."

"Well, the great thing is that you both escaped. It would have been very awkward for all of us if he'd been drowned."

"I thought I'd better come and tell you the facts before you saw Campion, sir. I fancy he's inclined to talk rather wildly about it. There's no use exaggerating."

"On the whole your stories agree pretty well," said Willis, with a little smile.

Izzart looked at him blankly.

"Haven't you seen Campion this morning? I heard from Goring that there'd been some trouble and I looked in last night on my way home from the Fort after dinner. You'd already gone to bed."

Izzart felt himself trembling and he made a great effort to preserve his composure.

"By the way, you got away first, didn't you?"

"I don't really know, sir. You see, there was a lot of confusion."

"You must have if you got over to the other side before he did."

"I suppose I did then."

"Well, thanks for coming to tell me," said Willis, rising from his chair.

As he did so he knocked some books on the floor. They fell with a sudden thud. The unexpected sound made Izzart start violently and he gave a gasp. The Resident looked at him quickly.

"I say, your nerves are in a pretty state."

Izzart could not control his trembling.

"I'm very sorry, sir," he murmured.

"I expect it's been a shock. You'd better take it easy for a few days. Why don't you get the doctor to give you something?"

"I didn't sleep very well last night."

The Resident nodded as though he understood. Izzart left the room, and as he passed out some man he knew stopped and congratulated him on his escape. They all knew of it. He walked back to the rest-house. And as he walked he repeated to himself the story he had told the Resident. Was it really the same story that Campion had told? He had never suspected that the Resident had already heard it from Campion. What a fool he had been to go to bed! He should never have let Campion out of his sight. Why had the Resident listened without telling him that he already knew? Now Izzart cursed himself for having suggested that Campion was drunk and had lost his head. He had said this in order to discredit him, but he knew now that it was a stupid thing to do. And why had Willis said that about his having got away first? Perhaps he was holding his hand too; perhaps he was going to make enquiries; Willis was very shrewd. But what exactly had Campion said? He must know that; at whatever cost he must know. Izzart's mind was seething so that he felt he could hardly keep a hold on his thoughts, but he must keep calm. He felt like a hunted animal. He did not believe that Willis liked him; once or twice in the office he had blamed him because he was careless; perhaps he was just waiting till he got all the facts. Izzart was almost hysterical.

He entered the rest-house and there, sitting on a long chair, with his legs stretched out, was Campion. He was reading the papers which had arrived during their absence in the jungle. Izzart felt a blind rush of hatred well up in him as he looked at the little, shabby man who held him in the hollow of his hand.

"Hulloa," said Campion, looking up. "Where have you been?"

To Izzart it seemed that there was in his eyes a mocking irony. He clenched his hands and his breath came fast.

"What have you been saying to Willis about me?" he asked abruptly.

The tone in which he put the unexpected question was so harsh that Campion gave him a glance of faint surprise.

"I don't think I've been saying anything very much about you. Why?"

"He came here last night."

Izzart looked at him intently. His brows were drawn together in an angry frown as he tried to read Campion's thoughts.

"I told him you'd gone to bed with a headache. He wanted to know about our mishap."

"I've just seen him."

Izzart walked up and down the large and shaded room; now, though it was still early, the sun was hot and dazzling. He felt himself in a net. He was blind with rage; he could have seized Campion by the throat and strangled him, and yet, because he did not know what he had to fight against, he felt himself powerless. He was tired and ill, and his nerves were shaken. On a sudden the anger which had given him a sort of strength left him and he was filled with despondency. It was as though water and not blood ran through his veins; his heart sank and his knees seemed to give way. He felt that if he did not take care he would begin to cry. He was dreadfully sorry for himself.

"Damn you, I wish to God I'd never set eyes on you," he cried pitifully.

"What on earth's the matter?" asked Campion, with astonishment.

"Oh, don't pretend. We've been pretending for two days and I'm fed up with it." His voice rose shrilly, it sounded odd in that robust and powerful man. "I'm fed up with it. I cut and run. I left you to drown. I know I behaved like a skunk. I couldn't help it."

Campion rose slowly from his chair.

"What *are* you talking about?"

His tone was so genuinely surprised that it gave Izzart a start. A cold shiver ran down his spine.

"When you called for help I was panic-stricken. I just caught hold of an oar and got Hassan to help me get away."

"That was the most sensible thing you could do."

"I couldn't help you. There wasn't a thing I could do."

"Of course not. It was damned silly of me to shout. It was waste of breath, and breath was the very thing I wanted "

"Do you mean to say you didn't know?"

"When those fellows got me the mattress I thought you were still clinging to the boat. I had an idea that I got away before you did."

Izzart put both his hands to his head and gave a hoarse cry of despair.

"My God, what a fool I've been."

The two men stood for a while staring at one another. The silence seemed endless.

"What are you going to do now?" asked Izzart at last.

"Oh, my dear fellow, don't worry. I've been frightened too often myself to blame any one who shows the white feather. I'm not going to tell a soul."

"Yes, but you *know*."

"I promise you, you can trust me. Besides, my job's done here and I'm going home. I want to catch the next boat to Singapore." There was a pause, and Campion looked for a while reflectively at Izzart. "There's only one thing I'd like to ask you: I've made a good many friends here, and there are one or two things I'm a little sensitive about; when you tell the story of our upset I should be grateful if you wouldn't make out that I had behaved badly. I wouldn't like the fellows here to think that I'd lost my nerve."

Izzart flushed darkly. He remembered what he had said to the Resident. It almost looked as though Campion had been listening over his shoulder. He cleared his throat.

"I don't know why you think I should do that."

Campion chuckled good-naturedly, and his blue eyes were gay with amusement.

"The yellow streak," he replied, and then, with a grin that showed his broken and discoloured teeth: "Have a cheroot, dear boy."

P. & O.

Mrs. HAMLYN lay on her long chair and lazily watched the passengers come along the gangway. The ship had reached Singapore in the night and since dawn had been taking on cargo; the winches had been grinding away all day, but by now her ears were accustomed to their insistent clamour. She had lunched at the Europe and for lack of anything better to do had driven in a rickshaw through the gay, multitudinous streets of the city. Singapore is the meeting-place of many races. The Malays, though natives of the soil, dwell uneasily in towns, and are few; and it is the Chinese, supple, alert and industrious, who throng the streets, the dark-skinned Tamils walk on their silent, naked feet as though they were but brief sojourners in a strange land, but the Bengalis, sleek and prosperous, are easy in their surroundings and self-assured; the sly and obsequious Japanese seem busy with pressing and secret affairs; and the English in their topees and white ducks, speeding past in motor-cars or at leisure in their rickshaws, wear a nonchalant and careless air. The rulers of these teeming peoples take their authority with a smiling unconcern. And now, tired and hot, Mrs. Hamlyn waited for the ship to set out again on her long journey across the Indian Ocean.

She waved a rather large hand, for she was a big woman, to the doctor and Mrs. Linsell as they came on board. She had been on the ship since she left Yokohama, and had watched with acid amusement the intimacy which had sprung up between the two. Linsell was a naval officer who had been attached to the British

Embassy at Tokio, and she had wondered at the indifference with which he took the attentions that the doctor paid his wife. Two men came along the gangway, new passengers, and she amused herself by trying to discover from their demeanour whether they were married or single. Close by, a group of men were sitting together on rattan chairs, planters she judged by their khaki suits and wide-brimmed double felt hats, and they kept the deck-steward busy with their orders. They were talking loudly and laughing, for they had all drunk enough to make them somewhat foolishly hilarious, and they were evidently giving one of their number a send-off; but Mrs. Hamlyn could not tell which it was that was to be a fellow-passenger. The time was growing short. More passengers arrived, and then Mr. Jephson with dignity strolled up the gangway. He was a consul and was going home on leave. He had joined the ship at Shanghai and had immediately set about making himself agreeable to Mrs. Hamlyn. But just then she was disinclined for anything in the nature of a flirtation. She frowned as she thought of the reason which was taking her back to England. She would be spending Christmas at sea, far from anyone who cared two straws for her, and for a moment she felt a little twist at her heartstrings; it vexed her that a subject which she was so resolute to put away from her should so constantly intrude on her unwilling mind.

But a warning bell clanged loudly and there was a general movement among the men who sat beside her.

"Well, if we don't want to be taken on we'd better be toddling," said one of them.

They rose and walked towards the gangway. Now that they were all shaking hands she saw who it was that they had come to see the last of. There was nothing very interesting about the man on whom Mrs. Hamlyn's eyes rested, but because she had nothing better to do she gave him more than a casual glance. He was a big fellow, well over six feet high, broad and stout; he was dressed in a bedraggled suit of khaki drill and his hat was battered and shabby. His friends left him, but they bandied chaff from the quay, and Mrs. Hamlyn noticed that he had a strong Irish brogue; his voice was full, loud and hearty.

Mrs. Linsell had gone below and the doctor came and sat down beside Mrs. Hamlyn. They told one another their small adventures of the day. The bell sounded again and presently the ship slid away from the wharf. The Irishman waved a last farewell to his friends and then sauntered towards the chair on which he had left papers and magazines. He nodded to the doctor.

"Is that some one you know?" asked Mrs. Hamlyn.

"I was introduced to him at the club before tiffin. His name is Gallagher. He's a planter."

After the hubbub of the port and the noisy bustle of departure, the silence of the ship was marked and grateful. They steamed slowly past green-clad, rocky cliffs (the P. & O. anchorage was in a charming and secluded cove), and came out into the main harbour. Ships of all nations lay at anchor, a great multitude, passenger boats, tugs, lighters, tramps; and beyond, behind the breakwater, you saw the crowded masts, a bare straight forest, of the native junks. In the soft light of the evening the busy scene was strangely touched with mystery, and you felt that all those vessels, their activity for the moment suspended, waited for some event of a peculiar significance.

Mrs. Hamlyn was a bad sleeper and when the dawn broke she was in the habit of going on deck. It rested her troubled heart to watch the last faint stars fade before the encroaching day and at that early hour the glassy sea had often an immobility which seemed to make all earthly sorrows of little consequence. The light was wan, and there was a pleasant shiver in the air. But next morning when she went to the end of the promenade deck, she found that some one was up before her. It was Gallagher. He was watching the low coast of Sumatra which the sunrise like a magician seemed to call forth from the dark sea. She was startled and a little vexed, but before she could turn away he had seen her and nodded.

"Up early," he said. "Have a cigarette?"

He was in pyjamas and slippers. He took his case from his coat pocket and handed it to her. She hesitated. She had on nothing but a dressing-gown and a little lace cap which she had put over her tousled hair, and she knew that she must look a sight; but she had her reasons for scourging her soul.

"I suppose a woman of forty has no right to mind how she looks," she smiled, as though he must know what vain thoughts occupied her. She took the cigarette. "But you're up early too."

"I'm a planter. I've had to get up at five in the morning for so many years that I don't know how I'm going to get out of the habit."

"You'll not find it will make you very popular at home."

She saw his face better now that it was not shadowed by a hat. It was agreeable without being handsome. He was of course much too fat, and his features which must have been good enough when he was a young man were thickened. His skin was red and bloated. But his dark eyes were merry; and though he could not have been less than five and forty his hair was black and thick. He gave you an impression of great strength. He was a heavy, ungraceful, commonplace man, and Mrs. Hamlyn, except for the promiscuity of shipboard, would never have thought it worth while to talk to him.

"Are you going home on leave?" she hazarded.

"No, I'm going home for good."

His black eyes twinkled. He was of a communicative turn, and before it was time for Mrs. Hamlyn to go below in order to have her bath he had told her a good deal about himself. He had been in the Federated Malay States for twenty-five years, and for the last ten had managed an estate in Selantan. It was a hundred miles from anything that could be described as civilization and the life had been lonely; but he had made money; during the rubber boom he had done very well and with an astuteness which was unexpected in a man who looked so happy-go-lucky he had invested his savings in Government stock. Now that the slump had come he was prepared to retire.

"What part of Ireland do you come from?" asked Mrs. Hamlyn.

"Galway."

Mrs. Hamlyn had once motored through Ireland and she had a vague recollection of a sad and moody town with great stone warehouses, deserted and crumbling, which faced the melancholy sea. She had a sensation of greenness and of soft rain, of silence and of resignation. Was it here that Mr. Gallagher meant to spend the rest of his life? He spoke of it with boyish eagerness. The thought of his vitality in that grey world of shadows was so incongruous that Mrs. Hamlyn was intrigued.

"Does your family live there?" she asked.

"I've got no family. My mother and father are dead. So far as I know I haven't a relation in the world."

He had made all his plans, he had been making them for twenty-five years, and he was pleased to have some one to talk to of all these things that he had been obliged for so long only to talk to himself about. He meant to buy a house and he would keep a motor-car. He was going to breed horses. He didn't

much care about shooting; he had shot a lot of big game during
his first years in the F.M.S.; but now he had lost his zest. He
didn't see why the beasts of the jungle should be killed; he had
lived in the jungle so long. But he could hunt.

"Do you think I'm too heavy?" he asked.

Mrs. Hamlyn, smiling, looked him up and down with appraising eyes.

"You must weigh a ton," she said.

He laughed. The Irish horses were the best in the world, and
he'd always kept pretty fit. You had a devil of a lot of walking
exercise on a rubber estate and he'd played a good deal of tennis.
He'd soon get thin in Ireland. Then he'd marry. Mrs. Hamlyn
looked silently at the sea, coloured now with the tenderness of
the sunrise. She sighed.

"Was it easy to drag up all your roots? Is there no one you
regret leaving behind? I should have thought after so many
years, however much you'd looked forward to going home, when
the time came at last to go it must have given you a pang."

"I was glad to get out. I was fed up. I never want to see the
country again or any one in it."

One or two early passengers now began to walk round the
deck and Mrs. Hamlyn, remembering that she was scantily
clad, went below.

During the next day or two she saw little of Mr. Gallagher
who passed his time in the smoking-room. Owing to a strike the
ship was not touching at Colombo and the passengers settled
down to a pleasant voyage across the Indian Ocean. They
played deck games, they gossiped about one another, they
flirted. The approach of Christmas gave them an occupation,
for some one had suggested that there should be a fancy-dress
dance on Christmas day, and the ladies set about making their
dresses. A meeting was held of the first-class passengers to decide whether the second-class passengers should be invited, and
notwithstanding the heat the discussion was animated. The
ladies said that the second-class passengers would only feel ill-
at-ease. On Christmas day it was to be expected that they
would drink more than was good for them and unpleasantness
might ensue. Every one who spoke insisted that there was in his
(or her) mind no idea of class distinction, no one would be so
snobbish as to think there was any difference between first- and
second-class passengers as far as that went, but it would really
be kinder to the second-class passengers not to put them in a

false position. They would enjoy themselves much more if they had a party of their own in the second-class cabin. On the other hand, no one wanted to hurt their feelings, and of course one had to be more democratic nowadays (this was in reply to the wife of a missionary in China who said she had travelled on the P. & O. for thirty-five years and she had never heard of the second-class passengers being invited to a dance in the first-class saloon) and even though they wouldn't enjoy it, they might like to come. Mr. Gallagher, dragged unwillingly from the card-table, because it had been foreseen that the voting would be close, was asked his opinion by the consul. He was taking home in the second-class a man who had been employed on his estate. He raised his massive bulk from the couch on which he sat.

"As far as I'm concerned I've only got this to say: I've got the man who was looking after our engines with me. He's a rattling good fellow and he's just as fit to come to your party as I am. But he won't come because I'm going to make him so drunk on Christmas day that by six o'clock he'll be fit for nothing but to be put to bed."

Mr. Jephson, the consul, gave a distorted smile. On account of his official position he had been chosen to preside at the meeting and he wished the matter to be taken seriously. He was a man who often said that if a thing was worth doing it was worth doing well.

"I gather from your observations," he said, not without acidity, "that the question before the meeting does not seem to you of great importance."

"I don't think it matters a tinker's curse," said Gallagher, with twinkling eyes.

Mrs. Hamlyn laughed. The scheme was at last devised to invite the second-class passengers, but to go to the captain privily and point out to him the advisability of withholding his consent to their coming into the first-class saloon. It was on the evening of the day on which this happened that Mrs. Hamlyn, having dressed for dinner, came on deck at the same time as Mr. Gallagher.

"Just in time for a cocktail, Mrs. Hamlyn," he said jovially.

"I'd like one. To tell you the truth I need cheering up."

"Why?" he smiled.

Mrs. Hamlyn thought his smile attractive, but she did not want to answer his question.

"I told you the other morning," she answered cheerfully. "I'm forty."

"I never met a woman who insisted on the fact so much."

They went into the lounge and the Irishman ordered a dry Martini for her and a gin pahit for himself. He had lived too long in the East to drink anything else.

"You've got hiccups," said Mrs. Hamlyn.

"Yes, I've had them all the afternoon," he answered carelessly. "It's rather funny, they came on just as we got out of sight of land."

"I daresay they'll pass off after dinner."

They drank, the second bell rang, and they went into the dining-saloon.

"You don't play bridge?" he said, as they parted.

"No."

Mrs. Hamlyn did not notice that she saw nothing of Gallagher for two or three days. She was occupied with her own thoughts. They crowded upon her when she was sewing; they came between her and the novel with which she sought to cheat their insistence. She had hoped that as the ship took her further away from the scene of her unhappiness the torment of her mind would be eased; but contrariwise, each day that brought her nearer England increased her distress. She looked forward with dismay to the bleak emptiness of the life that awaited her; and then, turning her exhausted wits from a prospect that made her flinch, she considered, as she had done she knew not how many times before, the situation from which she had fled.

She had been married for twenty years. It was a long time and of course she could not expect her husband to be still madly in love with her; she was not madly in love with him; but they were good friends and they understood one another. Their marriage, as marriages go, might very well have been looked upon as a success. Suddenly she discovered that he had fallen in love. She would not have objected to a flirtation, he had had those before, and she had chaffed him about them; he had not minded that, it somewhat flattered him, and they had laughed together at an inclination which was neither deep nor serious. But this was different. He was in love as passionately as a boy of eighteen. He was fifty-two. It was ridiculous. It was indecent. And he loved without sense or prudence: by the time the hideous fact was forced upon her all the foreigners in Yokohama knew it. After the first shock of astonished anger, for he was the last man from whom such a folly might have been expected, she tried to persuade herself that she could have understood, and so have forgiven, if he had fallen in love with a girl. Middle-aged men often make fools of themselves with flappers, and after twenty years in the Far East she knew that the fifties were the dangerous age for men. But he had no excuse. He was in love with a woman eight years older than herself, It was grotesque, and it made her, his wife, perfectly absurd. Dorothy Lacom was hard on fifty. He had known her for eighteen years, for Lacom, like her own husband, was a silk merchant in Yokohama. Year in, year out, they had seen one another three or four times a week, and once, when they happened to be in England together, had shared a house at the seaside. But nothing! Not till a year ago had there been anything between them but a chaffing friendship. It was incredible. Of course Dorothy was a handsome woman; she had a good figure, overdeveloped, perhaps, but still comely; with bold black eyes and a red mouth and lovely hair; but all that she had had years before. She was forty-eight. Forty-eight!

Mrs. Hamlyn tackled her husband at once. At first he swore that there was not a word of truth in what she accused him of, but she had her proofs; he grew sulky; and at last he admitted what he could no longer deny. Then he said an astonishing thing.

"Why should you care?" he asked.

It maddened her. She answered him with angry scorn. She was voluble, finding in the bitterness of her heart wounding things to say. He listened to her quietly.

"I've not been such a bad husband to you for the twenty years we've been married. For a long time now we've only been friends. I have a great affection for you and this hasn't altered it in the very smallest degree. I'm giving Dorothy nothing that I take away from you."

"But what have you to complain of in me?"

"Nothing. No man could want a better wife."

"How can you say that when you have the heart to treat me so cruelly?"

"I don't want to be cruel to you. I can't help myself."

"But what on earth made you fall in love with her?"

"How can I tell? You don't think I wanted to, do you?"

"Couldn't you have resisted?"

"I tried. I think we both tried."

"You talk as though you were twenty. Why, you're both middle-aged people. She's eight years older than I am. It makes me look such a perfect fool."

He did not answer. She did not know what emotions seethed in her heart. Was it jealousy that seemed to clutch at her throat, anger, or was it merely wounded pride?

"I'm not going to let it go on. If only you and she were concerned I would divorce you, but there's her husband and then there are the children. Good heavens, does it occur to you that if they were girls instead of boys she might be a grandmother by now?"

"Easily."

"What a mercy that we have no children!"

He put out an affectionate hand as though to caress her, but she drew back with horror.

"You've made me the laughing-stock of all my friends. For all our sakes I'm willing to hold my tongue, but only on the condition that everything stops now, at once, and for ever."

He looked down and played reflectively with a Japanese knickknack that was on the table.

"I'll tell Dorothy what you say," he replied at last.

She gave him a little bow, silently, and walked past him out of the room. She was too angry to observe that she was somewhat melodramatic.

She waited for him to tell her the result of his interview with Dorothy Lacom, but he made no further reference to the scene. He was quiet, polite, and silent; and at last she was obliged to ask him.

"Have you forgotten what I said to you the other day?" she enquired frigidly.

"No. I talked to Dorothy. She wishes me to tell you that she is desperately sorry that she has caused you so much pain. She would like to come and see you, but she is afraid you wouldn't like it."

"What decision have you come to?"

He hesitated. He was very grave, but his voice trembled a little.

"I'm afraid there's no use in our making a promise we shouldn't be able to keep."

"That settles it then," she answered.

"I think I should tell you that if you brought an action for

divorce we should have to contest it. You would find it impossible to get the necessary evidence and you would lose your
case."

"I wasn't thinking of doing that. I shall go back to England
and consult a lawyer. Nowadays these things can be managed
fairly easily and I shall throw myself on your generosity. I
daresay you will enable me to get my freedom without bringing
Dorothy Lacom into the matter."

He sighed.

"It's an awful muddle, isn't it? I don't want you to divorce
me, but of course I'll do anything I can to meet your wishes."

"What on earth do you expect me to do?" she cried, her
anger rising again. "Do you expect me to sit still and be made a
damned fool of?"

"I'm awfully sorry to put you in a humiliating position." He
looked at her with harassed eyes. "I'm quite sure we didn't
want to fall in love with one another. We're both of us very
conscious of our age. Dorothy, as you say, is old enough to be a
grandmother and I'm a baldish, stoutish gentleman of fifty-
two. When you fall in love at twenty you think your love will
last for ever, but at fifty you know so much, about life and
about love, and you know that it will last so short a time." His
voice was low and rueful. It was as though before his mind's
eye he saw the sadness of autumn and the leaves falling from
the trees. He looked at her gravely. "And at that age you feel
that you can't afford to throw away the chance of happiness
which a freakish destiny has given you. In five years it will
certainly be over, and perhaps in six months. Life is rather drab
and grey, and happiness is so rare. We shall be dead so long."

It gave Mrs. Hamlyn a bitter sensation of pain to hear her
husband, a matter-of-fact and practical man, speak in a strain
which was quite new to her. He had gained on a sudden a wistful
and tragic personality of which she knew nothing. The twenty
years during which they had lived together had no power over
him and she was helpless in face of his determination. She
could do nothing but go, and now, resentfully determined to
get the divorce with which she had threatened him, she was on
her way to England.

The smooth sea, upon which the sun beat down so that it
shone like a sheet of glass, was as empty and hostile as life in
which there was no place for her. For three days no other craft
had broken in upon the solitariness of that expanse. Now and

again its even surface was scattered for the twinkling of an eye by the scurry of flying fish. The heat was so great that even the most energetic of passengers had given up deck games and now (it was after luncheon) such as were not resting in their cabins lay about on chairs. Linsell strolled towards her and sat down.

"Where's Mrs. Linsell?" asked Mrs. Hamlyn.

"Oh, I don't know. She's about somewhere."

His indifference exasperated her. Was it possible that he did not see that his wife and the surgeon were falling in love with one another? Yet, not so very long ago, he must have cared. Their marriage had been romantic. They had become engaged when Mrs. Linsell was still at school and he little more than a boy. They must have been a charming, handsome pair, and their youth and their mutual love must have been touching. And now, after so short a time, they were tired of one another. It was heartbreaking. What had her husband said?

"I suppose you're going to live in London when you get home?" asked Linsell lazily, for something to say.

"I suppose so," said Mrs. Hamlyn.

It was hard to reconcile herself to the fact that she had nowhere to go and where she lived mattered not in the least to any one alive. Some association of ideas made her think of Gallagher. She envied the eagerness with which he was returning to his native land, and she was touched, and at the same time amused, when she remembered the exuberant imagination he showed in describing the house he meant to live in and the wife he meant to marry. Her friends in Yokohama, apprised in confidence of her determination to divorce her husband, had assured her that she would marry again. She did not much want to enter a second time upon a state which had once so disappointed her, and besides, most men would think twice before they suggested marriage to a woman of forty. Mr. Gallagher wanted a buxom young person.

"Where is Mr. Gallagher?" she asked the submissive Linsell.

"I haven't seen him for the last day or two."

"Didn't you know? He's ill."

"Poor thing. What's the matter with him?"

"He's got hiccups."

Mrs. Hamlyn laughed.

"Hiccups don't make one ill, do they?"

"The surgeon is rather worried. He's tried all sorts of things, but he can't stop them."

"How very odd."

She thought no more about it, but next morning, chancing upon the surgeon, she asked him how Mr. Gallagher was. She was surprised to see his boyish, cheerful face darken and grow perplexed.

"I'm afraid he's very bad, poor chap."

"With hiccups?" she cried in amazement.

It was a disorder that really it was impossible to take seriously.

"You see, he can't keep any food down. He can't sleep. He's fearfully exhausted. I've tried everything I can think of." He hesitated. "Unless I can stop them soon—I don't quite know what'll happen."

Mrs. Hamlyn was startled.

"But he's so strong. He seemed so full of vitality."

"I wish you could see him now."

"Would he like me to go and see him?"

"Come along."

Gallagher had been moved from his cabin into the ship's hospital, and as they approached it they heard a loud hiccup. The sound, perhaps owing to its connection with insobriety, had in it something ludicrous. But Gallagher's appearance gave Mrs. Hamlyn a shock. He had lost flesh and the skin hung about his neck in loose folds; under the sunburn his face was pale. His eyes, before, full of fun and laughter, were haggard and tormented. His great body was shaken incessantly by the hiccups, and now there was nothing ludicrous in the sound; to Mrs. Hamlyn, for no reason that she knew, it seemed strangely terrifying. He smiled when she came in.

"I'm sorry to see you like this," she said.

"I shan't die of it, you know," he gasped. "I shall reach the green shores of Erin all right."

There was a man sitting beside him and he rose as they entered.

"This is Mr. Pryce," said the surgeon. "He was in charge of the machinery on Mr. Gallagher's estate."

Mrs. Hamlyn nodded. This was the second-class passenger to whom Gallagher had referred when they had discussed the party which was to be given on Christmas day. He was a very small man, but sturdy, with a pleasantly impudent countenance and an air of self-assurance.

"Are you glad to be going home?" asked Mrs. Hamlyn.

"You bet I am, lady," he answered.

The intonation of the few words told Mrs. Hamlyn that he was a cockney and, recognizing the cheerful, sensible, good-humoured and careless type, her heart warmed to him.

"You're not Irish?" she smiled.

"Not me, miss. London's my 'ome and I shan't be sorry to see it again, I can tell you."

Mrs. Hamlyn never thought it offensive to be called miss.

"Well, sir, I'll be getting along," he said to Gallagher, with the beginning of a gesture as though he were going to touch a cap which he hadn't got on.

Mrs. Hamlyn asked the sick man whether she could do any-thing for him and in a minute or two left him with the doctor. The little cockney was waiting outside the door.

"Can I speak to you a minute or two, miss?" he asked.

"Of course."

The hospital cabin was aft and they stood, leaning against the rail, and looked down on the well-deck where lascars and stewards off duty were lounging about on the covered hatches.

"I don't know exactly 'ow to begin," said Pryce, uncertainly, a serious look strangely changing his lively, puckered face. "I've been with Mr. Gallagher for four years now and a better gentleman you wouldn't find in a week of Sundays."

He hesitated again.

"I don't like it and that's the truth."

"What don't you like?"

"Well, if you ask me 'e's for it, and the doctor don't know it. I told 'im, but 'e won't listen to a word I say."

"You mustn't be too depressed, Mr. Pryce. Of course the doctor's young, but I think he's quite clever, and people don't die of hiccups, you know. I'm sure Mr. Gallagher will be all right in a day or two."

"You know when it come on? Just as we was out of sight of land. She said 'e'd never see 'is 'ome."

Mrs. Hamlyn turned and faced him. She stood a good three inches taller than he.

"What do you mean?"

"My belief is, it's a spell been put on 'im, if you understand what I mean. Medicine's going to do 'im no good. You don't know them Malay women like what I do."

For a moment Mrs. Hamlyn was startled, and because she was startled she shrugged her shoulders and laughed.

"Oh, Mr. Pryce, that's nonsense."

"That's what the doctor said when I told 'im. But you mark my words, 'e'll die before we see land again."

The man was so serious that Mrs. Hamlyn, vaguely uneasy, was against her will impressed.

"Why should any one cast a spell on Mr. Gallagher?" she asked.

"Well, it's a bit awkward speakin' of it to a lady."

"Please tell me."

Pryce was so embarrassed that at another time Mrs. Hamlyn would have had difficulty in concealing her amusement.

"Mr. Gallagher's lived a long time up-country, if you under-stand what I mean, and of course it's lonely, and you know what men are, miss."

"I've been married for twenty years," she replied, smil-ing.

"I beg your pardon, ma'am. The fact is he had a Malay girl living with him. I don't know 'ow long, ten or twelve years, I think. Well, when he made up 'is mind to come 'ome for good she didn't say nothing. She just sat there. He thought she'd carry on no end, but she didn't. Of course 'e provided for 'er all right, 'e gave 'er a little 'ouse for herself, an' 'e fixed it up so as so much should be paid 'er every month; 'e wasn't mean, I will say that for 'im, an' she knew all along as 'e'd be going some time. She didn't cry or anything. When 'e packed up all 'is things and sent them off she just sat there an' watched 'em go. And when 'e sold 'is furniture to the Chinks she never said a word. He'd give 'er all she wanted. And when it was time for 'im to go so as to catch the boat she just kep' on sitting on the steps of the bungalow, you know, and she just looked an' said nothing. He wanted to say good-bye to 'er, same as any one would, an', would you believe it? she never even moved. 'Aren't you going to say good-bye to me?' he says. A rare funny look came over 'er face. And do you know what she says? 'You go,' she says; they 'ave a funny way of talking, them na-tives, not like we 'ave, 'you go,' she says, 'but I tell you that you will never come to your own country. When the land sinks into the sea death will come upon you, an' before them as goes with you sees the land again, death will have took you.' It gave me quite a turn."

"What did Mr. Gallagher say?" asked Mrs. Hamlyn.

"Oh, well, you know what 'e is. He just laughed. 'Always

merry an' bright,' he says and he jumps into the motor, an' off
we go."

Mrs. Hamlyn saw the bright and sunny road that ran
through the rubber estates, with their trim green trees, carefully spaced, and their silence, and then wound its way up hill
and down through the tangled jungle. The car raced on, driven
by a reckless Malay, with its white passengers, past Malay
houses that stood away from the road among the coconut trees,
sequestered and taciturn, and through busy villages where the
market-place was crowded with dark-skinned little people in
gay sarongs. Then towards evening it reached the trim, modern
town, with its clubs and its golf links, its well-ordered rest-
house, its white people, and its railway station, from which the
two men could take the train to Singapore. And the woman
sat on the steps of the bungalow, empty till the new manager
moved in, and watched the road down which the car had
panted, watched the car as it sped on, and watched till at last
it was lost in the shadow of the night.

"What was she like?" Mrs. Hamlyn asked.

"Oh, well, to my way of thinking them Malay women are all
very much alike, you know," Pryce answered. "Of course she
wasn't so young any more and you know what they are, them
natives, they run to fat something terrible."

"Fat?"

The thought, absurdly enough, filled Mrs. Hamlyn with dismay.

"Mr. Gallagher was always one to do himself well, if you
understand what I mean."

The idea of corpulence at once brought Mrs. Hamlyn back
to common sense. She was impatient with herself because for an
instant she had seemed to accept the little cockney's suggestion.

"It's perfectly absurd, Mr. Pryce. Fat women can't throw
spells on people at a distance of a thousand miles. In fact life is
very difficult for a fat woman anyway."

"You can laugh, miss, but unless something's done, you mark
my words, the governor's for it. And medicine ain't goin' to
save him, not white man's medicine."

"Pull yourself together, Mr. Pryce. This fat lady had no
particular grievance against Mr. Gallagher. As these things
are done in the East he seems to have treated her very well.
Why should she wish him any harm?"

"We don't know 'ow they look at things. Why, a man can

live there for twenty years with one of them natives, and d'you think 'e knows what's goin' on in that black heart of hers? Not 'im!"

She could not smile at his melodramatic language, for his intensity was impressive. And she knew, if any one did, that the hearts of men, whether their skins are yellow or white or brown, are incalculable.

"But even if she felt angry with him, even if she hated him and wanted to kill him, what could she do?" It was strange that Mrs. Hamlyn with her questions was trying now, unconsciously, to reassure herself. "There's no poison that could start working after six or seven days."

"I never said it was poison."

"I'm sorry, Mr. Pryce," she smiled, "but I'm not going to believe in a magic spell, you know."

"You've lived in the East."

"Off and on for twenty years."

"Well, if you can say what they can do and what they can't, it's more than I can." He clenched his fist and beat it on the rail with sudden, angry violence. "I'm fed up with the bloody country. It's got on my nerves, that's what it is. We're no match for them, us white men, and that's a fact. If you'll excuse me I think I'll go an' 'ave a tiddley. I've got the jumps."

He nodded abruptly and left her. Mrs. Hamlyn watched him, a sturdy, shuffling little man in shabby khaki, slither down the companion into the waist of the ship, walk across it with bent head, and disappear into the second-class saloon. She did not know why he left with her a vague uneasiness. She could not get out of her mind that picture of a stout woman, no longer young, in a sarong, a coloured jacket and gold ornaments, who sat on the steps of a bungalow looking at an empty road. Her heavy face was painted, but in her large, tearless eyes there was no expression. The men who drove in the car were like schoolboys going home for the holidays. Gallagher gave a sigh of relief. In the early morning, under the bright sky, his spirits bubbled. The future was like a sunny road that wandered through a wide-flung, wooded plain.

Later in the day Mrs. Hamlyn asked the doctor how his patient did. The doctor shook his head.

"I'm done. I'm at the end of my tether." He frowned unhappily. "It's rotten luck, striking a case like this. It would be bad enough at home, but on board ship . . ."

He was an Edinburgh man, but recently qualified, and he was taking this voyage as a holiday before settling down to practice. He felt himself aggrieved. He wanted to have a good time and, faced with this mysterious illness, he was worried to death. Of course he was inexperienced, but he was doing everything that could be done and it exasperated him to suspect that the passengers thought him an ignorant fool.

"Have you heard what Mr. Pryce thinks?" asked Mrs. Hamlyn.

"I never heard such rot. I told the captain and he's right up in the air. He doesn't want it talked about. He thinks it'll upset the passengers."

"I'll be as silent as the grave."

The surgeon looked at her sharply.

"Of course you don't believe that there can be any truth in nonsense of that sort?" he asked.

"Of course not." She looked out at the sea which shone, blue and oily and still, all round them. "I've lived in the East a long time," she added. "Strange things happen there."

"This is getting on my nerves," said the doctor.

Near them two little Japanese gentlemen were playing deck quoits. They were trim and neat in their tennis shirts, white trousers and buckram shoes. They looked very European, they even called the score to one another in English, and yet somehow to look at them filled Mrs. Hamlyn at that moment with a vague disquiet. Because they seemed to wear so easily a disguise there was about them something sinister. Her nerves too were on edge.

And presently, no one quite knew how, the notion spread through the ship that Gallagher was bewitched. While the ladies sat about on their deck-chairs, stitching away at the costumes they were making for the fancy-dress party on Christmas day, they gossiped about it in undertones, and the men in the smoking-room talked of it over their cocktails. A good many of the passengers had lived long in the East and from the recesses of their memory they produced strange and inexplicable stories. Of course it was absurd to think seriously that Gallagher was suffering from a malignant spell, such things were impossible, and yet this and that was a fact and no one had been able to explain it. The doctor had to confess that he could suggest no cause for Gallagher's condition, he was able to give a physiological explanation, but why these terrible spasms should have suddenly assailed him he did not say. Feeling vaguely to blame, he tried to defend himself.

"Why, it's the sort of case you might never come across in the whole of your practice," he said. "It's rotten luck."

He was in wireless communication with passing ships and suggestions for treatment came from here and there.

"I've tried everything they tell me," he said irritably. "The doctor of the Japanese boat advised adrenalin. How the devil does he expect me to have adrenalin in the middle of the Indian Ocean?"

There was something impressive in the thought of this ship speeding through a deserted sea while to her from all parts came unseen messages. She seemed at that moment strangely alone and yet the centre of the world. In the lazaret the sick man, shaken by the cruel spasms, gasped for life. Then the passengers became conscious that the ship's course was altered and they heard that the captain had made up his mind to put in at Aden. Gallagher was to be landed there and taken to the hospital where he could have attention which on board was impossible. The chief engineer received orders to force his engines. The ship was an old one and she throbbed with the greater effort. The passengers had grown used to the sound and feel of her engines and now the greater vibration shook their nerves with a new sensation. It would not pass into each one's unconsciousness, but beat on their sensibilities so that each felt a personal concern. And still the wide sea was empty of traffic so that they seemed to traverse an empty world. And now the uneasiness which had descended upon the ship, but which no one had been willing to acknowledge, became a definite malaise. The passengers grew irritable, and people quarrelled over trifles which at another time would have seemed insignificant. Mr. Jephson made his hackneyed jokes, but no one any longer repaid him with a smile. The Linsells had an altercation and Mrs. Linsell was heard late at night walking round the deck with her husband, and uttering in a low, tense voice a stream of vehement reproaches. There was a violent scene in the smoking-room one night over a game of bridge, and the reconciliation which followed it was attended with general intoxication. People talked little of Gallagher, but he was seldom absent from their thoughts. They examined the route map. The doctor said now that Gallagher could not live more than three or four days and they discussed acrimoniously what was the shortest time in which Aden could be reached. What happened to him after he was landed was no affair of theirs; they did not want him to die on board.

Mrs. Hamlyn saw Gallagher every day. With the suddenness with which after tropical rain in the spring you seem to see the herbage grow before your very eyes, she saw him go to pieces. Already his skin hung loosely on his bones and his double chin was like the wrinkled wattle of a turkey-cock. His cheeks were sunken. You saw now how large his frame was and through the sheet under which he lay his bony structure was like the skeleton of a prehistoric giant. For the most part he lay with his eyes closed, torpid with morphia, but shaken still with terrible spasms and when now and again he opened his eyes they were preternaturally large; they looked at you vaguely, perplexed and troubled, from the depths of their bony sockets. But when, emerging from his stupor, he recognized Mrs. Hamlyn he forced a gallant smile to his lips.

"How are you, Mr. Gallagher?" she said.

"Getting along, getting along. I shall be all right when we get out of this confounded heat. Lord, how I look forward to a dip in the Atlantic. I'd give anything for a good long swim. I want to feel the cold grey sea of Galway beating against my chest."

Then the hiccup shook him from the crown of his head to the sole of his foot. Mr. Pryce and the stewardess shared the care of him. The little cockney's face wore no longer its look of impudent gaiety, but instead was sullen.

"The captain sent for me yesterday," he told Mrs. Hamlyn when they were alone. "He gave me a rare talking to."

"What about?"

"He said 'e wouldn't 'ave all this hoodoo stuff. He said it was frightening the passengers and I'd better keep a watch on me tongue or I'd 'ave 'im to reckon with. It's not my doing. I never said a word except to you and the doctor."

"It's all over the ship."

"I know it is. D'you think it's only me that's saying it? All them lascars and the Chinese, they all know what's the matter with him. You don't think you can teach them much, do you? They know it ain't a natural illness."

Mrs. Hamlyn was silent. She knew through the amahs of some of the passengers that there was no one on the ship, except the whites, who doubted that the woman whom Gallagher had left in distant Selantau was killing him with her magic. All were convinced that as they sighted the barren rocks of Arabia his soul would be parted from his body.

"The captain says if he hears of me trying any hanky-panky he'll confine me to my cabin for the rest of the voyage," said Pryce suddenly, a surly frown on his puckered face.

"What do you mean by hanky-panky?"

He looked at her for a moment fiercely as though she too were an object of the anger he felt against the captain.

"The doctor's tried every damned thing he knows, and he's wirelessed all over the place, and what good 'as 'e done? Tell me that. Can't 'e see the man's dying? There's only one way to save him now."

"What do you mean?"

"It's magic what's killing 'im, and it's only magic what'll save him. Oh, don't you say it can't be done. I've seen it with me own eyes." His voice rose, irritable and shrill. "I've seen a man dragged from the jaws of death, as you might say, when they got in a *pawang*, what we call a witch-doctor, an' 'e did 'is little tricks. I seen it with me own eyes, I tell you."

Mrs. Hamlyn did not speak. Pryce gave her a searching look.

"One of them lascars on board, he's a witch-doctor, same as the *pawang* thet we 'ave in the F.M.S. An' 'e says he'll do it. Only he must 'ave a live animal. A cock would do."

"What do you want a live animal for?" Mrs. Hamlyn asked, frowning a little.

The cockney looked at her with quick suspicion.

"If you take my advice you won't know anything about it. But I tell you what, I'm going to leave no stone unturned to save my governor. An' if the captain 'ears of it and shuts me up in me cabin, well, let 'im."

At that moment Mrs. Linsell came up and Pryce with his quaint gesture of salute left them. Mrs. Linsell wanted Mrs. Hamlyn to fit the dress she had been making herself for the fancy-dress ball, and on the way down to the cabin she spoke to her anxiously about the possibility that Mr. Gallagher might die on Christmas day. They could not possibly have the dance if he did. She had told the doctor that she would never speak to him again if this happened, and the doctor had promised her faithfully that he would keep the man alive over Christmas day somehow.

"It would be nice for him, too," said Mrs. Linsell.

"For whom?" asked Mrs. Hamlyn.

"For poor Mr. Gallagher. Naturally no one likes to die on Christmas day. Do they?"

"I don't really know," said Mrs. Hamlyn.

That night, after she had been asleep a little while, she awoke weeping. It dismayed her that she should cry in her sleep. It was as though then the weakness of the flesh mastered her, and, her will broken, she was defenceless against a natural sorrow. She turned over in her mind, as so often before, the details of the disaster which had so profoundly affected her; she repeated the conversations with her husband, wishing she had said this and blaming herself because she had said the other. She wished with all her heart that she had remained in comfortable ignorance of her husband's infatuation, and asked herself whether she would not have been wiser to pocket her pride and shut her eyes to the unwelcome truth. She was a woman of the world and she knew too well how much more she lost in separating herself from her husband than his love; she lost the settled establishment and the assured position, the ample means and the support of a recognized background. She had known of many separated wives, living equivocally on smallish incomes, and knew how quickly their friends found them tiresome. And she was lonely. She was as lonely as the ship that throbbed her hasting way through an unpeopled sea, and lonely as the friendless man who lay dying in the ship's lazaret. Mrs. Hamlyn knew that her thoughts had got the better of her now and that she would not easily sleep again. It was very hot in her cabin. She looked at the time; it was between four and half-past; she must pass two mortal hours before broke the reassuring day.

She slipped into a kimono and went on deck. The night was sombre and although the sky was unclouded no stars were visible. Panting and shaking, the old ship under full steam lumbered through the darkness. The silence was uncanny. Mrs. Hamlyn with bare feet groped her way slowly along the deserted deck. It was so black that she could see nothing. She came to the end of the promenade deck and leaned against the rail. Suddenly she started and her attention was fixed, for on the lower deck she caught a fitful glow. She leaned forward cautiously. It was a little fire, and she saw only the glow because the naked backs of men, crouched round, hid the flame. At the edge of the circle she divined, rather than saw, a stocky figure in pyjamas. The rest were natives, but this was a European. It must be Pryce and she guessed immediately that some dark ceremony of exorcism was in progress. Straining her ears she heard a low voice muttering a string of secret words. She began to tremble. She was aware that they were too intent upon their business to think that any one was watching them, but she dared not move. Suddenly, rending the sultry silence of the night like a piece of silk violently torn in two, came the crowing of a cock. Mrs. Hamlyn almost shrieked. Mr. Pryce was trying to save the life of his friend and master by a sacrifice to the strange gods of the East. The voice went on, low and insistent. Then in the dark circle there was a movement, something was happening, she knew not what; there was a cluck-cluck from the cock, angry and frightened, and then a strange, indescribable sound; the magician was cutting the cock's throat; then silence; there were vague doings that she could not follow, and in a little while it looked as though some one was stamping out the fire. The figures she had dimly seen were dissolved in the night and all once more was still. She heard again the regular throbbing of the engines.

Mrs. Hamlyn stood still for a little while, strangely shaken, and then walked slowly along the deck. She found a chair and lay down in it. She was trembling still. She could only guess what had happened. She did not know how long she lay there, but at last she felt that the dawn was approaching. It was not yet day, but it was no longer night. Against the darkness of the sky she could now see the ship's rail. Then she saw a figure come towards her. It was a man in pyjamas.

"Who's that?" she cried nervously.

"Only the doctor," came a friendly voice.

"Oh! What are you doing here at this time of night?"

"I've been with Gallagher." He sat down beside her and lit a cigarette. "I've given him a good strong hypodermic and he's quiet now."

"Has he been very ill?"

"I thought he was going to pass out. I was watching him, and suddenly he started up on his bed and began to talk Malay. Of course I couldn't understand a thing. He kept on saying one word over and over again."

"Perhaps it was a name, a woman's name."

"He wanted to get out of bed. He's a damned powerful man

even now. By George, I had a struggle with him. I was afraid
he'd throw himself overboard. He seemed to think some one
was calling him."

"When was that?" asked Mrs. Hamlyn slowly.

"Between four and half-past. Why?"

"Nothing."

She shuddered.

Later in the morning when the ship's life was set upon its
daily round, Mrs. Hamlyn passed Pryce on the deck, but he
gave her a brief greeting and walked on with quickly averted
gaze. He looked tired and overwrought. Mrs. Hamlyn thought
again of that fat woman, with golden ornaments in her thick,
black hair, who sat on the steps of the deserted bungalow and
looked at the road which ran through the trim lines of the rubber trees.

It was fearfully hot. She knew now why the night had been so
dark. The sky was no longer blue, but a dead, level white; its
surface was too even to give the effect of cloud; it was as though
in the upper air the heat hung like a pall. There was no breeze
and the sea, as colourless as the sky, was smooth and shining
like the dye in a dyer's vat. The passengers were listless; when
they walked round the deck they panted and beads of sweat
broke out on their foreheads. They spoke in undertones. Something uncanny and disquieting brooded over the ship, and they
could not bring themselves to laugh. A feeling of resentment
arose in their hearts; they were alive and well, and it exasperated them that, so near, a man should be dying and by the
fact (which was after all no concern of theirs) so mysteriously
affect them. A planter in the smoking-room over a gin sling
said brutally what most of them felt, though none had confessed.

"Well, if he's going to peg out," he said, "I wish he'd hurry
up and get it over. It gives me the creeps."

The day was interminable. Mrs. Hamlyn was thankful when
the dinner hour arrived. So much time, at all events, was
passed. She sat at the doctor's table.

"When do we reach Aden?" she asked.

"Some time to-morrow. The captain says we shall sight land
between five and six in the morning."

She gave him a sharp look. He stared at her for a moment,
then dropped his eyes and reddened. He remembered that the
woman, the fat woman sitting on the bungalow steps, had said

that Gallagher would never see the land. Mrs. Hamlyn wondered whether he, the sceptical, matter-of-fact young doctor, was wavering at last. He frowned a little, and then, as though he sought to pull himself together, looked at her once more.

"I shan't be sorry to hand over my patient to the hospital people at Aden, I can tell you," he said.

Next day was Christmas eve. When Mrs. Hamlyn awoke from a troubled sleep the dawn was breaking. She looked out of her porthole and saw that the sky was clear and silvery; during the night the haze had melted, and the morning was brilliant. With a lighter heart she went on deck. She walked as far forward as she could go. A late star twinkled palely close to the horizon. There was a shimmer on the sea as though a loitering breeze passed playful fingers over its surface. The light was exquisitely soft, tenuous like a budding wood in spring, and crystalline so that it reminded you of the bubbling of water in a mountain brook. She turned to look at the sun rising rosy in the east, and saw coming towards her the doctor. He wore his uniform; he had not been to bed all night; he was dishevelled and he walked, with bowed shoulders, as though he were dog-tired. She knew at once that Gallagher was dead. When he came up to her she saw that he was crying. He looked so young then that her heart went out to him. She took his hand.

"You poor dear," she said. "You're tired out."

"I did all I could," he said. "I wanted so awfully to save him."

His voice shook and she saw that he was almost hysterical.

"When did he die?" she asked.

He closed his eyes, trying to control himself, and his lips trembled.

"A few minutes ago."

Mrs. Hamlyn sighed. She found nothing to say. Her gaze wandered across the calm, dispassionate and ageless sea. It stretched on all sides of them as infinite as human sorrow. But on a sudden her eyes were held, for there, ahead of them, on the horizon was something which looked like a precipitous and massy cloud. But its outline was too sharp to be a cloud's. She touched the doctor on the arm.

"What's that?"

He looked at it for a moment and under his sunburn she saw him grow white.

"Land."

Once more Mrs. Hamlyn thought of the fat Malay woman who sat silent on the steps of Gallagher's bungalow. Did she know?

They buried him when the sun was high in the heavens. They stood on the lower deck and on the hatches, the first- and second-class passengers, the white stewards and the European officers. The missionary read the burial service.

"Man that is born of woman hath but a short time to live, and is full of misery. He cometh up, and is cut down, like a flower; he fleeth as it were a shadow, and never continueth in one stay."

Pryce looked down at the deck with knit brows. His teeth were tightly clenched. He did not grieve, for his heart was hot with anger. The doctor and the consul stood side by side. The consul bore to a nicety the expression of an official regret, but the doctor, clean-shaven now, in his neat fresh uniform and his gold braid, was pale and harassed. From him Mrs. Hamlyn's eyes wandered to Mrs. Linsell. She was pressed against her husband, weeping, and he was holding her hand tenderly. Mrs. Hamlyn did not know why this sight singularly affected her. At that moment of grief, her nerves distraught, the little woman went by instinct to the protection and support of her husband. But then Mrs. Hamlyn felt a little shudder pass through her and she fixed her eyes on the seams in the deck, for she did not want to see what was toward. There was a pause in the reading. There were various movements. One of the officers gave an order. The missionary's voice continued.

"Forasmuch as it has pleased Almighty God of his great mercy to take unto himself the soul of our dear brother here departed; we therefore commend his body to the deep, to be turned into corruption, looking for the resurrection of the body when the sea shall give up its dead."

Mrs. Hamlyn felt the hot tears flow down her cheeks. There was a dull splash. The missionary's voice went on.

When the service was finished the passengers scattered; the second-class passengers returned to their quarters and a bell rang to summon them to luncheon. But the first-class passengers sauntered aimlessly about the promenade deck. Most of the men made for the smoking-room and sought to cheer themselves with whiskies and sodas and with gin slings. But the consul put up a notice on the board outside the dining-saloon summoning the passengers to a meeting. Most of them had an idea for what purpose it was called and at the appointed hour they assembled. They were more cheerful than they had been for a week and they chattered with a gaiety which was only subdued by a mannerly reserve. The consul, an eye-glass in his eye, said that he had gathered them together to discuss the question of the fancy-dress ball on the following day. He knew they all had the deepest sympathy for Mr. Gallagher and he would have proposed that they should combine to send an appropriate message to the deceased's relatives; but his papers had been examined by the purser and no trace could be found of any relative or friend with whom it was possible to communicate. The late Mr. Gallagher appeared to be quite alone in the world. Meanwhile he (the consul) ventured to offer his sincere sympathy to the doctor who, he was quite sure, had done everything that was possible in the circumstances.

"Hear, hear," said the passengers.

They had all passed through a very trying time, proceeded the consul, and to some it might seem that it would be more respectful to the deceased's memory if the fancy-dress ball were postponed till New Year's eve. This, however, he told them frankly was not his view, and he was convinced that Mr. Gallagher himself would not have wished it. Of course it was a question for the majority to decide. The doctor got up and thanked the consul and the passengers for the kind things that had been said of him, it had of course been a very trying time, but he was authorized by the captain to say that the captain expressly wished all the festivities to be carried out on Christmas day as though nothing had happened. He (the doctor) told them in confidence that the captain felt the passengers had got into a rather morbid state and thought it would do them all good if they had a jolly good time on Christmas day. Then the missionary's wife rose and said they mustn't think only of themselves; it had been arranged by the Entertainment Committee that there should be a Christmas tree for the children immediately after the first-class passengers' dinner, and the children had been looking forward to seeing every one in fancy dress; it would be too bad to disappoint them; she yielded to no one in her respect for the dead and she sympathized with any one who felt too sad to think of dancing just then. Her own heart was very heavy, but she did feel it would be merely selfish to give way to a feeling which could do no good to any one. Let them think of the little ones. This very much impressed the passengers. They wanted to forget the brooding terror which had hung over the boat for so many days, they were alive and they wanted to enjoy themselves; but they had an uneasy notion that it would be decent to exhibit a certain grief. It was quite another matter if they could do as they wished from altruistic motives. When the consul called for a show of hands every one, but Mrs. Hamlyn and one old lady who was rheumatic, held up an eager arm.

"The ayes have it," said the consul. "And I venture to congratulate the meeting on a very sensible decision."

It was just going to break up when one of the planters got on his feet and said he wished to offer a suggestion. In the circumstances didn't they all think it would be as well to invite the second-class passengers? They had all come to the funeral that morning. The missionary jumped up and seconded the motion. The events of the last few days had drawn them all together, he said, and in the presence of death all men were equal. The consul again addressed them. This matter had been discussed at a previous meeting and the conclusion had been reached that it would be pleasanter for the second-class passengers to have their own party, but circumstances alter cases, and he was distinctly of opinion that their previous decision should be reversed.

"Hear, hear," said the passengers.

A wave of democratic feeling swept over them and the motion was carried by acclamation. They separated light-heartedly, they felt charitable and kindly. Every one stood every one else drinks in the smoking-room.

And so, on the following evening, Mrs. Hamlyn put on her fancy-dress. She had no heart for the gaiety before her, and for a moment had thought of feigning illness, but she knew no one would believe her, and was afraid to be thought affected. She was dressed as Carmen and she could not resist the vanity of making herself as attractive as possible. She darkened her eyelashes and rouged her cheeks. The costume suited her. When the bugle sounded and she went into the saloon she was received with flattering surprise. The consul (always a humorist) was dressed as a ballet-girl and was greeted with shouts of delighted laughter. The missionary and his wife, self-conscious but pleased with themselves, were very grand as Manchus. Mrs. Linsell, as Columbine, showed all that was possible of her very pretty legs. Her husband was an Arab sheik and the doctor was a Malay sultan.

A subscription had been collected to provide champagne at
dinner and the meal was hilarious. The company had provided
crackers in which were paper hats of various shapes and these
the passengers put on. There were paper streamers too which
they threw at one another and little balloons which they beat
from one to the other across the room. They laughed and
shouted. They were very gay. No one could say that they were
not having a good time. As soon as dinner was finished they
went into the saloon where the Christmas tree, with candles lit,
was ready, and the children were brought in, shrieking with
delight, and given presents. Then the dance began. The second-
class passengers stood about shyly round the part of the deck
reserved for dancing and occasionally danced with one another.

"I'm glad we had them," said the consul, dancing with Mrs.
Hamlyn. "I'm all for democracy, and I think they're very
sensible to keep themselves to themselves."

But he noticed that Pryce was not to be seen, and when an
opportunity presented asked one of the second-class passengers
where he was.

"Blind to the world," was the answer. "We put him to bed
in the afternoon and locked him up in his cabin."

The consul claimed her for another dance. He was very
facetious. Suddenly Mrs. Hamlyn felt that she could not bear
it any more, the noise of the amateur band, the consul's jokes,
the gaiety of the dancers. She knew not why, but the merriment
of those people passing on their ship through the night and the
solitary sea affected her on a sudden with horror. When the
consul released her he slipped away and, with a look to see
that no one had noticed her, ascended the companion to the
boat-deck. Here everything was in darkness. She walked softly
to a spot where she knew she would be safe from all intrusion.
But she heard a faint laugh and she caught sight in a hidden
corner of a Columbine and a Malay sultan. Mrs. Linsell and the
doctor had resumed already the flirtation which the death of
Gallagher had interrupted.

Already all those people had put out of their minds with a
kind of ferocity the thought of that poor lonely man who had so
strangely died in their midst. They felt no compassion for him,
but resentment rather, because on his account they had been
ill-at-ease. They seized upon life avidly. They made their jokes,
they flirted, they gossiped. Mrs. Hamlyn remembered what
the consul had said, that among Mr. Gallagher's papers no

letter could be found, not the name of a single friend to whom
the news of his death might be sent, and she knew not why this
seemed to her unbearably tragic. There was something mysterious in a man who could pass through the world in such solitariness. When she remembered how he had come on deck in
Singapore, so short a while since, in such rude health, full of
vitality, and his arrogant plans for the future, she was seized
with dismay. Those words of the burial service filled her with a
solemn awe: *Man that is born of woman hath but a short time to
live, and is full of misery. He cometh up, and is cut down, like a
flower.* . . . Year in, year out, he had made his plans for the
future, he wanted to live so much and he had so much to live
for, and then just when he stretched out his hand—oh, it was
pitiful; it made all the other distresses of the world of small account. Death with its mystery was the only thing that really
mattered. Mrs. Hamlyn leaned over the rail and looked at the
starry sky. Why did people make themselves unhappy? Let
them weep for the death of those they loved, death was terrible
always, but for the rest, was it worth while to be wretched, to
harbour malice, to be vain and uncharitable? She thought again
of herself and her husband and the woman he so strangely
loved. He too had said that we live to be happy so short a time
and we are so long dead. She pondered long and intently, and
suddenly, as summer lightning flashes across the darkness of
the night, she made a discovery which filled her with tremulous
surprise; for she found that in her heart was no longer anger
with her husband nor jealousy of her rival. A notion dawned
on some remote horizon of her consciousness and like the
morning sun suffused her soul with a tender, blissful glow.
Out of the tragedy of that unknown Irishman's death she
gathered elatedly the courage for a desperate resolution. Her
heart beat quickly, she was impatient to carry it into effect. A
passion for self-sacrifice seized her.

The music had stopped, the ball was over; most of the passengers would have gone to bed and the rest would be in the
smoking-room. She went down to her cabin and met no one
on the way. She took her writing-pad and wrote a letter to her
husband.

*My dear. It is Christmas day and I want to tell you that my
heart is filled with kindly thoughts towards both of you. I have
been foolish and unreasonable. I think we should allow those we*

care for to be happy in their own way, and we should care for them enough not to let it make us unhappy. I want you to know that I grudge you none of the joy that has so strangely come into your life. I am no longer jealous, nor hurt, nor vindictive. Do not think I shall be unhappy or lonely. If ever you feel that you need me, come to me, and I will welcome you with a cheerful spirit and without reproach or ill-will. I am most grateful for all the years of happiness and of tenderness that you gave me, and in return I wish to offer you an affection which makes no claim on you and is, I hope, utterly disinterested. Think kindly of me and be happy, happy, happy.

She signed her name and put the letter into an envelope. Though it would not go till they reached Port Said she wanted to place it at once in the letter-box. When she had done this, beginning to undress, she looked at herself in the glass. Her eyes were shining and under her rouge her colour was bright. The future was no longer desolate, but bright with a fair hope. She slipped into bed and fell at once into a sound and dreamless sleep.

JANE

I REMEMBER very well the occasion on which I first saw Jane
Fowler. It is indeed only because the details of the glimpse I
had of her then are so clear that I trust my recollection at all,
for, looking back, I must confess that I find it hard to believe
that it has not played me a fantastic trick. I had lately returned
to London from China and was drinking a dish of tea with Mrs.
Tower. Mrs. Tower had been seized with the prevailing passion
for decoration; and with the ruthlessness of her sex had sacrificed chairs in which she had comfortably sat for years, tables,
cabinets, ornaments, on which her eyes had dwelt in peace
since she was married, pictures that had been familiar to her
for a generation; and delivered herself into the hands of an
expert. Nothing remained in her drawing-room with which she
had any association, or to which any sentiment was attached;
and she had invited me that day to see the fashionable glory in
which she now lived. Everything that could be pickled was
pickled and what couldn't be pickled was painted. Nothing
matched, but everything harmonized.

"Do you remember that ridiculous drawing-room suite that
I used to have?" asked Mrs. Tower.

The curtains were sumptuous yet severe; the sofa was covered with Italian brocade; the chair on which I sat was in *petit
point*. The room was beautiful, opulent without garishness and
original without affectation; yet to me it lacked something;
and while I praised with my lips I asked myself why I so much
preferred the rather shabby chintz of the despised suite, the
Victorian water-colours that I had known so long, and the

ridiculous Dresden china that had adorned the chimney-piece.
I wondered what it was that I missed in all these rooms that
the decorators were turning out with a profitable industry.
Was it heart? But Mrs. Tower looked about her happily.

"Don't you like my alabaster lamps?" she said. "They
give such a soft light."

"Personally I have a weakness for a light that you can see
by," I smiled.

"It's so difficult to combine that with a light that you can't
be too much seen by," laughed Mrs. Tower.

I had no notion what her age was. When I was quite a young
man she was a married woman a good deal older than I, but
now she treated me as her contemporary. She constantly said
that she made no secret of her age, which was forty, and then
added with a smile that all women took five years off. She
never sought to conceal the fact that she dyed her hair (it was
a very pretty brown with reddish tints), and she said she did
this because hair was hideous while it was going grey; as soon
as hers was white she would cease to dye it.

"Then they'll say what a young face I have."

Meanwhile it was painted, though with discretion, and her
eyes owed not a little of their vivacity to art. She was a handsome woman, exquisitely gowned, and in the sombre glow of the
alabaster lamps did not look a day more than the forty she
gave herself.

"It is only at my dressing-table that I can suffer the naked
brightness of a thirty-two-candle electric bulb," she added
with smiling cynicism. "There I need it to tell me first the hideous truth and then to enable me to take the necessary steps to
correct it."

We gossiped pleasantly about our common friends and Mrs.
Tower brought me up to date in the scandal of the day. After
roughing it here and there it was very agreeable to sit in a comfortable chair, the fire burning brightly on the hearth, charming
tea-things set out on a charming table, and talk with this amusing, attractive woman. She treated me as a prodigal returned
from his husks and was disposed to make much of me. She
prided herself on her dinner-parties; she took no less trouble
to have her guests suitably assorted than to give them excellent
food; and there were few persons who did not look upon it as
a treat to be bidden to one of them. Now she fixed a date and
asked me whom I would like to meet.

"There's only one thing I must tell you. If Jane Fowler is still here I shall have to put it off."

"Who is Jane Fowler?" I asked.

Mrs. Tower gave a rueful smile.

"Jane Fowler is my cross."

"Oh!"

"Do you remember a photograph that I used to have on the piano before I had my room done of a woman in a tight dress with tight sleeves and a gold locket, with her hair drawn back from a broad forehead and her ears showing and spectacles on a rather blunt nose? Well, that was Jane Fowler."

"You had so many photographs about the room in your unregenerate days," I said, vaguely.

"It makes me shudder to think of them. I've made them into a huge brown-paper parcel and hidden them in an attic."

"Well, who is Jane Fowler?" I asked again, smiling.

"She's my sister-in-law. She was my husband's sister and she married a manufacturer in the north. She's been a widow for many years, and she's very well-to-do."

"And why is she your cross?"

"She's worthy, she's dowdy, she's provincial. She looks twenty years older than I do and she's quite capable of telling anyone she meets that we were at school together. She has an overwhelming sense of family affection, and because I am her only living connection she's devoted to me. When she comes to London it never occurs to her that she should stay anywhere but here—she thinks it would hurt my feelings—and she'll pay me visits of three or four weeks. We sit here and she knits and reads. And sometimes she insists on taking me to dine at Claridge's and she looks like a funny old charwoman and everyone I particularly don't want to be seen by is sitting at the next table. When we are driving home she says she loves giving me a little treat. With her own hands she makes me tea-cozies that I am forced to use when she is here and doilies and centrepieces for the dining-room table."

Mrs. Tower paused to take breath.

"I should have thought a woman of your tact would find a way to deal with a situation like that."

"Ah, but don't you see, I haven't a chance. She's so immeasurably kind. She has a heart of gold. She bores me to death, but I wouldn't for anything let her suspect it."

"And when does she arrive?"

"To-morrow."

But the answer was hardly out of Mrs. Tower's mouth when the bell rang. There were sounds in the hall of a slight commotion and in a minute or two the butler ushered in an elderly lady.

"Mrs. Fowler," he announced.

"Jane!" cried Mrs. Tower, springing to her feet. "I wasn't expecting you to-day."

"So your butler has just told me. I certainly said to-day in my letter."

Mrs. Tower recovered her wits.

"Well, it doesn't matter. I'm very glad to see you whenever you come. Fortunately I'm doing nothing this evening."

"You mustn't let me give you any trouble. If I can have a boiled egg for my dinner that's all I shall want."

A faint grimace for a moment distorted Mrs. Tower's handsome features. A boiled egg!

"Oh, I think we can do a little better than that."

I chuckled inwardly when I recollected that the two ladies were contemporaries. Mrs. Fowler looked a good fifty-five. She was a rather big woman; she wore a black straw hat with a wide brim, and from it a black lace veil hung over her shoulders, a cloak that oddly combined severity with fussiness, a long black dress, voluminous as though she wore several petticoats under it, and stout boots. She was evidently short-sighted, for she looked at you through large gold-rimmed spectacles.

"Won't you have a cup of tea?" asked Mrs. Tower.

"If it wouldn't be too much trouble. I'll take off my mantle."

She began by stripping her hands of the black gloves she wore, and then took off her cloak. Round her neck was a solid gold chain from which hung a large gold locket in which I felt certain was a photograph of her deceased husband. Then she took off her hat and placed it neatly with her gloves and cloak on the sofa corner. Mrs. Tower pursed her lips. Certainly those garments did not go very well with the austere but sumptuous beauty of Mrs. Tower's redecorated drawing-room. I wondered where on earth Mrs. Fowler had found the extraordinary clothes she wore. They were not old, and the materials were expensive. It was astounding to think that dressmakers still made things that had not been worn for a quarter of a century. Mrs. Fowler's grey hair was very plainly done, showing all her forehead and her ears, with a parting in the middle. It had evidently never known the tongs of Monsieur Marcel. Now her eyes fell on the tea-table with its teapot of Georgian silver and its cups in old Worcester.

"What have you done with the tea-cozy I gave you last time I came up, Marion?" she asked. "Don't you use it?"

"Yes, I use it every day, Jane," answered Mrs. Tower glibly. "Unfortunately we had an accident with it a little while ago. It got burnt."

"But the last one I gave you got burnt."

"I'm afraid you'll think us very careless."

"It doesn't really matter," smiled Mrs. Fowler. "I shall enjoy making you another. I'll go to Liberty's to-morrow and buy some silks."

Mrs. Tower kept her face bravely.

"I don't deserve it, you know. Doesn't your vicar's wife need one?"

"Oh, I've just made her one," said Mrs. Fowler brightly.

I noticed that when she smiled she showed white, small and regular teeth. They were a real beauty. Her smile was certainly very sweet.

But I felt it high time for me to leave the two ladies to themselves, so I took my leave.

Early next morning Mrs. Tower rang me up, and I heard at once from her voice that she was in high spirits.

"I've got the most wonderful news for you," she said. "Jane is going to be married."

"Nonsense."

"Her fiancé is coming to dine here to-night to be introduced to me, and I want you to come too."

"Oh, but I shall be in the way."

"No, you won't. Jane suggested herself that I should ask you. Do come."

She was bubbling over with laughter.

"Who is he?"

"I don't know. She tells me he's an architect. Can you imagine the sort of man Jane would marry?"

I had nothing to do and I could trust Mrs. Tower to give me a good dinner.

When I arrived Mrs. Tower, very splendid in a tea-gown a little too young for her, was alone.

"Jane is putting the finishing touches to her appearance. I'm longing for you to see her. She's all in a flutter. She says

he adores her. His name is Gilbert and when she speaks of
him her voice gets all funny and tremulous. It makes me want
to laugh."

"I wonder what he's like."

"Oh, I'm sure I know. Very big and massive, with a bald
head and an immense gold chain across an immense tummy.
A large, fat, clean-shaven, red face and a booming voice."

Mrs. Fowler came in. She wore a very stiff black silk dress
with a wide skirt and a train. At the neck it was cut into a
timid V and the sleeves came down to the elbows. She wore a
necklace of diamonds set in silver. She carried in her hands a
long pair of black gloves and a fan of black ostrich feathers.
She managed (as so few people do) to look exactly what she was.
You could never have thought her anything in the world but
the respectable relict of a north-country manufacturer of ample
means.

"You've really got quite a pretty neck, Jane," said Mrs.
Tower with a kindly smile.

It was indeed astonishingly young when you compared it
with her weather-beaten face. It was smooth and unlined and
the skin was white. And I noticed then that her head was very
well placed on her shoulders.

"Has Marion told you my news?" she said, turning to me
with that really charming smile of hers as if we were already
old friends.

"I must congratulate you," I said.

"Wait to do that till you've seen my young man."

"I think it's too sweet to hear you talk of your young man,"
smiled Mrs. Tower.

Mrs. Fowler's eyes certainly twinkled behind her preposterous spectacles.

"Don't expect anyone too old. You wouldn't like me to
marry a decrepit old gentleman with one foot in the grave,
would you?"

This was the only warning she gave us. Indeed there was no
time for any further discussion, for the butler flung open the
door and in a loud voice announced:

"Mr. Gilbert Napier."

There entered a youth in a very well-cut dinner jacket. He
was slight, not very tall, with fair hair in which there was a
hint of a natural wave, clean-shaven and blue-eyed. He was not
particularly good-looking, but he had a pleasant, amiable face.

In ten years he would probably be wizened and sallow; but now, in extreme youth, he was fresh, and clean and blooming. For he was certainly not more than twenty-four. My first thought was that this was the son of Jane Fowler's fiancé (I had not known he was a widower) come to say that his father was prevented from dining by a sudden attack of gout. But his eyes fell immediately on Mrs. Fowler, his face lit up, and he went towards her with both hands outstretched. Mrs. Fowler gave him hers, a demure smile on her lips, and turned to her sister-in-law.

"This is my young man, Marion," she said.

He held out his hand.

"I hope you'll like me, Mrs. Tower," he said. "Jane tells me you're the only relation she has in the world."

Mrs. Tower's face was wonderful to behold. I saw then to admiration how bravely good breeding and social usage could combat the instincts of the natural woman. For the astonishment and then the dismay that for an instant she could not conceal were quickly driven away, and her face assumed an expression of affable welcome. But she was evidently at a loss for words. It was not unnatural if Gilbert felt a certain embarrassment, and I was too busy preventing myself from laughing to think of anything to say. Mrs. Fowler alone kept perfectly calm.

"I know you'll like him, Marion. There's no one enjoys good food more than he does." She turned to the young man. "Marion's dinners are famous."

"I know," he beamed.

Mrs. Tower made some quick rejoinder and we went downstairs. I shall not soon forget the exquisite comedy of that meal. Mrs. Tower could not make up her mind whether the pair of them were playing a practical joke on her or whether Jane by wilfully concealing her fiancé's age had hoped to make her look foolish. But then Jane never jested and she was incapable of doing a malicious thing. Mrs. Tower was amazed, exasperated and perplexed. But she had recovered her self-control, and for nothing would she have forgotten that she was a perfect hostess whose duty it was to make her party go. She talked vivaciously; but I wondered if Gilbert Napier saw how hard and vindictive was the expression of her eyes behind the mask of friendliness that she turned to him. She was measuring him. She was seeking to delve into the secret of his soul. I could see that she was in a passion, for under her rouge her cheeks glowed with an angry red.

"You've got a very high colour, Marion," said Jane, looking at her amiably through her great round spectacles.

"I dressed in a hurry. I daresay I put on too much rouge."

"Oh, is it rouge? I thought it was natural. Otherwise I shouldn't have mentioned it." She gave Gilbert a shy little smile. "You know, Marion and I were at school together. You would never think it to look at us now, would you? But of course I've lived a very quiet life."

I do not know what she meant by these remarks; it was almost incredible that she made them in complete simplicity; but anyhow they goaded Mrs. Tower to such a fury that she flung her own vanity to the winds. She smiled brightly.

"We shall neither of us see fifty again, Jane," she said.

If the observation was meant to discomfit the widow it failed.

"Gilbert says I mustn't acknowledge to more than forty-nine for his sake," she answered blandly.

Mrs. Tower's hands trembled slightly, but she found a retort.

"There is of course a certain disparity of age between you," she smiled.

"Twenty-seven years," said Jane. "Do you think it's too much? Gilbert says I'm very young for my age. I told you I shouldn't like to marry a man with one foot in the grave."

I was really obliged to laugh, and Gilbert laughed too. His laughter was frank and boyish. It looked as though he were amused at everything Jane said. But Mrs. Tower was almost at the end of her tether, and I was afraid that unless relief came she would for once forget that she was a woman of the world. I came to the rescue as best I could.

"I suppose you're very busy buying your trousseau," I said.

"No. I wanted to get my things from the dressmaker in Liverpool I've been to ever since I was first married. But Gilbert won't let me. He's very masterful, and of course he has wonderful taste."

She looked at him with a little affectionate smile, demurely, as though she were a girl of seventeen.

Mrs. Tower went quite pale under her make-up.

"We're going to Italy for our honeymoon. Gilbert has never had a chance of studying Renaissance architecture, and of

course it's important for an architect to see things for himself.
And we shall stop in Paris on the way and get my clothes there."

"Do you expect to be away long?"

"Gilbert has arranged with his office to stay away for six
months. It will be such a treat for him, won't it? You see, he's
never had more than a fortnight's holiday before."

"Why not?" asked Mrs. Tower in a tone that no effort of
will could prevent from being icy.

"He's never been able to afford it, poor dear."

"Ah!" said Mrs. Tower, and into the exclamation put
volumes.

Coffee was served and the ladies went upstairs. Gilbert and
I began to talk in the desultory way in which men talk who have
nothing whatever to say to one another; but in two minutes a
note was brought in to me by the butler. It was from Mrs.
Tower and ran as follows:

*Come upstairs quickly and then go as soon as you can. Take him
with you. Unless I have it out with Jane at once I shall have a fit.*

I told a facile lie.

"Mrs. Tower has a headache and wants to go to bed. I think
if you don't mind we'd better clear out."

"Certainly," he answered.

We went upstairs and five minutes later were on the doorstep.
I called a taxi and offered the young man a lift.

"No, thanks," he answered. "I'll just walk to the corner
and jump on a bus."

Mrs. Tower sprang to the fray as soon as she heard the front
door close behind us.

"Are you crazy, Jane?" she cried.

"Not more than most people who don't habitually live in a
lunatic asylum, I trust," Jane answered blandly.

"May I ask why you're going to marry this young man?"
asked Mrs. Tower with formidable politeness.

"Partly because he won't take no for an answer. He's asked
me five times. I grew positively tired of refusing him."

"And why do you think he's so anxious to marry you?"

"I amuse him."

Mrs. Tower gave an exclamation of annoyance.

"He's an unscrupulous rascal. I very nearly told him so to
his face."

"You would have been wrong, and it wouldn't have been very polite."

"He's penniless and you're rich. You can't be such a besotted fool as not to see that he's marrying you for your money."

Jane remained perfectly composed. She observed her sister-in-law's agitation with detachment.

"I don't think he is, you know," she replied. "I think he's very fond of me."

"You're an old woman, Jane."

"I'm at the same age as you are, Marion," she smiled.

"I've never let myself go. I'm very young for my age. No one would think I was more than forty. But even I wouldn't dream of marrying a boy twenty years younger than myself."

"Twenty-seven," corrected Jane.

"Do you mean to tell me that you can bring yourself to believe that it's possible for a young man to care for a woman old enough to be his mother?"

"I've lived very much in the country for many years. I daresay there's a great deal about human nature that I don't know. They tell me there's a man called Freud, an Austrian, I believe——"

But Mrs. Tower interrupted her without any politeness at all.

"Don't be ridiculous, Jane. It's so undignified. It's so ungraceful. I always thought you were a sensible woman. Really you're the last person I should ever have thought likely to fall in love with a boy."

"But I'm not in love with him. I've told him that. Of course I like him very much or I wouldn't think of marrying him. I thought it only fair to tell him quite plainly what my feelings were towards him."

Mrs. Tower gasped. The blood rushed to her head and her breathing oppressed her. She had no fan, but she seized the evening paper and vigorously fanned herself with it.

"If you're not in love with him why do you want to marry him?"

"I've been a widow a very long time and I've led a very quiet life. I thought I'd like a change."

"If you want to marry just to be married why don't you marry a man of your own age?"

"No man of my own age has asked me five times. In fact no man of my own age has asked me at all."

Jane chuckled as she answered. It drove Mrs. Tower to the final pitch of frenzy.

"Don't laugh, Jane. I won't have it. I don't think you can be right in your mind. It's dreadful."

It was altogether too much for her and she burst into tears. She knew that at her age it was fatal to cry; her eyes would be swollen for twenty-four hours and she would look a sight. But there was no help for it. She wept. Jane remained perfectly calm. She looked at Marion through her large spectacles and reflectively smoothed the lap of her black silk dress.

"You're going to be so dreadfully unhappy," Mrs. Tower sobbed, dabbing her eyes cautiously in the hope that the black on her lashes would not smudge.

"I don't think so, you know," Jane answered in those equable, mild tones of hers, as if there were a little smile behind the words. "We've talked it over very thoroughly. I always think I'm a very easy person to live with. I think I shall make Gilbert very happy and comfortable. He's never had anyone to look after him properly. We're only marrying after mature consideration. And we've decided that if either of us wants his liberty the other will place no obstacles in the way of his getting it."

Mrs. Tower had by now recovered herself sufficiently to make a cutting remark.

"How much has he persuaded you to settle on him?"

"I wanted to settle a thousand a year on him, but he wouldn't hear of it. He was quite upset when I made the suggestion. He says he can earn quite enough for his own needs."

"He's more cunning than I thought," said Mrs. Tower acidly.

Jane paused a little and looked at her sister-in-law with kindly but resolute eyes.

"You see, my dear, it's different for you," she said. "You've never been so very much a widow, have you?"

Mrs. Tower looked at her. She blushed a little. She even felt slightly uncomfortable. But of course Jane was much too simple to intend an innuendo. Mrs. Tower gathered herself together with dignity.

"I'm so upset that I really must go to bed," she said. "We'll resume the conversation to-morrow morning."

"I'm afraid that won't be very convenient, dear. Gilbert and I are going to get the license to-morrow morning."

Mrs. Tower threw up her hands in a gesture of dismay, but she found nothing more to say.

The marriage took place at a registrar's office. Mrs. Tower and I were the witnesses. Gilbert in a smart blue suit looked absurdly young and he was obviously nervous. It is a trying moment for any man. But Jane kept her admirable composure. She might have been in the habit of marrying as frequently as a woman of fashion. Only a slight colour on her cheeks suggested that beneath her calm was some faint excitement. It is a thrilling moment for any woman. She wore a very full dress of silver grey velvet, in the cut of which I recognized the hand of the dressmaker in Liverpool (evidently a widow of unimpeachable character), who had made her gowns for so many years; but she had so far succumbed to the frivolity of the occasion as to wear a large picture hat covered with blue ostrich feathers. Her gold-rimmed spectacles made it extraordinarily grotesque. When the ceremony was over the registrar (somewhat taken aback, I thought, by the difference of age between the pair he was marrying) shook hands with her, tendering his strictly official congratulations; and the bridegroom, blushing slightly, kissed her. Mrs. Tower, resigned but implacable, kissed her; and then the bride looked at me expectantly. It was evidently fitting that I should kiss her too. I did. I confess that I felt a little shy as we walked out of the registrar's office past loungers who waited cynically to see the bridal pairs, and it was with relief that I stepped into Mrs. Tower's car. We drove to Victoria Station, for the happy couple were to go over to Paris by the two o'clock train, and Jane had insisted that the wedding-breakfast should be eaten at the station restaurant. She said it always made her nervous not to be on the platform in good time. Mrs. Tower, present only from a strong sense of family duty, was able to do little to make the party go off well; she ate nothing (for which I could not blame her, since the food was execrable, and anyway I hate champagne at luncheon) and talked in a strained voice. But Jane went through the menu conscientiously.

"I always think one should make a hearty meal before starting out on a journey," she said.

We saw them off, and I drove Mrs. Tower back to her house.

"How long do you give it?" she said. "Six months?"

"Let's hope for the best," I smiled.

"Don't be so absurd. There can be no best. You don't think he's marrying her for anything but her money, do you? Of course it can't last. My only hope is that she won't have to go through as much suffering as she deserves."

I laughed. The charitable words were spoken in such a tone as to leave me in small doubt of Mrs. Tower's meaning.

"Well, if it doesn't last you'll have the consolation of saying 'I told you so,'" I said.

"I promise you I'll never do that."

"Then you'll have the satisfaction of congratulating yourself on your self-control in not saying 'I told you so.'"

"She's old and dowdy and dull."

"Are you sure she's dull?" I said. "It's true she doesn't say very much, but when she says anything it's very much to the point."

"I've never heard her make a joke in my life."

I was once more in the Far East when Gilbert and Jane returned from their honeymoon, and this time I remained away for nearly two years. Mrs. Tower was a bad correspondent and though I sent her an occasional picture-postcard I received no news from her. But I met her within a week of my return to London; I was dining out and found that I was seated next to her. It was an immense party—I think we were four-and-twenty like the blackbirds in the pie—and, arriving somewhat late, I was too confused by the crowd in which I found myself to notice who was there. But when we sat down, looking round the long table I saw that a good many of my fellow-guests were well known to the public from their photographs in the illustrated papers. Our hostess had a weakness for the persons technically known as celebrities, and this was an unusually brilliant gathering. When Mrs. Tower and I had exchanged the conventional remarks that two people make when they have not seen one another for a couple of years I asked about Jane.

"She's very well," said Mrs. Tower with a certain dryness.

"How has the marriage turned out?"

Mrs. Tower paused a little and took a salted almond from the dish in front of her.

"It appears to be quite a success."

"You were wrong, then?"

"I said it wouldn't last and I still say it won't last. It's contrary to human nature."

"Is she happy?"

"They're both happy."

"I suppose you don't see very much of them."

"At first I saw quite a lot of them. But now . . ." Mrs. Tower pursed her lips a little. "Jane is becoming very grand."

"What *do* you mean?" I laughed.

"I think I should tell you that she's here to-night."

"Here?"

I was startled. I looked round the table again. Our hostess was a delightful and an entertaining woman, but I could not imagine that she would be likely to invite to a dinner such as this the elderly and dowdy wife of an obscure architect. Mrs. Tower saw my perplexity and was shrewd enough to see what was in my mind. She smiled thinly.

"Look on the left of our host."

I looked. Oddly enough the woman who sat there had by her fantastic appearance attracted my attention the moment I was ushered into the crowded drawing-room. I thought I noticed a gleam of recognition in her eye, but to the best of my belief I had never seen her before. She was not a young woman, for her hair was iron-grey; it was cut very short and clustered thickly round her well-shaped head in tight curls. She made no attempt at youth, for she was conspicuous in that gathering by using neither lipstick, rouge nor powder. Her face, not a particularly handsome one, was red and weather-beaten; but because it owed nothing to artifice had a naturalness that was very pleasing. It contrasted oddly with the whiteness of her shoulders. They were really magnificent. A woman of thirty might have been proud of them. But her dress was extraordinary. I had not seen often anything more audacious. It was cut very low, with short skirts, which were then the fashion, in black and yellow; it had almost the effect of fancy-dress and yet so became her that though on anyone else it would have been outrageous, on her it had the inevitable simplicity of nature. And to complete the impression of an eccentricity in which there was no pose and of an extravagance in which there was no ostentation she wore, attached by a broad black ribbon, a single eye-glass.

"You're not going to tell me *that* is your sister-in-law," I gasped.

"That is Jane Napier," said Mrs. Tower icily.

At that moment she was speaking. Her host was turned towards her with an anticipatory smile. A baldish white-haired man, with a sharp, intelligent face, who sat on her left, was leaning forward eagerly, and the couple who sat opposite, ceasing to talk with one another, listened intently. She said her say and they all, with a sudden movement, threw themselves back in their chairs and burst into vociferous laughter. From the other side of the table a man addressed Mrs. Tower: I recognized a famous statesman.

"Your sister-in-law has made another joke, Mrs. Tower," he said.

Mrs. Tower smiled.

"She's priceless, isn't she?"

"Let me have a long drink of champagne and then for heaven's sake tell me all about it," I said.

Well, this is how I gathered it had all happened. At the beginning of their honeymoon Gilbert took Jane to various dressmakers in Paris and he made no objection to her choosing a number of "gowns" after her own heart; but he persuaded her to have a "frock" or two made according to his own design. It appeared that he had a knack for that kind of work. He engaged a smart French maid. Jane had never had such a thing before. She did her own mending and when she wanted "doing up" was in the habit of ringing for the housemaid. The dresses Gilbert had devised were very different from anything she had worn before; but he had been careful not to go too far too quickly, and because it pleased him she persuaded herself, though not without misgivings, to wear them in preference to those she had chosen herself. Of course she could not wear them with the voluminous petticoats she had been in the habit of using, and these, though it cost her an anxious moment, she discarded.

"Now, if you please," said Mrs. Tower, with something very like a sniff of disapproval, "she wears nothing but thin silk tights. It's a wonder to me she doesn't catch her death of cold at her age."

Gilbert and the French maid taught her how to wear her clothes, and, unexpectedly enough, she was very quick at learning. The French maid was in raptures over Madame's arms and shoulders. It was a scandal not to show anything so fine.

"Wait a little, Alphonsine," said Gilbert. "The next lot of clothes I design for Madame we'll make the most of her."

The spectacles of course were dreadful. No one could look really well in gold-rimmed spectacles. Gilbert tried some with tortoise-shell rims. He shook his head.

"They'd look all right on a girl," he said. "You're too old to wear spectacles, Jane." Suddenly he had an inspiration. "By George, I've got it. You must wear an eyeglass."

"Oh, Gilbert, I couldn't."

She looked at him, and his excitement, the excitement of the artist, made her smile. He was so sweet to her she wanted to do what she could to please him.

"I'll try," she said.

When they went to an optician and, suited with the right size, she placed an eyeglass jauntily in her eye Gilbert clapped his hands. There and then, before the astonished shopman, he kissed her on both cheeks.

"You look wonderful," he cried.

So they went down to Italy and spent happy months studying Renaissance and Baroque architecture. Jane not only grew accustomed to her changed appearance but found she liked it. At first she was a little shy when she went into the dining-room of a hotel and people turned round to stare at her—no one had ever raised an eyelid to look at her before—but presently she found that the sensation was not disagreeable. Ladies came up to her and asked her where she got her dress.

"Do you like it?" she answered demurely. "My husband designed it for me."

"I should like to copy it if you don't mind."

Jane had certainly for many years lived a very quiet life, but she was by no means lacking in the normal instincts of her sex. She had her answer ready.

"I'm so sorry, but my husband's very particular and he won't hear of anyone copying my frocks. He wants me to be unique."

She had an idea that people would laugh when she said this, but they didn't; they merely answered:

"Oh, of course I quite understand. You *are* unique."

But she saw them making mental notes of what she wore, and for some reason this quite "put her about." For once in her life when she wasn't wearing what everybody else did, she reflected, she didn't see why everybody else should want to wear what she did.

"Gilbert," she said, quite sharply for her, "next time you're designing dresses for me I wish you'd design things that people *can't* copy."

"The only way to do that is to design things that only you can wear."

"Can't you do that?"

"Yes, if you'll do something for me."

"What is it?"

"Cut off your hair."

I think this was the first time that Jane jibbed. Her hair was long and thick, and as a girl she had been quite vain of it; to cut it off was a very drastic proceeding. This really was burning her boats behind her. In her case it was not the first step that cost so much, it was the last; but she took it ("I know Marion will think me a perfect fool, and I shall *never* be able to go to Liverpool again," she said), and when they passed through Paris on their way home Gilbert led her (she felt quite sick, her heart was beating so fast) to the best hairdresser in the world. She came out of his shop with a jaunty, saucy, impudent head of crisp grey curls. Pygmalion had finished his fantastic masterpiece: Galatea was come to life.

"Yes," I said, "but that isn't enough to explain why Jane is here to-night amid this crowd of duchesses, cabinet ministers and such like; nor why she is sitting on one side of her host with an admiral of the Fleet on the other."

"Jane is a humorist," said Mrs. Tower. "Didn't you see them all laughing at what she said?"

There was no doubt now of the bitterness in Mrs. Tower's heart.

"When Jane wrote and told me they were back from their honeymoon I thought I must ask them both to dinner. I didn't much like the idea, but I felt it had to be done. I knew the party would be deadly and I wasn't going to sacrifice any of the people who really mattered. On the other hand I didn't want Jane to think I hadn't any nice friends. You know I never have more than eight, but on this occasion I thought it would make things go better if I had twelve. I'd been too busy to see Jane until the evening of the party. She kept us all waiting a little—that was Gilbert's cleverness—and at last she sailed in. You could have knocked me down with a feather. She made the rest of the women look dowdy and provincial. She made me feel like a painted old trollop."

Mrs. Tower drank a little champagne.

"I wish I could describe the frock to you. It would have been quite impossible on anyone else; on her it was perfect. And the eyeglass! I'd known her for thirty-five years and I'd never seen her without spectacles."

"But you knew she had a good figure."

"How should I? I'd never seen her except in the clothes you first saw her in. Did *you* think she had a good figure? She seemed not to be unconscious of the sensation she made but to take it as a matter of course. I thought of my dinner and I heaved a sigh of relief. Even if she was a little heavy in hand, with that appearance it didn't so very much matter. She was sitting at the other end of the table and I heard a good deal of laughter; I was glad to think that the other people were playing up well; but after dinner I was a good deal taken aback when no less than three men came up to me and told me that my sister-in-law was priceless, and did I think she would allow them to call on her. I didn't quite know whether I was standing on my head or my heels. Twenty-four hours later our hostess of to-night rang me up and said she had heard my sister-in-law was in London and she was priceless and would I ask her to luncheon to meet her. She has an infallible instinct, that woman: in a month everyone was talking about Jane. I am here to-night, not because I've known our hostess for twenty years and have asked her to dinner a hundred times, but because I'm Jane's sister-in-law."

Poor Mrs. Tower. The position was galling, and though I could not help being amused, for the tables were turned on her with a vengeance, I felt that she deserved my sympathy.

"People never can resist those who make them laugh," I said, trying to console her.

"She never makes *me* laugh."

Once more from the top of the table I heard a guffaw and guessed that Jane had said another amusing thing.

"Do you mean to say that you are the only person who doesn't think her funny?" I asked, smiling.

"Had it struck *you* that she was a humorist?"

"I'm bound to say it hadn't."

"She says just the same things as she's said for the last thirty-five years. I laugh when I see everyone else does because I don't want to seem a perfect fool, but I am not amused."

"Like Queen Victoria," I said.

It was a foolish jest and Mrs. Tower was quite right sharply to tell me so. I tried another tack.

"Is Gilbert here?" I asked, looking down the table.

"Gilbert was asked because she won't go out without him, but to-night he's at a dinner of the Architects' Institute or whatever it's called."

"I'm dying to renew my acquaintance with her."

"Go and talk to her after dinner. She'll ask you to her Tuesdays."

"Her Tuesdays?"

"She's at home every Tuesday evening. You'll meet there everyone you ever heard of. They're the best parties in London. She's done in one year what I've failed to do in twenty."

"But what you tell me is really miraculous. How has it been done?"

Mrs. Tower shrugged her handsome but adipose shoulders.

"I shall be glad if you'll tell me," she replied.

After dinner I tried to make my way to the sofa on which Jane was sitting, but I was intercepted and it was not till a little later that my hostess came up to me and said:

"I must introduce you to the star of my party. Do you know Jane Napier? She's priceless. She's much more amusing than your comedies."

I was taken up to the sofa. The admiral who had been sitting beside her at dinner was with her still. He showed no sign of moving, and Jane, shaking hands with me, introduced me to him.

"Do you know Sir Reginald Frobisher?"

We began to chat. It was the same Jane as I had known before, perfectly simple, homely and unaffected, but her fantastic appearance certainly gave a peculiar savour to what she said. Suddenly I found myself shaking with laughter. She had made a remark, sensible and to the point, but not in the least witty, which her manner of saying and the bland look she gave me through her eyeglass made perfectly irresistible. I felt light-hearted and buoyant. When I left her she said to me:

"If you've got nothing better to do, come and see us on Tuesday evening. Gilbert will be so glad to see you."

"When he's been a month in London he'll know that he *can* have nothing better to do," said the admiral.

So, on Tuesday but rather late, I went to Jane's. I confess I was a little surprised at the company. It was quite a remarkable collection of writers, painters and politicians, actors, great ladies and great beauties: Mrs. Tower was right, it was a grand party; I had seen nothing like it in London since Stafford House was sold. No particular entertainment was provided. The refreshments were adequate without being luxurious. Jane in her quiet way seemed to be enjoying herself; I could not see that she took a great deal of trouble with her guests, but they seemed to like being there, and the gay, pleasant party did not break up till two in the morning. After that I saw much of her. I not only went often to her house, but seldom went out to luncheon or to dinner without meeting her. I am an amateur of humour and I sought to discover in what lay her peculiar gift. It was impossible to repeat anything she said, for the fun, like certain wines, would not travel. She had no gift for epigram. She never made a brilliant repartee. There was no malice in her remarks nor sting in her rejoinders. There are those who think that impropriety, rather than brevity, is the soul of wit; but she never said a thing that could have brought a blush to a Victorian cheek. I think her humour was unconscious and I am sure it was unpremeditated. It flew like a butterfly from flower to flower, obedient only to its own caprice and pursuivant of neither method nor intention. It depended on the way she spoke and on the way she looked. Its subtlety gained by the flaunting and extravagant appearance that Gilbert had achieved for her; but her appearance was only an element in it. Now of course she was the fashion and people laughed if she but opened her mouth. They no longer wondered that Gilbert had married a wife so much older than himself. They saw that Jane was a woman with whom age did not count. They thought him a devilish lucky young fellow. The admiral quoted Shakespeare to me: "Age cannot wither her, nor custom stale her infinite variety." Gilbert was delighted with her success. As I came to know him better I grew to like him. It was quite evident that he was neither a rascal nor a fortune-hunter. He was not only immensely proud of Jane but genuinely devoted to her. His kindness to her was touching. He was a very unselfish and sweet-tempered young man.

"Well, what do you think of Jane now?" he said to me once, with boyish triumph.

"I don't know which of you is more wonderful," I said. "You or she."

"Oh, I'm nothing."

"Nonsense. You don't think I'm such a fool as not to see that it's you, and you only, who've made Jane what she is."

"My only merit is that I saw what was there when it wasn't obvious to the naked eye," he answered.

"I can understand your seeing that she had in her the possibility of that remarkable appearance, but how in the world have you made her into a humorist?"

"But I always thought the things she said a perfect scream. She was always a humorist."

"You're the only person who ever thought so."

Mrs. Tower, not without magnanimity, acknowledged that she had been mistaken in Gilbert. She grew quite attached to him. But notwithstanding appearances she never faltered in her opinion that the marriage could not last. I was obliged to laugh at her.

"Why, I've never seen such a devoted couple," I said.

"Gilbert is twenty-seven now. It's just the time for a pretty girl to come along. Did you notice the other evening at Jane's that pretty little niece of Sir Reginald's? I thought Jane was looking at them both with a good deal of attention, and I wondered to myself."

"I don't believe Jane fears the rivalry of any girl under the sun."

"Wait and see," said Mrs. Tower.

"You gave it six months."

"Well, now I give it three years."

When anyone is very positive in an opinion it is only human nature to wish him proved wrong. Mrs. Tower was really too cocksure. But such a satisfaction was not mine, for the end that she had always and confidently predicted to the ill-assorted match did in point of fact come. Still, the fates seldom give us what we want in the way we want it, and though Mrs. Tower could flatter herself that she had been right, I think after all she would sooner have been wrong. For things did not happen at all in the way she expected.

One day I received an urgent message from her and fortunately went to see her at once. When I was shown into the room Mrs. Tower rose from her chair and came towards me with the stealthy swiftness of a leopard stalking his prey. I saw that she was excited.

"Jane and Gilbert have separated," she said.

"Not really? Well, you were right after all."

Mrs. Tower looked at me with an expression I could not understand.

"Poor Jane," I muttered.

"Poor Jane!" she repeated, but in tones of such derision that I was dumbfounded.

She found some difficulty in telling me exactly what had occurred.

Gilbert had left her a moment before she leaped to the telephone to summon me. When he entered the room, pale and distraught, she saw at once that something terrible had happened. She knew what he was going to say before he said it.

"Marion, Jane has left me."

She gave him a little smile and took his hand.

"I knew you'd behave like a gentleman. It would have been dreadful for her for people to think that *you* had left her."

"I've come to you because I knew I could count on your sympathy."

"Oh, I don't blame you, Gilbert," said Mrs. Tower, very kindly. "It was bound to happen."

He sighed.

"I suppose so. I couldn't hope to keep her always. She was too wonderful and I'm a perfectly commonplace fellow."

Mrs. Tower patted his hand. He was really behaving beautifully.

"And what is going to happen now?"

"Well, she's going to divorce me."

"Jane always said she'd put no obstacle in your way if ever you wanted to marry a girl."

"You don't think it's likely I should ever be willing to marry anyone else after being Jane's husband," he answered.

Mrs. Tower was puzzled.

"Of course you mean that *you've* left Jane."

"I? That's the last thing I should ever do."

"Then why is she divorcing you?"

"She's going to marry Sir Reginald Frobisher as soon as the decree is made absolute."

Mrs. Tower positively screamed. Then she felt so faint that she had to get her smelling salts.

"After all you've done for her?"

"I've done nothing for her."

"Do you mean to say you're going to allow yourself to be made use of like that?"

"We arranged before we married that if either of us wanted his liberty the other should put no hindrance in the way."

"But that was done on your account. Because you were twenty-seven years younger than she was."

"Well, it's come in very useful for her," he answered bitterly.

Mrs. Tower expostulated, argued, and reasoned; but Gilbert insisted that no rules applied to Jane, and he must do exactly what she wanted. He left Mrs. Tower prostrate. It relieved her a good deal to give me a full account of this interview. It pleased her to see that I was as surprised as herself, and if I was not so indignant with Jane as she was she ascribed that to the criminal lack of morality incident to my sex. She was still in a state of extreme agitation when the door was opened and the butler showed in—Jane herself. She was dressed in black and white as no doubt befitted her slightly ambiguous position, but in a dress so original and fantastic, in a hat so striking, that I positively gasped at the sight of her. But she was as ever bland and collected. She came forward to kiss Mrs. Tower, but Mrs. Tower withdrew herself with icy dignity.

"Gilbert has been here," she said.

"Yes, I know," smiled Jane. "I told him to come and see you. I'm going to Paris to-night and I want you to be very kind to him while I am away. I'm afraid just at first he'll be rather lonely and I shall feel more comfortable if I can count on your keeping an eye on him."

Mrs. Tower clasped her hands.

"Gilbert has just told me something that I can hardly bring myself to believe. He tells me that you're going to divorce him to marry Reginald Frobisher."

"Don't you remember, before I married Gilbert you advised me to marry a man of my own age. The admiral is fifty-three."

"But, Jane, you owe everything to Gilbert," said Mrs. Tower indignantly. "You wouldn't exist without him. Without him to design your clothes, you'll be nothing."

"Oh, he's promised to go on designing my clothes," Jane answered blandly.

"No woman could want a better husband. He's always been kindness itself to you."

"Oh, I know he's been sweet."

"How *can* you be so heartless?"

"But I was never in love with Gilbert," said Jane. "I always told him that. I'm beginning to feel the need of the companionship of a man of my own age. I think I've probably been married to Gilbert long enough. The young have no conversation." She paused a little and gave us both a charming smile. "Of course I shan't lose sight of Gilbert. I've arranged that with Reginald. The admiral has a niece that would just suit him. As soon as we're married we'll ask them to stay with us at Malta—you know that the admiral is to have the Mediterranean Command—and I shouldn't be at all surprised if they fell in love with one another."

Mrs. Tower gave a little sniff.

"And have you arranged with the admiral that if you want your liberty neither should put any hindrance in the way of the other?"

"I suggested it," Jane answered with composure. "But the admiral says he knows a good thing when he sees it and he won't want to marry anyone else, and if anyone wants to marry me—he has eight twelve-inch guns on his flagship and he'll discuss the matter at short range." She gave us a look through her eyeglass which even the fear of Mrs. Tower's wrath could not prevent me from laughing at. "I think the admiral's a very passionate man."

Mrs. Tower indeed gave me an angry frown.

"I never thought you funny, Jane," she said, "I never understood why people laughed at the things you said."

"I never thought I was funny myself, Marion," smiled Jane, showing her bright, regular teeth. "I am glad to leave London before too many people come round to our opinion."

"I wish you'd tell me the secret of your astonishing success," I said.

She turned to me with that bland, homely look I knew so well.

"You know, when I married Gilbert and settled in London and people began to laugh at what I said no one was more surprised than I was. I'd said the same things for thirty years and no one ever saw anything to laugh at. I thought it must be my clothes or my bobbed hair or my eyeglass. Then I discovered it was because I spoke the truth. It was so unusual that people thought it humorous. One of these days someone else will discover the secret, and when people habitually tell the truth of course there'll be nothing funny in it."

"And why am I the only person not to think it funny?" asked
Mrs. Tower.

Jane hesitated a little as though she were honestly searching
for a satisfactory explanation.

"Perhaps you don't know the truth when you see it, Marion
dear," she answered in her mild good-natured way.

It certainly gave her the last word. I felt that Jane would
always have the last word. She *was* priceless.

THE ROUND DOZEN

I LIKE Elsom. It is a seaside resort in the south of England, not very far from Brighton, and it has something of the late Georgian charm of that agreeable town. But it is neither bustling nor garish. Ten years ago, when I used to go there not infrequently, you might still see here and there an old house, solid and pretentious in no unpleasing fashion (like a decayed gentlewoman of good family whose discreet pride in her ancestry amuses rather than offends you) which was built in the reign of the First Gentleman in Europe and where a courtier of fallen fortunes may well have passed his declining years. The main street had a lackadaisical air and the doctor's motor seemed a trifle out of place. The housewives did their housekeeping in a leisurely manner. They gossiped with the butcher as they watched him cut from his great joint of South Down a piece of the best end of the neck, and they asked amiably after the grocer's wife as he put half a pound of tea and a packet of salt into their string bag. I do not know whether Elsom was ever fashionable: it certainly was not so then; but it was respectable and cheap. Elderly ladies, maiden and widowed, lived there. Indian civilians and retired soldiers: they looked forward with little shudders of dismay to August and September which would bring holiday-makers; but did not disdain to let them their houses and on the proceeds spend a few worldly weeks in a Swiss pension. I never knew Elsom at that hectic time when the lodging-houses were full and young men in blazers sauntered along the front, when Pierrots performed on the beach and in the billiard-room at the Dolphin you heard the click of balls till eleven at night. I only knew it in winter. Then in every house on the sea-front, stucco houses with bow-windows built a hundred years ago, there was a sign to inform you that apartments were to let; and the guests of the Dolphin were waited on by a single waiter and the boots. At ten o'clock the porter came into the smoking-room and looked at you in so marked a manner that you got up and went to bed. Then Elsom was a restful place and the Dolphin a very comfortable inn. It was pleasing to think that the Prince Regent drove over with Mrs. Fitzherbert more than once to drink a dish of tea in its coffee-room. In the hall was a framed letter from Mr. Thackeray ordering a sitting-room and two bedrooms over-looking the sea and giving instructions that a fly should be sent to the station to meet him.

One November, two or three years after the war, having had a bad attack of influenza, I went down to Elsom to regain my strength. I arrived in the afternoon and when I had un-packed my things went for a stroll on the front. The sky was overcast and the calm sea grey and cold. A few seagulls flew close to the shore. Sailing boats, their masts taken down for the winter, were drawn up high on the shingly beach and the bathing huts stood side by side in a long, grey and tat-tered row. No one was sitting on the benches that the town council had put here and there, but a few people were trudging up and down for exercise. I passed an old colonel with a red nose who stamped along in plus fours followed by a terrier, two elderly women in short skirts and stout shoes and a plain girl in a Tam o' Shanter. I had never seen the front so deserted. The lodging-houses looked like bedraggled old maids waiting for lovers who would never return, and even the friendly Dolphin seemed wan and desolate. My heart sank. Life on a sudden seemed very drab. I returned to the hotel, drew the curtains of my sitting-room, poked the fire and with a book sought to dispel my melancholy. But I was glad enough when it was time to dress for dinner. I went into the coffee-room and found the guests of the hotel already seated. I gave them a casual glance. There was one lady of middle age by herself and there were two elderly gentlemen, golfers probably, with red faces and baldish heads, who ate their food in moody silence. The only other persons in the room were a group of three who sat in the bow-window, and they immediately at-

tracted my surprised attention. The party consisted of an old
gentleman and two ladies, one of whom was old and probably
his wife, while the other was younger and possibly his daughter.
It was the old lady who first excited my interest. She wore a
voluminous dress of black silk and a black lace cap; on her
wrists were heavy gold bangles and round her neck a substantial gold chain from which hung a large gold locket; at
her neck was a large gold brooch. I did not know that anyone
still wore jewelry of that sort. Often, passing second-hand
jewellers and pawnbrokers, I had lingered for a moment to
look at these strangely old-fashioned articles, so solid, costly
and hideous, and thought, with a smile in which there was a
tinge of sadness, of the women long since dead who had worn
them. They suggested the period when the bustle and the
flounce were taking the place of the crinoline and the pork-
pie hat was ousting the poke-bonnet. The British people liked
things solid and good in those days. They went to church on
Sunday morning and after church walked in the Park. They
gave dinner parties of twelve courses where the master of the
house carved the beef and the chickens, and after dinner the
ladies who could play favoured the company with Mendelssohn's Songs Without Words and the gentleman with the
fine baritone voice sang an old English ballad.

The younger woman had her back turned to me and at first
I could see only that she had a slim and youthful figure. She
had a great deal of brown hair which seemed to be elaborately arranged. She wore a grey dress. The three of them were
chatting in low tones and presently she turned her head so
that I saw her profile. It was astonishingly beautiful. The nose
was straight and delicate, the line of the cheek exquisitely
modelled; I saw then that she wore her hair after the manner
of Queen Alexandra. The dinner proceeded to its close and the
party got up. The old lady sailed out of the room, looking
neither to the right nor to the left, and the young one followed
her. Then I saw with a shock that she was old. Her frock was
simple enough. The skirt was longer than was at that time
worn, and there was something slightly old-fashioned in the
cut. I daresay the waist was more clearly indicated than was
then usual, but it was a girl's frock. She was tall, like a heroine
of Tennyson's, slight, with long legs and a graceful carriage.
I had seen the nose before: it was the nose of a Greek goddess;
her mouth was beautiful, and her eyes were large and blue.

Her skin was of course a little tight on the bones, and there were wrinkles on her forehead and about her eyes, but in youth it must have been lovely. She reminded you of those Roman ladies with features of an exquisite regularity whom Alma-Tadema used to paint, but who, notwithstanding their antique dress, were so stubbornly English. It was a type of cold perfection that one had not seen for five-and-twenty years. Now it is as dead as the epigram. I was like an archæologist who finds some long-buried statue and I was thrilled in so unexpected a manner to hit upon this survival of a past era. For no day is so dead as the day before yesterday.

The gentleman rose to his feet when the two ladies left, and then resumed his chair. A waiter brought him a glass of heavy port. He smelt it, sipped it, and rolled it round his tongue. I observed him. He was a little man, much shorter than his imposing wife, well-covered without being stout, with a fine head of curling grey hair. His face was much wrinkled and it bore a faintly humorous expression. His lips were tight and his chin was square. He was, according to our present notions, somewhat extravagantly dressed. He wore a black velvet jacket, a frilled shirt with a low collar and a large black tie, and very wide evening trousers. It gave you vaguely the effect of costume. Having drunk his port with deliberation, he got up and sauntered out of the room.

When I passed through the hall, curious to know who these singular people were, I glanced at the visitors' book. I saw, written in an angular feminine hand, the writing that was taught to young ladies in modish schools forty years or so ago, the names: Mr. and Mrs. Edwin St. Clair and Miss Porchester. Their address was given as 68, Leinster Square, Bayswater, London. These must be the names and this the address of the persons who had so much interested me. I asked the manageress who Mr. St. Clair was and she told me that she believed he was something in the City. I went into the billiard-room and knocked the balls about for a little while and then on my way upstairs passed through the lounge. The two red-faced gentlemen were reading the evening paper and the middle-aged lady was dozing over a novel. The party of three sat in a corner. Mrs. St. Clair was knitting, Miss Porchester was busy with embroidery, and Mr. St. Clair was reading aloud in a discreet but resonant tone. As I passed I discovered that he was reading *Bleak House*.

I read and wrote most of the next day, but in the afternoon I went for a walk and on my way home I sat down for a little on one of those convenient benches on the sea-front. It was not quite so cold as the day before and the air was pleasant. For want of anything better to do I watched a figure advancing towards me from a distance. It was a man and as he came nearer I saw that it was rather a shabby little man. He wore a thin black greatcoat and a somewhat battered bowler. He walked with his hands in his pockets and looked cold. He gave me a glance as he passed by, went on a few steps, hesitated, stopped and turned back. When he came up once more to the bench on which I sat he took a hand out of his pocket and touched his hat. I noticed that he wore shabby black gloves, and surmised that he was a widower in straitened circumstances. Or he might have been a mute recovering, like myself, from influenza.

"Excuse me, sir," he said, "but could you oblige me with a match?"

"Certainly."

He sat down beside me and while I put my hand in my pocket for matches he hunted in his for cigarettes. He took out a small packet of Goldflakes and his face fell.

"Dear, dear, how very annoying! I haven't got a cigarette left."

"Let me offer you one," I replied, smiling.

I took out my case and he helped himself.

"Gold?" he asked, giving the case a tap as I closed it. "Gold? That's a thing I never could keep. I've had three. All stolen."

His eyes rested in a melancholy way on his boots, which were sadly in need of repair. He was a wizened little man with a long thin nose and pale blue eyes. His skin was sallow and he was much lined. I could not tell what his age was; he might have been five-and-thirty or he might have been sixty. There was nothing remarkable about him except his insignificance. But though evidently poor he was neat and clean. He was respectable and he clung to respectability. No, I did not think he was a mute, I thought he was a solicitor's clerk who had lately buried his wife and been sent to Elsom by an indulgent employer to get over the first shock of his grief.

"Are you making a long stay, sir?" he asked me.

"Ten days or a fortnight."

"Is this your visit first to Elsom, sir?"

"I have been here before."

"I know it well, sir. I flatter myself there are very few sea-side resorts that I have not been to at one time or another. Elsom is hard to beat, sir. You get a very nice class of people here. There's nothing noisy or vulgar about Elsom if you understand what I mean. Elsom has very pleasant recollections for me, sir. I knew Elsom well in bygone days. I was married in St. Martin's Church, sir."

"Really," I said feebly.

"It was a very happy marriage, sir."

"I'm very glad to hear it," I returned.

"Nine months, that one lasted," he said reflectively.

Surely the remark was a trifle singular. I had not looked forward with any enthusiasm to the probability which I so clearly foresaw that he would favour me with an account of his matrimonial experiences, but now I waited if not with eagerness at least with curiosity for a further observation. He made none. He sighed a little. At last I broke the silence

"There don't seem to be very many people about," I remarked.

"I like it so. I'm not one for crowds. As I was saying just now I reckon I've spent a good many years at one seaside resort after the other, but I never came in the season. It's the winter I like."

"Don't you find it a little melancholy?"

He turned towards me and placed his black-gloved hand for an instant on my arm.

"It is melancholy. And because it's melancholy a little ray of sunshine is very welcome."

The remark seemed to me perfectly idiotic and I did not answer. He withdrew his hand from my arm and got up.

"Well, I mustn't keep you, sir. Pleased to have made your acquaintance."

He took off his dingy hat very politely and strolled away. It was beginning now to grow chilly and I thought I would return to the Dolphin. As I reached its broad steps a landau drove up, drawn by two scraggy horses, and from it stepped Mr. St. Clair. He wore a hat that looked like the unhappy result of a union between a bowler and a top-hat. He gave his hand to his wife and then to his niece. The porter carried in after them rugs and cushions. As Mr. St. Clair paid the driver

I heard him tell him to come at the usual time next day, and
I understood that the St. Clairs took a drive every afternoon
in a landau. It would not have surprised me to learn that
none of them had ever been in a motor-car.

The manageress told me that they kept very much to themselves and sought no acquaintance among the other persons
staying at the hotel. I rode my imagination on a loose rein. I
watched them eat three meals a day. I watched Mr. and Mrs.
St. Clair sit at the top of the hotel steps in the morning. He
read *The Times* and she knitted. I suppose Mrs. St. Clair had
never read a paper in her life, for they never took anything
but *The Times* and Mr. St. Clair of course took it with him
every day to the City. At about twelve Miss Porchester joined
them.

"Have you enjoyed your walk, Eleanor?" asked Mrs. St.
Clair.

"It was very nice, Aunt Gertrude," answered Miss Porchester.

And I understood that just as Mrs. St. Clair took "her drive"
every afternoon Miss Porchester took "her walk" every morning.

"When you have come to the end of your row, my dear,"
said Mr. St. Clair, with a glance at his wife's knitting, "we
might go for a constitutional before luncheon."

"That will be very nice," answered Mrs. St. Clair. She folded
up her work and gave it to Miss Porchester. "If you're going
upstairs, Eleanor, will you take my work?"

"Certainly, Aunt Gertrude."

"I daresay you're a little tired after your walk, my dear."

"I shall have a little rest before luncheon."

Miss Porchester went into the hotel and Mr. and Mrs. St.
Clair walked slowly along the sea-front, side by side, to a
certain point, and then walked slowly back.

When I met one of them on the stairs I bowed and received
an unsmiling, polite bow in return, and in the morning I ventured upon a good-day, but there the matter ended. It looked
as though I should never have a chance to speak to any of
them. But presently I thought that Mr. St. Clair gave me
now and then a glance, and thinking he had heard my name I
imagined, perhaps vainly, that he looked at me with curiosity.
And a day or two after that I was sitting in my room when
the porter came in with a message.

"Mr. St. Clair presents his compliments and could you oblige him with the loan of Whitaker's Almanack."

I was astonished.

"Why on earth should he think that I have a Whitaker's Almanack?"

"Well, sir, the manageress told him you wrote."

I could not see the connection.

"Tell Mr. St. Clair that I'm very sorry that I haven't got a Whitaker's Almanack, but if I had I would very gladly lend it to him."

Here was my opportunity. I was by now filled with eagerness to know these fantastic persons more closely. Now and then in the heart of Asia I have come upon a lonely tribe living in a little village among an alien population. No one knows how they came there or why they settled in that spot. They live their own lives, speak their own language, and have no communication with their neighbours. No one knows whether they are the descendants of a band that was left behind when their nation swept in a vast horde across the continent or whether they are the dying remnant of some great people that in that country once held empire. They are a mystery. They have no future and no history. This odd little family seemed to me to have something of the same character. They were of an era that is dead and gone. They reminded me of persons in one of those leisurely, old-fashioned novels that one's father read. They belonged to the eighties and they had not moved since then. How extraordinary it was that they could have lived through the last forty years as though the world stood still! They took me back to my childhood and I recollected people who are long since dead. I wonder if it is only distance that gives me the impression that they were more peculiar than anyone is now. When a person was described then as "quite a character," by heaven, it meant something.

So that evening after dinner I went into the lounge and boldly addressed Mr. St. Clair.

"I'm so sorry I haven't got a Whitaker's Almanack," I said, "but if I have any other book that can be of service to you I shall be delighted to lend it to you."

Mr. St. Clair was obviously startled. The two ladies kept their eyes on their work. There was an embarrassed hush.

"It does not matter at all, but I was given to understand by the manageress that you were a novelist."

I racked my brain. There was evidently some connection between my profession and Whitaker's Almanack that escaped me.

"In days gone by Mr. Trollope used often to dine with us in Leinster Square and I remember him saying that the two most useful books to a novelist were the Bible and Whitaker's Almanack."

"I see that Thackeray once stayed in this hotel," I remarked, anxious not to let the conversation drop.

"I never very much cared for Mr. Thackeray, though he dined more than once with my wife's father, the late Mr. Sargeant Saunders. He was too cynical for me. My niece has not read *Vanity Fair* to this day."

Miss Porchester blushed slightly at this reference to herself. A waiter brought in the coffee and Mrs. St. Clair turned to her husband.

"Perhaps, my dear, this gentleman would do us the pleasure to have his coffee with us."

Although not directly addressed, I answered promptly.

"Thank you very much."

I sat down.

"Mr. Trollope was always my favourite novelist," said Mr St. Clair. "He was so essentially a gentleman. I admire Charles Dickens. But Charles Dickens could never draw a gentleman. I am given to understand that young people nowadays find Mr. Trollope a little slow. My niece, Miss Porchester, prefers the novels of Mr. William Black."

"I'm afraid I've never read any," I said.

"Ah, I see that you are like me; you are not up-to-date. My niece once persuaded me to read a novel by a Miss Rhoda Broughton, but I could not manage more than a hundred pages of it."

"I did not say I liked it, Uncle Edwin," said Miss Porchester, defending herself, with another blush. "I told you it was rather fast, but everybody was talking about it."

"I'm quite sure it is not the sort of book your Aunt Gertrude would have wished you to read, Eleanor."

"I remember Miss Broughton telling me once that when she was young people said her books were fast and when she was old they said they were slow, and it was very hard, since she had written exactly the same sort of book for forty years."

"Oh, did you know Miss Broughton?" asked Miss Porchester, addressing me for the first time. "How very inter-esting! And did you know Ouida?"

"My dear Eleanor, what will you say next! I'm quite sure you've never read anything by Ouida."

"Indeed, I have, Uncle Edwin. I've read *Under Two Flags* and I liked it very much."

"You amaze and shock me. I don't know what girls are coming to nowadays."

"You always said that when I was thirty you gave me complete liberty to read anything I liked."

"There is a difference, my dear Eleanor, between liberty and license," said Mr. St. Clair, smiling a little in order not to make his reproof offensive, but with a certain gravity.

I do not know if in recounting this conversation I have managed to convey the impression it gave me of a charming and old-fashioned air. I could have listened all night to them discussing the depravity of an age that was young in the eighteen-eighties. I would have given a good deal for a glimpse of their large and roomy house in Leinster Square. I should have recognized the suite covered in red brocade that stood stiffly about the drawing-room, each piece in its appointed place; and the cabinets filled with Dresden china would have brought me back my childhood. In the dining-room, where they habitually sat, for the drawing-room was used only for parties, there was a Turkey carpet and a vast mahogany side-board "groaning" with silver. On the walls were the pictures that had excited the admiration of Mrs. Humphry Ward and her uncle Matthew in the Academy of eighteen-eighty.

Next morning, strolling through a pretty lane at the back of Elsom, I met Miss Porchester, who was taking "her walk." I should have liked to go a little way with her, but felt certain that it would embarrass this maiden of fifty to saunter alone with a man even of my respectable years. She bowed as I passed her, and blushed. Oddly enough, a few yards behind her I came upon the funny shabby little man in black gloves with whom I had spoken for a few minutes on the front. He touched his old bowler hat.

"Excuse me, sir, but could you oblige me with a match?" he said.

"Certainly," I retorted, "but I'm afraid I have no cigarettes on me."

"Allow me to offer you one of mine," he said, taking out

the paper case. It was empty. "Dear, dear, I haven't got one either. What a curious coincidence!"

He went on and I had a notion that he a little hastened his steps. I was beginning to have my doubts about him. I hoped he was not going to bother Miss Porchester. For a moment I thought of walking back, but I did not. He was a civil little man and I did not believe he would make a nuisance of himself to a single lady.

I saw him again that very afternoon. I was sitting on the front. He walked towards me with little, halting steps. There was something of a wind and he looked like a dried leaf being driven before it. This time he did not hesitate, but sat down beside me.

"We meet again, sir. The world is a small place. If it will not inconvenience you perhaps you will allow me to rest a few minutes. I am a wee bit tired."

"This is a public bench, and you have just as much right to sit on it as I."

I did not wait for him to ask me for a match, but at once offered him a cigarette.

"How very kind of you, sir! I have to limit myself to so many cigarettes a day, but I enjoy those I smoke. As one grows older the pleasures of life diminish, but my experience is that one enjoys more those that remain."

"That is a very consoling thought."

"Excuse me, sir, but am I right in thinking that you are the well-known author?"

"I am an author," I replied. "But what made you think it?"

"I have seen your portrait in the illustrated papers. I suppose you don't recognize me?"

I looked at him again, a weedy little man in neat but shabby black clothes, with a long nose and watery blue eyes.

"I'm afraid I don't."

"I daresay I've changed," he sighed. "There was a time when my photograph was in every paper in the United Kingdom. Of course, those press photographs never do you justice. I give you my word, sir, that if I hadn't seen my name underneath I should never have guessed that some of them were meant for me."

He was silent for a while. The tide was out, and beyond the shingle of the beach was a strip of yellow mud. The breakwaters were half buried in it like the backbones of prehistoric beasts.

"It must be a wonderfully interesting thing to be an author, sir. I've often thought I had quite a turn for writing myself. At one time and another I've done a rare lot of reading. I haven't kept up with it much lately. For one thing my eyes are not so good as they used to be. I believe I could write a book if I tried."

"They say anybody can write one," I answered.

"Not a novel, you know. I'm not much of a one for novels; I prefer histories and that like. But memoirs. If anybody was to make it worth my while I wouldn't mind writing my memoirs."

"It's very fashionable just now."

"There are not many people who've had the experiences I've had in one way and another. I did write to one of the Sunday papers about it some little while back, but they never answered my letter."

He gave me a long, appraising look. He had too respectable an air to be about to ask me for half a crown.

"Of course you don't know who I am, sir, do you?"

"I honestly don't."

He seemed to ponder for a moment, then he smoothed down his black gloves on his fingers, looked for a moment at a hole in one of them, and then turned to me not without self-consciousness.

"I am the celebrated Mortimer Ellis," he said.

"Oh?"

I did not know what other ejaculation to make, for to the best of my belief I had never heard the name before. I saw a look of disappointment come over his face, and I was a trifle embarrassed.

"Mortimer Ellis," he repeated. "You're not going to tell me you don't know."

"I'm afraid I must. I'm very often out of England."

I wondered to what he owed his celebrity. I passed over in my mind various possibilities. He could never have been an athlete, which alone in England gives a man real fame, but he might have been a faith-healer or a champion billiard-player. There is of course no one so obscure as a cabinet minister out of office and he might have been the President of the Board of

Trade in a defunct administration. But he had none of the look of a politician.

"That's fame for you," he said bitterly. "Why, for weeks I was the most talked-about man in England. Look at me. You must have seen my photograph in the papers. Mortimer Ellis."

"I'm sorry," I said, shaking my head.

He paused a moment to give his disclosure effectiveness.

"I am the well-known bigamist."

Now what are you to reply when a person who is practically a stranger to you informs you that he is a well-known bigamist? I will confess that I have sometimes had the vanity to think that I am not as a rule at a loss for a retort, but here I found myself speechless.

"I've had eleven wives, sir," he went on.

. "Most people find one about as much as they can manage."

"Ah, that's want of practice. When you've had eleven there's very little you don't know about women."

"But why did you stop at eleven?"

"There now, I knew you'd say that. The moment I set eyes on you I said to myself, he's got a clever face. You know, sir, that's the thing that always grizzles me. Eleven does seem a funny number, doesn't it? There's something unfinished about it. Now three anyone might have, and seven's all right, they say nine's lucky, and there's nothing wrong with ten. But eleven! That's the one thing I regret. I shouldn't have minded anything if I could have brought it up to the Round Dozen."

He unbuttoned his coat and from an inside pocket produced a bulging and very greasy pocketbook. From this he took a large bundle of newspaper cuttings; they were worn and creased and dirty. But he spread out two or three.

"Now just you look at those photographs, I ask you, are they like me? It's an outrage. Why, you'd think I was a criminal to look at them."

The cuttings were of imposing length. In the opinion of sub-editors Mortimer Ellis had obviously been a news item of value. One was headed, A Much Married Man; another, Heartless Ruffian Brought to Book; a third, Contemptible Scoundrel Meets His Waterloo.

"Not what you would call a good press," I murmured.

"I never pay any attention to what the newspapers say."

he answered, with a shrug of his thin shoulders. "I've known too many journalists myself for that. No, it's the judge I blame. He treated me shocking and it did him no good, mind you; he died within the year."

I ran my eyes down the report I held.

"I see he gave you five years."

"Disgraceful, I call it, and see what it says." He pointed to a place with his forefinger. "'Three of his victims pleaded for mercy to be shown to him.' That shows what they thought of me. And after that he gave me five years. And just look what he called me, a heartless scoundrel—me, the best-hearted man that ever lived—a pest of society and a danger to the public. Said he wished he had the power to give me the cat. I don't so much mind his giving me five years, though you'll never get me to say it wasn't excessive, but I ask you, had he the right to talk to me like that? No, he hadn't, and I'll never forgive him, not if I live to be a hundred."

The bigamist's cheeks flushed and his watery eyes were filled for a moment with fire. It was a sore subject with him.

"May I read them?" I asked him.

"That's what I gave them you for. I want you to read them, sir. And if you can read them without saying that I'm a much wronged man, well, you're not the man I took you for."

As I glanced through one cutting after another I saw why Mortimer Ellis had so wide an acquaintance with the seaside resorts of England. They were his hunting-ground. His method was to go to some place when the season was over and take apartments in one of the empty lodging-houses. Apparently it did not take him long to make acquaintance with some woman or other, widow or spinster, and I noticed that their ages at the time were between thirty-five and fifty. They stated in the witness-box that they had met him first on the sea-front. He generally proposed marriage to them within a fortnight of this and they were married shortly after. He induced them in one way or another to entrust him with their savings and in a few months, on the pretext that he had to go to London on business, he left them, never to return. Only one had ever seen him again till, obliged to give evidence, they saw him in the dock. They were women of a certain respectability; one was the daughter of a doctor and another of a clergyman; there was a lodging-house keeper, there was the widow of a commercial traveller, and there was a retired dressmaker. For the most part, their fortunes ranged from five hundred to a thousand pounds, but whatever the sum the misguided women were stripped of every penny. Some of them told really pitiful stories of the destitution to which they had been reduced. But they all acknowledged that he had been a good husband to them. Not only had three actually pleaded for mercy to be shown him; but one said in the witness-box that, if he was willing to come, she was ready to take him back. He noticed that I was reading this.

"And she'd have worked for me," he said, "there's no doubt about that. But I said, better let bygones be bygones. No one likes a cut off the best end of the neck better than I do, but I'm not much of a one for cold roast mutton, I will confess."

It was only by an accident that Mortimer Ellis did not marry his twelfth wife and so achieve the Round Dozen which I understand appealed to his love of symmetry. For he was engaged to be married to a Miss Hubbard—"two thousand pounds she had, if she had a penny, in war-loan," he confided to me—and the banns had been read, when one of his former wives saw him, made enquiries, and communicated with the police. He was arrested on the very day before his twelfth wedding.

"She was a bad one, she was," he told me. "She deceived me something cruel."

"How did she do that?"

"Well, I met her at Eastbourne, one December it was, on the pier, and she told me in course of conversation that she'd been in the millinery business and had retired. She said she'd made a tidy bit of money. She wouldn't say exactly how much it was, but she gave me to understand it was something like fifteen hundred pounds. And when I married her—would you believe it?—she hadn't got three hundred. And that's the one who gave me away. And mind you, I'd never blamed her. Many a man would have cut up rough when he found out he'd been made a fool of. I never showed her that I was disappointed even, I just went away without a word."

"But not without the three hundred pounds, I take it."

"Oh come, sir, you must be reasonable," he returned in an injured tone. "You can't expect three hundred pounds to last for ever, and I'd been married to her four months before she confessed the truth."

"Forgive my asking," I said, "and pray don't think my question suggests a disparaging view of your personal attractions, but—why did they marry you?"

"Because I asked them," he answered, evidently very much surprised at my enquiry.

"But did you never have any refusals?"

"Very seldom. Not more than four or five in the whole course of my career. Of course I didn't propose till I was pretty sure of my ground and I don't say I didn't draw a blank sometimes. You can't expect to click every time, if you know what I mean, and I've often wasted several weeks making up to a woman before I saw there was nothing doing."

I surrendered myself for a time to my reflections. But I noticed presently that a broad smile spread over the mobile features of my friend.

"I understand what you mean," he said. "It's my appearance that puzzles you. You don't know what it is they see in me. That's what comes of reading novels and going to the pictures. You think what women want is the cowboy type, or the romance-of-old-Spain touch, flashing eyes, an olive skin, and a beautiful dancer. You make me laugh."

"I'm glad," I said.

"Are you a married man, sir?"

"I am. But I only have one wife."

"You can't judge by that. You can't generalize from a single instance, if you know what I mean. Now, I ask you, what would you know about dogs if you'd never had anything but one bull-terrier?"

The question was rhetorical and I felt sure did not require an answer. He paused for an effective moment and went on.

"You're wrong, sir. You're quite wrong. They may take a fancy to a good-looking young fellow, but they don't want to marry him. They don't really care about looks."

"Douglas Jerrold, who was as ugly as he was witty, used to say that if he was given ten minutes' start with a woman he could cut out the handsomest man in the room."

"They don't want wit. They don't want a man to be funny; they think he's not serious. They don't want a man who's too handsome; they think he's not serious either. That's what they want, they want a man who's serious. Safety first. And then—attention. I may not be handsome and I may not be amusing, but believe me, I've got what every woman wants.

Poise. And the proof is, I've made every one of my wives happy."

"It certainly is much to your credit that three of them pleaded for mercy to be shown to you and that one was willing to take you back."

"You don't know what an anxiety that was to me all the time I was in prison. I thought she'd be waiting for me at the gate when I was released, and I said to the Governor, 'For God's sake, sir, smuggle me out so as no one can see me.'"

He smoothed his gloves again over his hands and his eye once more fell upon the hole in the first finger.

"That's what comes of living in lodgings, sir. How's a man to keep himself neat and tidy without a woman to look after him? I've been married too often to be able to get along without a wife. There are men who don't like being married. I can't understand them. The fact is, you can't do a thing really well unless you've got your heart in it, and I like being a married man. It's no difficulty to me to do the little things that women like and that some men can't be bothered with. As I was saying just now, it's attention a woman wants. I never went out of the house without giving my wife a kiss and I never came in without giving her another. And it was very seldom I came in without bringing her some chocolates or a few flowers. I never grudged the expense."

"After all, it was her money you were spending," I interposed.

"And what if it was? It's not the money that you've paid for a present that signifies, it's the spirit you give it in. That's what counts with women. No, I'm not one to boast, but I will say this for myself, I am a good husband."

I looked desultorily at the reports of the trial which I still held.

"I'll tell you what surprises me," I said. "All these women were very respectable, of a certain age, quiet, decent persons. And yet they married you without any enquiry after the shortest possible acquaintance."

He put his hand impressively on my arm.

"Ah, that's what you don't understand, sir. Women have got a craving to be married. It doesn't matter how young they are or how old they are, if they're short or tall, dark or fair, they've all got one thing in common: they want to be married. And mind you, I married them in church. No woman feels really safe unless she's married in church. You say I'm no beauty. Well, I never thought I was, but if I had one leg and a hump on my back I could find any number of women who'd jump at the chance of marrying me. It's not the man they care about, it's marriage. It's a mania with them. It's a disease. Why, there's hardly one of them who wouldn't have accepted me the second time I saw her only I like to make sure of my ground before I commit myself. When it all came out there was a rare to-do because I'd married eleven times. Eleven times? Why, it's nothing, it's not even a Round Dozen. I could have married thirty times if I'd wanted to. I give you my word, sir, when I consider my opportunities, I'm astounded at my moderation."

"You told me you were very fond of reading history."

"Yes, Warren Hastings said that, didn't he? It struck me at the time I read it. It seemed to fit me like a glove."

"And you never found these constant courtships a trifle monotonous?"

"Well, sir, I think I've got a logical mind, and it always gave me a rare lot of pleasure to see how the same effects followed on the same causes, if you know what I mean. Now, for instance, with a woman who'd never been married before I always passed myself off as a widower. It worked like a charm. You see, a spinster likes a man who knows a thing or two. But with a widow I always said I was a bachelor: a widow's afraid a man who's been married before knows too much."

I gave him back his cuttings; he folded them up neatly and replaced them in his greasy pocketbook.

"You know, sir, I always think I've been misjudged. Just see what they say about me: a pest of society, unscrupulous villain, contemptible scoundrel. Now just look at me. I ask you, do I look that sort of man? You know me, you're a judge of character, I've told you all about myself; do you think me a bad man?"

"My acquaintance with you is very slight," I answered with what I thought considerable tact.

"I wonder if the judge, I wonder if the jury, I wonder if the public ever thought about my side of the question. The public booed me when I was taken into court and the police had to protect me from their violence. Did any of them think what I'd done for these women?"

"You took their money."

"Of course I took their money. I had to live the same as
anybody has to live. But what did I give them in exchange for
their money?"

This was another rhetorical question, and though he looked
at me as though he expected an answer I held my tongue. Indeed I did not know the answer. His voice was raised and he
spoke with emphasis. I could see that he was serious.

"I'll tell you what I gave them in exchange for their money.
Romance. Look at this place." He made a wide, circular gesture
that embraced the sea and the horizon. "There are a hundred
places in England like this. Look at that sea and that sky;
look at these lodging-houses; look at that pier and the front.
Doesn't it make your heart sink? It's dead as mutton. It's all
very well for you who come down here for a week or two because you're run down. But think of all those women who live
here from one year's end to another. They haven't a chance.
They hardly know anyone. They've just got enough money to
live on and that's all. I wonder if you know how terrible their
lives are. Their lives are just like the front, a long, straight,
cemented walk that goes on and on from one seaside resort to
another. Even in the season there's nothing for them. They're
out of it. They might as well be dead. And then I come along.
Mind you, I never made advances to a woman who wouldn't
have gladly acknowledged to thirty-five. And I give them love.
Why, many of them had never known what it was to have a
man do them up behind. Many of them had never known what
it was to sit on a bench in the dark with a man's arm round
their waist. I bring them change and excitement. I give them
a new pride in themselves. They were on the shelf and I come
along quite quietly and I deliberately take them down. A
little ray of sunshine in those drab lives, that's what I was.
No wonder they jumped at me, no wonder they wanted me
to go back to them. The only one who gave me away was the
milliner. She said she was a widow. My private opinion is that
she'd never been married at all. You say I did the dirty on them;
why, I brought happiness and glamour into eleven lives that
never thought they had even a dog's chance of it again. You
say I'm a villain and a scoundrel. You're wrong. I'm a philanthropist. Five years, they gave me; they should have given me
the medal of the Royal Humane Society."

He took out his empty packet of Goldflakes and looked at
it with a melancholy shake of the head. When I handed him

my cigarette case he helped himself without a word. I watched
the spectacle of a good man struggling with his emotion.

"And what did I get out of it, I ask you?" he continued
presently. "Board and lodging and enough to buy cigarettes.
But I never was able to save, and the proof is that now, when
I'm not so young as I was, I haven't got half a crown in my
pocket." He gave me a sidelong glance. "It's a great come-
down for me to find myself in this position. I've always paid
my way and I've never asked a friend for a loan in all my life.
I was wondering, sir, if you could oblige me with a trifle. It's
humiliating to me to have to suggest it, but the fact is, if you
could oblige me with a pound it would mean a great deal to
me."

Well, I had certainly had a pound's worth of entertainment
out of the bigamist and I dived for my pocketbook.

"I shall be very glad," I said.

He looked at the notes I took out.

"I suppose you couldn't make it two, sir?"

"I think I could."

I handed him a couple of pound notes and he gave a little
sigh as he took them.

"You don't know what it means to a man who's used to the
comforts of home life not to know where to turn for a night's
lodging."

"But there is one thing I should like you to tell me," I said.
"I shouldn't like you to think me cynical, but I had a notion
that women on the whole take the maxim, it is more blessed
to give than to receive, as applicable exclusively to our sex.
How did you persuade these respectable, and no doubt thrifty,
women to entrust you so confidently with all their savings?"

An amused smile spread over his undistinguished features.

"Well, sir, you know what Shakespeare said about ambition
o'erleaping itself. That's the explanation. Tell a woman you'll
double her capital in six months if she'll give it you to handle
and she won't be able to give you the money quick enough.
Greed, that's what it is. Just greed."

It was a sharp sensation, stimulating to the appetite (like
hot sauce with ice cream) to go from this diverting ruffian to
the respectability, all lavender bags and crinolines, of the St.
Clairs and Miss Porchester. I spent every evening with them
now. No sooner had the ladies left him than Mr. St. Clair sent

his compliments to my table and asked me to drink a glass of port with him. When we had finished it we went into the lounge and drank coffee. Mr. St. Clair enjoyed his glass of old brandy. The hour I thus spent with them was so exquisitely boring that it had for me a singular fascination. They were told by the manageress that I had written plays.

"We used often to go to the theatre when Sir Henry Irving was at the Lyceum," said Mr. St. Clair. "I once had the pleasure of meeting him. I was taken to supper at the Garrick Club by Sir Everard Millais and I was introduced to Mr. Irving as he then was."

"Tell him what he said to you, Edwin," said Mrs. St. Clair.

Mr. St. Clair struck a dramatic attitude and gave not at all a bad imitation of Henry Irving.

"'You have the actor's face, Mr. St. Clair,' he said to me. 'If you ever think of going on the stage, come to me and I will give you a part.'" Mr. St. Clair resumed his natural manner. "It was enough to turn a young man's head."

"But it didn't turn yours," I said.

"I will not deny that if I had been otherwise situated I might have allowed myself to be tempted. But I had my family to think of. It would have broken my father's heart if I had not gone into the business."

"What is that?" I asked.

"I am a tea-merchant, sir. My firm is the oldest in the City of London. I have spent forty years of my life in combating to the best of my ability the desire of my fellow-countrymen to drink Ceylon tea instead of the China tea which was universally drunk in my youth."

I thought it charmingly characteristic of him to spend a lifetime in persuading the public to buy something they didn't want rather than something they did.

"But in his younger days my husband did a lot of amateur acting and he was thought very clever," said Mrs. St. Clair.

"Shakespeare, you know, and sometimes *The School for Scandal*. I would never consent to act trash. But that is a thing of the past. I had a gift. Perhaps it was a pity to waste it, but it's too late now. When we have a dinner-party I sometimes let the ladies persuade me to recite the great soliloquies of Hamlet. But that is all I do."

Oh! Oh! Oh! I thought with shuddering fascination of those dinner-parties and wondered whether I should ever be asked to one of them. Mrs. St. Clair gave me a little smile, half shocked, half prim.

"My husband was very bohemian as a young man," she said

"I sowed my wild oats. I knew quite a lot of painters and writers, Wilkie Collins, for instance, and even men who wrote for the papers. Watts painted a portrait of my wife, and I bought a picture of Millais. I knew a number of the pre-Raphaelites."

"Have you a Rossetti?" I asked.

"No. I admired Rossetti's talent, but I could not approve of his private life. I would never buy a picture by an artist whom I should not care to ask to dinner at my house."

My brain was reeling when Miss Porchester, looking at her watch, said: "Are you not going to read to us to-night, Uncle Edwin?"

I withdrew.

It was while I was drinking a glass of port with Mr. St. Clair one evening that he told me the sad story of Miss Porchester. She was engaged to be married to a nephew of Mrs. St. Clair, a barrister, when it was discovered that he had had an intrigue with the daughter of his laundress.

"It was a terrible thing," said Mr. St. Clair. "A terrible thing. But of course my niece took the only possible course. She returned him his ring, his letters and his photograph, and said that she could never marry him. She implored him to marry the young person he had wronged and said she would be a sister to her. It broke her heart. She has never cared for anyone since."

"And did he marry the young person?"

Mr. St. Clair shook his head and sighed.

"No, we were greatly mistaken in him. It has been a sore grief to my dear wife to think that a nephew of hers should behave in such a dishonourable manner. Some time later we heard that he was engaged to a young lady in a very good position with ten thousand pounds of her own. I considered it my duty to write to her father and put the facts before him. He answered my letter in a most insolent fashion. He said he would much rather his son-in-law had a mistress before marriage than after."

"What happened then?"

"They were married and now my wife's nephew is one of His Majesty's Judges of the High Court, and his wife is My

Lady. But we've never consented to receive them. When my
wife's nephew was knighted Eleanor suggested that we should
ask them to dinner, but my wife said that he should never
darken our doors and I upheld her."

"And the laundress's daughter?"

"She married in her own class of life and has a public-house
at Canterbury. My niece, who has a little money of her own,
did everything for her and is godmother to her eldest child."

Poor Miss Porchester. She had sacrificed herself on the altar
of Victorian morality, and I am afraid the consciousness that
she had behaved beautifully was the only benefit she had got
from it.

"Miss Porchester is a woman of striking appearance," I
said. "When she was younger she must have been perfectly
lovely. I wonder she never married somebody else."

"Miss Porchester was considered a great beauty. Alma-
Tadema admired her so much that he asked her to sit as a
model for one of his pictures, but of course we couldn't very
well allow that." Mr. St. Clair's tone conveyed that the suggestion had deeply outraged his sense of decency. "No, Miss
Porchester never cared for anyone but her cousin. She never
speaks of him and it is now thirty years since they parted, but
I am convinced that she loves him still. She is a true woman,
my dear sir, one life, one love, and though perhaps I regret
that she has been deprived of the joys of marriage and mother-
hood I am bound to admire her fidelity."

But the heart of woman is incalculable, and rash is the man
who thinks she will remain in one stay. Rash, Uncle Edwin.
You have known Eleanor for many years, for when, her mother
having fallen into a decline and died, you brought the orphan
to your comfortable and even luxurious house in Leinster
Square, she was but a child; but what, when it comes down to
brass tacks, Uncle Edwin, do you really know of Eleanor?

It was but two days after Mr. St. Clair had confided to me
the touching story which explained why Miss Porchester had
remained a spinster that, coming back to the hotel in the afternoon after a round of golf, the manageress came up to me in an
agitated manner.

"Mr. St. Clair's compliments and will you go up to number
twenty-seven the moment you come in."

"Certainly. But why?"

"Oh, there's a rare upset. They'll tell you."

I knocked at the door. I heard a "come in, come in," which reminded me that Mr. St. Clair had played Shakespearean parts in probably the most refined amateur dramatic company in London. I entered and found Mrs. St. Clair lying on the sofa with a handkerchief soaked in eau-de-Cologne on her brow and a bottle of smelling salts in her hand. Mr. St. Clair was standing in front of the fire in such a manner as to prevent anyone else in the room from obtaining any benefit from it.

"I must apologize for asking you to come up in this unceremonious fashion, but we are in great distress, and we thought you might be able to throw some light on what has happened."

His perturbation was obvious.

"What *has* happened?"

"Our niece, Miss Porchester, has eloped. This morning she sent in a message to my wife that she had one of her sick headaches. When she has one of her sick headaches she likes to be left absolutely alone, and it wasn't till this afternoon that my wife went to see if there was anything she could do for her. The room was empty. Her trunk was packed. Her dressing-case with silver fittings was gone. And on the pillow was a letter telling us of her rash act."

"I'm very sorry," I said. "I don't know exactly what I can do."

"We were under the impression that you were the only gentleman at Elsom with whom she had any acquaintance."

His meaning flashed across me.

"I see you haven't eloped with her. At the first moment we thought perhaps . . . but if it isn't you, who is it?"

"I'm sure I don't know."

"Show him the letter, Edwin," said Mrs. St. Clair from the sofa.

"Don't move, Gertrude. It will bring on your lumbago."

Miss Porchester had "her" sick headaches and Mrs. St. Clair had "her" lumbago. What had Mr. St. Clair? I was willing to bet a fiver that Mr. St. Clair had "his" gout. He gave me the letter and I read it with an air of decent commiseration.

DEAREST UNCLE EDWIN AND AUNT GERTRUDE:
When you receive this I shall be far away. I am going to be married this morning to a gentleman who is very dear to me. I know I am doing wrong in running away like this, but I was

*afraid you would endeavour to set obstacles in the way of my
marriage, and since nothing would induce me to change my
mind I thought it would save us all much unhappiness if I
did it without telling you anything about it. My fiancé is a
very retiring man, owing to his long residence in tropical countries not in the best of health, and he thought it much better that
we should be married quite privately. When you know how
radiantly happy I am I hope you will forgive me. Please send
my box to the luggage office at Victoria Station,*

Your loving niece,

ELEANOR.

"I will never forgive her," said Mr. St. Clair as I returned
him the letter. "She shall never darken my doors again. Gertrude, I forbid you ever to mention Eleanor's name in my
hearing."

Mrs. St. Clair began to sob quietly.

"Aren't you rather hard?" I said. "Is there any reason why
Miss Porchester shouldn't marry?"

"At her age?" he answered angrily. "It's ridiculous. We
shall be the laughing-stock of everyone in Leinster Square.
Do you know how old she is? She's fifty-one."

"Fifty-four," said Mrs. St. Clair through her sobs.

"She's been the apple of my eye. She's been like a daughter
to us. She's been an old maid for years. I think it's positively
improper for her to think of marriage."

"She was always a girl to us, Edwin," pleaded Mrs. St.
Clair.

"And who is this man she's married? It's the deception that
rankles. She must have been carrying on with him under our
very noses. She does not even tell us his name. I fear the very
worst."

Suddenly I had an inspiration. That morning after breakfast
I had gone out to buy myself some cigarettes and at the to-
bacconist's I ran across Mortimer Ellis. I had not seen him
for some days.

"You're looking very spruce," I said.

His boots had been repaired and were neatly blacked, his
hat was brushed, he was wearing a clean collar and new gloves.
I thought he had laid out my two pounds to advantage.

"I have to go to London this morning on business," he said.

I nodded and left the shop.

I remembered that a fortnight before, walking in the country, I had met Miss Porchester and, a few yards behind, Mortimer Ellis. Was it possible that they had been walking together and he had fallen back as they caught sight of me? By heaven, I saw it all.

"I think you said that Miss Porchester had money of her own," I said.

"A trifle. She has three thousand pounds."

Now I was certain. I looked at them blankly. Suddenly Mrs. St. Clair, with a cry, sprang to her feet.

"Edwin, Edwin, supposing he doesn't marry her?"

Mr. St. Clair at this put his hand to his head and in a state of collapse sank into a chair.

"The disgrace would kill me," he groaned.

"Don't be alarmed," I said. "He'll marry her all right. He always does. He'll marry her in church."

They paid no attention to what I said. I suppose they thought I'd suddenly taken leave of my senses. I was quite sure now. Mortimer Ellis had achieved his ambition after all. Miss Porchester completed the Round Dozen.

THE CREATIVE IMPULSE

I SUPPOSE that very few people know how Mrs. Albert Forrester came to write *The Achilles Statue;* and since it has been acclaimed as one of the great novels of our time I cannot but think that a brief account of the circumstances that gave it birth must be of interest to all serious students of literature; and indeed, if, as the critics say, this is a book that will live, the following narrative, serving a better purpose than to divert an idle hour, may be regarded by the historian of the future as a curious footnote to the literary annals of our day.

Everyone of course remembers the success that attended the publication of *The Achilles Statue*. Month after month printers were kept busy printing, binders were kept busy binding, edition after edition; and the publishers, both in England and America, were hard put to it to fulfil the pressing orders of the booksellers. It was promptly translated into every European tongue and it has been recently announced that it will soon be possible to read it in Japanese and in Urdu. But it had previously appeared serially in magazines on both sides of the Atlantic and from the editors of these Mrs. Albert Forrester's agent had wrung a sum that can only be described as thumping. A dramatization of the work was made, which ran for a season in New York, and there is little doubt that when the play is produced in London it will have an equal success. The film rights have been sold at a great price. Though the amount that Mrs. Albert Forrester is reputed (in literary circles) to have made is probably exaggerated, there can be no doubt that she will have earned enough money from this one book to save her for the rest of her life from any financial anxiety.

It is not often that a book meets with equal favour from the public and the critics, and that she, of all persons, had (if I may so put it) squared the circle must have proved the more gratifying to Mrs. Albert Forrester, since, though she had received the commendation of the critics in no grudging terms (and indeed had come to look upon it as her due) the public had always remained strangely insensible to her merit. Each work she published, a slender volume beautifully printed and bound in white buckram, was hailed as a masterpiece, always to the length of a column, and, in the weekly reviews which you see only in the dusty library of a very long-established club, even to the extent of a page; and all well-read persons read and praised it. But well-read persons apparently do not buy books, and she did not sell. It was indeed a scandal that so distinguished an author, with an imagination so delicate and a style so exquisite, should remain neglected of the vulgar. In America, she was almost completely unknown; and though Mr. Carl Van Vechten had written an article berating the public for its obtuseness, the public remained callous. Her agent, a warm admirer of her genius, had blackmailed an American publisher into taking two of her books by refusing, unless he did so, to let him have others (trashy novels, doubtless) that he badly wanted, and they had been duly published. The reception they received from the press was flattering and showed that in America the best minds were sensitive to her talent; but when it came to the third book the American publisher (in the coarse way publishers have) told the agent that any money he had to spare he preferred to spend on synthetic gin.

Since *The Achilles Statue* Mrs. Albert Forrester's previous books have been republished (and Mr. Carl Van Vechten has written another article pointing out sadly, but firmly, that he had drawn the attention of the reading world to the merits of this exceptional writer fully fifteen years ago), and they have been so widely advertised that they can scarcely have escaped the cultured reader's attention. It is unnecessary, therefore, for me to give an account of them; and it would certainly be no more than cold potatoes after those two subtle articles by Mr. Carl Van Vechten. Mrs. Albert Forrester began to write early. Her first work (a volume of elegies) appeared when she was a maiden of eighteen; and published, every two or three years, for she had too exalted a conception of her art to hurry her production, a volume either of verse or prose. When *The Achilles Statue* was written she had reached the respectable age of fifty-seven, so that it will be readily surmised that the number of her works was considerable. She had given the world half a dozen volumes of verse, published under Latin titles, such as *Felicitas, Pax Maris* and *Aes Triplex*, all of the graver kind, for her muse, disinclined to skip on a light, fantastic toe, trod a somewhat solemn measure. She remained faithful to the Elegy, and the Sonnet claimed much of her attention; but her chief distinction was to revive the Ode, a form of poetry that the poets of the present day somewhat neglect; and it may be asserted with confidence that her *Ode to President Fallières* will find a place in every anthology of English verse. It is admirable not only for the noble sonority of its rhythms, but also for its felicitous description of the pleasant land of France. Mrs. Albert Forrester wrote of the valley of the Loire with its memories of Du Bellay, of Chartres and the jewelled windows of its cathedral, of the sun-swept cities of Provence, with a sympathy all the more remarkable since she had never penetrated farther into France than Boulogne, which she visited shortly after her marriage on an excursion steamer from Margate. But the physical mortification of being extremely seasick and the intellectual humiliation of discovering that the inhabitants of that popular seaside resort could not understand her fluent and idiomatic French made her determine not to expose herself a second time to experiences which were at once undignified and unpleasant; and she never again embarked on the treacherous element which she however sang (*Pax Maris*) in numbers both grave and sweet.

There are some fine passages too in the *Ode to Woodrow Wilson*, and I regret that, owing to a change in her sentiments towards that no doubt excellent man, the author decided not to reprint it. But I think it must be admitted that Mrs. Albert Forrester's most distinguished work was in prose. She wrote several volumes of brief but perfectly constructed essays on such subjects as Autumn in Sussex, Queen Victoria, Death, Spring in Norfolk, Georgian Architecture, Monsieur de Diaghileff and Dante; she also wrote works, both erudite and whimsical, on the Jesuit Architecture of the XVIIth Century, and on the Literary Aspect of the Hundred Years' War. It was her prose that gained her that body of devoted admirers, fit though few as with her rare gift of phrase she herself put it, that proclaimed her the greatest master of the English language that this century has seen. She admitted herself that it was her style, sonorous yet racy, polished yet eloquent, that was her strong point; and it was only in her prose that she had occasion to exhibit the delicious but restrained humour that her readers found so irresistible. It was not a humour of ideas, nor even a humour of words; it was much more subtle than that, it was a humour of punctuation: in a flash of inspiration she had discovered the comic possibilities of the semicolon, and of this she had made abundant and exquisite use. She was able to place it in such a way that if you were a person of culture with a keen sense of humour, you did not exactly laugh through a horse-collar, but you giggled delightedly, and the greater your culture the more delightedly you giggled. Her friends said that it made every other form of humour coarse and exaggerated. Several writers had tried to imitate her; but in vain: whatever else you might say about Mrs. Albert Forrester you were bound to admit that she was able to get every ounce of humour out of the semicolon and no one else could get within a mile of her.

Mrs. Albert Forrester lived in a flat not far from the Marble Arch, which combined the advantage of a good address and a moderate rent. It had a handsome drawing-room on the street and a large bedroom for Mrs. Albert Forrester, a darkish dining-room at the back and a small poky bedroom, next door to the kitchen, for Mr. Albert Forrester, who paid the rent. It was in the handsome drawing-room that Mrs. Albert Forrester every Tuesday afternoon received her friends. It was a severe and chaste apartment. On the walls was a paper designed by William Morris himself and on this, in plain black frames, mezzotints collected before mezzotints grew expensive; the furniture was of the Chippendale period, but for the roll-top desk, vaguely Louis XVI in character, at which Mrs. Albert Forrester wrote her works. This was pointed out to visitors the first time they came to see her, and there were few who looked at it without emotion. The carpet was thick and the lights discreet. Mrs. Albert Forrester sat in a straight-backed grandfather's chair covered with red damask. There was nothing ostentatious about it, but since it was the only comfortable chair in the room it set her apart as it were and above her guests. Tea was dispensed by a female of uncertain age, silent and colourless, who was never introduced to anyone but who was known to look upon it as a privilege to be allowed to save Mrs. Albert Forrester from the irksome duty of pouring out tea. She was thus able to devote herself entirely to conversation, and it must be admitted that her conversation was excellent. It was not sprightly; and since it is difficult to indicate punctuation in speech it may have seemed to some slightly lacking in humour, but it was of wide range, solid, instructive and interesting. Mrs. Albert Forrester was well acquainted with social science, jurisprudence and theology. She had read much and her memory was retentive. She had a pretty gift for quotation, which is a serviceable substitute for wit, and having for thirty years known more or less intimately a great many distinguished people, she had a great many interesting anecdotes to tell, which she placed with tact and which she did not repeat more than was pardonable. Mrs. Albert Forrester had the gift of attracting the most varied persons, and you were liable at one and the same time to meet in her drawing-room an ex-prime minister, a newspaper proprietor and the ambassador of a First Class Power. I always imagined that these great people came because they thought that here they rubbed shoulders with Bohemia, but with a Bohemia sufficiently neat and clean for them to be in no danger that the dirt would come off on them. Mrs Albert Forrester was deeply interested in politics and I myself heard a cabinet minister tell her frankly that she had a masculine intelligence. She had been opposed to female suffrage, but when it was at last granted to women she began to dally with the idea of going into Parliament. Her difficulty was that she did not know which party to choose.

"After all," she said, with a playful shrug of her somewhat massive shoulders, "I cannot form a party of one."

Like many serious patriots, in her inability to know for certain which way the cat would jump she held her political opinions in suspense; but of late she had been definitely turning towards Labour as the best hope of the country, and if a safe seat were offered her it was felt fairly certain that she would not hesitate to come out into the open as a champion of the oppressed proletariat.

Her drawing-room was always open to foreigners, to Czecho-Slovaks, Italians and Frenchmen if they were distinguished and to Americans even if they were obscure. But she was not a snob and you seldom met there a duke unless he was of a peculiarly serious turn and a peeress only if in addition to her rank she had the passport of some small social solecism such as having been divorced, written a novel or forged a check, which might give her a claim on Mrs. Albert Forrester's Catholic Sympathies. She did not much care for painters, who were shy and silent; and musicians did not interest her: even if they consented to play—and if they were celebrated they were too often reluctant —their music was a hindrance to conversation: if people wanted to hear music they could go to a concert; for her part she preferred the more subtle music of the soul. But her hospitality to writers, especially if they were promising and little known, was warm and constant. She had an eye for budding talent and there were few of the famous writers who from time to time drank a dish of tea with her whose first efforts she had not encouraged and whose early steps she had not guided. Her own position was too well assured for her to be capable of envy, and she had heard the word genius attached to her name too often to feel a trace of jealousy because the talents of others brought them a material success that was denied to her.

Mrs. Albert Forrester, confident in the judgment of posterity, could afford to be disinterested. With these elements then it is no wonder that she had succeeded in creating something as near the French salon of the eighteenth century as our barbarous nation has ever reached. To be invited to "eat a bun and drink a cup of tea on Tuesday" was a privilege that few failed to recognize; and when you sat on your Chippendale chair in the discreetly lit but austere room, you could not but feel that you were living literary history. The American ambassador once said to Mrs. Albert Forrester:

"A cup of tea with you, Mrs. Forrester, is one of the richest intellectual treats which it has ever been my lot to enjoy."

It was indeed on occasion a trifle overwhelming. Mrs. Albert Forrester's taste was so perfect, she so inevitably admired the right thing and made the just observation about it, that sometimes you almost gasped for air. For my part I found it prudent to fortify myself with a cocktail or two before I exposed myself to the rarefied atmosphere of her society. Indeed, I very nearly found myself for ever excluded from it, for one afternoon, presenting myself at the door, instead of asking the maid who opened it: "Is Mrs. Forrester at home?" I asked: "Is there Divine Service to-day?"

Of course it was said in pure inadvertence, but it was unfortunate that the maid sniggered and one of Mrs. Albert

Forrester's most devoted admirers, Ellen Hannaway, happened to be at the moment in the hall taking off her galoshes. She told my hostess what I had said before I got into the drawing-room, and as I entered Mrs. Albert Forrester fixed me with an eagle eye.

"Why did you ask if there was Divine Service to-day?" she inquired.

I explained that I was absent-minded, but Mrs. Albert Forrester held me with a gaze that I can only describe as compelling.

"Do you mean to suggest that my parties are . . ." She searched for a word. "Sacramental?"

I did not know what she meant, but did not like to show my ignorance before so many clever people, and I decided that the only thing was to seize my trowel and the butter.

"Your parties are like you, dear lady, perfectly beautiful and perfectly divine."

A little tremor passed through Mrs. Albert Forrester's substantial frame. She was like a man who enters suddenly a room filled with hyacinths; the perfume is so intoxicating that he almost staggers. But she relented.

"If you were trying to be facetious," she said, "I should prefer you to exercise your facetiousness on my guests rather than on my maids. . . . Miss Warren will give you some tea."

Mrs. Albert Forrester dismissed me with a wave of the hand, but she did not dismiss the subject, since for the next two or three years whenever she introduced me to someone she never failed to add:

"You must make the most of him, he only comes here as a penance. When he comes to the door he always asks: 'Is there Divine Service to-day?' So amusing, isn't he?"

But Mrs. Albert Forrester did not confine herself to weekly tea-parties: every Saturday she gave a luncheon of eight persons; this according to her opinion being the perfect number for general conversation and her dining-room conveniently holding no more. If Mrs. Albert Forrester flattered herself upon anything it was not that her knowledge of English prosody was unique, but that her luncheons were celebrated. She chose her guests with care and an invitation to one of them was more than a compliment, it was a consecration. Over the luncheon-table it was possible to keep the conversation on a higher level than in the mixed company of a tea-party, and few can have left her dining-room without taking away with them an enhanced belief in Mrs. Albert Forrester's ability and a brighter faith in human nature. She only asked men, since, stout enthusiast for her sex as she was and glad to see women on other occasions, she could not but realize that they were inclined at table to talk exclusively to their next-door neighbours and thus hinder the general exchange of ideas that made her own parties an entertainment not only of the body but of the soul. For it must be said that Mrs. Albert Forrester gave you uncommonly good food, excellent wine and a first-rate cigar. Now to anyone who has partaken of literary hospitality this must appear very remarkable, since literary persons for the most part think highly and live plainly; their minds are occupied with the things of the spirit and they do not notice that the roast mutton is underdone and the potatoes cold: the beer is all right, but the wine has a sobering effect, and it is unwise to touch the coffee. Mrs. Albert Forrester was pleased enough to receive compliments on the fare she provided.

"If people do me the honour to break bread with me," she said, "it is only fair that I should give them as good food as they can get at home."

But if the flattery was excessive she deprecated it.

"You really embarrass me when you give me a meed of praise which is not my due. You must praise Mrs. Bulfinch."

"Who is Mrs. Bulfinch?"

"My cook."

"She's a treasure then, but you're not going to ask me to believe that she's responsible for the wine."

"Is it good? I'm terribly ignorant of such things; I put myself entirely in the hands of my wine-merchant."

But if mention was made of the cigars Mrs. Albert Forrester beamed.

"Ah, for them you must compliment Albert. It is Albert who chooses the cigars and I am given to understand that no one knows more about a cigar than Albert."

She looked at her husband, who sat at the end of the table, with the proud bright eyes of a pedigree hen (a Buff Orpington for choice) looking at her only chick. Then there was a quick flutter of conversation as the guests, anxious to be civil to their host and relieved at length to find an occasion, expressed their appreciation of his peculiar merit.

"You're very kind," he said. "I'm glad you like them."

Then he would give a little discourse on cigars, explaining the excellences he sought and regretting the deterioration in quality which had followed on the commercialization of the industry. Mrs. Albert Forrester listened to him with a complacent smile, and it was plain that she enjoyed this little triumph of his. Of course you cannot go on talking of cigars indefinitely, and as soon as she perceived that her guests were growing restive she broached a topic of more general, and it may be of more significant, interest. Albert subsided into silence. But he had had his moment.

It was Albert who made Mrs. Forrester's luncheons to some less attractive than her tea-parties, for Albert was a bore; but though without doubt perfectly conscious of the fact, she made a point that he should come to them and in fact had fixed upon Saturdays (for the rest of the week he was busy) in order that he should be able to. Mrs. Albert Forrester felt that her husband's presence on these festive occasions was an unavoidable debt that she paid to her own self-respect. She would never by a negligence admit to the world that she had married a man who was not spiritually her equal, and it may be that in the silent watches of the night she asked herself where indeed such could have been found. Mrs. Albert Forrester's friends were troubled by no such reticence and they said it was dreadful that such a woman should be burdened with such a man. They asked one another how she had ever come to marry him and (being most celibate) answered despairingly that no one ever knew why anybody married anybody else.

It was not that Albert was a verbose and aggressive bore; he did not buttonhole you with interminable stories or pester you with pointless jokes; he did not crucify you on a platitude or hamstring you with a commonplace; he was just dull. A cipher. Clifford Boyleston, for whom the French Romantics had no secrets and who was himself a writer of merit, had said that when you looked into a room into which Albert had just gone there was nobody there. This was thought very clever by Mrs. Albert Forrester's friends, and Rose Waterford, the well-known novelist and the most fearless of women, had ventured to repeat it to Mrs. Albert Forrester. Though she pretended to be annoyed, she had not been able to prevent the smile that rose to her lips. Her behaviour towards Albert could not but increase the respect in which her friends held her. She insisted that whatever in their secret hearts they thought of him, they should treat him with the decorum that was due to her husband. Her own demeanour was admirable. If he chanced to make an observation she listened to him with a pleasant expression, and when he fetched her a book that she wanted or gave her his pencil to make a note of an idea that had occurred to her, she always thanked him. Nor would she allow her friends pointedly to neglect him, and though, being a woman of tact, she saw that it would be asking too much of the world if she took him about with her always, and she went out much alone, yet her friends knew that she expected them to ask him to dinner at least once a year. He always accompanied her to public banquets when she was going to make a speech, and if she delivered a lecture she took care that he should have a seat on the platform.

Albert was, I believe, of average height, but perhaps because you never thought of him except in connection with his wife (of imposing dimensions) you only thought of him as a little man. He was spare and frail and looked older than his age. This was the same as his wife's. His hair, which he kept very short, was white and meagre, and he wore a stubby white moustache; his was a face, thin and lined, without a noticeable feature; and his blue eyes, which once might have been attractive, were now pale and tired. He was always very neatly dressed in pepper-and-salt trousers, which he chose always of the same pattern, a black coat and a grey tie with a small pearl pin in it. He was perfectly unobtrusive, and when he stood in Mrs. Albert Forrester's drawing-room to receive the guests whom she had asked to luncheon you noticed him as little as you noticed the quiet and gentlemanly furniture. He was well-mannered and it was with a pleasant, courteous smile that he shook hands with them.

"How do you do? I'm very glad to see you," he said if they were friends of some standing. "Keeping well, I hope?"

But if they were strangers of distinction coming for the first time to the house, he went to the door as they entered the drawing-room, and said:

"I am Mrs. Albert Forrester's husband. I will introduce you to my wife."

Then he led the visitor to where Mrs. Albert Forrester stood, with her back to the light, and she with a glad and eager gesture advanced to make the stranger welcome.

It was agreeable to see the demure pride he took in his wife's literary reputation and the self-effacement with which he furthered her interests. He was always there when he was wanted and never when he wasn't. His tact, if not deliberate, was instinctive. Mrs. Albert Forrester was the first to acknowledge his merits.

"I really don't know what I should do without him," she said. "He's invaluable to me. I read him everything I write and his criticisms are often very useful."

"Molière and his cook," said Miss Waterford.

"Is that funny, dear Rose?" asked Mrs. Forrester, somewhat acidly.

When Mrs. Albert Forrester did not approve of a remark, she had a way, that put many persons to confusion, of asking you whether it was a joke which she was too dense to see. But it was impossible to embarrass Miss Waterford. She was a lady who in the course of a long life had had many affairs, but only one passion, and this was for printer's ink. Mrs. Albert Forrester tolerated rather than approved her.

"Come, come, my dear," she replied, "you know very well that he wouldn't exist without you. He wouldn't know us. It must be wonderful to him to come in contact with all the best brains and the most distinguished people of our day."

"It may be that the bee would perish without the hive which shelters it, but the bee nevertheless has a significance of its own."

And since Mrs. Albert Forrester's friends, though they knew all about art and literature, knew little about natural history, they had no reply to this observation. She went on:

"He doesn't interfere with me. He knows subconsciously when I don't want to be disturbed and, indeed, when I am following out a train of thought I find his presence in the room a comfort rather than a hindrance to me."

"Like a Persian cat," said Miss Waterford.

"But like a very well-trained, well-bred, and well-mannered Persian cat," answered Mrs. Forrester severely, thus putting Miss Waterford in her place.

But Mrs. Albert Forrester had not finished with her husband.

"We who belong to the intelligentsia," she said, "are apt to live in a world too exclusively our own. We are interested in the abstract rather than in the concrete, and sometimes I think that we survey the bustling world of human affairs in too detached a manner and from too serene a height. Do you not think that we stand in danger of becoming a little inhuman? I shall

always be grateful to Albert because he keeps me in contact
with the man in the street."

It was on account of this remark, to which none of her friends
could deny the rare insight and subtlety that characterized so
many of her utterances, that for some time Albert was known
in her immediate circle as The Man in the Street. But this was
only for a while, and it was forgotten. He then became known as
The Philatelist. It was Clifford Boyleston, with his wicked wit,
who invented the name. One day, his poor brain exhausted by
the effort to sustain a conversation with Albert, he had asked in
desperation:

"Do you collect stamps?"

"No," answered Albert mildly. "I'm afraid I don't."

But Clifford Boyleston had no sooner asked the question than
he saw its possibilities. He had written a book on Baudelaire's
aunt by marriage, which had attracted the attention of all who
were interested in French literature, and was well known in his
exhaustive studies of the French spirit to have absorbed a
goodly share of the Gallic quickness and the Gallic brilliancy.
He paid no attention to Albert's disclaimer, but at the first opportunity informed Mrs. Albert Forrester's friends that he had
at last discovered Albert's secret. He collected stamps. He never
met him afterwards without asking him:

"Well, Mr. Forrester, how is the stamp collection?" Or:
"Have you been buying any stamps since I saw you last?"

It mattered little that Albert continued to deny that he collected stamps, the invention was too apt not to be made the
most of; Mrs. Albert Forrester's friends insisted that he did, and
they seldom spoke to him without asking him how he was getting on. Even Mrs. Albert Forrester, when she was in a specially
gay humour, would sometimes speak of her husband as The
Philatelist. The name really did seem to fit Albert like a
glove. Sometimes they spoke of him thus to his face and they
could not but appreciate the good nature with which he took it;
he smiled unresentfully and presently did not even protest that
they were mistaken.

Of course Mrs. Albert Forrester had too keen a social sense to
jeopardize the success of her luncheons by allowing her more
distinguished guests to sit on either side of Albert. She took care
that only her older and more intimate friends should do this,
and when the appointed victims came in she would say to them:

"I know you won't mind sitting by Albert, will you?"

They could only say that they would be delighted, but if
their faces too plainly expressed their dismay she would pat
their hands playfully and add:

"Next time you shall sit by me. Albert is so shy with strangers and you know so well how to deal with him."

They did: they simply ignored him. So far as they were concerned the chair in which he sat might as well have been empty.
There was no sign that it annoyed him to be taken no notice of
by persons who after all were eating food he paid for, since the
earnings of Mrs. Forrester could certainly not have provided
her guests with spring salmon and forced asparagus. He sat
quiet and silent, and if he opened his mouth it was only to give
a direction to one of the maids. If a guest were new to him he
would let his eyes rest on him in a stare that would have been
embarrassing if it had not been so childlike. He seemed to be
asking himself what this strange creature was; but what answer
his mild scrutiny gave him he never revealed. When the conversation grew animated he would look from one speaker to
the other, but again you could not tell from his thin, lined face
what he thought of the fantastic notions that were bandied
across the table.

Clifford Boyleston said that all the wit and wisdom he heard
passed over his head like water over a duck's back. He had given
up trying to understand and now only made a semblance of
listening. But Harry Oakland, the versatile critic, said that
Albert was taking it all in; he found it all too, too marvellous,
and with his poor, muddled brain he was trying desperately to
make head or tail of the wonderful things he heard. Of course in
the city he must boast of the distinguished persons he knew;
perhaps there he was a light of learning and letters, an authority
on the ideal; it would be perfectly divine to hear what he made
of it all. Harry Oakland was one of Mrs. Albert Forrester's
staunchest admirers, and had written a brilliant and subtle
essay on her style. With his refined and even beautiful features
he looked like a San Sebastian who had had an accident with a
hair restorer; for he was uncommonly hirsute. He was a very
young man, not thirty, but he had been in turn a dramatic
critic, and a critic of fiction, a musical critic and a critic of
painting. But he was getting a little tired of art and threatened
to devote his talents in future to the criticism of sport.

Albert, I should explain, was in the city and it was a misfortune that Mrs. Forrester's friends thought she bore with

meritorious fortitude that he was not even rich. There would have been something romantic in it if he had been a merchant prince who held the fate of nations in his hand or sent argosies, laden with rare spices, to those ports of the Levant the names of which have provided many a poet with so rich and rare a rhyme. But Albert was only a currant-merchant and was supposed to make no more than just enabled Mrs. Albert Forrester to conduct her life with distinction and even with liberality. Since his occupation kept him in his office till six o'clock he never managed to get to Mrs. Albert Forrester's Tuesdays till the most important visitors were gone. By the time he arrived, there were seldom more than three or four of her more intimate friends in the drawing-room, discussing with freedom and humour the guests who had departed, and when they heard Albert's key in the front-door they realized with one accord that it was late. In a moment he opened the door in his hesitating way and looked mildly in. Mrs. Albert Forrester greeted him with a bright smile.

"Come in, Albert, come in. I think you know everybody here."

Albert entered and shook hands with his wife's friends.

"Have you just come from the city?" she asked eagerly, though she knew there was nowhere else he could have come from. "Would you like a cup of tea?"

"No, thank you, my dear. I had tea in my office."

Mrs. Albert Forrester smiled still more brightly and the rest of the company thought she was perfectly wonderful with him.

"Ah, but I know you like a second cup. I will pour it out for you myself."

She went to the tea-table and, forgetting that the tea had been stewing for an hour and a half and was stone cold, poured him out a cup and added milk and sugar. Albert took it with a word of thanks, and meekly stirred it, but when Mrs. Forrester resumed the conversation which his apperance had interrupted, without tasting it he put it quietly down. His arrival was the signal for the party finally to break up, and one by one the remaining guests took their departure. On one occasion, however, the conversation was so absorbing and the point at issue so important that Mrs. Albert Forrester would not hear of their going.

"It must be settled once for all. And after all," she remarked in a manner that for her was almost arch, "this is a matter on which Albert may have something to say. Let us have the benefit of his opinion."

It was when women were beginning to cut their hair and the subject of discussion was whether Mrs. Albert Forrester should or should not shingle. Mrs. Albert Forrester was a woman of authoritative presence. She was large-boned and her bones were well covered; had she not been so tall and strong it might have suggested itself to you that she was corpulent. But she carried her weight gallantly. Her features were a little larger than life-size, and it was this that gave her face doubtless the look of virile intellectuality that it certainly possessed. Her skin was dark and you might have thought that she had in her veins some trace of Levantine blood: she admitted that she could not but think there was in her a gypsy strain and that would account, she felt, for the wild and lawless passion that sometimes characterized her poetry. Her eyes were large and black and bright, her nose like the great Duke of Wellington's, but more fleshy, and her chin square and determined. She had a big mouth, with full red lips, which owed nothing to cosmetics, for of these Mrs. Albert Forrester had never deigned to make use; and her hair, thick, solid and grey, was piled on the top of her head in such a manner as to increase her already commanding height. She was in appearance an imposing, not to say an alarming, female.

She was always very suitably dressed in rich materials of sombre hue and she looked every inch a woman of letters; but in her discreet way (being after all human and susceptible to vanity) she followed the fashions, and the cut of her gowns was modish. I think for some time she had hankered to shingle her hair, but she thought it more becoming to do it at the solicitation of her friends than on her own initiative.

"Oh, you must, you must," said Harry Oakland, in his eager, boyish way. "You'd look too, too wonderful."

Clifford Boyleston, who was now writing a book on Madame de Maintenon, was doubtful. He thought it a dangerous experiment.

"I think," he said, wiping his eyeglasses with a cambric handkerchief, "I think when one has made a type one should stick to it. What would Louis XIV have been without his wig?"

"I'm hesitating," said Mrs. Forrester. "After all, we must move with the times. I am of my day and I do not wish to lag behind. America, as Wilhelm Meister said, is here and now." She turned brightly to Albert. "What does my lord and master

say about it? What is your opinion, Albert? To shingle or not to
shingle, that is the question."

"I'm afraid my opinion is not of great importance, my dear,"
he answered mildly.

"To me it is of the greatest importance," answered Mrs.
Albert Forrester, flatteringly.

She could not but see how beautifully her friends thought
she treated The Philatelist.

"I insist," she proceeded, "I insist. No one knows me as you
do, Albert. Will it suit me?"

"It might," he answered. "My only fear is that with your—
statuesque appearance short hair would perhaps suggest, well,
shall we say, the Isle of Greece where burning Sappho loved and
sung."

There was a moment's embarrassed pause. Rose Waterford
smothered a giggle, but the others preserved a stony silence.
Mrs. Forrester's smile froze on her lips. Albert had dropped a
brick.

"I always thought Byron a very mediocre poet," said Mrs.
Albert Forrester at last.

The company broke up. Mrs. Albert Forrester did not shingle,
nor indeed was the matter ever again referred to.

It was towards the end of another of Mrs. Albert Forrester's
Tuesdays that the event occurred that had so great an influence
on her literary career.

It had been one of her most successful parties. The leader of
the Labour Party had been there and Mrs. Albert Forrester
had gone as far as she could without definitely committing
herself to intimate to him that she was prepared to throw in her
lot with Labour. The time was ripe and if she was ever to adopt
a political career she must come to a decision. A member of the
French Academy had been brought by Clifford Boyleston and,
though she knew he was wholly unacquainted with English, it
had gratified her to receive his affable compliment on her
ornate and yet pellucid style. The American ambassador had
been there and a young Russian prince whose authentic
Romanoff blood alone prevented him from looking a gigolo.
A duchess who had recently divorced her duke and married a
jockey had been very gracious; and her strawberry leaves,
albeit sere and yellow, undoubtedly added tone to the assembly

There had been quite a galaxy of literary lights. But now all, all were gone but Clifford Boyleston, Harry Oakland, Rose Waterford, Oscar Charles and Simmons. Oscar Charles was a little, gnome-like creature, young but with the wizened face of a cunning monkey, with gold spectacles, who earned his living in a government office but spent his leisure in the pursuit of literature. He wrote little articles for the sixpenny weeklies and had a spirited contempt for the world in general. Mrs. Albert Forrester liked him, thinking he had talent, but though he always expressed the keenest admiration for her style (it was indeed he who had named her the mistress of the semicolon), his acerbity was so general that she also somewhat feared him. Simmons was her agent; a round-faced man who wore glasses so strong that his eyes behind them looked strange and misshapen. They reminded you of the eyes of some uncouth crustacean that you had seen in an aquarium. He came regularly to Mrs. Albert Forrester's parties, partly because he had the greatest admiration for her genius and partly because it was convenient for him to meet prospective clients in her drawing-room.

Mrs. Albert Forrester, for whom he had long laboured with but a trifling recompense, was not sorry to put him in the way of earning an honest penny, and she took care to introduce him, with warm expressions of gratitude, to anyone who might be supposed to have literary wares to sell. It was not without pride that she remembered that the notorious and vastly lucrative memoirs of Lady St. Swithin had been first mooted in her drawing-room.

They sat in a circle of which Mrs. Albert Forrester was the centre and discussed brightly, and, it must be confessed, somewhat maliciously the various persons who had been that day present. Miss Warren, the pallid female who had stood for two hours at the tea-table, was walking silently round the room collecting cups that had been left here and there. She had some vague employment, but was always able to get off in order to pour out tea for Mrs. Albert Forrester, and in the evening she typed Mrs. Albert Forrester's manuscripts. Mrs. Albert Forrester did not pay her for this, thinking quite rightly that as it was she did a great deal for the poor thing; but she gave her the seats for the cinema that were sent her for nothing and often presented her with articles of clothing for which she had no further use.

Mrs. Albert Forrester in her rather deep, full voice was talking in a steady flow and the rest were listening to her with attention. She was in good form and the words that poured from her lips could have gone straight down on paper without alteration. Suddenly there was a noise in the passage as though something heavy had fallen, and then the sound of an altercation.

Mrs. Albert Forrester stopped and a slight frown darkened her really noble brow.

"I should have thought they knew by now that I will not have this devastating racket in the flat. Would you mind ringing the bell, Miss Warren, and asking what is the reason of this tumult?"

Miss Warren rang the bell and in a moment the maid appeared. Miss Warren at the door, in order not to interrupt Mrs. Albert Forrester, spoke to her in undertones. But Mrs. Albert Forrester somewhat irritably interrupted herself.

"Well, Carter, what is it? Is the house falling down or has the Red Revolution at last broken out?"

"If you please, ma'am, it's the new cook's box," answered the maid. "The porter dropped it as he was bringing it in and the cook got all upset about it."

"What do you mean by the new cook?"

"Mrs. Bulfinch went away this afternoon, ma'am," said the maid.

Mrs. Albert Forrester stared at her.

"This is the first I've heard of it. Had Mrs. Bulfinch given notice? The moment Mr. Forrester comes in tell him that I wish to speak to him."

"Very good, ma'am."

The maid went out and Miss Warren slowly returned to the tea-table. Mechanically, though nobody wanted them, she poured out several cups of tea.

"What a catastrophe!" cried Miss Waterford.

"You must get her back," said Clifford Boyleston. "She's a treasure, that woman, a remarkable cook, and she gets better and better every day."

But at that moment the maid came in again with a letter on a small plated salver and handed it to her mistress.

"What is this?" said Mrs. Albert Forrester.

"Mr. Forrester said I was to give you this letter when you asked for him, ma'am," said the maid.

"Where is Mr. Forrester then?"

"Mr. Forrester's gone, ma'am," answered the maid as though the question surprised her.

"Gone? That'll do. You can go."

The maid left the room and Mrs. Albert Forrester, with a look of perplexity on her large face, opened the letter. Rose Waterford has told me that her first thought was that Albert, fearful of his wife's displeasure at the departure of Mrs. Bulfinch, had thrown himself in the Thames. Mrs. Albert Forrester read the letter and a look of consternation crossed her face.

"Oh, monstrous," she cried. "Monstrous! Monstrous!"

"What is it, Mrs. Forrester?"

Mrs. Albert Forrester pawed the carpet with her foot like a restive, high-spirited horse pawing the ground, and crossing her arms with a gesture that is indescribable (but that you sometimes see in a fishwife who is going to make the very devil of a scene) bent her looks upon her curious and excessively startled friends.

"Albert has eloped with the cook."

There was a gasp of dismay. Then something terrible happened. Miss Warren, who was standing behind the tea-table, suddenly choked. Miss Warren, who never opened her mouth and whom no one ever spoke to, Miss Warren, whom not one of them, though he had seen her every week for three years, would have recognized in the street, Miss Warren suddenly burst into uncontrollable laughter. With one accord, aghast, they turned and stared at her. They felt as Balaam must have felt when his ass broke into speech. She positively shrieked with laughter. There was a nameless horror about the sight, as though something had on a sudden gone wrong with a natural phenomenon, and you were just as startled as though the chairs and tables without warning began to skip about the floor in an antic dance. Miss Warren tried to contain herself, but the more she tried the more pitilessly the laughter shook her, and seizing a handkerchief she stuffed it in her mouth and hurried from the room. The door slammed behind her.

"Hysteria," said Clifford Boyleston.

"Pure hysteria, of course," said Harry Oakland.

But Mrs. Albert Forrester said nothing.

The letter had dropped at her feet and Simmons, the agent, picked it up and handed it to her. She would not take it.

"Read it," she said. "Read it aloud."

Mr. Simmons pushed his spectacles up on his forehead and holding the letter very close to his eyes read as follows:

"MY DEAR,

"*Mrs. Bulfinch is in need of a change and has decided to leave, and as I do not feel inclined to stay on here without her I am going too. I have had all the literature I can stand and I am fed up with art.*

"*Mrs. Bulfinch does not care about marriage, but if you care to divorce me she is willing to marry me. I hope you will find the new cook satisfactory. She has excellent references. It may save you trouble if I inform you that Mrs. Bulfinch and I are living at 411, Kennington Road, S. E.*

"ALBERT."

No one spoke. Mr. Simmons slipped his spectacles back or to the bridge of his nose. The fact was that none of them, brilliant as they were and accustomed to find topics of conversation to suit every occasion, could think of an appropriate remark. Mrs. Albert Forrester was not the kind of woman to whom you could offer condolences, and each was too much afraid of the other's ridicule to venture upon the obvious. At last Clifford Boyleston came bravely to the rescue.

"One doesn't know what to say," he observed.

There was another silence and then Rose Waterford spoke.

"What does Mrs. Bulfinch look like?" she asked.

"How should I know?" answered Mrs. Albert Forrester, somewhat peevishly. "I have never looked at her. Albert always engaged the servants She just came in for a moment so that I could see if her aura was satisfactory."

"But you must have seen her every morning when you did the housekeeping."

"Albert did the housekeeping. It was his own wish, so that I might be free to devote myself to my work. In this life one has to limit oneself."

"Did Albert order your luncheons?" asked Clifford Boyleston.

"Naturally. It was his province."

Clifford Boyleston slightly raised his eyebrows. What a fool he had been never to guess that it was Albert who was responsible for Mrs. Forrester's beautiful food! And of course it was owing to him that the excellent Chablis was always just suffi-

ciently chilled to run coolly over the tongue, but never so cold
as to lose its bouquet and its savour.

"He certainly knew good food and good wine."

"I always told you he had his points," answered Mrs.
Albert Forrester, as though he were reproaching her. "You all
laughed at him. You would not believe me when I told you that
I owed a great deal to him."

There was no answer to this and once more silence, heavy
and ominous, fell on the party. Suddenly Mr. Simmons flung a
bombshell.

"You must get him back."

So great was her surprise that if Mrs. Albert Forrester had
not been standing against the chimney-piece she would undoubtedly have staggered two paces to the rear.

"What on earth do you mean?" she cried. "I will never see
him again as long as I live. Take him back? Never. Not even
if he came and begged me on his bended knees."

"I didn't say take him back; I said get him back."

But Mrs. Albert Forrester paid no attention to the misplaced
interruption.

"I have done everything for him. What would he be without
me? I ask you. I have given him a position which never in his
remotest dreams could he have aspired to."

None could deny that there was something magnificent in
the indignation of Mrs. Albert Forrester, but it appeared to
have little effect on Mr. Simmons.

"What are you going to live on?"

Mrs. Albert Forrester flung him a glance totally devoid of
amiability.

"God will provide," she answered in freezing tones.

"I think it very unlikely," he returned.

Mrs. Albert Forrester shrugged her shoulders. She wore an
outraged expression. But Mr. Simmons made himself as comfortable as he could on his chair and lit a cigarette.

"You know you have no warmer admirer of your art than
me," he said.

"Than I," corrected Clifford Boyleston.

"Or than you," went on Mr. Simmons blandly. "We all
agree that there is no one writing now who you need fear
comparison with. Both in prose and verse you are absolutely
first class. And your style—well, everyone knows your style."

"The opulence of Sir Thomas Browne with the limpidity of

Cardinal Newman," said Clifford Boyleston. "The raciness of
John Dryden with the precision of Jonathan Swift."

The only sign that Mrs. Albert Forrester heard was the smile
that hesitated for a brief moment at the corners of her tragic
mouth.

"And you have humour."

"Is there anyone in the world," cried Miss Waterford, "who
can put such a wealth of wit and satire and comic observation
into a semicolon?"

"But the fact remains that you don't sell," pursued Mr.
Simmons imperturbably. "I've handled your work for twenty
years and I tell you frankly that I shouldn't have grown fat on
my commission, but I've handled it because now and again I
like to do what I can for good work. I've always believed in you
and I've hoped that sooner or later we might get the public to
swallow you. But if you think you can make your living by
writing the sort of stuff you do I'm bound to tell you that you
haven't a chance."

"I have come into the world too late," said Mrs. Albert
Forrester. "I should have lived in the eighteenth century
when the wealthy patron rewarded a dedication with a hundred
guineas."

"What do you suppose the currant business brings in?"

Mrs. Albert Forrester gave a little sigh.

"A pittance. Albert always told me he made about twelve
hundred a year."

"He must be a very good manager. But you couldn't expect
him on that income to allow you very much. Take my word for
it, there's only one thing for you to do and that's to get him
back."

"I would rather live in a garret. Do you think I'm going to
submit to the affront he has put upon me? Would you have me
battle for his affections with my cook? Do not forget that there
is one thing which is more valuable to a woman like me than
her ease and that is her dignity."

"I was just coming to that," said Mr. Simmons coldly.

He glanced at the others and those strange, lopsided eyes of
his looked more than ever monstrous and fish-like.

"There is no doubt in my mind," he went on, "that you have
a very distinguished and almost unique position in the world of
letters. You stand for something quite apart. You never pros-
tituted your genius for filthy lucre and you have held high the

banner of pure art. You're thinking of going into Parliament. I
don't think much of politics myself, but there's no denying
that it would be a good advertisement, and if you get in I daresay we could get you a lecture tour in America on the strength
of it. You have ideals and this I can say, that even the people
who've never read a word you've written respect you. But in
your position there's one thing you can't afford to be and that's
a joke."

Mrs. Albert Forrester gave a distinct start.

"What on earth do you mean by that?"

"I know nothing about Mrs. Bulfinch and for all I know she's
a very respectable woman, but the fact remains that a man
doesn't run away with his cook without making his wife ridiculous. If it had been a dancer or a lady of title I daresay it
wouldn't have done you any harm, but a cook would finish you.
In a week you'd have all London laughing at you, and if there's
one thing that kills an author or a politician it is ridicule. You
must get your husband back and you must get him back pretty
damned quick."

A dark flush settled on Mrs. Albert Forrester's face, but she
did not immediately reply. In her ears there rang on a sudden
the outrageous and unaccountable laughter that had sent Miss
Warren flying from the room.

"We're all friends here and you can count on our discretion."

Mrs. Forrester looked at her friends and she thought that in
Rose Waterford's eyes there was already a malicious gleam.
On the wizened face of Oscar Charles was a whimsical look.
She wished that in a moment of abandon she had not betrayed
her secret. Mr. Simmons, however, knew the literary world and
allowed his eyes to rest on the company.

"After all, you are the centre and head of their set. Your
husband has not only run away from you but also from them.
It's not too good for them either. The fact is that Albert Forrester has made you all look a lot of damned fools."

"All," said Clifford Boyleston. "We're all in the same boat.
He's quite right, Mrs. Forrester, The Philatelist must come
back."

"*Et tu, Brute.*"

Mr. Simmons did not understand Latin and if he had would
probably not have been moved by Mrs. Albert Forrester's exclamation. He cleared his throat.

"My suggestion is that Mrs. Albert Forrester should go and

see him to-morrow—fortunately we have his address—and beg him to reconsider his decision. I don't know what sort of things a woman says on these occasions, but Mrs. Forrester has tact and imagination and she must say them. If Mr. Forrester makes any conditions she must accept them. She must leave no stone unturned."

"If you play your cards well there is no reason why you shouldn't bring him back here with you to-morrow evening," said Rose Waterford lightly.

"Will you do it, Mrs. Forrester?"

For two minutes, at least, turned away from them, she stared at the empty fireplace; then, drawing herself to her full height, she faced them.

"For my art's sake, not for mine. I will not allow the ribald laughter of the Philistine to besmirch all that I hold good and true and beautiful."

"Capital," said Mr. Simmons, rising to his feet, "I'll look in on my way home to-morrow and I hope to find you and Mr. Forrester billing and cooing side by side like a pair of turtle-doves."

He took his leave, and the others, anxious not to be left alone with Mrs. Albert Forrester and her agitation, in a body followed his example.

It was latish in the afternoon next day when Mrs. Albert Forrester, imposing in black silk and a velvet toque, set out from her flat in order to get a bus from the Marble Arch that would take her to Victoria Station. Mr. Simmons had explained to her by telephone how to reach the Kennington Road with expedition and economy. She neither felt nor looked like Delilah. At Victoria she took the tram that runs down the Vauxhall Bridge Road. When she crossed the river she found herself in a part of London more noisy, sordid and bustling than that to which she was accustomed, but she was too much occupied with her thoughts to notice the varied scene. She was relieved to find that the tram went along the Kennington Road, and asked the conductor to put her down a few doors from the house she sought. When it did and rumbled on, leaving her alone in the busy street, she felt strangely lost, like a traveller in an Eastern tale set down by a djinn in an unknown city. She walked slowly, looking to right and left, and notwithstanding the emotions of indignation and embarrassment that fought for the possession of her somewhat opulent bosom she could not but reflect that here was the material for a very pretty piece of prose. The little houses held about them the feeling of a bygone age when here it was still almost country, and Mrs. Albert Forrester registered in her retentive memory a note that she must look into the literary associations of the Kennington Road. Number 411 was one of a row of shabby houses that stood some way back from the street; in front of it was a narrow strip of shabby grass, and a paved way led up to a latticed wooden porch that badly needed a coat of paint. This and the straggling, stunted creeper that grew over the front of the house gave it a falsely rural air which was strange and even sinister in that road down which thundered a tumultuous traffic. There was something equivocal about the house that suggested that here lived women to whom a life of pleasure had brought an inadequate reward.

The door was opened by a scraggy girl of fifteen with long legs and a tousled head.

"Does Mrs. Bulfinch live here, do you know?"

"You've rung the wrong bell. Second floor." The girl pointed to the stairs and at the same time screamed shrilly: "Mrs. Bulfinch, a party to see you. Mrs. Bulfinch."

Mrs. Albert Forrester walked up the dingy stairs. They were covered with torn carpet. She walked slowly, for she did not wish to get out of breath. A door opened as she reached the second floor, and she recognized her cook.

"Good-afternoon, Bulfinch," said Mrs. Albert Forrester, with dignity. "I wish to see your master."

Mrs. Bulfinch hesitated for the shadow of a second, then held the door wide open.

"Come in, ma'am." She turned her head. "Albert, here's Mrs. Forrester to see you."

Mrs. Forrester stepped by quickly and there was Albert sitting by the fire in a leather-covered but rather shabby armchair, with his feet in slippers, and in shirt sleeves. He was reading the evening paper and smoking a cigar. He rose to his feet as Mrs. Albert Forrester came in. Mrs. Bulfinch followed her visitor into the room and closed the door.

"How are you, my dear?" said Albert cheerfully. "Keeping well, I hope."

"You'd better put on your coat, Albert," said Mrs. Bulfinch. "What *will* Mrs. Forrester think of you, finding you like that? I never."

She took the coat, which was hanging on a peg, and helped him into it; and, like a woman familiar with the peculiarities of masculine dress, pulled down his waistcoat so that it should not ride over his collar.

"I received your letter, Albert," said Mrs. Forrester.

"I supposed you had, or you wouldn't have known my address, would you?"

"Won't you sit down, ma'am?" said Mrs. Bulfinch, deftly dusting a chair, part of a suite covered in plum-coloured velvet, and pushing it forwards.

Mrs. Albert Forrester with a slight bow seated herself.

"I should have preferred to see you alone, Albert," she said.

His eyes twinkled.

"Since anything you have to say concerns Mrs. Bulfinch as much as it concerns me I think it much better that she should be present."

"As you wish."

Mrs. Bulfinch drew up a chair and sat down. Mrs. Albert Forrester had never seen her before but with a large apron over a print dress. She was wearing now an open-work blouse of white silk, a black skirt, and high-heeled, patent-leather shoes with silver buckles. She was a woman of about five-and-forty, with reddish hair and a reddish face, not pretty, but with a good-natured look, and buxom. She reminded Mrs. Albert Forrester of a serving-wench, somewhat overblown, in a jolly picture by an old Dutch master.

"Well, my dear, what have you to say to me?" asked Albert.

Mrs. Albert Forrester gave him her brightest and most affable smile. Her great black eyes shone with tolerant good-humour.

"Of course you know that this is perfectly absurd, Albert. I think you must be out of your mind."

"Do you, my dear? Fancy that."

"I'm not angry with you, I'm only amused, but a joke's a joke and should not be carried too far. I've come to take you home."

"Was my letter not quite clear?"

"Perfectly. I ask no questions and I will make no reproaches.

We will look upon this as a momentary aberration and say no more about it."

"Nothing will induce me ever to live with you again, my dear," said Albert in, however, a perfectly friendly fashion.

"You're not serious?"

"Quite."

"Do you love this woman?"

Mrs. Albert Forrester still smiled with an eager and somewhat metallic brightness. She was determined to take the matter lightly. With her intimate sense of values she realized that the scene was comic. Albert looked at Mrs. Bulfinch and a smile broke out on his withered face.

"We get on very well together, don't we, old girl?"

"Not so bad," said Mrs. Bulfinch.

Mrs. Albert Forrester raised her eyebrows; her husband had never in all their married life called *her* "old girl": nor indeed would she have wished it.

"If Bulfinch has any regard or respect for you she must know that the thing is impossible. After the life you've led and the society you've moved in she can hardly expect to make you permanently happy in miserable furnished lodging."

"They're not furnished lodgin's, ma'am," said Mrs. Bulfinch. "It's all me own furniture. You see, I'm very independent like and I've always liked to have a home of me own. So I keep these rooms on whether I'm in a situation or whether I'm not, and so I always have some place to go back to."

"And a very nice cozy little place it is," said Albert.

Mrs. Albert Forrester looked about her. There was a kitchen range in the fireplace on which a kettle was simmering, and on the mantelshelf was a black marble clock flanked by black marble candelabra. There was a large table covered with a red cloth, a dresser, and a sewing-machine. On the walls were photographs and framed pictures from Christmas supplements. A door at the back, covered with a red plush portière, led into what, considering the size of the house, Mrs. Albert Forrester (who in her leisure moments had made a somewhat extensive study of architecture) could not but conclude was the only bed-room. Mrs. Bulfinch and Albert lived in a contiguity that allowed no doubt about their relations.

"Have you not been happy with me, Albert?" asked Mrs. Forrester in a deeper tone.

"We've been married for thirty-five years, my dear. It's too

long. It's a great deal too long. You're a good woman in your
way, but you don't suit me. You're literary and I'm not.
You're artistic and I'm not."

"I've always taken care to make you share in all my interests. I've taken great pains that you shouldn't be overshadowed by my success. You can't say that I've ever left you
out of things."

"You're a wonderful writer, I don't deny it for a moment,
but the truth is I don't like the books you write."

"That, if I may be permitted to say so, merely shows that
you have very bad taste. All the best critics admit their power
and their charm."

"And I don't like your friends. Let me tell you a secret, my
dear. Often at your parties I've had an almost irresistible impulse to take off all my clothes just to see what would happen."

"Nothing would have happened," said Mrs. Albert Forrester
with a slight frown. "I should merely have sent for the doctor."

"Besides, you haven't the figure for that, Albert," said Mrs.
Bulfinch.

Mr. Simmons had hinted to Mrs. Albert Forrester that if the
need arose she must not hesitate to use the allurements of her
sex in order to bring back her erring husband to the conjugal
roof, but she did not in the least know how to do this. It would
have been easier, she could not but reflect, had she been in
evening dress.

"Does the fidelity of five-and-thirty years count for nothing?
I have never looked at another man, Albert. I'm used to you. I
shall be lost without you."

"I've left all my menus with the new cook, ma'am. You've
only got to tell her how many to luncheon and she'll manage,"
said Mrs. Bulfinch. "She's very reliable and she has as light a
hand with pastry as anyone I ever knew."

Mrs. Albert Forrester began to be discouraged. Mrs. Bulfinch's remark, well-meant no doubt, made it difficult to bring
the conversation onto the plane on which emotion could be
natural.

"I'm afraid you're only wasting your time, my dear," said
Albert. "My decision is irrevocable. I'm not very young any
more and I want someone to take care of me. I shall of course
make you as good an allowance as I can. Corinne wants me to
retire."

"Who is Corinne?" asked Mrs. Forrester with the utmost surprise.

"It's my name," said Mrs. Bulfinch. "My mother was half French."

"That explains a great deal," replied Mrs. Forrester, pursing her lips, for though she admired the literature of the French she knew that their morals left much to be desired.

"What I say is, Albert's worked long enough, and it's about time he started enjoying himself. I've got a little bit of property at Clacton-on-Sea. It's a very healthy neighbourhood and the air is wonderful. We could live there very comfortable. And what with the beach and the pier there's always something to do. They're a very nice lot of people down there. If you don't interfere with nobody, nobody'll interfere with you."

"I discussed the matter with my partners to-day and they're willing to buy me out. It means a certain sacrifice. When everything is settled I shall have an income of nine hundred pounds a year. There are three of us, so it gives us just three hundred a year apiece."

"How am I to live on that?" cried Mrs. Albert Forrester. "I have my position to keep up."

"You have a fluent, a fertile and a distinguished pen, my dear."

Mrs. Albert Forrester impatiently shrugged her shoulders.

"You know very well that my books don't bring me in anything but reputation. The publishers always say that they lose by them and in fact they only publish them because it gives them prestige."

It was then that Mrs. Bulfinch had the idea that was to have consequences of such magnitude.

"Why don't you write a good thrilling detective story?" she asked.

"Me?" exclaimed Mrs. Albert Forrester, for the first time in her life regardless of grammar.

"It's not a bad idea," said Albert. "It's not a bad idea at all."

"I should have the critics down on me like a thousand of bricks."

"I'm not so sure of that. Give the highbrow the chance of being lowbrow without demeaning himself and he'll be so grateful to you, he won't know what to do."

"For this relief much thanks," murmured Mrs. Albert Forrester reflectively.

"My dear, the critics'll eat it. And written in your beautiful English they won't be afraid to call it a masterpiece."

"The idea is preposterous. It's absolutely foreign to my genius. I could never hope to please the masses."

"Why not? The masses want to read good stuff, but they dislike being bored. They all know your name, but they don't read you, because you bore them. The fact is, my dear, you're dull."

"I don't know how you can say that, Albert," replied Mrs. Albert Forrester, with as little resentment as the equator might feel if someone called it chilly. "Everyone knows and acknowledges that I have an exquisite sense of humour and there is nobody who can extract so much good wholesome fun from a semicolon as I can."

"If you can give the masses a good thrilling story and let them think at the same time that they are improving their minds you'll make a fortune."

"I've never read a detective story in my life," said Mrs. Albert Forrester. "I once heard of a Mr. Barnes of New York and I was told that he had written a book called *The Mystery of a Hansom Cab*. But I never read it."

"Of course you have to have the knack," said Mrs. Bulfinch. "The first thing to remember is that you don't want any love-making—it's out of place in a detective story; what you want is murder, and sleuth-hounds, and you don't want to be able to guess who done it till the last page."

"But you must play fair with your reader, my dear," said Albert. "It always annoys me when suspicion has been thrown on the secretary or the lady of title and it turns out to be the second footman who's never done more than say, 'The carriage is at the door.' Puzzle your reader as much as you can, but don't make a fool of him."

"I love a good detective story," said Mrs. Bulfinch. "Give me a lady in evening dress, just streaming with diamonds, lying on the library floor with a dagger in her heart and I know I'm going to have a treat."

"There's no accounting for tastes," said Albert. "Personally, I prefer a respectable family solicitor, with side-whiskers, gold watch chain, and a benign appearance, lying dead in Hyde Park."

"With his throat cut?" asked Mrs. Bulfinch eagerly.

"No, stabbed in the back. There's something peculiarly attractive to the reader in the murder of a middle-aged gentleman of spotless reputation. It is pleasant to think that the most apparently blameless of us have a mystery in our lives."

"I see what you mean, Albert," said Mrs. Bulfinch. "He was the repository of a fatal secret."

"We can give you all the tips, my dear," said Albert, smiling mildly at Mrs. Albert Forrester. "I've read hundreds of detective stories."

"You!"

"That's what first brought Corinne and me together. I used to pass them on to her when I'd finished them."

"Many's the time I've heard him switch off the electric light as the dawn was creeping through the window and I couldn't help smiling to myself as I said: 'There, he's finished it at last, now he can have a good sleep.'"

Mrs. Albert Forrester rose to her feet. She drew herself up.

"Now I see what a gulf separates us," she said, and her fine contralto shook a little. "You have been surrounded for thirty years with all that was best in English literature and you read hundreds of detective novels."

"Hundreds and hundreds," interrupted Albert with a smile of satisfaction.

"I came here willing to make any reasonable concession so that you should come back to your home, but now I wish it no longer. You have shown me that we have nothing in common and never had. There is an abyss between us."

"Very well, my dear," said Albert gently, "I will submit to your decision. But you think over the detective story."

"I will arise and go now," she murmured, "and go to Innisfree."

"I'll just show you downstairs," said Mrs. Bulfinch. "One has to be careful of the carpet if one doesn't exactly know where the holes are."

With dignity, but not without circumspection, Mrs. Albert Forrester walked downstairs, and when Mrs. Bulfinch opened the door and asked her if she would like a taxi she shook her head.

"I shall take the tram."

"You need not be afraid that I won't take good care of Mr. Forrester, ma'am," said Mrs. Bulfinch pleasantly. "He shall have every comfort. I nursed Mr. Bulfinch for three years during his last illness and there's very little I don't know about invalids. Not that Mr. Forrester isn't very strong and active for

his years. And of course he'll have a hobby. I always think a
man should have a hobby. He's going to collect postage-
stamps."

Mrs. Albert Forrester gave a little start of surprise. But just
then a tram came in sight and, as a woman (even the greatest of
them) will, she hurried at the risk of her life into the middle of
the road and waved frantically. It stopped and she climbed in.
She did not know how she was going to face Mr. Simmons. He
would be waiting for her when she got home. Clifford Boyleston
would probably be there too. They would all be there and she
would have to tell them that she had miserably failed. At that
moment she had no warm feeling of friendship towards her
little group of devoted admirers. Wondering what the time was,
she looked up at the man sitting opposite her to see whether he
was the kind of person she could modestly ask, and suddenly
started; for sitting there was a middle-aged gentleman of the
most respectable appearance, with side-whiskers, a benign
expression and a gold watch chain. It was the very man whom
Albert had described lying dead in Hyde Park, and she could
not but jump to the conclusion that he was a family solicitor.
The coincidence was extraordinary and really it looked as
though the hand of fate were beckoning to her. He wore a silk
hat, a black coat and pepper-and-salt trousers, he was somewhat corpulent, of a powerful build, and by his side was a
despatch-case. When the tram was halfway down the Vauxhall
Bridge Road he asked the conductor to stop and she saw him go
down a small, mean street. Why? Ah, why? When it reached
Victoria, so deeply immersed in thought was she, until the
conductor somewhat roughly told her where she was, she did
not move. Edgar Allan Poe had written detective stories. She
took a bus. She sat inside, buried in reflection, but when it
arrived at Hyde Park Corner she suddenly made up her mind
to get out. She couldn't sit still any longer. She felt she must
walk. She entered the gates, walking slowly, and looked about
her with an air that was at once intent and abstracted. Yes,
there was Edgar Allan Poe; no one could deny that. After all,
he had invented the genre, and everyone knew how great his
influence had been on the Parnassians. Or was it the Symbolists?
Never mind. Baudelaire and all that. As she passed the Achilles
Statue she stopped for a minute and looked at it with raised
eyebrows.

At length she reached her flat and, opening the door, saw

several hats in the hall. They were all there. She went into the drawing-room.

"Here she is at last," cried Miss Waterford.

Mrs. Albert Forrester advanced, smiling with animation, and shook the proffered hands. Mr. Simmons and Clifford Boyleston were there, Harry Oakland and Oscar Charles.

"Oh, you poor things, have you had no tea?" she cried brightly. "I haven't an idea what the time is, but I know I'm fearfully late."

"Well?" they said. "Well?"

"My dears, I've got something quite wonderful to tell you. I've had an inspiration. Why should the devil have all the best tunes?"

"What *do* you mean?"

She paused in order to give full effect to the surprise she was going to spring upon them. Then she flung it at them without preamble:

"I'M GOING TO WRITE A DETECTIVE STORY."

They stared at her with open mouths. She held up her hand to prevent them from interrupting her, but indeed no one had the smallest intention of doing so.

"I am going to raise the detective story to the dignity of Art. It came to me suddenly in Hyde Park. It's a murder story and I shall give the solution on the very last page. I shall write it in an impeccable English, and since it's occurred to me lately that perhaps I've exhausted the possibilities of the semicolon, I am going to take up the colon. No one yet has explored its potentialities. Humour and mystery are what I aim at. I shall call it *The Achilles Statue*."

"What a title!" cried Mr. Simmons, recovering himself before any of the others. "I can sell the serial rights on the title and your name alone."

"But what about Albert?" asked Clifford Boyleston.

"Albert?" echoed Mrs. Forrester. "Albert?"

She looked at him as though for the life of her she could not think what he was talking about. Then she gave a little cry as if she had suddenly remembered.

"Albert! I knew I'd gone out on some errand and it absolutely slipped my memory. I was walking through Hyde Park and I had this inspiration. What a fool you'll all think me!"

"Then you haven't seen Albert?"

"My dear, I forgot all about him." She gave an amused laugh. "Let Albert keep his cook. I can't bother about Albert now. Albert belongs to the semicolon period. I am going to write a detective story."

"My dear, you're too, too wonderful," said Harry Oakland.

MISS KING

It was not till the beginning of September that Ashenden, a writer by profession, who had been abroad at the outbreak of the war, managed to get back to England. He chanced soon after his arrival to go to a party and was there introduced to a middle-aged Colonel whose name he did not catch. He had some talk with him. As he was about to leave this officer came up to him and asked:

"I say, I wonder if you'd mind coming to see me. I'd rather like to have a chat with you."

"Certainly," said Ashenden. "Whenever you like."

"What about to-morrow at eleven?"

"All right."

"I'll just write down my address. Have you a card on you?"

Ashenden gave him one and on this the Colonel scribbled in pencil the name of a street and the number of a house. When Ashenden walked along next morning to keep his appointment he found himself in a street of rather vulgar red-brick houses in a part of London that had once been fashionable, but was now fallen in the esteem of the house-hunter who wanted a good address. On the house at which Ashenden had been asked to call there was a board up to announce that it was for sale, the shutters were closed and there was no sign that anyone lived in it. He rang the bell and the door was opened by a non-commissioned officer so promptly that he was startled. He was not asked his business, but led immediately into a long room at the back, once evidently a dining-room, the florid decoration of which looked oddly out of keeping with the office furniture, shabby and sparse, that was in it. It gave Ashenden the impression of a room in which the brokers had taken possession. The Colonel, who was known in the Intelligence Department, as Ashenden later discovered, by the letter R., rose when he came in and shook hands with him. He was a man somewhat above the middle height, lean, with a yellow, deeply-lined face, thin grey hair and a toothbrush moustache. The thing immediately noticeable about him was the closeness with which his blue eyes were set. He only just escaped a squint. They were hard and cruel eyes, and very wary; and they gave him a cunning, shifty look. Here was a man that you could neither like nor trust at first sight. His manner was pleasant and cordial.

He asked Ashenden a good many questions and then, without further to-do, suggested that he had particular qualifications for the secret service. Ashenden was acquainted with several European languages and his profession was excellent cover; on the pretext that he was writing a book he could without attracting attention visit any neutral country. It was while they were discussing this point that R. said:

"You know you ought to get material that would be very useful to you in your work."

"I shouldn't mind that," said Ashenden.

"I'll tell you an incident that occurred only the other day and I can vouch for its truth. I thought at the time it would make a damned good story. One of the French ministers went down to Nice to recover from a cold and he had some very important documents with him that he kept in a dispatch-case. They were very important indeed. Well, a day or two after he arrived he picked up a yellow-haired lady at some restaurant or other where there was dancing, and he got very friendly with her. To cut a long story short he took her back to his hotel —of course it was a very imprudent thing to do—and when he came to himself in the morning the lady and the dispatch-case had disappeared. They had one or two drinks up in his room and his theory is that when his back was turned the woman slipped a drug into his glass."

R. finished and looked at Ashenden with a gleam in his close-set eyes.

"Dramatic, isn't it?" he asked.

"Do you mean to say that happened the other day?"

"The week before last."

"Impossible," cried Ashenden. "Why, we've been putting that incident on the stage for sixty years, we've written it in a thousand novels. Do you mean to say that life has only just caught up with us?"

R. was a trifle disconcerted.

"Well, if necessary, I could give you names and dates, and believe me, the Allies have been put to no end of trouble by the loss of the documents that the dispatch-case contained."

"Well, sir, if you can't do better than that in the secret service," sighed Ashenden, "I'm afraid that as a source of inspiration to the writer of fiction, it's a washout. We really *can't* write that story much longer."

It did not take them long to settle things and when Ashenden rose to go he had already made careful note of his instructions. He was to start for Geneva next day. The last words that R. said to him, with a casualness that made them impressive, were:

"There's just one thing I think you ought to know before you take on this job. And don't forget it. If you do well you'll get no thanks and if you get into trouble you'll get no help. Does that suit you?"

"Perfectly."

"Then I'll wish you good-afternoon."

Ashenden was on his way back to Geneva. The night was stormy and the wind blew cold from the mountains, but the stodgy little steamer plodded sturdily through the choppy waters of the lake. A scudding rain, just turning into sleet, swept the deck in angry gusts, like a nagging woman who cannot leave a subject alone. Ashenden had been to France in order to write and dispatch a report. A day or two before, about five in the afternoon, an Indian agent of his had come to see him in his rooms; it was only by a lucky chance that he was in, for he had no appointment with him, and the agent's instructions were to come to the hotel only in case of urgent importance. He told Ashenden that a Bengali in the German service had recently come from Berlin with a black cane trunk in which were a number of documents interesting to the British Government. At that time the Central Powers were doing their best to foment such an agitation in India as would make it necessary for Great Britain to keep their troops in the country and perhaps send others from France. It had been found possible to get the Bengali arrested in Berne on a charge that would keep

him out of harm's way for a while, but the black cane trunk
could not be found. Ashenden's agent was a very brave and
very clever fellow and he mixed freely with such of his countrymen as were disaffected to the interests of Great Britain. He
had just discovered that the Bengali before going to Berne had,
for greater safety, left the trunk in the cloak-room at Zürich
Station, and now that he was in jail, awaiting trial, was unable
to get the *bulletin* by which it might be obtained into the hands
of any of his confederates. It was a matter of great urgency
for the German Intelligence Department to secure the contents
of the trunk without delay, and since it was impossible for them
to get hold of it by the ordinary official means, they had decided to break into the station that very night and steal it.
It was a bold and ingenious scheme and Ashenden felt a pleasant
exhilaration (for a great deal of his work was uncommonly
dull) when he heard of it. He recognized the dashing and unscrupulous touch of the head of the German secret service at
Berne. But the burglary was arranged for two o'clock on the
following morning and there was not a moment to lose. He
could trust neither the telegraph nor the telephone to communicate with the British officer at Berne, and since the Indian agent could not go, (he was taking his life in his hands
by coming to see Ashenden and if he were noticed leaving his
room it might easily be that he would be found one day floating
in the lake with a knife thrust in his back,) there was nothing
for it but to go himself.

There was a train to Berne that he could just catch and he
put on his hat and coat as he ran downstairs. He jumped into a
cab. Four hours later he rang the bell of the headquarters of the
Intelligence Department. His name was known there but to
one person, and it was for him that Ashenden asked. A tall
tired-looking man, whom he had not met before, came out and
without a word led him into an office. Ashenden told him his
errand. The tall man looked at his watch.

"It's too late for us to do anything ourselves. We couldn't
possibly get to Zürich in time."

He reflected.

"We'll put the Swiss authorities on the job. They can telephone, and when your friends attempt their little burglary, I
have no doubt they'll find the station well-guarded. Anyhow
you had better get back to Geneva."

He shook hands with Ashenden and showed him out. Ashenden was well aware that he would never know what happened then. Being no more than a tiny rivet in a vast and complicated machine, he never had the advantage of seeing a completed action. He was concerned with the beginning or the end of it, perhaps, or with some incident in the middle, but what his own doings led to he had seldom a chance of discovering. It was as unsatisfactory as those modern novels that give you a number of unrelated episodes and expect you by piecing them together to construct in your mind a connected narrative.

Notwithstanding his fur coat and his muffler, Ashenden was chilled to the bone. It was warm in the saloon and there were good lights to read by, but he thought it better not to sit there in case some habitual traveller, recognizing him, wondered why he made these constant journeys between Geneva in Switzerland and Thonon in France; and so, making the best of what shelter could be found, he passed the tedious time in the darkness of the deck. He looked in the direction of Geneva, but could see no lights, and the sleet, turning into snow, prevented him from recognizing the landmarks. Lake Leman, on fine days so trim and pretty, artificial like a piece of water in a French garden, in this tempestuous weather was as secret and as menacing as the sea. He made up his mind that, on getting back to his hotel, he would have a fire lit in his sitting-room, a hot bath and dinner comfortably by the fireside in pyjamas and a dressing-gown. The prospect of spending an evening by himself with his pipe and a book was so agreeable that it made the misery of that journey across the lake positively worth while. Two sailors tramped past him heavily, their heads bent down to save themselves from the sleet that blew in their faces, and one of them shouted to him: *nous arrivons;* they went to the side and withdrew a bar to allow passage for the gangway, and looking again Ashenden through the howling darkness saw mistily the lights of the quay. A welcome sight. In two or three minutes the steamer was made fast and Ashenden joined himself to the little knot of passengers, muffled to the eyes, that waited to step ashore. Though he made the journey so often—it was his duty to cross the lake into France once a week to deliver his reports and to receive instructions—he had always a faint sense of trepidation when he stood among the crowd at the gangway and waited to land. There was nothing on his passport to show that he had been in France; the steamer went round the lake touching French soil at two places, but going from Switzerland to Switzerland, so that his journey might have been to Vevey or to Lausanne; but he could never be sure that the secret police had not taken note of him, and if he had been followed and seen to land in France, the fact that there was no stamp on his passport would be difficult to explain. Of course he had his story ready, but he well knew that it was not a very convincing one, and though it might be impossible for the Swiss authorities to prove that he was anything but a casual traveller he might nevertheless spend two or three days in jail, which would be uncomfortable, and then be firmly conducted to the frontier, which would be mortifying. The Swiss knew well that their country was the scene of all manner of intrigues; agents of the secret service, spies, revolutionaries and agitators infested the hotels of the principal towns and, jealous of their neutrality, they were determined to prevent conduct that might embroil them with any of the belligerent powers.

There were as usual two police officers on the quay to watch the passengers disembark and Ashenden, walking past them with as unconcerned an air as he could assume, was relieved when he had got safely by. The darkness swallowed him up and he stepped out briskly for his hotel. The wild weather with a scornful gesture had swept all the neatness from the trim promenade. The shops were closed and Ashenden passed only an occasional pedestrian who sidled along, scrunched up, as though he fled from the blind wrath of the unknown. You had a feeling in that black and bitter night that civilization, ashamed of its artificiality, cowered before the fury of elemental things. It was hail now that blew in Ashenden's face and the pavement was wet and slippery so that he had to walk with caution. The hotel faced the lake. When he reached it and a page-boy opened the door for him, he entered the hall with a flurry of wind that sent the papers on the porter's desk flying into the air. Ashenden was dazzled by the light. He stopped to ask the porter if there were letters for him. There was nothing, and he was about to get into the lift when the porter told him that two gentlemen were waiting in his room to see him. Ashenden had no friends in Geneva.

"Oh?" he answered, not a little surprised. "Who are they?"

He had taken care to get on friendly terms with the porter and his tips for trifling services had been generous. The porter gave a discreet smile.

"There is no harm in telling you. I think they are members of the police."

"What do they want?" asked Ashenden.

"They did not say. They asked me where you were, and I told them you had gone for a walk. They said they would wait till you came back."

"How long have they been there?"

"An hour."

Ashenden's heart sank, but he took care not to let his face betray his concern.

"I'll go up and see them," he said. The liftman stood aside to let him step into the lift, but Ashenden shook his head. "I'm so cold," he said, "I'll walk up."

He wished to give himself a moment to think, but as he ascended the three flights slowly his feet were like lead. There could be small doubt why two police officers were so bent upon seeing him. He felt on a sudden dreadfully tired. He did not feel he could cope with a multitude of questions. And if he were arrested as a secret agent he must spend at least the night in a cell. He longed more than ever for a hot bath and a pleasant dinner by his fireside. He had half a mind to turn tail and walk out of the hotel, leaving everything behind him; he had his passport in his pocket and he knew by heart the hours at which trains started for the frontier: before the Swiss authorities had made up their minds what to do he would be in safety. But he continued to trudge upstairs. He did not like the notion of abandoning his job so easily, he had been sent to Geneva, knowing the risks, to do work of a certain kind, and it seemed to him that he had better go through with it. Of course it would not be very nice to spend two years in a Swiss prison, but the chance of this was, like assassination to kings, one of the inconveniences of his profession. He reached the landing of the third floor and walked to his room. Ashenden had in him, it seems, a strain of flippancy (on account of which, indeed, the critics had often reproached him) and as he stood for a moment outside the door his predicament appeared to him on a sudden rather droll. His spirits went up and he determined to brazen the thing out. It was with a genuine smile on his lips that he turned the handle and entering the room faced his visitors.

"Good evening, gentlemen," said he.

The room was brightly lit, for all the lights were on, and a fire

burned in the hearth. The air was grey with smoke, since the
strangers, finding it long to wait for him, had been smoking
strong and inexpensive cigars. They sat in their great-coats and
bowler-hats as though they had only just that moment come
in; but the ashes in the little tray on the table would alone have
suggested that they had been long enough there to make themselves familiar with their surroundings. They were two powerful
men, with black moustaches, on the stout side, heavily built,
and they reminded Ashenden of Fafner and Fasolt, the giants
in the Rhinegold; their clumsy boots, the massive way they
sat in their chairs and the ponderous alertness of their expression, made it obvious that they were members of the detective
force. Ashenden gave his room an enveloping glance. He was
a neat creature and saw at once that his things, though not in
disorder, were not as he had left them. He guessed that an examination had been made of his effects. That did not disturb
him, for he kept in his room no document that would compromise him; his code he had learned by heart and destroyed
before leaving England, and such communications as reached
him from Germany were handed to him by third parties and
transmitted without delay to the proper places. There was nothing he need fear in a search, but the impression that it had been
made confirmed his suspicion that he had been denounced to
the authorities as a secret agent.

"What can I do for you, gentlemen?" he asked affably.
"It's warm in here, wouldn't you like to take off your coats—
and hats?"

It faintly irritated him that they should sit there with their
hats on.

"We're only staying a minute," said one of them. "We were
passing and as the *concierge* said you would be in at once, we
thought we would wait."

He did not remove his hat. Ashenden unwrapped his scarf
and disembarrassed himself of his heavy coat.

"Won't you have a cigar?" he asked, offering the box to
the two detectives in turn.

"I don't mind if I do," said the first, Fafner, taking one, upon
which the second, Fasolt, helped himself without a word, even
of thanks.

The name on the box appeared to have a singular effect on
their manners, for both now took off their hats.

"You must have had a very disagreeable walk in this bad

weather," said Fafner, as he bit half an inch off the end of his cigar and spat it in the fire-place.

Now it was Ashenden's principle (a good one in life as well as in the Intelligence Department) always to tell as much of the truth as he conveniently could; so he answered as follows:

"What do you take me for? I wouldn't go out in such weather if I could help it. I had to go to Vevey to-day to see an invalid friend and I came back by boat. It was bitter on the lake."

"We come from the police," said Fafner casually.

Ashenden thought they must consider him a perfect idiot if they imagined he had not long discovered that, but it was not a piece of information to which it was discreet to reply with a pleasantry.

"Oh, really," he said.

"Have you your passport on you?"

"Yes. In these war-times I think a foreigner is wise always to keep his passport on him."

"Very wise."

Ashenden handed the man the nice new passport which gave no information about his movements other than that he had come from London three months before and had since then crossed no frontier. The detective looked at it carefully and passed it on to his colleague.

"It appears to be all in order," he said.

Ashenden, standing in front of the fire to warm himself, a cigarette between his lips, made no reply. He watched the detectives warily, but with an expression, he flattered himself, of amiable unconcern. Fasolt handed back the passport to Fafner, who tapped it reflectively with a thick forefinger.

"The chief of police told us to come here," he said, and Ashenden was conscious that both of them now looked at him with attention, "to make a few enquiries of you."

Ashenden knew that when you have nothing apposite to say it is better to hold your tongue; and when a man has made a remark that calls to his mind for an answer, he is apt to find silence a trifle disconcerting. Ashenden waited for the detective to proceed. He was not quite sure, but it seemed to him that he hesitated.

"It appears that there have been a good many complaints lately of the noise that people make when they come out of the Casino late at night. We wish to know if you personally have been troubled by the disturbance. It is evident that as your rooms look on the lake and the revellers pass your windows, if the noise is serious, you must have heard it."

For an instant Ashenden was dumbfounded. What balderdash was this the detective was talking to him (boom, boom, he heard the big drum as the giant lumbered on the scene), and why on earth should the chief of police send to him to find out if his beauty sleep had been disturbed by vociferous gamblers? It looked very like a trap. But nothing is so foolish as to ascribe profundity to what on the surface is merely inept; it is a pitfall into which many an ingenuous reviewer has fallen headlong: Ashenden had a confident belief in the stupidity of the human animal, which in the course of his life had stood him in good stead. It flashed across him that if the detective asked him such a question it was because he had no shadow of proof that he was engaged in any illegal practice. It was clear that he had been denounced, but no evidence had been offered and the search of his rooms had been fruitless. But what a silly excuse was this to make for a visit and what a poverty of invention it showed! Ashenden immediately thought of three reasons the detectives might have given for seeking an interview with him and he wished that he were on terms sufficiently familiar with them to make the suggestions. This was really an insult to the intelligence. These men were even stupider than he thought; but Ashenden had always a soft corner in his heart for the stupid and now he looked upon them with a feeling of unexpected kindliness. He would have liked to pat them gently. But he answered the question with gravity.

"To tell you the truth, I am a very sound sleeper (the result doubtless of a pure heart and an easy conscience), and I have never heard a thing."

Ashenden looked at them for the faint smile that he thought his remark deserved, but their countenances remained stolid. Ashenden, as well as an agent of the British Government, was a humorist, and he stifled the beginnings of a sigh. He assumed a slightly imposing air and adopted a more serious tone.

"But even if I had been awakened by noisy people I should not dream of complaining. At a time when there is so much trouble, misery and unhappiness in the world, I cannot but think it very wrong to disturb the amusement of persons who are lucky enough to be able to amuse themselves."

"*En effet.*" said the detective. "But the fact remains that

people have been disturbed and the chief of police thought
the matter should be enquired into."

His colleague, who had hitherto preserved a silence that was
positively sphinx-like, now broke it.

"I notice by your passport that you are an author, *monsieur*,"
he said.

Ashenden in reaction from his previous perturbation was
feeling exceedingly debonair and he answered with good
humour.

"It is true. It is a profession full of tribulation, but it has
now and then its compensations."

"*La gloire*," said Fafner politely.

"Or shall we say notoriety?" hazarded Ashenden.

"And what are you doing in Geneva?"

The question was put so pleasantly that Ashenden felt it
behooved him to be on his guard. A police officer amiable is
more dangerous to the wise than a police officer aggressive.

"I am writing a play," said Ashenden.

He waved his hand to the papers on his table. Four eyes
followed his gesture. A casual glance told him that the detectives had looked and taken note of his manuscripts.

"And why should you write a play here rather than in your
own country?"

Ashenden smiled upon them with even more affability than
before, since this was a question for which he had long been
prepared, and it was a relief to give the answer. He was curious
to see how it would go down.

"*Mais*, *monsieur*, there is the war. My country is in a turmoil, it would be impossible to sit there quietly and write a
play."

"Is it a comedy or a tragedy?"

"Oh, a comedy, and a light one at that," replied Ashenden.
"The artist needs peace and quietness. How do you expect
him to preserve that detachment of spirit that is demanded
by creative work unless he can have perfect tranquillity?
Switzerland has the good fortune to be neutral, and it seemed
to me that in Geneva I should find the very surroundings I
wanted."

Fafner nodded slightly to Fasolt, but whether to indicate
that he thought Ashenden an imbecile or whether in sympathy
with his desire for a safe retreat from a turbulent world, Ashenden had no means of knowing. Anyhow the detective evidently

came to the conclusion that he could learn nothing more from
talking to Ashenden, for his remarks grew now desultory and
in a few minutes he rose to go.

When Ashenden, having warmly shaken their hands, closed
the door behind the pair he heaved a great sigh of relief. He
turned on the water for his bath, as hot as he thought he could
possibly bear it, and as he undressed reflected comfortably over
his escape.

The day before, an incident had occurred that had left him
on his guard. There was in his service a Swiss, known in the
Intelligence Department as Bernard, who had recently come
from Germany, and Ashenden had instructed him to go to a
certain café desiring to see him, at a certain time. Since he had
not seen him before, so that there might be no mistake he had
informed him through an intermediary what question he himself would ask and what reply he was to give. He chose the
luncheon hour for the meeting, since then the café was unlikely
to be crowded, and it chanced that on entering he saw but one
man of about the age he knew Bernard to be. He was by himself
and going up to him Ashenden casually put to him the pre-
arranged question. The pre-arranged answer was given, and
sitting down beside him, Ashenden ordered himself a Dubonnet.
The spy was a stocky little fellow, shabbily dressed, with a
bullet-shaped head, close-cropped, fair, with shifty blue eyes
and a sallow skin. He did not inspire confidence, and but that
Ashenden knew by experience how hard it was to find men
willing to go into Germany he would have been surprised that
his predecessor had engaged him. He was a German-Swiss
and spoke French with a strong accent. He immediately asked
for his wages and these Ashenden passed over to him in an
envelope. They were in Swiss francs. He gave a general account
of his stay in Germany and answered Ashenden's careful questions. He was by calling a waiter and had found a job in a
restaurant near one of the Rhine bridges, which gave him good
opportunity to get the information that was required of him.
His reasons for coming to Switzerland for a few days were
plausible and there could apparently be no difficulty in his
crossing the frontier on his return. Ashenden expressed his
satisfaction with his behaviour, gave him his orders and was
prepared to finish the interview.

"Very good," said Bernard. "But before I go back to Germany I want two thousand francs."

"Do you?"

"Yes, and I want them now, before you leave this café. It's a sum I have to pay, and I've got to have it."

"I'm afraid I can't give it to you."

A scowl made the man's face even more unpleasant to look at than it was before.

"You've got to."

"What makes you think that?"

The spy leaned forward and, not raising his voice, but speaking so that only Ashenden could hear, burst out angrily.

"Do you think I'm going on risking my life for that beggarly sum you give me? Not ten days ago a man was caught at Mainz and shot. Was that one of your men?"

"We haven't got anyone at Mainz," said Ashenden, carelessly, and for all he knew it was true. He had been puzzled not to receive his usual communications from that place and Bernard's information might afford the explanation. "You knew exactly what you were to get when you took on the job, and if you weren't satisfied you needn't have taken it. I have no authority to give you a penny more."

"Do you see what I've got here?" said Bernard.

He took a small revolver out of his pocket and fingered it significantly.

"What are you going to do with it? Pawn it?"

With an angry shrug of the shoulders he put it back in his pocket. Ashenden reflected that had he known anything of the technique of the theatre Bernard would have been aware that it was useless to make a gesture that had no ulterior meaning.

"You refuse to give me the money?"

"Certainly."

The spy's manner, which at first had been obsequious, was now somewhat truculent, but he kept his head and never for a moment raised his voice. Ashenden could see that Bernard, however big a ruffian, was a reliable agent, and he made up his mind to suggest to R. that his salary should be raised. The scene diverted him. A little way off two fat citizens of Geneva, with black beards, were playing dominoes, and on the other side a young man with spectacles was with great rapidity writing sheet after sheet of an immensely long letter. A Swiss family (who knows, perhaps Robinson by name), consisting of a father and mother and four children, were sitting round a

table making the best of two small cups of coffee. The *caissière*
behind the counter, an imposing brunette with a large bust en-
cased in black silk, was reading the local paper. The surroundings made the melodramatic scene in which Ashenden was
engaged perfectly grotesque. His own play seemed to him much
more real.

Bernard smiled. His smile was not engaging.

"Do you know that I have only to go to the police and tell
them about you to have you arrested? Do you know what a
Swiss prison is like?"

"No, I've often wondered lately. Do you?"

"Yes, and you wouldn't much like it."

One of the things that had bothered Ashenden was the
possibility that he would be arrested before he finished his play.
He disliked the notion of leaving it half done for an indefinite
period. He did not know whether he would be treated as a
political prisoner or as a common criminal and he had a mind
to ask Bernard whether in the latter case (the only one Bernard
was likely to know anything about) he would be allowed writing
materials. He was afraid Bernard would think the inquiry an
attempt to laugh at him. But he was feeling comparatively at
ease and was able to answer Bernard's threat without heat.

"You could of course get me sentenced to two years' imprisonment."

"At least."

"No, that is the maximum, I understand, and I think it is
quite enough. I won't conceal from you that I should find it
extremely disagreeable. But not nearly so disagreeable as you
would."

"What could you do?"

"Oh, we'd get you somehow. And after all, the war won't
last for ever. You are a waiter, you want your freedom of
action. I promise you that if I get into any trouble, you will
never be admitted into any of the allied countries for the rest
of your life. I can't help thinking it would cramp your style."

Bernard did not reply, but looked down sulkily at the marble-
topped table. Ashenden thought this was the moment to pay
for the drinks and go.

"Think it over, Bernard," he said. "If you want to go back
to your job, you have your instructions, and your usual wages
shall be paid through the usual channels."

The spy shrugged his shoulders, and Ashenden, though not

knowing in the least what was the result of their conversation, felt that it behoved him to walk out with dignity. He did so.

And now as he carefully put one foot into the bath, wondering if he could bear it, he asked himself what Bernard had in the end decided on. The water was just not scalding and he gradually let himself down into it. On the whole it seemed to him that the spy had thought it would be as well to go straight, and the source of his denunciation must be looked for elsewhere. Perhaps in the hotel itself. Ashenden lay back, and as his body grew used to the heat of the water gave a sigh of satisfaction.

"Really," he reflected, "there are moments in life when all this to-do that has led from the primeval slime to myself seems almost worth while."

Ashenden could not but think he was lucky to have wriggled out of the fix he had found himself in that afternoon. Had he been arrested and in due course sentenced R., shrugging his shoulders, would merely have called him a damned fool and set about looking for someone to take his place. Already Ashenden knew his chief well enough to be aware that when he had told him that if he got into trouble he need look for no help he meant exactly what he said.

Ashenden, lying comfortably in his bath, was glad to think that in all probability he would be able to finish his play in peace. The police had drawn a blank and though they might watch him from now on with some care it was unlikely that they would take a further step until he had at least roughed out his third act. It behooved him to be prudent (only a fortnight ago his colleague at Lausanne had been sentenced to a term of imprisonment), but it would be foolish to be alarmed: his predecessor in Geneva, seeing himself, with an exaggerated sense of his own importance, shadowed from morning till night, had been so affected by the nervous strain that it had been found necessary to withdraw him. Twice a week Ashenden had to go to the market to receive instructions that were brought to him by an old peasant woman from French Savoy who sold butter and eggs. She came in with the other market-women and the search at the frontier was perfunctory. It was barely dawn when they crossed and the officials were only too glad to have done quickly with these chattering noisy women and get back to their warm fires and their cigars. Indeed this old lady looked so bland and innocent, with her corpulence, her fat red face, and her smiling good-natured mouth, it would have been a very astute detective who could imagine that if he took the trouble to put his hand deep down between those voluminous breasts of hers, he would find a little piece of paper that would land in the dock an honest old woman (who kept her son out of the trenches by taking this risk) and an English writer approaching middle-age. Ashenden went to the market about nine when the housewives of Geneva for the most part had done their provisioning, stopped in front of the basket by the side of which, rain or wind, hot or cold, sat that indomitable creature and bought half a pound of butter. She slipped the note into his hand when he was given change for ten francs and he sauntered away. His only moment of risk was when he walked back to his hotel with the paper in his pocket, and after this scare he made up his mind to shorten as much as possible the period during which it could be found on him.

Ashenden sighed, for the water was no longer quite so hot; he could not reach the tap with his hand nor could he turn it with his toes (as every properly regulated tap should turn) and if he got up enough to add more hot water he might just as well get out altogether. On the other hand he could not pull out the plug with his foot in order to empty the bath and so force himself to get out, nor could he find in himself the will-power to step out of it like a man. He had often heard people tell him that he possessed character and he reflected that people judge hastily in the affairs of life because they judge on insufficient evidence: they had never seen him in a hot, but diminishingly hot, bath. His mind, however, wandered back to his play, and telling himself jokes and repartees that he knew by bitter experience would never look so neat on paper nor sound so well on the stage as they did then, he abstracted his mind from the fact that his bath was growing almost tepid, when he heard a knock at the door. Since he did not want anyone to enter, he had the presence of mind not to say come in, but the knocking was repeated.

"Who is it?" he cried irascibly.

"A letter."

"Come in then. Wait a minute."

Ashenden heard his bedroom-door open and getting out of the bath flung a towel round him and went in. A page-boy was waiting with a note. It needed only a verbal answer. It was from a lady staying in the hotel asking him to play bridge

after dinner and was signed in the continental fashion Baronne
de Higgins. Ashenden, longing for a cosy meal in his own room,
in slippers and with a book leaned up against a reading-lamp,
was about to refuse when it occurred to him that under the
circumstances it might be discreet to show himself in the dining-
room that night. It was absurd to suppose that in that hotel the
news would not have spread that he had been visited by the
police and it would be as well to prove to his fellow-guests that
he was not disconcerted. It had passed through his mind that
it might be someone in the hotel who had denounced him and
indeed the name of the sprightly baroness had not failed to
suggest itself to him. If it was she who had given him away there
would be a certain humour in playing bridge with her. He gave
the boy a message that he would be pleased to come and proceeded slowly to don his evening clothes.

The Baroness von Higgins was an Austrian, who on settling
in Geneva during the first winter of the war, had found it convenient to make her name look as French as possible. She spoke
English and French perfectly. Her surname, so far from Teutonic, she owed to her grandfather, a Yorkshire stable-boy, who
had been taken over to Austria by a Prince Blankenstein early
in the nineteenth century. He had had a charming and romantic
career; a very good-looking young man, he attracted the attention of one of the arch-duchesses and then made such good use
of his opportunities that he ended his life as a Baron and
minister plenipotentiary to an Italian court. The baroness, his
only descendant, after an unhappy marriage, the particulars of
which she was fond of relating to her acquaintance, had resumed her maiden name. She mentioned not infrequently the
fact that her grandfather had been an ambassador, but never
that he had been a stable-boy and Ashenden had learned this
interesting detail from Vienna; for as he grew friendly with her
he had thought it necessary to get a few particulars about her
past, and he knew among other things that her private income
did not permit her to live on the somewhat lavish scale on which
she was living in Geneva. Since she had so many advantages for
espionage, it was fairly safe to suppose that an alert secret
service had enlisted her services and Ashenden took it for
granted that she was engaged somehow on the same kind of
work as himself. It increased if anything the cordiality of his
relations with her.

When he went into the dining-room it was already full. He

sat down at his table and feeling jaunty after his adventure ordered himself (at the expense of the British Government) a bottle of champagne. The baroness gave him a flashing, brilliant smile. She was a woman of more than forty, but in a hard and glittering manner extremely beautiful. She was a high-coloured blonde with golden hair of a metallic lustre, lovely no doubt but not attractive, and Ashenden had from the first reflected that it was not the sort of hair you would like to find in your soup. She had fine features, blue eyes, a straight nose, and a pink and white skin, but her skin was stretched over her bones a trifle tightly; she was generously *décolletée* and her white and ample bosom had the quality of marble. There was nothing in her appearance to suggest the yielding tenderness that the susceptible find so alluring She was magnificently gowned, but scantily bejewelled, so that Ashenden, who knew something of these matters, concluded that the superior authority had given her *carte blanche* at a dress-maker's but had not thought it prudent or necessary to provide her with rings or pearls. She was notwithstanding so showy that but for R.'s story of the minister, Ashenden would have thought the sight of her alone must have aroused in anyone on whom she desired to exercise her wiles, the sense of prudence.

While he waited for his dinner to be served, Ashenden cast his eyes over the company. Most of the persons gathered were old friends by sight. At that time Geneva was a hot-bed of intrigue and its home was the hotel at which Ashenden was staying. There were Frenchmen there, Italians and Russians, Turks, Rumanians, Greeks and Egyptians. Some had fled their country, some doubtless represented it. There was a Bulgarian, an agent of Ashenden's, whom for greater safety he had never even spoken to in Geneva; he was dining that night with two fellow-countrymen and in a day or so, if he was not killed in the interval, might have a very interesting communication to make. Then there was a little German prostitute, with china-blue eyes and a doll-like face, who made frequent journeys along the lake and up to Berne, and in the exercise of her profession got little titbits of information over which doubtless they pondered with deliberation in Berlin. She was of course of a different class from the baroness and hunted much easier game. But Ashenden was surprised to catch sight of Count von Holzminden and wondered what on earth he was doing there. This was the German agent in Vevey and he came over to

Geneva only on occasion. Once Ashenden had seen him in the old quarter of the city, with its silent houses and deserted streets, talking at a corner to a man whose appearance very much suggested the spy and he would have given a great deal to hear what they said to one another. It had amused him to come across the Count, for in London before the war he had known him fairly well. He was of great family and indeed related to the Hohenzollerns. He was fond of England; he danced well, rode well and shot well; people said he was more English than the English. He was a tall, thin fellow, in well-cut clothes, with a close-cropped Prussian head, and that peculiar bend of the body as though he were just about to bow to a royalty that you feel, rather than see, in those who have spent their lives about a court. He had charming manners and was much interested in the Fine Arts. But now Ashenden and he pretended they had never seen one another before. Each of course knew on what work the other was engaged and Ashenden had had a mind to chaff him about it—it seemed absurd when he had dined with a man off and on for years and played cards with him, to act as though he did not know him from Adam— but refrained in case the German looked upon his behaviour as further proof of the British frivolity in face of war. Ashenden was perplexed: Holzminden had never set foot in that hotel before and it was unlikely that he had done so now without good reason.

Ashenden asked himself whether this event had anything to do with the unusual presence in the dining-room of Prince Ali. At that juncture it was imprudent to ascribe any occurrence, however accidental it looked, to the hazard of coincidence. Prince Ali was an Egyptian, a near relation of the Khedive, who had fled his country when the Khedive was deposed. He was a bitter enemy of the English and was known to be actively engaged in stirring up trouble in Egypt. The week before, the Khedive in great secrecy had passed three days at the hotel and the pair of them had held constant meetings in the Prince's apartments. He was a little fat man with a heavy black mous· tache. He was living with his two daughters and a certain Pasha, Mustapha by name, who was his secretary and managed his affairs. The four of them were now dining together; they drank a great deal of champagne, but sat in a stolid silence. The two princesses were emancipated young women who spent their nights dancing in restaurants with the bloods of Geneva. They were short and stout, with fine black eyes and heavy sallow faces; and they were dressed with a rich loudness that suggested the Fish-market at Cairo rather than the Rue de la Paix. His Highness usually ate upstairs, but the princesses dined every evening in the public dining-room: they were chaperoned vaguely by a little old Englishwoman, a Miss King, who had been their governess; but she sat at a table by herself and they appeared to pay no attention to her. Once Ashenden, going along a corridor, had come upon the elder of the two fat princesses berating the governess in French with a violence that took his breath away. She was shouting at the top of her voice and suddenly smacked the old woman's face. When she caught sight of Ashenden she gave him a furious look and flinging into her room slammed the door. He walked on as though he had noticed nothing.

On his arrival Ashenden had tried to scrape acquaintance with Miss King, but she had received his advances not merely with frigidity but with churlishness. He had begun by taking off his hat when he met her, and she had given him a stiff bow, then he had addressed her and she had answered with such brevity that it was evident that she wished to have nothing much to do with him. But it was not his business to be discouraged, so with what assurance he could muster he took the first opportunity to enter into conversation with her. She drew herself up and said in French, but with an English accent:

"I don't wish to make acquaintance with strangers."

She turned her back on him and next time he saw her, cut him dead.

She was a tiny old woman, just a few little bones in a bag of wrinkled skin, and her face was deeply furrowed. It was obvious that she wore a wig, it was of a mousy brown, very elaborate and not always set quite straight, and she was heavily made up, with great patches of scarlet on her withered cheeks and brilliantly red lips. She dressed fantastically in gay clothes that looked as though they had been bought higgledy-piggledy from an old-clothes shop and in the day-time she wore enormous, extravagantly girlish hats. She tripped along in very small smart shoes with very high heels. Her appearance was so grotesque that it created consternation rather than amusement. People turned in the street and stared at her with open mouths.

Ashenden was told that Miss King had not been to England since she was first engaged as governess of the prince's mother and he could not but be amazed to think of all she must have seen during those long years in the harems of Cairo. It was impossible to guess how old she was. How many of those short Eastern lives must have run their course under her eyes and what dark secrets must she have known! Ashenden wondered where she came from; an exile from her own country for so long, she must possess in it neither family nor friends: he knew that her sentiments were anti-English and if she had answered him so rudely he surmised that she had been told to be on her guard against him. She never spoke anything but French. Ashenden wondered what it was she thought of as she sat there, for luncheon and dinner, by herself. He wondered if she ever read. After meals she went straight upstairs and was never seen in the public sitting-rooms. He wondered what she thought of those two emancipated princesses who wore garish frocks and danced with strange men in second-rate cafés. But when Miss King passed him on her way out of the dining-room it seemed to Ashenden that her mask of a face scowled. She appeared actively to dislike him. Her gaze met his and the pair of them looked at one another for a moment; he imagined that she tried to put into her stare an unspoken insult. It would have been pleasantly absurd in that painted, withered visage if it had not been for some reason rather oddly pathetic.

But now the Baroness de Higgins, having finished her dinner, gathered up her handkerchief and her bag, and with waiters bowing on either side sailed down the spacious room. She stopped at Ashenden's table. She looked magnificent.

"I'm so glad you can play bridge to-night," she said in her perfect English, with no more than a trace of German accent. "Will you come to my sitting-room when you are ready and have your coffee?"

"What a lovely dress," said Ashenden.

"It is frightful. I have nothing to wear, I don't know what I shall do now that I cannot go to Paris. Those horrible Prussians," and her r's grew guttural as she raised her voice, "why did they want to drag my poor country into this terrible war?"

She gave a sigh, and a flashing smile, and sailed on. Ashenden was among the last to finish and when he left the dining-room it was almost empty. As he walked past Count Holzminden, Ashenden feeling very gay hazarded the shadow of a wink. The German agent could not be quite sure of it and if he suspected

it might rack his brains to discover what mystery it portended.
Ashenden walked up to the second floor and knocked at the
baroness's door.

"*Entrez, entrez,*" she said and flung it open.

She shook both his hands with cordiality and drew him into
the room. He saw that the two persons who were to make the
four had already arrived. They were Prince Ali and his secretary. Ashenden was astounded.

"Allow me to introduce Mr. Ashenden to your Highness,"
said the baroness, speaking in her fluent French.

Ashenden bowed and took the proffered hand. The Prince
gave him a quick look, but did not speak. Madame de Higgins
went on:

"I do not know if you have met the Pasha."

"I am delighted to make your acquaintance, Mr. Ashen-
den," said the Prince's secretary, warmly shaking his hand.
"Our beautiful baroness has talked to us of your bridge and His
Highness is devoted to the game. *N'est ce pas, Altesse?*"

"*Oui, oui,*" said the Prince.

Mustapha Pasha was a huge fat fellow, of forty-five perhaps,
with large mobile eyes and a big black moustache. He wore a
dinner-jacket with a large diamond in his shirt-front and the
tarboosh of his country. He was exceedingly voluble, and the
words tumbled out of his mouth tumultuously, like marbles
out of a bag. He took pains to be extremely civil to Ashenden.
The Prince sat in silence, looking at Ashenden quietly from
under his heavy eyelids. He seemed shy.

"I have not seen you at the club, *Monsieur,*" said the Pasha.
"Do you not like baccarat?"

"I play but seldom."

"The baroness, who has read everything, tells me that you
are a remarkable writer. Unfortunately I do not read English."

The baroness paid Ashenden some very fulsome compliments, to which he listened with a proper and grateful politeness, and then, having provided her guests with coffee and
liqueurs, she produced the cards. Ashenden could not but
wonder why he had been asked to play. He had (he flattered
himself) few illusions about himself, and so far as bridge was
concerned none. He knew that he was a good player of the
second class, but he had played often enough with the best
players in the world to know that he was not in the same street

with them. The game played now was contract, with which he was not very familiar, and the stakes were high; but the game was obviously but a pretext and Ashenden had no notion what other game was being played under the rose. It might be that knowing he was a British agent the Prince and his secretary had desired to see him in order to find out what sort of person he was. Ashenden had felt for a day or two that something was in the air and this meeting confirmed his suspicions, but he had not the faintest notion of what nature this something was. His spies had told him of late nothing that signified. He was now persuaded that he owed that visit of the Swiss police to the kindly intervention of the baroness and it looked as though the bridge-party had been arranged when it was discovered that the detectives had been able to do nothing. The notion was mysterious, but diverting, and as Ashenden played one rubber after another, joining in the incessant conversation, he watched what was said by himself no less closely than what was said by the others. The war was spoken of a good deal and the baroness and the Pasha expressed very anti-German sentiments. The baroness's heart was in England whence her family (the stable-boy from Yorkshire) had sprung and the Pasha looked upon Paris as his spiritual home. When the Pasha talked of Montmartre and its life by night the Prince was roused from his silence.

"*C'est une bien belle ville, Paris,*" he said.

"The Prince has a beautiful apartment there," said his secretary, "with beautiful pictures and life-sized statues."

Ashenden explained that he had the greatest sympathy for the national aspirations of Egypt and that he looked upon Vienna as the most pleasing capital in Europe. He was as friendly to them as they were to him. But if they were under the impression that they would get any information out of him that they had not already seen in the Swiss papers he had a notion that they were mistaken. At one moment he had a suspicion that he was being sounded upon the possibility of selling himself. It was done so discreetly that he could not be quite sure, but he had a feeling that a suggestion floated in the air that a clever writer could do his country a good turn and make a vast amount of money for himself if he cared to enter into an arrangement that would bring to a troubled world the peace that every humane man must so sincerely desire. It was plain that nothing very much would be said that first evening, but

Ashenden as evasively as he could, more by general amiability than by words, tried to indicate that he was willing to hear more of the subject. While he talked with the Pasha and the beautiful Austrian he was conscious that the watchful eyes of Prince Ali were upon him, and he had an uneasy suspicion that they read too much of his thoughts. He felt rather than knew that the Prince was an able and astute man. It was possible that after he left them the Prince would tell the other two that they were wasting their time and there was nothing to be done with Ashenden.

Soon after midnight, a rubber having been finished, the Prince rose from the table.

"It is getting late," he said, "and Mr. Ashenden has doubtless much to do to-morrow. We must not keep him up."

Ashenden looked upon this as a signal to take himself off. He left the three together to discuss the situation and retired not a little mystified. He could only trust that they were no less puzzled than he. When he got to his room he suddenly realized that he was dog-tired. He could hardly keep his eyes open while he undressed, and the moment he flung himself into bed he fell asleep.

He would have sworn that he had not been asleep five minutes when he was dragged back to wakefulness by a knocking at the door. He listened for a moment.

"Who is it?"

"It's the maid. Open. I have something to say to you."

Cursing, Ashenden turned on his light, ran a hand through his thinning and rumpled hair (for like Julius Cæsar he disliked exposing an unbecoming baldness) and unlocked and opened the door. Outside it stood a tousled Swiss maid. She wore no apron and looked as though she had thrown on her clothes in a hurry.

"The old English lady, the governess of the Egyptian princesses, is dying and she wants to see you."

"Me?" said Ashenden. "It's impossible. I don't know her. She was all right this evening."

He was confused and spoke his thoughts as they came to him.

"She asks for you. The doctor says, will you come. She cannot last much longer."

"It must be a mistake. She can't want me."

"She said your name and the number of your room. She says quick, quick."

Ashenden shrugged his shoulders. He went back into his room to put on slippers and a dressing-gown, and as an afterthought dropped a small revolver into his pocket. Ashenden believed much more in his acuteness than in a firearm, which is apt to go off at the wrong time and make a noise, but there are moments when it gives you confidence to feel your fingers round its butt, and this sudden summons seemed to him exceedingly mysterious. It was ridiculous to suppose that those two cordial stout Egyptian gentlemen were laying some sort of trap for him, but in the work upon which Ashenden was engaged the dullness of routine was apt now and again to slip quite shamelessly into the melodrama of the sixties. Just as passion will make use brazenly of the hackneyed phrase, so will chance show itself insensitive to the triteness of the literary convention.

Miss King's room was two floors higher than Ashenden's, and as he accompanied the chamber-maid along the corridor and up the stairs he asked her what was the matter with the old governess. She was flurried and stupid.

"I think she has had a stroke. I don't know. The nightporter woke me and said Monsieur Bridet wanted me to get up at once."

Monsieur Bridet was the assistant-manager.

"What is the time?" asked Ashenden.

"It must be three o'clock."

They arrived at Miss King's door and the maid knocked. It was opened by Monsieur Bridet. He had evidently been roused from his sleep; he wore slippers on his bare feet, grey trousers and a frock-coat over his pyjamas. He looked absurd. His hair as a rule plastered neatly on his head stood on end. He was extremely apologetic.

"A thousand excuses for disturbing you, Monsieur Ashenden, but she kept asking for you and the doctor said you should be sent for."

"It doesn't matter at all."

Ashenden walked in. It was a small back room and all the lights were on. The windows were closed and the curtains drawn. It was intensely hot. The doctor, a bearded, grizzled Swiss, was standing at the bedside. Monsieur Bridet, notwithstanding his costume and his evident harassment, found in himself the presence of mind to remain the attentive manager, and with ceremony effected the proper introduction.

"This is Mr. Ashenden, for whom Miss King has been asking. Dr. Arbos of the Faculty of Medicine of Geneva."

Without a word the doctor pointed to the bed. On it lay Miss King. It gave Ashenden a shock to look at her. She wore a large white cotton night-cap (on entering Ashenden had noticed the brown wig on a stand on the dressing-table) tied under the chin and a white, voluminous nightdress that came high up in the neck. Nightcap and nightdress belonged to a past age and reminded you of Cruikshank's illustrations to the novels of Charles Dickens. Her face was greasy still with the cream she had used before going to bed to remove her make-up, but she had removed it summarily and there were streaks of black on her eyebrows and of red on her cheeks. She looked very small, lying in the bed, no larger than a child, and immensely old.

"She must be well over eighty," thought Ashenden.

She did not look human, but like a doll, the caricature of an old, old witch that an ironic toymaker had amused himself with modelling. She lay perfectly still on her back, the tiny little body hardly marked under the flatness of the blanket, her face even smaller than usual because she had removed her teeth; and you would have thought she was dead but for the black eyes, strangely large in the shrunken mask, that stared unblinkingly. Ashenden thought their expression changed when she saw him.

"Well, Miss King, I'm sorry to see you like this," he said with forced cheerfulness.

"She cannot speak," said the doctor. "She had another little stroke when the maid went to fetch you. I have just given her an injection. She may partly recover the use of her tongue in a little while. She has something to say to you."

"I will gladly wait," said Ashenden.

He fancied that in those dark eyes he saw a look of relief. For a moment or two the four of them stood round the bed and stared at the dying woman.

"Well, if there is nothing I can do, I may just as well go back to bed," said Monsieur Bridet then.

"*Allez, mon ami,*" said the doctor. "You can do nothing."

Monsieur Bridet turned to Ashenden.

"May I have a word with you?" he asked.

"Certainly."

The doctor noticed a sudden fear in Miss King's eyes.

"Do not be alarmed," he said kindly. "Monsieur Ashenden is not going. He will stay as long as you wish."

The assistant-manager took Ashenden to the door and partly closed it so that those within should not hear his undertones.

"I can count on your discretion, Monsieur Ashenden, can I not? It is a very disagreeable thing to have anyone die in a hotel. The other guests do not like it and we must do all we can to prevent their knowing. I shall have the body removed the first possible moment and I shall be extremely obliged if you will not say that there has been a death."

"You can have every confidence in me," said Ashenden.

"It is very unfortunate that the manager should be away for the night. I am afraid he will be exceedingly displeased. Of course if it had been possible I would have sent for an ambulance and had her taken to the hospital, but the doctor said she might die before we got her downstairs and absolutely refused to let me. It is not my fault if she dies in the hotel."

"Death so often chooses its moments without consideration," murmured Ashenden.

"After all she is an old woman, she should have died years ago. What did this Egyptian prince want to have a governess of that age for? He ought to have sent her back to her own country. These Orientals, they are always giving trouble."

"Where is the Prince now?" asked Ashenden. "She has been in his service for many years. Ought you not to wake him?"

"He is not in the hotel. He went out with his secretary. He may be playing baccarat. I do not know. Anyhow I cannot send all over Geneva to find him."

"And the princesses?"

"They have not come in. They seldom return to the hotel till dawn. They are mad about dancing. I do not know where they are and in any case they would not thank me for dragging them away from their diversions, I know what they are, because their governess has had a stroke. The night-porter will tell them when they arrive and then they can please themselves. She does not want them. When the night-porter fetched me and I went into her room I asked where his highness was and she cried with all her strength: no, no."

"She could talk then?"

"Yes, after a fashion, but the thing that surprised me was

that she spoke in English. She always insisted on talking French. You know, she hated the English."

"What did she want with me?"

"That I cannot tell you. She said she had something that she must say to you at once. It is funny, she knew the number of your room. At first when she asked for you I would not let them send. I cannot have my clients disturbed in the middle of the night because a crazy old woman asks for them. You have the right to your sleep, I imagine. But when the doctor came he insisted. She gave us no peace and when I said she must wait till morning she cried."

Ashenden looked at the assistant-manager. He seemed to find nothing at all touching in the scene he related.

"The doctor asked who you were and when I told him he said that perhaps she wished to see you because you were a compatriot."

"Perhaps," said Ashenden drily.

"Well, I shall try to get a little sleep. I shall give the night-porter orders to wake me when everything is over. Fortunately the nights are long now and if everything goes well we may be able to get the body away before it is light."

Ashenden went back into the room and immediately the dark eyes of the dying woman fixed upon him. He felt that it was incumbent upon him to say something, but as he spoke he reflected on the foolish way in which one speaks to the sick.

"I'm afraid you're feeling very ill, Miss King."

It seemed to him that a flash of anger crossed her eyes and Ashenden could not but imagine that she was exasperated by his futile words.

"You do not mind waiting?" asked the doctor.

"Of course not."

It appeared that the night-porter had been roused by the ring-ing of the telephone from Miss King's room, but on listening could get no one to speak. The bell continued to ring, so he went upstairs and knocked at the door. He entered with his pass-key and found Miss King lying on the floor. The telephone had fallen too. It looked as though, feeling ill, she had taken off the receiver to call for help and then collapsed. The night-porter hurried to fetch the assistant-manager and together they had lifted her back into bed. Then the maid was wakened and the doctor sent for. It gave Ashenden a queer feeling to listen to the doctor giving him these facts in Miss King's hearing.

He spoke as though she could not understand his French. He spoke as though she were already dead.

Then the doctor said:

"Well, there is really nothing more that I can do. It is useless for me to stay. I can be rung up if there is any change."

Ashenden, knowing that Miss King might remain in that condition for hours, shrugged his shoulders.

"Very well."

The doctor patted her raddled cheek as though she were a child.

"You must try to sleep. I will come back in the morning."

He packed up the dispatch-case in which he had his medical appliances, washed his hands and shuffled himself into a heavy coat. Ashenden accompanied him to the door and as he shook hands the doctor gave his prognosis in a pout of his bearded mouth. Ashenden, coming back, looked at the maid. She sat on the edge of a chair, uneasily, as though in the presence of death she feared to presume. Her broad, ugly face was bloated with fatigue.

"There's no use in your staying up," Ashenden said to her. "Why don't you go to bed?"

"*Monsieur* wouldn't like to remain here alone. Somebody must stay with him."

"But, good heavens, why? You have your day's work to do to-morrow."

"In any case I have to get up at five."

"Then try to get a little sleep now. You can give me a look in when you get up. *Allez*."

She rose heavily to her feet.

"As the gentleman wishes. But I will stay very willingly."

Ashenden smiled and shook his head.

"*Bonsoir, ma pauvre mademoiselle*," said the maid.

She went out and Ashenden was left alone. He sat by the bedside and again his eyes met Miss King's. It was embarrassing to encounter that unshrinking stare.

"Don't worry yourself, Miss King. You've had a slight stroke. I'm sure your speech will come back to you in a minute."

He felt certain then that he saw in those dark eyes a desperate effort to speak. He could not be mistaken. The mind was shaken by desire, but the paralyzed body was incapable of obedience. For her disappointment expressed itself quite plainly, tears

came to her eyes and ran down her cheeks. Ashenden took out
his handkerchief and dried them.

"Don't distress yourself, Miss King. Have a little patience
and I'm sure you'll be able to say anything you want."

He did not know if it was his fancy that he read in her eyes
now the despairing thought that she had not the time to wait.
Perhaps it was only that he ascribed to her the notions that
came to himself. On the dressing-table were the governess's
poor little toilet things, silver-backed embossed brushes and a
silver mirror; in a corner stood a shabby black trunk and on
the top of the wardrobe a large hat-box in shiny leather. It
all looked poor and mean in that trim hotel room, with its
suite in highly varnished rose-wood. The glare was intolerable.

"Wouldn't you be more comfortable if I turned out some of
the lights?" asked Ashenden.

He put out all the lamps but the one by the bedside and then
sat down again. He had a longing to smoke. Once more his
eyes were held by those other eyes in which was all that remained alive of that old, old woman. He felt certain that she
had something that she wanted urgently to say to him. But
what was it? What was it? Perhaps she had asked him only because, feeling death near, she had had a sudden yearning, she
the exile of so many years, to die with someone of her own
people, so long forgotten, by her side. That was what the doctor
thought. But why should she have sent for him? There were
other English people in the hotel. There was an old pair, a
retired Indian Civilian and his wife, to whom it seemed more
natural that she should turn. No one could be more of a stranger
to her than Ashenden.

"Have you got something to say to me, Miss King?"

He tried to read an answer in her eyes. They continued to
stare at him meaningly, but what the meaning was he had no
notion.

"Don't be afraid I shall go. I will stay as long as you want
me."

Nothing, nothing. The black eyes, and as he looked at them
they seemed to glow mysteriously as though there were fire
behind them, the eyes continued to hold him with that insistent
stare. Then Ashenden asked himself if she had sent for him
because she knew that he was a British agent. Was it possible
that at that last moment she had had some unexpected revul-
sion of feeling from everything that had signified to her for so

many years? Perhaps at the moment of death a love for her country, a love that had been dead for half a century, awakened again in her—("I'm silly to fancy these idiotic things," thought Ashenden, "it's cheap and tawdry fiction.")—and she had been seized with a desire to do something for what was after all her own. No one was quite himself just then and patriotism (in peace-time an attitude best left to politicians, publicists and fools, but in the dark days of war an emotion that can wring the heart-strings) patriotism made one do odd things. It was curious that she had been unwilling to see the Prince and his daughters. Did she on a sudden hate them? Did she feel herself a traitor on their account and now at the last hour wish to make amends? ("It's all very improbable, she's just a silly old maid who ought to have died years ago.") But you couldn't ignore the improbable. Ashenden, his common sense protesting, became strangely convinced that she had some secret that she wished to impart to him. She had sent for him knowing who he was because he could make use of it. She was dying and feared nothing. But was it really important? Ashenden leaned forward trying more eagerly to read what her eyes had to say. Perhaps it was only some trivial thing that was important only in her addled old brain. Ashenden was sick of the people who saw spies in every inoffensive passer-by and plots in the most innocent combination of circumstances. It was a hundred to one that if Miss King recovered her speech she would tell him something that could be of no use to anybody.

But what must that old woman know! With her sharp eyes and sharp ears she must have had the chance to discover matters that were closely hidden from persons that seemed less insignificant. Ashenden thought again how he had had the impression that something of real consequence was being prepared round about him. It was curious that Holzminden should have come to the hotel that day; and why had Prince Ali and the Pasha, those wild gamblers, wasted an evening in playing contract-bridge with him? It might be that some new plan was in question, it might be that the very greatest affairs were afoot, and perhaps what the old woman had to say might make all the difference in the world. It might mean defeat or victory. It might mean anything. And there she lay powerless to speak. For a long time Ashenden stared at her in silence.

"Has it got anything to do with the war, Miss King?" he said on a sudden, loudly.

Something passed through her eyes and a tremor shot across her little old face. It was a distinct movement. Something strange and horrible was happening and Ashenden held his breath. The tiny frail body was suddenly convulsed and that old woman, as though by a final desperate effort of will, raised herself up in the bed. Ashenden sprang forward to support her.

"England," she said, just that one word, in a harsh cracked voice, and fell back in his arms.

When he laid her down on the pillow, he saw that she was dead.

THE HAIRLESS MEXICAN

"Do you like macaroni?" said R.

"What do you mean by macaroni?" answered Ashenden "It is like asking me if I like poetry. I like Keats and Wordsworth and Verlaine and Goethe. When you say macaroni, do you mean *spaghetti, tagliatelli, rigatoni, vermicelli, fettucini, tufali, farfalli,* or just macaroni?"

"Macaroni," replied R., a man of few words.

"I like all simple things, boiled eggs, oysters and caviare, *truite au bleu,* grilled salmon, roast lamb (the saddle by preference), cold grouse, treacle tart and rice pudding. But of all simple things the only one I can eat day in and day out, not only without disgust but with the eagerness of an appetite unimpaired by excess, is macaroni."

"I am glad of that because I want you to go down to Italy."

Ashenden had come from Geneva to meet R. at Lyons and having got there before him had spent the afternoon wandering about the dull, busy and prosaic streets of that thriving city. They were sitting now in a restaurant on the *place* to which Ashenden had taken R. on his arrival because it was reputed to give you the best food in that part of France. But since in so crowded a resort (for the Lyonese like a good dinner) you never knew what inquisitive ears were pricked up to catch any useful piece of information that might fall from your lips, they had contented themselves with talking of indifferent things. They had reached the end of an admirable repast.

"Have another glass of brandy?" said R.

"No, thank you," answered Ashenden, who was of an abstemious turn.

"One should do what one can to mitigate the rigours of war," remarked R. as he took the bottle and poured out a glass for himself and another for Ashenden.

Ashenden, thinking it would be affectation to protest, let the gesture pass, but felt bound to remonstrate with his chief on the unseemly manner in which he held the bottle.

"In my youth I was always taught that you should take a woman by the waist and a bottle by the neck," he murmured.

"I am glad you told me. I shall continue to hold a bottle by the waist and give women a wide berth."

Ashenden did not know what to reply to this and so remained silent. He sipped his brandy and R. called for his bill. It was true that he was an important person, with power to make or mar quite a large number of his fellows, and his opinions were listened to by those who held in their hands the fate of empires; but he could never face the business of tipping a waiter without an embarrassment that was obvious in his demeanour. He was tortured by the fear of making a fool of himself by giving too much or of exciting the waiter's icy scorn by giving too little. When the bill came he passed some hundred-franc notes over to Ashenden and said:

"Pay him, will you? I can never understand French figures."

The groom brought them their hats and coats.

"Would you like to go back to the hotel?" asked Ashenden.

"We might as well."

It was early in the year, but the weather had suddenly turned warm, and they walked with their coats over their arms. Ashenden knowing that R. liked a sitting-room had engaged one for him and to this, when they reached the hotel, they went. The hotel was old-fashioned and the sitting-room was vast. It was furnished with a heavy mahogany suite upholstered in green velvet and the chairs were set primly round a large table. On the walls, covered with a dingy paper, were large steel engravings of the battles of Napoleon, and from the ceiling hung an enormous chandelier once used for gas, but now fitted with electric bulbs. It flooded the cheerless room with a cold, hard light.

"This is very nice," said R., as they went in.

"Not exactly cosy," suggested Ashenden.

"No, but it looks as though it were the best room in the place.
It all looks very *good* to me."

He drew one of the green velvet chairs away from the table
and, sitting down, lit a cigar. He loosened his belt and unbuttoned his tunic.

"I always thought I liked a cheroot better than anything,"
he said, "but since the war I've taken quite a fancy to Havanas.
Oh, well, I suppose it can't last for ever." The corners of his
mouth flickered with the beginning of a smile. "It's an ill wind
that blows nobody any good."

Ashenden took two chairs, one to sit on and one for his feet,
and when R. saw him he said: "That's not a bad idea," and
swinging another chair out from the table with a sigh of relief
put his boots on it.

"What room is that next door?" he asked.

"That's your bedroom."

"And on the other side?"

"A banqueting hall."

R. got up and strolled slowly about the room and when he
passed the windows, as though in idle curiosity, peeped through
the heavy rep curtains that covered them, and then returning
to his chair once more comfortably put his feet up.

"It's just as well not to take any more risk than one need,"
he said.

He looked at Ashenden reflectively. There was a slight smile
on his thin lips, but the pale eyes, too closely set together, remained cold and steely. R.'s stare would have been embarrassing if Ashenden had not been used to it. He knew that R. was
considering how he would broach the subject that he had in
mind. The silence must have lasted for two or three minutes.

"I'm expecting a fellow to come and see me to-night," he
said at last. "His train gets in about ten." He gave his wrist-
watch a glance. "He's known as the Hairless Mexican."

"Why?"

"Because he's hairless and because he's a Mexican."

"The explanation seems perfectly satisfactory," said Ashenden.

"He'll tell you all about himself. He talks nineteen to the
dozen. He was on his uppers when I came across him. It appears
that he was mixed up in some revolution in Mexico and had to
get out with nothing but the clothes he stood up in. They were
rather the worse for wear when I found him. If you want to

please him you call him General. He claims to have been a general in Huerta's army, at least I think it was Huerta; anyhow he says that if things had gone right he would be minister of war now and no end of a big bug. I've found him very useful. Not a bad chap. The only thing I really have against him is that he will use scent."

"And where do I come in?" asked Ashenden.

"He's going down to Italy. I've got rather a ticklish job for him to do and I want you to stand by. I'm not keen on trusting him with a lot of money. He's a gambler and he's a bit too fond of the girls. I suppose you came from Geneva on your Ashenden passport."

"Yes."

"I've got another for you, a diplomatic one, by the way, in the name of Somerville with visas for France and Italy. I think you and he had better travel together. He's an amusing cove when he gets going, and I think you ought to get to know one another."

"What is the job?"

"I haven't yet quite made up my mind how much it's desirable for you to know about it."

Ashenden did not reply. They eyed one another in a detached manner, as though they were strangers who sat together in a railway carriage and each wondered who and what the other was.

"In your place I'd leave the General to do most of the talking. I wouldn't tell him more about yourself than you find absolutely necessary. He won't ask you any questions, I can promise you that, I think he's by way of being a gentleman after his own fashion."

"By the way, what is his real name?"

"I always call him Manuel, I don't know that he likes it very much, his name is Manuel Carmona."

"I gather by what you have not said that he's an unmitigated scoundrel."

R. smiled with his pale blue eyes.

"I don't know that I'd go quite so far as that. He hasn't had the advantages of a public-school education. His ideas of playing the game are not quite the same as yours or mine. I don't know that I'd leave a gold cigarette case about when he was in the neighbourhood, but if he lost money to you at poker and had pinched your cigarette case he would immediately pawn it to pay you. If he had half a chance he'd seduce your wife, but if you were up against it he'd share his last crust with you. The tears will run down his face when he hears Gounod's 'Ave Maria' on the gramophone, but if you insult his dignity he'll shoot you like a dog. It appears that in Mexico it's an insult to get between a man and his drink and he told me himself that once when a Dutchman who didn't know passed between him and the bar he whipped out his revolver and shot him dead."

"Did nothing happen to him?"

"No, it appears that he belongs to one of the best families. The matter was hushed up and it was announced in the papers that the Dutchman had committed suicide. He did practically. I don't believe the Hairless Mexican has a great respect for human life."

Ashenden who had been looking intently at R. started a little and he watched more carefully than ever his chief's tired, lined and yellow face. He knew that he did not make this remark for nothing.

"Of course a lot of nonsense is talked about the value of human life. You might just as well say that the counters you use at poker have an intrinsic value, their value is what you like to make it; for a general giving battle men are merely counters and he's a fool if he allows himself for sentimental reasons to look upon them as human beings."

"But, you see, they're counters that feel and think and if they believe they're being squandered they are quite capable of refusing to be used any more."

"Anyhow that's neither here nor there. We've had information that a man called Constantine Andreadi is on his way from Constantinople with certain documents that we want to get hold of. He's a Greek. He's an agent of Enver Pasha and Enver has great confidence in him. He's given him verbal messages that are too secret and too important to be put on paper. He's sailing from the Piræus, on a boat called the Ithaca, and will land at Brindisi on his way to Rome. He's to deliver his dispatches at the German embassy and impart what he has to say personally to the ambassador."

"I see."

At this time Italy was still neutral; the Central Powers were straining every nerve to keep her so; the Allies were doing what they could to induce her to declare war on their side.

"We don't want to get into any trouble with the Italian

authorities, it might be fatal, but we've got to prevent Andreadi from getting to Rome."

"At any cost?" asked Ashenden.

"Money's no object," answered R., his lips twisting into a sardonic smile.

"What do you propose to do?"

"I don't think you need bother your head about that."

"I have a fertile imagination," said Ashenden.

"I want you to go down to Naples with the Hairless Mexican. He's very keen on getting back to Cuba. It appears that his friends are organizing a show and he wants to be as near at hand as possible so that he can hop over to Mexico when things are ripe. He needs cash. I've brought money down with me, in American dollars, and I shall give it to you to-night. You'd better carry it on your person."

"Is it much?"

"It's a good deal, but I thought it would be easier for you if it wasn't bulky, so I've got it in thousand dollar notes. You will give the Hairless Mexican the notes in return for the documents that Andreadi is bringing."

A question sprang to Ashenden's lips, but he did not ask it. He asked another instead.

"Does this fellow understand what he has to do?"

"Perfectly."

There was a knock at the door. It opened and the Hairless Mexican stood before them.

"I have arrived. Good-evening, Colonel. I am enchanted to see you."

R. got up.

"Had a nice journey, Manuel? This is Mr. Somerville who's going to Naples with you. General Carmona."

"Pleased to meet you, sir."

He shook Ashenden's hand with such force that he winced.

"Your hands are like iron, General," he murmured.

The Mexican gave them a glance.

"I had them manicured this morning. I do not think they were very well done. I like my nails much more highly polished."

They were cut to a point, stained bright red, and to Ashenden's mind shone like mirrors. Though it was not cold the General wore a fur coat with an astrakhan collar and with his every movement a wave of perfume was wafted to your nose.

"Take off your coat, General. and have a cigar," said R.

The Hairless Mexican was a tall man, and though thinnish gave you the impression of being very powerful; he was smartly dressed in a blue serge suit, with a silk handkerchief neatly tucked in the breast pocket of his coat, and he wore a gold brace-let on his wrist. His features were good, but a little larger than life-size, and his eyes were brown and lustrous. He was quite hairless. His yellow skin had the smoothness of a woman's and he had no eyebrows nor eyelashes; he wore a pale brown wig, rather long, and the locks were arranged in artistic dis-order. This and the unwrinkled sallow face, combined with his dandified dress, gave him an appearance that was at first glance a trifle horrifying. He was repulsive and ridiculous, but you could not take your eyes from him. There was a sinister fascina-tion in his strangeness.

He sat down and hitched up his trousers so that they should not bag at the knee.

"Well, Manuel, have you been breaking any hearts to-day?" said R. with his sardonic joviality.

The General turned to Ashenden.

"Our good friend, the Colonel, envies me my successes with the fair sex. I tell him he can have just as many as I if he will only listen to me. Confidence, that is all you need. If you never fear a rebuff you will never have one."

"Nonsense, Manuel, one has to have your way with the girls. There's something about you that they can't resist."

The Hairless Mexican laughed with a self-satisfaction that he did not try to disguise. He spoke English very well, with a Spanish accent, but with an American intonation.

"But since you ask me, Colonel, I don't mind telling you that I got into conversation on the train with a little woman who was coming to Lyons to see her mother-in-law. She was not very young and she was thinner than I like a woman to be, but she was possible, and she helped me to pass an agreeable hour."

"Well, let's get to business," said R.

"I am at your service, Colonel." He gave Ashenden a glance. "Is Mr. Somerville a military man?"

"No," said R., "he's an author."

"It takes all sorts to make a world, as you say. I am happy to make your acquaintance, Mr. Somerville. I can tell you many stories that will interest you; I am sure that we shall get on well together. You have a sympathetic air. I am very sensitive to that. To tell you the truth I am nothing but a bundle of nerves and if I am with a person who is antipathetic to me I go all to pieces."

"I hope we shall have a pleasant journey," said Ashenden.

"When does our friend arrive at Brindisi?" asked the Mexican, turning to R.

"He sails from the Piræus in the Ithaca on the fourteenth. It's probably some old tub, but you'd better get down to Brindisi in good time."

"I agree with you."

R. got up and with his hands in his pocket sat on the edge of the table. In his rather shabby uniform, his tunic unbuttoned, he looked a slovenly creature beside the neat and well-dressed Mexican.

"Mr. Somerville knows practically nothing of the errand on which you are going and I do not desire you to tell him anything. I think you had much better keep your own counsel. He is instructed to give you the funds you need for your work, but your actions are your own affair. If you need his advice of course you can ask for it."

"I seldom ask other people's advice and never take it."

"And should you make a mess of things I trust you to keep Mr. Somerville out of it. He must on no account be compromised."

"I am a man of honour, Colonel," answered the Hairless Mexican with dignity, "and I would sooner let myself be cut in a thousand pieces than betray my friends."

"That is what I have already told Mr. Somerville. On the other hand if everything pans out O. K. Mr. Somerville is instructed to give you the sum we agreed on in return for the papers I spoke to you about. In what manner you get them is no business of his."

"That goes without saying. There is only one thing I wish to make quite plain; Mr. Somerville understands of course that I have not accepted the mission with which you have entrusted me on account of the money?"

"Quite," replied R., gravely, looking him straight in the eyes.

"I am with the Allies body and soul, I cannot forgive the Germans for outraging the neutrality of Belgium, and if I accept the money that you have offered me it is because I am first and foremost a patriot. I can trust Mr. Somerville implicitly, I suppose?"

R. nodded. The Mexican turned to Ashenden.

"An expedition is being arranged to free my unhappy country from the tyrants that exploit and ruin it and every penny that I receive will go on guns and cartridges. For myself I have no need of money; I am a soldier and I can live on a crust and a few olives. There are only three occupations that befit a gentleman, war, cards and women; it costs nothing to sling a rifle over your shoulder and take to the mountains—and that is real warfare, not this manœuvring of battalions and firing of great guns— women love me for myself, and I generally win at cards."

Ashenden found the flamboyance of this strange creature, with his scented handkerchief and his gold bracelet, very much to his taste. This was far from being just the man in the street (whose tyranny we rail at but in the end submit to) and to the amateur of the baroque in human nature he was a rarity to be considered with delight. He was a purple patch on two legs. Notwithstanding his wig and his hairless big face he had un- doubtedly an air; he was absurd, but he did not give you the impression that he was a man to be trifled with. His self- complacency was magnificent.

"Where is your kit, Manuel?" asked R.

It was possible that a frown for an instant darkened the Mexican's brow at the abrupt question that seemed a little contemptuously to brush to one side his eloquent statement, but he gave no other sign of displeasure. Ashenden suspected that he thought the Colonel a barbarian insensitive to the finer emotions.

"I left it at the station."

"Mr. Somerville has a diplomatic passport so that he can get it through with his own things at the frontier without examination if you like."

"I have very little, a few suits and some linen, but perhaps it would be as well if Mr. Somerville would take charge of it. I bought half a dozen suits of silk pyjamas before I left Paris."

"And what about you?" asked R., turning to Ashenden.

"I've only got one bag. It's in my room."

"You'd better have it taken to the station while there's someone about. Your train goes at one ten."

"Oh?"

This was the first Ashenden had heard that they were to start that night.

"I think you'd better get down to Naples as soon as possible."

"Very well."

R. got up.

"I'm going to bed. I don't know what you fellows want to do."

"I shall take a walk about Lyons," said the Hairless Mexican. "I am interested in life. Lend me a hundred francs, Colonel, will you? I have no change on me."

R. took out his pocket-book and gave the General the note he asked for. Then to Ashenden:

"What are you going to do? Wait here?"

"No," said Ashenden, "I shall go to the station and read."

"You'd both of you better have a whisky and soda before you go, hadn't you? What about it, Manuel?"

"It is very kind of you, but I never drink anything but champagne and brandy."

"Mixed?" asked R. drily.

"Not necessarily," returned the other with gravity.

R. ordered brandy and soda and when it came, whereas he and Ashenden helped themselves to both, the Hairless Mexican poured himself out three parts of a tumbler of neat brandy and swallowed it in two noisy gulps. He rose to his feet and put on his coat with the astrakhan collar, seized in one hand his bold black hat and, with the gesture of a romantic actor giving up the girl he loved to one more worthy of her, held out the other to R.

"Well, Colonel, I will bid you goodnight and pleasant dreams. I do not expect that we shall meet again so soon."

"Don't make a hash of things, Manuel, and if you do keep your mouth shut."

"They tell me that in one of your colleges where the sons of gentlemen are trained to become naval officers it is written in letters of gold: there is no such word as impossible in the British Navy. I do not know the meaning of the word failure."

"It has a good many synonyms," retorted R.

"I will meet you at the station, Mr. Somerville," said the Hairless Mexican, and with a flourish left them.

R. looked at Ashenden with that little smile of his that always made his face look so dangerously shrewd.

"Well, what d'you think of him?"

"You've got me beat," said Ashenden. "Is he a mountebank? He seems as vain as a peacock. And with that frightful appear-

ance can he really be the lady's man he pretends? What makes
you think you can trust him?"

R. gave a low chuckle and he washed his thin, old hands with
imaginary soap.

"I thought you'd like him. He's quite a character, isn't he?
I think we can trust him." R.'s eyes suddenly grew opaque.
"I don't believe it would pay him to double-cross us." He
paused for a moment. "Anyhow we've got to risk it. I'll give
you the tickets and the money and then you can take yourself
off; I'm all in and I want to go to bed."

Ten minutes later Ashenden set out for the station with his
bag on a porter's shoulder.

Having nearly two hours to wait he made himself comfortable
in the waiting-room. The light was good and he read a novel.
When the time drew near for the arrival of the train from Paris
that was to take them direct to Rome and the Hairless Mexican
did not appear Ashenden, beginning to grow a trifle anxious,
went out on the platform to look for him. Ashenden suffered
from that distressing malady known as train fever: an hour
before his train was due he began to have apprehensions lest
he should miss it; he was impatient with the porters who would
never bring his luggage down from his room in time and he could
not understand why the hotel bus cut it so fine; a block in the
street would drive him to frenzy and the languid movements
of the station porters infuriate him. The whole world seemed in
a horrid plot to delay him; people got in his way as he passed
through the barriers; others, a long string of them, were at
the ticket-office getting tickets for other trains than his and they
counted their change with exasperating care; his luggage took
an interminable time to register; and then if he was travelling
with friends they would go to buy newspapers, or would take a
walk along the platform and he was certain they would be left
behind, they would stop to talk to a casual stranger or suddenly
be seized with a desire to telephone and disappear at a run. In
fact the universe conspired to make him miss every train he
wanted to take and he was not happy unless he was settled in
his corner, his things on the rack above him, with a good half
hour to spare. Sometimes by arriving at the station too soon
he had caught an earlier train than the one he had meant to,
but that was nerve-racking and caused him all the anguish of
very nearly missing it.

The Rome express was signalled and there was no sign of
the Hairless Mexican, it came in and he was not to be seen.
Ashenden became more and more harassed. He walked quickly
up and down the platform, looked in all the waiting-rooms,
went to the *consigne* where the luggage was left; he could not
find him. There were no sleeping-cars, but a number of people
got out and he took two seats in a first-class carriage. He stood
at the door, looking up and down the platform and up at the
clock; it was useless to go if his travelling companion did not
turn up and Ashenden made up his mind to take his things
out of the carriage as the porter cried *en voiture;* but, by George!
he would give the brute hell when he found him. There were
three minutes more, then two minutes, then one; at that late
hour there were few persons about and all who were travelling
had taken their seats. Then he saw the Hairless Mexican, followed by two porters with his luggage and accompanied by a
man in a bowler-hat, walk leisurely on to the platform. He
caught sight of Ashenden and waved to him.

"Ah, my dear fellow, there you are, I wondered what had
become of you."

"Good God, man, hurry up or we shall miss the train."

"I never miss a train. Have you got good seats? The *chef
de gare* has gone for the night; this is his assistant."

The man in the bowler-hat took it off when Ashenden nodded
to him.

"But this is an ordinary carriage. I am afraid I could not
travel in that." He turned to the station-master's assistant with
an affable smile. "You must do better for me than that, *mon
cher.*"

"*Certainement, mon général,* I will put you into a *salon-lit.*
Of course."

The assistant station-master led them along the train and
put them in an empty compartment where there were two beds.
The Mexican eyed it with satisfaction and watched the porters
arrange the luggage.

"That will do very well. I am much obliged to you." He held
out his hand to the man in the bowler-hat. "I shall not forget
you and next time I see the Minister I will tell him with what
civility you have treated me."

"You are too good, General. I shall be very grateful."

A whistle was blown and the train started.

"This is better than an ordinary first-class carriage, I think,

Mr. Somerville," said the Mexican. "A good traveller should learn how to make the best of things."

But Ashenden was still extremely cross.

"I don't know why the devil you wanted to cut it so fine. We should have looked a pair of damned fools if we'd missed the train."

"My dear fellow, there was never the smallest chance of that. When I arrived I told the station-master that I was General Carmona, Commander-in-Chief of the Mexican Army, and that I had to stop off in Lyons for a few hours to hold a conference with the British Field-Marshal. I asked him to hold the train for me if I was delayed and suggested that my government might see its way to conferring an order on him. I have been to Lyons before, I like the girls here; they have not the *chic* of the Parisians, but they have something, there is no denying that they have something. Will you have a mouthful of brandy before you go to sleep?"

"No, thank you," said Ashenden morosely.

"I always drink a glass before going to bed, it settles the nerves."

He looked in his suit-case and without difficulty found a bottle. He put it to his lips and had a long drink, wiped his mouth with the back of his hand and lit a cigarette. Then he took off his boots and lay down. Ashenden dimmed the light.

"I have never yet made up my mind," said the Hairless Mexican reflectively, "whether it is pleasanter to go to sleep with the kisses of a beautiful woman on your mouth or with a cigarette between your lips. Have you ever been to Mexico? I will tell you about Mexico to-morrow. Goodnight."

Presently Ashenden heard from his steady breathing that he was asleep and in a little while himself dozed off. Presently he woke. The Mexican, deep in slumber, lay motionless; he had taken off his fur coat and was using it as a blanket; he still wore his wig. Suddenly there was a jolt and the train with a noisy grinding of brakes stopped; in the twinkling of an eye, before Ashenden could realize that anything had happened, the Mexican was on his feet with his hand to his hip.

"What is it?" he cried.

"Nothing. Probably only a signal against us."

The Mexican sat down heavily on his bed. Ashenden turned on the light.

"You wake quickly for such a sound sleeper," he said

"You have to in my profession."

Ashenden would have liked to ask him whether this was murder, conspiracy or commanding armies, but was not sure that it would be discreet. The General opened his bag and took out the bottle.

"Will you have a nip?" he asked. "There is nothing like it when you wake suddenly in the night."

When Ashenden refused he put the bottle once more to his lips and poured a considerable quantity of liquor down his throat. He sighed and lit a cigarette. Although Ashenden had seen him now drink nearly a bottle of brandy and it was probable that he had had a good deal more when he was going about the town he was certainly quite sober. Neither in his manner nor in his speech was there any indication that he had drunk during the evening anything but lemonade.

The train started and soon Ashenden again fell asleep. When he awoke it was morning and turning round lazily he saw that the Mexican was awake too. He was smoking a cigarette. The floor by his side was strewn with burnt-out butts and the air was thick and grey. He had begged Ashenden not to insist on opening a window, for he said the night air was dangerous.

"I did not get up, because I was afraid of waking you. Will you do your toilet first or shall I?"

"I'm in no hurry," said Ashenden.

"I am an old campaigner, it will not take me long. Do you wash your teeth every day?"

"Yes," said Ashenden.

"So do I. It is a habit I learned in New York. I always think that a fine set of teeth are an adornment to a man."

There was a wash-basin in the compartment and the General scrubbed his teeth, with gurglings and garglings, energetically. Then he got a bottle of eau-de-cologne from his bag, poured some of it on a towel and rubbed it over his face and hands. He took a comb and carefully arranged his wig; either it had not moved in the night or else he had set it straight before Ashenden awoke. He got another bottle out of his bag, with a spray attached to it, and squeezing a bulb covered his shirt and coat with a fine cloud of scent, did the same to his handkerchief, and then with a beaming face, like a man who has done his duty by the world and is well pleased, turned to Ashenden and said:

"Now I am ready to brave the day. I will leave my things for you, you need not be afraid of the eau-de-cologne, it is the best you can get in Paris."

"Thank you very much," said Ashenden. "All I want is soap and water."

"Water? I never use water except when I have a bath. Nothing can be worse for the skin."

When they approached the frontier, Ashenden, remembering the General's instructive gesture when he was suddenly awakened in the night, said to him:

"If you've got a revolver on you I think you'd better give it to me. With my diplomatic passport they're not likely to search me, but they might take it into their heads to go through you and we don't want to have any bothers."

"It is hardly a weapon, it is only a toy," returned the Mexican, taking out of his hip-pocket a fully loaded revolver of formidable dimensions. "I do not like parting with it even for an hour, it gives me the feeling that I am not fully dressed. But you are quite right, we do not want to take any risks; I will give you my knife as well. I would always rather use a knife than a revolver; I think it is a more elegant weapon."

"I daresay it is only a matter of habit," answered Ashenden. "Perhaps you are more at home with a knife."

"Anyone can pull a trigger, but it needs a man to use a knife."

To Ashenden it looked as though it were in a single movement that he tore open his waistcoat and from his belt snatched and opened a long knife of murderous aspect. He handed it to Ashenden with a pleased smile on his large, ugly and naked face.

"There's a pretty piece of work for you, Mr. Somerville. I've never seen a better bit of steel in my life, it takes an edge like a razor and it's strong; you can cut a cigarette-paper with it and you can hew down an oak. There is nothing to get out of order and when it is closed it might be the knife a schoolboy uses to cut notches in his desk."

He shut it with a click and Ashenden put it along with the revolver in his pocket.

"Have you anything else?"

"My hands," replied the Mexican with arrogance, "but those I daresay the custom officials will not make trouble about."

Ashenden remembered the iron grip he had given him when they shook hands and slightly shuddered. They were large and long and smooth; there was not a hair on them or on the wrists, and with the pointed, rosy, manicured nails there was really something sinister about them.

Ashenden and General Carmona went through the formalities at the frontier independently and when they returned to their carriage Ashenden handed back to his companion the revolver and the knife. He sighed.

"Now I feel more comfortable. What do you say to a game of cards?"

"I should like it," said Ashenden.

The Hairless Mexican opened his bag again and from a corner extracted a greasy pack of French cards. He asked Ashenden whether he played *écarté* and when Ashenden told him that he did not suggested piquet. This was a game that Ashenden was not unfamiliar with so they settled the stakes and began. Since both were in favour of quick action they played the game of four hands, doubling the first and last. Ashenden had good enough cards, but the General seemed notwithstanding always to have better. Ashenden kept his eyes open and he was not careless of the possibility that his antagonist might correct the inequalities of chance, but he saw nothing to suggest that everything was not above board. He lost game after game. He was capoted and rubiconed. The score against him mounted up and up till he had lost something like a thousand francs, which at that time was a tidy sum. The General smoked innumerable cigarettes. He made them himself with a twist of the finger, a lick of his tongue and incredible celerity. At last he flung himself against the back of his seat.

"By the way, my friend, does the British Government pay your card losses when you are on a mission?" he asked.

"It certainly doesn't."

"Well, I think you have lost enough. If it went down on your expense account I would have proposed playing till we reached Rome, but you are sympathetic to me. If it is your own money I do not want to win any more of it."

He picked up the cards and put them aside. Ashenden some-what ruefully took out a number of notes and handed them to the Mexican. He counted them and with his usual neatness put them carefully folded into his pocket-book. Then, leaning forward, he patted Ashenden almost affectionately on the knee.

"I like you, you are modest and unassuming, you have not the arrogance of your countrymen, and I am sure that you will take my advice in the spirit in which it is meant. Do not play piquet with people you don't know."

Ashenden was somewhat mortified and perhaps his face showed it, for the Mexican seized his hand.

"My dear fellow, I have not hurt your feelings? I would not do that for the world. You do not play piquet worse than most piquet players. It is not that. If we were going to be together longer I would teach you how to win at cards. One plays cards to win money and there is no sense in losing."

"I thought it was only in love and war that all things were fair," said Ashenden, with a chuckle.

"Ah, I am glad to see you smile. That is the way to take a loss. I see that you have good humour and good sense. You will go far in life. When I get back to Mexico and am in possession of my estates again you must come and stay with me. I will treat you like a king. You shall ride my best horses, we will go to bull-fights together, and if there are girls you fancy you have only to say the word and you shall have them."

He began telling Ashenden of the vast territories, the *haciendas* and the mines in Mexico, of which he had been dispossessed. He told him of the feudal state in which he lived. It did not matter whether what he said was true or not, for those sonorous phrases of his were fruity with the rich-distilled perfumes of romance. He described a spacious life that seemed to belong to another age and his eloquent gestures brought before the mind's eye tawny distances and vast green plantations, great herds of cattle and in the moonlit night the song of the blind singers that melted in the air and the twanging of guitars.

"Everything I lost, everything. In Paris I was driven to earn a pittance by giving Spanish lessons or showing Americans—*Americanos del Norte*, I mean—the night life of the city. I who have flung away a thousand *duros* on a dinner have been forced to beg my bread like a blind Indian. I who have taken pleasure in clasping a diamond bracelet round the wrist of a beautiful woman have been forced to accept a suit of clothes from a hag old enough to be my mother. Patience. Man is born to trouble as the sparks fly upward, but misfortune cannot last for ever. The time is ripe and soon we shall strike our blow."

He took up the greasy pack of cards and set them out in a number of little piles.

"Let us see what the cards say. They never lie. Ah, if I had only had greater faith in them I should have avoided the only action of my life that has weighed heavily on me. My conscience is at ease. I did what any man would do under the circumstances, but I regret that necessity forced upon me an action that I would willingly have avoided."

He looked through the cards, set some of them on one side on a system Ashenden did not understand, shuffled the remainder and once more put them in little piles.

"The cards warned me, I will never deny that, their warning was clear and definite. Love and a dark woman, danger, betrayal and death. It was as plain as the nose on your face. Any fool would have known what it meant and I have been using the cards all my life. There is hardly an action that I make without consulting them. There are no excuses. I was besotted. Ah, you of the Northern races do not know what love means, you do not know how it can prevent you from sleeping, how it can take your appetite for food away so that you dwindle as if from a fever, you do not understand what a frenzy it is so that you are like a madman and you will stick at nothing to satisfy your desire. A man like me is capable of every folly and every crime when he is in love, *si, Señor,* and of heroism. He can scale mountains higher than Everest and swim across seas broader than the Atlantic. He is god, he is devil. Women have been my ruin."

Once more the Hairless Mexican glanced at the cards, took some out of the little piles and left others in. He shuffled them again.

"I have been loved by multitudes of women. I do not say it in vanity. I offer no explanation. It is mere matter of fact. Go to Mexico City and ask them what they know of Manuel Carmona and of his triumphs. Ask them how many women have resisted Manuel Carmona."

Ashenden, frowning a little, watched him reflectively. He wondered whether R., that shrewd fellow. who chose his instruments with such a sure instinct, had not this time made a mistake, and he was uneasy. Did the Hairless Mexican really believe that he was irresistible or was he merely a blatant liar? In the course of his manipulations he had thrown out all the cards in the pack but four and these now lay in front of him face downwards and side by side. He touched them one by one but did not turn them up.

"There is fate," he said, "and no power on earth can change it. I hesitate. This is a moment that ever fills me with apprehension and I have to steel myself to turn over the cards that may tell me that disaster awaits me. I am a brave man, but sometimes I have reached this stage and not had the courage to look at the four fatal cards."

Indeed now he eyed the backs of them with an anxiety he did not try to hide.

"What was I saying to you?"

"You were telling me that women found your fascinations irresistible?" replied Ashenden dryly.

"Once all the same I found a woman who resisted me. I saw her first in a house, a *casa de mujeres* in Mexico City, she was going down the stairs as I went up; she was not very beautiful, I had had a hundred more beautiful, but she had something that took my fancy and 1 told the old woman who kept the house to send her to me. You will know her when you go to Mexico City; they call her La Marqueza. She said that the girl was not an inmate, but came there only from time to time and had left. I told her to have her there next evening and not to let her go till I came. But I was delayed and when I arrived La Marqueza told me that the girl had said she was not used to being kept waiting and had gone. I am a good-natured fellow and I do not mind if women are capricious and teasing, that is part of their charm, so with a laugh I sent her a note of a hundred *duros* and promised that on the following day I would be punctual. But when I went, on the minute, La Marqueza handed me back my hundred *duros* and told me the girl did not fancy me. I laughed at her impertinence. I took off the diamond ring I was wearing and told the old woman to give her that and see whether it would induce her to change her mind. In the morning La Marqueza brought me in return for my ring—a red carnation. I did not know whether to be amused or angry. I am not used to being thwarted in my passions, I never hesitate to spend money (what is it for but to squander on pretty women?), and I told La Marqueza to go to the girl and say that I would give her a thousand *duros* to dine with me that night. Presently she came back with the answer that the girl would come on the condition that I allowed her to go home immediately after dinner. I accepted with a shrug of the shoulders. I did not think she was serious. I thought that she was saying that only to make herself more desired. She came to dinner at my house. Did I say she was not beautiful? She was the most beautiful, the most exquisite creature I had ever met.

I was intoxicated. She had charm and she had wit. She had all
the *gracia* of the Andalusian. In one word she was adorable. I
asked her why she had treated me so casually and she laughed in
my face. I laid myself out to be agreeable. I exercised all my
skill. I surpassed myself. But when we finished dinner she rose
from her seat and bade me good-night. I asked her where she
was going. She said I had promised to let her go and she trusted
me as a man of honour to keep my word. I expostulated, I
reasoned, I raved, I stormed. She held me to my word. All I
could induce her to do was to consent to dine with me the following night on the same terms.

"You will think I was a fool, I was the happiest man alive;
for seven days I paid her a thousand silver *duros* to dine with
me. Every evening I waited for her with my heart in my mouth,
as nervous as a *novillero* at his first bull-fight, and every evening
she played with me, laughed at me, coquetted with me and
drove me frantic. I was madly in love with her. I have never
loved anyone so much before or since. I could think of nothing
else. I was distracted. I neglected everything. I am a patriot
and I love my country. A small band of us had got together
and made up our minds that we could no longer put up with the
misrule from which we were suffering. All the lucrative posts
were given to other people, we were being made to pay taxes
as though we were tradesmen, and we were exposed to abominable affronts. We had money and men. Our plans were made and
we were ready to strike. I had an infinity of things to do, meetings to go to, ammunition to get, orders to give; I was so besotted over this woman that I could attend to nothing.

"You would have thought that I should be angry with her
for making such a fool of me, me who had never known what
it was not to gratify my smallest whim; I did not believe that
she refused me to inflame my desires, I believed that she told
the plain truth when she said that she would not give herself to
me until she loved me. She said it was for me to make her love
me. I thought her an angel. I was ready to wait. My passion
was so consuming that sooner or later, I felt, at last it must communicate itself to her; it was like a fire on the prairie that de-
vours everything around it; and at last—at last she said she
loved me. My emotion was so terrific that I thought I should
fall down and die. Oh, what rapture, oh, what madness! I would
have given her everything I possessed in the world, I would
have torn down the stars from heaven to deck her hair; I

wanted to do something to prove to her the extravagance of
my love, I wanted to do the impossible, the incredible, I wanted
to give her myself, my soul, my honour, all, all I had and all I
was; and that night when she lay in my arms I told her of our
plot and who we were that were concerned in it. I felt her body
stiffen with attention, I was conscious of a flicker of her eyelids,
there was something, I hardly knew what, the hand that stroked
my face was dry and cold; a sudden suspicion seized me and all
at once I remembered what the cards had told me: love and a
dark woman, danger, betrayal and death. Three times they'd
said it and I wouldn't heed. I made no sign that I had noticed
anything. She nestled up against my heart and told me that
she was frightened to hear such things and asked me if so and
so was concerned. I answered her. I wanted to make sure. One
after the other, with infinite cunning, between her kisses she
cajoled me into giving every detail of the plot, and now I was
certain, as certain as I am that you sit before me, that she was
a spy. She was a spy of the president's and she had been set
to allure me with her devilish charm and now she had wormed
out of me all our secrets. The lives of all of us were in her hands
and I knew that if she left that room in twenty-four hours we
should be dead men. And I loved her, I loved her; oh, words
cannot tell you the agony of desire that burned my heart; love
like that is no pleasure, it is pain, pain, but the exquisite pain
that transcends all pleasure. It is that heavenly anguish that
the saints speak of when they are seized with a divine ecstasy.
I knew that she must not leave the room alive and I feared
that if I delayed my courage would fail me.

"'I think I shall sleep,' she said.

"'Sleep, my dove,' I answered.

"'*Alma de mi corazon*,' she called me. 'Soul of my heart.'
They were the last words she spoke. Those heavy lids of hers,
dark like a grape and faintly humid, those heavy lids of hers
closed over her eyes and in a little while I knew by the regular
movement of her breast against mine that she slept. You see,
I loved her, I could not bear that she should suffer, she was a
spy, yes, but my heart bade me spare her the terror of knowing
what must happen. It is strange, I felt no anger because she
had betrayed me, I should have hated her because of her vile-
ness, I could not, I only felt that my soul was enveloped in
night. Poor thing, poor thing, I could have cried for pity for her.
I drew my arm very gently from around her, my left arm that

was, my right was free, and raised myself on my hand. But she was so beautiful, I turned my face away when I drew the knife with all my strength across her lovely throat. Without awaking she passed from sleep to death."

He stopped and stared frowning at the four cards that still lay, their backs upward, waiting to be turned up.

"It was in the cards. Why did I not take their warning? I will not look at them. Damn them. Take them away."

With a violent gesture he swept the whole pack on to the floor.

"Though I am a free-thinker I had masses said for her soul." He leaned back and rolled himself a cigarette. He inhaled a long breathful of smoke. He shrugged his shoulders. "The Colonel said you were a writer. What do you write?"

"Stories," replied Ashenden.

"Detective stories?"

"No."

"Why not? They are the only ones I read. If I were a writer I should write detective stories."

"They are very difficult. You need an incredible amount of invention. I devised a murder story once, but the murder was so ingenious that I could never find a way of bringing it home to the murderer, and after all, one of the conventions of the detective story is that the mystery should in the end be solved and the criminal brought to justice."

"If your murder is as ingenious as you think the only means you have of proving the murderer's guilt is by the discovery of his motives. When once you have found a motive the chances are that you will hit upon evidence that till then had escaped you. If there is no motive the most damning evidence will be inconclusive. Imagine for instance that you went up to a man in a lonely street on a moonless night and stabbed him to the heart. Who would ever think of you? But if he was your wife's lover, or your brother, or had cheated or insulted you, then a scrap of paper, a bit of string or a chance remark would be enough to hang you. What were your movements at the time he was killed? Are there not a dozen people who saw you before and after? But if he was a total stranger you would never for a moment be suspected. It was inevitable that Jack the Ripper should escape unless he was caught in the act."

Ashenden had more than one reason to change the conversation. They were parting at Rome and he thought it necessary to come to an understanding with his companion about their respective movements. The Mexican was going to Brindisi and Ashenden to Naples. He meant to lodge at the Hotel de Belfast, which was a large second-rate hotel near the harbour frequented by commercial travellers and the thriftier kind of tripper. It would be as well to let the General have the number of his room so that he could come up if necessary without enquiring of the porter, and at the next stopping-place Ashenden got an envelope from the station-buffet and made him address it in his own writing to himself at the post-office in Brindisi. All Ashenden had to do then was to scribble a number on a sheet of paper and post it.

The Hairless Mexican shrugged his shoulders.

"To my mind all these precautions are rather childish. There is absolutely no risk. But whatever happens you may be quite sure that I will not compromise you."

"This is not the sort of job which I'm very familiar with," said Ashenden. "I'm content to follow the Colonel's instructions and know no more about it than it's essential I should."

"Quite so. Should the exigencies of the situation force me to take a drastic step and I get into trouble I shall of course be treated as a political prisoner. Sooner or later Italy is bound to come into the war on the side of the Allies and I shall be released. I have considered everything. But I beg you very seriously to have no more anxiety about the outcome of our mission than if you were going for a picnic on the Thames."

But when at last they separated and Ashenden found himself alone in a carriage on the way to Naples he heaved a great sigh of relief. He was glad to be rid of that chattering, hideous and fantastic creature. He was gone to meet Constantine Andreadi at Brindisi and if half of what he had told Ashenden was true, Ashenden could not but congratulate himself that he did not stand in the Greek spy's shoes. He wondered what sort of a man he was. There was a grimness in the notion of his coming across the blue Ionian, with his confidential papers and his dangerous secrets, all unconscious of the noose into which he was putting his head. Well, that was war, and only fools thought it could be waged with kid gloves on.

Ashenden arrived in Naples and having taken a room at the hotel, wrote its number on a sheet of paper in block letters and posted it to the Hairless Mexican. He went to the British Consulate where R. had arranged to send any instructions he might have for him and found that they knew about him and everything was in order. Then he put aside these matters and made up his mind to amuse himself. Here in the South the spring was well advanced and in the busy streets the sun was hot. Ashenden knew Naples pretty well. The Piazza di San Ferdinando, with its bustle, the Piazza del Plebiscito, with its handsome church, stirred in his heart pleasant recollections. The Strada di Chiaia was as noisy as ever. He stood at corners and looked up the narrow alleys that climbed the hill precipitously, those alleys of high houses with the washing set out to dry on lines across the street like pennants flying to mark a feast-day; and he sauntered along the shore, looking at the burnished sea with Capri faintly outlined against the day, till he came to Posilippo where there was an old, rambling and bedraggled *palazzo* in which in his youth he had spent many a romantic hour. He observed the curious little pain with which the memories of the past wrung his heart-strings. Then he took a fly drawn by a small and scraggy pony and rattled back over the stones to the *Galleria* where he sat in the cool and drank an *americano* and looked at the people who loitered there, talking, for ever talking with vivacious gestures, and, exercising his fancy, sought from their appearance to divine their reality.

For three days Ashenden led the idle life that fitted so well the fantastical, untidy and genial city. He did nothing from morning till night but wander at random, looking, not with the eye of the tourist who seeks for what ought to be seen, nor with the eye of the writer who looks for his own, (seeing in a sunset a melodious phrase or in a face the inkling of a character,) but with that of the tramp to whom whatever happens is absolute. He went to the museum to look at the statue of Agrippina the Younger, which he had particular reasons for remembering with affection, and took the opportunity to see once more the Titian and the Brueghel in the picture gallery. But he always came back to the church of Santa Chiara. Its grace, its gaiety, the airy persiflage with which it seemed to treat religion and at the back of this its sensual emotion; its extravagance, its elegance of line; to Ashenden it seemed to express, as it were in one absurd and grandiloquent metaphor, the sunny, dusty, lovely city and its bustling inhabitants. It said that life was charming and sad; it's a pity one hadn't any money, but money wasn't everything, and anyway why bother when we are here to-day and gone to-morrow, and it was all very exciting and amusing, and after all we must make the best of things: *facciamo una piccola combinazione.*

But on the fourth morning when Ashenden, having just stepped out of his bath, was trying to dry himself on a towel that absorbed no moisture, his door was quickly opened and a man slipped into his room.

"What d'you want?" cried Ashenden.

"It's all right. Don't you know me?"

"Good Lord, it's the Mexican. What have you done to yourself?"

He had changed his wig and wore now a black one, close cropped, that fitted on his head like a cap. It entirely altered the look of him and though this was still odd enough, it was quite different from that which he had borne before. He wore a shabby grey suit.

"I can only stop a minute. He's getting shaved."

Ashenden felt his cheeks suddenly redden.

"You found him then?"

"That wasn't difficult. He was the only Greek passenger on the ship. I went on board when she got in and asked for a friend who had sailed from the Piræus. I said I had come to meet a Mr. George Diogenidis. I pretended to be much puzzled at his not coming and I got into conversation with Andreadi. He's travelling under a false name. He calls himself Lombardos. I followed him when he landed and do you know the first thing he did? He went into a barber's and had his beard shaved. What do you think of that?"

"Nothing. Anyone might have his beard shaved."

"That is not what I think. He wanted to change his appearance. Oh, he's cunning. I admire the Germans, they leave nothing to chance, he's got his whole story pat, but I'll tell you that in a minute."

"By the way, you've changed your appearance too."

"Ah yes, this is a wig I'm wearing; it makes a difference, doesn't it?"

"I should never have known you."

"One has to take precautions. We are bosom friends. We had to spend the day in Brindisi and he cannot speak Italian. He was glad to have me help him and we travelled up together. I have brought him to this hotel. He says he is going to Rome to-morrow, but I shall not let him out of my sight; I do not want him to give me the slip. He says that he wants to see

Naples and I have offered to show him everything there is to
see."

"Why isn't he going to Rome to-day?"

"That is part of the story. He pretends he is a Greek business
man who has made money during the war. He says he was the
owner of two coasting steamers and has just sold them. Now
he means to go to Paris and have his fling. He says he has
wanted to go to Paris all his life and at last has the chance. He
is close. I tried to get him to talk. I told him I was a Spaniard
and had been to Brindisi to arrange communications with
Turkey about war material. He listened to me and I saw he
was interested, but he told me nothing and of course I did not
think it wise to press him. He has the papers on his person."

"How do you know?"

"He is not anxious about his grip, but he feels every now and
then round his middle, they're either in a belt or in the lining
of his vest."

"Why the devil did you bring him to this hotel?"

"I thought it would be more convenient. We may want to
search his luggage."

"Are you staying here too?"

"No, I am not such a fool as that, I told him I was going to
Rome by the night train and would not take a room. But I must
go, I promised to meet him outside the barber's in fifteen
minutes."

"All right."

"Where shall I find you to-night if I want you?"

Ashenden for an instant eyed the Hairless Mexican, then
with a slight frown looked away.

"I shall spend the evening in my room."

"Very well. Will you just see that there's nobody in the
passage."

Ashenden opened the door and looked out. He saw no one.
The hotel in point of fact at that season was nearly empty.
There were few foreigners in Naples and trade was bad.

"It's all right," said Ashenden.

The Hairless Mexican walked boldly out. Ashenden closed
the door behind him. He shaved and slowly dressed. The sun
was shining as brightly as usual on the square and the people
who passed, the shabby little carriages with their scrawny
horses, had the same air as before, but they did not any longer
fill Ashenden with gaiety. He was not comfortable. He went out

and called as was his habit at the Consulate to ask if there was
a telegram for him. Nothing. Then he went to Cook's and looked
out the trains to Rome: there was one soon after midnight and
another at five in the morning. He wished he could catch the
first. He did not know what were the Mexican's plans; if he
really wanted to get to Cuba he would do well to make his
way to Spain, and, glancing at the notices in the office, Ashenden saw that next day there was a ship sailing from Naples to
Barcelona.

Ashenden was bored with Naples. The glare in the streets
tired his eyes, the dust was intolerable, the noise was deafening.
He went to the *Galleria* and had a drink. In the afternoon he
went to a cinema. Then, going back to his hotel, he told the
clerk that since he was starting so early in the morning he preferred to pay his bill at once, and he took his luggage to the
station, leaving in his room only a dispatch-case in which were
the printed part of his code and a book or two. He dined. Then
returning to the hotel, he sat down to wait for the Hairless
Mexican. He could not conceal from himself the fact that he
was exceedingly nervous. He began to read, but the book was
tiresome, and he tried another: his attention wandered and he
glanced at his watch. It was desperately early; he took up his
book again, making up his mind that he would not look at his
watch till he had read thirty pages, but though he ran his eyes
conscientiously down one page after another he could not tell
more than vaguely what it was he read. He looked at the time
again. Good God, it was only half-past ten. He wondered where
the Hairless Mexican was, and what he was doing; he was afraid
he would make a mess of things. It was a horrible business.
Then it struck him that he had better shut the window and
draw the curtains. He smoked innumerable cigarettes. He
looked at his watch and it was a quarter past eleven. A thought
struck him and his heart began to beat against his chest; out
of curiosity he counted his pulse and was surprised to find that
it was normal. Though it was a warm night and the room was
stuffy his hands and feet were icy. What a nuisance it was, he
reflected irritably, to have an imagination that conjured up
pictures of things that you didn't in the least want to see!
From his standpoint as a writer he had often considered murder
and his mind went to that fearful description of one in *Crime
and Punishment*. He did not want to think of this topic, but it
forced itself upon him; his book dropped to his knees and staring

at the wall in front of him (it had a brown wall-paper with a pattern of dingy roses) he asked himself how, if one had to, one would commit a murder in Naples. Of course there was the Villa, the great leafy garden facing the bay in which stood the aquarium; that was deserted at night and very dark; things happened there that did not bear the light of day and prudent persons after dusk avoided its sinister paths. Beyond Posilippo the road was very solitary and there were byways that led up the hill in which by night you would never meet a soul, but how would you induce a man who had any nerves to go there? You might suggest a row in the bay, but the boatman who hired the boat would see you; it was doubtful indeed if he would let you go on the water alone; there were disreputable hotels down by the harbour where no questions were asked of persons who arrived late at night without luggage; but here again the waiter who showed you your room had the chance of a good look at you and you had on entering to sign an elaborate question-naire.

Ashenden looked once more at the time. He was very tired. He sat now not even trying to read, his mind a blank.

Then the door opened softly and he sprang to his feet. His flesh crept. The Hairless Mexican stood before him.

"Did I startle you?" he asked smiling. "I thought you would prefer me not to knock."

"Did anyone see you come in?"

"I was let in by the night-watchman; he was asleep when I rang and didn't even look at me. I'm sorry I'm so late, but I had to change."

The Hairless Mexican wore now the clothes he had travelled down in and his fair wig. It was extraordinary how different he looked. He was bigger and more flamboyant; the very shape of his face was altered. His eyes were shining and he seemed in excellent spirits. He gave Ashenden a glance.

"How white you are, my friend! Surely you're not nervous?"

"Have you got the documents?"

"No. He hadn't got them on him. This is all he had."

He put down on the table a bulky pocket-book and a pass-port.

"I don't want them," said Ashenden quickly. "Take them."

With a shrug of the shoulders the Hairless Mexican put the things back in his pocket.

"What was in his belt? You said he kept feeling round his middle."

"Only money. I've looked through the pocket-book. It contains nothing but private letters and photographs of women. He must have locked the documents in his grip before coming out with me this evening."

"Damn," said Ashenden.

"I've got the key of his room. We'd better go and look through his luggage."

Ashenden felt a sensation of sickness in the pit of his stomach. He hesitated. The Mexican smiled not unkindly.

"There's no risk, *amigo*," he said, as though he were reassuring a small boy, "but if you don't feel happy, I'll go alone."

"No, I'll come with you," said Ashenden.

"There's no one awake in the hotel and Mr. Andreadi won't disturb us. Take off your shoes if you like."

Ashenden did not answer. He frowned because he noticed that his hands were slightly trembling. He unlaced his shoes and slipped them off. The Mexican did the same.

"You'd better go first," he said. "Turn to the left and go straight along the corridor. It's number thirty-eight."

Ashenden opened the door and stepped out. The passage was dimly lit. It exasperated him to feel so nervous when he could not but be aware that his companion was perfectly at ease. When they reached the door the Hairless Mexican inserted the key, turned the lock and went in. He switched on the light. Ashenden followed him and closed the door. He noticed that the shutters were shut.

"Now we're all right. We can take our time."

He took a bunch of keys out of his pocket, tried one or two and at last hit upon the right one. The suitcase was filled with clothes.

"Cheap clothes," said the Mexican contemptuously as he took them out. "My own principle is that it's always cheaper in the end to buy the best. After all one is a gentleman or one isn't a gentleman."

"Are you obliged to talk?" asked Ashenden.

"A spice of danger affects people in different ways. It only excites me, but it puts you in a bad temper, *amigo*."

"You see I'm scared and you're not," replied Ashenden with candour.

"It's merely a matter of nerves."

Meanwhile he felt the clothes, rapidly but with care, as he took them out. There were no papers of any sort in the suit-case. Then he took out his knife and slit the lining. It was a cheap piece and the lining was gummed to the material of which the suit-case was made. There was no possibility of anything being concealed in it.

"They're not here. They must be hidden in the room."

"Are you sure he didn't deposit them in some office? At one of the consulates for example?"

"He was never out of my sight for a moment except when he was getting shaved."

The Hairless Mexican opened the drawers and the cupboard. There was no carpet on the floor. He looked under the bed, in it, and under the mattress. His dark eyes shot up and down the room, looking for a hiding-place, and Ashenden felt that nothing escaped him.

"Perhaps he left them in charge of the clerk downstairs?"

"I should have known it. And he wouldn't dare. They're not here. I can't understand it."

He looked about the room irresolutely. He frowned in the attempt to guess at a solution of the mystery.

"Let's get out of here," said Ashenden.

"In a minute."

The Mexican went down on his knees, quickly and neatly folded the clothes, and packed them up again. He locked the bag and stood up. Then, putting out the light, he slowly opened the door and looked out. He beckoned to Ashenden and slipped into the passage. When Ashenden had followed him he stopped and locked the door, put the key in his pocket and walked with Ashenden to his room. When they were inside it and the bolt drawn Ashenden wiped his clammy hands and his forehead.

"Thank God, we're out of that!"

"There wasn't really the smallest danger. But what are we to do now? The Colonel will be angry that the papers haven't been found."

"I'm taking the five o'clock train to Rome. I shall wire for instructions there."

"Very well, I will come with you."

"I should have thought it would suit you better to get out of the country more quickly. There's a boat to-morrow that goes to Barcelona. Why don't you take that and if necessary I can come to see you there?"

The Hairless Mexican gave a little smile.

"I see that you are anxious to be rid of me. Well, I won't thwart a wish that your inexperience in these matters excuses. I will go to Barcelona. I have a visa for Spain."

Ashenden looked at his watch. It was a little after two. He had nearly three hours to wait. His companion comfortably rolled himself a cigarette.

"What do you say to a little supper?" he asked. "I'm as hungry as a wolf."

The thought of food sickened Ashenden, but he was terribly thirsty. He did not want to go out with the Hairless Mexican, but neither did he want to stay in that hotel by himself.

"Where could one go at this hour?"

"Come along with me. I'll find you a place."

Ashenden put on his hat and took his dispatch-case in his hand. They went downstairs. In the hall the porter was sleeping soundly on a mattress on the floor. As they passed the desk, walking softly in order not to wake him, Ashenden noticed in the pigeon-hole belonging to his room a letter. He took it out and saw that it was addressed to him. They tiptoed out of the hotel and shut the door behind them. Then they walked quickly away. Stopping after a hundred yards or so under a lamp-post Ashenden took the letter out of his pocket and read it; it came from the Consulate and said: *The enclosed telegram arrived to-night and in case it is urgent I am sending it round to your hotel by messenger.* It had apparently been left some time before midnight while Ashenden was sitting in his room. He opened the telegram and saw that it was in code.

"Well, it'll have to wait," he said, putting it back in his pocket.

The Hairless Mexican walked as though he knew his way through the deserted streets and Ashenden walked by his side. At last they came to a tavern in a blind alley, noisome and evil, and this the Mexican entered.

"It's not the Ritz," he said, "but at this hour of the night it's only in a place like this that we stand a chance of getting something to eat."

Ashenden found himself in a long sordid room at one end of which a wizened young man sat at a piano; there were tables standing out from the wall on each side and against them benches. A number of persons, men and women, were sitting about. They were drinking beer and wine. The women were old,

painted, and hideous; and their harsh gaiety was at once noisy
and lifeless. When Ashenden and the Hairless Mexican came
in they all stared and when they sat down at one of the tables
Ashenden looked away in order not to meet the leering eyes,
just ready to break into a smile, that sought his insinuatingly.
The wizened pianist strummed a tune and several couples got
up and began to dance. Since there were not enough men to go
round some of the women danced together. The General ordered
two plates of spaghetti and a bottle of Capri wine. When the
wine was brought he drank a glassful greedily and then waiting
for the *pasta* eyed the women who were sitting at the other
tables.

"Do you dance?" he asked Ashenden. "I'm going to ask
one of these girls to have a turn with me."

He got up and Ashenden watched him go up to one who had
at least flashing eyes and white teeth to recommend her; she
rose and he put his arm round her. He danced well. Ashenden
saw him begin talking; the woman laughed and presently the
look of indifference with which she had accepted his offer
changed to one of interest. Soon they were chatting gaily. The
dance came to an end and putting her back at her table he
returned to Ashenden and drank another glass of wine.

"What do you think of my girl?" he asked. "Not bad, is she?
It does one good to dance. Why don't you ask one of them?
This is a nice place, is it not? You can always trust me to find
anything like this. I have an instinct."

The pianist started again. The woman looked at the Hairless
Mexican and when with his thumb he pointed to the floor she
jumped up with alacrity. He buttoned up his coat, arched his
back and standing up by the side of the table waited for her to
come to him. He swung her off, talking, smiling, and already he
was on familiar terms with everyone in the room. In fluent Italian, with his Spanish accent, he exchanged badinage with one
and the other. They laughed at his sallies. Then the waiter
brought two heaped platefuls of macaroni and when the Mexican saw them he stopped dancing without ceremony and allowing his partner to get back to her table as she chose hurried to
his meal.

"I'm ravenous," he said. "And yet I ate a good dinner.
Where did you dine? You're going to eat some macaroni,
aren't you?"

"I have no appetite," said Ashenden.

But he began to eat and to his surprise found that he was hungry. The Hairless Mexican ate with huge mouthfuls, enjoying himself vastly; his eyes shone and he was loquacious. The woman he had danced with had in that short time told him all about herself and he repeated now to Ashenden what she had said. He stuffed huge pieces of bread into his mouth. He ordered another bottle of wine.

"Wine?" he cried scornfully. "Wine is not a drink, only champagne; it does not even quench your thirst. Well, *amigo*, are you feeling better?"

"I'm bound to say I am," smiled Ashenden.

"Practice, that is all you want, practice."

He stretched out his hand to pat Ashenden on the arm.

"What's that?" cried Ashenden with a start. "What's that stain on your cuff?"

The Hairless Mexican gave his sleeve a glance.

"That? Nothing. It's only blood. I had a little accident and cut myself."

Ashenden was silent. His eyes sought the clock that hung over the door.

"Are you anxious about your train? Let me have one more dance and then I'll accompany you to the station."

The Mexican got up and with his sublime self-assurance seized in his arms the woman who sat nearest to him and danced away with her. Ashenden watched him moodily. He was a monstrous, terrible figure with that blond wig and his hairless face, but he moved with a matchless grace; his feet were small and seemed to hold the ground like the pads of a cat or a tiger; his rhythm was wonderful and you could not but see that the bedizened creature he danced with was intoxicated by his gestures. There was music in his toes and in the long arms that held her so firmly, and there was music in those long legs that seemed to move strangely from the hips. Sinister and grotesque though he was, there was in him now a feline elegance, even something of beauty, and you felt a secret, shameful fascination. To Ashenden he suggested one of those sculptures of the pre-Aztec hewers of stone, in which there is barbarism and vitality, something terrible and cruel, and yet withal a brooding and significant loveliness. All the same he would gladly have left him to finish the night by himself in that sordid dance-hall, but he knew that he must have a business conversation with him. He did not look forward to it without misgiving. He had been instructed to give Manuel Carmona certain sums in return for certain documents. Well, the documents were not forthcoming, and as for the rest—Ashenden knew nothing about that; it was no business of his. The Hairless Mexican waved gaily as he passed him.

"I will come the moment the music stops. Pay the bill and then I shall be ready."

Ashenden wished he could have seen into his mind. He could not even make a guess at its workings. Then the Mexican, with his scented handkerchief wiping the sweat from his brow, came back.

"Have you had a good time, General?" Ashenden asked him.

"I always have a good time. Poor white trash, but what do I care? I like to feel the body of a woman in my arms and see her eyes grow languid and her lips part as her desire for me melts the marrow in her bones like butter in the sun. Poor white trash, but women."

They sallied forth. The Mexican proposed that they should walk and in that quarter, at that hour, there would have been little chance of finding a cab; but the sky was starry. It was a summer night and the air was still. The silence walked beside them like the ghost of a dead man. When they neared the station the houses seemed on a sudden to take on a greyer, more rigid line, and you felt that the dawn was at hand. A little shiver trembled through the night. It was a moment of apprehension and the soul for an instant was anxious; it was as though, inherited down the years in their countless millions, it felt a witless fear that perhaps another day would not break. But they entered the station and the night once more enwrapped them. One or two porters lolled about like stage-hands after the curtain has rung down and the scene is struck. Two soldiers in dim uniforms stood motionless.

The waiting-room was empty, but Ashenden and the Hairless Mexican went to sit in the most retired part of it.

"I still have an hour before my train goes. I'll just see what this cable's about."

He took it out of his pocket and from the dispatch-case got his code. He was not then using a very elaborate one. It was in two parts, one contained in a slim book and the other, given him on a sheet of paper and destroyed by him before he left allied territory, committed to memory. Ashenden put on his spectacles and set to work. The Hairless Mexican sat in a corner of the seat, rolling himself cigarettes and smoking; he sat there placidly, taking no notice of what Ashenden did, and enjoyed his well-earned repose. Ashenden deciphered the groups of numbers one by one and as he got it out jotted down each word on a piece of paper. His method was to abstract his mind from the sense till he had finished, since he had discovered that if you took notice of the words as they came along you often jumped to a conclusion and sometimes were led into error. So he translated quite mechanically, without paying attention to the words as he wrote them one after the other. When at last he had done he read the complete message. It ran as follows:

Constantine Andreadi has been detained by illness at Piræus. He will be unable to sail. Return Geneva and await instructions.

At first Ashenden could not understand. He read it again. He shook from head to foot. Then, for once robbed of his self-possession, he blurted out, in a hoarse, agitated and furious whisper:

"You bloody fool, you've killed the wrong man."

GIULIA LAZZARI

ASHENDEN was in the habit of asserting that he was never bored. It was one of his notions that only such persons were as had no resources in themselves and it was but the stupid that depended on the outside world for their amusement. Ashenden had no illusions about himself and such success in current letters as had come to him had left his head unturned. He distinguished acutely between fame and the notoriety that rewards the author of a successful novel or a popular play; and he was indifferent to this except in so far as it was attended with tangible benefits. He was perfectly ready to take advantage of his familiar name to get a better state-room on a ship than he had paid for, and if a Customs-house officer passed his luggage unopened because he had read his short stories Ashenden was pleased to admit that the pursuit of literature had its compensations. He sighed when eager young students of the drama sought to discuss its technique with him, and when gushing ladies tremulously whispered in his ear their admiration of his books he often wished he was dead. But he thought himself intelligent and so it was absurd that he should be bored. It was a fact that he could talk with interest to persons commonly thought so excruciatingly dull that their fellows fled from them as though they owed them money. It may be that here he was but indulging the professional instinct that was seldom dormant in him; they, his raw material, did not bore him any more than fossils bore the geologist. And now he had everything that a reasonable man could want for his entertainment. He had

pleasant rooms in a good hotel and Geneva is one of the most
agreeable cities in Europe to live in. He hired a boat and rowed
on the lake or hired a horse and trotted sedately, for in that
neat and orderly Canton it is difficult to find a stretch of turf
where you can have a good gallop, along the macadamized
roads in the environs of the town. He wandered on foot about
its old streets, trying among those grey stone houses, so quiet
and dignified, to recapture the spirit of a past age. He read
again with delight Rousseau's *Confessions*, and for the second
or third time tried in vain to get on with *La Nouvelle Heloïse*.
He wrote. He knew few people, for it was his business to keep
in the background, but he had picked up a chatting acquaintance with several persons living in his hotel and he was not
lonely. His life was sufficiently filled, it was varied, and when he
had nothing else to do he could enjoy his own reflections; it
was absurd to think that under these circumstances he could
possibly be bored and yet, like a little lonely cloud in the sky,
he did see in the offing the possibility of boredom. There is a
story that Louis XIV, having summoned a courtier to attend
him on a ceremonial occasion, found himself ready to go as the
courtier appeared; he turned to him and with icy majesty said,
j'ai failli attendre, of which the only translation I can give, but a
poor one, is, I have but just escaped waiting: so Ashenden might
have admitted that he now but just escaped being bored.

It might be, he mused, as he rode along the lake on a dappled
horse with a great rump and a short neck, like one of those
prancing steeds that you see in old pictures, but this horse never
pranced and he needed a firm jab with the spur to break even
into a smart trot, it might be, he mused, that the great chiefs
of the secret service in their London offices, their hands on the
throttle of this great machine, led a life full of excitement; they
moved their pieces here and there, they saw the pattern woven
by the multitudinous threads (Ashenden was lavish with his
metaphors,) they made a picture out of the various pieces of
the jigsaw puzzle; but it must be confessed that for the small
fry like himself to be a member of the secret service was not as
adventurous an affair as the public thought. Ashenden's official
existence was as orderly and monotonous as a City clerk's. He
saw his spies at stated intervals and paid them their wages;
when he could get hold of a new one he engaged him, gave him
his instructions and sent him off to Germany; he waited for the
information that came through and dispatched it; he went into

France once a week to confer with his colleague over the frontier
and to receive his orders from London; he visited the market-
place on market-day to get any message the old butter-woman
had brought him from the other side of the lake; he kept his eyes
and ears open; and he wrote long reports which he was convinced no one read till having inadvertently slipped a jest into
one of them he received a sharp reproof for his levity. The work
he was doing was evidently necessary, but it could not be called
anything but monotonous. At one moment for something better
to do he had considered the possibility of a flirtation with the
Baroness von Higgins. He was confident now that she was an
agent in the service of the Austrian Government and he looked
forward to a certain entertainment in the duel he foresaw. It
would be amusing to set his wits against hers. He was quite
aware that she would lay snares for him and to avoid them
would give him something to keep his mind from rusting. He
found her not unwilling to play the game. She wrote him gushing little notes when he sent her flowers. She went for a row
with him on the lake and letting her long white hand drag
through the water talked of Love and hinted at a Broken Heart.
They dined together and went to see a performance in French
and in prose of *Romeo and Juliet*. Ashenden had not made up
his mind how far he was prepared to go when he received a sharp
note from R. to ask him what he was playing at: information
"had come to hand" that he (Ashenden) was much in the
society of a woman calling herself the Baroness de Higgins who
was known to be an agent of the Central Powers and it was
most undesirable that he should be on any terms with her but
those of frigid courtesy. Ashenden shrugged his shoulders. R.
did not think him as clever as he thought himself. But he was
intrigued to discover, what he had not known before, that there
was someone in Geneva part of whose duties at all events was
to keep an eye on him. There was evidently someone who had
orders to see that he did not neglect his work or get into mischief. Ashenden was not a little amused. What a shrewd, unscrupulous old thing was R.! He took no risks; he trusted
nobody; he made use of his instruments, but high or low, had
no opinion of them. Ashenden looked about to see whether he
could spot the person who had told R. what he was doing. He
wondered if it was one of the waiters in the hotel. He knew that
R. had a great belief in waiters; they had the chance of seeing
so much and could so easily get into places where information

was lying about to be picked up. He even wondered whether R. had got his news from the Baroness herself; it would not be so strange if after all she was employed by the secret service of one of the Allied nations. Ashenden continued to be polite to the Baroness, but ceased to be attentive.

He turned his horse and trotted gently back to Geneva. An ostler from the riding-stables was waiting at the hotel door and slipping out of the saddle Ashenden went into the hotel. At the desk the porter handed him a telegram. It was to the following effect:

Aunt Maggie not at all well. Staying at Hotel Lotti, Paris. If possible please go and see her. Raymond.

Raymond was one of R.'s facetious *noms de guerre*, and since Ashenden was not so fortunate as to possess an Aunt Maggie he concluded that this was an order to go to Paris. It had always seemed to Ashenden that R. had spent much of his spare time in reading detective fiction and especially when he was in a good humour he found a fantastic pleasure in aping the style of the shilling shocker. If R. was in a good humour it meant that he was about to bring off a coup, for when he had brought one off he was filled with depression and then vented his spleen on his subordinates.

Ashenden, leaving his telegram with deliberate carelessness on the desk, asked at what time the express left for Paris. He glanced at the clock to see whether he had time to get to the Consulate before it closed and secure his visa. When he went upstairs to fetch his passport the porter, just as the lift doors were closed, called him.

"*Monsieur* has forgotten his telegram," he said.

"How stupid of me," said Ashenden.

Now Ashenden knew that if an Austrian baroness by any chance wondered why he had so suddenly gone to Paris she would discover that it was owing to the indisposition of a female relative. In those troublous times of war it was just as well that everything should be clear and above board. He was known at the French Consulate and so lost little time there. He had told the porter to get him a ticket and on his return to the hotel bathed and changed. He was not a little excited at the prospect of this unexpected jaunt. He liked the journey. He slept well in a sleeping-car and was not disturbed if a sudden jolt awaked him, it was pleasant to lie a while smoking a cigarette and to feel oneself in one's little cabin so enchantingly alone; the

rhythmical sound as the wheels rattled over the points was an
agreeable background to the pattern of one's reflections, and
to speed through the open country and the night made one feel
like a star speeding through space. And at the end of the journey
was the unknown.

When Ashenden arrived in Paris it was chilly and a light rain
was falling, he felt unshaved and he wanted a bath and clean
linen; but he was in excellent spirits. He telephoned from the
station to R. and asked how Aunt Maggie was.

"I'm glad to see that your affection for her was great enough
to allow you to waste no time in getting here," answered R.,
with the ghost of a chuckle in his voice. "She's very low, but I'm
sure it'll do her good to see you."

Ashenden reflected that this was the mistake the amateur
humorist, as opposed to the professional, so often made; when
he made a joke he harped on it. The relations of the joker to his
joke should be as quick and desultory as those of a bee to its
flower. He should make his joke and pass on. There is of course
no harm if, like the bee approaching the flower, he buzzes a
little; for it is just as well to announce to a thick-headed world
that a joke is intended. But Ashenden, unlike most professional
humorists, had a kindly tolerance for other people's humour and
now he answered R. on his own lines.

"When would she like to see me, do you think?" he asked.
"Give her my love, won't you?"

Now R. quite distinctly chuckled. Ashenden sighed.

"She'll want to titivate a little before you come, I expect.
You know what she is, she likes to make the best of herself.
Shall we say half-past ten, and then when you've had a talk
to her we might go out and lunch together somewhere."

"All right," said Ashenden. "I'll come to the Lotti at ten-
thirty."

When Ashenden, clean and refreshed, reached the hotel an
orderly whom he recognized met him in the hall and took him
up to R.'s apartment. He opened the door and showed Ashenden
in. R. was standing with his back to a bright log fire dictating to
his secretary.

"Sit down," said R. and went on with his dictation.

It was a nicely furnished sitting-room and a bunch of roses
in a bowl gave the impression of a woman's hand. On a large
table was a litter of papers. R. looked older than when last
Ashenden had seen him. His thin yellow face was more lined

and his hair was greyer. The work was telling on him. He did not spare himself. He was up at seven every morning and he worked late into the night. His uniform was spick and span, but he wore it shabbily.

"That'll do," he said. "Take all this stuff away and get on with the typing. I'll sign before I go out to lunch." Then he turned to the orderly. "I don't want to be disturbed."

The secretary, a sub-lieutenant in the thirties, obviously a civilian with a temporary commission, gathered up a mass of papers and left the room. As the orderly was following R. said:

"Wait outside. If I want you I'll call."

"Very good, sir."

When they were alone R. turned to Ashenden with what for him was cordiality.

"Have a nice journey up?"

"Yes, sir."

"What do you think of this?" he asked, looking round the room. "Not bad, is it? I never see why one shouldn't do what one can to mitigate the hardships of war."

While he was idly chatting R. gazed at Ashenden with a singular fixity. The stare of those pale eyes of his, too closely set together, gave you the impression that he looked at your naked brain and had a very poor opinion of what he saw there. R. in rare moments of expansion made no secret of the fact that he looked upon his fellow men as fools or knaves. That was one of the obstacles he had to contend with in his calling. On the whole he preferred them knaves; you knew then what you were up against and could take steps accordingly. He was a professional soldier and had spent his career in India and the Colonies. At the outbreak of the war he was stationed in Jamaica and someone in the War Office who had had dealings with him, remembering him, brought him over and put him in the Intelligence Department. His astuteness was so great that he very soon occupied an important post. He had an immense energy and a gift for organization, no scruples, but resource, courage and determination. He had perhaps but one weakness. Throughout his life he had never come in contact with persons, especially women, of any social consequence, the only women he had ever known were the wives of his brother officers, the wives of Government officials and of business men; and when, coming to London at the beginning of the war, his work brought him into contact with brilliant, beautiful and distinguished women he was unduly dazzled. They made him feel shy, but he cultivated their society; he became quite a lady's man, and to Ashenden who knew more about him than R. suspected that bowl of roses told a story.

Ashenden knew that R. had not sent for him to talk about the weather and the crops, and wondered when he was coming to the point. He did not wonder long.

"You've been doing pretty well in Geneva," he said.

"I'm glad you think that, sir," replied Ashenden.

Suddenly R. looked very cold and stern. He had done with idle talk.

"I've got a job for you," he said.

Ashenden made no reply, but he felt a happy little flutter somewhere about the pit of his stomach.

"Have you ever heard of Chandra Lal?"

"No, sir."

A frown of impatience for an instant darkened the Colonel's brow. He expected his subordinates to know everything he wished them to know.

"Where have you been living all these years?"

"At 36 Chesterfield Street, Mayfair," returned Ashenden.

The shadow of a smile crossed R.'s yellow face. The somewhat impertinent reply was after his own sardonic heart. He went over to the big table and opened a dispatch-case that lay upon it. He took out a photograph and handed it to Ashenden.

"That's him."

To Ashenden, unused to Oriental faces, it looked like any one of a hundred Indians that he had seen. It might have been the photograph of one or other of the Rajahs who come periodically to England and are portrayed in the illustrated papers. It showed a fat-faced, swarthy man, with full lips and a fleshy nose; his hair was black, thick and straight, and his very large eyes even in the photograph were liquid and cow-like. He looked ill-at-ease in European clothes.

"Here he is in native dress," said R., giving Ashenden another photograph.

This was full-length, whereas the first had shown only the head and shoulders, and it had evidently been taken some years earlier. He was thinner and his great, serious eyes seemed to devour his face. It was done by a native photographer in Calcutta and the surroundings were naïvely grotesque. Chandra Lal stood against a background on which had been painted a

pensive palm tree and a view of the sea. One hand rested on a
heavily carved table on which was a rubber-plant in a flower-
pot. But in his turban and long, pale tunic he was not without
dignity.

"What d'you think of him?" asked R.

"I should have said he was a man not without personality.
There is a certain force there."

"Here's his dossier. Read it, will you."

R. gave Ashenden a couple of typewritten pages and Ashenden sat down. R. put on his spectacles and began to read the
letters that awaited his signature. Ashenden skimmed the report
and then read it a second time more attentively. It appeared
that Chandra Lal was a dangerous agitator. He was a lawyer by
profession, but had taken up politics and was bitterly hostile
to the British rule in India. He was a partisan of armed force
and had been on more than one occasion responsible for riots
in which life had been lost. He was once arrested, tried and
sentenced to two years' imprisonment; but he was at liberty at
the beginning of the war and seizing his opportunity began to
foment active rebellion. He was at the heart of plots to embarrass the British in India and so prevent them from transferring troops to the seat of war and with the help of immense
sums given to him by German agents he was able to cause a
great deal of trouble. He was concerned in two or three bomb
outrages which, though beyond killing a few innocent bystanders they did little harm, yet shook the nerves of the public and
so damaged its morale. He evaded all attempts to arrest him,
his activity was formidable, he was here and there; but the
police could never lay hands on him, and they only learned
that he had been in some city when, having done his work, he
had left it. At last a high reward was offered for his arrest on a
charge of murder, but he escaped the country, got to America,
from there went to Sweden and eventually reached Berlin.
Here he busied himself with schemes to create disaffection
among the native troops that had been brought to Europe. All
this was narrated drily, without comment or explanation, but
from the very frigidity of the narrative you got a sense of mystery and adventure, of hairbreadth escapes and dangers dangerously encountered. The report ended as follows:

"C. has a wife in India and two children. He is not known to
have anything to do with women. He neither drinks nor smokes.
He is said to be honest. Considerable sums of money have

passed through his hands and there has never been any question as to his not having made a proper (!) use of them. He has undoubted courage and is a hard worker. He is said to pride himself on keeping his word."

Ashenden returned the document to R.

"Well?"

"A fanatic." Ashenden thought there was about the man something rather romantic and attractive, but he knew that R. did not want any nonsense of that sort from him. "He looks like a very dangerous fellow."

"He is the most dangerous conspirator in or out of India. He's done more harm than all the rest of them put together. You know that there's a gang of these Indians in Berlin; well, he's the brains of it. If he could be got out of the way I could afford to ignore the others, he's the only one who has any guts. I've been trying to catch him for a year, I thought there wasn't a hope; but now at last I've got a chance, and by God, I'm going to take it."

"And what'll you do then?"

R. chuckled grimly.

"Shoot him and shoot him damn quick."

Ashenden did not answer. R. walked once or twice across the small room and then, again with his back to the fire, faced Ashenden. His thin mouth was twisted by a sarcastic smile.

"Did you notice at the end of that report I gave you, it said he wasn't known to have anything to do with women? Well, that *was* true, but it isn't any longer. The damned fool has fallen in love."

R. stepped over to his dispatch-case and took out a bundle tied up with pale blue ribbon.

"Look, here are his love letters. You're a novelist, it might amuse you to read them. In fact you should read them, it will help you to deal with the situation. Take them away with you."

R. flung the neat little bundle back into the dispatch-case.

"One wonders how an able man like that can allow himself to get besotted over a woman. It was the last thing I ever expected of him."

Ashenden's eyes travelled to that bowl of beautiful roses that stood on the table, but he said nothing. R. who missed little saw the glance and his look suddenly darkened. Ashenden knew that he felt like asking him what the devil he was staring at. At that moment R. had no friendly feelings towards his sub-

ordinate, but he made no remark. He went back to the subject
on hand.

"Anyhow that's neither here nor there. Chandra has fallen
madly in love with a woman called Giulia Lazzari. He's crazy
about her."

"Do you know how he picked her up?"

"Of course I do. She's a dancer, and she does Spanish dances,
but she happens to be an Italian. For stage purposes she calls
herself La Malagueña. You know the kind of thing. Popular
Spanish music and a mantilla, a fan and a high comb. She's
been dancing all over Europe for the last ten years."

"Is she any good?"

"No, rotten. She's been in the provinces in England and she's
had a few engagements in London. She never got more than ten
pounds a week. Chandra met her in Berlin in a Tingel-tangel,
you know what that is, a cheap sort of music-hall. I take it that
on the Continent she looked upon her dancing chiefly as a
means to enhance her value as a prostitute."

"How did she get to Berlin during the war?"

"She'd been married to a Spaniard at one time, I think she
still is though they don't live together, and she travelled on a
Spanish passport. It appears Chandra made a dead set for her."
R. took up the Indian's photograph again and looked at it
thoughtfully. "You wouldn't have thought there was anything
very attractive in that greasy little nigger. God, how they
run to fat! The fact remains that she fell very nearly as much
in love with him as he did with her. I've got her letters too, only
copies, of course, he's got the originals and I daresay he keeps
them tied up in pink ribbon. She's mad about him. I'm not a
literary man, but I think I know when a thing rings true, anyhow you'll be reading them, and you can tell me what you
think. And then people say there's no such thing as love at first
sight."

R. smiled with faint irony. He was certainly in a good humour
this morning.

"But how did you get hold of all these letters?"

"How did I get hold of them? How do you imagine? Owing
to her Italian nationality Giulia Lazzari was eventually ex-
pelled from Germany. She was put over the Dutch frontier.
Having an engagement to dance in England she was granted a
visa and"—R. looked up a date among the papers,—"and on
the twenty-fourth of October last sailed from Rotterdam to

Harwich. Since then she has danced in London, Birmingham, Portsmouth and other places. She was arrested a fortnight ago at Hull."

"What for?"

"Espionage. She was transferred to London and I went to see her myself at Holloway."

Ashenden and R. looked at one another for a moment without speaking and it may be that each was trying his hardest to read the other's thoughts. Ashenden was wondering where the truth in all this lay and R. wondered how much of it he could advantageously tell him.

"How did you get on to her?"

"I thought it odd that the Germans should allow her to dance quite quietly in Berlin for weeks and then for no particular reason decide to put her out of the country. It would be a good introduction for espionage. And a dancer who was not too careful of her virtue might make opportunities of learning things that it would be worth somebody's while in Berlin to pay a good price for. I thought it might be as well to let her come to England and see what she was up to. I kept track of her. I discovered that she was sending letters to an address in Holland two or three times a week and two or three times a week was receiving answers from Holland. Hers were written in a queer mixture of French, German and English, she speaks English a little and French quite well, but the answers were written entirely in English; it was good English, but not an Englishman's English, flowery and rather grandiloquent; I wondered who was writing them. They seemed to be just ordinary loveletters, but they were by way of being rather hot stuff. It was plain enough that they were coming from Germany and the writer was neither English, French, nor German. Why did he write in English? The only foreigners who know English better than any continental language are Orientals, and not Turks or Egyptians either; they know French. A Jap would write English and so would an Indian. I came to the conclusion that Giulia's lover was one of that gang of Indians that were making trouble for us in Berlin. I had no idea it was Chandra Lal till I found the photograph."

"How did you get that?"

"She carried it about with her. It was a pretty good bit of work. that. She kept it locked up in her trunk, with a lot of theatrical photographs, of comic singers and clowns and acrobats, it might easily have passed for the picture of some music-hall artiste in his stage dress. In fact, later, when she was arrested and asked who the photograph represented she said she didn't know, it was an Indian conjuror who had given it her and she had no idea what his name was. Anyhow I put a very smart lad on the job and he thought it queer that it should be the only photograph in the lot that came from Calcutta. He noticed that there was a number on the back, and he took it, the number, I mean; of course the photograph was replaced in the box."

"By the way, just as a matter of interest how did your very smart lad get at the photograph at all?"

R.'s eyes twinkled.

"That's none of your business. But I don't mind telling you that he was a good-looking boy. Anyhow it's of no consequence. When we got the number of the photograph we cabled to Calcutta and in a little while I received the grateful news that the object of Giulia's affections was no less a person than the incorruptible Chandra Lal. Then I thought it my duty to have Giulia watched a little more carefully. She seemed to have a sneaking fondness for naval officers. I couldn't exactly blame her for that, they are attractive, but it is unwise for ladies of easy virtue and doubtful nationality to cultivate their society in war-time. Presently I got a very pretty little body of evidence against her."

"How was she getting her stuff through?"

"She wasn't getting it through. She wasn't trying to. The Germans had turned her out quite genuinely, she wasn't working for them, she was working for Chandra. After her engagement was through in England she was planning to go to Holland again and meet him. She wasn't very clever at the work, she was nervous, but it looked easy, no one seemed to bother about her, it grew rather exciting, she was getting all sorts of interesting information without any risk. In one of her letters she said: 'I have so much to tell you, *mon petit chou* darling, and what you will be *extrêmement intéressé* to know,' and she underlined the French words."

R. paused and rubbed his hands together. His tired face bore a look of devilish enjoyment of his own cunning.

"It was espionage made easy. Of course I didn't care a damn

about her, it was him I was after. Well, as soon as I'd got the goods on her I arrested her. I had enough evidence to convict a regiment of spies."

R. put his hands in his pockets and his pale lips twisted to a smile that was almost a grimace.

"Holloway's not a very cheerful place, you know."

"I imagine no prison is," remarked Ashenden.

"I left her to stew in her own juice for a week before I went to see her. She was in a very pretty state of nerves by then. The wardress told me she'd been in violent hysterics most of the time. I must say she looked like the devil."

"Is she handsome?"

"You'll see for yourself. She's not my type. I daresay she's better when she's made up and that kind of thing. I talked to her like a Dutch uncle. I put the fear of God into her. I told her she'd get ten years. I think I scared her, I know I tried to. Of course she denied everything, but the proofs were there, I assured her she hadn't got a chance. I spent three hours with her. She went all to pieces and at last she confessed everything. Then I told her that I'd let her go scot free if she'd get Chandra to come to France. She absolutely refused, she said she'd rather die, she was very hysterical and tiresome, but I let her rave. I told her to think it over and said I'd see her in a day or two and we'd have another talk about it. In point of fact I left her for a week. She'd evidently had time to reflect, because when I came again she asked me quite calmly what it was exactly that I proposed. She'd been in jail a fortnight then and I expect she'd had about enough of it. I put it to her as plainly as I could and she accepted."

"I don't think I quite understand," said Ashenden.

"Don't you? I should have thought it was clear to the meanest intelligence. If she can get Chandra to cross the Swiss frontier and come into France she's to go free, either to Spain or to South America, with her passage paid."

"And how the devil is she to get Chandra to do that?"

"He's madly in love with her. He's longing to see her. His letters are almost crazy. She's written to him to say that she can't get a visa to Holland (I told you she was to join him there when her tour was over), but she can get one for Switzerland. That's a neutral country and he's safe there. He jumped at the chance. They've arranged to meet at Lausanne."

"Yes."

"When he reaches Lausanne he'll get a letter from her to say that the French authorities won't let her cross the frontier and that she's going to Thonon, which is just on the other side of the lake from Lausanne, in France, and she's going to ask him to come there."

"What makes you think he will?"

R. paused for an instant. He looked at Ashenden with a pleasant expression.

"She must make him if she doesn't want to go to penal servitude for ten years."

"I see."

"She's arriving from England this evening in custody and I should like you to take her down to Thonon by the night train."

"Me?" said Ashenden.

"Yes, I thought it the sort of job you could manage very well. Presumably you know more about human nature than most people. It'll be a pleasant change for you to spend a week or two at Thonon. I believe it's a pretty little place, fashionable too—in peace-time. You might take the baths there."

"And what do you expect me to do when I get the lady down to Thonon?"

"I leave you a free hand. I've made a few notes that may be useful to you. I'll read them to you, shall I?"

Ashenden listened attentively. R.'s plan was simple and explicit. Ashenden could not but feel unwilling admiration for the brain that had so neatly devised it.

Presently R. suggested that they should have luncheon and he asked Ashenden to take him to some place where they could see smart people. It amused Ashenden to see R. so sharp, sure of himself and alert in his office, seized as he walked into the restaurant with shyness. He talked a little too loud in order to show that he was at his ease and made himself somewhat unnecessarily at home. You saw in his manner the shabby and commonplace life he had led till the hazards of war raised him to a position of consequence. He was glad to be in that fashionable restaurant cheek by jowl with persons who bore great or distinguished names, but he felt like a school-boy in his first top-hat, and he quailed before the steely eye of the *maître d'hôtel*. His quick glance darted here and there and his sallow face beamed with a self-satisfaction of which he was slightly ashamed. Ashenden drew his attention to an ugly woman in black. with a lovely figure, wearing a long row of pearls.

"That is Madame de Brides. She is the mistress of the Grand
Duke Theodore. She's probably one of the most influential
women in Europe, she's certainly one of the cleverest."

R.'s clever eyes rested on her and he flushed a little.

"By George, this is life," he said.

Ashenden watched him curiously. Luxury is dangerous to
people who have never known it and to whom its temptations
are held out too suddenly. R., that shrewd, cynical man, was
captivated by the vulgar glamour and the shoddy brilliance of
the scene before him. Just as the advantage of culture is that it
enables you to talk nonsense with distinction so the habit of
luxury allows you to regard its frills and furbelows with a proper
contumely.

But when they had eaten their luncheon and were drinking
their coffee Ashenden, seeing that R. was mellowed by the good
meal and his surroundings, went back to the subject that was
in his thoughts.

"That Indian fellow must be a rather remarkable chap," he
said.

"He's got brains of course."

"One can't help being impressed by a man who had the
courage to take on almost single-handed the whole British
power in India."

"I wouldn't get sentimental about him if I were you. He's
nothing but a dangerous criminal."

"I don't suppose he'd use bombs if he could command a few
batteries and half a dozen battalions. He uses what weapons
he can. You can hardly blame him for that. After all, he's aiming at nothing for himself, is he? He's aiming at freedom for his
country. On the face of it it looks as though he were justified in
his actions."

But R. had no notion of what Ashenden was talking.

"That's very far-fetched and morbid," he said. "We can't
go into all that. Our job is to get him and when we've got him
to shoot him."

"Of course. He's declared war and he must take his chance.
I shall carry out your instructions, that's what I'm here for, but
I see no harm in realizing that there's something to be admired
and respected in him."

R. was once more the cool and astute judge of his fellows.

"I've not yet made up my mind whether the best men for this
kind of job are those who do it with passion or those who keep

their heads. Some of them are filled with hatred for the people we're up against and when we down them it gives them a sort of satisfaction like satisfying a personal grudge. Of course they're very keen on their work. You're different, aren't you? You look at it like a game of chess and you don't seem to have any feeling one way or the other. I can't quite make it out. Of course for some sort of jobs it's just what one wants."

Ashenden did not answer. He called for the bill and walked back with R. to the hotel.

The train started at eight. When he had disposed of his bag Ashenden walked along the platform. He found the carriage in which Giulia Lazzari was, but she sat in a corner, looking away from the light, so that he could not see her face. She was in charge of two detectives who had taken her over from English police at Boulogne. One of them worked with Ashenden on the French side of the Lake Geneva and as Ashenden came up he nodded to him.

"I've asked the lady if she will dine in the restaurant-car, but she prefers to have dinner in the carriage, so I've ordered a basket. Is that quite correct?"

"Quite," said Ashenden.

"My companion and I will go into the diner in turn so that she will not remain alone."

"That is very considerate of you. I will come along when we've started and have a chat with her."

"She's not disposed to be very talkative," said the detective.

"One could hardly expect it," replied Ashenden.

He walked on to get his ticket for the second service and then returned to his own carriage. Giulia Lazzari was just finishing her meal when he went back to her. From a glance at the basket he judged that she had not eaten with too poor an appetite. The detective who was guarding her opened the door when Ashenden appeared and at Ashenden's suggestion left them alone.

Giulia Lazzari gave him a sullen look.

"I hope you've had what you wanted for dinner," he said as he sat down in front of her.

She bowed slightly, but did not speak. He took out his case.

"Will you have a cigarette?"

She gave him a glance, seemed to hesitate, and then, still without a word, took one. He struck a match and, lighting it, looked at her. He was surprised. For some reason he had ex-

pected her to be fair, perhaps from some notion that an Oriental
would be more likely to fall for a blonde; but she was almost
swarthy. Her hair was hidden by a close-fitting hat, but her
eyes were coal-black. She was far from young, she might have
been thirty-five, and her skin was lined and sallow. She had at
the moment no makeup on and she looked haggard. There was
nothing beautiful about her but her magnificent eyes. She was
big, and Ashenden thought she must be too big to dance gracefully; it might be that in Spanish costume she was a bold and
flaunting figure, but there in the train, shabbily dressed, there
was nothing to explain the Indian's infatuation. She gave
Ashenden a long, appraising stare. She wondered evidently
what sort of man he was. She blew a cloud of smoke through her
nostrils and gave it a glance, then looked back at Ashenden.
He could see that her sullenness was only a mask, she was
nervous and frightened. She spoke in French with an Italian
accent.

"Who are you?"

"My name would mean nothing to you, *madame*. I am going
to Thonon. I have taken a room for you at the Hotel de la Place.
It is the only one open now. I think you will find it quite comfortable."

"Ah, it is you the Colonel spoke to me of. You are my jailer."

"Only as a matter of form. I shall not intrude upon you."

"All the same you are my jailer."

"I hope not for very long. I have in my pocket your passport
with all the formalities completed to permit you to go to Spain."

She threw herself back into the corner of the carriage. White,
with those great black eyes, in the poor light, her face was suddenly a mask of despair.

"It's infamous. Oh, I think I could die happy if I could only
kill that old Colonel. He has no heart. I'm so unhappy."

"I am afraid you have got yourself into a very unfortunate
situation. Did you not know that espionage was a dangerous
game?"

"I never sold any of the secrets. I did no harm."

"Surely only because you had no opportunity. I understand
that you signed a full confession."

Ashenden spoke to her as amiably as he could, a little as
though he were talking to a sick person, and there was no harsh-
ness in his voice.

"Oh, yes, I made a fool of myself. I wrote the letter the

Colonel said I was to write. Why isn't that enough? What is to
happen to me if he does not answer? I cannot force him to come
if he does not want to."

"He has answered," said Ashenden. "I have the answer with
me."

She gave a gasp and her voice broke.

"Oh, show it to me, I beseech you to let me see it."

"I have no objection to doing that. But you must return it
to me."

He took Chandra's letter from his pocket and gave it to her.
She snatched it from his hand. She devoured it with her eyes,
there were eight pages of it, and as she read the tears streamed
down her cheeks. Between her sobs she gave little exclamations
of love, calling the writer by pet names French and Italian.
This was the letter that Chandra had written in reply to hers
telling him, on R.'s instructions, that she would meet him in
Switzerland. He was mad with joy at the prospect. He told
her in passionate phrases how long the time had seemed to him
since they were parted, and how he had yearned for her, and
now that he was to see her again so soon he did not know how
he was going to bear his impatience. She finished it and let it
drop to the floor.

"You can see he loves me, can't you? There's no doubt about
that. I know something about it, believe me."

"Do you really love him?" asked Ashenden.

"He's the only man who's ever been kind to me. It's not very
gay the life one leads in these music halls, all over Europe,
never resting, and men—they are not much the men who haunt
those places. At first I thought he was just like the rest of
them."

Ashenden picked up the letter and replaced it in his pocket-
book.

"A telegram was sent in your name to the address in Holland
to say that you would be at the Hotel Gibbons at Lausanne on
the 14th."

"That is to-morrow."

"Yes."

She threw up her head and her eyes flashed.

"Oh, it is an infamous thing that you are forcing me to do. It
is shameful."

"You are not obliged to do it," said Ashenden.

"And if I don't?"

"I'm afraid you must take the consequences."

"I can't go to prison," she cried out suddenly, "I can't, I can't; I have such a short time before me; he said ten years. Is it possible I could be sentenced to ten years?"

"If the Colonel told you so it is very possible."

"Oh, I know him. That cruel face. He would have no mercy. And what should I be in ten years? Oh, no, no."

At that moment the train stopped at a station and the detective waiting in the corridor tapped on the window. Ashenden opened the door and the man gave him a picture-postcard. It was a dull little view of Pontarlier, the frontier station between France and Switzerland, and showed a dusty *place* with a statue in the middle and a few plane trees. Ashenden handed her a pencil.

"Will you write this postcard to your lover. It will be posted at Pontarlier. Address it to the hotel at Lausanne."

She gave him a glance, but without answering took it and wrote as he directed.

"Now on the other side write: 'delayed at frontier but everything all right. Wait at Lausanne.' Then add whatever you like, *tendresses*, if you like."

He took the postcard from her, read it to see that she had done as he directed and then reached for his hat.

"Well, I shall leave you now, I hope you will have a sleep. I will fetch you in the morning when we arrive at Thonon."

The second detective had now returned from his dinner and as Ashenden came out of the carriage the two men went in. Giulia Lazzari huddled back into her corner. Ashenden gave the postcard to an agent who was waiting to take it to Pontarlier and then made his way along the crowded train to his sleeping-car.

It was bright and sunny, though cold, next morning when they reached their destination. Ashenden, having given his bags to a porter, walked along the platform to where Giulia Lazzari and the two detectives were standing. Ashenden nodded to them.

"Well, good morning. You need not trouble to wait."

They touched their hats, gave a word of farewell to the woman, and walked away.

"Where are they going?" she asked.

"Off. You will not be bothered with them any more."

"Am I in your custody then?"

"You're in nobody's custody. I'm going to permit myself to take you to your hotel and then I shall leave you. You must try to get a good rest."

Ashenden's porter took her hand-luggage and she gave him the ticket for her trunk. They walked out of the station. A cab was waiting for them and Ashenden begged her to get in. It was a longish drive to the hotel and now and then Ashenden felt that she gave him a sidelong glance. She was perplexed. He sat without a word. When they reached the hotel the proprietor—it was a small hotel, prettily situated at the corner of a little promenade and it had a charming view—showed them the room that had been prepared for Madame Lazzari. Ashenden turned to him.

"That'll do very nicely, I think. I shall come down in a minute."

The proprietor bowed and withdrew.

"I shall do my best to see that you are comfortable, *Madame*," said Ashenden. "You are here absolutely your own mistress and you may order pretty well anything you like. To the proprietor you are just a guest of the hotel like any other. You are absolutely free."

"Free to go out?" she asked quickly.

"Of course."

"With a policeman on either side of me, I suppose."

"Not at all. You are as free in the hotel as though you were in your own house and you are free to go out and come in when you choose. I should like an assurance from you that you will not write any letters without my knowledge or attempt to leave Thonon without my permission."

She gave Ashenden a long stare. She could not make it out at all. She looked as though she thought it a dream.

"I am in a position that forces me to give you any assurance you ask. I give you my word of honour that I will not write a letter without showing it to you or attempt to leave this place."

"Thank you. Now I will leave you. I will do myself the pleasure of coming to see you to-morrow morning."

Ashenden nodded and went out. He stopped for five minutes at the police-station to see that everything was in order and then took the cab up the hill to a little secluded house on the outskirts of the town at which on his periodical visits to this place he stayed. It was pleasant to have a bath and a shave and get into slippers. He felt lazy and spent the rest of the morning reading a novel.

Soon after dark, for even at Thonon, though it was in France, it was thought desirable to attract attention to Ashenden as little as possible, an agent from the police-station came to see him. His name was Felix. He was a little dark Frenchman with sharp eyes and an unshaven chin, dressed in a shabby grey suit and rather down at heel, so that he looked like a lawyer's clerk out of work. Ashenden offered him a glass of wine and they sat down by the fire.

"Well, your lady lost no time," he said. "Within a quarter of an hour of her arrival she was out of the hotel with a bundle of clothes and trinkets that she sold in a shop near the market. When the afternoon boat came in she went down to the quay and bought a ticket to Evian."

Evian, it should be explained, was the next place along the lake in France and from there, crossing over, the boat went to Switzerland.

"Of course she hadn't a passport, so permission to embark was denied her."

"How did she explain that she had no passport?"

"She said she'd forgotten it. She said she had an appointment to see friends in Evian and tried to persuade the official in charge to let her go. She attempted to slip a hundred francs into his hand."

"She must be a stupider woman than I thought," said Ashenden.

But when next day he went about eleven in the morning to see her he made no reference to her attempt to escape. She had had time to arrange herself, and now, her hair elaborately done, her lips and cheeks painted, she looked less haggard than when he had first seen her.

"I've brought you some books," said Ashenden. "I'm afraid the time hangs heavy on your hands."

"What does that matter to you?"

"I have no wish that you should suffer anything that can be avoided. Anyhow I will leave them and you can read them or not as you choose."

"If you only knew how I hated you."

"It would doubtless make me very uncomfortable. But I really don't know why you should. I am only doing what I have been ordered to do."

"What do you want of me now? I do not suppose you have come only to ask after my health."

Ashenden smiled.

"I want you to write a letter to your lover telling him that owing to some irregularity in your passport the Swiss authorities would not let you cross the frontier, so you have come here where it is very nice and quiet, so quiet that one can hardly realize there is a war, and you propose that Chandra should join you."

"Do you think he is a fool? He will refuse."

"Then you must do your best to persuade him."

She looked at Ashenden a long time before she answered. He suspected that she was debating within herself whether by writing the letter and so seeming docile she could not gain time.

"Well, dictate and I will write what you say."

"I should prefer you to put it in your own words."

"Give me half an hour and the letter shall be ready."

"I will wait here," said Ashenden.

"Why?"

"Because I prefer to."

Her eyes flashed angrily, but controlling herself she said nothing. On the chest of drawers were writing materials. She sat down at the dressing-table and began to write. When she handed Ashenden the letter he saw that even through her rouge she was very pale. It was the letter of a person not much used to expressing herself by means of pen and ink, but it was well enough, and when towards the end, starting to say how much she loved the man, she had been carried away and wrote with all her heart, it had really a certain passion.

"Now add: The man who is bringing this is Swiss, you can trust him absolutely. I didn't want the censor to see it."

She hesitated an instant, but then wrote as he directed.

"How do you spell, absolutely?"

"As you like. Now address an envelope and I will relieve you of my unwelcome presence."

He gave the letter to the agent who was waiting to take it across the lake. Ashenden brought her the reply the same evening. She snatched it from his hands and for a moment pressed it to her heart. When she read it she uttered a little cry of relief.

"He won't come."

The letter, in the Indian's flowery, stilted English, expressed his bitter disappointment. He told her how intensely he had

looked forward to seeing her and implored her to do everything
in the world to smooth the difficulties that prevented her from
crossing the frontier. He said that it was impossible for him to
come, impossible, there was a price on his head, and it would be
madness for him to think of risking it. He attempted to be
jocular, she did not want her little fat lover to be shot, did
she?

"He won't come," she repeated, "he won't come."

"You must write and tell him that there is no risk. You must
say that if there were you would not dream of asking him. You
must say that if he loves you he will not hesitate."

"I won't. I won't."

"Don't be a fool. You can't help yourself."

She burst into a sudden flood of tears. She flung herself on
the floor and seizing Ashenden's knees implored him to have
mercy on her.

"I will do anything in the world for you if you will let me
go."

"Don't be absurd," said Ashenden. "Do you think I want to
become your lover? Come, come, you must be serious. You
know the alternative."

She raised herself to her feet and changing on a sudden to
fury flung at Ashenden one foul name after another.

"I like you much better like that," he said. "Now will you
write or shall I send for the police?"

"He will not come. It is useless."

"It is very much to your interest to make him come."

"What do you mean by that? Do you mean that if I do everything in my power and fail, that . . ."

She looked at Ashenden with wild eyes.

"Yes, it means either you or him."

She staggered. She put her hand to her heart. Then without
a word she reached for pen and paper. But the letter was not to
Ashenden's liking and he made her write it again. When she had
finished she flung herself on the bed and burst once more into
passionate weeping. Her grief was real, but there was something
theatrical in the expression of it that prevented it from being
peculiarly moving to Ashenden. He felt his relation to her as
impersonal as a doctor's in the presence of a pain that he cannot
alleviate. He saw now why R. had given him this peculiar task;
it needed a cool head and an emotion well under control.

He did not see her next day. The answer to the letter was not delivered to him till after dinner when it was brought to Ashenden's little house by Felix.

"Well, what news have you?"

"Our friend is getting desperate," smiled the Frenchman. "This afternoon she walked up to the station just as a train was about to start for Lyons. She was looking up and down uncertainly so I went to her and asked if there was anything I could do. I introduced myself as an agent of the Sureté. If looks could kill I should not be standing here now."

"Sit down, *mon ami*," said Ashenden.

"*Merci*. She walked away, she evidently thought it was no use to try to get on the train, but I have something more interesting to tell you. She has offered a boatman on the lake a thousand francs to take her across to Lausanne."

"What did he say to her?"

"He said he couldn't risk it."

"Yes?"

The little agent gave his shoulders a slight shrug and smiled.

"She's asked him to meet her on the road that leads to Evian at ten o'clock to-night so that they can talk of it again, and she's given him to understand that she will not repulse too fiercely the advances of a lover. I have told him to do what he likes so long as he comes and tells me everything that is of importance."

"Are you sure you can trust him?" asked Ashenden.

"Oh, quite. He knows nothing, of course, but that she is under surveillance. You need have no fear about him. He is a good boy, I have known him all his life."

Ashenden read Chandra's letter. It was eager and passionate. It throbbed strangely with the painful yearning of his heart. Love? Yes, if Ashenden knew anything of it there was the real thing. He told her how he spent long long hours walking by the lakeside and looking towards the coast of France. How near they were and yet so desperately parted! He repeated again and again that he could not come, and begged her not to ask him, he would do everything in the world for her, but that he dared not do, and yet if she insisted how could he resist her? He besought her to have mercy on him. And then he broke into a long wail at the thought that he must go away without seeing her, he asked her if there were not some means by which she could slip over, he swore that if he could ever hold her in his arms again he would never let her go. Even the forced and elaborate language in which it was written could not dim the hot fire that burned the pages; it was the letter of a madman.

"When will you hear the result of her interview with the boatman?" asked Ashenden.

"I have arranged to meet him at the landing-stage between eleven and twelve."

Ashenden looked at his watch.

"I will come with you."

They walked down the hill and reaching the quay for shelter from the cold wind stood in the lea of the custom-house. At last they saw a man approaching and Felix stepped out of the shadow that hid them.

"Antoine."

"*Monsieur Félix?* I have a letter for you; I promised to take it to Lausanne by the first boat tomorrow."

Ashenden gave the man a brief glance, but did not ask what had passed between him and Giulia Lazzari. He took the letter and by the light of Felix's electric torch read it. It was in faulty German.

"*On no account come. Pay no attention to my letters. Danger. I love you. Sweetheart. Don't come.*"

He put it in his pocket, gave the boatman fifty francs, and went home to bed. But the next day when he went to see Giulia Lazzari he found her door locked. He knocked for some time, there was no answer. He called her.

"Madame Lazzari, you must open the door. I want to speak to you."

"I am in bed. I am ill and can see no one."

"I am sorry, but you must open the door. If you are ill I will send for a doctor."

"No, go away. I will see no one."

"If you do not open the door I shall send for a locksmith and have it broken open."

There was a silence and then he heard the key turned in the lock. He went in. She was in a dressing-gown and her hair was dishevelled. She had evidently just got out of bed.

"I am at the end of my strength. I can do nothing more. You have only to look at me to see that I am ill. I have been sick all night."

"I shall not keep you long. Would you like to see a doctor?"

"What good can a doctor do me?"

He took out of his pocket the letter she had given the boatman and handed it to her.

"What is the meaning of this?" he asked.

She gave a gasp at the sight of it and her sallow face went green.

"You gave me your word that you would neither attempt to escape nor write a letter without my knowledge."

"Did you think I would keep my word?" she cried, her voice ringing with scorn.

"No. To tell you the truth it was not entirely for your convenience that you were placed in a comfortable hotel rather than in the local jail, but I think I should tell you that though you have your freedom to go in and out as you like you have no more chance of getting away from Thonon than if you were chained by the leg in a prison cell. It is silly to waste your time writing letters that will never be delivered."

"*Cochon.*"

She flung the opprobrious word at him with all the violence that was in her.

"But you must sit down and write a letter that *will* be delivered."

"Never. I will do nothing more. I will not write another word."

"You came here on the understanding that you would do certain things."

"I will not do them. It is finished."

"You had better reflect a little."

"Reflect! I have reflected. You can do what you like; I don't care."

"Very well, I will give you five minutes to change your mind."

Ashenden took out his watch and looked at it. He sat down on the edge of the unmade bed.

"Oh, it has got on my nerves, this hotel. Why did you not put me in the prison? Why, why? Everywhere I went I felt that spies were on my heels. It is infamous what you are making me do. Infamous! What is my crime? I ask you, what have I done? Am I not a woman? It is infamous what you are asking me to do. Infamous."

She spoke in a high shrill voice. She went on and on. At last the five minutes were up. Ashenden had not said a word. He rose.

"Yes, go, go," she shrieked at him.

She flung foul names at him.

"I shall come back," said Ashenden.

He took the key out of the door as he went out of the room and locked it behind him. Going downstairs he hurriedly scribbled a note, called the boots and dispatched him with it to the police-station. Then he went up again. Giulia Lazzari had thrown herself on her bed and turned her face to the wall. Her body was shaken with hysterical sobs. She gave no sign that she heard him come in. Ashenden sat down on the chair in front of the dressing-table and looked idly at the odds and ends that littered it. The toilet things were cheap and tawdry and none too clean. There were little shabby pots of rouge and cold-cream and little bottles of black for the eyebrows and eyelashes. The hairpins were horrid and greasy. The room was untidy and the air was heavy with the smell of cheap scent. Ashenden thought of the hundreds of rooms she must have occupied in third-rate hotels in the course of her wandering life from provincial town to provincial town in one country after another. He wondered what had been her origins. She was a coarse and vulgar woman, but what had she been when young? She was not the type he would have expected to adopt that career, for she seemed to have no advantages that could help her, and he asked himself whether she came of a family of entertainers (there are all over the world families in which for generations the members have become dancers or acrobats or comic singers) or whether she had fallen into the life accidentally through some lover in the business who had for a time made her his partner. And what men must she have known in all these years, the comrades of the shows she was in, the agents and managers who looked upon it as a perquisite of their position that they should enjoy her favours, the merchants or well-to-do tradesmen, the young sparks of the various towns she played in, who were attracted for the moment by the glamour of the dancer or the blatant sensuality of the woman! To her they were the paying customers and she accepted them indifferently as the recognized and admitted supplement to her miserable salary, but to them perhaps she was romance. In her bought arms they caught sight for a moment of the brilliant world of the capitals, and ever so distantly and however shoddily of the adventure and the glamour of a more spacious life.

There was a sudden knock at the door and Ashenden immediately cried out:

"*Entrez.*"

Giulia Lazzari sprang up in bed to a sitting posture.

"Who is it?" she called.

She gave a gasp as she saw the two detectives who had brought her from Boulogne and handed her over to Ashenden at Thonon.

"You! What do you want?" she shrieked.

"*Allons, levez vous,*" said one of them, and his voice had a sharp abruptness that suggested that he would put up with no nonsense.

"I'm afraid you must get up, Madame Lazzari," said Ashenden. "I am delivering you once more to the care of these gentlemen."

"How can I get up! I'm ill, I tell you. I cannot stand. Do you want to kill me?"

"If you won't dress yourself, we shall have to dress you, and I'm afraid we shouldn't do it very cleverly. Come, come, it's no good making a scene."

"Where are you going to take me?"

"They're going to take you back to England."

One of the detectives took hold of her arm.

"Don't touch me, don't come near me," she screamed furiously.

"Let her be," said Ashenden. "I'm sure she'll see the necessity of making as little trouble as possible."

"I'll dress myself."

Ashenden watched her as she took off her dressing-gown and slipped a dress over her head. She forced her feet into shoes obviously too small for her. She arranged her hair. Every now and then she gave the detectives a hurried, sullen glance. Ashenden wondered if she would have the nerve to go through with it. R. would call him a damned fool, but he almost wished she would. She went up to the dressing-table and Ashenden stood up in order to let her sit down. She greased her face quickly and then rubbed off the grease with a dirty towel, she powdered herself and made up her eyes. But her hand shook. The three men watched her in silence. She rubbed the rouge on her cheeks and painted her mouth. Then she crammed a hat down on her head. Ashenden made a gesture to the first detective and he took a pair of handcuffs out of his pocket and advanced towards her.

At the sight of them she started back violently and flung her arms wide.

"*Non, non, non. Je ne veux pas.* No, not them. No. No."

"Come, *ma fille,* don't be silly," said the detective roughly.

As though for protection (very much to his surprise) she flung her arms round Ashenden.

"Don't let them take me, have mercy on me, I can't, I can't."

Ashenden extricated himself as best he could.

"I can do nothing more for you."

The detective seized her wrists and was about to affix the handcuffs when with a great cry she threw herself down on the floor.

"I will do what you wish. I will do everything."

On a sign from Ashenden the detectives left the room. He waited for a little till she had regained a certain calm. She was lying on the floor, sobbing passionately. He raised her to her feet and made her sit down.

"What do you want me to do?" she gasped.

"I want you to write another letter to Chandra."

"My head is in a whirl. I could not put two phrases together. You must give me time."

But Ashenden felt that it was better to get her to write a letter while she was under the effect of her terror. He did not want to give her time to collect herself.

"I will dictate the letter to you. All you have to do is to write exactly what I tell you."

She gave a deep sigh, but took the pen and the paper and sat down before them at the dressing-table.

"If I do this and . . . and you succeed, how do I know that I shall be allowed to go free?"

"The Colonel promised that you should. You must take my word for it that I shall carry out his instructions."

"I *should* look a fool if I betrayed my friend and then went to prison for ten years."

"I'll tell you your best guarantee of our good faith. Except by reason of Chandra you are not of the smallest importance to us. Why should we put ourselves to the bother and expense of keeping you in prison when you can do us no harm?"

She reflected for an instant. She was composed now. It was as though, having exhausted her emotion, she had become on a sudden a sensible and practical woman.

"Tell me what you want me to write."

Ashenden hesitated. He thought he could put the letter more or less in the way she would naturally have put it, but he had to give it consideration. It must be neither fluent nor literary. He knew that in moments of emotion people are inclined to be melodramatic and stilted. In a book or on the stage this always rings false and the author has to make his people speak more simply and with less emphasis than in fact they do. It was a serious moment, but Ashenden felt that there were in it elements of the comic.

"I didn't know I loved a coward," he started. "If you loved me you couldn't hesitate when I ask you to come. . . . Underline *couldn't* twice." He went on. "When I promise you there is no danger. If you don't love me, you are right not to come. Don't come. Go back to Berlin where you are in safety. I am sick of it. I am alone here. I have made myself ill by waiting for you and every day I have said he is coming. If you loved me you would not hesitate so much. It is quite clear to me that you do not love me. I am sick and tired of you. I have no money. This hotel is impossible. There is nothing for me to stay for. I can get an engagement in Paris. I have a friend there who has made me serious propositions. I have wasted long enough over you and look what I have got from it. It is finished. Good-bye. You will never find a woman who will love you as I have loved you. I cannot afford to refuse the proposition of my friend, so I have telegraphed to him and as soon as I shall receive his answer I go to Paris. I do not blame you because you do not love me, that is not your fault, but you must see that I should be a stupid to go on wasting my life. One is not young for ever. Good-bye. Giulia."

When Ashenden read over the letter he was not altogether satisfied. But it was the best he could do. It had an air of verisimilitude which the words lacked because, knowing little English, she had written phonetically, the spelling was atrocious and the handwriting like a child's; she had crossed out words and written them over again. Some of the phrases he had put in French. Once or twice tears had fallen on the pages and blurred the ink.

"I leave you now," said Ashenden. "It may be that when next you see me I shall be able to tell you that you are free to go where you choose. Where do you want to go?"

"Spain."

"Very well, I will have everything prepared."

She shrugged her shoulders. He left her.

There was nothing now for Ashenden to do but wait. He sent

a messenger to Lausanne in the afternoon, and next morning
went down to the quay to meet the boat. There was a waiting-
room next to the ticket-office and here he told the detectives
to hold themselves in readiness. When a boat arrived the
passengers advanced along the pier in line and their passports
were examined before they were allowed to go ashore. If Chandra came and showed his passport, and it was very likely that
he was travelling with a false one, issued probably by a neutral
nation, he was to be asked to wait and Ashenden was to identify
him. Then he would be arrested. It was with some excitement
that Ashenden watched the boat come in and the little group
of people gathered at the gangway. He scanned them closely
but saw no one who looked in the least like an Indian. Chandra
had not come. Ashenden did not know what to do. He had
played his last card. There were not more than half a dozen
passengers for Thonon and when they had been examined and
gone their way he strolled slowly along the pier.

"Well, it's no go," he said to Felix who had been examining
the passports. "The gentleman I expected hasn't turned up."

"I have a letter for you."

He handed Ashenden an envelope addressed to Madame
Lazzari on which he immediately recognized the spidery handwriting of Chandra Lal. At that moment the steamer from
Geneva which was going to Lausanne and the end of the lake
hove in sight. It arrived at Thonon every morning twenty
minutes after the steamer going in the opposite direction had
left. Ashenden had an inspiration.

"Where is the man who brought it?"

"He's in the ticket-office."

"Give him the letter and tell him to return to the person who
gave it to him. He is to say that he took it to the lady and she
sent it back. If the person asks him to take another letter he is
to say that it is not much good as she is packing her trunk and
leaving Thonon."

He saw the letter handed over and the instructions given and
then walked back to his little house in the country.

The next boat on which Chandra could possibly come arrived
about five and having at that hour an important engagement
with an agent working in Germany he warned Felix that he
might be a few minutes late. But if Chandra came he could
easily be detained; there was no great hurry since the train in
which he was to be taken to Paris did not start till shortly after

eight. When Ashenden had finished his business he strolled leisurely down to the lake. It was light still and from the top of the hill he saw the steamer pulling out. It was an anxious moment and instinctively he quickened his steps. Suddenly he saw someone running towards him and recognized the man who had taken the letter.

"Quick, quick," he cried. "He's there."

Ashenden's heart gave a great thud against his chest.

"At last."

He began to run too and as they ran the man, panting, told him how he had taken back the unopened letter. When he put it in the Indian's hand he turned frightfully pale ("I should never have thought an Indian could turn that colour," he said) and turned it over and over in his hand as though he could not understand what his own letter was doing there. Tears sprang to his eyes and rolled down his cheeks. ("It was grotesque, he's fat, you know.") He said something in a language the man did not understand and then in French asked him when the boat went to Thonon. When he got on board he looked about, but did not see him, then he caught sight of him, huddled up in an ulster with his hat drawn down over his eyes, standing alone in the bows. During the crossing he kept his eyes fixed on Thonon.

"Where is he now?" asked Ashenden.

"I got off first and Monsieur Felix told me to come for you."

"I suppose they're holding him in the waiting-room."

Ashenden was out of breath when they reached the pier. He burst into the waiting-room. A group of men, talking at the top of their voices and gesticulating wildly, were clustered round a man lying on the ground.

"What's happened?" he cried.

"Look," said Monsieur Felix.

Chandra Lal lay there, his eyes wide open and a thin line of foam on his lips, dead. His body was horribly contorted.

"He's killed himself. We've sent for the doctor. He was too quick for us."

A sudden thrill of horror passed through Ashenden.

When the Indian landed Felix recognized from the description that he was the man they wanted. There were only four passengers. He was the last. Felix took an exaggerated time to examine the passports of the first three, and then took the Indian's. It was a Spanish one and it was all in order. Felix

asked the regulation questions and noted them on the official
sheet. Then he looked at him pleasantly and said:

"Just come into the waiting-room for a moment. There are
one or two formalities to fulfil."

"Is my passport not in order?" the Indian asked.

"Perfectly."

Chandra hesitated, but then followed the official to the
door of the waiting-room. Felix opened it and stood aside.

"*Entrez.*"

Chandra went in and the two detectives stood up. He must
have suspected at once that they were police-officers and realized that he had fallen into a trap.

"Sit down," said Felix. "I have one or two questions to put
to you."

"It is hot in here," he said, and in point of fact they had a
little stove there that kept the place like an oven. "I will take
off my coat if you permit."

"Certainly," said Felix graciously.

He took off his coat, apparently with some effort, and he
turned to put it on a chair, and then before they realized what
had happened they were startled to see him stagger and fall
heavily to the ground. While taking off his coat Chandra had
managed to swallow the contents of a bottle that was still
clasped in his hand. Ashenden put his nose to it. There was a
very distinct odour of almonds.

For a little while they looked at the man who lay on the
floor. Felix was apologetic.

"Will they be very angry?" he asked nervously.

"I don't see that it was your fault," said Ashenden. "Anyhow
he can do no more harm. For my part I am just as glad he killed
himself. The notion of his being executed did not make me very
comfortable."

In a few minutes the doctor arrived and pronounced life
extinct.

"Prussic acid," he said to Ashenden.

Ashenden nodded.

"I will go and see Madame Lazzari," he said. "If she wants
to stay a day or two longer I shall let her. But if she wants to go
to-night of course she can. Will you give the agents at the
station instructions to let her pass?"

"I shall be at the station myself," said Felix.

Ashenden once more climbed the hill. It was night now, a

cold, bright night with an unclouded sky and the sight of the
new moon, a white shining thread, made him turn three times
the money in his pocket. When he entered the hotel he was
seized on a sudden with distaste for its cold banality. It smelt
of cabbage and boiled mutton. On the walls of the hall were
coloured posters of railway companies advertising Grenoble,
Carcassonne and the bathing places of Normandy. He went upstairs and after a brief knock opened the door of Giulia Lazzari's room. She was sitting in front of her dressing-table, looking at herself in the glass, just idly or despairingly, apparently
doing nothing, and it was in this that she saw Ashenden as he
came in. Her face changed suddenly as she caught sight of his
and she sprang up so vehemently that the chair fell over.

"What is it? Why are you so white?" she cried.

She turned round and stared at him and her features were
gradually twisted to a look of horror.

"*Il est pris*," she gasped.

"*Il est mort*," said Ashenden.

"Dead! He took the poison. He had the time for that. He's
escaped you after all."

"What do you mean? How did you know about the poison?"

"He always carried it with him. He said that the English
should never take him alive."

Ashenden reflected for an instant. She had kept that secret
well. He supposed the possibility of such a thing should have
occurred to him. How was he to anticipate these melodramatic
devices?

"Well, now you are free. You can go wherever you like and no
obstacle shall be put in your way. Here are your ticket and your
passport and here is the money that was in your possession
when you were arrested. Do you wish to see Chandra?"

She started.

"No, no."

"There is no need. I thought you might care to."

She did not weep. Ashenden supposed that she had exhausted
all her emotion. She seemed apathetic.

"A telegram will be sent to-night to the Spanish frontier to
instruct the authorities to put no difficulties in your way. If you
will take my advice you will get out of France as soon as you
can."

She said nothing, and since Ashenden had no more to say
he made ready to go.

"I am sorry that I have had to show myself so hard to you. I am glad to think that now the worst of your troubles are over and I hope that time will assuage the grief that I know you must feel for the death of your friend."

Ashenden gave her a little bow and turned to the door. But she stopped him.

"One little moment," she said. "There is one thing I should like to ask. I think you have some heart."

"Whatever I can do for you, you may be sure I will."

"What are they going to do with his things?"

"I don't know. Why?"

Then she said something that confounded Ashenden. It was the last thing he expected.

"He had a wrist-watch that I gave him last Christmas. It cost twelve pounds. Can I have it back?"

THE TRAITOR

WHEN Ashenden, given charge of a number of spies working from Switzerland, was first sent there, R., wishing him to see the sort of reports that he would be required to obtain, handed him the communications, a sheaf of typewritten documents, of a man known in the secret service as Gustav.

"He's the best fellow we've got," said R. "His information is always very full and circumstantial. I want you to give his reports your very best attention. Of course Gustav is a clever little chap, but there's no reason why we shouldn't get just as good reports from the other agents. It's merely a question of explaining exactly what we want."

Gustav, who lived at Basle, represented a Swiss firm with branches at Frankfort, Mannheim and Cologne, and by virtue of his business was able to go in and out of Germany without risk. He travelled up and down the Rhine, and gathered material about the movement of troops, the manufacture of munitions, the state of mind of the country (a point on which R. laid stress) and other matters upon which the Allies desired information. His frequent letters to his wife hid an ingenious code and the moment she received them in Basle she sent them to Ashenden in Geneva, who extracted from them the important facts and communicated these in the proper quarter. Every two months Gustav came home and prepared one of the reports that served as models to the other spies in this particular section of the secret service.

His employers were pleased with Gustav and Gustav had

reason to be pleased with his employers. His services were so useful that he was not only paid more highly than the others but for particular scoops had received from time to time a handsome bonus.

This went on for more than a year. Then something aroused R.'s quick suspicions: he was a man of an amazing alertness, not so much of mind, as of instinct, and he had suddenly a feeling that some hankey-pankey was going on. He said nothing definite to Ashenden (whatever R. surmised he was disposed to keep to himself) but told him to go to Basle, Gustav being then in Germany, and have a talk with Gustav's wife. He left it to Ashenden to decide the tenor of the conversation.

Having arrived at Basle, and leaving his bag at the station, for he did not yet know whether he would have to stay or not, he took a tram to the corner of the street in which Gustav lived and, with a quick look to see that he was not followed, walked along to the house he sought. It was a block of flats that gave you the impression of decent poverty and Ashenden conjectured that they were inhabited by clerks and small tradespeople. Just inside the door was a cobbler's shop and Ashenden stopped.

"Does Herr Grabow live here?" he asked in his none too fluent German.

"Yes, I saw him go up a few minutes ago. You'll find him in."

Ashenden was startled, for he had but the day before received through Gustav's wife a letter addressed from Mannheim in which Gustav by means of his code gave the numbers of certain regiments that had just crossed the Rhine. Ashenden thought it unwise to ask the cobbler the question that rose to his lips, so thanked him and went up to the third floor on which he knew already that Gustav lived. He rang the bell and heard it tinkle within. In a moment the door was opened by a dapper little man with a close-shaven round head and spectacles. He wore carpet slippers.

"Herr Grabow?" asked Ashenden.

"At your service," said Gustav.

"May I come in?"

Gustav was standing with his back to the light and Ashenden could not see the look on his face. He felt a momentary hesitation and gave the name under which he received Gustav's letters from Germany.

"Come in, come in. I am very glad to see you."

Gustav led the way into a stuffy little room, heavy with carved oak furniture, and on the large table covered with a table-cloth of green velveteen was a typewriter. Gustav was apparently engaged in composing one of his invaluable reports. A woman was sitting at the open window darning socks, but at a word from Gustav rose, gathered up her things and left. Ashenden had disturbed a pretty picture of connubial bliss.

"Sit down, please. How very fortunate that I was in Basle! I have long wanted to make your acquaintance. I have only just this minute returned from Germany." He pointed to the sheets of paper by the typewriter. "I think you will be pleased with the news I bring. I have some very valuable information." He chuckled. "One is never sorry to earn a bonus."

He was very cordial, but to Ashenden his cordiality rang false. Gustav kept his eyes, smiling behind the glasses, fixed watchfully on Ashenden and it was possible that they held a trace of nervousness.

"You must have travelled quickly to get here only a few hours after your letter, sent here and then sent on by your wife, reached me in Geneva."

"That is very probable. One of the things I had to tell you is that the Germans suspect that information is getting through by means of commercial letters and so they have decided to hold up all mail at the frontier for eight and forty hours."

"I see," said Ashenden amiably. "And was it on that account that you took the precaution of dating your letter forty-eight hours after you sent it?"

"Did I do that? That was very stupid of me. I must have mistaken the day of the month."

Ashenden looked at Gustav with a smile. That was very thin; Gustav, a business man, knew too well how important in his particular job was the exactness of a date. The circuitous routes by which it was necessary to get information from Germany made it difficult to transmit news quickly and it was essential to know precisely on what days certain events had taken place.

"Let me look at your passport a minute," said Ashenden.

"What do you want with my passport?"

"I want to see when you went into Germany and when you came out."

"But you do not imagine that my comings and goings are

marked on my passport? I have methods of crossing the frontier."

Ashenden knew a good deal of this matter. He knew that both the Germans and the Swiss guarded the frontier with severity.

"Oh? Why should you not cross in the ordinary way? You were engaged because your connection with a Swiss firm supplying necessary goods to Germany made it easy for you to travel backwards and forwards without suspicion. I can understand that you might get past the German sentries with the connivance of the Germans, but what about the Swiss?"

Gustav assumed a look of indignation.

"I do not understand you. Do you mean to suggest that I am in the service of the Germans? I give you my word of honour . . . I will not allow my straightforwardness to be impugned."

"You would not be the only one to take money from both sides and provide information of value to neither."

"Do you pretend that my information is of no value? Why then have you given me more bonuses than any other agent has received? The Colonel has repeatedly expressed the highest satisfaction with my services."

It was Ashenden's turn now to be cordial.

"Come, come, my dear fellow, do not try to ride the high horse. You do not wish to show me your passport and I will not insist. You are not under the impression that we leave the statements of our agents without corroboration or that we are so foolish as not to keep track of their movements? Even the best of jokes cannot bear an indefinite repetition. I am in peace-time a humorist by profession and I tell you that from bitter experience." Now Ashenden thought the moment had arrived to attempt his bluff; he knew something of the excellent but difficult game of poker. "We have information that you have not been to Germany now, nor since you were engaged by us, but have sat here quietly in Basle, and all your reports are merely due to your fertile imagination."

Gustav looked at Ashenden and saw a face expressive of nothing but tolerance and good humour. A smile slowly broke on his lips and he gave his shoulders a little shrug.

"Did you think I was such a fool as to risk my life for fifty pounds a month? I love my wife."

Ashenden laughed outright.

"I congratulate you. It is not everyone who can flatter himself that he has made a fool of our secret service for a year."

"I had the chance of earning money without any difficulty. My firm stopped sending me into Germany at the beginning of the war, but I learned what I could from the other travellers, I kept my ears open in restaurants and beer-cellars, and I read the German papers. I got a lot of amusement out of sending you reports and letters."

"I don't wonder," said Ashenden.

"What are you going to do?"

"Nothing. What can we do? You are not under the impression that we shall continue to pay you a salary?"

"No, I cannot expect that."

"By the way, if it is not indiscreet, may I ask if you have been playing the same game with the Germans?"

"Oh, no," Gustav cried vehemently. "How can you think it? My sympathies are absolutely pro-ally. My heart is entirely with you."

"Well, why not?" asked Ashenden. "The Germans have all the money in the world and there is no reason why you should not get some of it. We could give you information from time to time that the Germans would be prepared to pay for."

Gustav drummed his fingers on the table. He took up a sheet of the now useless report.

"The Germans are dangerous people to meddle with."

"You are a very intelligent man. And after all, even if your salary is stopped, you can always earn a bonus by bringing us news that can be useful to us. But it will have to be substantiated; in future we pay only by results."

"I will think of it."

For a moment or two Ashenden left Gustav to his reflections. He lit a cigarette and watched the smoke he had inhaled fade into the air. He thought too.

"Is there anything particular you want to know?" asked Gustav suddenly.

Ashenden smiled.

"It would be worth a couple of thousand Swiss francs to you if you could tell me what the Germans are doing with a spy of theirs in Lucerne. He is an Englishman and his name is Grantley Caypor."

"I have heard the name," said Gustav. He paused a moment. "How long are you staying here?"

"As long as necessary. I will take a room at the hotel and let you know the number. If you have anything to say to me you can be sure of finding me in my room at nine every morning and at seven every night."

"I should not risk coming to the hotel. But I can write."

"Very well."

Ashenden rose to go and Gustav accompanied him to the door.

"We part without ill-feeling then?" he asked.

"Of course. Your reports will remain in our archives as models of what a report should be."

Ashenden spent two or three days visiting Basle. It did not much amuse him. He passed a good deal of time in the bookshops turning over the pages of books that would have been worth reading if life were a thousand years long. Once he saw Gustav in the street. On the fourth morning a letter was brought up with his coffee. The envelope was that of a commercial firm unknown to him and inside it was a typewritten sheet. There was no address and no signature. Ashenden wondered if Gustav was aware that a typewriter could betray its owner as certainly as a handwriting. Having twice carefully read the letter, he held the paper up to the light to see the watermark, (he had no reason for doing this except that the sleuths of detective novels always did it,) then struck a match and watched it burn. He scrunched up the charred fragments in his hand.

He got up, for he had taken advantage of his situation to breakfast in bed, packed his bag and took the next train to Berne. From there he was able to send a code telegram to R. His instructions were given to him verbally two days later, in the bedroom of his hotel at an hour when no one was likely to be seen walking along a corridor, and within twenty-four hours, though by a circuitous route, he arrived at Lucerne.

Having taken a room at the hotel at which he had been instructed to stay Ashenden went out; it was a lovely day, early in August, and the sun shone in an unclouded sky. He had not been to Lucerne since he was a boy and but vaguely remembered a covered bridge, a great stone lion and a church in which he had sat, bored yet impressed, while they played an organ; and now wandering along a shady quay (and the lake

looked just as tawdry and unreal as it looked on the picture-
postcards) he tried not so much to find his way about a half-
forgotten scene as to reform in his mind some recollection of
the shy and eager lad, so impatient for life (which he saw not
in the present of his adolescence but only in the future of his
manhood), who so long ago had wandered there. But it seemed
to him that the most vivid of his memories was not of himself,
but of the crowd; he seemed to remember sun and heat and
people; the train was crowded and so was the hotel, the lake
steamers were packed and on the quays and in the streets you
threaded your way among the throng of holiday makers. They
were fat and old and ugly and odd, and they stank. Now, in
wartime, Lucerne was as deserted as it must have been before
the world at large discovered that Switzerland was the play-
ground of Europe. Most of the hotels were closed, the streets
were empty, the rowing boats for hire rocked idly at the water's
edge and there was none to take them, and in the avenues by
the lake the only persons to be seen were serious Swiss taking
their neutrality, like a dachshund, for a walk with them. Ashenden felt exhilarated by the solitude, and sitting down on a
bench that faced the water surrendered himself deliberately
to the sensation. It was true that the lake was absurd, the water
was too blue, the mountains too snowy, and its beauty, hitting
you in the face, exasperated rather than thrilled; but all the
same there was something pleasing in the prospect, an artless
candour, like one of Mendelssohn's *Songs Without Words*, that
made Ashenden smile with complacency. Lucerne reminded
him of wax flowers under glass cases and cuckoo clocks and
fancy work in Berlin wool. So long at all events as the fine
weather lasted he was prepared to enjoy himself. He did not
see why he should not at least try to combine pleasure to himself with profit to his country. He was travelling with a brand-
new passport in his pocket, under a borrowed name, and this
gave him an agreeable sense of owning a new personality. He
was often slightly tired of himself and it diverted him for a
while to be merely a creature of R.'s facile invention. The experience he had just enjoyed appealed to his acute sense of the
absurd. R., it is true, had not seen the fun of it: what humour
R. possessed was of a sardonic turn and he had no facility for
taking in good part a joke at his own expense. To do that you
must be able to look at yourself from the outside and be at
the same time spectator and actor in the pleasant comedy of

life. R. was a soldier and regarded introspection as unhealthy,
unenglish and unpatriotic.

Ashenden got up and strolled slowly to his hotel. It was a
small German hotel, of the second class, spotlessly clean, and
his bedroom had a nice view; it was furnished with brightly
varnished pitch-pine, and though on a cold wet day it would
have been wretched, in that warm and sunny weather it was
gay and pleasing. There were tables in the hall and he sat
down at one of these and ordered a bottle of beer. The landlady was curious to know why in that dead season he had come
to stay and he was glad to satisfy her curiosity. He told her
that he had recently recovered from an attack of typhoid and
had come to Lucerne to get back his strength. He was employed
in the Censorship Department and was taking the opportunity
to brush up his rusty German. He asked her if she could recommend to him a German teacher. The landlady was a blond and
blowsy Swiss, good-humoured and talkative, so that Ashenden
felt pretty sure that she would repeat in the proper quarter
the information he gave her. It was his turn now to ask a few
questions. She was voluble on the subject of the war on account of which the hotel, in that month so full that rooms had
to be found for visitors in neighbouring houses, was nearly
empty. A few people came in from outside to eat their meals
en pension, but she had only two lots of resident guests. One
was an old Irish couple who lived in Vevey and passed their
summers in Lucerne and the other was an Englishman and his
wife. She was a German and they were obliged on that account
to live in a neutral country. Ashenden took care to show little
curiosity about them—he recognized in the description Grantley Caypor—but of her own accord she told him that they
spent most of the day walking about the mountains. Herr
Caypor was a botanist and much interested in the flora of the
country. His lady was a very nice woman and she felt her
position keenly. Ah, well, the war could not last for ever. The
landlady bustled away and Ashenden went upstairs.

Dinner was at seven, and, wishing to be in the dining-room
before anyone else so that he could take stock of his fellow-
guests as they entered, he went down as soon as he heard the
bell. It was a very plain, stiff, whitewashed room, with chairs
of the same shiny pitchpine as in his bedroom, and on the walls
were oleographs of Swiss lakes. On each little table was a bunch
of flowers. It was all neat and clean and presaged a bad din-

ner. Ashenden would have liked to make up for it by ordering a bottle of the best Rhine-wine to be found in the hotel, but did not venture to draw attention to himself by extravagance (he saw on two or three tables half-empty bottles of table hock, which made him surmise that his fellow-guests drank thriftily, and so contented himself with ordering a pint of lager. Presently one or two persons came in, single men with some occupation in Lucerne and obviously Swiss, and sat down each at his own little table and untied the napkins that at the end of luncheon they had neatly tied up. They propped newspapers against their water-jugs and read while they somewhat noisily ate their soup. Then entered a very old tall bent man, with white hair and a drooping white moustache, accompanied by a little old white-haired lady in black. These were certainly the Irish colonel and his wife of whom the landlady had spoken. They took their seats and the colonel poured out a thimbleful of wine for his wife and a thimbleful for himself. They waited in silence for their dinner to be served to them by the buxom, hearty maid.

At last the persons arrived for whom Ashenden had been waiting. He was doing his best to read a German book and it was only by an exercise of self-control that he allowed himself only for one instant to raise his eyes as they came in. His glance showed him a man of about forty-five with short dark hair, somewhat grizzled, of middle height, but corpulent, with a broad red clean-shaven face. He wore a shirt open at the neck, with a wide collar, and a grey suit. He walked ahead of his wife, and of her Ashenden only caught the impression of a German woman self-effaced and dusty. Grantley Caypor sat down and began in a loud voice explaining to the waitress that they had taken an immense walk. They had been up some mountain the name of which meant nothing to Ashenden but which excited in the maid expressions of astonishment and enthusiasm. Then Caypor, still in fluent German but with a marked English accent, said that they were so late they had not even gone up to wash, but had just rinsed their hands outside. He had a resonant voice and a jovial manner.

"Serve me quick, we're starving with hunger, and bring beer, bring three bottles. *Lieber Gott*, what a thirst I have!"

He seemed to be a man of exuberant vitality. He brought into that dull, overclean dining-room the breath of life and everyone in it appeared on a sudden more alert. He began to talk to his wife, in English, and everything he said could be heard by all; but presently she interrupted him with a remark made in an undertone. Caypor stopped and Ashenden felt that his eyes were turned in his direction. Mrs. Caypor had noticed the arrival of a stranger and had drawn her husband's attention to it. Ashenden turned the page of the book he was pretending to read, but he felt that Caypor's gaze was fixed intently upon him. When he addressed his wife again it was in so low a tone that Ashenden could not even tell what language he used, but when the maid brought them their soup Caypor, his voice still low, asked her a question. It was plain that he was enquiring who Ashenden was. Ashenden could catch of the maid's reply but the one word *länder*.

One or two people finished their dinner and went out picking their teeth. The old Irish colonel and his old wife rose from their table and he stood aside to let her pass. They had eaten their meal without exchanging a word. She walked slowly to the door; but the colonel stopped to say a word to a Swiss who might have been a local attorney, and when she reached it she stood there, bowed and with a sheep-like look, patiently waiting for her husband to come and open it for her. Ashenden realized that she had never opened a door for herself. She did not know how to. In a minute the colonel with his old, old gait came to the door and opened it; she passed out and he followed. The little incident offered a key to their whole lives, and from it Ashenden began to reconstruct their histories, circumstances and characters; but he pulled himself up: he could not allow himself the luxury of creation. He finished his dinner.

When he went into the hall he saw tied to the leg of a table a bull-terrier and in passing mechanically put down his hand to fondle the dog's drooping, soft ears. The landlady was standing at the foot of the stairs.

"Whose is this lovely beast?" asked Ashenden.

"He belongs to Herr Caypor. Fritzi, he is called. Herr Caypor says he has a longer pedigree than the King of England."

Fritzi rubbed himself against Ashenden's leg and with his nose sought the palm of his hand. Ashenden went upstairs to fetch his hat, and when he came down saw Caypor standing at the entrance of the hotel talking with the landlady. From the sudden silence and their constrained manner he guessed that Caypor had been making enquiries about him. When he passed

between them, into the street, out of the corner of his eye
he saw Caypor give him a suspicious stare. That frank, jovial
red face bore then a look of shifty cunning.

Ashenden strolled along till he found a tavern where he
could have his coffee in the open and to compensate himself
for the bottle of beer that his sense of duty had urged him to
drink, at dinner ordered the best brandy the house provided.
He was pleased at last to have come face to face with the man
of whom he had heard so much and in a day or two hoped to
become acquainted with him. It is never very difficult to get
to know anyone who has a dog. But he was in no hurry; he
would let things take their course: with the object he had in
view he could not afford to be hasty.

Ashenden reviewed the circumstances. Grantley Caypor was
an Englishman, born according to his passport in Birmingham,
and he was forty-two years of age. His wife, to whom he had
been married for eleven years, was of German birth and parent-
age. That was public knowledge. Information about his antecedents was contained in a private document. He had started
life, according to this, in a lawyer's office in Birmingham and
then had drifted into journalism. He had been connected with
an English paper in Cairo and with another in Shanghai. There
he got into trouble for attempting to get money on false pre-
tences and was sentenced to a short term of imprisonment.
All trace of him was lost for two years after his release, when
he reappeared in a shipping-office in Marseilles. From there,
still in the shipping business, he went to Hamburg, where he
married, and to London. In London he set up for himself, in
the export business, but after some time failed and was made
a bankrupt. He returned to journalism. At the outbreak of
war he was once more in the shipping business and in August
1914 was living quietly with his German wife at Southampton.
In the beginning of the following year he told his employers
that owing to the nationality of his wife his position was intolerable; they had no fault to find with him and, recognizing
that he was in an awkward fix, granted his request that he
should be transferred to Genoa. Here he remained till Italy
entered the war, but then gave notice and with his papers
in perfect order crossed the border and took up his residence
in Switzerland.

All this indicated a man of doubtful honesty and unsettled
disposition, with no background and of no financial standing;

but the facts were of no importance to anyone till it was discovered that Caypor, certainly from the beginning of the war
and perhaps sooner, was in the service of the German Intelligence Department. He had a salary of forty pounds a month.
But though dangerous and wily no steps would have been
taken to deal with him if he had contented himself with trans-
mitting such news as he was able to get in Switzerland. He
could do no great harm there and it might even be possible to
make use of him to convey information that it was desirable to
let the enemy have. He had no notion that anything was
known of him. His letters, and he received a good many, were
closely censored; there were few codes that the people who dealt
with such matters could not in the end decipher and it might
be that sooner or later through him it would be possible to
lay hands on the organization that still flourished in England.
But then he did something that drew R.'s attention to him. Had
he known it none could have blamed him for shaking in his
shoes: R. was not a very nice man to get on the wrong side of.
Caypor scraped acquaintance in Zürich with a young Spaniard,
Gomez by name, who had lately entered the British secret
service, by his nationality inspired him with confidence, and
managed to worm out of him the fact that he was engaged in
espionage. Probably the Spaniard, with a very human desire
to seem important, had done no more than talk mysteriously;
but on Caypor's information he was watched when he went to
Germany and one day caught just as he was posting a letter
in a code that was eventually deciphered. He was tried, convicted and shot. It was bad enough to lose a useful and disinterested agent, but it entailed besides the changing of a safe
and simple code. R. was not pleased. But R. was not the man
to let any desire of revenge stand in the way of his main object and it occurred to him that if Caypor was merely betraying
his country for money it might be possible to get him to take
more money to betray his employers. The fact that he had
succeeded in delivering into their hands an agent of the Allies
must seem to them an earnest of his good faith. He might be
very useful. But R. had no notion what kind of man Caypor
was, he had lived his shabby, furtive life obscurely, and the
only photograph that existed of him was one taken for a passport. Ashenden's instructions were to get acquainted with
Caypor and see whether there was any chance that he would
work honestly for the British: if he thought there was, he was

entitled to sound him and if his suggestions were met with favour to make certain propositions. It was a task that needed tact and a knowledge of men. If on the other hand Ashenden came to the conclusion that Caypor could not be bought he was to watch and report his movements. The information he had obtained from Gustav was vague, but important; there was only one point in it that was interesting, and this was that the head of the German Intelligence Department in Berne was growing restive at Caypor's lack of activity. Caypor was asking for a higher salary and Major von P. had told him that he must earn it. It might be that he was urging him to go to England. If he could be induced to cross the frontier Ashenden's work was done.

"How the devil do you expect *me* to persuade him to put his head in a noose?" asked Ashenden.

"It won't be a noose, it'll be a firing squad," said R.

"Caypor's clever."

"Well, be cleverer, damn your eyes."

Ashenden made up his mind that he would take no steps to make Caypor's acquaintance, but allow the first advances to be made by him. If he was being pressed for results it must surely occur to him that it would be worth while to get into conversation with an Englishman who was employed in the Censorship Department. Ashenden was prepared with a supply of information that it could not in the least benefit the Central Powers to possess. With a false name and a false passport he had little fear that Caypor would guess that he was a British agent.

Ashenden did not have to wait long. Next day he was sitting in the doorway of the hotel, drinking a cup of coffee and already half asleep after a substantial *mittagessen*, when the Caypors came out of the dining-room. Mrs. Caypor went upstairs and Caypor released his dog. The dog bounded along and in a friendly fashion leaped up against Ashenden.

"Come here, Fritzi," cried Caypor, and then to Ashenden: "I'm so sorry. But he's quite gentle."

"Oh, that's all right. He won't hurt me."

Caypor stopped at the doorway.

"He's a bull-terrier. You don't often see them on the Continent." He seemed while he spoke to be taking Ashenden's measure; he called to the maid, "A coffee, please, *fräulein.* You've just arrived, haven't you?"

"Yes, I came yesterday."

"Really? I didn't see you in the dining-room last night. Are you making a stay?"

"I don't know. I've been ill and I've come here to recuperate."

The maid came with the coffee and seeing Caypor talking to Ashenden put the tray on the table at which he was sitting. Caypor gave a laugh of faint embarrassment.

"I don't want to force myself upon you. I don't know why the maid put my coffee on your table."

"Please sit down," said Ashenden.

"It's very good of you. I've lived so long on the Continent that I'm always forgetting that my countrymen are apt to look upon it as confounded cheek if you talk to them. Are you English, by the way, or American?"

"English," said Ashenden.

Ashenden was by nature a very shy person, and he had in vain tried to cure himself of a failing that at his age was unseemly, but on occasion he knew how to make effective use of it. He explained now in a hesitating and awkward manner the facts that he had the day before told the landlady and that he was convinced she had already passed on to Caypor.

"You couldn't have come to a better place than Lucerne. It's an oasis of peace in this war-weary world. When you're here you might almost forget that there is such a thing as a war going on. That is why I've come here. I'm a journalist by profession."

"I couldn't help wondering if you wrote," said Ashenden, with an eagerly timid smile.

It was clear that he had not learnt that "oasis of peace in a war-weary world" at the shipping-office.

"You see, I married a German lady," said Caypor gravely.

"Oh, really?"

"I don't think anyone could be more patriotic than I am, I'm English through and through and I don't mind telling you that in my opinion the British Empire is the greatest instrument for good that the world has ever seen, but having a German wife I naturally see a good deal of the reverse of the medal. You don't have to tell me that the Germans have faults, but frankly I'm not prepared to admit that they're devils incarnate. At the beginning of the war my poor wife had a very rough time in England and I for one couldn't have

blamed her if she'd felt rather bitter about it. Everyone
thought she was a spy. It'll make you laugh when you know
her. She's the typical German *hausfrau* who cares for nothing
but her house and her husband and our only child Fritzi."
Caypor fondled his dog and gave a little laugh. "Yes, Fritzi,
you are our child, aren't you? Naturally it made my position
very awkward, I was connected with some very important
papers, and my editors weren't quite comfortable about it.
Well, to cut a long story short I thought the most dignified
course was to resign and come to a neutral country till the
storm blew over. My wife and I never discuss the war, though
I'm bound to tell you that it's more on my account than hers,
she's much more tolerant than I am and she's more willing to
look upon this terrible business from my point of view than I
am from hers."

"That is strange," said Ashenden. "As a rule women are
so much more rabid than men."

"My wife is a very remarkable person. I should like to introduce you to her. By the way, I don't know if you know my
name. Grantley Caypor."

"My name is Somerville," said Ashenden.

He told him then of the work he had been doing in the Censorship Department, and he fancied that into Caypor's eyes
came a certain intentness. Presently he told him that he was
looking for someone to give him conversation-lessons in German so that he might rub up his rusty knowledge of the language; and as he spoke a notion flashed across his mind: he gave
Caypor a look and saw that the same notion had come to him.
It had occurred to them at the same instant that it would be
a very good plan for Ashenden's teacher to be Mrs. Caypor.

"I asked our landlady if she could find me someone and
she said she thought she could. I must ask her again. It ought
not to be very hard to find a man who is prepared to come and
talk German to me for an hour a day."

"I wouldn't take anyone on the landlady's recommendation," said Caypor. "After all you want someone with a good
north-German accent and she only talks Swiss. I'll ask my
wife if she knows anyone. My wife's a very highly educated
woman and you could trust her recommendation."

"That's very kind of you."

Ashenden observed Grantley Caypor at his ease. He noticed
how the small, grey-green eyes, which last night he had not

been able to see, contradicted the red good-humoured frankness of the face. They were quick and shifty, but when the mind behind them was seized by an unexpected notion they were suddenly still. It gave one a peculiar feeling of the working of the brain. They were not eyes that inspired confidence; Caypor did that with his jolly, good-natured smile, the openness of his broad, weather-beaten face, his comfortable obesity and the cheeriness of his loud, deep voice. He was doing his best now to be agreeable. While Ashenden talked to him, a little shyly still but gaining confidence from that breezy, cordial manner, capable of putting anyone at his ease, it intrigued him to remember that the man was a common spy. It gave a tang to his conversation to reflect that he had been ready to sell his country for no more than forty pounds a month. Ashenden had known Gomez, the young Spaniard whom Caypor had betrayed. He was a high-spirited youth, with a love of adventure, and he had undertaken his dangerous mission not for the money he earned by it, but from a passion for romance. It amused him to outwit the clumsy German and it appealed to his sense of the absurd to play a part in a shilling shocker. It was not very nice to think of him now six feet underground in a prison yard. He was young and he had a certain grace of gesture. Ashenden wondered whether Caypor had felt a qualm when he delivered him up to destruction.

"I suppose you know a little German?" asked Caypor, interested in the stranger.

"Oh, yes, I was a student in Germany, and I used to talk it fluently, but that is long ago and I have forgotten. I can still read it very comfortably."

"Oh, yes, I noticed you were reading a German book last night."

Fool! It was only a little while since he had told Ashenden that he had not seen him at dinner. He wondered whether Caypor had observed the slip. How difficult it was never to make one! Ashenden must be on his guard; the thing that made him most nervous was the thought that he might not answer readily enough to his assumed name of Somerville. Of course there was always the chance that Caypor had made the slip on purpose to see by Ashenden's face whether he noticed anything. Caypor got up.

"There is my wife. We go for a walk up one of the mountains

every afternoon. I can tell you some charming walks. The flowers even now are lovely."

"I'm afraid I must wait till I'm a bit stronger," said Ashenden, with a little sigh.

He had naturally a pale face and never looked as robust as he was. Mrs. Caypor came downstairs and her husband joined her. They walked down the road, Fritzi bounding round them, and Ashenden saw that Caypor immediately began to speak with volubility. He was evidently telling his wife the results of his interview with Ashenden. Ashenden looked at the sun shining so gaily on the lake; the shadow of a breeze fluttered the green leaves of the trees; everything invited to a stroll: he got up, went to his room and throwing himself on his bed had a very pleasant sleep.

He went into dinner that evening as the Caypors were finishing, for he had wandered melancholy about Lucerne in the hope of finding a cocktail that would enable him to face the potato salad that he foresaw, and on their way out of the dining-room Caypor stopped and asked him if he would drink coffee with them. When Ashenden joined them in the hall Caypor got up and introduced him to his wife. She bowed stiffly and no answering smile came to her face to respond to Ashenden's civil greeting. It was not hard to see that her attitude was definitely hostile. It put Ashenden at his ease. She was a plainish woman, nearing forty, with a muddy skin and vague features; her drab hair was arranged in a plait round her head like that of Napoleon's Queen of Prussia; and she was squarely built, plump rather than fat, and solid. But she did not look stupid; she looked on the contrary a woman of character and Ashenden, who had lived enough in Germany to recognize the type, was ready to believe that though capable of doing the housework, cooking the dinner and climbing a mountain, she might be also prodigiously well-informed. She wore a white blouse that showed a sunburned neck, a black skirt and heavy walking boots. Caypor addressing her in English told her in his jovial way, as though she did not know it already, what Ashenden had told him about himself. She listened grimly.

"I think you told me you understood German," said Caypor, his big red face wreathed in polite smiles but his little eyes darting about restlessly.

"Yes, I was for some time a student in Heidelberg."

"Really?" said Mrs. Caypor in English, an expression oi faint interest for a moment chasing away the sullenness from her face. "I know Heidelberg very well. I was at school there for one year."

Her English was correct, but throaty, and the mouthing emphasis she gave her words was disagreeable. Ashenden was diffuse in praise of the old university town and the beauty of the neighbourhood. She heard him, from the standpoint of her Teutonic superiority, with toleration rather than with enthusiasm.

"It is well known that the valley of the Neckar is one of the beauty places of the whole world," she said.

"I have not told you, my dear," said Caypor then, "that Mr. Somerville is looking for someone to give him conversation lessons while he is here. I told him that perhaps you could suggest a teacher."

"No, I know no one whom I could conscientiously recommend," she answered. "The Swiss accent is hateful beyond words. It could do Mr. Somerville only harm to converse with a Swiss."

"If I were in your place, Mr. Somerville, I would try and persuade my wife to give you lessons. She is, if I may say so, a very cultivated and highly educated woman."

"*Ach*, Grantley, I have not the time. I have my own work to do."

Ashenden saw that he was being given his opportunity. The trap was prepared and all he had to do was to fall in. He turned to Mrs. Caypor with a manner that he tried to make shy, deprecating and modest.

"Of course it would be too wonderful if you would give me lessons. I should look upon it as a real privilege. Naturally I wouldn't want to interfere with your work, I am just here to get well, with nothing in the world to do, and I would suit my time entirely to your convenience."

He felt a flash of satisfaction pass from one to the other and in Mrs. Caypor's blue eyes he fancied that he saw a dark glow.

"Of course it would be a purely business arrangement," said Caypor. "There's no reason that my good wife shouldn't earn a little pin-money. Would you think ten francs an hour too much?"

"No," said Ashenden, "I should think myself lucky to get a first-rate teacher for that."

"What do you say, my dear? Surely you can spare an hour, and you would be doing this gentleman a kindness. He would learn that all Germans are not the devilish fiends that they think them in England."

On Mrs. Caypor's brow was an uneasy frown and Ashenden could not but think with apprehension of that hour's conversation a day that he was going to exchange with her. Heaven only knew how he would have to rack his brain for subjects of discourse with that heavy and morose woman. Now she made a visible effort.

"I shall be very pleased to give Mr. Somerville conversation lessons."

"I congratulate you, Mr. Somerville," said Caypor noisily. "You're in for a treat. When will you start, to-morrow at eleven?"

"That would suit me very well if it suits Mrs. Caypor."

"Yes, that is as good an hour as another," she answered.

Ashenden left them to discuss the happy outcome of their diplomacy. But when, punctually at eleven next morning, he heard a knock at his door (for it had been arranged that Mrs. Caypor should give him his lesson in his room) it was not without trepidation that he opened it. It behooved him to be frank, a trifle indiscreet, but obviously wary of a German woman, sufficiently intelligent, and impulsive. Mrs. Caypor's face was dark and sulky. She plainly hated having anything to do with him. But they sat down and she began, somewhat peremptorily, to ask him questions about his knowledge of German literature. She corrected his mistakes with exactness and when he put before her some difficulty in German construction explained it with clearness and precision. It was obvious that though she hated giving him a lesson she meant to give it conscientiously. She seemed to have not only an aptitude for teaching, but a love of it, and as the hour went on she began to speak with greater earnestness. It was already only by an effort that she remembered that he was a brutal Englishman. Ashenden, noticing the unconscious struggle within her, found himself not a little entertained; and it was with truth that, when later in the day Caypor asked him how the lesson had gone, he answered that it was highly satisfactory; Mrs. Caypor was an excellent teacher and a most interesting person.

"I told you so. She's the most remarkable woman I know."

And Ashenden had a feeling that when in his hearty, laughing way Caypor said this he was for the first time entirely sincere.

In a day or two Ashenden guessed that Mrs. Caypor was giving him lessons only in order to enable Caypor to arrive at a closer intimacy with him, for she confined herself strictly to matters of literature, music and painting; and when Ashenden, by way of experiment, brought the conversation round to the war, she cut him short.

"I think that is a topic that we had better avoid, Herr Somerville," she said.

She continued to give her lessons with the greatest thoroughness, and he had his money's worth, but every day she came with the same sullen face and it was only in the interest of teaching that she lost for a moment her instinctive dislike of him. Ashenden exercised in turn, but in vain, all his wiles. He was ingratiating, ingenuous, humble, grateful, flattering, simple and timid. She remained coldly hostile. She was a fanatic. Her patriotism was aggressive, but disinterested, and obsessed with the notion of the superiority of all things German she loathed England with a virulent hatred because in that country she saw the chief obstacle to their diffusion. Her ideal was a German world in which the rest of the nations under a hegemony greater than that of Rome should enjoy the benefits of German science and German art and German culture. There was in the conception a magnificent impudence that appealed to Ashenden's sense of humour. She was no fool. She had read much, in several languages, and she could talk of the books she had read with good sense. She had a knowledge of modern painting and modern music that not a little impressed Ashenden. It was amusing once to hear her before luncheon play one of those silvery little pieces of Debussy: she played it disdainfully because it was French and so light, but with an angry appreciation of its grace and gaiety. When Ashenden congratulated her she shrugged her shoulders.

"The decadent music of a decadent nation," she said. Then with powerful hands she struck the first resounding chords of a sonata by Beethoven; but she stopped. "I cannot play, I am out of practice, and you English, what do you know of music? You have not produced a composer since Purcell!"

"What do you think of that statement?" Ashenden, smiling, asked Caypor who was standing near.

"I confess its truth. The little I know of music my wife taught me. I wish you could hear her play when she is in practice." He put his fat hand, with its square, stumpy fingers, on her shoulder. "She can wring your heartstrings with pure beauty."

"*Dummer Kerl,*" she said, in a soft voice. "Stupid fellow," and Ashenden saw her mouth for a moment quiver, but she quickly recovered. "You English, you cannot paint, you cannot model, you cannot write music."

"Some of us can at times write pleasing verses," said Ashenden, with good humour, for it was not his business to be put out, and, he did not know why, two lines occurring to him he said them:

> "*Whither, O splendid ship, thy white sails crowding,*
> *Leaning across the bosom of the urgent West.*"

"Yes," said Mrs. Caypor, with a strange gesture, "you can write poetry. I wonder why."

And to Ashenden's surprise she went on, in her guttural English, to recite the next two lines of the poem he had quoted.

"Come, Grantley, *mittagessen* is ready, let us go into the dining-room."

They left Ashenden reflective.

Ashenden admired goodness, but was not outraged by wickedness. People sometimes thought him heartless because he was more often interested in others than attached to them, and even in the few to whom he was attached his eyes saw with equal clearness the merits and the defects. When he liked people it was not because he was blind to their faults, he did not mind their faults but accepted them with a tolerant shrug of the shoulders, or because he ascribed to them excellencies that they did not possess; and since he judged his friends with candour they never disappointed him and so he seldom lost one. He asked from none more than he could give. He was able to pursue his study of the Caypors without prejudice and without passion. Mrs. Caypor seemed to him more of a piece and therefore the easier of the two to understand; she obviously detested him; though it was so necessary for her to be civil to him her antipathy was strong enough to wring from her now and then an expression of rudeness; and had she been safely able to do so she would have killed him without a qualm

But in the pressure of Caypor's chubby hand on his wife's shoulder and in the fugitive trembling of her lips Ashenden had divined that this unprepossessing woman and that mean fat man were joined together by a deep and sincere love. It was touching. Ashenden assembled the observations that he had been making for the past few days and little things that he had noticed but to which he had attached no significance returned to him. It seemed to him that Mrs. Caypor loved her husband because she was of a stronger character than he and because she felt his dependence on her; she loved him for his admiration of her, and you might guess that till she met him this dumpy, plain woman with her dullness, good sense and want of humour could not have much enjoyed the admiration of men; she enjoyed his heartiness and his noisy jokes, and his high spirits stirred her sluggish blood; he was a great big bouncing boy and he would never be anything else and she felt like a mother towards him; she had made him what he was, and he was her man and she was his woman, and she loved him, notwithstanding his weakness (for with her clear head she must always have been conscious of that), she loved him, *ach, was,* as Isolde loved Tristan. But then there was the espionage. Even Ashenden with all his tolerance for human frailty could not but feel that to betray your country for money is not a very pretty proceeding. Of course she knew of it, indeed it was probably through her that Caypor had first been approached; he would never have undertaken such work if she had not urged him to it. She loved him and she was an honest and an upright woman. By what devious means had she persuaded herself to force her husband to adopt so base and dishonourable a calling? Ashenden lost himself in a labyrinth of conjecture as he tried to piece together the actions of her mind.

Grantley Caypor was another story. There was little to admire in him, but at that moment Ashenden was not looking for an object of admiration; but there was much that was singular and much that was unexpected in that gross and vulgar fellow. Ashenden watched with entertainment the suave manner in which the spy tried to inveigle him in his toils. It was a couple of days after his first lesson that Caypor after dinner, his wife having gone upstairs, threw himself heavily into a chair by Ashenden's side. His faithful Fritzi came up to him and put his long muzzle with its black nose on his knee.

"He has no brain," said Caypor, "but a heart of gold. Look at those little pink eyes. Did you ever see anything so stupid? And what an ugly face, but what incredible charm!"

"Have you had him long?" asked Ashenden.

"I got him in 1914 just before the outbreak of war. By the way, what do you think of the news to-day? Of course my wife and I never discuss the war. You can't think what a relief to me it is to find a fellow-countryman to whom I can open my heart."

He handed Ashenden a cheap Swiss cigar and Ashenden, making a rueful sacrifice to duty, accepted it.

"Of course they haven't got a chance, the Germans," said Caypor, "not a dog's chance. I knew they were beaten the moment we came in."

His manner was earnest, sincere and confidential. Ashenden made a commonplace rejoinder.

"It's the greatest grief of my life that owing to my wife's nationality I was unable to do any war work. I tried to enlist the day war broke out, but they wouldn't have me on account of my age, but I don't mind telling you, if the war goes on much longer, wife or no wife, I'm going to do something. With my knowledge of languages I ought to be of some service in the Censorship Department. That's where you were, wasn't it?"

That was the mark at which he had been aiming and in answer now to his well-directed questions Ashenden gave him the information that he had already prepared. Caypor drew his chair a little nearer and dropped his voice.

"I'm sure you wouldn't tell me anything that anyone shouldn't know, but after all these Swiss are absolutely pro-German and we don't want to give anyone the chance of over-hearing."

Then he went on another tack. He told Ashenden a number of things that were of a certain secrecy.

"I wouldn't tell this to anybody else, you know, but I have one or two friends who are in pretty influential positions, and they know they can trust me."

Thus encouraged Ashenden was a little more deliberately indiscreet and when they parted both had reason to be satisfied. Ashenden guessed that Caypor's typewriter would be kept busy next morning and that that extremely energetic Major in Berne would shortly receive a most interesting report.

One evening, going upstairs after dinner, Ashenden passed an open bath-room. He caught sight of the Caypors.

"Come in," cried Caypor in his cordial way. "We're washing our Fritzi."

The bull-terrier was constantly getting himself very dirty, and it was Caypor's pride to see him clean and white. Ashenden went in. Mrs. Caypor with her sleeves turned up and a large white apron was standing at one end of the bath, while Caypor, in a pair of trousers and a singlet, his fat, freckled arms bare, was soaping the wretched hound.

"We have to do it at night," he said, "because the Fitzgeralds use this bath and they'd have a fit if they knew we washed the dog in it. We wait till they go to bed. Come along, Fritzi, show the gentleman how beautifully you behave when you have your face scrubbed."

The poor brute, woe-begone but faintly wagging his tail to show that however foul was this operation performed on him he bore no malice to the god who did it, was standing in the middle of the bath in six inches of water. He was soaped all over and Caypor, talking the while, shampooed him with his great fat hands.

"Oh, what a beautiful dog he's going to be when he's as white as the driven snow. His master will be as proud as Punch to walk out with him and all the little lady-dogs will say: good gracious, who's that beautiful aristocratic-looking bull-terrier walking as though he owned the whole of Switzerland? Now stand still while you have your ears washed. You couldn't bear to go out into the street with dirty ears, could you? Like a nasty little Swiss schoolboy. *Noblesse oblige.* Now the black nose. Oh, and all the soap is going into his little pink eyes and they'll smart."

Mrs. Caypor listened to this nonsense with a good-humoured sluggish smile on her broad, plain face, and presently gravely took a towel.

"Now he's going to have a ducking. Upsie-daisy."

Caypor seized the dog by the fore legs and ducked him once and ducked him twice. There was a struggle, a flurry and a splashing. Caypor lifted him out of the bath.

"Now go to mother and she'll dry you."

Mrs. Caypor sat down and taking the dog between her strong legs rubbed him till the sweat poured off her forehead. And Fritzi, a little shaken and breathless, but happy it was all over stood, with his sweet stupid face, white and shining.

"Blood will tell," cried Caypor exultantly. "He knows the names of no less than sixty-four of his ancestors, and they were all nobly born."

Ashenden was faintly troubled. He shivered a little as he walked upstairs.

Then, one Sunday, Caypor told him that he and his wife were going on an excursion and would eat their luncheon at some little mountain restaurant; and he suggested that Ashenden, each paying his share, should come with them. After three weeks at Lucerne Ashenden thought that his strength would permit him to venture the exertion. They started early, Mrs. Caypor businesslike in her walking boots and Tyrolese hat and alpenstock, and Caypor in stockings and plus-fours looking very British. The situation amused Ashenden and he was prepared to enjoy his day; but he meant to keep his eyes open; it was not inconceivable that the Caypors had discovered what he was and it would not do to go too near a precipice: Mrs. Caypor would not hesitate to give him a push and Caypor for all his jolliness was an ugly customer. But on the face of it there was nothing to mar Ashenden's pleasure in the golden morning. The air was fragrant. Caypor was full of conversation. He told funny stories. He was gay and jovial. The sweat rolled off his great red face and he laughed at himself because he was so fat. To Ashenden's astonishment he showed a peculiar knowledge of the mountain flowers. Once he went out of the way to pick one he saw a little distance from the path and brought it back to his wife. He looked at it tenderly.

"Isn't it lovely?" he cried, and his shifty grey-green eyes for a moment were as candid as a child's. "It's like a poem by Walter Savage Landor."

"Botany is my husband's favourite science," said Mrs. Caypor. "I laugh at him sometimes. He is devoted to flowers. Often when we have hardly had enough money to pay the butcher he has spent everything in his pocket to bring me a bunch of roses."

"*Qui fleurit sa maison fleurit son cœur*," said Grantley Caypor.

Ashenden had once or twice seen Caypor, coming in from a walk, offer Mrs. Fitzgerald a nosegay of mountain flowers with an elephantine courtesy that was not entirely displeasing; and what he had just learned added a certain significance to the pretty little action. His passion for flowers was genuine and when he gave them to the old Irish lady he gave her something he valued. It showed a real kindness of heart. Ashenden had always thought botany a tedious science, but Caypor, talking exuberantly as they walked along, was able to impart to it life and interest. He must have given it a good deal of study.

"I've never written a book," he said. "There are too many books already and any desire to write I have is satisfied by the more immediately profitable and quite ephemeral composition of an article for a daily paper. But if I stay here much longer I have half a mind to write a book about the wild flowers of Switzerland. Oh, I wish you'd been here a little earlier. They were marvellous. But one wants to be a poet for that, and I'm only a poor newspaper man."

It was curious to observe how he was able to combine real emotion with false fact.

When they reached the inn, with its view of the mountains and the lake, it was good to see the sensual pleasure with which he poured down his throat a bottle of ice-cold beer. You could not but feel sympathy for a man who took so much delight in simple things. They lunched deliciously off scrambled eggs and mountain trout. Even Mrs. Caypor was moved to an unwonted gentleness by her surroundings; the inn was in an agreeably rural spot, it looked like a picture of a Swiss châlet in a book of early nineteenth century travels; and she treated Ashenden with something less than her usual hostility. When they arrived she had burst into loud German exclamations on the beauty of the scene, and now, softened perhaps too by food and drink, her eyes, dwelling on the grandeur before her, filled with tears. She stretched out her hand.

"It is dreadful and I am ashamed, notwithstanding this horrible and unjust war I can feel in my heart at the moment nothing but happiness and gratitude."

Caypor took her hand and pressed it and, an unusual thing with him, addressing her in German, called her little pet-names. It was absurd, but touching. Ashenden, leaving them to their emotions, strolled through the garden and sat down on a bench that had been prepared for the comfort of the tourist. The view was of course spectacular, but it captured you; it was like a piece of music that was obvious and meretricious, but for the moment shattered your self-control.

And as Ashenden lingered idly in that spot he pondered over

the mystery of Grantley Caypor's treachery. If he liked strange
people he had found in him one who was strange beyond
belief. It would be foolish to deny that he had amiable traits.
His joviality was not assumed, he was without pretence a hearty
fellow, and he had real good nature. He was always ready to
do a kindness. Ashenden had often watched him with the old
Irish Colonel and his wife who were the only other residents of
the hotel; he would listen good-humouredly to the old man's
tedious stories of the Egyptian war, and he was charming with
her. Now that Ashenden had arrived at terms of some familiarity with Caypor he found that he regarded him less with
repulsion than with curiosity. He did not think that he had
become a spy merely for the money; he was a man of modest
tastes and what he had earned in a shipping-office must have
sufficed to so good a manager as Mrs. Caypor; and after war
was declared there was no lack of remunerative work for men
over the military age. It might be that he was one of those men
who prefer devious ways to straight for some intricate pleasure
they get in fooling their fellows; and that he had turned spy,
not from hatred of the country that had imprisoned him, not
even from love of his wife, but from a desire to score off the
big-wigs who never even knew of his existence. It might be
that it was vanity that impelled him, a feeling that his talents
had not received the recognition they merited, or just a puckish,
impish desire to do mischief. He was a crook. It is true that
only two cases of dishonesty had been brought home to him,
but if he had been caught twice it might be surmised that he
had often been dishonest without being caught. What did Mrs.
Caypor think of this? They were so united that she must be
aware of it. Did it make her ashamed, for her own uprightness
surely none could doubt, or did she accept it as an inevitable
kink in the man she loved? Did she do all she could to prevent
it or did she close her eyes to something she could not help?

How much easier life would be if people were all black or
all white and how much simpler it would be to act in regard
to them! Was Caypor a good man who loved evil or a bad man
who loved good? And how could such unreconcilable elements
exist side by side and in harmony within the same heart? For
one thing was clear, Caypor was disturbed by no gnawing of
conscience; he did his mean and despicable work with gusto.
He was a traitor who enjoyed his treachery. Though Ashenden
had been studying human nature more or less consciously all

his life, it seemed to him that he knew as little about it now in middle age as he had done when he was a child. Of course R. would have said to him: why the devil do you waste your time with such nonsense? The man's a dangerous spy and your business is to lay him by the heels.

That was true enough. Ashenden had decided that it would be useless to attempt to make any arrangement with Caypor. Though doubtless he would have no feeling about betraying his employers he could certainly not be trusted. His wife's influence was too strong. Besides, notwithstanding what he had from time to time told Ashenden, he was in his heart convinced that the Central Powers must win the war, and he meant to be on the winning side. Well, then Caypor must be laid by the heels, but how he was to effect that Ashenden had no notion. Suddenly he heard a voice.

"There you are. We've been wondering where you had hidden yourself."

He looked round and saw the Caypors strolling towards him. They were walking hand in hand.

"So this is what has kept you so quiet," said Caypor as his eyes fell on the view. "What a spot!"

Mrs. Caypor clasped her hands.

"*Ach Gott, wie schön!*" she cried. "*Wie schön.* When I look at that blue lake and those snowy mountains I feel inclined, like Goëthe's Faust, to cry to the passing moment: tarry."

"This is better than being in England with the excursions and alarums of war, isn't it?" said Caypor.

"Much," said Ashenden.

"By the way, did you have any difficulty in getting out?"

"No, not the smallest."

"I'm told they make rather a nuisance of themselves at the frontier nowadays."

"I came through without the smallest difficulty. I don't fancy they bother much about the English. I thought the examination of passports was quite perfunctory."

A fleeting glance passed between Caypor and his wife. Ashenden wondered what it meant. It would be strange if Caypor's thoughts were occupied with the chances of a journey to England at the very moment when he was himself reflecting on its possibility. In a little while Mrs. Caypor suggested that they had better be starting back and they wandered together in the shade of trees down the mountain paths.

Ashenden was watchful. He could do nothing (and his inactivity irked him) but wait with his eyes open to seize the opportunity that might present itself. A couple of days later an incident occurred that made him certain something was in the wind. In the course of his morning lesson Mrs. Caypor remarked:

"My husband has gone to Geneva to-day. He had some business to do there."

"Oh," said Ashenden, "will he be gone long?"

"No, only two days."

It is not everyone who can tell a lie and Ashenden had the feeling, he hardly knew why, that Mrs. Caypor was telling one then. Her manner perhaps was not quite as indifferent as you would have expected when she was mentioning a fact that could be of no interest to Ashenden. It flashed across his mind that Caypor had been summoned to Berne to see the redoubtable head of the German secret service. When he had the chance he said casually to the waitress:

"A little less work for you to do, *fräulein*. I hear that Herr Caypor has gone to Berne."

"Yes. But he'll be back to-morrow."

That proved nothing, but it was something to go upon. Ashenden knew in Lucerne a Swiss who was willing on emergency to do odd jobs and, looking him up, asked him to take a letter to Berne. It might be possible to pick up Caypor and trace his movements. Next day Caypor appeared once more with his wife at the dinner-table, but merely nodded to Ashenden and afterwards both went straight upstairs. They looked troubled. Caypor, as a rule so animated, walked with bowed shoulders and looked neither to the right nor to the left. Next morning Ashenden received a reply to his letter: Caypor had seen Major von P. It was possible to guess what the Major had said to him. Ashenden well knew how rough he could be: he was a hard man and a brutal, clever and unscrupulous and he was not accustomed to mince his words. They were tired of paying Caypor a salary to sit still in Lucerne and do nothing; the time was come for him to go to England. Guess-work? Of course it was guess-work, but in that trade it mostly was: you had to deduce the animal from its jaw-bone. Ashenden knew from Gustav that the Germans wanted to send someone to England. He drew a long breath; if Caypor went he would have to get busy.

When Mrs. Caypor came in to give him his lesson she was dull and listless. She looked tired and her mouth was set obstinately. It occurred to Ashenden that the Caypors had spent most of the night talking. He wished he knew what they had said. Did she urge him to go or did she try to dissuade him? Ashenden watched them again at luncheon. Something was the matter, for they hardly spoke to one another and as a rule they found plenty to talk about. They left the room early, but when Ashenden went out he saw Caypor sitting in the hall by himself.

"Hulloa," he cried jovially, but surely the effort was patent, "how are you getting on? I've been to Geneva."

"So I heard," said Ashenden.

"Come and have your coffee with me. My poor wife's got a headache. I told her she'd better go and lie down." In his shifty green eyes was an expression that Ashenden could not read. "The fact is, she's rather worried, poor dear; I'm thinking of going to England."

Ashenden's heart gave a sudden leap against his ribs, but his face remained impassive.

"Oh, are you going for long? We shall miss you."

"To tell you the truth, I'm fed up with doing nothing. The war looks as though it were going on for years and I can't sit here indefinitely. Besides, I can't afford it, I've got to earn my living. I may have a German wife, but I am an Englishman, hang it all, and I want to do my bit. I could never face my friends again if I just stayed here in ease and comfort till the end of the war and never attempted to do a thing to help the country. My wife takes her German point of view and I don't mind telling you that she's a bit upset. You know what women are."

Now Ashenden knew what it was that he saw in Caypor's eyes. Fear. It gave him a nasty turn. Caypor didn't want to go to England, he wanted to stay safely in Switzerland; Ashenden knew now what the major had said to him when he went to see him in Berne. He had got to go or lose his salary. What was it that his wife had said when he told her what had happened? He had wanted her to press him to stay, but, it was plain, she hadn't done that; perhaps he had not dared tell her how frightened he was; to her he had always been gay, bold, adventurous and devil-may-care; and now, the prisoner of his own lies, he had not found it in him to confess himself the mean and sneaking coward he was.

"Are you going to take your wife with you?" asked Ashenden.

"No, she'll stay here."

It had been arranged very neatly. Mrs. Caypor would receive his letters and forward the information they contained to Berne.

"I've been out of England so long that I don't quite know how to set about getting war-work. What would you do in my place?"

"I don't know; what sort of work are you thinking of?"

"Well, you know, I imagine I could do the same thing as you did. I wonder if there's anyone in the Censorship Department that you could give me a letter of introduction to."

It was only by a miracle that Ashenden saved himself from showing by a smothered cry or by a broken gesture how startled he was; but not by Caypor's request, by what had just dawned upon him. What an idiot he had been! He had been disturbed by the thought that he was wasting his time at Lucerne, he was doing nothing, and though in fact, as it turned out, Caypor was going to England it was due to no cleverness of his. He could take to himself no credit for the result. And now he saw that he had been put in Lucerne, told how to describe himself and given the proper information, so that what actually had occurred should occur. It would be a wonderful thing for the German secret service to get an agent into the Censorship Department; and by a happy accident there was Grantley Caypor, the very man for the job, on friendly terms with someone who had worked there. What a bit of luck! Major von P. was a man of culture and, rubbing his hands, he must surely have murmured: *stultum facit fortuna quem vult perdere*. It was a trap of that devilish R. and the grim major at Berne had fallen into it. Ashenden had done his work just by sitting still and doing nothing. He almost laughed as he thought what a fool R. had made of him.

"I was on very good terms with the chief of my department, I could give you a note to him if you liked."

"That would be just the thing."

"But of course I must give the facts. I must say I've met you here and only known you a fortnight."

"Of course. But you'll say what else you can for me, won't you?"

"Oh, certainly."

"I don't know yet if I can get a visa. I'm told they're rather fussy."

"I don't see why. I shall be very sick if they refuse me one when I want to go back."

"I'll go and see how my wife is getting on," said Caypor suddenly, getting up. "When will you let me have that letter?"

"Whenever you like. Are you going at once?"

"As soon as possible."

Caypor left him. Ashenden waited in the hall for a quarter of an hour so that there should appear in him no sign of hurry. Then he went upstairs and prepared various communications. In one he informed R. that Caypor was going to England; in another he made arrangements through Berne that wherever Caypor applied for a visa it should be granted to him without question; and these he despatched forthwith. When he went down to dinner he handed Caypor a cordial letter of introduction.

Next day but one Caypor left Lucerne.

Ashenden waited. He continued to have his hour's lesson with Mrs. Caypor and under her conscientious tuition began now to speak German with ease. They talked of Goethe and Winckelmann, of art and life and travel. Fritzi sat quietly by her chair.

"He misses his master," she said, pulling his ears. "He only really cares for him, he suffers me only as belonging to him."

After his lesson Ashenden went every morning to Cook's to ask for his letters. It was here that all communications were addressed to him. He could not move till he received instructions, but R. could be trusted not to leave him idle long; and meanwhile there was nothing for him to do but have patience. Presently he received a letter from the consul in Geneva to say that Caypor had there applied for his visa and had set out for France. Having read this Ashenden went on for a little stroll by the lake and on his way back happened to see Mrs. Caypor coming out of Cook's office. He guessed that she was having her letters addressed there too. He went up to her.

"Have you had news of Herr Caypor?" he asked her.

"No," she said. "I suppose I could hardly expect to yet."

He walked along by her side. She was disappointed, but not yet anxious; she knew how irregular at that time was the post. But next day during the lesson he could not but see that she was impatient to have done with it. The post was delivered at noon and at five minutes to she looked at her watch and him. Though Ashenden knew very well that no letter would ever come for her he had not the heart to keep her on tenter-hooks.

"Don't you think that's enough for the day? I'm sure you want to go down to Cook's," he said.

"Thank you. That is very amiable of you."

When a little later he went there himself he found her standing in the middle of the office. Her face was distraught. She addressed him wildly.

"My husband promised to write from Paris. I am sure there is a letter for me, but these stupid people say there's nothing. They're so careless, it's a scandal."

Ashenden did not know what to say. While the clerk was looking through the bundle to see if there was anything for him she came up to the desk again.

"When does the next post come in from France?" she asked.

"Sometimes there are letters about five."

"I'll come then."

She turned and walked rapidly away. Fritzi followed her with his tail between his legs. There was no doubt of it, already the fear had seized her that something was wrong. Next morning she looked dreadful; she could not have closed her eyes all night; and in the middle of the lesson she started up from her chair.

"You must excuse me, Herr Somerville, I cannot give you a lesson to-day. I am not feeling well."

Before Ashenden could say anything she had flung nervously from the room, and in the evening he got a note from her to say that she regretted that she must discontinue giving him conversation lessons. She gave no reason. Then Ashenden saw no more of her; she ceased coming in to meals; except to go morning and afternoon to Cook's she spent apparently the whole day in her room. Ashenden thought of her sitting there hour after hour with that hideous fear gnawing at her heart. Who could help feeling sorry for her? The time hung heavy on his hands too. He read a good deal and wrote a little, he hired a canoe and went for long leisurely paddles on the lake;

and at last one morning the clerk at Cook's handed him a letter. It was from R. It had all the appearance of a business communication, but between the lines he read a good deal.

Dear Sir, it began, *The goods, with accompanying letter, despatched by you from Lucerne have been duly delivered. We are obliged to you for executing our instructions with such promptness.*

It went on in this strain. R. was exultant. Ashenden guessed that Caypor had been arrested and by now had paid the penalty of his crime. He shuddered. He remembered a dreadful scene. Dawn. A cold, grey dawn, with a drizzling rain falling. A man, blindfolded, standing against a wall, an officer very pale giving an order, a volley, and then a young soldier, one of the firing-party, turning round and holding on to his gun for support, vomiting. The officer turned paler still, and he, Ashenden, feeling dreadfully faint. How terrified Caypor must have been! It was awful when the tears ran down their faces. Ashenden shook himself. He went to the ticket-office and obedient to his orders bought himself a ticket for Geneva.

As he was waiting for his change Mrs. Caypor came in. He was shocked at the sight of her. She was blowsy and dishevelled and there were heavy rings round her eyes. She was deathly pale. She staggered up to the desk and asked for a letter. The clerk shook his head.

"I'm sorry, madam, there's nothing yet."

"But look, look. Are you sure? Please look again."

The misery in her voice was heart-rending. The clerk with a shrug of the shoulders took out the letters from a pigeon-hole and sorted them once more.

"No, there's nothing, madam."

She gave a hoarse cry of despair and her face was distorted with anguish.

"Oh, God, oh, God," she moaned.

She turned away, the tears streaming from her weary eyes, and for a moment she stood there like a blind man groping and not knowing which way to go. Then a fearful thing happened. Fritzi, the bull-terrier, sat down on his haunches and threw back his head and gave a long, long melancholy howl. Mrs. Caypor looked at him with terror; her eyes seemed really to start from her head. The doubt, the gnawing doubt that had tortured her during those dreadful days of suspense, was a doubt no longer. She knew. She staggered blindly into the street.

HIS EXCELLENCY

When Ashenden was sent to X and looked about him he could not but see that his situation was equivocal. X was the capital of an important belligerent state; but a state divided against itself; there was a large party antagonistic to the war and revolution was possible if not imminent. Ashenden was instructed to see what under the circumstances could best be done; he was to suggest a policy and, if it was approved by the exalted personages who had sent him, to carry it out. A vast amount of money was put at his disposal. The ambassadors of Great Britain and the United States had been directed to afford him such facilities as were at their command, but Ashenden had been told privately to keep himself to himself; he was not to make difficulties for the official representatives of the two powers by divulging to them facts that it might be inconvenient for them to know; and since it might be necessary for him to give support under cover to a party that was at daggers drawn with that in office and with which the relations of the United States and Great Britain were extremely cordial it was just as well that Ashenden should keep his own counsel. The exalted personages did not wish the ambassadors to suffer the affront of discovering that an obscure agent had been sent to work at cross-purposes with them. On the other hand it was thought just as well to have a representative in the opposite camp, who in the event of a sudden upheaval would be at hand with adequate funds and in the confidence of the new leaders of the country.

But ambassadors are sticklers for their dignity and they have a keen nose to scent any encroachment on their authority. When Ashenden on his arrival at X paid an official call on Sir Herbert Witherspoon, the British ambassador, he was received with a politeness to which no exception could be taken, but with a frigidity that would have sent a little shiver down the spine of a polar bear. Sir Herbert was a diplomat *de carrière* and he cultivated the manner of his profession to a degree that filled the observer with admiration. He did not ask Ashenden anything about his mission because he knew that Ashenden would reply evasively, but he allowed him to see that it was a perfectly foolish one. He talked with acidulous tolerance of the exalted personages who had sent Ashenden to X. He told Ashenden that he had instructions to meet any demands for help that he made and stated that if Ashenden at any time desired to see him he had only to say so.

"I have received the somewhat singular request to despatch telegrams for you in a private code which I understand has been given to you and to hand over to you telegrams in code as they arrive."

"I hope they will be few and far between, sir," answered Ashenden. "I know nothing so tedious as coding and decoding."

Sir Herbert paused for an instant. Perhaps that was not quite the answer he expected. He rose.

"If you will come into the Chancellery I will introduce you to the Counsellor and to the Secretary to whom you can take your telegrams."

Ashenden followed him out of the room, and after handing him over to the Counsellor the ambassador gave him a limp hand to shake.

"I hope I shall have the pleasure of seeing you again one of these days," he said, and with a curt nod left him.

Ashenden bore his reception with composure. It was his business to remain in obscurity and he did not wish any official attentions to attract notice to him. But when on the afternoon of the same day he made his call at the American Embassy he discovered why Sir Herbert Witherspoon had shown him so much coldness. The American ambassador was Mr. Wilbur Schäfer; he came from Kansas City and had been given his post, when few suspected that a war was on the point of breaking out, as a reward for political services. He was a big stout man, no longer young, for his hair was white, but well-preserved and exceedingly robust. He had a square, red face, clean-shaven, with a little snub nose and a determined chin. His face was very mobile and he twisted it continually into odd and amusing grimaces. It looked as though it were made out of the red india-rubber from which they make hot-water bottles. He greeted Ashenden with cordiality. He was a hearty fellow.

"I suppose you've seen Sir Herbert. I reckon you've got his dander up. What do they mean in Washington and London by telling us to despatch your code telegrams without knowing what they're all about? You know, they've got no right to do that."

"Oh, Your Excellency, I think it was only done to save time and trouble," said Ashenden.

"Well, what is this mission anyway?"

This of course was a question that Ashenden was not prepared to answer, but not thinking it politic to say so, he determined to give a reply from which the ambassador could learn little. He had already made up his mind from the look of him that Mr. Schäfer, though doubtless possessed of the gifts that enable a man to swing a presidential election this way or that, had not, at least nakedly for all men to see, the acuteness that his position perhaps demanded. He gave you the impression of a bluff, good-humoured creature who liked good cheer. Ashenden would have been wary when playing poker with him, but where the matter in hand was concerned felt himself fairly safe. He began to talk in a loose, vague way of the world at large and before he had gone far managed to ask the ambassador his opinion of the general situation. It was the sound of the trumpet to the war-horse: Mr. Schäfer made him a speech that lasted without a break for twenty-five minutes, and when at last he stopped in exhaustion, Ashenden with warm thanks for his friendly reception was able to take his leave.

Making up his mind to give both the ambassadors a wide berth, he set about his work and presently devised a plan of campaign. But by chance he was able to do Sir Herbert Wither-spoon a good turn and so was thrown again into contact with him. It has been suggested that Mr. Schäfer was more of a politician than a diplomat, and it was his position rather than his personality that gave weight to his opinions. He looked upon the eminence to which he had risen as an opportunity to enjoy the good things of life and his enthusiasm led him to lengths that his constitution could ill support. His ignorance of foreign

affairs would in any case have made his judgment of doubtful
value, but his state at meetings of the allied ambassadors so
often approached the comatose that he seemed hardly capable
of forming a judgment at all. He was known to have succumbed
to the fascination of a Swedish lady of undoubted beauty, but
of antecedents that from the point of view of a secret service
agent were suspect. Her relations with Germany were such as
to make her sympathy with the Allies dubious. Mr. Schäfer saw
her every day and was certainly much under her influence. Now
it was noticed that there was from time to time a leakage of
very secret information and the question arose whether Mr.
Schäfer did not in these daily interviews inadvertently say
things that were promptly passed on to the headquarters of
the enemy. No one could have doubted Mr. Schäfer's honesty
and patriotism, but it was permissible to be uncertain of his
discretion. It was an awkward matter to deal with, but the
concern was as great in Washington as in London and Paris,
and Ashenden was instructed to deal with it. He had of course
not been sent to X without help to do the work he was expected
to do, and among his assistants was an astute, powerful and
determined man, a Galician Pole, named Herbartus. After con-
sultation with him it happened by one of those fortunate coin-
cidences that occasionally come about in the secret service that
a maid in the service of the Swedish lady fell ill and in her place
the Countess (for such she was) was very luckily able to engage
an extremely respectable person from the neighbourhood of
Cracow. The fact that before the war she had been secretary
to an eminent scientist made her doubtless no less competent a
housemaid.

The result of this was that Ashenden received every two
or three days a neat report upon the goings-on at this charming
lady's apartment, and though he learned nothing that could
confirm the vague suspicions that had arisen he learned something else of no little importance. From conversations held at
the cosy little *tête-à-tête* dinners that the countess gave the ambassador it appeared that his excellency was harbouring a bitter
grievance against his English colleague. He complained that
the relations between himself and Sir Herbert were deliberately
maintained on a purely official level. In his blunt way he said
he was sick of the frills that damned Britisher put on. He was a
he-man and a hundred per cent American and he had no more
use for protocol and etiquette than for a snowball in hell.

Why didn't they get together, like a couple of regular fellows, and have a good old crack? Blood was thicker than water, he'd say, and they'd do more towards winning the war by sitting down in their shirt-sleeves and talking things out over a bottle of rye than by all their diplomacy and white spats. Now it was obviously very undesirable that there should not exist between the two ambassadors a perfect cordiality, so Ashenden thought it well to ask Sir Herbert whether he might see him.

He was ushered into Sir Herbert's library.

"Well, Mr. Ashenden, what can I do for you? I hope you're quite satisfied with everything. I understand that you've been keeping the telegraph lines busy."

Ashenden, as he sat down, gave the ambassador a glance. He was beautifully dressed in a perfectly cut tail-coat that fitted his slim figure like a glove, in his black silk tie was a handsome pearl, there was a perfect line in his grey trousers, with their quiet and distinguished stripe, and his neat, pointed shoes looked as though he had never worn them before. You could hardly imagine him sitting in his shirt-sleeves over a whisky high-ball. He was a tall, thin man, with exactly the figure to show off modern clothes, and he sat in his chair, rather upright, as though he were sitting for an official portrait. In his cold and uninteresting way he was really a very handsome fellow. His neat grey hair was parted on one side, his pale face was clean-shaven, he had a delicate, straight nose and grey eyes under grey eyebrows, his mouth in youth might have been sensual and well-shaped, but now it was set to an expression of sarcastic determination and the lips were pallid. It was the kind of face that suggested centuries of good breeding, but you could not believe it capable of expressing emotion. You would never expect to see it break into the hearty distortion of laughter, but at the most be for a moment frigidly moved by an ironic smile.

Ashenden was uncommonly nervous.

"I'm afraid you'll think I'm meddling in what doesn't concern me, sir. I'm quite prepared to be told to mind my own business."

"We'll see. Pray go on."

Ashenden told his story and the ambassador listened attentively. He did not turn his cold, grey eyes from Ashenden's face, and Ashenden knew that his embarrassment was obvious.

"How did you find out all this?"

"I have means of getting hold of little bits of information that are sometimes useful," said Ashenden.

"I see."

Sir Herbert maintained his steady gaze, but Ashenden was surprised to see on a sudden in the steely eyes a little smile. The bleak, supercilious face became for an instant quite attractive.

"There is another little bit of information that perhaps you'd be good enough to give me. What does one do to be a regular fellow?"

"I am afraid one can do nothing, Your Excellency," replied Ashenden gravely. "I think it is a gift of God."

The light vanished from Sir Herbert's eyes, but his manner was slightly more urbane than when Ashenden was brought into the room. He rose and held out his hand.

"You did quite right to come and tell me this, Mr. Ashenden. I have been very remiss. It is inexcusable on my part to offend that inoffensive old gentleman. But I will do my best to repair my error. I will call at the American Embassy this afternoon."

"But not in too great state, sir, if I may venture a suggestion."

The ambassador's eyes twinkled. Ashenden began to think him almost human.

"I can do nothing but in state, Mr. Ashenden. That is one of the misfortunes of my temperament." Then as Ashenden was leaving he added: "Oh, by the way, I wonder if you'd care to come to dinner with me tomorrow night. Black tie. At eight-fifteen."

He did not wait for Ashenden's assent, but took it for granted, and with a nod of dismissal sat down once more at his great writing-table.

Ashenden looked forward with misgiving to the dinner to which Sir Herbert Witherspoon had invited him. The black tie suggested a small party, perhaps only Lady Anne, the ambassador's wife, whom Ashenden did not know, or one or two young secretaries. It did not presage a hilarious evening. It was possible that they might play bridge after dinner, but Ashenden knew that professional diplomats do not play bridge with skill: it may be supposed that they find it difficult to bend their great minds to the triviality of a parlour game. On the other hand he was interested to see a little more of the ambassador in circumstances of less formality. For it was evident that Sir Herbert Witherspoon was not an ordinary person. He was in appearance and manner a perfect specimen of his class and it is always entertaining to come upon good examples of a well-known type. He was exactly what you expected an ambassador to be. If any of his characteristics had been ever so slightly exaggerated he would have been a caricature. He escaped being ridiculous only by a hair's breadth and you watched him with a kind of breathlessness as you might watch a tight-rope dancer doing perilous feats at a dizzy height. He was certainly a man of character. His rise in the diplomatic service had been rapid and though doubtless it had helped him to be connected by marriage with powerful families his rise had been due chiefly to his merit. He knew how to be determined when determination was necessary and conciliatory when conciliation was opportune. His manners were perfect; he could speak half a dozen languages with ease and accuracy; he had a clear and logical brain. He was never afraid to think out his thoughts to the end, but was wise enough to suit his actions to the exigencies of the situation. He had reached his post at X at the early age of fifty-three and had borne himself in the exceedingly difficult conditions created by the war and contending parties within the state with tact, confidence and once at least with courage. For on one occasion a riot having arisen a band of revolutionaries forced their way into the British Embassy and Sir Herbert from the head of his stairs had harangued them and notwithstanding revolvers flourished at him had persuaded them to go to their homes. He would end his career in Paris. That was evident. He was a man whom you could not but admire but whom it was not easy to like. He was a diplomat of the school of those Victorian ambassadors to whom could confidently be entrusted great affairs and whose self-reliance, sometimes it must be admitted tinctured with arrogance, was justified by its results.

When Ashenden drove up to the doors of the Embassy they were flung open and he was received by a stout and dignified English butler and three footmen. He was ushered up that magnificent flight of stairs on which had taken place the dramatic incident just related and shown into an immense room, dimly lit with shaded lamps, in which at the first glance he caught sight of large pieces of stately furniture and over the chimney-piece an immense portrait in coronation robes of King George IV. But there was a bright fire blazing on the hearth and from a deep sofa by the side of it his host as his

name was announced slowly rose. Sir Herbert looked very
elegant as he came towards him. He wore his dinner-jacket, the
most difficult costume for a man to look well in, with incredible
distinction.

"My wife has gone to a concert, but she'll come in later.
She wants to make your acquaintance. I haven't asked anybody
else. I thought I would give myself the pleasure of enjoying
your company *en tête-à-tête.*"

Ashenden murmured a civil rejoinder, but his heart sank.
He wondered how he was going to pass at least a couple of hours
alone with this man who made him, he was bound to confess,
feel extremely shy.

The door was opened again and the butler and a footman
entered bearing very heavy silver salvers.

"I always have a glass of sherry before my dinner," said the
ambassador, "but in case you have acquired the barbarous custom of drinking cocktails I can offer you what I believe is called
a dry Martini."

Shy though he might be Ashenden was not going to give in
to this sort of thing with complete tameness.

"I move with the times," he replied. "To drink a glass of
sherry when you can get a dry Martini is like taking a stage-
coach when you can travel by the Orient Express."

A little desultory conversation after this fashion was interrupted by the throwing open of two great doors and the announcement that His Excellency's dinner was served. They
went into the dining-room. This was a vast apartment in which
sixty people might have comfortably dined, but there was now
only a small round table in it so that Sir Herbert and Ashenden
sat intimately. There was an immense mahogany sideboard
on which were massive pieces of gold plate, and above it, facing
Ashenden, was a fine picture by Canaletto. Over the chimney-
piece was a three-quarter length portrait of Queen Victoria as a
girl with a little gold crown on her small, prim head. Dinner was
served by the corpulent butler and the three very tall English
footmen. Ashenden had the impression that the ambassador
enjoyed in his well-bred way the sensation of ignoring the pomp
in which he lived. They might have been dining in one of the
great country houses of England; it was a ceremony they performed, sumptuous without ostentation, and it was saved from
a trifling absurdity only because it was in a tradition; but the
experience gained for Ashenden a kind of savour from the

thought that dwelt with him that on the other side of the wall
was a restless, turbulent population that might at any moment
break into bloody revolution, while not two hundred miles
away men in the trenches were sheltering in their dug-outs from
the bitter cold and the pitiless bombardment.

Ashenden need not have feared that the conversation would
proceed with difficulty and the notion he had had that Sir
Herbert had asked him in order to question him about his
secret mission was quickly dispelled. The ambassador behaved
to him as though he were a travelling Englishman who had
presented a letter of introduction and to whom he desired to
show civility. You would hardly have thought that a war was
raging, for he made to it only such references as showed that
he was not deliberately avoiding a distressing subject. He spoke
of art and literature, proving himself to be a diligent reader of
catholic taste, and when Ashenden talked to him, from personal
acquaintance, of the writers whom Sir Herbert knew only
through their works, he listened with the friendly condescension
which the great ones of the earth affect towards the artist.
(Sometimes, however, they paint a picture or write a book, and
then the artist gets a little of his own back.) He mentioned in
passing a character in one of Ashenden's novels, but did not
make any other reference to the fact that his guest was a writer.
Ashenden admired his urbanity. He disliked people to talk to
him of his books, in which indeed, once written, he took small
interest, and it made him self-conscious to be praised or blamed
to his face. Sir Herbert Witherspoon flattered his self-esteem by
showing that he had read him, but spared his delicacy by withholding his opinion of what he had read. He spoke too of the
various countries in which during his career he had been stationed and of various persons, in London and elsewhere, that
he and Ashenden knew in common. He talked well, not without
a pleasant irony that might very well have passed for humour,
and intelligently. Ashenden did not find his dinner dull, but
neither did he find it exhilarating. He would have been more interested if the ambassador had not so invariably said the right,
wise and sensible thing upon every topic that was introduced.
Ashenden was finding it something of an effort to keep up with
this distinction of mind and he would have liked the conversation to get into its shirt-sleeves, so to speak, and put its feet on
the table. But of this there was no chance and Ashenden once or
twice caught himself wondering how soon after dinner he could

decently take his leave. At eleven he had an appointment with
Herbartus at the Hotel de Paris.

The dinner came to an end and coffee was brought in. Sir
Herbert knew good food and good wine and Ashenden was
obliged to admit that he had fared excellently. Liqueurs were
served with the coffee, and Ashenden took a glass of brandy.

"I have some very old Benedictine," said the ambassador.
"Won't you try it?"

"To tell you the honest truth I think brandy is the only
liqueur worth drinking."

"I'm not sure that I don't agree with you. But in that case
I must give you something better than that."

He gave an order to the butler who presently brought in a
cobwebbed bottle and two enormous glasses.

"I don't really want to boast," said the ambassador as he
watched the butler pour the golden liquid into Ashenden's glass,
"but I venture to think that if you like brandy you'll like this.
I got it when I was Counsellor for a short time in Paris."

"I've had a good deal to do lately with one of your successors
there."

"Byring?"

"Yes."

"What do you think of the brandy?"

"I think it's marvellous."

"And of Byring?"

The question came so oddly on the top of the other that it
sounded faintly comic.

"Oh, I think he's a damned fool."

Sir Herbert leaned back in his chair, holding the huge glass
with both hands in order to bring out the aroma, and looked
slowly round the stately and spacious room. The table had
been cleared of superfluous things. There was a bowl of roses
between Ashenden and his host. The servants switched off the
electric light as they finally left the room and it was lit now
only by the candles that were on the table and by the fire.
Notwithstanding its size it had an air of sober comfort. The
ambassador's eyes rested on the really distinguished portrait of
Queen Victoria that hung over the chimneypiece.

"I wonder," he said at last.

"He'll have to leave the diplomatic service."

"I'm afraid so."

Ashenden gave him a quick glance of enquiry. He was the

last man from whom he would have expected sympathy for Byring.

"Yes, in the circumstances," he proceeded, "I suppose it's inevitable that he should leave the service. I'm sorry. He's an able fellow and he'll be missed. I think he had a career before him."

"Yes, that is what I've heard. I'm told that at the F.O. they thought very highly of him."

"He has many of the gifts that are useful in this rather dreary trade," said the ambassador, with a slight smile, in his cold and judicial manner. "He's handsome, he's a gentleman, he has nice manners, he speaks excellent French and he has a good head on his shoulders. He'd have done well."

"It seems a pity that he should waste such golden opportunities."

"I understand he's going into the wine business at the end of the war. Oddly enough he's going to represent the very firm from whom I got this brandy."

Sir Herbert raised the glass to his nose and inhaled the fragrance. Then he looked at Ashenden. He had a way of looking at people, when he was thinking of something else perhaps, that suggested that he thought them somewhat peculiar but rather disgusting insects.

"Have you ever seen the woman?" he asked.

"I dined with her and Byring at Larue's."

"How very interesting. What is she like?"

"Charming."

Ashenden tried to describe her to his host, but meanwhile with another part of his mind he recollected the impression she had made on him at the restaurant when Byring had introduced him to her. He had been not a little interested to meet a woman of whom for some years he had heard so much. She called herself Rose Auburn, but what her real name was few knew. She had gone to Paris originally as one of a troupe of dancers, called the Glad Girls, who performed at the Moulin Rouge, but her astonishing beauty had soon caused her to be noticed and a wealthy French manufacturer fell in love with her. He gave her a house and loaded her with jewels, but could not long meet the demands she made upon him, and she passed in rapid succession from lover to lover. She became in a short time the best known courtesan in France. Her expenditure was prodigal and she ruined her admirers with cynical unconcern. The richest men found themselves unable to cope with her extravagance. Ashenden, before the war, had seen her once at Monte Carlo lose a hundred and eighty thousand francs at a sitting and that then was an important sum. She sat at the big table, surrounded by curious onlookers, throwing down packets of thousand franc notes with a self-possession that would have been admirable if it had been her own money that she was losing.

When Ashenden met her she had been leading this riotous life, dancing and gambling all night, racing most afternoons a week, for twelve or thirteen years and she was no longer very young; but there was hardly a line on that lovely brow, scarcely a crowsfoot round those liquid eyes, to betray the fact. The most astonishing thing about her was that notwithstanding this feverish and unending round of senseless debauchery she had preserved an air of virginity. Of course she cultivated the type. She had an exquisitely graceful and slender figure, and her innumerable frocks were always made with a perfect simplicity. Her brown hair was very plainly done. With her oval face, charming little nose and large blue eyes she had all the air of one or other of Anthony Trollope's charming heroines. It was the keepsake style raised to such rareness that it made you catch your breath. She had a lovely skin, very white and red, and if she painted it was not from necessity but from wantonness. She irradiated a sort of dewy innocence that was as attractive as it was unexpected.

Ashenden had heard of course that Byring for a year or more had been her lover. Her notoriety was such that a hard light of publicity was shed on everyone with whom she had any affair, but in this instance the gossips had more to say than usual because Byring had no money to speak of and Rose Auburn had never been known to grant her favours for anything that did not in some way represent hard cash. Was it possible that she loved him? It seemed incredible and yet what other explanation was there? Byring was a young man with whom any woman might have fallen in love. He was somewhere in the thirties, very tall and good-looking, with a singular charm of manner and of an appearance so debonair that people turned round in the street to look at him; but unlike most handsome men he seemed entirely unaware of the impression he created. When it became known that Byring was the *amant de cœur* (a prettier phrase than our English fancy man) of this famous harlot he became an object of admiration to many women and of envy

to many men; but when a rumour spread abroad that he was
going to marry her consternation seized his friends and ribald
laughter everyone else. It became known that Byring's chief
had asked him if it was true and he had admitted it. Pressure
was put upon him to relinquish a plan that could only end in
disaster. It was pointed out to him that the wife of a diplomat
has social obligations that Rose Auburn could not fulfil. Byring
replied that he was prepared to resign his post whenever by so
doing he would not cause inconvenience. He brushed aside
every expostulation and every argument; he was determined to
marry.

When first Ashenden met Byring he did not very much take
to him. He found him slightly aloof. But as the hazards of his
work brought him from time to time into contact with him he
discerned that the distant manner was due merely to shyness
and as he came to know him better he was charmed by the uncommon sweetness of his disposition. Their relations, however,
remained purely official so that it was a trifle unexpected when
Byring one day asked him to dinner to meet Miss Auburn, and
he could not but wonder whether it was because already people
were beginning to turn the cold shoulder on him. When he went
he discovered that the invitation was due to the lady's curiosity.
But the surprise he got on learning that she had found time to
read (with admiration, it appeared) two or three of his novels
was not the only surprise he got that evening. Leading on the
whole a quiet and studious life he had never had occasion to
penetrate into the world of the higher prostitution and the great
courtesans of the period were known to him only by name. It
was somewhat astonishing to Ashenden to discover that Rose
Auburn differed so little in air and manner from the smart
women of Mayfair with whom through his books he had become
more or less intimately acquainted. She was perhaps a little
more anxious to please (indeed one of her agreeable traits was
the interest she took in whomever she was talking to), but she
was certainly no more made-up and her conversation was as
intelligent. It lacked only the coarseness that society has lately
affected. Perhaps she felt instinctively that those lovely lips
should never disfigure themselves with foul words; perhaps
only she was at heart still a trifle suburban. It was evident that
she and Byring were madly in love with one another. It was
really moving to see their mutual passion. When Ashenden
took his leave of them, as he shook hands with her (and she held

his hand a moment and with her blue, starry eyes looked into his) she said to him:

"You will come and see us when we're settled in London, won't you? You know we're going to be married."

"I heartily congratulate you," said Ashenden.

"And him?" she smiled, and her smile was like an angel's; it had the freshness of dawn and the tender rapture of a southern spring.

"Have you never looked at yourself in the glass?"

Sir Herbert Witherspoon watched him intently while Ashenden (he thought not without a trace of humour) described the dinner-party. No flicker of a smile brightened his cold eyes.

"Do you think it'll be a success?" he asked now.

"No."

"Why not?"

The question took Ashenden aback.

"A man not only marries his wife, he marries her friends. Do you realize the sort of people Byring will have to mix with, painted women of tarnished reputation and men who've gone down in the social scale, parasites and adventurers? Of course they'll have money, her pearls must be worth a hundred thousand pounds, and they'll be able to cut a dash in the smart Bohemia of London. Do you know the gold fringe of society? When a woman of bad character marries she earns the admiration of her set, she has worked the trick, she's caught a man and become respectable, but he, the man, only earns its ridicule. Even her own friends, the old hags with their gigolos and the abject men who earn a shabby living by introducing the unwary to tradesmen on a ten per cent commission, even they despise him. He is the mug. Believe me, to conduct yourself gracefully in such a position you need either great dignity of character or an unparalleled effrontery. Besides, do you think there's a chance of its lasting? Can a woman who's led that wild career settle down to domestic life? In a little while she'll grow bored and restless. And how long does love last? Don't you think Byring's reflections will be bitter when, caring for her no longer, he compares what he is with what he might have been?"

Witherspoon helped himself to another drop of his old brandy. Then he looked up at Ashenden with a curious expression.

"I'm not sure if a man isn't wiser to do what he wants very

much to do and let the consequences take care of themselves."

"It must be very pleasant to be an ambassador," said Ashenden.

Sir Herbert smiled thinly.

"Byring rather reminds me of a fellow I knew when I was a very junior clerk at the F.O. I won't tell you his name because he's by way of being very well-known now and highly respected. He's made a great success of his career. There is always something a little absurd in success."

Ashenden slightly raised his eyebrows at this statement, somewhat unexpected in the mouth of Sir Herbert Witherspoon, but did not say anything.

"He was one of my fellow clerks. He was a brilliant creature, I don't think anyone ever denied that, and everyone prophesied from the beginning that he would go far. I venture to say that he had pretty well all the qualifications necessary for a diplomatic career. He was of a family of soldiers and sailors, nothing very grand, but eminently respectable, and he knew how to behave in the great world without bumptiousness or timidity. He was well-read. He took an interest in painting. I dare say he made himself a trifle ridiculous; he wanted to be in the movement, he was very anxious to be modern, and at a time when little was known of Gauguin and Cézanne he raved over their pictures. There was perhaps a certain snobbishness in his attitude, a desire to shock and astonish the conventional, but at heart his admiration of the arts was genuine and sincere. He adored Paris and whenever he had the chance ran over and put up at a little hotel in the Latin Quarter where he could rub shoulders with painters and writers. As is the habit with gentry of that sort they patronized him a little because he was nothing but a diplomat and laughed at him a little because he was evidently a gentleman. But they liked him because he was always ready to listen to their speeches, and when he praised their works they were even willing to admit that, though a philistine, he had a certain instinct for the Right Stuff."

Ashenden noted the sarcasm and smiled at the fling at his own profession. He wondered what this long description was leading to. The ambassador seemed to linger over it partly because he liked it, but also because for some reason he hesitated to come to the point.

"But my friend was modest. He enjoyed himself enormously and he listened open-mouthed when these young painters and unknown scribblers tore to pieces established reputations and talked with enthusiasm of persons of whom the sober but cultured secretaries in Downing Street had never even heard. At the back of his mind he knew that they were rather a common, second-rate lot, and when he went back to his work in London it was with no regret, but with the feeling that he had been witnessing an odd and diverting play; now the curtain had fallen he was quite ready to go home. I haven't told you that he was ambitious. He knew that his friends expected him to do considerable things and he had no notion of disappointing them. He was perfectly conscious of his abilities. He meant to succeed. Unfortunately he was not rich, he had only a few hundreds a year, but his father and mother were dead and he had neither brother nor sister. He was aware that this freedom from close ties was an asset. His opportunity to make connections that would be of use to him was unrestricted. Do you think he sounds a very disagreeable young man?"

"No," said Ashenden in answer to the sudden question. "Most clever young men are aware of their cleverness, and there is generally a certain cynicism in their calculations with regard to the future. Surely young men should be ambitious."

"Well, on one of these little trips to Paris my friend became acquainted with a talented young Irish painter called O'Malley. He's an R.A. now and paints highly paid portraits of Lord Chancellors and Cabinet Ministers. I wonder if you remember one he did of my wife, which was exhibited a couple of years ago."

"No, I don't. But I know his name."

"My wife was delighted with it. His art always seems to me very refined and agreeable. He's able to put on canvas the distinction of his sitters in a very remarkable way. When he paints a woman of breeding you know that it is a woman of breeding and not a trollop."

"It is a charming gift," said Ashenden. "Can he also paint a slut and make her look like one?"

"He could. Now doubtless he would scarcely wish to. He was living then in a small and dirty studio in the rue du Cherche Midi with a little Frenchwoman of the character you describe and he painted several portraits of her which were extremely like."

It seemed to Ashenden that Sir Herbert was going into somewhat excessive detail, and he asked himself whether the friend of whom he was telling a story that till now seemed to lead no whither was in point of fact himself. He began to give it more of his attention.

"My friend liked O'Malley. He was good company, the type of the agreeable rattle, and he had a truly Irish gift of the gab. He talked incessantly and in my friend's opinion brilliantly. He found it very amusing to go and sit in the studio while O'Malley was painting and listen to him chattering away about the technique of his art. O'Malley was always saying that he would paint a portrait of him and his vanity was tickled. O'Malley thought him—far from plain and said it would do him good to exhibit the portrait of someone who at least looked like a gentleman."

"By the way, when was all this?" asked Ashenden.

"Oh, thirty years ago. . . . They used to talk of their future and when O'Malley said the portrait he was going to paint of my friend would look very well in the National Portrait Gallery, my friend had small doubt in the back of his mind, whatever he modestly said, that it would eventually find its way there. One evening when my friend—shall we call him Brown?— was sitting in the studio and O'Malley, desperately taking advantage of the last light of day, was trying to get finished for the Salon that portrait of his mistress which is now in the Tate Gallery, O'Malley asked him if he would like to come and dine with them. He was expecting a friend of hers, she was called Yvonne by the way, and he would be glad if Brown would make a fourth. This friend of Yvonne's was an acrobat and O'Malley was anxious to get her to pose for him in the nude. Yvonne said she had a marvellous figure. She had seen O'Malley's work and was willing enough to sit and dinner was to be devoted to settling the matter. She was not performing then, but was about to open at the Gaîtés Montparnasses and with her days free was not disinclined to oblige a friend and earn a little money. The notion amused Brown, who had never met an acrobat, and he accepted. Yvonne suggested that he might find her to his taste and if he did she could promise him that he would not find her very difficult to persuade. With his grand air and English clothes she would take him for a *milord anglais*. My friend laughed. He did not take the suggestion very seriously. "*On ne sait jamais*," he said. Yvonne looked at him with mischievous eyes. He sat on. It was Easter time and cold, but the studio was comfortably warm, and though it was small and everything was higgledy-piggledy and the dust lay heavy on the rim of the window, it was most friendly and cosy. Brown had a tiny flat in Waverton Street, in London, with very good mezzotints on the walls and several pieces of early Chinese pottery here and there, and he wondered to himself why his tasteful sitting-room had none of the comforts of home nor the romance that he found in that disorderly studio.

"Presently there was a ring at the door and Yvonne ushered in her friend. Her name, it appeared, was Alix and she shook hands with Brown, uttering a stereotyped phrase, with the mincing politeness of a fat woman in a *bureau de tabac*. She wore a long cloak in imitation mink and an enormous scarlet hat. She looked incredibly vulgar. She was not even pretty. She had a broad flat face, a wide mouth and an upturned nose. She had a great deal of hair, golden, but obviously dyed, and large china-blue eyes. She was heavily made-up."

Ashenden began to have no doubt that Witherspoon was narrating an experience of his own, for otherwise he could never have remembered after thirty years what hat the young woman wore and what coat, and he was amused at the ambassador's simplicity in thinking that so thin a subterfuge could disguise the truth. Ashenden could not but guess how the story would end and it tickled him to think that this cold, distinguished and exquisite person should ever have had anything like an adventure.

"She began to talk away to Yvonne and my friend noticed that she had one feature that oddly enough he found very attractive: she had a deep and husky voice as though she were just recovering from a bad cold and, he didn't know why, it seemed to him exceedingly pleasant to listen to. He asked O'Malley if that was her natural voice and O'Malley said she had it as long as ever he had known her. He called it a whisky voice. He told her what Brown said about it and she gave him a smile of her wide mouth and said it wasn't due to drink, it was due to standing so much on her head. That was one of the inconveniences of her profession. Then the four of them went to a beastly little restaurant off the boulevard St. Michel where for two francs fifty including wine my friend ate a dinner that seemed to him more delicious than any he had ever eaten at the Savoy or Claridge's. Alix was a very chatty young person and Brown listened with amusement, with amazement even, while in her rich, throaty voice she talked of the varied incidents of the day. She had a great command of slang and though he could not understand half of it he was immensely tickled with its picturesque vulgarity. It was pungent of the heated asphalt, the zinc bars of cheap taverns and racy of the crowded squares in the poorer districts of Paris. There was an energy in those apt and vivid metaphors that went like champagne to his anæmic head. She was a guttersnipe, yes, that's what she was, but she had a vitality that warmed you like a blazing fire. He was conscious that Yvonne had told her that he was an unattached Englishman, with plenty of money; he saw the appraising glance she gave him and then, pretending that he had noticed nothing, he caught the phrase, *il n'est pas mal.* It faintly amused him: he had a notion himself that he was not so bad. There were places, indeed, where they went further than that. She did not pay much attention to him, in point of fact they were talking of things of which he was ignorant and he could do little more than show an intelligent interest, but now and again she gave him a long look, passing her tongue quickly round her lips, that suggested to him that he only had to ask for her to give. He shrugged a mental shoulder. She looked healthy and young, she had an agreeable vivacity, but beyond her husky voice there was nothing particularly attractive in her. But the notion of having a little affair in Paris did not displease him, it was life, and the thought that she was a music-hall artiste was mildly diverting: in middle age it would doubtless amuse him to remember that he had enjoyed the favours of an acrobat. Was it la Rochefaucauld or Oscar Wilde who said that you should commit errors in youth in order to have something to regret in old age? At the end of dinner (and they sat over their coffee and brandy till late) they went out into the street and Yvonne proposed that he should take Alix home. He said he would be delighted. Alix said it was not far and they walked. She told him that she had a little apartment, of course mostly she was on tour, but she liked to have a place of her own, a woman, you know, had to be in her furniture, without that she received no consideration; and presently they reached a shabby house in a bedraggled street. She rang the bell for the *concièrge* to open the door. She did not press him to enter. He did not know if she looked upon it as a matter of course. He was seized with timidity. He racked his brains, but could not think of a single thing to say. Silence fell upon them. It was absurd. With a little click the door opened; she looked at him expectantly;

she was puzzled; a wave of shyness swept over him. Then she held out her hand, thanked him for bringing her to the door, and bade him goodnight. His heart beat nervously. If she had asked him to come in he would have gone. He wanted some sign that she would like him to. He shook her hand, said goodnight, raised his hat and walked away. He felt a perfect fool. He could not sleep; he tossed from side to side of his bed, thinking for what a noodle she must take him, and he could hardly wait for the day that would permit him to take steps to efface the contemptible impression he must have made on her. His pride was lacerated. Wanting to lose no time he went round to her house at eleven to ask her to lunch with him, but she was out; he sent round some flowers and later in the day called again. She had been in, but was gone out once more. He went to see O'Malley on the chance of finding her, but she was not there, and O'Malley facetiously asked him how he had fared. To save his face he told him that he had come to the conclusion that she did not mean very much to him and so like a perfect gentleman he had left her. But he had an uneasy feeling that O'Malley saw through his story. He sent her a *pneumatique* asking her to dine with him next day. She did not answer. He could not understand it, he asked the porter of his hotel a dozen times if there was nothing for him, and at last, almost in desperation, just before dinner went to her house. The *concièrge* told him she was in and he went up. He was very nervous, inclined to be angry because she had treated his invitation so cavalierly, but at the same time anxious to appear at his ease. He climbed the four flights of stairs, dark and smelly, and rang at the door to which he had been directed. There was a pause, he heard sounds within and rang again. Presently she opened. He had an absolute certitude that she did not in the least know who he was. He was taken aback, it was a blow to his vanity; but he assumed a cheerful smile.

"'I came to find out if you were going to dine with me to-night. I sent you a *pneumatique*.'

"Then she recognized him. But she stood at the door and did not ask him in.

"'Oh, no, I can't dine with you to-night. I have terrible megrim and I am going to bed. I couldn't answer your *pneumatique*, I mislaid it, and I'd forgotten your name. Thank you for the flowers. It was nice of you to send them.'

"'Then won't you come and dine with me to-morrow night?'

"'*Justement*, I have an engagement to-morrow night. I'm sorry.'

"'There was nothing more to say. He had not the nerve to ask her to anything else and so bade her goodnight and went. He had the impression that she was not vexed with him, but that she had entirely forgotten him. It was humiliating. When he went back to London, without having seen her again, it was with a curious sense of dissatisfaction. He was not in the least in love with her, he was annoyed with her, but he could not get her quite out of his mind. He was honest enough to realize that he was suffering from nothing more than wounded vanity.

"During that dinner at the little restaurant off the Boul' Mich' she had mentioned that her troupe was going to London in the spring and in one of his letters to O'Malley he slipped in casually a phrase to the effect that if his young friend Alix happened to be coming to town he (O'Malley) might let him know and he would look her up. He would like to hear from her own ingenuous lips what she thought of the nude O'Malley had painted of her. When the painter some time afterwards wrote and told him that she was appearing a week later at the Metropolitan in the Edgware Road he felt a sudden rush of blood to his head. He went to see her play. If he had not taken the precaution to go earlier in the day and look at the programme he would have missed her, for her turn was the first on the list. There were two men, a stout one and a thin one, with large black moustaches, and Alix. They were dressed in ill-fitting pink tights with green satin trunks. The men did various exercises on twin trapezes while Alix tripped about the stage, giving them handkerchiefs to wipe their hands on, and occasionally turned a somersault. When the fat man raised the thin one on his shoulders she climbed up and stood on the shoulders of the second kissing her hand to the audience. They did tricks with safety bicycles. There is often grace, and even beauty, in the performance of clever acrobats, but this one was so crude, so vulgar that my friend felt positively embarrassed. There is something shameful in seeing grown men publicly make fools of themselves. Poor Alix, with a fixed and artificial smile on her lips, in her pink tights and green satin trunks, was so grotesque that he wondered how he could have let himself feel a moment's annoyance because when he went to her apartment she had not recognized him. It was with a shrug of the shoulders, condescendingly, that he went round to the stage door afterwards and gave the doorkeeper a shilling to take her his card. In a few minutes she came out. She seemed delighted to see him.

"'Oh, how good it is to see the face of someone you know in this sad city,' she said. 'Ah, now you can give me that dinner you asked me to in Paris. I'm dying of hunger. I never eat before the show. Imagine that they should have given us such a bad place on the programme. It's an insult. But we shall see the agent to-morrow. If they think they can put upon us like that they are mistaken. *Ah, non, non et non!* And what an audience! No enthusiasm, no applause, nothing.'

"My friend was staggered. Was it possible that she took her performance seriously? He almost burst out laughing. But she still spoke with that throaty voice that had such a queer effect on his nerves. She was dressed all in red and wore the same red hat in which he had first seen her. She looked so flashy that he did not fancy the notion of asking her to a place where he might be seen and so suggested Soho. There were hansoms still in those days and the hansom was more conducive to love-making, I imagine, than is the taxi of the present time. My friend put his arm round Alix's waist and kissed her. It left her calm, but on the other hand did not wildly excite him. While they ate a late dinner he made himself very gallant and she played up to him agreeably; but when they got up to go and he proposed that she should come round to his rooms in Waverton Street she told him that a friend had come over from Paris with her and that she had to meet him at eleven: she had only been able to dine with Brown because her companion had a business engagement. Brown was exasperated, but did not want to show it, and when, as they walked down Wardour Street, (for she said she wanted to go to the Café Monico), pausing in front of a pawnbroker's to look at the jewellery in the window, she went into ecstasies over a bracelet of sapphires and diamonds that Brown thought incredibly vulgar, he asked her if she would like it.

"'But it's marked fifteen pounds,' she said.

"He went in and bought it for her. She was delighted. She made him leave her just before they came to Piccadilly Circus.

"'Now listen, *mon petit*,' she said, 'I cannot see you in London because of my friend, he is jealous as a wolf, that is why I think it is more prudent for you to go now, but I am playing at Boulogne next week, why do you not come over? I shall be alone there. My friend has to go back to Holland where he lives.'

"'All right,' said Brown, 'I'll come.'

"When he went to Boulogne—he had two days' leave—it was with the one idea of salving the wound to his pride. It was odd that he should care. I daresay to you it seems inexplicable. He could not bear the notion that Alix looked upon him as a fool and he felt that when once he had removed that impression from her he would never bother about her again. He thought of O'Malley too, and Yvonne. She must have told them and it galled him to think that people whom in his heart he despised should laugh at him behind his back. Do you think he was very contemptible?"

"Good gracious, no," said Ashenden. "All sensible people know that vanity is the most devastating, the most universal and the most ineradicable of the passions that afflict the soul of man, and it is only vanity that makes him deny its power. It is more consuming than love. With advancing years, mercifully, you can snap your fingers at the terror and the servitude of love, but age cannot free you from the thraldom of vanity. Time can assuage the pangs of love, but only death can still the anguish of wounded vanity. Love is simple and seeks no subterfuge, but vanity cozens you with a hundred disguises. It is part and parcel of every virtue: it is the mainspring of courage and the strength of ambition; it gives constancy to the lover and endurance to the stoic; it adds fuel to the fire of the artist's desire for fame and is at once the support and the compensation of the honest man's integrity; it leers even cynically in the humility of the saint. You cannot escape it, and should you take pains to guard against it, it will make use of those very pains to trip you up. You are defenceless against its onslaught because you know not on what unprotected side it will attack you. Sincerity cannot protect you from its snare nor humour from its mockery."

Ashenden stopped, not because he had said all he had to say, but because he was out of breath. He noticed also that the ambassador, desiring to talk rather than to listen, heard him with a politeness that was strained. But he had made this speech not so much for his host's edification as for his own entertainment.

"It is vanity finally that makes man support his abominable lot."

For a minute Sir Herbert was silent. He looked straight in front of him as though his thoughts lingered distressfully on some far horizon of memory.

"When my friend came back from Boulogne he knew that he was madly in love with Alix and he had arranged to meet her again in a fortnight's time when she would be performing at Dunkirk. He thought of nothing else in the interval and the night before he was to start, he only had thirty-six hours this time, he could not sleep so devouring was the passion that consumed him. Then he went over for a night to Paris to see her and once when she was disengaged for a week he persuaded her to come to London. He knew that she did not love him. He was just a man among a hundred others and she made no secret of the fact that he was not her only lover. He suffered agonies of jealousy but knew that it would only excite her ridicule or her anger if he showed it. She had not even a fancy for him. She liked him because he was a gentleman and well-dressed. She was quite willing to be his mistress so long as the claims he made on her were not irksome. But that was all. His means were not large enough to enable him to make her any serious offers, but even if they had been, liking her freedom, she would have refused."

"But what about the Dutchman?" asked Ashenden.

"The Dutchman? He was a pure invention. She made him up on the spur of the moment because for one reason or another she did not just then want to be bothered with Brown. What should one lie more or less matter to her? Don't think he didn't struggle against his passion. He knew it was madness; he knew that a permanent connection between them could only lead to disaster for him. He had no illusions about her: she was common, coarse and vulgar. She could talk of none of the things that interested him, nor did she try, she took it for granted that he was concerned with her affairs and told him interminable stories of her quarrels with fellow performers, her disputes with managers and her wrangles with hotel-keepers. What she said bored him to death, but the sound of her throaty voice made his heart beat so that sometimes he thought he would suffocate."

Ashenden sat uneasily in his chair. It was a Sheraton chair very good to look at, but hard and straight; and he wished that Sir Herbert had had the notion of going back to the other room where there was a comfortable sofa. It was quite plain now that the story he was telling was about himself and Ashenden felt a certain indelicacy in the man's stripping his soul before him so nakedly. He did not desire this confidence to be forced upon him. Sir Herbert Witherspoon meant nothing to him. By the light of the shaded candles Ashenden saw that he was deathly pale and there was a wildness in his eyes that in that cold and composed man was strangely disconcerting. He poured himself out a glass of water; his throat was dry so that he could hardly speak. But he went on pitilessly.

"At last my friend managed to pull himself together. He was disgusted by the sordidness of his intrigue; there was no beauty in it, nothing but shame; and it was leading to nothing. His passion was as vulgar as the woman for whom he felt it. Now it happened that Alix was going to spend six months in the North of Africa with her troupe and for that time at least it would be impossible for him to see her. He made up his mind that he must seize the opportunity and make a definite break. He knew bitterly that it would mean nothing to her. In three weeks she would have forgotten him.

"And then there was something else. He had come to know very well some people, a man and his wife, whose social and political connections were extremely important. They had an only daughter and, I don't know why, she fell in love with him. She was everything that Alix was not, pretty in the real English way, with blue eyes and pink and white cheeks, tall and fair; she might have stepped out of one of du Maurier's pictures in *Punch*. She was clever and well-read, and since she had lived all her life in political circles she could talk intelligently of the sort of things that interested him. He had reason to believe that if he asked her to marry him she would accept. I have told you that he was ambitious. He knew that he had great abilities and he wanted the chance to use them. She was related to some of the greatest families in England and he would have been a fool not to realize that a marriage of this kind must make his path infinitely easier. The opportunity was golden. And what a relief to think that he could put behind him definitely that ugly little episode, and what a happiness, instead of that wall of cheerful indifference and matter of fact good nature against which in his passion for Alix he had vainly battered his head, what a happiness to feel that to someone else he really meant something! How could he help being flattered and touched when he saw her face light up as he came into the room? He wasn't in love with her, but he thought her charming, and he wanted to forget Alix and the vulgar life into which she had led him. At last he made up his mind. He asked her to marry him and was accepted. Her family was delighted. The marriage was to take place in the autumn, since her father had to go on some political errand to South America and was taking his wife and daughter with him. They were to be gone the whole summer. My friend Brown was transferring from the F.O. to the diplomatic service and had been promised a post at Lisbon. He was to go there immediately.

"He saw his *fiancée* off. Then it happened that owing to some hitch the man whom Brown was going to replace was kept at Lisbon three months longer and so for that period my friend found himself at a loose end. And just when he was making up his mind what to do with himself he received a letter from Alix. She was coming back to France and had a tour booked; she gave him a long list of the places she was going to, and in her casual, friendly way said that they would have fun if he could manage to run over for a day or two. An insane, a criminal notion seized him. If she had shown any eagerness for him to come he might have resisted, it was her airy, matter-of-fact indifference that took him. On a sudden he longed for her. He did not care if she was gross and vulgar, he had got her in his bones, and it was his last chance. In a little while he was going to be married. It was now or never. He went down to Marseilles and met her as she stepped off the boat that had brought her from Tunis. His heart leaped at the pleasure she showed on seeing him. He knew he loved her madly. He told her that he was going to be married in three months and asked her to spend the last of his freedom with him. She refused to abandon her tour. How could she leave her companions in the lurch? He offered to compensate them, but she would not hear of it; they could not find someone to take her place at a moment's notice, nor could they afford to throw over a good engagement that might lead to others in the future; they were honest people, and they kept their word, they had their duty to their managers and their duty to their public. He was exasperated; it seemed absurd that his whole happiness should be sacrificed to that wretched tour. And at the end of the three months? What was to happen to her then? Oh, no, he was asking something that wasn't reasonable. He told her that he adored her. He did not know till then how insanely he loved her. Well, then, she said, why did he not come with her and make the tour with them? She would be glad of his company; they could have a good time together and at the end of three months he could go and marry his heiress and neither of them would be any the worse. For a moment he hesitated, but now that he saw her again he could not bear the thought of being parted from her so soon. He accepted. And then she said:

"'But listen, my little one, you mustn't be silly, you know. The managers won't be too pleased with me if I make a lot of *chichi*, I have to think of my future, and they won't be so anxious to have me back if I refuse to please old customers of the house. It won't be very often, but it must be understood that you are not to make me scenes if now and then I give myself to someone whose fancy I take. It will mean nothing, that is business, you will be my *amant de cœur*.'

"He felt a strange, excruciating pain in his heart, and I think he went so pale that she thought he was going to faint. She looked at him curiously.

"'Those are the terms,' she said. 'You can either take them or leave them.'

"He accepted."

Sir Herbert Witherspoon leaned forward in his chair and he was so white that Ashenden thought too that he was going to faint. His skin was drawn over his skull so that his face looked like a death's head, but the veins on his forehead stood out like knotted cords. He had lost all reticence. And Ashenden once more wished that he would stop, it made him shy and nervous to see the man's naked soul: no one has the right to show himself to another in that destitute state. He was inclined to cry:

"Stop, stop. You mustn't tell me any more. You'll be so ashamed."

But the man had lost all shame.

"For three months they travelled together from one dull provincial town to another, sharing a filthy little bedroom in frousy hotels; Alix would not let him take her to good hotels, she said she had not the clothes for them and she was more comfortable in the sort of hotel she was used to; she did not want her companions in the business to say that she was putting on side. He sat interminable hours in shabby cafés. He was treated as a brother by members of the troupe, they called him by his Christian name and chaffed him coarsely and slapped

him on the back. He ran errands for them when they were busy
with their work. He saw the good-humoured contempt in the
eyes of managers and was obliged to put up with the familiarity
of stage-hands. They travelled third-class from place to place
and he helped to carry the luggage. He with whom reading was
a passion never opened a book because Alix was bored by reading and thought that anyone who did was just giving himself
airs. Every night he went to the music-hall and watched her go
through that grotesque and ignoble performance. He had to fall
in with her pathetic fancy that it was artistic. He had to congratulate her when it had gone well and condole with her when
some feat of agility had gone amiss. When she had finished he
went to a café and waited for her while she changed, and sometimes she would come in rather hurriedly and say:

"'Don't wait for me to-night, *mon chou*, I'm busy.'

"And then he would undergo agonies of jealousy. He would
suffer as he never knew a man could suffer. She would come
back to the hotel at three or four in the morning. She wondered
why he was not asleep. Sleep! How could he sleep with that
misery gnawing at his heart? He had promised he would not
interfere with her. He did not keep his promise. He made her
terrific scenes. Sometimes he beat her. Then she would lose
her patience and tell him she was sick of him, she would pack
her things to go, and then he would go grovelling to her, promising anything, any submission, vowing to swallow any humiliation, if she would not leave him. It was horrible and degrading.
He was miserable. Miserable? No, he was happier than he'd
ever been in his life. It was the gutter that he wallowed in,
but he wallowed in it with delight. Oh, he was so bored with the
life he'd led hitherto, and this one seemed to him amazing and
romantic. This was reality. And that frousy, ugly woman with
the whisky voice, she had such a splendid vitality, such a zest
for life that she seemed to raise his own to some more vivid level.
It really did seem to him to burn with a pure, gem-like flame.
Do people still read Pater?"

"I don't know," said Ashenden. "I don't."

"There was only three months of it. Oh, how short the time
seemed and how quickly the weeks sped by! Sometimes he had
wild dreams of abandoning everything and throwing in his lot
with the acrobats. They had come to have quite a liking for him
and they said he could easily train himself to take a part in the
turn. He knew they said it more in jest than in earnest, but the

notion vaguely tickled him. But these were only dreams and he knew that nothing would come of them. He never really chaffered with the thought that when the three months came to an end he would not return to his own life with its obligations. With his mind, that cold, logical mind of his, he knew it would be absurd to sacrifice everything for a woman like Alix; he was ambitious, he wanted power; and besides, he could not break the heart of that poor child who loved and trusted him. She wrote to him once a week. She was longing to get back, the time seemed endless to her and he, he had a secret wish that something would happen to delay her arrival. If he could only have a little more time! Perhaps if he had six months he would have got over his infatuation. Already sometimes he hated Alix.

"The last day came. They seemed to have little to say to one another. They were both sad; but he knew that Alix only regretted the breaking of an agreeable habit, in twenty-four hours she would be as gay and full of spirits with her stray companions as though he had never crossed her path; he could only think that next day he was going to Paris to meet his *fiancée* and her family. They spent their last night in one another's arms weeping. If she'd asked him then not to leave her it may be that he would have stayed; but she didn't, it never occurred to her, she accepted his going as a settled thing, and she wept not because she loved him, she wept because he was unhappy.

"In the morning she was sleeping so soundly that he had not the heart to wake her to say good-bye. He slipped out very quietly, with his bag in his hand, and took the train to Paris."

Ashenden turned away his head for he saw two tears form themselves in Witherspoon's eyes and roll down his cheeks. He did not even try to hide them. Ashenden lit another cigar.

"In Paris they cried out when they saw him. They said he looked like a ghost. He told them he'd been ill and hadn't said anything about it in order not to worry them. They were very kind. A month later he was married. He did very well for himself. He was given opportunities to distinguish himself and he distinguished himself. His rise was spectacular. He had the well-ordered and distinguished establishment that he had wanted. He had the power for which he had craved. He was loaded with honours. Oh, he made a success of life and there were hundreds who envied him. It was all ashes. He was bored, bored to distraction, bored by that distinguished, beautiful lady he had married, bored by the people his life forced him to live with; it was a comedy he was playing and sometimes it seemed intolerable to live for ever and ever behind a mask; sometimes he felt he couldn't bear it. But he bore it. Sometimes he longed for Alix so fiercely that he felt it would be better to shoot himself than to suffer such anguish. He never saw her again. Never. He heard from O'Malley that she had married and left her troupe. She must be a fat old woman now and it doesn't matter any more. But he had wasted his life. And he never even made that poor creature whom he married happy. How could he go on hiding from her year after year that he had nothing to give her but pity? Once in his agony he told her about Alix and she tortured him ever after with her jealousy. He knew that he should never have married her; in six months she would have got over her grief if he had told her he could not bear it, and in the end would have happily married somebody else. So far as she was concerned his sacrifice was vain. He was terribly conscious that he had only one life and it seemed so sad to think that he had wasted it. He could never surmount his immeasurable regret. He laughed when people spoke of him as a strong man: he was as weak and unstable as water. And that's why I tell you that Byring is right. Even though it only lasts five years, even though he ruins his career, even though this marriage of his ends in disaster, it will have been worth while. He will have been satisfied. He will have fulfilled himself."

At that moment the door opened and a lady came in. The ambassador glanced at her and for an instant a look of cold hatred crossed his face, but it was only for an instant; then, rising from the table, he composed his ravaged features to an expression of courteous suavity. He gave the incomer a haggard smile.

"Here is my wife. This is Mr. Ashenden."

"I couldn't imagine where you were. Why didn't you go and sit in your study? I'm sure Mr. Ashenden's been dreadfully uncomfortable."

She was a tall, thin woman of fifty, rather drawn and faded, but she looked as though she had once been pretty. It was obvious that she was very well-bred. She vaguely reminded you of an exotic plant, reared in a hot-house, that had begun to lose its bloom. She was dressed in black.

"What was the concert like?" asked Sir Herbert.

"Oh, not bad at all. They gave a Brahms' Concerto and the Fire-music from the *Walküre*, and some Hungarian dances of

Dvořák. I thought them rather showy." She turned to Ashenden. "I hope you haven't been bored all alone with my husband. What have you been talking about? Art and Literature?"

"No, its raw material," said Ashenden.

He took his leave.

MR. HARRINGTON'S
WASHING

WHEN Ashenden went on deck and saw before him a low-lying coast and a white town he felt a pleasant flutter of excitement. It was early and the sun had not long risen, but the sea was glassy and the sky was blue; it was warm already and one knew that the day would be sweltering. Vladivostok. It really gave one the sensation of being at the end of the world. It was a long journey that Ashenden had made from New York to San Francisco, across the Pacific in a Japanese boat to Yokohama, then from Tsuruki in a Russian boat, he the only Englishman on board, up the Sea of Japan. From Vladivostok he was to take the Trans-Siberian to Petrograd. It was the most important mission that he had ever had and he was pleased with the sense of responsibility that it gave him. He had no one to give him orders, unlimited funds (he carried in a belt next to his skin bills of exchange for a sum so enormous that he was staggered when he thought of them), and though he had been set to do something that was beyond human possibility he did not know this and was prepared to set about his task with confidence. He believed in his own astuteness. Though he had both esteem and admiration for the sensibility of the human race he had little respect for their intelligence: man has always found it easier to sacrifice his life than to learn the multiplication table.

Ashenden did not much look forward to ten days on a Russian train and in Yokohama he had heard rumours that in one or two places bridges had been blown up and the line cut. He was told that the soldiers, completely out of hand, would rob him of everything he possessed and turn him out on the steppe to shift for himself. It was a cheerful prospect. But the train was certainly starting and whatever happened later (and Ashenden had always a feeling that things never turned out as badly as you expected) he was determined to get a place on it. His intention on landing was to go at once to the British Consulate and find out what arrangements had been made for him; but as they neared the shore and he was able to discern the untidy and bedraggled town he felt not a little forlorn. He knew but a few words of Russian. The only man on the ship who spoke English was the purser and though he promised Ashenden to do anything he could to help him Ashenden had the impression that he must not too greatly count upon him. It was a relief then, when they docked, to have a young man, small and with a mop of untidy hair, obviously a Jew, come up to him and ask if his name was Ashenden.

"Mine is Benedict. I'm the interpreter at the British Consulate. I've been told to look after you. We've got you a place on the train to-night."

Ashenden's spirits went up. They landed. The little Jew looked after his luggage and had his passport examined and then, getting into a car that waited for them, they drove off to the Consulate.

"I've had instructions to offer you every facility," said the Consul, "and you've only got to tell me what you want. I've fixed you up all right on the train, but God knows if you'll ever get to Petrograd. Oh, by the way, I've got a travelling companion for you. He's a man called Harrington, an American, and he's going to Petrograd for a firm in Philadelphia. He's trying to fix up some deal with the Provisional Government."

"What's he like?" asked Ashenden.

"Oh, he's all right. I wanted him to come with the American Consul to luncheon, but they've gone for an excursion in the country. You must get to the station a couple of hours before the train starts. There's always an awful scrimmage and if you're not there in good time someone will pinch your seat."

The train started at midnight and Ashenden dined with Benedict at the station restaurant which was, it appeared, the only place in that slatternly town where you could get a decent meal. It was crowded. The service was intolerably slow. Then they went on to the platform, where, though they had still two hours to spare, there was already a seething mob.

Whole families, sitting on piles of luggage, seemed to be camped there. People rushed to and fro, or stood in little groups violently arguing. Women screamed. Others were silently weeping. Here two men were engaged in a fierce quarrel. It was a scene of indescribable confusion. The light in the station was wan and cold and the white faces of all those people were like the white faces of the dead waiting, patient or anxious, distraught or penitent, for the judgment of the last day. The train was made up and most of the carriages were already filled to overflowing. When at last Benedict found that in which Ashenden had his place a man sprang out of it excitedly.

"Come in and sit down," he said. "I've had the greatest difficulty in keeping your seat. A fellow wanted to come in here with a wife and two children. My Consul has just gone off with him to see the station-master."

"This is Mr. Harrington," said Benedict.

Ashenden stepped into the carriage. It had two berths in it. The porter stowed his luggage away. He shook hands with his travelling companion.

Mr. John Quincy Harrington was a very thin man of somewhat less than middle height, he had a yellow, bony face, with large, pale-blue eyes and when he took off his hat to wipe his brow wet from the perturbation he had endured he showed a large, bald skull; it was very bony and the ridges and protuberances stood out disconcertingly. He wore a bowler hat, a black coat and waistcoat, and a pair of striped trousers; a very high white collar and a neat, unobtrusive tie. Ashenden did not know precisely how you should dress in order to take a ten days' journey across Siberia, but he could not but think that Mr. Harrington's costume was eccentric. He spoke with precision in a high-pitched voice and in an accent that Ashenden recognized as that of New England.

In a minute the station-master came accompanied by a bearded Russian, suffering evidently from profound emotion, and followed by a lady holding two children by the hand. The Russian, tears running down his face, was talking with quivering lips to the station-master and his wife between her sobs was apparently telling him the story of her life. When they arrived at the carriage the altercation became more violent and Benedict joined in with his fluent Russian. Mr. Harrington did not know a word of the language, but being obviously of an excitable turn broke in and explained in voluble English that these

seats had been booked by the Consuls of Great Britain and the
United States respectively, and though he didn't know about
the King of England, he could tell them straight and they could
take it from him that the President of the United States would
never permit an American citizen to be done out of a seat on
the train that he had duly paid for. He would yield to force, but
to nothing else, and if they touched him he would register a
complaint with the Consul at once. He said all this and a great
deal more to the station-master, who of course had no notion
what he was talking about, but with much emphasis and a
good deal of gesticulation made him in reply a passionate
speech. This roused Mr. Harrington to the utmost pitch of
indignation, for shaking his fist in the station-master's face, his
own pale with fury, he cried out:

"Tell him I don't understand a word he says and I don't
want to understand. If the Russians want us to look upon them
as a civilized people why don't they talk a civilized language?
Tell him that I am Mr. John Quincy Harrington and I'm travelling on behalf of Messrs Crewe and Adams of Philadelphia with
a special letter of introduction to Mr. Kerensky and if I'm
not left in peaceful possession of this carriage, Mr. Crewe will
take the matter up with the Administration in Washington."

Mr. Harrington's manner was so truculent and his gestures
so menacing that the station-master, throwing up the sponge,
turned on his heel without another word and walked moodily
away. He was followed by the bearded Russian and his wife
arguing heatedly with him and the two apathetic children.
Mr. Harrington jumped back into the carriage.

"I'm terribly sorry to have to refuse to give up my seat to
a lady with two children," he said. "No one knows better than
I the respect due to a woman and a mother, but I've got to
get to Petrograd by this train if I don't want to lose a very
important order and I'm not going to spend ten days in a corridor for all the mothers in Russia."

"I don't blame you," said Ashenden.

"I am a married man and I have two children myself. I
know that travelling with your family is a difficult matter, but
there's nothing that I know to prevent you from staying at
home."

When you are shut up with a man for ten days in a railway
carriage you can hardly fail to learn most of what there is to
know about him, and for ten days (for eleven to be exact)

Ashenden spent twenty-four hours a day with Mr. Harrington. It is true that they went into the dining-room three times a day for their meals, but they sat opposite to one another; it is true that the train stopped for an hour morning and afternoon so that they were able to have a tramp up and down the platform, but they walked side by side. Ashenden made acquaintance with some of his fellow-travellers and sometimes they came into the compartment to have a chat, but if they only spoke French or German Mr. Harrington would watch them with acidulous disapproval and if they spoke English he would never let them get a word in. For Mr. Harrington was a talker. He talked as though it were a natural function of the human being, automatically, as men breathe or digest their food; he talked not because he had something to say, but because he could not help himself, in a high-pitched, nasal voice, without inflection, at one dead level of tone. He talked with precision, using a copious vocabulary and forming his sentences with deliberation; he never used a short word when a longer one would do; he never paused. He went on and on. It was not a torrent, for there was nothing impetuous about it, it was like a stream of lava pouring irresistibly down the side of a volcano. It flowed with a quiet and steady force that overwhelmed everything that was in its path.

Ashenden thought he had never known as much about anyone as he knew about Mr. Harrington, and not only about him, with all his opinions, habits and circumstances, but about his wife and his wife's family, his children and their schoolfellows, his employers and the alliances they had made for three or four generations with the best families of Philadelphia. His own family had come from Devonshire early in the eighteenth century and Mr. Harrington had been to the village where the graves of his forebears were still to be seen in the churchyard. He was proud of his English ancestry, but proud too of his American birth, though to him America was a little strip of land along the Atlantic coast and Americans were a small number of persons of English or Dutch origin whose blood had never been sullied by foreign admixture. He looked upon the Germans, Swedes, Irish and the inhabitants of Central and Eastern Europe who for the last hundred years have descended upon the United States as interlopers. He turned his attention away from them as a maiden lady who lived in a secluded manor might avert her eyes from the factory chimneys that had trespassed upon her retirement.

When Ashenden mentioned a man of vast wealth who owned some of the finest pictures in America Mr. Harrington said:

"I've never met him. My great-aunt Maria Penn Warmington always said his grandmother was a very good cook. My great-aunt Maria was terribly sorry when she left her to get married. She said she never knew anyone who could make an apple pancake as she could."

Mr. Harrington was devoted to his wife and he told Ashenden at unbelievable length how cultivated and what a perfect mother she was. She had delicate health and had undergone a great number of operations all of which he described in detail. He had had two operations himself, one on his tonsils and one to remove his appendix and he took Ashenden day by day through his experiences. All his friends had had operations and his knowledge of surgery was encyclopædic. He had two sons, both at school, and he was seriously considering whether he would not be well-advised to have them operated on. It was curious that one of them should have enlarged tonsils, and he was not at all happy about the appendix of the other. They were more devoted to one another than he had ever seen two brothers be and a very good friend of his, the brightest surgeon in Philadelphia, had offered to operate on them both together so that they should not be separated. He showed Ashenden photographs of the boys and their mother. This journey of his to Russia was the first time in their lives that he had been separated from them and every morning he wrote a long letter to his wife telling her everything that had happened and a good deal of what he had said during the day. Ashenden watched him cover sheet after sheet of paper with his neat, legible and precise handwriting.

Mr. Harrington had read all the books on conversation and knew its technique to the last detail. He had a little book in which he noted down the stories he heard and he told Ashenden that when he was going out to dinner he always looked up half a dozen so that he should not be at a loss. They were marked with a G if they could be told in general society and with an M (for men) if they were more fit for rough masculine ears. He was a specialist in that peculiar form of anecdote that consists in narrating a long serious incident, piling detail upon detail, till a comic end is reached. He spared you nothing and Ashenden foreseeing the point long before it arrived would clench his hands and knit his brows in the strenuous effort not to betray his impatience and at last force from his unwilling mouth a grim and hollow laugh. If someone came into the compartment in the middle Mr. Harrington would greet him with cordiality.

"Come right in and sit down. I was just telling my friend a story. You must listen to it, it's one of the funniest things you ever heard."

Then he would begin again from the very beginning and repeat it word for word, without altering a single apt epithet, till he reached the humorous end. Ashenden suggested once that they should see whether they could find two people on the train who played cards so that they might while away the time with a game of bridge, but Mr. Harrington said he never touched cards and when Ashenden in desperation began to play patience he pulled a wry face.

"It beats me how an intelligent man can waste his time card playing, and of all the unintellectual pursuits I have ever seen it seems to me that solitaire is the worst. It kills conversation. Man is a social animal and he exercises the highest part of his nature when he takes part in social intercourse."

"There is a certain elegance in wasting time," said Ashenden. "Any fool can waste money, but when you waste time you waste what is priceless. Besides," he added with bitterness, "you can still talk."

"How can I talk when your attention is taken up by whether you are going to get a black seven to put on a red eight? Conversation calls forth the highest powers of the intellect and if you have made a study of it you have the right to expect that the person you're talking to will give you the fullest attention he is capable of."

He did not say this acrimoniously, but with the good-humoured patience of a man who has been much tried. He was just stating a plain fact and Ashenden could take it or leave it. It was the claim of the artist to have his work taken seriously.

Mr. Harrington was a diligent reader. He read pencil in hand, underlining passages that attracted his attention and on the margin making in his neat writing comments on what he read. This he was fond of discussing and when Ashenden himself was reading and felt on a sudden that Mr. Harrington, book in one hand and pencil in the other, was looking at him with his large pale eyes he began to have violent palpitations of the heart. He dared not look up, he dared not even turn the page, for he knew that Mr. Harrington would regard this as ample excuse to break into a discourse, but remained with his eyes fixed desperately on a single word, like a chicken with its beak to a chalk line, and only ventured to breathe when he realized that Mr. Harrington, having given up the attempt, had resumed his reading. He was then engaged on a History of the American Constitution in two volumes and for recreation was perusing a stout volume that purported to contain all the great speeches of the world. For Mr. Harrington was an after-dinner speaker and had read all the best books on speaking in public. He knew exactly how to get on good terms with his audience, just where to put in the serious words that touched their hearts, how to catch their attention by a few apt stories and finally with what degree of eloquence, suiting the occasion, to deliver his peroration.

Mr. Harrington was very fond of reading aloud. Ashenden had had frequent occasion to observe the distressing propensity of Americans for this pastime. In hotel drawing-rooms at night after dinner he had often seen the father of a family seated in a retired corner and surrounded by his wife, his two sons and his daughter, reading to them. On ships crossing the Atlantic he had sometimes watched with awe the tall, spare gentleman of commanding aspect who sat in the centre of fifteen ladies no longer in their first youth and in a resonant voice read to them the history of Art. Walking up and down the promenade deck he had passed honeymooning couples lying on deck-chairs and caught the unhurried tones of the bride as she read to her young husband the pages of a popular novel. It had always seemed to him a curious way of showing affection. He had had friends who had offered to read to him and he had known women who had said they loved being read to, but he had always politely refused the invitation and firmly ignored the hint. He liked neither reading aloud nor being read aloud to. In his heart he thought the national predilection for this form of entertainment the only flaw in the perfection of the American character. But the immortal gods love a good laugh at the expense of human beings and now delivered him, bound and helpless, to the knife of the high priest. Mr. Harrington flattered himself that he was a very good reader and he explained to Ashenden the theory and practice of the art. Ashenden learned that there were two schools, the dramatic and the natural: in the first you imitated the voices of those who spoke (if you were reading a novel) and when the heroine wailed you wailed and when emotion choked her you choked too; but in the other you read as impassively as though you were reading the price-list of a mail-order house in Chicago. This was the school Mr. Harrington belonged to. In the seventeen years of his married life he had read aloud to his wife, and to his sons as soon as they were old enough to appreciate them, the novels of Sir Walter Scott, Jane Austen, Dickens, the Brontë Sisters, Thackeray, George Eliot, Nathaniel Hawthorne and W. J. Howells. Ashenden came to the conclusion that it was second nature with Mr. Harrington to read aloud and to prevent him from doing so made him as uneasy as cutting off his tobacco made the confirmed smoker. He would take you unawares.

"Listen to this," he would say, "you must listen to this," as though he were suddenly struck by the excellence of a maxim or the neatness of a phrase. "Now just tell me if you don't think this is remarkably well put. It's only three lines."

He read them and Ashenden was willing to give him a moment's attention, but having finished them, without pausing for a moment to take breath, he went on. He went right on. On and on. In his measured high-pitched voice, without emphasis or expression, he read page after page. Ashenden fidgeted, crossed and uncrossed his legs, lit cigarettes and smoked them sat first in one position, then in another. Mr. Harrington went on and on. The train went leisurely through the interminable steppes of Siberia. They passed villages and crossed rivers. Mr. Harrington went on and on. When he finished a great speech by Edmund Burke he put down the book in triumph.

"Now that in my opinion is one of the finest orations in the English language. It is certainly a part of our common heritage that we can look upon with genuine pride."

"Doesn't it seem to you a little ominous that the people to whom Edmund Burke made that speech are all dead?" asked Ashenden gloomily.

Mr. Harrington was about to reply that this was hardly to be wondered at since the speech was made in the eighteenth century when it dawned upon him that Ashenden (bearing up wonderfully under affliction as any unprejudiced person could not fail to admit) was making a joke. He slapped his knee and laughed heartily.

"Gee, that's a good one," he said. "I'll write that down in my little book. I see exactly how I can bring it in one time when I have to speak at our luncheon club."

Mr. Harrington was a highbrow; but that appellation, invented by the vulgar as a term of abuse, he had accepted like the instrument of a saint's martyrdom, the gridiron of Saint Laurence for instance or the wheel of Saint Catherine, as an honorific title. He gloried in it.

"Emerson was a highbrow," he said. "Longfellow was a highbrow. Oliver Wendell Holmes was a highbrow. James Russell Lowell was a highbrow."

Mr. Harrington's study of American literature had taken him no further down the years than the period during which those eminent, but not precisely thrilling, authors flourished.

Mr. Harrington was a bore. He exasperated Ashenden, and enraged him; he got on his nerves, and drove him to frenzy. But Ashenden did not dislike him. His self-satisfaction was enormous but so ingenuous that you could not resent it; his conceit was so childlike that you could only smile at it. He was so well-meaning, so thoughtful, so deferential, so polite that though Ashenden would willingly have killed him he could not but own that in that short while he had conceived for Mr. Harrington something very like affection. His manners were exquisite, formal, a trifle elaborate perhaps (there is no harm in that, for good manners are the product of an artificial state of society and so can bear a touch of the powdered wig and the lace ruffle) but though natural to his good breeding they gained a pleasant significance from his good heart. He was ready to do anyone a kindness and seemed to find nothing too much trouble if he could thereby oblige his fellow man. He was eminently *serviable*. And it may be that this is a word for which there is no exact translation because the charming quality it denotes is not very common among our practical people. When Ashenden was ill for a couple of days Mr. Harrington nursed him with devotion. Ashenden was embarrassed by the care he took of him and though racked with pain could not help laughing at the fussy attention with which Mr. Harrington took his temperature, from his neatly packed valise extracted a whole regiment of tabloids and firmly doctored him; and he was touched by the trouble he gave himself to get from the dining-car the things that he thought Ashenden could eat. He did everything in the world for him but stop talking.

It was only when he was dressing that Mr. Harrington was silent, for then his maidenly mind was singly occupied with the problem of changing his clothes before Ashenden without indelicacy. He was extremely modest. He changed his linen every day, neatly taking it out of his suit-case and neatly putting back what was soiled; but he performed miracles of dexterity in order during the process not to show an inch of bare skin. After a day or two Ashenden gave up the struggle to keep neat and clean in that dirty train, with one lavatory for the whole carriage, and soon was as grubby as the rest of the passengers; but Mr. Harrington refused to yield to the difficulties. He performed his toilet with deliberation, notwithstanding the impatient persons who rattled the door-handle, and returned from the lavatory every morning washed, shining and smelling of soap. Once dressed, in his black coat, striped trousers and well-polished shoes, he looked as spruce as though he had just stepped out of his tidy little red-brick house in Philadelphia and was about to board the street-car that would take him down town to his office. At one point of the journey it was announced that an attempt had been made to blow up a bridge and that there were disturbances at the next station over the river; it might be that the train would be stopped and the passengers turned adrift or taken prisoners. Ashenden, thinking he might be separated from his luggage, took the precaution to change into his thickest clothes so that if he had to pass the winter in Siberia he need suffer as little as necessary from the cold; but Mr. Harrington would not listen to reason; he made no preparations for the possible experience and Ashenden had the conviction that if he spent three months in a Russian prison he would still preserve that smart and natty appearance. A troop of Cossacks boarded the train and stood on the platform of each carriage with their guns loaded, and the train rattled gingerly over the damaged bridge; then they came to the station at which they had been warned of danger, put on steam and dashed straight through it. Mr. Harrington was mildly satirical when Ashenden changed back into a light summer suit.

Mr. Harrington was a keen business man. It was obvious that it would need someone very astute to over-reach him and Ashenden was sure that his employers had been well-advised to send him on this errand. He would safeguard their interests with all his might and if he succeeded in driving a bargain with the

Russians it would be a hard one. His loyalty to his firm demanded that. He spoke of the partners with affectionate reverence. He loved them and was proud of them; but he did not envy them because their wealth was great. He was quite content to work on a salary and thought himself adequately paid; so long as he could educate his boys and leave his widow enough to live on what was money to him? He thought it a trifle vulgar to be rich. He looked upon culture as more important than money. He was careful of it and after every meal put down in his note-book exactly what it had cost him. His firm might be certain that he would not charge a penny more for his expenses than he had spent. But having discovered that poor people came to the station at the stopping places of the train to beg and seeing that the war had really brought them to destitution he took care before each halt to supply himself with ample small change and in a shame-faced way, mocking himself for being taken in by such impostors, distributed everything in his pocket.

"Of course I know they don't deserve it," he said, "and I don't do it for them. I do it entirely for my own peace of mind. I should feel so terribly badly if I thought some man really was hungry and I'd refused to give him the price of a meal."

Mr. Harrington was absurd, but lovable. It was inconceivable that anyone should be rude to him, it would have seemed as dreadful as hitting a child; and Ashenden, chafing inwardly but with a pretence of amiability, suffered meekly and with a truly Christian spirit the affliction of the gentle, ruthless creature's society. It took eleven days at that time to get from Vladivostok to Petrograd and Ashenden felt that he could not have borne another day. If it had been twelve he would have killed Mr. Harrington.

When at last (Ashenden tired and dirty, Mr. Harrington neat, sprightly and sententious) they reached the outskirts of Petrograd and stood at the window looking at the crowded houses of the city, Mr. Harrington turned to Ashenden and said:

"Well, I never would have thought that eleven days in the train would pass so quickly. We've had a wonderful time. I've enjoyed your company and I know you've enjoyed mine. I'm not going to pretend I don't know that I'm a pretty good conversationalist. But now we've come together like this we must.

take care to stay together. We must see as much of one another as we can while I'm in Petrograd."

"I shall have a great deal to do," said Ashenden. "I'm afraid my time won't be altogether my own."

"I know," answered Mr. Harrington cordially. "I expect to be pretty busy myself, but we can have breakfast together anyway and we'll meet in the evening and compare notes. It would be too bad if we drifted apart now."

"Too bad," sighed Ashenden.

When Ashenden found himself alone in his bedroom for the first time, he sat down and looked about him. It had seemed an age. He had not the energy to start immediately to unpack. How many of these hotel bedrooms had he known since the beginning of the war, grand or shabby, in one place and one land after another! It seemed to him that he had been living in his luggage for as long as he could remember. He was weary. He asked himself how he was going to set about the work that he had been sent to do. He felt lost in the immensity of Russia and very solitary. He had protested when he was chosen for this mission, it looked too large an order, but his protests were ignored. He was chosen not because those in authority thought him particularly suited for the job, but because there was no one to be found who was more suited. There was a knock at the door and Ashenden, pleased to make use of the few words of the language he knew, called out in Russian. The door was opened. He sprang to his feet.

"Come in, come in," he cried. "I'm awfully glad to see you."

Three men entered. He knew them by sight, since they had travelled on the same boat with him from San Francisco to Yokohama, but following their instructions no communications had passed between them and Ashenden. They were Czechs, exiled from their country for their revolutionary activity and long settled in America, who had been sent over to Russia to help Ashenden in his mission and put him in touch with Professor Z. whose authority over the Czechs in Russia was absolute. Their chief was a certain Dr. Egon Orth, a tall thin man, with a little grey head; he was minister to some church in the Middle West and a doctor of divinity; but had abandoned his cure to work for the liberation of his country, and Ashenden had the impression that he was an intelligent fellow who would not put too fine a point on matters of conscience. A parson with a fixed idea has this advantage over common men that he can persuade himself of the Almighty's approval for almost any goings on. Dr. Orth had a merry twinkle in his eye and a dry humour.

Ashenden had had two secret interviews with him in Yokohama and had learnt that Professor Z., though eager to free his country from the Austrian rule and since he knew that this could only come about by the downfall of the Central Powers with the allies body and soul, yet had scruples; he would not do things that outraged his conscience, all must be straightforward and above board, and so some things that it was necessary to do had to be done without his knowledge. His influence was so great that his wishes could not be disregarded, but on occasion it was felt better not to let him know too much of what was going on.

Dr. Orth had arrived in Petrograd a week before Ashenden and now put before him what he had learned of the situation. It seemed to Ashenden that it was critical and if anything was to be done it must be done quickly. The army was dissatisfied and mutinous, the Government under the weak Kerensky was tottering and held power only because no one else had the courage to seize it, famine was staring the country in the face and already the possibility had to be considered that the Germans would march on Petrograd. The ambassadors of Great Britain and the United States had been apprised of Ashenden's coming, but his mission was secret even from them, and there were particular reasons why he could demand no assistance from them. He arranged with Dr. Orth to make an appointment with Professor Z. so that he could learn his views and explain to him that he had the financial means to support any scheme that seemed likely to prevent the catastrophe that the Allied governments foresaw of Russia's making a separate peace. But he had to get in touch with influential persons in all classes. Mr. Harrington with his business proposition and his letters to Ministers of State would be thrown in contact with members of the Government and Mr. Harrington wanted an interpreter. Dr. Orth spoke Russian almost as well as his own language and it struck Ashenden that he would be admirably suited to the post. He explained the circumstances to him and it was arranged that while Ashenden and Mr. Harrington were at luncheon Dr. Orth should come in, greeting Ashenden as though he had not seen him before, and be introduced to Mr. Harrington; then Ashenden, guiding the conversation, would suggest to Mr.

Harrington that the heavens had sent in Dr. Orth the ideal man for his purpose.

But there was another person on whom Ashenden had fixed as possibly useful to him and now he said:

"Have you ever heard of a woman called Anastasia Alexandrovna Leonidov? She's the daughter of Alexander Denisiev."

"I know all about him of course."

"I have reason to believe she's in Petrograd. Will you find out where she lives and what she's doing."

"Certainly."

Dr. Orth spoke in Czech to one of the two men who accompanied him. They were sharp-looking fellows both of them, one was tall and fair and the other was short and dark, but they were younger than Dr. Orth and Ashenden understood that they were there to do as he bade them. The man nodded, got up, shook hands with Ashenden and went out.

"You shall have all the information possible this afternoon."

"Well, I think there's nothing more we can do for the present," said Ashenden. "To tell you the truth I haven't had a bath for eleven days and I badly want one."

Ashenden had never quite made up his mind whether the pleasure of reflection was better pursued in a railway carriage or in a bath. So far as the act of invention was concerned he was inclined to prefer a train that went smoothly and not too fast, and many of his best ideas had come to him when he was thus traversing the plains of France; but for the delight of reminiscence or the entertainment of embroidery upon a theme already in his head he had no doubt that nothing could compare with a hot bath. He considered now, wallowing in soapy water like a water-buffalo in a muddy pond, the grim pleasantry of his relations with Anastasia Alexandrovna Leonidov.

In these stories no more than the barest suggestion has been made that Ashenden was capable on occasions of the passion ironically called tender. The specialists in this matter, those charming creatures who make a business of what philosophers know is but a diversion, assert that writers, painters and musicians, all in short who are connected with the arts, in the relation of love cut no very conspicuous figure. There is much cry but little wool. They rave or sigh, make phrases and strike many a romantic attitude, but in the end, loving art or themselves (which with them is one and the same thing) better than the object of their emotion offer a shadow when the said object, with the practical common sense of the sex, demands a substance. It may be so and this may be the reason (never before suggested) why women in their souls look upon art with such a virulent hatred. Be this as it may Ashenden in the last twenty years had felt his heart go pit-a-pat because of one charming person after another. He had had a good deal of fun and had paid for it with a great deal of misery, but even when suffering most acutely from the pangs of unrequited love he had been able to say to himself, albeit with a wry face, after all, it's grist to the mill.

Anastasia Alexandrovna Leonidov was the daughter of a revolutionary who had escaped from Siberia after being sentenced to penal servitude for life and had settled in England. He was an able man and had supported himself for thirty years by the activity of a restless pen and had even made himself a distinguished position in English letters. When Anastasia Alexandrovna reached a suitable age she married Vladimir Semenovich Leonidov, also an exile from his native country, and it was after she had been married to him for some years that Ashenden made her acquaintance. It was at the time when Europe discovered Russia. Everyone was reading the Russian novelists, the Russian dancers captivated the civilized world, and the Russian composers set shivering the sensibility of persons who were beginning to want a change from Wagner. Russian art seized upon Europe with the virulence of an epidemic of influenza. New phrases became the fashion, new colours, new emotions, and the highbrows described themselves without a moment's hesitation as members of the intelligentsia. It was a difficult word to spell but an easy one to say. Ashenden fell like the rest, changed the cushions of his sitting-room, hung an eikon on the wall, read Chekoff and went to the ballet.

Anastasia Alexandrovna was by birth, circumstances and education very much a member of the intelligentsia. She lived with her husband in a tiny house near Regent's Park and here all the literary folk in London might gaze with humble reverence at pale-faced bearded giants who leaned against the wall like caryatids taking a day off; they were revolutionaries to a man and it was a miracle that they were not in the mines of Siberia. Women of letters tremulously put their lips to a glass of vodka. If you were lucky and greatly favoured you might shake hands there with Diaghileff and now and again, like a

peach-blossom wafted by the breeze, Pavlova herself hovered
in and out. At this time Ashenden's success had not been so
great as to affront the highbrows, he had very distinctly been
one of them in his youth, and though some already looked
askance, others (optimistic creatures with a faith in human
nature) still had hopes of him. Anastasia Alexandrovna told
him to his face that he was a member of the intelligentsia.
Ashenden was quite ready to believe it. He was in a state when
he was ready to believe anything. He was thrilled and excited.
It seemed to him that at last he was about to capture that il-
lusive spirit of romance that he had so long been chasing.
Anastasia Alexandrovna had fine eyes and a good, though for
these days, too voluptuous figure, high cheek bones and a snub
nose (this was very Tartar), a wide mouth full of large square
teeth and a pale skin. She dressed somewhat flamboyantly. In
her dark melancholy eyes Ashenden saw the boundless steppes
of Russia, and the Kremlin with its pealing bells, and the
solemn ceremonies of Easter at St. Isaac's, and forests of silver
beeches and the Nevsky Prospekt; it was astonishing how
much he saw in her eyes. They were round and shining and
slightly protuberant like those of a Pekinese. They talked together of Alyósha in the *Brothers Karamazov*, of Natasha in
War and Peace, of Anna Karenina and of *Fathers and Sons*.

Ashenden soon discovered that her husband was quite unworthy of her and presently learned that she shared his opinion.
Vladimir Semenovich was a little man with a large, long head
that looked as though it had been pulled like a piece of liquorice,
and he had a great shock of unruly Russian hair. He was a
gentle, unobtrusive creature and it was hard to believe that the
Czarist government had really feared his revolutionary activities. He taught Russian and wrote for papers in Moscow. He
was amiable and obliging. He needed these qualities for Anastasia Alexandrovna was a woman of character: when she had
a toothache Vladimir Semenovich suffered the agonies of the
damned and when her heart was wrung by the suffering of her
unhappy country Vladimir Semenovich might well have wished
he had never been born. Ashenden could not help admitting
that he was a poor thing, but he was so harmless that he conceived quite a liking for him, and when in due course he had
disclosed his passion to Anastasia Alexandrovna and to his
joy found it was returned he was puzzled to know what to do
about Vladimir Semenovich. Neither Anastasia Alexandrovna

nor he felt that they could live another minute out of one another's pockets, and Ashenden feared that with her revolutionary views and all that she would never consent to marry him; but somewhat to his surprise, and very much to his relief, she accepted the suggestion with alacrity.

"Would Vladimir Semenovich let himself be divorced, do you think?" he asked, as he sat on the sofa, leaning against cushions the colour of which reminded him of raw meat just gone bad, and held her hand.

"Vladimir adores me," she answered. "It'll break his heart."

"He's a nice fellow, I shouldn't like him to be very unhappy. I hope he'll get over it."

"He'll never get over it. That is the Russian spirit. I know that when I leave him he'll feel that he has lost everything that made life worth living for him. I've never known anyone so wrapped up in a woman as he is in me. But of course he wouldn't want to stand in the way of my happiness. He's far too great for that. He'll see that when it's a question of my own self-development I haven't the right to hesitate. Vladimir will give me my freedom without question."

At that time the divorce law in England was even more complicated and absurd than it is now and in case she was not acquainted with its peculiarities Ashenden explained to Anastasia Alexandrovna the difficulties of the case. She put her hand gently on his.

"Vladimir would never expose me to the vulgar notoriety of the divorce court. When I tell him that I have decided to marry you he will commit suicide."

"That would be terrible," said Ashenden.

He was startled, but thrilled. It was really very much like a Russian novel and he saw the moving and terrible pages, pages and pages, in which Dostoievsky would have described the situation. He knew the lacerations his characters would have suffered, the broken bottles of champagne, the visits to the gipsies, the vodka, the swoonings, the catalepsy and the long, long speeches everyone would have made. It was all very dreadful and wonderful and shattering.

"It would make us horribly unhappy," said Anastasia Alexandrovna, "but I don't know what else he could do. I couldn't ask him to live without me. He would be like a ship without a rudder or a car without a carburettor. I know Vladimir so well. He will commit suicide."

"How?" asked Ashenden, who had the realist's passion for the exact detail.

"He will blow his brains out."

Ashenden remembered *Rosmerholm*. In his day he had been an ardent Ibsenite and had even flirted with the notion of learning Norwegian so that he might, by reading the master in the original, get at the secret essence of his thought. He had once seen Ibsen in the flesh drink a glass of Munich beer.

"But do you think we could ever pass another easy hour if we had the death of that man on our conscience?" he asked. "I have a feeling that he would always be between us."

"I know we shall suffer, we shall suffer dreadfully," said Anastasia Alexandrovna, "but how can we help it? Life is like that. We must think of Vladimir. There is his happiness to be considered too. He will prefer to commit suicide."

She turned her face away and Ashenden saw that the heavy tears were coursing down her cheeks. He was much moved. For he had a soft heart and it was dreadful to think of poor Vladimir lying there with a bullet in his brain.

These Russians, what fun they have!

But when Anastasia Alexandrovna had mastered her emotion she turned to him gravely. She looked at him with her humid, round and slightly protuberant eyes.

"We must be quite sure that we're doing the right thing," she said. "I should never forgive myself if I'd allowed Vladimir to commit suicide and then found I'd made a mistake. I think we ought to make sure that we really love one another."

"But don't you know?" exclaimed Ashenden in a low, tense voice. "I know."

"Let's go over to Paris for a week and see how we get on. Then we shall know."

Ashenden was a trifle conventional and the suggestion took him by surprise. But only for a moment. Anastasia was wonderful. She was very quick and she saw the hesitation that for an instant troubled him.

"Surely you have no bourgeois prejudices?" she said.

"Of course not," he assured her hurriedly, for he would much sooner have been thought knavish than bourgeois, "I think it's a splendid idea."

"Why should a woman hazard her whole life on a throw? It's impossible to know what a man is really like till you've lived with him. It's only fair to give her the opportunity to change her mind before it's too late."

"Quite so," said Ashenden.

Anastasia Alexandrovna was not a woman to let the grass grow under her feet and so having made their arrangements forthwith on the following Saturday they started for Paris.

"I shall not tell Vladimir that I am going with you," she said. "It would only distress him."

"It would be a pity to do that," said Ashenden.

"And if at the end of the week I come to the conclusion that we've made a mistake he need never know anything about it."

"Quite so," said Ashenden.

They met at Victoria station.

"What class have you got?" she asked him.

"First."

"I'm glad of that. Father and Vladimir travel third on account of their principles, but I always feel sick on a train and I like to be able to lean my head on somebody's shoulder. It's easier in a first-class carriage."

When the train started Anastasia Alexandrovna said she felt dizzy, so she took off her hat and leaned her head on Ashenden's shoulder. He put his arm round her waist.

"Keep quite still, won't you?" she said.

When they got on to the boat she went down to the ladies' cabin and at Calais was able to eat a very hearty meal, but when they got into the train she took off her hat again and rested her head on Ashenden's shoulder. He thought he would like to read and took up a book.

"Do you mind not reading?" she said. "I have to be held and when you turn the pages it makes me feel all funny."

Finally they reached Paris and went to a little hotel on the Left Bank that Anastasia Alexandrovna knew of. She said it had atmosphere. She could not bear those great big grand hotels on the other side; they were hopelessly vulgar and bourgeois.

"I'll go anywhere you like," said Ashenden, "as long as there's a bathroom."

She smiled and pinched his cheek.

"How adorably English you are. Can't you do without a bathroom for a week? My dear, my dear, you have so much to learn."

They talked far into the night about Maxim Gorki and Karl

Marx, human destiny, love and the brotherhood of man; and drank innumerable cups of Russian tea, so that in the morning Ashenden would willingly have breakfasted in bed and got up for luncheon; but Anastasia Alexandrovna was an early riser. When life was so short and there was so much to do it was a sinful thing to have breakfast a minute after half-past eight. They sat down in a dingy little dining-room the windows of which showed no signs of having been opened for a month. It was full of atmosphere. Ashenden asked Anastasia Alexandrovna what she would have for breakfast.

"Scrambled eggs," she said.

She ate heartily. Ashenden had already noticed that she had a healthy appetite. He supposed it was a Russian trait: you could not picture Anna Karenina making her midday meal off a bath-bun and a cup of coffee, could you?

After breakfast they went to the Louvre and in the afternoon they went to the Luxembourg. They dined early in order to go to the Comédie Française; then they went to a Russian cabaret where they danced. When next morning at eight-thirty they took their places in the dining-room and Ashenden asked Anastasia Alexandrovna what she fancied, her reply was:

"Scrambled eggs."

"But we had scrambled eggs yesterday," he expostulated.

"Let's have them again to-day," she smiled.

"All right."

They spent the day in the same manner except that they went to the Carnavalet instead of the Louvre and the Musée Guimet instead of the Luxembourg. But when the morning after in answer to Ashenden's enquiry Anastasia Alexandrovna again asked for scrambled eggs, his heart sank.

"But we had scrambled eggs yesterday and the day before," he said.

"Don't you think that's a very good reason to have them again to-day?"

"No, I don't."

"Is it possible that your sense of humour is a little deficient this morning?" she asked. "I eat scrambled eggs every day. It's the only way I like them."

"Oh, very well. In that case of course we'll have scrambled eggs."

But the following morning he could not face them.

"Will you have scrambled eggs as usual?" he asked her.

"Of course," she smiled affectionately, showing him two rows of large square teeth.

'All right, I'll order them for you, I shall have mine fried." The smile vanished from her lips.

"Oh?" She paused a moment. "Don't you think that's rather inconsiderate? Do you think it's fair to give the cook unnecessary work? You English, you're all the same, you look upon servants as machines. Does it occur to you that they have hearts like yours, the same feelings and the same emotions? How can you be surprised that the proletariat are seething with discontent when the bourgeoisie like you are so monstrously selfish?"

"Do you really think that there'll be a revolution in England if I have my eggs in Paris fried rather than scrambled?"

She tossed her pretty head in indignation.

"You don't understand. It's the principle of the thing. You think it's a jest, of course I know you're being funny, I can laugh at a joke as well as anyone, Chekoff was well-known in Russia as a humorist; but don't you see what is involved? Your whole attitude is wrong. It's a lack of feeling. You wouldn't talk like that if you had been through the events of 1905 in Petersburg. When I think of the crowds in front of the Winter Palace kneeling in the snow while the Cossacks charged them, women and children! No, no, no."

Her eyes filled with tears and her face was all twisted with pain. She took Ashenden's hand.

"I know you have a good heart. It was just thoughtless on your part and we won't say anything more about it. You have imagination. You're very sensitive. I know. You'll have your eggs done in the same way as mine, won't you?"

"Of course," said Ashenden.

He ate scrambled eggs for breakfast every morning after that. The waiter said: "*Monsieur aime les œufs brouillés.*" At the end of the week they returned to London. He held Anastasia Alexandrovna in his arms, her head resting on his shoulder, from Paris to Calais and again from Dover to London. He reflected that the journey from New York to San Francisco took five days. When they arrived at Victoria and stood on the platform waiting for a cab she looked at him with her round, shining and slightly protuberant eyes.

"We've had a wonderful time, haven't we?" she said.

"Wonderful."

"I've quite made up my mind. The experiment has justified itself. I'm willing to marry you whenever you like."

But Ashenden saw himself eating scrambled eggs every morning for the rest of his life. When he had put her in a cab, he called another for himself, went to the Cunard office and took a berth on the first ship that was going to America. No immigrant, eager for freedom and a new life, ever looked upon the statue of Liberty with more heartfelt thankfulness than did Ashenden, when on that bright and sunny morning his ship steamed into the harbour of New York.

Some years had passed since then and Ashenden had not seen Anastasia Alexandrovna again. He knew that on the outbreak of the revolution in March she and Vladimir Semenovich had gone to Russia. It might be that they would be able to help him, in a way Vladimir Semenovich owed him his life, and he made up his mind to write to Anastasia Alexandrovna to ask if he might come to see her.

When Ashenden went down to lunch he felt somewhat rested. Mr. Harrington was waiting for him and they sat down. They ate what was put before them.

"Ask the waiter to bring us some bread," said Mr. Harrington.

"Bread?" replied Ashenden. "There's no bread."

"I can't eat without bread," said Mr. Harrington.

"I'm afraid you'll have to. There's no bread, no butter, no sugar, no eggs, no potatoes. There's fish and meat and green vegetables, and that's all."

Mr. Harrington's jaw dropped.

"But this is war," he said.

"It looks very much like it."

Mr. Harrington was for a moment speechless; then he said: "I'll tell you what I'm going to do, I'm going to get through with my business as quick as I can and then I'm going to get out of this country. I'm sure Mrs. Harrington wouldn't like me to go without sugar or butter. I've got a very delicate stomach. The firm would never have sent me here if they'd thought I wasn't going to have the best of everything."

In a little while Dr. Egon Orth came in and gave Ashenden an envelope. On it was written Anastasia Alexandrovna's address. He introduced him to Mr. Harrington. It was soon clear that he was pleased with Dr. Egon Orth and so without further to do he suggested that here was the perfect interpreter for him.

"He talks Russian like a Russian. But he's an American citizen so that he won't do you down. I've known him a considerable time and I can assure you that he's absolutely trustworthy."

Mr. Harrington was pleased with the notion and after luncheon Ashenden left them to settle the matter by themselves. He wrote a note to Anastasia Alexandrovna and presently received an answer to say that she was going to a meeting, but would look in at his hotel about seven. He awaited her with apprehension. Of course he knew now that he had not loved her, but Tolstoi and Dostoievsky, Rimsky-Korsakoff, Stravinsky and Bakst; but he was not quite sure if the point had occurred to her. When between eight and half-past she arrived he suggested that she should join Mr. Harrington and him at dinner. The presence of a third party, he thought, would prevent any awkwardness their meeting might have; but he need not have had any anxiety, for five minutes after they had sat down to a plate of soup it was borne in upon him that the feelings of Anastasia Alexandrovna towards him were as cool as were his towards her. It gave him a momentary shock. It is very hard for a man, however modest, to grasp the possibility that a woman who has once loved him may love him no longer, and though of course he did not imagine that Anastasia Alexandrovna had languished for five years with a hopeless passion for him, he did think that by a heightening of colour, a flutter of the eyelashes, or a quiver of the lips she would betray the fact that she had still a soft place in her heart for him. Not at all. She talked to him as though he were a friend she was very glad to see again after an absence of a few days, but whose intimacy with her was purely social. He asked after Vladimir Semenovich.

"He has been a disappointment to me," she said. "I never thought he was a clever man, but I thought he was an honest one. He's going to have a baby."

Mr. Harrington who was about to put a piece of fish into his mouth, stopped, his fork in the air, and stared at Anastasia Alexandrovna with astonishment. In extenuation it must be explained that he had never read a Russian novel in his life. Ashenden, slightly perplexed too, gave her a questioning look.

"I'm not the mother," she said with a laugh. "I am not

interested in that sort of thing. The mother is a friend of mine
and a well-known writer on Political Economy. I do not think
her views are sound, but I should be the last to deny that
they deserve consideration. She has a good brain, quite a good
brain." She turned to Mr. Harrington. "Are you interested in
Political Economy?"

For once in his life Mr. Harrington was speechless. Anastasia
Alexandrovna gave them her views on the subject and they
began to speak on the situation in Russia. She seemed to be
on intimate terms with the leaders of the various political
parties and Ashenden made up his mind to sound her on the
possibility of her working with him. His infatuation had not
blinded him to the fact that she was an extremely intelligent
woman. After dinner he told Mr. Harrington that he wished
to talk business with Anastasia Alexandrovna and took her
to a retired corner of the lounge. He told her all he thought
necessary and found her interested and anxious to help. She
had a passion for intrigue and a desire for power. When he
hinted that he had command of large sums of money she saw
at once that through him she might acquire an influence in the
affairs of Russia. It tickled her vanity. She was immensely
patriotic, but like many patriots she had an impression that
her own aggrandisement tended to the good of her country.
When they parted they had come to a working agreement.

"That was a very remarkable woman," said Mr. Harrington
next morning when they met at breakfast.

"Don't fall in love with her," smiled Ashenden.

This, however, was not a matter on which Mr. Harrington
was prepared to jest.

"I have never looked at a woman since I married Mrs. Harrington," he said. "That husband of hers must be a bad man."

"I could do with a plate of scrambled eggs," said Ashenden,
irrelevantly, for their breakfast consisted of a cup of tea without
milk and a little jam instead of sugar.

With Anastasia Alexandrovna to help him and Dr. Orth in
the background, Ashenden set to work. Things in Russia were
going from bad to worse. Kerensky, the head of the Provisional
Government, was devoured by vanity and dismissed any minister who gave evidence of a capacity that might endanger his
own position. He made speeches. He made endless speeches.
At one moment there was a possibility that the Germans
would make a dash for Petrograd. Kerensky made speeches.

The food shortage grew more serious, the winter was approaching and there was no fuel. Kerensky made speeches. In the background the Bolsheviks were active, Lenin was hiding in Petrograd, it was said that Kerensky knew where he was, but dared not arrest him. He made speeches.

It amused Ashenden to see the unconcern with which Mr. Harrington wandered through this turmoil. History was in the making and Mr. Harrington minded his own business. It was uphill work. He was made to pay bribes to secretaries and underlings under the pretence that the ear of great men would be granted to him. He was kept waiting for hours in antechambers and then sent away without ceremony. When at last he saw the great men he found they had nothing to give him but idle words. They made him promises and in a day or two he discovered that the promises meant nothing. Ashenden advised him to throw in his hand and return to America; but Mr. Harrington would not hear of it; his firm had sent him to do a particular job, and by gum, he was going to do it or perish in the attempt. Then Anastasia Alexandrovna took him in hand. A singular friendship had arisen between the pair. Mr. Harrington thought her a very remarkable and deeply wronged woman; he told her all about his wife and his two sons, he told her all about the Constitution of the United States; she on her side told him all about Vladimir Semenovich, and she told him about Tolstoi, Turgenieff and Dostoievsky. They had great times together. He said he couldn't manage to call her Anastasia Alexandrovna, it was too much of a mouthful; so he called her Delilah. And now she placed her inexhaustible energy at his service and they went together to the persons who might be useful to him. But things were coming to a head. Riots broke out and the streets were growing dangerous. Now and then armoured cars filled with discontented reservists careered wildly along the Nevsky Prospekt and in order to show that they were not happy took pot-shots at the passers-by. On one occasion when Mr. Harrington and Anastasia Alexandrovna were in a tram together shots peppered the windows and they had to lie down on the floor for safety. Mr. Harrington was highly indignant.

"An old fat woman was lying right on top of me and when I wriggled to get out Delilah caught me a clip on the side of the head and said, stop still, you fool. I don't like your Russian ways, Delilah."

"Anyhow you stopped still," she giggled.

"What you want in this country is a little less art and a little more civilization."

"You are bourgeoisie, Mr. Harrington, you are not a member of the intelligentsia."

"You are the first person who's ever said that, Delilah. If I'm not a member of the intelligentsia I don't know who is," retorted Mr. Harrington with dignity.

Then one day when Ashenden was working in his room there was a knock at the door and Anastasia Alexandrovna stalked in followed, somewhat sheepishly, by Mr. Harrington. Ashenden saw that she was excited.

"What's the matter?" he asked.

"Unless this man goes back to America he'll get killed. You really must talk to him. If I hadn't been there something very unpleasant might have happened to him."

"Not at all, Delilah," said Mr. Harrington, with asperity. "I'm perfectly capable of taking care of myself and I wasn't in the smallest danger."

"What is it all about?" asked Ashenden.

"I'd taken Mr. Harrington to the Lavra of Alexander Nevsky to see Dostoievsky's grave," said Anastasia Alexandrovna, "and on our way back we saw a soldier being rather rough with an old woman."

"Rather rough!" cried Mr. Harrington. "There was an old woman walking along the side-walk with a basket of provisions on her arm. Two soldiers came up behind her and one of them snatched the basket from her and walked off with it. She burst out screaming and crying, I don't know what she was saying, but I can guess, and the other soldier took his gun and with the butt-end of it hit her over the head. Isn't that right, Delilah?"

"Yes," she answered, unable to help smiling. "And before I could prevent it Mr. Harrington jumped out of the cab and ran up to the soldier who had the basket, wrenched it from him and began to abuse the pair of them like pickpockets. At first they were so taken aback they didn't know what to do and then they got in a rage. I ran after Mr. Harrington and explained to them that he was a foreigner and drunk."

"Drunk?" cried Mr. Harrington.

"Yes, drunk. Of course a crowd collected. It looked as though it wasn't going to be very nice."

Mr. Harrington smiled with those large pale-blue eyes of his.

"It sounded to me as though you were giving them a piece of your mind, Delilah. It was as good as a play to watch you."

"Don't be stupid, Mr. Harrington," cried Anastasia, in a sudden fury, stamping her foot. "Don't you know that those soldiers might very easily have killed you and me too, and not one of the bystanders would have raised a finger to help us?"

"Me? I'm an American citizen, Delilah. They wouldn't dare touch a hair of my head."

"They'd have difficulty in finding one," said Anastasia Alexandrovna, who when she was in a temper had no manners. "But if you think Russian soldiers are going to hesitate to kill you because you're an American citizen you'll get a big surprise one of these days."

"Well, what happened to the old woman?" asked Ashenden.

"The soldiers went off after a little and we went back to her."

"Still with the basket?"

"Yes. Mr. Harrington clung on to that like grim death. She was lying on the ground with the blood pouring from her head. We got her into the cab and when she could speak enough to tell us where she lived we drove her home. She was bleeding dreadfully and we had some difficulty in staunching the blood."

Anastasia Alexandrovna gave Mr. Harrington an odd look and to his surprise Ashenden saw him turn scarlet.

"What's the matter now?"

"You see, we had nothing to bind her up with. Mr. Harrington's handkerchief was soaked. There was only one thing about me that I could get off quickly and so I took off my . . ."

But before she could finish Mr. Harrington interrupted her.

"You need not tell Mr. Ashenden what you took off. I'm a married man and I know ladies wear them, but I see no need to refer to them in general society."

Anastasia Alexandrovna giggled.

"Then you must kiss me, Mr. Harrington. If you don't I shall say."

Mr. Harrington hesitated a moment, considering evidently the pros and cons of the matter, but he saw that Anastasia Alexandrovna was determined.

"Go on then, you may kiss me, Delilah, though I'm bound to say I don't see what pleasure it can be to you."

She put her arms round his neck and kissed him on both

cheeks, then without a word of warning burst into a flood of tears.

"You're a brave little man, Mr. Harrington. You're absurd but magnificent," she sobbed.

Mr. Harrington was less surprised than Ashenden would have expected him to be. He looked at Anastasia with a thin, quizzical smile and gently patted her.

"Come, come, Delilah, pull yourself together. It gave you a nasty turn, didn't it? You're quite upset. I shall have terrible rheumatism in my shoulder if you go on weeping all over it."

The scene was ridiculous and touching, Ashenden laughed, but he had the beginnings of a lump in his throat.

When Anastasia Alexandrovna had left them Mr. Harrington sat in a brown study.

"They're very queer, these Russians. Do you know what Delilah did?" he said, suddenly. "She stood up in the cab, in the middle of the street, with people passing on both sides, and took her pants off. She tore them in two and gave me one to hold while she made a bandage of the other. I was never so embarrassed in my life."

"Tell me what gave you the idea of calling her Delilah?" smiled Ashenden.

Mr. Harrington reddened a little.

"She's a very fascinating woman, Mr. Ashenden. She's been deeply wronged by her husband and I naturally felt a great deal of sympathy for her. These Russians are very emotional people and I did not want her to mistake my sympathy for anything else. I told her I was very much attached to Mrs. Harrington."

"You're not under the impression that Delilah was Potiphar's wife?" asked Ashenden.

"I don't know what you mean by that, Mr. Ashenden," replied Mr. Harrington. "Mrs. Harrington has always given me to understand that I'm very fascinating to women, and I thought if I called our little friend Delilah it would make my position quite clear."

"I don't think Russia's any place for you, Mr. Harrington," said Ashenden smiling. "If I were you I'd get out of it as quick as I could."

"I can't go now. I've got them to agree to my terms at last and we're going to sign next week. Then I shall pack my grip and go."

"I wonder if your signatures will be worth the paper they're written on," said Ashenden.

He had at length devised a plan of campaign. It took him twenty-four hours' hard work to code a telegram in which he put his scheme before the persons who had sent him to Petrograd. It was accepted and he was promised all the money he needed. Ashenden knew he could do nothing unless the Provisional Government remained in power for another three months; but winter was at hand and food was getting scarcer every day. The army was mutinous. The people clamoured for peace. Every evening at the Europe Ashenden drank a cup of chocolate with Professor Z. and discussed with him how best to make use of his devoted Czechs. Anastasia Alexandrovna had a flat in a retired spot and here he had meetings with all manner of persons. Plans were drawn up. Measures were taken. Ashenden argued, persuaded, promised. He had to overcome the vacillation of one and wrestle with the fatalism of another. He had to judge who was resolute and who was self-sufficient, who was honest and who was infirm of purpose. He had to curb his impatience with the Russian verbosity; he had to be good-tempered with people who were willing to talk of everything but the matter in hand; he had to listen sympathetically to ranting and rhodomontade. He had to beware of treachery. He had to humour the vanity of fools and elude the greed of the ambitious. Time was pressing. The rumours grew hot and many of the activities of the Bolsheviks. Kerensky ran hither and thither like a frightened hen.

Then the blow fell. On the night of November 7th, 1917, the Bolsheviks rose, Kerensky's ministers were arrested and the Winter Palace was sacked by the mob; the reins of power were seized by Lenin and Trotsky.

Anastasia Alexandrovna came to Ashenden's room at the hotel early in the morning. Ashenden was coding a telegram. He had been up all night, first at the Smolny, and then at the Winter Palace. He was tired out. Her face was white and her shining brown eyes were tragic.

"Have you heard?" she asked Ashenden.

He nodded.

"It's all over then. They say Kerensky has fled. They never even showed fight." Rage seized her. "The buffoon!" she screamed.

At that moment there was a knock at the door and Anastasia Alexandrovna looked at it with sudden apprehension.

"You know the Bolsheviks have got a list of people they've decided to execute. My name is on it, and it may be that yours is too."

"If it's they and they want to come in they only have to turn the handle," said Ashenden, smiling, but with ever so slightly odd a feeling at the pit of his stomach. "Come in."

The door was opened and Mr. Harrington stepped into the room. He was as dapper as ever, in his short black coat and striped trousers, his shoes neatly polished and a derby on his bald head. He took it off when he saw Anastasia Alexandrovna.

"Oh, fancy finding you here so early. I looked in on my way out, I wanted to tell you my news. I tried to find you yesterday evening, but couldn't. You didn't come in to dinner."

"No, I was at a meeting," said Ashenden.

"You must both congratulate me, I got my signatures yesterday, and my business is done."

Mr. Harrington beamed on them, the picture of self-satisfaction, and he arched himself like a bantam-cock who has chased away all rivals. Anastasia Alexandrovna burst into a sudden shriek of hysterical laughter. He stared at her in perplexity.

"Why, Delilah, what is the matter?" he said.

Anastasia laughed till the tears ran from her eyes and then began to sob in earnest. Ashenden explained.

"The Bolsheviks have overthrown the Government. Kerensky's ministers are in prison. The Bolsheviks are out to kill. Delilah says her name is on the list. Your minister signed your documents yesterday because he knew it did not matter what he did then. Your contracts are worth nothing. The Bolsheviks are going to make peace with Germany as soon as they can."

Anastasia Alexandrovna had recovered her self-control as quickly as she had lost it.

"You had better get out of Russia as soon as you can, Mr. Harrington. It's no place for a foreigner now and it may be that in a few days you won't be able to."

Mr. Harrington looked from one to the other.

"O my," he said. "O my!" It seemed inadequate. "Are you going to tell me that that Russian minister was just making a fool of me?"

Ashenden shrugged his shoulders.

"How can one tell what he was thinking of? He may have

a keen sense of humour and perhaps he thought it funny to sign a fifty million dollar contract yesterday when there was every chance of his being stood against the wall and shot to-day. Anastasia Alexandrovna's right, Mr. Harrington, you'd better take the first train that'll get you to Sweden."

"And what about you?"

"There's nothing for me to do here any more. I'm cabling for instructions and I shall go as soon as I get leave. The Bolsheviks have got in ahead of us and the people I was working with will have their work cut out to save their lives."

"Boris Petrovich was shot this morning," said Anastasia Alexandrovna with a frown.

They both looked at Mr. Harrington and he stared at the floor. His pride in this achievement of his was shattered and he sagged like a pricked balloon. But in a minute he looked up. He gave Anastasia Alexandrovna a little smile and for the first time Ashenden noticed how attractive and kindly his smile was. There was something peculiarly disarming about it.

"If the Bolsheviks are after you, Delilah, don't you think you'd better come with me? I'll take care of you and if you like to come to America I'm sure Mrs. Harrington would be glad to do anything she could for you."

"I can see Mrs. Harrington's face if you arrived in Philadelphia with a Russian refugee," laughed Anastasia Alexandrovna. "I'm afraid it would need more explaining than you could ever manage. No, I shall stay here."

"But if you're in danger?"

"I'm a Russian. My place is here. I will not leave my country when most my country needs me."

"That is the bunk, Delilah," said Mr. Harrington very quietly.

Anastasia Alexandrovna had spoken with deep emotion, but now with a little start she shot a sudden quizzical look at him.

"I know it is, Samson," she answered. "To tell you the truth I think we're all going to have a hell of a time, God knows what's going to happen, but I want to see; I wouldn't miss a minute of it for the world."

Mr. Harrington shook his head.

"Curiosity is the bane of your sex, Delilah," he said.

"Go along and do your packing, Mr. Harrington," said Ashenden, smiling; "and then we'll take you to the station. The train will be besieged."

"Very well, I'll go. And I shan't be sorry either. I haven't had a decent meal since I came here and I've done a thing I never thought I should have to do in my life, I've drunk my coffee without sugar and when I've been lucky enough to get a little piece of black bread I've had to eat it without butter. Mrs. Harrington will never believe me when I tell her what I've gone through. What this country wants is organization."

When he left them Ashenden and Anastasia Alexandrovna talked over the situation. Ashenden was depressed because all his careful schemes had come to nothing, but Anastasia Alexandrovna was excited and she hazarded every sort of guess about the outcome of this new revolution. She pretended to be very serious, but in her heart she looked upon it all very much as a thrilling play. She wanted more and more things to happen. Then there was another knock at the door and before Ashenden could answer Mr. Harrington burst in.

"Really the service at this hotel is a scandal," he cried heatedly, "I've been ringing my bell for fifteen minutes and I can't get anyone to pay the smallest attention to me."

"Service?" exclaimed Anastasia Alexandrovna. "There is not a servant left in the hotel."

"But I want my washing. They promised to let me have it back last night."

"I'm afraid you haven't got much chance of getting it now," said Ashenden.

"I'm not going to leave without my washing. Four shirts, two union suits, a pair of pyjamas, and four collars. I wash my handkerchiefs and socks in my room. I want my washing and I'm not going to leave this hotel without it."

"Don't be a fool," cried Ashenden. "What you've got to do is to get out of here while the going's good. If there are no servants to get it you'll just have to leave your washing behind you."

"Pardon me, sir, I shall do nothing of the kind. I'll go and fetch it myself. I've suffered enough at the hands of this country and I'm not going to leave four perfectly good shirts to be worn by a lot of dirty Bolsheviks. No, sir. I do not leave Russia till I have my washing."

Anastasia Alexandrovna stared at the floor for a moment; then with a little smile looked up. It seemed to Ashenden that there was something in her that responded to Mr. Harrington's futile obstinacy. In her Russian way she understood that Mr.

Harrington could not leave Petrograd without his washing. His insistence had given it the value of a symbol.

"I'll go downstairs and see if I can find anybody about who knows where the laundry is and if I can, I'll go with you and you can bring your washing away with you."

Mr. Harrington unbent. He answered with that sweet and disarming smile of his.

"That's terribly kind of you, Delilah. I don't mind if it's ready or not, I'll take it just as it is."

Anastasia Alexandrovna left them.

"Well, what do you think of Russia and the Russians now?" Mr. Harrington asked Ashenden.

"I'm fed up with them. I'm fed up with Tolstoi, I'm fed up with Turgeniev and Dostoievski, I'm fed up with Chekov. I'm fed up with the Intelligentsia. I hanker after people who know their mind from one minute to another, who mean what they say an hour after they've said it, whose word you can rely on; I'm sick of fine phrases, and oratory and attitudinizing."

Ashenden, bitten by the prevailing ill, was about to make a speech when he was interrupted by a rattle as of peas on a drum. In the city, so strangely silent, it sounded abrupt and odd.

"What's that?" asked Mr. Harrington.

"Rifle firing. On the other side of the river I should think."

Mr. Harrington gave a funny little look. He laughed, but his face was a trifle pale; he did not like it, and Ashenden did not blame him.

"I think it's high time I got out. I shouldn't so much mind for myself, but I've got a wife and children to think of. I haven't had a letter from Mrs. Harrington for so long I'm a bit worried." He paused an instant. "I'd like you to know Mrs. Harrington, she's a very wonderful woman. She's the best wife a man ever had. Until I came here I'd not been separated from her for more than three days since we were married."

Anastasia Alexandrovna came back and told them that she had found the address.

"It's about forty minutes' walk from here and if you'll come now I'll go with you," she said.

"I'm ready."

"You'd better look out," said Ashenden. "I don't believe the streets are very healthy to-day."

Anastasia Alexandrovna looked at Mr. Harrington.

"I must have my washing, Delilah," he said. "I should never rest in peace if I left it behind me and Mrs. Harrington would never let me hear the last of it."

"Come on then."

They set out and Ashenden went on with the dreary business of translating into a very complicated code the shattering news he had to give. It was a long message, and then he had to ask for instructions upon his own movements. It was a mechanical job and yet it was one in which you could not allow your attention to wander. The mistake of a single figure might make a whole sentence incomprehensible.

Suddenly his door was burst open and Anastasia Alexandrovna flung into the room. She had lost her hat and was dishevelled. She was panting. Her eyes were starting out of her head and she was obviously in a state of great excitement.

"Where's Mr. Harrington?" she cried. "Isn't he here?"

"No."

"Is he in his bedroom?"

"I don't know. Why, what's the matter? We'll go and look if you like. Why didn't you bring him along with you?"

They walked down the passage and knocked at Mr. Harrington's door; there was no answer; they tried the handle; the door was locked.

"He's not there."

They went back to Ashenden's room. Anastasia Alexandrovna sank into a chair.

"Give me a glass of water, will you. I'm out of breath. I've been running."

She drank the water Ashenden poured out for her. She gave a sudden sob.

"I hope he's all right. I should never forgive myself if he was hurt. I was hoping he would have got here before me. He got his washing all right. We found the place. There was only an old woman there and they didn't want to let us take it, but we insisted. Mr. Harrington was furious because it hadn't been touched. It was exactly as he had sent it. They'd promised it last night and it was still in the bundle that Mr. Harrington had made himself. I said that was Russia and Mr. Harrington said he preferred coloured people. I'd led him by side streets because I thought it was better, and we started to come back again. We passed at the top of a street and at the bottom of it I saw a little crowd. There was a man addressing them.

"'Let's go and hear what he's saying,' I said.

"I could see they were arguing. It looked exciting. I wanted to know what was happening.

"'Come along, Delilah,' he said. 'Let us mind our own business.'

"'You go back to the hotel and do your packing. I'm going to see the fun,' I said.

"I ran down the street and he followed me. There were about two or three hundred people there and a student was addressing them. There were some working men and they were shouting at him. I love a row and I edged my way into the crowd. Suddenly we heard the sound of shots and before you could realize what was happening two armoured cars came dashing down the street. There were soldiers in them and they were firing as they went. I don't know why. For fun, I suppose, or because they were drunk. We all scattered like a lot of rabbits. We just ran for our lives. I lost Mr. Harrington. I can't make out why he isn't here. Do you think something has happened to him?"

Ashenden was silent for a while.

"We'd better go out and look for him," he said. "I don't know why the devil he couldn't leave his washing."

"I understand, I understand so well."

"That's a comfort," said Ashenden irritably. "Let's go."

He put on his hat and coat, and they walked downstairs. The hotel seemed strangely empty. They went out into the street. There was hardly anyone to be seen. They walked along. The trams were not running and the silence in the great city was uncanny. The shops were closed. It was quite startling when a motor car dashed by at breakneck speed. The people they passed looked frightened and downcast. When they had to go through a main thoroughfare they hastened their steps. A lot of people were there and they stood about irresolutely as though they did not know what to do next. Reservists in their shabby grey were walking down the middle of the roadway in little bunches. They did not speak. They looked like sheep looking for their shepherd. Then they came to the street down which Anastasia Alexandrovna had run, but they entered it from the opposite end. A number of windows had been broken by the wild shooting. It was quite empty. You could see where the people had scattered, for strewn about were articles they had dropped in their haste, books, a man's hat, a lady's bag and a basket. Anastasia Alexandrovna touched Ashenden's arm to draw his attention: sitting on the pavement, her head bent right down to her lap, was a woman and she was dead. A little way on two men had fallen together. They were dead too. The wounded, one supposed, had managed to drag themselves away or their friends had carried them. Then they found Mr. Harrington. His derby had rolled in the gutter. He lay on his face, in a pool of blood, his bald head, with its prominent bones, very white; his neat black coat smeared and muddy. But his hand was clenched tight on the parcel that contained four shirts, two union suits, a pair of pyjamas and four collars. Mr. Harrington had not let his washing go.

FOOTPRINTS IN THE JUNGLE

THERE is no place in Malaya that has more charm than Tanah Merah. It lies on the sea and the sandy shore is fringed with casuarinas. The government offices are still in the old Raad Huis that the Dutch built when they owned the land, and on the hill stand the grey ruins of the fort by aid of which the Portuguese maintained their hold over the unruly natives. Tanah Merah has a history and in the vast labyrinthine houses of the Chinese merchants, backing on the sea so that in the cool of the evening they may sit in their loggias and enjoy the salt breeze, families dwell that have been settled in the country for three centuries. Many have forgotten their native language and hold intercourse with one another in Malay and pidgin English. The imagination lingers here gratefully, for in the Federated Malay States the only past is within the memory for the most part of the fathers of living men.

Tanah Merah was for long the busiest mart of the Middle East and its harbour was crowded with shipping when the clipper and the junk still sailed the China seas. But now it is dead. It has the sad and romantic air of all places that have once been of importance and live now on the recollection of a vanished grandeur. It is a sleepy little town and strangers that come to it, losing their native energy, insensibly drop into its easy and lethargic ways. Successive rubber booms bring it no prosperity and the ensuing slumps hasten its decay.

The European quarter is very silent. It is trim and neat and clean. The houses of the white men—Government servants

641

and agents of companies—stand round an immense padang, agreeable and roomy bungalows shaded by great cassias, and the padang is vast and green and well cared for, like the lawn of a cathedral close, and indeed there is in the aspect of this corner of Tanah Merah something quiet and delicately secluded that reminds you of the precincts of Canterbury.

The Club faces the sea; it is a spacious but shabby building; it has an air of neglect and when you enter you feel that you intrude. It gives you the impression that it is closed really, for alterations and repairs, and that you have taken indiscreet advantage of an open door to go where you are not wanted. In the morning you may find there a couple of planters who have come in from their estates on business and are drinking a gin-sling before starting back again; and latish in the afternoon a lady or two may perhaps be seen looking with a furtive air through old numbers of the Illustrated London News. At nightfall a few men saunter in and sit about the billiard-room watching the play and drinking sukus. But on Wednesdays there is a little more animation. On that day the gramophone is set going in the large room upstairs and people come in from the surrounding country to dance. There are sometimes no less than a dozen couples and it is even possible to make up two tables of bridge.

It was on one of these occasions that I met the Cartwrights. I was staying with a man called Gaze who was head of the police and he came into the billiard-room, where I was sitting, and asked me if I would make up a four. The Cartwrights were planters and they came in to Tanah Merah on Wednesdays because it gave their girl a chance of a little fun. They were very nice people, said Gaze, quiet and unobtrusive, and played a very pleasant game of bridge. I followed Gaze into the card-room and was introduced to them. They were already seated at a table and Mrs. Cartwright was shuffling the cards. It inspired me with confidence to see the competent way in which she did it. She took half the pack in each hand, and her hands were large and strong, deftly inserted the corners of one half under the corners of the others, and with a click and a neat bold gesture cascaded the cards together.

It had all the effect of a conjuring trick. The card-player knows that it can be done perfectly only after incessant practice. He can be fairly sure that anyone who can so shuffle a pack of cards loves cards for their own sake.

"Do you mind if my husband and I play together?" asked Mrs. Cartwright. "It's no fun for us to win one another's money."

"Of course not."

We cut for deal and Gaze and I sat down.

Mrs. Cartwright drew an ace and while she dealt, quickly and neatly, chatted with Gaze of local affairs. But I was aware that she took stock of me. She looked shrewd but good-natured.

She was a woman somewhere in the fifties (though in the East, where people age quickly, it is difficult to tell their ages), with white hair very untidily arranged, and a constant gesture with her was an impatient movement of the hand to push back a long wisp of hair that kept falling over her forehead. You wondered why she did not, by the use of a hairpin or two, save herself so much trouble. Her blue eyes were large, but pale and a little tired; her face was lined and sallow; I think it was her mouth that gave it the expression which I felt was characteristic of caustic but tolerant irony. You saw that here was a woman who knew her mind and was never afraid to speak it. She was a chatty player (which some people object to strongly, but which does not disconcert me, for I do not see why you should behave at the card-table as though you were at a memorial service) and it was soon apparent that she had an effective knack of badinage. It was pleasantly acid, but it was amusing enough to be offensive only to a fool. If now and then she uttered a remark so sarcastic that you wanted all your sense of humour to see the fun in it, you could not but quickly see that she was willing to take as much as she gave. Her large, thin mouth broke into a dry smile and her eyes shone brightly when by a lucky chance you brought off a repartee that turned the laugh against her.

I thought her a very agreeable person. I liked her frankness. I liked her quick wit. I liked her plain face. I never met a woman who obviously cared so little how she looked. It was not only her head that was untidy, everything about her was slovenly; she wore a high-necked silk blouse, but for coolness had unbuttoned the top buttons and showed a gaunt and withered neck; the blouse was crumpled and none too clean, for she smoked innumerable cigarettes and covered herself with ash. When she got up for a moment to speak to somebody I saw that her blue skirt was rather ragged at the hem and badly needed a brush, and she wore heavy, low-heeled boots. But none of this mattered. Everything she wore was perfectly in character.

And it was a pleasure to play bridge with her. She played very quickly, without hesitation, and she had not only knowledge but flair. Of course she knew Gaze's game, but I was a stranger and she soon took my measure. The team-work between her husband and herself was admirable; he was sound and cautious, but knowing him, she was able to be bold with assurance and brilliant with safety. Gaze was a player who founded a foolish optimism on the hope that his opponents would not have the sense to take advantage of his errors, and the pair of us were no match for the Cartwrights. We lost one rubber after another, and there was nothing to do but smile and look as if we liked it.

"I don't know what's the matter with the cards," said Gaze at last, plaintively. "Even when we have every card in the pack we go down."

"It can't be anything to do with your play," answered Mrs. Cartwright, looking him full in the face with those pale blue eyes of hers, "it must be bad luck pure and simple. Now if you hadn't had your hearts mixed up with your diamonds in that last hand you'd have saved the game."

Gaze began to explain at length how the misfortune, which had cost us dear, occurred, but Mrs. Cartwright, with a deft flick of the hand, spread out the cards in a great circle so that we should cut for deal. Cartwright looked at the time.

"This will have to be the last, my dear," he said.

"Oh, will it?" She glanced at her watch and then called to a young man who was passing through the room. "Oh, Mr. Bullen, if you're going upstairs tell Olive that we shall be going in a few minutes." She turned to me. "It takes us the best part of an hour to get back to the estate and poor Theo has to be up at the crack of dawn."

"Oh, well, we only come in once a week," said Cartwright, "and it's the one chance Olive gets of being gay and abandoned."

I thought Cartwright looked tired and old. He was a man of middle height, with a bald, shiny head, a stubbly grey moustache, and gold-rimmed spectacles. He wore white ducks and a black-and-white tie. He was rather neat and you could see he took much more pains with his clothes than his untidy wife. He talked little, but it was plain that he enjoyed his wife's caustic humour and sometimes he made quite a neat retort.

They were evidently very good friends. It was pleasing to see so solid and tolerant an affection between two people who were almost elderly and must have lived together for so many years.

It took but two hands to finish the rubber and we had just ordered a final gin and bitters when Olive came down.

"Do you really want to go already, Mumsey?" she asked.

Mrs. Cartwright looked at her daughter with fond eyes.

"Yes, darling. It's nearly half-past eight. It'll be ten before we get our dinner."

"Damn our dinner," said Olive, gaily.

"Let her have one more dance before we go," suggested Cartwright.

"Not one. You must have a good night's rest."

Cartwright looked at Olive with a smile.

"If your mother has made up her mind, my dear, we may just as well give in without any fuss."

"She's a determined woman," said Olive, lovingly stroking her mother's wrinkled cheek.

Mrs. Cartwright patted her daughter's hand, and kissed it.

Olive was not very pretty, but she looked extremely nice. She was nineteen or twenty, I suppose, and she had still the plumpness of her age; she would be more attractive when she had fined down a little. She had none of the determination that gave her mother's face so much character, but resembled her father; she had his dark eyes and slightly aquiline nose, and his look of rather weak good nature. It was plain that she was strong and healthy. Her cheeks were red and her eyes bright. She had a vitality that he had long since lost. She seemed to be the perfectly normal English girl, with high spirits, a great desire to enjoy herself, and an excellent temper.

When we separated, Gaze and I set out to walk to his house.

"What did you think of the Cartwrights?" he asked me.

"I liked them. They must be a great asset in a place like this."

"I wish they came oftener. They live a very quiet life."

"It must be dull for the girl. The father and mother seem very well satisfied with one another's company."

"Yes, it's been a great success."

"Olive is the image of her father, isn't she?"

Gaze gave me a sidelong glance.

"Cartwright isn't her father. Mrs. Cartwright was a widow when he married her. Olive was born four months after her father's death."

"Oh!"

I drew out the sound in order to put in it all I could of sur-prise, interest and curiosity. But Gaze said nothing and we walked the rest of the way in silence. The boy was waiting at the door as we entered the house and after a last gin pahit we sat down to dinner.

At first Gaze was inclined to be talkative. Owing to the re-striction of the output of rubber there had sprung up a con-siderable activity among the smugglers and it was part of his duty to circumvent their knavishness. Two junks had been captured that day and he was rubbing his hands over his suc-cess. The go-downs were full of confiscated rubber and in a little while it was going to be solemnly burnt. But presently he fell into silence and we finished without a word. The boys brought in coffee and brandy and we lit our cheroots. Gaze leaned back in his chair. He looked at me reflectively and then looked at his brandy. The boys had left the room and we were alone.

"I've known Mrs. Cartwright for over twenty years," he said slowly. "She wasn't a bad-looking woman in those days. Always untidy, but when she was young it didn't seem to matter so much. It was rather attractive. She was married to a man called Bronson. Reggie Bronson. He was a planter. He was manager of an estate up in Selantan and I was stationed at Alor Lipis. It was a much smaller place than it is now; I don't suppose there were more than twenty people in the whole community, but they had a jolly little club, and we used to have a very good time. I remember the first time I met Mrs. Bronson as though it was yesterday. There were no cars in those days and she and Bronson had ridden in on their bicycles. Of course then she didn't look so determined as she looks now. She was much thinner, she had a nice colour, and her eyes were very pretty—blue, you know—and she had a lot of dark hair. If she'd only taken more trouble with herself she'd have been rather stunning. As it was she was the best-looking woman there."

I tried to construct in my mind a picture of what Mrs. Cart-wright—Mrs. Bronson as she was then—looked like from what she was now and from Gaze's not very graphic description. In the solid woman, with her well-covered bones, who sat rather heavily at the bridge-table, I tried to see a slight young thing with buoyant movements and graceful, easy gestures. Her chin now was square and her nose decided, but the roundness of youth must have masked this: she must have been charming with a pink and white skin and her hair carelessly dressed, brown and abundant. At that period she wore a long skirt, a tight waist and a picture hat. Or did women in Malaya still wear the topis that you see in old numbers of the illustrated papers?

"I hadn't seen her for—oh, nearly twenty years," Gaze went on. "I knew she was living somewhere in the F.M.S., but it was a surprise when I took this job and came here to run across her in the club just as I had up in Selantan so many years before. Of course she's an elderly woman now and she's changed out of all recognition. It was rather a shock to see her with a grown-up daughter, it made me realize how the time had passed; I was a young fellow when I met her last and now, by Jingo, I'm due to retire on the age limit in two or three years. Bit thick, isn't it?"

Gaze, a rueful grin on his ugly face, looked at me with faint indignation, as though I could help the hurrying march of the years as they trod upon one another's heels.

"I'm no chicken myself," I replied.

"You haven't lived out East all your life. It ages one before one's time. One's an elderly man at fifty and at fifty-five one's good for nothing but the scrap heap."

But I did not want Gaze to wander off into a disquisition on old age.

"Did you recognize Mrs. Cartwright when you saw her again?" I asked.

"Well, I did and I didn't. At the first glance I thought I knew her, but couldn't quite place her. I thought perhaps she was someone I'd met on board ship when I was going on leave and had known only by sight. But the moment she spoke I remembered at once. I remembered the dry twinkle in her eyes and the crisp sound of her voice. There was something in her voice that seemed to mean: you're a bit of a damned fool, my lad, but you're not a bad sort and upon my soul I rather like you."

"That's a good deal to read into the sound of a voice," I smiled.

"She came up to me in the club and shook hands with me. 'How do you do, Major Gaze? Do you remember me?' she said.

"'Of course I do.'

"'A lot of water has passed under the bridge since we met

last. We're none of us as young as we were. Have you seen
Theo?'

"For a moment I couldn't think whom she meant. I suppose
I looked rather stupid, because she gave a little smile, that
chaffing smile that I knew so well, and explained.

"'I married Theo, you know. It seemed the best thing to do.
I was lonely and he wanted it.'

"'I heard you married him,' I said. 'I hope you've been very
happy.'

"'Oh, very. Theo's a perfect duck. He'll be here in a minute.
He'll be so glad to see you.'

"I wondered. I should have thought I was the last man Theo
would wish to see. I shouldn't have thought she would wish it
very much either. But women are funny."

"Why shouldn't she wish to see you?" I asked.

"I'm coming to that later," said Gaze. "Then Theo turned
up. I don't know why I call him Theo; I never called him anything but Cartwright, I never thought of him as anything but
Cartwright. Theo was a shock. You know what he looks like
now; I remembered him as a curly-headed youngster, very
fresh and clean looking; he was always neat and dapper, he had
a good figure and he held himself well, like a man who's used
to taking a lot of exercise. Now I come to think of it he wasn't
bad looking, not in a big, massive way, but graceful, you know,
and lithe. When I saw this bowed, cadaverous, bald-headed
old buffer with spectacles I could hardly believe my eyes. I
shouldn't have known him from Adam. He seemed pleased to
see me, at least, interested; he wasn't effusive, but he'd always
been on the quiet side and I didn't expect him to be.

"'Are you surprised to find us here?' he asked me.

"'Well, I hadn't the faintest notion where you were.'

"'We've kept track of your movements more or less. We've
seen your name in the paper every now and then. You must
come out one day and have a look at our place. We've been
settled there a good many years, and I suppose we shall stay
there till we go home for good. Have you ever been back to
Alor Lipis?'

"'No, I haven't,' I said.

"'It was a nice little place. I'm told it's grown. I've never
been back.'

"'It hasn't got the pleasantest recollections for us,' said Mrs.
Cartwright.

"I asked them if they'd have a drink and we called the boy. I daresay you noticed that Mrs. Cartwright likes her liquor; I don't mean that she gets tight or anything like that, but she drinks her stengah like a man. I couldn't help looking at them with a certain amount of curiosity. They seemed perfectly happy; I gathered that they hadn't done at all badly, and I found out later that they were quite well off. They had a very nice car, and when they went on leave they denied themselves nothing. They were on the best of terms with one another. You know how jolly it is to see two people who've been married a great many years obviously better pleased with their own company than anyone else's. Their marriage had evidently been a great success. And they were both of them devoted to Olive and very proud of her, Theo especially."

"Although she was only his step-daughter?" I said.

"Although she was only his step-daughter," answered Gaze. "You'd think that she would have taken his name. But she hadn't. She called him Daddy, of course, he was the only father she'd ever known, but she signed her letters, Olive Bronson."

"What was Bronson like, by the way?"

"Bronson? He was a great big fellow, very hearty, with a loud voice and a bellowing laugh, beefy, you know, and a fine athlete. There was not very much to him but he was as straight as a die. He had a red face and red hair. Now I come to think of it I remember that I never saw a man sweat as much as he did. Water just poured off him, and when he played tennis he always used to bring a towel on the court with him."

"It doesn't sound very attractive."

"He was a handsome chap. He was always fit. He was keen on that. He hadn't much to talk about but rubber and games, tennis, you know, and golf and shooting; and I don't suppose he read a book from year's end to year's end. He was the typical public-school boy. He was about thirty-five when I first knew him, but he had the mind of a boy of eighteen. You know how many fellows when they come out East seem to stop growing."

I did indeed. One of the most disconcerting things to the traveller is to see stout, middle-aged gentlemen, with bald heads, speaking and acting like schoolboys. You might almost think that no idea has entered their heads since they first passed through the Suez Canal. Though married and the fathers of children, and perhaps in control of a large business, they continue to look upon life from the standpoint of the sixth form.

"But he was no fool," Gaze went on. "He knew his work from A to Z. His estate was one of the best managed in the country and he knew how to handle his labour. He was a damned good sort, and if he did get on your nerves a little you couldn't help liking him. He was generous with his money, and always ready to do anybody a good turn. That's how Cartwright happened to turn up in the first instance."

"Did the Bronsons get on well together?"

"Oh, yes, I think so. I'm sure they did. He was good natured and she was very jolly and gay. She was very outspoken, you know. She can be very amusing when she likes even now, but there's generally a sting lurking in the joke; when she was a young woman and married to Bronson it was just pure fun. She had high spirits and liked having a good time. She never cared a hang what she said, but it went with her type, if you understand what I mean; there was something so open and frank and careless about her that you didn't care what she said to you. They seemed very happy.

"Their estate was about five miles from Alor Lipis. They had a trap and they used to drive in most evenings about five. Of course it was a very small community and men were in the majority. There were only about six women. The Bronsons were a god-send. They bucked things up the moment they arrived. We used to have very jolly times in that little club. I've often thought of them since and I don't know that on the whole I've ever enjoyed myself more than I did when I was stationed there. Between six and eight-thirty the club at Alor Lipis twenty years ago was about as lively a place as you could find between Aden and Yokohama.

"One day Mrs. Bronson told us that they were expecting a friend to stay with them and a few days later they brought Cartwright along. It appeared that he was an old friend of Bronson's, they'd been at school together, Marlborough, or some place like that, and they'd first come out East on the same ship. Rubber had taken a toss and a lot of fellows had lost their jobs. Cartwright was one of them. He'd been out of work for the greater part of a year and he hadn't anything to fall back on. In those days planters were even worse paid than they are now and a man had to be very lucky to put by something for a rainy day. Cartwright had gone to Singapore. They all go there when there's a slump, you know. It's awful then, I've seen it; I've known of planters sleeping in the street because they hadn't the price of a night's lodging. I've known them stop strangers outside the Europe and ask for a dollar to get a meal, and I think Cartwright had had a pretty rotten time.

"At last he wrote to Bronson and asked him if he couldn't do something for him. Bronson asked him to come and stay till things got better, at least it would be free board and lodging, and Cartwright jumped at the chance, but Bronson had to send him the money to pay his railway fare. When Cartwright arrived at Alor Lipis he hadn't ten cents in his pocket. Bronson had a little money of his own, two or three hundred a year, I think, and though his salary had been cut, he'd kept his job, so that he was better off than most planters. When Cartwright came Mrs. Bronson told him that he was to look upon the place as his home and stay as long as he liked."

"It was very nice of her, wasn't it?" I remarked.

"Very."

Gaze lit himself another cheroot and filled his glass. It was very still and but for the occasional croak of the chik-chak the silence was intense. We seemed to be alone in the tropical night and heaven only knows how far from the habitations of men. Gaze did not speak for so long that at last I was forced to say something.

"What sort of a man was Cartwright at that time?" I asked. "Younger, of course, and you told me rather nice looking; but in himself?"

"Well, to tell you the truth, I never paid much attention to him. He was pleasant and unassuming. He's very quiet now, as I daresay you noticed; well, he wasn't exactly lively then. But he was perfectly inoffensive. He was fond of reading and he played the piano rather nicely. You never minded having him about, he was never in the way, but you never bothered very much about him. He danced well and the women rather liked that, but he also played billiards quite decently and he wasn't bad at tennis. He fell into our little groove very naturally. I wouldn't say that he ever became wildly popular, but everybody liked him. Of course we were sorry for him, as one is for a man who's down and out, but there was nothing we could do, and, well, we just accepted him and then forgot that he hadn't always been there. He used to come in with the Bronsons every evening and pay for his drinks like everyone else, I suppose Bronson had lent a bit of money for current expenses, and he was always very civil. I'm rather vague about him, because really he didn't make any particular impression on me; in the East one meets such a lot of people, and he seemed very much like anybody else. He did everything he could to get something to do, but he had no luck; the fact is, there were no jobs going, and sometimes he seemed rather depressed about it. He was with the Bronsons for over a year. I remember his saying to me once:

"'After all I can't live with them for ever. They've been most awfully good to me, but there are limits.'

"'I should think the Bronsons would be very glad to have you,' I said. 'It's not particularly gay on a rubber estate, and as far as your food and drink go, it must make precious little difference if you're there or not.'"

Gaze stopped once more and looked at me with a sort of hesitation.

"What's the matter?" I asked.

"I'm afraid I'm telling you this story very badly," he said. "I seem to be just rambling on. I'm not a damned novelist, I'm a policeman, and I'm just telling you the facts as I saw them at the time; and from my point of view all the circumstances are important; it's important, I mean, to realize what sort of people they were."

"Of course. Fire away."

"I remember someone, a woman, I think it was, the doctor's wife, asking Mrs. Bronson if she didn't get tired sometimes of having a stranger in the house. You know, in places like Alor Lipis there isn't very much to talk about, and if you didn't talk about your neighbours there'd be nothing to talk about at all.

"'Oh, no,' she said, 'Theo's no trouble.' She turned to her husband who was sitting there mopping his face. 'We like having him, don't we?'

"'He's all right,' said Bronson.

"'What does he do with himself all day long?'

"'Oh, I don't know,' said Mrs. Bronson. 'He walks round the estate with Reggie sometimes, and he shoots a bit. He talks to me.'

"'He's always glad to make himself useful,' said Bronson. 'The other day when I had a go of fever, he took over my work and I just lay in bed and had a good time.'"

"Hadn't the Bronsons any children?" I asked.

"No," Gaze answered. "I don't know why, they could well have afforded it."

Gaze leant back in his chair. He took off his glasses and wiped them. They were very strong and hideously distorted his eyes. Without them he wasn't so homely. The chik-chak on the ceiling gave its strangely human cry. It was like the cackle of an idiot child.

"Bronson was killed," said Gaze suddenly.

"Killed?"

"Yes, murdered. I shall never forget that night. We'd been playing tennis, Mrs. Bronson and the doctor's wife, Theo Cartwright and I; and then we played bridge. Cartwright had been off his game and when we sat down at the bridge-table Mrs. Bronson said to him: 'Well, Theo, if you play bridge as rottenly as you played tennis we shall lose our shirts.'

"We'd just had a drink, but she called the boy and ordered another round.

"'Put that down your throat,' she said to him, 'and don't call without top honours and an outside trick.'

"Bronson hadn't turned up, he'd cycled in to Kabulong to get the money to pay his coolies their wages and was to come along to the club when he got back. The Bronsons' estate was nearer Alor Lipis than it was to Kabulong, but Kabulong was a more important place commercially, and Bronson banked there.

"'Reggie can cut in when he turns up,' said Mrs. Bronson.

"'He's late, isn't he?' said the doctor's wife.

"'Very. He said he wouldn't get back in time for tennis, but would be here for a rubber. I have a suspicion that he went to the club at Kabulong instead of coming straight home and is having drinks, the ruffian.'

"'Oh, well, he can put away a good many without their having much effect on him,' I laughed.

"'He's getting fat, you know. He'll have to be careful.'

"We sat by ourselves in the card-room and we could hear the crowd in the billiard-room talking and laughing. They were all on the merry side. It was getting on to Christmas Day and we were all letting ourselves go a little. There was going to be a dance on Christmas Eve.

"I remembered afterwards that when we sat down the doctor's wife asked Mrs. Bronson if she wasn't tired.

"'Not a bit,' she said. 'Why should I be?'

"I didn't know why she flushed.

"'I was afraid the tennis might have been too much for you,' said the doctor's wife.

"'Oh, no,' answered Mrs. Bronson, a trifle abruptly, I thought, as though she didn't want to discuss the matter.

"I didn't know what they meant, and indeed it wasn't till later that I remembered the incident.

"We played three or four rubbers and still Bronson didn't turn up.

"'I wonder what's happened to him,' said his wife. 'I can't think why he should be so late.'

"Cartwright was always silent, but this evening he had hardly opened his mouth. I thought he was tired and asked him what he'd been doing.

"'Nothing very much,' he said. 'I went out after tiffin to shoot pigeon.'

"'Did you have any luck?' I asked.

"'Oh, I got half a dozen. They were very shy.'

"But now he said: 'If Reggie got back late, I daresay he thought it wasn't worth while to come here. I expect he's had a bath and when we get in we shall find him asleep in his chair.'

"'It's a good long ride from Kabulong,' said the doctor's wife.

"'He doesn't take the road, you know,' Mrs. Bronson explained. 'He takes the short cut through the jungle.'

"'Can he get along on his bicycle?' I asked.

"'Oh, yes, it's a very good track. It saves about a couple of miles.'

"We had just started another rubber when the barboy came in and said there was a police-sergeant outside who wanted to speak to me.

"'What does he want?' I asked.

"The boy said he didn't know, but he had two coolies with him.

"'Curse him,' I said. 'I'll give him hell if I find he's disturbed me for nothing.'

"I told the boy I'd come and I finished playing the hand. Then I got up.

"'I won't be a minute,' I said. 'Deal for me, will you?' I added to Cartwright.

"I went out and found the sergeant with two Malays waiting for me on the steps. I asked him what the devil he wanted.

You can imagine my consternation when he told me that the
Malays had come to the police-station and said there was a
white man lying dead on the path that led through the jungle
to Kabulong. I immediately thought of Bronson.

"'Dead?' I cried.

"'Yes, shot. Shot through the head. A white man with red
hair.'

"Then I knew it was Reggie Bronson, and indeed, one of
them naming his estate said he'd recognized him as the tuan.
It was an awful shock. And there was Mrs. Bronson in the card-
room waiting impatiently for me to sort my cards and make a
bid. For a moment I really didn't know what to do. I was
frightfully upset. It was dreadful to give her such a terrible
and unexpected blow without a word of preparation, but I
found myself quite unable to think of any way to soften it.
I told the sergeant and the coolies to wait and went back into
the club. I tried to pull myself together. As I entered the card-
room Mrs. Bronson said: 'You've been an awful long time.'
Then she caught sight of my face. 'Is anything the matter?'
I saw her clench her fists and go white. You'd have thought
she had a presentiment of evil.

"'Something dreadful has happened,' I said, and my throat
was all closed up so that my voice sounded even to myself
hoarse and uncanny. 'There's been an accident. Your husband's
been wounded.'

"She gave a long gasp, it was not exactly a scream, it reminded me oddly of a piece of silk torn in two.

"'Wounded?'

"She leapt to her feet and with her eyes starting from her
head stared at Cartwright. The effect on him was ghastly, he
fell back in his chair and went as white as death.

"'Very, very badly, I'm afraid,' I added.

"I knew that I must tell her the truth, and tell it then, but
I couldn't bring myself to tell it all at once.

"'Is he,' her lips trembled so that she could hardly form the
words, 'is he—conscious?'

"I looked at her for a moment without answering. I'd have
given a thousand pounds not to have to.

"'No, I'm afraid he isn't.'

"Mrs. Bronson stared at me as though she were trying to see
right into my brain.

"'Is he dead?'

"I thought the only thing was to get it out and have done with it.

"'Yes, he was dead when they found him.'

"Mrs. Bronson collapsed into her chair and burst into tears.

"'Oh, my God,' she muttered. 'Oh, my God.'

"The doctor's wife went to her and put her arms round her. Mrs. Bronson with her face in her hands swayed to and fro weeping hysterically. Cartwright, with that livid face, sat quite still, his mouth open, and stared at her. You might have thought he was turned to stone.

"'Oh, my dear, my dear,' said the doctor's wife, 'you must try and pull yourself together.' Then, turning to me, 'Get her a glass of water and fetch Harry.'

"Harry was her husband and he was playing billiards. I went in and told him what had happened.

"'A glass of water be damned,' he said. 'What she wants is a good long peg of brandy.'

"We took it in to her and forced her to drink it and gradually the violence of her emotion exhausted itself. In a few minutes the doctor's wife was able to take her into the ladies' lavatory to wash her face. I'd made up my mind now what had better be done. I could see that Cartwright wasn't good for much; he was all to pieces. I could understand that it was a fearful shock to him, for after all Bronson was his greatest friend and had done everything in the world for him.

"'You look as though you'd be all the better for a drop of brandy yourself, old man,' I said to him.

"He made an effort.

"'It's shaken me, you know,' he said. 'I . . . I didn't . . .,' He stopped as though his mind was wandering; he was still fearfully pale; he took out a packet of cigarettes and struck a match, but his hand was shaking so that he could hardly manage it.

"'Yes, I'll have a brandy.'

"'Boy,' I shouted, and then to Cartwright: 'Now, are you fit to take Mrs. Bronson home?'

"'Oh, yes,' he answered.

"'That's good. The doctor and I will go along with the coolies and some police to where the body is.'

"'Will you bring him back to the bungalow?' asked Cartwright.

"'I think he'd better be taken straight to the mortuary,'

said the doctor before I could answer. 'I shall have to do a P.M.'

"When Mrs. Bronson, now so much calmer that I was amazed, came back, I told her what I suggested. The doctor's wife, kind woman, offered to go with her and spend the night at the bungalow, but Mrs. Bronson wouldn't hear of it. She said she would be perfectly all right, and when the doctor's wife insisted—you know how bent some people are on forcing their kindness on those in trouble—she turned on her almost fiercely.

"'No, no, I must be alone,' she said. 'I really must. And Theo will be there.'

"They got into the trap. Theo took the reins and they drove off. We started after them, the doctor and I, while the sergeant and the coolies followed. I had sent my seis to the police-station with instructions to send two men to the place where the body was lying. We soon passed Mrs. Bronson and Cartwright.

"'All right?' I called.

"'Yes,' he answered.

"For some time the doctor and I drove without saying a word; we were both of us deeply shocked. I was worried as well. Somehow or other I'd got to find the murderers and I foresaw that it would be no easy matter.

"'Do you suppose it was gang robbery?' said the doctor at last.

"He might have been reading my thoughts.

"'I don't think there's a doubt of it,' I answered. 'They knew he'd gone into Kabulong to get the wages and lay in wait for him on the way back. Of course he should never have come alone through the jungle when everyone knew he had a packet of money with him.'

"'He'd done it for years,' said the doctor. 'And he's not the only one.'

"'I know. The question is, how we're going to get hold of the fellows that did it.'

"'You don't think the two coolies who say they found him could have had anything to do with it?'

"'No. They wouldn't have the nerve. I think a pair of Chinks might think out a trick like that, but I don't believe Malays would. They'd be much too frightened. Of course we'll keep an eye on them. We shall soon see if they seem to have any money to fling about.'

"'It's awful for Mrs. Bronson,' said the doctor. 'It would have been bad enough at any time, but now she's going to have a baby . . .'

"'I didn't know that,' I said, interrupting him.

"'No, for some reason she wanted to keep it dark. She was rather funny about it, I thought.'

"I recollected then that little passage between Mrs. Bronson and the doctor's wife. I understood why that good woman had been so anxious that Mrs. Bronson should not overtire herself.

"'It's strange her having a baby after being married so many years.'

"'It happens, you know. But it was a surprise to her. When first she came to see me and I told her what was the matter she fainted, and then she began to cry. I should have thought she'd be as pleased as Punch. She told me that Bronson didn't like children and he'd be awfully bored at the idea, and she made me promise to say nothing about it till she had had a chance of breaking it to him gradually.'

"I reflected for a moment.

"'He was the kind of breezy, hearty cove whom you'd expect to be as keen as mustard on having kids.'

"'You never can tell. Some people are very selfish and just don't want the bother.'

"'Well, how did he take it when she did tell him? Wasn't he rather bucked?'

"'I don't know that she ever told him. Though she couldn't have waited much longer; unless I'm very much mistaken she ought to be confined in about five months.'

"'Poor devil,' I said. 'You know, I've got a notion that he'd have been most awfully pleased to know.'

"We drove in silence for the rest of the way and at last came to the point at which the short cut to Kabulong branched off from the road. Here we stopped and in a minute or two my trap, in which were the police-sergeant and the two Malays, came up. We took the head-lamps to light us on our way. I left the doctor's seis to look after the ponies and told him that when the policemen came they were to follow the path till they found us. The two coolies, carrying the lamps, walked ahead and we followed them. It was a fairly broad track, wide enough for a small cart to pass, and before the road was built it had been the highway between Kabulong and Alor Lipis. It was

firm to the foot and good walking. The surface here and there
was sandy and in places you could see quite plainly the mark
of a bicycle wheel. It was the track Bronson had left on his
way to Kabulong.

"We walked twenty minutes, I should think, in single file,
and on a sudden the coolies, with a cry, stopped sharply. The
sight had come upon them so abruptly that notwithstanding
they were expecting it they were startled. There, in the middle
of the pathway lit dimly by the lamps the coolies carried, lay
Bronson; he'd fallen over his bicycle and lay across it in an ungainly heap. I was too shocked to speak, and I think the doctor
was, too. But in our silence the din of the jungle was deafening;
those damned cicadas and the bull-frogs were making enough
row to wake the dead. Even under ordinary circumstances the
noise of the jungle at nights always seems to me uncanny;
because you feel that at that hour there should be an utter
silence it has an odd effect on you, that ceaseless and invisible
uproar that beats upon your nerves. It surrounds you and hems
you in. But just then, believe me, it was terrifying. That poor
fellow lay dead and all round him the restless life of the jungle
pursued its indifferent and ferocious course.

"He was lying face downwards. The sergeant and the coolies
looked at me as though awaiting an order. I was a young fellow
then and I'm afraid I felt a little frightened. Though I couldn't
see the face I had no doubt that it was Bronson, but I felt that
I ought to turn the body over to make sure. I suppose we all
have our little squeamishnesses; you know, I've always had a
horrible distaste for touching dead bodies. I've had to do it
fairly often now, but it still makes me feel slightly sick.

"'It's Bronson, all right,' I said.

"The doctor—by George, it was lucky for me he was there—
the doctor bent down and turned the head. The sergeant directed the lamp on the dead face.

"'My God, half his head's been shot away,' I cried.

"'Yes.'

"The doctor stood up straight and wiped his hands on the
leaves of a tree that grew beside the path.

"'Is he quite dead?' I asked.

"'Oh, yes. Death must have been instantaneous. Whoever
shot him must have fired at pretty close range.'

"'How long has he been dead, d'you think?'

"'Oh, I don't know, several hours.'

"'He would have passed here about five o'clock, I suppose, if he was expecting to get to the club for a rubber at six.'

"'There's no sign of any struggle,' said the doctor.

"'No, there wouldn't be. He was shot as he was riding along.'

"I looked at the body for a little while. I couldn't help thinking how short a time ago it was since Bronson, noisy and loud-voiced, had been so full of hearty life.

"'You haven't forgotten that he had the coolies' wages on him,' said the doctor.

"'No, we'd better search him.'

"'Shall we turn him over?'

"'Wait a minute. Let us just have a look at the ground first.'

"I took the lamp and as carefully as I could looked all about me. Just where he had fallen the sandy pathway was trodden and confused; there were our footprints and the footprints of the coolies who had found him. I walked two or three paces and then saw quite clearly the mark of his bicycle wheels; he had been riding straight and steadily. I followed it to the spot where he had fallen, to just before that rather, and there saw very distinctly the prints on each side of the wheels of his heavy boots. He had evidently stopped there and put his feet to the ground, then he'd started off again, there was a great wobble of the wheel, and he'd crashed.

"'Now let's search him,' I said.

"The doctor and the sergeant turned the body over and one of the coolies dragged the bicycle away. They laid Bronson on his back. I supposed he would have had the money partly in notes and partly in silver. The silver would have been in a bag attached to the bicycle and a glance told me that it was not there. The notes he would have put in a wallet. It would have been a good thick bundle. I felt him all over, but there was nothing; then I turned out the pockets, they were all empty except the right trouser pocket, in which there was a little small change.

"'Didn't he always wear a watch?' asked the doctor.

"'Yes, of course he did.'

"I remembered that he wore the chain through the button-hole in the lapel of his coat and the watch and some seals and things in his handkerchief pocket. But watch and chain were gone.

"'Well, there's not much doubt now, is there?' I said.

"It was clear that he had been attacked by gang robbers

who knew he had money on him. After killing him they had
stripped him of everything. I suddenly remembered the footprints that proved that for a moment he had stood still. I saw
exactly how it had been done. One of them had stopped him
on some pretext and then, just as he started off again, another,
slipping out of the jungle behind him, had emptied the two
barrels of a gun into his head.

"'Well,' I said to the doctor, 'it's up to me to catch them,
and I'll tell you what, it'll be a real pleasure to me to see them
hanged.'

"Of course there was an inquest. Mrs. Bronson gave evidence,
but she had nothing to say that we didn't know already.
Bronson had left the bungalow about eleven, he was to have
tiffin at Kabulong and was to be back between five and six.
He asked her not to wait for him, he said he would just put the
money in the safe and come straight to the club. Cartwright
confirmed this. He had lunched alone with Mrs. Bronson and
after a smoke had gone out with a gun to shoot pigeon. He
had got in about five, a little before perhaps, had a bath and
changed to play tennis. He was shooting not far from the place
where Bronson was killed, but never heard a shot. That, of
course, meant nothing; what with the cicadas and the frogs,
and the other sounds of the jungle he would have had to be very
near to hear anything; and besides, Cartwright was probably
back in the bungalow before Bronson was killed. We traced
Bronson's movements. He had lunched at the club, he had got
money at the bank just before it closed, had gone back to the
club and had one more drink, and then started off on his bicycle.
He had crossed the river by the ferry, the ferryman remembered
distinctly seeing him, but was positive that no one else with a
bicycle had crossed. That looked as though the murderers were
not following, but lying in wait for him. He rode along the main
road for a couple of miles and then took the path which was a
short cut to his bungalow.

"It looked as though he had been killed by men who knew
his habits, and suspicion, of course, fell immediately on the
coolies of his estate. We examined them all—pretty carefully—
but there was not a scrap of evidence to connect any of them
with the crime. In fact, most of them were able satisfactorily
to account for their actions and those who couldn't seemed to
me for one reason and another out of the running. There were
a few bad characters among the Chinese at Alor Lipis and I

had them looked up. But somehow I didn't think it was the
work of the Chinese; I had a feeling that Chinese would have
used revolvers and not a shot gun. Anyhow, I could find out
nothing there. So then we offered a reward of a thousand dollars
to anyone who could put us in the way of discovering the murderers. I thought there were a good many people to whom it
would appeal to do a public service and at the same time earn
a tidy sum. But I knew that an informer would take no risks,
he wouldn't want to tell what he knew till he knew he could tell
it safely, and I armed myself with patience. The reward had
brightened the interest of my police and I knew they would
use every means they had to bring the criminals to trial. In a
case like this they could do more than I.

"But it was strange, nothing happened; the reward seemed
to tempt no one. I cast my net a little wider. There were two or
three kampongs along the road and I wondered if the murderers
were there; I saw the headmen, but got no help from them. It
was not that they would tell me nothing, I was sure they had
nothing to tell. I talked to the bad hats, but there was absolutely
nothing to connect them with the murder. There was not the
shadow of a clue.

"'Very well, my lads,' I said to myself, as I drove back to
Alor Lipis, 'there's no hurry; the rope won't spoil by keeping.'

"The scoundrels had got away with a considerable sum, but
money is no good unless you spend it. I felt I knew the native
temperament enough to be sure that the possession of it was a
constant temptation. The Malays are an extravagant race, and
a race of gamblers, and the Chinese are gamblers, too; sooner or
later someone would start flinging his money about, and then
I should want to know where it came from. With a few well-
directed questions I thought I could put the fear of God into
the fellow and then, if I knew my business, it shouldn't be hard
to get a full confession.

"The only thing now was to sit down and wait till the hue
and cry had died down and the murderers thought the affair
was forgotten. The itch to spend those ill-gotten dollars would
grow more and more intolerable till at last it could be resisted
no longer. I would go about my business, but I meant never to
relax my watch, and one day, sooner or later, my time must
come.

"Cartwright took Mrs. Bronson down to Singapore. The
company Bronson had worked for asked him if he would care

to take Bronson's place, but he said, very naturally, that he didn't like the idea of it; so they put another man in and told Cartwright that he could have the job that Bronson's successor had vacated. It was the management of the estate that Cartwright lives cn now. He moved in at once. Four months after this Olive was born at Singapore, and a few months later, when Bronson had been dead just over a year, Cartwright and Mrs. Bronson were married. I was surprised; but on thinking it over I couldn't help confessing that it was very natural. After the trouble Mrs. Bronson had leant much on Cartwright and he had arranged everything for her; she must have been lonely, and rather lost, and I daresay she was grateful for his kindness, he did behave like a brick; and so far as he was concerned I imagined he was sorry for her, it was a dreadful position for a woman, she had nowhere to go, and all they'd gone through must have been a tie between them. There was every reason for them to marry and it was probably the best thing for them both.

"It looked as though Bronson's murderers would never be caught, for that plan of mine didn't work; there was no one in the district who spent more money than he could account for, and if anyone had that hoard buried away under his floor he was showing a self-control that was super-human. A year had passed and to all intents and purposes the thing was forgotten. Could anyone be so prudent as after so long not to let a little money dribble out? It was incredible. I began to think that Bronson had been killed by a couple of wandering Chinese who had got away, to Singapore perhaps, where there would be small chance of catching them. At last I gave it up. If you come to think of it, as a rule, it's just those crimes, crimes of robbery, in which there is least chance of getting the culprit; for there's nothing to attach suspicion to him, and if he's caught it can only be by his own carelessness. It's different with crimes of passion or vengeance, then you can find out who had a motive to put the victim out of the way.

"It's no use grizzling over one's failures, and bringing my common sense to bear I did my best to put the matter out of my mind. No one likes to be beaten, but beaten I was and I had to put as good a face on it as I could. And then a Chinaman was caught trying to pawn poor Bronson's watch.

"I told you that Bronson's watch and chain had been taken, and of course Mrs. Bronson was able to give us a fairly accurate description of it. It was a half-hunter, by Benson, there was a gold chain, three or four seals and a sovereign purse. The pawn-broker was a smart fellow and when the Chinaman brought the watch he recognized it at once. On some pretext he kept the man waiting and sent for a policeman. The man was arrested and immediately brought to me. I greeted him like a long-lost brother. I was never so pleased to see anyone in my life. I have no feeling about criminals, you know; I'm rather sorry for them, because they're playing a game in which their opponents hold all the aces and kings; but when I catch one it gives me a little thrill of satisfaction, like bringing off a neat finesse at bridge. At last the mystery was going to be cleared up, for if the China-man hadn't done the thing himself we were pretty sure through him to trace the murderers. I beamed on him.

"I asked him to account for his possession of the watch. He said he had bought it from a man he didn't know. That was very thin. I explained the circumstances briefly and told him he would be charged with murder. I meant to frighten him and I did. He said then that he'd found the watch.

"'Found it?' I said. 'Fancy that. Where?'

"His answer staggered me; he said he'd found it in the jungle; I laughed at him; I asked him if he thought watches were likely to be left lying about in the jungle; then he said he'd been coming along the pathway that led from Kabulong to Alor Lipis, and had gone into the jungle and caught sight of some-thing gleaming and there was the watch. That was odd. Why should he have said he found the watch just there? It was either true or excessively astute. I asked him where the chain and the seals were, and he produced them immediately. I'd got him scared, and he was pale and shaking; he was a knock-kneed little fellow and I should have been a fool not to see that I hadn't got hold of the murderer there. But his terror suggested that he knew something.

"I asked him when he'd found the watch.

"'Yesterday,' he said.

"I asked him what he was doing on the short-cut from Kabu-long to Alor Lipis. He said that he'd been working in Singapore and had gone to Kabulong because his father was ill, and that he himself had come to Alor Lipis to work. A friend of his father, a carpenter by trade, had given him a job. He gave me the name of the man with whom he had worked in Singapore and the name of the man who had engaged him at Alor Lipis. All he said seemed plausible and could so easily be verified that it was hardly likely to be false. Of course it occurred to me that if he had found the watch as he said it must have been lying in the jungle for more than a year. It could hardly be in very good condition; I tried to open it, but couldn't. The pawnbroker had come to the police-station and was waiting in the next room. Luckily he was also something of a watchmaker. I sent for him and asked him to look at the watch; when he opened it he gave a little whistle, the works were thick with rust.

"'This watch no good,' he said, shaking his head. 'Him never go now.'

"I asked him what had put it in such a state, and without a word from me he said that it had been long exposed to wet. For the moral effect I had the prisoner put in a cell and I sent for his employer. I sent a wire to Kabulong and another to Singapore. While I waited I did my best to put two and two together. I was inclined to believe the man's story true; his fear might be ascribed to no more guilt than consisted in his having found something and tried to sell it. Even quite innocent persons are apt to be nervous when they're in the hands of the police; I don't know what there is about a policeman, people are never very much at their ease in his company. But if he really had found the watch where he said, someone had thrown it there. Now that was funny. Even if the murderers had thought the watch a dangerous thing to possess, one would have expected them to melt down the gold case; that would be a very simple thing for any native to do; and the chain was of so ordinary a pattern they could hardly have thought it possible to trace that. There were chains like it in every jeweller's shop in the country. Of course there was the possibility that they had plunged into the jungle and having dropped the watch in their hurry had been afraid to go back and look for it. I didn't think that very likely: the Malays are used to keeping things tucked away in their sarongs, and the Chinese have pockets in their coats. Besides, the moment they got into the jungle they knew there was no hurry; they probably waited and divided the swag then and there.

"In a few minutes the man I had sent for came to the police-station and confirmed what the prisoner had said, and in an hour I got an answer from Kabulong. The police had seen his father who told them that the boy had gone to Alor Lipis to get a job with a carpenter. So far everything he had said seemed

true. I had him brought in again, and told him I was going to
take him to the place where he said he had found the watch
and he must show me the exact spot. I handcuffed him to a
policeman, though it was hardly necessary, for the poor devil
was shaking with fright, and took a couple of men besides. We
drove out to where the track joined the road and walked along
it; within five yards of the place where Bronson was killed the
Chinaman stopped.

"'Here,' he said.

"He pointed to the jungle and we followed him in. We went in
about ten yards and he pointed to a chink between two large
boulders and said that he found the watch there. It could only
have been by the merest chance that he noticed it, and if he
really had found it there it looked very much as though someone had put it there to hide it."

Gaze stopped and gave me a reflective look.

"What would you have thought then?" he asked.

"I don't know," I answered.

"Well, I'll tell you what I thought. I thought that if the
watch was there the money might be there, too. It seemed
worth while having a look. Of course, to look for something in
the jungle makes looking for a needle in a bundle of hay a
drawing-room pastime. I couldn't help that. I released the
Chinaman, I wanted all the help I could get, and set him to
work. I set my three men to work and I started in myself. We
made a line—there were five of us—and we searched from the
road; for fifty yards on each side of the place at which Bronson
was murdered and for a hundred yards in we went over the
ground foot by foot. We routed among dead leaves and peered
in bushes, we looked under boulders and in the hollows of trees.
I knew it was a foolish thing to do, for the chances against us
were a thousand to one; my only hope was that anyone who
had just committed a murder would be rattled and if he wanted
to hide anything would hide it quickly; he would choose the
first obvious hiding-place that offered itself. That is what he
had done when he hid the watch. My only reason for looking in
so circumscribed an area was that as the watch had been found
so near the road, the person who wanted to get rid of the things
must have wanted to get rid of them quickly.

"We worked on. I began to grow tired and cross. We were
sweating like pigs. I had a maddening thirst and nothing in the
world to drink. At last I came to the conclusion that we must

give it up as a bad job, for that day at least, when suddenly the
Chinaman—he must have had sharp eyes, that young man—
uttered a guttural cry. He stooped down and from under the
winding root of a tree drew out a messy, mouldering, stinking
thing. It was a pocket-book that had been out in the rain for a
year, that had been eaten by ants and beetles and God knows
what, that was sodden and foul, but it was a pocket-book all
right, Bronson's, and inside were the shapeless, mushed-up,
fetid remains of the Singapore notes he had got from the bank
at Kabulong. There was still the silver and I was convinced that
it was hidden somewhere about, but I wasn't going to bother
about that. I had found out something very important; whoever
had murdered Bronson had made no money out of it.

"Do you remember my telling you that I'd noticed the print
of Bronson's feet on each side of the broad line of the pneumatic
tyre, where he had stopped, and presumably spoken to someone? He was a heavy man and the prints were well marked.
He hadn't just put his feet on the soft sand and taken them off,
but must have stopped at least for a minute or two. My explanation was that he had stopped to chat with a Malay or
a Chinaman, but the more I thought of it the less I liked it.
Why the devil should he? Bronson wanted to get home, and
though a jovial chap, he certainly was not hail-fellow-well-met
with the natives. His relations towards them were those of
master and servants. Those footprints had always puzzled me.
And now the truth flashed across me. Whoever had murdered
Bronson hadn't murdered him to rob and if he'd stopped to
talk with someone it could only be with a friend. I knew at
last who the murderer was."

I have always thought the detective story a most diverting
and ingenious variety of fiction, and have regretted that I
never had the skill to write one, but I have read a good many,
and I flatter myself it is rarely that I have not solved the mystery before it was disclosed to me; and now for some time I had
foreseen what Gaze was going to say, but when at last he said
it I confess that it gave me, notwithstanding, somewhat of a
shock.

"The man he met was Cartwright. Cartwright was pigeon-
shooting. He stopped and asked him what sport he had had,
and as he rode on Cartwright raised his gun and discharged
both barrels into his head. Cartwright took the money and the
watch in order to make it look like the work of gang robbers

and hurriedly hid them in the jungle, then made his way along
the edge till he got to the road, went back to the bungalow,
changed into his tennis things and drove with Mrs. Bronson
to the club.

"I remembered how badly he'd played tennis, and how he'd
collapsed when, in order to break the news more gently to
Mrs. Bronson, I said Bronson was wounded and not dead. If
he was only wounded he might have been able to speak. By
George, I bet that was a bad moment. The child was Cartwright's. Look at Olive: why, you saw the likeness yourself.
The doctor had said that Mrs. Bronson was upset when he
told her she was going to have a baby and made him promise
not to tell Bronson. Why? Because Bronson knew that he
couldn't be the father of the child."

"Do you think that Mrs. Bronson knew what Cartwright
had done?" I asked.

"I'm sure of it. When I look back on her behaviour that
evening at the club I am convinced of it. She was upset, but
not because Bronson was killed; she was upset because I said
he was wounded; on my telling her that he was dead when they
found him she burst out crying, but from relief. I know that
woman. Look at that square chin of hers and tell me that she
hasn't got the courage of the devil. She has a will of iron. She
made Cartwright do it. She planned every detail and every
move. He was completely under her influence; he is now."

"But do you mean to tell me that neither you nor anyone
else ever suspected that there was anything between them?"

"Never. Never."

"If they were in love with one another and knew that she
was going to have a baby, why didn't they just bolt?"

"How could they? It was Bronson who had the money; she
hadn't a bean and neither had Cartwright. He was out of a job.
Do you think he would have got another with that story round
his neck? Bronson had taken him in when he was starving and
he'd stolen his wife from him. They wouldn't have had a dog's
chance. They couldn't afford to let the truth come out, their
only chance was to get Bronson out of the way, and they got
him out of the way."

"They might have thrown themselves on his mercy."

"Yes, but I think they were ashamed. He'd been so good to
them, he was such a decent chap, I don't think they had the
heart to tell him the truth. They preferred to kill him."

There was a moment's silence while I reflected over what Gaze said.

"Well, what did you do about it?" I asked.

"Nothing. What was there to do? What was the evidence? That the watch and notes had been found? They might easily have been hidden by someone who was afterwards afraid to come and get them. The murderer might have been quite content to get away with the silver. The footprints? Bronson might have stopped to light a cigarette or there might have been a tree trunk across the path and he waited while the coolies he met there by chance moved it away. Who could prove that the child that a perfectly decent, respectable woman had had four months after her husband's death was not his child? No jury would have convicted Cartwright. I held my tongue and the Bronson murder was forgotten."

"I don't suppose the Cartwrights have forgotten," I suggested.

"I shouldn't be surprised. Human memory is astonishingly short and if you want my professional opinion I don't mind telling you that I don't believe remorse for a crime ever sits very heavily on a man when he's absolutely sure he'll never be found out."

I thought once more of the pair I had met that afternoon, the thin, elderly, bald man with gold-rimmed spectacles, and that white-haired untidy woman with her frank speech and kindly, caustic smile. It was almost impossible to imagine that in the distant past they had been swayed by so turbulent a passion, for that alone made their behaviour explicable, that it had brought them in the end to such a pass that they could see no other issue than a cruel and cold-blooded murder.

"Doesn't it make you feel a little uncomfortable to be with them?" I asked Gaze. "For, without wishing to be censorious, I'm bound to say that I don't think they can be very nice people."

"That's where you're wrong. They are very nice people; they're about the pleasantest people here. Mrs. Cartwright is a thoroughly good sort and a very amusing woman. It's my business to prevent crime and to catch the culprit when crime is committed, but I've known far too many criminals to think that on the whole they're worse than anybody else. A perfectly decent fellow may be driven by circumstances to commit a crime and if he's found out he's punished; but he may very well remain a perfectly decent fellow. Of course society punishes him if he breaks its laws, and it's quite right, but it's not always his actions that indicate the essential man. If you'd been a policeman as long as I have, you'd know it's not what people do that really matters, it's what they are. Luckily a policeman has nothing to do with their thoughts, only with their deeds; if he had, it would be a very different, a much more difficult matter."

Gaze flicked the ash from his cheroot and gave me his wry, sardonic, but agreeable smile.

"I'll tell you what, there's one job I *shouldn't* like," he said.

"What is that?" I asked.

"God's, at the Judgment Day," said Gaze. "No, sir."

THE HUMAN ELEMENT

I SEEM never to find myself in Rome but at the dead season. I pass through in August or September on my way somewhere or other and spend a couple of days revisiting places or pictures that are endeared to me by old associations. It is very hot then and the inhabitants of the city spend their day interminably strolling up and down the Corso. The Caffé Nazionale is crowded with people sitting at little tables for long hours with an empty cup of coffee in front of them and a glass of water. In the Sistine Chapel you see blond and sunburned Germans, in knickerbockers and shirts open at the neck, who have walked down the dusty roads of Italy with knapsacks on their shoulders; and in St. Peter's little groups of the pious, tired but eager, who have come on pilgrimage (at an inclusive rate) from some distant country. They are under the charge of a priest and they speak strange tongues. The Hotel Plaza then is cool and restful. The public rooms are dark, silent and spacious. In the lounge at teatime the only persons are a young, smart officer and a woman with fine eyes, drinking iced lemonade, and they talk intimately, in low tones, with the unwearying fluency of their race. You go up to your room and read and write letters and come down again two hours later and they are still talking. Before dinner a few people saunter into the bar, but for the rest of the day it is empty and the barman has time to tell you of his mother in Switzerland and his experiences in New York. You discuss life and love and the high cost of liquor.

And on this occasion too I found that I had the hotel almost

671

to myself. When the reception clerk took me to my room he told me that they were pretty full, but when, having bathed and changed, I came down again to the hall, the liftman, an old acquaintance, informed me that there were not more than a dozen people staying there. I was tired after a long and hot journey down Italy and had made up my mind to dine quietly in the hotel and go to bed early. It was late when I went into the dining-room, vast and brightly lit, but not more than three or four tables were occupied. I looked round me with satisfaction. It is very agreeable to find yourself alone in a great city which is yet not quite strange to you and in a large empty hotel. It gives you a delectable sense of freedom. I felt the wings of my spirit give a little flutter of delight. I had paused for ten minutes in the bar and had a dry Martini. I ordered myself a bottle of good red wine. My limbs were weary, but my soul responded wonderfully to food and drink and I began to feel a singular lightness of heart. I ate my soup and my fish and pleasant thoughts filled my mind. Scraps of dialogue occurred to me and my fancy played happily with the persons of a novel I was then at work on. I rolled a phrase on my tongue and it tasted better than the wine. I began to think of the difficulty of describing the looks of people in such a way as to make the reader see them as you see them. To me it has always been one of the most difficult things in fiction. What does the reader really get when you describe a face feature by feature? I should think nothing. And yet the plan some writers adopt of taking a salient characteristic, a crooked smile or shifty eyes, and emphasizing that, though effective, avoids rather than solves the problem. I looked about me and wondered how I would describe the people at the tables round me. There was one man by himself just opposite and for practice I asked myself in what way I should treat him. He was a tall, spare fellow, and what I believe is generally called loose-limbed. He wore a dinner-jacket and a boiled shirt. He had a rather long face and pale eyes; his hair was fairish and wavy, but it was growing thin, and the baldness of his temples gave him a certain nobility of brow. His features were undistinguished. His mouth and nose were like everybody else's; he was clean-shaven; his skin was naturally pale, but at the moment sunburned. His appearance suggested an intellectual but slightly commonplace distinction. He looked as though he might have been a lawyer or a don who played a pretty game of golf. I felt that he had good taste and was well-read and would

be a very agreeable guest at a luncheon party in Chelsea. But
how the devil one was to describe him so as in a few lines to give
a vivid, interesting and accurate picture I could not imagine.
Perhaps it would be better to let all the rest go and dwell only
on that rather fatigued distinction which on the whole was the
most definite impression he gave. I looked at him reflectively.
Suddenly he leaned forwards and gave me a stiff but courtly
little bow. I have a ridiculous habit of flushing when I am taken
aback and now I felt my cheeks redden. I was startled. I had
been staring at him for several minutes as though he were a
dummy. He must have thought me extremely rude. I nodded
with a good deal of embarrassment and looked away. Fortunately at that moment the waiter was handing me a dish. To the
best of my belief I had never seen the fellow before. I asked
myself whether his bow was due to my insistent stare, which
made him think that he had met me somewhere, or whether I
had really run across him and completely forgotten. I have a
bad memory for faces and I had in this case the excuse that he
looked exactly like a great many other people. You saw a dozen
of him at every golf course round London on a fine Sunday.

He finished his dinner before me. He got up, but on his way
out stopped at my table. He stretched out his hand.

"How d'you do," he said. "I didn't recognize you when you
first came in. I wasn't meaning to cut you."

He spoke in a pleasant voice with the tones cultivated at
Oxford and copied by many who have never been there. It was
evident that he knew me, and evident too that he had no notion
that I did not also know him. I had risen, and since he was a
good deal taller than I he looked down on me. He held himself
with a sort of languor. He stooped a little which added to the
impression he gave me of having about him an air that was
vaguely apologetic. His manner was a trifle condescending and
at the same time a trifle shy.

"Won't you come and have your coffee with me?" he said.
"I'm quite alone."

"Yes, I shall be glad to."

He left me and I still had no notion who he was or where I
had met him. I had noticed one curious thing about him. Not
once during the few sentences we exchanged, when we shook
hands, or when with a nod he left me, did even the suspicion of
a smile cross his face. Seeing him more closely I observed that
he was in his way good-looking: his features were regular, his

grey eyes were handsome, he had a slim figure; but it was a way that I found uninteresting. A silly woman would say he looked romantic. He reminded you of one of the knights of Burne-Jones though he was on a larger scale and there was no suggestion that he suffered from the chronic colitis that afflicted those unfortunate creatures. He was the sort of man whom you expected to look wonderful in fancy dress till you saw him in it and then you found that he looked absurd.

Presently I finished my dinner and went into the lounge. He was sitting in a large armchair and when he saw me he called a waiter. I sat down. The waiter came up and he ordered coffee and liqueurs. He spoke Italian very well. I was wondering by what means I could find out who he was without offending him. People are always a little disconcerted when you do not recognize them; they are so important to themselves, it is a shock to discover of what small importance they are to others. The excellence of his Italian recalled him to me. I remembered who he was and remembered at the same time that I did not like him. His name was Humphrey Carruthers. He was in the Foreign Office and he had a position of some importance. He was in charge of I know not what department. He had been attached to various embassies, and I supposed that a sojourn in Rome accounted for his idiomatic Italian. It was stupid of me not to have seen at once that he was connected with the diplomatic service. He had all the marks of the profession. He had the supercilious courtesy that is so well calculated to put up the backs of the general public, and the aloofness due to the consciousness the diplomat has that he is not as other men are, joined with the shyness occasioned by his uneasy feeling that other men do not quite realize it. I had known Carruthers for a good many years, but had met him infrequently, at luncheon parties where I said no more than "How do you do" to him, and at the opera where he gave me a cool nod. He was generally thought intelligent; he was certainly cultured. He could talk of all the right things. It was inexcusable of me not to have remembered him, for he had lately acquired a very considerable reputation as a writer of short stories. They had appeared first in one or other of those magazines that are founded now and then by well-disposed persons to give the intelligent reader something worthy of his attention, and that die when their proprietors have lost as much money as they want to; and in their discreet and handsomely printed pages had excited as much attention as an exiguous circulation permitted. Then they were published in book form. They created a sensation. I have seldom read such unanimous praise in the weekly papers. Most of them gave the book a column, and the Literary Supplement of *The Times* reviewed it not among the common ruck of novels but in a place by itself cheek by jowl with the memoirs of a distinguished statesman. The critics welcomed Humphrey Carruthers as a new star in the firmament. They praised his distinction, his subtlety, his delicate irony and his insight. They praised his style, his sense of beauty and his atmosphere. Here at last was a writer who had raised the short story from the depths into which in English-speaking countries it had fallen, and here was work to which an Englishman could point with pride; it bore comparison with the best compositions in this manner of Finland, Russia and Czecho-Slovakia.

Three years later Humphrey Carruthers brought out his second book and the critics commented on the interval with satisfaction. Here was no hack prostituting his talent for money! The praise it received was perhaps a little cooler than that which welcomed his first volume—the critics had had time to collect themselves—but it was enthusiastic enough to have delighted any common writer who earns his living by his pen, and there was no doubt that his position in the world of letters was secure and honourable. The story that attracted most commendation was called "The Shaving Mop" and all the best critics pointed out with what beauty the author in three or four pages had laid bare the tragic soul of a barber's assistant.

But his best-known story, which was also his longest, was called "Week-End." It gave its title to his first book. It narrated the adventures of a number of people who left Paddington Station on Saturday afternoon to stay with friends at Taplow and on Monday morning returned to London. It was so delicate that it was a little difficult to know exactly what happened. A young man, parliamentary secretary to a cabinet minister, very nearly proposed to a baronet's daughter, but didn't. Two or three others went on the river in a punt. They all talked a great deal in an allusive way, but none of them ever finished a sentence, and what they meant was very subtly indicated by dots and dashes. There were a good many descriptions of flowers in the garden and a sensitive picture of the Thames under the rain.

It was all seen through the eyes of the German governess, and everyone agreed that Carruthers had conveyed her outlook on the situation with quite delicious humour.

I read both Humphrey Carruthers' books. I think it part of the writer's business to make himself aware of what is being written by his contemporaries. I am very willing to learn, and I thought I might discover in them something that would be useful to me. I was disappointed. I like a story to have a beginning, a middle, and an end. I have a weakness for a point. I think atmosphere is all very well, but atmosphere without anything else is like a frame without a picture; it has not much significance. But it may be that I could not see the merit of Humphrey Carruthers on account of defects in myself, and if I have described his two most successful stories without enthusiasm the cause perhaps lies in my own wounded vanity. For I was perfectly conscious that Humphrey Carruthers looked upon me as a writer of no account. I am convinced that he had never read a word I had written. The popularity I enjoyed was sufficient to persuade him that there was no occasion for him to give me any of his attention. For a moment, such was the stir he created, it looked as though he might himself be faced with that ignominy, but it soon appeared that his exquisite work was above the heads of the public. One can never tell how large the intelligentsia is, but one can tell fairly well how many of its members are prepared to pay money to patronize the arts they cherish. The plays that are of too fine a quality to attract the patrons of the commercial theatre can count on an audience of ten thousand, and the books that demand from their readers more comprehension than can be expected from the common herd sell twelve hundred copies. For the intelligentsia, notwithstanding their sensitiveness to beauty, prefer to go to the theatre on the nod and to get a book from the library.

I am sure this did not distress Carruthers. He was an artist. He was also a clerk in the Foreign Office. His reputation as a writer was distinguished; he was not interested in the vulgar, and to sell well would possibly have damaged his career. I could not surmise what had induced him to invite me to have coffee with him. It is true he was alone, but I should have supposed he found his thoughts excellent company, and I could not believe he imagined that I had anything to say that would interest him. Nevertheless I could not but see that he was doing his dreary best to be affable. He reminded me of where we had last met, and we talked for a moment of common friends in London. He asked me how I came to be in Rome at this season, and I told him. He volunteered the information that he had arrived that morning from Brindisi. Our conversation did not go easily, and I made up my mind that as soon as I civilly could I would get up and leave him. But presently I had an odd sensation—I hardly know what caused it—that he was conscious of this and was desperately anxious not to give me the opportunity. I was surprised. I gathered my wits about me. I noticed that whenever I paused he broke in with a new topic. He was trying to find something to interest me so that I should stay. He was straining every nerve to be agreeable. Surely he could not be lonely; with his diplomatic connections he must know plenty of people with whom he could have spent the evening. I wondered indeed that he was not dining at the Embassy; even though it was summer there must be someone there he knew. I noticed also that he never smiled. He talked with a sort of harsh eagerness as though he were afraid of a moment's silence and the sound of his voice shut out of his mind something that tortured him. It was very strange. Though I did not like him, though he meant nothing to me and to be with him irked me somewhat, I was against my will a trifle interested. I gave him a searching glance. I wondered if it was my fancy that I saw in those pale eyes of his the cowed look of a hunted dog, and notwithstanding his neat features and his expression so civilly controlled, in his aspect something that suggested the grimace of a soul in pain. I could not understand. A dozen absurd notions flashed through my mind. I was not particularly sympathetic: like an old war horse scenting the fray I roused myself. I had been feeling very tired, but now I grew alert. My sensibilities put out tentacles. I was suddenly alive to every expression of his face and every gesture. I put aside the thought that had come to me that he had written a play and wanted my advice. These exquisite persons succumb strangely to the glamour of the footlights, and they are not averse from getting a few tips from the craftsman whose competence they superciliously despise. No, it was not that. A single man in Rome, of æsthetic leanings, is liable to get into trouble, and I asked myself whether Carruthers had got into some difficulty to extricate himself from which the Embassy was the last place he could go to. The idealist, I have noticed, is apt at times to be imprudent in the affairs of the flesh. He sometimes finds love in places which the police

inconveniently visit. I tittered in my heart. Even the gods laugh
when a prig is caught in an equivocal situation.

Suddenly Carruthers said something that staggered me.

"I'm so desperately unhappy," he muttered.

He said it without warning. He obviously meant it. There
was in his tone a sort of gasp. It might very well have been a
sob. I cannot describe what a shock it was to me to hear him
say those words. I felt as you do when you turn a corner of the
street and on a sudden a great blast of wind meets you, takes
your breath away, and nearly blows you off your feet. It was
so unexpected. After all, I hardly knew the fellow. We were not
friends. I did not like him; he did not like me. I had never looked
on him as quite human. It was amazing that a man so self-
controlled, so urbane, accustomed to the usages of polite society,
should break in upon a stranger with such a confession. I am
naturally reticent. I should be ashamed, whatever I was suffering, to disclose my pain to another. I shivered. His weakness
outraged me. For a moment I was filled with a passion of anger.
How dared he thrust the anguish of his soul on me? I very
nearly cried:

"What the hell do I care?"

But I didn't. He was sitting huddled up in the big armchair.
The solemn nobility of his features, which reminded one of the
marble statue of a Victorian statesman, had strangely crumpled
and his face sagged. He looked almost as though he were going
to cry. I hesitated. I faltered. I had flushed when he spoke and
now I felt my face go white. He was a pitiable object.

"I'm awfully sorry," I said.

"Do you mind if I tell you about it?"

"No."

It was not the moment for many words. I suppose Carruthers
was in the early forties. He was a well-made man, athletic in
his way, and with a confident bearing. Now he looked twenty
years older and strangely shrivelled. He reminded me of the
dead soldiers I had seen during the war and how oddly small
death had made them. I was embarrassed and looked away, but
I felt his eyes claiming mine and I looked back.

"Do you know Betty Welldon-Burns?" he asked me.

"I used to meet her sometimes in London years ago. I've not
seen her lately."

"She lives in Rhodes now, you know. I've just come from
there. I've been staying with her."

"Oh?"

He hesitated.

"I'm afraid you'll think it awfully strange of me to talk to you like this. I'm at the end of my tether. If I don't talk to somebody I shall go off my head."

He had ordered double brandies with the coffee and now, calling the waiter, he ordered himself another. We were alone in the lounge. There was a little shaded lamp on the table between us. Because it was a public room he spoke in a low voice. The place gave one, oddly enough, a sense of intimacy. I cannot repeat all that Carruthers said to me in the words he said it; it would be impossible for me to remember them; it is more convenient for me to put it in my own fashion. Sometimes he could not bring himself to say a thing right out and I had to guess at what he meant. Sometimes he had not understood, and it seemed to me that in certain ways I saw the truth more clearly than he. Betty Welldon-Burns had a very keen sense of humour and he had none. I perceived a good deal that had escaped him.

I had met her a good many times, but I knew her chiefly from hearsay. In her day she had made a great stir in the little world of London, and I had heard of her often before I met her. This was at a dance in Portland Place soon after the war. She was then already at the height of her celebrity. You could not open an illustrated paper without seeing in it a portrait of her, and her mad pranks were a staple of conversation. She was twenty-four. Her mother was dead, her father, the Duke of St. Erth, old and none too rich, spent most of the year in his Cornish castle, and she lived in London with a widowed aunt. At the outbreak of the war she went to France. She was just eighteen. She was a nurse in a hospital at the base and then drove a car. She acted in a theatrical tour designed to amuse the troops; she posed in tableaux at home for charitable purposes, held auctions for this object and that and sold flags in Piccadilly. Every one of her activities was widely advertised and in every new rôle she was profusely photographed. I suppose that she managed to have a very good time. But now that the war was over she was having her fling with a vengeance. Just then everybody a little lost his head. The young, relieved of the burden that for five years had oppressed them, indulged in one wild escapade after another. Betty took part in them all. Sometimes, for one reason or another, an account of them found its way into the newspapers, and her name was always in the headline. At that time night clubs were in the first flush of their success, and she was to be seen at them every night. She lived a life of hectic gaiety. It can only be described in a hackneyed phrase, because it was a hackneyed thing. The British public in its odd way took her to its heart, and Lady Betty was a sufficient description of her throughout the British islands. Women mobbed her when she went to a wedding, and the gallery applauded her at first nights as though she were a popular actress. Girls copied the way she did her hair, and manufacturers of soap and face cream paid her money to use her photograph to advertise their wares.

Of course dull, stodgy people, the people who remembered and regretted the old order, disapproved of her. They sneered at her constant appearance in the limelight. They said she had an insane passion for self-advertisement. They said she was fast. They said she drank too much. They said she smoked too much. I will admit that nothing I had heard of her had pre-disposed me to think very well of her. I held cheap the women who seemed to look upon the war as an occasion to enjoy themselves and be talked about. I am bored by the papers in which you see photographs of persons in society walking in Cannes or playing golf at St. Andrew's. I have always found the Bright Young People extremely tedious. The gay life seems dull and stupid to the onlooker, but the moralist is unwise to judge it harshly. It is as absurd to be angry with the young things who lead it as with a litter of puppies scampering aimlessly around, rolling one another over and chasing their tails. It is well to bear it with fortitude if they cause havoc in the flower beds or break a piece of china. Some of them will be drowned because their points are not up to the mark, and the rest will grow up into well-behaved dogs. Their unruliness is due only to the vitality of youth.

And it was vitality that was Betty's most shining characteristic. The urge of life flowed through her with a radiance that dazzled you. I do not think I shall ever forget the impression she made on me at the party at which I first saw her. She was like a maenad. She danced with an abandon that made you laugh, so obvious was her intense enjoyment of the music and the movement of her young limbs. Her hair was brown, slightly disordered by the vigour of her gestures, but her eyes were deep blue, and her skin was milk and roses. She was a great beauty, but she had none of the coldness of great beauty. She laughed constantly, and when she was not laughing she smiled and her eyes danced with the joy of living. She was like a milkmaid on the farmstead of the gods. She had the strength and health of the people; and yet the independence of her bearing, a sort of noble frankness of carriage, suggested the great lady. I do not quite know how to put the feeling she gave me, that though so simple and unaffected she was not unconscious of her station. I fancied that if occasion arose she could get on her dignity and be very grand indeed. She was charming to everybody because, probably without being quite aware of it, in the depths of her heart she felt that the rest of the world was perfectly insignificant. I understood why the factory girls in the East End adored her and why half a million people who had never seen her except in a photograph looked upon her with the intimacy of personal friendship. I was introduced to her and she spent a few minutes talking to me. It was extraordinarily flattering to see the interest she showed in you; you knew she could not really be so pleased to meet you as she seemed, or so delighted with what you said, but it was very attractive. She had the gift of being able to jump over the first difficult phases of acquaintance, and you had not known her for five minutes before you felt you had known her all her life. She was snatched away from me by someone who wanted to dance with her, and she surrendered herself to her partner's arms with just the same eager happiness as she had shown when she sank into a chair by my side. I was surprised, when I met her at luncheon a fortnight later, to find that she remembered exactly what we had talked about during those noisy ten minutes at the dance. A young woman with all the social graces.

I mentioned the incident to Carruthers.

"She was no fool," he said. "Very few people knew how intelligent she was. She wrote some very good poetry. Because she was so gay, because she was so reckless and never cared a damn for anybody, people thought she was scatter-brained. Far from it. She was as clever as a monkey. You would never have thought she'd had the time to read all the things she had. I don't suppose anyone knew that side of her as well as I did. We used to take walks together, in the country at week-ends, and in London we'd drive out to Richmond Park and walk there, and talk. She loved flowers and trees and grass. She was interested in everything. She had a lot of information and a lot of sense. There was nothing she couldn't talk about. Sometimes when we'd been for a walk in the afternoon and we met at a night club and she'd had a couple of glasses of champagne—

that was enough to make her completely buffy, you know—and she was the life and soul of the party, I couldn't help thinking how amazed the rest of them would be if they knew how seriously we'd been talking only a few hours before. It was an extraordinary contrast. There seemed to be two entirely different women in her."

Carruthers said all this without a smile. He spoke with the melancholy he might have used if he had been speaking of some person snatched from the pleasant company of the living by untimely death. He gave a deep sigh.

"I was madly in love with her. I proposed to her half a dozen times. Of course I knew I hadn't a chance, I was only a very junior clerk at the F. O., but I couldn't help myself. She refused me, but she was always frightfully nice about it. It never made any difference to our friendship. You see, she really liked me. I gave her something that other people didn't. I always thought that she was really fonder of me than of anybody. I was crazy about her."

"I don't suppose you were the only one," I said, having to say something.

"Far from it. She used to get dozens of love letters from men she'd never seen or heard of, farmers in Africa, miners, and policemen in Canada. All sorts of people proposed to her. She could have married anyone she liked."

"Even royalty, one heard."

"Yes, she said she couldn't stand the life. And then she married Jimmie Welldon-Burns."

"People were rather surprised, weren't they?"

"Did you ever know him?"

"No, I don't think so. I may have met him, but he left no impression on me."

"He wouldn't. He was the most insignificant fellow that ever breathed. His father was a big manufacturer up in the north. He'd made a lot of money during the war and bought a baronetcy. I believe he hadn't an aitch to his name. Jimmie was at Eton with me—they'd tried hard to make a gentleman of him—and in London after the war he was about a good deal. He was always willing to throw a party. No one ever paid any attention to him. He just paid the bill. He was the most crashing bore. You know, rather prim, terribly polite; he made you rather uncomfortable because he was so anxious not to do the wrong thing. He always wore his clothes as though he'd just put them on for the first time and they were a little too tight for him.'

When Carruthers innocently opened his *Times* one morning and, casting his eyes down the fashionable intelligence of the day, saw that a marriage had been arranged between Elizabeth, only daughter of the Duke of St. Erth, and James, eldest son of Sir John Welldon-Burns, Bart, Bart., he was dumbfounded. He rang Betty up and asked if it was true.

"Of course," she said.

He was so shocked that for the moment he found nothing to say. She went on speaking.

"He's bringing his family to luncheon to-day to meet Father. I daresay it'll be a bit grim. You might stand me a cocktail at Claridge's to fortify me, will you?"

"At what time?" he asked.

"One."

"All right. I'll meet you there."

He was waiting for her when she came in. She walked with a sort of spring as though her eager feet itched to break into a dance. She was smiling. Her eyes shone with the joy that suffused her because she was alive and the world was such a pleasant place to live in. People recognizing her whispered to one another as she came in. Carruthers really felt that she brought sunshine and the scent of flowers into the sober but rather overwhelming splendour of Claridge's lounge. He did not wait to say "How do you do" to her.

"Betty, you can't do it," he said. "It's simply out of the question."

"Why?"

"He's awful."

"I don't think he is. I think he's rather nice."

A waiter came up and took their order. Betty looked at Carruthers with those beautiful blue eyes of hers that managed to be at the same time so gay and so tender.

"He's such a frightful bounder, Betty."

"Oh, don't be so silly, Humphrey. He's just as good as anybody else. I think you're rather a snob."

"He's so dull."

"No, he's rather quiet. I don't know that I want a husband who's too brilliant. I think he'll make a very good background. He's quite good-looking and he has nice manners."

"My God, Betty."

"Oh, don't be idiotic, Humphrey."

"Are you going to pretend you're in love with him?"

"I think it would be tactful, don't you?"

"Why are you going to marry him?"

She looked at him coolly.

"He's got pots of money. I'm nearly twenty-six."

There was nothing much more to be said. He drove her back to her aunt's house. She had a very grand marriage, with dense crowds lining the approach to St. Margaret's, Westminster, presents from practically all the royal family, and the honeymoon was passed on the yacht her father-in-law had lent them. Carruthers applied for a post abroad and was sent to Rome (I was right in guessing that he had thus acquired his admirable Italian) and later to Stockholm. Here he was counsellor and here he wrote the first of his stories.

Perhaps Betty's marriage had disappointed the British public who expected much greater things of her, perhaps only that as a young married woman she no longer appealed to the popular sense of romance; the fact was plain that she soon lost her place in the public eye. You ceased to hear very much about her. Not long after her marriage it was rumoured that she was going to have a baby and a little later that she had had a miscarriage. She did not drop out of society; I suppose she continued to see her friends, but her activities were no longer spectacular. She was certainly but seldom seen any more in those raffish assemblies where the members of a tarnished aristocracy hob-nob with the hangers-on of the arts and flatter themselves that they are being at once smart and cultured. People said she was settling down. They wondered how she was getting on with her husband, and no sooner did they do this than they concluded that she was not getting on very well. Presently gossip said that Jimmie was drinking too much and then, a year or two later, one heard that he had contracted tuberculosis. The Welldon-Burns spent a couple of winters in Switzerland. Then the news spread that they had separated and Betty had gone to live in Rhodes. An odd place to choose.

"It must be deadly," her friends said.

A few of them went to stay with her now and then and came back with reports of the beauty of the island and the leisurely charm of the life. But of course it was very lonely. It seemed strange that Betty, with her brilliance and her energy, should be content to settle there. She had bought a house. She knew no one but a few Italian officials, there was indeed no one to know; but she seemed perfectly happy. Her visitors could not make it out. But the life of London is busy and memories are short. People ceased to concern themselves with her. She was forgotten. Then, a few weeks before I met Humphrey Carruthers in Rome, *The Times* announced the death of Sir James Welldon-Burns, second baronet. His younger brother succeeded him in the title. Betty had never had a child.

Carruthers continued to see her after her marriage. Whenever he came to London they lunched together. She had the ability to take up a friendship after a long separation as though no passage of time had intervened, so that there was never any strangeness in their meetings. Sometimes she asked him when he was going to marry.

"You're getting on, you know, Humphrey. If you don't marry soon you'll get rather old-maidish."

"D'you recommend marriage?"

It was not a very kindly thing to say, because like everyone else he had heard that she was not getting on too well with her husband, but her remark piqued him.

"On the whole. I think probably an unsatisfactory marriage is better than no marriage at all."

"You know quite well that nothing would induce me to marry and you know why."

"Oh my dear, you're not going to pretend that you're still in love with me?"

"I am."

"You are a damned fool."

"I don't care."

She smiled at him. Her eyes always had that look, partly bantering, partly tender, that gave him such a happy pain in his heart. Funny, he could almost localize it.

"You're rather sweet, Humphrey. You know I'm devoted to you, but I wouldn't marry you even if I were free."

When she left her husband and went to live in Rhodes Carruthers ceased to see her. She never came to England. They maintained an active correspondence.

"Her letters were wonderful," he said. "You seemed to hear her talking. They were just like her. Clever and witty, inconsequent and yet so shrewd."

He suggested coming to Rhodes for a few days, but she

thought he had better not. He understood why. Everyone knew he had been madly in love with her. Everyone knew he was still. He did not know in what circumstances exactly the Welldon-Burns had separated. It might be that there had been a good deal of bad feeling. Betty might think that his presence on the island would compromise her.

"She wrote a charming letter to me when my first book came out. You know I dedicated it to her. She was surprised that I had done anything so good. Everyone was very nice about it, and she was delighted with that. I think her pleasure was the chief thing that pleased me. After all I'm not a professional writer, you know: I don't attach much importance to literary success."

Fool, I thought, and liar. Did he think I had not noticed the self-satisfaction that consumed him on account of the favourable reception of his books? I did not blame him for feeling that; nothing could be more pardonable; but why be at such pains to deny it? But it was doubtless true that it was mostly for Betty's sake that he relished the notoriety they had brought him. He had a positive achievement to offer her. He could lay at her feet now not only his love, but a distinguished reputation. Betty was not very young any more, she was thirty-four; her marriage, her sojourn abroad, had changed things; she was no longer surrounded by suitors; she had lost the halo with which the public admiration had surrounded her. The distance between them was no longer insuperable. He alone had remained faithful through the years. It was absurd that she should continue to bury her beauty, her wit, her social grace in an island in a corner of the Mediterranean. He knew she was fond of him. She could hardly fail to be touched by his long devotion. And the life he had to offer her now was one that he knew would appeal to her. He made up his mind to ask her once more to marry him. He was able to get away towards the end of July. He wrote and said that he was going to spend his leave in the Greek islands and if she would be glad to see him he would stop off at Rhodes for a day or two where he had heard the Italians had opened a very good hotel. He put his suggestion in this casual way out of delicacy. His training at the Foreign Office had taught him to eschew abruptness. He never willingly put himself in a position from which he could not if necessary withdraw with tact. Betty sent him a telegram in reply. She said it was too marvellous that he was coming to Rhodes and of course he must come and stay with her, for at least a fortnight, and he was to wire what boat he was coming by.

He was in a state of wild excitement when at last the ship he had taken at Brindisi steamed, soon after sunrise, into the neat and pretty harbour of Rhodes. He had hardly slept a wink all night, and getting up early had watched the island loom grandly out of the dawn and the sun rise over the summer sea. Boats came out as the ship dropped her anchor. The gangway was lowered. Humphrey, leaning over the rail, watched the doctor and the port officials and the hotel couriers swarm up it. He was the only Englishman on board. His nationality was obvious. A man came on deck and immediately walked up to him.

"Are you Mr. Carruthers?"

"Yes."

He was about to smile and put out his hand, but he perceived in the twinkling of an eye that the person who addressed him, an Englishman like himself, was not a gentleman. Instinctively his manner, remaining exceedingly polite, became a trifle stiff. Of course Carruthers did not tell me this, but I see the scene so clearly that I have no hesitation in describing it.

"Her ladyship hopes you don't mind her not coming to meet you, but the boat got in so early and it's more than an hour's drive to where we live."

"Oh, of course. Her ladyship well?"

"Yes, thank you. Got your luggage ready?"

"Yes."

"If you'll show me where it is I'll tell one of these fellows to put it in a boat. You won't have any difficulty at the Customs. I've fixed that up all right, and then we'll get off. Have you had breakfast?"

"Yes, thank you."

The man was not quite sure of his aitches. Carruthers wondered who he was. You could not say he was uncivil, but he was certainly a little offhand. Carruthers knew that Betty had rather a large estate; perhaps he was her agent. He seemed very competent. He gave the porters instructions in fluent Greek. and when they got in the boat and the boatmen asked for more money than he gave them, he said something that made them laugh and they shrugged their shoulders, satisfied. The luggage was passed through the Customs without examination, Humphrey's guide shaking hands with the officials, and they went into a sunny place where a large yellow car was standing.

"Are you going to drive me?" asked Carruthers.

"I'm her ladyship's chauffeur."

"Oh, I see. I didn't know."

He was not dressed like a chauffeur. He wore white duck trousers and espadrilles on his bare feet, a white tennis shirt, with no tie and open at the neck, and a straw hat. Carruthers frowned. Betty oughtn't to let her chauffeur drive the car like that. It was true that he had had to get up before daybreak and it looked like being a hot drive up to the villa. Perhaps under ordinary conditions he wore uniform. Though not so tall as Carruthers, who was six feet one in his socks, he was not short; but he was broad-shouldered and squarely built, so that he looked stocky. He was not fat, but plump rather; he looked as though he had a hearty appetite and ate well. Young still, thirty perhaps or thirty-one, he had already a massive look and one day would be very beefy. Now he was a hefty fellow. He had a broad face deeply sunburned, a short thickish nose and a somewhat sullen look. He wore a short fair moustache. Oddly enough Carruthers had a vague feeling that he had seen him before.

"Have you been with her ladyship long?" he asked.

"Well, I have, in a manner of speaking."

Carruthers became a trifle stiffer. He did not quite like the manner in which the chauffeur spoke. He wondered why he did not say "sir" to him. He was afraid Betty had let him get a little above himself. It was like her to be a bit careless about such things. But it was a mistake. He'd give her a hint when he got a chance. Their eyes met for an instant and he could have sworn that there was a twinkle of amusement in the chauffeur's. Carruthers could not imagine why. He was not aware that there was anything amusing in him.

"That, I suppose, is the old city of the Knights," he said distantly, pointing to the battlemented walls.

"Yes. Her ladyship'll take you over. We get a rare lot of tourists here in the season."

Carruthers wished to be affable. He thought it would be nicer of him to offer to sit by the chauffeur rather than behind by himself and was just going to suggest it, when the matter was taken out of his hands. The chauffeur told the porters to put Carruthers' bags at the back, and settling himself at the wheel said:

"Now if you'll hop in we'll get along."

Carruthers sat down beside him and they set off along a white road that ran by the sea. In a few minutes they were in the open country. They drove in silence. Carruthers was a little on his dignity. He felt that the chauffeur was inclined to be familiar and he did not wish to give him occasion to be so. He flattered himself that he had a manner with him that put his inferiors in their place. He thought with sardonic grimness that it would not be long before the chauffeur would be calling him "sir." But the morning was lovely; the white road ran between olive groves, and the farmhouses they passed now and then, with their white walls and flat roofs, had an oriental look that took the fancy. And Betty was waiting for him. The love in his heart disposed him to kindliness towards all men, and lighting himself a cigarette he thought it would be a generous act to offer the chauffeur one too. After all, Rhodes was very far away from England and the age was democratic. The chauffeur accepted the gift and stopped the car to light up.

"Have you got the baccy?" he asked suddenly.

"Have I got what?"

The chauffeur's face fell.

"Her ladyship wired to you to bring two pounds of Player's Navy Cut. That's why I fixed it up with the Customs people not to open your luggage."

"I never got the wire."

"Damn!"

"What on earth does her ladyship want with two pounds of Player's Navy Cut?"

He spoke with hauteur. He did not like the chauffeur's exclamation. The fellow gave him a sidelong glance in which Carruthers read a certain insolence.

"We can't get it here," he said briefly.

He threw away with what looked very like exasperation the Egyptian cigarette Carruthers had given him and started off again. He looked sulky. He said nothing more. Carruthers felt that his efforts at sociability had been a mistake. For the rest of the journey he ignored the chauffeur. He adopted the frigid manner that he had used so successfully as secretary at the Embassy when a member of the British public came to him for assistance. For some time they had been running up hill, and now they came to a long low wall and then to an open gate. The chauffeur turned in.

"Have we arrived?" cried Carruthers.

"Sixty-five kilometres in fifty-seven minutes," said the chauffeur, a smile suddenly showing his fine white teeth. "Not so bad, considering the road."

He sounded his klaxon shrilly. Carruthers was breathless with excitement. They drove up a narrow road through an olive grove, and came to a low, white, rambling house. Betty was standing at the door. He jumped out of the car and kissed her on both cheeks. For a moment he could not speak. But subconsciously he noticed that at the door stood an elderly butler in white ducks and a couple of footmen in the fustanellas of their country. They were smart and picturesque. Whatever Betty permitted her chauffeur, it was evident that the house was run in the civilized style suited to her station. She led him through the hall, a large apartment with whitewashed walls in which he was vaguely conscious of handsome furniture, into the drawing-room. This also was large and low, with the same whitewashed walls, and he had immediately an impression of comfort and luxury.

"The first thing you must do is to come and look at my view," she said.

"The first thing I must do is to look at you."

She was dressed in white. Her arms, her face, her neck, were deeply burned by the sun; her eyes were bluer than he had ever seen them, and the whiteness of her teeth was startling. She looked extremely well. She was very trim and neat. Her hair was waved, her nails were manicured; he had had a moment's anxiety that in the easy life she led on this romantic isle she had let herself go.

"Upon my word you look eighteen, Betty. How do you manage it?"

"Happiness," she smiled.

It gave him a momentary pang to hear her say this. He did not want her to be too happy. He wanted to give her happiness. But now she insisted on taking him out on the terrace. The drawing-room had five long windows that led out to it and from the terrace the olive-clad hill tumbled steeply to the sea. There was a tiny bay below in which a white boat, mirrored on the calm water, lay at anchor. On a farther hill, round the corner you saw the white houses of a Greek village, and beyond it a huge grey crag surmounted by the battlements of a medieval castle.

"It was one of the strongholds of the Knights," she said. "I'll take you up there this evening."

The scene was exquisitely lovely. It took your breath away. It was peaceful and yet it had a strange air of life. It moved you not to contemplation, but stirred you to activity.

"You've got the tobacco all right, I suppose."

He started.

"I'm afraid I haven't. I never got your wire."

"But I wired to the Embassy and I wired to the Excelsior."

"I stayed at the Plaza."

"What a bore! Albert'll be furious."

"Who is Albert?"

"He drove you out. Player's is the only tobacco he likes and he can't get it here."

"Oh, the chauffeur." He pointed to the boat that lay gleaming beneath them. "Is that the yacht I've heard about?"

"Yes."

It was a large caïque that Betty had bought, fitted with a motor auxiliary and smartened up. In it she wandered about the Greek islands. She had been as far north as Athens and as far south as Alexandria.

"We'll take you for a trip if you can spare the time," she said. "You ought to see Cos while you're here."

"Who runs it for you?"

"Of course I have a crew, but Albert chiefly. He's very clever with motors and all that."

He did not know why it gave him a vague discomfort to hear her speak of the chauffeur again. Carruthers wondered if she did not leave too much in his hands. It was a mistake to give a servant too much leeway.

"You know, I couldn't help thinking I'd seen Albert before somewhere. But I can't place him."

She smiled brightly, her eyes shining, with that sudden gaiety of hers that gave her face its delightful frankness.

"You ought to remember him. He was the second footman at Aunt Louise's. He must have opened the door to you hundreds of times."

Aunt Louise was the aunt with whom Betty had lived before her marriage.

"Oh, is that who he is? I suppose I must have seen him there without noticing him. How does he happen to be here?"

"He comes from our place at home. When I married he

wanted to come with me, so I took him. He was Jimmie's valet
for some time and then I sent him to some motor works; he was
mad about cars, and eventually I took him on as my chauffeur.
I don't know what I should do without him now."

"Don't you think it's rather a mistake to get too dependent
on a servant?"

"I don't know. It never occurred to me."

Betty showed him the rooms that had been got ready for him,
and when he had changed they strolled down to the beach. A
dinghy was waiting for them and they rowed out to the caïque
and bathed from there. The water was warm and they sunned
themselves on the deck. The caïque was roomy, comfortable
and luxurious. Betty showed him over and they came upon
Albert tinkering with the engines. He was in filthy overalls, his
hands were black and his face was smeared with grease.

"What's the matter, Albert?" said Betty.

He raised himself and faced her respectfully.

"Nothing, m'lady. I was just 'aving a look round."

"There are only two things Albert loves in the world. One
is the car and the other's the yacht. Isn't that true, Albert?"

She gave him a gay smile, and Albert's rather stolid face lit
up. He showed his beautiful white teeth.

"That's true, m'lady."

"He sleeps on board, you know. We rigged up a very nice
cabin for him aft."

Carruthers fell into the life very easily. Betty had bought
the estate from a Turkish pasha exiled to Rhodes by Abdul
Hamid, and she had added a wing to the picturesque house.
She had made a wild garden of the olive grove that surrounded
it. It was planted with rosemary and lavender and asphodel,
broom that she had had sent from England and the roses for
which the island was famous. In the spring, she told him, the
ground was carpeted with anemones. But when she showed him
her property, telling him her plans and what alterations she had
in mind, Carruthers could not help feeling a little uneasy.

"You talk as though you were going to live here all your life,"
he said.

"Perhaps I am," she smiled.

"What nonsense! At your age."

"I'm getting on for forty, old boy," she answered lightly.

He discovered with satisfaction that Betty had an excellent

cook, and it gratified his sense of propriety to dine with her in the splendid dining-room, with its Italian furniture, and be waited on by the dignified Greek butler and the two handsome footmen in their flamboyant uniforms. The house was furnished with taste; the rooms contained nothing that was not essential, but every piece was exquisite. Betty lived in considerable state. When, the day after his arrival, the Governor with several members of his staff came over to dinner she displayed all the resources of the household. The Governor, entering the house, passed between a double row of flunkeys magnificent in their starched petticoats, embroidered jackets and velvet caps. It was almost a bodyguard. Carruthers liked the grand style. The dinner-party was very gay. Betty's Italian was fluent and Carruthers spoke it perfectly. The young officers in the Governor's suite were uncommonly smart in their uniforms. They were very attentive to Betty and she treated them with easy cordiality. She chaffed them. After dinner the gramophone was turned on and they danced with her one after the other.

When they were gone Carruthers asked her:

"Aren't they all madly in love with you?"

"I don't know about that. They hint occasionally at alliances permanent or otherwise, but they take it very good-naturedly when I decline with thanks."

They were not serious. The young ones were callow and the not so young were fat and bald. Whatever they might feel about her, Carruthers could not for a moment believe that Betty would make a fool of herself with a middle-class Italian. But a day or two later a curious thing happened. He was in his rooms dressing for dinner; he heard a man's voice outside in the passage, he could not hear what was said or what language was spoken, and then ringing out suddenly Betty's laughter. It was a charming laugh, rippling and gay, like a young girl's, and it had a joyous abandon that was infectious. But whom could she be laughing with? It was not the way you would laugh with a servant. It had a curious intimacy. It may seem strange that Carruthers read all this into a peal of laughter, but it must be remembered that Carruthers was very subtle. His stories were remarkable for such touches.

When they met presently on the terrace and he was shaking a cocktail he sought to gratify his curiosity.

"What were you laughing your head off over just now? Has anyone been here?"

"No."

She looked at him with genuine surprise.

"I thought one of your Italian officers had come to pass the time of day."

"No."

Of course the passage of years had had its effect on Betty. She was beautiful, but her beauty was mature. She had always had assurance, but now she had repose; her serenity was a feature, like her blue eyes and her candid brow, that was part of her beauty. She seemed to be at peace with all the world; it rested you to be with her as it rested you to lie among the olives within sight of the wine-coloured sea. Though she was as gay and witty as ever, the seriousness which once he had been alone to know was now patent. No one could accuse her any longer of being scatter-brained; it was impossible not to perceive the fineness of her character. It had even nobility. That was not a trait it was usual to find in the modern woman, and Carruthers said to himself that she was a throw-back; she reminded him of the great ladies of the eighteenth century. She had always had a feeling for literature, the poems she wrote as a girl were graceful and melodious, and he was more interested than surprised when she told him that she had undertaken a solid historical work. She was getting materials together for an account of the Knights of St. John in Rhodes. It was a story of romantic incidents. She took Carruthers to the city and showed him the noble battlements, and together they wandered through austere and stately buildings. They strolled up the silent Street of the Knights with the lovely stone façades and the great coats of arms that recalled a dead chivalry. She had a surprise for him here. She had bought one of the old houses and with affectionate care had restored it to its old state. When you entered the little courtyard, with its carved stone stairway, you were taken back into the Middle Ages. It had a tiny walled garden in which a fig tree grew and roses. It was small and secret and silent. The old Knights had been in contact with the East long enough to have acquired oriental ideas of privacy.

"When I'm tired of the villa I come here for two or three days and picnic. It's a relief sometimes not to be surrounded by people."

"But you're not alone here?"

"Practically."

There was a little parlour austerely furnished.

"What is this?" said Carruthers, pointing with a smile to a copy of *The Sporting Times* that lay on a table.

"Oh, that's Albert's. I suppose he left it here when he came to meet you. He has *The Sporting Times* and *The News of the World* sent him every week. That is how he keeps abreast of the great world."

She smiled tolerantly. Next to the parlour was a bedroom with nothing much in it but a large bed.

"The house belonged to an Englishman. That's partly why I bought it. He was a Sir Giles Quern, and one of my ancestors married a Mary Quern who was a cousin of his. They were Cornish people."

Finding that she could not get on with her history without such a knowledge of Latin as would enable her to read the medieval documents with ease, Betty had set about learning the classical language. She troubled to acquire only the elements of grammar and then started, with a translation by her side, to read the authors that interested her. It is a very good method of learning a language and I have often wondered that it is not used in schools. It saves all the endless turning over of dictionaries and the fumbling search for meaning. After nine months Betty could read Latin as fluently as most of us can read French. It seemed a trifle ridiculous to Carruthers that this lovely, brilliant creature should take her work so seriously and yet he was moved; he would have liked to snatch her in his arms and kiss her, not at that moment as a woman, but as a precocious child whose cleverness suddenly enchants you. But later he reflected upon what she had told him. He was of course a very clever man, otherwise he could not have attained the position he held in the Foreign Office, and it would be silly to claim that those two books of his could have made so much stir without some merit; if I have made him look a bit of a fool it is only because I did not happen to like him, and if I have derided his stories it is merely because stories of that sort seem to me rather silly. He had tact and insight. He had a conviction that there was but one way to win her. She was in a groove and happy in it, her plans were definite; but her life at Rhodes was so well-ordered, so complete and satisfying, that for that very reason its hold over her could be combated. His chance was to arouse in her the restlessness that lies deep in the heart of the English. So he talked to Betty of England and London, their common friends and the painters, writers and musicians with whom his literary success had brought him acquaintance. He talked of the bohemian parties in Chelsea, and of the opera, of trips to Paris *en bande* for a fancy-dress ball or to Berlin to see the new plays. He recalled to her imagination a life rich and easy, varied, cultured, intelligent and highly civilized. He tried to make her feel that she was stagnating in a backwater. The world was hurrying on, from one new and interesting phase to another, and she was standing still. They were living in a thrilling age and she was missing it. Of course he did not tell her this; he left her to infer it. He was amusing and spirited, he had an excellent memory for a good story, he was whimsical and gay. I know I have not made Humphrey Carruthers witty any more than I have shown Lady Betty brilliant. The reader must take my word for it that they were. Carruthers was generally reckoned an entertaining companion, and that is half the battle; people were willing to find him amusing and they vowed the things he said were marvellous. Of course his wit was social. It needed a particular company, who understood his allusions and shared his exclusive sense of humour. There are a score of journalists in Fleet Street who could knock spots off the most famous of the society wits; it is their business to be witty and brilliance is in their day's work. There are few of the society beauties whose photographs appear in the papers who could get a job at three pounds a week in the chorus of a song-and-dance show. Amateurs must be judged with tolerance. Carruthers knew that Betty enjoyed his society. They laughed a great deal together. The days passed in a flash.

"I shall miss you terribly when you go," she said in her frank way. "It's been a treat having you here. You are a sweet, Humphrey."

"Have you only just discovered it?"

He patted himself on the back. His tactics had been right. It was interesting to see how well his simple plan had worked. Like a charm. The vulgar might laugh at the Foreign Office, but there was no doubt it taught you how to deal with difficult people. Now he had but to choose his opportunity. He felt that Betty had never been more attached to him. He would wait till the end of his visit. Betty was emotional. She would be sorry that he was going. Rhodes would seem very dull without him. Whom would she have to talk to when he was gone? After dinner they usually sat on the terrace looking at the starry sea; the air was warm and balmy and vaguely scented: it was then

he would ask her to marry him, on the eve of his departure. He
felt it in his bones that she would accept him.

One morning when he had been in Rhodes a little over a week,
he happened to be coming upstairs as Betty was walking along
the passage.

"You've never shown me your room, Betty," he said.

"Haven't I? Come in and have a look now. It's rather nice."

She turned back and he followed her in. It was over the
drawing-room and nearly as large. It was furnished in the
Italian style, and as is the present way more like a sitting-
room than a bedroom. There were fine Paninis on the walls and
one or two handsome cabinets. The bed was Venetian and
beautifully painted.

"That's a couch of rather imposing dimensions for a widow
lady," he said facetiously.

"It is enormous, isn't it? But it was so lovely, I had to buy
it. It cost a fortune."

His eye took in the bed-table by the side. There were two or
three books on it, a box of cigarettes, and on an ash-tray a briar
pipe. Funny! What on earth had Betty got a pipe by her bed
for?

"Do look at this *cassone*. Isn't the painting marvellous? I
almost cried when I found it."

"I suppose that cost a fortune too.'

"I daren't tell you what I paid."

When they were leaving the room he cast another glance at
the bed-table. The pipe had vanished.

It was odd that Betty should have a pipe in her bedroom;
she certainly didn't smoke one herself, and if she had would
have made no secret of it; but of course there were a dozen
reasonable explanations. It might be a present she was making
to somebody, one of the Italians or even Albert—he had not
been able to see if it was new or old—or it might be a pattern
that she was going to ask him to take home to have others of
the same sort sent out to her. After the moment's perplexity,
not altogether unmingled with amusement, he put the matter
out of his mind. They were going for a picnic that day, taking
their luncheon with them, and Betty was driving him herself.
They had arranged to go for a cruise of a couple of days before
he left, so that he should see Patmos and Cos, and Albert was
busy with the engines of the caïque. They had a wonderful

day. They visited a ruined castle and climbed a mountain on
which grew asphodel, hyacinth and narcissus, and returned
dead beat. They separated not long after dinner and Carruthers
went to bed. He read for a little while and then turned out his
light. But he could not sleep. It was hot under his mosquito
net. He turned and tossed. Presently he thought he would go
down to the little beach at the foot of the hill and bathe. It was
not more than three minutes' walk. He put on his espadrilles
and took a towel. The moon was full and he saw it shining on the
sea through the olive trees. But he was not alone to have
thought that this radiant night would be lovely to bathe in,
for just before he came out on to the beach sounds reached his
ears. He muttered a little damn of vexation; some of Betty's
servants were bathing, and he could not very well disturb them.
The olive trees came almost to the water's edge and, undecided,
he stood in their shelter. He heard a voice that gave him a sudden start.

"Where's my towel?"

English. A woman waded out of the water and stood for a
moment at its edge. From the darkness a man came forward
with nothing but a towel round his loins. The woman was
Betty. She was stark naked. The man wrapped a bath-robe
round her and began drying her vigorously. She leaned on him
while she put on first one shoe and then the other, and to support her he placed his arm round her shoulders. The man was
Albert.

Carruthers turned and fled up the hill. He stumbled blindly.
Once he nearly fell. He was gasping like a wounded beast.
When he got into his room he flung himself on the bed and
clenched his fists, and the dry, painful sobs that tore his chest
broke into tears. He evidently had a violent attack of hysterics.
It was all clear to him, clear with the ghastly vividness with
which on a stormy night a flash of lightning can disclose a
ravaged landscape, clear, horribly clear. The way the man had
dried her and the way she leaned against him pointed not to
passion, but to a long continued intimacy, and the pipe by the
bedside, the pipe had a hideously conjugal air. It suggested the
pipe a man might smoke while he was reading in bed before
going to sleep. *The Sporting Times!* That was why she had that
little house in the Street of the Knights, so that they could
spend two or three days together in domestic familiarity. They
were like an old married couple. Humphrey asked himself how

long the hateful thing had lasted and suddenly he knew the answer; for years. Ten, twelve, fourteen: it had started when the young footman first came to London—he was a boy then, and it was obvious enough that it was not he who had made the advances; all through those years when she was the idol of the British public, when everyone adored her and she could have married anyone she liked, she was living with the second footman at her aunt's house. She took him with her when she married. Why had she made that surprising marriage? And the still-born child that came before its time. Of course that was why she had married Jimmie Welldon-Burns, because she was going to have a child by Albert. Oh shameless, shameless! And then, when Jimmie's health broke down she had made him take Albert as his valet. And what had Jimmie known and what had he suspected? He drank, that was what had started his tuberculosis; but why had he started drinking? Perhaps it was to still a suspicion that was so ugly that he could not face it. And it was to live with Albert that she had left Jimmie, and it was to live with Albert that she had settled in Rhodes. Albert, his hands with their broken nails stained by his work on the motors, coarse of aspect and stocky, rather like a butcher with his high colour and clumsy strength, Albert not even very young any more and running to fat, uneducated and vulgar, with his common way of speaking. Albert, Albert, how could she?

Carruthers got up and drank some water. He threw himself into a chair. He could not bear his bed. He smoked cigarette after cigarette. He was a wreck in the morning. He had not slept at all. They brought him in his breakfast; he drank the coffee but could eat nothing. Presently there was a brisk knock on his door.

"Coming down to bathe, Humphrey?"

That cheerful voice sent the blood singing through his head. He braced himself and opened the door.

"I don't think I will to-day. I don't feel very well."

She gave him a look.

"Oh my dear, you look all in. What's the matter with you?"

"I don't know, I think I must have got a touch of the sun."

His voice was dead and his eyes were tragic. She looked at him more closely. She did not say anything for a moment. He thought she went pale. *He knew.* Then a faintly mocking smile crossed her eyes; she thought the situation comic.

"Poor old boy, go and lie down. I'll send you in some aspirin. Perhaps you'll feel better at luncheon."

He lay in his darkened room. He would have given anything to get away then so that he need not set eyes on her again, but there was no means of that; the ship that was to take him back to Brindisi did not touch at Rhodes till the end of the week. He was a prisoner. And the next day they were to go to the islands. There was no escape from her there; in the caïque they would be in one another's pockets all day long. He couldn't face that. He was so ashamed. But she wasn't ashamed. At that moment when it had been plain to her that nothing was hidden from him any longer she had smiled. She was capable of telling him all about it. He could not bear that. That was too much. After all, she couldn't be certain that he knew, at best she could only suspect; if he behaved as if nothing had happened, if at luncheon and during the days that remained he was as gay and jolly as usual, she would think she had been mistaken. It was enough to know what he knew; he would not suffer the crowning humiliation of hearing from her own lips the disgraceful story. But at luncheon the first thing she said was:

"Isn't it a bore, Albert says something's gone wrong with the motor, we shan't be able to go on our trip after all. I daren't trust to sail at this time of the year. We might be becalmed for a week."

She spoke lightly and he answered in the same casual fashion.

"Oh, I'm sorry, but still I don't really care. It's so lovely here, I really didn't much want to go."

He told her that the aspirin had done him good and he felt much better; to the Greek butler and the two footmen in fustanellas it must have seemed that they talked as vivaciously as usual. That night the British consul came to dinner, and the night after, some Italian officers. Carruthers counted the days, he counted the hours. Oh, if the moment would only come when he could step on the ship and be free from the horror that, every moment of the day, obsessed him! He was growing so tired. But Betty's manner was so self-possessed that sometimes he asked himself if she really knew that he was aware of her secret. Was it the truth that she had told about the caïque and not, as had at once struck him, an excuse; and was it an accident that a succession of visitors prevented them from ever being alone together? The worst of having so much tact was that you never quite knew whether other people were acting naturally or being tactful too. When he looked at her, so easy and calm, so obviously happy, he could not believe the odious truth. And yet he had seen with his own eyes. And the future. What would her future be? It was horrible to think of. Sooner or later the truth must become notorious. And to think of Betty a mock and an outcast, in the power of a coarse and common man, growing older, losing her beauty; and the man was five years younger than she. One day he would take a mistress, one of her own maids, perhaps, with whom he would feel at home as he had never felt with the great lady, and what could she do then? What humiliation then must she be prepared to put up with! He might be cruel to her. He might beat her. Betty. Betty.

Carruthers wrung his hands. And on a sudden an idea came to him that filled him with a painful exultation; he put it away from him, but it returned; it would not let him be. He must save her; he had loved her too much and too long to let her sink, sink as she was sinking; a passion of self-sacrifice welled up in him. Notwithstanding everything, though his love now was dead and he felt for her an almost physical repulsion, he would marry her. He laughed mirthlessly. What would his life be? He couldn't help that. He didn't matter. It was the only thing to do. He felt wonderfully exalted, and yet very humble, for he was awed at the thought of the heights which the divine spirit of man could reach.

His ship was to sail on Saturday, and on Thursday, when the guests who had been dining left them, he said:

"I hope we're going to be alone to-morrow."

"As a matter of fact I've asked some Egyptians who spend the summer here. She's a sister of the ex-Khedive and very intelligent. I'm sure you'll like her."

"Well, it's my last evening. Couldn't we spend it alone?"

She gave him a glance. There was a faint amusement in her eyes, but his were grave.

"If you like. I can put them off."

"Then do."

He was to start early in the morning and his luggage was packed. Betty had told him not to dress, but he had answered that he preferred to. For the last time they sat down to dinner facing one another. The dining-room, with its shaded lights, was bare and formal, but the summer night flooding in through the great open windows gave it a sober richness. It had the effect of the private refectory in a convent to which a royal lady had retired in order to devote the remainder of her life to a piety not too austere. They had their coffee on the terrace. Carruthers drank a couple of liqueurs. He was feeling very nervous.

"Betty my dear, I've got something I want to say to you," he began.

"Have you? I wouldn't say it if I were you."

She answered gently. She remained perfectly calm, watching him shrewdly, but with the glimmer of a smile in her blue eyes.

"I must."

She shrugged her shoulders and was silent. He was conscious that his voice trembled a little and he was angry with himself.

"You know I've been madly in love with you for many years. I don't know how many times I've asked you to marry me. But after all, things change and people change too, don't they? We're neither of us so young as we were. Won't you marry me now, Betty?"

She gave him the smile that had always been such an attractive thing in her; it was so kindly, so frank and still, still so wonderfully innocent.

"You're very sweet, Humphrey. It's awfully nice of you to ask me again. I can't tell you how touched I am. But you know, I'm a creature of habit, I've got in the habit of saying no to you now, and I can't change it."

"Why not?"

There was something aggressive in his tone, something almost ominous, that made her give him a quick look. Her face blanched with sudden anger, but she immediately controlled herself.

"Because I don't want to," she smiled.

"Are you going to marry anyone else?"

"I? No. Of course not."

For a moment she seemed to draw herself up as though a wave of ancestral pride swept through her, and then she began to laugh. But whether she laughed at the thought that had passed through her mind or because something in Humphrey's proposal had amused her none but she could have told.

"Betty, I implore you to marry me."

"Never."

"You can't go on living this life."

He put into his voice all the anguish of his heart, and his face was drawn and tortured. She smiled affectionately.

"Why not? Don't be such a donkey. You know I adore you, Humphrey, but you are rather an old woman."

"Betty, Betty."

Did she not see that it was for her sake that he wanted it? It was not love that made him speak, but human pity and shame. She got up.

"Don't be tiresome, Humphrey. You'd better go to bed. You know you have to be up with the lark. I shan't see you in the morning. Good-bye and God bless you. It's been wonderful having you here."

She kissed him on both cheeks.

Next morning, early, for he had to be on board at eight, when Carruthers stepped out of the front door he found Albert waiting for him in the car. He wore a singlet, duck trousers and a beret basque. Carruthers' luggage was in the back. He turned to the butler.

"Put my bags beside the chauffeur," he said. "I'll sit behind."

Albert made no remark. Carruthers got in and they drove off. When they arrived at the harbour porters ran up. Albert got out of the car. Carruthers looked down at him from his greater height.

"You need not see me on board. I can manage perfectly well by myself. Here's a tip for you."

He gave him a five-pound note. Albert flushed. He was taken aback; he would have liked to refuse it, but did not know how to, and the servility of years asserted itself. Perhaps he did not know what he said.

"Thank you, sir."

Carruthers gave him a curt nod and walked away. He had forced Betty's lover to call him "sir." It was as though he had struck her a blow across that smiling mouth of hers and flung in her face an opprobrious word. It filled him with a bitter satisfaction.

He shrugged his shoulders and I could see that even this small triumph now seemed vain. For a little while we were silent. There was nothing for me to say. Then he began again.

"I daresay you think it's very strange that I should tell you all this. I don't care. You know, I feel as if nothing mattered any more. I feel as if decency no longer existed in the world.

Heaven knows, I'm not jealous. You can't be jealous unless you love, and my love is dead. It was killed in a flash. After all those years. I can't think of her now without horror. What destroys me, what makes me so frightfully unhappy, is to think of her unspeakable degradation."

So it has been said that it was not jealousy that caused Othello to kill Desdemona, but an agony that the creature that he believed angelic should be proved impure and worthless. What broke his noble heart was that virtue should so fall.

"I thought there was no one like her. I admired her so much. I admired her courage and her frankness, her intelligence and her love of beauty. She's just a sham and she's never been anything else."

"I wonder if that's true. Do you think any of us are all of a piece? Do you know what strikes me? I should have said that Albert was only the instrument, her toll to the solid earth, so to speak, that left her soul at liberty to range the empyrean. Perhaps the mere fact that he was so far below her gave her a sense of freedom in her relations with him that she would have lacked with a man of her own class. The spirit is very strange; it never soars so high as when the body has wallowed for a period in the gutter."

"Oh, don't talk such rot," he answered angrily.

"I don't think it is rot. I don't put it very well, but the idea's sound."

"Much good it does me. I'm broken and done for. I'm finished."

"Oh, nonsense. Why don't you write a story about it?"

"I?"

"You know that's the great pull a writer has over other people. When something has made him terribly unhappy, and he's tortured and miserable, he can put it all into a story and it's astonishing what a comfort and relief it is."

"It would be monstrous. Betty was everything in the world to me. I couldn't do anything so caddish."

He paused for a little and I saw him reflect. I saw that notwithstanding the horror that my suggestion caused him he did for one minute look at the situation from the standpoint of the writer. He shook his head.

"Not for her sake, for mine. After all, I have some self-respect. Besides, there's no story there."

VIRTUE

THERE are few things better than a good Havana. When I was young and very poor and smoked a cigar only when somebody gave me one, I determined that if ever I had money I would smoke a cigar every day after luncheon and after dinner. This is the only resolution of my youth that I have kept. It is the only ambition I have achieved that has never been embittered by disillusion. I like a cigar that is mild, but full-flavoured, neither so small that it is finished before you have become aware of it nor so large as to be irksome, rolled so that it draws without consciousness of effort on your part, with a leaf so firm that it doesn't become messy on your lips and in such condition that it keeps its savour to the very end. But when you have taken the last pull and put down the shapeless stump and watched the final cloud of smoke dwindle blue in the surrounding air it is impossible, if you have a sensitive nature, not to feel a certain melancholy at the thought of all the labour, the care and pains that have gone, the thought, the trouble, the complicated organization that have been required, to provide you with half an hour's delight. For this men have sweltered long years under tropical suns and ships have scoured the seven seas. These reflections become more poignant still when you are eating a dozen oysters (with half a bottle of dry white wine) and they become almost unbearable when it comes to a lamb cutlet. For these are animals, and there is something that inspires awe in the thought that since the surface of the earth became capable of supporting life from generation to generation for millions upon millions of years creatures have come into existence, to end at last upon a plate of crushed ice or on a silver grill. It may be that a sluggish fancy cannot grasp the dreadful solemnity of eating an oyster and evolution has taught us that the bivalve has through the ages kept itself to itself in a manner that inevitably alienates sympathy. There is an aloofness in it that is offensive to the aspiring spirit of man, and a self-complacency that is obnoxious to his vanity. But I do not know how anyone can look upon a lamb cutlet without thoughts too deep for tears: here man himself has taken a hand, and the history of the race is bound up with the tender morsel on your plate.

And sometimes even the fate of human beings is curious to consider. It is strange to look upon this man or that, the quiet ordinary persons of every day, the bank clerk, the dustman, the middle-aged girl in the second row of the chorus, and think of the interminable history behind them and of the long, long series of hazards by which from the primeval slime the course of events has brought them at this moment to such and such a place. When such tremendous vicissitudes have been needed to get them here at all, one would have thought some huge significance must be attached to them; one would have thought that what befell them must matter a little to the Life Spirit or whatever else it is that has produced them. An accident befalls them. The thread is broken. The story that began with the world is finished abruptly, and it looks as though it meant nothing at all. A tale told by an idiot. And is it not odd that this event, of an importance so dramatic, may be brought about by a cause so trivial?

An incident of no moment, that might easily not have happened, has consequences that are incalculable. It looks as though blind chance ruled all things. Our smallest actions may affect profoundly the whole lives of people who have nothing to do with us. The story I have to tell would never have happened if one day I had not walked across the street. Life is really very fantastic, and one has to have a peculiar sense of humour to see the fun of it.

I was strolling down Bond Street one spring morning and, having nothing much to do till lunch time, thought I would look in at Sotheby's, the auction rooms, to see whether there was anything on show that interested me. There was a block in the traffic and I threaded my way through the cars. When I reached the other side I ran into a man I had known in Borneo coming out of a hatter's.

"Hullo, Morton," I said. "When did you come home?"

"I've been back about a week."

He was a District Officer. The Governor had given me a letter of introduction to him, and I wrote and told him I meant to spend a week at the place he lived at and should like to put up at the government rest-house. He met me on the ship when I arrived and asked me to stay with him. I demurred. I did not see how I could spend a week with a total stranger, I did not want to put him to the expense of my board, and besides I thought I should have more freedom if I were on my own. He would not listen to me.

"I've got plenty of room," he said, "and the rest-house is beastly. I haven't spoken to a white man for six months and I'm fed to the teeth with my own company."

But when Morton had got me and his launch had landed us at the bungalow and he had offered me a drink, he did not in the least know what to do with me. He was seized on a sudden with shyness, and his conversation, which had been fluent and ready, ran dry. I did my best to make him feel at home (it was the least I could do, considering that it was his own house) and asked him if he had any new records. He turned on the gramophone, and the sound of ragtime gave him confidence.

His bungalow overlooked the river, and his living-room was a large verandah. It was furnished in the impersonal fashion that characterized the dwellings of government officials who were moved here and there at little notice according to the exigencies of the service. There were native hats as ornaments on the walls and the horns of animals, blow-pipes and spears. In the book-shelf were detective novels and old magazines. There was a cottage piano with yellow keys. It was very untidy, but not uncomfortable.

Unfortunately I cannot very well remember what he looked like. He was young, twenty-eight, I learnt later, and he had a boyish and attractive smile. I spent an agreeable week with him. We went up and down the river and we climbed a mountain. We had tiffin one day with some planters who lived twenty miles away, and every evening we went to the club. The only members were the manager of a kutch factory and his assistants, but they were not on speaking terms with one another and it was only on Morton's representations that they must not let him down when he had a visitor that we could get up a rubber of bridge The atmosphere was strained. We came back to dinner, listened to the gramophone and went to bed. Morton had little office work, and one would have thought the time hung heavy on his hands, but he had energy and high spirits; it was his first post of the sort and he was happy to be independent. His only anxiety was lest he should be transferred before he had finished a road he was building. This was the joy of his heart. It was his own idea and he had wheedled the government into giving him the money to make it; he had surveyed the country himself and traced the path. He had solved unaided the technical problems that presented themselves. Every morning, before he went to his office, he drove out in a rickety old Ford to where the coolies were working and watched the progress that had been made since the day before. He thought of nothing else. He dreamt of it at night. He reckoned that it would be finished in a year and he did not want to take his leave till then. He could not have worked with more zest if he had been a painter or a sculptor creating a work of art. I think it was this eagerness that made me take a fancy to him. I liked his zeal. I liked his ingenuousness. And I was impressed by the passion for achievement that made him indifferent to the solitariness of his life, to promotion and even to the thought of going home. I forget how long the road was, fifteen or twenty miles, I think, and I forget what purpose it was to serve. I don't believe Morton cared very much. His passion was the artist's and his triumph was the triumph of man over nature. He learnt as he went along. He had the jungle to contend against, torrential rains that destroyed the labour of weeks, accidents of topography; he had to collect his labour and hold it together; he had inadequate funds. His imagination sustained him. His labours gained a sort of epic quality, and the vicissitudes of the work were a great saga that unrolled itself with an infinity of episodes.

His only complaint was that the day was too short. He had office duties, he was judge and tax collector, father and mother (at twenty-eight) of the people in his district; he had now and then to make tours that took him away from home. Unless he were on the spot nothing was done. He would have liked to be there twenty-four hours a day driving the reluctant coolies to further effort. It so happened that shortly before I arrived

an incident had occurred that filled him with jubilation. He
had offered a contract to a Chinese to make a certain section
of the road, and the Chinese had asked more than Morton
could afford to pay. Notwithstanding interminable discussions
they had been unable to arrive at an agreement, and Morton
with rage in his heart saw his work held up. He was at his wit's
end. Then, going down to his office one morning, he heard that
there had been a row in one of the Chinese gambling houses
the night before. A coolie had been badly wounded and his
assailant was under arrest. This assailant was the contractor.
He was brought into court, the evidence was clear and Morton
sentenced him to eighteen months' hard labour.

"Now he'll have to build the blasted road for nothing,"
said Morton, his eyes glistening when he told me the story.

We saw the fellow at work one morning, in the prison sarong,
unconcerned. He was taking his misfortunes in good part.

"I've told him I'll remit the rest of his sentence when the
road's finished," said Morton, "and he's as pleased as Punch.
Bit of a snip for me, eh, what?"

When I left Morton I asked him to let me know when he
came to England, and he promised to write to me as soon as he
landed. On the spur of the moment one gives these invitations
and one is perfectly sincere about them. But when one is taken
at one's word a slight dismay seizes one. People are so different
at home from what they are abroad. There they are easy, cordial and natural. They have interesting things to tell you. They
are immensely kind. You are anxious, when your turn comes,
to do something in return for the hospitality you have received. But it is not easy. The persons who were so entertaining
in their own surroundings are very dull in yours. They are constrained and shy. You introduce them to your friends, and your
friends find them a crashing bore. They do their best to be
civil, but sigh with relief when the strangers go and the conversation can once more run easily in its accustomed channels.
I think the residents in far places early in their careers understand the situation pretty well, as the result maybe of bitter
and humiliating experiences, for I have found that they seldom
take advantage of the invitation which on some outstation on
the edge of the jungle has been so cordially extended to them
and by them as cordially accepted. But Morton was different.
He was a young man and single. It is generally the wives that
are the difficulty; other women look at their drab clothes, in a

glance take in their provincial air, and freeze them with their indifference. But a man can play bridge and tennis, and dance. Morton had charm. I had no doubt that in a day or two he would find his feet.

"Why didn't you let me know you were back?" I asked him.

"I thought you wouldn't want to be bothered with me," he smiled.

"What nonsense!"

Of course now as we stood in Bond Street on the curb and chatted for a minute he looked strange to me. I had never seen him in anything but khaki shorts and a tennis shirt, except when we got back from the club at night and he put on a pajama jacket and a sarong for dinner. It is as comfortable a form of evening dress as has ever been devised. He looked a bit awkward in his blue serge suit. His face against a white collar was very brown.

"How about the road?" I asked him.

"Finished. I was afraid I'd have to postpone my leave. We struck one or two snags towards the end, but I made 'em hustle and the day before I left I drove the Ford to the end and back without stopping."

I laughed. His pleasure was charming

"What have you been doing with yourself in London?"

"Buying clothes."

"Been having a good time?"

"Marvellous. A bit lonely, you know, but I don't mind that. I've been to a show every night. The Palmers, you know—I think you met them in Sarawak—were going to be in town and we were going to do the plays together, but they had to go to Scotland because her mother's ill."

His words, said so breezily, cut me to the quick. His was the common experience. It was heart-breaking. For months, for long months before it was due, these people planned their leave, and when they got off the ship they were in such spirits they could hardly contain themselves. London. Shops and clubs and theatres and restaurants. London. They were going to have the time of their lives. London. It swallowed them. A strange, turbulent city, not hostile but indifferent, and they were lost in it. They had no friends. They had nothing in common with the acquaintances they made. They were more lonely than in the jungle. It was a relief when at a theatre they ran across someone they had known in the East (and perhaps been

bored stiff by or disliked) and they could fix up an evening together and have a good laugh and tell one another what a grand
time they were having and talk of common friends and at last
confide to one another a little shyly that they would not be
sorry when their leave was up and they were once again in
harness. They went to see their families and of course they
were glad to see them, but it wasn't the same as it had been;
they did feel a bit out of it, and when you came down to brass
tacks the life people led in England was deadly. It was grand
fun to come home, but you couldn't live there any more, and
sometimes you thought of your bungalow overlooking the river
and your tours of the district and what a lark it was to run
over once in a blue moon to Sandakan or Kuching or Singapore

And because I remembered what Morton had looked forward to when, the road finished and off his chest, he went on
leave, I could not but feel a pang when I thought of him dining
by himself in a dismal club where he knew nobody, or alone in
a restaurant in Soho and then going off to see a play with no
one by his side with whom he could enjoy it, and no one to
have a drink with during the interval. And at the same time
I reflected that even if I had known he was in London I could
have done nothing much for him, for during the last week I
had not had a moment free. That every evening I was dining
with friends and going to a play, and the next day I was going
abroad.

"What are you doing to-night?" I asked him.

"I'm going to the Pavilion. It's packed jammed full, but
there's a fellow over the road who's wonderful and he's got me
a ticket that had been returned. You can often get one seat,
you know, when you can't get two."

"Why don't you come and have supper with me? I'm taking
some people to the Haymarket and we're going on to Ciro's
afterwards."

"I'd love to."

We arranged to meet at eleven, and I left him to keep an
engagement.

I was afraid the friends I had asked him to meet would not
amuse Morton very much, for they were distinctly middle-
aged, but I could not think of anyone young that at this
season of the year I should be likely to get hold of at the last
moment. None of the girls I knew would thank me for asking

her to supper to dance with a shy young man from Malaya.
I could trust the Bishops to do their best for him, and after
all it must be jollier for him to have supper in a club with a
good band where he could see pretty women dancing than to
go home to bed at eleven because he had nowhere else in the
world to go. I had known Charlie Bishop first when I was a
medical student. He was then a thin little fellow with sandy hair
and blunt features; he had fine eyes, dark and gleaming, but he
wore spectacles. He had a round, merry, red face. He was very
fond of the girls. I suppose he had a way with him, for with
no money and no looks, he managed to pick up a succession of
young persons who gratified his roving desires. He was clever
and bumptious, argumentative and quick-tempered. He had
a caustic tongue. Looking back, I should say he was a rather
disagreeable young man, but I do not think he was a bore. Now,
halfway through the fifties, he was inclined to be stout and he
was very bald, but his eyes behind the gold-rimmed spectacles
were still bright and alert. He was dogmatic and somewhat
conceited, argumentative still and caustic, but he was good-
natured and amusing. After you have known a person so long
his idiosyncrasies cease to trouble you. You accept them as
you accept your own physical defects. He was by profession
a pathologist, and now and then he sent me a slim book he
had just published. It was severe and extremely technical and
grimly illustrated with photographs of bacteria. I did not read
it. I gathered from what I sometimes heard that Charlie's
views on the subjects with which he dealt were unsound. I do
not believe that he was very popular with the other members
of his profession—he made no secret of the fact that he looked
upon them as a set of incompetent idiots—but he had his job,
it brought him in six or eight hundred a year, I think, and he
was completely indifferent to other people's opinion of him.

I liked Charlie Bishop because I had known him for thirty
years, but I liked Margery, his wife, because she was very nice.
I was extremely surprised when he told me he was going to be
married. He was hard on forty at the time, and so fickle in his
affections that I had made up my mind he would remain
single. He was very fond of women, but he was not in the least
sentimental, and his aims were loose. His views on the female
sex would in these idealistic days be thought crude. He knew
what he wanted and he asked for it, and if he couldn't get it
for love or money he shrugged his shoulders and went his way.

To be brief, he did not look to women to gratify his ideal but to provide him with fornication. It was odd that, though small and plain, he found so many who were prepared to grant his wishes. For his spiritual needs he found satisfaction in unicellular organisms. He had always been a man who spoke to the point, and when he told me he was going to marry a young woman called Margery Hobson I did not hesitate to ask him why. He grinned.

"Three reasons. First, she won't let me go to bed with her without. Second, she makes me laugh like a hyena. And third, she's alone in the world, without a single relation, and she must have someone to take care of her."

"The first reason is just swank and the second is eyewash. The third is the real one and it means that she's got you by the short hairs."

His eyes gleamed softly behind his large spectacles.

"I shouldn't be surprised if you weren't dead right."

"She's not only got you by the short hairs but you're as pleased as Punch that she has."

"Come and lunch to-morrow and have a look at her. She's easy on the eye."

Charlie was a member of a cock-and-hen club which at that time I used a good deal, and we arranged to lunch there. I found Margery a very attractive young woman. She was then just under thirty. She was a lady. I noticed the fact with satisfaction, but with a certain astonishment, for it had not escaped my notice that Charlie was attracted as a rule by women whose breeding left something to be desired. She was not beautiful, but comely, with fine dark hair and fine eyes, a good colour and a look of health. She had a pleasant frankness and an air of candour that was very taking. She looked honest, simple and dependable. I took an immediate liking to her. She was easy to talk to, and though she did not say anything very brilliant she understood what other people were talking about; she was quick to see a joke and she was not shy. She gave you the impression of being competent and businesslike. She had a happy placidity that suggested a good temper and an excellent digestion.

They seemed extremely pleased with one another. I had asked myself when I first saw her why Margery was marrying this irritable little man, baldish already and by no means young, but I discovered very soon that it was because she was

in love with him. They chaffed one another a good deal and
laughed a lot, and every now and then their eyes met more
significantly and they seemed to exchange a little private message. It was really rather touching.

A week later they were married at a registrar's office. It was
a very successful marriage. Looking back now after sixteen
years I could not but chuckle sympathetically at the thought
of the lark they had made of their life together. I had never
known a more devoted couple. They had never had very much
money. They never seemed to want any. They had no ambitions. Their life was a picnic that never came to an end. They
lived in the smallest flat I ever saw, in Panton Street, a small
bedroom, a small sitting-room and a bathroom that served also
as a kitchen. But they had no sense of home, they ate their
meals in restaurants, and only had breakfast in the flat. It
was merely a place to sleep in. It was comfortable, though a
third person coming in for a whisky and soda crowded it, and
Margery with the help of a charwoman kept it as neat as
Charlie's untidiness permitted, but there was not a single thing
in it that had a personal note. They had a tiny car, and whenever Charlie had a holiday they took it across the Channel and
started off, with a bag each for all their luggage, to drive where-
ever the fancy took them. Breakdowns never disturbed them,
bad weather was part of the fun, a puncture was no end of a
joke, and if they lost their way and had to sleep out in the open
they thought they were having the time of their lives.

Charlie continued to be irascible and contentious, but nothing he did ever disturbed Margery's lovely placidity. She could
calm him with a word. She still made him laugh. She typed his
monographs on obscure bacteria and corrected the proofs of
his articles in the scientific magazines. Once I asked them if
they ever quarrelled.

"No," she said, "we never seem to have anything to quarrel
about. Charlie has the temper of an angel."

"Nonsense," I said, "he's an overbearing, aggressive, and
cantankerous fellow. He always has been."

She looked at him and giggled, and I saw that she thought
I was being funny.

"Let him rave," said Charlie. "He's an ignorant fool and
he uses words of whose meaning he hasn't the smallest idea."

They were sweet together. They were very happy in one
another's company and were never apart if they could help

it. Even after the long time they had been married Charlie used to get into the car every day at luncheon time to come west and meet Margery at a restaurant. People used to laugh at them, not unkindly, but perhaps with a little catch in the throat, because when they were asked to go and spend a week-end in the country Margery would write to the hostess and say they would like to come if they could be given a double bed. They had slept together for so many years that neither of them could sleep alone. It was often a trifle awkward. Husbands and wives as a rule not only demanded separate rooms, but were inclined to be peevish if asked to share the same bathroom. Modern houses were not arranged for domestic couples, but among their friends it became an understood thing that if you wanted the Bishops you must give them a room with a double bed. Some people of course thought it a little indecent and it was never convenient, but they were a pleasant pair to have to stay and it was worth while to put up with their crankiness. Charlie was always full of spirits and in his caustic way extremely amusing, and Margery was peaceful and easy. They were no trouble to entertain. Nothing pleased them more than to be left to go out together for a long ramble in the country.

When a man marries, his wife sooner or later estranges him from his old friends, but Margery on the contrary increased Charlie's intimacy with them. By making him more tolerant she made him a more agreeable companion. They gave you the impression not of a married couple, but, rather amusingly, of two middle-aged bachelors living together; and when Margery, as was the rule, found herself the only woman among half a dozen men, ribald, argumentative and gay, she was not a bar to good-fellowship but an asset. Whenever I was in England I saw them. They generally dined at the club of which I have spoken, and if I happened to be alone I joined them.

When we met that evening for a snack before going to the play I told them I had asked Morton to come to supper.

"I'm afraid you'll find him rather dull," I said. "But he's a very decent sort of boy and he was awfully kind to me when I was in Borneo."

"Why didn't you let me know sooner?" cried Margery. "I'd have brought a girl along."

"What do you want a girl for?" said Charlie. "There'll be you."

"I don't think it can be much fun for a young man to dance with a woman of my advanced years," said Margery.

"Rot. What's your age got to do with it?" He turned to me. "Have you ever danced with anyone who danced better?"

I had, but she certainly danced very well. She was light on her feet and she had a good sense of rhythm.

"Never," I said heartily.

Morton was waiting for us when we reached Ciro's. He looked very sunburned in his evening clothes. Perhaps it was because I knew that they had been wrapped away in a tin box with moth balls for four years that I felt he did not look quite at home in them. He was certainly more at ease in khaki shorts. Charlie Bishop was a good talker and liked to hear himself speak. Morton was shy. I gave him a cocktail and ordered some champagne. I had a feeling that he would be glad to dance, but was not quite sure whether it would occur to him to ask Margery. I was acutely conscious that we all belonged to another generation.

"I think I should tell you that Mrs. Bishop is a beautiful dancer," I said.

"Is she?" He flushed a little. "Will you dance with me?"

She got up and they took the floor. She was looking peculiarly nice that evening, not at all smart, and I do not think her plain black dress had cost more than six guineas, but she looked a lady. She had the advantage of having extremely good legs, and at that time skirts were still being worn very short. I suppose she had a little make-up on, but in contrast with the other women there she looked very natural. Shingled hair suited her; it was not even touched with white and it had an attractive sheen. She was not a pretty woman, but her kindliness, her wholesome air, her good health, gave you, if not the illusion that she was, at least the feeling that it didn't at all matter. When she came back to the table her eyes were bright and she had a heightened colour.

"How does he dance?" asked her husband.

"Divinely."

"You're very easy to dance with," said Morton.

Charlie went on with his discourse. He had a sardonic humour and he was interesting because he was himself so interested in what he said. But he spoke of things that Morton knew nothing about, and though he listened with a civil show of interest I could see that he was too much excited by the gaiety of the

scene, the music and the champagne to give his attention to
conversation. When the music struck up again his eyes immediately sought Margery's. Charles caught the look and
smiled.

"Dance with him, Margery. Good for my figure to see you
take exercise."

They set off again, and for a moment Charlie watched her
with fond eyes.

"Margery's having the time of her life. She loves dancing,
and it makes me puff and blow. Not a bad youth."

My little party was quite a success, and when Morton and
I, having taken leave of the Bishops, walked together towards
Piccadilly Circus he thanked me warmly. He had really enjoyed
himself. I said good-bye to him. Next morning I went abroad.

I was sorry not to have been able to do more for Morton,
and I knew that when I returned he would be on his way back
to Borneo. I gave him a passing thought now and then, but by
the autumn when I got home he had slipped my memory. After
I had been in London a week or so I happened to drop in one
night at the club to which Charlie Bishop also belonged. He
was sitting with three or four men I knew and I went up. I
had not seen any of them since my return. One of them, a man
called Bill Marsh, whose wife, Janet, was a great friend of
mine, asked me to have a drink.

"Where have you sprung from?" asked Charlie. "Haven't
seen you about lately."

I noticed at once that he was drunk. I was astonished.
Charlie had always liked his liquor, but he carried it well and
never exceeded. In years gone by, when we were very young,
he got tight occasionally, but probably more than anything to
show what a great fellow he was, and it is unfair to bring up
against a man the excesses of his youth. But I remembered that
Charlie had never been very nice when he was drunk: his
natural aggressiveness was exaggerated then and he talked
too much and too loud; he was very apt to be quarrelsome. He
was very dogmatic now, laying down the law and refusing to
listen to any of the objections his rash statements called forth.
The others knew he was drunk and were struggling between
the irritation his cantankerousness aroused in them and the
good-natured tolerance which they felt his condition demanded.
He was not an agreeable object. A man of that age, bald and

fattish, with spectacles, is disgusting drunk. He was generally
rather dapper, but he was untidy now and there was tobacco
ash all over him. Charlie called the waiter and ordered another
whisky. The waiter had been at the club for thirty years.

"You've got one in front of you, sir."

"Mind your own damned business," said Charlie Bishop.
"Bring me a double whisky right away or I'll report you to
the secretary for insolence."

"Very good, sir," said the waiter.

Charlie emptied his glass at a gulp, but his hand was unsteady and he spilled some of the whisky over himself.

"Well, Charlie, old boy, we'd better be toddling along,"
said Bill Marsh. He turned to me. "Charlie's staying with us
for a bit."

I was more surprised still. But I felt that something was
wrong and thought it safer not to say anything.

"I'm ready," said Charlie. "I'll just have another drink before I go. I shall have a better night if I do."

It did not look to me as though the party would break up
for some time, so I got up and announced that I meant to stroll
home.

"I say," said Bill, as I was about to go, "you wouldn't come
and dine with us to-morrow night, would you, just me and
Janet and Charlie?"

"Yes, I'll come with pleasure," I said.

It was evident that something was up.

The Marshes lived in a terrace on the east side of Regent's
Park. The maid who opened the door for me asked me to go in
to Mr. Marsh's study. He was waiting for me there.

"I thought I'd better have a word with you before you went
upstairs," he said as he shook hands with me. "You know
Margery's left Charlie?"

"No?"

"He's taken it very hard. Janet thought it was so awful
for him alone in that beastly little flat that we asked him to
stay here for a bit. We've done everything we could for him.
He's been drinking like a fish. He hasn't slept a wink for a
fortnight."

"But she hasn't left him for good?"

"Yes. She's crazy about a fellow called Morton."

I was astounded.

"Morton. Who's he?"

It never struck me it was my friend from Borneo.

"Damn it all, you introduced him, and a pretty piece of work you did. Let's go upstairs. I thought I'd better put you wise."

He opened the door and we went out. I was thoroughly confused.

"But look here——" I said.

"Ask Janet. She knows the whole thing. It beats me. I've got no patience with Margery, and he must be a mess."

He preceded me into the drawing-room. Janet Marsh rose as I entered, and came forward to greet me. Charlie was sitting at the window, reading the evening paper; he put it aside as I went up to him and shook his hand. He was quite sober and he spoke in his usual rather perky manner, but I noticed that he looked very ill. We had a glass of sherry and went down to dinner. Janet was a woman of spirit. She was tall and fair and good to look at. She kept the conversation going with alertness. When she left us to drink a glass of port it was with instructions not to stay more than ten minutes. Bill, as a rule somewhat taciturn, exerted himself now to talk. I tumbled to the game. I was hampered by my ignorance of what exactly had happened, but it was plain that the Marshes wanted to prevent Charlie from brooding, and I did my best to interest him. He seemed willing to play his part, he was always fond of holding forth, and he discussed, from the pathologist's standpoint, a murder that was just then absorbing the public. But he spoke without life. He was an empty shell, and one had the feeling that though for the sake of his host he forced himself to speak, his thoughts were elsewhere. It was a relief when a knocking on the floor above indicated to us that Janet was getting impatient. This was an occasion when a woman's presence eased the situation. We went upstairs and played family bridge. When it was time for me to go Charlie said he would walk with me as far as the Marylebone Road.

"Oh, Charlie, it's so late, you'd much better go to bed," said Janet.

"I shall sleep better if I have a stroll before turning in," he replied.

She gave him a worried look. You cannot forbid a middle-aged professor of pathology from going for a little walk if he wants to. She glanced brightly at her husband.

"I daresay it'll do Bill no harm."

I think the remark was tactless. Women are often a little too managing. Charlie gave her a sullen look.

"There's absolutely no need to drag Bill out," he said with some firmness.

"I haven't the smallest intention of coming," said Bill, smiling. "I'm tired out and I'm going to hit the hay."

I fancy we left Bill Marsh and his wife to a little argument.

"They've been frightfully kind to me," said Charlie, as we walked along by the railings. "I don't know what I should have done without them. I haven't slept for a fortnight."

I expressed regret but did not ask the reason, and we walked for a little in silence. I presumed that he had come with me in order to talk to me of what had happened, but I felt that he must take his own time. I was anxious to show my sympathy, but afraid of saying the wrong thing; I did not want to seem eager to extract confidences from him. I did not know how to give him a lead. I was sure he did not want one. He was not a man given to beating about the bush. I imagined that he was choosing his words. We reached the corner.

"You'll be able to get a taxi at the church," he said. "I'll walk on a bit farther. Good-night."

He nodded and slouched off. I was taken aback. There was nothing for me to do but to stroll on till I found a cab. I was having my bath next morning when a telephone call dragged me out of it, and with a towel round my wet body I took up the receiver. It was Janet.

"Well, what do you think of it all?" she said. "You seem to have kept Charlie up pretty late last night. I heard him come home at three."

"He left me at the Marylebone Road," I answered. "He said nothing to me at all."

"Didn't he?"

There was something in Janet's voice that suggested that she was prepared to have a long talk with me. I suspected she had a telephone by the side of her bed.

"Look here," I said quickly, "I'm having my bath."

"Oh, have you got a telephone in your bathroom?" she answered eagerly, and I think with envy.

"No, I haven't." I was abrupt and firm. "And I'm drippng all over the carpet."

"Oh!" I felt disappointment in her tone and a trace of irritation. "Well, when can I see you? Can you come here at twelve?"

It was inconvenient, but I was not prepared to start an ar-gument.

"Yes, good-bye."

I rang off before she could say anything more. In heaven when the blessed use the telephone they will say what they have to say and not a word besides.

I was devoted to Janet, but I knew that there was nothing that thrilled her more than the misfortunes of her friends. She was only too anxious to help them, but she wanted to be in the thick of their difficulties. She was the friend in adversity. Other people's business was meat and drink to her. You could not enter upon a love affair without finding her somehow your confidante, nor be mixed up in a divorce case without discover-ing that she too had a finger in the pie. Withal she was a very nice woman. I could not help, then, chuckling in my heart when at noon I was shown in to Janet's drawing-room and observed the subdued eagerness with which she received me. She was very much upset by the catastrophe that had befallen the Bishops, but it was exciting, and she was tickled to death to have someone fresh to whom she could tell all about it. Janet had just that businesslike expectancy that a mother has when she is discussing with the family doctor her married daughter's first confinement. Janet was conscious that the matter was very serious, and she would not for a moment have been thought to regard it flippantly, but she was determined to get every ounce of value out of it.

"I mean, no one could have been more horrified than I was when Margery told me she'd finally made up her mind to leave Charlie," she said, speaking with the fluency of a person who has said the same thing in the same words a dozen times at least. "They were the most devoted couple I'd ever known. It was a perfect marriage. They got on like a house on fire. Of course Bill and I are devoted to one another, but we have awful rows now and then. I mean, I could kill him sometimes."

"I don't care a hang about your relations with Bill," I said. "Tell me about the Bishops. That's what I've come here for."

"I simply felt I must see you. After all, you're the only person who can explain it."

"Oh, God, don't go on like that. Until Bill told me last night I didn't know a thing about it."

"That was my idea. It suddenly dawned on me that perhaps you didn't know and I thought you might put your foot in it too awfully."

"Supposing you begin at the beginning," I said.

"Well, you're the beginning. After all you started the trouble. You introduced the young man. That's why I was so crazy to see you. You know all about him. I never saw him. All I know is what Margery has told me about him."

"At what time are you lunching?" I asked.

"Half-past one."

"So am I. Get on with the story."

But my remark had given Janet an idea.

"Look here, will you get out of your luncheon if I get out of mine? We could have a snack here. I'm sure there's some cold meat in the house, and then we needn't hurry. I don't have to be at the hair-dresser's till three.'"

"No, no, no," I said. "I hate the notion of that. I shall leave here at twenty minutes past one at the latest."

"Then I shall just have to race through it. What do *you* think of Gerry?"

"Who's Gerry?"

"Gerry Morton. His name's Gerald."

"How should I know that?"

"You stayed with him. Weren't there any letters lying about?"

"I daresay, but I didn't happen to read them," I answered somewhat tartly.

"Oh, don't be so stupid. I meant the envelopes. What's he like?"

"All right. Rather the Kipling type, you know. Very keen on his work. Hearty. Empire-builder and all that sort of thing."

"I don't mean that," cried Janet, not without impatience. "I mean, what does he look like?"

"More or less like everybody else, I think. Of course I should recognize him if I saw him again, but I can't picture him to myself very distinctly. He looks clean."

"Oh, my God," said Janet. "Are you a novelist or are you not? What's the colour of his eyes?"

"I don't know."

"You must know. You can't spend a week with anyone without knowing if their eyes are blue or brown. Is he fair or dark?"

"Neither."

"Is he tall or short?"

"Average, I should say."

"Are you trying to irritate me?"

"No. He's just ordinary. There's nothing in him to attract your attention. He's neither plain nor good-looking. He looks quite decent. He looks a gentleman."

"Margery says he has a charming smile and a lovely figure."

"I daresay."

"He's absolutely crazy about her."

"What makes you think that?" I asked dryly.

"I've seen his letters."

"Do you mean to say she's shown them to you?"

"Why, of course."

It is always difficult for a man to stomach the want of reticence that women betray in their private affairs. They have no shame. They will talk to one another without embarrassment of the most intimate matters. Modesty is a masculine virtue. But though a man may know this theoretically, each time he is confronted with women's lack of reserve he suffers a new shock. I wondered what Morton would think if he knew that not only were his letters read by Janet Marsh as well as by Margery, but that she had been kept posted from day to day with the progress of his infatuation. According to Janet he had fallen in love with Margery at first sight. The morning after they had met at my little supper party at Ciro's he had rung up and asked her to come and have tea with him at some place where they could dance. While I listened to Janet's story I was conscious of course that she was giving me Margery's view of the circumstances, and I kept an open mind. I was interested to observe that Janet's sympathies were with Margery. It was true that when Margery left her husband it was her idea that Charlie should come to them for two or three weeks rather than stay on in miserable loneliness in the deserted flat, and she had been extraordinarily kind to him. She lunched with him almost every day, because he had been accustomed to lunch every day with Margery; she took him for walks in Regent's Park and made Bill play golf with him on Sundays. She listened with wonderful patience to the story of his unhappiness and did what she could to console him. She was terribly sorry for him. But all the same she was definitely on Margery's side, and when I expressed my disapproval of her she came down on me like a thousand of bricks. The affair thrilled her. She had been in it from the beginning, when Margery, smiling, flattered and a little doubtful, came and told her that she had a young man, to the final scene when Margery, exasperated and distraught, announced that she could not stand the strain any more and had packed her things and moved out of the flat.

"Of course, at first I couldn't believe my ears," she said. "You know how Charlie and Margery were. They simply lived in one another's pockets. One couldn't help laughing at them, they were so devoted to one another. I never thought him a very nice little man, and heaven knows he wasn't very attractive physically, but one couldn't help liking him because he was so awfully nice to Margery. I rather envied her sometimes. They had no money and they lived in a hugger-mugger sort of way, but they were frightfully happy. Of course I never thought anything would come of it. Margery was rather amused. 'Naturally I don't take it very seriously,' she told me, 'but it is rather fun to have a young man at my time of life. I haven't had any flowers sent me for years. I had to tell him not to send any more because Charlie would think it so silly. He doesn't know a soul in London and he loves dancing and he says I dance like a dream. It's miserable for him going to the theatre by himself all the time, and we've done two or three matinees together. It's pathetic to see how grateful he is when I say I'll go out with him.' 'I must say,' I said, 'he sounds rather a lamb.' 'He is,' she said. 'I knew you'd understand. You don't blame me, do you?' 'Of course not, darling,' I said, 'surely you know me better than that. I'd do just the same in your place.'"

Margery made no secret of her outings with Morton, and her husband chaffed her good-naturedly about her beau. But he thought him a very civil, pleasant-spoken young man and was glad that Margery had someone to play with while he was busy. It never occurred to him to be jealous. The three of them dined together several times and went to a show. But presently Gerry Morton begged Margery to spend an evening with him alone; she said it was impossible, but he was persuasive, he gave her no peace; and at last she went to Janet and asked her to ring up Charlie one day and ask him to come to dinner and make a fourth at bridge. Charlie would never go anywhere without his wife, but the Marshes were old friends.

and Janet made a point of it. She invented some cock-and-bull story that made it seem important that he should consent. Next day Margery and she met. The evening had been wonderful. They had dined at Maidenhead and danced there and then had driven home through the summer night.

"He says he's crazy about me," Margery told her.

"Did he kiss you?" asked Janet.

"Of course," Margery chuckled. "Don't be silly, Janet. He is awfully sweet and, you know, he has such a nice nature. Of course I don't believe half the things he says to me."

"My dear, you're not going to fall in love with him."

"I have," said Margery.

"Darling, isn't it going to be rather awkward?"

"Oh, it won't last. After all, he's going back to Borneo in the autumn."

"Well, one can't deny that it's made you look years younger."

"I know, and I feel years younger."

Soon they were meeting every day. They met in the morning and walked in the park together or went to a picture gallery. They separated for Margery to lunch with her husband and after lunch met again and motored into the country or to some place on the river. Margery did not tell her husband. She very naturally thought he would not understand.

"How was it you never met Morton?" I asked Janet.

"Oh, she didn't want me to. You see, we belong to the same generation, Margery and I. I quite understand that."

"I see."

"Of course I did everything I could. When she went out with Gerry she was always supposed to be with me."

I am a person who likes to cross a t and dot an i.

"Were they having an affair?" I asked.

"Oh, no. Margery isn't that sort of woman at all."

"How do you know?"

"She would have told me."

"I suppose she would."

"Of course I asked her. But she denied it point-blank and I'm sure she was telling me the truth. There's never been anything of that sort between them at all."

"It seems rather odd to me."

"Well, you see, Margery is a very good woman."

I shrugged my shoulders.

"She was absolutely loyal to Charlie She wouldn't have

deceived him for anything in the world. She couldn't bear the thought of having any secret from him. As soon as she knew she was in love with Gerry she wanted to tell Charlie. Of course I begged her not to. I told her it wouldn't do any good and it would only make Charlie miserable. And after all, the boy was going away in a couple of months; it didn't seem much good to make a lot of fuss about a thing that couldn't possibly last."

But Gerry's imminent departure was the cause of the crash. The Bishops had arranged to go abroad as usual and proposed to motor through Belgium, Holland and the north of Germany. Charlie was busy with maps and guides. He collected information from friends about hotels and roads. He looked forward to his holiday with the bubbling excitement of a schoolboy. Margery listened to him discussing it with a sinking heart. They were to be away four weeks, and in September Gerry was sailing. She could not bear to lose so much of the short time that remained to them, and the thought of the motor tour filled her with exasperation. As the interval grew shorter and shorter she grew more and more nervous. At last she decided that there was only one thing to do.

"Charlie, I don't want to come on this trip," she interrupted him suddenly, one day when he was talking to her of some restaurant he had just heard of. "I wish you'd get someone else to go with you."

He looked at her blankly. She was startled at what she had said, and her lips trembled a little.

"Why, what's the matter?"

"Nothing's the matter. I don't feel like it. I want to be by myself for a bit."

"Are you ill?"

She saw the sudden fear in his eyes. His concern drove her beyond her endurance.

"No. I've never been better in my life. I'm in love."

"You? Who with?"

"Gerry."

He looked at her in amazement. He could not believe his ears. She mistook his expression.

"It's no good blaming me. I can't help it. He's going away in a few weeks. I'm not going to waste the little time he has left."

He burst out laughing.

"Margery, how can you make such a damned fool of yourself? You're old enough to be his mother."

She flushed.

"He's just as much in love with me as I am with him."

"Has he told you so?"

"A thousand times."

"He's a bloody liar, that's all."

He chuckled. His fat stomach rippled with mirth. He thought
it a huge joke. I daresay Charlie did not treat his wife in the
proper way. Janet seemed to think he should have been tender
and compassionate. *He should have understood.* I saw the scene
that was in her mind's eye, the stiff upper lip, the silent sorrow,
and the final renunciation. Women are always sensitive to the
beauty of the self-sacrifice of others. Janet would have sympathized also if he had flown into a violent passion, broken
one or two pieces of furniture (which he would have had to
replace), or given Margery a sock in the jaw. But to laugh at
her was unpardonable. I did not point out that it is very
difficult for a rather stout and not very tall professor of pathology, aged fifty-five, to act all of a sudden like a caveman.
Anyhow, the excursion to Holland was given up and the Bishops
stayed in London through August. They were not very happy.
They lunched and dined together every day because they had
been in the habit of doing so for so many years, and the rest
of the time Margery spent with Gerry. The hours she passed
with him made up for all she had to put up with, and she had
to put up with a good deal. Charlie had a ribald and sarcastic
humour and he made himself very funny at her expense and
at Gerry's. He persisted in refusing to take the matter seriously. He was vexed with Margery for being so silly, but apparently it never occurred to him that she might have been
unfaithful to him. I commented upon this to Janet.

"He never suspected it even," she said. "He knew Margery
much too well."

The weeks passed and at last Gerry sailed. He went from
Tilbury and Margery saw him off. When she came back she
cried for forty-eight hours. Charlie watched her with increasing
exasperation. His nerves were much frayed.

"Look here, Margery," he said at last, "I've been very
patient with you, but now you must pull yourself together.
This is getting past a joke."

"Why can't you leave me alone?" she cried. "I've lost everything that made life lovely to me."

"Don't be such a fool," he said.

I do not know what else he said. But he was unwise enough to tell her what he thought of Gerry, and I gather that the picture he drew was virulent. It started the first violent scene they had ever had. She had borne Charlie's jibes when she knew that she would see Gerry in an hour or next day, but now that she had lost him for ever she could bear them no longer. She had held herself in for weeks: now she flung her self-control to the winds. Perhaps she never knew exactly what she said to Charlie. He had always been irascible, and at last he hit her. They were both frightened when he had. He seized a hat and flung out of the flat. During all that miserable time they had shared the same bed, but when he came back, in the middle of the night, he found that she had made herself up a shake-down on the sofa in the sitting-room.

"You can't sleep there," he said. "Don't be so silly. Come to bed."

"No, I won't, let me alone."

For the rest of the night they wrangled, but she had her way and now made up her bed every night on the sofa. But in that tiny flat they could not get away from one another; they could not even get out of sight or out of hearing of one another. They had lived in such intimacy for so many years that it was an instinct for them to be together. He tried to reason with her. He thought her incredibly stupid and argued with her interminably in the effort to show her how wrong-headed she was. He could not leave her alone. He would not let her sleep, and he talked half through the night till they were both exhausted. He thought he could talk her out of love. For two or three days at a time they would not speak to one another. Then one day, coming home, he found her crying bitterly; the sight of her tears distracted him; he told her how much he loved her and sought to move her by the recollection of all the happy years they had spent together. He wanted to let bygones be bygones. He promised never to refer to Gerry again. Could they not forget the nightmare they had been through? But the thought of all that a reconciliation implied revolted her. She told him she had a racking headache and asked him to give her a sleeping draught. She pretended to be still asleep when he went out next morning, but the moment he was gone she packed up her things and left. She had a few trinkets that she had inherited, and by selling them she got a little money. She took a room at a cheap boarding-house and kept her address a secret from Charlie.

It was when he found she had left him that he went all to pieces. The shock of her flight broke him. He told Janet that his loneliness was intolerable. He wrote to Margery imploring her to come back, and asked Janet to intercede for him; he was willing to promise anything; he abased himself. Margery was obdurate.

"Do you think she'll ever go back?" I asked Janet.

"She says not."

I had to leave then, for it was nearly half-past one and I was bound for the other end of London.

Two or three days later I got a telephone message from Margery asking if I could see her. She suggested coming to my rooms. I asked her to tea. I tried to be nice to her; her affairs were no business of mine, but in my heart I thought her a very silly woman and I daresay my manner was cold. She had never been handsome and the passing years had changed her little. She had still those fine dark eyes and her face was astonishingly unlined. She was very simply dressed, and if she wore make-up it was so cunningly put on that I did not perceive it. She had still the charm she had always had of perfect naturalness and of a kindly humour.

"I want you to do something for me if you will," she began without beating about the bush.

"What is it?"

"Charlie is leaving the Marshes to-day and going back to the flat. I'm afraid his first few days there will be rather difficult; it would be awfully nice of you if you'd ask him to dinner or something."

"I'll have a look at my book."

"I'm told he's been drinking heavily. It's such a pity. I wish you could give him a hint."

"I understand he's had some domestic worries of late," I said perhaps acidly.

Margery flushed. She gave me a pained look. She winced as though I had struck her.

"Of course you've known him ever so much longer than you've known me. It's natural that you should take his part."

"My dear, to tell you the truth I've known him all these years chiefly on your account. I have never very much liked him, but I thought you were awfully nice."

She smiled at me and her smile was very sweet. She knew that I meant what I said.

"Do you think I was a good wife to him?"

"Perfect."

"He used to put people's backs up. A lot of people didn't like him, but I never found him difficult."

"He was awfully fond of you."

"I know. We had a wonderful time together. For sixteen years we were perfectly happy." She paused and looked down. "I had to leave him. It became quite impossible. That cat-and-dog life we were leading was too awful."

"I never see why two persons should go on living together if they don't want to."

"You see, it was awful for us. We'd always lived in such close intimacy. We could never get away from one another. At the end I hated the sight of him."

"I don't suppose the situation was easy for either of you."

"It wasn't my fault that I fell in love. You see, it was quite a different love from the one I'd felt for Charlie. There was always something maternal in that and protective. I was so much more reasonable than he was. He was unmanageable, but I could always manage him. Gerry was different." Her voice grew soft and her face was transfigured with glory. "He gave me back my youth. I was a girl to him and I could depend on his strength and be safe in his care."

"He seemed to me a very nice lad," I said slowly. "I imagine he'll do well. He was very young for the job he had when I ran across him. He's only twenty-nine now, isn't he?"

She smiled softly. She knew quite well what I meant.

"I never made any secret of my age to him. He says it doesn't matter."

I knew this was true. She was not the woman to have lied about her age. She had found a sort of fierce delight in telling him the truth about herself.

"How old are you?"

"Forty-four."

"What are you going to do now?"

"I've written to Gerry and told him I've left Charlie. As soon as I hear from him I'm going out to join him."

I was staggered.

"You know, it's a very primitive little colony he's living in. I'm afraid you'll find your position rather awkward."

"He made me promise that if I found my life impossible after he left I'd go to him."

"Are you sure you're wise to attach so much importance to the things a young man says when he's in love?"

Again that really beautiful look of exaltation came into her face.

"Yes, when the young man happens to be Gerry."

My heart sank. I was silent for a moment. Then I told her the story of the road Gerry Morton had built. I dramatized it, and I think I made it rather effective.

"What did you tell me that for?" she asked when I finished.

"I thought it rather a good story."

She shook her head and smiled.

"No, you wanted to show me that he was very young and enthusiastic, and so keen on his work that he hadn't much time to waste on other interests. I wouldn't interfere with his work. You don't know him as I do. He's incredibly romantic. He looks upon himself as a pioneer. I've caught from him something of his excitement at the idea of taking part in the opening up of a new country. It *is* rather splendid, isn't it? It makes life here seem very humdrum and commonplace. But of course it's very lonely there. Even the companionship of a middle-aged woman may be worth having."

"Are you proposing to marry him?" I asked.

"I leave myself in his hands. I want to do nothing that he does not wish."

She spoke with so much simplicity, there was something so touching in her self-surrender, that when she left me I no longer felt angry with her. Of course I thought her very foolish, but if the folly of men made one angry one would pass one's life in a state of chronic ire. I thought all would come right. She said Gerry was romantic. He was, but the romantics in this workaday world only get away with their nonsense because they have at bottom a shrewd sense of reality: the mugs are the people who take their vapourings at their face value. The English are romantic; that is why other nations think them hypocritical; they are not: they set out in all sincerity for the Kingdom of God, but the journey is arduous and they have reason to pick up any gilt-edged investment that offers itself by the way. The British soul, like Wellington's armies, marches on its belly. I supposed that Gerry would go through a bad quarter of an hour when he received Margery's letter. My sympathies were not deeply engaged in the matter and I was only curious to see how he would extricate himself from the pass he was in. I thought Margery would suffer a bitter disappointment—well, that would do her no great harm, and then she would go back to her husband and I had no doubt the pair of them, chastened, would live in peace, quiet and happiness for the rest of their lives.

The event was different. It happened that it was quite impossible for me to make any sort of engagement with Charlie Bishop for some days, but I wrote to him and asked him to dine with me one evening in the following week. I proposed, though with misgiving, that we should go to a play; I knew he was drinking like a fish, and when tight he was noisy. I hoped he would not make a nuisance of himself in the theatre. We arranged to meet at our club and dine at seven because the piece we were going to began at a quarter past eight. I arrived. I waited. He did not come. I rang up his flat, but could get no reply, so concluded that he was on his way. I hate missing the beginning of a play and I waited impatiently in the hall so that when he came we could go straight upstairs. To save time I had ordered dinner. The clock pointed to half-past seven, then a quarter to eight; I did not see why I should wait for him any longer, so walked up to the dining-room and ate my dinner alone. He did not appear. I put a call through from the dining-room to the Marshes and presently was told by a waiter that Bill Marsh was at the end of the wire.

"I say, do you know anything about Charlie Bishop?" I said. "We were dining together and going to a play and he hasn't turned up."

"He died this afternoon."

"What?"

My exclamation was so startled that two or three people within earshot looked up. The dining-room was full and the waiters were hurrying to and fro. The telephone was on the cashier's desk, and a wine waiter came up with a bottle of hock and two long-stemmed glasses on a tray and gave the cashier a chit. The portly steward showing two men to a table jostled me.

"Where are you speaking from?" asked Bill.

I suppose he heard the clatter that surrounded me. When I told him he asked me if I could come round as soon as I had finished my dinner. Janet wanted to speak to me.

"I'll come at once," I said.

I found Janet and Bill sitting in the drawing-room. He was reading the paper and she was playing patience. She came forward swiftly when the maid showed me in. She walked with a sort of spring, crouching a little, on silent feet, like a panther stalking his prey. I saw at once that she was in her element. She gave me her hand and turned her face away to hide her eyes brimming with tears. Her voice was low and tragic.

"I brought Margery here and put her to bed. The doctor has given her a sedative. She's all in. Isn't it awful?" She gave a sound that was something between a gasp and a sob. "I don't know why these things always happen to me."

The Bishops had never kept a servant, but a charwoman went in every morning, cleaned the flat and washed up the breakfast things. She had her own key. That morning she had gone in as usual and done the sitting-room. Since his wife had left him Charlie's hours had been irregular and she was not surprised to find him asleep. But the time passed and she knew he had his work to go to. She went to the bedroom door and knocked. There was no answer. She thought she heard him groaning. She opened the door softly. He was lying in bed, on his back, and was breathing stertorously. He did not wake. She called him. Something about him frightened her. She went to the flat on the same landing. It was occupied by a journalist. He was still in bed when she rang, and opened the door to her in pajamas.

"Beg pardon, sir," she said, "but would you just come and 'ave a look at my gentleman? I don't think he's well."

The journalist walked across the landing and into Charlie's flat. There was an empty bottle of veronal by the bed.

"I think you'd better fetch a policeman," he said.

A policeman came and rang through to the police station for an ambulance. They took Charlie to Charing Cross Hospital. He never recovered consciousness. Margery was with him at the end.

"Of course there'll have to be an inquest," said Janet. "But it's quite obvious what happened. He'd been sleeping awfully badly for the last three or four weeks and I suppose he'd been taking veronal. He must have taken an overdose by accident."

"Is that what Margery thinks?" I asked.

"She's too upset to think anything, but I told her I was positive he hadn't committed suicide. I mean, he wasn't that sort of a man. Am I right, Bill?"

"Yes, dear," he answered.

"Did he leave any letter?"

"No, nothing. Oddly enough Margery got a letter from him this morning—well, hardly a letter, just a line. 'I'm so lonely without you, darling.' That's all. But of course that means nothing and she's promised to say nothing about it at the inquest. I mean, what is the use of putting ideas in people's heads? Everyone knows that you never can tell with veronal—I wouldn't take it myself for anything in the world—and it was quite obviously an accident. Am I right, Bill?"

"Yes, dear," he answered.

I saw that Janet was quite determined to believe that Charlie Bishop had not committed suicide, but how far in her heart she believed what she wanted to believe I was not sufficiently expert in female psychology to know. And of course it might be that she was right. It is unreasonable to suppose that a middle-aged scientist should kill himself because his middle-aged wife leaves him, and it is extremely plausible that, exasperated by sleeplessness, and in all probability far from sober, he took a larger dose of the sleeping draught than he realized. Anyhow that was the view the coroner took of the matter. It was indicated to him that of late Charles Bishop had given way to habits of intemperance which had caused his wife to leave him, and it was quite obvious that nothing was further from his thoughts than to put an end to himself. The coroner expressed his sympathy with the widow and commented very strongly on the dangers of sleeping draughts.

I hate funerals, but Janet begged me to go to Charlie's. Several of his colleagues at the hospital had intimated their desire to come, but at Margery's wish they were dissuaded; and Janet and Bill, Margery and I were the only persons who attended it. We were to fetch the hearse from the mortuary, and they offered to call for me on their way. I was on the lookout for the car, and when I saw it drive up went downstairs, but Bill got out and met me just inside the door.

"Half a minute," he said. "I've got something to say to you. Janet wants you to come back afterwards and have tea. She says it's no good Margery moping and after tea we'll play a few rubbers of bridge. Can you come?"

"Like this?" I asked.

I had a tail coat on and a black tie and my evening dress trousers.

"Oh, that's all right. It'll take Margery's mind off."

"Very well."

But we did not play bridge after all. Janet, with her fair hair, was very smart in her deep mourning and she played the part of the sympathetic friend with amazing skill. She cried a little, wiping her eyes delicately so as not to disturb the black on her eyelashes, and, when Margery sobbed broken-heartedly, put her arm tenderly through hers. She was a very present help in trouble. We returned to the house. There was a telegram for Margery. She took it and went upstairs. I presumed it was a message of condolence from one of Charlie's friends who had just heard of his death. Bill went to change and Janet and I went up to the drawing-room and got the bridge table out. She took off her hat and put it on the piano.

"It's no good being hypocritical," she said. "Of course Margery has been frightfully upset, but she must pull herself together now. A rubber of bridge will help her to get back to her normal state. Naturally I'm dreadfully sorry about poor Charlie, but as far as he was concerned I don't believe he'd ever have got over Margery's leaving him, and one can't deny that it has made things much easier for her. She wired to Gerry this morning."

"What about?"

"To tell him about poor Charlie."

At that moment the maid came to the room.

"Will you go up to Mrs. Bishop, please, ma'am. She wants to see you."

"Yes, of course."

She went out of the room quickly and I was left alone. Bill joined me presently and we had a drink. At last Janet came back. She handed a telegram to me. It read as follows:

For God's sake await letter. Gerry.

"What do you think it means?" she asked me.

"What it says," I replied.

"Idiot! Of course I've told Margery that it doesn't mean anything, but she's rather worried. It must have crossed her cable telling him that Charles was dead. I don't think she feels very much like bridge after all. I mean, it would be rather bad form to play on the very day her husband has been buried."

"Quite," I said.

"Of course he may wire in answer to the cable. He's sure to do that, isn't he? The only thing we can do now is to sit tight and wait for his letter."

I saw no object in continuing the conversation. I left. In a couple of days Janet rang me up to tell me that Margery had received a telegram of condolence from Morton. She repeated it to me:

Dreadfully distressed to hear sad news. Deeply sympathize with your great grief. Love. Gerry.

"What do you think of it?" she asked me.

"I think it's very proper."

"Of course he couldn't say he was as pleased as Punch, could he?"

"Not with any delicacy."

"And he did put in *love*."

I imagined how those women had examined the two telegrams from every point of view and scrutinized every word to press from it every possible shade of meaning. I almost heard their interminable conversations.

"I don't know what'll happen to Margery if he lets her down now," Janet went on. "Of course it remains to be seen if he's a gentleman."

"Rot," I said and rang off quickly.

In the course of the following days I dined with the Marshes a couple of times. Margery looked tired. I guessed that she awaited the letter that was on the way with sickening anxiety. Grief and fear had worn her to a shadow; she seemed very fragile now, and she had acquired a spiritual look that I had never seen in her before. She was very gentle, very grateful for every kindness shown her, and in her smile, unsure and a little timid, was an infinite pathos. Her helplessness was very appealing. But Morton was several thousand miles away. Then one morning Janet rang me up.

"The letter has come. Margery says I can show it to you. Will you come round?"

Her tense voice told me everything. When I arrived Janet gave it to me. I read it. It was a very careful letter and I guessed that Morton had written it a good many times. It was very kind and he had evidently taken great pains to avoid saying anything that could possibly wound Margery; but what transpired was his terror. It was obvious that he was shaking in his shoes. He had felt apparently that the best way to cope with the situation was to be mildly facetious, and he made very good fun of the white people in the colony. What would they say if Margery suddenly turned up? He would be given the order of the boot pretty damn quick. People thought the East was free and easy; it wasn't, it was more suburban than Clapham. He loved Margery far too much to bear the thought of those horrible women out there turning up their noses at her. And besides he had been sent to a station ten days from anywhere; she couldn't live in his bungalow exactly, and of course there wasn't a hotel, and his work took him out into the jungle for days at a time. It was no place for a woman anyhow. He told her how much she meant to him, but she mustn't bother about him and he couldn't help thinking it would be better if she went back to her husband. He would never forgive himself if he thought he had come between her and Charlie. Yes, I am quite sure it had been a difficult letter to write.

"Of course he didn't know then that Charlie was dead. I've told Margery that changes everything."

"Does she agree with you?"

"I think she's being rather unreasonable. What do you make of the letter?"

"Well, it's quite plain that he doesn't want her."

"He wanted her badly enough two months ago."

"It's astonishing what a change of air and a change of scene will do for you. It must seem to him already like a year since he left London. He's back among his old friends and his old interests. My dear, it's no good Margery kidding herself, the life there has taken him back and there's no place for her."

"I've advised her to ignore the letter and go straight out to him."

"I hope she's too sensible to expose herself to a very terrible rebuff."

"But then what's to happen to her? Oh, it's too cruel. She's the best woman in the world. She has real goodness."

"It's funny, if you come to think of it, it's her goodness that has caused all the trouble. Why on earth didn't she have an affair with Morton? Charlie would have known nothing about it and wouldn't have been a penny the worse. She and Morton could have had a grand time, and when he went away they could have parted with the consciousness that a pleasant episode had come to a graceful end. It would have been a jolly recollection, and she could have gone back to Charlie satisfied and rested and continued to make him the excellent wife she had always been."

Janet pursed her lips. She gave me a look of disdain.

"There is such a thing as virtue, you know."

"Virtue be damned. A virtue that only causes havoc and unhappiness is worth nothing. You can call it virtue if you like. I call it cowardice."

"The thought of being unfaithful to Charlie while she was living with him revolted her. There are women like that, you know."

"Good gracious, she could have remained faithful to him in spirit while she was being unfaithful to him in the flesh. That is a feat of legerdemain that women find it easy to accomplish."

"What an odious cynic you are."

"If it's cynical to look truth in the face and exercise common-sense in the affairs of life, then certainly I'm a cynic and odious, if you like. Let's face it: Margery's a middle-aged woman, Charlie was fifty-five and they'd been married for sixteen years. It was natural enough that she should lose her head over a young man who made a fuss of her. But don't call it love. It was physiology. She was a fool to take anything he said seriously. It wasn't himself speaking, it was his starved sex; he'd suffered from sexual starvation, at least as far as white women are concerned, for four years; it's monstrous that she should seek to ruin his life by holding him to the wild promises he made then. It was an accident that Margery took his fancy; he wanted her, and because he couldn't get her wanted her more. I daresay he thought it love; believe me, it was only letch. If they'd gone to bed together Charlie would be alive to-day. It's her damned virtue that caused the whole trouble."

"How stupid you are. Don't you see that she couldn't help herself? She just doesn't happen to be a loose woman."

"I prefer a loose woman to a selfish one and a wanton to a fool."

"Oh, shut up. I didn't ask you to come here in order to make yourself absolutely beastly."

"What did you ask me to come here for?"

"Gerry is your friend. You introduced him to Margery. If she's in the soup it's on his account. But *you* are the cause of the whole trouble. It's your duty to write to him and tell him he must do the right thing by her."

"I'm damned if I will," I said.

"Then you'd better go."

I started to do so.

"Well, at all events it's a mercy that Charlie's life was insured," said Janet.

Then I turned on her.

"And you have the nerve to call me a cynic."

I will not repeat the opprobrious word I flung at her as I slammed the door behind me. But Janet is all the same a very nice woman. I often think it would be great fun to be married to her.

THE ALIEN CORN

I HAD known the Blands a long time before I discovered that they had any connection with Ferdy Rabenstein. Ferdy must have been nearly fifty when I first knew him, and at the time of which I write he was well over seventy. He had altered little. His hair, coarse but abundant and curly, was white, but he had kept his figure and held himself as gallantly as ever. It was not hard to believe that in youth he had been as beautiful as people said. He had still his fine Semitic profile and the lustrous black eyes that had caused havoc in so many a Gentile breast. He was very tall, lean, with an oval face and a clear skin. He wore his clothes very well, and in evening dress, even now, he was one of the handsomest men I had ever seen. He wore then large black pearls in his shirt front and platinum and sapphire rings on his fingers. Perhaps he was rather flashy, but you felt it was so much in character that it would have ill become him to be anything else.

"After all, I am an Oriental," he said. "I can carry a certain barbaric magnificence."

I have often thought that Ferdy Rabenstein would make an admirable subject for a biography. He was not a great man, but within the limits he set himself he made of his life a work of art. It was a masterpiece in little, like a Persian miniature, and derived its interest from its perfection. Unfortunately the materials are scanty. They would consist of letters that may very well have been destroyed and the recollections of people who are old now and will soon be dead. His memory is extraordinary, but he would never write his memoirs, for he looks upon his past as a source of purely private entertainment; and he is a man of the most perfect discretion. Nor do I know anyone who could do justice to the subject but Max Beerbohm. There is no one else in this hard world of to-day who can look upon the trivial with such tender sympathy and wring such a delicate pathos from futility. I wonder that Max, who must have known Ferdy much better than I, and long before, was never tempted to exercise his exquisite fancy on such a theme. He was born for Max to write about. And who should have illustrated the elegant book that I see in my mind's eye but Aubrey Beardsley? Thus would have been erected a monument of triple brass and the ephemera imprisoned to succeeding ages in the amber's exquisite translucency.

Ferdy's conquests were social and his venue was the great world. He was born in South Africa and did not come to England till he was twenty. For some time he was on the Stock Exchange, but on the death of his father he inherited a considerable fortune, and retiring from business devoted himself to the life of a man about town. At that period English society was still a closed body and it was not easy for a Jew to force its barriers, but to Ferdy they fell like the walls of Jericho. He was handsome, he was rich, he was a sportsman and he was good company. He had a house in Curzon Street, furnished with the most beautiful French furniture, and a French chef, and a brougham. It would be interesting to know the first steps in his wonderful career: they are lost in the dark abysm of time. When I first met him he had been long established as one of the smartest men in London: this was at a very grand house in Norfolk to which I had been asked as a promising young novelist by the hostess who took an interest in letters, but the company was very distinguished and I was overawed. We were sixteen, and I felt shy and alone among these cabinet ministers, great ladies and peers of the realm who talked of people and things of which I knew nothing. They were civil to me, but indifferent, and I was conscious that I was somewhat of a burden to my hostess. Ferdy saved me. He sat with me, walked with me and talked with me. He discovered that I was a writer and we discussed the drama and the novel; he learnt that I had lived much on the continent and he talked to me pleasantly of France, Germany and Spain. He seemed really to seek my society. He gave me the flattering impression that he and I stood apart from the other

members of the company and by our conversation upon affairs
of the spirit made that of the rest of them, the political situation, the scandal of somebody's divorce and the growing dis-
inclination of pheasants to be killed, seem a little ridiculous.
But if Ferdy had at the bottom of his heart a feeling of ever so
faint a contempt for the hearty British gentry that surrounded
us I am sure that it was only to me that he allowed an inkling
of it to appear, and looking back I cannot but wonder whether
it was not after all a suave and very delicate compliment that
he paid me. I think of course that he liked to exercise his charm,
and I daresay the obvious pleasure his conversation gave me
gratified him, but he could have had no motive for taking so
much trouble over an obscure novelist other than his real interest in art and letters. I felt that he and I at bottom were
equally alien in that company, I because I was a writer and he
because he was a Jew, but I envied the ease with which he bore
himself. He was completely at home. Everyone called him
Ferdy. He seemed to be always in good spirits. He was never at
a loss for a quip, a jest or a repartee. They liked him in that
house because he made them laugh but never made them uncomfortable by talking above their heads. He brought a faint
savour of Oriental romance into their lives, but so cleverly that
they only felt more English. You could never be dull when he
was by and with him present you were safe from the fear of
the devastating silences that sometimes overwhelm a British
company. A pause looked inevitable and Ferdy Rabenstein had
broken into a topic that interested everyone. An invaluable
asset to any party. He had an inexhaustible fund of Jewish
stories. He was a very good mimic and he assumed the Yiddish
accent and reproduced the Jewish gestures to perfection; his
head sank into his body, his face grew cunning, his voice oily,
and he was a rabbi or an old-clothes merchant or a smart commercial traveller or a fat procuress in Frankfort. It was as good
as a play. Because he was himself a Jew and insisted on it you
laughed without reserve, but for my own part not without an
undercurrent of discomfort. I was not quite sure of a sense of
humour that made such cruel fun of his own race. I discovered
afterwards that Jewish stories were his speciality, and I seldom
met him anywhere without hearing him tell sooner or later the
last he had heard.

But the best story he told me on this occasion was not a
Jewish one. It struck me so that I have never forgotten it, but

for one reason or another I have never had occasion to tell it
again. I give it here because it is a curious little incident con-
cerning persons whose names at least will live in the social history of the Victorian Era and I think it would be a pity if it
were lost. He told me then that once when quite a young man
he was staying in the country in a house where Mrs. Langtry,
at that time at the height of her beauty and astounding reputation, was also a guest. It happened to be within driving distance
of that in which lived the Duchess of Somerset, who had been
Queen of Beauty at the Eglinton Tournament, and knowing
her slightly, it occurred to him that it would be interesting to
bring the two women together. He suggested it to Mrs. Langtry,
who was willing, and forthwith wrote to the Duchess asking if
he might bring the celebrated beauty to call on her. It was fitting, he said, that the loveliest woman of this generation (this
was in the eighties) should pay her respects to the loveliest
woman of the last. 'Bring her by all means,' answered the
Duchess, 'but I warn you that it will be a shock to her.' They
drove over in a carriage and pair, Mrs. Langtry in a close-
fitting blue bonnet with long satin strings, which showed the exquisite shape of her head and made her blue eyes even bluer,
and were received by a little ugly old hag who looked with irony
out of her beady eyes at the radiant beauty who had come to
see her. They had tea, they talked and they drove home again.
Mrs. Langtry was very silent and when Ferdy looked at her he
saw that she was quietly weeping. When they got back to the
house she went to her room and would not come down to dinner
that night. For the first time she had realized that beauty dies.

Ferdy asked me for my address and a few days after I got
back to London invited me to dinner. There were only six of us,
an American woman married to an English peer, a Swedish
painter, an actress and a well-known critic. We ate very good
food and drank excellent wine. The conversation was easy and
intelligent. After dinner Ferdy was persuaded to play the
piano. He only played Viennese waltzes—I discovered later
that they were his speciality—and the light, tuneful and sensual
music seemed to accord well with his discreet flamboyance. He
played without affectation, with a lilt, and he had a graceful
touch. This was the first of a good many dinners I had with him;
he would ask me two or three times a year, and as time passed I
met him more and more frequently at other people's houses. I

rose in the world and perhaps he came down a little. Of late years I had sometimes found him at parties where other Jews were, and I fancied that I read in his shining liquid eyes, resting for a moment on these members of his race, a certain good-natured amusement at the thought of what the world was coming to. There were people who said he was a snob, but I do not think he was; it just happened that in his early days he had never met any but the great. He had a real passion for art, and in his commerce with those that produced it was at his best. With them he had never that faint air of persiflage which when he was with very grand persons made you suspect that he was never quite the dupe of their grandeur. His taste was exquisite and many of his friends were glad to avail themselves of his knowledge. He was one of the first to value old furniture, and he rescued many an exquisite piece from the attics of ancestral mansions and gave it an honourable place in the drawing-room. It amused him to saunter round the auction rooms, and he was always willing to give his advice to great ladies who desired at once to acquire a beautiful thing and make a profitable investment. He was rich and good-natured. He liked to patronize the arts and would take a great deal of trouble to get commissions for some young painter whose talent he admired or an engagement to play at a rich man's house for a violinist who could in no other way get a hearing. But he never let his rich man down. His taste was too good to deceive, and civil though he might be to the mediocre he would not lift a finger to help him. His own musical parties, very small and carefully chosen, were a treat.

He never married.

"I am a man of the world," he said, "and I flatter myself that I have no prejudices, *tous les goûts sont dans la nature*, but I do not think I could bring myself to marry a Gentile. There's no harm in going to the opera in a dinner-jacket, but it just would never occur to me to do so."

"Then why didn't you marry a Jewess?"

(I did not hear this conversation, but the lively and audacious creature who thus tackled him told me of it.)

"Oh, my dear, our women are so prolific. I could not bear the thought of peopling the world with a little Ikey and a little Jacob and a little Rebecca and a little Leah and a little Rachel."

But he had had affairs of note and the glamour of past romance still clung to him. He was in his youth of an amorous complexion. I have met old ladies who told me that he was irresistible, and when in reminiscent mood they talked to me of this woman and that who had completely lost her head over him, I divined that, such was his beauty, they could not find it in their hearts to blame them. It was interesting to hear of great ladies that I had read of in the memoirs of the day or had met as respectable dowagers garrulous over their grandsons at Eton or making a mess of a hand at bridge and bethink myself that they had been consumed with sinful passion for the handsome Jew. Ferdy's most notorious amour was with the Duchess of Hereford, the loveliest, the most gallant and dashing of the beauties of the end of Queen Victoria's reign. It lasted for twenty years. He had doubtless flirtations meanwhile, but their relations were stable and recognized. It was proof of his marvellous tact that when at last they ended he exchanged an aging mistress for a loyal friend. I remember meeting the pair not so very long ago at luncheon. She was an old woman, tall and of a commanding presence, but with a mask of paint on a ravaged face. We were lunching at the Carlton and Ferdy, our host, came a few minutes late. He offered us a cocktail and the Duchess told him we had already had one.

"Ah, I wondered why your eyes were so doubly bright," he said.

The old raddled woman flushed with pleasure.

My youth passed, I grew middle-aged, I wondered how soon I must begin to describe myself as elderly; I wrote books and plays, I travelled, I underwent experiences, I fell in love and out of it; and still I kept meeting Ferdy at parties. War broke out and was waged, millions of men were killed and the face of the world was changed. Ferdy did not like the war. He was too old to take part in it, and his German name was awkward, but he was discreet and took care not to expose himself to humiliation. His old friends were faithful to him, and he lived in a dignified but not too strict seclusion. But then peace came and with courage he set himself to making the best of changed conditions. Society was mixed now, parties were rowdy, but Ferdy fitted himself to the new life. He still told his funny Jewish stories, he still played charmingly the waltzes of Strauss, he still went round auction rooms and told the new rich what they ought to buy. I went to live abroad, but whenever I was in London I saw Ferdy, and now there was something a little uncanny in him. He did not give in. He had never known a day's illness. He seemed never to grow tired. He still dressed beautifully. He was interested in everybody. His mind was alert and people asked him to dinner, not for old times' sake, but because he was worth his salt. He still gave charming little concerts at his house in Curzon Street.

It was when he invited me to one of these that I made the discovery that started the recollections of him I have here set down. We were dining at a house in Hill Street, a large party, and the women having gone upstairs Ferdy and I found ourselves side by side. He told me that Lea Makart was coming to play for him on the following Friday evening and he would be glad if I would come.

"I'm awfully sorry," I said, "but I'm going down to the Blands."

"What Blands?"

"They live in Sussex at a place called Tilby."

"I didn't know you knew them."

He looked at me rather strangely. He smiled. I didn't know what amused him.

"Oh, yes, I've known them for years. It's a very nice house to stay at."

"Adolph is my nephew."

"Sir Adolphus?"

"It suggests one of the bucks of the Regency, doesn't it? But I will not conceal from you that he was named Adolph."

"Everyone I know calls him Freddy."

"I know, and I understand that Miriam, his wife, only answers to the name of Muriel."

"How does he happen to be your nephew?"

"Because Hannah Rabenstein, my sister, married Alphonse Bleikogel, who ended life as Sir Alfred Bland, first baronet and Adolph, their only son, in due course became Sir Adolphus Bland, second baronet."

"Then Freddy Bland's mother, the Lady Bland who lives in Portland Place, is your sister?"

"Yes, my sister Hannah. She was the eldest of the family. She's eighty, but in full possession of her faculties and a remarkable woman."

"I've never met her."

"I think your friends the Blands would just as soon you didn't. She has never lost her German accent."

"Do you never see them?" I asked.

"I haven't spoken to them for twenty years. I am such a

Jew and they are so English." He smiled. "I could never remember that their names were Freddy and Muriel. I used to come out with an Adolph or a Miriam at awkward moments. And they didn't like my stories. It was better that we should not meet. When the war broke out and I would not change my name it was the last straw. It was too late. I could never have accustomed my friends to think of me as anything but Ferdy Rabenstein. I was quite content. I was not ambitious to be a Smith, a Brown, or a Robinson."

Though he spoke facetiously, there was in his tone the faintest possible derision and I felt, hardly felt even, the sensation was so shadowy, that, as it had often vaguely seemed to me before, there was in the depth of his impenetrable heart a cynical contempt for the Gentiles he had conquered.

"Then you don't know the two boys?" I said.

"No."

"The eldest is called George, you know. I don't think he's so clever as Harry, the other one, but he's an engaging youth. I think you'd like him."

"Where is he now?"

"Well, he's just been sent down from Oxford. I suppose he's at home. Harry's still at Eton."

"Why don't you bring George to lunch with me?"

"I'll ask him. I should think he'd love to come."

"It has reached my ears that he's been a little troublesome."

"Oh, I don't know. He wouldn't go into the army, which is what they wanted. They rather fancied the Guards. And so he went to Oxford instead. He didn't work and he spent a great deal of money and he painted the town red. It was all quite normal."

"What was he sent down for?"

"I don't know. Nothing of any consequence."

At that moment our host rose and we went upstairs. When Ferdy bade me good-night he asked me not to forget about his great-nephew.

"Ring me up," he said. "Wednesday would suit me. Or Friday."

Next day I went down to Tilby. It was an Elizabethan mansion standing in a spacious park, in which roamed fallow deer, and from its windows you had wide views of rolling downs. It seemed to me that as far as the eye could reach the land be-

longed to the Blands. His tenants must have found Sir Adolphus
a wonderful landlord, for I never saw farms kept in such order,
the barns and cow-sheds were spick and span and the pigsties
were a picture; the public-houses looked like old English water-
colours and the cottages he had built on the estate combined
admirably picturesqueness and convenience. It must have cost
him a pot of money to run the place on these lines. Fortunately
he had it. The park with its grand old trees (and its nine-hole
golf course) was tended like a garden, and the wide-stretching
gardens were the pride of the neighbourhood. The magnificent
house, with its steep roofs and mullioned windows, had been
restored by the most celebrated architect in England and furnished by Lady Bland, with taste and knowledge, in a style that
perfectly fitted it.

"Of course it's very simple," she said. "Just an English
house in the country."

The dining-room was adorned with old English sporting
pictures, and the Chippendale chairs were of incredible value.
In the drawing-room were portraits by Reynolds and Gains-
borough and landscapes by Old Crome and Richard Wilson.
Even in my bedroom with its four-post bed were water-colours
by Birket Foster. It was very beautiful and a treat to stay
there, but though it would have distressed Muriel Bland beyond anything to know it, it missed oddly enough entirely the
effect she had sought. It did not give you for a moment the
impression of an English house. You had the feeling that every
object had been bought with a careful eye to the general
scheme. You missed the dull Academy portraits that hung in
the dining-room beside a Carlo Dolci that an ancestor had
brought back from the grand tour, and the water-colours
painted by a great-aunt that cluttered up the drawing-room so
engagingly. There was no ugly Victorian sofa that had always
been there and that it never occurred to anybody to take away,
and no needlework chairs that an unmarried daughter had so
painstakingly worked at about the time of the Great Exhibition.
There was beauty but no sentiment.

And yet how comfortable it was and how well looked after
you were! And what a cordial greeting the Blands gave you!
They seemed really to like people. They were generous and
kindly. They were never happier than when they were entertaining the county, and though they had not owned the property for more than twenty years they had established them-

selves firmly in the favour of their neighbours. Except perhaps
in their splendour and the competent way in which the estate
was run there was nothing to suggest that they had not been
settled there for centuries.

Freddy had been at Eton and Oxford. He was now in the
early fifties. He was quiet in manner, courtly, very clever, I
imagine, but a trifle reserved. He had great elegance, but it was
not an English elegance; he had grey hair and a short pointed
grey beard, fine dark eyes and an aquiline nose. He was just
above middle height; I don't think you would have taken him
for a Jew, but rather for a foreign diplomat of some distinction.
He was a man of character, but gave you, strangely enough,
notwithstanding the success he had had in life, an impression
of faint melancholy. His successes had been financial and
political; in the world of sport, for all his perseverance, he had
never shone. For many years he had followed hounds, but he
was a bad rider and I think it must have been a relief to him
when he could persuade himself that middle-age and pressure
of business forced him to give up hunting. He had excellent
shooting and gave grand parties for it, but he was a poor shot;
and despite the course in his park he never succeeded in being
more than an indifferent golfer. He knew only too well how
much these things meant in England, and his incapacity was a
bitter disappointment to him. However, George would make up
for it.

George was scratch at golf, and though tennis was not his
game he played much better than the average; the Blandshad
had him taught to shoot as soon as he was old enough to hold a
gun, and he was a fine shot; they had put him on a pony when
he was two, and Freddy, watching him mount his horse, knew
that out hunting when the boy came to a fence he felt exhilaration and not that sickening feeling in the pit of his stomach
which, though he had chased the fox with such grim determination, had always made the sport a torture to him. George was so
tall and slim, his curly hair, of a palish brown, was so fine, his
eyes were so blue, he was the perfect type of the young Englishman. He had the engaging candour of the breed. His nose was
straight, though perhaps a trifle fleshy, and his lips were perhaps
a little full and sensual, but he had beautiful teeth, and his
smooth skin was like ivory. George was the apple of his father's
eye. He did not like Harry, his second son, so well. He was
rather stocky, broad-shouldered and strong for his age, but his

black eyes, shining with cleverness, his coarse dark hair and his big nose revealed his race. Freddy was severe with him, and often impatient, but with George he was all indulgence. Harry would go into the business, he had brains and push, but George was the heir. George would be an English gentleman.

George had offered to motor me down in the roadster his father had given him as a birthday present. He drove very fast and we arrived before the rest of the guests. The Blands were sitting on the lawn and tea was laid out under a magnificent cedar.

"By the way," I said presently, "I saw Ferdy Rabenstein the other day and he wants me to bring George to lunch with him."

I had not mentioned the invitation to George on the way because I thought that if there had been a family coldness I had better address his parents as well.

"Who in God's name is Ferdy Rabenstein?" said George.

How brief is human glory! A generation back such a question would have seemed grotesque.

"He's by way of being your great-uncle," I replied.

A glance had passed from father to mother when I first spoke. "He's a horrid old man," said Muriel.

"I don't think it's in the least necessary for George to resume relationships that were definitely severed before he was born," said Freddy with decision.

"Anyhow I've delivered the message," said I, feeling somewhat snubbed.

"I don't want to see the old blighter," said George.

The conversation was broken off by the arrival of other guests, and in a little while George went off to play golf with one of his Oxford friends.

It was not till next day that the matter was referred to again. I had played an indifferent round with Freddy Bland in the morning, and several sets of what is known as country-house tennis in the afternoon, and was sitting alone with Muriel on the terrace. In England we have so much bad weather that it is only fair that a beautiful day should be more beautiful than anywhere in the world, and this June evening was perfect. The blue sky was cloudless and the air was balmy; before us stretched green rolling downs, and woods, and in the distance you saw red roofs of a little village and the grey tower of the

village church. It was a day when to be alive was sufficient
happiness. Detached lines of poetry hovered vaguely in my
memory. Muriel and I had been chatting desultorily.

"I hope you didn't think it rather horrid of us to refuse to let
George lunch with Ferdy," she said suddenly. "He's such a
fearful snob, isn't he?"

"D'you think so? He's always been very nice to me."

"We haven't been on speaking terms for twenty years.
Freddy never forgave him for his behaviour during the war.
So unpatriotic, I thought, and one really must draw the line
somewhere. You know, he absolutely refused to drop his horrible German name. With Freddy in Parliament and running
munitions and all that sort of thing it was quite impossible.
I don't know why he should want to see George. He can't mean
anything to him."

"He's an old man. George and Harry are his great-nephews.
He must leave his money to some one."

"We'd rather not have his money," said Muriel coldly.

Of course I didn't care a row of pins whether George went to
lunch with Ferdy Rabenstein, and I was quite willing to let the
matter drop, but evidently the Blands had talked it over and
Muriel felt that some explanation was due to me.

"Of course you know that Freddy has Jewish blood in him,"
she said.

She looked at me sharply. Muriel was rather a big blonde
woman and she spent a great deal of time trying to keep down
the corpulence to which she was predisposed. She had been
very pretty when young and even now was a comely person;
but her round blue eyes, slightly prominent, her fleshy nose,
the shape of her face and the back of her neck, her exuberant
manner, betrayed her race. No Englishwoman, however fair-
haired, ever looked like that. And yet her observation was designed to make me take it for granted that she was a Gentile. I
answered discreetly.

"So many people have nowadays."

"I know. But there's no reason to dwell on it, is there? After
all, we're absolutely English; no one could be more English
than George, in appearance and manner and everything; I
mean, he's such a fine sportsman and all that sort of thing. I
can't see any object in his knowing Jews just because they happen to be distant connections of his."

"It's very difficult in England now not to know Jews, isn't it?"

"Oh, I know, in London one does meet a good many, and I think some of them are very nice. They're so artistic. I don't go so far as to say that Freddy and I deliberately avoid them—of course I wouldn't do that—but it just happens that we don't really know any of them very well. And down here, there simply aren't any to know."

I could not but admire the convincing manner in which she spoke. It would not have surprised me to be told that she really believed every word she said.

"You say that Ferdy might leave George his money. Well, I don't believe it's so very much anyway; it was quite a comfortable fortune before the war, but that's nothing nowadays. Besides, we're hoping that George will go in for politics when he's a little older, and I don't think it would do him any good in the constituency to inherit money from a Mr. Rabenstein."

"Is George interested in politics?" I asked, to change the conversation.

"Oh, I hope so. After all, there's the family constituency waiting for him. It's a safe Conservative seat and one can't expect Freddy to go on with the grind of the House of Commons indefinitely."

Muriel was grand. She talked already of the constituency as though twenty generations of Blands had sat for it. Her remark, however, was my first intimation that Freddy's ambition was not satisfied.

"I suppose Freddy would go to the House of Lords when George was old enough to stand."

"We've done a good deal for the party," said Muriel.

Muriel was a Catholic and she often told you that she had been educated in a convent—"Such sweet women, those nuns. I always said that if I had a daughter I should have sent her to a convent too"—but she liked her servants to be Church of England, and on Sunday evenings we had what was called supper because the fish was cold and there was ice cream, so that they could go to church, and we were waited on by two footmen instead of four. It was still light when we finished, and Freddy and I, smoking our cigars, walked up and down the terrace in the gloaming. I suppose Muriel had told him of her conversation with me, and it may be that his refusal to let George see his great-uncle still troubled him, but being subtler than she he attacked the question more indirectly. He told me that he had been very much worried about George. It had been a great disappointment that he had refused to go into the army.

"I should have thought he'd have loved the life," he said.

"And he would certainly have looked marvellous in his Guards' uniform."

"He would, wouldn't he?" returned Freddy, ingenuously. "I wonder he could resist that."

He had been completely idle at Oxford; although his father had given him a very large allowance, he had got monstrously into debt; and now he had been sent down. But though he spoke so tartly I could see that he was not a little proud of his scape-grace son, he loved him with, oh, such an un-English love, and in his heart it flattered him that George had cut such a dash.

"Why should you worry?" I said. "You don't really care if George has a degree or not."

Freddy chuckled.

"No, I don't suppose I do really. I always think the only important thing about Oxford is that people know you were there, and I daresay that George isn't any wilder than the other young men in his set. It's the future I'm thinking of. He's so damned idle. He doesn't seem to want to do anything but have a good time."

"He's young, you know."

"He's not interested in politics, and though he's so good at games he's not even very keen on sport. He seems to spend most of his time strumming the piano."

"That's a harmless amusement."

"Oh, yes, I don't mind that, but he can't go on loafing indefinitely. You see, all this will be his one day." Freddy gave a sweeping gesture that seemed to embrace the whole country, but I knew that he did not own it all yet. "I'm very anxious that he should be fit to assume his responsibilities. His mother is very ambitious for him, but I only want him to be an English gentleman."

Freddy gave me a sidelong glance as though he wanted to say something but hesitated in case I thought it ridiculous; but there is one advantage in being a writer, that, since people look upon you as of no account, they will often say things to you that they would not to their equals. He thought he would risk it.

"You know, I've got an idea that nowhere in the world now is the Greek ideal of life so perfectly cultivated as by the

English country gentleman living on his estates. I think his life has the beauty of a work of art."

I could not but smile when I reflected that it was impossible for the English country gentleman in these days to do anything of the sort without a packet of money safely invested in American bonds, but I smiled with sympathy. I thought it rather touching that this Jewish financier should cherish so romantic a dream.

"I want him to be a good landlord. I want him to take his part in the affairs of the country. I want him to be a thorough sportsman."

"Poor mutt," I thought, but said: "Well, what are your plans for George now?"

"I think he has a fancy for the diplomatic service. He's suggested going to Germany to learn the language."

"A very good idea, I should have thought."

"For some reason he's got it into his head that he wants to go to Munich."

"A nice place."

Next day I went back to London and shortly after my arrival rang up Ferdy.

"I'm sorry, but George isn't able to come to lunch on Wednesday."

"What about Friday?"

"Friday's no good either." I thought it useless to beat about the bush. "The fact is, his people aren't keen on his lunching with you."

There was a moment's silence. Then:

"I see. Well, will you come on Wednesday anyway?"

"Yes, I'd like to," I answered.

So on Wednesday at half-past one I strolled round to Curzon Street. Ferdy received me with the somewhat elaborate graciousness that he cultivated. He made no reference to the Blands. We sat in the drawing-room and I could not help reflecting what an eye for beautiful objects that family had. The room was more crowded than the fashion of to-day approves and the gold snuff-boxes in vitrines, the French china, appealed to a taste that was not mine; but they were no doubt choice pieces; and the Louis XV suite, with its beautiful *petit pcint*, must have been worth an enormous lot of money. The pictures on the walls by Lancret, Pater and Watteau did not greatly interest me, but I recognized their intrinsic excellence. It was a proper setting for this aged man of the world. It fitted his period. Suddenly the door opened and George was announced. Ferdy saw my surprise and gave me a little smile of triumph.

"I'm very glad you were able to come after all," he said as he shook George's hand.

I saw him in a glance take in his great-nephew whom he saw to-day for the first time. George was very elegantly dressed. He wore a short black coat, striped trousers and the grey double-breasted waistcoat which at that time was the mode. You could only wear it with elegance if you were tall and thin and your belly was slightly concave. I felt sure that Ferdy knew exactly who George's tailor was and what haberdasher he went to, and approved of them. George, so smart and trim, wearing his clothes so beautifully, certainly looked very handsome. We went down to luncheon. Ferdy had the social graces at his fingers' ends and he put the boy at his ease, but I saw that he was carefully appraising him; then, I do not know why, he began to tell some of his Jewish stories. He told them with gusto and with his wonderful mimicry. I saw George flush, and though he laughed at them, I could see that it was with embarrassment. I wondered what on earth had induced Ferdy to be so tactless. But he was watching George and he told story after story. It looked as though he would never stop. I wondered if for some reason I could not grasp he was taking a malicious pleasure in the boy's obvious discomfiture. At last we went upstairs, and to make things easier I asked Ferdy to play the piano. He played us three or four little waltzes. He had lost none of his exquisite lightness nor his sense of their lilting rhythm. Then he turned to George.

"Do you play?" he asked him.

"A little."

"Won't you play something?"

"I'm afraid I only play classical music. I don't think it would interest you."

Ferdy smiled slightly, but did not insist. I said it was time for me to go and George accompanied me.

"What a filthy old Jew," he said as soon as we were in the street. "I hated those stories of his."

"They're his great stunt. He always tells them."

"Would you if you were a Jew?"

I shrugged my shoulders.

"How is it you came to lunch after all?" I asked George.

He chuckled. He was a light-hearted creature, with a sense of humour, and he shook off the slight irritation his great-uncle had caused him.

"He went to see Granny. You don't know Granny, do you?"

"No."

"She treats Daddy like a kid in Etons. Granny said I was to go to lunch with Great-uncle Ferdy, and what Granny says goes."

"I see."

A week or two later George went to Munich to learn German. I happened then to go on a journey, and it was not till the following spring that I was again in London. Soon after my arrival I found myself sitting next to Muriel Bland at dinner. I asked after George.

"He's still in Germany," she said.

"I see in the papers that you're going to have a great beano at Tilby for his coming of age."

"We're going to entertain the tenants and they're making George a presentation."

She was less exuberant than usual, but I did not pay much attention to the fact. She led a strenuous life and it might be that she was tired. I knew she liked to talk of her son, so I continued.

"I suppose George has been having a grand time in Germany," I said.

She did not answer for a moment and I gave her a glance. I was surprised to see that her eyes were filled with tears.

"I'm afraid George has gone mad," she said.

"What *do* you mean?"

"We've been so frightfully worried. Freddy's so angry, he won't even discuss it. I don't know what we're going to do."

Of course it immediately occurred to me that George, who, I supposed, like most young Englishmen sent to learn the language, had been put with a German family, had fallen in love with the daughter of the house and wanted to marry her. I had a pretty strong suspicion that the Blands were intent on his making a very grand marriage.

"Why, what's happened?" I asked.

"He wants to become a pianist."

"A what?"

"A professional pianist."

"What on earth put that idea in his head?"

"Heaven knows. We didn't know anything about it. We thought he was working for his exam. I went out to see him. I thought I'd like to know that he was getting on all right. Oh, my dear. He looks like nothing on earth. And he used to be so smart; I could have cried. He told me he wasn't going in for the exam and had never had any intention of doing so; he'd only suggested the diplomatic service so that we'd let him go to Germany and he'd be able to study music."

"But has he any talent?"

"Oh, that's neither here nor there. Even if he had the genius of Paderewski we couldn't have George traipsing around the country playing at concerts. No one can deny that I'm very artistic, and so Freddy—we love music and we've always known a lot of artists—but George will have a very great position; it's out of the question. We've set our hearts on his going into Parliament. He'll be very rich one day. There's nothing he can't aspire to."

"Did you point all that out to him?"

"Of course I did. He laughed at me. I told him he'd break his father's heart. He said his father could always fall back on Harry. Of course I'm devoted to Harry, and he's as clever as a monkey, but it was always understood that he was to go into the business; even though I am his mother I can see that he hasn't got the advantages that George has. Do you know what he said to me? He said that if his father would settle five pounds a week on him he would resign everything in Harry's favour and Harry could be his father's heir and succeed to the baronetcy and everything. It's too ridiculous. He said that if the Crown Prince of Roumania could abdicate a throne he didn't see why he couldn't abdicate a baronetcy. But you can't do that. Nothing can prevent him from being third baronet and, if Freddy should be granted a peerage, from succeeding to it at Freddy's death. Do you know, he even wants to drop the name of Bland and take some horrible German name."

I could not help asking what.

"Bleikogel or something like that," she answered.

That was a name I recognized. I remembered Ferdy telling me that Hannah Rabenstein had married Alphonse Bleikogel, who became eventually Sir Alfred Bland, first baronet. It was all very strange. I wondered what had happened to the charming and so typically English boy whom I had seen only a few months before.

"Of course when I came home and told Freddy he was furious. I've never seen him so angry. He foamed at the mouth. He wired to George to come back immediately, and George wired back to say he couldn't on account of his work."

"Is he working?"

"From morning till night. That's the maddening part of it. He never did a stroke of work in his life. Freddy used to say he was born idle."

"H'm."

"Then Freddy wired to say that if he didn't come he'd stop his allowance, and George wired back: 'Stop it.' That put the lid on. You don't know what Freddy can be when his back is up."

I knew that Freddy had inherited a large fortune, but I knew also that he had immensely increased it, and I could well imagine that behind the courteous and amiable Squire of Tilby there was a ruthless man of affairs. He had been used to having his own way, and I could believe that when crossed he would be hard and cruel.

"We'd been making George a very handsome allowance, but you know how frightfully extravagant he was. We didn't think he'd be able to hold out long, and in point of fact within a month he wrote to Ferdy and asked him to lend him a hundred pounds. Ferdy went to my mother-in-law—she's his sister, you know—and asked her what it meant. Though they hadn't spoken for twenty years Freddy went to see him and begged him not to send George a penny, and he promised he wouldn't. I don't know how George has been making both ends meet. I'm sure Freddy's right, but I can't help being rather worried. If I hadn't given Freddy my word of honour that I wouldn't send him anything I think I'd have slipped a few notes in a letter in case of accident. I mean, it's awful to think that perhaps he hasn't got enough to eat."

"It'll do him no harm to go short for a bit."

"We were in an awful hole, you know. We'd made all sorts of preparations for his coming of age, and I'd issued hundreds of invitations. Suddenly George said he wouldn't come. I was simply frantic. I wrote and wired. I would have gone over to Germany, only Freddy wouldn't let me. I practically went down on my bended knees to George. I begged him not to put us in such a humiliating position. I mean, it's the sort of thing it's so difficult to explain. Then my mother-in-law stepped in. You don't know her, do you? She's an extraordinary old woman. You'd never think she was Freddy's mother. She was German originally but of very good family."

"Oh?"

"To tell you the truth I'm rather frightened of her. She tackled Freddy and then she wrote to George herself. She said that if he'd come home for his twenty-first birthday she'd pay any debts he had in Munich and we'd all give a patient hearing to anything he had to say. He agreed to that and we're expecting him one day next week. But I'm not looking forward to it I can tell you."

She gave a deep sigh. When we were walking upstairs after dinner Freddy addressed me.

"I see Muriel has been telling you about George. The damned fool! I have no patience with him. Fancy wanting to be a pianist! It's so ungentlemanly."

"He's very young, you know," I said soothingly.

"He's had things too easy for him. I've been much too indulgent. There's never been a thing he wanted that I haven't given him. I'll learn him."

The Blands had a discreet apprehension of the uses of advertisement, and I gathered from the papers that the celebrations at Tilby of George's twenty-first birthday were conducted in accordance with the usage of English county families. There were a dinner party and ball for the gentry and a collation and a dance in marquees on the lawn for the tenants. Expensive bands were brought down from London. In the illustrated papers were pictures of George, surrounded by his family being presented with a solid silver tea set by the tenantry. They had subscribed to have his portrait painted, but since his absence from the country had made it impossible for him to sit, the tea service had been substituted. I read in the columns of the gossip writers that his father had given him a hunter, his mother a gramophone that changed its own records, his grandmother the dowager Lady Bland an Encyclopædia Britannica and his great-uncle Ferdinand Rabenstein a Virgin and Child by Pellegrino da Modena. I could not help observing that these gifts were bulky and not readily convertible into cash. From Ferdy's presence at the festivities I concluded that George's unaccountable vagary had effected a reconciliation between uncle and nephew. I was right. Ferdy did not at all like the notion of his great-nephew becoming a professional pianist. At the first hint of danger to its prestige the family drew together and a united front was presented to oppose George's designs. Since I was not there I only know from hearsay what happened when the birthday celebrations were over. Ferdy told me something and so did Muriel, and later George gave me his version. The Blands had very much the impression that when George came home and found himself occupying the centre of the stage, when, surrounded by splendour, he saw for himself once more how much it meant to be the heir of a great estate, he would weaken. They surrounded him with love. They flattered him. They hung on his words. They counted on the goodness of his heart and thought that if they were very kind to him he would not have the courage to cause them pain. They seemed to take it for granted that he had no intention of going back to Germany, and in conversation included him in all their plans. George did not say very much. He seemed to be enjoying himself. He did not open a piano. Things looked as though they were going very well. Peace descended on the troubled house. Then one day at luncheon when they were discussing a garden party to which they had all been asked for one day of the following week, George said pleasantly:

"Don't count on me. I shan't be here."

"Oh, George, why not?" asked his mother.

"I must get back to my work. I'm leaving for Munich on Monday."

There was an awful pause. Everyone looked for something to say, but was afraid of saying the wrong thing, and at last it seemed impossible to break it. Luncheon was finished in silence. Then George went into the garden and the others, old Lady Bland and Ferdy, Muriel and Sir Adolphus, into the morning-room. There was a family council. Muriel wept. Freddy flew into a temper. Presently from the drawing-room they heard the sound of someone playing a nocturne of Chopin. It was George. It was as though, now he had announced his decision, he had gone for comfort, rest and strength to the instrument he loved. Freddy sprang to his feet.

"Stop that noise," he cried. "I won't have him play the piano in my house."

Muriel rang for a servant and gave him a message.

"Will you tell Mr. Bland that her ladyship has a bad head‑ache and would he mind not playing the piano."

Ferdy, the man of the world, was deputed to have a talk with George. He was authorized to make him certain promises if he would give up the idea of becoming a pianist. If he did not wish to go into the diplomatic service his father would not insist, but if he would stand for Parliament he was prepared to pay his election expenses, give him a flat in London and make him an allowance of five thousand a year. I must say it was a handsome offer. I do not know what Ferdy said to the boy. I suppose he painted to him the life that a young man could lead in London on such an income. I am sure he made it very alluring. It availed nothing. All George asked was five pounds a week to be able to continue his studies and to be left alone. He was indiffer‑ent to the position that he might some day enjoy. He didn't want to hunt. He didn't want to shoot. He didn't want to be a Member of Parliament. He didn't want to be a millionaire. He didn't want to be a baronet. He didn't want to be a peer. Ferdy left him, defeated and in a state of considerable exasperation.

After dinner that evening there was a battle royal. Freddy was a quick-tempered man, unused to opposition, and he gave George the rough side of his tongue. I gather that it was very rough indeed. The women who sought to restrain his violence were sternly silenced. Perhaps for the first time in his life Freddy would not listen to his mother. George was obstinate and sullen. He had made up his mind and if his father didn't like it he could lump it. Freddy was peremptory. He forbade George to go back to Germany. George answered that he was twenty-one and his own master. He would go where he chose. Freddy swore he would not give him a penny.

"All right, I'll earn money."

"You! You've never done a stroke of work in your life. What do you expect to do to earn money?"

"Sell old clothes," grinned George.

There was a gasp from all of them. Muriel was so taken aback that she said a stupid thing.

"Like a Jew?"

"Well, aren't I a Jew? And aren't you a Jewess and isn't Daddy a Jew? We're all Jews, the whole gang of us, and every‑one knows it and what the hell's the good of pretending we're not?"

Then a very dreadful thing happened. Freddy burst suddenly

into tears. I'm afraid he didn't behave very much like Sir
Adolphus Bland, Bart., M.P., and the good old English gentleman he so much wanted to be, but like an emotional Adolph
Bleikogel who loved his son and wept with mortification because
the great hopes he had set on him were brought to nothing and
the ambition of his life was frustrated. He cried noisily with
great loud sobs and pulled his beard and beat his breast and
rocked to and fro. Then they all began to cry, old Lady Bland
and Muriel, and Ferdy, who sniffed and blew his nose and
wiped the tears streaming down his face, and even George cried.
Of course it was very painful, but to our rough Anglo-Saxon
temperament I am afraid it must seem also a trifle ridiculous.
No one tried to console anybody else. They just sobbed and
sobbed. It broke up the party.

But it had no result on the situation. George remained
obdurate. His father would not speak to him. There were more
scenes. Muriel sought to excite his pity; he was deaf to her
piteous entreaties, he did not seem to mind if he broke her
heart, he did not care two hoots if he killed his father. Ferdy
appealed to him as a sportsman and a man of the world.
George was flippant and indeed personally offensive. Old Lady
Bland with her guttural German accent and strong common
sense argued with him, but he would not listen to reason. It
was she, however, who at last found a way out. She made
George acknowledge that it was no use to throw away all the
beautiful things the world laid at his feet unless he had talent.
Of course he thought he had, but he might be mistaken. It
was not worth while to be a second-rate pianist. His only excuse, his only justification, was genius. If he had genius his
family had no right to stand in his way.

"You can't expect me to show genius already," said George.
"I shall have to work for years."

"Are you sure you are prepared for that?"

"It's my only wish in the world. I'll work like a dog. I only
want to be given my chance."

This was the proposition she made. His father was determined
to give him nothing, and obviously they could not let the boy
starve. He had mentioned five pounds a week. Well, she was
willing to give him that herself. He could go back to Germany
and study for two years. At the end of that time he must come
back and they would get some competent and disinterested
person to hear him play, and if then that person said he showed

promise of becoming a first-rate pianist no further obstacles
would be placed in his way. He would be given every advantage, help and encouragement. If on the other hand that person
decided that his natural gifts were not such as to ensure ultimate
success he must promise faithfully to give up all thoughts of
making music his profession and in every way accede to his
father's wishes. George could hardly believe his ears.

"Do you mean that, Granny?"

"I do."

"But will Daddy agree?"

"I vill see dat he does," she answered.

George seized her in his arms and impetuously kissed her on
both cheeks.

"Darling," he cried.

"Ah, but de promise?"

He gave her his solemn word of honour that he would faithfully abide by the terms of the arrangement. Two days later he
went back to Germany. Though his father consented unwillingly
to his going, and indeed could not help doing so, he would not
be reconciled to him and when he left refused to say good-bye to
him. I imagine that in no other manner could he have caused
himself such pain. I permit myself a trite remark. It is strange
that men, inhabitants for so short a while of an alien and inhuman world, should go out of their way to cause themselves
so much unhappiness.

George had stipulated that during his two years of study his
family should not visit him, so that when Muriel heard some
months before he was due to come home that I was passing
through Munich on my way to Vienna, whither business called
me, it was not unnatural that she should ask me to look him up.
She was anxious to have first-hand information about him. She
gave me George's address and I wrote ahead, telling him I was
spending a day in Munich, and asked him to lunch with me. His
answer awaited me at the hotel. He said he worked all day and
could not spare the time to lunch with me, but if I would come
to his studio about six he would like to show me that and if I
had nothing better to do would love to spend the evening with
me. So soon after six I went to the address he gave me. He
lived on the second floor of a large block of flats and when I
came to his door I heard the sound of piano-playing. It stopped
when I rang and George opened the door for me. I hardly rec-

ognized him. He had grown very fat. His hair was extremely long, it curled all over his head in picturesque confusion; and he had certainly not shaved for three days. He wore a grimy pair of Oxford bags, a tennis shirt and slippers. He was not very clean and his fingernails were rimmed with black. It was a startling change from the spruce, slim youth so elegantly dressed in such beautiful clothes that I had last seen. I could not but think it would be a shock to Ferdy to see him now. The studio was large and bare; on the walls were three or four unframed canvases of a highly cubist nature; there were several armchairs much the worse for wear, and a grand piano. Books were littered about and old newspapers and art magazines. It was dirty and untidy and there was a frousty smell of stale beer and stale smoke.

"Do you live here alone?" I asked.

"Yes, I have a woman who comes in twice a week and cleans up. But I make my own breakfast and lunch."

"Can you cook?"

"Oh, I only have bread and cheese and a bottle of beer for lunch. I dine at a *bier stube*."

It was pleasant to discover that he was very glad to see me. He seemed in great spirits and extremely happy. He asked after his relations and we talked of one thing and another. He had a lesson twice a week and for the rest of the time practised. He told me that he worked ten hours a day.

"That's a change," I said.

He laughed.

"Daddy said I was born tired. I wasn't really lazy. I didn't see the use of working at things that bored me."

I asked him how he was getting on with the piano. He seemed to be satisfied with his progress and I begged him to play to me.

"Oh, not now. I'm all in, I've been at it all day. Let's go out and dine and come back here later and then I'll play. I generally go to the same place; there are several students I know there, and it's rather fun."

Presently we set out. He put on socks and shoes and a very old golf coat, and we walked together through the wide quiet streets. It was a brisk cold day. His step was buoyant. He looked round him with a sigh of delight.

"I love Munich," he said. "It's the only city in the world where there's art in the very air you breathe. After all, art is the only thing that matters, isn't it? I loathe the idea of going home."

"All the same I'm afraid you'll have to."

"I know. I'll go all right, but I'm not going to think about it till the time comes."

"When you do, you might do worse than get a haircut. If you don't mind my saying so you look almost too artistic to be convincing."

"You English, you're such Philistines," he said.

He took me to a rather large restaurant in a side street, crowded even at that early hour with people dining and furnished heavily in the German medieval style. A table covered with a red cloth, well away from the air, was reserved for George and his friends, and when we went to it four or five youths were at it. There was a Pole studying Oriental languages, a student of philosophy, a painter—I suppose the author of George's cubist picture—a Swede, and a young man who introduced himself to me, clicking his heels, as Hans Reiting, *dichter*, namely Hans Reiting, poet. Not one of them was more than twenty-two and I felt a trifle out of it. They all addressed George as *du* and I noticed that his German was extremely fluent. I had not spoken it for some time and mine was rusty, so that I could not take much part in the lively conversation. But nevertheless I thoroughly enjoyed myself. They ate sparingly, but drank a good deal of beer. They talked of art and literature and life and ethics and motor-cars and women. They were very revolutionary, and though gay very much in earnest. They were contemptuous of everyone you had ever heard of, and the only point on which they all agreed was that in this topsy-turvy world only the vulgar could hope for success. They argued points of technique with animation, and contradicted one another, and shouted and were obscene. They had a grand time.

At about eleven George and I walked back to his studio. Munich is a city that frolics demurely, and except about the Marienplatz the streets were still and empty. When we got in he took off his coat and said:

"Now I'll play to you."

I sat in one of the dilapidated armchairs, and a broken spring stuck into my behind, but I made myself as comfortable as I could. George played Chopin. I know very little of music, and that is one of the reasons for which I have found this story difficult to write. When I go to a concert at the Queen's Hall and in the intervals read the programme it is all Greek to me. I know nothing of harmony and counterpoint. I shall never forget how humiliated I felt once when, having come to Munich for a Wagner Festival, I went to a wonderful performance of *Tristan und Isolde* and never heard a note of it. The first few bars sent me off and I began to think of what I was writing, my characters leapt into life and I heard their long conversations, I suffered their pains and was a party to their joy; the years swept by and all sorts of things happened to me, the spring brought me its rapture and in the winter I was cold and hungry; and I loved and I hated and I died. I suppose there were intervals in which I walked round and round the garden and probably ate *schinken brödchen* and drank beer, but I have no recollection of them. The only thing I know is that when the curtain for the last time fell I woke with a start. I had had a wonderful time, but I could not help thinking it was very stupid of me to come such a long way and spend so much money if I couldn't pay attention to what I heard and saw.

I knew most of the things George played. They were the familiar pieces of concert programmes. He played with a great deal of dash. Then he played Beethoven's *Appassionata*. I used to play it myself when I played the piano (very badly) in my far distant youth and I still knew every note of it. Of course it is a classic and a great work, it would be foolish to deny it, but I confess that at this time of day it leaves me cold. It is like *Paradise Lost*, splendid, but a trifle stolid. This too George played with vigour. He sweated profusely. At first I could not make out what was the matter with his playing, something did not seem to me quite right, and then it struck me that the two hands did not exactly synchronize, so that there was ever so slight an interval between the bass and the treble; but I repeat, I am ignorant of these things; what disconcerted me might have been merely the effect of his having drunk a good deal of beer that evening, or indeed only my fancy. I said all I could think of to praise him.

"Of course I know I need a lot more work. I'm only a beginner, but I know I can do it. I feel it in my bones. It'll take me ten years, but then I shall be a pianist."

He was tired and came away from the piano. It was after midnight and I suggested going, but he would not hear of it. He opened a couple of bottles of beer and lit his pipe. He wanted to talk.

"Are you happy here?" I asked him.

"Very," he answered gravely. "I'd like to stay for ever. I've never had such fun in my life. This evening for instance. Wasn't it grand?"

"It was very jolly. But one can't go on leading the student's life. Your friends here will grow older and go away."

"Others'll come. There are always students here and people like that."

"Yes, but you'll grow older too. Is there anything more lamentable than the middle-aged man who tries to go on living the undergraduate's life? The old fellow who wants to be a boy among boys, and tries to persuade himself that they'll accept him as one of themselves—how ridiculous he is. It can't be done."

"I feel so at home here. My poor father wants me to be an English gentleman. It gives me gooseflesh. I'm not a sportsman. I don't care a damn for hunting and shooting and playing cricket. I was only acting."

"You gave a very natural performance."

"It wasn't till I came here that I knew it wasn't real. I loved Eton and Oxford was a riot, but all the same I knew I didn't belong. I played the part all right, because acting's in my blood, but there was always something in me that wasn't satisfied. The house in Grosvenor Square is a freehold, and Daddy paid a hundred and eighty thousand pounds for Tilby; I don't know if you understand what I mean, I felt they were just furnished houses we'd taken for the season and one of these days we'd pack up and the real owners would come back."

I listened to him attentively, but I wondered how much he was describing what he had obscurely felt and how much he imagined now in his changed circumstances that he had felt.

"I used to hate hearing Great-uncle Ferdy tell his Jewish stories. I thought it so damned mean. I understand now; it was a safety valve. My God, the strain of being a man about town. It's easier for Daddy, he can play the old English squire at Tilby, but in the city he can be himself. He's all right. I've taken the make-up off and my stage clothes and at last I can be my real self too. What a relief! You know, I don't like English people. I never really know where I am with you. You're so dull and conventional. You never let yourselves go. There's no freedom in you, freedom of the soul, and you're such funks. There's nothing in the world you're so frightened of as doing the wrong thing "

"Don't forget that you're English yourself, George," I murmured.

He laughed.

"I? I'm not English. I haven't got a drop of English blood in me. I'm a Jew and you know it, and a German Jew into the bargain. I don't want to be English. I want to be a Jew. My friends are Jews. You don't know how much more easy I feel with them. I can be myself. We did everything we could to avoid Jews at home; Mummy because she was blonde thought she could get away with it and pretended she was a Gentile. What rot! D'you know, I have a lot of fun wandering about the Jewish parts of Munich and looking at the people. I went to Frankfort once—there are a lot of them there—and I walked about and looked at the frowsy old men with their hooked noses and the fat women with their false hair. I felt such a sympathy for them, I felt I belonged to them, I could have kissed them. When they looked at me I wondered if they knew that I was one of them. I wish to God I knew Yiddish. I'd like to become friends with them, and go into their houses and eat Kosher food and all that sort of thing. I wanted to go to a synagogue, but I was afraid I'd do the wrong thing and be kicked out. I like the smell of the Ghetto and the sense of life, and the mystery and the dust and the squalor and the romance. I shall never get the longing for it out of my head now. That's the real thing. All the rest is only pretence."

"You'll break your father's heart," I said.

"It's his or mine. Why can't he let me go? There's Harry. Harry would love to be squire of Tilby. He'd be an English gentleman all right. You know, Mummy's set her heart on my marrying a Christian. Harry would love to. He'll found the good old English family all right. After all, I ask so little. I only want five pounds a week, and they can keep the title and the park and the Gainsboroughs and the whole bag of tricks."

"Well, the fact remains that you gave your solemn word of honour to go back after two years."

"I'll go back all right," he said sullenly. "Lea Makart has promised to come and hear me play."

"What'll you do if she says you're no good?"

"Shoot myself," he said gaily.

"What nonsense," I answered in the same tone.

"Do *you* feel at home in England?"

"No," I said, "but then I don't feel at home anywhere else."

But he was quite naturally not interested in me.

"I loathe the idea of going back. Now that I know what life has to offer I wouldn't be an English country gentleman for anything in the world. My God, the boredom of it!"

"Money's a very nice thing and I've always understood it's very pleasant to be an English peer."

"Money means nothing to me. I want none of the things it can buy, and I don't happen to be a snob."

It was growing very late and I had to get up early next day. It seemed unnecessary for me to pay too much attention to what George said. It was the sort of nonsense a young man might very well indulge in when thrown suddenly among painters and poets. Art is strong wine and needs a strong head to carry. The divine fire burns most efficiently in those who temper its fury with horse sense. After all, George was not twenty-three yet. Time teaches. And when all was said and done his future was no concern of mine. I bade him good-night and walked back to my hotel. The stars were shining in the indifferent sky. I left Munich in the morning.

I did not tell Muriel on my return to London what George had said to me, or what he looked like, but contented myself with assuring her that he was well and happy, working very hard, and seemed to be leading a virtuous and sober life. Six months later he came home. Muriel asked me to go down to Tilby for the week-end: Ferdy was bringing Lea Makart to hear George play and he particularly wished me to be there. I accepted. Muriel met me at the station.

"How did you find George?" I asked.

"He's very fat, but he seems in great spirits. I think he's pleased to be back again. He's been very sweet to his father."

"I'm glad of that."

"Oh, my dear, I do hope Lea Makart will say he's no good. It'll be such a relief to all of us."

"I'm afraid it'll be a terrible disappointment to him."

"Life is full of disappointments," said Muriel crisply. "But one learns to put up with them."

I gave her a smile of amusement. We were sitting in a Rolls, and there was a footman as well as a chauffeur on the box. She wore a string of pearls that had probably cost forty thousand pounds. I recollected that in the birthday honours Sir Adolphus Bland had not been one of the three gentlemen on whom the King had been pleased to confer a peerage.

Lea Makart was able to make only a flying visit. She was playing that evening at Brighton and would motor over to Tilby on the Sunday morning for luncheon. She was returning to London the same day because she had a concert in Manchester on the Monday. George was to play in the course of the afternoon.

"He's practising very hard," his mother told me. "That's why he didn't come with me to meet you."

We turned in at the park gates and drove up the imposing avenue of elms that led to the house. I found that there was no party.

I met the dowager Lady Bland for the first time. I had always been curious to see her. I had had in my mind's eye a somewhat sensational picture of an old, old Jewish woman who lived alone in her grand house in Portland Place and, with a finger in every pie, ruled her family with a despotic hand. She did not disappoint me. She was of a commanding presence, rather tall, and stout without being corpulent. Her countenance was markedly Hebraic. She wore a rather heavy moustache and a wig of a peculiarly metallic brown. Her dress was very grand, of black brocade, and she had a row of large diamond stars on her breast and round her neck a chain of diamonds. Diamond rings gleamed on her wrinkled hands. She spoke in a rather loud harsh voice and with a strong German accent. When I was introduced to her she fixed me with shining eyes. She summed me up with despatch and to my fancy at all events made no attempt to conceal from me that the judgment she formed was unfavourable.

"You have known my brother Ferdinand for many years, is it not so?" she said, rolling a guttural *r*. "My brother Ferdinand has always moved in very good society. Where is Sir Adolphus, Muriel? Does he know your guest is arrived? And will you not send for George? If he does not know his pieces by now he will not know them by to-morrow."

Muriel explained that Freddy was finishing a round of golf with his secretary and that she had had George told I was there. Lady Bland looked as though she thought Muriel's replies highly unsatisfactory and turned again to me.

"My daughter tells me you have been in Italy?"

"Yes, I've only just come back."

"It is a beautiful country. How is the King?"

I said I did not know.

"I used to know him when he was a little boy. He was not very strong then. His mother, Queen Margarita, was a great friend of mine. They thought he would never marry. The Duchess of Aosta was very angry when he fell in love with that Princess of Montenegro."

She seemed to belong to some long past period of history, but she was very alert and I imagine that little escaped her beady eyes. Freddy, very spruce in plus fours, presently came in. It was amusing and yet a little touching to see this grey-bearded man, as a rule somewhat domineering, so obviously on his best behaviour with the old lady. He called her Mamma. Then George came in. He was as fat as ever, but he had taken my advice and had his hair cut; he was losing his boyish looks, but he was a powerful and well-set-up young man. It was good to see the pleasure he took in his tea. He ate quantities of sandwiches and great hunks of cake. He had still a boy's appetite. His father watched him with a tender smile, and as I looked at him I could not be surprised at the attachment which they all so obviously felt for him. He had an ingenuousness, a charm and an enthusiasm which were certainly very pleasant. There was about him a generosity of demeanour, a frankness and a natural cordiality which could not but make people take to him. I do not know whether it was owing to a hint from his grandmother or merely of his own good nature, but it was plain that he was going out of his way to be nice to his father; and in his father's soft eyes, in the way he hung upon the boy's words, in his pleased, proud and happy look, you felt how bitterly the estrangement of the last two years had weighed on him. He adored George.

We played golf in the morning, a three-ball match, since Muriel, having to go to Mass, could not join us, and at one Ferdy arrived in Lea Makart's car. We sat down to luncheon. Of course Lea Makart's reputation was well-known to me. She was acknowledged to be the greatest woman pianist in Europe. She was a very old friend of Ferdy's, who with his interest and patronage had greatly helped her at the beginning of her career.

and it was he who had arranged for her to come and give her opinion of George's chances. At one time I went as often as I could to hear her play. She had no affectations; she played as a bird sings, without any appearance of effort, very naturally, and the silvery notes dripped from her light fingers in a curiously spontaneous manner, so that it gave you the impression that she was improvising those complicated rhythms. They used to tell me that her technique was wonderful. I could never make up my mind how much the delight her playing gave me was due to her person. In those days she was the most ethereal thing you could imagine, and it was surprising that a creature so sylphlike should be capable of so much power. She was very slight, pale, with enormous eyes and magnificent black hair, and at the piano she had a childlike wistfulness that was most appealing. She was very beautiful in a hardly human way, and when she played, a little smile on her closed lips, she seemed to be remembering things she had heard in another world. Now, however, a woman in the early forties, she was sylphlike no more; she was stout and her face had broadened; she had no longer that lovely remoteness, but the authority of her long succession of triumphs. She was brisk, businesslike and somewhat overwhelming. Her vitality lit her with a natural spotlight as his sanctity surrounds the saint with a halo. She was not interested in anything very much but her own affairs, but since she had humour and knew the world she was able to invest them with gaiety. She held the conversation, but did not absorb it. George talked little. Every now and then she gave him a glance, but did not try to draw him in. I was the only Gentile at the table. All but old Lady Bland spoke perfect English, yet I could not help feeling that they did not speak like English people; I think they rounded their vowels more than we do, they certainly spoke louder, and the words seemed not to fall, but to gush from their lips. I think if I had been in another room where I could hear the tone but not the words of their speech I should have thought it was in a foreign language that they were conversing. The effect was slightly disconcerting.

Lea Makart wished to set out for London at about six, so it was arranged that George should play at four. Whatever the result of the audition, I felt that I, a stranger in the circle which her departure must render exclusively domestic, would be in the way and so, pretexting an early engagement in town next morning, I asked her if she would take me with her in her car.

At a little before four we all wandered into the drawing-room. Old Lady Bland sat on a sofa with Ferdy; Freddy, Muriel and I made ourselves comfortable in armchairs; and Lea Makart sat by herself. She chose instinctively a high-backed Jacobean chair that had somewhat the air of a throne, and in a yellow dress, with her olive skin, she looked very handsome. She had magnificent eyes. She was very much made up and her mouth was scarlet.

George gave no sign of nervousness. He was already seated at the piano when I went in with his father and mother, and he watched us quietly settling ourselves down. He gave me the shadow of a smile. When he saw that we were all at our ease he began to play. He played Chopin. He played two waltzes that were familiar to me, a polonaise and an *étude*. He played with a great deal of *brio*. I wish I knew music well enough to give an exact description of his playing. It had strength and a youthful exuberance, but I felt that he missed what to me is the peculiar charm of Chopin, the tenderness, the nervous melancholy, the wistful gaiety and the slightly faded romance that reminds me always of an early Victorian keepsake. And again I had the vague sensation, so slight that it almost escaped me, that the two hands did not quite synchronize. I looked at Ferdy and saw him give his sister a look of faint surprise. Muriel's eyes were fixed on the pianist, but presently she dropped them and for the rest of the time stared at the floor. His father looked at him too, and his eyes were steadfast, but unless I was much mistaken he went pale and his face betrayed something like dismay. Music was in the blood of all of them, all their lives they had heard the greatest pianists in the world, and they judged with instinctive precision. The only person whose face betrayed no emotion was Lea Makart. She listened very attentively. She was as still as an image in a niche.

At last he stopped and turning round on his seat faced her. He did not speak.

"What is it you want me to tell you?" she asked.

They looked into one another's eyes.

"I want you to tell me whether I have any chance of becoming in time a pianist in the first rank."

"Not in a thousand years."

For a moment there was a dead silence. Freddy's head sank and he looked down at the carpet at his feet. His wife put out her hand and took his. But George continued to look steadily at Lea Makart.

"Ferdy has told me the circumstances," she said at last. "Don't think I'm influenced by them. Nothing of this is very important." She made a great sweeping gesture that took in the magnificent room with the beautiful things it contained and all of us. "If I thought you had in you the makings of an artist I shouldn't hesitate to beseech you to give up everything for art's sake. Art is the only thing that matters. In comparison with art, wealth and rank and power are not worth a row of pins." She gave us a look so sincere that it was void of insolence. "We are the only people who count. We give the world significance. You are only our raw material."

I was not too pleased to be included with the rest under that heading, but that is neither here nor there.

"Of course I can see that you've worked very hard. Don't think it's been wasted. It will always be a pleasure to you to be able to play the piano, and it will enable you to appreciate great playing as no ordinary person can hope to do. Look at your hands. They're not a pianist's hands."

Involuntarily I glanced at George's hands. I had never noticed them before. I was astounded to see how podgy they were and how short and stumpy the fingers.

"Your ear is not quite perfect. I don't think you can ever hope to be more than a very competent amateur. In art the difference between the amateur and the professional is immeasurable."

George did not reply. Except for his pallor no one would have known that he was listening to the blasting of all his hopes. The silence that fell was quite awful. Lea Makart's eyes suddenly filled with tears.

"But don't take my opinion alone," she said. "After all, I'm not infallible. Ask somebody else. You know how good and generous Paderewski is. I'll write to him about you and you can go down and play to him. I'm sure he'll hear you."

George now gave a little smile. He had very good manners and, whatever he was feeling, did not want to make the situation too difficult for others.

"I don't think that's necessary. I am content to accept your verdict. To tell you the truth it's not so very different from my master's in Munich."

He got up from the piano and lit a cigarette. It eased the

strain. The others moved a little in their chairs. Lea Makart smiled at George.

"Shall I play to you?" she said.

"Yes, do."

She got up and went to the piano. She took off the rings with which her fingers were laden. She played Bach. I do not know the names of the pieces, but I recognized the stiff ceremonial of the frenchified little German courts and the sober, thrifty comfort of the burghers, and the dancing on the village green, the green trees that looked like Christmas trees, and the sunlight on the wide German country, and a tender coziness; and in my nostrils there was a warm scent of the soil and I was conscious of a sturdy strength that seemed to have its roots deep in mother earth, and of an elemental power that was timeless and had no home in space. She played exquisitely, with a soft brilliance that made you think of the full moon shining at dusk in the summer sky. With another part of me I watched the others and I saw how intensely they were conscious of the experience. They were rapt. I wished with all my heart that I could get from music the wonderful exaltation that possessed them. She stopped, a smile hovered on her lips, and she put on her rings. George gave a little chuckle.

"That clinches it, I fancy," he said.

The servants brought in tea, and after tea Lea Makart and I bade the company farewell and got into the car. We drove up to London. She talked all the way, if not brilliantly at all events with immense gusto, she told me of her early years in Manchester and of the struggle of her beginnings. She was very interesting. She never even mentioned George; the episode was of no consequence; it was finished and she thought of it no more.

We little knew what was happening at Tilby. When we left, George went out on the terrace and presently his father joined him. Freddy had won the day, but he was not happy. With his more than feminine sensitiveness he felt all that George was feeling, and George's anguish simply broke his heart. He had never loved his son more than then. When he appeared George greeted him with a little smile. Freddy's voice broke. In a sudden and overwhelming emotion he found it in him to surrender the fruits of his victory.

"Look here, old boy," he said, "I can't bear to think that you've had such a disappointment. Would you like to go back to Munich for another year and then see?"

George shook his head.

"No, it wouldn't be any good. I've had my chance. Let's call it a day."

"Try not to take it too hard."

"You see, the only thing in the world I want is to be a pianist. And there's nothing doing. It's a bit thick if you come to think of it."

George, trying so hard to be brave, smiled wanly.

"Would you like to go round the world? You can get one of your Oxford pals to go with you and I'll pay all the expenses. You've been working very hard for a long time."

"Thanks awfully, Daddy, we'll talk about it. I'm just going for a stroll now."

"Shall I come with you?"

"I'd rather go alone."

Then George did a strange thing. He put his arm round his father's neck and kissed him on the lips. He gave a funny little moved laugh and walked away. Freddy went back to the drawing-room. His mother, Ferdy and Muriel were sitting there.

"Freddy, why don't you marry the boy?" said the old lady. "He is twenty-three. It would take his mind off his troubles and when he is married and has a baby he will soon settle down like everybody else."

"Who is he to marry, Mamma?" asked Sir Adolphus, smiling.

"That's not so difficult. Lady Frielinghausen came to see me the other day with her daughter Violet. She is a very nice maiden and she will have money of her own. Lady Frielinghausen gave me to understand that her Sir Jacob would come down very handsome if Violet made a good match."

Muriel flushed.

"I hate Lady Frielinghausen. George is much too young to marry. He can afford to marry anyone he likes."

Old Lady Bland gave her daughter a strange look.

"You are a very foolish girl, Miriam," she said, using the name Muriel had long discarded. "As long as I am here I shall not allow you to commit a foolishness."

She knew as well as if Muriel had said it in so many words that she wanted George to marry a Gentile, but she knew also that so long as she was alive neither Freddy nor his wife would dare to suggest it.

But George did not go for a walk. Perhaps because the

shooting season was about to open he took it into his head to go into the gun-room. He began to clean the gun that his mother had given him on his twentieth birthday. No one had used it since he went to Germany. Suddenly the servants were startled by a report. When they went into the gun-room they found George lying on the floor shot through the heart. Apparently the gun had been loaded and George while playing about with it had accidentally shot himself. One reads of such accidents in the paper often.

THE BOOK-BAG

SOME people read for instruction, which is praiseworthy, and
some for pleasure, which is innocent, but not a few read from
habit, and I suppose that this is neither innocent nor praiseworthy. Of that lamentable company am I. Conversation after
a time bores me, games tire me and my own thoughts, which
we are told are the unfailing resource of a sensible man, have
a tendency to run dry. Then I fly to my book as the opium-
smoker to his pipe. I would sooner read the catalogue of the
Army and Navy Stores or Bradshaw's Guide than nothing at all,
and indeed I have spent many delightful hours over both these
works. At one time I never went out without a second-hand
bookseller's list in my pocket. I know no reading more fruity.
Of course to read in this way is as reprehensible as doping, and
I never cease to wonder at the impertinence of great readers
who, because they are such, look down on the illiterate. From
the standpoint of what eternity is it better to have read a
thousand books than to have ploughed a million furrows? Let
us admit that reading with us is just a drug that we cannot do
without—who of this band does not know the restlessness that
attacks him when he has been severed from reading too long,
the apprehension and irritability, and the sigh of relief which the
sight of a printed page extracts from him?—and so let us be no
more vainglorious than the poor slaves of the hypodermic
needle or the pint-pot.

And like the dope-fiend who cannot move from place to place
without taking with him a plentiful supply of his deadly balm

I never venture far without a sufficiency of reading matter. Books are so necessary to me that when in a railway train I have become aware that fellow-travellers have come away without a single one I have been seized with a veritable dismay. But when I am starting on a long journey the problem is formidable. I have learnt my lesson. Once, imprisoned by illness for three months in a hill-town in Java, I came to the end of all the books I had brought with me, and knowing no Dutch was obliged to buy the school-books from which intelligent Javanese, I suppose, acquired knowledge of French and German. So I read again after five and twenty years the frigid plays of Goethe, the fables of La Fontaine and the tragedies of the tender and exact Racine. I have the greatest admiration for Racine, but I admit that to read his plays one after the other requires a certain effort in a person who is suffering from colitis. Since then I have made a point of travelling with the largest sack made for carrying soiled linen and filling it to the brim with books to suit every possible occasion and every mood. It weighs a ton and strong porters reel under its weight. Customhouse officials look at it askance, but recoil from it with consternation when I give them my word that it contains nothing but books. Its inconvenience is that the particular work I suddenly hanker to read is always at the bottom and it is impossible for me to get it without emptying the book-bag's entire contents upon the floor. Except for this, however, I should perhaps never have heard the singular history of Olive Hardy.

I was wandering about Malaya, staying here and there, a week or two if there was a rest-house or a hotel, and a day or so if I was obliged to inflict myself on a planter or a District Officer whose hospitality I had no wish to abuse; and at the moment I happened to be at Penang. It is a pleasant little town, with a hotel that has always seemed to me very agreeable, but the stranger finds little to do there and time hung a trifle heavily on my hands. One morning I received a letter from a man I knew only by name. This was Mark Featherstone. He was Acting Resident, in the absence on leave of the Resident, at a place called Tenggarah. There was a sultan there and it appeared that a water festival of some sort was to take place which Featherstone thought would interest me. He said that he would be glad if I would come and stay with him for a few days. I wired to tell him that I should be delighted and next day took the train to Tenggarah. Featherstone met me at the station.

He was a man of about thirty-five, I should think, tall and handsome, with fine eyes and a strong, stern face. He had a wiry black moustache and bushy eyebrows. He looked more like a soldier than a government official. He was very smart in white ducks, with a white topi, and he wore his clothes with elegance. He was a little shy, which seemed odd in a strapping fellow of resolute mien, but I surmised that this was only because he was unused to the society of that strange fish, a writer, and I hoped in a little to put him at his ease.

"My boys'll look after your barang," he said. "We'll go down to the club. Give them your keys and they'll unpack before we get back."

I told him that I had a good deal of luggage and thought it better to leave everything at the station but what I particularly wanted. He would not hear of it.

"It doesn't matter a bit. It'll be safer at my house. It's always better to have one's barang with one."

"All right."

I gave my keys and the ticket for my trunk and my book-bag to a Chinese boy who stood at my host's elbow. Outside the station a car was waiting for us and we stepped in.

"Do you play bridge?" asked Featherstone.

"I do."

"I thought most writers didn't."

"They don't," I said. "It's generally considered among authors a sign of deficient intelligence to play cards."

The club was a bungalow, pleasing but unpretentious; it had a large reading-room, a billiard-room with one table, and a small card-room. When we arrived it was empty but for one or two persons reading the English weeklies, and we walked through to the tennis courts where a couple of sets were being played. A number of people were sitting on the verandah, looking on, smoking and sipping long drinks. I was introduced to one or two of them. But the light was failing and soon the players could hardly see the ball. Featherstone asked one of the men I had been introduced to if he would like a rubber. He said he would. Featherstone looked about for a fourth. He caught sight of a man sitting a little by himself, paused for a second, and went up to him. The two exchanged a few words and then came towards us. We strolled in to the card-room. We had a very nice game. I did not pay much attention to the two men who made up the four. They stood me drinks, and I, a temporary member of the club, returned the compliment. The drinks were very small, quarter whiskies, and in the two hours we played each of us was able to show his open-handedness without an excessive consumption of alcohol. When the advancing hour suggested that the next rubber must be the last we changed from whisky to gin pahits. The rubber came to an end. Featherstone called for the book and the winnings and losings of each one of us were set down. One of the men got up.

"Well, I must be going," he said.

"Going back to the Estate?" asked Featherstone.

"Yes," he nodded. He turned to me. "Shall you be here to-morrow?"

"I hope so."

He went out of the room.

"I'll collect my mem and get along home to dinner," said the other.

"We might be going too," said Featherstone.

"I'm ready whenever you are," I replied.

We got into the car and drove to his house. It was a longish drive. In the darkness I could see nothing much, but presently I realized that we were going up a rather steep hill. We reached the Residency.

It had been an evening like any other, pleasant, but not at all exciting, and I had spent I don't know how many just like it. I did not expect it to leave any sort of impression on me.

Featherstone led me into his sitting-room. It looked comfortable, but it was a trifle ordinary. It had large basket armchairs covered with cretonne and on the walls were a great many framed photographs; the tables were littered with papers, magazines and official reports, with pipes, yellow tins of straight-cut cigarettes and pink tins of tobacco. In a row of shelves were untidily stacked a good many books, their bindings stained with damp and the ravages of white ants. Featherstone showed me my room and left me with the words:

"Shall you be ready for a gin pahit in ten minutes?"

"Easily," I said.

I had a bath and changed and went downstairs. Featherstone, ready before me, mixed our drink as he heard me clatter down the wooden staircase. We dined. We talked. The festival which I had been invited to see was the next day but one, but Featherstone told me he had arranged for me before that to be received by the Sultan.

"He's a jolly old boy," he said. "And the palace is a sight for sore eyes."

After dinner we talked a little more, Featherstone put on the gramophone, and we looked at the latest illustrated papers that had arrived from England. Then we went to bed. Featherstone came to my room to see that I had everything I wanted.

"I suppose you haven't any books with you," he said. "I haven't got a thing to read."

"Books?" I cried.

I pointed to my book-bag. It stood upright, bulging oddly, so that it looked like a humpbacked gnome somewhat the worse for liquor.

"Have you got books in there? I thought that was your dirty linen or a camp-bed or something. Is there anything you can lend me?"

"Look for yourself."

Featherstone's boys had unlocked the bag, but quailing before the sight that then discovered itself had done no more. I knew from long experience how to unpack it. I threw it over on its side, seized its leather bottom and, walking backwards, dragged the sack away from its contents. A river of books poured on to the floor. A look of stupefaction came upon Featherstone's face.

"You don't mean to say you travel with as many books as that? By George, what a snip."

He bent down and turning them over rapidly looked at the titles. There were books of all kinds. Volumes of verse, novels, philosophical works, critical studies (they say books about books are profitless, but they certainly make very pleasant reading), biographies, history; there were books to read when you were ill and books to read when your brain, all alert, craved for something to grapple with, there were books that you had always wanted to read, but in the hurry of life at home had never found time to, there were books to read at sea when you were meandering through narrow waters on a tramp steamer, and there were books for bad weather when your whole cabin creaked and you had to wedge yourself in your bunk in order not to fall out; there were books chosen solely for their length, which you took with you when on some expedition you had to travel light, and there were the books you could read when you could read nothing else. Finally Featherstone picked out a life of Byron that had recently appeared.

"Hullo, what's this?" he said. "I read a review of it some time ago."

"I believe it's very good," I replied. "I haven't read it yet."

"May I take it? It'll do me for to-night at all events."

"Of course. Take anything you like."

"No, that's enough. Well, good-night. Breakfast at eight-thirty."

When I came down next morning the head boy told me that Featherstone, who had been at work since six, would be in shortly. While I waited for him I glanced at his shelves.

"I see you've got a grand library of books on bridge," I remarked as we sat down to breakfast.

"Yes, I get every one that comes out. I'm very keen on it."

"That fellow we were playing with yesterday plays a good game."

"Which? Hardy?"

"I don't know. Not the one who said he was going to collect his wife. The other."

"Yes, that was Hardy. That was why I asked him to play. He doesn't come to the club very often."

"I hope he will to-night."

"I wouldn't bank on it. He has an estate about thirty miles away. It's a longish ride to come just for a rubber of bridge."

"Is he married?"

"No. Well, yes. But his wife is in England."

"It must be awfully lonely for those men who live by themselves on those estates," I said.

"Oh, he's not so badly off as some. I don't think he much cares about seeing people. I think he'd be just as lonely in London."

There was something in the way Featherstone spoke that struck me as a little strange. His voice had what I can only describe as a shuttered tone. He seemed suddenly to have moved away from me. It was as though one were passing along a street at night and paused for a second to look in at a lighted window that showed a comfortable room and suddenly an invisible hand pulled down a blind. His eyes, which habitually met those of the person he was talking to with frankness, now avoided mine and I had a notion that it was not only my fancy that read in his face an expression of pain. It was drawn for a moment as it might be by a twinge of neuralgia. I could not think of anything to say and Featherstone did not speak. I was conscious that his thoughts, withdrawn from me and what we were about, were turned upon a subject unknown to me. Presently he gave a little sigh, very slight, but unmistakable, and seemed with a deliberate effort to pull himself together.

"I'm going down to the office immediately after breakfast," he said. "What are you going to do with yourself?"

"Oh, don't bother about me. I shall slack around. I'll stroll down and look at the town."

"There's not much to see."

"All the better. I'm fed up with sights."

I found that Featherstone's verandah gave me sufficient entertainment for the morning. It had one of the most enchanting views I had seen in the F.M.S. The Residency was built on the top of a hill and the garden was large and well-cared for. Great trees gave it almost the look of an English park. It had vast lawns and there Tamils, black and emaciated, were scything with deliberate and beautiful gestures. Beyond and below, the jungle grew thickly to the bank of a broad, winding and swiftly flowing river, and on the other side of this, as far as the eye could reach, stretched the wooded hills of Tenggarah. The contrast between the trim lawns, so strangely English, and the savage growth of the jungle beyond pleasantly titillated the fancy. I sat and read and smoked. It is my business to be curious about people and I asked myself how the peace of this scene, charged nevertheless with a tremulous and dark significance, affected Featherstone who lived with it. He knew it under every aspect: at dawn when the mist rising fror the river shrouded it with a ghostly pall; in the splendour of noon; and at last when the shadowy gloaming crept softly out of the jungle, like an army making its way with caution in unknown country, and presently enveloped the green lawns and the great flowering trees and the flaunting cassias in the silent night. I wondered whether, unbeknownst to him, the tender and yet strangely sinister aspect of the scene, acting on his nerves and his loneliness, imbued him with some mystical quality so that the life he led, the life of the capable administrator, the sportsman and the good fellow, on occasion seemed to him not quite real. I smiled at my own fancies, for certainly the conversation we had had the night before had not indicated in him any stirrings of the soul. I had thought him quite nice. He had been at Oxford and was a member of a good London club. He seemed to attach a good deal of importance to social things. He was a gentleman

and slightly conscious of the fact that he belonged to a better
class than most of the Englishmen his life brought him in contact with. I gathered from the various silver pots that adorned
his dining-room that he excelled in games. He played tennis
and billiards. When he went on leave he hunted and, anxious
to keep his weight down, he dieted carefully. He talked a good
deal of what he would do when he retired. He hankered after
the life of a country gentleman. A little house in Leicestershire,
a couple of hunters and neighbours to play bridge with. He
would have his pension and he had a little money of his own.
But meanwhile he worked hard and did his work, if not brilliantly, certainly with competence. I have no doubt that he
was looked upon by his superiors as a reliable officer. He was
cut upon a pattern that I knew too well to find very interesting.
He was like a novel that is careful, honest and efficient, yet a
little ordinary, so that you seem to have read it all before, and
you turn the pages listlessly knowing that it will never afford
you a surprise or move you to excitement.

But human beings are incalculable and he is a fool who tells
himself that he knows what a man is capable of.

In the afternoon Featherstone took me to see the Sultan.
We were received by one of his sons, a shy, smiling youth who
acted as his A.D.C. He was dressed in a neat blue suit, but
round his waist he wore a sarong, white flowers on a yellow
ground, on his head a red fez, and on his feet knobby American
shoes. The palace, built in the Moorish style, was like a very
big doll's house and it was painted bright yellow, which is the
royal colour. We were led into a spacious room, furnished with
the sort of furniture you would find in an English lodging-house
at the seaside, but the chairs were covered with yellow silk.
On the floor was a Brussels carpet and on the walls photographs
in very grand gilt frames of the Sultan at various state functions. In a cabinet was a large collection of all kinds of fruit
done entirely in crochet work. The Sultan came in with several
attendants. He was a man of fifty, perhaps, short and stout,
dressed in trousers and tunic of a large white and yellow check;
round his middle he wore a very beautiful yellow sarong and on
his head a white fez. He had large, handsome, friendly eyes. He
gave us coffee to drink, sweet cakes to eat and cheroots to
smoke. Conversation was not difficult, for he was affable, and
he told me that he had never been to a theatre or played cards,
for he was very religious, and he had four wives and twenty-

four children. The only bar to the happiness of his life seemed
to be that common decency obliged him to divide his time
equally between his four wives. He said that an hour with one
was a month and with another five minutes. I remarked that
Professor Einstein—or was it Bergson?—had made similar
observations upon time and indeed on this question had given
the world much to ponder over. Presently we took our leave and
the Sultan presented me with some beautiful white Malaccas.

In the evening we went to the club. One of the men we had
played with the day before got up from his chair as we entered.

"Ready for a rubber?" he said.

"Where's our fourth?" I asked.

"Oh, there are several fellows here who'll be glad to play."

"What about that man we played with yesterday?" I had
forgotten his name.

"Hardy? He's not here."

"It's not worth while waiting for him," said Featherstone.

"He very seldom comes to the club. I was surprised to see
him last night."

I did not know why I had the impression that behind the
very ordinary words of these two men there was an odd sense
of embarrassment. Hardy had made no impression on me and
I did not even remember what he looked like. He was just a
fourth at the bridge table. I had a feeling that they had something against him. It was no business of mine and I was quite
content to play with a man who at that moment joined us. We
certainly had a more cheerful game than before. A good deal of
chaff passed from one side of the table to the other. We played
less serious bridge. We laughed. I wondered if it was only that
they were less shy of the stranger who had happened in upon
them or if the presence of Hardy had caused in the other two
a certain constraint. At half-past eight we broke up and Featherstone and I went back to dine at his house.

After dinner we lounged in arm-chairs and smoked cheroots.
For some reason our conversation did not flow easily. I tried
topic after topic, but could not get Featherstone to interest
himself in any of them. I began to think that in the last twenty-
four hours he had said all he had to say. I fell somewhat discouraged into silence. It prolonged itself and again, I did not
know why, I had a faint sensation that it was charged with a
significance that escaped me. I felt slightly uncomfortable. I
had that queer feeling that one sometimes has when sitting in

an empty room that one is not by oneself. Presently I was conscious that Featherstone was steadily looking at me. I was sitting by a lamp, but he was in shadow so that the play of his features was hidden from me. But he had very large brilliant eyes and in the half darkness they seemed to shine dimly. They were like new boot-buttons that caught a reflected light. I wondered why he looked at me like that. I gave him a glance and catching his eyes insistently fixed upon me faintly smiled.

"Interesting book that one you lent me last night," he said suddenly, and I could not help thinking his voice did not sound quite natural. The words issued from his lips as though they were pushed from behind.

"Oh, the Life of Byron?" I said breezily. "Have you read it already?"

"A good deal of it. I read till three."

"I've heard it's very well done. I'm not sure that Byron interests me so much as all that. There was so much in him that was so frightfully second-rate. It makes one rather uncomfortable."

"What do you think is the real truth of that story about him and his sister?"

"Augusta Leigh? I don't know very much about it. I've never read Astarte."

"Do you think they were really in love with one another?"

"I suppose so. Isn't it generally believed that she was the only woman he ever genuinely loved?"

"Can you understand it?"

"I can't really. It doesn't particularly shock me. It just seems to me very unnatural. Perhaps 'unnatural' isn't the right word. It's incomprehensible to me. I can't throw myself into the state of feeling in which such a thing seems possible. You know, that's how a writer gets to know the people he writes about, by standing himself in their shoes and feeling with their hearts."

I knew I did not make myself very clear, but I was trying to describe a sensation, an action of the subconscious, which from experience was perfectly familiar to me, but which no words I knew could precisely indicate. I went on.

"Of course she was only his half-sister, but just as habit kills love I should have thought habit would prevent its arising. When two persons have known one another all their lives and lived together in close contact I can't imagine how or why that sudden spark should flash that results in love. The probabilities are that they would be joined by mutual affection and I don't know anything that is more contrary to love than affection."

I could just see in the dimness the outline of a smile flicker for a moment on my host's heavy, and it seemed to me then, somewhat saturnine face.

"You only believe in love at first sight?"

"Well, I suppose I do, but with the proviso that people may have met twenty times before seeing one another. 'Seeing' has an active side and a passive one. Most people we run across mean so little to us that we never bestir ourselves to look at them. We just suffer the impression they make on us."

"Oh, but one's often heard of couples who've known one another for years and it's never occurred to one they cared two straws for each other and suddenly they go and get married. How do you explain that?"

"Well, if you're going to bully me into being logical and consistent, I should suggest that their love is of a different kind. After all, passion isn't the only reason for marriage. It may not even be the best one. Two people may marry because they're lonely or because they're good friends or for convenience' sake. Though I said that affection was the greatest enemy of love, I would never deny that it's a very good substitute. I'm not sure that a marriage founded on it isn't the happiest."

"What did you think of Tim Hardy?"

I was a little surprised at the sudden question, which seemed to have nothing to do with the subject of our conversation.

"I didn't think of him very much. He seemed quite nice. Why?"

"Did he seem to you just like everybody else?"

"Yes. Is there anything peculiar about him? If you'd told me that I'd have paid more attention to him."

"He's very quiet, isn't he? I suppose no one who knew nothing about him would give him a second thought."

I tried to remember what he looked like. The only thing that had struck me when we were playing cards was that he had fine hands. It passed idly through my mind that they were not the sort of hands I should have expected a planter to have. But why a planter should have different hands from anybody else I did not trouble to ask myself. His were somewhat large, but very well formed, with peculiarly long fingers, and the nails were of an admirable shape. They were virile and yet oddly sensitive hands. I noticed this and thought no more about it. But if you are a writer, instinct and the habit of years enable you to store up impressions that you are not aware of. Sometimes of course they do not correspond with the facts and a woman for example may remain in your subconsciousness as a dark, massive and ox-eyed creature when she is indeed rather small and of a nondescript colouring. But that is of no consequence. The impression may very well be more exact than the sober truth. And now, seeking to call up from the depths of me a picture of this man I had a feeling of some ambiguity. He was clean-shaven and his face, oval but not thin, seemed strangely pale under the tan of long exposure to the tropical sun. His features were vague. I did not know whether I remembered it or only imagined now that his rounded chin gave one the impression of a certain weakness. He had thick brown hair, just turning grey, and a long wisp fell down constantly over his forehead. He pushed it back with a gesture that had become habitual. His brown eyes were rather large and gentle, but perhaps a little sad; they had a melting softness which, I could imagine, might be very appealing.

After a pause Featherstone continued:

"It's rather strange that I should run across Tim Hardy here after all these years. But that's the way of the F.M.S. People move about and you find yourself in the same place as a man you'd known years before in another part of the country. I first knew Tim when he had an estate near Sibuku. Have you ever been there?"

"No. Where is it?"

"Oh, it's up north. Towards Siam. It wouldn't be worth your while to go. It's just like every other place in the F.M.S. But it was rather nice. It had a very jolly little club and there were some quite decent people. There was the schoolmaster and the head of the police, the doctor, the padre and the government engineer. The usual lot, you know. A few planters. Three or four women. I was A.D.O. It was one of my first jobs. Tim Hardy had an estate about twenty-five miles away. He lived there with his sister. They had a bit of money of their own and he'd bought the place. Rubber was pretty good then and he wasn't doing at all badly. We rather cottoned on to one another. Of course it's a toss-up with planters. Some of them are very good fellows, but they're not exactly . . ." he sought for a word or a phrase that did not sound snobbish. "Well, they're not the sort of people you'd be likely to meet at home. Tim and Olive were of one's own class, if you understand what I mean."

"Olive was the sister?"

"Yes. They'd had a rather unfortunate past. Their parents had separated when they were quite small, seven or eight, and the mother had taken Olive and the father had kept Tim. Tim went to Clifton, they were West Country people, and only came home for the holidays. His father was a retired naval man who lived at Fowey. But Olive went with her mother to Italy. She was educated in Florence; she spoke Italian perfectly and French too. For all those years Tim and Olive never saw one another once, but they used to write to one another regularly. They'd been very much attached when they were children. As far as I could understand, life when their people were living together had been rather stormy with all sorts of scenes and upsets, you know the sort of thing that happens when two people who are married don't get on together, and that had thrown them on their own resources. They were left a good deal to themselves. Then Mrs. Hardy died and Olive came home to England and went back to her father. She was eighteen then and Tim was seventeen. A year later the war broke out, Tim joined up and his father, who was over fifty, got some job at Portsmouth. I take it he had been a hard liver and a heavy drinker. He broke down before the end of the war and died after a lingering illness. They don't seem to have had any relations. They were the last of a rather old family; they had a fine old house in Dorsetshire that had belonged to them for a good many generations, but they had never been able to afford to live in it and it was always let. I remember seeing photographs of it. It was very much a gentleman's house, of grey stone and rather stately, with a coat of arms carved over the front door and mullioned windows. Their great ambition was to make enough money to be able to live in it. They used to talk about it a lot. They never spoke as though either of them would marry, but always as though it were a settled thing that they would remain together. It was rather funny considering how young they were."

"How old were they then?" I asked.

"Well, I suppose he was twenty-five or twenty-six and she was a year older. They were awfully kind to me when I first went up to Sibuku. They took a fancy to me at once. You see, we had more in common than most of the people there. I think they were glad of my company. They weren't particularly popular."

"Why not?" I asked.

"They were rather reserved and you couldn't help seeing that they liked their own society better than other people's. I don't know if you've noticed it, but that always seems to put people's backs up. They resent it somehow if they have a feeling that you can get along very well without them."

"It's tiresome, isn't it?" I said.

"It was rather a grievance to the other planters that Tim was his own master and had private means. They had to put up with an old Ford to get about in, but Tim had a real car. Tim and Olive were very nice when they came to the club and they played in the tennis tournaments and all that sort of thing, but you had an impression that they were always glad to get away again. They'd dine out with people and make themselves very pleasant, but it was pretty obvious that they'd just as soon have stayed at home. If you had any sense you couldn't blame them. I don't know if you've been much to planters' houses. They're a bit dreary. A lot of gimcrack furniture and silver ornaments and tiger skins. And the food's uneatable. But the Hardys had made their bungalow rather nice. There was nothing very grand in it; it was just easy and homelike and comfortable. Their living-room was like a drawing-room in an English country house. You felt that their things meant something to them and that they had had them a long time. It was a very jolly house to stay at. The bungalow was in the middle of the estate, but it was on the brow of a little hill and you looked right over the rubber trees to the sea in the distance. Olive took a lot of trouble with her garden and it was really topping. I never saw such a show of cannas. I used to go there for week-ends. It was only about half an hour's drive to the sea and we'd take our lunch with us and bathe and sail. Tim kept a small boat there. Those days were grand. I never knew one could enjoy oneself so much. It's a beautiful bit of coast and it was really extraordinarily romantic. Then in the evenings we'd play patience and chess or turn on the gramophone. The cooking was damned good too. It was a change from what one generally got. Olive had taught their cook to make all sorts of Italian dishes and we used to have great wallops of macaroni and risotto and gnocchi and things like that. I couldn't help envying them their life, it was so jolly and peaceful, and when they talked of what they'd do when they went back to England for good I used to tell them they'd always regret what they'd left.

"'We've been very happy here,' said Olive.

"She had a way of looking at Tim, with a slow, sidelong glance from under her long eyelashes, that was rather engaging.

"In their own house they were quite different from what they were when they went out. They were so easy and cordial. Everybody admitted that and I'm bound to say that people enjoyed going there. They often asked people over. They had the gift of making you feel at home. It was a very happy house, if you know what I mean. Of course no one could help seeing how attached they were to one another. And whatever people said about their being standoffish and self-centred, they were bound to be rather touched by the affection they had for one another. People said they couldn't have been more united if they were married, and when you saw how some couples got on you couldn't help thinking they made most marriages look rather like a wash-out. They seemed to think the same things at the same time. They had little private jokes that made them laugh like children. They were so charming with one another, so gay and happy, that really to stay with them was, well, a spiritual refreshment. I don't know what else you could call it. When you left them, after a couple of days at the bungalow, you felt that you'd absorbed some of their peace and their sober gaiety. It was as though your soul had been sluiced with cool clear water. You felt strangely purified."

It was singular to hear Featherstone talking in this exalted strain. He looked so spruce in his smart white coat, technically known as a bum-freezer, his moustache was so trim, his thick curly hair so carefully brushed, that his high-flown language made me a trifle uncomfortable. But I realized that he was trying to express in his clumsy way a very sincerely felt emotion.

"What was Olive Hardy like?" I asked.

"I'll show you. I've got quite a lot of snapshots."

He got up from his chair and going to a shelf brought me a large album. It was the usual thing, indifferent photographs of people in groups and unflattering likenesses of single figures. They were in bathing dress or in shorts or tennis things, generally with their faces all screwed up because the sun blinded them, or puckered by the distortion of laughter. I recognized

Hardy, not much changed after ten years, with his wisp of hair hanging across his forehead. I remembered him better now that I saw the snapshots. In them he looked nice and fresh and young. He had an alertness of expression that was attractive and that I certainly had not noticed when I saw him. In his eyes was a sort of eagerness for life that danced and sparkled through the fading print. I glanced at the photographs of his sister. Her bathing dress showed that she had a good figure, well-developed, but slender; and her legs were long and slim.

"They look rather alike," I said.

"Yes, although she was a year older they might have been twins, they were so much alike. They both had the same oval face and that pale skin without any colour in the cheeks, and they both had those soft brown eyes, very liquid and appealing, so that you felt whatever they did you could never be angry with them. And they both had a sort of careless elegance that made them look charming whatever they wore and however untidy they were. He's lost that now, I suppose, but he certainly had it when I first knew him. They always rather reminded me of the brother and sister in Twelfth Night. You know whom I mean."

"Viola and Sebastian."

"They never seemed to belong quite to the present. There was something Elizabethan about them. I don't think it was only because I was very young then that I couldn't help feeling they were strangely romantic somehow. I could see them living in Illyria."

I gave one of the snapshots another glance.

"The girl looks as though she had a good deal more character than her brother," I remarked.

"She had. I don't know if you'd have called Olive beautiful, but she was awfully attractive. There was something poetic in her, a sort of lyrical quality as it were, that coloured her movements, her acts and everything about her. It seemed to exalt her above common cares. There was something so candid in her expression, so courageous and independent in her bearing, that—oh, I don't know, it made mere beauty just flat and dull."

"You speak as if you'd been in love with her," I interrupted.

"Of course I was. I should have thought you'd guessed that at once. I was frightfully in love with her."

"Was it love at first sight?" I smiled.

"Yes, I think it was, but I didn't know it for a month or so.

When it suddenly struck me that what I felt for her—I don't know how to explain it, it was a sort of shattering turmoil that affected every bit of me—that that was love, I knew I'd felt it all along. It was not only her looks, though they were awfully alluring, the smoothness of her pale skin and the way her hair fell over her forehead and the grave sweetness of her brown eyes, it was more than that; you had a sensation of well-being when you were with her, as though you could relax and be quite natural and needn't pretend to be anything you weren't. You felt she was incapable of meanness. It was impossible to think of her as envious of other people or catty. She seemed to have a natural generosity of soul. One could be silent with her for an hour at a time and yet feel that one had had a good time."

"A rare gift," I said.

"She was a wonderful companion. If you made a suggestion to do something she was always glad to fall in with it. She was the least exacting girl I ever knew. You could throw her over at the last minute and however disappointed she was it made no difference. Next time you saw her she was just as cordial and serene as ever."

"Why didn't you marry her?"

Featherstone's cheroot had gone out. He threw the stub away and deliberately lit another. He did not answer for a while. It may seem strange to persons who live in a highly civilized state that he should confide these intimate things to a stranger; it did not seem strange to me. I was used to it. People who live so desperately alone, in the remote places of the earth, find it a relief to tell someone whom in all probability they will never meet again the story that has burdened perhaps for years their waking thoughts and their dreams at night. And I have an inkling that the fact of your being a writer attracts their confidence. They feel that what they tell you will excite your interest in an impersonal way that makes it easier for them to discharge their souls. Besides, as we all know from our own experience, it is never unpleasant to talk about oneself.

"Why didn't you marry her?" I had asked him.

"I wanted to badly enough," Featherstone answered at length. "But I hesitated to ask her. Although she was always so nice to me and so easy to get on with, and we were such good friends, I always felt that there was something a little mysterious in her. Although she was so simple, so frank and

natural, you never quite got over the feeling of an inner kernel
of aloofness, as if deep in her heart she guarded, not a secret,
but a sort of privacy of the soul that not a living person would
ever be allowed to know. I don't know if I make myself clear."

"I think so."

"I put it down to her upbringing. They never talked of
their mother, but somehow I got the impression that she was
one of those neurotic, emotional women who wreck their own
happiness and are a pest to everyone connected with them. I
had a suspicion that she'd led rather a hectic life in Florence
and it struck me that Olive owed her beautiful serenity to a
disciplined effort of her own will and that her aloofness was a
sort of citadel she'd built to protect herself from the knowledge
of all sorts of shameful things. But of course that aloofness was
awfully captivating. It was strangely exciting to think that
if she loved you, and you were married to her, you would
at last pierce right into the hidden heart of that mystery; and
you felt that if you could share that with her it would be as it
were a consummation of all you'd ever desired in your life.
Heaven wouldn't be in it. You know, I felt about it just like
Bluebeard's wife about the forbidden chamber in the castle.
Every room was open to me, but I should never rest till I had
gone into that last one that was locked against me."

My eye was caught by a chik-chak, a little brown house
lizard with a large head, high up on the wall. It is a friendly
little beast and it is good to see it in a house. It watched a fly.
It was quite still. On a sudden it made a dart and then as
the fly flew away fell back with a sort of jerk into a strange
immobility.

"And there was another thing that made me hesitate. I
couldn't bear the thought that if I proposed to her and she
refused me she wouldn't let me come to the bungalow in the
same old way. I should have hated that, I enjoyed going there
so awfully. It made me so happy to be with her. But you know,
sometimes one can't help oneself. I did ask her at last, but it was
almost by accident. One evening, after dinner, when we were
sitting on the verandah by ourselves, I took her hand. She withdrew it at once.

"'Why did you do that?" I asked her.

"'I don't very much like being touched,' she said. She
turned her head a little and smiled. 'Are you hurt? You mustn't
mind, it's just a funny feeling I have. I can't help it.'

"'I wonder if it's ever occurred to you that I'm frightfully fond of you,' I said.

"I expect I was terribly awkward about it, but I'd never proposed to anyone before." Featherstone gave a little sound that was not quite a chuckle and not quite a sigh. "For the matter of that, I've never proposed to anyone since. She didn't say anything for a minute. Then she said:

"'I'm very glad, but I don't think I want you to be anything more than that.'

"'Why not?' I asked.

"'I could never leave Tim.'

"'But supposing he marries?'

"'He never will.'

"I'd gone so far then that I thought I'd better go on. But my throat was so dry that I could hardly speak. I was shaking with nervousness.

"'I'm frightfully in love with you, Olive. I want to marry you more than anything in the world.'

"She put her hand very gently on my arm. It was like a flower falling to the ground.

"'No, dear, I can't,' she said.

"I was silent. It was difficult for me to say what I wanted to. I'm naturally rather shy. She was a girl. I couldn't very well tell her that it wasn't quite the same thing living with a husband and living with a brother. She was normal and healthy; she must want to have babies; it wasn't reasonable to starve her natural instincts. It was such waste of her youth. But it was she who spoke first.

"'Don't let's talk about this any more,' she said. 'D'you mind? It did strike me once or twice that perhaps you cared for me. Tim noticed it. I was sorry because I was afraid it would break up our friendship. I don't want it to do that, Mark. We do get on so well together, the three of us, and we have such jolly times. I don't know what we should do without you now.'

"'I thought of that too,' I said.

"'D'you think it need?' she asked me.

"'My dear, I don't want it to,' I said. 'You must know how much I love coming here. I've never been so happy anywhere before!'

"'You're not angry with me?'

"'Why should I be? It's not your fault. It only means that

you're not in love with me. If you were you wouldn't care a
hang about Tim.'

"'You are rather sweet,' she said.

"She put her arm round my neck and kissed me lightly on
the cheek. I had a notion that in her mind it settled our relation. She adopted me as a second brother.

"A few weeks later Tim went back to England. The tenant
of their house in Dorset was leaving and though there was
another in the offing, he thought he ought to be on the spot to
conduct negotiations. And he wanted some new machinery for
the estate. He thought he'd get it at the same time. He didn't
expect to be gone more than three months and Olive made
up her mind not to go. She knew hardly anyone in England,
and it was practically a foreign country to her, she didn't mind
being left alone, and she wanted to look after the estate. Of
course they could have put a manager in charge, but that wasn't
the same thing. Rubber was falling and in case of accidents
it was just as well that one or other of them should be there. I
promised Tim I'd look after her and if she wanted me she
could always call me up. My proposal hadn't changed anything.
We carried on as though nothing had happened. I don't know
whether she'd told Tim. He made no sign that he knew. Of
course I loved her as much as ever, but I kept it to myself. I
have a good deal of self-control, you know. I had a sort of feeling
I hadn't a chance. I hoped eventually my love would change
into something else and we could just be wonderful friends.
It's funny, it never has, you know. I suppose I was hit too
badly ever to get quite over it.

"She went down to Penang to see Tim off and when she
came back I met her at the station and drove her home. I
couldn't very well stay at the bungalow while Tim was away,
but I went over every Sunday and had tiffin and we'd go
down to the sea and have a bathe. People tried to be kind to
her and asked her to stay with them, but she wouldn't. She
seldom left the estate. She had plenty to do. She read a lot.
She was never bored. She seemed quite happy in her own
company, and when she had visitors it was only from a sense
of duty. She didn't want them to think her ungracious. But
it was an effort and she told me she heaved a sigh of relief
when she saw the last of them and could again enjoy without
disturbance the peaceful loneliness of the bungalow. She was
a very curious girl. It was strange that at her age she should

be so indifferent to parties and the other small gaieties the station afforded. Spiritually, if you know what I mean, she was entirely self-supporting. I don't know how people found out that I was in love with her; I thought I'd never given myself away in anything, but I had hints here and there that they knew. I gathered they thought Olive hadn't gone home with her brother on my account. One woman, a Mrs. Sergison, the policeman's wife, actually asked me when they were going to be able to congratulate me. Of course I pretended I didn't know what she was talking about, but it didn't go down very well. I couldn't help being amused. I meant so little to Olive in that way that I really believe she'd entirely forgotten that I'd asked her to marry me. I can't say she was unkind to me, I don't think she could have been unkind to anyone; but she treated me with just the casualness with which a sister might treat a younger brother. She was two or three years older than I. She was always terribly glad to see me, but it never occurred to her to put herself out for me, she was almost amazingly intimate with me; but unconsciously, you know, as you might be with a person you'd known so well all your life that you never thought of putting on frills with him. I might not have been a man at all, but an old coat that she wore all the time because it was easy and comfortable and she didn't mind what she did in it. I should have been crazy not to see that she was a thousand miles away from loving me.

"Then one day, three or four weeks before Tim was due back, when I went to the bungalow I saw she'd been crying. I was startled. She was always so composed. I'd never seen her upset over anything.

"'Hullo, what's the matter?' I said.

"'Nothing.'

"'Come off it, darling,' I said. 'What have you been crying about?'

"She tried to smile.

"'I wish you hadn't got such sharp eyes,' she said. 'I think I'm being silly. I've just had a cable from Tim to say he's postponed his sailing.'

"'Oh, my dear, I am sorry,' I said. 'You must be awfully disappointed.'

"'I've been counting the days. I want him back so badly.'

"'Does he say why he's postponing?' I asked.

"'No, he says he's writing. I'll show you the cable.'

"I saw that she was very nervous. Her slow quiet eyes were filled with apprehension and there was a little frown of anxiety between her brows. She went into her bedroom and in a moment came back with the cable. I felt that she was watching me anxiously as I read. So far as I remember it ran: *Darling, I cannot sail on the seventh after all. Please forgive me. Am writing fully. Fondest love. Tim.*

"'Well, perhaps the machinery he wanted isn't ready and he can't bring himself to sail without it,' I said.

"'What could it matter if it came by a later ship? Anyhow, it'll be hung up at Penang.'

"'It may be something about the house.'

"'If it is why doesn't he say so? He must know how frightfully anxious I am.'

"'It wouldn't occur to him,' I said. 'After all, when you're away you don't realize that the people you've left behind don't know something that you take as a matter of course.'

"She smiled again, but now more happily.

"'I daresay you're right. In point of fact Tim is a little like that. He's always been rather slack and casual. I daresay I've been making a mountain out of a molehill. I must just wait patiently for his letter.'

"Olive was a girl with a lot of self-control and I saw her by an effort of will pull herself together. The little line between her eyebrows vanished and she was once more her serene, smiling and kindly self. She was always gentle: that day she had a mildness so heavenly that it was shattering. But for the rest of the time I could see that she kept her restlessness in check only by the deliberate exercise of her common sense. It was as though she had a foreboding of ill. I was with her the day before the mail was due. Her anxiety was all the more pitiful to see because she took such pains to hide it. I was always busy on mail day, but I promised to go up to the estate later on and hear the news. I was just thinking of starting when Hardy's seis came along in the car with a message from the amah asking me to go at once to her mistress. The amah was a decent, elderly woman to whom I had given a dollar or two and said that if anything went wrong on the estate she was to let me know at once. I jumped into my car. When I arrived I found the amah waiting for me on the steps.

"'A letter came this morning,' she said.

"I interrupted her. I ran up the steps. The sitting-room was empty.

"'Olive,' I called.

"I went into the passage and suddenly I heard a sound that froze my heart. The amah had followed me and now she opened the door of Olive's room. The sound I had heard was the sound of Olive crying. I went in. She was lying on her bed, on her face, and her sobs shook her from head to foot. I put my hand on her shoulder.

"'Olive, what is it?' I asked.

"'Who's that?' she cried. She sprang to her feet suddenly, as though she were scared out of her wits. And then: 'Oh, it's you,' she said. She stood in front of me, with her head thrown back and her eyes closed, and the tears streamed from them. It was dreadful. 'Tim's married,' she gasped, and her face screwed up in a sort of grimace of pain.

"I must admit that for one moment I had a thrill of exultation, it was like a little electric shock tingling through my heart; it struck me that now I had a chance, she might be willing to marry me; I know it was terribly selfish of me; you see, the news had taken me by surprise; but it was only for a moment, after that I was melted by her awful distress and the only thing I felt was deep sorrow because she was unhappy. I put my arm round her waist.

"'Oh, my dear, I'm so sorry,' I said. 'Don't stay here. Come into the sitting-room and sit down and we'll talk about it. Let me give you something to drink.'

"She let me lead her into the next room and we sat down on the sofa. I told the amah to fetch the whisky and syphon and I mixed her a good strong stengah and made her drink a little. I took her in my arms and rested her head on my shoulder. She let me do what I liked with her. The great tears streamed down her poor face.

"'How could he?' she moaned. 'How could he?'

"'My darling,' I said, 'it was bound to happen sooner or later. He's a young man. How could you expect him never to marry? It's only natural.'

"'No, no, no,' she gasped.

"Tight-clenched in her hand I saw that she had a letter and I guessed that it was Tim's.

"'What does he say?' I asked.

"She gave a frightened movement and clutched the letter to her heart as though she thought I would take it from her.

"'He says he couldn't help himself. He says he had to. What does it mean?'

"'Well, you know, in his way he's just as attractive as you are. He has so much charm. I suppose he just fell madly in love with some girl and she with him.'

"'He's so weak,' she moaned.

"'Are they coming out?' I asked.

"'They sailed yesterday. He says it won't make any difference. He's insane. How *can* I stay here?'

"She began to cry hysterically. It was torture to see that girl, usually so calm, utterly shattered by her emotion. I had always felt that her lovely serenity masked a capacity for deep feeling. But the abandon of her distress simply broke me up. I held her in my arms and kissed her, her eyes and her wet cheek and her hair. I don't think she knew what I was doing. I was hardly conscious of it myself. I was so deeply moved.

"'What shall I do?' she wailed.

"'Why won't you marry me?' I said.

"She tried to withdraw herself from me, but I wouldn't let her go.

"'After all, it would be a way out,' I said.

"'How can I marry you?' she moaned. 'I'm years older than you are.'

"'Oh, what nonsense, two or three. What do I care?'

"'No, no.'

"'Why not?' I said.

"'I don't love you,' she said.

"'What does that matter? I love you.'

"I don't know what I said. I told her that I'd try to make her happy. I said I'd never ask anything from her but what she was prepared to give me. I talked and talked. I tried to make her see reason. I felt that she didn't want to stay there, in the same place as Tim, and I told her that I'd be moved soon to some other district. I thought that might tempt her. She couldn't deny that we'd always got on awfully well together. After a time she did seem to grow a little quieter. I had a feeling that she was listening to me. I had even a sort of feeling that she knew that she was lying in my arms and that it comforted her. I made her drink a drop more whisky. I gave her a cigarette. At last I thought I might be just mildly facetious.

"'You know, I'm not a bad sort really,' I said. 'You might do worse.'

"'You don't know me,' she said. 'You know nothing whatever about me.'

"'I'm capable of learning,' I said.

"She smiled a little.

"'You're awfully kind, Mark,' she said.

"'Say yes, Olive,' I begged.

"She gave a deep sigh. For a long time she stared at the ground. But she did not move and I felt the softness of her body in my arms. I waited. I was frightfully nervous and the minutes seemed endless.

"'All right,' she said at last, as though she were not conscious that any time had passed between my prayer and her answer.

"I was so moved that I had nothing to say. But when I wanted to kiss her lips, she turned her face away, and wouldn't let me. I wanted us to be married at once, but she was quite firm that she wouldn't. She insisted on waiting till Tim came back. You know how sometimes you see so clearly in people's thoughts that you're more certain of them than if they'd spoken them; I saw that she couldn't quite believe that what Tim had written was true and that she had a sort of miserable hope that it was all a mistake and he wasn't married after all. It gave me a pang, but I loved her so much, I just bore it. I was willing to bear anything. I adored her. She wouldn't even let me tell anyone that we were engaged. She made me promise not to say a word till Tim's return. She said she couldn't bear the thought of the congratulations and all that. She wouldn't even let me make any announcement of Tim's marriage. She was obstinate about it. I had a notion that she felt if the fact were spread about it gave it a certainty that she didn't want it to have.

"But the matter was taken out of her hands. News travels mysteriously in the East. I don't know what Olive had said in the amah's hearing when first she received the news of Tim's marriage; anyhow, the Hardys' seis told the Sergisons' and Mrs. Sergison attacked me the next time I went into the club.

"'I hear Tim Hardy's married,' she said.

"'Oh?' I answered, unwilling to commit myself.

"She smiled at my blank face, and told me that her amah

having told her the rumour she had rung up Olive and asked her if it was true. Olive's answer had been rather odd. She had not exactly confirmed it, but said that she had received a letter from Tim telling her he was married.

"'She's a strange girl,' said Mrs. Sergison. 'When I asked her for details she said she had none to give and when I said: "Aren't you thrilled?" she didn't answer.'

"'Olive's devoted to Tim, Mrs. Sergison,' I said. 'His marriage has naturally been a shock to her. She knows nothing about Tim's wife. She's nervous about her.'

"'And when are you two going to be married?' she asked me abruptly.

"'What an embarrassing question!' I said, trying to laugh it off.

"She looked at me shrewdly.

"'Will you give me your word of honour that you're not engaged to her?'

"I didn't like to tell her a deliberate lie, nor to ask her to mind her own business, and I'd promised Olive faithfully that I would say nothing till Tim got back. I hedged.

"'Mrs. Sergison,' I said, 'when there's anything to tell I promise that you'll be the first person to hear it. All I can say to you now is that I do want to marry Olive more than anything in the world.'

"'I'm very glad that Tim's married,' she answered. 'And I hope she'll marry you very soon. It was a morbid and unhealthy life that they led up there, those two, they kept far too much to themselves and they were far too much absorbed in one another.'

"I saw Olive practically every day. I felt that she didn't want me to make love to her, and I contented myself with kissing her when I came and when I went. She was very nice to me, kindly and thoughtful; I knew she was glad to see me and sorry when it was time for me to go. Ordinarily, she was apt to fall into silence, but during this time she talked more than I had ever heard her talk before. But never of the future and never of Tim and his wife. She told me a lot about her life in Florence with her mother. She had led a strange lonely life, mostly with servants and governesses, while her mother, I suspected, engaged in one affair after another with vague Italian counts and Russian princes. I guessed that by the time she was fourteen there wasn't much she didn't know. It was natural for her to be quite unconventional: in the only world she knew till she was eighteen conventions weren't mentioned because they didn't exist. Gradually, Olive seemed to regain her serenity and I should have thought that she was beginning to accustom herself to the thought of Tim's marriage if it hadn't been that I couldn't but notice how pale and tired she looked. I made up my mind that the moment he arrived I'd press her to marry me at once. I could get short leave whenever I asked for it, and by the time that was up I thought I could manage a transfer to some other post. What she wanted was change of air and fresh scenes.

"We knew, of course, within a day when Tim's ship would reach Penang, but it was a question whether she'd get in soon enough for him to catch the train and I wrote to the P. & O. agent asking him to telegraph as soon as he had definite news. When I got the wire and took it up to Olive I found that she'd just received one from Tim. The ship had docked early and he was arriving next day. The train was supposed to get in at eight o'clock in the morning, but it was liable to be anything from one to six hours late, and I bore with me an invitation from Mrs. Sergison asking Olive to come back with me to stay the night with her so that she would be on the spot and need not go to the station till the news came through that the train was coming.

"I was immensely relieved. I thought that when the blow at last fell Olive wouldn't feel it so much. She had worked herself up into such a state that I couldn't help thinking that she must have a reaction now. She might take a fancy to her sister-in-law. There was no reason why they shouldn't all three get on very well together. To my surprise Olive said she wasn't coming down to the station to meet them.

"'They'll be awfully disappointed,' I said.

"'I'd rather wait here,' she answered. She smiled a little. 'Don't argue with me, Mark, I've quite made up my mind.'

"'I've ordered breakfast in my house,' I said.

"'That's all right. You meet them and take them to your house and give them breakfast, and then they can come along here afterwards. Of course I'll send the car down.'

"'I don't suppose they'll want to breakfast if you're not there,' I said.

"'Oh, I'm sure they will. If the train gets in on time they wouldn't have thought of breakfasting before it arrived and they'll be hungry. They won't want to take this long drive without anything to eat.'

"I was puzzled. She had been looking forward so intensely to Tim's coming, it seemed strange that she should want to wait all by herself while the rest of us were having a jolly breakfast. I supposed she was nervous and wanted to delay as long as possible meeting the strange woman who had come to take her place. It seemed unreasonable. I couldn't see that an hour sooner or an hour later could make any difference, but I knew women were funny, and anyhow I felt Olive wasn't in the mood for me to press it.

"'Telephone when you're starting so that I shall know when to expect you,' she said.

"'All right,' I said, 'but you know I shan't be able to come with them. It's my day for going to Lahad.'

"This was a town that I had to go to once a week to take cases. It was a good way off and one had to ferry across a river which took some time, so that I never got back till late. There were a few Europeans there and a club. I generally had to go on there for a bit to be sociable and see that things were getting along all right.

"'Besides,' I added, 'with Tim bringing his wife home for the first time I don't suppose he'll want me about. But if you'd like to ask me to dinner I'll be glad to come to that.'

"Olive smiled.

"'I don't think it'll be my place to issue any more invitations, will it?' she said. 'You must ask the bride.'

"She said this so lightly that my heart leaped. I had a feeling that at last she had made up her mind to accept the altered circumstances and, what was more, was accepting them with cheerfulness. She asked me to stay to dinner. Generally I left about eight and dined at home. She was very sweet, almost tender, and I was happier than I'd been for weeks. I had never been more desperately in love with her. I had a couple of gin pahits and I think I was in rather good form at dinner. I know I made her laugh. I felt that at last she was casting away the load of misery that had oppressed her. That was why I didn't let myself be very much disturbed by what happened at the end.

"'Don't you think it's about time you were leaving a presumably maiden lady?' she said.

"She spoke in a manner that was so quietly gay that I answered without hesitation:

"'Oh, my dear, if you think you've got a shred of reputation left you deceive yourself. You're surely not under the impression that the ladies of Sibuku don't know that I've been coming to see you every day for a month. The general feeling is that if we're not married it's high time we were. Don't you think it would be just as well if I broke it to them that we're engaged?'

"'Oh, Mark, you mustn't take our engagement very seriously,' she said.

"I laughed.

"'How else do you expect me to take it? It is serious.'

"She shook her head a little.

"'No. I was upset and hysterical that day. You were being very sweet to me. I said yes because I was too miserable to say no. But now I've had time to collect myself. Don't think me unkind. I made a mistake. I've been very much to blame. You must forgive me.'

"'Oh, darling, you're talking nonsense. You've got nothing against me.'

"She looked at me steadily. She was quite calm. She had even a little smile at the back of her eyes.

"'I can't marry you. I can't marry anyone. It was absurd of me ever to think I could.'

"I didn't answer at once. She was in a queer state and I thought it better not to insist.

"'I suppose I can't drag you to the altar by main force,' I said.

"I held out my hand and she gave me hers. I put my arm round her, and she made no attempt to withdraw. She suffered me to kiss her as usual on her cheek.

"Next morning I met the train. For once in a way it was punctual. Tim waved to me as his carriage passed the place where I was standing, and by the time I had walked up he had already jumped out and was handing down his wife. He grasped my hand warmly.

"'Where's Olive?' he said, with a glance along the platform. 'This is Sally.'

"I shook hands with her and at the same time explained why Olive was not there.

"'It was frightfully early, wasn't it?' said Mrs. Hardy.

"I told them that the plan was for them to come and have a bit of breakfast at my house and then drive home.

"'I'd love a bath,' said Mrs. Hardy.

"'You shall have one,' I said.

"She was really an extremely pretty little thing, very fair, with enormous blue eyes and a lovely little straight nose. Her skin, all milk and roses, was exquisite. A little of the chorus girl type, of course, and you may happen to think that rather namby-pamby, but in that style she was enchanting. We drove to my house, they both had a bath and Tim a shave; I just had two minutes alone with him. He asked me how Olive had taken his marriage. I told him she'd been upset.

"'I was afraid so,' he said, frowning a little. He gave a short sigh. 'I couldn't do anything else.'

"I didn't understand what he meant. At that moment Mrs. Hardy joined us and slipped her arm through her husband's. He took her hand in his and gently pressed it. He gave her a look that had in it something pleased and humorously affectionate, as though he didn't take her quite seriously, but enjoyed his sense of proprietorship and was proud of her beauty. She really was lovely. She was not at all shy, she asked me to call her Sally before we'd known one another ten minutes, and she was quick in the uptake. Of course, just then she was excited at arriving. She'd never been East and everything thrilled her. It was quite obvious that she was head over heels in love with Tim. Her eyes never left him and she hung on his words. We had a jolly breakfast and then we parted. They got into their car to go home and I into mine to go to Lahad. I promised to go straight to the estate from there and in point of fact it was out of my way to pass by my house. I took a change with me. I didn't see why Olive shouldn't like Sally very much, she was frank and gay, and ingenuous; she was extremely young, she couldn't have been more than nineteen, and her wonderful prettiness couldn't fail to appeal to Olive. I was just as glad to have had a reasonable excuse to leave the three of them by themselves for the day, but as I started out from Lahad I had a notion that by the time I arrived they would all be pleased to see me. I drove up to the bungalow and blew my horn two or three times, expecting someone to appear. Not a soul. The place was in total darkness. I was surprised. It was absolutely silent. I couldn't make it out. They must be in. Very odd, I thought. I waited a moment, then got out of the car and walked up the steps. At the top of them I stumbled over something. I swore and bent down to see what it was; it had felt like a body. There was a cry and I saw it was the amah. She shrank back cowering as I touched her and broke into loud wails.

"'What the hell's the matter?' I cried, and then I felt a hand on my arm and heard a voice. Tuan, Tuan. I turned and in the darkness recognized Tim's head boy. He began to speak in little frightened gasps. I listened to him with horror. What he told me was unspeakable. I pushed him aside and rushed into the house. The sitting-room was dark. I turned on the light. The first thing I saw was Sally huddled up in an armchair. She was startled by my sudden appearance and cried out. I could hardly speak. I asked her if it was true. When she told me it was I felt the room suddenly going round and round me. I had to sit down. As the car that bore Tim and Sally drove up the road that led to the house and Tim sounded the claxon to announce their arrival and the boys and the amah ran out to greet them there was the sound of a shot. They ran to Olive's room and found her lying in front of the looking-glass in a pool of blood. She had shot herself with Tim's revolver.

"'Is she dead?' I said.

"'No, they sent for the doctor, and he took her to the hospital.'

"I hardly knew what I was doing. I didn't even trouble to tell Sally where I was going. I got up and staggered to the door. I got into the car and told my seis to drive like hell to the hospital. I rushed in. I asked where she was. They tried to bar my way, but I pushed them aside. I knew where the private rooms were. Someone clung to my arm, but I shook him off. I vaguely understood that the doctor had given instructions that no one was to go into the room. I didn't care about that. There was an orderly at the door; he put out his arm to prevent me from passing. I swore at him and told him to get out of my way. I suppose I made a row, I was beside myself; the door was opened and the doctor came out.

"'Who's making all this noise?' he said. 'Oh, it's you. What do you want?'

"'Is she dead?' I asked.

"'No. But she's unconscious. She never regained consciousness. It's only a matter of an hour or two.'

"'I want to see her.'

"'You can't.'

"'I'm engaged to her.'

"'You?' he cried, and even at that moment I was aware that he looked at me strangely. 'That's all the more reason.'

"I didn't know what he meant. I was stupid with horror.

"'Surely you can do something to save her,' I cried.

"He shook his head.

"'If you saw her you wouldn't wish it,' he said.

"I stared at him aghast. In the silence I heard a man's convulsive sobbing.

"'Who's that?' I asked.

"'Her brother.'

"Then I felt a hand on my arm. I looked round and saw it was Mrs. Sergison.

"'My poor boy,' she said, 'I'm so sorry for you.'

"'What on earth made her do it?' I groaned.

"'Come away, my dear,' said Mrs. Sergison. 'You can do no good here.'

"'No, I must stay,' I said.

"'Well, go and sit in my room,' said the doctor.

"I was so broken that I let Mrs. Sergison take me by the arm and lead me into the doctor's private room. She made me sit down. I couldn't bring myself to realize that it was true. I thought it was a horrible nightmare from which I must awake. I don't know how long we sat there. Three hours. Four hours. At last the doctor came in.

"'It's all over,' he said.

"Then I couldn't help myself, I began to cry. I didn't care what they thought of me. I was so frightfully unhappy.

"We buried her next day.

"Mrs. Sergison came back to my house and sat with me for a while. She wanted me to go to the club with her. I hadn't the heart. She was very kind, but I was glad when she left me by myself. I tried to read, but the words meant nothing to me. I felt dead inside. My boy came in and turned on the lights. My head was aching like mad. Then he came back and said that a lady wished to see me. I asked who it was. He wasn't quite sure, but he thought it must be the new wife of the tuan at Putatan. I couldn't imagine what she wanted. I got up and went to the door. He was right. It was Sally. I asked her to come in. I noticed that she was deathly white. I felt sorry for her. It was a frightful experience for a girl of that age and for a bride a miserable home-coming. She sat down. She was very nervous. I tried to put her at her ease by saying conventional things. She made me very uncomfortable because she stared at me with those enormous blue eyes of hers, and they were simply ghastly with horror. She interrupted me suddenly.

"'You're the only person here I know,' she said. 'I had to come to you. I want you to get me away from here.'

"I was dumbfounded.

"'What *do* you mean?' I said.

"'I don't want you to ask me any questions. I just want you to get me away. At once. I want to go back to England!'

"'But you can't leave Tim like that just now,' I said. 'My dear, you must pull yourself together. I know it's been awful for you. But think of Tim. I mean, he'll be miserable. If you have any love for him the least you can do is to try and make him a little less unhappy.'

"'Oh, you don't know,' she cried. 'I can't tell you. It's too horrible. I beseech you to help me. If there's a train to-night let me get on it. If I can only get to Penang I can get a ship. I can't stay in this place another night. I shall go mad.'

"I was absolutely bewildered.

"'Does Tim know?' I asked her.

"'I haven't seen Tim since last night. I'll never see him again. I'd rather die.'

"I wanted to gain a little time.

"'But how can you go without your things? Have you got any luggage?'

"'What does that matter?' she cried impatiently. 'I've got what I want for the journey.'

"'Have you any money?'

"'Enough. Is there a train to-night?'

"'Yes,' I said. 'It's due just after midnight.'

"'Thank God. Will you arrange everything? Can I stay here till then?'

"'You're putting me in a frightful position,' I said. 'I don't know what to do for the best. You know, it's an awfully serious step you're taking.'

"'If you knew everything you'd know it was the only possible thing to do.'

"'It'll create an awful scandal here. I don't know what people'll say. Have you thought of the effect on Tim?' I was worried and unhappy. 'God knows I don't want to interfere in what isn't my business. But if you want me to help you I ought to know enough to feel justified in doing so. You must tell me what's happened.'

"'I can't. I can only tell you that I know everything.'

"She hid her face with her hands and shuddered. Then she gave herself a shake as though she were recoiling from some frightful sight.

"'He had no right to marry me. It was monstrous.'

"And as she spoke her voice rose shrill and piercing. I was afraid she was going to have an attack of hysterics. Her pretty doll-like face was terrified and her eyes stared as though she could never close them again.

"'Don't you love him any more?' I asked.

"'After that?'

"'What will you do if I refuse to help you?' I said.

"'I suppose there's a clergyman here or a doctor. You can't refuse to take me to one of them.'

"'How did you get here?'

"'The head boy drove me. He got a car from somewhere.'

"'Does Tim know you've gone?'

"'I left a letter for him.'

"'He'll know you're here.'

"'He won't try to stop me. I promise you that. He daren't. For God's sake don't you try either. I tell you I shall go mad if I stay here another night.'

"I sighed. After all she was of an age to decide for herself."

I, the writer of this, hadn't spoken for a long time.

"Did you know what she meant?" I asked Featherstone.

He gave me a long, haggard look.

"There was only one thing she could mean. It was unspeakable. Yes, I knew all right. It explained everything. Poor Olive. Poor sweet. I suppose it was unreasonable of me, at that moment I only felt a horror of that little pretty fair-haired thing with her terrified eyes. I hated her. I didn't say anything for a while. Then I told her I'd do as she wished. She didn't even say thank you. I think she knew what I felt about her. When it was dinner time I made her eat something and then she asked me if there was a room she could go and lie down in till it was time to go to the station. I showed her into my spare room and left her. I sat in the sitting-room and waited. My God, I don't think the time has ever passed so slowly for me. I thought twelve would never strike. I rang up the station and was told the train wouldn't be in till nearly two. At midnight she came back to the sitting-room and we sat there for an hour and a half. We had nothing to say to one another and we didn't speak. Then I took her to the station and put her on the train."

"Was there an awful scandal?"

Featherstone frowned.

"I don't know. I applied for short leave. After that I was moved to another post. I heard that Tim had sold his estate and bought another. But I didn't know where. It was a shock to me at first when I found him here."

Featherstone, getting up, went over to a table and mixed himself a whiskey and soda. In the silence that fell now I heard the monotonous chorus of the croaking frogs. And suddenly the bird that is known as the fever-bird, perched in a tree close to the house, began to call. First, three notes in a descending, chromatic scale, then five, then four. The varying notes of the scale succeeded one another with maddening persistence. One was compelled to listen and to count them, and because one did not know how many there would be it tortured one's nerves.

"Blast that bird," said Featherstone. "That means no sleep for me to-night."

THE VESSEL OF WRATH

THERE are few books in the world that contain more meat than the Sailing Directions published by the Hydrographic Department by order of the Lords Commissioners of the Admiralty. They are handsome volumes, bound (very flimsily) in cloth of different colours, and the most expensive of them is cheap. For four shillings you can buy the Yangtse Kiang Pilot, "containing a description of, and sailing directions for, the Yangtse Kiang from the Wusung River to the highest navigable point, including the Han Kiang, the Kialing Kiang, and the Min Kiang"; and for three shillings you can get Part III of the Eastern Archipelago Pilot, "comprising the N. E. end of Celebes, Molucca and Gilolo passages, Banda and Arafura Seas, and North, West, and South-West coasts of New Guinea." But it is not very safe to do so if you are a creature of settled habits that you have no wish to disturb or if you have an occupation that holds you fast to one place. These business-like books take you upon enchanted journeys of the spirit; and their matter-of-fact style, the admirable order, the concision with which the material is set before you, the stern sense of the practical that informs every line, cannot dim the poetry that, like the spice-laden breeze that assails your senses with a more than material languor when you approach some of those magic islands of the Eastern seas, blows with so sweet a fragrance through the printed pages. They tell you the anchorages and the landing places, what supplies you can get at each spot, and where you can get water; they tell you the lights and buoys, tides, winds and weather that you will find there. They give you brief information about the population and the trade. And it is strange when you think how sedately it is all set down, with no words wasted, that so much else is given you besides. What? Well, mystery and beauty, romance and the glamour of the unknown. It is no common book that offers you casually turning its pages such a paragraph as this: "Supplies. A few jungle fowl are preserved, the island is also the resort of vast numbers of sea birds. Turtle are found in the lagoon, as well as quantities of various fish, including grey mullet, shark, and dog-fish; the seine cannot be used with any effect; but there is a fish which may be taken on a rod. A small store of tinned provisions and spirits is kept in a hut for the relief of shipwrecked persons. Good water may be obtained from a well near the landing place." Can the imagination want more material than this to go on a journey through time and space?

In the volume from which I have copied this passage, the compilers with the same restraint have described the Alas Islands. They are composed of a group or chain of islands, "for the most part low and wooded, extending about 75 miles east and west, and 40 miles north and south." The information about them, you are told, is very slight; there are channels between the different groups, and several vessels have passed through them, but the passages have not been thoroughly explored, and the positions of many of the dangers not yet determined; it is therefore advisable to avoid them. The population of the group is estimated at about 8000, of whom 200 are Chinese and 400 Mohammedans. The rest are heathen. The principal island is called Baru, it is surrounded by a reef, and here lives a Dutch Controleur. His white house with its red roof on the top of a little hill is the most prominent object that the vessels of the Royal Netherlands Steam Packet Company see when every other month on their way up to Macassar and every four weeks on their way down to Merauke in Dutch New Guinea they touch at the island.

At a certain moment of the world's history the Controleur was Mynheer Evert Gruyter and he ruled the people who inhabited the Alas Islands with firmness tempered by a keen sense of the ridiculous. He had thought it a very good joke to be placed at the age of twenty-seven in a position of such consequence and at thirty he was still amused by it. There was no cable communication between his islands and Batavia, and

the mail arrived after so long a delay that even if he asked
advice, by the time he received it, it was useless, and so he
equably did what he thought best and trusted to his good
fortune to keep out of trouble with the authorities. He was
very short, not more than five feet four in height, and extremely
fat; he was of a florid complexion. For coolness' sake he kept his
head shaved and his face was hairless. It was round and red.
His eyebrows were so fair that you hardly saw them; and he
had little twinkling blue eyes. He knew that he had no dignity,
but for the sake of his position made up for it by dressing very
dapperly. He never went to his office, nor sat in court, nor
walked abroad but in spotless white. His stengah-shifter, with
its bright brass buttons, fitted him very tightly and displayed
the shocking fact that, young though he was, he had a round
and protruding belly. His good-humoured face shone with
sweat and he constantly fanned himself with a palm-leaf fan.

But in his house Mr. Gruyter preferred to wear nothing but
a sarong and then with his white podgy little body he looked
like a fat funny boy of sixteen. He was an early riser and his
breakfast was always ready for him at six. It never varied. It
consisted of a slice of papaia, three cold fried eggs, Edam cheese,
sliced thin, and a cup of black coffee. When he had eaten it, he
smoked a large Dutch cigar, read the papers if he had not read
them through and through already, and then dressed to go
down to his office.

One morning while he was thus occupied his head boy came
into his bedroom and told him that Tuan Jones wanted to
know if he could see him. Mr. Gruyter was standing in front
of a looking-glass. He had his trousers on and was admiring
his smooth chest. He arched his back in order to throw it out
and throw in his belly and with a good deal of satisfaction gave
his breast three or four resounding slaps. It was a manly chest.
When the boy brought the message he looked at his own eyes
in the mirror and exchanged a slightly ironic smile with them.
He asked himself what the devil his visitor could want. Evert
Gruyter spoke English, Dutch and Malay with equal facility,
but he thought in Dutch. He liked to do this. It seemed to him
a pleasantly ribald language.

"Ask the Tuan to wait and say I shall come directly." He
put on his tunic, over his naked body, buttoned it up, and
strutted into the sitting-room. The Rev. Owen Jones got up.

"Good-morning, Mr. Jones," said the Controleur. "Have

you come in to have a peg with me before I start my day's work?"

Mr. Jones did not smile.

"I've come to see you upon a very distressing matter, Mr. Gruyter," he answered.

The Controleur was not disconcerted by his visitor's gravity nor depressed by his words. His little blue eyes beamed amiably.

"Sit down, my dear fellow, and have a cigar."

Mr. Gruyter knew quite well that the Rev. Owen Jones neither drank nor smoked, but it tickled something prankish in his nature to offer him a drink and a smoke whenever they met. Mr. Jones shook his head.

Mr. Jones was in charge of the Baptist Mission on the Alas Islands. His headquarters were at Baru, the largest of them, with the greatest population, but he had meeting-houses under the care of native helpers in several other islands of the group. He was a tall, thin melancholy man, with a long face, sallow and drawn, of about forty. His brown hair was already white on the temples and it receded from the forehead. This gave him a look of somewhat vacuous intellectuality. Mr. Gruyter both disliked and respected him. He disliked him because he was narrow-minded and dogmatic. Himself a cheerful pagan who liked the good things of the flesh and was determined to get as many of them as his circumstances permitted, he had no patience with a man who disapproved of them all. He thought the customs of the country suited its inhabitants and had no patience with the missionary's energetic efforts to destroy a way of life that for centuries had worked very well. He respected him because he was honest, zealous and good. Mr. Jones, an Australian of Welsh descent, was the only qualified doctor in the group and it was a comfort to know that if you fell ill you need not rely only on a Chinese practitioner, and none knew better than the Controleur how useful to all Mr. Jones's skill had been and with what charity he had given it. On the occasion of an epidemic of influenza the missionary had done the work of ten men and no storm short of a typhoon could prevent him from crossing to one island or another if his help was needed.

He lived with his sister in a little white house about half a mile from the village and when the Controleur had arrived, came on board to meet him and begged him to stay till he could get his own house in order. The Controleur had accepted

and soon saw for himself with what simplicity the couple lived.
It was more than he could stand. Tea at three sparse meals a
day and when he lit his cigar Mr. Jones politely but firmly asked
him to be good enough not to smoke since both his sister and he
strongly disapproved of it. In twenty-four hours Mr. Gruyter
moved into his own house. He fled, with panic in his heart, as
though from a plague-stricken city. The Controleur was fond
of a joke and he liked to laugh; to be with a man who took your
nonsense in deadly earnest and never even smiled at your
best story was more than flesh and blood could stand. The
Rev. Owen Jones was a worthy man, but as a companion he
was impossible. His sister was worse. Neither had a sense of
humour, but whereas the missionary was of a melancholy turn,
doing his duty so conscientiously, with the obvious conviction
that everything in the world was hopeless, Miss Jones was
resolutely cheerful. She grimly looked on the bright side of
things. With the ferocity of an avenging angel she sought out
the good in her fellow men. Miss Jones taught in the mission
school and helped her brother in his medical work. When he did
operations she gave the anæsthetic and was matron, dresser
and nurse of the tiny hospital which on his own initiative Mr.
Jones had added to the mission. But the Controleur was an
obstinate little fellow and he never lost his capacity of extract-
ing amusement from the Rev. Owen's dour struggle with the
infirmities of human nature, and Miss Jones's ruthless optimism. He had to get his fun where he could. The Dutch boats
came in three times in two months for a few hours and then he
could have a good old crack with the captain and chief engineer, and once in a blue moon a pearling lugger came in from
Thursday Island or Port Darwin and for two or three days he
had a grand time. They were rough fellows, the pearlers, for
the most part, but they were full of guts, and they had plenty
of liquor on board, and good stories to tell, and the Controleur
had them up to his house and gave them a fine dinner and the
party was only counted a success if they were all too drunk to
get back on the lugger again that night. But besides the missionary the only white man who lived on Baru was Ginger
Ted, and he, of course, was a disgrace to civilization. There
was not a single thing to be said in his favour. He cast discredit
on the white race. All the same, but for Ginger Ted the Controleur sometimes thought he would find life on the island of
Baru almost more than he could bear.

Oddly enough it was on account of this scamp that Mr. Jones, when he should have been instructing the pagan young in the mysteries of the Baptist faith, was paying Mr. Gruyter this early visit.

"Sit down, Mr. Jones," said the Controleur. "What can I do for you?"

"Well, I've come to see you about the man they call Ginger Ted. What are you going to do now?"

"Why, what's happened?"

"Haven't you heard? I thought the sergeant would have told you."

"I don't encourage the members of my staff to come to my private house unless the matter is urgent," said the Controleur rather grandly. "I am unlike you, Mr. Jones, I only work in order to have leisure and I like to enjoy my leisure without disturbance."

But Mr. Jones did not care much for small talk and he was not interested in general reflections.

"There was a disgraceful row in one of the Chinese shops last night. Ginger Ted wrecked the place and half killed a Chinaman."

"Drunk again, I suppose," said the Controleur placidly.

"Naturally. When is he anything else? They sent for the police and he assaulted the sergeant. They had to have six men to get him to the gaol."

"He's a hefty fellow," said the Controleur.

"I suppose you'll send him to Macassar."

Evert Gruyter returned the missionary's outraged look with a merry twinkle. He was no fool and he knew already what Mr. Jones was up to. It gave him considerable amusement to tease him a little.

"Fortunately my powers are wide enough to enable me to deal with the situation myself," he answered.

"You have power to deport anyone you like, Mr. Gruyter, and I'm sure it would save a lot of trouble if you got rid of the man altogether."

"I have the power of course, but I am sure you would be the last person to wish me to use it arbitrarily."

"Mr. Gruyter, the man's presence here is a public scandal. He's never sober from morning till night; it's notorious that he has relations with one native woman after another."

"That is an interesting point, Mr. Jones. I had always heard that alcoholic excess, though it stimulated sexual desire, prevented its gratification. What you tell me about Ginger Ted does not seem to bear out this theory."

The missionary flushed a dull red.

"These are physiological matters which at the moment I have no wish to go into," he said, frigidly. "The behaviour of this man does incalculable damage to the prestige of the white race, and his example seriously hampers the efforts that are made in other quarters to induce the people of these islands to lead a less vicious life. He's an out and out bad lot."

"Pardon my asking, but have you made any attempts to reform him?"

"When he first drifted here I did my best to get in touch with him. He repelled all my advances. When there was that first trouble I went to him and talked to him straight from the shoulder. He swore at me."

"No one has a greater appreciation than I of the excellent work that you and other missionaries do on these islands, but are you sure that you always exercise your calling with all the tact possible?"

The Controleur was rather pleased with this phrase. It was extremely courteous and yet contained a reproof that he thought worth administering. The missionary looked at him gravely. His sad brown eyes were full of sincerity.

"Did Jesus exercise tact when he took a whip and drove the money-changers from the Temple? No, Mr. Gruyter. Tact is the subterfuge the lax avail themselves of to avoid doing their duty."

Mr. Jones's remark made the Controleur feel suddenly that he wanted a bottle of beer. The missionary leaned forward earnestly.

"Mr. Gruyter, you know this man's transgressions just as well as I do. It's unnecessary for me to remind you of them. There are no excuses for him. Now he really has overstepped the limit. You'll never have a better chance than this. I beg you to use the power you have and turn him out once for all."

The Controleur's eyes twinkled more brightly than ever. He was having a lot of fun. He reflected that human beings were much more amusing when you did not feel called upon in dealing with them to allot praise or blame.

"But Mr. Jones, do I understand you right? Are you asking me to give you an assurance to deport this man before I've heard the evidence against him and listened to his defence?"

"I don't know what his defence can be."

The Controleur rose from his chair and really he managed to get quite a little dignity into his five feet four inches.

"I am here to administer justice according to the laws of the Dutch Government. Permit me to tell you that I am exceedingly surprised that you should attempt to influence me in my judicial functions."

The missionary was a trifle flustered. It had never occurred to him that this little whipper-snapper of a boy, ten years younger than himself, would dream of adopting such an attitude. He opened his mouth to explain and apologize, but the Controleur raised a podgy little hand.

"It is time for me to go to my office, Mr. Jones. I wish you good-morning."

The missionary, taken aback, bowed and without another word walked out of the room. He would have been surprised to see what the Controleur did when his back was turned. A broad grin broke on his lips and he put his thumb to his nose and cocked a snook at the Rev. Owen Jones.

A few minutes later he went down to his office. His head clerk, who was a Dutch half-caste, gave him his version of the previous night's row. It agreed pretty well with Mr. Jones's. The Court was sitting that day.

"Will you take Ginger Ted first, sir?" asked the clerk.

"I see no reason to do that. There are two or three cases held over from the last sitting. I will take him in his proper order."

"I thought perhaps as he was a white man you would like to see him privately, sir."

"The majesty of the law knows no difference between white and coloured, my friend," said Mr. Gruyter, somewhat pompously.

The Court was a big square room with wooden benches on which, crowded together, sat natives of all kinds, Polynesians, Bugis, Chinese, Malays, and they all rose when a door was opened and a sergeant announced the arrival of the Controleur. He entered with his clerk and took his place on a little dais at a table of varnished pitch pine. Behind him was a large engraving of Queen Wilhelmina. He despatched half a dozen cases and then Ginger Ted was brought in. He stood in the dock, handcuffed, with a warder on either side of him. The Controleur looked at him with a grave face, but he could not keep the amusement out of his eyes.

Ginger Ted was suffering from a hangover. He swayed a little as he stood and his eyes were vacant. He was a man still young, thirty perhaps, of somewhat over the middle height, rather fat, with a bloated red face and a shock of curly red hair. He had not come out of the tussle unscathed. He had a black eye and his mouth was cut and swollen. He wore khaki shorts, very dirty and ragged, and his singlet had been almost torn off his back. A great rent showed the thick mat of red hair with which his chest was covered, but showed also the astonishing whiteness of his skin. The Controleur looked at the charge sheet. He called the evidence. When he had heard it, when he had seen the Chinaman whose head Ginger Ted had broken with a bottle, when he had heard the agitated story of the sergeant who had been knocked flat when he tried to arrest him, when he had listened to the tale of the havoc wrought by Ginger Ted who in his drunken fury had smashed everything he could lay hands on, he turned and addressed the accused in English.

"Well, Ginger, what have you got to say for yourself?"

"I was blind. I don't remember a thing about it. If they say I half killed 'im I suppose I did. I'll pay the damage if they'll give me time."

"You will, Ginger," said the Controleur, "but it's me who'll give you time."

He looked at Ginger Ted for a minute in silence. He was an unappetizing object. A man who had gone completely to pieces. He was horrible. It made you shudder to look at him and if Mr. Jones had not been so officious, at that moment the Controleur would certainly have ordered him to be deported.

"You've been a trouble ever since you came to the islands, Ginger. You're a disgrace. You're incorrigibly idle. You've been picked up in the street dead drunk time and time again. You've kicked up row after row. You're hopeless. I told you the last time you were brought here that if you were arrested again I should deal with you severely. You've gone the limit this time and you're for it. I sentence you to six months' hard labour."

"Me?"

"You."

"By God, I'll kill you when I come out."

He burst into a string of oaths both filthy and blasphemous.

Mr. Gruyter listened scornfully. You can swear much better in Dutch than in English and there was nothing that Ginger Ted said that he could not have effectively capped.

"Be quiet," he ordered. "You make me tired."

The Controleur repeated his sentence in Malay and the prisoner was led struggling away.

Mr. Gruyter sat down to tiffin in high good humour. It was astonishing how amusing life could be if you exercised a little ingenuity. There were people in Amsterdam, and even in Batavia and Surabaya, who looked upon his island home as a place of exile. They little knew how agreeable it was and what fun he could extract from unpromising material. They asked him whether he did not miss the club and the races and the cinema, the dances that were held once a week at the Casino and the society of Dutch ladies. Not at all. He liked comfort. The substantial furniture of the room in which he sat had a satisfying solidity. He liked reading French novels of a frivolous nature and he appreciated the sensation of reading one after the other without the uneasiness occasioned by the thought that he was wasting his time. It seemed to him a great luxury to waste time. When his young man's fancy turned to thoughts of love his head boy brought to the house a little dark-skinned bright-eyed creature in a sarong. He took care to form no connection of a permanent nature. He thought that change kept the heart young. He enjoyed freedom and was not weighed down by a sense of responsibility. He did not mind the heat. It made a sluice over with cold water half a dozen times a day a pleasure that had almost an æsthetic quality. He played the piano. He wrote letters to his friends in Holland. He felt no need for the conversation of intellectual persons. He liked a good laugh, but he could get that out of a fool just as well as out of a professor of philosophy. He had a notion that he was a very wise little man.

Like all good Dutchmen in the Far East he began his lunch with a small glass of Hollands gin. It has a musty acrid flavour, and the taste for it must be acquired, but Mr. Gruyter preferred it to any cocktail. When he drank it he felt besides that he was upholding the traditions of his race. Then he had *rystafel*. He had it every day. He heaped a soup-plate high with rice, and then, his three boys waiting on him, helped himself to the curry that one handed him, to the fried egg that another brought, and to the condiment presented by the third. Then each one brought another dish, of bacon, or bananas, or pickled fish, and presently his plate was piled high in a huge pyramid. He stirred it all together and began to eat. He ate slowly and with relish. He drank a bottle of beer.

He did not think while he was eating. His attention was applied to the mass in front of him and he consumed it with a happy concentration. It never palled on him. And when he had emptied the great plate it was a compensation to think that next day he would have *rystafel* again. He grew tired of it as little as the rest of us grow tired of bread. He finished his beer and lit his cigar. The boy brought him a cup of coffee. He leaned back in his chair then and allowed himself the luxury of reflection.

It tickled him to have sentenced Ginger Ted to the richly deserved punishment of six months' hard labour, and he smiled when he thought of him working on the roads with the other prisoners. It would have been silly to deport from the island the one man with whom he could occasionally have a heart-to-heart talk, and besides, the satisfaction it would have given the missionary would have been bad for that gentleman's character. Ginger Ted was a scamp and a scallywag, but the Controleur had a kindly feeling for him. They had drunk many a bottle of beer in one another's company and when the pearl fishers from Port Darwin came in and they all made a night of it, they had got gloriously tight together. The Controleur liked the reckless way in which Ginger Ted squandered the priceless treasure of life.

Ginger Ted had wandered in one day on the ship that was going up from Merauke to Macassar. The captain did not know how he had found his way there, but he had travelled steerage with the natives, and he stopped off at the Alas Islands because he liked the look of them. Mr. Gruyter had a suspicion that their attraction consisted perhaps in their being under the Dutch flag and so out of British jurisdiction. But his papers were in order, so there was no reason why he should not stay. He said that he was buying pearl-shell for an Australian firm, but it soon appeared that his commercial undertakings were not serious. Drink, indeed, took up so much of his time that he had little left over for other pursuits. He was in receipt of two pounds a week, paid monthly, which came regularly to him from England. The Controleur guessed that this sum was paid only so long as he kept well away from the persons who sent it. It was anyway too small to permit him any liberty of movement. Ginger Ted was reticent. The Controleur discovered that he was an Englishman, this he learnt from his passport, which described him as Edward Wilson, and that he had been in Australia. But why he had left England and what he had done in Australia he had no notion. Nor could he ever quite tell to what class Ginger Ted belonged. When you saw him in a filthy singlet and a pair of ragged trousers, a battered topi on his head, with the pearl fishers and heard his conversation, coarse, obscene and illiterate, you thought he must be a sailor before the mast who had deserted his ship, or a labourer, but when you saw his handwriting you were surprised to find that it was that of a man not without at least some education, and on occasion when you got him alone, if he had had a few drinks but was not yet drunk, he would talk of matters that neither a sailor nor a labourer would have been likely to know anything about. The Controleur had a certain sensitiveness and he realized that Ginger Ted did not speak to him as an inferior to a superior but as an equal. Most of his remittance was mortgaged before he received it, and the Chinamen to whom he owed money were standing at his elbow when the monthly letter was delivered to him, but with what was left he proceeded to get drunk. It was then that he made trouble, for when drunk he grew violent and was then likely to commit acts that brought him into the hands of the police. Hitherto Mr. Gruyter had contented himself with keeping him in gaol till he was sober and giving him a talking to. When he was out of money he cadged what drink he could from anyone who would give it him. Rum, brandy, arak, it was all the same to him. Two or three times Mr. Gruyter had got him work on plantations run by Chinese in one or other of the islands, but he could not stick to it, and in a few weeks was back again at Baru on the beach. It was a miracle how he kept body and soul together. He had, of course, a way with him. He picked up the various dialects spoken on the islands, and knew how to make the natives laugh. They despised him, but they respected his physical strength, and they liked his company. He was as a result never at a loss for a meal or a mat to sleep on. The strange thing was, and it was this that chiefly outraged the Rev. Owen Jones, that he could do anything he liked with a woman. The Controleur could not imagine what it was they saw in him. He was casual with them and rather brutal. He took what they gave him, but

seemed incapable of gratitude. He used them for his pleasure
and then flung them indifferently away. Once or twice this had
got him into trouble, and Mr. Gruyter had had to sentence
an angry father for sticking a knife in Ginger Ted's back one
night, and a Chinese woman had sought to poison herself by
swallowing opium because he had deserted her. Once Mr.
Jones came to the Controleur in a great state because the beach-
comber had seduced one of his converts. The Controleur agreed
that it was very deplorable, but could only advise Mr. Jones to
keep a sharp eye on these young persons. The Controleur liked
it less when he discovered that a girl whom he fancied a good
deal himself and had been seeing for several weeks had all the
time been according her favours also to Ginger Ted. When he
thought of this particular incident he smiled again at the
thought of Ginger Ted doing six months' hard labour. It is
seldom in this life that in the process of doing your bounden
duty you can get back on a fellow who has played you a dirty
trick.

A few days later Mr. Gruyter was taking a walk, partly for
exercise and partly to see that some job he wanted done was
being duly proceeded with, when he passed a gang of prisoners
working under the charge of a warder. Among them he saw
Ginger Ted. He wore the prison sarong, a dingy tunic called in
Malay a baju, and his own battered topi. They were repairing
the road, and Ginger Ted was wielding a heavy pick. The way
was narrow and the Controleur saw that he must pass within
a foot of him. He remembered his threats. He knew that Ginger
Ted was a man of violent passion and the language he had
used in the dock made it plain that he had not seen what a good
joke it was of the Controleur's to sentence him to six months'
hard labour. If Ginger Ted suddenly attacked him with the
pick, nothing on God's earth could save him. It was true that
the warder would immediately shoot him down, but meanwhile
the Controleur's head would be bashed in. It was with a funny
little feeling in the pit of his stomach that Mr. Gruyter walked
through the gang of prisoners. They were working in pairs a few
feet from one another. He set his mind on neither hastening his
pace nor slackening it. As he passed Ginger Ted, the man swung
his pick into the ground and looked up at the Controleur and
as he caught his eye winked. The Controleur checked the smile
that rose to his lips and with official dignity strode on. But that
wink, so lusciously full of sardonic humour, filled him with satis-

faction. If he had been the Caliph of Bagdad instead of a junior official in the Dutch Civil Service, he would forthwith have released Ginger Ted, sent slaves to bathe and perfume him, and having clothed him in a golden robe entertained him to a sumptuous repast.

Ginger Ted was an exemplary prisoner and in a month or two the Controleur, having occasion to send a gang to do some work on one of the outlying islands, included him in it. There was no gaol there, so the ten fellows he sent, under the charge of a warder, were billeted on the natives and after their day's work lived like free men. The job was sufficient to take up the rest of Ginger Ted's sentence. The Controleur saw him before he left.

"Look here, Ginger," he said to him, "here's ten guilder for you so that you can buy yourself tobacco when you're gone."

"Couldn't you make it a bit more? There's eight pounds a month coming in regularly."

"I think that's enough. I'll keep the letters that come for you, and when you get back you'll have a tidy sum. You'll have enough to take you anywhere you want to go."

"I'm very comfortable here," said Ginger Ted.

"Well, the day you come back, clean yourself up and come over to my house. We'll have a bottle of beer together."

"That'll be fine. I guess I'll be ready for a good crack then."

Now chance steps in. The island to which Ginger Ted had been sent was called Maputiti, and like all the rest of them it was rocky, heavily wooded and surrounded by a reef. There was a village among coconuts on the sea-shore opposite the opening of the reef and another village on a brackish lake in the middle of the island. Of this some of the inhabitants had been converted to Christianity. Communication with Baru was effected by a launch that touched at the various islands at irregular intervals. It carried passengers and produce. But the villagers were seafaring folk, and if they had to communicate urgently with Baru, manned a prahu and sailed the fifty miles or so that separated them from it. It happened that when Ginger Ted's sentence had but another fortnight to run the Christian headman of the village on the lake was taken suddenly ill. The native remedies availed him nothing and he writhed in agony. Messengers were sent to Baru imploring the missionary's help; but as ill luck would have it Mr. Jones was suffering at the moment from an attack of malaria. He was in bed and unable to move. He talked the matter over with his sister.

"It sounds like acute appendicitis," he told her.

"You can't go, Owen," she said.

"I can't let the man die."

Mr. Jones had a temperature of a hundred and four. His head was aching like mad. He had been delirious all night. His eyes were shining strangely and his sister felt that he was holding on to his wits by a sheer effort of will.

"You couldn't operate in the state you're in."

"No, I couldn't. Then Hassan must go."

Hassan was the dispenser.

"You couldn't trust Hassan. He'd never dare to do an operation on his own responsibility. And they'd never let him. I'll go. Hassan can stay here and look after you."

"You can't remove an appendix?"

"Why not? I've seen you do it. I've done lots of minor operations."

Mr. Jones felt he didn't quite understand what she was saying.

"Is the launch in?"

"No, it's gone to one of the islands. But I can go in the prahu the men came in."

"You? I wasn't thinking of you. You can't go."

"I'm going, Owen."

"Going where?" he said.

She saw that his mind was wandering already. She put her hand soothingly on his dry forehead. She gave him a dose of medicine. He muttered something and she realized that he did not know where he was. Of course she was anxious about him, but she knew that his illness was not dangerous, and she could leave him safely to the mission boy who was helping her nurse him and to the native dispenser. She slipped out of the room. She put her toilet things, a night-dress, and a change of clothes into a bag. A little chest with surgical instruments, bandages and antiseptic dressings was kept always ready. She gave them to the two natives who had come over from Maputiti, and telling the dispenser what she was going to do gave him instructions to inform her brother when he was able to listen. Above all he was not to be anxious about her. She put on her topi and sallied forth. The mission was about half a mile from the village. She walked quickly. At the end of the jetty the prahu was waiting. Six men manned it. She took her place in the stern and they set off with a rapid stroke. Within the reef the sea was calm, but when they crossed the bar they came upon a long swell. But this was not the first journey of the sort Miss Jones had taken and she was confident in the seaworthiness of the boat she was in. It was noon and the sun beat down from a sultry sky. The only thing that harassed her was that they could not arrive before dark, and if she found it necessary to operate at once she could count only on the light of hurricane lamps.

Miss Jones was a woman of hard on forty. Nothing in her appearance would have prepared you for such determination as she had just shown. She had an odd drooping gracefulness, which suggested that she might be swayed by every breeze; it was almost an affectation; and it made the strength of character which you soon discovered in her seem positively monstrous. She was flat-chested, tall and extremely thin. She had a long sallow face and she was much afflicted with prickly heat. Her lank brown hair was drawn back straight from her forehead. She had rather small eyes, grey in colour, and because they were somewhat too close they gave her face a shrewish look. Her nose was long and thin and a trifle red. She suffered a good deal from indigestion. But this infirmity availed nothing against her ruthless determination to look upon the bright side of things. Firmly persuaded that the world was evil and men unspeakably vicious, she extracted any little piece of decency she could find in them with the modest pride with which a conjurer extracts a rabbit from a hat. She was quick, resourceful and competent. When she arrived on the island she saw that there was not a moment to lose if she was to save the headman's life. Under the greatest difficulties, showing a native how to give the anæsthetic, she operated, and for the next three days nursed the patient with anxious assiduity. Everything went very well and she realized that her brother could not have made a better job of it. She waited long enough to take out the stitches and then prepared to go home. She could flatter herself that she had not wasted her time. She had given medical attention to such as needed it, she had strengthened the small Christian community in its faith, admonished such as were lax and cast the good seed in places where it might be hoped under divine providence to take root.

The launch, coming from one of the other islands, put in somewhat late in the afternoon, but it was full moon and they expected to reach Baru before midnight. They brought her things down to the wharf and the people who were seeing her off stood about repeating their thanks. Quite a little crowd collected. The launch was loaded with sacks of copra, but Miss Jones was used to its strong smell and it did not incommode her. She made herself as comfortable a place to sit in as she could, and waiting for the launch to start, chatted with her grateful flock. She was the only passenger. Suddenly a group of natives emerged from the trees that embowered the little village on the lagoon and she saw that among them was a white man. He wore a prison sarong and a baju. He had long red hair. She at once recognized Ginger Ted. A policeman was with him. They shook hands and Ginger Ted shook hands with the villagers who accompanied him. They bore bundles of fruit and a jar which Miss Jones guessed contained native spirit, and these they put in the launch. She discovered to her surprise that Ginger Ted was coming with her. His term was up and instructions had arrived that he was to be returned to Baru in the launch. He gave her a glance, but did not nod—indeed Miss Jones turned away her head—and stepped in. The mechanic started his engine and in a moment they were jug-jugging through the channel in the lagoon. Ginger Ted clambered on to a pile of sacks and lit a cigarette.

Miss Jones ignored him. Of course she knew him very well. Her heart sank when she thought that he was going to be once more in Baru, creating a scandal and drinking, a peril to the women and a thorn in the flesh of all decent people. She knew the steps her brother had taken to have him deported and she had no patience with the Controleur, who would not see a duty that stared him so plainly in the face. When they had crossed the bar and were in the open sea Ginger Ted took the stopper out of the jar of arak and putting his mouth to it took a long pull. Then he handed the jar to the two mechanics who formed the crew. One was a middle-aged man and the other a youth.

"I do not wish you to drink anything while we are on the journey," said Miss Jones sternly to the elder one.

He smiled at her and drank.

"A little arak can do no one any harm," he answered. He passed the jar to his companion, who drank also.

"If you drink again I shall complain to the Controleur," said Miss Jones.

The elder man said something she could not understand,

but which she suspected was very rude, and passed the jar back
to Ginger Ted. They went along for an hour or more. The sea
was like glass and the sun set radiantly. It set behind one of the
islands and for a few minutes changed it into a mystic city of
the skies. Miss Jones turned round to watch it and her heart
was filled with gratitude for the beauty of the world.

"And only man is vile," she quoted to herself.

They went due east. In the distance was a little island which
she knew they passed close by. It was uninhabited. A rocky
islet thickly grown with virgin forest. The boatman lit his lamps.
The night fell and immediately the sky was thick with stars.
The moon had not yet risen. Suddenly there was a slight jar
and the launch began to vibrate strangely. The engine rattled.
The head mechanic, calling to his mate to take the helm, crept
under the housing. They seemed to be going more slowly. The
engine stopped. She asked the youth what was the matter, but
he did not know. Ginger Ted got down from the top of the copra
sacks and slipped under the housing. When he reappeared she
would have liked to ask him what had happened, but her dignity
prevented her. She sat still and occupied herself with her
thoughts. There was a long swell and the launch rolled slightly.
The mechanic emerged once more into view and started the
engine. Though it rattled like mad they began to move. The
launch vibrated from stem to stern. They went very slowly.
Evidently something was amiss, but Miss Jones was exasperated rather than alarmed. The launch was supposed to do six
knots, but now it was just crawling along; at that rate they
would not get into Baru till long, long after midnight. The mechanic, still busy under the housing, shouted out something
to the man at the helm. They spoke in Bugi, of which Miss
Jones knew very little. But after a while she noticed that they
had changed their course and seemed to be heading for the little
uninhabited island a good deal to the lee of which they should
have passed.

"Where are we going?" she asked the helmsman with sudden
misgiving.

He pointed to the islet. She got up and went to the housing
and called to the man to come out.

"You're not going there? Why? What's the matter?"

"I can't get to Baru," he said.

"But you must. I insist. I order you to go to Baru."

The man shrugged his shoulders. He turned his back on her

and slipped once more under the housing. Then Ginger Ted addressed her.

"One of the blades of the propeller has broken off. He thinks he can get as far as that island. We shall have to stay the night there and he'll put on a new propeller in the morning when the tide's out."

"I can't spend the night on an uninhabited island with three men," she cried.

"A lot of women would jump at it."

"I insist on going to Baru. Whatever happens we must get there to-night."

"Don't get excited, old girl. We've got to beach the boat to put a new propeller on, and we shall be all right on the island."

"How dare you speak to me like that! I think you're very insolent."

"You'll be O.K. We've got plenty of grub and we'll have a snack when we land. You have a drop of arak and you'll feel like a house on fire."

"You're an impertinent man. If you don't go to Baru I'll have you all put in prison."

"We're not going to Baru. We can't. We're going to that island and if you don't like it you can get out and swim."

"Oh, you'll pay for this."

"Shut up, you old cow," said Ginger Ted.

Miss Jones gave a gasp of anger. But she controlled herself. Even out there, in the middle of the ocean, she had too much dignity to bandy words with that vile wretch. The launch, the engine rattling horribly, crawled on. It was pitch dark now, and she could no longer see the island they were making for. Miss Jones, deeply incensed, sat with lips tight shut and a frown on her brow; she was not used to being crossed. Then the moon rose and she could see the bulk of Ginger Ted sprawling on the top of the piled sacks of copra. The glimmer of his cigarette was strangely sinister. Now the island was vaguely outlined against the sky. They reached it and the boatman ran the launch on to the beach. Suddenly Miss Jones gave a gasp. The truth had dawned on her and her anger changed to fear. Her heart beat violently. She shook in every limb. She felt dreadfully faint. She saw it all. Was the broken propeller a put-up job or was it an accident? She could not be certain; anyhow, she knew that Ginger Ted would seize the opportunity. Ginger Ted would rape her. She knew his character. He was mad about

women. That was what he had done, practically, to the girl at
the mission, such a good little thing she was and an excellent
sempstress; they would have prosecuted him for that and he
would have been sentenced to years of imprisonment only very
unfortunately the innocent child had gone back to him several
times and indeed had only complained of his ill usage when he
left her for somebody else. They had gone to the Controleur
about it, but he had refused to take any steps, saying in that
coarse way of his that even if what the girl said was true, it
didn't look very much as though it had been an altogether unpleasant experience. Ginger Ted was a scoundrel. And she was a
white woman. What chance was there that he would spare her?
None. She knew men. But she must pull herself together. She
must keep her wits about her. She must have courage. She was
determined to sell her virtue dearly, and if he killed her—well,
she would rather die than yield. And if she died she would rest
in the arms of Jesus. For a moment a great light blinded her eyes
and she saw the mansions of her Heavenly Father. They were
a grand and sumptuous mixture of a picture palace and a railway station. The mechanics and Ginger Ted jumped out of the
launch and, waist deep in water, gathered round the broken
propeller. She took advantage of their preoccupation to get her
case of surgical instruments out of the box. She took out the four
scalpels it contained and secreted them in her clothing. If
Ginger Ted touched her she would not hesitate to plunge a
scalpel in his heart.

"Now then, miss, you'd better get out," said Ginger Ted.
"You'll be better off on the beach than in the boat."

She thought so too. At least there she would have freedom
of action. Without a word she clambered over the copra sacks.
He offered her his hand.

"I don't want your help," she said coldly.

"You can go to hell," he answered.

It was a little difficult to get out of the boat without showing
her legs, but by the exercise of considerable ingenuity she
managed it.

"Damned lucky we've got something to eat. We'll make a
fire and then you'd better have a snack and a nip of arak."

"I want nothing. I only want to be left alone."

"It won't hurt me if you go hungry."

She did not answer. She walked, with head erect, along the
beach. She held the largest scalpel in her closed fist. The

moon allowed her to see where she was going. She looked for a place to hide. The thick forest came down to the very edge of the beach; but, afraid of its darkness (after all, she was but a woman), she dared not plunge into its depth. She did not know what animals lurked there or what dangerous snakes. Besides, her instinct told her that it was better to keep those three bad men in sight; then if they came towards her she would be prepared. Presently she found a little hollow. She looked round. They seemed to be occupied with their own affairs and they could not see her. She slipped in. There was a rock between them and her so that she was hidden from them and yet could watch them. She saw them go to and from the boat carrying things. She saw them build a fire. It lit them luridly and she saw them sit around it and eat, and she saw the jar of arak passed from one to the other. They were all going to get drunk. What would happen to her then? It might be that she could cope with Ginger Ted, though his strength terrified her, but against three she would be powerless. A mad idea came to her to go to Ginger Ted and fall on her knees before him and beg him to spare her. He must have some spark of decent feeling in him and she had always been so convinced that there was good even in the worst of men. He must have had a mother. Perhaps he had a sister. Ah, but how could you appeal to a man blinded with lust and drunk with arak? She began to feel terribly weak. She was afraid she was going to cry. That would never do. She needed all her self-control. She bit her lip. She watched them, like a tiger watching his prey; no, not like that, like a lamb watching three hungry wolves. She saw them put more wood on the fire and Ginger Ted, in his sarong, silhouetted by the flames. Perhaps after he had had his will of her he would pass her on to the others. How could she go back to her brother when such a thing had happened to her? Of course he would be sympathetic, but would he ever feel quite the same to her again? It would break his heart. And perhaps he would think that she ought to have resisted more. For his sake perhaps it would be better if she said nothing about it, naturally the men would say nothing. It would mean twenty years in prison for them. But then supposing she had a baby. Miss Jones instinctively clenched her hands with horror and nearly cut herself with the scalpel. Of course it would only infuriate them if she resisted.

"What shall I do?" she cried. "What have I done to deserve this?"

She flung herself down on her knees and prayed to God to save her. She prayed long and earnestly. She reminded God that she was a virgin and just mentioned, in case it had slipped the divine memory, how much St. Paul had valued that excellent state. And then she peeped round the rock again. The three men appeared to be smoking and the fire was dying down. Now was the time that Ginger Ted's lewd thoughts might be expected to turn to the woman who was at his mercy. She smothered a cry, for suddenly he got up and walked in her direction. She felt all her muscles grow taut, and though her heart was beating furiously she clenched the scalpel firmly in her hand. But it was for another purpose that Ginger Ted had got up. Miss Jones blushed and looked away. He strolled slowly back to the others and sitting down again raised the jar of arak to his lips. Miss Jones, crouching behind the rock, watched with straining eyes. The conversation round the fire grew less and presently she divined, rather than saw, that the two natives wrapped themselves in blankets and composed themselves to slumber. She understood. This was the moment Ginger Ted had been waiting for. When they were fast asleep he would get up cautiously and without a sound, in order not to wake the others, creep stealthily towards her. Was it that he was unwilling to share her with them or did he know that his deed was so dastardly that he did not wish them to know of it? After all, he was a white man and she was a white woman. He could not have sunk so low as to allow her to suffer the violence of natives. But his plan, which was so obvious to her, had given her an idea; when she saw him coming she would scream, she would scream so loudly that it would wake the two mechanics. She remembered now that the elder, though he had only one eye, had a kind face. But Ginger Ted did not move. She was feeling terribly tired. She began to fear that she would not have the strength now to resist him. She had gone through too much. She closed her eyes for a minute.

When she opened them it was broad daylight. She must have fallen asleep and, so shattered was she by emotion, have slept till long after dawn. It gave her quite a turn. She sought to rise, but something caught in her legs. She looked and found that she was covered with two empty copra sacks. Someone had come in the night and put them over her. Ginger Ted. She gave a little scream. The horrible thought flashed through her mind that he had outraged her in her sleep. No. It was impossible. And yet he had had her at his mercy. Defenceless. And he had spared her. She blushed furiously. She raised herself to her feet, feeling a little stiff, and arranged her disordered dress. The scalpel had fallen from her hand and she picked it up. She took the two copra sacks and emerged from her hiding-place. She walked towards the boat. It was floating in the shallow water of the lagoon.

"Come on, Miss Jones," said Ginger Ted. "We've finished. I was just going to wake you up."

She could not look at him, but she felt herself as red as a turkey cock.

"Have a banana?" he said.

Without a word she took it. She was very hungry, and ate it with relish.

"Step on this rock and you'll be able to get in without wetting your feet."

Miss Jones felt as though she could sink into the ground with shame, but she did as he told her. He took hold of her arm —good heavens, his hand was like an iron vice, never, never could she have struggled with him—and helped her into the launch. The mechanic started the engine and they slid out of the lagoon. In three hours they were at Baru.

That evening, having been officially released, Ginger Ted went to the Controleur's house. He wore no longer the prison uniform, but the ragged singlet and the khaki shorts in which he had been arrested. He had had his hair cut and it fitted his head now like a little curly red cap. He was thinner. He had lost his bloated flabbiness and looked younger and better. Mr. Gruyter, a friendly grin on his round face, shook hands with him and asked him to sit down. The boy brought two bottles of beer.

"I'm glad to see you hadn't forgotten my invitation, Ginger," said the Controleur.

"Not likely. I've been looking forward to this for six months."

"Here's luck, Ginger Ted."

"Same to you, Controleur."

They emptied their glasses and the Controleur clapped his hands. The boy brought two more bottles.

"Well, you don't bear me any malice for the sentence I gave you, I hope."

"No bloody fear. I was mad for a minute, but I got over it. I didn't have half a bad time, you know. Nice lot of girls o that island, Controleur. You ought to give 'em a look over one of these days."

"You're a bad lot, Ginger."

"Terrible."

"Good beer, isn't it?"

"Fine."

"Let's have some more."

Ginger Ted's remittance had been arriving every month and the Controleur now had fifty pounds for him. When the damage he had done to the Chinaman's shop was paid for there would still be over thirty.

"That's quite a lot of money, Ginger. You ought to do something useful with it."

"I mean to," answered Ginger. "Spend it."

The Controleur sighed.

"Well, that's what money's for, I guess."

The Controleur gave his guest the news. Not much had happened during the last six months. Time on the Alas Islands did not matter very much and the rest of the world did not matter at all.

"Any wars anywhere?" asked Ginger Ted.

"No. Not that I've noticed. Harry Jervis found a pretty big pearl. He says he's going to ask a thousand quid for it."

"I hope he gets it."

"And Charlie McCormack's married."

"He always was a bit soft."

Suddenly the boy appeared and said Mr. Jones wished to know if he might come in. Before the Controleur could give an answer Mr. Jones walked in.

"I won't detain you long," he said. "I've been trying to get hold of this good man all day and when I heard he was here I thought you wouldn't mind my coming."

"How is Miss Jones?" asked the Controleur politely. "None the worse for her night in the open, I trust."

"She's naturally a bit shaken. She had a temperature and I've insisted on her going to bed, but I don't think it's serious."

The two men had got up on the missionary's entrance, and now the missionary went up to Ginger Ted and held out his hand.

"I want to thank you. You did a great and noble thing. My sister is right, one should always look for the good in their fellow men; i am afraid I misjudged you in the past: I beg your pardon."

He spoke very solemnly. Ginger Ted looked at him with amazement. He had not been able to prevent the missionary taking his hand. He still held it.

"What the hell are you talking about?"

"You had my sister at your mercy and you spared her. I thought you were all evil and I am ashamed. She was defenceless. She was in your power. You had pity on her. I thank you from the bottom of my heart. Neither my sister nor I will ever forget. God bless and guard you always."

Mr. Jones's voice shook a little and he turned his head away. He released Ginger Ted's hand and strode quickly to the door. Ginger Ted watched him with a blank face.

"What the blazes does he mean?" he asked.

The Controleur laughed. He tried to control himself, but the more he did the more he laughed. He shook and you saw the folds of his fat belly ripple under the sarong. He leaned back in his long chair and rolled from side to side. He did not laugh only with his face, he laughed with his whole body, and even the muscles of his podgy legs shook with mirth. He held his aching ribs. Ginger Ted looked at him frowning, and because he did not understand what the joke was he grew angry. He seized one of the empty beer bottles by the neck.

"If you don't stop laughing, I'll break your bloody head open," he said.

The Controleur mopped his face. He swallowed a mouthful of beer. He sighed and groaned because his sides were hurting him.

"He's thanking you for having respected the virtue of Miss Jones," he spluttered at last.

"Me?" cried Ginger Ted.

The thought took quite a long time to travel through his head, but when at last he got it he flew into a violent rage. There flowed from his mouth such a stream of blasphemous obscenities as would have startled a marine.

"That old cow," he finished. "What does he take me for?"

"You have the reputation of being rather hot stuff with the girls, Ginger," giggled the little Controleur.

"I wouldn't touch her with the fag end of a barge-pole. It never entered my head. The nerve. I'll wring his blasted neck. Look here, give me my money, I'm going to get drunk."

"I don't blame you," said the Controleur.

"That old cow," repeated Ginger Ted. "That old cow."

He was shocked and outraged. The suggestion really shattered his sense of decency.

The Controleur had the money at hand and having got Ginger Ted to sign the necessary papers gave it to him.

"Go and get drunk, Ginger Ted," he said, "but I warn you. if you get into mischief it'll be twelve months next time."

"I shan't get into mischief," said Ginger Ted sombrely. He was suffering from a sense of injury. "It's an insult," he shouted at the Controleur. "That's what it is, it's a bloody insult."

He lurched out of the house, and as he went he muttered to himself: "dirty swine, dirty swine." Ginger Ted remained drunk for a week. Mr. Jones went to see the Controleur again.

"I'm very sorry to hear that poor fellow has taken up his evil course again," he said. "My sister and I are dreadfully disappointed. I'm afraid it wasn't very wise to give him so much money at once."

"It was his own money. I had no right to keep it back."

"Not a legal right, perhaps, but surely a moral right."

He told the Controleur the story of that fearful night on the island. With her feminine instinct, Miss Jones had realized that the man, inflamed with lust, was determined to take advantage of her, and, resolved to defend herself to the last, had armed herself with a scalpel. He told the Controleur how she had prayed and wept and how she had hidden herself. Her agony was indescribable, and she knew that she could never have survived the shame. She rocked to and fro and every moment she thought he was coming. And there was no help anywhere and at last she had fallen asleep; she was tired out, poor thing, she had undergone more than any human being could stand, and then when she awoke she found that he had covered her with copra sacks. He had found her asleep, and surely it was her innocence, her very helplessness that had moved him, he hadn't the heart to touch her; he covered her gently with two copra sacks and crept silently away.

"It shows you that deep down in him there is something sterling. My sister feels it's our duty to save him. We must do something for him."

"Well, in your place I wouldn't try till he's got through all his money," said the Controleur, "and then if he's not in gaol you can do what you like."

But Ginger Ted didn't want to be saved. About a fortnight after his release from prison he was sitting on a stool outside a Chinaman's shop looking vacantly down the street when he saw Miss Jones coming along. He stared at her for a minute and once more amazement seized him. He muttered to himself and there can be little doubt that his mutterings were disrespectful. But then he noticed that Miss Jones had seen him and he quickly turned his head away; he was conscious, notwithstanding, that she was looking at him. She was walking briskly, but she sensibly diminished her pace as she approached him. He thought she was going to stop and speak to him. He got up quickly and went into the shop. He did not venture to come out for at least five minutes. Half an hour later Mr. Jones himself came along and he went straight up to Ginger Ted with outstretched hand.

"How do you do, Mr. Edward? My sister told me I should find you here."

Ginger Ted gave him a surly look and did not take the proffered hand. He made no answer.

"We'd be so very glad if you'd come to dinner with us next Sunday. My sister's a capital cook and she'll make you a real Australian dinner."

"Go to hell," said Ginger Ted.

"That's not very gracious," said the missionary, but with a little laugh to show that he was not affronted. "You go and see the Controleur from time to time, why shouldn't you come and see us? It's pleasant to talk to white people now and then. Won't you let bygones be bygones? I can assure you of a very cordial welcome."

"I haven't got clothes fit to go out in," said Ginger Ted sulkily.

"Oh, never mind about that. Come as you are."

"I won't."

"Why not? You must have a reason."

Ginger Ted was a blunt man. He had no hesitation in saying what we should all like to when we receive unwelcome invitations.

"I don't want to."

"I'm sorry. My sister will be very disappointed."

Mr. Jones, determined to show that he was not in the least offended, gave him a breezy nod and walked on. Forty-eight hours later there mysteriously arrived at the house in which

Ginger Ted lodged a parcel containing a suit of ducks, a tennis shirt, a pair of socks and some shoes. He was unaccustomed to receiving presents and next time he saw the Controleur asked him if it was he who had sent the things.

"Not on your life," replied the Controleur. "I'm perfectly indifferent to the state of your wardrobe."

"Well, then, who the hell can have?"

"Search me."

It was necessary from time to time for Miss Jones to see Mr. Gruyter on business and shortly after this she came to see him one morning in his office. She was a capable woman and though she generally wanted him to do something he had no mind to, she did not waste his time. He was a little surprised then to discover that she had come on a very trivial errand. When he told her that he could not take cognizance of the matter in question, she did not as was her habit try to convince him, but accepted his refusal as definite. She got up to go and then as though it were an afterthought said:

"Oh, Mr. Gruyter, my brother is very anxious that we should have the man they call Ginger Ted to supper with us and I've written him a little note inviting him for the day after to-morrow. I think he's rather shy, and I wonder if you'd come with him."

"That's very kind of you."

"My brother feels that we ought to do something for the poor fellow."

"A woman's influence and all that sort of thing," said the Controleur demurely.

"Will you persuade him to come? I'm sure he will if you make a point of it, and when he knows the way he'll come again. It seems such a pity to let a young man like that go to pieces altogether."

The Controleur looked up at her. She was several inches taller than he. He thought her very unattractive. She reminded him strangely of wet linen hung on a clothes-line to dry. His eyes twinkled, but he kept a straight face.

"I'll do my best," he said.

"How old is he?" she asked.

"According to his passport he's thirty-one."

"And what is his real name?"

"Wilson."

"Edward Wilson," she said softly.

"It's astonishing that after the life he's led he should be so strong," murmured the Controleur. "He has the strength of an ox."

"Those red-headed men sometimes are very powerful," said Miss Jones, but spoke as though she were choking.

"Quite so," said the Controleur.

Then for no obvious reason Miss Jones blushed. She hurriedly said good-bye to the Controleur and left his office.

"*Godverdomme!*" said the Controleur.

He knew now who had sent Ginger Ted the new clothes.

He met him during the course of the day and asked him whether he had heard from Miss Jones. Ginger Ted took a crumpled ball of paper out of his pocket and gave it to him. It was the invitation. It ran as follows:

Dear Mr. Wilson,—

My brother and I would be so very glad if you would come and have supper with us next Thursday at 7.30. The Controleur has kindly promised to come. We have some new records from Australia which I am sure you will like. I am afraid I was not very nice to you last time we met, but I did not know you so well then, and I am big enough to admit it when I have committed an error. I hope you will forgive me and let me be your friend.

Yours sincerely,
Martha Jones.

The Controleur noticed that she addressed him as Mr. Wilson and referred to his own promise to go, so that when she told him she had already invited Ginger Ted she had a little anticipated the truth.

"What are you going to do?"

"I'm not going, if that's what you mean. Damned nerve."

"You must answer the letter."

"Well, I won't."

"Now look here, Ginger, you put on those new clothes and you come as a favour to me. I've got to go, and damn it all, you can't leave me in the lurch. It won't hurt you just once."

Ginger Ted looked at the Controleur suspiciously, but his face was serious and his manner sincere; he could not guess that within him the Dutchman bubbled with laughter.

"What the devil do they want me for?"

"I don't know. The pleasure of your society, I suppose."

"Will there be any booze?"

"No, but come up to my house at seven, and we'll have a tiddly before we go."

"Oh, all right," said Ginger Ted sulkily.

The Controleur rubbed his little fat hands with joy. He was expecting a great deal of amusement from the party. But when Thursday came and seven o'clock Ginger Ted was dead drunk and Mr. Gruyter had to go alone. He told the missionary and his sister the plain truth. Mr. Jones shook his head.

"I'm afraid it's no good, Martha, the man's hopeless."

For a moment Miss Jones was silent and the Controleur saw two tears trickle down her long thin nose. She bit her lip.

"No one is hopeless. Everyone has some good in him. I shall pray for him every night. It would be wicked to doubt the power of God."

Perhaps Miss Jones was right in this, but the divine providence took a very funny way of effecting its ends. Ginger Ted began to drink more heavily than ever. He was so troublesome that even Mr. Gruyter lost patience with him. He made up his mind that he could not have the fellow on the islands any more and resolved to deport him on the next boat that touched at Baru. Then a man died under mysterious circumstances after having been for a trip to one of the islands and the Controleur learnt that there had been several deaths on the same island. He sent the Chinese who was the official doctor of the group to look into the matter, and very soon received intelligence that the deaths were due to cholera. Two more took place at Baru and the certainty was forced upon him that there was an epidemic.

The Controleur cursed freely. He cursed in Dutch, he cursed in English and he cursed in Malay. Then he drank a bottle of beer and smoked a cigar. After that he took thought. He knew the Chinese doctor would be useless. He was a nervous little man from Java and the natives would refuse to obey his orders. The Controleur was efficient and knew pretty well what must be done, but he could not do everything single-handed. He did not like Mr. Jones, but just then he was thankful that he was at hand, and he sent for him at once. In ten minutes Mr. Jones was in the office. He was accompanied by his sister.

"You know what I want to see you about, Mr. Jones," he said abruptly.

"Yes. I've been expecting a message from you. That is why my sister has come with me. We are ready to put all our resources at your disposal. I need not tell you that my sister is as competent as a man."

"I know. I shall be very glad of her assistance."

They set to without further delay to discuss the steps that must be taken. Hospital huts would have to be erected and quarantine stations. The inhabitants of the various villages on the islands must be forced to take proper precautions. In a good many cases the infected villages drew their water from the same well as the uninfected, and in each case this difficulty would have to be dealt with according to circumstances. It was necessary to send round people to give orders and make sure that they were carried out. Negligence must be ruthlessly punished. The worst of it was that the natives would not obey other natives, and orders given by native policemen, themselves unconvinced of their efficacy, would certainly be disregarded. It was advisable for Mr. Jones to stay at Baru where the population was largest and his medical attention most wanted; and what with the official duties that forced him to keep in touch with his headquarters, it was impossible for Mr. Gruyter to visit all the other islands himself. Miss Jones must go; but the natives of some of the outlying islands were wild and treacherous; the Controleur had had a good deal of trouble with them. He did not like the idea of exposing her to danger.

"I'm not afraid," she said.

"I daresay. But if you have your throat cut I shall get into trouble, and besides, we're so short-handed I don't want to risk losing your help."

"Then let Mr. Wilson come with me. He knows the natives better than anyone and can speak all their dialects."

"Ginger Ted?" The Controleur stared at her. "He's just getting over an attack of D.T.'s."

"I know," she answered.

"You know a great deal, Miss Jones."

Even though the moment was so serious Mr. Gruyter could not but smile. He gave her a sharp look, but she met it coolly.

"There's nothing like responsibility for bringing out what there is in a man, and I think something like this may be the making of him."

"Do you think it would be wise to trust yourself for days at a time to a man of such infamous character?" said the missionary.

"I put my trust in God," she answered gravely.

"Do you think he'd be any use?" asked the Controleur. "You know what he is."

"I'm convinced of it." Then she blushed. "After all, no one knows better than I that he's capable of self-control."

The Controleur bit his lip.

"Let's send for him."

He gave a message to the sergeant and in a few minutes Ginger Ted stood before them. He looked ill. He had evidently been much shaken by his recent attack and his nerves were all to pieces. He was in rags and he had not shaved for a week. No one could have looked more disreputable.

"Look here, Ginger," said the Controleur, "it's about this cholera business. We've got to force the natives to take precautions and we want you to help us."

"Why the hell should I?"

"No reason at all. Except philanthropy."

"Nothing doing, Controleur. I'm not a philanthropist."

"That settles that. That was all. You can go."

But as Ginger Ted turned to the door Miss Jones stopped him.

"It was my suggestion, Mr. Wilson. You see, they want me to go to Labobo and Sakunchi, and the natives there are so funny I was afraid to go alone. I thought if you came I should be safer."

He gave her a look of extreme distaste.

"What do you suppose I care if they cut your throat?"

Miss Jones looked at him and her eyes filled with tears. She began to cry. He stood and watched her stupidly.

"There's no reason why you should." She pulled herself together and dried her eyes. "I'm being silly. I shall be all right. I'll go alone."

"It's damned foolishness for a woman to go to Labobo."

She gave him a little smile.

"I daresay it is, but you see, it's my job and I can't help myself. I'm sorry if I offended you by asking you. You must forget about it. I daresay it wasn't quite fair to ask you to take such a risk."

For quite a minute Ginger Ted stood and looked at her. He shifted from one foot to the other. His surly face seemed to grow black.

"Oh, hell, have it your own way," he said at last. "I'll come with you. When d'you want to start?"

They set out next day, with drugs and disinfectants, in the government launch. Mr. Gruyter as soon as he had put the necessary work in order was to start off in a prahu in the other direction. For four months the epidemic raged. Though everything possible was done to localize it one island after another was attacked. The Controleur was busy from morning to night. He had no sooner got back to Baru from one or other of the islands to do what was necessary there than he had to set off again. He distributed food and medicine. He cheered the terrified people. He supervised everything. He worked like a dog. He saw nothing of Ginger Ted, but he heard from Mr. Jones that the experiment was working out beyond all hopes. The scamp was behaving himself. He had a way with the natives; and by cajolery, firmness and on occasion the use of his fist, managed to make them take the steps necessary for their own safety. Miss Jones could congratulate herself on the success of the scheme. But the Controleur was too tired to be amused. When the epidemic had run its course he rejoiced because out of a population of eight thousand only six hundred had died.

Finally he was able to give the district a clean bill of health.

One evening he was sitting in his sarong on the verandah of his house and he read a French novel with the happy consciousness that once more he could take things easy. His head boy came in and told him that Ginger Ted wished to see him. He got up from his chair and shouted to him to come in. Company was just what he wanted. It had crossed the Controleur's mind that it would be pleasant to get drunk that night, but it is dull to get drunk alone, and he had regretfully put the thought aside. And heaven had sent Ginger Ted in the nick of time. By God, they would make a night of it. After four months they deserved a bit of fun. Ginger Ted entered. He was wearing a clean suit of white ducks. He was shaved. He looked another man.

"Why, Ginger, you look as if you'd been spending a month at a health resort instead of nursing a pack of natives dying of cholera. And look at your clothes. Have you just stepped out of a band-box?"

Ginger Ted smiled rather sheepishly. The head boy brought two bottles of beer and poured them out.

"Help yourself, Ginger," said the Controleur as he took his glass.

"I don't think I'll have any, thank you."

The Controleur put down his glass and looked at Ginger Ted with amazement.

"Why, what's the matter? Aren't you thirsty?"

"I don't mind having a cup of tea."

"A cup of what?"

"I'm on the wagon. Martha and I are going to be married."

"Ginger!"

The Controleur's eyes popped out of his head. He scratched his shaven pate.

"You can't marry Miss Jones," he said. "No one could marry Miss Jones."

"Well, I'm going to. That's what I've come to see you about. Owen's going to marry us in chapel, but we want to be married by Dutch law as well."

"A joke's a joke, Ginger. What's the idea?"

"She wanted it. She fell for me that night we spent on the island when the propeller broke. She's not a bad old girl when you get to know her. It's her last chance, if you understand what I mean, and I'd like to do something to oblige her. And she wants someone to take care of her, there's no doubt about that."

"Ginger, Ginger, before you can say knife she'll make you into a damned missionary."

"I don't know that I'd mind that so much if we had a little mission of our own. She says I'm a bloody marvel with the natives. She says I can do more with a native in five minutes than Owen can do in a year. She says she's never known anyone with the magnetism I have. It seems a pity to waste a gift like that."

The Controleur looked at him without speaking and slowly nodded his head three or four times. She'd nobbled him all right.

"I've converted seventeen already," said Ginger Ted.

"You? I didn't know you believed in Christianity."

"Well, I don't know that I did exactly, but when I talked to 'em and they just came into the fold like a lot of blasted sheep, well, it gave me quite a turn. Blimey, I said, I daresay there's something in it after all."

"You should have raped her, Ginger. I wouldn't have been

hard on you. I wouldn't have given you more than three years and three years is soon over."

"Look here, Controleur, don't you ever let on that the thought never entered my head. Women are touchy, you know, and she'd be as sore as hell if she knew that."

"I guessed she'd got her eye on you, but I never thought it would come to this." The Controleur in an agitated manner walked up and down the verandah. "Listen to me, old boy," he said after an interval of reflection, "we've had some grand times together and a friend's a friend. I'll tell you what I'll do, I'll lend you the launch and you can go and hide on one of the islands till the next ship comes along and then I'll get 'em to slow down and take you on board. You've only got one chance now and that's to cut and run."

Ginger Ted shook his head.

"It's no good, Controleur, I know you mean well, but I'm going to marry the blasted woman, and that's that. You don't know the joy of bringing all them bleeding sinners to repentance, and Christ, that girl can make a treacle pudding. I haven't eaten a better one since I was a kid."

The Controleur was very much disturbed. The drunken scamp was his only companion on the islands and he did not want to lose him. He discovered that he had even a certain affection for him. Next day he went to see the missionary.

"What's this I hear about your sister marrying Ginger Ted?" he asked him. "It's the most extraordinary thing I've ever heard in my life."

"It's true nevertheless."

"You must do something about it. It's madness."

"My sister is of full age and entitled to do as she pleases."

"But you don't mean to tell me you approve of it. You know Ginger Ted. He's a bum and there are no two ways about it. Have you told her the risk she's running? I mean, bringing sinners to repentance and all that sort of thing's all right, but there are limits. And does the leopard ever change his spots?"

Then for the first time in his life the Controleur saw a twinkle in the missionary's eye.

"My sister is a very determined woman, Mr. Gruyter," he replied. "From that night they spent on the island he never had a chance."

The Controleur gasped. He was as surprised as the prophet when the Lord opened the mouth of the ass, and she said unto

Balaam, "What have I done unto thee, that thou hast smitten me these three times?" Perhaps Mr. Jones was human after all.

"*Allejesus!*" muttered the Controleur.

Before anything more could be said Miss Jones swept into the room. She was radiant. She looked ten years younger. Her cheeks were flushed and her nose was hardly red at all.

"Have you come to congratulate me, Mr. Gruyter?" she cried, and her manner was sprightly and girlish. "You see, I was right after all. Everyone has some good in them. You don't know how splendid Edward has been all through this terrible time. He's a hero. He's a saint. Even I was surprised."

"I hope you'll be very happy, Miss Jones."

"I know I shall. Oh, it would be wicked of me to doubt it. For it is the Lord who has brought us together."

"Do you think so?"

"I know it. Don't you see? Except for the cholera Edward would never have found himself. Except for the cholera we should never have learnt to know one another. I have never seen the hand of God more plainly manifest."

The Controleur could not but think that it was rather a clumsy device to bring those two together that necessitated the death of six hundred innocent persons, but not being well versed in the ways of omnipotence he made no remark.

"You'll never guess where we're going for our honeymoon," said Miss Jones, perhaps a trifle archly.

"Java?"

"No, if you'll lend us the launch, we're going to that island where we were marooned. It has very tender recollections for both of us. It was there that I first guessed how fine and good Edward was. It's there I want him to have his reward."

The Controleur caught his breath. He left quickly, for he thought that unless he had a bottle of beer at once he would have a fit. He was never so shocked in his life.

THE DOOR OF OPPORTUNITY

THEY got a first-class carriage to themselves. It was lucky, because they were taking a good deal in with them, Alban's suit-case and a hold-all, Anne's dressing-case and her hat-box. They had two trunks in the van, containing what they wanted immediately, but all the rest of their luggage Alban had put in the care of an agent who was to take it up to London and store it till they had made up their minds what to do. They had a lot, pictures and books, curios that Alban had collected in the East, his guns and saddles. They had left Sondurah for ever. Alban, as was his way, tipped the porter generously and then went back to the book-stall and bought papers. He bought The New Statesman and The Nation, and The Tatler and The Sketch, and the last number of The London Mercury. He came back to the carriage and threw them on the seat.

"It's only an hour's journey," said Anne.

"I know, but I wanted to buy them. I've been starved so long. Isn't it grand to think that to-morrow morning we shall have to-morrow's Times, and The Express and The Mail?"

She did not answer and he turned away, for he saw coming towards them two persons, a man and his wife, who had been fellow-passengers from Singapore.

"Get through the customs all right?" he cried to them cheerily.

The man seemed not to hear, for he walked straight on, but the woman answered.

"Yes, they never found the cigarettes."

She saw Anne, gave her a friendly little smile, and passed on. Anne flushed.

"I was afraid they'd want to come in here," said Alban. "Let's have the carriage to ourselves if we can."

She looked at him curiously.

"I don't think you need worry," she answered. "I don't think anyone will come in."

He lit a cigarette and lingered at the carriage door. On his face was a happy smile. When they had passed through the Red Sea and found a sharp wind in the Canal, Anne had been surprised to see how much the men who had looked presentable enough in the white ducks in which she had been accustomed to see them, were changed when they left them off for warmer clothes. They looked like nothing on earth then. Their ties were awful and their shirts all wrong. They wore grubby flannel trousers and shabby old golf-coats that had too obviously been bought off the nail, or blue serge suits that betrayed the provincial tailor. Most of the passengers had got off at Marseilles, but a dozen or so, either because after a long period in the East they thought the trip through the Bay would do them good, or, like themselves, for economy's sake, had gone all the way to Tilbury, and now several of them walked along the platform. They wore solar topis or double-brimmed terais, and heavy greatcoats, or else shapeless soft hats or bowlers, not too well brushed, that looked too small for them. It was a shock to see them. They looked suburban and a trifle second-rate. But Alban had already a London look. There was not a speck of dust on his smart greatcoat, and his black Homburg hat looked brand-new. You would never have guessed that he had not been home for three years. His collar fitted closely round his neck and his foulard tie was neatly tied. As Anne looked at him she could not but think how good-looking he was. He was just under six feet tall, and slim, and he wore his clothes well, and his clothes were well cut. He had fair hair, still thick, and blue eyes and the faintly yellow skin common to men of that complexion after they have lost the pink and white freshness of early youth. There was no colour in his cheeks. It was a fine head, well-set on rather a long neck, with a somewhat prominent Adam's apple; but you were more impressed with the distinction than with the beauty of his face. It was because his features were so regular, his nose so straight, his brow so broad that he photographed so well. Indeed, from his photographs you would have thought him extremely handsome. He was not that, perhaps because his eyebrows and his eyelashes were pale, and his lips thin, but he looked very intellectual. There was refinement in his face and a spirituality that was oddly moving. That was how you thought a poet should look; and when Anne became engaged to him she told her girl friends who asked her about him that he looked like Shelley. He turned to her now with a little smile in his blue eyes. His smile was very attractive.

"What a perfect day to land in England!"

It was October. They had steamed up the Channel on a grey sea under a grey sky. There was not a breath of wind. The fishing boats seemed to rest on the placid water as though the elements had forever forgotten their old hostility. The coast was incredibly green, but with a bright cosy greenness quite un-like the luxuriant, vehement verdure of Eastern jungles. The red towns they passed here and there were comfortable and homelike. They seemed to welcome the exiles with a smiling friendliness. And when they drew into the estuary of the Thames they saw the rich levels of Essex and in a little while Chalk Church on the Kentish shore, lonely in the midst of weather-beaten trees, and beyond it the woods of Cobham. The sun, red in a faint mist, set on the marshes, and night fell. In the station the arc-lamps shed a light that spotted the dark-ness with cold hard patches. It was good to see the porters lum-bering about in their grubby uniforms and the station-master fat and important in his bowler hat. The stationmaster blew a whistle and waved his arm. Alban stepped into the carriage and seated himself in the corner opposite to Anne. The train started.

"We're due in London at six-ten," said Alban. "We ought to get to Jermyn Street by seven. That'll give us an hour to bath and change and we can get to the Savoy for dinner by eight-thirty. A bottle of pop to-night, my pet, and a slap-up dinner." He gave a chuckle. "I heard the Strouds and the Maundys ar-ranging to meet at the Trocadero Grill-Room."

He took up the papers and asked if she wanted any of them. Anne shook her head.

"Tired?" he smiled.

"No."

"Excited?"

In order not to answer she gave a little laugh. He began to look at the papers, starting with the publishers' advertisements, and she was conscious of the intense satisfaction it was to him to feel himself through them once more in the middle of things. They had taken in those same papers in Sondurah, but they arrived six weeks old, and though they kept them abreast of what was going on in the world that interested them both, they emphasized their exile. But these were fresh from the press. They smelt different. They had a crispness that was almost voluptuous. He wanted to read them all at once. Anne looked out of the window. The country was dark, and she could see little but the lights of their carriage reflected on the glass, but very soon the town encroached upon it, and then she saw little sordid houses, mile upon mile of them, with a light in a window here and there, and the chimneys made a dreary pattern against the sky. They passed through Barking and East Ham and Bromley—it was silly that the name on the platform as they went through the station should give her such a tremor—and then Stepney. Alban put down his papers.

"We shall be there in five minutes now."

He put on his hat and took down from the racks the things the porter had put in them. He looked at her with shining eyes and his lips twitched. She saw that he was only just able to control his emotion. He looked out of the window, too, and they passed over brightly lighted thoroughfares, close packed with tram-cars, buses and motor-vans, and they saw the streets thick with people. What a mob! The shops were all lit up. They saw the hawkers with their barrows at the curb.

"London," he said.

He took her hand and gently pressed it. His smile was so sweet that she had to say something. She tried to be facetious.

"Does it make you feel all funny inside?"

"I don't know if I want to cry or if I want to be sick."

Fenchurch Street. He lowered the window and waved his arm for a porter. With a grinding of brakes the train came to a standstill. A porter opened the door and Alban handed him out one package after another. Then in his polite way, having jumped out, he gave his hand to Anne to help her down to the platform. The porter went to fetch a barrow and they stood by the pile of their luggage. Alban waved to two passengers from the ship who passed them. The man nodded stiffly.

"What a comfort it is that we shall never have to be civil to those awful people any more," said Alban lightly.

Anne gave him a quick glance. He was really incomprehensible. The porter came back with his barrow, the luggage was put on and they followed him to collect their trunks. Alban took his wife's arm and pressed it.

"The smell of London. By God, it's grand."

He rejoiced in the noise and the bustle, and the crowd of people who jostled them; the radiance of the arc-lamps and the black shadows they cast, sharp but full-toned, gave him a sense of elation. They got out into the street and the porter went off to get them a taxi. Alban's eyes glittered as he looked at the buses and the policemen trying to direct the confusion. His distinguished face bore a look of something like inspiration. The taxi came. Their luggage was stowed away and piled up beside the driver, Alban gave the porter half-a-crown, and they drove off. They turned down Grace-church Street and in Cannon Street were held up by a block in the traffic. Alban laughed out loud.

"What's the matter?" said Anne.

"I'm so excited."

They went along the Embankment. It was relatively quiet there. Taxis and cars passed them. The bells of the trams were music in his ears. At Westminster Bridge they cut across Parliament Square and drove through the green silence of St. James's Park. They had engaged a room at a hotel just off Jermyn Street. The reception clerk took them upstairs and a porter brought up their luggage. It was a room with twin beds and a bathroom.

"This looks all right," said Alban. "It'll do us till we can find a flat or something."

He looked at his watch.

"Look here, darling, we shall only fall over one another if we try to unpack together. We've got oodles of time and it'll take you longer to get straight and dress than me. I'll clear out. I want to go to the club and see if there's any mail for me. I've got my dinner-jacket in my suit-case and it'll only take me twenty minutes to have a bath and dress. Does that suit you?"

"Yes. That's all right."

"I'll be back in an hour."

"Very well."

He took out of his pocket the little comb he always carried and passed it through his long fair hair. Then he put on his hat. He gave himself a glance in the mirror.

"Shall I turn on the bath for you?"

"No, don't bother."

"All right. So long."

He went out.

When he was gone Anne took her dressing-case and her hat-box and put them on the top of her trunk. Then she rang the bell. She did not take off her hat. She sat down and lit a cigarette. When a servant answered the bell she asked for the porter. He came. She pointed to the luggage.

"Will you take those things and leave them in the hall for the present. I'll tell you what to do with them presently."

"Very good, ma'am."

She gave him a florin. He took the trunk out and the other packages and closed the door behind him. A few tears slid down Anne's cheeks, but she shook herself; she dried her eyes and powdered her face. She needed all her calm. She was glad that Alban had conceived the idea of going to his club. It made things easier and gave her a little time to think them out.

Now that the moment had come to do what she had for weeks determined, now that she must say the terrible things she had to say, she quailed. Her heart sank. She knew exactly what she meant to say to Alban, she had made up her mind about that long ago, and had said the very words to herself a hundred times, three or four times a day every day of the long journey from Singapore, but she was afraid that she would grow confused. She dreaded an argument. The thought of a scene made her feel slightly sick. It was something at all events to have an hour in which to collect herself. He would say she was heartless and cruel and unreasonable. She could not help it.

"No, no, no," she cried aloud.

She shuddered with horror. And all at once she saw herself again in the bungalow, sitting as she had been sitting when the whole thing started. It was getting on towards tiffin time and in a few minutes Alban would be back from the office. It gave her pleasure to reflect that it was an attractive room for him to come back to, the large verandah which was their parlour, and she knew that though they had been there eighteen months he was still alive to the success she had made of it. The jalousies were drawn now against the midday sun and the mellowed light filtering through them gave an impression of cool silence. Anne was house-proud, and though they were moved from district to district according to the exigencies of the Service and seldom

stayed anywhere very long, at each new post she started with
new enthusiasm to make their house cosy and charming. It
amused her to devise fresh schemes of decoration. She was very
modern. People were surprised because there were no knick-
knacks. They were taken aback by the bold colour of her curtains and they could not at all make out the tinted reproduc-
tions of pictures by Marie Laurencin and Gauguin in silvered
frames which were placed on the walls with such cunning skill.
She was conscious that few of them quite approved and the good
ladies of Port Wallace and Pemberton thought such arrangements odd, affected and out of place; but this left her calm.
They would learn. It did them good to get a bit of a jolt. And
now she looked round the long, spacious verandah with the
complacent sigh of the artist satisfied with his work. It was gay.
It was bare. It was restful. It refreshed the spirit and gently
excited the fancy. Three immense bowls of yellow cannas completed the colour scheme. Her eyes lingered for a moment on
the bookshelves filled with books; that was another thing that
disconcerted the colony, all the books they had, and strange
books too, heavy they thought them for the most part; and
she gave them a little affectionate look as though they were
living things. Then she gave the piano a glance. A piece of
music was still open on the rack, it was something of Debussy,
and Alban had been playing it before he went to the office.

Her friends in the colony had condoled with her when Alban
was appointed D.O. at Daktar, for it was the most isolated district in Sondurah. It was connected with the town which was
the headquarters of the government neither by telegraph nor
telephone. But she liked it. They had been there for some time
and she hoped they would remain till Alban went home on leave
in another twelve months. It was as large as an English county,
with a long coast line, and the sea was dotted with little islands.
A broad, winding river ran through it and on each side of this
stretched hills densely covered with virgin forest. The station, a
good way up the river, consisted of a row of Chinese shops and a
little native village nestling amid coconut trees, the District
Office, the D.O.'s bungalow, the Clerk's quarters and the bar-
racks. Their only neighbours were the manager of a rubber estate
a few miles up the river and the manager and his assistant,
Dutchmen both, of a timber camp on one of the river's tribu-
taries. The rubber estate's launch went up and down twice a

month and was their only means of regular communication with the outside world. But though they were lonely they were not dull. Their days were full. Their ponies waited for them at dawn and they rode while the day was still fresh and in the bridle-paths through the jungle lingered the mystery of the tropical night. They came back, bathed, changed and had breakfast, and Alban went to the office. Anne spent the morning writing letters and working. She had fallen in love with the country from the first day she arrived in it and had taken pains to master the common language spoken. Her imagination was inflamed by the stories she heard of love and jealousy and death. She was told romantic tales of a time that was only just past. She sought to steep herself in the lore of those strange people. Both she and Alban read a great deal. They had for the country a considerable library and new books came from London by nearly every mail. Little that was noteworthy escaped them. Alban was fond of playing the piano. For an amateur he played very well. He had studied rather seriously, and he had an agreeable touch and a good ear; he could read music with ease, and it was always a pleasure to Anne to sit by him and follow the score when he tried something new. But their great delight was to tour the district. Sometimes they would be away for a fortnight at a time. They would go down the river in a prahu and then sail from one little island to another, bathe in the sea, and fish, or else row upstream till it grew shallow and the trees on either bank were so close to one another that you only saw a slim strip of sky between. Here the boatmen had to pole and they would spend the night in a native house. They bathed in a river pool so clear that you could see the sand shining silver at the bottom and the spot was so lovely, so peaceful and remote, that you felt you could stay there for ever. Sometimes, on the other hand, they would tramp for days along the jungle paths, sleeping under canvas, and notwithstanding the mosquitoes that tormented them and the leeches that sucked their blood, enjoy every moment. Who ever slept so well as on a camp bed? And then there was the gladness of getting back, the delight in the comfort of the well-ordered establishment, the mail that had arrived with letters from home and all the papers, and the piano.

Alban would sit down to it then, his fingers itching to feel the keys, and in what he played, Stravinsky, Ravel, Darius Milhaud, she seemed to feel that he put in something of his own, the sounds of the jungle at night, dawn over the estuary, the starry nights, and the crystal clearness of the forest pools.

Sometimes the rain fell in sheets for days at a time. Then Alban worked at Chinese. He was learning it so that he could communicate with the Chinese of the country in their own language, and Anne did the thousand and one things for which she had not had time before. Those days brought them even more closely together; they always had plenty to talk about, and when they were occupied with their separate affairs they were pleased to feel in their bones that they were near to one another. They were wonderfully united. The rainy days that shut them up within the walls of the bungalow made them feel as if they were one body in face of the world.

On occasion they went to Port Wallace. It was a change, but Anne was always glad to get home. She was never quite at her ease there. She was conscious that none of the people they met liked Alban. They were very ordinary people, middle-class and suburban and dull, without any of the intellectual interests that made life so full and varied to Alban and her, and many of them were narrow-minded and ill-natured; but since they had to pass the better part of their lives in contact with them, it was tiresome that they should feel so unkindly towards Alban. They said he was conceited. He was always very pleasant with them, but she was aware that they resented his cordiality. When he tried to be jovial they said he was putting on airs, and when he chaffed them they thought he was being funny at their expense.

Once they stayed at Government House, and Mrs. Hannay, the Governor's wife, who liked her, talked to her about it. Perhaps the Governor had suggested that she should give Anne a hint.

"You know, my dear, it's a pity your husband doesn't try to be more come-hither with people. He's very intelligent; don't you think it would be better if he didn't let others see he knows it quite so clearly? My husband said to me only yesterday: of course I know that Alban Torel is the cleverest young man in the Service, but he does manage to put my back up more than anyone I know. I am the Governor, but when he talks to me he always gives me the impression that he looks upon me as a damned fool."

The worst of it was that Anne knew how low an opinion Alban had of the Governor's parts.

"He doesn't mean to be superior," Anne answered, smiling. "And he really isn't in the least conceited. I think it's only because he has a straight nose and high cheek-bones."

"You know, they don't like him at the club. They call him Powder-Puff Percy."

Anne flushed. She had heard that before and it made her very angry. Her eyes filled with tears.

"I think it's frightfully unfair."

Mrs. Hannay took her hand and gave it an affectionate little squeeze.

"My dear, you know I don't want to hurt your feelings. Your husband can't help rising very high in the Service. He'd make things so much easier for himself if he were a little more human. Why doesn't he play football?"

"It's not his game. He's always only too glad to play tennis."

"He doesn't give that impression. He gives the impression that there's no one here who's worth his while to play with."

"Well, there isn't," said Anne, stung.

Alban happened to be an extremely good tennis player. He had played a lot of tournaments in England and Anne knew that it gave him a grim satisfaction to knock those beefy, hearty men all over the court. He could make the best of them look foolish. He could be maddening on the tennis court and Anne was aware that sometimes he could not resist the temptation.

"He does play to the gallery, doesn't he?" said Mrs. Hannay.

"I don't think so. Believe me, Alban has no idea he isn't popular. As far as I can see he's always pleasant and friendly with everybody."

"It's then he's most offensive," said Mrs. Hannay dryly.

"I know people don't like us very much," said Anne, smiling a little. "I'm very sorry, but really I don't know what we can do about it."

"Not you, my dear," cried Mrs. Hannay. "Everybody adores you. That's why they put up with your husband. My dear, who could help liking you?"

"I don't know why they should adore me," said Anne.

But she did not say it quite sincerely. She was deliberately playing the part of the dear little woman and within her she bubbled with amusement. They disliked Alban because he had such an air of distinction, and because he was interested in art and literature; they did not understand these things and so thought them unmanly; and they disliked him because his

capacity was greater than theirs. They disliked him because he
was better bred than they. They thought him superior; well,
he was superior, but not in the sense they meant. They forgave
her because she was an ugly little thing. That was what she
called herself, but she wasn't that, or if she was it was with an
ugliness that was most attractive. She was like a little monkey,
but a very sweet little monkey and very human. She had a
neat figure. That was her best point. That and her eyes. They
were very large, of a deep brown, liquid and shining; they were
full of fun, but they could be tender on occasion with a charming sympathy. She was dark, her frizzy hair was almost black,
and her skin was swarthy; she had a small fleshy nose, with
large nostrils, and much too big a mouth. But she was alert
and vivacious. She could talk with a show of real interest to the
ladies of the colony about their husbands and their servants
and their children in England, and she could listen appreci-
atively to the men who told her stories that she had often heard
before. They thought her a jolly good sort. They did not know
what clever fun she made of them in private. It never occurred
to them that she thought them narrow, gross and pretentious.
They found no glamour in the East because they looked at it
vulgarly with material eyes. Romance lingered at their threshold and they drove it away like an importunate beggar. She
was aloof. She repeated to herself Landor's line:
"Nature I loved, and next to nature, art."
She reflected on her conversation with Mrs. Hannay, but on
the whole it left her unconcerned. She wondered whether she
should say anything about it to Alban; it had always seemed a
little odd to her that he should be so little aware of his unpopu-
larity; but she was afraid that if she told him of it he would
become self-conscious.
He never noticed the coldness of the men at the club. He
made them feel shy and therefore uncomfortable. His appearance there caused a sort of awkwardness, but he, happily
insensible, was breezily cordial to all and sundry. The fact was
that he was strangely unconscious of other people. She was in
a class by herself, she and a little group of friends they had in
London, but he could never quite realize that the people of
the colony, the government officials and the planters and their
wives, were human beings. They were to him like pawns in a
game. He laughed with them, chaffed them, and was amiably
tolerant of them; with a chuckle Anne told herself that he was

rather like a master of a preparatory school taking little boys
out on a picnic and anxious to give them a good time.

She was afraid it wasn't much good telling Alban. He was
incapable of the dissimulation which, she happily realized, came
so easily to her. What was one to do with these people? The
men had come out to the colony as lads from second-rate
schools, and life had taught them nothing. At fifty they had the
outlook of hobbledehoys. Most of them drank a great deal too
much. They read nothing worth reading. Their ambition was
to be like everybody else. Their highest praise was to say that
a man was a damned good sort. If you were interested in the
things of the spirit you were a prig. They were eaten up with
envy of one another and devoured by petty jealousies. And the
women, poor things, were obsessed by petty rivalries. They
made a circle that was more provincial than any in the smallest
town in England. They were prudish and spiteful. What did
it matter if they did not like Alban? They would have to put
up with him because his ability was so great. He was clever and
energetic. They could not say that he did not do his work well.
He had been successful in every post he had occupied. With his
sensitiveness and his imagination he understood the native
mind and he was able to get the natives to do things that no
one in his position could. He had a gift for languages, and he
spoke all the local dialects. He knew not only the common
tongue that most of the government officials spoke, but was
acquainted with the niceties of the language and on occasion
could make use of a ceremonial speech that flattered and impressed the chiefs. He had a gift for organization. He was not
afraid of responsibility. In due course he was bound to be made
a Resident. Alban had some interest in England; his father
was a brigadier-general killed in the war, and though he had no
private means he had influential friends. He spoke of them with
pleasant irony.

"The great advantage of democratic government," he said,
"is that merit, with influence to back it, can be pretty sure of
receiving its due reward."

Alban was so obviously the ablest man in the Service that
there seemed no reason why he should not eventually be made
Governor. Then, thought Anne, his air of superiority, of which
they complained, would be in place. They would accept him as
their master and he would know how to make himself respected
and obeyed. The position she foresaw did not dazzle her. She

accepted it as their right. It would be fun for Alban to be Governor and for her to be the Governor's wife. And what an opportunity! They were sheep, the government servants and the planters; when Government House was the seat of culture they would soon fall into line. When the best way to the Governor's favour was to be intelligent, intelligence would become the fashion. She and Alban would cherish the native arts and collect carefully the memorials of a vanished past. The country would make an advance it had never dreamed of. They would develop it, but along lines of order and beauty. They would instil into their subordinates a passion for that beautiful land and a loving interest in these romantic races. They would make them realize what music meant. They would cultivate literature. They would create beauty. It would be the golden age.

Suddenly she heard Alban's footstep. Anne awoke from her day-dream. All that was far away in the future. Alban was only a District Officer yet and what was important was the life they were living now. She heard Alban go into the bath-house and splash water over himself. In a minute he came in. He had changed into a shirt and shorts. His fair hair was still wet.

"Tiffin ready?" he asked.

"Yes."

He sat down at the piano and played the piece that he had played in the morning. The silvery notes cascaded coolly down the sultry air. You had an impression of a formal garden with great trees and elegant pieces of artificial water and of leisurely walks bordered with pseudo-classical statues. Alban played with an exquisite delicacy. Lunch was announced by the head boy. He rose from the piano and gave her his hand. They walked into the dining-room hand in hand. A punkah lazily fanned the air. Anne gave the table a glance. With its bright-coloured tablecloth and the amusing plates it looked very gay.

"Anything exciting at the office this morning?" she asked.

"No, nothing much. A buffalo case. Oh, and Prynne has sent along to ask me to go up to the estate. Some coolies have been damaging the trees and he wants me to come along and look into it."

Prynne was manager of the rubber estate up the river and now and then they spent a night with him. Sometimes when he wanted a change he came down to dinner and slept at the D.O.'s bungalow. They both liked him. He was a man of five and thirty, with a red face, with deep furrows in it, and very black hair. He was quite uneducated, but cheerful and easy, and being the only Englishman within two days' journey they could not but be friendly with him. He had been a little shy of them at first. News spreads quickly in the East and long before they arrived in the district he heard that they were highbrows. He did not know what he would make of them. He probably did not know that he had charm, which makes up for many more commendable qualities, and Alban with his almost feminine sensibilities was peculiarly susceptible to this. He found Alban much more human than he expected, and of course Anne was stunning. Alban played ragtime for him, which he would not have done for the Governor, and played dominoes with him. When Alban was making his first tour of the district with Anne, and suggested that they would like to spend a couple of nights on the estate, he had thought it as well to warn him that he lived with a native woman and had two children by her. He would do his best to keep them out of Anne's sight, but he could not send them away, there was nowhere to send them. Alban laughed.

"Anne isn't that sort of woman at all. Don't dream of hiding them. She loves children."

Anne quickly made friends with the shy, pretty little native woman and soon was playing happily with the children. She and the girl had long confidential chats. The children took a fancy to her. She brought them lovely toys from Port Wallace. Prynne, comparing her smiling tolerance with the disapproving acidity of the other white women in the colony, described himself as knocked all of a heap. He could not do enough to show his delight and gratitude.

"If all highbrows are like you," he said, "give me highbrows every time."

He hated to think that in another year they would leave the district for good and the chances were that, if the next D.O. was married, his wife would think it dreadful that, rather than live alone, he had a native woman to live with him and, what was more, was much attached to her.

But there had been a good deal of discontent on the estate of late. The coolies were Chinese and infected with communist ideas. They were disorderly. Alban had been obliged to sentence several of them for various crimes to terms of imprisonment.

"Prynne tells me that as soon as their term is up he's going

to send them all back to China and get Javanese instead," said
Alban. "I'm sure he's right. They're much more amenable."

"You don't think there's going to be any serious trouble?"

"Oh, no. Prynne knows his job and he's a pretty determined
fellow. He wouldn't put up with any nonsense and with me and
our policemen to back him up I don't imagine they'll try any
monkey tricks." He smiled. "The iron hand in the velvet
glove."

The words were barely out of his mouth when a sudden shouting arose. There was a commotion and the sound of steps. Loud
voices and cries.

"Tuan, Tuan."

"What the devil's the matter?"

Alban sprang from his chair and went swiftly on to the verandah. Anne followed him. At the bottom of the steps was a group
of natives. There was the sergeant, and three or four policemen,
boatmen and several men from the kampong.

"What is it?" called Alban.

Two or three shouted back in answer. The sergeant pushed
others aside and Alban saw lying on the ground a man in a
shirt and khaki shorts. He ran down the steps. He recognized
the man as the assistant manager of Prynne's estate. He was a
half-caste. His shorts were covered with blood and there was
clotted blood all over one side of his face and head. He was unconscious.

"Bring him up here," called Anne.

Alban gave an order. The man was lifted up and carried on
to the verandah. They laid him on the floor and Anne put a
pillow under his head. She sent for water and for the medicine-
chest in which they kept things for emergency.

"Is he dead?" asked Alban.

"No."

"Better try to give him some brandy."

The boatmen brought ghastly news. The Chinese coolies had
arisen suddenly and attacked the manager's office. Prynne was
killed and the assistant manager, Oakley by name, had escaped
only by the skin of his teeth. He had come upon the rioters
when they were looting the office, he had seen Prynne's body
thrown out of the window, and had taken to his heels. Some of
the Chinese saw him and gave chase. He ran for the river and
was wounded as he jumped into the launch. The launch managed to put off before the Chinese could get on board and they

had come down stream for help as fast as they could go. As they went they saw flames rising from the office buildings. There was no doubt that the coolies had burned down everything that would burn.

Oakley gave a groan and opened his eyes. He was a little, dark-skinned man, with flattened features and thick coarse hair. His great native eyes were filled with terror.

"You're all right," said Anne. "You're quite safe."

He gave a sigh and smiled. Anne washed his face and swobbed it with antiseptics. The wound on his head was not serious.

"Can you speak yet?" said Alban.

"Wait a bit," she said. "We must look at his leg."

Alban ordered the sergeant to get the crowd out of the verandah. Anne ripped up one leg of the shorts. The material was clinging to the coagulated wound.

"I've been bleeding like a pig," said Oakley.

It was only a flesh wound. Alban was clever with his fingers, and though the blood began to flow again they stanched it. Alban put on a dressing and a bandage. The sergeant and a policeman lifted Oakley on to a long chair. Alban gave him a brandy and soda, and soon he felt strong enough to speak. He knew no more than the boatmen had already told. Prynne was dead and the estate was in flames.

"And the girl and the children?" asked Anne.

"I don't know."

"Oh, Alban."

"I must turn out the police. Are you sure Prynne is dead?"

"Yes, sir. I saw him."

"Have the rioters got firearms?"

"I don't know, sir."

"How d'you mean, you don't know?" Alban cried irritably. "Prynne had a gun, hadn't he?"

"Yes, sir."

"There must have been more on the estate. You had one, didn't you? The head overseer had one."

The half-caste was silent. Alban looked at him sternly.

"How many of those damned Chinese are there?"

"A hundred and fifty."

Anne wondered that he asked so many questions. It seemed waste of time. The important thing was to collect coolies for the transport up river, prepare the boats and issue ammunition to the police.

"How many policemen have you got, sir?" asked Oakley.

"Eight and the sergeant."

"Could I come too? That would make ten of us. I'm sure I shall be all right now I'm bandaged."

"I'm not going," said Alban.

"Alban, you must," cried Anne. She could not believe her ears.

"Nonsense. It would be madness. Oakley's obviously useless. He's sure to have a temperature in a few hours. He'd only be in the way. That leaves nine guns. There are a hundred and fifty Chinese and they've got firearms and all the ammunition in the world."

"How d'you know?"

"It stands to reason they wouldn't have started a show like this unless they had. It would be idiotic to go."

Anne stared at him with open mouth. Oakley's eyes were puzzled.

"What are you going to do?"

"Well, fortunately we've got the launch. I'll send it to Port Wallace with a request for reinforcements."

"But they won't be here for two days at least."

"Well, what of it? Prynne's dead and the estate burned to the ground. We couldn't do any good by going up now. I shall send a native to reconnoitre so that we can find out exactly what the rioters are doing." He gave Anne his charming smile. "Believe me, my pet, the rascals won't lose anything by waiting a day or two for what's coming to them."

Oakley opened his mouth to speak, but perhaps he hadn't the nerve. He was a half-caste assistant manager and Alban, the D.O., represented the power of the Government. But the man's eyes sought Anne's and she thought she read in them an earnest and personal appeal.

"But in two days they're capable of committing the most frightful atrocities," she cried. "It's quite unspeakable what they may do."

"Whatever damage they do they'll pay for. I promise you that."

"Oh, Alban, you can't sit still and do nothing. I beseech you to go yourself at once."

"Don't be so silly. I can't quell a riot with eight policemen and a sergeant. I haven't got the right to take a risk of that sort. We'd have to go in boats. You don't think we could get up unobserved. The lalang along the banks is perfect cover and they could just take pot shots at us as we came along. We shouldn't have a chance."

"I'm afraid they'll only think it weakness if nothing is done for two days, sir," said Oakley.

"When I want your opinion I'll ask for it," said Alban acidly. "So far as I can see when there was danger the only thing you did was to cut and run. I can't persuade myself that your assistance in a crisis would be very valuable."

The half-caste reddened. He said nothing more. He looked straight in front of him with troubled eyes.

"I'm going down to the office," said Alban. "I'll just write a short report and send it down the river by launch at once."

He gave an order to the sergeant who had been standing all this time stiffly at the top of the steps. He saluted and ran off. Alban went into a little hall they had to get his topi. Anne swiftly followed him.

"Alban, for God's sake listen to me a minute," she whispered.

"I don't want to be rude to you, darling, but I am pressed for time. I think you'd much better mind your own business."

"You can't do nothing, Alban. You must go. Whatever the risk."

"Don't be such a fool," he said angrily.

He had never been angry with her before. She seized his hand to hold him back.

"I tell you I can do no good by going."

"You don't know. There's the woman and Prynne's children. We must do something to save them. Let me come with you. They'll kill them."

"They've probably killed them already."

"Oh, how can you be so callous! If there's a chance of saving them it's your duty to try."

"It's my duty to act like a reasonable human being. I'm not going to risk my life and my policemen's for the sake of a native woman and her half-caste brats. What sort of a damned fool do you take me for?"

"They'll say you were afraid."

"Who?"

"Everyone in the colony."

He smiled disdainfully.

"If you only knew what a complete contempt I have for the opinion of everyone in the colony."

She gave him a long searching look. She had been married to him for eight years and she knew every expression of his face and every thought in his mind. She stared into his blue eyes as if they were open windows. She suddenly went quite pale. She dropped his hand and turned away. Without another word she went back on to the verandah. Her ugly little monkey face was a mask of horror.

Alban went to his office, wrote a brief account of the facts, and in a few minutes the motor launch was pounding down the river.

The next two days were endless. Escaped nahois brought them news of happenings on the estate. But from their excited and terrified stories it was impossible to get an exact impression of the truth. There had been a good deal of bloodshed. The head overseer had been killed. They brought wild tales of cruelty and outrage. Anne could hear nothing of Prynne's woman and the two children. She shuddered when she thought of what might have been their fate. Alban collected as many natives as he could. They were armed with spears and swords. He commandeered boats. The situation was serious, but he kept his head. He felt that he had done all that was possible and nothing remained but for him to carry on normally. He did his official work. He played the piano a great deal. He rode with Anne in the early morning. He appeared to have forgotten that they had had the first serious difference of opinion in the whole of their married life. He took it that Anne had accepted the wisdom of his decision. He was as amusing, cordial and gay with her as he had always been. When he spoke of the rioters it was with grim irony: when the time came to settle matters a good many of them would wish they had never been born.

"What'll happen to them?" asked Anne.

"Oh, they'll hang." He gave a shrug of distaste. "I hate having to be present at executions. It always makes me feel rather sick."

He was very sympathetic to Oakley, whom they had put to bed and whom Anne was nursing. Perhaps he was sorry that in the exasperation of the moment he had spoken to him offensively, and he went out of his way to be nice to him.

Then on the afternoon of the third day, when they were

drinking their coffee after luncheon, Alban's quick ears caught the sound of a motor boat approaching. At the same moment a policeman ran up to say that the government launch was sighted.

"At last," cried Alban.

He bolted out of the house. Anne raised one of the jalousies and looked out at the river. Now the sound was quite loud and in a moment she saw the boat come round the bend. She saw Alban on the landing-stage. He got into a prahu and as the launch dropped her anchor he went on board. She told Oakley that the reinforcements had come.

"Will the D.O. go up with them when they attack?" he asked her.

"Naturally," said Anne coldly.

"I wondered."

Anne felt a strange feeling in her heart. For the last two days she had had to exercise all her self-control not to cry. She did not answer. She went out of the room.

A quarter of an hour later Alban returned to the bungalow with the captain of constabulary who had been sent with twenty Sikhs to deal with the rioters. Captain Stratton was a little red-faced man with a red moustache and bow legs, very hearty and dashing, whom she had met often at Port Wallace.

"Well, Mrs. Torel, this is a pretty kettle of fish," he cried, as he shook hands with her, in a loud jolly voice. "Here I am, with my army all full of pep and ready for a scrap. Up, boys, and at 'em. Have you got anything to drink in this benighted place?"

"Boy," she cried, smiling.

"Something long and cool and faintly alcoholic, and then I'm ready to discuss the plan of campaign."

His breeziness was very comforting. It blew away the sullen apprehension that had seemed ever since the disaster to brood over the lost peace of the bungalow. The boy came in with a tray and Stratton mixed himself a stengah. Alban put him in possession of the facts. He told them clearly, briefly and with precision.

"I must say I admire you," said Stratton. "In your place I should never have been able to resist the temptation to take my eight cops and have a whack at the blighters myself."

"I thought it was a perfectly unjustifiable risk to take."

"Safety first, old boy, eh, what?" said Stratton jovially.

"I'm jolly glad you didn't. It's not often we get the chance of a scrap. It would have been a dirty trick to keep the whole show to yourself."

Captain Stratton was all for steaming straight up the river and attacking at once, but Alban pointed out to him the inadvisability of such a course. The sound of the approaching launch would warn the rioters. The long grass at the river's edge offered them cover and they had enough guns to make a landing difficult. It seemed useless to expose the attacking force to their fire. It was silly to forget that they had to face a hundred and fifty desperate men and it would be easy to fall into an ambush. Alban expounded his own plan. Stratton listened to it. He nodded now and then. The plan was evidently a good one. It would enable them to take the rioters on the rear, surprise them, and in all probability finish the job without a single casualty. He would have been a fool not to accept it.

"But why didn't you do that yourself?" asked Stratton.

"With eight men and a sergeant?"

Stratton did not answer.

"Anyhow it's not a bad idea and we'll settle on it. It gives us plenty of time, so with your permission, Mrs. Torel, I'll have a bath."

They set out at sunset, Captain Stratton and his twenty Sikhs, Alban with his policemen and the natives he had collected. The night was dark and moonless. Trailing behind them were the dug-outs that Alban had gathered together and into which after a certain distance they proposed to transfer their force. It was important that no sound should give warning of their approach. After they had gone for about three hours by launch they took to the dug-outs and in them silently paddled up stream. They reached the border of the vast estate and landed. Guides led them along a path so narrow that they had to march in single file. It had been long unused and the going was heavy. They had twice to ford a stream. The path led them circuitously to the rear of the coolie lines, but they did not wish to reach them till nearly dawn and presently Stratton gave the order to halt. It was a long cold wait. At last the night seemed to be less dark; you did not see the trunks of the trees, but were vaguely sensible of them against its darkness. Stratton had been sitting with his back to a tree. He gave a whispered order to a sergeant and in a few minutes the column was once more on the march. Suddenly they found themselves on a road. They formed fours.

The dawn broke and in the ghostly light the surrounding objects were wanly visible. The column stopped on a whispered order. They had come in sight of the coolie lines. Silence reigned in them. The column crept on again and again halted. Stratton, his eyes shining, gave Alban a smile.

"We've caught the blighters asleep."

He lined up his men. They inserted cartridges in their guns. He stepped forward and raised his hand. The carbines were pointed at the coolie lines.

"Fire."

There was a rattle as the volley of shots rang out. Then suddenly there was a tremendous din and the Chinese poured out, shouting and waving their arms, but in front of them, to Alban's utter bewilderment, bellowing at the top of his voice and shaking his fist at them, was a white man.

"Who the hell's that?" cried Stratton.

A very big, very fat man, in khaki trousers and a singlet, was running towards them as fast as his fat legs would carry him and as he ran shaking both fists at them and yelling:

"*Smerige flikkers! Verlockte ploerten!*"

"My God, it's Van Hasseldt," said Alban.

This was the Dutch manager of the timber camp which was situated on a considerable tributary of the river about twenty miles away.

"What the hell do you think you're doing?" he puffed as he came up to them.

"How the hell did you get here?" asked Stratton in turn.

He saw that the Chinese were scattering in all directions and gave his men instructions to round them up. Then he turned again to Van Hasseldt.

"What's it mean?"

"Mean? Mean?" shouted the Dutchman furiously. "That's what I want to know. You and your damned policemen. What do you mean by coming here at this hour in the morning and firing a damned volley? Target practice? You might have killed me. Idiots!"

"Have a cigarette," said Stratton.

"How did you get here, Van Hasseldt?" asked Alban again, very much at sea. "This is the force they've sent from Port Wallace to quell the riot."

"How did I get here? I walked. How did you think I got here? Riot be damned. I quelled the riot. If that's what you came for you can take your damned policemen home again. A bullet came within a foot of my head."

"I don't understand," said Alban.

"There's nothing to understand," spluttered Van Hasseldt, still fuming. "Some coolies came to my estate and said the chinks had killed Prynne and burned the bally place down, so I took my assistant and my head overseer and a Dutch friend I had staying with me and came over to see what the trouble was."

Captain Stratton opened his eyes wide.

"Did you just stroll in as if it was a picnic?" he asked.

"Well, you don't think after all the years I've been in this country I'm going to let a couple of hundred chinks put the fear of God into me? I found them all scared out of their lives. One of them had the nerve to pull a gun on me and I blew his bloody brains out. And the rest surrendered. I've got the leaders tied up. I was going to send a boat down to you this morning to come up and get them."

Stratton stared at him for a minute and then burst into a shout of laughter. He laughed till the tears ran down his face. The Dutchman looked at him angrily, then began to laugh too; he laughed with the big belly laugh of a very fat man and his coils of fat heaved and shook. Alban watched them sullenly. He was very angry.

"What about Prynne's girl and the kids?" he asked.

"Oh, they got away all right."

It just showed how wise he had been not to let himself be influenced by Anne's hysteria. Of course the children had come to no harm. He never thought they would.

Van Hasseldt and his little party started back for the timber camp, and as soon after as possible Stratton embarked his twenty Sikhs and leaving Alban with his sergeant and his policemen to deal with the situation departed for Port Wallace. Alban gave him a brief report for the Governor. There was much for him to do. It looked as though he would have to stay for a considerable time; but since every house on the estate had been burned to the ground and he was obliged to install himself in the coolie lines he thought it better that Anne should not join him. He sent her a note to that effect. He was glad to be able to reassure her of the safety of poor Prynne's girl. He set to work at once to make his preliminary enquiry. He examined a host of witnesses. But a week later he received an order to go to Port

Wallace at once. The launch that brought it was to take him and he was able to see Anne on the way down for no more than an hour. Alban was a trifle vexed.

"I don't know why the Governor can't leave me to get things straight without dragging me off like this. It's extremely inconvenient."

"Oh, well, the Government never bothers very much about the convenience of its subordinates, does it?" smiled Anne.

"It's just red tape. I would offer to take you along, darling, only I shan't stay a minute longer than I need. I want to get my evidence together for the Sessions Court as soon as possible. I think in a country like this it's very important that justice should be prompt."

When the launch came in to Port Wallace one of the harbour police told him that the harbour-master had a chit for him. It was from the Governor's secretary and informed him that His Excellency desired to see him as soon as convenient after his arrival. It was ten in the morning. Alban went to the club, had a bath and shaved, and then in clean ducks, his hair neatly brushed, he called a rickshaw and told the boy to take him to the Governor's office. He was at once shown in to the secretary's room. The secretary shook hands with him.

"I'll tell H.E. you're here," he said. "Won't you sit down?"

The secretary left the room and in a little while came back.

"H.E. will see you in a minute. Do you mind if I get on with my letters?"

Alban smiled. The secretary was not exactly come-hither. He waited, smoking a cigarette, and amused himself with his own thoughts. He was making a good job of the preliminary enquiry. It interested him. Then an orderly came in and told Alban that the Governor was ready for him. He rose from his seat and followed him into the Governor's room.

"Good-morning, Torel."

"Good-morning, sir."

The Governor was sitting at a large desk. He nodded to Alban and motioned to him to take a seat. The Governor was all grey. His hair was grey, his face, his eyes; he looked as though the tropical suns had washed the colour out of him; he had been in the country for thirty years and had risen one by one through all the ranks of the Service; he looked tired and depressed. Even his voice was grey. Alban liked him because he was quiet; he did not think him clever, but he had an unrivalled knowledge

of the country, and his great experience was a very good substitute for intelligence. He looked at Alban for a full moment
without speaking and the odd idea came to Alban that he was
embarrassed. He very nearly gave him a lead.

"I saw Van Hasseldt yesterday," said the Governor suddenly.

"Yes, sir?"

"Will you give me your account of the occurrences at the
Alud Estate and of the steps you took to deal with them."

Alban had an orderly mind. He was self-possessed. He mar-
shalled his facts well and was able to state them with precision.
He chose his words with care and spoke them fluently.

"You had a sergeant and eight policemen. Why did you not
immediately go to the scene of the disturbance?"

"I thought the risk was unjustifiable."

A thin smile was outlined on the Governor's grey face.

"If the officers of this government had hesitated to take unjustifiable risks it would never have become a province of the
British Empire."

Alban was silent. It was difficult to talk to a man who spoke
obvious nonsense.

"I am anxious to hear your reasons for the decision you took."

Alban gave them coolly. He was quite convinced of the right-
ness of his action. He repeated, but more fully, what he had said
in the first place to Anne. The Governor listened attentively.

"Van Hasseldt, with his manager, a Dutch friend of his, and a
native overseer, seems to have coped with the situation very
efficiently," said the Governor.

"He had a lucky break. That doesn't prevent him from
being a damned fool. It was madness to do what he did."

"Do you realize that by leaving a Dutch planter to do what
you should have done yourself, you have covered the Government with ridicule?"

"No, sir."

"You've made yourself a laughing-stock in the whole
colony."

Alban smiled.

"My back is broad enough to bear the ridicule of persons to
whose opinion I am entirely indifferent."

"The utility of a government official depends very largely
on his prestige, and I'm afraid his prestige is likely to be incon-
siderable when he lies under the stigma of cowardice."

Alban flushed a little.

"I don't quite know what you mean by that, sir."

"I've gone into the matter very carefully. I've seen Captain Stratton, and Oakley, poor Prynne's assistant, and I've seen Van Hasseldt. I've listened to your defence."

"I didn't know that I was defending myself, sir."

"Be so good as not to interrupt me. I think you committed a grave error of judgment. As it turns out the risk was very small, but whatever it was, I think you should have taken it. In such matters promptness and firmness are essential. It is not for me to conjecture what motive led you to send for a force of constabulary and do nothing till they came. I am afraid, however, that I consider that your usefulness in the Service is no longer very great."

Alban looked at him with astonishment.

"But would you have gone under the circumstances?" he asked him.

"I should."

Alban shrugged his shoulders.

"Don't you believe me?" rapped out the Governor.

"Of course I believe you, sir. But perhaps you will allow me to say that if you had been killed the colony would have suffered an irreparable loss."

The Governor drummed on the table with his fingers. He looked out of the window and then looked again at Alban. When he spoke it was not unkindly.

"I think you are unfitted by temperament for this rather rough and tumble life, Torel. If you'll take my advice you'll go home. With your abilities I feel sure that you'll soon find an occupation much better suited to you."

"I'm afraid I don't understand what you mean, sir."

"Oh, come, Torel, you're not stupid. I'm trying to make things easy for you. For your wife's sake as well as for your own I do not wish you to leave the colony with the stigma of being dismissed from the Service for cowardice. I'm giving you the opportunity of resigning."

"Thank you very much, sir. I'm not prepared to avail myself of the opportunity. If I resign I admit that I committed an error and that the charge you make against me is justified. I don't admit it."

"You can please yourself. I have considered the matter very carefully and I have no doubt about it in my mind. I am forced to discharge you from the Service. The necessary papers will reach you in due course. Meanwhile you will return to your post and hand over to the officer appointed to succeed you on his arrival."

"Very good, sir," replied Alban, a twinkle of amusement in his eyes. "When do you desire me to return to my post?"

"At once."

"Have you any objection to my going to the club and having tiffin before I go?"

The Governor looked at him with surprise. His exasperation was mingled with an unwilling admiration.

"Not at all. I'm sorry, Torel, that this unhappy incident should have deprived the Government of a servant whose zeal has always been so apparent and whose tact, intelligence and industry seemed to point him out in the future for very high office."

"Your Excellency does not read Schiller, I suppose. You are probably not acquainted with his celebrated line: *mit der dummheit kämpfen die Götter selbst vergebens.*"

"What does it mean?"

"Roughly, against stupidity the gods themselves battle in vain."

"Good-morning."

With his head in the air, a smile on his lips, Alban left the Governor's office. The Governor was human, and he had the curiosity to ask his secretary later in the day if Alban Torel had really gone to the club.

"Yes, sir. He had tiffin there."

"It must have wanted some nerve."

Alban entered the club jauntily and joined the group of men standing at the bar. He talked to them in the breezy, cordial tone he always used with them. It was designed to put them at their ease. They had been discussing him ever since Stratton had come back to Port Wallace with his story, sneering at him and laughing at him, and all that had resented his superciliousness, and they were the majority, were triumphant because his pride had had a fall. But they were so taken aback at seeing him now, so confused to find him as confident as ever, that it was they who were embarrassed.

One man, though he knew perfectly, asked him what he was doing in Port Wallace.

"Oh, I came about the riot on the Alud Estate. H.E. wanted

to see me. He does not see eye to eye with me about it. The silly old ass has fired me. I'm going home as soon as he appoints a D.O. to take over."

There was a moment of awkwardness. One, more kindly disposed than the others, said:

"I'm awfully sorry."

Alban shrugged his shoulders. "My dear fellow, what can you do with a perfect damned fool? The only thing is to let him stew in his own juice."

When the Governor's secretary had told his chief as much of this as he thought discreet, the Governor smiled.

"Courage is a queer thing. I would rather have shot myself than go to the club just then and face all those fellows."

A fortnight later, having sold to the incoming D.O. all the decorations that Anne had taken so much trouble about, with the rest of their things in packing-cases and trunks, they arrived at Port Wallace to await the local steamer that was to take them to Singapore. The padre's wife invited them to stay with her, but Anne refused; she insisted that they should go to the hotel. An hour after their arrival she received a very kind little letter from the Governor's wife asking her to go and have tea with her. She went. She found Mrs. Hannay alone, but in a minute the Governor joined them. He expressed his regret that she was leaving and told her how sorry he was for the cause.

"It's very kind of you to say that," said Anne, smiling gaily, "but you mustn't think I take it to heart. I'm entirely on Alban's side. I think what he did was absolutely right and if you don't mind my saying so I think you've treated him most unjustly."

"Believe me, I hated having to take the step I took."

"Don't let's talk about it," said Anne.

"What are your plans when you get home?" asked Mrs. Hannay.

Anne began to chat brightly. You would have thought she had not a care in the world. She seemed in great spirits at going home. She was jolly and amusing and made little jokes. When she took leave of the Governor and his wife she thanked them for all their kindness. The Governor escorted her to the door.

The next day but one, after dinner, they went on board the clean and comfortable little ship. The padre and his wife saw them off. When they went into their cabin they found a large parcel on Anne's bunk. It was addressed to Alban. He opened it and saw that it was an immense powder-puff.

"Hullo, I wonder who sent us this," he said, with a laugh. "It must be for you, darling."

Anne gave him a quick look. She went pale. The brutes! How could they be so cruel? She forced herself to smile.

"It's enormous, isn't it? I've never seen such a large powder-puff in my life."

But when he had left the cabin and they were out at sea, she threw it passionately overboard.

And now, now that they were back in London and Sondurah was nine thousand miles away, she clenched her hands as she thought of it. Somehow, it seemed the worst thing of all. It was so wantonly unkind to send that absurd object to Alban, Powder-puff Percy; it showed such a petty spite. Was that their idea of humour? Nothing had hurt her more and even now she felt that it was only by holding on to herself that she could prevent herself from crying. Suddenly she started, for the door opened and Alban came in. She was still sitting in the chair in which he had left her.

"Hullo, why haven't you dressed?" He looked about the room. "You haven't unpacked."

"No."

"Why on earth not?"

"I'm not going to unpack. I'm not going to stay here. I'm leaving you."

"What are you talking about?"

"I've stuck it out till now. I made up my mind I would till we got home. I set my teeth, I've borne more than I thought it possible to bear, but now it's finished. I've done all that could be expected of me. We're back in London now and I can go."

He looked at her in utter bewilderment.

"Are you mad, Anne?"

"Oh, my God, what I've endured! The journey to Singapore, with all the officers knowing, and even the Chinese stewards. And at Singapore, the way people looked at us at the hotel, and the sympathy I had to put up with, the bricks they dropped and their embarrassment when they realized what they'd done. My God, I could have killed them. That interminable journey home. There wasn't a single passenger on the ship who didn't know. The contempt they had for you and the kindness they went out of their way to show me. And you so self-complacent and so pleased with yourself, seeing nothing, feeling nothing. You must have the hide of a rhinoceros. The misery of seeing you so chatty and agreeable. Pariahs, that's what we were. You seemed to ask them to snub you. How can anyone be so shameless?"

She was flaming with passion. Now that at last she need not wear the mask of indifference and pride that she had forced herself to assume she cast aside all reserve and all self-control. The words poured from her trembling lips in a virulent stream.

"My dear, how can you be so absurd?" he said good-naturedly, smiling. "You must be very nervous and high-strung to have got such ideas in your head. Why didn't you tell me? You're like a country bumpkin who comes to London and thinks everyone is staring at him. Nobody bothered about us and if they did what on earth did it matter? You ought to have more sense than to bother about what a lot of fools say. And what do you imagine they were saying?"

"They were saying you'd been fired."

"Well, that was true," he laughed.

"They said you were a coward."

"What of it?"

"Well, you see, that was true too."

He looked at her for a moment reflectively. His lips tightened a little.

"And what makes you think so?" he asked acidly.

"I saw it in your eyes, that day the news came, when you refused to go to the estate and I followed you into the hall when you went to fetch your topi. I begged you to go, I felt that whatever the danger you must take it, and suddenly I saw the fear in your eyes. I nearly fainted with the horror."

"I should have been a fool to risk my life to no purpose. Why should I? Nothing that concerned me was at stake. Courage is the obvious virtue of the stupid. I don't attach any particular importance to it."

"How do you mean that nothing that concerned you was at stake? If that's true then your whole life is a sham. You've given away everything you stood for, everything we both stand for. You've let all of us down. We did set ourselves up on a pinnacle, we did think ourselves better than the rest of them because we loved literature and art and music, we weren't content to live a life of ignoble jealousies and vulgar tittle-tattle, we did cherish the things of the spirit, and we loved beauty. It was our food and drink. They laughed at us and sneered at us. That was inevitable. The ignorant and the com-

mon naturally hate and fear those who are interested in things
they don't understand. We didn't care. We called them Philistines. We despised them and we had a right to despise them.
Our justification was that we were better and nobler and wiser
and braver than they were. And you weren't better, you weren't
nobler, you weren't braver. When the crisis came you slunk
away like a whipped cur with his tail between his legs. You of all
people hadn't the right to be a coward. They despise *us* now
and they have the right to despise *us*. Us and all we stood for.
Now they can say that art and beauty are all rot; when it
comes to a pinch people like us always let you down. They never
stopped looking for a chance to turn and rend us and you gave
it to them. They can say that they always expected it. It's a
triumph for them. I used to be furious because they called you
Powder-Puff Percy. Did you know they did?"

"Of course. I thought it very vulgar, but it left me entirely
indifferent."

"It's funny that their instinct should have been so right."

"Do you mean to say you've been harbouring this against
me all these weeks? I should never have thought you capable of
it."

"I couldn't let you down when everyone was against you. I
was too proud for that. Whatever happened I swore to myself
that I'd stick to you till we got home. It's been torture."

"Don't you love me any more?"

"Love you? I loathe the very sight of you."

"Anne."

"God knows I loved you. For eight years I worshipped the
ground you trod on. You were everything to me. I believed in
you as some people believe in God. When I saw the fear in your
eyes that day, when you told me that you weren't going to risk
your life for a kept woman and her half-caste brats, I was shattered. It was as though someone had wrenched my heart out
of my body and tramped on it. You killed my love there and
then, Alban. You killed it stone dead. Since then when you've
kissed me I've had to clench my hands so as not to turn my face
away. The mere thought of anything else makes me feel physically sick. I loathe your complacence and your frightful insensi-
tiveness. Perhaps I could have forgiven it if it had been just a
moment's weakness and if afterwards you'd been ashamed. I
should have been miserable, but I think my love was so great
that I should only have felt pity for you. But you're incapable

of shame. And now I believe in nothing. You're only a silly, pretentious, vulgar poseur. I would rather be the wife of a second-rate planter so long as he had the common human virtues of a man than the wife of a fake like you."

He did not answer. Gradually his face began to discompose. Those handsome, regular features of his horribly distorted and suddenly he broke out into loud sobs. She gave a little cry.

"Don't, Alban, don't."

"Oh, darling, how can you be so cruel to me? I adore you. I'd give my whole life to please you. I can't live without you."

She put out her arms as though to ward off a blow.

"No, no, Alban, don't try to move me. I can't. I must go. I can't live with you any more. It would be frightful. I can never forget. I must tell you the truth, I have only contempt for you and repulsion."

He sank down at her feet and tried to cling to her knees. With a gasp she sprang up and he buried his head in the empty chair. He cried painfully with sobs that tore his chest. The sound was horrible. The tears streamed from Anne's eyes and, putting her hands to her ears to shut out that dreadful, hysterical sobbing, blindly stumbling she rushed to the door and ran out.

THE BACK OF BEYOND

GEORGE MOON was sitting in his office. His work was finished, and he lingered there because he hadn't the heart to go down to the club. It was getting on towards tiffin time, and there would be a good many fellows hanging about the bar. Two or three of them would offer him a drink. He could not face their heartiness. Some he had known for thirty years. They had bored him, and on the whole he disliked them, but now that he was seeing them for the last time it gave him a pang. To-night they were giving him a farewell dinner. Everyone would be there and they were presenting him with a silver tea-service that he did not in the least want. They would make speeches in which they would refer eulogistically to his work in the colony, express their regret at his departure and wish him long life to enjoy his well-earned leisure. He would reply suitably. He had prepared a speech in which he surveyed the changes that had taken place in the F.M.S., since first, a raw cadet, he had landed at Singapore. He would thank them for their loyal co-operation with him during the term which it had been his privilege to serve as Resident at Timbang Belud, and draw a glowing picture of the future that awaited the country as a whole, and Timbang Belud in particular. He would remind them that he had known it as a poverty-stricken village with a few Chinese shops and left it now a prosperous town with paved streets down which ran trams, with stone houses, a rich Chinese settlement and a club-house second in splendour only to that of Singapore. They would sing For he's a jolly good fellow and

Auld Lang Syne. Then they would dance and a good many of
the younger men would get drunk. The Malays had already
given him a farewell party and the Chinese an interminable
feast. To-morrow a vast concourse would see him off at the
station and that would be the end of him. He wondered what
they would say of him. The Malays and the Chinese would
say that he had been stern, but acknowledge that he had been
just. The planters had not liked him. They thought him hard
because he would not let them ride roughshod over their labour.
His subordinates had feared him. He drove them. He had no
patience with slackness or inefficiency. He had never spared
himself and saw no reason why he should spare others. They
thought him inhuman. It was true that there was nothing come-
hither in him. He could not throw off his official position when
he went to the club and laugh at bawdy stories, chaff and be
chaffed. He was conscious that his arrival cast a gloom, and to
play bridge with him (he liked to play every day from six to
eight) was looked upon as a privilege rather than an entertainment. When at some other table a young man's four as the
evening wore on grew hilarious, he caught glances thrown in his
direction and sometimes an older member would stroll up to
the noisy ones and in an undertone advise them to be quiet.
George Moon sighed a little. From an official standpoint his
career had been a success, he had been the youngest Resident
ever appointed in the F.M.S., and for exceptional services a
C.M.G. had been conferred upon him; but from the human it
had perhaps been otherwise. He had earned respect, respect for
his ability, industry and trustworthiness, but he was too clear-
sighted to think for a moment that he had inspired affection.
No one would regret him. In a few months he would be forgotten.

He smiled grimly. He was not sentimental. He had enjoyed
his authority, and it gave him an austere satisfaction to know
that he had kept everyone up to the mark. It did not displease
him to think that he had been feared rather than loved. He
saw his life as a problem in higher mathematics, the working-
out of which had required intense application of all his powers,
but of which the result had not the least practical consequence.
Its interest lay in its intricacy and its beauty in its solution.
But like pure beauty it led nowhither. His future was blank.
He was fifty-five, and full of energy, and to himself his mind
seemed as alert as ever, his experience of men and affairs was

wide: all that remained to him was to settle down in a country town in England or in a cheap part of the Riviera and play bridge with elderly ladies and golf with retired colonels. He had met, when on leave, old chiefs of his, and had observed with what difficulty they adapted themselves to the change in their circumstances. They had looked forward to the freedom that would be theirs when they retired and had pictured the charming uses to which they would put their leisure. Mirage. It was not very pleasant to be obscure after having been distinguished, to live in a poky villa after having dwelt in a spacious residency, to make do with a couple of maids when you had been accustomed to the service of half a dozen Chinese boys; and above all, it was not pleasant to realize that you did not matter a row of beans to anyone when you had grown used to the delicate flattery of knowing that a word of praise could delight and a frown humiliate all sorts and conditions of men.

George Moon stretched out his hand and helped himself to a cigarette from the box on his desk. As he did so he noticed all the little lines on the back of his hand and the thinness of his shrivelled fingers. He frowned with distaste. It was the hand of an old man. There was in his office a Chinese mirror-picture that he had bought long ago and that he was leaving behind. He got up and looked at himself in it. He saw a thin yellow face, wrinkled and tight-lipped, thin grey hair and grey tired eyes. He was tallish, very spare, with narrow shoulders, and he held himself erect. He had always played polo and even now could beat most of the younger men at tennis. When you talked to him he kept his eyes fixed on your face, listening attentively, but his expression did not change, and you had no notion what effect your words had on him. Perhaps he did not realize how disconcerting this was. He seldom smiled.

An orderly came in with a name written on a chit. George Moon looked at it and told him to show the visitor in. He sat down once more in his chair and looked with his cold eyes at the door through which in a moment the visitor would come. It was Tom Saffary, and he wondered what he wanted. Presumably something to do with the festivity that night. It had amused him to hear that Tom Saffary was the head of the committee that had organized it, for their relations during the last year had been far from cordial. Saffary was a planter and one of his Tamil overseers had lodged a complaint against him for assault. The Tamil had been grossly insolent to him and

Saffary had given him a thrashing. George Moon realized that
the provocation was great, but he had always set his face
against the planters taking the law in their own hands, and
when the case was tried he sentenced Saffary to a fine. But
when the court rose, to show that there was no ill-feeling he
asked Saffary to luncheon: Saffary, resentful of what he thought
an unmerited affront, curtly refused and since then had declined
to have any social relations with the Resident. He answered
when George Moon, casually, but resolved not to be affronted,
spoke to him; but would neither play bridge nor tennis with him.
He was manager of the largest rubber estate in the district, and
George Moon asked himself sardonically whether he had arranged the dinner and collected subscriptions for the representation, because he thought his dignity required it or whether,
now that his Resident was leaving, it appealed to his sentimentality to make a noble gesture. It tickled George Moon's
frigid sense of humour to think that it would fall to Tom Saffary
to make the principal speech of the evening, in which he would
enlarge upon the departing Resident's admirable qualities, and
voice the community's regret at their irreparable loss.

Tom Saffary was ushered in. The Resident rose from his
chair, shook hands with him and thinly smiled.

"How do you do? Sit down. Won't you have a cigarette?"

"How do you do?"

Saffary took the chair to which the Resident motioned him,
and the Resident waited for him to state his business. He had
a notion that his visitor was embarrassed. He was a big, burly
stout fellow, with a red face and a double chin, curly black hair
and blue eyes. He was a fine figure of a man, strong as a horse,
but it was plain that he did himself too well. He drank a good
deal and ate too heartily. But he was a good business man and
a hard worker. He ran his estate efficiently. He was popular
in the community. He was generally known as a good chap.
He was free with his money and ready to lend a helping hand
to anyone in distress. It occurred to the Resident that Saffary
had come in order, before the dinner, to compose the difference
between them. The emotion that might have occasioned such
a desire excited in the Resident's sensibility a very faint, good-
humoured contempt. He had no enemies because individuals
did not mean enough to him for him to hate any of them, but
if he had, he thought, he would have hated them to the end.

"I daresay you're a bit surprised to see me here this morning, and I expect, as it's your last day and all that, you're pretty busy."

George Moon did not answer, and the other went on.

"I've come on rather an awkward business. The fact is that my wife and I won't be able to come to the dinner to-night, and after that unpleasantness we had together last year I thought it only right to come and tell you that it has nothing to do with that. I think you treated me very harshly; it's not the money I minded, it was the indignity, but bygones are bygones. Now that you're leaving I don't want you to think that I bear any more ill-feeling towards you."

"I realized that when I heard that you were chiefly responsible for the send-off you're giving me," answered the Resident civilly. "I'm sorry that you won't be able to come to-night."

"I'm sorry, too. It's on account of Knobby Clarke's death." Saffary hesitated for a moment. "My wife and I were very much upset by it."

"It was very sad. He was a great friend of yours, wasn't he?"

"He was the greatest friend I had in the colony."

Tears shone in Tom Saffary's eyes. Fat men are very emotional, thought George Moon.

"I quite understand that in that case you should have no heart for what looks like being a rather uproarious party," he said kindly. "Have you heard anything of the circumstances?"

"No, nothing but what appeared in the paper."

"He seemed all right when he left here."

"As far as I know he'd never had a day's illness in his life."

"Heart, I suppose. How old was he?"

"Same age as me. Thirty-eight."

"That's young to die."

Knobby Clarke was a planter and the estate he managed was next door to Saffary's. George Moon had liked him. He was a rather ugly man, sandy, with high cheek-bones and hollow temples, large pale eyes in deep sockets and a big mouth. But he had an attractive smile and an easy manner. He was amusing and could tell a good story. He had a careless good humour that people found pleasing. He played games well. He was no fool. George Moon would have said he was somewhat colourless. In the course of his career he had known a good many men like him. They came and went. A fortnight before he had left for

England on leave and the Resident knew that the Saffarys had given a large dinner-party on his last night. He was married and his wife of course went with him.

"I'm sorry for her," said George Moon. "It must have been a terrible blow. He was buried at sea, wasn't he?"

"Yes. That's what it said in the paper."

The news had reached Timbang the night before. The Singapore papers arrived at six just as people were getting to the club, and a good many men waited to play bridge or billiards till they had had a glance at them. Suddenly one fellow had called out:

"I say, do you see this? Knobby's dead."

"Knobby who? Not Knobby Clarke?"

There was a three-line paragraph in a column of general intelligence.

"*Messrs. Star, Moseley & Co. have received a cable informing them that Mr. Harold Clarke of Timbang Batu died suddenly on his way home and was buried at sea.*"

A man came up and took the paper from the speaker's hand, and incredulously read the note for himself. Another peered over his shoulder. Such as happened to be reading the paper turned to the page in question and read the three indifferent lines.

"By George," cried one.

"I say, what tough luck," said another.

"He was as fit as a fiddle when he left here."

A shiver of dismay pierced those hearty, jovial, careless men, and each one for a moment remembered that he too was mortal. Other members came in and as they entered, braced by the thought of the six o'clock drink, and eager to meet their friends, they were met by the grim tidings.

"I say, have you heard? Poor Knobby Clarke's dead."

"No? I say, how awful!"

"Rotten luck, isn't it?"

"Rotten."

"Damned good sort."

"One of the best."

"It gave me quite a turn when I saw it in the paper just by chance."

"I don't wonder."

One man with the paper in his hand went into the billiard-room to break the news. They were playing off the handicap for the Prince of Wales's Cup. That august personage had presented it to the club on the occasion of his visit to Timbang Belud. Tom Saffary was playing against a man called Douglas, and the Resident, who had been beaten in the previous round, was seated with about a dozen others watching the game. The marker was monotonously calling out the score. The newcomer waited for Saffary to finish his break and then called out to him.

"I say, Tom, Knobby's dead."

"Knobby? It's not true."

The other handed him the paper. Three or four gathered round to read with him.

"Good God!"

There was a moment's awed silence. The paper was passed from hand to hand. It was odd that none seemed willing to believe till he saw it for himself in black and white.

"Oh, I am sorry."

"I say, it's awful for his wife," said Tom Saffary. "She was going to have a baby. My poor missus'll be upset."

"Why, it's only a fortnight since he left here."

"He was all right then."

"In the pink."

Saffary, his fat red face sagging a little, went over to a table and, seizing his glass, drank deeply.

"Look here, Tom," said his opponent, "would you like to call the game off?"

"Can't very well do that." Saffary's eye sought the score board and he saw that he was ahead. "No, let's finish. Then I'll go home and break it to Violet."

Douglas had his shot and made fourteen. Tom Saffary missed an easy in-off, but left nothing. Douglas played again, but did not score and again Saffary missed a shot that ordinarily he could have been sure of. He frowned a little. He knew his friends had betted on him pretty heavily and he did not like the idea of failing them. Douglas made twenty-two. Saffary emptied his glass and by an effort of will that was quite patent to the sympathetic onlookers settled down to concentrate on the game. He made a break of eighteen and when he just failed to do a long Jenny they gave him a round of applause. He was sure of himself now and began to score quickly. Douglas was playing well too, and the match grew exciting to watch. The few minutes during which Saffary's attention wandered had allowed his opponent to catch up with him, and now it was anybody's game.

"Spot two hundred and thirty-five," called the Malay, in his queer clipped English. "Plain two hundred and twenty-eight. Spot to play."

Douglas made eight, and then Saffary, who was plain, drew up to two hundred and forty. He left his opponent a double balk. Douglas hit neither ball, and so gave Saffary another point.

"Spot two hundred and forty-three," called the marker. "Plain two hundred and forty-one. Plain to play."

Saffary played three beautiful shots off the red and finished the game.

"A popular victory," the bystanders cried.

"Congratulations, old man," said Douglas.

"Boy," called Saffary, "ask these gentlemen what they'll have. Poor old Knobby."

He sighed heavily. The drinks were brought and Saffary signed the chit. Then he said he'd be getting along. Two others had already begun to play.

"Sporting of him to go on like that," said someone when the door was closed on Saffary.

"Yes, it shows grit."

"For a while I thought his game had gone all to pieces."

"He pulled himself together in grand style. He knew there were a lot of bets on him. He didn't want to let his backers down."

"Of course it's a shock, a thing like that."

"They were great pals. I wonder what he died of."

"Good shot, sir."

George Moon, remembering this scene, thought it strange that Tom Saffary, who on hearing of his friend's death had shown such self-control, should now apparently take it so hard. It might be that just as in the war a man when hit often did not know it till some time afterwards, Saffary had not realized how great a blow to him Harold Clarke's death was till he had had time to think it over. It seemed to him, however, more probable that Saffary, left to himself, would have carried on as usual, seeking sympathy for his loss in the company of his fellows, but that his wife's conventional sense of propriety had insisted that it would be bad form to go to a party when the grief they were suffering from made it only decent for them to eschew, for a little, festive gatherings. Violet Saffary was a nice little woman, three or four years younger than her husband; not very pretty, but pleasant to look at and always becomingly dressed; amiable, ladylike and unassuming. In the days when he had been on friendly terms with the Saffarys the Resident had from time to time dined with them. He had found her agreeable, but not very amusing. They had never talked but of commonplace things. Of late he had seen little of her. When they chanced to meet she always gave him a friendly smile, and on occasion he said one or two civil words to her. But it was only by an effort of memory that he distinguished her from half a dozen of the other ladies in the community whom his official position brought him in contact with.

Saffary had presumably said what he had come to say and the Resident wondered why he did not get up and go. He sat heaped up in his chair oddly, so that it gave you the feeling that his skeleton had ceased to support him and his considerable mass of flesh was falling in on him. He looked dully at the desk that separated him from the Resident. He sighed deeply.

"You must try not to take it too hard, Saffary," said George Moon. "You know how uncertain life is in the East. One has to resign oneself to losing people one's fond of."

Saffary's eyes slowly moved from the desk, and he fixed them on George Moon's. They stared unwinking. George Moon liked people to look him in the eyes. Perhaps he felt that when he thus held their vision he held them in his power. Presently two tears formed themselves in Saffary's blue eyes and slowly ran down his cheeks. He had a strangely puzzled look. Something had frightened him. Was it death? No. Something that he thought worse. He looked cowed. His mien was cringing so that he made you think of a dog unjustly beaten.

"It's not that," he faltered. "I could have borne that."

George Moon did not answer. He held that big, powerful man with his cold level gaze and waited. He was pleasantly conscious of his absolute indifference. Saffary gave a harassed glance at the papers on the desk.

"I'm afraid I'm taking up too much of your time."

"No, I have nothing to do at the moment."

Saffary looked out of the window. A little shudder passed between his shoulders. He seemed to hesitate.

"I wonder if I might ask your advice," he said at last.

"Of course," said the Resident, with the shadow of a smile, "that's one of the things I'm here for."

"It's a purely private matter."

"You may be quite sure that I shan't betray any confidence you place in me."

"No, I know you wouldn't do that, but it's rather an awkward thing to speak about, and I shouldn't feel very comfortable meeting you afterwards. But you're going away to-morrow, and that makes it easier, if you understand what I mean."

"Quite."

Saffary began to speak, in a low voice, sulkily, as though he were ashamed, and he spoke with the awkwardness of a man unused to words. He went back and said the same thing over again. He got mixed up. He started a long, elaborate sentence and then broke off abruptly because he did not know how to finish it. George Moon listened in silence, his face a mask, smoking, and he only took his eyes off Saffary's face to reach for another cigarette from the box in front of him and light it from the stub of that which he was just finishing. And while he listened he saw, as it were a background, the monotonous round of the planter's life. It was like an accompaniment of muted strings that threw into sharper relief the calculated dissonances of an unexpected melody.

With rubber at so low a price every economy had to be exercised and Tom Saffary, notwithstanding the size of the estate, had to do work which in better times he had had an assistant for. He rose before dawn and went down to the lines where the coolies were assembled. When there was just enough light to see he read out the names, ticking them off according to the answers, and assigned the various squads to their work. Some tapped, some weeded, and others tended the ditches. Saffary went back to his solid breakfast, lit his pipe and sallied forth again to inspect the coolies' quarters. Children were playing and babies sprawling here and there. On the sidewalks Tamil women cooked their rice. Their black skins shone with oil. They were draped about in dull red cotton and wore gold ornaments in their hair. There were handsome creatures among them, upright of carriage, with delicate features and small, exquisite hands; but Saffary looked upon them only with distaste. He set out on his rounds. On his well-grown estate the trees planted in rows gave one a charming feeling of the prim forest of a German fairy-tale. The ground was thick with dead leaves. He was accompanied by a Tamil overseer, his long black hair done in a chignon, barefooted, in sarong and baju, with a showy ring on his finger. Saffary walked hard, jumping the ditches when he came to them, and soon he dripped with sweat. He examined the trees to see that they were properly tapped, and when he came across a coolie at work looked at the shavings and if they were too thick swore at him and docked him half a day's pay. When a tree was not to be tapped any more he told the overseer to take away the cup and the wire that held it to the trunk. The weeders worked in gangs.

At noon Saffary returned to the bungalow and had a drink of beer which, because there was no ice, was lukewarm. He stripped the khaki shorts, the flannel shirt, the heavy boots and stockings in which he had been walking, and shaved and bathed. He lunched in a sarong and baju. He lay off for half an hour, and then went down to his office and worked till five; he had tea and went to the club. About eight he started back for the bungalow, dined, and half an hour after went to bed.

But last night he went home immediately he had finished his match. Violet had not accompanied him that day. When the Clarkes were there they had met at the club every afternoon but now they had gone home she came less often. She said there was no one there who much amused her and she had heard everything everyone had to say till she was fed to the teeth. She did not play bridge and it was dull for her to wait about while he played. She told Tom he need not mind leaving her alone. She had plenty of things to do in the house.

As soon as she saw him back so early she guessed that he had come to tell her that he had won his match. He was like a child in his self-satisfaction over one of these small triumphs. He was a kindly, simple creature and she knew that his pleasure at winning was not only on his own account, but because he thought it must give her pleasure too. It was rather sweet of him to hurry home in order to tell her all about it without delay.

"Well, how did your match go?" she said as soon as he came lumbering into the sitting-room.

"I won."

"Easily?"

"Well, not as easily as I should have. I was a bit ahead, and then I stuck, I couldn't do a thing, and you know what Douglas is, not at all showy, but steady, and he pulled up with me. Then I said to myself, well, if I don't buck up I shall get a licking. I had a bit of luck here and there, and then, to cut a long story short, I beat him by seven."

"Isn't that splendid? You ought to win the cup now, oughtn't you?"

"Well, I've got three matches more. If I can get into the semi-finals I ought to have a chance."

Violet smiled. She was anxious to show him that she was as much interested as he expected her to be.

"What made you go to pieces when you did?"

His face sagged.

"That's why I came back at once. I'd have scratched only I thought it wasn't fair on the fellows who'd backed me. I don't know how to tell you, Violet."

She gave him a questioning look.

"Why, what's the matter? Not bad news?"

"Rotten. Knobby's dead."

For a full minute she stared at him, and her face, her neat friendly little face, grew haggard with horror. At first it seemed as though she could not understand.

"What *do* you mean?" she cried.

"It was in the paper. He died on board. They buried him at sea."

Suddenly she gave a piercing cry and fell headlong to the floor. She had fainted dead away.

"Violet," he cried, and threw himself down on his knees and took her head in his arms. "Boy, boy."

A boy, startled by the terror in his master's voice, rushed in and Saffary shouted to him to bring brandy. He forced a little between Violet's lips. She opened her eyes, and as she remembered they grew dark with anguish. Her face was screwed up like a little child's when it is just going to burst into tears. He lifted her up in his arms and laid her on the sofa. She turned her head away.

"Oh, Tom, it isn't true. It can't be true."

"I'm afraid it is."

"No, no, no."

She burst into tears. She wept convulsively. It was dreadful to hear her. Saffary did not know what to do. He knelt beside her and tried to soothe her. He sought to take her in his arms, but with a sudden gesture she repelled him.

"Don't touch me," she cried, and she said it so sharply that he was startled.

He rose to his feet.

"Try not to take it too hard, sweetie," he said. "I know it's been an awful shock. He was one of the best."

She buried her face in the cushions and wept despairingly. It tortured him to see her body shaken by those uncontrollable sobs. She was beside herself. He put his hand gently on her shoulder.

"Darling, don't give way like that. It's so bad for you."

She shook herself free from his hand.

"For God's sake leave me alone," she cried. "Oh, Hal, Hal." He had never heard her call the dead man that before. Of course his name was Harold, but everyone called him Knobby. "What shall I do?" she wailed. "I can't bear it. I can't bear it."

Saffary began to grow a trifle impatient. So much grief did seem to him exaggerated. Violet was not normally so emotional. He supposed it was the damned climate. It made women nervous and high-strung. Violet hadn't been home for four years. She was not hiding her face now. She lay, almost falling off the sofa, her mouth open in the extremity of her pain, and the tears streamed from her staring eyes. She was distraught.

"Have a little more brandy," he said. "Try and pull yourself together, darling. You can't do Knobby any good by getting in such a state."

With a sudden gesture she sprang to her feet and pushed him aside. She gave him a look of hatred.

"Go away, Tom. I don't want your sympathy. I want to be left alone."

She walked swiftly over to an armchair and threw herself down in it. She flung back her head and her poor white face was wrenched into a grimace of agony.

"Oh, it's not fair," she moaned. "What's to become of me now? Oh, God, I wish I were dead."

"Violet."

His voice quavered with pain. He was very nearly crying too. She stamped her foot impatiently.

"Go away, I tell you. Go away."

He started. He stared at her and suddenly gasped. A shudder passed through his great bulk. He took a step towards her and stopped, but his eyes never left her white, tortured face; he stared as though he saw in it something that appalled him.

Then he dropped his head and without a word walked out of the room. He went into a little sitting-room they had at the back, but seldom used, and sank heavily into a chair. He thought. Presently the gong sounded for dinner. He had not had his bath. He gave his hands a glance. He could not be bothered to wash them. He walked slowly into the dining-room. He told the boy to go and tell Violet that dinner was ready. The boy came back and said she did not want any.

"All right. Let me have mine then," said Saffary.

He sent Violet in a plate of soup and a piece of toast, and when the fish was served put some on a plate for her and gave it to the boy. But the boy came back with it at once.

"Mem, she say no wantchee," he said.

Saffary ate his dinner alone. He ate from habit, stolidly, through the familiar courses. He drank a bottle of beer. When he had finished the boy brought him a cup of coffee and he lit a cheroot. Saffary sat still till he had finished it. He thought. At last he got up and went back into the large verandah which was where they always sat. Violet was still huddled in the chair in which he had left her. Her eyes were closed, but she opened them when she heard him come. He took a light chair and sat down in front of her.

"What *was* Knobby to you, Violet?" he said.

She gave a slight start. She turned away her eyes, but did not speak.

"I can't quite make out why you should have been so frightfully upset by the news of his death."

"It was an awful shock."

"Of course. But it seems very strange that anyone should go simply all to pieces over the death of a friend."

"I don't understand what you mean," she said.

She could hardly speak the words and he saw that her lips were trembling.

"I've never heard you call him Hal. Even his wife called him Knobby."

She did not say anything. Her eyes, heavy with grief, were fixed on vacancy.

"Look at me, Violet."

She turned her head slightly and listlessly gazed at him.

"Was he your lover?"

She closed her eyes and tears flowed from them. Her mouth was strangely twisted.

"Haven't you got anything to say at all?"

She shook her head.

"You must answer me, Violet."

"I'm not fit to talk to you now," she moaned. "How can you be so heartless?"

"I'm afraid I don't feel very sympathetic at the moment. We must get this straight now. Would you like a drink of water?"

"I don't want anything."

"Then answer my question."

"You have no right to ask it. It's insulting."

"Do you ask me to believe that a woman like you who hears of the death of someone she knew is going to faint dead away and then, when she comes to, is going to cry like that? Why, one wouldn't be so upset over the death of one's only child. When we heard of your mother's death you cried of course, anyone would, and I know you were utterly miserable, but you came to me for comfort and you said you didn't know what you'd have done without me."

"This was so frightfully sudden."

"Your mother's death was sudden, too."

"Naturally I was very fond of Knobby."

"How fond? So fond that when you heard he was dead you didn't know and you didn't care what you said? Why did you say it wasn't fair? Why did you say, 'What's going to become of me now?'"

She sighed deeply. She turned her head this way and that like a sheep trying to avoid the hands of the butcher.

"You mustn't take me for an utter fool, Violet. I tell you it's impossible that you should be so shattered by the blow if there hadn't been something between you."

"Well, if you think that why do you torture me with questions?"

"My dear, it's no good shilly-shallying. We can't go on like this. What d'you think I'm feeling?"

She looked at him when he said this. She hadn't thought of him at all. She had been too much absorbed in her own misery to be concerned with his.

"I'm so tired," she sighed.

He leaned forward and roughly seized her wrist.

"Speak," he cried.

"You're hurting me."

"And what about me? D'you think you're not hurting me? How can you have the heart to let me suffer like this?"

He let go of her arm and sprang to his feet. He walked to the end of the room and back again. It looked as though the movement had suddenly roused him to fury. He caught her by the shoulders and dragged her to her feet. He shook her.

"If you don't tell me the truth I'll kill you," he cried.

"I wish you would," she said.

"He was your lover?"

"Yes."

"You swine."

With one hand still on her shoulder so that she could not move he swung back his other arm and with a flat palm struck her repeatedly, with all his strength, on the side of her face. She quivered under the blows, but did not flinch or cry out. He struck her again and again. All at once he felt her strangely inert, he let go of her and she sank unconscious to the floor. Fear seized him. He bent down and touched her, calling her name. She did not move. He lifted her up and put her back into the chair from which a little while before he had pulled her. The brandy that had been brought when first she fainted was still in the room and he fetched it and tried to force it down her throat. She choked and it spilt over her chin and neck. One side of her pale face was livid from the blows of his heavy hand. She sighed a little and opened her eyes. He held the glass again to her lips, supporting her head, and she sipped a little of the neat spirit. He looked at her with penitent, anxious eyes.

"I'm sorry, Violet. I didn't mean to do that. I'm dreadfully ashamed of myself. I never thought I could sink so low as to hit a woman."

Though she was feeling very weak and her face was hurting, the flicker of a smile crossed her lips. Poor Tom. He did say things like that. He felt like that. And how scandalized he would be if you asked him why a man shouldn't hit a woman. But Saffary, seeing the wan smile, put it down to her indomitable courage. By God, she's a plucky little woman, he thought. Game isn't the word.

"Give me a cigarette," she said.

He took one out of his case and put it in her mouth. He made two or three ineffectual attempts to strike his lighter. It would not work.

"Hadn't you better get a match?" she said.

For the moment she had forgotten her heart-rending grief and was faintly amused at the situation. He took a box from the table and held the lighted match to her cigarette. She inhaled the first puff with a sense of infinite relief.

"I can't tell you how ashamed I am, Violet," he said. "I'm disgusted with myself. I don't know what came over me."

"Oh, that's all right. It was very natural. Why don't you have a drink? It'll do you good."

Without a word, his shoulders all hunched up as though the burden that oppressed him were material, he helped himself to a brandy and soda. Then, still silent, he sat down. She watched the blue smoke curl into the air.

"What are you going to do?" she said at last.

He gave a weary gesture of despair.

"We'll talk about that to-morrow. You're not in a fit state to-night. As soon as you've finished your cigarette you'd better go to bed."

"You know so much, you'd better know everything."

"Not now, Violet."

"Yes, now."

She began to speak. He heard her words, but could hardly make sense of them. He felt like a man who has built himself a house with loving care and thought to live in it all his life, and then, he does not understand why, sees the housebreakers come and with their picks and heavy hammers destroy it room by room, till what was a fair dwelling-place is only a heap of rubble. What made it so awful was that it was Knobby Clarke who had done this thing. They had come out to the F.M.S. on the same ship and had worked at first on the same estate. They call the young planter a creeper and you can tell him in the streets of Singapore by his double felt hat and his khaki coat turned up at the wrists. Callow youths who saunter about staring and are inveigled by wily Chinese into buying worthless truck from Birmingham which they send home as Eastern curios, sit in the lounges of cheap hotels drinking innumerable stengahs, and after an evening at the pictures get into rickshaws and finish the night in the Chinese quarter. Tom and Knobby were inseparable. Tom, a big, powerful fellow, simple, very honest, hard-working; and Knobby, ungainly, but curiously attractive, with his deep-set eyes, hollow cheeks and large humorous mouth. It was Knobby who made the jokes and Tom who laughed at them. Tom married first. He met Violet when he went on leave. The daughter of a doctor killed in the war, she was governess in the house of some people who lived in the same place as his father. He fell in love with her because she was alone in the world, and his tender heart was touched by the thought of the drab life that lay before her. But Knobby married, because Tom had and he felt lost without him, a girl who had come East to spend the winter with relations. Enid Clarke had been very pretty then in her blonde way, and full face she was pretty still, though her skin, once so clear and fresh, was already faded; but she had a very weak, small, insignificant chin and in profile reminded you of a sheep. She had pretty flaxen hair, straight, because in the heat it would not keep its wave, and china-blue eyes. Though but twenty-six, she had already a tired look. A year after marriage she had a baby, but it died when only two years old. It was after this that Tom Saffary managed to get Knobby the post of manager of the estate next his own. The two men pleasantly resumed their old familiarity, and their wives, who till then had not known one another very well, soon made friends. They copied one another's frocks and lent one another servants and crockery when they gave a party. The four of them met every day. They went everywhere together. Tom Saffary thought it grand.

The strange thing was that Violet and Knobby Clarke lived on these terms of close intimacy for three years before they fell in love with one another. Neither saw love approaching. Neither suspected that in the pleasure each took in the other's company there was anything more than the casual friendship of two persons thrown together by the circumstances of life. To be together gave them no particular happiness, but merely a quiet sense of comfort. If by chance a day passed without their meeting they felt unaccountably bored. That seemed very natural. They played games together. They danced together. They chaffed one another. The revelation came to them by what looked like pure accident. They had all been to a dance at the club and were driving home in Saffary's car. The Clarke's estate was on the way and he was dropping them at their bungalow. Violet and Knobby sat in the back. He had had a good deal to drink, but was not drunk; their hands touched by chance, and he took hers and held it. They did not speak. They were all tired. But suddenly the exhilaration of the champagne left him and he was cold sober. They knew in a flash that they were madly in love with one another and at the same moment they realized that they had never been in love before. When they reached the Clarkes' Tom said:

"You'd better hop in beside me, Violet."

"I'm too exhausted to move," she said.

Her legs seemed so weak that she thought she would never be able to stand.

When they met next day neither referred to what had happened, but each knew that something inevitable had passed. They behaved to one another as they had always done, they continued to behave so for weeks, but they felt that everything was different. At last flesh and blood could stand it no longer and they became lovers. But the physical tie seemed to them the least important element in their relation, and indeed their way of living made it impossible for them, except very seldom, to enjoy any intimate connection. It was enough that they saw one another, though in the company of others, every day; a glance, a touch of the hand, assured them of their love, and that was all that mattered. The sexual act was no more than an affirmation of the union of their souls.

They very seldom talked of Tom or Enid. If sometimes they laughed together at their foibles it was not unkindly. It might have seemed odd to them to realize how completely these two people whom they saw so constantly had ceased to matter to them if they had given them enough thought to consider the matter. Their relations with them fell into the routine of life that nobody notices, like shaving oneself, dressing and eating three meals a day. They felt tenderly towards them. They even took pains to please them, as you would with a bed-ridden invalid, because their own happiness was so great that in charity they must do what they could for others less fortunate. They had no scruples. They were too much absorbed in one another to be touched even for a moment by remorse. Beauty now excitingly kindled the pleasant humdrum life they had led so long.

But then an event took place that filled them with consternation. The company for which Tom worked entered into negotiations to buy extensive rubber plantations in British North Borneo and invited Tom to manage them. It was a better job than his present one, with a higher salary, and since he would have assistants under him he would not have to work so hard. Saffary welcomed the offer. Both Clarke and Saffary were due for leave and the two couples had arranged to travel home together. They had already booked their passages. This changed everything. Tom would not be able to get away for at least a year. By the time the Clarkes came back the Saffarys would be settled in Borneo. It did not take Violet and Knobby long to decide that there was only one thing to do. They had been willing enough to go on as they were, notwithstanding the hindrances to the enjoyment of their love, when they were certain of seeing one another continually; they felt that they had endless time before them and the future was coloured with a happiness that seemed to have no limit; but neither could suffer for an instant the thought of separation. They made up their minds to run away together, and then it seemed to them on a sudden that every day that passed before they could be together always and all the time was a day lost. Their love took another guise. It flamed into a devouring passion that left them no emotion to waste on others. They cared little for the pain they must cause Tom and Enid. It was unfortunate, but inevitable. They made their plans deliberately. Knobby on the pretence of business would go to Singapore and Violet, telling Tom that she was going to spend a week with friends on an estate down the line, would join him there. They would go over to Java and thence take ship to Sydney. In Sydney Knobby would look for a job. When Violet told Tom that the Mackenzies had asked her to spend a few days with them, he was pleased.

"That's grand. I think you want a change, darling," he said. "I've fancied you've been looking a bit peaked lately."

He stroked her cheek affectionately. The gesture stabbed her heart.

"You've always been awfully good to me, Tom," she said, her eyes suddenly filled with tears.

"Well, that's the least I could be. You're the best little woman in the world."

"Have you been happy with me these eight years?"

"Frightfully."

"Well, that's something, isn't it? No one can ever take that away from you."

She had told herself that he was the kind of man who would soon console himself. He liked women for themselves and it would not be long after he had regained his freedom before he found someone that he would wish to marry. And he would be just as happy with his new wife as he had been with her. Perhaps he would marry Enid. Enid was one of those dependent little things that somewhat exasperated her and she did not think her capable of deep feeling. Her vanity would be hurt; her heart would not be broken. But now that the die was cast, everything settled and the day fixed, she had a qualm. Remorse beset her. She wished that it had been possible not to cause those two people such fearful distress. She faltered.

"We've had a very good time here, Tom," she said. "I wonder if it's wise to leave it all. We're giving up a certainty for we don't know what."

"My dear child, it's a chance in a million and much better money."

"Money isn't everything. There's happiness."

"I know that, but there's no reason why we shouldn't be just as happy in B.N.B. And besides, there was no alternative. I'm not my own master. The directors want me to go and I must, and that's all there is to it."

She sighed. There was no alternative for her either. She shrugged her shoulders. It was hateful to cause others pain; sometimes you couldn't help yourself. Tom meant no more to her than the casual man on the voyage out who was civil to you: it was absurd that she should be asked to sacrifice her life for him.

The Clarkes were due to sail for England in a fortnight and this determined the date of their elopement. The days passed. Violet was restless and excited. She looked forward with a joy that was almost painful to the peace that she anticipated when they were once on board the ship and could begin the life which she was sure would give her at last perfect happiness.

She began to pack. The friends she was supposed to be going to stay with entertained a good deal and this gave her an excuse to take quite a lot of luggage. She was starting next day. It was eleven o'clock in the morning and Tom was making his round of the estate. One of the boys came to her room and told her that Mrs. Clarke was there and at the same moment she heard Enid calling her. Quickly closing the lid of her trunk, she went out on to the verandah. To her astonishment Enid came up to her, flung her arms round her neck and kissed her eagerly. She looked at Enid and saw that her cheeks, usually pale, were flushed and that her eyes were shining. Enid burst into tears.

"What on earth's the matter, darling?" she cried.

For one moment she was afraid that Enid knew everything. But Enid was flushed with delight and not with jealousy or anger.

"I've just seen Dr. Harrow," she said. "I didn't want to say anything about it. I've had two or three false alarms, but this time he says it's all right."

A sudden coldness pierced Violet's heart.

"What do you mean? You're not going to . . ."

She looked at Enid and Enid nodded.

"Yes, he says there's no doubt about it at all. He thinks I'm at least three months gone. Oh, my dear, I'm so wildly happy."

She flung herself again into Violet's arms and clung to her, weeping.

"Oh, darling, don't."

Violet felt herself grow pale as death and knew that if she didn't keep a tight hold of herself she would faint.

"Does Knobby know?"

"No, I didn't say a word. He was so disappointed before. He was so frightfully cut up when baby died. He's wanted me to have another so badly."

Violet forced herself to say the things that were expected of her, but Enid was not listening. She wanted to tell the whole story of her hopes and fears, of her symptoms, and then of her interview with the doctor. She went on and on.

"When are you going to tell Knobby?" Violet asked at last. "Now, when he gets in?"

"Oh, no, he's tired and hungry when he gets back from his round. I shall wait till to-night after dinner."

Violet repressed a movement of exasperation; Enid was going to make a scene of it and was choosing her moment; but after all, it was only natural. It was lucky, for it would give her the chance to see Knobby first. As soon as she was rid of her she rang him up. She knew that he always looked in at his office on his way home, and she left a message asking him to call her. She was only afraid that he would not do so till Tom was back, but she had to take her chance of that. The bell rang and Tom had not yet come in.

"Hal?"

"Yes."

"Will you be at the hut at three?"

"Yes. Has anything happened?"

"I'll tell you when I see you. Don't worry."

She rang off. The hut was a little shelter on Knobby's estate which she could get to without difficulty and where they occasionally met. The coolies passed it while they worked and it had no privacy; but it was a convenient place for them without exciting comment to exchange a few minutes' conversation. At three Enid would be resting and Tom at work in his office.

When Violet walked up Knobby was already there. He gave a gasp.

"Violet, how white you are."

She gave him her hand. They did not know what eyes might be watching them and their behaviour here was always such as anyone could observe.

"Enid came to see me this morning. She's going to tell you to-night. I thought you ought to be warned. She's going to have a baby."

"Violet!"

He looked at her aghast. She began to cry. They had never talked of the relations they had, he with his wife and she with her husband. They ignored the subject because it was to each exquisitely painful. Violet knew what her own life was; she satisfied her husband's appetite; but, with a woman's strange nonchalance, because to do so gave her no pleasure, attached no importance to it; but somehow she had persuaded herself that with Hal it was different. He felt now instinctively how bitterly what she had learned wounded her. He tried to excuse himself.

"Darling, I couldn't help myself."

She cried silently and he watched her with miserable eyes.

"I know it seems beastly," he said, "but what could I do? It wasn't as if I had any reason to . . ."

She interrupted him.

"I don't blame you. It was inevitable. It's only because I'm stupid that it gives me such a frightful pain in my heart."

"Darling!"

"We ought to have gone away together two years ago. It was madness to think we could go on like this."

"Are you sure Enid's right? She thought she was in the family way three or four years ago."

"Oh, yes, she's right. She's frightfully happy. She says you wanted a child so badly."

"It's come as such an awful surprise. I don't seem able to realize it yet."

She looked at him. He was staring at the leaf-strewn earth with harassed eyes. She smiled a little.

"Poor Hal." She sighed deeply. "There's nothing to be done about it. It's the end of us."

"What do you mean?" he cried.

"Oh, my dear, you can't very well leave her now, can you? It was all right before. She would have been unhappy, but she would have got over it. But now it's different. It's not a very nice time for a woman anyhow. For months she feels more or less ill. She wants affection. She wants to be taken care of. It would be frightful to leave her to bear it all alone. We couldn't be such beasts."

"Do you mean to say you want me to go back to England with her?"

She nodded gravely.

"It's lucky you're going. It'll be easier when you get away and we don't see one another every day."

"But I can't live without you now."

"Oh, yes, you can. You must. I can. And it'll be worse for me, because I stay behind and I shall have nothing."

"Oh, Violet, it's impossible."

"My dear, it's no good arguing. The moment she told me I saw it meant that. That's why I wanted to see you first. I thought the shock might lead you to blurt out the whole truth. You know I love you more than anything in the world. She's never done me any harm. I couldn't take you away from her now. It's bad luck on both of us, but there it is, I simply wouldn't dare to do a filthy thing like that."

"I wish I were dead," he moaned.

"That wouldn't do her any good, or me either," she smiled.

"What about the future? Have we got to sacrifice our whole lives?"

"I'm afraid so. It sounds rather grim, darling, but I suppose sooner or later we shall get over it. One gets over everything."

She looked at her wrist-watch.

"I ought to be getting back. Tom will be in soon. We're all meeting at the club at five."

"Tom and I are supposed to be playing tennis." He gave her a pitiful look. "Oh, Violet, I'm so frightfully unhappy."

"I know. So am I. But we shan't do any good by talking about it."

She gave him her hand, but he took her in his arms and kissed her, and when she released herself her cheeks were wet with his tears. But she was so desperate she could not cry.

Ten days later the Clarkes sailed.

While George Moon was listening to as much of this story as Tom Saffary was able to tell him, he reflected in his cool, detached way how odd it was that these commonplace people, leading lives so monotonous, should have been convulsed by such a tragedy. Who would have thought that Violet Saffary, so neat and demure, sitting in the club reading the illustrated papers or chatting with her friends over a lemon squash, should have been eating her heart out for love of that ordinary man? George Moon remembered seeing Knobby at the club the evening before he sailed. He seemed in great spirits. Fellows envied him because he was going home. Those who had recently come back told him by no means to miss the show at the Pavilion. Drink flowed freely. The Resident had not been asked to the farewell party the Saffarys gave for the Clarkes, but he knew very well what it had been like, the good cheer, the cordiality, the chaff, and then after dinner the gramophone turned on and everyone dancing. He wondered what Violet and Clarke had felt as they danced together. It gave him an odd sensation of dismay to think of the despair that must have filled their hearts while they pretended to be so gay.

And with another part of his mind George Moon thought of his own past. Very few knew that story. After all, it had happened twenty-five years ago.

"What are you going to do now, Saffary?" he asked.

"Well, that's what I wanted you to advise me about. Now that Knobby's dead I don't know what's going to happen to Violet if I divorce her. I was wondering if I oughtn't to let her divorce me."

"Oh, you want to divorce?"

"Well, I must."

George Moon lit another cigarette and watched for a moment the smoke that curled away into the air.

"Did you ever know that I'd been married?"

"Yes, I think I'd heard. You're a widower, aren't you?"

"No, I divorced my wife. I have a son of twenty-seven. He's farming in New Zealand. I saw my wife the last time I was home on leave. We met at a play. At first we didn't recognize one another. She spoke to me. I asked her to lunch at the Berkeley."

George Moon chuckled to himself. He was alone. It was a musical comedy. He found himself sitting next to a large fat dark woman whom he vaguely thought he had seen before, but the play was just beginning and he did not give her a second look. When the curtain fell after the first act she looked at him with bright eyes and spoke.

"How are you, George?"

He gave a start. It was his wife. She had a bold, friendly manner and was very much at her ease.

"It's a long time since we met," she said.

"It is."

"How has life been treating you?"

"Oh, all right."

"I suppose you're a Resident now. You're still in the Service, aren't you?"

"Yes. I'm retiring soon, worse luck."

"Why? You look very fit."

"I'm reaching the age limit. I'm supposed to be an old buffer and no good any more."

"You're lucky to have kept so thin. I'm terrible, aren't I?"

"You don't look as though you were wasting away."

"I know. I'm stout and I'm growing stouter all the time. I can't help it and I love food. I can't resist cream and bread and potatoes."

George Moon laughed, but not at what she said; at his own thoughts. In years gone by it had sometimes occurred to him that he might meet her, but he had never thought that the meeting would take his turn. When the play was ended and with a smile she bade him good-night, he said:

"I suppose you wouldn't lunch with me one day?"

"Any day you like."

They arranged a date and duly met. He knew that she had married the man on whose account he had divorced her, and he judged by her clothes that she was in comfortable circumstances. They drank a cocktail. She ate the *hors-d'œuvres* with gusto. She was fifty if she was a day, but she carried her years with spirit. There was something jolly and careless about her, she was quick in the uptake, chatty, and she had the hearty, infectious laugh of the fat woman who has let herself go. If he had not known that her family had for a century been in the Indian Civil Service he would have thought that she had been a chorus girl. She was not flashy, but she had a sort of flamboyance of nature that suggested the stage. She was not in the least embarrassed.

"You never married again, did you?" she asked him.

"No."

"Pity. Because it wasn't a success the first time there's no reason why it shouldn't have been the second."

"There's no need for me to ask if you've been happy."

"I've got nothing to complain of. I think I've got a happy nature. Jim's always been very good to me; he's retired no~ you know, and we live in the country, and I adore Bett. I'm

"Who's Betty?"

"Oh, she's my daughter. She got married t~ expecting to be a grandmother almost an~

"That ages us a bit."   ~r you to ask me to lunch,
She gave a laugh.   ~ay to have any feelings about
"Betty's twenty-two. It ~ong ago as all that."
George. After all, it w~
something that ha~~ted to one another and it's lucky we found
"Idiotic."   ~it was too late. Of course I was foolish, but then
"We w~ young. Have you been happy too?"
it on~~ry
~ ~ think I can say I've been a success."

"Oh, well, that's probably all the happiness you were capable of."

He smiled in appreciation of her shrewdness. And then, putting the whole matter aside easily, she began to talk of other things. Though the courts had given him custody of their son, he, unable to look after him, had allowed his mother to have him. The boy had emigrated at eighteen and was now married. He was a stranger to George Moon, and he was aware that if he met him in the street he would not recognize him. He was too sincere to pretend that he took much interest in him. They talked of him, however, for a while, and then they talked of actors and plays.

"Well," she said at last, "I must be running away. I've had a lovely lunch. It's been fun meeting you, George. Thanks so much."

He put her into a taxi and taking off his hat walked down Piccadilly by himself. He thought her quite a pleasant, amusing woman: he laughed to think that he had ever been madly in love with her. There was a smile on his lips when he spoke again to Tom Saffary.

"She was a damned good-looking girl when I married her. That was the trouble. Though, of course, if she hadn't been I'd never have married her. They were all after her like flies round a honey-pot. We used to have awful rows. And at last I caught her out. Of course I divorced her."

"Of course."

"Yes, but I know I was a damned fool to do it." He leaned forward. "My dear Saffary, I know now that if I'd had any ʌI'd have shut my eyes. She'd have settled down and made it had sellent wife."

comfortable ʌwere able to explain to his visitor how grotesque made so much fussʰ when he sat and talked with that jolly, little. moured woman that he should have

"But one has one's honoṳ now seemed to him to matter so

"Honour be damned. One has ᴜ of," said Saffary.
Is one's honour really concerned becaᴜ piness to think of.
bed with another man? We're not crusadeᴜ wife hops into
Spanish grandees. I *liked* my wife. I don't say ɪ and I, or
other women. I have. But she had just that something ᴛᴜ had
of the others could give me. What a fool I was to throw aʍ
what I wanted more than anything in the world because I
couldn't enjoy exclusive possession of it!"

"You're the last man I should ever have expected to hear speak like that."

George Moon smiled thinly at the embarrassment that was so clearly expressed on Saffary's fat troubled face.

"I'm probably the first man you've heard speak the naked truth," he retorted.

"Do you mean to say that if it were all to do over again you would act differently?"

"If I were twenty-seven again I suppose I should be as big a fool as I was then. But if I had the sense I have now I'll tell you what I'd do if I found my wife had been unfaithful to me. I'd do just what you did last night: I'd give her a damned good hiding and let it go at that."

"Are you asking me to forgive Violet?"

The Resident shook his head slowly and smiled.

"No. You've forgiven her already. I'm merely advising you not to cut off your nose to spite your face."

Saffary gave him a worried look. It disconcerted him to know that this cold precise man should see in his heart emotions which seemed so unnatural to himself that he thrust them out of his consciousness.

"You don't know the circumstances," he said. "Knobby and I were almost like brothers. I got him this job. He owed everything to me. And except for me Violet might have gone on being a governess for the rest of her life. It seemed such a waste; I couldn't help feeling sorry for her. If you know what I mean, it was pity that first made me take any notice of her. Don't you think it's a bit thick that when you've been thoroughly decent with people they should go out of their way to do the dirty on you? It's such awful ingratitude."

"Oh, my dear boy, one mustn't expect gratitude. It's a thing that no one has a right to. After all, you do good because it gives you pleasure. It's the purest form of happiness there is. To expect thanks for it is really asking too much. If you get it, well, it's like a bonus on shares on which you've already received a dividend; it's grand, but you mustn't look upon it as your due."

Saffary frowned. He was perplexed. He could not quite make it out that George Moon should think so oddly about things that it had always seemed to him there were no two ways of thinking about. After all there were limits. I mean, if you had any sense of decency you had to behave like a tuan. There was your own self-respect to think of. It was funny that George Moon should give reasons that looked so damned plausible for doing something that, well, damn it, you had to admit you'd be only too glad to do if you could see your way to it. Of course George Moon was queer. No one ever quite understood him.

"Knobby Clarke is dead, Saffary. You can't be jealous of him any more. No one knows a thing except you and me and your wife, and to-morrow I'm going away for ever. Why don't you let bygones be bygones?"

"Violet would only despise me."

George Moon smiled, and unexpectedly on that prim, fastidious face, his smile had a singular sweetness.

"I know her very little. I always thought her a very nice woman. Is she as detestable as that?"

Saffary gave a start and reddened to his ears.

"No, she's an angel of goodness. It's me who's detestable for saying that of her." His voice broke and he gave a little sob. "God knows I only want to do the right thing."

"The right thing is the kind thing."

Saffary covered his face with his hands. He could not curb the emotion that shook him.

"I seem to be giving, giving all the time, and no one does a God-damned thing for me. It doesn't matter if my heart is broken, I must just go on." He drew the back of his hand across his eyes and sighed deeply. "I'll forgive her."

George Moon looked at him reflectively for a little.

"I wouldn't make too much of a song and dance about it, if I were you," he said. "You'll have to walk warily. She'll have a lot to forgive too."

"Because I hit her, you mean? I know, that was awful of me."

"Not a bit. It did her a power of good. I didn't mean that. You're behaving very generously, old boy, and you know, one needs a devil of a lot of tact to get people to forgive one one's generosity. Fortunately women are frivolous and they very quickly forget the benefits conferred upon them. Otherwise, of course, there'd be no living with them."

Saffary looked at him open-mouthed.

"Upon my word you're a rum 'un, Moon," he said. "Sometimes you seem as hard as nails and then you talk so that one thinks you're almost human, and then, just as one thinks one's misjudged you and you have a heart after all, you come out with something that just shocks one. I suppose that's what they call a cynic."

"I haven't deeply considered the matter," smiled George Moon, "but if to look truth in the face and not resent it when it's unpalatable, and take human nature as you find it, smiling when it's absurd and grieved without exaggeration when it's pitiful, is to be cynical, then I suppose I'm a cynic. Mostly human nature is both absurd and pitiful, but if life has taught you tolerance you find in it more to smile at than to weep."

When Tom Saffary left the room the Resident lit himself with deliberation the last cigarette he meant to smoke before tiffin. It was a new rôle for him to reconcile an angry husband with an erring wife and it caused him a discreet amusement. He continued to reflect upon human nature. A wintry smile hovered upon his thin and pallid lips. He recalled with what interest in the dry creeks of certain places along the coast he had often stood and watched the Jumping Johnnies. There were hundreds of them sometimes, from little things of a couple of inches long to great fat fellows as long as your foot. They were the colour of the mud they lived in. They sat and looked at you with large round eyes and then with a sudden dash buried themselves in their holes. It was extraordinary to see them scudding on their flappers over the surface of the mud. It teemed with them. They gave you a fearful feeling that the mud itself was mysteriously become alive and an atavistic terror froze your heart when you remembered that such creatures, but gigantic and terrible, were once the only inhabitants of the earth. There was something uncanny about them, but something amusing too. They reminded you very much of human beings. It was quite entertaining to stand there for half an hour and observe their gambols.

George Moon took his topi off the peg and not displeased with life stepped out into the sunshine.

NEIL MACADAM

CAPTAIN BREDON was good-natured. When Angus Munro, the Curator of the museum at Kuala Solor, told him that he had advised Neil MacAdam, his new assistant, on his arrival at Singapore to put up at the Van Dyke Hotel, and asked him to see that the lad got into no mischief during the few days he must spend there, he said he would do his best. Captain Bredon commanded the Sultan Ahmed, and when he was at Singapore always stayed at the Van Dyke. He had a Japanese wife and kept a room there. It was his home. When he got back after his fortnight's trip along the coast of Borneo the Dutch manager told him that Neil had been there for two days. The boy was sitting in the little dusty garden of the hotel reading old numbers of The Straits Times. Captain Bredon took a look at him first and then went up.

"You're MacAdam, aren't you?"

Neil rose to his feet, flushed to the roots of his hair and answered shyly: "I am."

"My name's Bredon. I'm skipper of the Sultan Ahmed. You're sailing with me next Tuesday. Munro asked me to look after you. What about a stengah? I suppose you've learned what that means by now."

"Thank you very much, but I don't drink." He spoke with a broad Scots accent.

"I don't blame you. Drink's been the ruin of many a good man in this country."

He called the Chinese boy and ordered himself a double whisky and a small soda.

"What have you been doing with yourself since you got in?"

"Walking about."

"There's nothing much to see in Singapore."

"I've found plenty."

Of course the first thing he had done was to go to the museum. There was little that he had not seen at home, but the fact that those beasts and birds, those reptiles, moths, butterflies and insects, were native to the country excited him. There was one section devoted to that part of Borneo of which Kuala Solor was the capital, and since these were the creatures that for the next three years would chiefly concern him, he examined them with attention. But it was outside, in the streets, that it was most thrilling, and except that he was a grave and sober young man he would have laughed aloud with joy. Everything was new to him. He walked till he was footsore. He stood at the corner of a busy street and wondered at the long line of rickshaws and the little men between the shafts running with dogged steps. He stood on a bridge over a canal, and looked at the sampans wedged up against one another like sardines in a tin. He peered into the Chinese shops in Victoria Road where so many strange things were sold. Bombay merchants, fat and exuberant, stood at their shop doors and sought to sell him silks and tinsel jewellery. He watched the Tamils, pensive and forlorn, who walked with a sinister grace, and the bearded Arabs, in white skull-caps, who bore themselves with scornful dignity. The sun shone upon the varied scene with a hard, acrid brilliance. He was confused. He thought it would take him years to find his bearings in this multi-coloured and excessive world.

After dinner that night Captain Bredon asked him if he would like to go round the town.

"You ought to see a bit of life while you're here," he said.

They stepped into rickshaws and drove to the Chinese quarter. The Captain, who never drank at sea, had been making up for his abstinence during the day. He was feeling good. The rickshaws stopped at a house in a side street and they knocked at the door. It was opened and they passed through a narrow passage into a large room with benches all round it covered with red plush. A number of women were sitting about. French, Italian and American. A mechanical piano was grinding out

harsh music and a few couples were dancing. Captain Bredon
ordered drinks. Two or three women, waiting for an invitation,
gave them inciting glances.

"Well, young feller, is there anyone you fancy here?" the
Captain asked facetiously.

"To sleep with, d'you mean? No."

"No white girls where you're going, you know."

"Oh, well."

"Like to go an' see some natives?"

"I don't mind."

The Captain paid for the drinks and they strolled on. They
went to another house. Here the girls were Chinese, small and
dainty, with tiny feet and hands like flowers, and they wore
suits of flowered silk. But their painted faces were like masks.
They looked at the strangers with black derisive eyes. They
were strangely inhuman.

"I brought you here because I thought you ought to see the
place," said Captain Bredon, with the air of a man doing
his bounden duty, "but just look see is all. They don't like
us for some reason. In some of these Chinese joints they won't
even let a white man in. Fact is, they say we stink. Funny,
ain't it? They say we smell of corpses."

"We?"

"Give me Japs," said the Captain. "They're fine. My wife's
a Jap, you know. You come along with me and I'll take you
to a place where they have Japanese girls, and if you don't
see something you like there I'm a Dutchman."

Their rickshaws were waiting and they stepped into them.
Captain Bredon gave a direction and the boys started off.
They were let into the house by a stout middle-aged Japanese
woman, who bowed low as they entered. She took them into a
neat, clean room furnished only with mats on the floor; they
sat down and presently a little girl came in with a tray on which
were two bowls of pale tea. With a shy bow she handed one
to each of them. The Captain spoke to the middle-aged woman
and she looked at Neil and giggled. She said something to
the child, who went out, and presently four girls tripped in.
They were sweet in their kimonos, with their shining black hair
artfully dressed; they were small and plump, with round
faces and laughing eyes. They bowed low as they came in
and with good manners murmured polite greetings. Their
speech sounded like the twittering of birds. Then they knelt,

one on each side of the two men, and charmingly flirted with
them. Captain Bredon soon had his arms round two slim waists.
They all talked nineteen to the dozen. They were very gay.
It seemed to Neil that the Captain's girls were mocking him,
for their gleaming eyes were mischievously turned towards
him, and he blushed. But the other two cuddled up to him,
smiling, and spoke in Japanese as though he understood every
word they said. They seemed so happy and guileless that he
laughed. They were very attentive. They handed him the bowl
so that he should drink his tea, and then took it from him so
that he should not have the trouble of holding it. They lit
his cigarette for him and one put out a small, delicate hand
to take the ash so that it should not fall on his clothes. They
stroked his smooth face and looked with curiosity at his large
young hands. They were as playful as kittens.

"Well, which is it to be?" said the Captain after a while.
"Made your choice yet?"

"What d'you mean?"

"I'll just wait and see you settled and then I'll fix myself up."

"Oh, I don't want either of them. I'm going home to bed."

"Why, what's the matter? You're not scared, are you?"

"No, I just don't fancy it. But don't let me stand in your
way. I'll get back to the hotel all right."

"Oh, if you're not going to do anything I won't either. I
only wanted to be matey."

He spoke to the middle-aged woman and what he said
caused the girls to look at Neil with sudden surprise. She
answered and the Captain shrugged his shoulders. Then one
of the girls made a remark that set them all laughing.

"What does she say?" asked Neil.

"She's pulling your leg," replied the Captain, smiling.

But he gave Neil a curious look. The girl, having made them
laugh once, now said something directly to Neil. He could not
understand, but the mockery of her eyes made him blush
and frown. He did not like to be made fun of. Then she laughed
outright and throwing her arm round his neck lightly kissed
him.

"Come on, let's be going," said the Captain.

When they dismissed their rickshaws and walked into the
hotel Neil asked him:

"What was it that girl said that made them all laugh?"

"She said you were a virgin."

"I don't see anything to laugh at in that," said Neil, with his slow Scots accent.

"Is it true?"

"I suppose it is."

"How old are you?"

"Twenty-two."

"What are you waiting for?"

"Till I marry."

The Captain was silent. At the top of the stairs he held out his hand. There was a twinkle in his eyes when he bade the lad good-night, but Neil met it with a level, candid and un-troubled gaze.

Three days later they sailed. Neil was the only white pas, senger. When the Captain was busy he read. He was reading again Wallace's Malay Archipelago. He had read it as a boy, but now it had a new and absorbing interest for him. When the Captain was at leisure they played cribbage or sat in long chairs on the deck, smoking, and talked. Neil was the son of a country doctor, and he could not remember when he had not been interested in natural history. When he had done with school he went to the University of Edinburgh and there took a B. Sc. with Honours. He was looking out for a job as demon-strator in biology when he chanced to see in Nature an ad-vertisement for an assistant curator of the museum at Kuala Solor. The Curator, Angus Munro, had been at Edinburgh with his uncle, a Glasgow merchant, and his uncle wrote to ask him if he would give the boy a trial. Though Neil was es-pecially interested in entomology he was a trained taxidermist, which the advertisement said was essential; he enclosed cer-tificates from Neil's old teachers; he added that Neil had played football for his university. In a few weeks a cable arrived en-gaging him and a fortnight later he sailed.

"What's Mr. Munro like?" asked Neil.

"Good fellow. Everybody likes him."

"I looked out his papers in the scientific journals. He had one in the last number of The Ibis on the Gymnathidæ."

"I don't know anything about that. I know he's got a Russian wife. They don't like her much."

"I got a letter from him at Singapore saying they'd put me up for a bit till I could look round and see what I wanted to do."

Now they were steaming up the river. At the mouth was a

straggling fishermen's village standing on piles in the water; on the bank grew thickly nipah palm and the tortured mangrove; beyond stretched the dense green of the virgin forest. In the distance, darkly silhouetted against the blue sky, was the rugged outline of a mountain. Neil, his heart beating with the excitement that possessed him, devoured the scene with eager eyes. He was surprised. He knew his Conrad almost by heart and he was expecting a land of brooding mystery. He was not prepared for the blue milky sky. Little white clouds on the horizon, like sailing boats becalmed, shone in the sun. The green trees of the forest glittered in the brilliant light. Here and there, on the banks, were Malay houses with thatched roofs, and they nestled cosily among fruit trees. Natives in dugouts rowed, standing, up the river. Neil had no feeling of being shut in, nor in that radiant morning, of gloom, but of space and freedom. The country offered him a gracious welcome. He knew he was going to be happy in it. Captain Bredon from the bridge threw a friendly glance at the lad standing below him. He had taken quite a fancy to him during the four days the journey had lasted. It was true he did not drink, and when you made a joke he was as likely as not to take you seriously, but there was something very taking in his seriousness; everything was interesting and important to him—that, of course, was why he did not find your jokes amusing; but even though he didn't see them he laughed, because he felt you expected it. He laughed because life was grand. He was grateful for every little thing you told him. He was very polite. He never asked you to pass him anything without saying "please" and always said "thank you" when you gave it. And he was a good-looking fellow, no one could deny that. Neil was standing with his hands on the rail, bare-headed, looking at the passing bank. He was tall, six foot two, with long, loose limbs, broad shoulders and narrow hips; there was something charmingly coltish about him, so that you expected him at any moment to break into a caper. He had brown curly hair with a peculiar shine in it; sometimes when the light caught it, it glittered like gold. His eyes, large and very blue, shone with good humour. They reflected his happy disposition. His nose was short and blunt and his mouth big, his chin determined; his face was rather broad, But his most striking feature was his skin; it was very white and smooth, with a lovely patch

of red on either cheek. It would have been a beautiful skin
even for a woman. Captain Bredon made the same joke to him
every morning.

"Well, my lad, have you shaved to-day?"

Neil passed his hand over his chin.

"No, d'you think I need it?"

The Captain always laughed at this.

"Need it? Why, you've got a face like a baby's bottom."

And invariably Neil reddened to the roots of his hair.

"I shave once a week," he retorted.

But it wasn't only his looks that made you like him. It was
his ingenuousness, his candour and the freshness with which he
confronted the world. For all his intentness and the solemn way
in which he took everything, and his inclination to argue upon
every point that came up, there was something strangely simple
in him that gave you quite an odd feeling. The Captain couldn't
make it out.

"I wonder if it's because he's never had a woman," he said
to himself. "Funny. I should have thought the girls never left
him alone. With a complexion like that."

But the Sultan Ahmed was nearing the bend after rounding
which Kuala Solor would be in sight and the Captain's reflections were interrupted by the necessities of his work. He rang
down to the engine room. The ship slackened to half speed.
Kuala Solor straggled along the left bank of the river, a white
neat and trim little town, and on the right on a hill were the
fort and the Sultan's Palace. There was a breeze and the Sultan's flag, at the top of a tall staff, waved bravely against the
sky. They anchored in midstream. The doctor and a police
officer came on board in the government launch. They were
accompanied by a tall thin man in white ducks. The Captain
stood at the head of the gangway and shook hands with them.
Then he turned to the last comer.

"Well, I've brought you your young hopeful safe and sound."
And with a glance at Neil: "This is Munro."

The tall thin man held out his hand and gave Neil an appraising look. Neil flushed a little and smiled. He had beautiful
teeth.

"How do you do, sir?"

Munro did not smile with his lips, but faintly with his grey
eyes. His cheeks were hollow and he had a thin aquiline nose
and pale lips. He was deeply sunburned. His face looked tired,

but his expression was very gentle, and Neil immediately felt confidence in him. The Captain introduced him to the doctor and the policeman and suggested that they should have a drink. When they sat down and the boy brought bottles of beer Munro took off his topi. Neil saw that he had close-cropped brown hair turning grey. He was a man of forty, quiet, self-possessed in manner, with an intellectual air that distinguished him from the brisk little doctor and the heavy swaggering police officer.

"MacAdam doesn't drink," said the Captain when the boy poured out four glasses of beer.

"All the better," said Munro. "I hope you haven't been trying to lure him into evil ways."

"I tried to in Singapore," returned the Captain, with a twinkle in his eyes, "but there was nothing doing."

When he had finished his beer Munro turned to Neil.

"Well, we'll be getting ashore, shall we?"

Neil's baggage was put in charge of Munro's boy and the two men got into a sampan. They landed.

"Do you want to go straight up to the bungalow or would you like to have a look round first? We've got a couple of hours before tiffin."

"Couldn't we go to the museum?" said Neil.

Munro's eyes smiled gently. He was pleased. Neil was shy and Munro not by nature talkative, so they walked in silence. By the river were the native huts and here, living their immemorial lives, dwelt the Malays. They were busy, but without haste, and you were conscious of a happy, normal activity. There was a sense of the rhythm of life of which the pattern was birth and death, love and the affairs common to mankind. They came to the bazaars, narrow streets with arcades, when the teeming Chinese, working and eating, noisily talking, as is their way, indefatigably strove with eternity.

"It's not much after Singapore," said Munro, "but I always think it's rather picturesque."

He spoke with an accent less broad than Neil's, but the Scots burr was there and it put Neil at his ease. He could never quite get it out of his head that the English of English people was affected.

The museum was a handsome stone building and as they entered its portals Munro instinctively straightened himself. The attendant at the door saluted and Munro spoke to him in

Malay, evidently explaining who Neil was, for the attendant
gave him a smile and saluted again. It was cool in there in comparison with the heat without and the light was pleasant after
the glare of the street.

"I'm afraid you'll be disappointed," said Munro. "We
haven't got half the things we ought to have, but up to now
we've been handicapped by lack of money. We've had to do the
best we could. So you must make allowances."

Neil stepped in like a swimmer diving confidently into a summer sea. The specimens were admirably arranged. Munro
had sought to please as well as to instruct, and birds and beasts
and reptiles were presented, as far as possible in their natural
surroundings, in such a way as to give a vivid impression of life.
Neil lost his shyness and began with boyish enthusiasm to talk
of this and that. He asked an infinity of questions. He was excited. Neither of them was conscious of the passage of time,
and when Munro glanced at his watch he was surprised to see
what the hour was. They got into rickshaws and drove to the
bungalow.

Munro led the young man into a drawing-room. A woman was
lying on a sofa reading a book and as they came in she slowly
rose.

"This is my wife. I'm afraid we're dreadfully late, Darya."

"What does it matter?" she smiled. "What is more unim-
portant than time?"

She held out her hand, a rather large hand, to Neil and gave
him a long, reflective, but friendly look.

"I suppose you've been showing him the museum."

She was a woman of five and thirty, of medium height, with a
pale brown face of a uniform colour and pale blue eyes. Her hair,
parted in the middle and wound into a knot on the nape of her
neck, was untidy; it had a moth-like quality and was of a curious pale brown. Her face was broad, with high cheek-bones, and
she had a rather fleshy nose. She was not a pretty woman, but
there was in her slow movements a sensual grace and in her
manner as it were a physical casualness that only very dull
people could have failed to find interesting. She wore a frock
of green cotton. She spoke English perfectly, but with a slight
accent.

They sat down to tiffin. Neil was overcome once more with
shyness, but Darya did not seem to notice it. She talked freely
and easily. She asked him about his journey and what he had

thought of Singapore. She told him about the people he would have to meet. That afternoon Munro was to take him to call on the Resident, the Sultan being away, and later they would go to the club. There he would see everybody.

"You will be popular," she said, her pale blue eyes resting on him with attention. A man less ingenuous than Neil might have noticed that she took stock of his size and youthful virility, his shiny, curling hair and his lovely skin. "They don't think much of us."

"Oh, nonsense, Darya. You're too sensitive. They're English, that's all."

"They think it's rather funny of Angus to be a scientist and they think it's rather vulgar of me to be a Russian. I don't care. They're fools. They're the most commonplace, the most narrow-minded, the most conventional people it has ever been my misfortune to live amongst."

"Don't put MacAdam off the moment he arrives. He'll find them kind and hospitable."

"What is your first name?" she asked the boy.

"Neil."

"I shall call you by it. And you must call me Darya. I hate being called Mrs. Munro. It makes me feel like a minister's wife."

Neil blushed. He was embarrassed that she should ask him so soon to be so familiar. She went on.

"Some of the men are not bad."

"They do their jobs competently and that's what they're ˜ere for," said Munro.

get òhey shoot. They play football and tennis and cricket. I
are jealoústhem quite well. The women are intolerable. They
If you introducespiteful and lazy. They can talk of nothing.
noses as though youintellectual subject they look down their
They're interested in noùindecent. What can they talk about?
think you improper, and if yù If you speak of the body they
you priggish." ˜peak of the soul they think

"You mustn't take what my wife say ˜oo literally," smiled Munro, in his gentle, tolerant way. "The cˮmunity here is just like any other in the East, neither very cle˳ nor very stupid, but amiable and kindly. And that's a good deˠ "

"I don't want people to be amiable and kindly. I want ˑem to be vital and passionate. I want them to be interested iˑ

mankind. I want them to attach more importance to the things of the spirit than to a gin pahit or a curry tiffin. I want art to matter to them and literature." She addressed herself abruptly to Neil: "Have you got a soul?"

"Oh, I don't know. I don't know exactly what you mean."

"Why do you blush when I ask you? Why should you be ashamed of your soul? It is what is important in you. Tell me about it. I am interested in you and I want to know."

It seemed very awkward to Neil to be tackled in this way by a perfect stranger. He had never met anyone like this. But he was a serious young man and when he was asked a question straight out he did his best to answer it. It was Munro's presence that embarrassed him.

"I don't know what you mean by the soul. If you mean an immaterial or spiritual entity, separately produced by the creator, in temporary conjunction with the material body, then my answer is in the negative. It seems to me that such a radically dualistic view of human personality cannot be defended by anyone who is able to take a calm view of the evidence. If, on the other hand, you mean by soul the aggregate of psychic elements which form what we know as the personality of the individual, then, of course, I have."

"You're very sweet and you're wonderfully handsome," she said, smiling. "No, I mean the heart with its longings and the body with its desires and the infinite in us. Tell me, what did you read on the journey, or did you only play deck tennis?"

Neil was taken aback at the inconsequence of her reply. He would have been a little affronted except for the good humed in her eyes and the naturalness in her manner. Munro ed the quietly at the young man's bewilderment. When he corners of lines that ran from the wings of his nostrils
his mouth became deep furrows.

"I read a lot of Conrad."　　　　　　mind?"

"For pleasure or to improve

"Both. I admire him awf　　　s in an extravagant gesture of pro-
Darya threw up her
test.

"That Pole," she cried. "How can you English ever have let yourselves e taken in by that wordy mountebank? He has all the superficiality of his countrymen. That stream of words, the e involved sentences, the showy rhetoric, that affectation of profundity: when you get through all that to the thought at the bottom, what do you find but a commonplace? He was like a second-rate actor who puts on a romantic dress and declaims a play by Victor Hugo. For five minutes you say this is heroic, and then your whole soul revolts and you cry, no, this is false, false, false."

She spoke with a passion that Neil had never known anyone show when speaking of art or literature. Her cheeks, usually colourless, flushed and her pale eyes glowed.

"There's no one who got atmosphere like Conrad," said Neil. "I can smell and see and feel the East when I read him."

"Nonsense. What do you know about the East? Everyone will tell you that he made the grossest blunders. Ask Angus."

"Of course he was not always accurate," said Munro, in his measured, reflective way. "The Borneo he described is not the Borneo we know. He saw it from the deck of a merchant vessel and he was not an acute observer even of what he saw. But does it matter? I don't know why fiction should be hampered by fact. I don't think it's a mean achievement to have created a country, a dark, sinister, romantic and heroic country of the soul."

"You're a sentimentalist, my poor Angus." And then again to Neil: "You must read Turgeniev, you must read Tolstoi, you must read Dostoevsky."

Neil did not in the least know what to make of Darya Munro. She skipped over the first stages of acquaintance and treated him at once like someone she had known intimately all her life. It puzzled him. It seemed so reckless. When he met anyone his own instinct was to go cautiously. He was amiable, but he did not like to step too far before he saw his way before him. He did not want to give anyone his confidence before he thought himself justified. But with Darya you could not help yourself; she forced your confidence. She poured out the feelings and thoughts that most people keep to themselves like a prodigal flinging gold pieces to a scrambling crowd. She did not talk, she did not act like anyone he had ever known. She did not mind what she said. She would speak of the natural functions of the human animal in a way that brought the blushes coursing to his cheeks. They excited her ridicule.

"Oh, what a prig you are! What is there indecent in it? When I'm going to take a purge, why shouldn't I say so and when I think you want one, why shouldn't I tell you?"

"Theoretically I daresay you're right," said Neil, always judicious and reasonable.

She made him tell her of his father and mother, his brothers, his life at school and at the university. She told him about herself. Her father was a general killed in the war and her mother a Princess Lutchkov. They were in Eastern Russia when the Bolsheviks seized power, and fled to Yokohama. Here they had subsisted miserably on the sale of their jewels and such objects of art as they had been able to save, and here she married a fellow exile. She was unhappy with him and in two years divorced him. Her mother died and, penniless, she was driven to earn her living as best she could. She was employed by an American relief organization. She taught in a mission school. She worked in a hospital. She made Neil's blood boil, and at the same time embarrassed him very much, when she spoke of the men who tried to take advantage of her defencelessness and her poverty. She spared him no details.

"Brutes," he said.

"Oh, all men are like that," she replied, with a shrug of her shoulders.

She told him how once she protected her virtue at the point of her revolver.

"I swore I'd kill him if he took another step, and if he had I'd have shot him like a dog."

"Gosh!" said Neil.

It was at Yokohama that she met Angus. He was spending his leave in Japan. She was captivated by his straightforwardness, the decency which was so obvious in him, his tenderness and his consideration. He was not a business man; he was a scientist, and science is milk brother to art. He offered her peace. He offered her security. And she was tired of Japan. Borneo was a land of mystery. They had been married for five years.

She gave Neil the Russian novelists to read. She gave him Fathers and Sons, Anna Karenina and The Brothers Karamazoff.

"Those are the three peaks of our literature. Read them. They are the greatest novels the world has ever seen."

Like many of her countrymen she talked as though no other literature counted, and as though a few novels and stories, some indifferent poetry and a half a dozen good plays had made whatever else the world has produced negligible. Neil was fascinated and overwhelmed.

"You're rather like Alyosha yourself, Neil," she said, looking at him with eyes that were now so soft and tender, "an Alyosha

with a Scotch dourness, suspicious and prudent, that will not
let the soul in you, the spiritual beauty, come out."

"I'm not a bit like Alyosha," he answered self-consciously.

"You don't know what you're like. You don't know anything
about yourself. Why are you a naturalist? Is it for money? You
could have made much more money by going into your uncle's
office in Glasgow. I feel in you something strange and unearthly. I could bow down at your feet as Father Zossima did to
Dimitri."

"Please don't," he said, smiling, but flushing a little too.

But the novels he read made her seem a little less strange to
him. They gave her an environment and he recognized in her
traits which, however unusual in the women he knew in Scotland, his mother and the daughters of his uncle in Glasgow, were
common to many of the characters in Russian fiction. He no
longer wondered that she should like to sit up so late, drinking
innumerable cups of tea, and lie on the sofa nearly all day long
reading and incessantly smoking cigarettes. She could do nothing at all for days on end without being bored. She had a curious
mixture of languor and zest. She often said, with a shrug of her
shoulders, that she was an Oriental and a European only by
chance. She had a feline grace that indeed suggested the Oriental. She was immensely untidy and it did not seem to affect
her that cigarette ends, old papers and empty tins should lie
about their living-room. But he thought she had something of
Anna Karenina in her, and he transferred to her the sympathy
he felt for that pathetic creature. He understood her arrogance.
It was not unnatural that she despised the women of the community, whose acquaintance little by little he made; they *were*
commonplace; her mind was quicker than theirs, she had a
wider culture, and she had above all a sort of tremulous sensi-
tivenesss that made *them* extraordinarily colourless. She certainly took no pains to conciliate them. Though at home she
slopped about in a sarong and baju, when she and Angus went
out to dinner she dressed with a splendour that was somewhat
out of place. She liked to display her ample bosom and her
shapely back. She painted her cheeks and made up her eyes
like an actress for the footlights. Though it made Neil angry
to see the amused or outraged glances that her appearance pro-
voked, he could not in his heart but think it a pity that she
should make such an object of herself. She looked grand, of
course, but if you hadn't known who she was you would have

thought she wasn't respectable. There were things about her that he could never get over. She had an enormous appetite and it fashed him that she ate more than he and Angus put together. He could never quite get used to the bluntness with which she discussed sexual matters. She took it for granted that at home and in Edinburgh he had had affairs with a host of women. She pressed him for details of his adventures. His Scotch pawkiness helped him to parry her thrusts and he evaded her questions with native caution. She laughed at his reticence.

Sometimes she shocked him. He grew accustomed to the frankness with which she admired his looks, and when she told him that he was as beautiful as a young Norse god he did not turn a hair. Flattery fell off him like water from a duck's back. But he did not like it when she ran her hand, though large, very soft, with caressing fingers, through his curly hair or, a smile on her lips, stroked his smooth face. He couldn't bear being mussed about. One day she wanted a drink of tonic water and began pouring some out in a glass that stood on the table.

"That's my glass," he said quickly. "I've just been drinking out of it."

"Well, what of it? You haven't got syphilis, have you?"

"I hate drinking out of other people's glasses myself."

She was funny about cigarettes too. Once, when he hadn't been there very long, he had just lit one, when she passed and said:

"I want that."

She took it out of his mouth and began to smoke it. After two or three puffs, she said she did not want any more and handed it back to him. The end she had had in her mouth was red from the rouge on her lips, and he didn't want to go on smoking it at all. But he was afraid she would think it rude if he threw it away. It somewhat disgusted him. Often she would ask him for a cigarette and when he handed it to her, say:

"Oh, light it for me, will you?"

When he did so, and held it out to her, she opened her mouth so that he should put it in. He hadn't been able to help wetting the end a little. He wondered she could bear to put it in her mouth after it had been in his. The whole thing seemed to him awfully familiar. He was sure Munro wouldn't like it. She had even done this once or twice at the club. Neil had felt himself go purple. He wished she hadn't got these rather unpleasant habits, but he supposed they were Russian, and one couldn't deny

He was also studying mimicry and instilled into Neil his absorbed interest in this controversial subject. They had interminable talks about it. Neil was astonished at the Curator's wonderful knowledge. It was encyclopædic, and he was abashed at his own ignorance. But it was when Munro spoke of the trips into the country to collect specimens that his enthusiasm was most contagious. That was the perfect life, a life of hardship, difficulty, often of privation and sometimes of danger, but rewarded by the thrill of finding a rare, or even a new species, by the beauty of the scenery and the intimate observation of nature, and above all by the sense of freedom from every tie. It was for this part of the work that Neil had been chiefly engaged. Munro was occupied in research work that made it difficult for him to be away from home for several weeks at a time, and Darya had always refused to accompany him. She had an unreasoning fear of the jungle. She was terrified of wild beasts, snakes and venomous insects. Though Munro had told her over and over again that no animal hurt you unless you molested or frightened it, she could not get over her instinctive horror. He did not like leaving her. She cared little for the local society and with him away he realized that life for her must be intolerably dull. But the Sultan was keenly interested in natural history and was anxious that the museum should be completely representative of the country's fauna. One expedition Munro and Neil were to make together, so that Neil should learn how to go to work, and the plans for this were discussed by them for months. Neil looked forward to it as he had never looked forward to anything in his life.

Meanwhile he learned Malay and acquired a smattering of the dialects that would be useful to him on future journeys. He played tennis and football. He soon knew everyone in the community. On the football field he threw off his absorption in science and his interest in Russian fiction and gave himself up to the pleasure of the game. He was strong, quick and active. After it was all over it was grand to have a sluice down and a long tonic with a slice of lemon and go over it all with the other fellows. It had never been intended that Neil should live permanently with the Munros. There was a roomy Rest House at Kuala Solor, but the rule was that no one should stay in it for more than a fortnight and such of the bachelors as had no official quarters clubbed together and took a house between them. When Neil arrived it so happened that there was no

that she was wonderfully good company. Her conversation w
very stimulating. It was like champagne (which Neil had tast
once and thought wretched stuff) "metaphorically speaking
There was nothing she couldn't talk about. She didn't ta
like a man; with a man you generally knew what he would s
next, but with her you never did; her intuition was quite
markable. She gave you ideas. She enlarged your mind and
cited your imagination. Neil felt alive as he had never felt ali
before. He seemed to walk on mountain peaks and the horizc
of the spirit were unbounded. Neil felt a certain complacen
when he stopped to reflect on what an exalted plane his mi
communed with hers. Such conversations made very small b
of the vaunted pleasure of sense. She was in many ways (he v
of a cautious nature and seldom made a statement even to hi
self that he did not qualify) the most intelligent woman he I
ever met. And besides, she was Angus Munro's wife.

For, whatever Neil's reservations were about Darya, he I
none about Munro, and she would have had to be a much I
remarkable woman not to profit by the enormous admirat
he conceived for her husband. With him Neil let himself
He felt for him what he had never felt for anyone before.
was so sane, so balanced, so tolerant. This was the sort of n
he would himself like to be when he was older. He talked lit
but when he did, with good sense. He was wise. He had a
humour that Neil understood. It made the hearty English
of the men at the club seem inane. He was kind and pati
He had a dignity that made it impossible to conceive of any
taking a liberty with him, but he was neither pompous
solemn. He was honest and absolutely truthful. But Neil
mired him no less as a scientist than as a man. He had imag
tion. He was careful and painstaking. Though his interest
in research he did the routine work of the museum consc
tiously. He was just then much interested in stick-insects
intended to write a paper on their powers of parthenogen
reproduction. An incident occurred in connection with the
periments he was making that made a great impression on I
One day, a little captive gibbon escaped from its chain and
up all the larvæ and so destroyed the whole of Munro's
dence. Neil nearly cried. Angus Munro took the gibbon ir
arms and, smiling, stroked it.

"Diamond, Diamond," he said, quoting Sir Isaac New
"you little know the damage you have done."

vacancy in any of these messes. One evening, however, when he had been about four months in the colony, two men, Waring and Jonson, when they were sitting together after a game of tennis, told him that one member of their mess was going home and if he would like to join them they would be glad to have him. They were young fellows of his own age, in the football team, and Neil liked them both. Waring was in the customs and Jonson in the police. He jumped at the suggestion. They told him how much it would cost and fixed a day, a fortnight later, when it would be convenient for him to move in.

At dinner he told the Munros.

"It's been awfully good of you to let me stay so long. It's made me very uncomfortable planting myself on you like this, I've been quite ashamed, but now there's no excuse for me."

"But we like having you here," said Darya. "You don't need an excuse."

"I can hardly go on staying here indefinitely?"

"Why not? Your salary's miserable, what's the use of wasting it on board and lodging? You'd be bored stiff with Jonson and Waring. Stupids. They haven't an idea in their heads outside playing the gramophone and knocking balls about."

It was true that it had been very convenient to live free of cost. He had saved the greater part of his salary. He had a thrifty soul and had never been used to spending money when it wasn't necessary, but he was proud. He could not go on living at other people's expense. Darya looked at him with her quiet, observant eyes.

"Angus and I have got used to you now. I think we'd miss you. If you like, you can pay us for your board. You don't cost anything, but if it'll make you easier I'll find out exactly what difference you make in cookie's book and you can pay that."

"It must be an awful nuisance having a stranger in the house," he answered uncertainly.

"It'll be miserable for you there. Good heavens, the filth they eat."

It was true also that at the Munros' you ate better than any-where else at Kuala Solor. He had dined out now and then, and even at the Resident's you didn't get a very good dinner. Darya liked her food and kept the cook up to the mark. He made Russian dishes which were a fair treat. That cabbage soup of Darya's was worth walking five miles for. But Munro hadn't said anything.

"I'd be glad if you'd stay here," he said now. "It's very convenient to have you on the spot. If anything comes up we can talk it over there and then. Waring and Jonson are very good fellows, but I daresay you'd find them rather limited after a bit."

"Oh, well, then I'll be very pleased. Heaven knows, I couldn't want anything better than this. I was only afraid I was in the way."

Next day it was raining cats and dogs and it was impossible to play tennis or football, but towards six Neil put on a mackintosh and went to the club. It was empty, but for the Resident, who was sitting in an armchair reading The Fortnightly. His name was Trevelyan, and he claimed to be related to the friend of Byron. He was a tall fat man, with close-cropped white hair and the large red face of a comic actor. He was fond of amateur theatricals, and specialized in cynical dukes and facetious butlers. He was a bachelor, but generally supposed to be fond of the girls, and he liked his gin pahit before dinner. He owed his position to the Sultan's friendship. He was a slack, complacent man, a great talker, not very fond of work, who wanted everything to go smoothly and no one to give trouble. Though not considered especially competent he was popular in the community because he was easy-going and hospitable, and he certainly made life more comfortable than if he had been energetic and efficient. He nodded to Neil.

"Well, young fellow, how are bugs to-day?"

"Feeling the weather, sir," said Neil gravely.

"Hi-hi."

In a few minutes Waring, Jonson and another man, called Bishop, came in. He was in the civil service. Neil did not play bridge, so Bishop went up to the Resident.

"Would you care to make a fourth, sir?" he asked him. "There's nobody much in the club to-day."

The Resident gave the others a glance.

"All right. I'll just finish this article and join you. Cut for me and deal. I shall only be five minutes."

Neil went up to the three men.

"Oh, I say, Waring, thanks awfully, but I can't move over to you after all. The Munros have asked me to stay on with them for good."

A broad smile broke on Waring's face.

"Fancy that."

"It's awfully nice of them, isn't it? They made rather a point
of it. I couldn't very well refuse."

"What did I tell you?" said Bishop.

"I don't blame the boy," said Waring.

There was something in their manner that Neil did not like.
They seemed to be amused. He flushed.

"What the hell are you talking about?" he cried.

"Oh, come off it," said Bishop. "We know our Darya. You're
not the first good-looking fellow she's had a romp with, and
you won't be the last."

The words were hardly out of his mouth before Neil's
clenched fist shot out like a flash. He hit Bishop on the face
and he fell heavily to the floor. Jonson sprang at Neil and
seized him round the middle, for he was beside himself.

"Let me go," he shouted. "If he doesn't withdraw that I'll
kill him."

The Resident, startled by the commotion, looked up and
rose to his feet. He walked heavily towards them.

"What's this? What's this? What the hell are you boys
playing at?"

They were taken aback. They had forgotten him. He was
their master. Jonson let go of Neil and Bishop picked himself
up. The Resident, a frown on his face, spoke to Neil sharply.

"What's the meaning of this? Did you hit Bishop?"

"Yes, sir."

"Why?"

"He made a foul suggestion reflecting on a woman's honour,"
said Neil, very haughtily, and still white with rage.

The Resident's eyes twinkled, but he kept a grave face.

"What woman?"

"I refuse to answer," said Neil, throwing back his head and
drawing himself up to his full imposing height.

It would have been more effective if the Resident hadn't been
a good two inches taller, and very much stouter.

"Don't be a damned young fool."

"Darya Munro," said Jonson.

"What did you say, Bishop?"

"I forget the exact words I used. I said she'd hopped into
bed with a good many young chaps here, and I supposed she
hadn't missed the chance of doing the same with MacAdam."

"It was a most offensive suggestion. Will you be so good as to
apologize and shake hands. Both of you."

"I've had a hell of a biff, sir. My eye's going to look like the devil. I'm damned if I apologize for telling the truth."

"You're old enough to know that the fact that your statement is true only makes it more offensive, and as far as your eye is concerned I'm told that a raw beefsteak is very efficacious in these circumstances. Though I put my desire that you should apologize in the form of a request out of politeness, it is in point of fact an order."

There was a moment's silence. The Resident looked bland.

"I apologize for what I said, sir," Bishop said sulkily.

"Now then, MacAdam."

"I'm sorry I hit him, sir. I apologize, too."

"Shake hands."

The two young men solemnly did so.

"I shouldn't like this to go any further. It wouldn't be very nice for Munro, whom I think we all like. Can I count on you all holding your tongues?"

They nodded.

"Now be off with you. You stay, MacAdam, I want to have a few words with you."

When the two of them were left alone, the Resident sat down and lit himself a cheroot. He offered one to Neil, but he only smoked cigarettes.

"You're a very violent young man," said the Resident, with a smile. "I don't like my officers to make scenes in a public place like this."

"Mrs. Munro is a great friend of mine. She's been kindness itself to me. I won't hear a word said against her."

"Then I'm afraid you'll have your job cut out for you if you stay here much longer."

Neil was silent for a moment. He stood, tall and slim, before the Resident, and his grave young face was guileless. He flung back his head defiantly. His emotion made him speak in broader Scots even than usual.

"I've lived with the Munros for four months, and I give you my word of honour that so far as I am concerned there is not an iota of truth in what that beast said. Mrs. Munro has never treated me with anything that you could call undue familiarity. She's never by word or deed given me the smallest hint that she had an improper idea in her head. She's been like a mother to me or an elder sister."

The Resident watched him with ironical eyes.

"I'm very glad to hear it. That's the best thing I've heard about her for a long time."

"You believe me, sir, don't you?"

"Of course. Perhaps you've reformed her." He called out. "Boy. Bring me a gin pahit." And then to Neil. "That'll do. You can go now if you want to. But no more fighting, mind you, or you'll get the order of the boot."

When Neil walked back to the Munros' bungalow the rain had stopped and the velvet sky was bright with stars. In the garden the fire-flies were flitting here and there. From the earth rose a scented warmth and you felt that if you stopped you would hear the growth of that luxuriant vegetation. A white flower of the night gave forth an overwhelming perfume. In the verandah Munro was typing some notes and Darya, lying at full length on a long chair, was reading. The lamp behind her lit her smoky hair so that it shone like an aureole. She looked up at Neil and putting down her book, smiled. Her smile was very friendly.

"Where have you been, Neil?"

"At the club."

"Anybody there?"

The scene was so cosy and domestic, Darya's manner so peaceful and quietly assured, that it was impossible not to be touched. The two of them there, each occupied with his own concerns, seemed so united, their intimacy so natural, that no one could have conceived that they were not perfectly happy in one another. Neil did not believe a single word of what Bishop had said and the Resident had hinted. It was incredible. After all, he knew that what they had suspected of *him* was untrue, so what reason was there to think that the rest was any truer? They had dirty minds, all those people; because they were a lot of swine they thought everyone else as bad as they were. His knuckle hurt him a little. He was glad he had hit Bishop. He wished he knew who had started that filthy story. He'd wring his neck.

But now Munro fixed a date for the expedition that they had so much discussed, and in his careful way began to make preparations so that at the last moment nothing should be forgotten. The plan was to go as far up the river as possible and then make their way through the jungle and hunt for specimens on the little-known Mount Hitam. They expected to be away two months. As the day on which they were to start grew nearer

Munro's spirits rose, and though he did not say very much, though he remained quiet and self-controlled, you could tell by the light in his eyes and the jauntiness of his step how much he looked forward to it. One morning, at the museum, he was almost sprightly.

"I've got some good news for you," he said suddenly to Neil, after they had been looking at some experiments they were making, "Darya's coming with us."

"Is she? That's grand."

Neil was delighted. That made it perfect.

"It's the first time I've ever been able to induce her to accompany me. I told her she'd enjoy it, but she would never listen to me. Queer cattle, women. I'd given it up and never thought of asking her to come this time, and suddenly, last night, out of a blue sky she said she'd like to."

"I'm awfully glad," said Neil.

"I didn't much like the idea of leaving her by herself so long; now we can stay just as long as we want to."

They started early one morning in four prahus, manned by Malays, and besides themselves the party consisted of their servants and four Dyak hunters. The three of them lay on cushions side by side, under an awning; in the other boats were the Chinese servants and the Dyaks. They carried bags of rice for the whole party, provisions for themselves, clothes, books and all that was necessary for their work. It was heavenly to leave civilization behind them and they were all excited. They talked. They smoked. They read. The motion of the river was exquisitely soothing. They lunched on a grassy bank. Dusk fell and they moored for the night. They slept at a long house and their Dyak hosts celebrated their visit with arak, eloquence and a fantastic dance. Next day the river, narrowing, gave them more definitely the feeling that they were adventuring into the unknown, and the exotic vegetation that crowded the banks to the water's edge, like an excited mob pushed from behind by a multitude, caused Neil a breathless ravishment. O wonder and delight! On the third day, because the water was shallower and the stream more rapid, they changed into lighter boats, and soon it grew so strong that the boatmen could paddle no longer, and they poled against the current with powerful and magnificent gestures. Now and then they came to rapids and had to disembark, unload and haul the boats through a rock-strewn passage. After five days

they reached a point beyond which they could go no further.
There was a government bungalow there, and they settled in
for a couple of nights while Munro made arrangements for their
excursion into the interior. He wanted bearers for their baggage,
and men to build a house for them when they reached Mount
Hitam. It was necessary for Munro to see the headman of a
village in the vicinity and thinking it would save time if he
went himself rather than let the headman come to him, the day
after they arrived he set out at dawn with a guide and a couple
of Dyaks. He expected to be back in a few hours. When he had
seen him off Neil thought he would have a bathe. There was a
pool a little way from the bungalow, and the water was so clear
that you saw every grain of the sandy bottom. The river was so
narrow there that the trees over-arched it. It was a lovely spot.
It reminded Neil of the pools in Scotch streams he had bathed
in as a boy, and yet it was strangely different. It had an air of
romance, a feeling of virgin nature, that filled him with sensa-
tions that he found hard to analyze. He tried, of course, but
older heads than his have found it difficult to anatomize happiness. A kingfisher was sitting on an overhanging branch and its
vivid blue was reflected as bluely in the crystal stream. It flew
away with a flashing glitter of jewelled wings when Neil, slipping off his sarong and baju, scrambled down into the water.
It was fresh without being cold. He splashed and tumbled
about. He enjoyed the movement of his strong limbs. He
floated and looked at the blue sky peeping through the leaves
and the sun that here and there gilded the water. Suddenly he
heard a voice.

"How white your body is, Neil."

With a gasp he let himself sink and turning round saw Darya
standing on the bank.

"I say, I haven't got any clothes on."

"So I saw. It's much nicer bathing without. Wait a minute,
I'll come in, it looks lovely."

She also was wearing a sarong and baju. He turned away his
head quickly for he saw that she was taking them off. He
heard her splash into the water. He gave two or three strokes
in order that she should have room to swim about at a good
distance from him, but she swam up to him.

"Isn't the feel of the water on one's body lovely?" she said.

She laughed and opening her hand splashed water in his face.
He was so embarrassed he did not know which way to look.

In that limpid water it was impossible not to see that she was stark naked. It was not so bad now, but he could not help thinking how difficult it would be to get out. She seemed to be having a grand time.

"I don't care if I do get my hair wet," she said.

She turned over on her back and with strong strokes swam round the pool. When she wanted to get out, he thought, the best thing would be if he turned his back, and when she was dressed she could go and he would get out later. She seemed quite unconscious of the awkwardness of the situation. He was vexed with her. It really was rather tactless to behave like that. She kept on talking to him just as if they were on dry land and properly dressed. She even called his attention to herself.

"Does my hair look awful? It's so fine it gets like rat tails when it's wet. Hold me under the shoulders a moment while I try to screw it up."

"Oh, it's all right," he said. "You'd better leave it now."

"I'm getting frightfully hungry," she said presently. "What about breakfast?"

"If you'll get out first and put on your things, I'll follow you in a minute."

"All right."

She swam the two strokes needed to bring her to the side, and he modestly looked away so that he should not see her get out nude from the water.

"I can't get up," she cried. "You'll have to help me."

It had been easy enough to get in, but the bank overhung the water and one had to lift oneself up by the branch of a tree.

"I can't. I haven't got a stitch of clothing on."

"I know that. Don't be so Scotch. Get up on the bank and give me a hand."

There was no help for it. Neil swung himself up and pulled her after him. She had left her sarong beside his. She took it up unconcernedly and began to dry herself with it. There was nothing for him but to do the same, but for decency's sake he turned his back on her.

"You really have a most lovely skin," she said. "It's as smooth and white as a woman's. It's funny on such a manly virile figure. And you haven't got a hair on your chest."

Neil wrapped the sarong round him and slipped his arms into the baju.

"Are you ready?"

She had porridge for breakfast, and eggs and bacon, cold
meat and marmalade. Neil was a trifle sulky. She was really
almost too Russian. It was stupid of her to behave like that; of
course there was no harm in it, but it was just that sort of
thing that made people think the things they did about her.
The worst of it was that you couldn't give her a hint. She'd only
laugh at you. But the fact was that if any of those men at
Kuala Solor had seen them bathing like that together, stark
naked, nothing would have persuaded them that something
improper hadn't happened. In his judicious way Neil admitted
to himself that you could hardly blame them. It was too bad of
her. She had no right to put a fellow in such a position. He had
felt such a fool. And say what you liked it was indecent.

Next morning, having seen their carriers on the way, a long
procession in single file, each man carrying his load in a creel
on his back, with their servants, guides and hunters, they
started to walk. The path ran over the foothills of the mountain,
through scrub and tall grass, and now and then they came to
narrow streams which they crossed by rickety bridges of bamboo. The sun beat on them fiercely. In the afternoon they
reached the shade of a bamboo forest, grateful after the glare,
and the bamboos in their slender elegance rose to incredible
heights, and the green light was like the light under the sea.
At last they reached the primeval forest, huge trees swathed
in luxuriant creepers, an inextricable tangle, and awe descended
upon them. They cut their way through the undergrowth. They
walked in twilight and only now and then caught through the
dense foliage above them a glimpse of sunshine. They saw
neither man nor beast, for the denizens of the jungle are shy
and at the first sound of footsteps vanish from sight. They
heard birds up high in the tall trees, but saw none save the
twittering sunbirds that flew in the underwoods and delicately
coquetted with the wild flowers. They halted for the night.
The carriers made a floor of branches and on this spread waterproof sheets. The Chinese cook made them their dinner and
then they turned in.

It was the first night Neil had ever spent in the jungle and
he could not sleep. The darkness was profound. The noise was
deafening of innumerable insects, but like the roar of traffic in
a great city it was so constant that in a little while it was like
an impenetrable silence, and when on a sudden he heard the
shriek of a monkey seized by a snake or the scream of a night-

bird he nearly jumped out of his skin. He had a mysterious sensation that all around creatures were watching them. Over there, beyond the camp fires, savage warfare was waged and they three on their bed of branches were defenceless and alone in face of the horror of nature. By his side Munro was breathing quietly in his deep sleep.

"Are you awake, Neil?" Darya whispered.

"Yes. Is anything the matter?"

"I'm terrified."

"It's all right. There's nothing to be afraid of."

"The silence is so awful. I wish I hadn't come."

She lit a cigarette.

Neil, having at last dozed off, was awakened by the hammering of a woodpecker, and its complacent laugh as it flew from one tree to another seemed to mock the sluggards. A hurried breakfast and the caravan started. The gibbons swung from branch to branch, gathering in the dawn dew from the leaves, and their strange cry was like the call of a bird. The light had driven away Darya's fears, and notwithstanding a sleepless night she was alert and gay. They continued to climb. In the afternoon they reached the spot that the guides had told them would be a good camping place, and here Munro decided to build a house. The men set to work. With their long knives they cut palm leaves and saplings and soon had erected a two-roomed hut raised on piles from the ground. It was neat and fresh and green. It smelt good.

The Munros, he from old habit, she because she had for years wandered about the world and had a catlike knack of making herself comfortable wherever she went, were at home anywhere. In a day they had arranged everything and settled down. Their routine was invariable. Every morning early Neil and Munro started out separately, collecting. The afternoon was devoted to pinning insects in boxes, placing butterflies between sheets of paper and skinning birds. When dusk came they caught moths. Darya busied herself with the hut and the servants, sewed and read and smoked innumerable cigarettes. The days passed very pleasantly, monotonous but eventful. Neil was enraptured. He explored the mountain in all directions. One day, to his pride, he found a new species of stick-insect. Munro named it Cuniculina MacAdami. This was fame. Neil (at twenty-two) realized that he had not lived in vain. But another day he only just escaped being bitten by a viper. Owing to its green colour he had not seen it and was only saved from lurching against it by the Dyak hunter who was with him. They killed it and brought it back to camp. Darya shuddered at the sight of it. She had a terror of the wild creatures of the jungle that was almost hysterical. She would never go more than a few yards from the camp for fear of being lost.

"Has Angus ever told you how he was lost?" she asked Neil one evening when they were sitting quietly together after dinner.

"It wasn't a very pleasant experience," he smiled.

"Tell him, Angus."

He hesitated a little. It was not a thing he liked to recall.

"It was some years ago, I'd gone out with my butterfly net and I'd been very lucky, I'd got several rare specimens that I'd been looking for a long time. After a while I thought I was getting hungry so I turned back. I walked for some time and it struck me I'd come a good deal farther than I knew. Suddenly I caught sight of an empty match-box. I swore. I knew at once what had happened. I'd thrown it away when I started to come back, I'd been walking in a circle and was exactly where I was an hour before. I was not pleased. But I had a look round and set off again. It was fearfully hot, and I was simply dripping with sweat. I knew more or less the direction the camp was in and I looked about for traces of my passage to see if I had come that way. I thought I found one or two and went on hopefully. I was frightfully thirsty. I walked on and on, picking my way over snags and trailing plants, and suddenly I knew I was lost. I couldn't have gone so far in the right direction without hitting the camp. I can tell you I was startled. I knew I must keep my head, so I sat down and thought the situation over. I was tortured by thirst. It was long past midday and in three or four hours it would be dark. I didn't like the idea of spending a night in the jungle at all. The only thing I could think of was to try and find a stream; if I followed its course, it would eventually bring me to a larger stream and sooner or later to the river. But of course it might take a couple of days. I cursed myself for being such a fool, but there was nothing better to do and I began walking. At all events if I found a stream I should be able to get a drink. I couldn't find a trickle of water anywhere, not the smallest brook that might lead to something like a stream. I began to be alarmed. I saw myself wandering on till at last I fell exhausted. I knew there was a lot of game in the forest and if I came upon a rhino I was done for. The maddening thing was I knew I couldn't be more than ten miles from my camp. I forced myself to keep my head. The day was waning and in the depths of the jungle it was growing dark already. If I'd brought a gun I could have fired it. In the camp they must have realized I was lost and would be looking for me. The undergrowth was so thick that I couldn't see six feet into it and presently, I don't know if it was nerves or not, I had the sensation that some animal was walking stealthily beside me. I stopped and it stopped too. I went on and it went on. I couldn't see it. I could see no movement in the undergrowth. I didn't even hear the breaking of a twig or the brushing of a body through leaves, but I knew how silently those beasts could move, and I was positive something was stalking me. My heart beat so violently against my ribs that I thought it would break. I was scared out of my wits. It was only by the exercise of all the self-control I had that I prevented myself from breaking into a run. I knew if I did that I was lost. I should be tripped up before I had gone twenty yards by a tangled root and when I was down it would spring on me. And if I started to run God knew where I should get to. And I had to husband my strength. I felt very like crying. And that intolerable thirst. I've never been so frightened in my life. Believe me, if I'd had a revolver I think I'd have blown my brains out. It was so awful I just wanted to finish with it. I was so exhausted I could hardly stagger. If I had an enemy who'd done me a deadly injury I wouldn't wish him the agony I endured then. Suddenly I heard two shots. My heart stood still. They were looking for me. Then I did lose my head. I ran in the direction of the sound, screaming at the top of my voice, I fell, I picked myself up again, I ran on, I shouted till I thought my lungs would burst, there was another shot, nearer, I shouted again, I heard answering shouts; there was a scramble of men in the undergrowth. In a minute I was surrounded by Dyak hunters. They wrung and kissed my hands. They laughed and cried. I very nearly cried too. I was down and out, but they gave me a drink. We were only three miles from the camp. It was pitch dark when we got back. By God, it was a near thing."

A convulsive shudder passed through Darya.

"Believe me, I don't want to be lost in the jungle again."

"What would have happened if you hadn't been found?"

"I can tell you. I should have gone mad. If I hadn't been

stung by a snake or attacked by a rhino I should have gone on
blindly till I fell exhausted. I should have starved to death. I
should have died of thirst. Wild beasts would have eaten my
body and ants cleaned my bones."

Silence fell upon them.

Then it happened, when they had spent nearly a month on
Mount Hitam, that Neil, notwithstanding the quinine Munro
had made him take regularly, was stricken with fever. It was
not a bad attack, but he felt very sorry for himself and was
obliged to stay in bed. Darya nursed him. He was ashamed to
give her so much trouble, but she would not listen to his protests. She was certainly very capable. He resigned himself to
letting her do things for him that one of the Chinese boys could
have done just as well. He was touched. She waited on him
hand and foot. But when the fever was at its height and she
sponged him all over with cold water, though the comfort was
indescribable, he was excessively embarrassed. She insisted on
washing him night and morning.

"I wasn't in the British hospital at Yokohama for six months
without learning at least the routine of nursing," she said,
smiling.

She kissed him on the lips each time after she had finished.
It was friendly and sweet of her. He rather liked it, but attached
no importance to it; he even went so far, a rare thing for him,
as to be facetious on the subject.

"Did you always kiss your patients at the hospital?" he
asked her.

"Don't you like me to kiss you?" she smiled.

"It doesn't do me any harm."

"It may even hasten your recovery," she mocked.

One night he dreamt of her. He awoke with a start. He was
sweating profusely. The relief was wonderful, and he knew that
his temperature had fallen; he was well. He did not care. For
what he had dreamt filled him with shame. He was horrified.
That he should have such thoughts, even in his sleep, made him
feel awful. He must be a monster of depravity. Day was breaking, and he heard Munro getting up in the room next door that
he occupied with Darya. She slept late, and he took care not
to disturb her. When he passed through Neil's room, Neil in a
low voice called him.

"Hullo, are you awake?"

"Yes, I've had the crisis. I'm all right now."

"Good. You'd better stay in bed to-day. To-morrow you'll
be as fit as a fiddle."

"Send Ah Tan to me when you've had your breakfast, will
you?"

"Right-ho."

He heard Munro start out. The Chinese boy came and asked
him what he wanted. An hour later Darya awoke. She came in
to bid him good-morning. He could hardly look at her.

"I'll just have my breakfast and then I'll come in and wash
you," she said.

"I'm washed. I got Ah Tan to do it."

"Why?"

"I wanted to spare you the trouble."

"It isn't a trouble. I like doing it."

She came over to the bed and bent down to kiss him, but he
turned away his head.

"Oh, don't," he said.

"Why not?"

"It's silly."

She looked at him for a moment, surprised, and then with a
slight shrug of the shoulders left him. A little later she came
back to see if there was anything he wanted. He pretended to
be asleep. She very gently stroked his cheek.

"For God's sake don't do that," he cried.

"I thought you were sleeping. What's the matter with you
to-day?"

"Nothing."

"Why are you being horrid to me? Have I done anything to
offend you?"

"No."

"Tell me what it is."

She sat down on the bed and took his hand. He turned his
face to the wall. He was so ashamed he could hardly speak.

"You seem to forget I'm a man. You treat me as if I was a
boy of twelve."

"Oh?"

He was blushing furiously. He was angry with himself and
vexed with her. She really should be more tactful. He plucked
nervously at the sheet.

"I know it means nothing to you and it ought not to mean
anything to me. It doesn't when I'm well and up and about.

One can't help one's dreams, but they are an indication of what is going on in the subconscious."

"Have you been dreaming about me? Well, I don't think there's any harm in that."

He turned his head and looked at her. Her eyes were gleaming, but his were sombre with remorse.

"You don't know men," he said.

She gave a little burble of laughter. She bent down and threw her arms round his neck. She had nothing on but her sarong and baju.

"You darling," she cried. "Tell me, what did you dream?"

He was startled out of his wits. He pushed her violently aside.

"What are you doing? You're crazy."

He jumped half out of bed.

"Don't you know that I'm madly in love with you?" she said.

"What *are* you talking about?"

He sat down on the side of the bed. He was frankly bewildered. She chuckled.

"Why do you suppose I came up to this horrible place? To be with you, ducky. Don't you know I'm scared stiff of the jungle? Even in here I'm frightened there'll be snakes or scorpions or something. I adore you."

"You have no right to speak to me like that," he said sternly.

"Oh, don't be so prim," she smiled.

"Let's get out of here."

He walked out on to the verandah and she followed him. He threw himself into a chair. She knelt by his side and tried to take his hands, but he withdrew them.

"I think you must be mad. I hope to God you don't mean what you say."

"I do. Every word of it," she smiled.

It exasperated him that she seemed unconscious of the frightfulness of her confession.

"Have you forgotten your husband?"

"Oh, what does he matter?"

"Darya."

"I can't be bothered about Angus now."

"I'm afraid you're a very wicked woman," he said slowly, a frown darkening his smooth brow.

She giggled.

"Because I've fallen in love with you? Darling, you shouldn't be so absurdly good-looking."

"For God's sake don't laugh."

"I can't help it; you're comic—but still adorable. I love your white skin and your shining curly hair. I love you because you're so prim and Scotch and humourless. I love your strength. I love your youth."

Her eyes glowed and her breath came quickly. She stooped and kissed his naked feet. He drew them away quickly, with a cry of protest, and in the agitation of his gesture nearly over-threw the rickety chair.

"Woman, you're insane. Have you no shame?"

"No."

"What do you want of me?" he asked fiercely.

"Love."

"What sort of a man do you take me for?"

"A man like any other," she replied calmly.

"Do you think after all that Angus Munro has done for me I could be such a damned beast as to play about with his wife? I admire him more than any man I've ever known. He's grand. He's worth a dozen of me and you put together. I'd sooner kill myself than betray him. I don't know how you can think me capable of such a dastardly act."

"Oh, my dear, don't talk such bilge. What harm is it going to do him? You mustn't take that sort of thing so tragically. After all life is very short; we're fools if we don't take what pleasure we can out of it."

"You can't make wrong right by talking about it."

"I don't know about that. I think that's a very controvertible statement."

He looked at her with amazement. She was sitting at his feet, cool to all appearance and collected, and she seemed to be en-joying the situation. She seemed quite unconscious of its serious-ness.

"Do you know that I knocked a fellow down at the club be-cause he made an insulting remark about you?"

"Who?"

"Bishop."

"Dirty dog. What did he say?"

"He said you'd had affairs with men."

"I don't know why people won't mind their own busi-ness. Anyhow, who cares what they say? I love you. I've never loved anyone like you. I'm absolutely sick with love for you."

"Be quiet. Be quiet."

"Listen, to-night when Angus is asleep, I'll slip into your room. He sleeps like a rock. There's no risk."

"You mustn't do that."

"Why not?"

"No, no, no."

He was frightened out of his wits. Suddenly she sprang to her feet and went into the house.

Munro came back at noon, and in the afternoon they busied themselves as usual. Darya, as she sometimes did, worked with them. She was in high spirits. She was so gay that Munro suggested that she was beginning to enjoy the life.

"It's not so bad," she admitted. "I'm feeling happy to-day."

She teased Neil. She seemed not to notice that he was silent and kept his eyes averted from her.

"Neil's very quiet," said Munro. "I suppose you're feeling a bit weak still."

"No, I just don't feel very talkative."

He was harassed. He was convinced that Darya was capable of anything. He remembered the hysterical frenzy of Nastasya Filipovna in The Idiot, and felt that she too could behave with that unfortunate lack of balance. He had seen her more than once fly into a temper with one of the Chinese servants and he knew how completely she could lose her self-control. Resistance only exasperated her. If she did not immediately get what she wanted she would go almost insane with rage. Fortunately she lost interest in a thing with the same suddenness with which she hankered for it, and if you could distract her attention for a minute she forgot all about it. It was in such situations that Neil had most admired Munro's tact. He had often been slyly amused to see with what a pawky and yet tender cunning he appeased her feminine tantrums. It was on Munro's account that Neil's indignation was so great. Munro was a saint, and from what a state of humiliation and penury and random shifts had he not taken her to make her his wife? She owed everything to him. His name protected her. She had respectability. The commonest gratitude should have made it impossible for her to harbour such thoughts as she had that morning expressed. It was all very well for men to make advances, that was what men did, but for women to do so was disgusting. His modesty

was outraged. The passion he had seen in her face, and the indelicacy of her gestures, scandalized him.

He wondered whether she would really carry out her threat
to come to his room. He didn't think she would dare. But when
night came and they all went to bed, he was so terrified that
he could not sleep. He lay there listening anxiously. The silence
was broken only by the repeated and monotonous cry of an
owl. Through the thin wall of woven palm leaves he heard
Munro's steady breathing. Suddenly he was conscious that
someone was stealthily creeping into his room. He had already
made up his mind what to do.

"Is that you, Mr. Munro?" he called in a loud voice.

Darya stopped suddenly. Munro awoke.

"There's someone in my room. I thought it was you."

"It's all right," said Darya. "It's only me. I couldn't sleep,
so I thought I'd go and smoke a cigarette on the verandah."

"Oh, is that all?" said Munro. "Don't catch cold."

She walked through Neil's room and out. He saw her light
a cigarette. Presently she went back and he heard her get into
bed.

He did not see her next morning, for he started out collecting
before she was up, and he took care not to get in till he was
pretty sure Munro also would be back. He avoided being alone
with her till it was dark and Munro went down for a few minutes
to arrange the moth-traps.

"Why did you wake Angus last night?" she said in a low
angry whisper.

He shrugged his shoulders and going on with his work did not
answer.

"Were you frightened?"

"I have a certain sense of decency."

"Oh, don't be such a prig."

"I'd rather be a prig than a dirty swine."

"I hate you."

"Then leave me alone."

She did not answer, but with her open hand smartly slapped
his face. He flushed, but did not speak. Munro returned and
they pretended to be intent on whatever they were doing.

For the next few days Darya, except at meal-times and in the
evenings, never spoke to Neil. Without pre-arrangement they
exerted themselves to conceal from Munro that their relations
were strained. But the effort with which Darya roused herself

from a brooding silence would have been obvious to anyone more suspicious than Angus, and sometimes she could not help herself from being a trifle sharp with Neil. She chaffed him, but in her chaff was a sting. She knew how to wound and caught him on the raw, but he took care not to let her see it. He had an inkling that the good humour he affected infuriated her.

Then, one day when Neil came back from collecting, though he had delayed till the last possible minute before tiffin, he was surprised to find that Munro had not yet returned. Darya was lying on a mattress on the verandah, sipping a gin pahit and smoking. She did not speak to him when he passed through to wash. In a minute the Chinese boy came into his room and told him that tiffin was ready. He walked out.

"Where's Mr. Munro?" he asked.

"He's not coming," said Darya. "He sent a message to say that the place he's at is so good he won't come down till night."

Munro had set out that morning for the summit of the mountain. The lower levels had yielded poor results in the way of mammals, and Munro's idea was, if he could find a good place higher up, with a supply of water, to transfer the camp. Neil and Darya ate their meal in silence. After they had finished he went into the house and came out again with his topi and his collecting gear. It was unusual for him to go out in the afternoon.

"Where are you going?" she asked abruptly.

"Out."

"Why?"

"I don't feel tired. I've got nothing much else to do this afternoon."

Suddenly she burst into tears.

"How can you be so unkind to me?" she sobbed. "Oh, it is cruel to treat me like this."

He looked down at her from his great height, his handsome, somewhat stolid face bearing a harassed look.

"What have *I* done?"

"You've been beastly to me. Bad as I am I haven't deserved to suffer like this. I've done everything in the world for you. Tell me one single little thing I could do that I haven't done gladly. I'm so terribly unhappy."

He moved on his feet uneasily. It was horrible to hear her say that. He loathed and feared her, but he had still the respect for her that he had always felt, not only because she was a woman, but because she was Angus Munro's wife. She wept uncontrollably. Fortunately the Dyak hunters had gone that morning with Munro. There was no one about the camp but the three Chinese servants and they, after tiffin, were asleep in their own quarters fifty yards away. They were alone.

"I don't want to make you unhappy. It's all so silly. It's absurd of a woman like you to fall in love with a fellow like me. It makes me look such a fool. Haven't you got any self-control?"

"Oh, God. Self-control!"

"I mean, if you really cared for me you couldn't want me to be such a cad. Doesn't it mean anything to you that your husband trusts us implicitly? The mere fact of his leaving us alone like this puts us on our honour. He's a man who would never hurt a fly. I should never respect myself again if I betrayed his confidence."

She looked up suddenly.

"What makes you think he would never hurt a fly? Why, all those bottles and cases are full of the harmless animals he's killed."

"In the interests of science. That's quite another thing."

"Oh, you fool, you fool."

"Well, if I am a fool I can't help it. Why do you bother about me?"

"Do you think I wanted to fall in love with you?"

"You ought to be ashamed of yourself."

"Ashamed? How stupid! My God, what have I done that I should eat my heart out for such a pretentious ass?"

"You talk about what you've done for me. What has Munro done for you?"

"Munro bores me to death. I'm sick of him. Sick to death of him."

"Then I'm not the first?"

Ever since her amazing avowal he had been tortured by the suspicion that what those men at Kuala Solor had said of her was true. He had refused to believe a word of it, and even now he could not bring himself to think that she could be such a monster of depravity. It was frightful to think that Angus Munro, so trusting and tender, should have lived in a fool's paradise. She could not be as bad as that. But she misunderstood him. She smiled through her tears.

"Of course not. How can you be so silly? Oh, darling, don't be so desperately serious. I love you."

Then it was true. He had sought to persuade himself that what she felt for him was exceptional, a madness that together they could contend with and vanquish. But she was simply promiscuous.

"Aren't you afraid Munro will find out?"

She was not crying any more. She adored talking about herself, and she had a feeling that she was inveigling Neil into a new interest in her.

"I sometimes wonder if he doesn't know, if not with his mind, then with his heart. He's got the intuition of a woman and a woman's sensitiveness. Sometimes I've been certain he suspected and in his anguish I've sensed a strange, spiritual exaltation. I've wondered if in his pain he didn't find an infinitely subtle pleasure. There are souls, you know, that feel a voluptuous joy in laceration."

"How horrible!" Neil had no patience with these conceits. "The only excuse for you is that you're insane."

She was now much more sure of herself. She gave him a bold look.

"Don't you think I'm attractive? A good many men have. You must have had dozens of women in Scotland who weren't so well made as I am."

She looked down at her shapely, sensual figure with calm pride.

"I've never had a woman," he said gravely.

"Why not?"

She was so surprised that she sprang to her feet. He shrugged his shoulders. He could not bring himself to tell her how disgusting the idea of such a thing was to him, and how vile he had thought the haphazard amours of his fellow students at Edinburgh. He took a mystical joy in his purity. Love was sacred. The sexual act horrified him. Its excuse was the procreation of children and its sanctification marriage. But Darya, her whole body rigid, stared at him, panting; and suddenly, with a sobbing cry in which there was exultation and at the same time wild desire, she flung herself on her knees and seizing his hand passionately kissed it.

"Alyosha," she gasped. "Alyosha."

And then, crying and laughing, she crumpled up in a heap

at his feet. Strange, hardly human sounds issued from her throat and convulsive tremors passed through her body so that you would have thought she was receiving one electric shock after another. Neil did not know if it was an attack of hysteria or an epileptic fit.

"Stop it," he cried. "Stop it."

He took her up in his strong arms and laid her in the chair. But when he tried to leave her she would not let him. She flung her arms round his neck and held him. She covered his face with kisses. He struggled. He turned his face away. He put his hand between her face and his to protect himself. Suddenly she dug her teeth into it. The pain was so great that, without thinking, he gave her a great swinging blow.

"You devil," he cried.

His violent gesture had forced her to release him. He held his hand and looked at it. She had caught him by the fleshy part on the side and it was bleeding. Her eyes blazed. She was feeling alert and active.

"I've had enough of this. I'm going out," he said.

She sprang to her feet.

"I'll come with you."

He put on his topi and, snatching up his collecting gear, without a word turned on his heel. With one stride he leaped down the three steps that led from the floor of the house to the ground. She followed him.

"I'm going into the jungle," he said.

"I don't care."

In the ravening desire that possessed her she forgot her morbid fear of the jungle. She recked nothing of snakes and wild beasts. She did not mind the branches that hit her face or the creepers that entangled her feet. For a month Neil had explored all that part of the forest and he knew every yard of it. He told himself grimly that he'd teach her to come with him. He forced his way through the undergrowth with rapid strides; she followed him, stumbling but determined; he crashed on, blind with rage, and she crashed after him. She talked; he did not listen to what she said. She besought him to have pity on her. She bemoaned her fate. She made herself humble. She wept and wrung her hands. She tried to cajole him. The words poured from her lips in an unceasing stream. She was like a mad woman. At last in a little clearing he stopped suddenly and turning round faced her.

"This is impossible," he cried. "I'm fed up. When Angus comes back I must tell him I've got to go. I shall go back to Kuala Solor to-morrow morning and go home."

"He won't let you go, he wants you. He finds you invaluable."

"I don't care. I'll fake up something."

"What?"

He mistook her.

"Oh, you needn't be frightened, I shan't tell him the truth. You can break his heart if you want to; I'm not going to."

"You worship him, don't you? That dull, phlegmatic man."

"He's worth a hundred of you."

"It would be rather funny if I told him you'd gone because I wouldn't yield to your advances."

He gave a slight start and looked at her to see if she was serious.

"Don't be such a fool. You don't think he'd believe that, do you? He knows it would never occur to me."

"Don't be too sure."

She had spoken carelessly, with no particular intention other than to continue the argument, but she saw that he was frightened and some instinct of cruelty made her press the advantage.

"Do you expect mercy from me? You've humiliated me beyond endurance. You've treated me like dirt. I swear that if you make any suggestion of going I shall go straight to Angus and say that you took advantage of his absence to try and assault me."

"I can deny it. After all it's only your word against mine."

"Yes, but my word'll count. I can prove what I say."

"What do you mean?"

"I bruise easily. I can show him the bruise where you struck me. And look at your hand." He turned and gave it a sudden glance. "How did those teeth marks get there?"

He stared at her stupidly. He had gone quite pale. How could he explain that bruise and that scar? If he was forced to in self-defence he could tell the truth, but was it likely that Angus would believe it? He worshipped Darya. He would take her word against anyone's. What monstrous ingratitude it would seem for all Munro's kindness and what treachery in return for so much confidence! He would think him a filthy skunk and from his standpoint with justice. That was what shattered him, the thought that Munro, for whom he would willingly have laid down his life, should think ill of him. He was so unhappy that tears, unmanly tears that he hated, came to his eyes. Darya saw that he was broken. She exulted. She was paying him back for the misery he had made her suffer. She held him now. He was in her power. She savoured her triumph and in the midst of her anguish laughed in her heart because he was such a fool. At that moment she did not know whether she loved or despised him.

"Now will you be good?" she said.

He gave a sob and blindly, with a sudden instinct of escape from that abominable woman, took to his heels and ran as hard as he could. He plunged through the jungle, like a wounded animal, not looking where he was going, till he was out of breath. Then, panting, he stopped. He took out his handkerchief and wiped away the sweat that was pouring into his eyes and blinding him. He was exhausted and he sat down to rest.

"I must take care I don't get lost," he said to himself.

That was the least of his troubles, but all the same he was glad that he had a pocket compass, and he knew in which direction he must go. He heaved a deep sigh and rose wearily to his feet. He started walking. He watched his way and with another part of his mind miserably asked himself what he should do. He was convinced that Darya would do what she had threatened. They were to be another three weeks in that accursed place. He dared not go; he dared not stay. His mind was in a whirl. The only thing was to get back to camp and think it out quietly. In about a quarter of an hour he came to a spot that he recognized. In an hour he was back. He flung himself miserably into a chair. And it was Angus who filled his thoughts. His heart bled for him. Neil saw now all sorts of things that before had been dark to him. They were revealed to him in a flash of bitter insight. He knew why the women at Kuala Solor were so hostile to Darya and why they looked at Angus so strangely. They treated him with a sort of affectionate levity. Neil thought it was because Angus was a man of science and so in their foolish eyes somewhat absurd. He knew now it was because they were sorry for him and at the same time found him ridiculous. Darya had made him the laughing stock of the community. If ever there was a man who hadn't deserved ill usage at a woman's hands it was he. Suddenly Neil gasped and began to tremble all over. It had suddenly occurred to him that Darya did not know her way through the jungle; in his anguish he had hardly been conscious of where they went. Supposing she could not find her way home? She would be terrified. He remembered the ghastly story Angus had told them of being lost in the forest. His first instinct was to go back and find her, and he sprang to his feet. Then a fierce anger seized him. No, let her shift for herself. She had gone of her own free will. Let her find her own way back. She was an abominable woman and deserved all that might come to her. Neil threw back his head defiantly, a frown of indignation on his smooth young brow, and clenched his hands. Courage. He made up his mind. It would be better for Angus if she never returned. He sat down and began trying to make a skin of a Mountain Trogon. But the Trogon has a skin like wet tissue paper and his hands trembled. He tried to apply his mind to the work he was doing, but his thoughts fluttered desperately, like moths in a trap, and he could not control them. What was happening over there in the jungle? What had she done when he suddenly bolted? Every now and then, against his will, he looked up. At any moment she might appear in the clearing and walk calmly up to the house. He was not to blame. It was the hand of God. He shuddered. Storm clouds were gathering in the sky and night fell quickly.

Just after dusk Munro arrived.

"Just in time," he said. "There's going to be a hell of a storm."

He was in great spirits. He had come upon a fine plateau, with lots of water, from which there was a magnificent view to the sea. He had found two or three rare butterflies and a flying squirrel. He was full of plans to move the camp to this new place. All about it he had seen abundant evidence of animal life. Presently he went into the house to take off his heavy walking boots. He came out at once.

"Where's Darya?"

Neil stiffened himself to behave with naturalness.

"Isn't she in her room?"

"No. Perhaps she's gone down to the servants' quarters for something."

He walked down the steps and strolled a few yards.

"Darya," he called. "Darya." There was no answer. "Boy."

A Chinese servant came running up and Angus asked him where his mistress was. He did not know. He had not seen her since tiffin.

"Where can she be?" asked Munro, coming back, puzzled. He went to the back of the house and shouted.

"She can't have gone out. There's nowhere to go. When did you see her last, Neil?"

"I went out collecting after tiffin. I'd had a rather unsatisfactory morning and I thought I'd try my luck again."

"Strange."

They hunted everywhere round the camp. Munro thought she might have made herself comfortable somewhere and gone to sleep.

"It's too bad of her to frighten one like this."

The whole party joined in the search. Munro began to grow alarmed.

"It's not possible that she should have gone for a stroll in the jungle and lost her way. She's never moved more than a hundred yards from the house to the best of my knowledge since we've been here."

Neil saw the fear in Munro's eyes and looked down.

"We'd better get everyone along and start hunting. There's one thing, she can't be far. She knows that if you get lost the best thing is to stay where you are and wait for people to come and find you. She'll be scared out of her wits, poor thing."

He called out the Dyak hunters and told the Chinese servants to bring lanterns. He fired his gun as a signal. They separated into two parties, one under Munro, the other under Neil, and went down the two rough paths that in the course of the month they had made in their comings and goings. It was arranged that whoever found Darya should fire three shots in quick succession. Neil walked with his face stern and set. His conscience was clear. He seemed to bear in his hands the decree of imminent justice. He knew that Darya would never be found. The two parties met. It was not necessary to look at Munro's face. He was distracted. Neil felt like a surgeon who is forced to perform a dangerous operation without assistance or appliances to save the life of someone he loves. It behoved him to be firm.

"She could never have got so far as this," said Munro. "We must go back and beat the jungle within the radius of a mile from the house inch by inch. The only explanation is that she was frightened by something or fainted or was stung by a snake."

Neil did not answer. They started out again and, making

lines, combed the undergrowth. They shouted. Every now and
then they fired a gun and listened for a faint call in answer.
Birds of the night flew with a whirring of wings, frightened,
as they advanced with their lanterns; and now and then they
half saw, half guessed at an animal, deer, boar or rhino, that
fled at their approach. The storm broke suddenly. A great wind
blew and then the lightning rent the darkness, like the scream
of a woman in pain, and the tortured flashes, quick, quick, one
on the heels of the other, like demon dancers in a frantic reel,
wriggled down the night. The horror of the forest was revealed
in an unearthly day. The thunder crashed down the sky in huge
rollers, peal upon peal, like vast, primeval waves dashing against
the shores of eternity. That fearful din hurtled through space as
though sound had size and weight. The rain pelted in fierce
torrents. Rocks and gigantic trees came tumbling down the
mountain. The tumult was awful. The Dyak hunters cowered,
gibbering in terror of the angry spirits who spoke in the storm,
but Munro urged them on. The rain fell all night, with lightning
and thunder, and did not cease till dawn. Wet through and
shivering they returned to the camp. They were exhausted.
When they had eaten Munro meant to resume the desperate
search. But he knew that it was hopeless. They would never
see her alive again. He flung himself down wearily. His face
was tired and white and anguished.

"Poor child. Poor child."

THE END